EDITH THE CAPTIVE:

OR,

THE ROBBERS OF EPPING FOREST.

BY THE AUTHOR OF "JANE BRIGHTWELL."

WITH FIFTY-TWO ILLUSTRATIONS.

DRAWN BY F. GILBERT, G. F. SARGENT, AND G. STANDFAST.

VOL. II.

LONDON:
PUBLISHED BY JOHN DICKS, 25, WELLINGTON STREET, STRAND.

1862.

INDEX TO VOL II.

INDEX TO THE ENGRAVINGS.

EDITH THE CAPTIVE;

OR,

THE ROBBERS OF EPPING FOREST.

CHAPTER CXVI.

EDITH ESCAPES FROM JONATHAN WILD.

AFTER the brief parley with Captain Heron, which we have already recorded, Jonathan Wild swung a heavy sofa against the door so as to prevent it from being broken open.

On to that sofa he cast himself at full length, to add by his weight to its value as a barricade; and the sword-blade of Captain Heron, when it came through the panel of the door, passed about a foot above the head of Jonathan Wild

"Ah," said Wild, "one might have been in the way of that, and afforded the first example of a man being killed by a sword thrust from one side of a door while his opponent was on the other."

Wild then tapped on the panel to command the attention of Captain Heron.

"Hilloa! hilloa!" he said.

"Villain!"

"Come, come! You receive with great insensibility the kindness I intend you. I was merely going to say that as you may possibly take it into your head to fire your pistols through the door——"

"Ah, yes!"

"No. Wait a moment. I was going to add, that as a bullet is no respecter of persons, you might lodge one in the heart or brain of Edith Tarleton."

"Oh, heaven!"

"Ah, I thought that would do!"

The violent ringing at the bell, which hung over the old gates of Castleneau House, had been heard by Wild, as well as by Captain Heron; but the former thought it much more likely to be some of his own men, than any assistance to Heron or to Edith.

"Come, now, Captain," he called out, after a few moments of silence; "I will make terms with you."

"What terms? What terms, ruffian?"

"You are abusive. You are not at all careful, Captain Heron, about your epithets. I say again that I will make a bargain with you."

"What would you say, Jonathan Wild? I hear you; but I warn you, at the same time, that if Edith suffers from you the remotest harm——"

The emotion of Heron choked his further utterance now, and he could say no more.

"You need fear nothing," replied Wild; "and if you will pay me a couple of thousand pounds, Edith shall be delivered up to you free. It is to be likewise understood in the arrangement, that you are to permit me to leave these rooms and the house freely."

"Bring her to me—bring her to me at once; and villain as you are, the money shall be yours!"

"Very well. Have you it about you?"

"No. But I can procure it, and it shall be deposited at any place you wish. Ah, who comes! I hear the sound of footsteps! My sword is broken! Yet am I one whom it would be dangerous to attack! Hold off, as you value your lives!"

"Why," thought Jonathan Wild, "surely that is some of my bull dogs! Hoy! Blueskin, is that you?"

"Oh, what has happened?" cried Lady Castleneau, who, with two gentlemen following her, now appeared in that fourth room, where, with looks of rage and fear for Edith, Captain Heron was engaged in that terrible parley with Wild.

"Ah, it is you," said Heron. "Oh, Lady Castleneau, what form of words shall I put the information in, when I tell you our dear Edith is——is——"

"Oh, what? Speak!—speak!"

"In the power of the villain Wild, and I am here helpless to save or aid her!"

"What does all this mean?" asked one of the gentlemen, advancing.

"Ah, my Lord Bridgewater!" cried Captain Heron; "you can, perhaps, feel for me!"

"And I, too, I hope," said Colonel Trelawney, who was the other gentleman with the young Earl; for after leaving the field in which the contest with Lord Warringdale had taken place, the Earl of Bridgewater had proposed to the Colonel that they should call upon Lady Castleneau, to inform her of what had happened.

"Sir, I do not know you," said Captain Heron; "but there is a young lady in the power of a villain, in the room that lies on the other side of this door."

"This is Colonel Trelawney," said the Earl of Bridgewater; "and this——"

He was about to introduce Heron to the Colonel, but it struck him, on the moment, that he might probably be disclosing who Heron was when he had no right to do so, and he paused.

"My name is Felix," said Captain Heron; "and if Colonel Trelawney will be so good as to consent only to know me by that name, while as a soldier and a gentleman he aids in the rescue of a lady, he will be but acting up to his well-known character."

"I seek to know no more," said the Colonel. "Surely we three men can force a door!"

"No!" cried Wild, in a loud voice, from the other side of the panel. "No! I have effectually secured the door; and I, a constable, bearing his Majesty's order to arrest all felons, call upon you, my Lord Bridgewater, and upon you, Colonel Trelawney, to aid me in the King's name in the performance of my duty!"

"Who is this man?" said the Colonel.

"I think I know," said the Earl.

"It is the villain Jonathan Wild!" said Captain Heron. "He is too well known!"

"I call upon you both, gentlemen, in the name of the King," cried Wild, "to arrest the notorious highwayman, called commonly Captain Felix Heron!"

"We don't see him," said the Earl; "but if you will come out, Mr. Wild, we will see about this affair."

"My lord, I have a prisoner here!"

"No, no!" said Heron; "whoever and whatever I may be, Edith Tarleton can be no prisoner to Jonathan Wild! She is no felon!"

"Yes!" said Wild; "it is a felony to aid, advise, comfort, and assist a felon; and if she has not done all that to you, why, I am blind and deaf!"

"Come away," said the Earl of Bridgewater, as he placed his hand kindly upon the arm of Captain Heron,—"come away!"

"No, no, I cannot! My Edith is here, and I will stay while life remains to me!"

Captain Heron now made another violent effort to force the door; but it was unsuccessful, although he bruised himself much in the attempt.

Colonel Trelawney had stepped aside, and was speaking to Lady Castleneau in a low tone, while she, with tears in her eyes, was explaining to him the exact state of the case.

"Very good," said the Colonel; "I think we can manage all this. It reminds me of when I was a prisoner once at Metz, and how I escaped."

"Escaped, Colonel?"

"Yes; allow me to take the conduct of this affair."

The Colonel stepped forward, and spoke in a

low tone to Captain Heron, for Wild to hear what he said from the other side of the door.

"If, Mr. Felix," he said, "you will follow some advice that I shall give you, I think I can show you how to rescue the young lady, without being beholden to anything but your own strength, perseverance, and courage."

"Oh, sir, if you can do that!"

"Hush!—come away!"

"On that promise, I will."

"Well, gentlemen," said Wild; "have you apprehended the highwayman, Captain Heron?"

"No," said Colonel Trelawney; "but we intend to consult about the matter."

"Very good!" said Wild. "Don't hurry yourselves in the least; I am very well contented here, and the young lady is fair, and good company!"

"Wretch!" cried Heron.

"Ha! ha!" responded Wild.

"There, there—that will do!" said the Colonel. "Come away at once!"

Captain Heron, although not without some resistance, suffered himself to be led away from the door by the Colonel.

The whole party reached one of the ante-rooms of the suite, and then Colonel Trelawney spoke freely.

"I am informed by Lady Castleneau," he said, "that Miss Edith Tarleton, the daughter of Sir John Tarleton, one of the judges, is in the hands of the notorious rascal, Wild."

"Yes, yes—oh, yes!"

"I am likewise informed that at the end of this suite of rooms there is one apartment which is a secret one. Now I may state that when I was a prisoner I was confined in a small room with an apartment adjoining it in which was my guard; but some faithful followers of mine got into the lower part of the place and got at me through the floor."

"Ah!" cried Captain Heron, "if we could only do that now!"

"We may, and can," said Lady Castleneau: "there will be but little difficulty. The flooring of the secret room is in small, short, thin pieces of plank, and surely they may soon be reached from the room below."

There was a bright look of hope now about the eyes of Captain Heron, and he almost ran out of the suite of rooms and down the grand staircase of the house in his eagerness.

But he paused a moment at the door of the breakfast-room, and waited for Lady Castleneau.

"Tell me, dear madam," he said, "is Sir John Tarleton still in the house?"

"No, I sent him away; and Anthony is with him in the coach, to see him in safety to his own door, where he has my directions to leave him."

"That is well—that is well!"

Lady Castleneau now led her guests to the room which was immediately under the small, narrow recess in the wall of the mansion above.

"This ceiling," she said, "is but paper; and although there are joists, of course they are wide apart, and the thin planking is just above."

"Then there is hope indeed!" cried Captain Heron. "Pray, Lady Castleneau, get, by your orders, assembled here, what tools that you think will help me, and I will soon work my way."

Anthony had not had time to return, but the young girl who attended on Lady Castleneau soon brought to Captain Heron various implements by which he could set to work.

Then Colonel Trelawney and the young Earl of Bridgewater helping him, he placed a table beneath the part of the ceiling against which he meant to operate, and on that table a chair.

When Captain Heron stood on the chair he could reach the ceiling easily.

As Lady Castleneau had said, there was nothing but some ornamental paper over that portion of the ceiling, and when Captain Heron tore it away the open space between the joists of the floor above could be seen.

Heron then intimated that he wished them all to be silent.

Then, amid the profound stillness of the whole party, he tapped on the under side of the boards, gently.

He thought that if Edith were there, it would be, to her, a sufficient signal that friends were at hand.

It was so.

Edith heard those light taps, and she felt confident that they could come from none but a friend, since the only foe she had in that house was Jonathan Wild; and he was not in a position to make them.

It might be said, that the knowledge which Edith had that some succour was at hand, was intuitive, and certainly it came to her mind without the shadow of a doubt.

The light and gentle manner in which the knocking was made, betrayed an evident desire that it should only reach her ears, and not those of the relentless foe who was close at hand.

A moment's thought, too, let her know that Lady Castleneau must be well aware of the exact place in the ceiling below, that was beneath the flooring of the secret recess; and that her situation as the prisoner of Jonathan Wild was known she had every reason to believe, for she had heard Wild's voice in evident altercation with some one, although the distance that Captain Heron had been from her was too great to permit her to recognise whose tones they were that challenged the attention of her gaoler.

And so Edith replied to the knocks, as gently as they had been given by Captain Heron.

"She is there," said the Captain, in a voice of pleasure and exultation—"she is there; and this answer to my signal is a sufficient proof that she is not even in the detested presence of Jonathan Wild."

"It must be so," said Lady Castleneau. "Work, Felix, work; and we shall rescue the dear girl yet."

Little did Captain Heron need any incentive to exertion; the thought that Edith was now only separated from him by a few thin and almost loose planks of wood, gave him a strength, awkwardly situated as he was for the exercise of it, which enabled him soon to cut a passage through the woodwork.

Then the voice of Edith was heard, as she said in low tones, "I am here, in danger, and in darkness. Speak to me, if you be indeed the friends I hope!"

"It is I, Edith—it is I," said Captain Heron.

Even at the risk of alarming Jonathan Wild, and letting him know that she was in communication with those who would save her from him, Edith uttered a cry of joy.

Wild was lying upon the sofa, still adding by his weight to its powers of resistance; but he heard that cry; and there was something so hopeful and joyous about it, that he began to fear his fair hostage would elude his grasp.

"I must and will see her," said Jonathan, as he sprang to his feet. "She hides from me in that secret room, but for my own safety's sake, I must have her more in my power."

Wild went into the huge chimney-piece, and made another attempt to make his way into the secret room by its regular entrance, but he soon found, by the solid feel of the door, that all his efforts would be futile; and with rage swelling in his heart, he sought the room again, and glared about him in the hope of some practical suggestion coming to his aid.

It did come!

"Ah, the wall!" he cried—"the wall! Many a wall is easier to break through than a door."

On the side of the wall, which appeared to be the end of the house, but which was, in reality, the partition which separated this narrow apartment from the larger room, hung a full length portrait of a lady, with most voluminous skirts and a ruff of portentous dimensions.

It was one of those dim, old family portraits, which our ancestors seem to have executed of everybody, as a sort of social duty. The frame was thin and meagre; and in the ingenuity of Jonathan Wild's intellect it struck him that he had heard of such portraits, hiding doors and recesses, in walls of old mansions.

The moment this idea struck Jonathan's mind, he seized upon the picture to tear it from its place, and its resistance to his efforts convinced him that it was placed there for a purpose.

He gave but one glance towards the door of the room, in order again to assure himself that it could not be readily forced without his perfect cognizance of the commencement of hostilities against it; and then drawing his hanger, he attacked the portrait as though it were a living person whom he wished to cut down and destroy.

Edith uttered a cry of dismay from within the next chamber.

Sharp splinters came away from the panel on which the portrait was painted, at each stroke of Jonathan Wild's hanger; but concurrent with those efforts of Edith, her best and dearest friend worked from the room below, and with a broad chisel was working his way through the floor-boards to her rescue.

But thin and light as they were, the boards were of oak; and Captain Heron worked at a great disadvantage above his head, while Jonathan Wild cut away the old, dry panel of the picture with facility.

Before Captain Heron could effect an entrance between the joists of the floor, Jonathan Wild had cut away space enough of the picture panel to project his head and shoulders into the apartment.

So much, too, of the light of that early morning as had found its way through the shutter which Wild had opened, straggled into the secret room; and Wild saw Edith kneeling on the floor, and with her hands clasped as if in entreaty, and her eyes fixed upon him in terror.

"Come away, girl!" he said. "I will not

have you here. You are my prisoner, and, for good or for evil, shall remain so!"

"Help, oh, help!" cried Edith. "Help me, Felix, now!"

"I am here—I come!" cried Captain Heron, and his voice sounded like the ring of a trumpet.

"Where? where?" shouted Wild, for he was bewildered and astonished for a moment to hear the voice of Heron; but the practical ingenuity of his mind soon suggested to him what was really the case.

"Ah!" he cried; "I see it now—but it shall be too late!"

He sprang away from the opening in the wall, and in a moment dashed his hanger through one of the panes of glass of the window he had released from its shutter; then placing the silver whistle he always carried with him, to his lips, he blew three such ear-piercing blasts, that they must have been heard over the entire neighbourhood.

"That will do," he said. "A dozen of my men are scattered about Bloomsbury, and they will now know I want them. Blueskin, without doubt, holds his post in the hall below; and whether or not, my bull-dogs are not the sort of men to wait patiently for admittance to any house, when they know I'm within it, and want them!"

He darted back again now from the window to the jagged and splintered opening he had made in the panel of the picture.

"Now, fair Edith," he said, "we will secure ourselves in another of these deserted rooms; and I really think, considering all the trouble I take about you, you should bestow upon me one of your sweetest caresses. Ha! ha! Jonathan Wild is not baffled yet."

Wild had dragged a chair after him, and it was his evident intention to scramble through the hole in the wall, and seize upon Edith for the purpose of retreating with her in the same direction; but at the moment he was about to put his head through the opening, he recoiled with terror, for Edith stood on one side of it, armed with a ponderous bar she had taken from its staples across the door, and which she now held in such a position that its mere weight in falling would crush all before it.

"Advance at your peril," she said. "Your death be on your own head."

Wild saw in a moment how utterly helpless he was against this defence, and he felt now that time was the principal element in all that was taking place, and that in a few moments all his pains and dangers would be thrown away, if he did not secure possession of Edith as a hostage for his safety. He raised one of his ordinary yells of passion, and drawing a pistol from his breast, he levelled it at the head of Edith.

"Girl," he said, "you know not your own danger. You're young, and should be fond of life. One touch of the finger to the trigger of this weapon, and you are hopelessly wounded. Fling down the bar, and yield yourself."

"Never!"

"Are you mad, girl?"

"I might well be thought so, could I yield to the villain Jonathan Wild."

There had not, from the moment that he levelled his pistol at her, been the slightest intention on the part of Wild to fire at Edith.

MARRIAGE OF CAPTAIN HRON AND EDITH TARLETON.

Presented Gratis with No. 53 of the New Edition ; Edith the Captive; or, the Robbers of Epping Forest.

EACH WEEK IS PRESENTED GRATIS A COLOURED ENGRAVING.

It was not that such a man as Wild had, in reality, any scruples about the commission of murder, or the sort of murder that might come to hand to him to commit; but well he knew that if he were to be guilty of so dastardly an act as the murder of Edith, his own life would not be worth an hour's purchase.

Even Colonel Trelawney or the young Earl of Bridgewater would soon have taken the most exemplary vengeance upon him for such a deed.

And well might Jonathan Wild know and feel that time was now such an element against him, that the lapse of a few minutes must alter the whole aspect of affairs.

Those few minutes elapsed, and the change that Wild expected, as well as the change that Edith looked for, took place. With a sharp, crackling noise the piece of flooring that Captain Heron had been at work upon, gave way.

Edith uttered a cry of delight, and dropped the heavy bar which had been her means of defence against Jonathan Wild.

"I am saved! I am saved!" she cried.

"I am here!" shouted Captain Heron, as, by a wonderful exertion of strength, he drew himself up through the small aperture he had made in the floor, and bounded into the room.

"That's over!" cried Wild.

As he spoke, he levelled the pistol at Heron and fired, calling out, in a yelling voice, "The shot was meant for you, Captain. I spared her——"

"And missed me," said Heron, as he sprang towards the opening in the wall.

Wild, in the confusion and smoke of the discharged pistol, had immediately turned and fled; and before Heron could scramble through the small jagged orifice that Wild had made in the panel of the portrait, the active thief-taker had reached the sofa which he had run across the door, and, upon the chance of it being unlocked on the other side, he turned the handle.

"Good!" he cried; "they were not likely to lock it, when she wanted to get in once more; and here, my gallant knight of the road, I hold you at bay!"

Wild slammed the door shut with a terrific bang, and instantly locked it.

"Now for my men," he said. "They will be assembling about the house by this time; and if I can but get to them to tell them how to act, the capture of Heron is still a certainty. I wonder, too, where that rascal Warringdale has got all this time."

With his hanger in his hand, for he yet dreaded some opposition, Wild now ran through that suite of rooms, dark as they were, and no one for a single moment impeded his progress.

The door of the first one that opened on to the landing at the head of the grand staircase was not quite closed, and through the narrow partial opening there came a stream of daylight.

"All's well!" said Wild—and he thrust his hanger into its sheath with a clang; then, dashing the door open, he was about to make a rush on to the landing, when, to his astonishment and dismay, a couple of sword-points met his throat, and he was met face to face by Colonel Trelawney and the Earl of Bridgewater.

Wild shrunk back for a moment as if he expected instant death; but then, as he saw who his opponents were, his old and habitual assurance came back to him, and he cried out, "Gentlemen—gentlemen, do not obstruct an officer in the discharge of his duty. I am on police service."

"You are a great scoundrel, Jonathan Wild," said the Earl of Bridgewater; "and you are here so much more upon your own service, and that of some rascally employers you have, than upon your duty as a constable, that we mean to impede you."

"Gentlemen—gentlemen, at your peril!" cried Wild. "I am a specially sworn officer under the Secretary of State, acting for his Majesty, whose representative I am."

Colonel Trelawney laughed.

"You're an insolent rascal," he said; "but were you a sworn constable of his satanic majesty, who is your real master, and which you may be, for all I know, you shall no longer disturb the peace of this house."

"March, Mr. Wild!" said the Earl of Bridgewater. "You will please to walk down stairs."

"My lord—my lord, I warn you——"

"And so do I you," said the Earl; "only my mode of warning is the most practical of the two."

The Earl accompanied these words with a slight lunge of his sword in Wild's back; who, the moment he felt the point, sprung half down the stairs at a single bound.

"Blueskin! Blueskin!" he cried. "Where are you? Sound your whistle, and call the men! Janissaries! Hoy, there!"

But no Blueskin responded to Jonathan Wild's call; and pursued by the Earl of Bridgewater, while Colonel Trelawney followed laughing, the thief-taker was compelled to run out of the house, and across the court-yard, as quickly as he could.

On the other side of the iron gates several men were collected, and Jonathan Wild recognised them as some of his bull-dogs.

"Help! help!" he cried. "Come over! Are you going to see me slaughtered before your eyes, you scoundrels, by a parcel of highwaymen?"

"Bless you, Mr. Wild," said a voice, "those are not highwaymen. One of them's the Earl of Bridgewater, and the other's Colonel Trelawney, in command of his Majesty's guard!"

Wild darted an angry look at the speaker, and saw that it was his old acquaintance, Ogle, who, with his hands in his pockets, quietly emerged from a little half-ruinous porter's lodge which was just within the gate.

Jonathan Wild's janissaries knew Ogle well enough; but perhaps they would not have been entirely inclined to take his word for the rank of the gentlemen who had been stigmatised by Jonathan Wild as highwaymen, had it not been that one of their number knew Colonel Trelawney perfectly well by sight, and intimated as much to his comrades.

In those days, it was no trifle to offend a man of rank, and one connected with the Court; and therefore, for the first time, perhaps, in his experience, Wild found his bull-dogs hanging back from his service.

The rage which began to convulse his countenance excited nothing but the disdain of the Earl of Bridgewater, who was determined that Jonathan Wild should leave the premises; and in order to ensure that result as quickly as possible, he made a feint of attacking him with his rapier, insisting at the same time on his climbing the gate, which

Jonathan Wild would have inevitably had to do but for the opportune arrival of old Anthony, on his return from seeing Judge Tarleton to his own house.

Anthony had his key of the outer gate, which he was never without; and as he let himself in, Jonathan Wild took the opportunity of slipping out.

When once on the other side, the thief-taker shook his hand angrily at Castleneau House and its inhabitants.

"I bide my time!" he said. "I may be de-defeated for the present, but my day of triumph will approach; and then woe be to those who have crossed me!"

With these words, Wild darted off at a rapid pace, and was quickly followed by his men.

CHAPTER CXVI.

CAPTAIN HERON SEEKS THE SHADES OF THE OLD FOREST ONCE AGAIN.

A STRANGE party was assembled within one hour of that time within the old breakfast-room of Lady Castleneau's mansion.

There was the ancient gentlewoman herself, with much excitement in her manner; and there was her much loved and persecuted Edith.

The young Earl of Bridgewater and Colonel Trelawney made up the third and fourth persons of the group, and Captain Heron the fifth.

Heron is speaking, and both the Earl and his friend, the Colonel, are listening with the greatest attention to his words.

It has appeared to Heron that the time has come when he should take every opportunity of making persons of rank and influence acquainted with what he thought was the secret of his life.

There was a look of animation upon Heron's countenance; and as he warmed upon his subject, and became eloquent in regard to it, that look deepened until it became one which might almost be called beautiful.

"The time has come," he said, "when I feel that I ought to declare who and what I think myself to be. In justice to this young lady, whom I have pursued with my affections, and to whose service I have much devoted myself of late, it is fit that I should say I do not believe myself to be the nameless adventurer my enemies would call me, or the fortune-hunter that others will not scruple to call me."

"No, no Felix; cried Edith; "no one who knows you will declare you that."

"But there are many, dear one, who know me not; and as I have the dear hope, soon, of making you my own, I would much prefer that these gentlemen should know who and what I think I am, in case some bullet should lay me low; in which case, I would not have you, Edith, con-sidered as the mourning widow of Heron the Highwayman, but as one who may rank with the highest and noblest of the land."

"You may speak freely to us," said the Earl of Bridgewater; "for I speak for my friend as well as for myself, when I declare we have a thousand times more inclination to befriend you than to harm you."

"Most assuredly," said Colonel Trelawney.

"Then I will speak freely, and perhaps surprise you, gentlemen, when I tell you that I believe myself to be the son of that Earl of Whitcombe who so recently expired at his house in St. James's Street."

"Can this be possible?" exclaimed Colonel Trelawney.

"Even so," added Heron; "and not only have I evidence sufficient in my own mind to convince me of that fact, but I am assured that my mother was married to the Earl, and that my birth is legitimate and prior to that of the man who has called himself for so long, Lord Warringdale."

"Then he is your half-brother, in that case," said the Earl of Bridgewater.

"I regret to say it. It is a humiliation to me to feel that such can be the case; but as I have reason to believe that the Earl, my father, con-tracted his second marriage even while my poor mother lived—alas! for aught I know, she may live yet—it is this man Warringdale whose birth is illegitimate, and who can have no legal right even to the name he bears."

"This is a strange story, Captain Heron," said Colonel Trelawney; "and so perfect a conviction have I of the villany of Lord Warringdale, as he calls himself, that I would give much to see you prove your claims."

"It is the business and study of my life to do so," said Heron. "And if you hear that the hunted knight of the road has wedded Judge Tarleton's daughter, believe that, from his inmost heart, he thinks he is making her a countess, and not the mere bride of an adventurer."

"Countess or no countess," said Edith, "you, Felix, alone have my heart, and you alone shall have my hand."

"Why, this," said Colonel Trelawney, "is as pretty a romance as ever I have heard or read of. If I were in the Church, fair Edith, I would not desire a pleasanter quarter of an hour than that in which I would unite you and your gallant lover here."

Edith clung to the arm of Heron, and there was something affecting in the whole scene which touched Lady Castleneau's heart, so that she shed tears abundantly.

"Indeed, indeed, Edith," she said, "I wish that you were the wife of Felix, for no one could then have even the pretence to tear you asunder."

Captain Heron smiled, and then, to the surprise of Edith, he spoke as follows:—"You are not yet of age, dear Edith; and there might be some cavil at your marriage—on account of your father's refusal to consent to it—with Felix Heron, the highwayman; and therefore, dearest, I have be-thought me to advise you what to do."

Edith looked anxiously in the face of Felix, for she could not imagine what he had to say. In-deed, his words seemed to bear some impression to her mind that he rather wished to postpone their union than urge it onwards.

"Will you pardon me, Edith," he said, "the advice I shall tender to you?"

"Yes, Felix—oh, yes!"

"Then listen, loved and dear one. Your father has registered his consent to your union with Lord Warringdale."

"Alas, yes; and he will not retract it for an-other."

Heron smiled.

"Let me then, Edith, advise you," he said, "to marry this Lord Warringdale; and so, with your father's consent, be happy."

"Marry him? Oh, Felix, Felix!"

"Marry him?" cried Lady Castleneau. "No, never, never!"

"And this from you!" sobbed Edith, as she looked reproachfully at Heron.

"Alas, alas!" said Lady Castleneau; "come to me, my child. In me alone you will find no change."

"Nay, Lady Castleneau," said the young Earl of Bridgewater, stepping forward, with a smile upon his face; "I think I can unravel this mystery."

"And I," said Colonel Trelawney.

"I think I see you do, gentlemen," remarked Captain Heron.

"Our friend here," added the young Earl, pointing to Felix, "claims to be the eldest son of the Earl of Whitcombe; and we all know that the title of courtesy taken by that eldest son is Lord Warringdale."

Edith uttered a cry of joy.

Lady Castleneau sprang forward, and clasped Heron by the hands.

"Yes," he said, "as the eldest son of the Earl of Whitcombe, I claim to call myself Lord Warringdale; and as such, I offer my hand and heart to Edith Tarleton."

"This is brave," cried Colonel Trelawney. "What say you, my Lord Bridgewater? The consent of Judge Tarleton has been given—a special license has no doubt been granted, which will be on record at the proper authorities. By Jove, my lord, I think the chaplain of our regiment would, at half a word from me, unite this fair couple."

"If it take a whole word," said the Earl, "pray let it be spoken."

"No, no!" cried Edith.

"No?" said Captain Heron.

"No?" exclaimed Lady Castleneau.

Edith hid her face upon Captain Heron's breast.

"She means yes," said the Earl.

"Of course she does," said Colonel Trelawney. "Excuse me, all of you. I feel a special pride and pleasure in this matter. I will but run down to Whitehall, and be back quickly with our reverend friend, who is as good a chaplain, as good a trooper, and as jolly a comrade as any in the regiment."

"And I will give the bride away," said the young Earl.

"Oh, what a wedding this will be!" cried Lady Castleneau. "Come, my dear Edith, I, as your mother's sister, sanction your nuptials."

"It must be so," said Edith. "I cannot so belie my heart and mind as to say 'no,' even to this sudden marriage. Had all been fair and cloudless as a summer's day with our love, dear Felix, how gladly would I have given you my hand; and shall I refuse it now, when the storms of fate beset us? No, Felix, I am yours—whether our home be in a gilded saloon—a humble cottage—or beneath the silver glades of the forest, where first I saw you."

There shone in the eyes of Captain Heron a sparkling joy; and as Lady Castleneau led Edith from the apartment in order to make such preparations for the hasty bridal as she had in her power, Heron looked after her as though the better part of his existence darted from his eyes to follow her.

"On my life, sir," said the young Earl, "you have as fair a bride as ever the light of day shone upon."

Heron sighed deeply.

"And yet," he said, "what can I offer her? Her last words, perchance, were spoken truly; and beneath the silver shades of old Epping Forest may be our only home."

"Hope for better things!" cried the Earl, with impetuosity. "Look you here now, sir! I will advise you as a friend to collect what proofs you can of your birth, and petition the King, who must perforce submit the matter to the Privy Council."

"You forget, my lord, I am a proscribed, hunted man. There is even a price upon my head." •

"Heed it not—heed it not! Many a brave soldier of fortune has taken to the road."

Heron shook his head.

"Look you here now!" added the Earl of Bridgewater—and he spoke with rapidity and enthusiasm. "There is to be a grand Court ball on this day week. Several of the principal saloons of the Palace are being now thrown into one for the purpose, for the whole affair is to be on an unexampled scale of splendour. You shall go."

"I, my lord?"

"Even you. I will arrange it. You shall have a ticket from me. The King will be present; and you shall take the opportunity yourself of presenting your petition or statement of rights and facts. By that means, you see, it reaches him directly, and cannot be intercepted by any creature of Lord Warringdale's on the way. Say that you will go."

"I will."

"Your hand on it."

"It is there, my lord, and freely. To say I thank you, is so little that I will leave it unsaid; but this generous kindness sinks deep into my heart."

"It is nothing—it is nothing! Where shall I send you the ticket?"

"Here—to Lady Castleneau's. Neither I nor Edith have a dearer friend than she has been to us."

"It shall be done—it shall be done!"

While this brief conversation was proceeding between the Earl of Bridgewater and Captain Heron, Lady Castleneau was taking a delight in adorning Edith for her wedding; and although, perhaps, the fashion of the rich old brocaded dress, in which she would insist in attiring her, was somewhat out of date, yet no caprice of taste or time could deteriorate from the value of the rich and rare jewels which the old gentlewoman drew from many a hidden store for the adornment of her darling niece.

And although Lady Castleneau was as well pleased as any one could possibly be with this union of her dear Edith with Felix Heron, yet was there something about the surrounding circumstances that seemed to call for tears; and from the moment that the strangely-hurried nuptials had been determined upon, poor old Lady Castleneau might be said to see everything and everybody through a mist of pearly drops, which welled up from her kind heart to her eyes.

And Captain Heron, too, was deeply touched by all that had taken place, and more particularly by the kindness of the Earl of Bridgewater and Colonel Trelawney, upon neither of whom had he any special claims for sympathy or support.

And yet what an abundance of both they were according to him by their presence and countenance at his marriage with Edith.

Begging the Earl to excuse him for a few moments, Captain Heron went into the hall of Castleneau House, where he knew that Ogle was waiting; for he was anxious about his band of attached followers, to whom he had sent, in so eccentric a manner, a message by old Anthony, the serving-man of the Lady Castleneau.

Ogle was delighted to see Captain Heron, and at once began to explain to him how he came to show himself in the court-yard of Castleneau House, when he (the Captain) might well expect that by that time he was more than half-way towards old Epping Forest.

"Captain," he said, "the fact is, I thought you might be in want of some one who would be as ready as I should be to give my life for you, if it were needed. So I just let the band go on, and remained behind."

"Then you all got my message?"

"Oh, yes, Captain. I was on the look-out, and saw the order on one of the railings of Montague House, and then the whole band went at once what we call homewards. But something has happened, Captain."

"What? No misfortunes, I hope?"

"Oh, no, no! Tom Ripon, though, has taken upon himself to come from the forest, and to bring Daisy with him."

"Indeed!"

"Yes. I have no doubt at all, Captain, but the boy has some good reason for it. He all but told me that if he had not done so he thought that Daisy would have fallen into the hands of some enemy; but you will hear his own account of the matter, Captain, soon."

"Be it what it may," said Heron, "I am well pleased to have Daisy in London. Where have you and Tom bestowed her?"

"She is with Tom at a stable in Bury Street, and could be easily brought round to the gates here in two minutes."

"It is well. I may want her. Have you, too, Ogle, kept a horse in town?"

"I have, Captain."

"Perhaps, then, this is providential. I may want my gallant Daisy, for all I can say to the contrary; and whether I do or not, I feel always as if safety were doubly assured when she is close at hand, and at my service."

There was a ring at this moment at the great bell over the iron gates; and upon Ogle and Captain Heron looking from the hall to see who it was, the Captain was well pleased to see Colonel Trelawney, who had arrived with a portly personage, who, he had no doubt, was the chaplain of the Colonel's regiment.

"Ogle," said Heron; "save old Anthony, and walk across the court, and let in those gentlemen. They are friends of mine."

Ogle did so; and the Colonel, with a smile, crossed the court, and ascended the steps of the mansion.

"Permit me," he said, "to introduce my very worthy friend and chaplain, the Reverend Peter Warren."

Captain Heron bowed.

"Your hand, sir," cried the chaplain. "I am right glad to have an opportunity of doing you a service, sir. The Colonel has explained all about it, and I shall not hesitate a moment about performing the ceremony. The man, sir, who would not lend a hand towards the union of a likely young fellow such as you are, and a fair lady, is—a—a——What is he, Colonel?"

"A Dutchman!" said Colonel Trelawney. "I think that both you and I have a bad opinion of the Hollanders, after their conduct at Metz and Spolsburgh, while we were campaigning there."

"To be sure we have—to be sure we have! But I cannot help thinking Lady Castleneau must be an old friend of mine. Upon my life, it is very strange how thirsty I always get upon a wedding!"

The Colonel laughed.

"I assure you, Warren," he said, "that Lady Castleneau has some of the finest old claret in the world, in her cellars!"

"In her cellars!" exclaimed the chaplain. "What is the use of it in her cellars? It should be somewhere else! Ah, it shall be somewhere else!"

The chaplain laid his capacious hand upon his capacious chest, as he spoke; and then followed Colonel Trelawney into the breakfast-room, where the young Earl of Bridgewater was waiting.

The Earl knew the Reverend Peter Warren perfectly well, and greeted him kindly; but in the midst of some account which the chaplain was giving of some campaign he had gone through in Flanders, where, for more than a fortnight, nothing could be got to drink but milk and water, the door of the breakfast-room was opened, and Anthony, who had put on what the old man called his state livery, announced—"The Lady Castleneau!"

Then he took breath, and added—"Miss Edith Tarleton!"

Captain Heron sprang forward, and gently lifting the lace net that covered Edith's face, he kissed her fair cheek.

"My Edith!" he whispered to her.

"Yes, Felix, yours ever and ever!"

"Ever and ever!" responded Heron.

Both the Earl of Bridgewater and Colonel Trelawney made low bows; and then the Reverend Peter Warren, with a loud prefatory "Hem!" took from one of his capacious pockets a large book.

Another moment, and Captain Heron and his Edith were side by side.

The Earl of Bridgewater and Colonel Trelawney took up their situations.

Lady Castleneau burst into tears.

"Dear, dear aunt!" cried Edith; "you do not weep for me! I shall be happy!"

"They are not tears of grief, child; they are of feeling. God bless you!"

"Hem!" cried the chaplain.

All was still.

"Hem! As I am informed by a gentleman, whose word I know I can take, that this young lady, who is the daughter of Sir John Tarleton, one of his Majesty's judges, has received her father's full and free consent to wed with Lord

Warringdale, I have no hesitation in performing the marriage ceremony between these two persons. I am further informed that the proper authorities have without doubt the special license from the Archbishop for the performance of these nuptials in any place, within the period laid down by the Rubric. And, therefore, I shall proceed to unite the Lady Edith Tarleton to Lord Warringdale without hesitation, and in the full belief that I am doing what is right."

No one dissented from all this; and then the chaplain, with another loud "hem!" which might be to intimate how thirsty he was sure to be after the ceremony, proceeded to tie those bands between Edith and Captain Heron, which no man should have power to force asunder.

In seven minutes and a half exactly, Felix Heron and Edith Tarleton were man and wife.

A rich, old, antique, gold ring had been pre-
No. 54.—EDITH.

sented by Lady Castleneau to Heron to put upon the finger of his bride.

The ceremony was over.

Then Edith could control her pent-up feelings no longer, but relieved her heart by a passion of tears; but she looked up at the handsome face of her young husband, and a smile like a gleam of sunshine in the midst of an April shower broke from her lips.

"My Edith," said Heron, "may these be the last tears I shall ever see you shed."

"I can never shed a tear of grief, Felix, while I am assured of your affection."

"Permit me now," said the Earl of Bridgewater, as he took the hand of Edith in his own, and gallantly kissed it,—"permit me to wish you all happiness for many and many a long year."

"And from my heart I too subscribe to that wish," said Colonel Trelawney; "hoping that the long years will prove short by the happiness which will make their days pass swiftly by."

"Hem!" said the chaplain. "I am quite sure that I, too, reciprocate that wish; and I will drink to the health and happiness of the bride and bridegroom in any old claret that Lady Castleneau may think proper to produce."

Lady Castleneau, in truth, did not require so very tangible a hint as this, for she had given full orders to Anthony, and to the girl who waited on her, and the door of the breakfast-room was now flung open, and they appeared loaded with two trays, on which were ample refreshments.

Some of the oldest claret was produced; and when the Reverend Peter Warren tasted it, his eyes began to dilate, and Lady Castleneau was surprised at the sudden friendly manner in which he insisted upon shaking hands with her.

"My dear madam," he said, "have you much of this?"

"Of the wine?"

"Yes, yes."

"Oh, there is a large bin full of it, I think."

"Good gracious!"

"Permit me," said Colonel Trelawney, as he now raised his glass above his head, "to propose health, long life, and happiness, to the bride and bridegroom."

"Hurrah! hurrah!" shouted the Earl of Bridgewater and the chaplain.

Then they all started, for a loud knocking at the front door of the house was heard, which at once overpowered all other sounds.

"What is that?" said the Earl.

"Danger!" cried Captain Heron.

"Oh, Felix! Felix!"

"Nay, dear Edith; all are not lost who are in danger. It is a word I am well accustomed to. Ah, here is my man, Ogle!"

Ogle had dashed into the room without any ceremony, and he cried out loudly and rapidly, "Captain, there is Jonathan Wild in the courtyard, with, I fancy, not less than twenty men at his heels; and one of them has a paper in his hand, which he keeps flaunting about as if it were a flag!"

"The rascal!" said Colonel Trelawney. "He has been to the Secretary of State's office, and got a pursuivant at arms, with a general warrant, to come with him."

CHAPTER CXVII.

HERON AND HIS EDITH FIND DAISY A MOST EFFI-
CIENT FRIEND.

QUITE up to the period of which we write, it had been a custom, which had grown out of the Jacobite persecutions in the two preceding reigns, to send a State messenger, or pursuivant, as he was called, along with the ordinary officers when any important capture had to be made, and more particularly if that capture had about it anything of a political significance.

Defeated and baffled as he had been at Castleneau House, Jonathan Wild, when compelled to leave it in the manner we have recorded, had resolved upon making one grand attempt to overcome all resistance, passive or active, for the arrest of Captain Heron.

The powers of a pursuivant, although not originally great, had yet grown by practice to be so; and in hunting Jesuits and persons suspected of Jacobitical plots, the Government pursuivant had assumed the authority of ordering the arrest of any persons impeding the principal capture—or whom he might think, in his discretion, implicated in the guilt, real or presumed, of the person against whom he proceeded.

The practice of sending such a State messenger was nearly abandoned; and it would be only on the requisition of some person high in authority that one of the under secretaries of state would feel inclined to bring such an officer into action.

Jonathan Wild knew all this very well. His intimate connexion with the Government in the persecutions of what were then called sedition-mongers, let him know exactly what could be done and what could not.

To procure a pursuivant, with the unlimited and arbitrary authority of such an officer, was, Wild saw, the only mode of overcoming the obstacles presented in the way of the capture of Captain Heron, by two such men as the Earl of Bridgewater and Colonel Trelawney.

It would have been a stretch of Wild's authority to take them into custody, but the pursuivant need not hesitate about it for a second; and any resistance to him involved troublesome and serious pains and penalties.

How well Jonathan Wild knew he could take liberties with his friend, the Right Honourable Sir John Tarleton, Baron of the Exchequer; how well he knew that what he, Wild, chose to do in his name, Sir John Tarleton dared not falsify or repudiate.

This, then, was Wild's plan.

He proceeded at once to Whitehall, and saw one of the under secretaries, to whom he pretended he brought a distinct message from Sir John Tarleton, justifying the aid of a pursuivant for the purpose of overcoming resistance to the capture of a dangerous felon at Castleneau House.

Hence was it, then, that he found his way back again to the scene of his defeat, armed with a much larger authority than when he had so precipitately left it.

Wild and his men had contrived to get open the outer gates, and hence was it that they were enabled to make a loud application for admission at the massive front door of the mansion.

It was Colonel Trelawney who now turned to Captain Heron, and in a tone of regret spoke to him.

"The villain Wild has stolen a march upon us, I fear. I do not see that the Earl and myself need acknowledge the presence of a pursuivant until we choose to see him; but as that time cannot be far distant, may it not be possible for you to make your escape?"

"The house is probably surrounded," said Heron; "but neither the pursuivant nor Wild can be in two places at once; and as they are together, one of them will not be able to act without the other."

"Then we will amuse them for a time at the front of the house," said the Earl of Bridgewater, "while you escape by the back."

"And must I indeed," said Heron, "leave you again, my Edith, in this, the first brief hour of our union?"

"No," said Edith, as she clung to his arm; "it must not and shall not be."

"Nay, surely, lady," said Colonel Trelawney, "you would not detain him in such danger! We can and will protect you, but we are powerless to resist authority against your husband."

"I will not detain him," cried Edith. "No Felix, I do not and will not detain you; but I can go with you. Your danger shall be my danger, your flight my flight, your refuge my refuge."

"By heaven! she is right," cried the young Earl of Bridgewater, as he drew his sword; "and were there twenty pursuivants in my path, I would see them off in safety."

"And I too," cried the chaplain. "Did I not charge the Walloons at Metz along with the regiment, Trelawney? and is a rascally pursuivant to stand in our way? I'll excommunicate the knave."

"A thousand thanks, a thousand thanks!" said Heron; "but I think I have a friend near at hand, who, if she once takes charge of me and Edith, will enable us to laugh at Jonathan Wild, and all the force he can bring against us."

"She!" cried Lady Castleneau. "Good gracious! who can that be?"

"Daisy, my gallant steed, who has carried me through so many dangers. Ogle, you know where to find her. Can you manage to take a trot round the garden? Edith, dear one, Daisy has before carried us both, leaving a host of enemies behind us; shall she do it again?"

"With you, Felix, yes—with you anywhere and anyhow."

"Then," said the Earl of Bridgewater, "I shall have a chance of seeing that noble creature which my poor father offered you so large a sum for, and in pursuit of which he really lost his life."

"It was so, my lord," said Heron sadly; "and yet no fault of mine. Ah! I see, Ogle is off. Cheer up my Edith; hope for the best. We shall soon be free."

Ogle had felt the impossibility of getting out of the house by the front door; so, with a brief nod to the occupants of that breakfast-room, he slipt open one of the casements, and was out on to the terrace, and into the garden in a moment.

Jonathan Wild was getting impatient, and was knocking thundering knocks at the outer door; and then they heard him cry out in a yelling voice, "Mr. Pursuivant, do your duty, and I will do mine."

"They will break their way in now," said the Colonel.

No sooner had the words escaped his lips, than a tremendous assault was made against the outer door.

Then a slight accession of colour came to the face of Captain Heron, and twining his arm round the waist of Edith, he said, "Come, then, dearest, since my danger is to be your danger, my safety shall be your safety."

"At once—at once!" cried Edith.

"By heaven, I will see you safe!" said the Earl of Bridgewater.

"It is well to be quick about it," added the Colonel; "for the house is not a fortress, and we must not see the pursuivant, or we are from that moment defenceless. Lady Castleneau, adieu! I

hope to have the pleasure, with my friend Bridgewater, of visiting you in more peaceful times."

"Which we shall assuredly do," said the Earl.

Edith flung her arms for a moment about her aunt, but her heart was too full to speak; and Captain Heron, as he shook the old lady by the hand, could only say, in a voice of much emotion, "I have no words in which to thank you. Should it ever happen that deeds can do, you will then only discover, Lady Castleneau, how deeply and sincerely I feel the part you have taken in promoting the happiness of myself and Edith! Farewell!"

Lady Castleneau could not utter a word; and, in another moment, the party of four had stepped out of the breakfast-room on to the terrace, and from thence made their way into the garden.

It was broad daylight now, and whatever had to be done, or whatever contest had to take place, would have to be beneath the sunlight, which was gleaming with beauty upon every object, and in each moment increasing in intensity and fervour.

Some shouts and cries seemed to be coming from the fields immediately over the wall of Lady Castleneau's garden; and as he heard them, Captain Heron felt confident that there were those without, who would not permit him to leave the place without some contest.

A look of animation came over his face, and his eyes flashed with that fire which was wont to irradiate them at the commencement of any enterprise which promised more danger than usual, or the result of which was important to his honour, or to his feelings.

He spoke hastily to the Earl of Bridgewater and to Colonel Trelawney.

"Gentlemen," he said, "I leave in your care, for a few moments, a treasure I would scarcely leave to the care of any other two men living. Edith, will you remain with these kind and noble friends for a few seconds, while I survey the state of affairs on the other side of the wall?"

"Yes, Felix, yes! But you will not run into needless danger?"

"In truth, I will not."

"Here! here!" cried old Anthony, at this moment running up one of the garden paths, and balancing a ladder of some twelve feet in length upon his shoulder. "Here, Captain Heron, are the means of scaling the wall. It is the ladder I keep to help me in pruning the wall-fruit."

"The very thing!" said Heron. "It gets me over my greatest difficulty."

Even while he spoke, the blows of the assailants at the front door of the house sounded fast and furious, and some slight feeling of surprise came over the mind of Captain Heron that Jonathan Wild should be so long in forcing the door.

It almost seemed as if some *ruse* were intended; but as Captain Heron had ordered Ogle to take Daisy round by the back of the garden wall, he did not feel that he was exactly at liberty to make any change in his intentions.

Both Colonel Trelawney and the Earl of Bridgewater had their swords drawn, and well did Captain Heron know and feel that Edith was as safe under their protection, as though in the inmost recesses of Epping Forest, surrounded by his faithful band.

Heron took the ladder from old Anthony, and

ran with it towards a particular part of the garden wall, which he knew looked over into a part of Bloomsbury Fields close at hand to a small cluster of trees.

He felt that if there were any contest to take place with Jonathan Wild or his myrmidons, that would be by far the best place he could select for the purpose of holding his own against superior numbers.

"Be mindful of yourself," said the Colonel; "they may fire at you."

Captain Heron waved his disengaged hand, to signify that he heard him; and then he placed the ladder against the garden wall, where his weight, as he ascended it, made it sink at least a foot deep in the soft soil.

Another moment, and heedless of all caution, Heron's head and shoulders were above the wall, and he saw at once a sight that would have struck any ordinary observer with dismay.

No less than four of Wild's bull-dogs, as he called them, were upon the spot. They were armed with bludgeons and hangers, but did not seem to have fire-arms; while just at the entrance to the little copse, or cluster of trees, was Ogle on horseback. The reins were hanging on his horse's neck, but the creature stood still, obedient to the wishes of his rider; while Ogle presented with each hand a pistol at Wild's men, who shrunk back, disinclined to be the victims of the first shot.

Standing—actually standing—upon the saddle, immediately behind Ogle, so as to project an arm over each of his shoulders, was Tom Ripon; and he, too, was pointing a pistol in each hand at the janissaries of the thief-taker, who might well hesitate at encountering such a volley.

Captain Heron saw at a glance that the pistols in Tom's hands were the long-barrelled, beautiful weapons from the holsters of Daisy's saddle.

A pang shot across his heart at this moment at the idea that something might have happened to the beautiful, courageous, and docile creature, who for years had been his friend and his companion.

"Daisy! Daisy!" cried Heron. "Where is Daisy?"

This loud call on the part of Captain Heron attracted all eyes towards him.

"All right, Captain," said Tom,—"all right!"

The particular jerk of the head that Tom gave seemed in Heron's apprehension to imply that Daisy was among the trees, where, indeed, she might very well be concealed, since four or five of them grew so closely together as to form a tolerable barrier.

This question, however, of Heron's attracted the attention of Wild's bull-dogs, as well as that of Ogle and Tom Ripon, and they shouted out with one voice, "There he is!—there he is!"

"And do you think," cried the Captain, as he scrambled up on to the top of the wall, "that I am to be hindered by such as you are? Keep them off, Ogle; and fire if they advance another step!"

Tom Ripon now sprung lightly on to the ground, and was about to run into the wood, but Heron called out to him, "The pistols, Tom—the pistols!"

"One for the Captain, and one for Tom," cried the boy, as he ran up to the wall and flung one of he pistols up to Heron, who caught it with diffi-

culty and placed it in his breast. Tom then ran in among the trees, and in a moment after, to the great joy of Heron, he appeared, leading Daisy by the bridle.

Then it was that Felix looked back into the garden, and with pleasure in his countenance, cried out, "Edith, we are saved—we are saved! All is well now. Gentlemen, I thank you from my soul, and will trouble you no further but to assist Edith up to me. Your hand, dearest—your hand! Ah, that is well done! Quick, Tom, quick! Ho! Daisy—my gallant Daisy, we have met again, and the greenwood glade will soon be beneath your feet."

Something between a shout and a cheer burst from Wild's four men at this moment, and both Edith and Heron, following the direction of their eyes, saw, just turning an angle of the garden-wall, Jonathan Wild and the pursuivant approaching at a rapid pace.

"Fire!—fire!" cried Wild. "Shoot him down, you villains, or I will be the death of you!"

But these men were without fire-arms, and had not therefore the power to obey the orders of their savage chief. Encouraged, however, by his presence, and by the assurance that he would be upon the spot, they drew their hangers and made a show of attacking Ogle, who would have fired at them but that he thought the pistols he had loaded might be useful as against Jonathan Wild.

Never, then, was the docility and almost reasoning instinct of Daisy more exhibited than upon this occasion; and when Captain Heron called out to her, "Hither—hither, gallant Daisy! Closer—closer still!" the creature seemed to understand that he wished to get upon her back from the wall, and she got so close to it that he had no difficulty in dropping into the saddle.

"Fling yourself upon me, Edith," he said, "and all will be well."

With a cry of mingled fear and joy, Edith might be almost said to have precipitated herself from the top of the wall into the arms of Heron; who, clasping his left arm about her, held her firmly in front of him.

It was at this moment that Wild thought himself near enough to be mischievous and deadly. He stopped short, and drawing a pistol from his coat pocket he took aim and fired at Heron, heedless now if the bullet struck Edith or not; and had not Daisy swerved at the moment, and made a slight plunge under her double burden, one or the other of these beings, who trusted so much to the love and devotion of each other, might have been mortally wounded.

"Dastardly villain!" cried Heron; "war with me as you will; but that was so foul a shot, that it disgraces even Jonathan Wild!"

Even as he spoke, Felix drew the pistol Tom had thrown to him from his breast, and fired it at Wild, who, with a yell that was awful to hear, fell upon his back, and then rolled over and over upon the grass.

The moment the pursuivant saw this, he turned and ran off with his utmost speed across the fields, heedless of everything in his way, and calling out "Murder!" as loudly as he could; until, having thrust himself through a hedge, he fell into a ditch, where he stuck fast, and still yelled "Murder!"

"Bravo!" shouted Ogle; "we've beat them

CAPTAIN HERON BEARS OFF HIS BIDE IN SAFETY FROM THE MIDST OF HIS FEMIES.

Presented Gratis with No. 54, of the New Edition Edith the Captive; or, the Robbers of Epping Forest.

EACH WEEK IS PRESENTED WITS A COLOURED ENGRAVING.

at last, Captain! Jump up, Tom! That will do!"

Tom was behind Ogle in a moment, and raised as lusty a cheer as he could; and yet Wild's men would probably have attempted to stop the flight of the fugitives, but that Colonel Trelawney and the Earl of Bridgewater had by this time reached the top of the wall, and dropped down into the field, sword in hand.

This reinforcement decided the contest, and Wild's men took to flight.

Captain Heron waved his arm once towards Castleneau House; and the word "Farewell!" seemed to be upon his lips. Another moment, and Daisy was off like the wind, followed by Ogle, who was pretty well mounted, although he could not make the speed that Daisy aspired to, even with her double burden.

CHAPTER CXVIII.

CAPTAIN HERON IS AT HOME UNDER THE GREEN-WOOD TREE.

IT was yet early in the day, when Daisy dashed over a little common that adjoined Epping Forest, and in another moment bounded into one of those beautiful open glades which both she and her master knew so well.

"Welcome, my Edith—welcome," cried Heron, "to your forest home! Here, at least, you will be free as the bounding fawn, and safe from all who would molest you."

"With you, Felix, anywhere!—anywhere with you!"

The sight of the greenwood tree, and the feel of elastic turf beneath her feet, appeared to inspire Daisy with fresh courage, and she dashed along with a speed that seemed to take no heed of the miles she had traversed with the double burden of Edith and the Captain; and then, with two or three graceful bounds, she came to a pause at the borders of a dense shrubbery, and Captain Heron sprang to the ground; but still with one arm he held Edith to the saddle, while he raised a peculiar bird-like cry, which would at any time, in the solitudes of that forest, call his men to his aid.

The cry was answered upon several sides at once; and as if the gigantic trees about had borne such fruit, three of Heron's men dropped from the boughs on to the greensward beneath.

"That is well, my men," said Heron; "you keep good watch and ward. See to the comfort of my gallant Daisy, for to her, this day, I owe my liberty and life—ay, and ten times more than that! Now, my Edith!"

He lifted her gently from the saddle; and then he raised a strange cry, which startled Edith, for it was like that of some wounded bird.

"Be not alarmed," he said, with a smile. "It is but one of our forest calls, and brings the whole of my men about me; and see, yonder, in good time, too, come Ogle and Tom Ripon up the glade. They have not been above a mile behind us."

The peculiar call of Captain Heron was well understood by his band; and in a few moments, from various deep recesses in the forest, they came into the open glade; and as Ogle had now ar-

rived, Captain Heron ran his eye over the assemblage, and saw that all were there. Raising, then, his hat for a moment, he spoke loudly and clearly.

"Comrades and companions, in many an adventure and bold exploit upon the heath and on the road, this lady whom you see with me now beneath the greenwood tree, is my wife. You will respect her, honour her, and obey her, as you would myself. Let her wants, her wishes, and her safety be ever precious to you all, far above my own."

A cheer rang from the band, which echoed far and wide in the whole wood.

Heron bowed slightly, and then taking Edith by the hand, he said, "Come, my Edith; I will show you now your forest home."

In another moment he had plunged with her into the recesses of the darkling wood.

We left our disreputable acquaintance, Jonathan Wild, rolling over in the long grass of Bloomsbury Fields, in anything but a pleasant state of mind.

That the bullet from Captain Heron's pistol had found a lodgment in his brain, Jonathan as fully believed as he believed in the daylight; and certainly the curious injury that had happened to him was highly calculated to convey that impression.

Nothing could stop him for some few minutes, and it was not until two or three of his men actually pounced upon him, and held him still by his arms and legs, that Jonathan's evolutions and contortions on the grass came to an end.

"Mr. Wild! Mr. Wild!" cried one. "What is the matter, sir?"

"I'm killed! I'm killed!"

There was certainly blood upon Jonathan Wild's face, and it seemed to be oozing from his head in a very singular manner; but now, as he sat up, supported by his men, and found that he could look about him much as usual, he began to think that a plug of lead in his brains might not be such a serious inconvenience, after all.

"I'm sure I was hit," he said; "I felt it!"

"Bless me, Mr. Wild!" said the man who had already spoken; "I see how it is. There's a clean furrow right along the top of your head, as if it was half cut in two; but I dare say, sir, in consequence of the hardness and thickness of the bone, it hasn't done any harm."

Wild put up his hand and felt his head—he then felt it with both hands, and shook it to and fro; after which, being satisfied that, with the exception of a furrow right through the scalp to the bone, and a tolerable rub on the bone itself by the passage of the bullet, he was as whole as usual, he scrambled to his feet.

"Wretches! cowards! dolts and beasts!" he cried. "So you've let him escape, have you? I'll hang every one of you next sessions, as sure as you're alive! There shall be stolen property found at all your lodgings, and I'll get people to swear you've committed a dozen highway robberies, each of you!"

"Oh, Mr. Wild!"

"Don't 'Oh!' me! The oaths only cost half-a-crown apiece, and I shan't grudge the money. Where's the pursuivant? I'll apprehend Lady Castleneau, and everybody else I can find in the house!"

"Are you not gone yet, Mr. Wild?" said a voice from over the wall.

Wild looked up, and he saw Anthony seated on the wall, and the head of Lady Castleneau herself just projected over its parapet. But the sight of neither of these persons would have been very alarming to Jonathan Wild, had he not seen likewise, in a direct line with him, there was the muzzle of that carbine of which Anthony had already made use, to the annoyance of Jonathan and his men.

The thief-taker only shook his clenched fist towards the garden; and then, muttering divers original oaths of the most discursive and terrible character, he slowly left the spot, followed by his men.

"I must seek out Lord Warringdale," he said, "and see what can be done."

Wild took his way, with what expedition he could, to his own house in Newgate Street, where, in truth, he was almost a stranger of late; for he had occupied his time so much in hunting Captain Heron, and in carrying out the projects of Sir John Tarleton and Lord Warringdale, that what might be called his ordinary affairs had been much neglected.

Those ordinary affairs of Jonathan Wild's were of a peculiar character, and such as it would be perfectly impossible for any person connected with the modern system of police to carry on; in fact, he was just what he had always accused Mrs. Ripon of being—namely, a "fence," that is, a receiver of stolen goods.

It was quite common for persons whose houses were robbed of portable and valuable property, to forego all thoughts of a prosecution, but to apply to Mr. Wild, who, for a consideration, generally had the means of procuring a restitution of the plunder.

There can be no doubt that he amassed what might be called wealth by this process; and had he not been cut short in his career, as he was, there is no doubt but that he would have become a very worshipful gentleman in the City, where wealth is the only true divinity.

Wild reached his house, however, in no very amiable frame of mind; and it would have fared very bad indeed with those who were in his power, had he not been soon mollified by a circumstance which yet promised him ample revenge, as well as holding out a prospect of large profit.

He had not been in his house above an hour, when one of his men, whose name was Shorts, came to him in a hasty manner, showing evident signs of having made good speed through the streets, for he was liberally splashed with mud.

"Mr. Wild," he said, "I have something to tell you you will like to hear."

"Out with it at once then, idiot," was the sharp rejoinder.

The feelings of Wild's bull-dogs were not very sensitive; and without taking any notice of the unflattering epithet that had been applied to him, the man, with an air of great importance, proceeded with what he had to say.

"I was one of the little party," he said, "you know, Mr. Wild, in Bloomsbury Fields a while ago; and when the pursuivant ran away, and I thought you were shot, I didn't see that I could do anything, so I left the place as quick as I could, and waited round by the wall of Montague

House; when who should come past, talking rather loud together, but the two gentlemen who had come over Lady Castleneau's garden wall."

"My malediction on them!" growled Wild. "But I will be even with them yet. I will take care, by some false testimony, to have them involved in the very next plot that turns up. Oh, yes, my fine Lord Bridgewater—and you, my gallant Colonel Trelawney—you shall rue the day you made an enemy of Jonathan Wild. Now, knave, what more have you to say?"

"Why, Mr. Wild, as they were speaking loud, and I heard them mention your name, I thought perhaps you would like to know what they were talking about."

"Ah, to be sure," cried Jonathan, with an air of interest.

"So, you see, sir, as they had only casually seen me for a moment, it was not likely they would know me, and I dogged their footsteps, keeping near enough to hear what they said."

Wild dashed his hand into his pocket, and pulled out two or three guineas, which the bull-dog was nothing loth to take.

"Now go on," said Wild: "I have oiled your tongue."

"Thank you, sir. It was the young Earl who said to the other gentleman, 'I have promised Heron a card from the Chamberlain's office, for the great Court ball, at which I have advised him to take an opportunity of taking to the King in person a statement of his claim to the Whitcombe peerage.' Then, Mr. Wild, the other gentleman said, 'But won't that be dangerous for him, in case Sir John Tarleton or that villain Wild should hear of it, or see him?'"

"Ha! ha!" cried Wild. "Go on. What next?"

"Why, then, sir, the young Earl said, 'I do not see how that can be, Colonel, for the secret will rest with you, me, and Heron himself. My idea will be to be close at hand when the King receives the petition—so close, indeed, that, as a Privy Councillor, it will be etiquette to hand it to me, so that I shall then be able in a regular way to try and see justice done.'"

"Was that all?" cried Wild.

"Well, sir, that was about all I heard, for the Colonel turned sharp round, and seemed to fancy I was dogging them, and so kicked me at once into the kennel."

Wild clapped his hands together.

"Ha! ha!" he cried. "I have them!—I have them!—I have them now! Shorts, you have done good service, and I will not fail to reward you."

Shorts expressed his acknowledgments, and left Jonathan to himself, who then walked up and down the room, rubbing his hands together with great expressions of delight.

"Yes," he cried, "I have them all now nicely. I will not spoil sport, by giving this information a day or an hour too soon. I will wait till the very evening of the ball at St. James's, and then I fancy I can make a little sensation at the Secretary of State's office. Let me see! I will call it a plot—a Jacobite conspiracy, in which the Earl of Bridgewater and Colonel Trelawney shall be the chiefs, and I will say that this Captain Heron is, under the pretence of presenting a petition to the King, to assassinate him. Ha! ha! This affair shall make a noise. It's a capital thing to have men about me who will swear to anything; and to what he really did overhear, Shorts, for a consideration, will willingly add whatever I please. So, so, my gallant Captain Heron, I have you now! I feel assured I have you now. But what on earth can have become of Warringdale? I feel uneasy about him, for his life is precious to me, inasmuch as how I am to get my bonds and securities, with his name attached to them, paid, unless he become Earl of Whitcombe?"

Wild began to get so uneasy about Lord Warrangdale, that he hastily sent for a hackney-coach, and drove at once to St. James's Street.

At Whitcombe House, he was informed that his lordship had not returned since the preceding evening; and Jonathan 'then sought his companion in iniquity at the suite of chambers on the other side of the way, which Warringdale had occupied during his father's lifetime.

There he found him.

Pale, wretched, and looking more like a spectre than a living man, Lord Warringdale met Wild, and detailed to him how he had been persecuted by the Earl of Bridgewater, and compelled to fight with him.

This was news for Wild,—at the same time, very pleasant news; because the wider apart those against whom he had vowed vengeance stood from Lord Warringdale, the more he, Wild, knew that he could count upon his aid against them.

"I know the young Earl well," said Wild. "He will kill you."

The cheek of Warringdale blanched with fear.

"What shall I do? what can I do?" he said. "Am I never to stir abroad without my sword in my hand, with which to fight this pestilent young noble?"

Wild shrugged his shoulders.

"Come, come, Jonathan," said Warringdale. "You're a man of experience, and can surely tell me what to do."

Wild put on an air of great gravity.

"My Lord Warringdale," he said, "you murdered this man's father!"

"Hush! hush!—oh, hush!"

"He will persecute you to the death."

"Then I must fly the country."

"No."

"But what else? what else can I do?"

"You will trust to me. I will manage all for you. What will you give, if, within one week from this time, I free you from all dread of the Earl of Bridgewater, and include into the bargain his friend Colonel Trelawney?"

"I owe you so much already!"

"I know that; and in order that you shall pay me, you must be Earl of Whitcombe. When that is the case, you will please to recollect that there is a pretty little manor called Rood, close to the Duke of Buckingham's estates, and his great property of Stowe. You will give me that."

"A little property, Mr. Wild! It is as pretty a manor——"

"Well, well," interrupted Wild; "as you please. Fight the Earl, and make an end of it. Kill, or be killed, I care not."

Warringdale drew a long breath, and then in a gasping sort of way, he said, "You shall have the manor—you shall have the manor."

"That'll do," said Wild. "And now tell me, was it you who fired a shot in the garden at Castleneau House?"

"I did. I thought it was at Captain Heron."

"And instead of that, you shot the Judge, your father-in-law that was to be."

"Alas! alas! I seem to get deeper in perplexities each moment of my life, and at times I am almost weary of it."

"And I," said Jonathan, "am weary of sitting so long without wine, since I know you have some of choice vintages in these rooms. Come, my lord, be hospitable."

"Do not speak so loud, Mr. Wild; I've an old man from over the way since my Swiss valet has left me, and although he is half deaf, yet he may hear too much."

Warringdale struck upon a bell, and ordered wine; and Wild had no fear, now, of poison in drinking with the dissipated nobleman.

Jonathan raised a full glass in his hand, and while a hideous grin distorted his features, he said, "Pledge me, my Lord Warringdale! Let us touch glasses, and be of good cheer; for I promise you, as sure as you and I are living men, that I will ruin the Earl of Bridgewater and Colonel Trelawney, and be the death of Captain Heron."

CHAPTER CXIX.

CAPTAIN HERON RETURNS FROM A DANGEROUS EXPEDITION.

IT was on a bright and beautiful morning some few days after the events we have related, that Captain Heron, mounted on Daisy, might have been seen trotting gently down one of the old glades of Epping Forest.

The hour of nine was struck by some distant church clock, and Heron paused as he listened to it.

"It is well," he said. "I have done the journey quickly. Here have I been to Finsbury and back within three mortal hours. And I bring news that will be welcome to my Edith; for Sir John Tarleton, they say, is better of his wound, and likely to recover. So, so, Daisy, you will canter up the old glade as though this swift gallop to London and back again had not touched your speed or strength!"

And, indeed, such seemed to be the case; for although Captain Heron, in order to calm the fears of Edith in regard to the condition of her father, of which he had informed her, had on that early morning himself visited London, the noble creature seemed as fresh and willing as when it started.

"Oh! how lovely is this morning!" cried Heron, as he watched the sunlight playing among the leaves, and heard the ceaseless twitter of the birds, as they flew rustling from bough to bough. "I almost wish I could live for ever in this forest with Edith, and have no thought beyond it!"

Heron had really been upon a dangerous enterprise; for, in order to satisfy Edith that a true account was brought her of the condition of her father, he had actually had the audacity to ride to Finsbury, and with the bridle of Daisy over his arm, to knock at the Judge's door, and get news of his health.

Perhaps the very boldness of this ride brought with it its own safety, for no one thought of looking for Captain Heron, the highwayman, upon whose head was a heavy price, in the solitary horseman who trotted through the City.

Heron now paused, as he was accustomed to do in that forest glade, and at his signal, Ogle, who had been waiting for him, appeared to take charge of Daisy.

"Is the old Judge dead, Captain?" said Ogle.

"No; nor likely to be so."

At this moment Tom emerged from one of the bushes, and calling out to Heron, he asked if he had happened to go round by Little Swallow Street.

"No, Tom," replied Heron; "but I fancy the house was burnt down. Your mother, however, is safe, no doubt, with some neighbour."

"Oh, I dare say, Captain," said Tom, "the old gal is all right! Let me take Daisy, Mr. Ogle. Now, Daisy, there you go again, pulling off my hat! Don't now—don't; you'll tear my jacket!"

Captain Heron smiled as Tom and Daisy went off frolicking together through the bushes; and then turning to Ogle, he said, "On the fourth night from this I have important business in London, but until then I shall pursue my old career upon the road or on the heath. Heaven only knows what may be my fate, for I feel I shall run great risks in following the advice of one in London who is a true friend to me; and as I make no doubt that Edith's fortune is already, or will be, entirely dissipated by her father, I would fain do what I can, in case of accident to me, to leave her well provided. I will go upon the road to-night, Ogle."

"Bravo, Captain! There's nothing like it!"

"Numbers One, Two, Three and Four of our men must remain here as scouts to guard the approaches to the forest, and to conduct Edith to the most secret recesses of the old foundations of Hinchcliffe Manor, in case of danger."

"Then I go with you, Captain?"

"Assuredly."

"I feared not; but since that's the case, it's all right. What road do we take?"

"I am scarcely decided; but I think of riding across the country to the Western Road, and I think, after all, it is best if we cry 'Stand!' to a traveller, that it should be as far away from here as possible. So we will say the Western Road; there should be some sport, Ogle, on Ealing Common?"

"To be sure!" said Ogle; "unless you like to ride over to Barnes, and try the gentry as they come from Kew and the Royal Lodge at Richmond."

"Be it so, then, Ogle. See that all is in readiness, and let my band follow me. When the sun dips below the trees we will be off, and by midnight we may be back again amid the shadows of old Epping Forest."

Captain Heron dived down an excessively narrow path in the midst of some luxuriant underwood. It was a path that would lead him to that portion of the old ruined manor of Hinchcliffe, which he and his men had long since made habitable, and where Edith was anxiously expecting him.

"No, no!" he said, in a low tone, as he pushed aside the overhanging branches which impeded his progress,—"no, no! she shall not know that I am going upon the road, and so will be spared many an anxious thought. I will not tell her. And yet, for a time, what can I do but continue my old adventurous life, with all its perils and all its pleasures. I may fall; but I would fain, if such should be the case, that Edith, even if she return to her aunt, Lady Castleneau, should not do so as a needy claimant on her bounty. Yes, the road—the road again for me! And come what may, at least for the sake of those brave hearts who have clung to me through so many strange adventures, I will yet do something which shall place means at their command."

It was probably as much that he required some relief of a violent and exciting character from the restlessness that beset him, which induced Captain Heron, for the few days which were to intervene before he could avail himself of the kind offer of the Earl of Bridgewater, to take to the road.

It has been formerly stated that during the time he and his band had occupied Epping Forest he had succeeded in accumulating a considerable sum, which he intended expressly to make use of for the purpose of attempting to substantiate his birthright; but Captain Heron had a liberal hand, and he had made up amply to his men for the dearth of profitable adventures of late by dispensing large sums among them.

Hence it was that he had widely scattered this fund, since he had not seen his way to use it in a mass, in consequence of the treachery of the attorney, with whom it will be recollected he had some interviews in the Temple.

It could not be, however, that Edith should fail to observe that there was some pre-occupation in the mind of Heron; and when the twilight was near at hand, and he told her gently that probably he would be absent until past midnight, she more than guessed his purpose.

But she sought not to dissuade him from it. She had a faith in him, which went the length of making her believe that for what he wished to do, there must be all-sufficing reasons.

"You will not run into danger, Felix," she said, "for my sake!"

"Indeed, I will not; and be assured that you will see me return even as I go forth—although, perchance, somewhat the richer."

This was so open an acknowledgment of what he meant to do, that Edith felt it to be equal to a distinct statement of the subject; and so, when the twilight came, she let him go, and watched his fading form as it disappeared through the mazes of the forest.

But Edith had made her resolves likewise, and what they were we shall quickly perceive.

CHAPTER CXX.

CAPTAIN HERON MEETS WITH A STRANGE ADVENTURE AND AN OLD FRIEND.

IN one of the prettiest glades of the old forest of Epping, while there yet lingered sufficient of twilight to let each man dimly see his neighbour's face, Captain Heron and his band assembled.

With the exception of the four men whose duty it was to remain as scouts in the different outlets

of the forest, the whole of the band was present, marshalled by Ogle, who it was generally understood acted on these occasions as a sort of lieutenant to Captain Heron.

Most reluctantly, Tom Ripon was persuaded to remain behind; and he and Mrs. Ogle were the only persons who were in the ruins of the old Manor House with Edith.

There was no cheer as Captain Heron made his appearance in that forest glade, for caution and silence were habitual characteristics of the men who followed his fortunes.

And now as the last rays of twilight seemed to draw away, or be condensed amidst the dense foliage of the trees; horses, men, accoutrements and costume blended together in an indistinguishable mass of a dull grey colour.

From the damp ground, a faint floating vapour had arisen, which, by gathering around Captain

Heron and his band, gave them all a strange spectral looking appearance.

Heron spoke in those slow measured accents which he usually used in addressing his followers beneath the greenwood tree.

"This is no special expedition," he said; "we go upon old Barnes Common to seek our fortune. Too much, I am well aware, my gallant friends and comrades, have I been absorbed of late, in matters near and dear to my affections and my fortunes, but yet, until greater changes ensue, I am the same Captain Heron, of Epping Forest, who has led you into many an adventure, which has filled your pockets. Follow me now, and between this time and midnight we are as we used to be, knights of the road."

Strange cries, in imitation of the various birds who inhabited the forest, came from Heron's band, and as he stooped with Daisy beneath the overhanging branches of a majestic oak, and then, at a rapid trot, made his way down the forest glade, the band followed him two and two, until, at the turn of a copse, they came upon a shady lane which wound round a hollow, and crossing a little stream, led them to the high road to London. Heron then paused a moment, and Ogle trotted up to his side.

"Disperse the band, Ogle, in the usual way," he said, "or we shall scare our prey before us, instead of entrapping it."

"All's right, Captain. What's to be the word to-night?"

"Starlings. All who use that pass-word go free. We are gentlemanly thieves, Ogle, and rob but once."

Ogle laughed, and went to give the necessary directions to the band; and then, as if by magic, they seemed to melt away, some riding on in advance, and some lingering in the rear of Ogle and Heron.

And yet, a few sharp calls in the peculiar fashion of the party, would quickly have brought the scattered force together, for any enterprise requiring strength, or to carry off a wounded comrade, or prevent any single one, or even two, from being unexpectedly overpowered and captured.

This was the way, in fact, in which Captain Heron and his men took systematic possession of a road or heath; so that no traveller or carriage that was worth the stopping could by any possibility escape them; and who ever was once stopped and made pay toll upon the road, was told the password for the night, so that he might pass unquestioned by all the rest of the band.

And now, seeming to be all alone, although in reality so well guarded and surrounded, Captain Heron and Ogle trotted briskly onward to town, like two gentlemen returning to London from their country house.

"It's cheering, Captain," said Ogle, "to be once again beneath the night sky on an expedition like this."

"It is," said Heron. "And yet, Ogle, I have matters on my mind that occupy it much; and there is one thing that I must adventure, and would even now at once, but that I feel assured it would be suspected by my enemies, and I should be waited for in force."

"What is that, Captain?"

"It is the rescue of Sir Dominick Browne from his bondage in that asylum at Highgate, if he be still there; and then again, from all the varied information I can collect, the conviction forces itself upon my mind, hour by hour, as I live, that the Countess of Whitcombe must be still in life."

"Who is that?" said Ogle, with surprise.

"My poor mother."

"A thousand pardons, Captain! Of course, if you are the son of the late Earl of Whitcombe, your mother was his countess."

"I am as certain," said Heron, elevating his hand,—"I am as certain that she was married to him as that there are stars in heaven!"

At that moment, even as if Captain Heron's words had invoked the presence of some bright constellation, a drift of clouds floated away, and brightly and clearly shone out some brilliant stars, as though they would have borne witness at once and for ever to the truth of his words.

"By heavens, Captain," said Ogle; "I would go through fire and water, and back again, to help you in this matter! What was the lady's name before she was married to the Earl?"

Captain Heron involuntarily touched the bridle of Daisy, and the obedient creature came to a halt. He then passed his hand abstractedly across the silken mane of his gallant steed, as he said in a voice of deep emotion, "Her name, Ogle?—her name was Amelia Staunton."

At that moment, a shrill, half-screaming voice startled both Heron and Ogle, and made even Daisy give a sudden leap that would have unhorsed a less skilful rider.

"Who speaks of Amelia Staunton?" cried a shrill voice. "Stand, that I may know if you be friend or foe to her who has suffered cruel wrong."

From a cluster of brushwood, that had at one time been connected with Epping Forest, and, in fact, was now a kind of straggling suburb of it, there darted a ragged, wild-looking figure, bearing in its hand a long, forked bough of a tree; and while the rags which fluttered around the emaciated form seemed almost to float away in the light evening air, she cried out again, "Who speaks of Amelia Staunton beneath the chesnuts and acorns of old Epping Forest? It was not here they tore her from her home to a living death!"

"Gracious heavens!" said Ogle. "Who is that?"

"Poor creature!" said Heron. "Do you not know her? We, who have been long in the forest, call her the 'Maniac of the Well.' Her son suffered on the triple-tree, and she accuses Hanging Judge Tarleton of his death. Good mother, do you not know me?"

"Ah, yes," cried the poor maniac, "I know you now. But you are like the rest, cruel—cruel—cruel!"

"I cruel?"

"Yes. I begged you not to call me that; for I have no son now, and am no mother. I should die, you see, but I have to beat away the ravens from his eyes; and I am bound, you see, to outlive Judge Tarleton. I am to see him die, too: and were he thousands of miles off, at his last hour he would be brought to me, or I should be taken to him, on a cloud by the night-wind, or on the far-reaching black wings of the storm."

"Here is money for you," said Heron. "Get better clothing, and food, and fire."

"Stop! Hush! Did you hear it?"

"Hear what?"

"There was a voice in the forest, and it whispered the name of Amelia Staunton."

"Alas, it was my voice!"

"No, no! What know you, or what care you, for Amelia Staunton? Woe, woe is me! We think of our own griefs, and forget those of others! You see, it was before my boy was doomed to death by the wicked Judge——Farewell, farewell! heaven speed you, brave heart! Should you see a vulture stooping low, and with its carrion bill seeking for its prey, will you kill it?"

"Indeed I will."

"That is well—that is well! Ha! ha! I can laugh now, for that is well! That one will not peck my poor boy's eyes out, and I can fight with all the rest! Yes, with all the rest—with all the rest!"

With wild laughter and maniacal screams, she fled raving into the wood.

"Tell me, Ogle, I pray you," said Captain Heron, "what is your thought of this matter? Was the repetition of the name I uttered but the mere raving of insanity, or some dim recollection of the past?"

"In good faith, Captain," said Ogle, "it is hard to say, but she had it pat enough."

"I will seek her, and question her," said Heron, "ere four and twenty hours be over my head. Let us push on now, Ogle, for the night wanes fast, and the highwayman's time, you know, expires at midnight; for after that time, you know, the birds that are abroad are not worth the plucking."

"That's true, Captain. On we go!"

Captain Heron and Ogle, in half an hour's active trot, now found themselves on the verge of Barnes Common, and there they found the same white mist which had been gathering up in the neighbourhood of Epping Forest.

It could not be called a fog, but yet it was sufficient to give every object a shadowy uncertain aspect.

"We shall be puzzled to-night, Ogle," said Heron, "to see who and what it is we cry 'Stand!' to."

"Not for long, though, Captain—not for long. There's a young moon. I'll be bound, the moment it gets above the tree tops, this mist will take itself off at once. Only look how clear the stars look down out of the rifts."

"You are right, Ogle. We shall have a clear night, although that is not exactly what a highwayman looks for. For, like a hunter, you know, what we want is a clear air, but a cloudy sky."

"There's the moon," cried Ogle.

There came a faint stream of clear, white light over the common, as a crescent moon just slightly showed itself over a distant clump of trees. And then, as Ogle had predicted, the white mist began to roll off and disappear, as if those cold, faint moonbeams had consumed it.

A bat took its headlong flight within a hand's breadth of the heads of Ogle and Captain Heron; and from a shrubbery at a little distance there came the faint hoot of an owl.

"Ah, now, indeed," said Captain Heron, "I see we shall have a fair and pleasant night! The owl is on a mousing expedition, and the bat is abroad—sure signs of fair weather."

"Hush, Captain! Do you hear nothing?"

Heron paused and listened.

"Yes," he said,—"the regular trot of horses' feet."

"And the wheels of a carriage," said Ogle. "Your humble servant, Captain. I suppose you take this adventure to yourself?"

"Yes; it is not worth while troubling more than one. I think they come along the highway, across the Common. Ah! to be sure. I see the lights now, as they mount a rise in the ground. Why, what is the meaning of that? There goes one light, and there goes the other."

"Well," said Ogle, "that's a strange manœuvre, to put out your carriage lamps at the moment you come to the dreariest and darkest portion of the road."

"It's for a purpose," said Captain Heron; "but be they whom they may, I will bring them to a standstill. Wait here, Ogle, and keep clear of the road. I see the carriage is on the highway across the Common. Ho, Daisy!—forward, my gallant Daisy! This is some of our old work."

Daisy shook her head so as to produce a pleasant jingle of her bit and reins, and then darted forward, covering an immense space of ground in a few strides, or what might be called leaps, in the direction of the carriage.

That there was something strange and mysterious about this carriage, that was so rapidly approaching to meet him on the road across the Common, Captain Heron could not but believe, for it seemed so unaccountable a thing to put out the carriage lamps at a time when any one would imagine they were most needed.

There was not much time for reflection, however, upon the subject, and Captain Heron had but just time to rein up a little out of the direct course of the vehicle before it reached him.

He adopted, then, a course which generally brought a coachman or a postilion to a standstill.

"Hold!" he cried, in a loud voice, "or you are a dead man!"

Ninety-nine drivers out of a hundred would have involuntarily pulled up at such a summons, from sheer alarm and doubt, and uncertainty as to where the danger lay, or what it was. The habit, likewise, of obeying prompt and loudly uttered orders would go some way towards inducing an instant stoppage of the horses on the part of the coachman.

It was that involuntary and sudden stoppage which Captain Heron was in the habit of taking advantage of, and when alone on those occasions he invariably made a dash at the horses' heads and turned them off the road, so that they were at right angles with the vehicle which they had been drawing; but in the present instance, the driver of this carriage must have had some peculiar motive for resisting a command to stop, and he made an instant attempt to lash on his horses to increased speed.

"Ah!" cried Heron, "then you will cast away your life. The act is yours, not mine."

Rapidly drawing one of the holster pistols from the saddle, Captain Heron fired, but he was quite sure that the bullet went not within killing distance of the coachman, who then immediately pulled up, crying out, somewhat to the surprise of Captain Heron, "I give it up, my lord—I give it up! I'm a poor fellow, and only obey orders!"

Not knowing what to make of this address, Heron dashed up to the horses' heads, and carried out his practice of turning them aside, so that the fore-wheels of the carriage ran under its body, and the vehicle could by no means be suddenly started again.

"Keep your seat," cried Heron fiercely to the coachman, "or the next shot may indeed be fatal."

"I will, my lord, I will."

"What on earth does he mean," said Heron to himself, "by 'my lording' me?" But all speculations with regard to the strange conduct of the coachman were quickly put an end to, by the still stranger conduct of some one who was riding in the carriage.

This person, who seemed, in the imperfect light of the young moon, to be a tall, slender, gentlemanly-looking young man, suddenly dashed open the door of the carriage, and sprang right into the roadway. In his hand he held his drawn sword, and turning to face Captain Heron, he put himself on his guard, crying out as he did so, "Now, my Lord Belessis, we will fight it out like gentlemen— if indeed, after your conduct, you deserve to be called by such a title! Dismount, sir, and draw your sword, and I will rid Lady Cleveland of her worst foe! Dismount, sir, and come on!"

Captain Heron could see the long glittering sword-blade of this mysterious young man, shining in the moonlight, which seemed to concentrate itself upon the bright steel; and although the tones in which the stranger spoke were high and passionate, there was a something about them which rang familiarly upon the ears of Captain Heron.

"Stand, Daisy, stand," he said, as he instantly dimounted; and drawing his sword, he added, "Sir, I know not why you give me a name and title which do not belong to me. I am no Lord Belessis, and have nothing to fight out with you, except you feel inclined to defend your purse—for I am one who cries out upon the highway, 'Stand and deliver!'"

It seemed that the young stranger hardly heard these words, for his attention was at the moment directed towards the coach. from which, to the further surprise of Heron, there now sprang a young lady, who, clasping the arm of the passionate young gentleman, cried out, "Oh, no, no! Let there be no bloodshed on my account. My Lord Belessis, you have no right to interfere with my actions."

"What on earth do you both mean," said Heron good humouredly, and lowering the point of his sword, "by calling me Lord Belessis?"

Blinded by passion, however, the young gentleman had rushed forward, and made a furious pass at Heron, by which they came almost face to face.

"Come, young sir, be careful, be careful. If I were a hasty man, now, I might do you an injury."

"Good heavens!" cried the young gentleman, at this moment, as he tore a half mask that he wore from his face, and cast it to the ground. "Good heavens, it is Captain Heron!"

The pale moonlight fell upon the face of the passionate young stranger; and, to his intense surprise, Captain Heron recognised him to be none other than his new and impulsive young friend, the Earl of Bridgewater.

But the young lady, who knew nothing of Captain Heron, only saw, or fancied she saw, a struggle for life and death taking place; and then she screamed aloud for help, when it suddenly seemed to occur to her that she could help herself; and springing back to the coach, she took from it a pistol, which she levelled at Captain Heron's head, and instantly discharged.

The ball passed through Heron's hat; but an inch lower, and it would have plunged into his brain.

"Harriet! Harriet!" cried the Earl of Bridgewater, "if you have another shot, let it be at me; for this gentleman is one of my best friends!"

"Oh, wretched me!" cried the young lady; "and I have killed him!"

"By no means, madam," said Heron; "you only tried to do so. Believe me, it is always desirable to look twice, and listen at least once, before sending a bullet upon its errand."

The young lady burst into some hysterical weeping.

"Nay, there is no harm done," cried Heron. "My Lord Bridgewater, you can easily believe that I had not the slightest idea this vehicle was yours, or it would have passed unmolested by me. You are on some business, I see, of secrecy and importance. Pray accept from me a thousand excuses, and let me place your horses right upon the road again."

"Good heavens!" cried the Earl of Bridgewater, "this is the strangest encounter I could possibly have looked for. Harriet, this is the gentleman I spoke of to you; and who, from my soul, I believe has a veritable right to the Earldom of Whitcombe. Nay, my dear girl, do not be terrified; but get into the coach again in peace. We have found a friend instead of a foe; although, perhaps, we have lost precious time. Captain Heron, do you think you can hold this road for half an hour?"

Heron smiled. "My Lord Bridgewater," he said, "I mean to hold it till midnight; and if you would pass over the heath without further inconvenience, which I trust and hope you will, please to call out as a watchword, 'Starlings,' to any one who may oppose your progress."

"Till midnight, say you? Dear Harriet, then we are safe; for if pursued by Belessis, he will surely come this way."

"Who is this Lord Belessis, you took me for?" said Heron. "And yet no—forget that I asked you, my lord; for I will not detain you so long as to answer me."

"Nay," said the young Earl, "I can tell you in a moment, if you will allow me to do so from the coach window, so that we can be off if we hear the tramp of horses' feet; for I do not court a contest with the man, since he stands in an invidious kind of relationship to this young lady, who is the only daughter of the Countess of Cleveland. We have been long attached; and but that my father has made a large excavation into the Bridgewater property by his unfortunate speculations on the turf, the Countess would have had no objection to our marriage, for she is poor as Job herself."

"Oh, listen — listen!" said the young Lady Cleveland—"I think I hear pursuers!"

"No," said Heron. "Trust to me, madam, there is nothing yet upon the road."

"Dear Harriet!" said Lord Bridgewater, "I am the most thoughtless fellow alive; for here, without your consent, I was telling all your story!"

"Oh, let it all be told," she said, "to any friend of yours. Besides, this gentleman who is going to help us, has a right to know."

"He has. You must know, Heron, that the Countess of Cleveland was brought up at the Court of Versailles, where she imbibed some of its lax notions of morals; and we—I mean Harriet and myself—have the best reason to know that, in combination with Lord Belessis, whom she has recently married, she was speculating upon the beauty of her own child with the highest personage at the Court of St. James's."

"Alas! alas!" said the young Lady Cleveland.

"And so you see, Heron, this is an elopement from Kew to-night; and we expect to be pursued by Lord Belessis, and probably some companions of his."

CAPTAIN HERON FALLS INTO THE HANDS OF HIS ENEMIES.

Presented Gratis with No. 55 of the New Edition of Edith the Captive; or, the Robbers of Epping Forest.

EACH WEEK IS PRESENTED GRATIS A COLOURED ENGRAVING.

" I sincerely hope so," said Captain Heron.

" You hope so ?" exclaimed Lady Harriet Cleveland.

" Yes, madam ; because, from what my Lord Bridgewater has just told me, there is no man whom I shall have greater pleasure in crying ' Stand !' to, to-night, than this same Lord Belessis. Pass on in safety—the road is mine; and if he follow you one inch beyond this spot, it will be over all that shall remain of Captain Heron, the highwayman !"

" Oh, listen—listen again !" cried Lady Harriet.

" Yes," added Heron. " Now, you are right, madam ; there are horses on the road. Good night—good night, my lord! Good night !"

" We meet on Saturday," cried Lord Bridgewater.

" Most surely, if I am alive."

" Good night, then, and good fortune attend you."

The carriage dashed forward, and Captain Heron was once more alone upon that road across the Common. Daisy had waited for him still as a statue; and now, as he heard the rapid sound of horses' feet approaching, he sprang lightly to the saddle, and placing one hand to his mouth, he hooted through it in imitation of an owl, and the sound echoed dismally far and wide over the whole common.

CHAPTER CXXI.

CAPTAIN HERON MAKES A RICH BOOTY BEFORE MIDNIGHT.

HARDLY had the sound which Captain Heron made as a signal to his men partially died away upon the night air, when, as if they had risen like spectres out of the very ground, or as if the pale moonbeams had consolidated into men and horses, there dashed up to the spot ten mounted men.

One was somewhat in advance of the rest, and he called out briefly, " Starlings signal, I take it, Captain ?"

" Yes, Ogle—yes, my men. Here are horsemen coming on the road, and I have pledged my word that not one of them shall pass a line which we will take up here in the roadway. They should be men with pockets well lined."

The band received the intelligence in silence ; and then, as if each man, by some intuition, knew his place, they ranked up across the roadway.

The sound of approaching horsemen, now, was so distinct and clear, that it was evident they would be in a few moments in sight.

" Follow me, Ogle," said Heron. " We can fall back if we find them too many for us."

" All right, Captain! I am with you."

At an ordinary trot the Captain and Ogle now went forward ; and they soon saw the dusky forms of some seven or eight horsemen coming along the road at a swinging trot. They seemed all to be talking together ; and there could be no doubt that they were the persons in pursuit of the young Earl of Bridgewater ; for his name, and that of the Countess of Cleveland, and Lady Harriet, flew from mouth to mouth.

They were, in fact, the dissolute set of gamblers and roués who were wont night after night to assemble either at the Countess of Cleveland's Lodge at Kew or her town house, to fleece each other, or any unwary man of fortune whom they could get into their clutches.

" Halt!" cried Captain Heron; and the word was uttered in such a tone, that every horseman drew rein, and the loud conversation ceased in a moment.

" I want to know," added Heron, " if Lord Belessis is here ; for if so, I have something to say to him ?"

" I am Lord Belessis," cried one of the horsemen as he spurred forward ; " and who may you you be, scoundrel, who dares to cry halt on the King's highway ?"

" Oh, my lord," cried Heron, " you need not have named yourself, for your manner of speech would have at once proclaimed you to be who and what you are—Lord Belessis, poltroon and villain."

" S'death, my lords, are we to put up with this ?" cried Belessis. " Cut the fellow down."

" No," said Heron as he drew his sword, " I want to know. my Lord Belessis, what you will do, if I can bring you face to face with the young Earl of Bridgewater ?"

" Ah! that's another thing. Perhaps, my friend, you were only repeating something that he had said. Only bring us up to him, and two of my kind friends, here, will hold him tight, while I pass my rapier through his heart."

" Bravo ! bravo !" cried several of Belessis' companions. " Bravo! that's the way to do it !"

" I regret, my lord," added Heron, " that I cannot in myself fulfil all the conditions you would impose upon the Earl, because I stand here as his substitute ; and if you do not alight and fight with me at once, I proclaim you a cowardly ruffian, and faint-hearted bully."

Lord Belessis had a straight cavalry sword by his side, and without a word of warning he made a slash at Heron with it ; but the quick eye of the Captain was upon him, and one touch to Daisy cleared him from the passage of the sword.

For a moment, now, Heron was on one side of the way, and Ogle on the other ; so that the seven horsemen of whom Lord Belessis was one, had an opportunity of sweeping past them, of which they instantly availed themselves.

" Let them go," said Heron quietly—" the band will stop them ; and I am averse to use firearms, as it is clear they have none."

" Yes," said Ogle, " or they wouldn't be half so scrupulous."

There can be no doubt that Lord Belessis and his companions thought that they had got over the obstructions on the roadway, and that there would be no further difficulty in their pursuit of the Earl of Bridgewater, since the road into town was long and tedious, even after passing the Common ; and our readers will recollect that the line of road from Barnes to Hammersmith over the Suspension Bridge had no existence, nor was a bridge at that part of the river dreamt of at the period of our tale.

But all too soon for their equanimity did the vicious roysterers from Lady Cleveland's Lodge at Kew come upon Captain Heron's men ; and the calm, stern attitude of the band from Epping

Forest seemed as alarming to Lord Belessis as if he had suddenly come upon a battery of great guns.

The seven gamblers, courtiers, and *rouès* turned to fly in the opposite direction again; but there they were immediately met by Captain Heron and Ogle; and the latter materially added to the panic, by calling out, "You are my prisoners! and I will pistol the first man of you who attempts to make his escape!"

"We give up! we give up!" cried one. "What do you want of us? And who, in the name of all that's desperate and dangerous, are you?"

"Ogle," said Heron, "you and your comrades can see to these fellows. My business is with Lord Belessis alone."

Ogle was well pleased with the part of the business that fell to his lot; and, assisted by a couple of the band, he quickly relieved the whole seven horsemen of a considerable sum of money in the aggregate, since they were all notorious gamblers, and carried their capital about them.

They were, however, with a few exceptions, profligate men of title; so that Ogle got possession likewise of several valuable watches, rings, and brooches.

Heron stood aside calmly, waiting until this little part of the business was concluded; he then called out aloud, "My Lord Belessis, since you informed me that it was your intention to have the young Earl of Bridgewater held fast by two of your companions, while you plunged your sword into his heart, it has become my fixed resolve to fight with you!"

"No! no!" said Belessis. "I did not mean it."

"In truth," added Heron, "I can scarcely believe that even among your associates you would have found one or two who would have aided you in such a murder. Therefore, I challenge you to a fair fight on equal terms."

"No, I will not fight. I have been stopped on the highway and robbed. Surely, that is sufficient!"

"Will you proclaim yourself a coward, then, and permit your own sword to be broken above your head?"

"No, never! I dare not! I could not live! But yet I am a gentleman and a nobleman, and I may not demean myself by crossing swords with a highway robber!"

"Are you a peer, my lord?"

"No—but my brother is a Scotch peer."

"Then I am more than your equal; and as a peer of England, I challenge you. Doubt my word, and it is an offence so deadly that your blood alone can atone for it!"

"I see," cried Belessis, as he alighted from his horse, "that I must fight with you. I take you all to witness, gentlemen, that if I am killed, it is a murder, and no fair fight!"

"My lord," said Heron, "the unfairness of the fight consists in your sword being a much more formidable weapon than my own; but I waive the objection. Draw, and come on! Defend your worthless life, or you will lose it!"

Lord Belessis drew his sword with much more alacrity than Captain Heron had expected; and as the weapons clashed together, the dissolute companions of the noble cried out in various tones, "Press him home, Belessis!" "Don't give way,

my lord!" "Give him the double thrust!" "Keep the high ground!" "Cut him down!" and such like encouragements; but they did not seem to have a favourable effect upon the issue of the contest, as regarded Lord Belessis; for, with a sudden cry, he dropped his sword, and fell to the ground.

"I am a dead man!" he cried: "the villain has killed me!"

Heron kept on his guard with some degree of surprise; for although he had made a vigorous thrust at Belessis, he had fancied it a failure, and that his sword point had only perforated one of the lappels of his coat.

"It's murder," cried the companions of the discomfited Scotch noble.

"No, gentlemen," said Heron, "it is not murder. It seems I am the victor, and such being the case, I dictate terms to you; and if you do not pick up your wounded friend, and be off at once on the road whence you came, I will order my men to fire upon you; for I will not tolerate your presence longer upon the Common."

This threat was of a sufficiently alarming character to have its full effect upon the companions of Lord Belessis; and they picked him up, notwithstanding all his heavy groanings, and placed him on his horse; then turning without a word, they all galloped off towards Kew. But there was a suspicious stop on the part of one of them, and then there ensued the sharp report of a pistol, which proved that one of them at least had firearms, if the others were unprovided with them.

"I am hit," cried one of Captain Heron's men. "Help! help me, some one, from the saddle. I am hit."

"A most treacherous shot," cried Heron. "I will, indeed, avenge it. Forward, my men. We will have them yet."

The distance travelled in a short space of time by tolerable horses, and going at full gallop, is incredibly great; so that before Captain Heron and his band had actually started into motion, Lord Belessis' party must have been at least half a mile ahead.

In the excitement of his feelings, however, Captain Heron did not calculate that he was so much better mounted than any of his band; and it was not until he had cleared the heath, and was on rather a narrow roadway that skirted the village of Mortlake, that he found he was leaving his men far behind him.

He then brought Daisy to a standstill at the corner of a winding lane which came out again about a mile and a half forward into the high road.

"Pass on—pass on," he cried, "and keep on their track. I will take Daisy at speed by the lane, and confront them; for I will have the man that fired that shot."

"All right, Captain," cried Ogle; "I will come with you."

"No, no, don't scatter,—your horse can't do it; I shall only leave you in the lane. Forward, forward!"

The band swept on, and Captain Heron, for a moment, stooping low in the saddle, seemed almost to be whispering his wishes to the ears of Daisy, who, then, at a tremendous pace, swept up the lane.

This lane was one of those narrow beautiful,

sylvan roads, which are to be found in such abundance in England, and in no other country under the sun. They are the small veins of communication, so to speak, which connect the farm-houses, homesteads, villas and mansions of so densely a populated country as our own, with the main arteries of communication, the high roads.

Tall trees in the hedge, now, stretched their branches right over the way; and in many cases Captain Heron had to stoop low, or his head would have struck against the low-arching of the green canopy above him.

There did not seem to be a living thing in this lane but himself and his horse; or if there were, it was but the timid hare, which cowered aside out of the path, or some startled bird, who half fell from its perch, as the rushing apparition of man and horse passed beneath it.

At such a speed, the lane, which was possibly a mile and a half in length, was traversed almost before a thought could be given to the distance; and out at once, into the high road, again dashed Captain Heron upon a broad patch of moonlight that fell upon its surface.

He was not a moment too soon, for almost at the instant that he appeared, he heard the clatter of horses' feet, but it was a clatter that puzzled him, for at the moment he could not decide in his own mind from whence it came. At first, as he stood in the middle of the road with Daisy in bold and clear relief, in that patch of moonlight, he thought the sounds came from his right, as he expected they would, since that way lay the road from the Common; and then, again, they seemed to come directly from his left hand.

"Can one of these tramping sounds," he said, "be but the echo of the other?"

This was a possible solution of the mystery; but a much more commonplace one soon presented itself; for two parties of horsemen, one in each direction, came at a brisk trot upon the road.

Then Captain Heron felt that his position was untenable, and like a man between two fires, he would fain have retreated in any direction that lay open to him; and there would have been the lane along which again Daisy would have carried him fleetly and safely, but unfortunately he had trotted about a hundred yards from its entrance towards London; and the horsemen, who were advancing from the country, passed the narrow opening before he could regain it.

High banks, with luxuriant hedge-rows above them, were on each side of the road—escape was impossible. For one moment, a pang of anguish came across the heart of Captain Heron; and then he made up his mind to do just what might have been expected from so brave a spirit.

He resolved to fight his way, sword in hand, through one or other of the group of horsemen that were approaching.

But, for once in his life, Captain Heron was undecided in an emergency. He had his choice, either to fight through the troop of horsemen who were coming from the country, and so regain the lane; or to make a dash at Lord Belessis' party, and effect a junction with his own men.

Both these plans presented advantages. He might take the strange horsemen by surprise, and so get through them easily; in fact, having no motive so to do, they might not even strive to detain him; but then there would surely be a battle between his band and both parties; and what an anxiety and pang it would be to him not to be present! Should he be galloping down a lane, while his faithful followers were, perchance, engaged in deadly conflict?

No; that thought decided him. He turned at once, and pursued the party of libertine nobles, whom he had eased of their purses on the Common, and who would know him well.

With his sword drawn, he charged forward, and in another moment was among them.

The shout they raised at the sight of him—for they could but dimly see him—must have reached the ears of the other party of horse; but Heron would have fought his way through gallantly, only that his sword-blade, in consequence of striking against some hard substance, he could not tell what, was shivered. Half a dozen hands were immediately upon him, and some one clung round his waist with desperate energy, shouting out, "Ha! ha! I have him—I have him! I shall live to see this fellow hung! I have him now! Hilloa! Gentlemen, welcome, whoever you be! Help us to secure a desperate highwayman!"

Captain Heron fought furiously, and blows rained thick and fast upon him. The other party of horsemen from the country at once surrounded the fighting group, and Heron was a prisoner.

Then it was Lord Belessis who cried out, "Whoever you are, gentlemen, a thousand thanks, for you have helped us to capture a notorious highwayman. I myself have had a desperate conflict with him!"

"And pretended to be killed, coward!" said Heron.

"Ha! ha!" laughed Lord Belessis; "I have made up my mind, my fine fellow, to see you hanged; and it will be much more agreeable to do so without a sword-thrust in my lungs than with one! But what's that I hear? Why it must be the fellow's comrades on the road still! Gentlemen all, there's neither profit nor glory to be got by a pitched battle with a set of desperadoes! Let us push on to Mortlake or Sheen, where we will rouse the constables."

This advice of Lord Belessis seemed to be acceptable as well to the new-comers as to Lord Belessis and his friends. A scarf had been hastily tied through Captain Heron's elbows, so that he was comparatively helpless; and as two of his captors, one on each side, held Daisy by the rein, there was nothing for it but to gallop on with them.

Then a feeling of anguish and desertion came over Captain Heron, for he felt certain that Ogle would not bring the band past the entrance to the lane; and, that missing his presence, they would all, more than probably, trot down the narrow, verdant lane to look for him.

"I fear I am lost!" he said to himself. "Oh, what will Edith think, when I return not to the forest?"

These thoughts, for a few moments, produced a deep dejection at his heart—a dejection that he had never felt before; but then, never before had he one waiting for him in his forest home to whom his safety was life and happiness; and to leave whom to the chances of a thousand dangers, brought more anguish to his heart than he had ever yet felt or knew there was to feel.

But there was another surprise and another bitterness in store for Captain Heron; for, after the party had proceeded about a mile, one of the strange group of horsemen called out, " I rejoice, my Lord Belessis, that you have caught a highwayman upon the Common; but I would give ten thousand pounds if it were the highwayman I should like to see caught !"

It was with difficulty that Captain Heron forbore uttering a cry of surprise and anguish; for too well did he recognise those tones.

They were the tones of his half-brother, the remorseless Lord Warringdale.

This was a discovery at once replete with danger and inquietude to Captain Heron; for he had scruples, which the readers of this narrative well know Lord Warringdale had not, against raising his hand with hostile intent to one so nearly related to him.

Lord Warringdale was ever willing to forget, except in the sense of rivalry, that they were sons of the same father; but it was a fact which, when Captain Heron had once ascertained and believed, saved Warringdale for ever from any danger at his hands.

"Now, indeed," thought Heron, " have I fallen upon evil fortune; for although he knows me not as yet, I shall soon be recognised by my most malignant foe on earth—and that foe, too, one whom I may not resist as I would any other who sought my life."

The cavalcade trotted onward, and Captain Heron thought it strange that Warringdale should never suspect who was the prisoner. But when recent events come to be considered, it will be seen that Warringdale might well suppose his half-brother to be more intent upon substantiating his rights than in seeking adventures on the road. In fact, he made no doubt that he was still in hiding at Lady Castleneau's.

But the present posture of affairs was not to last long, and the party of horsemen soon drew up in the little straggling village of Mortlake, where they halted beneath the glaring light of an inn door; and on the alarm being given that the road was infested with highwaymen, one of whom had been caught, and was there in his own proper person, there was a general rush of landlord, landlady, boots, chambermaid, and ostler, to look at the prisoner.

"Good gracious !" cried the landlord, " let me get a look at him. We had a cow stolen three years and a half ago, and I should like to see whether he seems the sort of a man to have taken it !"

"He's a murdering villain," said the landlady, " whoever he is. Dear me, no, he ain't; he's quite good-looking ! What a pity, to be sure !"

"Good-looking, however, as he is," said Lord Belessis, " he will grace the gallows."

As he spoke, Belessis struck off Captain Heron's hat, and then Warringdale uttered a cry of surprise and exultation.

"Why, my lords and gentlemen all," he said, " this is the famous highwayman, Captain Felix Heron !"

"I have another name, my Lord Warringdale," said Heron. "which you, of all men, know full well."

CHAPTER CXXII.

CAPTAIN HERON IS MADE A CLOSE PRISONER IN THE CAGE AT MORTLAKE.

UPON the announcement that the prisoner was none other than the celebrated highwayman, the excitement about the inn door was immense; and if the parish constable of Mortlake had not, at that moment, made his appearance, the Captain would have run the risk of almost being suffocated by the pressure of people on foot and on horseback to see him.

"Come, come—here—make way !" said a little, fat man. "Make way, in the King's name ! I'm the constable ! My name's Bumpus ! Now, gentlemen, if you please, where's the villain ? Where's the ruffian that robs his Majesty's subjects on his Majesty's highway ? Oh, that's him, is it ? Ha ! ha ! rascal ! So, we've caught you, have we ? You are my prisoner !"

"Not exactly, Mr. Constable," said Lord Belessis. "We caught him; and I shall not be satisfied until he is taken before the nearest magistrate. Or perhaps some of you gentlemen may be in the commission of the peace ?"

No one spoke.

Then Mr. Bumpus flourished his constable's staff, with the little brass crown at the end of it, before the eyes of Lord Belessis.

"I tell you what, sir," he said; " I'm a constable ! I know my duty, sir, I can tell you, and my name is Bumpus ! I'd just as soon think of disturbing Sir William Rose, who is the nearest magistrate, at this time of night, as of eating this staff; but I'll put him in the cage."

"It is late, my Lord Belessis," said Warringdale; " and if the cage be secure, perhaps it would be as well to let him remain there till morning."

"A lord !" cried Mr. Bumpus, the constable. "I begs ten thousand pardons, my lord, and only humbly mention the cage !"

"Is it strong and secure, fellow ?" said Belessis.

"Humbly, yes, my lord ! Nobody can get in, and nobody can get out ! There isn't such a cage in the country !"

"Be it so, then, my Lord Warringdale. Suppose we see this fellow properly secured, and then ride back to Kew ? We can easily canter over here again in the morning. I had an errand on this road to-night, but it is too late now; and the runaways I chased are, no doubt, housed in London."

"Be it so," said Lord Warringdale, gloomily.

"Now, Mr. Constable, lead the way, then, and put this night-bird in the cage you speak of."

"This way, my lord—this way. It's a wonderful cage, my lord; and if he gets out, I'll eat my staff. Our cage, my lord's, a fine idea."

"What do you mean ?"

"Why, my lord, it's in the middle of the parish pound, my lord.; and there's generally two donkeys, a pig and a cow, prowling about all night. It's a wonderful cage !"

"Cease your silly gabble, fellow, and lead on quickly."

"Certainly, my lord, certainly ! Here you are !"

The cavalcade reached a rather extensive en-

closure, which was the parish pound; and in the centre of which was a round stone building, with one low, arched doorway, and a conical roof. Mr. Bumpus produced a key of the pound, and likewise one of the cage; the small, low door of which was further secured by a heavy iron bar, and a couple of bolts.

It was Warringdale, then, who spoke in an assumed, careless tone.

"I don't see the necessity of leaving the fellow his horse: I think I will lead it on to Kew."

"Is horse-stealing," said Heron, "one of the accomplishments of my Lord Warringdale? My opinion is, that this respectable and energetic officer, Mr. Bumpus, has proper custody of both me and my horse."

"To be sure—to be sure!" cried the constable. "He's not such a fool as he looks, this highwayman. I'll put his horse in the pound, and him in the

No. 56.—EDITH.

cage; and if we don't find them both safe in the morning, I'll eat my staff."

"Be it so," said Belessis. "I don't think we are warranted in any other course. Now, fellow, in with you; and take this consolation—that I would have treated you to a bullet long ago, but that I anticipate the much greater satisfaction of seeing you hanged."

Captain Heron said not a word. He had accomplished his object, at least, of having Daisy near him; and although he did not see his way exactly, as yet, to freedom—yet the mere proximity of that friend and companion was a hopeful circumstance.

He was made to dismount within the enclosure of the pound, and then the little door of the cage was opened, and he was thrust into a narrow chamber that felt cold and damp, and the door was banged shut, and secured behind him.

"Good night!" said Mr. Bumpus. "You'd better go to sleep; and as you're a man of judgment, I'll bring you a pot of spiced ale in the morning, and a toast, before you go before his lordship. Ah! if you get out of that, I'll eat my staff."

Heron listened intently, and he heard the high paling which surrounded the pound, closed and locked.

The height was some fifteen feet, and so, far beyond a leap, even with Daisy's powers in that line; so that Captain Heron had to give himself some time to reflect in regard to what he could do in the present posture of affairs.

He knew that it would be about five o'clock in the morning before daylight, and he fancied, now, it was about a quarter past twelve; but the darkness in the cage at Mortlake was too great to enable him to see the hands of his watch. One thing, however, very much surprised him—which was, that his captors had not searched him; but probably they had been satisfied by seeing that only the scabbard of his sword was by his side, and he had observed that Lord Belessis had taken out the holster-pistols from Daisy's saddle.

Then it was that Heron began to feel about in his own pockets, to see what means he might have of helping himself in his present predicament.

A pair of small pocket-pistols, a powder-flask, with a receptacle for bullets, and a clasp-knife, were all the weapons, offensive and defensive, that he had about him.

While, however, he was making this inquiry, some changes took place in the aspect of his prison; and as his eyes got accustomed to the darkness, he saw that in one of the walls there was a narrow grating about the height of his face; and as he began slowly to define its outlines, the moon, which must have been hidden by some clouds or some building, suddenly emerged, and a stream of silvery light fell through the grating into the cage.

Captain Heron placed his lips close to the iron bars, and called out in a low voice, "Daisy, Daisy!"

There was a rush of feet, and a sudden squeal from a pig; and in another moment, Daisy's head was close to the grating.

"That's right, my gentle Daisy," said Heron. "All are not lost that are in danger, and we shall yet have many a gallop in the green glades of Epping."

Heron could just get his hand through the grating, but scarcely sufficiently to pat the neck of his gallant steed. Then Daisy uttered a short, peculiar cry, which he well knew she never used when they were alone. It was a warning to him of the approach of some one; and with the fine instinct of the creature, she seemed to know that it was an enemy.

"What can this mean?" said Heron.

Even as he spoke, he heard the heavy sound of some one leaping or dropping from the top of the palisade that surrounded the pound.

Heron would not speak, but he listened intently.

Daisy uttered another sound; but it was aggressive, and one, whoever was approaching, they might well take heed of.

"Peace, Daisy, peace!" whispered Heron.

"Peace! quiet—quiet! You can do me no good now; and I would not have you hurt for a thousand pounds! Peace! peace! Woa, sweetheart! woa!"

Daisy well understood she was not required to assume the offensive; and as Heron pushed her face gently with his fingers, she retreated some half-dozen paces from the grating, and was lost to sight in the deep shadow of the cage.

Then there was another squeak from that unlucky pig, which had been pounded, and which seemed to be continually in the way of something or somebody.

A loud oath proclaimed that whoever had penetrated into the pound had fallen over the pig; and then a great scrambling of feet ensued, and various maledictions were uttered in a low tone.

Captain Heron stood by the grating, in that narrow gleam of moonlight, and all his senses seemed concentrated in the one of hearing.

There was a footstep just outside the cage; and then the streak of moonlight was intercepted by something exactly without the narrow grating.

"Felix Heron," said a voice, "I have thought of what I hope will end our differences at once, and for ever; and have slipt away from my friends, in order to come back here in secrecy to tell it you."

The voice was that of Lord Warringdale.

A strange sickness of heart came over Heron as he heard him speak, and he began to have a loathing of the man, who, at one moment, it was evident, was intent upon taking his life in any treacherous manner he could; and at another, came to him with pretended motives of amity and good-will.

"Felix Heron," added Warringdale, "answer me, if you are still here, as I am assured you are; for I have not been far enough off to lose sight of this place, and escape is impossible."

"I am here," said Heron.

"Ah! that is well. Let me, now, speak to you—for I, too, am weary of this mortal strife between us; and thinking that in our veins runs the same blood, I would fain say something amicable to you, if you will listen."

"I listen."

"By one act, it seems to me that I can satisfy both you and myself. Come to this narrow grating, for I would not have my words travel far into the night air."

Captain Heron could never explain to himself, even afterwards, how it was that a terrible suspicion of treachery came over him; and he took his hat, with the long drooping feather, in his hand—that hat which had been struck off at the inn door by Lord Belessis, but civilly enough handed back to him by the constable, when the scarf was taken from his arms, as he was thrust into the cage;—he took that hat then in his hand, and held it suddenly on the inner side of the grating.

"I am here," he said.

In a moment, without a word, Lord Warringdale plunged between two of the bars of the grating, up to the very hilt, a long glistening sword, which passed through the hat, and led him to believe that he had killed at once, or mortally wounded, Felix Heron.

"That," he cried, "is what I hope will put an end for ever to all rivalry between us! I hope you think the proposition a good one! It is sharp, pointed, and to the purpose!"

Warringdale then indulged himself in a fiendish laugh, which echoed round the walls of the old cage.

And what were the feelings now of Felix Heron at this unexampled and atrocious treachery?

Anger and grief struggled for pre-eminence; and he wrung his hands, as he cried, " No, I cannot—I cannot kill this man! Even now, I cannot kill this man, villain that he is! Worse villain than tongue can tell!—I cannot kill him! My father was his father, and his spirit should ever stand between us."

" Dead?" cried Warringdale, as he placed his face close to the grating, and tried to look into the cage.

" No!"

" Badly hurt, then, and bleeding fast?"

" No, I am unhurt; but my heart bleeds for you, wretched, wretched man! It was but my hat I held up to your rapier's point!"

Warringdale uttered a cry of rage; and frantic with disappointment, he kept dashing his sword through the narrow grating, in the hope of yet inflicting some injury upon Heron.

This was too much for human endurance, this fearful perseverance in murder. Heron called out aloud, " Daisy, Daisy! seize him! Help! ho, my Daisy!"

There was a fearful scuffle just without the narrow grating. Warringdale shrieked aloud, and then Heron heard Daisy plunging with her feet, and shaking something to and fro as a mastiff would a rat.

" No, no, Daisy!" he cried. " No! Back! Off! off! Away with you!"

Another moment, and he heard Daisy galloping round and round the cage, but Warringdale uttered not a word: and then, amid the stillness of the night, only broken by the hoof-strokes of Daisy, Heron heard the village clock of Mortlake strike the hour of three.

" Oh, will this night never pass?" he said. " I must and will escape from this place. The air suffocates me. Edith, Edith, what will you think? And oh, what a fearful tragedy might have been enacted in this dreary hole! I will—I must escape!"

Heron felt cautiously around him, and he stumbled over a rude wooden bench which was in the cage, no doubt intended for a sleeping-place for any one who was there confined.

" Ah!" he cried, " I have it! I have it! The walls and door may be impregnable, and yon narrow opening far too small, even if the grating were removed, to permit me to pass through: but I will try the roof—yes, I will try the roof!"

Heron found that by standing upon the rude bench, he was not above a foot from the interior concavity of that conical-shaped roof.

But how was he to work at it—how reach it—and what weapon had he fit for such a purpose? What but the sheath of his sword, which had been so incautiously left him, and which was as well adapted as might be, to enable him to work his way to freedom.

The roof was composed of radiating beams of timber, meeting at the apex of the roof, and resting upon the top of the circular wall of which the cage was composed. Above these, again, were ordinary flat tiles in concentric circles; and, in fact, they formed the principal obstacle between Captain Heron and the daylight, which was now fast approaching.

The sheath of the sword was of steel, and of sufficient substantiality to form a good weapon in strong hands; and Heron, in the impatience of the moment, made vigorous thrusts with it at the tiles, so that two or three soon gave way, and came rattling down into the pound.

After this, the progress of disencumbering the roof of the cage of a sufficient number of tiles to leave a reasonable opening through which he, Captain Heron, could make his way, was a task of comparative ease; and all he feared was, that the early dawn would disturb him in his operations, and bring his enemies upon him.

Half an hour, however, of this work was sufficient to show a large gap, through which the moonlight streamed pleasantly and sweetly. There was hope and freedom in the very sight of the open air, and it was with great satisfaction that Captain Heron, by extending his arms above his head, and springing suddenly upwards from the wooden bench, caught the edge of the orifice, and drew his head and shoulders fairly through.

From this tolerably elevated position, he had a good view of the surrounding country; and he saw by the aspect of the eastern sky that the early morning would soon be struggling for supremacy with the faint moonlight.

There was no time to lose—and never did man with more alacrity disengage himself from a prison-house than did Captain Heron draw himself up on to the roof of the cage at Mortlake, preparatory to dropping into the circular pound that surrounded it.

In that pound were two objects which would excite his warmest interest: the one was his gallant and noble Daisy—the other, that man whose name he could never mention to himself without a shudder, and who sought his life with such relentless pertinacity.

Lord Warringdale neither by word nor gesture gave signs of existence; but Daisy saw her master on the roof of the cage, and seemed almost inclined to clamber up its roof to get at him.

" Close, Daisy, close!" cried Heron. " Quiet, now, quiet! This will be a better drop than to the ground."

Daisy stood close to the wall, and Heron let himself drop on to the saddle, from which his feet were not far off, as he hung by the edge of the circular roof.

That mode of descending broke his fall, for he alighted springingly upon the saddle, and then leaped to the ground.

He felt that he was comparatively free, although still within the high palisade that encircled the cage. There was quite light enough for him to see what he was about, and he ran at once to the doorway of cross-beams which shut in the pound. It was only secured by a common lock, which Heron felt was at his mercy at any moment; but then, although his own safety was so much at stake, he could not make up his mind to leave that place until he had ascertained the actual condition of Lord Warringdale.

With Daisy's bridle cast over his left arm, Captain Heron slowly paced round the circular pace between the palisade and the cage, until he reached that spot where what might be called his contest with Warringdale had taken place — a contest, however, which had nothing but violence and treachery on one side, and passive resistance upon the other.

Lying, then, on the ground, just beneath the little grated window, was that half-brother of Heron's, to whom, had he been at all worthy, the brave and gifted Felix would have accorded so freely his esteem.

"Speak!—speak!" he cried. "I would rather have you live to repent, and to feel what grievous wrong you do me, than that you should die in this fashion."

It was sullenness, or rage, which had hitherto kept Lord Warringdale silent. No doubt he was badly bruised, and would have found it difficult to rise; but he must have felt very sure indeed of the forbearance of Heron, to give him courage to utter the words that now came from his lips.

"It is your turn now—it may yet be mine to sweep you from my path. You do not know me yet."

"Alas!" said Heron, "I but too well perceive that you know me, or you would not dare to utter those words. For a time, at least, villain as you are, you are incapable of mischief. I leave you to reflections, which should be such as no honest heart would feel for the world's wealth. Farewell!"

"Ay, farewell!" howled Warringdale; "but we shall meet again!"

"Alas! I feel that we shall!"

Heron turned aside, and as he did so his foot struck against the sword—that very sword with which Lord Warringdale would have taken his life. His own good blade had perished on his encounter with the horsemen in the road; so now he picked this one of his half-brother's from the ground, and strode with it in his hand towards the door of the pound.

With that sword, then, he wrenched off the lock; but the weapon broke in the effort, although it accomplished its work; and then Heron cast the handle and the blade towards Warringdale, and without another word he led Daisy out of the pound.

"I am free—I am free!" he cried. "One should be imprisoned in a place like that, to feel the freshness of the air without. Edith, to thee!—to thee now, Edith!"

Heron sprung upon the back of Daisy, and had just wheeled into the high road, when round the corner of some buildings, a short distance off, there came at a sharp trot some half-dozen mounted men.

Heron must have been much absorbed in what had taken place at the pound and in the cage, not to have heard the tramp of these men upon the road; so that they came upon him, at a distance not exceeding a hundred paces, with all the effect of a surprise.

The only arms he had, were those two pocket-pistols in the breast of his apparel; but what need of arms when he was mounted upon his faithful Daisy, whose speed would surely be far more than a match for any of the horses that were approaching?

"Seize him!—seize him!" cried several voices: "he is escaping! My mind misgave me that he would! Seize him!—seize him!"

The morning had now sufficiently advanced, that a dim white light was over and about all objects, so that the approaching horsemen had no difficulty at all in recognising Captain Heron, with his scarlet coat, and rich half military costume, which he was fond of wearing on the road.

For a moment the gallant highwayman cast a glance over his opponents, and saw that they comprised some of those men who had been his captors a few hours since. Then he turned Daisy in the opposite direction, and crying out, "Off, and away!—off, and away, my gallant Daisy! for life and liberty now!" he fled from the spot.

CHAPTER CXXIII.

CAPTAIN HERON EFFECTS A WONDERFUL ESCAPE, AND FANCIES HE SEES AN APPARITION IN THE MEADOWS.

AH! what is this? What can this mean? What new and worse calamity than ever yet occurred, has fate produced? Where is the swift, rushing speed of that gallant creature, who was wont to leave pursuers far behind? Where are those rapid hoof-strokes that ever seemed to spurn the road beneath them?

Daisy lags but slowly and drearily along.

She is lame.

She places one fore-foot painfully to the ground; a cold dew is upon her beautiful mane. Almost with an articulate voice, the creature utters a cry of pain.

"I am lost!" said Heron. "I am lost!"

He sprung from the saddle, and lifted the wounded foot in his hand.

"Ah, yes," he cried; "I see it now, and I understand it. In her attack on the villain Warringdale, she has dashed her foot upon the point of his sword. My Daisy, we are surely lost now once again!"

And yet Daisy had made a gallant effort to carry her master free of his pursuers. With her usual speed she had gone about half a mile, and so had placed an abrupt turn of the road between Heron and his foes.

Then with a sudden inspiration, the highwayman saw what was his only chance.

It was to get through the hedge, and into the meadows, before the horsemen could come up, and so allow them to gallop on, believing him before them.

But the difficulty was great. There was a high bank, and the hedge was of thorn and holly; it was too much for Daisy, at her best of times, to clear with a leap, and how could she now, with her wounded foot, even attempt to do so?

There was not a moment to lose. From the ample pocket of his scarlet coat, Heron took his riding gloves; and as he almost tore them on to his hands, he sprung up the bank, and began beating aside the bushes to make a passage to the field beyond.

The sharp thorns pierced even the stout buff leather of the gloves; but Heron was not to be deterred in his work, and by grasping some of the younger stems close to the ground, he tore them bodily out, and flung them into the field, so **that**

EDITH RESCUES FELIX FROM A POSITION OF GREAT DANGER.

Presented Gratis with No. 56, of the New Edition Edith the Captive ; or, the Robbers of Epping Forest.

EACH WEEK IS PRESENTED GRATIS A COLOURED ENGRAVING.

in an incredibly short space of time he effected a slight, but yet what he thought would be sufficient, gap in the hedge.

"Daisy, Daisy!" he cried. "Follow, follow!"

Daisy came towards the bank on three legs.

Heron stooped and got hold of the bridle. She knew well what he wanted her to do, and although with difficulty, scrambled up the bank. Another moment, and, at the expense of some scratches on her sleek coat, she was through the hedge.

"Down—down, my Daisy, down!" cried Heron.

He gave her the slight pat on the chest, which she was accustomed to receive from him as a signal to lie down, and instantly she was on her side in the field with the docility of a dog.

Heron flung himself beside her. There was no time to mend the gap in the hedge, for he heard his pursuers close at hand; but he held up with both his hands the pieces of thorn and holly that he had torn out; and from the road nothing but a most critical examination could have led to a discovery of what had occurred.

The horsemen came rattling on; and as they passed the turning which, for those few moments, had so providentially hidden Captain Heron and Daisy from their view, they came to a halt, for the road beyond that point was very straight for more than a mile, and the morning light had so far advanced that it was plainly enough visible for the whole of that distance.

Therefore was it a subject of surprise to these mounted men that they saw nothing of the man and horse on whose heels they had pressed so closely.

"Where is he?" cried one of them. "I am certain his horse was lame, for I saw it drooping, and hardly able to stagger on."

"Yes," said another. "And there are spots of blood on the road, for some distance from the pound."

"By all that's infernal," cried Lord Belessis, "he must be in hiding somewhere!"

Captain Heron at once recognised the coarse, ferocious voice of this man.

"But where? where?" cried another, in sharp tones. "There is no lane or by-way near enough; and as to getting over the hedge on either side, I should like to see any horse try it, with these thorn hedges and that bank, to say nothing of a lame one."

"Then he's in league with the fiend himself," said Belessis, "and has been swallowed up in the earth!"

"Or gone up into the air!" said another.

"Who knows?" cried a third; "he may be invisible when he likes, horse and all, and is perhaps laughing at us, not fifty paces off!"

"Confound all your surmises!" said Belessis. "I am at my wits' end; and what on earth could have induced Lord Warringdale to give us the slip last night in that mysterious manner?"

Hardly had these words escaped the lips of Lord Belessis, when, with one voice, the other horsemen raised a simultaneous cry.

"There he is!" "There he is!" "There's the rascal!" "Fire at him!" "Fire at him!" "He's over the hedge!" "There he is!" "There he is!"

The instant impression upon Captain Heron's mind was, that by some fatality either he or Daisy had been seen, or perhaps both; and yet

he could not tell how that could be. So low down the road as the horsemen were, it was a wonder, though, that he did not spring to his feet with his pistols in his hand; but he controlled the impulse, and only raised his head sufficiently to look sharply through the hedge.

The whole party of horsemen had turned their backs upon him; and what words can paint his intense surprise to see the object that attracted their attention, and which had raised their outcries.

In the meadow on the opposite side of the road, and on sufficiently high ground to overlook the hedge and the bank, was a horseman, so exactly the counterpart of him, Captain Heron, in dress and appointments, that he could have believed it to have been the reflected image of himself.

The scarlet coat—the hat with the slouching feather—the rich cravat—the heavy buff gauntlets, and the half silk mask upon the face, all proclaimed the dashing knight of the road, and the counterpart of Captain Heron.

"There he is!" shouted all the horsemen at once, "again!"

"Surrender, rascal!" roared Lord Belessis.

Then a couple of pistol-shots were fired; but they seemed to take no effect upon the strange horseman, who then, making a waving motion with the right arm, stooped slightly, and seemed to pat the neck of the horse, which in another moment was galloping across the meadows.

"After him!—after him!" cried Lord Belessis. "After the villain!"

"It's well enough, my lord, to cry 'after him,'" said one of the others; "but we must trot or gallop down the road until we come to a lane, or turning; for my horse has not wings, to get over fifteen feet of hedge and bank."

"On, on!" cried Belessis. "We will raise the country! I will not give him up yet! Follow me!"

They all started off at a very rapid pace, and in a few seconds a deep silence was upon the road, and in the fields.

"This is all a dream—this must be a dream," said Captain Heron, as he clasped his hands over his eyes. "What else can it mean? Or was that some apparition I saw in the meadows, so like myself that it must surely be a presage of my death?"

He rose to his feet, and looked long and wistfully about him. Neither friend nor foe was to be seen; but in a few moments he thought he heard some one whistling, and slowly tramping along the road, in the fashion of some labourer going to his work.

Heron had not had time to arrange his thoughts, after the surprise of the singular circumstance that had taken place; but from a sort of instinct, rather than from reflection, he sunk down behind the hedge again, in order that this man, be he whom he might, should pass on his way without observing him.

The whistling continued, and was louder than before; and Heron somehow had an impression on his mind that either the tones or the air were familiar to his ears.

Through the hedge he could command a good view of this man who was approaching, and certainly his actions were somewhat curious and worth observing.

He had on one of those green-coloured, capacious smock-frocks, so common in country districts, and a capacious slouched hat, which covered a good part of his face. He carried a thick hedge-stake in his hand, and seemed a sturdy fellow.

Walking in the very centre of the road, this man looked as carefully to the right and to the left as though he expected to find some lurking foe beneath every blade of grass, or behind every wild flower in the hedge-row.

And still he kept up that pertinacious whistle; and as Captain Heron watched him, he scrambled up the bank on the other side of the road, and holding on by the stem of an alder tree, he took a long look around him, and in order to do so more effectually he took off the slouched hat.

Then Heron saw plainly his head and face.

It was Ogle.

Heron sprung to his feet again.

" You are looking for me, Ogle, I'm sure!"

"Bless us, and save us, Captain, and so I was! Hurrah for our side! Why, then, you are safe, after all! And where's Daisy? I hope she's all right, Captain."

"Only a little lame of the fore-foot. She is lying down by me now."

" Then something has happened; but my heart's a thousand pounds lighter now, to hear your voice again, Captain. We missed you all of a sudden last night, and couldn't make out what had become of you. So I sent a couple of the men home to the forest, to say to Miss Edith that you mightn't be back for a few hours."

" You were right, Ogle; but you must not call her Miss Edith."

" Well, nor more I oughtn't; but I shall never get into the habit of calling her anything else. But suppose I call her Lady Edith?"

"That will do, Ogle. And now come over here at once, and look at Daisy's foot: she has struck it on a sword point, and got lamed."

"That I will, Captain. But where are all those who were in pursuit of you?—for I heard, as I came down the road, that the country was being scoured in all directions in search of a highwayman,"

" I rather think, Ogle, something has happened which has sent my enemies off on a false scent; and to my surprise, there seems to be two Captain Herons in the field; for if ever a man saw a reflection or double of himself in this world, I have seen mine to-day. But come up at once: my present anxiety is all for Daisy."

Ogle scrambled up the hedge, and was quickly in the meadow through the gap which Captain Heron had made, and which he no longer hid, by holding up the branches of the bushes.

Ogle carefully looked at Daisy's foot.

"It is but a cut," he said, "and will soon be well; but she might be lamed for life without some rest."

"Then am I at my wits' ends," said Heron; "for rest in safety she can only have at Epping; and how to get her there is a question I cannot answer. I tell you, Ogle, that those who have been in hot pursuit of me, are still within the circuit of a mile or two."

Ogle looked thoughtful.

"Something must be done, Captain, and that at once," he said. "I am well disguised, as you see; for I met a countryman, and paid him for this frock and hat; but I'm afraid Daisy's a too valuable creature for me to be able to account for the possession of her, if you were to go home, even, and leave her to my care."

" I know not what to do. Home to the forest I ought to go; and yet to abandon this faithful creature, to whom I have on so many occasions owed my life, cuts me to the heart."

"Hush!" said Ogle; "do you hear nothing?"

Heron listened, and Daisy, too, pricked up her ears, and evidently heard some sound upon the road.

It was the slow, creaking revolution of wheels; and as Heron glanced through the hedge, he saw a small covered cart—a kind of half-waggon, indeed—for the covering was an awning upon hoops, after the waggon fashion.

This vehicle was drawn by one horse, which was proceeding at a walking pace, and looked the picture of laziness. A man in the dress of a labourer walked by the horse's head, with his hands deep in his pockets. By the droning gait and manner of both horse and man, they might be supposed to be half asleep, and the only thing that kept them from dropping off into a profound slumber, seemed to be a little bell, something like a sheep bell, that was connected to the horse's head-gear, and kept up a low tinkling sound as he walked.

"There's a picture of laziness," said Ogle. "A mile and a half an hour, and nothing to think about."

"Hush!" said Heron; "I have it. Stay with Daisy a moment."

Heron stepped through the gap in the hedge, and jumped into the road.

"Stop, my friend," he said. "A word with you."

But the man went on, droning the burden of some miserable song; and the horse's footsteps, and the little tinkling bell, appeared together to keep up the measure of the time.

"Stop, I say!" added Heron. "Are you deaf, or asleep?"

But still on went the man, and on went the horse; and Captain Heron, as the only expedient to bring them to a standstill, placed himself exactly in the way of the man, who, coming up to him in the same dreamy manner, was nearly thrown down by the sudden shock of encountering Heron.

That seemed to awaken him.

"Woa! Dobbin, woa!" he said. "Danged if I arn't been and run agin a postes! Woa, Dobbin!"

The horse stopped, and the little bell ceased to tinkle, when the creature, settling itself as firmly as it could upon its four legs, went right off into a sound sleep.

The driver rubbed his eyes then, and looked at Captain Heron with a stare of astonishment.

"Who be ye?" he said. "Ye bean't a post, like?"

"Where are you going?" said Heron.

The man looked at his horse, and then at his questioner.

" I should like to go to sleep," he said. "I've been up a hour."

"What have you in the cart?"

"Wuzzle."

"What do you mean by wuzzle? Oh, I see!— mangold wortzel."

"Danged if he knows what wuzzle is!"

The horse began audibly to snore

"Ah!" said the countryman. "Dobbin's off It's hard times, these here, maister. A man's obligated to get up when he wants to go to sleep."

"Look you, my fine fellow! I see that there is nothing so dear to you as repose."

"Eh? What do you mean?"

"I mean that you are fond of sleep."

"Danged if I bean't. I always wants to go to sleep, and I never wants to wake up; and Dobbin he always wants to go to sleep, and never wants to wake up; and Maister Thrup, as I works for, says I bees a lazy one, and is a going to have a bell above my head, like Dobbin's, to keep I awake."

"Look here," said Heron, as he held a couple of guineas in the palm of his hand. "Have you any objection to shoot your whole load of mangold wortzel by the side of the road, and then have your cart and horse taken away from you by a highwayman, while you take these two guineas, and go somewhere, and fall quietly asleep, and know nothing more about it?"

"Eh? Stop a bit! You say so many things at once to I."

"Ogle?" cried Heron.

"Yes, Captain."

"Take this fellow out of sight, and secure him in any way you like. Put these two guineas in his pocket, and I daresay he will be fast asleep in five minutes."

The countryman looked at Heron, and looked at Ogle, and then at the horse, and then up at the sky; after which he rubbed his eyes, and allowed Ogle to lead him away, without a word of remonstrance.

Ogle came back in about five minutes, laughing.

"The fellow's gone fast asleep, at the foot of a tree, Captain," he said. "I never met with such a man in all my life."

"Nor such a horse," said Heron. "Only look at the creature."

"Oh, I'll soon waken him up," said Ogle; and advancing to the horse's head, he rang the little bell, while he at the same time bawled in his ear, "Come up! Gee up! Come up!"

The horse started into a spasmodic sort of wakefulness, and began marching deliberately onwards.

"Woa!" cried Ogle. "Confound you! you've trod on my toe, now! Was there ever such a wretch of an animal? Woa! woa! will you?"

The horse looked at Ogle out of one eye only, and then closing it up, fell fast asleep again.

Captain Heron had run round to the back of the cart, and saw that far from being a load of mangold wortzel in it, there were not above fifty roots, which could easily be pushed aside, and leave ample room beneath the awning for a passenger.

And who was that passenger to be, but the gallant Daisy, who was thus to be transported to Epping Forest, without injury to her wounded foot.

"Let us be off as quickly as we can, Ogle," said Heron, "lest some more troublesome person than our sleepy friend should come along the road."

"All's right, Captain. If we take the way down the lane, we shall meet with the eight of our own fellows, who are still there."

"That is well—that is well. Keep a sharp look-out, Ogle, and I will get Daisy down."

Captain Heron made his way to the meadow again, and carefully tied up Daisy's foot with his handkerchief and one of his gloves. She could then place it to the ground without pain; and never was the docility of that faithful creature more truly exhibited than by the manner in which she followed Heron through the gap in the hedge, and down the bank, and finally, with a perfect understanding of what he wanted her to do, made her way into the covered cart, and laid down there quietly and securely.

"Ogle," cried Heron, "you are in capital costume for a driver; and I see the whip of our sleepy friend lying in the road, so let us start at once. I will get inside with Daisy, as well to keep her quiet, as that my costume would at once betray us."

"All's right, Captain."

"But where is your horse, Ogle?"

"Oh, the other fellows have got it somewhere down the lane."

"Then let us be moving at once."

Ogle stepped up to the horse's head again, and placing his mouth close to his ear, he bawled out, "When it's quite convenient to you, we'll go on!"

The horse gave a sort of start, and looked in a surprised manner at Ogle.

"I say if you've no objection, we'll go on!"

Ogle gave a crack with the whip in the air as he spoke, upon which the horse, with an air of dogged determination, began to step out and shake its head, and jingle the little bell, as much as to say, "There, I'm going—there's no occasion for any violence!"

And so off went the little party, the bell making a jingling sound, and Ogle trudging by the horse's head, while Daisy within the cart looked with her fine, sparkling eyes into the face of Heron.

CHAPTER CXXIV.

EDITH STARTS ON A PERILOUS EXPEDITION.

IT will be remembered that Captain Heron had felt a disinclination to trouble Edith with the intelligence that he was out upon the road on that night; and Edith had not questioned him, because, perhaps, she felt and guessed why it was he was not more communicative.

But she had not united herself to Felix Heron for the purpose of allowing him to encounter possible danger and disaster, in which she should be no sharer; and hence was it that so soon as she felt certain that he and his men were clear of Epping Forest, she formed a determination at once romantic and perilous.

It was a determination which would have brought back Captain Heron at a gallop, had the faintest suspicion of it once entered his mind.

She resolved to follow him on his expedition; to watch over his safety, to the extent of her ability, and to share any danger that he might be encountering.

She felt that she could not be wholly and truly his, unless his perils were her perils, his successes her successes; and perhaps, too, there lay at the bottom of this resolve, a hope that her determination to share with him the adventures of the road might wholly deter him from such a pursuit, or infuse an amount of caution into it that would strip it of its fears.

Edith knew well that she was properly guarded and cared for in the depths of that forest, although the only two persons immediately within her call were Mrs. Ogle and Tom Ripon.

From neither of them could she expect, for a moment, any opposition to her will, be it what it might; but their concurrence and assistance would be much more valuable than a mere obedient acquiescence.

Mrs. Ogle was startled at the proposition, and tried to dissuade Edith from it, until she found her resolved, and then she gave up remonstrance, merely saying, "Lady Edith, we have but one order from the Captain, and that is to obey you in all things; but I'm sure Ogle wouldn't thank me to be following him about upon the road."

"Say no more—say no more," said Edith. "I know you mean well, but I am resolved upon this course of action, and something seems to tell me I shall be useful. I have a presentiment that there is more than common danger to-night, and I would fain share it with him who is encountering it for my sake. With your assistance, Mrs. Ogle, I can easily make such an appearance on the road as will save me from molestation."

Such, indeed, was the fact. For in those secret old rooms in the ruins of Hinchcliffe Manor, Captain Heron had abundance of clothing and appointments; and there were arms, too, of all descriptions, so that Edith had no difficulty in equipping herself as so exact the counterpart of Captain Heron, that no wonder, when he saw her on the other side of the roadway, where he and Daisy lay concealed, he was struck with astonishment, and believed he saw an apparition of himself.

Tom Ripon was summoned, and at the sight of Edith, thus equipped for the road, he was lost in astonishment, which soon gave way to admiration.

"Bravo! Hurrah!" said Tom. "We'll all be highwaymen! Tom will go, too! Mother Ogle, lend me one of the Captain's coats. Hurrah for the road!

> On a moonlight night,
> But not too bright,
> With the clouds all scudding over,
> 'Stand! stand!' I cry,
> 'Or the bullets fly,
> For I'm a bold night rover!'"

"Get out, you little imp!" cried Mrs. Ogle, "and tell us at once what horse can be got for Lady Edith, and which way the Captain has gone."

"Trooper," said Tom, "and Barnes Common."

"What do you mean," cried Mrs. Ogle, "by 'Trooper' and 'Barnes Common?'"

"Why," said Tom, "there's a nice horse hidden in the wood, and his name's Trooper. He's not like our Daisy, though—oh, dear, no! Bless your heart, Miss Edith and Mrs. Ogle, only look at the top of my head! You see, Daisy, in her funny way, will pull off my cap with her teeth, and she's such a thoughtless creature, she is! She doesn't know she gets hold of a lot of my hair as well, so I shan't have any on the top of my head, soon!"

"Tom," said Edith, "get this horse you speak of, and bring it as near to this place as you can. I will ride to Barnes Common to-night."

"Goodness gracious!" said Mrs. Ogle, "do you know the way?"

"I know the general direction, and will find it."

"But do you mean to stop everybody," said Tom, "coaches and all, and give 'em a bullet in their nob, if they won't stand still and deliver?"

"No, no," said Edith. "My errand is of a different character. I may render assistance in some way—perhaps draw off a pursuit at some critical moment. Who shall say?—who shall say?"

It was strange, indeed, that in her conjectures of how she might possibly be useful to Captain Heron, Edith had hit upon the very circumstance that did actually occur. She was useful in drawing off a pursuit; for there can be little doubt but that Heron and Daisy would have been discovered over the hedge by the roadside, had it not been for the most opportune appearance of Edith, so exactly in the costume of the prisoner who had escaped from the cage at Mortlake; but not the slightest question of her identity occurred to Lord Belessis and the horsemen who were with him.

It would have been quite impossible for either Tom or Mrs. Ogle to have directed Edith from Epping Forest to Barnes Common at that hour of the night; and, in fact, they knew no more than she herself, which merely consisted in the general direction of the road.

It would be impossible to say that Edith did not feel some flutter at the heart as she trotted down one of the glades of the forest that led into the highway, but still there was a sense of pride and exultation in what she was about, which nerved her to her task; and the feeling, conviction, or presentiment—call it what we may—which had come over her, that that night she was to be useful to Felix Heron, never deserted her.

Just as she emerged from the trees of the forest, she heard a voice call out, "Why, it's the Captain himself; and he's mounted on Trooper! Hawks, ho! Hawks away!"

"Herons!" cried Edith; for she had been acquainted with the fact that those were the passwords of the forest.

There was much emotion at her heart, and yet she could not but smile to think that already she was so far fulfilling the character she had assigned to herself on that night, that one of the scouts who had been left to guard one of the entrances to the forest, actually mistook her for Captain Heron himself.

"I will accept this," she said, "as a promise of happy fortune to-night. But now, in good truth, I must ask my way; and yonder I see a light, which I fancy is at a mill I observed on my journey hither. They will, no doubt, be able to put me on the proper path."

The horse that Edith rode was a well-trained and docile creature. It carried her steadily, and at a good pace, towards the little glimmering light, which, in truth, came from an ale-house, which was nestled by the roadside, close to the mill.

At the sound of the horse's feet, a man came

out to the door, and shading his eyes with his hand, he looked down the road to see who it was.

At that moment, some clock chimed the half-hour past eleven, and then the man at the door of the little alehouse ran some paces towards her as he called out, "Captain, Captain, anything amiss? You know you can depend upon us; and the old crib is as safe as ever."

It was a gratification to Edith to find that she was so easily mistaken for Captain Heron; and pulling the half mask over her face, she resolved to try if she could succeed in keeping up the delusion until she should get past this man, who was evidently on good terms with her husband.

Imitating the voice of Heron as closely as she could—and no wonder that she could do it well, since its tones were never absent from her imagination—she called out, as she rode up to the door of the house, "All is well! all is well! But I

No. 57.—EDITH.

am dubious of my direct road to Barnes Common."

"You, Captain!" said the man, with an air of surprise. "Why, you've nothing to do but to go straight on, and get across the river by the old bridge, near to Battersea. But you're jesting with me, Captain; and there's no one on a dark night I would trust to more than yourself to show the way."

"Perhaps so," said Edith. "But one forgets, at times. Good night! Good night!"

"Nay, Captain; you don't go by the old crib in that kind of fashion. I've got the silver tankard you know so well all about; and the old October is humming in the cask below, like a kettle of water on a hot grate! I won't be a moment, Captain!"

Curiosity retained Edith for a few moments at the door of this little hostel; and when the landlord, after a short disappearance, came forth again with a silver tankard of old ale, she placed it to her lips.

"I am on service of importance to-night," she said, "and may not drink. Drain the tankard yourself, my good friend, and wish me good speed and happy fortune. Farewell!"

Edith trotted away from the door of the little road-side house of entertainment; and the landlord looked after her with some surprise, as he shook his head, saying, "Ah, I can see there is something the matter with the lad to-night. His voice is lower and softer than usual, and he won't drink his ale. There's not a worse sign going than when a man won't drink his ale."

Edith rode onward at a tolerably quick pace, but she felt the necessity of procuring more information in regard to her route, for it was not to be supposed that she was at all well acquainted with the environs of London. Still, however, as the landlord of the little hostel had said something about going straight on until she came to the old bridge at Battersea, she thought she could not be far wrong; and after about half an hour's riding, she fairly crossed the river, and struck into a country road that she thought would surely take her in the right direction, although she made up her mind to inquire of the first person she met more particularly the direct way to the common.

It was strange that throughout all this route the conviction never deserted Edith for a moment that she was doing something which would be beneficial to the safety of Heron.

But as she rode onward, the road, either by lying low and damp, was covered by a misty, cold air, or some actual sudden change in the temperature had taken place; for Edith felt cold and chilled, and she unstrapped the cloak which was at the back of the saddle, and wrapped it carefully about her.

It was one of those well-known travelling cloaks of the period, which fastened by a clasp round the neck, and had large sleeves, so that, when on, it completely hid the costume of the wearer; and now, Edith, as she felt both the comfort and the disguise of such a mantle, wondered to herself that she had not donned it before, since it was so much less likely to provoke observation on the road, than the picturesque and somewhat startling costume she wore beneath it.

"I can at any time," she said, "aid Felix as effectually, if it be necessary, as a supposed man in a cloak, as well as if I appeared in the costume of the road."

Edith had hardly made this observation to herself, when she became conscious that she was overtaking two persons on horseback, who were upon the road some short distance before her.

It did not enter into the imagination of Edith, to suppose that these persons might be enemies of either herself or Captain Heron; and she accelerated the speed of her horse, in order that she might reach them, and inquire her way.

The two horsemen, hearing the clatter of some rider behind them, paused until she came up; and then she spoke in a tone which, although not at all imitative of Captain Heron's, was yet a sufficient disguise of her own voice to deprive it of its most feminine character.

"Gentlemen," she said, "am I on the right way for London, through Barnes Common?"

There must have been something youthful and boyish about these assumed tones of Edith, for one of the horsemen replied in a low, snarling tone, "And pray, young sir, what brings you so much out of your way, if you want to reach London by Barnes Common?"

At that moment, Edith felt as if she could have fallen from the horse, so struck with sudden confusion and terror was she, to recognise by that voice that it was none other than Jonathan Wild who spoke to her.

For a moment she felt inclined to fly; but a second thought convinced her that that would be but to bespeak an instant pursuit, that might be fatal to her.

By an extraordinary exercise of resolution, she controlled her fears, and, so to speak, commanded her nerves to be still.

"If I were not out of my track," she said, "I should hardly accost strangers on my way, to put me into it."

"Are you in a hurry?" said Wild.

Before Edith could reply, she heard the other horseman say to Wild in a low voice, "Engage him if you can. I dare say it's some spark who would be glad of a few gold pieces. Engage him if you can, Mr. Wild, to come with us, for I'm mortally afraid."

"You always are," growled Wild; and then in a louder voice he said to Edith, "We'll put you upon your way with pleasure, young fellow; and you may ride to London with half a dozen guineas in your pocket, if you don't mind a trot of two or three miles of cross country, to do us a little service."

Edith hesitated a moment, and then the thought came strongly upon her, that Wild and his companion might possibly be upon some expedition inimical to the welfare of her Felix.

For all she knew, this might be some rare chance—some interposition of heaven itself, which was to place her in the way of carrying out that strong impression she had upon her mind, that on that night she was to be of some signal service to Captain Heron.

This thought, passing quick as lightning through her brain, decided her.

"I am one not overburdened with guineas," she said, keeping up the assumed tone in which she had spoken; "and if I might earn half a dozen, on conditions, I should have no objection."

"What conditions?" said Wild.

"First of all, a whole skin."

"Oh, certainly! There's no danger to you."

"Secondly, then, some lawful duty."

"Oh, perfectly lawful!"

"I can assure you, young gentleman," said Wild's companion, "that what you'll be asked to do is perfectly lawful—perfectly legal. I am myself in the law, and it is not likely that I should be interested in any act which was not perfectly within the law."

"Then, gentlemen," said Edith, "I am at your service."

"Come on, then," said Wild; "and I will tell you, as we go along, what I wish you to do."

"I am all attention."

"Did you ever hear of one Captain Heron, a highwayman?"

"Captain Heron, a highwayman?" replied Edith, in a dubious tone. "Did I ever hear of

Captain Heron, a highwayman? Well, now you mention the name, I seem to feel as if I had."

"Where?"

"Ah! There I can't tell you. Perhaps it was in some newspaper."

"But," said Wild's companion, "did you ever hear, young sir, of the great and famous Mr. Jonathan Wild?"

"No," said Edith.

"No?" exclaimed both Jonathan and his companions together. "Is that possible?"

"I never heard," added Edith, "of the great and famous Mr. Jonathan Wild; but I have heard of a notorious and bloodthirsty scoundrel of that name."

"Hold, young sir!" cried Jonathan Wild. "Never abuse any man to a stranger on a dark road until you can see his face! I am a friend of Mr. Wild's, and can assure you you have very wrong impressions in regard to him."

"Have I?"

"Most assuredly. But that is of little consequence. Let me tell you now what I want you to do. In another half-hour's trot we shall reach an old country house, which was once in the occuption of an old Sir Dominick Browne."

"Ah!" exclaimed Edith.

"What? Do you know that name, too?"

"No; but Browne, you know, is such a common name. Pray go on. I am all attention."

"I am an officer of police, then, and my name is Smith; and I, with this gentleman, who is in the law, have full authority to search that house for some papers that we require in the course of justice. We have, however, reason to think or to suspect that it may be occupied—guarded—or garrisoned by some lawless people; and what we want is to ascertain that fact."

"But I do not yet comprehend," said Edith, "what you want with me."

"Just this. If there are people in that house, they are those who know me, and likewise this gentleman, who is in the law, so that we should be in great danger by approaching it; whereas a stranger, do you see, would be in none, for he would be simply challenged, and probably warned off. Now you comprehend?"

"I do."

"Exactly, young gentleman," said Wild's companion, who was no other than that very attorney from the Temple who had behaved so treacherously to Captain Heron. "Exactly so. You understand, young gentleman, that we want you to make what military men call the—the——What is it, Mr. Smith?"

"Reconnaissance," said Wild.

"Exactly so. I will do it," said Edith; "and I am to have half a dozen guineas?"

"Yes, and welcome," added Jonathan. "You see, I take this gentleman, learned in the law, with me, in order that he may decide, at once, when we have found the papers we require."

"That's it," said the attorney; and then he muttered to himself, "And I will take good care, too, that I will get possession of them, if they are there to be had."

Wild, at the same moment, was indulging himself in a little aside, to the effect that he fully intended to give his friend the attorney a bullet, so soon as he had answered his purpose by authenticating the documents he was in search of.

Wild little suspected that his actions on that night were so clearly comprehended by the chance companion he had picked up on the road; but Edith, from what she had heard herself, and from what Felix Heron had told her, was able fully to comprehend that Wild still harboured the impression that, concealed in Sir Dominick's house, documents and papers essential to the claim of Heron to the Whitcombe peerage, were to be found.

A chance remark now of Wild's to his companion, not only assured Edith that Sir Dominick Browne still lived, but furnished her with a key to the secret of his preservation.

"So soon," muttered Wild, "as I find what papers the old man had, he shall die; but until I do, I cannot tell if he has told the truth or not with regard to where they are; and I must have that information from him before he draws his last breath."

We should be wronging human nature, and setting up Edith for a greater heroine than she was, if we were to say that she rode between Jonathan Wild and his villanous companion without fears and tremors—for many there were—and they were only overcome by the more powerful feeling that she was about something acceptable to the interests, and possibly to the life, of Heron.

"Here we are," said Wild, as they suddenly emerged from a narrow lane, and came in view of a heavy pile of building, which Edith recognised as Sir Dominick Browne's house.

"Oh, is this the place?" she said, with as much composure as she could assume.

"Yes," said Wild. "Speak low. There is a gap in the wall close to the old front gate, and you can ride in right to the hall-door. What I want you to do is to knock loudly, and under any pretence you like, discover if the place is tenanted. If any one answers you, inquire your way, and then come to us, for we will wait for you beneath these trees; and then, young sir, your guineas will be earned, and you are nearer London than as if you took the route by Barnes."

"I will do it," said Edith. "Stir not, and I will soon be back to you with news."

Edith had had ample time to make up her mind what course to pursue. If, indeed, in that old house of Sir Dominick Browne's there were documents of essential service to Felix, it was quite evident that Jonathan Wild, in his own interests, and in those of his villanous employer, Lord Warringdale, wanted to get possession of them.

It was equally evident that he could be scared away, if he thought that Heron kept that house under guard.

And so Edith made up her mind that she would once more try the efficacy of her disguise, even upon one who had encountered Heron so often, and who knew him so well as Jonathan Wild.

The gap in the ruined wall in front of the house was sufficient to admit Edith and her horse, and it was with strange sensations of familiarity with the old place that she made her way up to its doorway: for there had she already undergone an adventure with Wild, and passed many hours of repose under the protection of Felix.

Without the pause of a moment, she unclasped from around her neck the cloak which covered up the well-known costume of the knight of the road;

and divesting herself entirely of that outward covering, she again restored it to its place behind the saddle.

Then, to give a colour to what she was about to do, Edith raised the ponderous knocker upon the oaken door of the mansion, and awakened dismal echoes within it, by two or three heavy blows.

She then took one of the holster-pistols from the saddle and fired it in the air; immediately after which, she raised a wild, frantic kind of cry, and then turning her horse's head from the hall door, she gallopped out into the roadway; shouting loudly, in as near an approach to the voice of Captain Heron as she could produce, " Forward! Ho, Daisy! Forward!—forward! Follow me, my men, and down with the rascals! On my soul, I believe this is some *ruse* or attack of Jonathan Wild's."

Wild uttered an awful execration; and then he just saw, as he thought, in the dim light, the figure of Heron on horseback, and he fully believed he had all his band at his heels.

" Confusion on the fellow!" he said. " He's here himself! I'm off!"

" Murder! murder!" cried the attorney. " Don't desert me, Mr. Wild!"

" Do you want me to carry you?" cried Wild. " I always look after number one."

" Help! help! Murder! I came here to please you, and to tell you if the papers were legal or not. He's sure to murder me! Help! help!"

Wild paid not the slightest attention to the cries of the attorney, but gallopped off towards town, soothing his disappointed feelings by such volleys of oaths and execrations, that the mere invention of them did credit to his fancy.

Edith completed the rout of her enemies by firing the other pistol, which had such an effect upon the nerves of the attorney, that he slipped off his horse at once, and left it without a rider, to gallop where it would.

" Mercy! mercy!" he cried. " Spare my life, my dear Mr. Felix, and I will tell you all I know, and a great deal more! I'll come over to your side altogether, and tell you all about Lord Warringdale, and never ask you for a farthing of costs—only spare my wretched life! I suppose you've killed that young man who knocked at the door—and serve him right! I'm here in the middle of the road, my dear sir, on my knees in the mud—yours to command!"

" Wretch!" said Edith.

" Ah, yes—just so; I'm all that! If there's a little perjury wanted, my dear sir, I'll do it, with pleasure! How do you do, my dear Mr. Felix? I thought you looked a little pale when last I had the pleasure of seeing you in the Temple! And how is your charming horse? I think Buttercup's the name, isn't it?"

CHAPTER CXXV.

EDITH LEADS OFF A PURSUIT ACROSS THE FIELDS.

EDITH was by no means inclined to make a prisoner, or to hold any communication with this man who was cringing at her feet, which might have a tendency to enable him to discover her real character. She was, in fact, far too anxious to get on her road to Barnes Common, even to pause for the purpose of terrifying, to a greater extent, this old enemy of Captain Heron's.

It was a temptation, however, to dash past him on horseback so closely, that he fully believed his life to be in danger; and so, without a word in reply to the long speech, so profuse in doubtful service, which this man had made to her, Edith went on her way; and to her own relief, no doubt, as well as to his, there was soon an ample space of road between them.

This strange encounter with Jonathan Wild afforded to Edith ample food for reflection; and she went some miles now upon her road with a feeling of congratulation that she met no one, and was permitted in peace to arrange the information which she had casually become possessed of on the road that night.

That information consisted evidently in the fact that Jonathan Wild fully believed in the existence of documents important to the succession to the earldom of Whitcombe.

His anxiety to possess himself of these documents could only be in the interests of Lord Warringdale, with which interests his own were so intimately connected.

From the few words, likewise, which had been spoken, regarding Sir Dominick Browne, it was evident that his life hung upon a thread, and that the only reason why he was still permitted to survive the persecutions which had been directed against him, consisted in the fact that his enemies, and the enemies of Captain Heron, had not yet succeeded in getting possession of documents which they believed to be in the old gentleman's posession ; and therefore, the secret of where they were hidden might die with him.

" Ah!" cried Edith, " I will tell all this to Felix, and he will not blame me for the enterprise of this night, which brings him information of importance."

The encounter with Wild, and the little adventure at Sir Dominick's house, had occupied a considerable portion of the night, and Edith began to fancy, from the look of the eastern sky, that the morning was near at hand.

She had just emerged from a narrow lane, deeply cut up by cart tracks, when she heard voices; and she turned her horse's head, to seek the shadow of the tall trees at the entrance of the lane, while she again wrapped that cloak closely about her which had before been so effectual a disguise, even from the lynx eyes of Jonathan Wild.

The voices merely appeared to be those of people passing upon the road, so that Edith, now that she felt her appearance was not calculated to create observation or excite alarm, had no hesitation in asking them where she was.

" Why, this is Mortlake," said a man, in answer to the inquiry. " Be you one of them, sir, as took the great highwayman?"

" What highwayman?" cried Edith, with her heart beating violently; and forgetting all disguise of her natural tones, in the alarm of the moment.

" Why, the great Captain Heron, to be sure."

" No, no; oh, do not say so!"

" Well, sir, it's odd you should cry out in that sort of way. But I heard he was taken, and

EDITH HAS A DESPERATE ENCUNTER WITH HER MORTAL FOE.

Presented Gratis with No. 57 of the New Edition Edith the Captive; or, the Robbers of Epping Forest.

EACH WEEK IS PRESENTED RATIS A COLOURED ENGRAVING.

made an end of by my Lord Belessis, and some gentlemen from Kew."

Edith's head dropped upon the mane of her horse, and it seemed to her at that moment as if she would be glad if those men were to discover who and what she was, and make an end of her likewise, that she might follow Felix quickly from a world which no longer presented to her a single charm or association.

But this state of despair only lasted for a few seconds, and with indescribable joy she heard another of the men say, "Nay, mate, you're quite wrong there; for I saw them put him in the cage, and his horse in the pound; and he didn't seem to me to be hurt a bit, though I think there was a sort of fight."

"The cage! What cage?" cried Edith startlingly.

"The pound cage, away yonder, by Jukes's fields."

"Show me the way—show me the way."

"Why, sir, you've only got to go round there by Darby's cottage, and then you pass Leek's stables, and that brings you to Mr. Bumpus's garden wall."

Edith had started off before this direction, complicated as it was, had come to an end; and as she cleared the village, she was more and more certain that the morning was close at hand: but just as she was upon the point of emerging from the shadows of the last few cottages, she heard the rapid beat and trample of horses' feet; and down another thoroughfare than that in which she was, although only divided from it by a thin line of cottages, there evidently went at speed, first a single horseman, and then a troop of some half-dozen, or more, thundering at his rear.

"What can all this mean?" said Edith. "I have a terrible feeling that it in some way concerns Felix. Where, oh, where, is this cage, in which they said they had imprisoned him? I cannot bear this terrible suspense! It may be fatigue, or it may be confusion of brain; but I begin to feel like one in the midst of some confusing dream."

The horse had walked forward about some twenty paces of its own accord, while Edith was thus communing with herself; and then she could not forbear uttering a cry, partly of hope, and partly of fear, for she recollected the expression that had been used of a cage and a pound; and there, directly before her, was such an object, so clearly according to the description, that it could not be mistaken.

"Felix, Felix!" she cried, as she looked between the tall palisades,—"Felix, Felix, if you are here, speak to me! It is your Edith who addresses you!"

A low moaning sound from within the palisade was the only reply. But that moaning sound struck like a dagger to the heart of Edith; and seeing close to her what seemed to be a door in the palisade, she hastily dismounted, and summoned all her strength to try to force it.

She found, then, that this door or gate would have yielded to a touch; and she was nearly precipitated into the pound by the unrequired force which she used to the gate.

Then she saw a figure lying upon the ground, and imagination at once converted it into Felix Heron.

"I am here—I am here! Your own Edith! I am here to save you, or to perish with you!"

She dropped on her knees by the side of the prostrate figure; and then, by a violent exertion, no doubt attended with great pain, the figure rose to a sitting posture; and by the faint, grey light of that early morning, Edith and Lord Warringdale recognised each other.

"Ah!" shrieked Warringdale, "this repays me for all!"—and he made a clutch at the cloak which Edith wore; but with a feeling of loathing, she tore herself away from his grasp.

"You!" she cried. "It is you—worst enemy of my Felix, and would-be murderer of him whom I love! Oh, no, no! This cannot be! It is all a dream—a dream!"

"You shall wake to its reality, Edith Tarleton," cried Lord Warringdale; and in spite of his hurts and bruises, he tried to struggle to his feet, making, at the same time, repeated grasps at the heavy cloak which Edith wore, in order to detain her, and even assist him in rising from the ground.

"He has escaped me," he cried, "and left me here in pain and danger, incapable of following him; but you—you have come, by some infatuation, to surrender yourself in his place, and for the time present I am well satisfied with the exchange."

This was the most imprudent speech that my Lord Warringdale could possibly have made; and it at once cleared the mind of Edith of all doubt and anxiety in regard to Felix.

She seemed to see and comprehend everything of that night's adventure, as though she had been a spectator of all that had happened. Felix had been set upon by numbers, and captured; and then had made his escape, after a personal conflict with Warringdale. Surely that was the translation of his words; and as Edith felt a full conviction that such was the fact, she was doubly armed to resist the attack of her persevering enemy.

"He is free! he is free!" she said. "For once, I will even take the word of my Lord Warringdale. Unhand me, villain, or the peril be upon your own head!"

"Help! help!" cried Warringdale. "A hundred pounds for help!"

"Ah!" cried Edith; "then you will court destruction! Can you fancy for a moment that, with the means of resistance in my hands, I will yield to such as you are?"

"Help! help! rescue! To the cage! A hundred pounds reward!" again screamed Warringdale.

He still clung to the cloak; and Edith felt that there was instant danger if she did not free herself. With her disengaged right hand, then, she drew the sword she wore; and as it flashed before the eyes of the villain Warringdale, he made a grasp with one of his hands at the bare steel; but Edith felt the exigency of the moment too acutely to allow herself thus to be baffled. A sharp wound in the neck warned Lord Warringdale that the next thrust of the weapon might be fatal.

He recoiled in terror right to the wall of the cage.

Edith was free.

She sought not to pursue her advantage, but hastily leaving the pound, she mounted her horse, and with the drawn sword still in her hand, she gallopped from the spot.

Warringdale had not the strength to pursue her personally, but he did so with cries and yells, until they were lost in the distance.

And Edith might indeed have a well-grounded alarm that these cries would raise the village against her, particularly as the rapidly increasing morning light would be summoning the rustics to their labour.

She saw, a little in advance, a wide cattle gate, open, which led into the meadows; and the idea struck her that it would be wise to take that route for awhile, even if she made her way into the high road again, at some point clear of the village.

But Edith was yet to meet with another interruption, although not of a very alarming character.

Approaching the direction of the cage, at great speed, over a bit of waste ground, appeared a rather ludicrous individual, without a coat, and a nightcap on his head.

He flourished something in his right hand, which, as he neared her, Edith saw was a constable's staff.

"Stop! stop!" he cried. "Stop, everybody! I take up everybody at once, in the King's name! I hear cries—I hear shouts! There's a row! I'm Bumpus!"

Edith made up her mind, at once, to overawe this specimen of parochial authority; and she said sharply, "Fellow! how dare you appear before a nobleman of my rank, without your coat?"

Bumpus was awed into submission in a moment.

"I beg your pardon! Really, my lord, I beg your pardon; but I heard—that is, I thought I heard—and my wife hit me such a blow on my back with the frying-pan! 'Bumpus,' said she, 'there's something wrong with the cage!' And so, out I came, my lord, without my coat!"

"I accept your excuses for once. Go to the cage, and look after your prisoner."

"Yes, my lord!—most humbly, my lord! I will go with pleasure—anywhere but home; for Mrs. Bumpus, you see, my lord, when once she gets the frying-pan in her hand, never knows when to put it down again; and, even then, is apt to take up the bellows, my lord!"

"Away, fellow! and the next time you address me, I will trouble you not to say 'my lord.' That is not my title!"

"Oh, gracious! It's a Duke!" said Bumpus. "I humbly beg your Grace's pardon."

"Impertinent scoundrel!" said Edith. "Would you lower me to a dukedom?"

"Merciful providence!" said Bumpus, dropping on his knees. "He's a Royal Highness!"

"Ah!" said Edith, as if at last that was something satisfactory; and leaving Bumpus, then, on his knees in the middle of the road, she trotted through the gate.

"Hurrah!" said Bumpus. "My fortune's made! I've been spoken to by a Royal Highness, and been called an impertinent scoundrel!"

Edith found that a long stretch of open meadow lay before her, which she would have no difficulty in traversing, and keep, at the same time, within tolerable proximity of the road.

Then, as the morning brightened still further, and she could hear the birds singing merrily upon the branches of the trees, and see them darting in and out from the hedge-rows, she began to ask

herself what would be Captain Heron's feelings should he arrive at Epping Forest and find her absent.

This idea grew upon her minute by minute, until it became too painful to endure; and she resolved to make her way into the high road as soon as possible, as she was by no means sufficiently well acquainted with the neighbourhood to make her way with any certainty across the fields, where she might ride a long way before meeting any one who could direct her.

Imagine, then, Edith, in that brightening morning light, making her way towards the hedge-row that bounded the road, in the hope that she should find some gap there, through which to make her way.

The heavy cloak she had found cumbrous and warm, so she had folded it into the space which it was meant to occupy, when out of use, at the back of the saddle, and there securely strapped it.

To avoid the possibility of recognition or danger as she neared the hedge-row which divided her from the road, she replaced the half-mask upon her face; and thus, attired in Captain Heron's full costume, she had appeared on horseback on the other side of that hedge-row where she had so astonished Heron, and led his pursuers upon so false a track.

For one bewildering moment, Edith, from her elevated position in the meadows, caught a glance of something on the field-side of the opposite hedge which, by a sort of perception, without seeing it sufficiently for a stranger to have come to such a conclusion, she felt certain that it was Captain Heron and Daisy. Then it was that she told herself the idea or presentiment with which she had started upon that night expedition had come true, and that, after all, she was destined to save Heron from a great calamity, in the shape of the danger which awaited him.

To draw off the pursuit across the fields was, of course, the mode by which this was to be accomplished; and Edith did not hesitate for a moment, but, as we have before related, she turned her horse's head towards the meadows, and gallopped off at full speed.

Edith had but a vague idea that her proper route lay to the north of where she was; and at that early hour, while the sun was yet in the eastern sky, there was no danger whatever in deciding where that lay. And surely some good genius must have assisted Edith in her flight, for several turnings that she took at random, after regaining the highways and by-ways of the country, all turned out to be correct.

In an hour and a half, and just as nine o'clock came booming through the still air, from a village church clock, Edith began to see familiar signs and tokens of the neighbourhood of the forest.

"Safe! I am safe!" she cried; "and surely I have done some good, if that were indeed Felix I saw crouching by a prostrate horse, and so well hidden from the road by the hedge-row. I have left him at liberty to save himself; for his pursuers certainly came after me. If it were not Felix, then is he at home in the old forest ruin, and I shall at least bring him some intelligence that will be welcome to him."

Edith trotted slowly, for the horse was evidently jaded, not so much from the actual distance it had traversed, as from the number of hours it had been on foot.

And now the creature seemed to know that it was approaching its home and a place of rest; for as Edith entered one of the glades of the forest, it threw off its previous somewhat lagging gait, and with an air of alacrity trotted up the greensward.

"Whoop! whoop!" cried a voice, in imitation of an owl.

Edith knew the signal well.

"Hawks and herons!" she cried, as she looked about her, but could see no one.

"That's it!" cried a voice; and then, after hanging by his arms for a few moments from the branch of a tree, Tom Ripon dropped down dexterously enough upon the greensward beneath.

"Ah, Tom!" cried Edith; "tell me, has Felix returned?"

"The Captain, Lady Edith?" said Tom.

"Yes! oh, yes!"

"Well," said Tom, "I never took the liberty of calling him Felix, yet; but he hasn't come back, Lady Edith—I can tell you that; for when he does, whichever way he comes into the forest, the four scouts call out to each other, so that they all know of it; and they haven't said a word for many a long hour."

"Heaven send him back, then, in safety!" said Edith. "I feel that it is better I should return first. And something seems to tell me now that he will be safe. It was my mission to be of use to him this night, and I have performed it."

CHAPTER CXXVI.

CAPTAIN HERON AND OGLE REACH HOME THROUGH SOME DIFFICULTIES.

"Ogle," said Heron, as he looked out from the cart in which he was ensconced with Daisy, "I think we are all alone upon the road now, and may trust our voices."

"To be sure, Captain; but we shan't be all alone for long, for as soon as we get to the other entrance of the lane, I can run down and get my horse, and bring our fellows back with me."

"That is well! that is well!" said Heron. "We shall certainly be in too strong force, then, to be interfered with."

"Ah, you may well say that, Captain. We shall not meet anybody between this and old Epping Forest who will be inclined to dispute the road with ten mounted men, to say nothing of yourself, in the cart with Daisy. And here we are, Captain; so I'll leave you all to yourself for a little while."

"Fear not for me, Ogle, and do not hurry. Our four-footed friend here will no doubt take the opportunity of going fast asleep again; but he can be wakened up when you come back."

Ogle waved his arm, and then darted down the lane, in the shady recesses of which he had told Heron's band to wait until he came to them with some news.

The horse and cart had been drawn up close to the side of the road, and for a few moments the drowsy creature cropped the soft, sweet herbage from the bank.

But this was a philosophic horse, and must have heard somewhere of the Spanish proverb, "that he who sleeps over the dinner-hour dines;" and no doubt, by a subtle process of reasoning, he at once applied that to breakfast as well as to dinner, for after a few mouthfuls he gave it up, and fell fast asleep.

"I never, in all my life," said Heron, "came near such an animal! Why, Daisy, I don't think you sleep as much in a week as this fellow-creature of yours does in four-and-twenty hours!"

Daisy made a quick movement of her head at the mention of her name by Captain Heron, and he was about again to speak in those tones to his faithful steed, which, although she could not know the meaning of them, had the sound of that universal language of kindness about them which no creature misunderstood, when he heard the rapid trot of a horse, and the sound of wheels approaching.

Heron kept himself far back in the cart, and only projected his head sufficiently to command a view of the road.

He saw a low-hung chaise approaching, with one person in it; and this person seemed to have not only his hands occupied, inasmuch as in one of them was the whip, and in the other was a pocket-handkerchief with a lace border, but one of his eyes was fully engaged, by having a gold eye-glass stuck into it by muscular contraction, through which he seemed to be trying to observe with accuracy the covered cart.

Probably Captain Heron would have allowed the exquisite—for such he was, being dressed in the height of the reigning mode, and having an air of ineffable affectation and vanity about him—to pass unnoticed; but the traveller in the chaise would not have it so, and pulled up abruptly abreast of the cart.

"Yokel, and low fellow," he said, with a drawl, "is this a high road, or a cross road, that will take me to the Palace at Kew?"

"It's a high road," said Heron.

"Oh, very well, low fellow; but whenever you speak to a gentleman, who condescends to ask you a question, you should say 'sir,' or 'your worship,' and take off your hat."

"Really!" said Heron.

"Yes; and I'm sorry there's no constable here, and the stocks, low rustic, to teach you better manners."

"So am I," said Heron.

"Ah! as soon as one gets out of the atmosphere of St. James's, one's nerves become assailed by common vulgar odours in the country. Hay-stacks, flowers, and bean-fields, are really too much for a delicate organization; and I'm forced to carry a scented handkerchief in my hand, saturated with the last new fashionable perfume, which all the ladies are so delighted with. It is called *bouquet de tous les rois*."

"Why," said Heron, "you are perfectly entertaining! I've not met such a funny fellow as you for a month."

"Funny!" ejaculated the exquisite. "Low, vulgar fellow! I never was funny in my life. What a ridiculous country idea, to suppose that anybody who has breathed the air of a Court can be funny! I shall make all the ladies of my acquaintance die with laughing when I tell them I was called funny. Adieu, rustic! Adieu, low man!"

"Stop!" said Captain Heron. "You have forgotten——"

"Eh, vulgarian?"

"You've forgot something, idiot!"

"Eh?"

"The toll."

"The what?"

"There's a toll on this road, and you've forgot to pay it."

"A toll? Insolent and low companion of cows, wheel-barrows, carts, and bad pigs, what do you mean? I don't see any toll-bar."

"I'm the toll-bar."

"You? You a toll-bar?"

"Yes; and this cart holds the money. If anybody refuses to pay, I let them just get past a little way, and then lodge a couple of bullets in their back. After that, their dead bodies are sold by the road trustees to the highest bidder. Now, sir, if you please!"

Captain Heron levelled one of those long, handsome pistols of which he had a tolerable stock in Epping Forest, and with two of which Ogle had provided him, in lieu of those which had been taken from Daisy's saddle, right in the face of the exquisite, whose alarm was so great that he opened his mouth so wide it seemed as if he thought the safest plan would be to catch the bullet there at once, and prevent it going any further.

"Now, sir," said Heron, "I will trouble you to get out of that chaise, and to bring me, in a respectful manner, what money and valuables you have about you."

"Good gracious! Spare my money, and take my life! I'm only a poor fellow, and travel for Mr. Dobbs, the haberdasher, with samples of needles and pins! Have mercy upon me, good Mr. Toll-bar, and take threepence! I believe it's the usual charge."

"Quick!" said Heron, sharply. "I can hear some friends of mine approaching, who all keep toll-bars beside myself; and if they catch you, they will hang you, to a certainty!"

"In a terrible state of fright, the exquisite handed to Captain Heron a tolerably well-filled purse, and likewise a paste-board box, which he took from the chaise."

"What is here?" said Heron.

"The samples of needles and pins, Mr. Toll-bar, if you please."

"Well, I don't want them," said Heron.

"They'll be useful to you."

As he spoke, Captain Heron hit the exquisite a crack on the head with the paste-board box, and in a moment he was enveloped in a shower of pins and needles, of all sorts and sizes.

"Now go on," said Heron; "and you can tell the ladies, when you see them, that you've really been funny for once in a way, for I never saw anybody look so ridiculous in all my life."

Captain Heron then made a sharp sound with his mouth, and likewise whistled aloud, which had the full effect he intended it—namely, to start the horse in the chaise, which went on at a good hard trot down the road, with the exquisite rushing after it, calling out in vain to the animal to stop.

Captain Heron had hardly time to laugh at this ridiculous little adventure, when Ogle appeared with the band from the lane.

"All's right, Captain," he said. "I hope no one has interfered with you while I have been away?"

"Nothing of consequence," said Heron, "and all's well."

"Bless me," said Ogle, "the road's strewed with pins and needles."

Heron laughed.

"They are the result of a little adventure of mine," he said, "which, at all events, has been productive of something more substantial. All's fish that comes to my net, Ogle, upon the road. Take care of this purse."

"That I will, Captain. It feels heavy too. Hilloa! is this the sort of fish worth the taking?"

"What is it?"

Ogle had looked into the purse, and then he fixed his eyes on Heron's face, with a comical expression, as he said, "Buttons!"

For a moment, Heron looked grave, and then he burst into a laugh.

"Bravo!" he said; "the fellow has got the better of me, after all; and if ever I meet him again; for all his affectation and nonsense, he shall go free for this clever trick. Buttons—actually buttons!"

"Oh, there's no doubt of that," said Ogle, as he poured some out into his hand.

"Never mind," cried Alkins, "they'll be useful. I want one on my waistcoat, now."

The rest of the band laughed, and then Heron called out, "The morning wears on. Lead the way, Ogle, and let us feel that each step we take, now, nears us to old Epping Forest. I have had a night of strange adventures, and have passed through as much peril as ever I did in all my life. Lead the way, Ogle. Four of you then follow; and the others will form a rear guard behind the cart; for I cannot desert Daisy, however slow may be our progress. Forward, my men, forward!"

"Yes, Captain," said Ogle, "it's all very well to say forward, but don't you see that horse is fast asleep?"

"So he is—so he is! We shall never get on with him."

"I don't think he's a bad horse," said Ogle, "when once he's awake."

Ogle then advanced, and bawled in the horse's ear, "If you please, Dobbin, we want to go."

Heron at the same time gave him a dig with the handle of the whip, and the horse, in consequence of these two inducements, woke up with a spasmodic sort of start and trotted on; but they had not proceeded above a couple of hundred yards, when loud cries of "Stop, Stop! Woa! Stop! Where are you going?" resounded on the road, and the horse and chaise of the exquisite, flew past at a hard gallop, with that gentleman himself pursuing it with all the speed he could muster. His hat was gone, and his eye-glass flew out perpendicularly behind his back; while he seemed, by the state of his apparel, to have had two or three good rolls in the road.

"That's the button-man," cried Heron: "some one has turned his horse, and they're going towards now."

Captain Heron's band raised a whooping cry, such as they had often made the glades of Epping Forest resound with; and the horse in the chaise hearing the shout, burst into a furious gallop, and still pursued by the button-man, disappeared from view.

Ogle, without sacrificing much distance to do so, took all the by-ways he could towards Epping; but at the rate of progress that the horse which drew the cart went, it was eleven o'clock before the cavalcade reached the confines of the forest.

Scarcely ever before, at such an hour, had Captain Heron shown himself and his men with such force to the eye of day; but no one seemed to observe them, and it was a great relief to Heron when he plunged beneath the overhanging boughs, which had formed to him a home and a refuge for many a day.

Then his thoughts, which had really never wandered from her, flew with renewed vigour to Edith.

"Ogle," he said, "I leave you to take care of Daisy. See to her well, and let me know how she is in an hour. I fear my long absence must greatly have alarmed Edith."

In truth, Edith had been greatly alarmed, but

the action of the night had tended, by occupying her mind, to diminish very much the suffering she would have undergone had she been waiting for the whole of that night in the deep silence of Epping Forest, full of anxiety for the return of Felix.

It was with some amazement and terror, that he heard her account of her night's adventure.

"Ah, then, Edith," he said, it, was, you who saved me at that critical moment when I could not desert Daisy—when the slightest examination of the hedge would surely have discovered me."

"Felix, Felix!" cried Edith—"may I not rejoice at that?"

"Ah, yes; but still you fill me with a thousand fears; for now I shall never turn my back upon the old Forest, to seek adventures on the heath, or on the road, but I shall fancy in each bush or young tree-sapling that I see before me in the dim night, that my eyes rest upon you; and whenever there is tumult or danger, I shall be full of a thousand fears, lest you are secretly a sharer in it."

"No, no!" said Edith. "That must not be."

"And yet, my Edith, it will be, if you pursue this course."

"Then I dare not."

"No, Edith. Rather let me hear you say you will promise me, that this night that has passed away, has been the first and the last of your adventures on the road."

"I will promise; for now I feel that any danger I might be the chance means of rescuing you from, would be more than counterbalanced by the thousand fears you would continually have for my safety."

"Indeed, and in truth it would be so. Let me but feel that you are in safety, and I shall be freed from an anxiety that would paralyze my arm, and disorder my judgment!"

"I do promise—I do promise, Felix; and be assured that I will keep my word."

"A thousand, thousand thanks!"

"But yet, Felix, the information I have received from this chance meeting with Jonathan Wild is important."

"It is—it is, Edith; and, at the same time, it fills me with many reproaches."

"Reproaches, Felix?"

"Yes—oh, yes! I feel that my first care, when I was free myself, ought to have been to rescue poor Sir Dominick Browne from the clutches of those infamous Whalleys at Highgate; and I will not engage in any new adventure until I have made the attempt. On Saturday, you know, Edith, takes place that ball at St. James's Palace, at which, in compliance with the advice and wishes of our good friend the Earl of Bridgewater, I am to appear, and present my written statement to the King."

"Alas! alas, Felix! whenever you mention that, I seem to be possessed with a thousand fears!"

"Nay, nay—courage, and dismiss them."

"I cannot—I cannot! You will be surrounded by many enemies; and there will be such force at hand that resistance will be futile."

"Nay, do not despair. I feel assured that nothing will happen to me, by following the advice of one so noble and generous-hearted as the young Earl; and it is a great thing, my Edith, to have made a friend and supporter of a nobleman of such rank, and a member of the Privy Council at Court."

"It is—it is; and yet——"

"Think not of it—speak not of it, Edith. Take now the rest you so much need. I have some business in the forest."

"Away again, Felix? Away again?" said Edith, in a reproachful tone.

"Only in the forest, dear one. As I sallied forth last night, I met that poor demented creature who long since would have starved but that I have taken care her wants should be supplied. My men call her the 'Maniac of the Well,' because she resides in an ancient excavation close to one of the springs in the old forest; and that her griefs have made her maniacal, poor thing, there cannot be a doubt."

"Go, then, Felix. It is an errand of mercy."

"Not entirely, Edith, although I will myself carry her food enough to supply her simple wants for a week or more. But in her frenzy she let drop some expressions, which seemed to imply that she had known my mother."

"Can that be possible? Surely, they were but some accidental words of her disordered brain."

"I should have thought so, Edith, but that she named my mother by the name she bore before she became the wife of the Earl of Whitcombe. No frenzy, you know, Edith, could have taught her that."

"You are right, Felix; and I have but one request: it is, that you will take me with you. Indeed, I do not feel fatigued; and if I go not with you, I shall but watch for your return with a weariness that will be at once denied sleep and relaxation."

"Come, my Edith, then, come. The sun is climbing high in the heavens, and the sylvan glades of our forest home are full of a thousand pleasant sights and sounds. We will walk together to the old spring, and seek this poor creature, whom misfortune has crazed."

CHAPTER CXXVII.

THE REVELATION OF THE MANIAC OF THE WELL.

IT would have been a pleasant sight to any one who had wished well to Captain Heron and fair Edith, to have seen them walking through that pretty woodland scene in the then deep and dusky forest of Epping. There were deer, too, in the forest at that period; and many a creature made its home in the deep tangled brushwood that in some places linked the trees together in a mass of rich vegetation.

And if the sight of that fair young wife and her gallant husband would have been pleasant to the eyes of those who wished them well, what gall and wormwood would it have been to those who for so long had tried all in their power to make them unhappy, and who had resisted their union to the utmost extremity of mortal power!

Like a monarch of some fair dominion which he knew to be well guarded by those who set a real and loveable value upon his life, Captain Heron, with Edith by his side, walked gently down the green aisles of the forest.

Edith was well enough acquainted with all that Heron himself knew concerning the poor old Maniac of the Well, and she could not forget that, in the wild ravings of the unfortunate creature, it was her own father who was accused, by the name of "Hanging Judge Tarleton," of being the cause of all her woes.

The distance was not about half a mile through some of the narrow openings of the wood to the old well, where the maniac had taken up her abode. There was an abrupt knoll or hillock, and in old times no doubt much labour had been expended in removing a portion of the sloping ground, so as to make a perpendicular face of earth, some thirty feet in height.

A number of very ancient trees grew upon and about that spot; and in the cavernous recess behind the little bubbling spring in which the maniac lived, there seemed abundant evidence of the oft-asserted fact, that in its mature age the roots of a tree very nearly equalled that portion of the tree itself which is above the ground.

Certain it is that the interior of the cavern in the occupation of the maniac was perfectly interlaced by these roots, many of which were of great size and thickness, so that any fall of earth within was quite out of the question.

The spring was one of those "holy wells," which in monastic times were taken abundant care of, and which it is a thousand pities to see now neglected, and in so many of the fair districts of England, choked up by rubbish and the *débris* of many summers.

You descended from the surface of the earth to this well by a flight of about six stone steps, and then you came to a large slab of fair, grey marble, in the centre of which was a rudely-shaped hollow, deep enough to dip a cup or drinking-horn in; and as the water in the well, from some subterranean source, always rose rippling over the surface of this marble slab, a pure draught from the clear cold spring was ever to be obtained.

As Captain Heron approached near to the spot, he looked anxiously for some indication of the maniac's presence, but he could see nothing of her.

A very old tree, which had been struck by lightning many years since—the charred and blackened stump of which was all overgrown with ivy and wild flowers—stood near the mouth of the cavern; and it was not until Edith, by an exclamation, directed Captain Heron's attention to this stump of tree, that he saw, crouched down close to it, the object of his search.

"Yes," he said; "I see her now. She is either asleep, or in one of those long fits of meditation to which she is subject."

"Should we disturb her, Felix?"

"Perhaps it will be a mercy to do so, for I can see her now, at times, shuddering. And do you not hear that she moans as though suffering from some disturbing dream?"

"Yes—ah, yes. Let us leave this basket, with the provisions, in the cavern."

"Do so, while I arouse her. She knows my voice well; and is ever glad for me to speak to her, provided I do not call her mother. It is a name that comes naturally to one's lips in addressing one so aged as she is; but it evidently awakens too many sympathies and recollections for her endurance, and I will avoid it."

"Do so—oh, do so! Let us be careful not to add one pang to those which have driven her to be what she is."

Captain Heron slowly approached the crouching figure of the maniac. He laid his hand lightly on her shoulder, as he said, in low and gentle tones, "Did I not tell you I would visit you?"

She sprung to her feet with a wild cry.

"Who speaks? who speaks?" she cried. "Do you bring what they call a pardon—a reprieve? No! no! No pardon! They only shall be pardoned who are guilty; and my boy is innocent!"

"Do you not know me?" said Heron.

The poor creature clasped her hands over her eyes for a few moments; and when she again looked at Heron, she said, more quietly, "Yes, I know you—I know you! You are the good genius —the genius of the wood; and so long as there are a thousand trees in the forest you will be among them."

"There are many more than that now," said Heron, who was glad to see her so calm and collected. "But do you not recollect, not many hours since, when I met you, I spoke to you, and you then mentioned a name which I wish to hear from your lips again?"

"Hush! hush!" cried the maniac, and she put herself into an attitude of listening. "Hush! Do you hear nothing?"

"Nothing but the sighing of the wind among the leaves of the old forest."

"Then I will tell you the name again. It was the cruel Judge Tarleton; for, although he hanged my son, you see, and killed me, I came to life again, because I had a mission—which was, to keep the vultures from his eyes. They sleep now— they always do at the noonday sun."

"Oh, what a wreck is this!" said Edith. "Can it be possible that my father has produced all this misery?"

"Let me speak to her, Edith," said Heron, "or we shall have her wandering from the point on which I fain would question her."

There was a wild, strange look gathering in the eyes of the maniac; and before Heron could prevent her, even if he had felt so inclined, she rushed into the cavern, and reappeared with the long, forked branch of a tree, with which she was seldom without.

"Ah!" cried Heron, "I shall lose her again; for now she will make her way to the common, and be full of wild ravings for many an hour."

This seemed indeed probable enough, for the Maniac of the Well uttered some strange cries, and waved the forked branch of a tree high above her head.

Heron then thought that some sudden impulse alone would change her purpose, and he cried out loudly and almost fiercely, "It is of Amelia Staunton I came to speak."

The name seemed to act like a spell upon the faculties of the maniac, and she cowered down as if she had been struck a blow.

"Amelia Staunton?" she said. "Amelia Staunton? Who speaks of Amelia Staunton?"

"I speak of her," said Heron, "and you should speak of her. You know me well, and that I am not among those who would be your persecutors, or hers. Tell me then, I conjure you, what you know of Amelia Staunton."

The poor maniac seemed for a few moments so utterly confused and bewildered between the present and the past, as to be quite incapable of action: then, to the surprise and consternation of Captain Heron and Edith, she fell forward upon her face, and they thought for a few moments that she was dead.

Edith ran down the little steps that led to the well, for she had observed that upon the lowest of them was a small earthen vessel, and in another moment she had returned with it filled with clear water. Captain Heron was supporting the head of the maniac, and Edith dashed some of the water on her face, and placed the earthen vessel to her lips.

Some very strange revulsion of feeling seemed to have come over the poor woman. The wild, uncertain light of insanity had left her eyes, and her features were composed to such gentleness and peace, as Heron had never seen them wear before.

"Who spoke of Amelia Staunton?" she said

gently. "Did some one mention her, or was it only a dream?"

"It was I," said Heron.

The poor creature looked wistfully in his face for a few moments, and then turned her gaze upon Edith, as she added mildly, "And you, too?"

"I likewise would mention her," said Edith, "and implore you to tell all you know of her."

"Will you help her?"

"With all our hearts."

"Then I will tell you. Strange things have happened to me since I looked upon Amelia Staunton, or else I have dreamt or imagined them, for at times, you see, I almost think that my wits are much deranged, and I know not what I say or what I do. Amelia Staunton, then, was the young bride of Lord Warringdale."

"Warringdale?" whispered Edith to Heron. "What does she mean?"

"She's right," said Heron in the same tone. "It is the title of courtesy which the heir presumptive to the earldom of Whitcombe always bears, and when the late Earl was married to my mother, he had not yet come to the title."

The maniac clasped her hands together, and looked down upon the bright spring grass of the forest glade, and for a few moments her thoughts seemed to be far away.

"Speak again," whispered Heron—"speak again of Amelia Staunton."

"I will, I will!" she said in an abstracted tone, as if communing with herself. "Lord Warringdale married her. He was not a very young man then, but his father was old—old, so very old, and he had been waiting long for the earldom, when the bright eyes and sunny looks of Amelia Staunton fell upon his heart, and he married her. I alone, as the confidential servant, who had tended her from childhood, tried in vain to dissuade her from the match; for I thought the man was cold and heartless; and he talked too much of her beauty to be constant to her. But when I found that she was bent upon it, and would not be turned aside, I would not quit her, although she looked coldly upon me, and the Lord Warringdale spoke harshly to me; for he knew I was no friend of his. But he married her—yes, he married her!"

"Where?" said Heron.

"At the old church at Barnes."

"She speaks lucidly, and I will believe all. Edith, Edith, let me not forget a single word she utters."

"Yes," added the maniac; "and contrary to his wish, I was there. It was contrary to hers, too, then; although she clung to me in many an hour of grief, since; and for a time, all went well —yes, all went well!"

The maniac covered her face with her hands, and swayed to and fro in silence.

Heron was afraid that this gentle period, this peaceful calm of the brain, was passing away, and that he should hear no more.

He spoke to her very gently and persuasively.

"You interest me greatly. Try calmly and gently to collect your thoughts, and to tell me more of Amelia Staunton. You say that all went well for a time : what then happened? You know I am your friend. Speak to me, I beg of you."

"The old man was dead, and he was Earl of Whitcombe then; and it was rarely he came to the pretty villa, and when he did, it was but to rave, and wish the child was dead!"

"What child?"

"Amelia Staunton's. I nursed the babe; till one night there was a fire, and the red flames turned all the beauteous trees to the colour of molten copper; the honeysuckle upon the ancient porch crackled up, and was scorched in the fiery flame in a moment; and from that time to now I have seen nothing, and know nothing, of the fair Countess and her boy."

"Nay," cried Heron, "you must know more. Had the Earl no visitors that you could think of? Was there no friend who visited at this place, whose name you can mention to me?"

"Once, yes—once, yes, only—there came one with him, but he spoke kindly and tenderly, and he seemed to feel that some great misfortune was about the place. He never came again."

"Can you recollect his name?"

"Yes—in a moment. It was Sir Dominick Browne."

"Ah!" cried Heron, "now this story unravels itself. Like some tangled skein, my Edith, to which you get the clue piece by piece, it spreads itself before your eyes. Do you not see it all plainly? My poor mother married for her beauty, and to be the plaything of an hour; then deserted as an encumbrance to the new state of the Earl of Whitcombe—perhaps murdered."

"Alas, alas!"

"Yes, Edith, do you not see?—and that simple-hearted, unsuspicious Sir Dominick Browne, persuaded by the Earl, that I, the child, had no real claim to his name or dignities, took me, as a waif and stray in the great world, to his own home, where passed all my early days."

"And your mother?" said Edith.

"Oh, if I could but know the truth! If I knew in whose breast it lay locked, pity or fear should wring the hidden secret forth, and I would know all."

At this moment, the maniac sprang to her feet, and brandishing aloft the forked branch of a tree, she cried aloud with all her old distempered fury, "Time, time—it is time! I hear the clapping of the heavy wings, and the sharp rattle of the beaks steeped in gore. It may be they come from distant climes, where the battle rages, but still they seek my boy's eyes, and I must fly to save him. Away, away!—vultures, away! They shall not touch him! Help, help! I hear you, now, upon the fair morning air. You hear me coming, and you scream to feel that you are baulked in your dainty prey."

With these wild cries, and many others of similar import, the Maniac of the Well fled through the forest.

"Felix," said Edith, "all this is but a confirmation of what you knew. What can be done? Oh! what can be done to rid your heart of the load of anxiety that oppresses it?"

"Indeed, indeed, I know not! But little dreamt I that this poor creature, who has been the object of my bounty for so long, was in any way connected with my mother. I have but one hope, Edith, and that is in the course suggested to me by the Earl of Bridgewater; and oh! how I wish that Saturday were come, which would carry me to the Court ball; and I will extinguish those hopes for ever, or raise them higher."

THE MANIAC OF THE WELL REVEALS IMPORTANT SECRETS.

Presented Gratis with No. 58, of the New Edition of Ela the Captive; or, the Robbers of Epping Forest.

EACH WEEK IS PRESENTED GRATIS A COLOURED ENGRAVING.

"Felix, Felix," said Edith now, in a suppressed tone, "I fancy I hear voices in the wood."

"Ah, in what direction?"

"From yonder glade; and see, if my eyes do not deceive me, there are some persons approaching among the trees."

"Come into the cavern, Edith. Strangers will, at times, walk through the forest, and we let them do so, keeping, however, an eye upon their movements; for, after all, I am not so much the King of old Epping, that I can close it up against all wayfarers. Come into the cavern, and we shall observe them secretly."

"They seem to be making towards the well."

"Indeed it would seem so; but here we are safe."

At first sight the cavern did not seem to present any very great facilities for hiding; but Heron knew a great deal more of it than that first sight would have induced any one to believe there was to know, for at its further extremity there was an irregular jagged-like opening among the old roots of the trees, beyond which all seemed dark as midnight, and it would have required a bold man indeed to have ventured into that recess without a knowledge of where it would lead him.

Captain Heron, however, did not see the necessity of immediately taking refuge in this place, as his object was to watch the strangers, and see what manner of men they were.

As they approached through the trees he could see that one of them was in a ragged and wretched suit of soldier's regimentals—while the other had a staid and steady look about him, which suggested the idea that he was some small tradesman, or chapman, in some petty way of business.

There was a solemnity about his air and manner which likewise betokened extraordinary self-conceit, and it seemed to Heron as if he were haranguing his companion in some way which made that companion exceedingly impatient.

This strangely assorted pair made their way in a straggling sort of way towards the well, whereupon the staid and solemn-looking personage, waving his arm about in an oratorical manner, exclaimed, "Tummus, Tummus, I told you so! Here is balm—here is balm!"

"What do you mean by balm?" said the other. "It's something else, master, that I want, that begins with B—and that's brandy."

"Nay, nay," cried the other, with a strong conventicle twang; "here is comfort, and here are cooling draughts for the inward man; and yea, I will sit upon this stone, Tummus, and make some remarks upon your sinful life—yea, will I."

"And do you mean to tell me," growled "Tummus," "that I'm to get nothing but cold spring water?"

"Did you not say you were athirst?"

"Yes; but it was for something strong."

"Water is strong. It beareth ships upon its heaving surface, and the mighty whale gambolleth therein."

"Oh, bother!" cried Tummus. "How can you go on in that sort of way? It's all along of you, master, I had to enlist for a soldier; and now I'm a deserter, and I don't know what will become of me."

"Yea, Tummus; thou wert my apprentice, and I feel for thee. But for me thou would'st have been caught this morning, and then the cat with the nine tails would have descended on thy back, Tummus."

"But what's it all owing to?" growled Tummus. "You know I helped you to set fire to your house, and you got ever such a lot of money by it, and it all fell upon me."

"Tummus, Tummus, Tummus! if you listen not to the moral precepts I shall propound, while sitting upon this stone, the fire that was in my house and shop at Brentford will be as nothing to the fire into which thou will topple in time to come. Amen!"

"A pretty pair!" said Heron, in a low tone, to Edith.

————

CHAPTER CXXVIII.

CAPTAIN HERON RECEIVES NEWS FROM LONDON.

SOME similar conversation to that which we have recorded took place between these two eccentric persons, Tummus and his master, and then they both started, with an appearance of alarm, as coming rapidly down the forest glade in which they were, there appeared a mounted man.

Edith and Captain Heron could only know from their place of concealment that some one was approaching, by the eager looks of both the deserter and his master in that direction.

"Tummus," said the latter, "I advise you to take to the trees."

"And I would advise you, too, master," said Tummus; "for since you've been seen with me, they may say you helped me to desert."

"Nay; but who shall say I've been seen with thee, Tummus?"

"You will be seen soon enough, master; there's a man on horseback coming on as fast as he can through the forest."

"Even so—even so," said Tummus's master. "I have a suspicion, Tummus, that thou art, for once in a way, in the right. Come on. Let us get among the trees."

These two strange persons hid themselves now with alacrity some distance off; and hardly had they done so, when the mounted man, who was in the dress of a groom, or outrider, to some person of destinction, reached the spot.

This man, when he saw the old well, and the tree that had been stricken by lightning, and the cavern in the hillock, drew rein, and called out in a loud voice, "I have a letter for Captain Heron."

He seemed to know that eyes, invisible to him, might be upon him; and to substantiate what he said, he took a letter from his waist-belt, and held it up in his right hand.

"I will go out to this man," said Heron: "he may bring me news of consequence."

"Oh, be cautious, Felix—be cautious! There may be more treachery in all this than you dream of."

"It would be dangerous, then, to the projector. There is but one man, and if he knows sufficient of me to seek me in this place, his knowledge will likewise extend to the fact that he seeks far more danger himself than he can bring to me. Keep in hiding, Edith, yet for a few moments, and all will be well."

Edith still remained in the cavern, but Captain

Heron, in the most leisurely manner in the world, strolled out of it, to meet the man who was approaching on horseback.

"You inquired for Captain Heron," he said. "I am he. What would you with me?"

The groom touched his hat respectfully.

"I am the Earl of Bridgewater's groom, sir," he said, "and his lordship trusts me, as he has known me from a boy; so he told me to ride haste to Epping Forest, and to tell no one of my errand, but to deliver into the hands of Captain Heron himself this letter."

"I see you hesitate," said Heron, "because you cannot know that I am the person you seek."

"Well, sir, I think it's all right, because I can see you're a gentleman, and I will give you the letter.'

"I am, indeed, the person you seek, although I have no ready means of proving it. I was to have seen the Earl on Saturday, but perhaps this note alters the arrangement."

"Ah, sir!" said the groom. "Now I know it's all right, for the Earl himself made the same remark—that he was to have seen Captain Heron on Saturday."

Heron opened the letter hastily, and found it to contain the following words:—

"There is an alteration of day on which the great Court ball will be held at St. James's. It takes place to-night. I have seen Lady Castleneau, and she will expect you there not later than nine o'clock. Do not let this opportunity go by of getting possibly a step forward in your affairs.

"I do not sign this, for fear of accidents."

"Then I have little time to spare," said Heron. "Will you take a verbal message back to the good Lord Bridgewater, and tell him you have seen Captain Heron, who will attend strictly to the advice contained in his letter. Take this guinea for yourself, and when you get a mile clear of the forest get refreshment both for yourself and horse."

The groom touched his hat, and cantered off up the forest glade; and Heron turned again into the cavern to communicate with Edith in regard to this sudden summons to London.

Edith then looked so imploringly in his face, without speaking, that he saw her heart was full of some request or resolution.

"I see you would say something, Edith. What is it?"

"Let me go to town with you. I shall be safe at my aunt's house; for be assured that in that old mansion there are other secret chambers and recesses besides that which has become by accident known to Jonathan Wild. Let me go to town with you, and I shall feel a thousand times more content. While here, so far from what cannot but be a scene of danger, I should suffer a martyrdom of fears!"

Heron smiled.

"And probably, dear Edith, whether I would or no, I should have you galloping to St. James's?"

"No, no! Never again, without your consent!"

"Then, Edith, you shall come with me. We will take Ogle, and ride in the dusk of the evening. I fancy, too, it will be much better and safer if you keep the same attire which carried you through the adventures of last night in safety."

"Yes," said Edith. "There shall again be two Captain Herons in the field, to puzzle and confound his enemies!"

"Be it so, Edith—be it so. In five hours from now, the shades of evening will gather among the old trees. Until that time, you shall rest, for so much fatigue will tell upon you suddenly. For some nights, kept up by the excitement of adventure, I have been upon the road without a thought of sleep; and then, as if Nature were intent upon avenging herself for such a slight upon her behests, I have dropped into a profound slumber upon the back of Daisy; and if the world had been offered me to do so, I could not have unclosed my weary eyes!"

Edith was but too willing to adopt any suggestion of Heron's that would not interfere with her journey to London. And now we will suppose that those few hours that intervened between that time and sunset have passed away, and near the mouth of one of the narrow openings which led in from the open country, there might have been seen a man, mounted upon one horse, and holding the bridles of two others.

This man was attired in a dark suit, and the horse he rode was of considerable strength and symmetry.

Indeed, the two horses whose bridles he held, were animals of value, and by the impatience with which they pawed the turf beneath their feet, it would seem that they were able and willing to undertake an instant journey.

The mounted man was our old acquaintance, Ogle, and he held these two horses in waiting for Edith and Captain Heron.

Daisy was not yet sufficiently recovered from the wound in her foot to enable her to take to the road; but in the possession of Captain Heron's band there were some very choice animals, from which he could pick and choose, and those that Ogle held were two of the best and most docile.

The slant rays of sunlight fell with golden beauty through the branches of the old trees; and then just as Heron, with Edith by his side, reached the spot where the horses were in waiting, the sun sunk beneath the horizon; and the change upon the face of nature seemed little less than magical.

A gloomy obscurity seemed to rise up in the forest like a cloud from the very earth; and over the tree-tops there swept a sighing sound, which seemed as if it took from them at once all the golden beauty the bright sunbeams had lent them.

"It is time, Edith," said Heron; "and there is Ogle with the horses. It seems so strange to me, to go on any expedition of moment without Daisy."

"Yes, Felix; but she will be well cared for in your absence."

"I am sure of that—I am sure of that! The difficulty would be to get Tom Ripon to leave her stable. Is all right, Ogle?"

"Quite, Captain, I think."

"You only think?"

"Well, I thought I saw two men, Captain, lurking about the wood."

"What do they look like?"

"One rather startled me, for he seemed like a soldier."

"Then I, too, have seen them; and although I hardly know yet what to make of them, I do not think they bring us any positive danger. Now, off we go! I think you had better ride in advance Ogle, some fifty paces. You know the road well, and can pay the toll-bars for us all. Make direct for Bloomsbury, since it is Lady Castleneau's house we wish to reach as early as possible."

Both Edith and Heron wore cloaks, so that they were not likely to excite any particular observation on the road to London; and for once in the way, Captain Felix Heron, the highwayman, rode the entire distance from Epping Forest to town without an adventure.

As they neared London, they passed, of course, many passengers and vehicles; but it was no part of the policy of Heron now to dispute the way with any one; and unless some adventurous knight of the road had cried " Stand!" to him and to Edith, they were not likely to be embroiled in any affair of that description.

It was with a sensation of great relief to Edith, that they drew up to the iron gates of Lady Castleneau's mansion.

Ogle had already set the old bell in motion; and then they saw Anthony, the ancient serving man, making his way with speed over the fore-court to admit them.

"Anthony," said Heron, " is all well at this house?"

"Oh, dear me, Captain, yes; but don't speak. My lady has been in a thousand fidgets ever since young Lord Bridgewater came and said you would be here."

"I'm in good time, though, Anthony."

"Yes, to be sure; but you know when people get anxious, they don't calculate about the time. Ah! that's you, Mr. Ogle, is it? And how do you do? I hope your good lady's quite well?"

"I shouldn't wonder," said Ogle.

Anthony had swung the gate open, and let the three mounted men enter the court, and as he secured it again, he added, "And, Captain, how is our dear Edith? Bless the child, I've done nothing but think about her!"

"Oh, she's quite well," said Heron; "and sends her best love to you, Anthony."

"No, really, though! Now that's very thoughtful of her! But I say, Captain—Captain——"

"What is it?"

"Stoop down, and speak low. Who is this strange gentleman on the brown horse?"

"A highwayman."

"A which?"

"A highwayman. You know, Anthony."

"Good gracious! What did you bring him here for?"

"I couldn't help it. The fact is, Anthony, he's rather caught me than not, and I can't very well get away from him."

"You don't say so? I'll tell you what, Captain. Get him into a convenient corner of the hall, and I'll have the blunderbuss ready."

"No, Anthony; I think it's better to let him alone."

"He seems a surly fellow, and don't speak."

"Take the horses, Anthony, round to one of the old sheds. All is well, believe me. I will not carry on a jest at the expense of your fears. Edith, here is Anthony wishes to treat you with a charge from the blunderbuss."

"Edith?" cried Anthony. "Miss Edith? Providence protect us! and she's gone for a highwayman at last! I feel that I've lived long enough in this world. Bless us and save us! how well she looks, too!"

Edith laughed; and as the party had now reached the hall of the mansion, she turned to the right, and opened that well-known door which led into the apartment always occupied by her aunt.

Lady Castleneau had heard the sound of horses' feet in the fore-court, and had just taken off her spectacles, as she always did upon an arrival, and had risen from the perusal of a book with which she had been trying to cheat the time of its weariness.

Edith had flung the cloak off her, and strode into the apartment in the full costume of a knight of the road. "Lady Castleneau," she said, in an assumed deep-toned voice, "your money or a kiss."

Lady Castleneau uttered a short scream; but when Edith ran forward and caught the old lady in her arms, she thought that the end of the world had surely come; but then she knew Edith's voice in a moment, as, in a natural tone, the seeming highwayman cried out, "And so you, too, do not know me since I have taken to the road?"

Poor old Lady Castleneau looked for a moment as if she were about to faint, and Edith regretted the surprise she had given her.

"Nay, aunt," she cried, "do not be alarmed; I have not taken to the road; but this is a suit belonging to Felix, and I wear it at my own wish, on the possibility that I may be useful to him in distracting the attention of his enemies. All is well, dear aunt, believe me; and I am very, very happy."

"My dear child," said Lady Castleneau, much affected, "I did not expect to see you; but still it is new life for me to do so. Where is your husband? Where is Captain Heron?"

"I am here, dear Lady Castleneau," said Heron, as he entered the room; "and I grieve much that I should be this perpetual trouble to you. It seems as if I were always bringing riot and confusion into your house."

"No, no; nothing can be a trouble to me that concerns the happiness of my dear Edith. Make her happy, and no one can be more welcome to this house than yourself. But I have a message for you from the young Lord Bridgewater, and he has left this card, signed by the Lord Chamberlain, which admits whoever presents it to the Court ball to-night at St. James's."

"I am to use it." said Heron. "In half an hour before I start from here, I can write a brief statement of my claim to the Whitcombe peerage, which I am to hand to the King, while the Earl of Bridgewater will be so close at hand, that his Majesty cannot but place it in his hands, he being a member of the Privy Council, and the Committee of Privileges."

"Yes, Felix, yes," said Lady Castleneau. "Lord Bridgewater was good enough to explain all that to me; and he is quite right, for it is the only direct means by which your claims can be put in course of examination."

"It is so. And now excuse me a moment, Lady Castleneau, while I give directions to my man Ogle, who must get me a costume necessary to appear at Court with."

Heron left the room, and encountering Ogle in

the hall, he said to him, " As quickly as you can, you may get me a complete suit of Court mourning. My father, the Earl of Whitcombe, is too recently dead for me to appear otherwise. You know my size, and will be able to get it to fit sufficiently well. Spare no expense, and see that you bring with you a Court sword with jet ornaments. I must awaken no suspicions by any lapse in costume."

" I shall be back in half an hour, Captain," said Ogle.

" Have you money?"

" I think yes, Captain."

" Be sure you have sufficient. Here is more gold; and see that you hire a coach for me, to be at the iron gates here, at ten o'clock. I would not go until the saloons are well filled, for I court not particular attention, and wish but to perform my errand, and then come away."

Ogle instantly left Castleneau House, and Captain Heron, returning to the breakfast-room, begged writing materials of Lady Castleneau, and she and Edith then left him to himself, while he sat down to make a rapid sketch of the eventful circumstances of his birth.

Captain Heron had no intention whatever of stating any evidences upon which he founded his claim—he merely wished to assert it, so that it might be put in course of investigation.

In half an hour, his task was accomplished; and then, as he looked up from the paper, he could not but reflect upon his strange, mysterious life, and upon the possibilities of the many incidents, dangerous, romantic, and startling, which might still attend his career.

CHAPTER CXXIX.

DETAILS SOME IMPORTANT EVENTS WHICH TOOK PLACE AT THE COURT BALL AT ST. JAMES'S.

OGLE was as prompt as he could possibly be, in carrying out the instructions he had received from Captain Heron, so that by ten o'clock everything was in readiness; and by the light of the oil lamp which was commonly kept burning in the hall of Castleneau House, Captain Heron appeared fully equipped for that Court ball, to which he was invited by his friend, the Earl of Bridgewater, and where his presence, had it but been known to many of the gay flutterers in that scene of rank and splendour, would have produced the most intense consternation.

Poor Lady Castleneau was nervous, but yet hopeful on the occasion, for she had what may be called a sort of fanatical faith in what she thought was sure to attend any one whose cause was just.

The experience of a long life had not been sufficient to dislodge that belief from the mind of the old gentlewoman.

But Edith, although in the most hopeful age of youth, was full of a thousand fears.

She could not but recall to her mind what perils had attended the last visit of Captain Heron to St. James's Palace, when he ought to have had every reason to expect a contrary reception to that which he received.

She seemed to dread the moment when the door of Castleneau House should close upon him, and he would go forth alone to place himself in the presence of throngs of people, every one of whom would be armed against him, with the exception of the youthful noble who had taken up his cause, and who believed in his pretensions.

But the coach which Ogle had hired was in the court-yard, and it was time to go. Captain Heron put on a look of courage and composure, which probably, as regarded the latter feeling, was to some extent feigned; but in respect to courage, he never faltered for a moment in carrying out the resolution to which he had pledged himself.

"Edith," he said, "be hopeful and trustful. Two short hours will soon pass away, and then I shall return to you, having accomplished this one preliminary act, so necessary to my rights. I will not say good bye, for that is a sound which has a too large signification for two hours' absence."

And now Edith made an effort, and controlled the too agitating burst of feeling which would have sent Heron distressfully from that house. She, too, assumed a composure she was far from feeling; and it was not until the roll of carriage-wheels announced that Heron was gone, that she permitted herself to shed tears upon the breast of Lady Castleneau.

Never was the fact more fully exemplified, that in a great city like London everything and anything may be had for money, and that, too, at the shortest notice, than by this equipment of Captain Heron for the Court ball at St. James's.

He was attired in an elegant Court suit of mourning, and all his equipments were faultless, even to the sword, with its black bugle ornaments, and the lace ruffles of the most costly fabric.

The carriage, too, was such as any nobleman might have used on such an occasion; and the coachman and footmen, in the splendid liveries, made up altogether such an appearance that no possible suspicion could attach to it.

It would be difficult to analyze the feelings of Captain Heron, as he sat in that costly vehicle which was making its way towards St. James's Palace. Perhaps he wondered if he should ever really go as the acknowledged Earl of Whitcombe, instead of in the surreptitious manner in which he was on the present occasion gaining admittance; but be this as it may, his whole attention was soon engrossed by the stirring scene in the midst of which he found himself.

St. James's Street and the end of Pall Mall were in a complete blaze of light, for almost every house had links and flambeaux at the doors, stuck into those extinguisher-looking sconces which are still to be seen attached to the railings of some of the older houses of London.

Carriages, sedan-chairs, and equipages of every possible shape, size, and fashion, thronged St. James's Street,—pouring on in one uninterrupted stream down the left side of it, to deposit visitors at the Palace, and then creeping up the right side to assume what station they could until their owners required them,—wedging themselves into that compact mass from which was sure to ensue the confusion incident on such an occasion.

The smashed panels, the broken lamps, the oaths and expostulations of the coachmen, and the pitched battles of the footmen, made up upon all these occasions a scene of confusion and riot, which, from its frequency and continuance, ap-

No. 59.—EDITH.

peared to be considered properly incidental to a great entertainment of any kind, particularly at Court.

Captain Heron found that there was a magnificent carriage in front of him, the horses of which could only proceed at a creeping pace; while, from the frequent bumps upon the back of his own coach, and the loud expostulations of the footmen, he was aware how hardly pressed they were by some vehicle in the rear.

But still, slow as the pace was, it was progress; and now as the Palace was neared, he could hear the banging of the coach doors, and the loud cries of "Move on—move on!" from the link-men, porters, footmen, and royal servitors, who crowded about the gateway.

The faint sound of music, too, came upon his ears; and then, with a sudden jerk, the carriage stopped, and in the midst of a blaze of light, a flashing of uniforms, and a bustling crowd, through which it was difficult to make his way, Captain Heron alighted; and in three steps was within the precincts of the Palace.

As he passed from the carriage, he felt certain that he heard a voice cry out suddenly, "There he goes!"

Did this apply to him, or to some other person, or was it but some casual expression from some of the crowd collected about the spot, to watch the uniforms of the various guests?

Captain Heron had no means of deciding these questions. It was too late to retreat now if he had so wished it, and he had no such wish.

The usual cries of "Move on—move on!" had sent his carriage from the gate, and another visitor was alighting in a moment.

This ball was a popular and political one, at which it might be said that all manner of people were to be found.

One of the Lord Chamberlain's officers received the cards, and gave in return what might be called a voucher, consisting of another card with the one word "Pass" upon it; and this second card had to be delivered up in an apartment through which every guest had to pass, and in which there was a strong body of the Yeomen of the Guard; so that even if, in the confusion about the first officer, any one should step past without a ticket, he would inevitably be stopped in this chamber.

But Captain Heron had his pass, and the halberts of the Yeomen of the Guard, which were crossed over some heavy curtains of purple velvet, were moved aside.

He stepped forward, and found himself, for about six paces, amid a great mass of beautiful flowering shrubs, which formed a small kind of ante-room, which led to the large saloons in which was held the ball.

Another moment, and his ears were saluted by a crash of music, as he stood in the larger of the suite of rooms of the old Palace, where was assembled all the rank, beauty, and fashion then in the metropolis.

The scene was one of great magnificence; and having passed so much of his life, as Captain Heron had done, under the old trees in Epping Forest, that splendid interior had for him all the charms of novelty.

The magnificent chandeliers, all blazing, scintillating with wax-lights—the gorgeous silken hangings from every window—the profuse gilding that was laid on with no sparing hand on every cornice, ornament, or projection of the apartments—the exquisite columns of green porphyry—the oaken floors, painted with ornamental designs, in imitation of the richest carpets—the echoing din of music—the glitter of splendid costumes, radiant with jewels—and that confused, hustling sound, which never can be subdued in a large assemblage, although tempered to its lowest by the presence of royalty,—made up an aggregation of sights and sounds such as Captain Heron had never before witnessed.

And now there was a sudden cessation of the music, but only to be immediately succeeded by a few notes on a trumpet, which rang loud and clear through the saloons.

That was the signal for another dance. Some two hundred couple filled the floor, and in another moment a whirl of flashing costumes and a patter of many feet succeeded.

Captain Heron stood close to one of the columns, and surveyed the scene before him with eyes of interest and curiosity. He was most anxious to discover his friend the Earl of Bridgewater, but he could see nothing of him; and then he asked himself whether it would be better to wait in one spot, or to glide about among the guests.

He was about to decide upon the latter course as the one most likely to distract individual attention from himself, when he saw a gentleman, in a magnificent Court costume, approaching him.

A second glance told him that it was the Earl, and Heron advanced a few paces towards him.

"You see I'm here, my lord. How am I to act?"

"I rejoice to see you. All is well. His Majesty and the royal family are not yet in the saloons. They seldom come in till eleven; but you see we have a goodly throng here."

"Indeed you have. But tell me, my Lord Bridgewater, among all these glittering guests of royalty, is Lord Warringdale to be found—for I would fain avoid his eyes?"

"I think not. There is a rumour that he is laid up with serious hurts at his old lodgings opposite Whitcombe House."

"It may be so—it may be so; and, in truth, is probable enough: but were he able to crawl, he would soon be here, if he thought but my shadow was upon the gilding of these walls."

"No doubt of that—no doubt of that. Ah, the King!"

The dance, the music, had suddenly ceased; and the bands of the two regiments of Guards that were stationed in the saloons began to play the "National Anthem."

Two large, heavily-gilt folding doors were thrown open, and, preceded by several officers of state, the King, with some members of the royal family, entered the room.

"Your time of action will soon come," whispered the Earl of Bridgewater. "His Majesty will make a gossiping sort of tour round the rooms. I will keep pretty close to you."

"I will then deliver to him the statement."

"Do so; and I will instantly obtrude myself upon his notice, so that he cannot but hand me the paper. I think we had better not speak to each other more at present, as it will look like collusion between us."

"Be it so. I have the statement here."

"Is it small?"

"Oh, yes—only in the form of a letter."

"That is well. I see he is beginning his tour. It will be ten minutes before he reaches here. By heavens, he *is* here!"

"Who? Who?"

"Lord Warringdale."

"Ah! Then I must look to my safety."

"Nay; perhaps not. He might make an effort to come to the ball merely to see his name in the list, and without having a thought of you. Indeed, I do not see how it is possible he can know of your presence, for you may be sure Colonel Trelawney and myself kept the secret well."

"Oh, yes; I'm assured of that; but where is he? I do not see him."

"There—to the right. Now he glides along past those two ladies. How ghastly pale he is, and I see he walks with difficulty."

Lord Warringdale was in a magnificent suit, covered with embroidery; but as the Earl of Bridgewater had said, he was ghastly pale, and he moved with difficulty. Nothing but some powerful motive could have induced a man in such a state of physical depression to present himself at a Court festivity.

And now will the reader recollect that brief interview which Jonathan Wild and Lord Warringdale had held together, when, like boon companions, they chinked their glasses, and Wild, with abundance of exultation, had informed his companion in iniquity that he had information that would enable him certainly to destroy Captain Heron.

It was with the hope of seeing that destruction there and then accomplished that Lord Warringdale had risen from a couch of pain, and attired himself in that magnificent costume to make one at the Court ball at St. James's.

Slowly and insidiously, like some snake winding his way among fair flowers, Lord Warringdale crept onwards towards the thick porphyry column close to which stood Heron.

"He comes this way," said Bridgewater.

"Is it to attack me?"

"Nay, that is scarcely possible. I think he does not see you even, and his progress in this direction is accidental."

"It may be so—it may be so; and yet it looks as if it had a purpose in it. Where is the King?"

"Do you not see that group of ladies bowing so low? There he is, in the midst of them. Do you not see him as the feathers wave about him? He comes this way."

"And Warringdale the other. My lord, they will meet at this spot."

An expression of great anxiety began to creep over the young Earl.

"Impossible! impossible!" he murmured. "Warringdale cannot have any suspicion of *your* presence here; and if he had, the scandal and *éclat* of a quarrel with you here, in the presence of royalty, would be more hurtful to him than it could be to you."

"I am sure," said Heron, as he laid his hand lightly upon the hilt of his sword,—"I am sure the villain knows I am here."

"How can you be sure?"

"Because he keeps his eyes averted from this spot, while they seem to wander to every other;

and, at the same time, he slowly makes his way towards me."

"By Jove, Heron, it looks like it!"

"My Lord Bridgewater, I will not compromise you in this matter. You have kindly enabled me to come hither with a view to my own benefit. Unexpected circumstances seem to be about to occur, which might be prejudicial to any one who would befriend me. Leave me, my lord, to my own devices; and come what may, believe me, I thank you from my inmost heart for all you have striven to do for me."

"Never, never!" said the Earl. "I will not leave you now."

"I pray you to do so."

"Nay, Heron, do not ask me to fall so low in my own esteem! I cannot—will not leave you! And, after all, this danger may be imaginary."

The King was making his tour of the rooms, and had now reached to within twenty paces of where Captain Heron was standing. The King came from the left, while from the right, step by step, as it appeared, and in a studied manner, at the same rate of progression, came that ghastly, malevolent Lord Warringdale.

"Get your letter ready," whispered the Earl of Bridgewater.

"I have it."

Heron stepped a few paces on one side, so as to get close to the column, and he had hardly executed the movement when the King approached him within half a dozen paces on the one side, and Lord Warringdale to about the same distance on the other.

"Now!" said Bridgewater.

"Yes, now!" replied Heron.

At that moment, when Captain Heron stepped forward a pace, and the Earl of Bridgewater moved a little aside, so as not to seem immediately connected with him, Lord Warringdale placed his hand upon the hilt of his sword, and half drawing it, he cried out in a shrill, yelling voice, "Treason! treason! There is one in this assembly who, under pretence of presenting a written paper to the King, aims at his life! Treason! treason!"

It would have been possible, perhaps, to have counted ten hurriedly, during which time not a sound of any kind or description broke the unnatural stillness that reigned over that large assembly.

It seemed as if these words of Warringdale's had paralyzed everybody; and the last twice that he uttered that cry of treason, a word so terrible to kings and in palaces, the echo of the sound seemed to fall upon every heart with a crushing, deadening influence, which deprived them of the power of action.

CHAPTER CXXX.

CAPTAIN HERON IS SURROUNDED BY MANY PERILS.

It was impossible for Heron to come to any other conclusion, now that Lord Warringdale had spoken out in the fashion he had, but that by some strange accident, which at once baffled all experience and inquiry, he had become acquainted with the fact of his presence at the Court ball, and had adopted this heartless mode for his destruction.

It was more than probable that some zealous courtier, on such an occasion, would turn at once at the life of the man who was thus denounced as a would-be regicide; and on such an occurrence, Lord Warringdale would at once be rid of his enemy and the thousand fears which would always assail him so long as his half-brother lived.

It would be impossible to describe the confusion that immediately ensued at the Court ball when the first stunning shock of surprise was over, and people were able to act in any manner upon the words which had been uttered by Warringdale.

The music abruptly ceased—swords were drawn in all directions—ladies screamed and fainted, and such an uproar ensued as surely old St. James's Palace had never witnessed since it came into the hands of royalty as a residence.

Captain Heron was pale, but determined. He still stood close by that column where he had held his conference with Lord Bridgewater, and drew his sword.

His whole attitude and aspect were not such as to make it encouraging to any one to attack him.

The state of alarm and affright into which the King was thrown had something ludicrous about it, for he made a sudden rush to escape from the saloons by a small and what might almost be called a secret door, since it was one very rarely opened.

But that door was well known to Lord Warringdale, and immediately behind it he had stationed no less a personage than Jonathan Wild, who was to act as occasion should require.

If Captain Heron were killed in the scuffle and *melee* which occurred in the ball-room, Jonathan would not be wanted; but if, on the contrary, Heron should be making his escape, or be simply so much hemmed in by the swords of the courtiers and nobles as to become a prisoner, then Wild was to make his appearance, and take effectual care that he was lodged safely in durance.

And so Jonathan waited with his ear flat against the panel of the door, in anxious expectation of hearing sufficient to enable him to determine upon his course of action.

The rush which his Majesty made in that direction was mistaken by Wild for just the sort of alarm which justified his making an incursion into the ball-room, and he opened the door and darted forward just in time to receive the King almost in his arms.

Then it was Lord Warringdale who cried out, "For the King! For the King! Will no one strike a blow for the King?"

As he spoke, he made a treacherous pass with his sword at the back of Captain Heron; but there was another weapon which crossed his at the moment, and the young Earl of Bridgewater cried out, "No, my Lord Warringdale! That was a foul thrust, and it shall not take effect!"

"Beware, my lord!" said Warringdale, bitterly, "or you may find yourself compromised in the charges against a highwayman and a traitor, who has sought the life of his King!"

"Forbear my lord!" replied Bridgewater. "It is useless to add falsehood to treachery!"

"I have him!" said Wild; and he plunged forward to seize Captain Heron.

Lying between him and the column, close to which Heron stood, was the deep fringe of a Turkey carpet that lay on the floor of a deep recess, almost equal to the size of an apartment, in the saloon.

Wild was in his heavy riding-boots, for he seemed to have taken a kind of pleasure in coming to that Court ball in his roughest costume. His foot caught in the fringe, and he fell heavily; while the thick-thonged riding-whip he held in his hand, flew a considerable distance from him.

The young Earl of Bridgewater was close to Captain Heron, and in an anxious, sharp whisper, he said to him, "Quick! quick! through yonder door! You may save yourself yet."

Heron was as rapid in resolve as he was in action. He took a sharp run forward, and then with a leap cleared the prostrate figure of Jonathan Wild, and brought himself within two inches of the partially opened door. To dash through it, and instantly close it on the other side, was the work of an instant; and so complete was the change from those gay and glittering saloons of the Palace, all ablaze with light, and thronged with that brilliant company, to the narrow, intensely dark passage in which Captain Heron found himself, that he involuntarily stretched out his arms as though some deep pit might be yawning before him, into which another step might precipitate him to destruction.

And still he heard the cries and shouts of the courtiers and the screams of the ladies, from the dazzling scene he had left; and he could not but feel how very insecure was his position within a few paces only of a door on the other side of which was a host of enemies, and, at the least, two who would be ready at any moment to run some risk of their own lives in order to ensure the destruction of his.

But Captain Heron was safer than he thought himself.

The door only closed with a latch, but it was a heavy and strong one, and had no communication whatever with any handle, or means of acting upon it, from what may be called the saloon side of the panel of which it was composed.

But still the danger was great, and it was not likely that a piece of panelling, however strong, would prove any effectual bar to pursuit in that direction.

He felt that he must proceed, and as a moment's reflection told him that however intricate might be the ways of the old Palace, they must be a great deal more mysterious than dangerous, he slowly and carefully made his way along the narrow passage.

For some distance he kept his drawn sword in his hand, and carefully felt the flooring before him with its point before he trod upon it; but after a time he dismissed this caution as unnecessary, and only advanced slowly, with the sword directed before him, in order that he might not strike against some obstacle in his way.

By stretching out his left hand he found that the wall of the passage in that direction was not above a foot distant, and soon the point of the sword met with an obstruction which, by carefully inspecting with his hands, Heron felt certain was a door.

Where it might lead to was a matter far beyond any conjectures, but he was most anxious to open

CAPTAIN HERON ATTNDS THE COURT BALL.

Presented Gratis with No. 59 of the New Edition Edith the Captive; or, the Robbers of Epping Forest.

EACH WEEK IS PRESENTED RATIS A COLOURED ENGRAVING.

it, and at length lit upon a small handle, upon turning which, the door immediately yielded.

This door opened towards the passage in which he was, and immediately beyond it, to his surprise, he saw a well-lighted apartment, with a table in its centre, on which were refreshments.

A couple of chairs were close to the table, as if two guests had been partaking of the good cheer that was upon it; and close to a decanter of ruddy wine there lay a pair of heavy pistols, of precisely the sort and pattern Heron had often seen in the possession of Jonathan Wild.

This then was doubtless an apartment in which Wild had waited until it should be time for him to make his appearance in the ball-room.

Scarcely, however, had Heron time to make himself acquainted with these details when a loud crash at the door through which he had so providentially escaped from the ball-room, convinced him that the panel had yielded to the violence of Wild, and the eagerness, probably, of the courtiers to show their zeal in defence of the royal person.

"Now, then," said Captain Heron, "for perhaps the strangest hunt of all that was ever made after living highwayman, for it will be through the chambers and corridors of St. James's Palace."

Heron strode across the room towards a door which he saw at the extremity, but there he paused a moment, and turned quickly to the table, and took from it the pistols, which no doubt belonged to Jonathan.

A confused rush of feet, and various cries indicative of pursuit, came upon his ears, and he felt the necessity of instant action. He opened the door we have mentioned, and passed through into a similar apartment. A key was fortunately in the lock on that side, which he turned instantly; and still he sped onward through room after room, until he paused, with the hope that, having completely distanced his pursuers, he might be able to find some means of leaving the Palace.

He knew well that he was upon a floor that was not high in the building, and he thought if he could reach any window he might find a means of letting himself down in safety to one of the courts.

While these thoughts were passing through his mind, and while he had paused in a room which was lit by some wax candles, a door suddenly opened, and he saw the halberts of a couple of the Yeomen of the Guard projected into the apartment, preparatory to the entrance of two portly specimens of that corps.

Heron had just time to dart behind some heavy crimson cloth curtains which hung from one of the windows, and then a courtier, carrying a gilt wand, came backwards into the room.

There could be no possible mistake as to what this meant. No one would be preceded in such a fashion but the King himself; and accordingly, in another moment, Captain Heron saw the royal personage cross the threshold of the apartment.

"There, there, my lord!" said the King; "that will do. We are surely in safety now. There must be an investigation—a very full investigation."

"Yes, your Majesty," said the courtier with the gilt wand; "and there can be no doubt but that the villain will be caught."

"Caught!" said the King. "Yes, of course, he must be caught! There, that will do! Good night, my lord!"

The gentleman with the gilt wand bowed very low, and retreated backward from the room. The two Yeomen of the Guard went through the same process, retreating backwards, and drawing their halberts after them.

The door was closed.

"What can be the meaning of it?" said the King. "Is it a plot, or only a surprise, or an accident? I will send for my Lord Lauderdale, and take his advice about it. Yes, my Lord Lauderdale is the man—cool, calm, and no imagination."

The King crossed the room, and was about to leave it by a beautifully decorated door, the handles of which were of crystal, when Captain Heron stepped forward from behind the curtain, and bowing low, he said, "Let me intrude upon your Majesty's leisure for a moment. I am neither regicide nor treasonable plotter, but attended the Court ball for the purpose——"

Captain Heron had only got thus far when the fright of the King assumed so ludicrous a character that he was compelled to pause.

His Majesty leaped twice off the ground, and then, tottering back, he strove to reach a chair, which he just missed by about an inch, and came to the floor heavily.

"Help! Murder! Guard! Fire! Treason!"

"Nay, your Majesty," said Heron. "I doubt if you could be in better safety than in my presence, for I have a strong arm and a ready hand, and will willingly defend you in case of necessity. My object was to present a written paper to your Majesty."

"No, no! Don't! That's what he said—under pretence of presenting a written statement, some one was to take my life."

"Your Majesty alludes to one who calls himself Lord Warringdale, but who is a most unexampled villain. I shall ask but two favours now of your Majesty."

"Murder!"

"Nay, not so! The one is, to receive this paper, and the other is, to permit me to leave St. James's unquestioned and unassailed. Will it please your Majesty to take the paper?"

The King glared at Captain Heron for a few moments in silence, and held out his hand in a very reluctant manner, as though he supposed the paper must of necessity have contained some explosive substance, which would prove his instant destruction.

"There is no danger, your Majesty," added Heron, "but to me; and that danger is, that the events of this night, and the manner in which I almost compel your Majesty to receive this paper, may militate against the just statements it contains."

"No," said the King, faintly.

"Then I trust that my second request—namely, that I may be permitted to leave the Palace unmolested, will be granted."

"But how came you here? How can I—how ought I——"

"I came here at your Majesty's invitation."

"Our invitation?"

"Yes. I'm your Majesty's guest, and, as such, should be allowed to depart freely, in the same manner that I should be allowed to depart by any of your Majesty's judges from a court of justice, in which I might give evidence."

"Ah!" cried the King. "I know you now. You're a highwayman."

"I was, and shall be, if your Majesty will not take the trouble to see that I become what I really ought to be—a peer of the realm. But I claim your Majesty's promise, that I should be permitted to depart in peace."

"We are a King."

"I claim the promise, not from a king, but from a private gentleman, whose bidden guest I am."

"Nay, that cannot be. We never invited you."

"When your Majesty gives a popular ball, and allows to be distributed among the nobles of your Court cards of invitation, which they may make use of at their discretion, every one coming here, by virtue of such a card, is your Majesty's guest, were he the veriest beggar that walked the street."

The King was silenced, and looked confused.

"But it is not wholly for myself," said Captain Heron, with a lofty air, as he touched the hilt of his sword,—"it is not wholly for myself that I ask a safe conduct from St. James's, for I am armed; and, as sure as the sun will rise to-morrow, lives will be lost among those who will stay my progress. I may be overpowered, and fall, for I am but one man against many; nevertheless, I would ask your Majesty if it be worth while that your Palace should be stained by the blood of your servants, and possibly encumbered with the corpse of one of your guests, whose only offence towards you has been that he has adopted a somewhat romantic mode of presenting a petition of right?"

"Who gave you a card of admission to the Court ball?" said the King evasively.

"That your Majesty must permit me to decline to answer."

"Come, then," said the King as he scrambled to his feet, "I will take you out by the ambassadors' entrance. Follow us, and no one will molest you."

Heron bowed low, and followed the King, who opened the door with the crystal handles, and passed through a small cabinet, the walls of which were covered with books, and from thence they came to one of the old galleries of the Palace, at the further extremity of which, a couple of the Yeomen of the Guard were on duty.

"Pass this gentleman," said the King in a loud voice.

Heron bowed again.

"I have the honour of bidding your Majesty good night."

Immediately past the two Yeomen of the Guard, there was a small square hall, and then a door which opened into the Ambassador's Court of St. James's Palace.

That court was crowded up by carriages and sedan chairs, and as Heron issued forth in his rich costume, he was rather at a loss what to do; inasmuch as it was not a dress in which to walk the streets, without exciting a great deal too much attention.

A rather singular accident or mistake seemed to relieve him of this difficulty, for one of the men in charge of a sedan-chair touched his hat as he said, "Was it for your honour we were to wait?"

"Just so," said Heron, as he stepped into the chair. "Get away at once, now, and you shall have a guinea each."

The chair-men, incited by this reward, fought and hustled their way out of the Ambassadors' Court, and got into Pall Mall, by the side of Marlborough House.

Heron had just time to lean back in the chair as he saw Lord Warringdale standing, with his sword drawn, on the pavement of Pall Mall.

"Who is that?" he cried. "Who have you in the chair, my men?"

"The Brazilian Consul!" said Heron, rapidly.

"The Blazing Consul!" said the chair-men.

"Brazilian, idiot!" said Heron again.

"Who is it?" added Warringdale, as he advanced his sword.

"The Brazilian idiot!" said the chair-men.

"Oh, it's all right!" said a person who was with Warringdale, and who was in the dress of one of the inferior officers of the Palace. "They mean the Brazilian Consul."

"Oh!" said Warringdale, as he stepped back; and in another moment Captain Heron was past him, and out of danger.

CHAPTER CXXXI.

CAPTAIN HERON DETERMINES UPON THE RESCUE OF SIR DOMINICK BROWNE.

THE two men who carried the sedan-chair in which Heron had effected so adroit an escape from St. James's Palace, had no doubt brought to the Court ball the personage for whom they mistook him, for they jogged on comfortably for the whole length of Pall Mall without asking him a single question of where they were to go.

But it would not at all suit Captain Heron to be carried to the house of the Brazilian Consul, and he began to think upon the best mode of getting rid of his kind friends the chair-men, who, by their foolish blunder, had probably saved him considerable inconvenience.

But still, every step that they now took him from St. James's Palace was a step towards safety, and he thought he would let them go a little further, since of course he could alight at any moment.

But this resolve was brought to an abrupt termination by the chair-men halting suddenly at the steps of a large house, from which no doubt they had brought the exalted personage for whom they had mistaken Captain Heron.

"Here you are, your honour," said one of the chair-men, as he lifted up the roof so as to release the door,—"here you are, your honour; and I hope your honour won't forget the couple of guineas you were so good as to promise Mike and me."

"Certainly not," said Heron. "There they are. Hold! Do not do that!"

Heron was just too late; for the other chair-man, to show his efficiency, executed a thundering knock at the house door.

"Very well," said Heron. "I am not going in;" and then, as he walked away, he just saw, by a sidelong glance, that the door of the house was flung open, and from a well-lighted hall there appeared several servants, who looked at the chair-men and the sedan-chair, and then gazed after him, Heron, in undisguised astonishment.

It was no part of Captain Heron's wish to provoke discussion or to enter into any explanations, and he walked up the Haymarket quickly, taking good care to keep his hand near the hilt of his sword; for at present the streets of London were anything but safe after nightfall, and there had been recently some attempts on the part of dissolute young men to re-establish those parties which in a preceding reign were wont to traverse the metropolis, committing all sorts of excesses under the name of Mohawks.

But it was not from dissolute street-loungers of this description that Captain Heron had to look for any danger.

He had got just about half-way up the Haymarket when he heard, coming from the neighbourhood of Pall Mall, cries and shouts as of persons in full pursuit, accompanied by the springing of watchmen's rattles, as well as by the still more alarming sounds, the clatter of horses' feet.

For a few moments Captain Heron doubted whether it could be possible that this hue and cry was after him, but when he saw a stream of people at the lower end of the Haymarket, and felt convinced that some twenty or thirty of them were commencing to scamper up it, he thought it high time to look to his safety.

There were some cries, too, which left it no longer a matter of doubt that he was the person pursued.

"Catch him—seize him! Cut him down! A thousand pounds for him, dead or alive! A highwayman! A highwayman!"

"Indeed!" said Heron to himself. "This is my good Lord Warringdale's doing, I fancy, in some fashion; or can it be the King, in defiance of his word, has sent this hue and cry at my heels? It is like enough; it is like enough. But it is one thing to hunt me, and another to catch me. Let him who crosses my path, with a hostile intent, beware!"

There was a narrow court, with an entrance not larger than a doorway; all was profoundly dark within it, and Heron thought it was just possible that his pursuers might pass, while he was in hiding a few paces down the narrow entry.

Hardly had he stepped out of the open street into the deep gloom of the place, when several of them who were foremost in chase of him came closely up.

"Are you sure," cried one, "you saw him come up the Haymarket?"

"Quite—quite! You run on, Sir Charles, and I will look into the courts."

From these words, as well as from the tone in which they were uttered, Captain Heron felt certain that he was pursued by some of the Court gallants who thought to advance their interests by showing zeal upon the occasion.

"Don't run into danger, Sir Henry," cried the other. "He is a desperate fellow."

"Pshaw, Sir Charles!—these highwaymen are all cowards when it comes to the push. They trade upon people's timidity; but show them a bold front, and the rascals howl for mercy. If he be in any of these courts, I will prick him out with the end of my rapier—'pon honour, I will."

The one who was called Sir Charles ran on; but the last speaker stepped into the court, crying out, as he fenced through the dark air with his rapier, "Come out, Sir Knave, if you be here! Come out, Sir Knave! Or must I hook you out like periwinkle from shell, for something seems to tell me you are here?"

"You are quite right," said Heron; "and if you won't run away, I will cross swords with you with pleasure; and then, in two minutes, you will consider the meanest periwinkle, either in or out of a shell, an object of envy."

"Ha! ha! So, so! That's it, is it? Help! Watch! Here he is! I've got him! I've got him!"

Sir Henry backed out of the court with the utmost precipitation, but Heron darted after him, and he was compelled to defend himself. The swords rang together for a few moments, and then the courtier fell, with a cry of dismay; for Captain Heron had passed that slender triangular Court sword through his shoulder.

And now, in truth, there was no time to lose, if Heron would give himself a chance of safety; and he fled up the Haymarket, in the hope of baffling his pursuers by crossing over the way, and getting into some of the obscure regions of Soho.

They were close at his heels, however; and he felt that his only chance was by rapid turnings up and down short streets, at each corner of which they might lose sight of him.

Crossing over, then, from the top of the Haymarket, he dashed onwards, and heedless which way he went, so that he made many turnings, he at length paused a moment to listen, with the hope that he had baffled his foes.

But such was not the case, as he heard their footsteps close at hand; and then, for the first time, he became fully aware that Jonathan Wild was in close pursuit.

Heron knew the husky, ferocious voice at once, as Wild cried out, "We must have him! we must have him! He's in full Court suit, and you can't miss him."

Captain Heron darted down another court, and to his surprise, he nearly fell over a sedan-chair, which was in it, but which it was impossible to see for the darkness that prevailed.

"Can it be possible," thought Heron, "that, twice in one night, a sedan-chair is to prove my safety? No, I will say nothing to it."

He ran on, but found that the court had no outlet. In feeling with his hands, however, he found a door, which yielded before him; and just as he heard Wild cry out, from the mouth of the court, "Hilloa! who's down here?" he stepped into a dark passage, and closed the door behind him.

A soft, female voice immediately said, in the darkness, "Why, really, sir, you're late!"

"Am I?" replied Heron. "I believe I couldn't help it."

"Well, it isn't what my lady expects, I can tell you, sir; and if you were not so near a relation, she would be angry enough."

"And very right, too!" said Heron.

"What on earth," he thought, "can all this mean? I am mistaken for a near relation of somebody, who is late; but under my present circumstances, I cannot afford to be particular as to what sort of refuge I seek, for those who chase me, outside, aim more at my life, even, than at my capture."

"Now, sir," said the soft female voice, "follow me."

"With the utmost pleasure," replied Heron, "to the end of the world!"

"Now, really," said the female voice, "that's always the way you go on!"

"That's lucky," thought Heron, "for it keeps up my supposed identity."

"And if my lady should hear you," added the voice, "I should be discharged at once."

"I wouldn't have anything of the sort happen for the world," said Heron.

"Hush, sir! Now don't say another word, but come on."

"I'm coming."

"Keep to the right."

"I do—I am. But don't you think a light, now, would be a convenience?"

"Why, you know, it would ruin us all!"

"Would it, really? Then, I've not the slightest desire to have it."

"Hush!"

"Yes, I am hushed."

"Not another word, or you'll waken them up."

"The deuce I shall!" thought Heron. "Who are to be awakened up, I wonder?"

Cautiously and carefully he trod onwards in the dark, until a door was opened, through which came a stream of light, and in that stream of light he saw standing a smart enough looking girl, in the costume of a waiting-maid.

Heron stepped forward right to the threshold of the door; and it was not till then that the girl saw there must be some mistake, and she cried out, "You are not the Major—you are not the Major!"

The moment these words were uttered, a lady, with a travelling cloak about her, appeared at the door of the room, and clasping her hands, exclaimed, "I see I am betrayed, and that all is discovered; but there is no shame in aiding the escape of one so near to me. Let my Lord Belfond come, and let him blame himself that I was compelled to adopt these measures after appealing to him in vain."

"Madam," said Heron, as he bowed gracefully, "there is a mistake in all ways. I am not the gentleman you expected; but I have no more to do with betraying you to Lord Belfond, than I have any right to intrude upon you; nor do I know his lordship from the Grand Turk."

"Good heavens!" said the lady; "then who are you?"

"Yes," cried the waiting-maid; "wretch! who are you?"

"I am not a wretch, at all events," said Heron.

"Peace, Martha!" said the lady. "Let this gentleman speak!"

"I have enemies, madam, and ran down the court. A door opened to my touch, and I was requested by this young lady, whose name it appears is Martha, to 'come on,' and here I am."

"Then, sir, you're very indiscreet," said the lady, "and I beg you'll go away again, directly."

"But, madam——"

The lady began to shed tears, and wring her hands.

Captain Heron bowed low.

"Madam, I will go at once. At the entrance of this court, which I find is a *cul-de-sac*, I shall have a contest for my life: probably I shall kill two or three of those who seek it; but they are in number, and will overpower me. I shall then be murdered within twenty-five paces of where you stand; but since you wish it, and have the right to demand it, I will go now."

"Oh, no, no!"

"Farewell, madam!"

"No! I pray you do not! I do not wish it—I do not demand it! And yet—and yet——"

The distress of the lady seemed to increase.

"Perhaps," said Heron, "I unwittingly exaggerate my danger, and I may escape. Let me try it, madam; and be the issue what it may, I will not blame you."

"No, no, certainly not. On the contrary, I will tell you who and what I am, and why I'm here; for I can perceive you are a gentleman, and belong to the Court."

"I hope I am a gentleman, madam; but I do not belong to the Court at present, although I believe there is a singular anxiety to get me there!"

"You are mysterious, sir! But I will tell you that I am Lady Belfond, the wife of Lord Belfond, whose life is one perpetual scene of the most furious jealousy."

"His lordship is sixty," said Martha, "and my lady's twenty-two!"

"How dare you speak, Martha? Be silent!"

"But facts, you know, my lady, account for circumstances. My lord's got a cork leg, too, if you please, sir!"

"Martha! Martha!" said Lady Belfond; "this is cruel of you. I have been a kind mistress to you; but you fancy I cannot resent your intrusive speech. Sir, as I was saying, my lord is fearfully jealous, but without cause: and he's as penurious as he is jealous; for, although his fortune is immense, it is with the greatest difficulty I have got together one hundred guineas, to give to my brother, who has unfortunately killed an opponent in a duel, and must fly the country for a time. It is to meet him that I am here, for I am sure my Lord Belfond would gladly give him up to the authorities, even if it were to death."

"Madam," said Heron, "I have not sought this explanation from you; but I felt convinced, from the first moment that I looked upon you, that you had some just and honourable purpose in being here."

At this moment, a loud knocking came at the door of the house, and Lady Belfond with difficulty suppressed a scream.

"Fear nothing," said Heron, as he unsheathed his sword. "No harm shall come to you. This knocking portends the arrival of my enemies, or yours. If mine, you at least, are safe, madam; if yours, be assured, I will defend you with my life."

"Oh, if it should be Lord Belfond!" said Martha. "He's got but one eye, sir!"

The knocking continued violently.

"Keep within the room," said Heron, "and I will listen. Who is there in the lower part of this house?"

"I grieve to say," said Lady Belfond, "that I suspect them to be persons of bad character. An old discharged servant pretended that she resided here, and could give me the temporary accommodation of her roof to see my brother; but since we have been here, Martha and I have heard things

said which make us think that the place is little better than a den of thieves."

The knocking was repeated a third time at the door, and then Heron heard a harsh voice cry out, "Who are you? and what do you want?"

"Open! open! open!" said some one from without.

"Oh, it's the Major!" cried Martha.

"Fly, Martha! and let him in," cried Lady Belfond. "Why did you close the door?"

"Because I thought, my lady, this gentleman was the Major, and nobody else was expected."

A female voice at this moment echoed through the passage, crying out, "And what is it to you, I should like to know, who knocks at my door? Marry come up, and how dare you interfere?"

Martha now made her way down the passage, and the door was immediately opened to admit two persons, one of whom cried out, "Is this you, Martha? And is my sister here? There is not a

moment to lose. I must be off to Holland to-night."

The door was closed with a loud sound, and Martha as she flew back to her mistress, exclaimed, "It is the Major, madam—it is the Major; but he has got somebody with him."

"Oh, how imprudent—how very imprudent!" said Lady Belfond.

"Not at all, sister," said the young man, advancing, and who was attired in a military undress,—"not at all, sister. I think I have done, for once in my life, a prudent action, by bringing with me a gentleman of unblemished honour and reputation, who will be able to witness, should it ever be necessary, to the jealous-pated old Lord Belfond, that it was your brother you came to meet, and none other. Ah! who have we here?"

"A gentleman," said Lady Belfond.

"Yes," cried Martha, "quite a gentleman, and with two eyes in his head."

The young officer stroked his moustache.

"Sister, sister," he said, "am I too soon or too late?"

"This indeed is ungenerous," said Lady Belfond. "Oh! when will the troubles of this night end?"

"Let us hope," said the friend of the young officer, who now stepped forward, "that they are over already, or that they will never fairly begin."

The surprise and joy of Captain Heron was intense, when he recognised in this officer, his young friend the Earl of Bridgewater.

CHAPTER CXXXII.

CAPTAIN HERON GETS IN SAFETY TO CASTLENEAU HOUSE.

THE recognition between Captain Heron and the young Earl of Bridgewater was mutual; although neither spoke for a moment, so intensely surprised were they that a combination of strange accidents should bring them to a meeting in such a place.

Indeed, it was the Major who first broke the silence, by saying, "I can very well perceive, gentlemen, that you know each other, and therefore I have nothing further to say. Pray pardon me, sister, for my hasty expressions; but I do think that abominable husband of yours has affected everybody with a thousand doubts and suspicions."

"Say no more about it," replied Lady Belfond. "Here is money sufficient for your present exigences. Take it at once, and place yourself in safety as soon as possible."

"I will, sister, and with many thanks; but I feel confident we shall have to fight our way out of this court, for there are suspicious people hanging about the mouth of it, whose appearance I don't like at all."

"It may be," said the Earl of Bridgewater, "that those suspicious people have an eye to my friend, here, Captain Heron."

"Never mind," said the young Major, in his usual impetuous manner. "We are three, and, I fancy, good swordsmen all. I propose, then, that we sally out, and clear the court, and the street beyond, likewise, if necessary."

"I am willing," said the Earl of Bridgewater.

"And I," said Captain Heron, "cannot but be willing, since I have, indeed, a most special object in getting to Bloomsbury Fields as soon as possible."

"You have a sedan, sister," added the Major, "and we will put you in it, and see you safe off."

An evident attempt was made, either by the enemies of the young Major or of Captain Heron, to break in the door of the house; and, indeed, the probability was that those two parties had combined their forces, which turned out to be the case; for Jonathan Wild, who had so far followed up the pursuit of Heron, finding old Lord Belfond in a state of great fury, had suggested to him that Lady Belfond had an assignation with Heron, who, for his own purposes, on that occasion Jonathan chose to designate the handsome highwayman.

If anything was wanting to turn the whole mass of blood in the veins of old Lord Belfond into the veriest possible vinegar, this would surely suffice to do so; and, accompanied by a couple of men, whom he had brought with him, he aided Wild in making a furious onslaught upon the door of the house.

The other, and what might be called *amateur*, pursuers of Captain Heron had given up the chase, and Wild himself was alone, with the exception of a watchman, if he could be called any assistance, whom he had called to his aid, and stationed, as a kind of beacon, at the extreme end of the court.

Such was the state of affairs outside this house, in which Lady Belfond had, certainly most indiscreetly, trusted herself.

Three such persons as the young Lord Bridgewater, Captain Heron, and the hasty, hot-headed Major, were not likely to let much time elapse between the idea of such a sortie as they contemplated and its actual accomplishment. Drawing their swords, then, they marched down the passage, followed by the trembling Lady Belfond and her maid, Martha.

"Be at ease, sister," said the Major. "We will put you in the sedan-chair in safety, although where your chair-men are I cannot pretend to determine."

"I saw none such," remarked Heron, "as I came down the court."

"They were told they might return in half-an-hour, and may now be there."

"Forward, then," said the Earl of Bridgewater, and he flung the door open.

Jonathan Wild made a rush forward, but when he saw three swords opposed to him, a feeling of discretion came over him, and he retreated backward, calling out, "My Lord Belfond, her ladyship has three gallants, and as you and your men make up the same number, it will be a fair fight."

But Lord Belfond's two men ran off in a moment, and his lordship himself, either from being unsteady on the cork leg which Martha had mentioned, or from the inequality of the ground in the badly-paved court, fell on his hands and knees.

Heron pressed forward between the Major and the Earl of Bridgewater, calling out to Wild, "I fancy you seek me, Jonathan. You are armed, and, for once in a way, I will give you the advantage of fighting like a gentleman, and with one."

"Thank you for nothing," said Wild. "We shall meet again, and at a more favourable opportunity."

Jonathan was afraid to do other than face Captain Heron, and keep on his guard, so that he inevitably fell over Lord Belfond.

The Major laughed as he put his sister into the sedan-chair; and the two chair-men, who had been to refresh themselves at a neighbouring public-house, fortunately appearing, they trotted off with the lady, while Martha accompanied the vehicle, with her hand upon the door.

"I'm off to Holland," said the Major, as he sheathed his sword. "Good night, gentlemen."

"I am with you, Felix Heron," said the Earl of Bridgewater.

"And you can guess my destination, my lord," said Heron. "I am for home."

"Hush! You must say no more; for there may be ears abroad who will gladly catch the slightest sound that will indicate to them your whereabouts. Lead on, and I will follow you a pace or two behind, but woe be to him who seeks to follow me."

Jonathan Wild was not hurt in the least; but he felt quite confident that his wisest plan, since he was not in force sufficient to ensure a victory, was to remain at peace.

Captain Heron, then with the Earl of Bridgewater, were in perfect freedom, and at a very rapid pace indeed they made their way towards Castleneau House.

The hour was a very late one now—indeed, two o'clock had struck; but Heron knew well that his appearance even at any hour would be far indeed from an intrusion or disturbance at Castleneau House; and yet, now that the excitements of that evening were over, and he had carried out as far as he possibly could the advice of the young Earl in regard to placing a statement of his claims in the hands of the King, a feeling of great depression began to creep over him

"My Lord Bridgewater," he said, "I owe you more thanks than living man can well repay you; but I begin to feel that this struggle is something worse than fruitless. What progress do I make? How much nearer am I to the object in which you have so kindly helped me? I feel more than half inclined to abandon all hope and expectation of being acknowledged as what I really am. I was comparatively happy with my gallant steed and my free companions on the road."

"I have but one reply to make to you," said Lord Bridgewater, " and it is contained in two words."

" What can they be?"

" Remember Edith!"

"Ah, my lord! indeed those are two words which carry with them a potent spell. Gladly indeed would I place her in that position which she would grace, and which should surround her with the social distinctions she so well deserves. Yes, for the love I bear to thee, dear Edith, I will yet battle for my rights; and the first duty I shall now seek to perform will be the rescue of Sir Dominick Browne from his, no doubt, sad captivity."

"I do not see," remarked the Earl of Bridgewater, "that you can do any further at present as regards the peerage claims."

"Yet stay—how remiss of me—I have not yet told you, my lord, that the King actually has the paper."

The Earl of Bridgewater was, up to that moment, under the impression that Captain Heron had just contrived to make his escape from the Palace in some ordinary way, and he was not a little surprised when Heron narrated to him his interview with the King, and the peculiar manner in which he had succeeded in leaving the royal residence.

"Then more than ever," said the Earl, "must the affair be left to work its own way for the present. We shall soon see whether the King will suppress the document, or lay it before the Privy Council. Be assured that I will keep a watch over your interests, and I can always communicate with you through Lady Castleneau."

"Be it so," said Heron, as he gave a sigh, more of relief than anxiety; "be it so, and I will to my forest home in Epping again; there I know well I can preserve Edith in peace and safety. We are both young, and can afford to wait. Believe me my lord, that I feel as if a load were lifted off my heart at the idea of escaping, even for a time, further collisions with that man whom I dare not kill, and who even contends with me at the advantage that he has no scruples about my life, while my sword point dare not touch his breast."

"You mean Lord Warringdale?"

"Yes, yes! Would that he were not my brother. Oh, had he the soul of an honest man, or a gentleman, and had met me freely and justly, I could have left him the bauble of a coronet which I covet not; but I feel that the wealth which should descend to me from my father, should be mine, and with it I would gild the days of my Edith."

Without interruption, the Earl and Captain Heron had now reached close to the neighbourhood of Lady Castleneau's house; and then Ogle darted out from the shadow of the gate pediments, and raised a very imprudent cry of triumph at the sight of Captain Heron safe and unharmed.

"Why, Ogle," said Heron, "you did not expect me to be swallowed up by the courtiers at St. James's?"

"No, Captain, no. But still you were alone, and I have heard that those sort of people are a bad lot, and the hour is getting late."

"All is well—all is well with me," added Captain Heron. "Heaven send that all is well within this house. And yet I will not and do not doubt that it is so, for you, Ogle, have, I am sure, kept good guard."

"In truth I have, Captain."

Heron was soon once more in that ancient breakfast room, where he had last parted from Edith, and it was with a cry of joy that she flew to his arms.

"Safe, safe!" she cried. "You are safely returned to me. Oh, how much I have to be thankful for!"

"Dearest Edith!"

Lady Castleneau was forgotten for the moment, but she did not grudge to those young loving hearts their pre-occupation. It was the only real and true delight that she had left, to see the happiness of those who were so dear to her.

It was impossible but that Captain Heron must have observed a certain appearance of excitement, half joyous, half anxious, about the manner of the young Earl of Bridgewater; but, with a natural delicacy, he had forborne asking him a question on the subject; and the rapidity of the events that had taken place at the Court ball, had prevented them holding sufficient conversation together, even to allude to their previous singular meeting on the high road.

That singular meeting, it will be recollected, involved the rescue of the young Earl, with the young lady who was under his charge, from the pursuit and persecutions of Lord Belessis.

In fact, the hazardous night which Captain Heron had passed, partly in the cage at Mortlake, and partly in the hands of his enemies, had in a great measure resulted from his interference in favour of the young Earl.

And now, before either Heron, or Edith, or Lady Castleneau could say much to each other, there came a slight tap at the door of the apartment in which they were.

Another moment, and Lord Bridgewater entered

the room, with the familiarity of a friend of the house.

"I have a thousand fears of intruding," he said; "but I am so afraid you will be making preparations for departure, that I hazard breaking in upon you to say a word."

"You never can intrude, my Lord Bridgewater," said Heron.

"Never!" added Edith. "Oh, my lord, how much do we owe you!"

"So little, that you may pay it all off, and yet leave me largely your debtor, by remaining in London until after twelve o'clock to-morrow."

"It shall be done," said Heron.

"Most certainly," added Edith.

"Yes, my dear children," said Lady Castleneau; "any request of our kind, young, noble friend becomes a law. You shall remain here, and old Castleneau House may yet find some secret place which will defy the utmost malice of our enemies to discover."

"And you all consent to this," said Lord Bridgewater, "without asking me a single question?"

"It is sufficient," said Heron, "that it is your wish."

The young Earl clasped the hand of Heron fervently. "In the midst of all your dangers," he said, "surrounded by bitter foes as you are, you do not hesitate to make this sacrifice to friendship; but I will tell you why it is I ask it of you. Montague House, one side of which adjoins that of this mansion, is in possession of the old Lord Somers. He merely holds it until the royal commissioners take possession of it, in order to form, it is reported, a national museum in the mansion."

"Yes," said Lady Castleneau, "I have heard that; but I have not seen Lord Somers for many a long day."

"In that national museum," added the Earl, "there will be enshrined many beautiful objects of nature and art; but as old Lord Somers was one of my guardians, I have anticipated the royal commissioners, and placed in his care a beautiful object of nature, which I think will not be equalled by anything that the future museum will contain."

"I comprehend," said Heron.

"And I, too," said Edith.

"But I don't, in the least," said Lady Castleneau. "Is it a jewel?"

"It is a jewel, Lady Castleneau, and one so rare and precious, that I want my good friend here, Felix Heron, and his fair wife, your niece, to assist me to wear it, since I have won it!"

Lady Castleneau looked surprised, but the Earl quickly added, "My friends here are aware that I have eloped with a young lady, I have had the good fortune to take from a bad home to give a good one to. I did not intend to have taken her to Montague House—it was an after-thought to do so; but when I considered the rank and unblemished reputation of my Lord Somers, and the particular relation in which he stood to me, I felt I could not do better than take the Lady Cleveland to his house."

"You did well, my lord," said Lady Castleneau, "although you know I would gladly have received her."

"That I know well. But what I now want is, that you should all be present at my marriage to-morrow morning, which will be celebrated by the private chaplain to Lord Somers, at Montague House."

"Yes," said Heron, "with most abundant pleasure."

"I will go to Montague House now, if you wish it," said Edith.

"No, no," interposed Lady Castleneau, "that might indeed be dangerous; for how can we know who is lurking about this mansion? We can easily find our way there in the morning; and if Lord Somers does not object, I dare say we can get from one garden to another without the necessity of going out into the street."

"Admirable! most admirable!" cried the Earl of Bridgewater. "I will take care that everything is arranged, so that may be done with ease and safety. And now, Lady Castleneau, as I am in the begging vein to-night, may I ask another favour of you?"

"It is granted, my lord, before it is asked; only do not call it a favour."

"Lady Castleneau, I want you to let me lie down here somewhere for the remainder of the night, for I would fain not go abroad again into the streets of London until I have made the young Lady Cleveland the Countess of Bridgewater. It is now nearly five o'clock, and we are all in need of repose."

It is needless to say that old Lady Castleneau was delighted to accommodate the Earl beneath her roof, and in the course of another half-hour there was silence and sleep within the walls of that lordly mansion.

One quiet, stealthy figure only kept watch and ward in the old court-yard, and occasionally extended its noiseless peregrinations to the garden.

Insensible to fatigue, Captain Heron's friend and companion thus watched over his safety.

——

CHAPTER CXXXIII.

THE MARRIAGE AT OLD MONTAGUE HOUSE.

WITHIN two hours of the utterance of the last words we have recorded as coming from the lips of the young Earl of Bridgewater, a bright sun was shining upon the old garden, the gable ends, turrets, and extensive roof of Castleneau House.

Ogle crept into the hall, and, since daylight, had allowed himself a few moments' repose.

No one, however, was as yet stirring of the inmates of the house, and it was not until ten o'clock had pealed forth from Bloomsbury Church that there appeared in the breakfast room our little party of the previous night.

Old Anthony was in a terrible bustle, for in that quiet establishment three guests seemed to him quite a party.

The breakfast was laid with all that old-fashioned amplitude of material which our ancestors thought necessary for the first meal of the day; but scarcely had a few words passed between the attached friends who sat at that early meal, when a loud ringing at the outer gate somewhat disturbed their serenity.

The Earl of Bridgewater and Captain Heron at once started to their feet.

EDITH AGAIN FALLS INTO THE CLUTCHES OF JONATHAN WILD.

Presented Gratis with No. 60, of the New Edition Edith the Captive; or, the Robbers of Epping Forest.

EACH WEEK IS PRESENTED A COLOURED ENGRAVING.

An expression of alarm came over the countenance of Lady Castleneau.

"We are like evil doers," said Edith, "for we seem to dread each knock or ring that announced a visitor."

No one had time to utter a reply to this remark before Ogle made his appearance.

"There is a visitor," he said; "and I scarcely know whether or not you would wish me to admit him, although he is certainly alone, and therefore can scarcely be dangerous."

"Who is it?" asked Heron.

"It is Lord Warringdale."

"Impossible!"

"Nay, Captain. I saw him with my own eyes. There he is, in a coach at the door; although the liveries are not his, for they are grey and silver, and the Whitcombe liveries are crimson."

"Grey and silver!" exclaimed Edith. "Those are the colours of my father's liveries! Oh, tell me, is Lord Warringdale indeed alone, or is my father with him?"

"Your father, Edith," said Heron, "is too much hurt, you may depend, to be abroad thus early."

"I assure you all he is alone," said Ogle, "for I looked right into the coach, through the iron bars of the gate."

"Who did he ask for?" said Lady Castleneau.

"For you, madam."

"I will see him—I will see him. It is far better to see such a man as Warringdale, and hear what he has to say, than to avoid him."

"But the Captain," said Ogle, "and Lady Edith?"

"Oh, certainly not—certainly not. He shall not see them, nor you, too, my Lord Bridgewater."

"Nay, Lady Castleneau. Permit me to judge whether or not I would see this man. If, now, we could all be placed somewhere from whence we could overhear his words, this visit might turn out to be in the interests of truth and justice, instead of, as he no doubt intends it, quite the contrary."

"Once before," said Lady Castleneau, "dear friends of mine were hidden behind that Indian screen, while Judge Tarleton paid me a visit."

"Yes," said Heron; "and there is no reason on earth why we should not hide there again. Oh, that this man were not my brother; even now I would sally out to him, and the same spot of earth should not hold us both in life!"

There was a flush of excitement upon the face of Captain Heron; and well there might be, for the very sound of his name brought to his recollection the many injuries he had suffered at his hands;—how often, with a determined malice, he had sought his life—how he had tried to entangle him in the meshes of some plot which should surrender him to his enemies—and how, with diabolical fraud and recklessness, he had warred against the peace and happiness of Edith.

No wonder that there was a flush of excitement on the brow of Captain Heron at the sound of the name of Warringdale.

"Be calm—oh, be calm!" said Edith.

"I will—I will!"

"He is surely powerless to harm you," said Lady Castleneau.

"I will act calmly," added Heron, "let me feel what I may."

Ogle was then directed to admit Lord Warring-

dale; and as it would take several minutes to repair to the iron gates, and introduce him to the house, there was ample time for the little party to ensconce themselves behind the immense screen which shut off a considerable portion of a large breakfast room at the end furthest from the door.

Lord Warringdale must have recovered considerably from his bruises, for although somewhat pale, and with a certain difficulty in his movements, he walked erectly enough into Castleneau House.

This man was a coward—a coward at heart, or he never could have been guilty of the acts which we have related of him. And yet, there he was, venturing alone into a house in which he verily believed was to be found the man whom he had endeavoured to hunt to death, and whose implacable enemy he had become.

But how well Lord Warringdale knew that he was safe from Captain Heron!

He had no shame in meeting the eyes of one whom he had so deeply injured, provided he did not meet his sword.

That he knew he was safe from.

Hence the seeming courage of my Lord Warringdale.

But his purpose was neither to ask for nor to insinuate that he thought Captain Heron was there; he had another object, which we shall soon see.

Cold, stately, and with a certain flash of the eyes which showed in what light she regarded her visitor, Lady Castleneau stood by the high-backed chair which she usually occupied, and confronted him.

There was a silence of a few moments' duration, and Lord Warringdale took advantage of it to glance round the room, while he made the pretence of executing a low bow to the old gentlewoman.

"Madam," he said, "I come to you upon an errand which may be useless, and but a waste of precious time."

Lady Castleneau made no answer, but looked coldly and sternly into the face of Lord Warringdale.

"And yet, madam, I do sincerely hope that neither you, nor I, nor any one, would wish to carry our resentments beyond the grave!"

Still neither answer nor remark from Lady Castleneau.

"When the mortal pilgrimage is nearly over—when life is about to close, and the mists of futurity are before the dying eyes, let us hope that animosities, jealousies—ay, even injuries, may be forgotten—forgotten, madam, and pardoned!"

"I don't see that you're dying yet," said Lady Castleneau. "When you are, you can send word."

"Ah! madam, I allude not to myself. I hope to repent of my little sins in this life!"

"The sooner you begin, the better."

"Sage counsel—sage counsel, madam. We all are but as the flowers of the field, which the reaper Death strikes prostrate!"

"My Lord Warringdale," said Lady Castleneau impatiently, "I neither want your company nor your homilies upon life and death. You have been an intruder here before, and you are one now. If you have aught to say to me, say it, and go your way, in such peace as your own troubled conscience will permit."

"Minutes may be precious," said Warringdale. "I hope you know where at once to communicate with Edith."

"I decline to answer that question," said Lady Castleneau.

"Then, madam, the consequences be upon your own head, and upon hers. I shall at least have done my duty and at least redeemed my word."

"Your word? Your duty?'

"Yes, Lady Castleneau. And by what I am about to say, I give you a duty—which is to inform Edith, as speedily as you can, that her father is dying; and, in his last moments of despair, shrieks for his child, that she may forgive him. Oh, you should hear him, Lady Castleneau! Such cries! such sobs! such groans!"

"I am here—I am here!" cried Edith, as she darted from behind the screen. "Yes, I am here! I cannot resist an appeal like that. I am here!"

Lady Castleneau sunk back in her chair with a sigh.

A look of malignant satisfaction flashed from the eyes of Lord Warringdale; and then he bowed low to Edith, as he said, "You have heard me. I have done my duty."

"And I will do mine," said Edith. "Oh, Lady Castleneau, do not look upon me with those sorrowing eyes! You heard what he said?"

"Yes," said Lady Castleneau. "What he *said*, I heard."

Edith clasped her hands, and looked from one to the other.

"None but a fiend—no, surely none but a fiend would play with human feeling thus. Speak again, Lord Warringdale! Did I hear aright?"

In a harsh, slow voice, Warringdale spoke. "Sir John Tarleton is at his last gasp. He received a hurt, which, acting on a feeble frame, has brought him to death. He calls—no, that is not the proper word—he shrieks for his child."

"Oh, heaven! I will go," said Edith.

"No!" said Lady Castleneau, springing to her feet with unwonted agility. "No, not with that man."

"Ah!" cried Edith, as she shrunk back.

"No, not with him, my dear child. There is treachery in his every look—in his every action."

"I expected this," said Lord Warringdale. "I was prepared for these doubts. Step into the hall, Lady Castleneau, and you, Edith; from there you will see the liveries of your father's coach. He lent it me to come here to seek you."

Edith moved two steps to the door.

There was a slight rustling behind the Indian screen.

Lady Castleneau caught her by the wrist.

"No," she cried—and she intended others should hear beside Edith and Warringdale—"no, Edith, you shall not go with that man."

"Oh! heaven guide me!" cried Edith.

"I never intended," said Lord Warringdale, "to ask the Lady Edith to accompany me. I could have guessed her reluctance. But as I really wish this dying man to leave the world with what comfort he may, I remove myself as an obstacle, and Edith may go alone."

"Yes—yes," cried Edith. "I will go alone."

"And you?" said Lady Castleneau to Warringdale.

"Madam, if you will permit me, I will remain here as a hostage for her safe return."

"You will?"

"In all faith, I will."

"Very well," said the Earl of Bridgewater, as he stepped from behind the screen at this moment; "remain, and I will take care of you."

Lord Warringdale uttered a cry of surprise and fear. He had fully expected that Captain Heron would be there, but from death or danger at his hands he knew he would be safe. With the young Earl of Bridgewater, however, who had already accused him of his father's murder, the case was widely different.

The jaundiced hue of terror spread itself over the face of Warringdale. He shook in every limb, and, as he retreated backward to the door, he said, "No, no! Not with you—not with you! You seek my life—you make a false charge against me —you—you—you are my enemy! I cannot—will not—dare not stay with you! Help! help! His eyes look murder at me!"

"Villain!"

"No, no! I will not stay. Let it pass. Let the old man die, or recover. He may not, after all, be so bad. I will go, and tell him Edith will not, cannot come."

"No, no!" cried Edith. "I will go."

"Murderer!" cried the Earl of Bridgewater.

Warringdale had reached the door, but instead of passing into the hall, he fell into the arms of Ogle.

"Is he to go, my lord?" said Ogle.

Warringdale recoiled from Ogle, with another cry of alarm.

"No," said the Earl, "he shall stay. He offered himself as a hostage, and he shall be one. He trembles to look into my eyes, because he well knows the cause of quarrel my very soul has with him; but since he came here on such an errand as he has declared, and since this is not my house, but one in which I am but a visitor, I will for the present waive all personal feeling, and hold him but as a hostage for the safety of the Lady Edith. It is now half-past ten. Let her go to Finsbury. If she return not by twelve, let my Lord Warringdale look to it."

"No," said Warringdale. "I refuse—I retract. Let her do as she pleases. I will not stay."

"Then," said the Earl of Bridgewater, as he drew his sword, "you lose your character as a hostage, and I will follow you from this house; and so soon as the blue vault of heaven alone is above us, I will again assail you as my father's murderer."

Warringdale staggered against the wall, with a deep groan.

"Yes, yes!" cried Edith. "I will go. Minutes may be precious: he may die before I reach him. I will go, my Lord Bridgewater, and be assured I will return by mid-day. I must go—I will go, or this hour may perchance bring the regret of a life."

Edith flew to the hall. She saw the well-known liveries of her father's coach: the last doubt vanished from her mind. She rushed across the court-yard, and entered the vehicle.

"Quick—oh, quick!" she cried. "To Finsbury —to my father!"

The coach drove off. It reached two streets from Castleneau House, and then, from a terribly cramped-up position under one of the seats, Jonathan Wild put up his head.

"So, charming Edith," he said, "you're my helpless prisoner once again!"

CHAPTER CXXXIV.

EDITH FINDS HERSELF A HOSTAGE OF DISTINCTION.

AND this plot, or plan, of Lord Warringdale's had succeeded. By acting upon the affections of Edith, he had managed to place her in the hands of his unscrupulous agent and accomplice, Jonathan Wild.

Well he knew that he would succeed in nothing that would, in any way, depend for its success by an appeal to the fears of Edith.

But he might reach her through her heart.

The affections and the feelings of the great, the good, the brave, and the noble, are their vulnerable part.

There may be found "the crevice in the steel" through which they may be pierced.

The plot was diabolical, but it had succeeded, and Edith was a prisoner.

Whose brain hatched the device—Jonathan Wild's or Lord Warringdale's—it is needless to imagine.

It succeeded, and Edith fell into the snare.

They had neither of them taken the trouble even to inquire into the condition of Judge Tarleton. He might be worse—he might be better—he might be dead, or dying, for all they knew or cared; but they thought that such a device would bring Edith away from her refuge at Lady Castleneau's.

Jonathan Wild and Lord Warringdale both were of opinion that Captain Heron was with Edith at Castleneau House; but Wild felt that it would be too dangerous for him to attempt to play the part of the messenger from the Judge at Finsbury.

Warringdale ran no such danger.

Well the villain knew that he could count upon the forbearance of Heron; but the presence of one whom he had such cause to shun as the young Earl of Bridgewater, took him, indeed, by surprise.

And so the plot had succeeded so far—and succeeded, too, beyond Jonathan Wild's expectations.

The fact was that Jonathan had had no idea that Captain Heron would allow Edith to go alone to her father's house.

Neither he nor Lord Warringdale had any idea of the kind of feeling which was likely to come over the mind of Heron on such an account. They could not comprehend the delicacy which Captain Heron would feel in regard to any interference between Edith and that most unworthy father.

It was this very delicacy which had kept Heron behind the screen which Edith issued from, and held that brief parley with the villain Warringdale.

The Earl of Bridgewater had, with whispered entreaties, begged that he would let him act in the matter, and still keep himself concealed; and Heron had yielded to the wish.

And Edith, through her feelings and her affections, was betrayed.

We return now to that coach which, at a rapid pace, was making its way, not towards Finsbury, but in a directly contrary direction.

It would be difficult, nay, impossible, to analyse the feelings of Edith at that moment, when from his terribly cramped-up position under one of the seats of the coach Jonathan Wild let his head appear, and spoke.

"So, my charming Edith, you are once more my helpless prisoner!"

It seemed as if a gulf had opened at her feet, down which she had no resource but to fall to her destruction.

Terror froze her faculties for a few moments, and then the idea that it was all but a dream brought with it a few moments of anxious relief.

But that could not last long. The terrible realities of her position were before her, and Edith began to see them all in their vivid horrors.

The prisoner of Jonathan Wild!

His prisoner after all that had passed, and after the campaign, so to speak, of hate and despair, that he had carried on against her and her Felix!

Oh, the thought was too terrible to support!

"No! no! help! mercy! no! And I am unarmed, too!"

"To be sure you are!" said Wild.

He sprung to his feet, and seated himself on the seat opposite to Edith, and began to rub his knees.

"Infernally cramped," he said, "underneath that seat! I feel as if I had been fastened up for a month in a bandbox! Oh, yes, you are my prisoner!"

"No! help! My father's servants will know me, and help me."

"Your what?"

"My father's servants. Help! help!"

"Oh, you mean the coachman and footman. Bless you, Edith, they are two of my bull-dogs in livery, for once in a way!"

Edith's heart sunk within her.

"And this coach," added Wild, "is one that I borrowed of my excellent friend, Sir John Tarleton, some time ago!"

"Oh, heaven!"

"Eh?"

"Monster!"

"Well, now, that's scarcely civil, considering all the pains you have cost me from time to time; but we will not dispute about mere words, Edith. You are my prisoner, and with an ease, too, that should make you and yours dread my power."

"I do not dread it—I defy it!"

"Ah, say you so?"

"Yes, I do defy it; and from the chance passengers in the streets, I will demand, and doubtless shall procure, aid."

Edith, as she spoke, made an effort to let down one of the coach windows; but Wild was too quick for her, and grasped her arm.

"A truce! a truce!" he said, through his clenched teeth. "Hear me, Edith Tarleton, or Edith Heron, whichever you may choose to call yourself! I will treat you with all distance and respect up to one point—and that is, until you make so much noise or attempt so much resistance as shall compel me to act otherwise."

"Help! help!"

"Ah, you will have it, then! This handkerchief will effectually stop your cries."

The arm of Jonathan Wild was all but cast

about her neck, as, with the other hand, he began to put into her mouth, like the bit of a horse, a rolled up handkerchief.

Edith felt that she was helpless in his hands, and that he might inflict upon her any indignity. Indeed, what could be well more terrible than the mere touch of his hands?

"No, no!" she half cried, half sobbed,—"do not approach me, and I will be still."

"Very good!"

Edith shuddered almost convulsively.

"Beware! oh, beware, Jonathan Wild!" she said. "This can be but a temporary triumph to you, and will be as dangerous as it is temporary! My husband will avenge the slightest insult you subject me to most fearfully!"

"Your husband? Ah, then, you have married him! You are, after all, the wife of a highwayman!"

Edith disdained to answer.

"Look you here!" added Wild, in a careless, common-place kind of tone. "Now that we understand each other better than we did, I have no objection on earth to let you know exactly what is the object of this little affair, which has had so auspicious a commencement."

"What do you mean?"

"The object of making you a prisoner."

"I hear you."

"Well, then, this husband of yours, Captain Felix Heron, the highwayman of Epping Forest, is getting troublesome to a friend of mine—the noble, the gallant, and the tender-hearted Lord Warringdale!"

Wild coughed as he spoke.

"Well," he added, "such being the case, and as he and I am, both of us, too tender-hearted to take his life, we thought that we would bring him to terms by taking you prisoner, and making the price of your release, unharmed and safe, the terms we wish to make with him."

"Never—never!" said Edith.

"Ah, it is early times!" said Wild.

"Never, I say!" added Edith. "Felix will not barter his rights to either you or the base Lord Warringdale; but I bid you both beware, for the temporary success of this vile plot will fall in thunder upon your own heads!"

"Very good," said Wild.

"If you consulted, for one moment, your own safety, you would release me now."

"Indeed!"

"Yes; and I will make these terms and conditions with you—that if you set me free now and at once, this affair shall add nothing to the list of injuries which you have inflicted upon me and mine. Set me free at once, and much even of the past may be forgotten and forgiven."

"Oh, dear, no! You cannot imagine how safe I feel with you as my prisoner. When Captain Heron agrees to abandon his ridiculous claims to the peerage of Whitcombe, and to leave England at once and for ever, you may accompany him, but until then you are our prisoner."

"Our prisoner?"

"Yes, mine and the Lord Warringdale, who will soon change his title for that of the Earl of Whitcombe."

"And you are paid for all this, Mr. Wild! For the love of gold you inflict all this injury, and perpetrate all this injustice!"

Wild laughed.

"Do you think, Edith, that I should be so foolish as to give myself all this trouble without being well paid?"

"Alas! alas!"

The coach had proceeded to the West End of London, and had turned into some of the most populous streets. Jonathan Wild could see that Edith was looking through the coach windows with anxious eyes to recognise where she was.

"Come!" he said. "This will not do. You will please to tie this handkerchief over your eyes, or permit me to do so for you."

It was not for a moment doubtful which Edith preferred. She took the handkerchief, and with a sigh of despair, she tied it over her eyes. Then Jonathan Wild took hold of the edge of it, and gave it a jerk downwards, for he mistrusted Edith having so tied it that she could not see.

"That will do!" he said.

In a few moments the coach stopped.

Edith had no idea of where she was. She could only fancy by hearing the rattle of carriage wheels, and the confused sort of noise that the busy streets of London always produce, that she was in anything but a lonely situation, and she could hardly imagine how Wild should have the temerity to bring her right into the town.

Then she wondered if it was to his own house in Newgate Street that he had now brought her;—that terrible house in which she had once before been a prisoner, and which contained so many secrets and so many iniquities.

But Edith felt compelled to dismiss that idea.

She had seen that the streets which the coach was traversing were those of the West End of the town; and since her eyes had been bandaged, there had not elapsed anything like sufficient time for the vehicle to reach the vicinity of Newgate.

"Now!" said Wild, suddenly.

She felt that he grasped her by the arm.

The idea came across the mind of Edith now to scream aloud for help. Wild seemed to fancy that such a notion would present itself to her mind, and he whispered to her, "One cry now, and Captain Heron is a dead man!"

There was nothing reasonable — nothing that could be called in any way rational about this statement; but where the name of one who is loved is so used, the imagination and the feelings are startled into sudden compliance with the mandate.

There is no time for the reason to exert its influence, and come to a decision.

Edith was silent—silent for a few moments, and that was all Jonathan Wild wanted; for in those few moments she had been made to descend from the coach, and had reached the threshold of a house.

She heard a door closed behind her.

The closing of that door shut out, at once, the external world; and then Edith bitterly repented that she had let what, perhaps, was a most precious moment escape her— a moment in which she might have called for help, and received it.

She raised her voice.

"Help! help! Murder!"

"Ah, you are too late!" said Wild.

Another moment, and she felt something tied over her mouth; and then she was hurried onwards, and she felt that she trod upon a carpet

of thickness.   No voice sounded in the place but that of Jonathan Wild.

In a few seconds she ceased to be urged forward by Wild, and then he spoke again. "You have arrived," he said. "Your treatment while in this place depends upon yourself. Your period of captivity will depend upon the reasonableness of Captain Heron. Escape is possible; but it will bring you into such hands that you would think a lifetime of prayers only sufficient to restore you to this place again, where, if you stay, you will be unharmed, and subject neither to insult nor danger."

As he spoke, Wild removed from the eyes and mouth of Edith the handkerchiefs which had blinded and gagged her.

She looked round her with terror and with curiosity.

She was in a small room, the shutters to the windows of which were closed. On a round table

close to the door was a lamp which shed but a faint light over the apartment. By that faint light Edith could see that the room was furnished in rather a costly fashion, and that there were book-cases or cabinets all around its walls.

She saw, too, that those cabinets assumed a very singular shape, as though the walls were eccentrically formed.

A very large table was in the middle of the room, and some heavy ancient chairs were about the floor.

Little did Edith suspect that she was now in Whitcombe House, St. James's Street, and that the very apartment which was designed to be her prison had been the private cabinet of the late Earl of Whitcombe, the father of her own Felix.

But such was the case.

Since that terrible night when the Lord Warringdale had been so terrified in that very room, he had discharged the few remaining servants in

Whitcombe House, and had locked it up. To Jonathan Wild, however, he had entrusted the key, in order that he might carry Edith there, in case the villanous plan for her abduction from Castleneau House should be successful.

They both thought that a better place in which to hold Edith a prisoner could not be found than that house, inasmuch as no one would suspect Jonathan Wild to be in possession of it, and the slightest inquiry would meet with the answer that he, Warringdale, had had it locked up, and never set foot in it.

"Where am I?" said Edith.

"In safety, if you please."

"But what house is this?"

"That I decline to answer; except that, for the present, it is my house."

"Jonathan Wild, I again appeal to you!"

"Well?"

"If you value your life you will yet listen to reason, and let me free. Even up to now I will promise you immunity for this outrage, if you will set me free!"

"No; I will take my chance, Edith. But since you are so fond of proposals and conditions, I will make you one."

"What is it?"

"I will promise that Captain Felix Heron shall, as long as he pleases, be at liberty to do what he likes, and defy the law, if you will come to my house in Newgate Street, and be Mrs. Wild the—what will it be?—oh, well, we will say the fourth."

Edith disdained a reply to the speech, and Wild, with one of his sneering laughs, moved to the door. He took up the light.

"Will you leave me in darkness?" she said.

"Oh, no!"

"But you take the light."

"I leave you the sparkling light of your fair eyes, you know. Ha! ha!"

Bang went the door, and Edith was alone—alone in the darkness of that room; a darkness so absolute that it realized the idea of a darkness that could be felt, for it seemed to roll and heave about her in dense masses.

But this feeling soon passed away.

"Welcome, welcome darkness," said Edith, "rather than the presence of that man."

But there is no darkness on the face of the earth so absolute but that after a time the human eyes will get accustomed to it, and gather some faint power of vision from those minute particles of light which must come in upon the invisible air.

In about half an hour, Edith could just manage to distinguish objects in the room.

She felt then that she could move about without danger.

Again and again she congratulated herself that Wild had not thought proper to chain or manacle her in any way. She was free to move—to act as best she could, in that place; and now she resolved upon as thorough an examination of the room as the darkness would permit her to indulge in.

She felt round the walls until she came to its one window. The shutters were so tight, so perfectly immoveable, that it was evident they were fastened by some more secure method than ordinarily belonged to them. It was not likely that Jonathan Wild would leave them in a state that they could be tampered with in any way.

They were as fast as a portion of the wall itself.

Then Edith reached the door, but the moment she touched the lock a deep sepulchral voice, from the other side, said, "Beware!"

Edith shrunk back.

All was still again.

The darkness—the excitement of mind that had ensued upon the whole transaction, and now this strange manner in which she seemed to be guarded, began powerfully to affect the mind and the spirits of Edith. But the feelings that strove to come over her were not those to which she would give way: she battled bravely with them.

"No, no!" she said. "I will be strong—I will be resolute. This is but a temporary victory over my personal liberty—it shall be no victory over my mind. No, Felix, no! I will think of you, and still be strong and calm."

It required an effort, though, to command her feelings; and then she determined upon testing the fact of whether or not the strange voice, from the outside of the door, would come again.

She once more touched the lock.

All was still.

She rattled at it.

No sound came from without.

Then Edith felt that she knew what it was that had alarmed her. Jonathan Wild had lingered by the door, in the expectation that she would try the lock, and then had easily disguised his voice to the utterance of that dismal sound.

Having done so, he had left the place, perhaps satisfied that he had added so much terror to the imprisonment and the darkness, that she would not be able to make even the faintest effort at release.

Jonathan was mistaken.

———

CHAPTER CXXXV.

RETURNS TO THE HOSTAGE AT LADY CASTLE-NEAU'S.

THE state of affairs at Castleneau House was most peculiar.

Lord Warringdale was so completely thrown out in all his calculations, and so utterly calamitous appeared to him the success of the scheme by which he had placed Edith in the power of Jonathan Wild, that after she had gone, he bitterly regretted he had not, by a full and free confession, placed himself at the mercy of the Earl of Bridgewater.

Surely, that mercy would have been a better reliance than his vengeance. And what could he, Lord Warringdale, expect, when the hour of midday should approach, but that Captain Heron would appear, and exact some fearful account from him, in regard to Edith's disappearance?

But Warringdale had not to wait so long for the purpose of confronting one whom he had so deeply injured.

No sooner had Edith left Castleneau House, than, with a look of dejection and melancholy upon his face, Captain Heron came from behind the screen.

He heeded not the groan of dismay that Warringdale greeted him with, but turning to the Earl of Bridgewater, and to Lady Castleneau, he said, "Dear friends, have I done right? Or shall I ever reproach myself for allowing Edith to go alone to her father's?"

"You have done right," said the Earl of Bridgewater; "for your presence with her could but have involved you in a thousand dangers; whereas what human being has a right for a moment to interfere with the liberty of Edith?"

Lord Warringdale made an uneasy gesture.

"None," said Heron; "I grant it. None has such a right. And yet I feel that I should have been more content to have run all the risks of accompanying her."

"No, Felix, no," said Lady Castleneau; "for her sake, it is better not. If this message from her father be true and sincere, there is nothing to fear: if it be false, and but a snare, I shall almost begin to believe that Lord Warringdale has the courage of revengeful despair, for what can he look forward to as his fate?"

"I must go—I must go!" said Warringdale, faintly. "I am sick and ill. Edith will return. Alas! alas! this comes of attempting to interfere in the feelings and affections of families! She will return—she will return; but I cannot stay!"

"You are the hostage," said the Earl of Bridgewater, "and you shall not cross this threshold in life, until we look again upon the face of the Lady Edith."

Lord Warringdale began to give himself up for lost; and yet he had that lingering faith in the nobility of soul of both of his antagonists, that he could not quite make up his mind they would take his life under any circumstances whatever.

But oh, how devoutly he wished himself out of Castleneau House!

"She may be detained," he said, faintly; "she may be detained. It will be a hard case, if I am to be made the victim of an accidental delay, which may prevent her getting here by twelve o'clock."

"I cannot bear this state of doubt and uncertainty," said Captain Heron, suddenly. "I will go to Finsbury. The danger of my going there, alone, will be far less."

"No, Felix, no!" said Lady Castleneau. "Let me prevail upon you to forego that enterprise. Some one shall go that will be able to do so with perfect impunity. I will send Anthony. He is in no danger, and we may rely upon the intelligence he will bring us. If she be there, all is well. If otherwise, Felix, it will not be in that direction you will have to seek her."

"I thank you from my heart!" said Heron. "Let the old man go."

Lord Warringdale uttered another groan.

One by one, all the safeguards by which he tried to surround himself were passing away. Half an hour would take the old servant, either on horseback or in some carriage, to Finsbury. Another half-hour would bring him back, and what intelligence would he bring? Probably that Sir John Tarleton was better; and certainly that no Edith had been sent for, or was there.

"I am lost!" muttered Lord Warringdale to himself.

Lady Castleneau summoned old Anthony; and then, as a last resource, the baffled villain Warringdale spoke. "Who shall say," he cried, "that Jonathan Wild will not encounter Edith, and take her prisoner? Will that be fault of mine? No, surely not; and yet I am so surrounded by enemies in this house, that every act and every word will be tortured to my injury! I cannot—will not stay!"

"Wretch!" said the Earl of Bridgewater, "by each word you speak, by each malignant look that flashes from your eyes, I can see your falsehood! Confess all at once, or by the heaven above me, I will rid the world of a monster, who but lives to produce wretchedness and woe to those who else would know all the happiness that life would give!"

The young Earl impetuously tore his sword from its scabbard; and, at that moment, Lord Warringdale expected nothing but death.

It was desperation alone, then, that lent him vigour and courage to try to defend his worthless life.

He drew his sword, and with a yelling fierceness shrieked out, "Kill me, then, assassins both! Kill me, if you will and dare! At least, I will try not to die unavenged!"

"No," said Heron calmly, as he placed himself with two steps between Bridgewater and Warringdale,—"no, this must not be. You will but stain your sword, my noble friend, with the blood of such a recreant; but he shall tell all. Keep the point of your weapon to his throat, and should he hesitate, I will not interfere to save him!"

"This is murder!" cried Warringdale, as he made a furious lunge at the breast of the Earl of Bridgewater. "You mean to murder me, and I have a right to do what mischief I can!"

Captain Heron interposed his arm, and the sword-blade of Warringdale passed harmlessly the breast of the Earl of Bridgewater. Another moment, and the active young nobleman had closed with him, and Warringdale was disarmed.

"I am weak from hurts," he said, "or you would not get this advantage of me. I will fight you, my Lord Bridgewater, in any way you please when I am well."

"Villain! Murderer!"

"I know you accuse me of your father's murder, and with a wild sense of what you consider justice, dare me to the ordeal of combat; and I will meet you when I am well. Even you, my lord, would not choose the easy victory over an injured man, who cannot wield his weapon in his own defence!"

"I give you a minute to live," said the Earl of Bridgewater. "Cast away your life, if you please; it will be suicide on your part—not killing on mine. Confess what has become of Edith."

"You extort a confession."

"No. We feel that there is some plot, but I will deal more fairly with you. Consent to die upon the report of him who has gone to Finsbury, should it be adverse to you, or purchase your life by a free confession now."

Lord Warringdale saw the predicament in which he was placed. There was just a chance of escape, if he told the truth. There might be none, if, for one hour more, he adhered to the falsehood that Edith had been summoned by a dying father.

He hesitated for several seconds. A cold dew appeared upon his forehead, and he glanced uneasily at Captain Heron. A craven fear was at his heart, in regard to what effect the words he was about to utter would have on one to whom

Edith was so dear; and yet there he was, fairly at bay, with every defence beaten down—his life, so to speak, hanging upon a thread; that life which ever appears to be so much dearer to those to whom iniquity is a habit, than to the good, the gentle, and the true.

"I will tell all," he gasped. "That is, I will say that I think—that I am afraid that the Lady Edith may fall into the hands of Jonathan Wild. Save me—save me from him, Lord Bridgewater! I feel myself safer now with you than with him."

There was a look upon the face of Captain Heron which seemed almost enough to strike dead with fear the dastard whose eyes were gazing on him.

"He means to kill me! He means to kill me!" cried Warringdale. "I can see it in every feature of his face—he means to kill me!"

"Edith! Edith!" cried Lady Castleneau. "My poor child, Edith!"

The Earl of Bridgewater stepped back.

Heron stepped forward to the same degree, and his sword seemed by even a touch at its hilt to leap half-way from the scabbard.

Warringdale uttered a shriek, and dropped upon his knees.

"Mercy!"

"Fiend!"

"Brother!"

Captain Heron staggered back. "Heaven help me!" he said.

"Brother! brother!" shrieked Warringdale. "By that name I invoke you not to kill me!"

"This is terrible," said the Earl of Bridgewater, as he paced up the large apartment.

Lady Castleneau could not control her tears.

Captain Heron looked as pale as death, and he let his sword fall back into its sheath with a hollow clank.

"Save me! Oh, heaven!" he said, "save me from myself! Take thou the punishment of this man, and let me not have his blood upon my hands! Edith! Edith! where art thou? Torn from me by this shallow, flimsy device, and in the hands of another such villain even as thou art, Warringdale! Edith! Edith! where shall I seek for thee?"

"He shall tell all," said the Earl of Bridgewater. "If I take his guilty heart out from his breast, and read its secrets, we will know them. He shall tell all."

"I will—I will!" cried Warringdale. "I need no urging. You know the worst. All else is as nothing. Wild will treat the Lady Edith with all respect. He dare not do otherwise. But the plan was to keep her as a hostage, in order that I might make terms with you respecting the disputed peerage. I have now told you all. I have fulfilled your own terms, complied with your own conditions, and now you will set me free."

"Where is she?" said Heron faintly.

Warringdale hesitated a moment.

"She's at Mr. Wild's house in Newgate Street."

A slight accession of colour came to his wan cheeks as he spoke. After all, he thought, perhaps Heron would seek her there, heedlessly, and on the spur of the moment, and be himself apprehended.

Heron moved at once towards the door.

"Oh, Felix! Felix!" cried Lady Castleneau.

"Whither would you go? You will destroy yourself, without saving her. Be calm, and have fortitude, and all may yet be well. It is not you, Felix, who must seek Edith at the house of Jonathan Wild."

"Who should seek her but myself?"

"I will do so. Let that be my task. I am free. There is no price upon my life or liberty. I will seek her."

"Ah, you know not the villain you speak of! Jonathan Wild will defy you."

"No! I will go armed with such authority, that even he cannot resist."

"That is well, and wisely spoken," said the Earl of Bridgewater. "Listen to it, Heron, and be guided by this good counsel. Let Lady Castleneau go, and in her own way and fashion. She is a gentlewoman, and known well to the higher authorities of the country. Let her go, and claim of them the power to rescue her own niece from the clutches of Jonathan Wild, who can have no possible charge against her."

Bewildered, and agonized in heart and brain as he was, Captain Heron had not so far lost all power of reflection, as not to perceive that in this proposed course there lay much hope and much safety, while by any precipitate action of his own, he might not succeed in rescuing Edith, but might place himself in an equal, if not a much greater, danger.

"Be it so," he said. "I will wait here. I will wait here. Oh, Lady Castleneau, how much am I beholden to you!"

"Not a word of that—not a word of that! It is nearly twelve o'clock, and Anthony should return. I will have my carriage at once."

A clock struck twelve.

Heron turned to the Earl of Bridgewater.

"My dear friend," he said, "you have business at Montague House."

"I have, and will repair there at once. But I know that there is abundant faith in me, and that my absence until now will be attributed to some great necessity."

"And I may go?" said Warringdale in a low tone.

"No! I should advise that this man be detained. I will consider whether or not to charge him distinctly with the murder of my father. Lady Castleneau, is there no room in this house, which we can convert for a short time into a prison for this criminal?"

"Oh, yes, yes!"

The door of the breakfast room opened at this moment, and Anthony appeared.

"My lady," he said, "Sir John Tarleton is rather better, and nothing has been heard of the Lady Edith."

"My coach at once, Anthony," said Lady Castleneau. "Be as quick as you can, for I must visit the Secretary of State."

"One moment, Anthony," said the Earl of Bridgewater. "Have you any secure place we can put this man in for a few hours?"

"My Lord Warringdale?" exclaimed Anthony.

"Exactly so."

"I think there's one of the old cellars below. I dare say the rats will run away!"

"This is monstrous!" said Warringdale. "I have told you all you want to know, and yet you seek to keep me a prisoner."

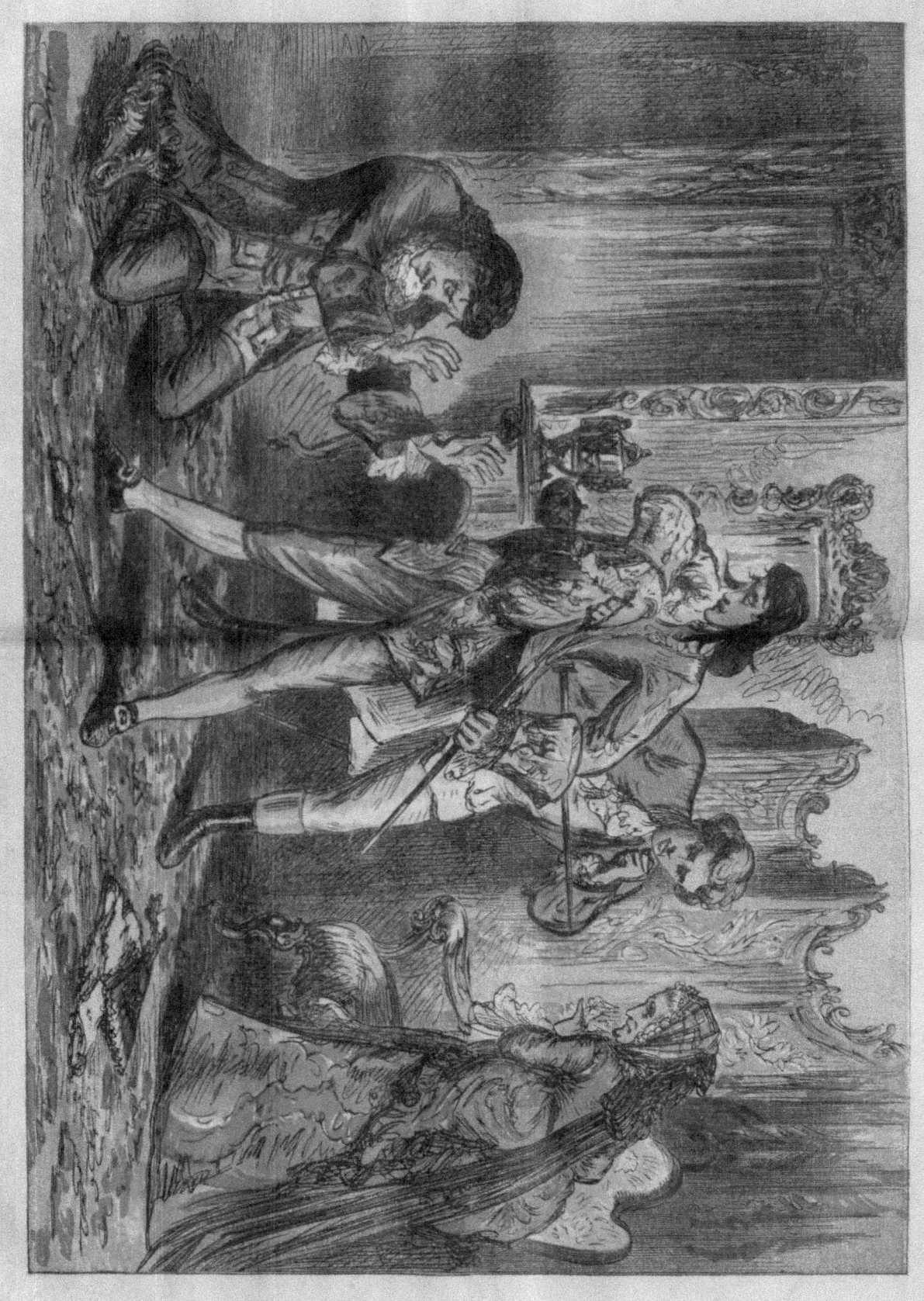

CAPTAIN HERON DETAINS LORD WARBEGDALE AS A HOSTAGE FOR THE SAFETY OF DITH.

Presented Gratis with No. 61 of the New Edition of Edith the Captive; or, the Robbers of Epping Forest.

EACH WEEK IS PRESENTED GATIS A COLOURED ENGRAVING.

"Yes," interposed Lady Castleneau; "and a prisoner you shall remain."

"Till when, and wherefore, madam?"

"Until Edith is in safety and freedom."

"Yes," cried the Earl of Bridgewater, "that will do,—hostage for hostage. We will keep my Lord Warringdale until the Lady Edith is released; and then comes my turn to call him to account on my own separate quarrel."

"Come on," said old Anthony. "Don't you hear my lady wants her carriage, and there is no time to waste on you? Come into the cellar, my lord, at once, and don't give us any trouble."

Warringdale looked at old Anthony furiously, and possibly he might have had some ideas of overcoming him; but if so, they quickly vanished when he found Ogle just outside the door, who seized him very scientifically by his cuff and his collar.

Warringdale had not a chance of escape; and in a few minutes he found himself an inmate of a very uncomfortable cellar, a great number of which were among the foundations of old Castleneau House.

Old Anthony then proceeded, at once, to get his mistress's carriage in order, while Captain Heron and the Earl of Bridgewater made their way over the garden wall into the grounds of Montague House.

Heron was in the same Court suit which had served him so well to make an appearance at the Court ball at St. James's.

The Earl of Bridgewater merely introduced him as Captain Heron, and so he was present at the nuptials of the young nobleman with the youthful Lady Cleveland, whom he had rescued from such cruel associations and persecutions of the dissolute and abandoned Lord Belessis.

To be sure, Captain Heron was but a gloomy and sorrowful attendant at a bridal, for his heart was full of distress on account of Edith; and yet he tried to reason with himself, and to be convinced, as in good truth he had reason to be, that all was being done that could be done; and that by far the safest and most effectual course for her release was that which had been adopted by the Lady Castleneau.

We will now follow that courageous and true-hearted gentlewoman upon her mission for the rescue of Edith; but the reader is well aware that Lord Warringdale has kept up his character for deception to the last, by stating that Edith was to be conveyed to Jonathan Wild's house, when such was not the case.

Little did Lady Castleneau or Captain Heron suspect that she had been conveyed to Whitcombe House, in St. James's, and that she was actually and absolutely at that moment alone in the extensive mansion, and could have been rescued at the cost of breaking down a couple of doors, which only stood between her and freedom.

Lady Castleneau had no difficulty in procuring an audience of the Secretary of State, who, at first, listened to her with a smile of incredulity, as she stated the somewhat romantic circumstances under which Jonathan Wild had taken possession of Edith.

Lady Castleneau, however, had well considered the posture of affairs while in her coach, on her route to the cabinet of the Secretary of State; and she thought that while he possibly might find some difficulty in rescuing Edith from Jonathan Wild, he would probably see none in ordering the instant release of Lord Warringdale from the cellar at Castleneau House.

She therefore resolved, as that fact had nothing to do with the demand for Edith's release, that she would not mention it.

But Lady Castleneau was too ingenuous to pretend that she told all while she kept anything back; and she said at once to the Secretary, "There are family circumstances with which I need not trouble you. It is sufficient that my niece, by name Edith Tarleton, has been seized upon by Jonathan Wild for his own purposes and those of some of his employers, and I demand power immediately to release her."

"It is an outrage," said the Secretary, "which we cannot countenance for a moment. The young lady shall not only be released, but a severe account shall be exacted from Wild for these illegal transactions. I cannot believe that he has any just grounds for her apprehension."

"And if so," said Lady Castleneau, "she should be taken before a magistrate, and not illegally confined in the cellars of Jonathan Wild's house, which, I am informed, extend right under Newgate Street, and form a little subterranean gaol, of which he has the entire control; and, I must say, I am surprised how any administration could give such power to such a man."

"My Lady Castleneau," said the Secretary, "we live in such ticklish times that really we men in office, who dare not do illegal things ourselves, are forced to connive at them sometimes in others. But this man Wild is growing insolent, and going too far. We shall have to check his little career. And besides, in course of time a man like that, who is so very useful, gets to—to——"

"Know too much," said Lady Castleneau.

"Well, that may be the case. But there is the order you require. It is imperative, you see, and orders Jonathan Wild instantly to deliver up to you your niece; and should he refuse, you can call upon any constables to search his place, and all its ins and outs, and recover her."

"I thank you," said Lady Castleneau; and "it will be for me to consider, when I have recovered my niece, what I can do to ensure the punishment of the perpetrator of this outrage."

The Secretary bowed, and Lady Castleneau took her departure to Jonathan Wild's house in Newgate Street.

But the old gentlewoman had a full appreciation of Wild's character, and from the dubious manner in which the Secretary of State had spoken, she was afraid that Wild was too useful to the authorities to be lightly got rid of; so, with her usual firmness of character and straightforward manner of doing things, the moment she alighted from her coach at Jonathan Wild's house in Newgate Street, she collected quite a little crowd about her, by calling out, "I want a constable— I want a constable! My name is Castleneau. I am Lady Castleneau, of Castleneau House, in Bloomsbury Fields; and I want a constable to accompany me into the house of Jonathan Wild, as I have an order from the Secretary of State for the release of my niece, who has been illegally taken into custody by him. A constable! a constable, good people, if you please!"

By this means, Lady Castleneau not only procured a parish constable, but she gave so much publicity to her visit to Jonathan Wild's house, that it would be quite impossible for him to detain her; and, in fact, the little crowd that had collected round the door showed no disposition to go away until they saw the end of the matter.

If anything could be obnoxious or annoying to Jonathan Wild more than another, it was publicity of this kind; and he made a rush on to his doorstep like a bull-dog in a state of exasperation, and scowled right and left upon the people.

"There he is—there he is!" cried everybody. "There's the rascal! Down with him! Burn him out! There's Jonathan!"

Wild was perfectly bewildered. He could know nothing of what had happened at Castleneau House, and the appearance of the old gentlewoman at his door, accompanied by a crowd of people, filled him with as much astonishment as rage.

CHAPTER CXXXVI.

EDITH MEETS WITH A SINGULAR ADVENTURE AT WHITCOMBE HOUSE.

A SENSATION of utter loneliness crept over the mind of Edith, as she listened in vain even for that terrifying response which, when she had first heard it, made her believe she was guarded, perhaps, by the beings of another world.

There was such an intense stillness in the air—a stillness only rendered the more remarkable by a faint hushing sound as if from far off, and which reminded her somewhat of the sighing of the wind among the trees of old Epping Forest.

That hushing sound was the subdued murmur of the life of the great city so close at hand to her. It only tended to make her own solitude the more profound, and to fill her mind with sadder thoughts.

It could not be said that she felt any personal fears as regarded her actual safety, but she could well guess that the object of her imprisonment was that the fears and the affection of Felix Heron might be worked upon in her name.

She could not doubt but that Wild had spoken the truth, when he intimated to her that she would be treated with all respect, and yet, at the same time, used as a means of goading and terrifying her husband into such terms as would render him no longer an object of fear to Lord Warringdale.

Along with these thoughts came the strong desire to escape, if possible, and so defeat this most terrible machination of her enemies.

We know that Edith was capable of surprise, and of the most lively and excitable feelings where her affections were concerned; but we know likewise that she possessed the courage of a real heroine, and that no ordinary danger would deter her from any attempt that promised success, by which she could rejoin Felix Heron.

She felt, however, that she had reached the limit of the visual observation she was able to make of the place in which she was.

She had been long enough in it for her eyes to make use of the smallest particles of light that made their way into that gloomy apartment, and still it was but dusky and shadowy.

The heavy articles of furniture only looked a little blacker than the air which surrounded them; and if she strove to fix one of the walls in her gaze, the dim haze of darkness in which she saw it, made it appear to advance and recede, like the figures in a phantasmagoria.

Then she crept slowly round the room, and she was not only able to localise, but to feel the shape, of the objects she encountered.

The panels of the door, the recess of the window, the carved moulding of the old cabinets, all passed before her observation twice; and then she crept towards the centre of the room, and placed her hands carefully upon the table which was there, and felt that there were books and papers; and then her touch lighted upon the arms and back of one of the antique chairs, and Edith sunk upon it with a deep sigh.

"Who will help me? Who can help me now?" she said. "Oh, Felix, Felix, why is it that I cannot raise my voice, so that you may hear it? I suffer, but what must you suffer? For I feel that you are in safety, and with those who love you, while your thoughts of me will be associated with a thousand agonies, because you will imagine me encompassed by a thousand dangers! Felix! Felix! Felix! shall I ever look upon your face again?"

Edith clasped her hands over her eyes, and gave way for a few moments to deep grief, but then she struggled to repress the tears that forced their way from her saddened heart.

"Oh, how weak, how weak I was to live at the mercy of the first specious tale that was brought to me on the lips of such a man as Warringdale!"

Hardly had these words escaped from Edith, when she was startled into attention by a sound that resembled a deep-drawn sigh.

So close did it seem to her, that she could almost have imagined it agitated the air about her face. A vague feeling of terror came over her, and she almost stilled the beating of her heart, in order to listen for a repetition of the sound.

The stillness about her was positively painful for a few moments, but it was broken then by a soft voice, which in the lowest and gentlest tone, pronounced these words:—"Who is it that, in the darkness of this place, gives way to lamentation?"

A feeling of alarm struggled with one of hope in the breast of Edith,—alarm for a moment that she was not alone; and then a hope that whoever could utter those gentle tones might be to her a friend: yet it was a few moments before she could gather nerve and strength to reply; and the voice spoke again, at the instant that her lips parted to ask a question.

"You are silent," said the voice, "and perhaps you dread that it is an enemy who speaks to you. Be assured it is not so, for he who has been long his own enemy has no disposition to be a foe to you."

"Your voice is assuring," said Edith, faintly. "Who and what are you? I am a prisoner here, and beseech your kindness."

"I am one, not now mentioned as among the living, but I can feel for you."

"Your accents breathe kindness and sympathy."

"I would that they should do so. Tell me your name, and by what strange accident I find you here."

"My name is Edith. I am daughter of Sir

John Tarleton, and the wife of one who will mourn for me, and who will unite with me in blessing the kind hand that sets me free."

"You are Edith Tarleton," said the voice, in a low tone of deep emotion,—"Edith Tarleton, who, according to report, was to be united with Lord Warringdale?"

"It was a false report. My father, I grieve to say, made some such compact with the false Lord Warringdale; but my heart never sanctioned it, and where I gave my love I have bestowed my hand."

"And upon whom has this love and this hand been bestowed?"

"Men call him Felix Heron."

"Ah! Is this possible?"

"Yes; but in reality he owns a nobler name."

"Just heaven! just heaven!" said the voice; and the tones were so low that it seemed to be fading away in the distance, conveying an impression to Edith that she should never hear its sound again.

"Oh, stay, stay!" she cried. "I know not why it is, but while I listen to you I feel an assurance that I am not alone and friendless. Your voice sinks deep into my heart; and, losing the care and affection of him who should have been my father, I feel as if heaven had raised you up in his stead, be you whom you may. Stay—oh, stay!"

"I am here," said the voice, but the tones were those of deep emotion,—"I am here; but bear with me a moment. I have much to say to you."

"I will listen. You shall ask me nothing I will not tell you. It is for the wicked and the designing to live in a haze of secrets and suspicions. I have none."

It was some few minutes now before the voice again addressed Edith, and then it said, abruptly, "How came you hither?"

"I was at Lady Castleneau's, my aunt's, when the false and cruel Lord Warringdale came, with a specious tale that my father lay at the point of death, and required my presence at his house in Finsbury. I did not think—I did not reason; but, on the impulse of the words, I fell into a snare, and blindfold, and with many threats, I was conducted hither."

"By whom?"

"By Jonathan Wild, the associate of the wicked Lord Warringdale."

"Alas! alas! alas!" said the voice. "It was even so. Know you where you are?"

"Indeed I do not."

"You are in Whitcombe House, in St. James's Street, and this is the cabinet of the late Earl."

Edith uttered a cry of surprise.

"Is this possible?" she said. "Is it to be believed that my first entrance into this house, the name of which is so intimately associated with that of my husband, has been as a prisoner?"

"Even so."

The more the tones of this strange voice lingered in the ears of Edith, the more the conviction pressed itself upon her that it was one which spoke to her but in friendly accents. She felt an irresistible desire to pour out all the thoughts and feelings of her soul to this most mysterious and hidden confidant; and it was with so much feeling and emotion in her tones that no doubt they expressed more than her words, she again spoke to her invisible visitant.

"I know not who you are," she said, "or if you be of this world or not, but I feel constrained to speak to you. Tell me—oh, tell me, if indeed you know—why I am here, and how I can procure my release?"

"Will you speak to me, in answer to questions I would fain put to you, first?" added the voice, in the lowest and gentlest of accents.

"I will. Indeed, and in truth, I will," replied Edith.

"How came you acquainted with him who calls himself Captain Felix Heron?"

"He saved more than my life, for he saved my happiness, at a time when I seemed deserted by the one person who should have held my future felicity most dear. Felix Heron saved me; and from that moment, thinking of him as my only friend, hearing ever the echo of his voice in my heart, he became dear to me; and I am his, and his only."

"Know you not," said the mysterious voice, in reply to these last words of Edith,—"know you not that this man, who calls himself Felix Heron, makes some pretensions to a higher birth and a more exalted destiny than that which has been his?"

"I know well," said Edith, "that there is no destiny he would not adorn; there is no rank which would not well become him; and I know and feel that his pretensions are true."

"Tell me then, Edith, since such is your name, what is your own opinion of your imprisonment in this place?"

"The cause of it is patent to my understanding. Lord Warringdale and Jonathan Wild have interests in common. They know that there is but one way of reaching the heart of Felix Heron, and that is through me. Hence the device which has made me a prisoner in this place, and which will fill him with despair."

"Be hopeful—be hopeful," said the voice. "There is one who will watch over you. Be hopeful, and you may yet achieve a happiness beyond your wildest dreams; but there must be no doubts, no misgivings, not a word or action upon which can hang a selfish thought. Farewell for a time!"

"Ah! you will not help me! I know not who you are. I cannot guess by what means you obtain admittance to this place. Darkness is about me, and I cannot see you; but if, indeed, you do, as your words indicate, feel for Felix Heron and myself, you will release me and let me fly to him."

"I cannot do so yet. Oh, be patient!"

"No, no; I cannot be patient. Each minute is an hour—each hour a day. You are surely human, and have human feeling. I speak not for myself, but for him. He is safe, but he knows not what I may be enduring."

"Means shall be taken," said the voice. "He shall not suffer; but the tests of truth and of affection must be made. I too have suffered! I too have suffered!"

The voice seemed to be dying away in the distance; and Edith, with all the agony of abandonment again in that lonely place, made her way through the darkness to that part of the room from whence the voice had proceeded, but there was nothing but the pannelled walls and the sharp arved edges of the cabinets to be felt.

"Speak! Oh, speak again!" she cried.

There was no reply.

Edith felt herself to be alone.

There was something altogether so strange, and out of the path of all experience, in the singular circumstance of a voice in that prison-house in which Edith found herself, that she was, for the first time in her life, on the verge of a belief in the supernatural.

With double darkness and with double solitude that place seemed to oppress her spirits. A sense almost of suffocation came over her; and amid the dim obscurity of the room she could almost believe that the walls were contracting, and that the space about her was narrowing.

No wonder then that she screamed for help.

It was her own voice, however, which recovered her from the dreamy, imaginative state into which she had fallen.

The echo of her own tones brought her back to the world, and to the realities of life again.

And then Edith got calmer, and she began to reason with herself.

"Surely," she said, "that voice was full of friendly sympathy towards both me and Felix. The questions that it asked all seemed to be dictated by a wish to gather fresh material for some sympathetic action in my behalf. Oh, yes; I will be patient—I will be patient, and I will be hopeful!"

Edith, then, rather for the purpose of keeping her mind employed, than that she had any idea it would evolve any usefulness, once again examined by the touch the whole of the room.

This time, however, she must have let her hands stray somewhat lower down the walls; for in one of the corners, she felt some cold metallic object encounter her hand.

The examination of another moment let her know that it was a sword-hilt that she touched.

She had reached the corner of that room where there was the collection of swords of different sorts, and for different occasions, which had belonged to the late Lord Whitcombe.

"Ah!" cried Edith, "I shall feel now that I am not so entirely helpless! I am now armed, and will defend myself!"

She at once possessed herself of one of those swords, and then she made her way to one of the old arm-chairs, and drew it close to that corner of the apartment where she had found the deadly weapons.

With considerable difficulty, then, Edith removed the large table likewise in that direction, and so bestowed it as well as she could in the darkness, that it formed a kind of rampart or fortification before her and the old arm-chair.

Edith began then to think that she was safer than she had been.

Hour after hour, however, passed away, and no one came to disturb the intense silence and solitude of that house.

Edith began, then, to wonder if she would be left to starve in Whitcombe House.

And, in good truth, the situation in which she was now placed was one of rather a critical character.

It had been the intention of Lord Warringdale, and it was so agreed upon between him and Jonathan Wild, that so soon as Edith should be a safe prisoner at Whitcombe House, he, Warringdale, would go there, and strive to make the terms with her, the enforcing of which had been the object of her imprisonment.

But that object was entirely set aside by the incarceration of Lord Warringdale in one of the old cellars of Castleneau House.

Hence Edith was left for so long to her own reflections, in the cabinet of the late Earl of Whitcombe; for it was not until rather late in the day that Jonathan Wild found that something had gone amiss with his villanous associate.

We must now leave Edith in the silence and solitude of the room, in which she keeps guard as best she can, behind the massive table, with a sword in her hand, while we proceed again to Newgate Street, to narrate what befel Lady Castleneau on her visit to Jonathan Wild's house.

CHAPTER CXXXVII.

LADY CASTLENEAU RESCUES ANOTHER PRISONER FROM MR. WILD.

THE sort of riot and confusion that Lady Castleneau made at Wild's house was almost sufficient to drive him frantic; for there was nothing in the world that he so much dreaded as a popular tumult about the mysterious residence he made so much of, close to Newgate.

Jonathan ran out on to the door-step, with such an unpleasant look of passion about his eyes, that any one with less courage than Lady Castleneau would have hesitated to encounter him.

"What is all this?" he cried,—"what is the reason of this disturbance?"

"I make the disturbance," said Lady Castleneau, "and I make it purposely!"

"Purposely, madam?"

"Yes, Jonathan Wild. I come with the Secretary of State's order for the release of Edith Tarleton."

"Ah!"

"You start!—you look guilty! You are guilty! I demand her release!"

"And you think she is here?"

"I do."

"Then, madam, I can only say that if you will honour my humble abode so far, you may examine it from the cellars to the attics, and you will find no Lady Edith here."

"I cannot believe you."

"Look then, madam, for yourself; but it will not help you to make a crowd round my door."

"I do not know that," said Lady Castleneau. "If I were about to go into the den of any noxious animal to seek for a victim, I should like as many people as possible to know of it."

"Ah!" sneered Wild. "Lady Castleneau likes her heroism to be popular."

"No; but I do not feel justified in making my actions unsafe. Now that there are plenty of witnesses to the fact that I entered your house, they will be impatient for my return."

Wild ground his teeth with rage.

Lady Castleneau detached from her waist the heavy gold watch she wore, and handed it to old Anthony, as she said, "Anthony, if I do not come out of this house in half an hour, call upon all good people to look for me."

"Confound you and all good people besides!" growled Wild.

"Now, Mr. Constable," added Lady Castleneau to the parish constable, who had made his appearance; "now, if you please, I will trouble you to come with me."

The constable looked, indeed, as he was, terribly scared at the idea that he was requested to make his way into the house of Jonathan Wild, of whom he had a most complete dread and terror.

"Mr. Wild," he said, aside, "I cannot help it, you see."

Jonathan uttered a growl like an angry bear; and indeed he seemed to be fully intent upon carrying out the simile of Lady Castleneau, when she had likened his house to the den of some noxious animal.

But he felt that to resist the examination of his house would be far more dangerous than to submit to it.

No. 62.—EDITH.

"Come on, then, my lady," he said. "My little page will go with you."

"Page! What page?"

"Blueskin, he sometimes calls himself, my lady, on account of his charming colour. You see, my Lady Castleneau, he was blown up once by incautiously sitting on a barrel of gunpowder while he was smoking."

"Here you are!" said Blueskin, as he made his appearance on hearing his name mentioned. "Here you are, Mr. Wild!

"'The rope was short—three kicks he gave—
"Row, dow, dow," says he;
Jack Ketch cried out, "Pull, pull his legs,
And all right he will be."
Row de dow.'"

"Hold your noise," said Jonathan Wild, "will you, and show Lady Castleneau over the house. She wants some one she thinks we have here, and let her ladyship take who she likes."

PUBLISHER'S NOTE

VOL.2. PP.74-75 ARE MISSING.

beginning to get very uneasy indeed at the absence of his mistress.

The mob raised a shout when the old gentlewoman appeared, and Jack Sheppard chose to take some of the cheers to himself, and executed a mock bow, which delighted the people.

"Get up on the coach-box," said Lady Castleneau to Jack. "You will go to my house."

"All's right, my lady!" said Jack; "and though folks say I'm a careless fellow, and though you found me in an odd place, it can never be said of Jack Sheppard that he forgot a kindness. God bless and thank you, lady!"

There was a tear in Jack's eye, as he clambered up to the coach-box; and old Anthony, as he made room for him, said, "I hope you are an honest boy?"

"The same to you, old pump," said Jack.

Anthony did not know what to make of this rather ambiguous reply, but drove off with a dignified look, and did not exchange another word with Jack Sheppard.

Poor Lady Castleneau's heart was very sad. She could not divine what had become of Edith.

"What shall I do now?" she said. "What can I do? How shall I seek to comfort or console Felix, after this failure to restore his Edith to him?"

Jonathan Wild, in the passage of his house, was in as great a state of doubt and perplexity, in regard to Lord Warringdale, as Lady Castleneau, in her carriage, was, as regarded Edith.

"What can have happened to him?" said Wild, as he stood in his favourite attitude when he was reflecting, of his hands behind his back. "What can have gone amiss, to make him say anything at all? I must find out all about it. I will be off to his rooms opposite to Whitcombe House, and then I will go and see if Edith is still safe. Well, well; so long as I can keep her a prisoner, the game, I fancy, is pretty well in my own hands."

Jonathan Wild then took his way to that suite of chambers in which he had often before seen and held council with his villanous employer, Lord Warringdale.

The only person there was an old woman, who had been employed to clean the rooms, and she had neither heard nor seen anything of Warringdale.

Wild was puzzled, and knew not what to do; so he hired a hackney coach, and told it to wait for him at the corner of St. James's Street, for he intended to go to Finsbury, to see Judge Tarleton; but first he resolved upon a visit to Edith, at Whitcombe House.

CHAPTER CXXXVIII.

THE EARL OF BRIDGEWATER FORCES LORD WARRINGDALE TO FIGHT.

IT was getting late in the day when Lady Castleneau reached home again; and as she neared her ancient mansion, she felt almost inclined to prolong the time, so saddened was her heart at the idea of the tale she had to tell, of disappointment to Captain Heron.

But still she could not but feel that the sooner some immediate action was taken, that would lead to the restoration of Edith, the happier it would be for all parties.

With all her anxieties and all her terrors, Lady Castleneau could scarcely believe that Edith was in any positive danger; for the circumstances attending her departure from Castleneau House were of too public a character to render it at all safe for Jonathan Wild to traffic with her life, or even her liberty, long.

Knowing, however, the affection which had become a part of the nature of Felix Heron, she might well fear the effect upon him of the intelligence that they had been deceived, and that she had searched in vain in Jonathan Wild's house for Edith.

Ogle was on the anxious watch for the approach of the carriage; and as it rolled into the courtyard of Castleneau House, he was not a little surprised to see the companion that old Anthony had on the coach-box.

"Why, if my eyes don't deceive me, that is Jack Sheppard, the young carpenter, who, they say, has already cracked several cribs about London, and yet kept clear of Jonathan Wild!"

"Why, Ogle," said Jack Sheppard, as he came down from the coach-box, "who would have thought of seeing you here?"

"And you, Jack—what brings you to Castleneau House?"

"Why, you see, Ogle, the old lady and I have made friends. But how is the Captain, and my little acquaintance, Tom Ripon?"

"He is all right; but I can see, by the look of Lady Castleneau's countenance, that she has failed in finding Edith."

"If she came to look for her," said Jack, "at Jonathan Wild's house, she might well fail; for I'm quite certain she isn't there. To be sure, I was shut up in one of his 'little jugs,' as he calls the cells under Newgate Street; but I'm reckoned rather a sharp one, you see, Ogle, and there was little that passed in Jonathan's house that I was not aware of."

It did not, indeed, need for Lady Castleneau to say anything to Ogle respecting her disappointment, in not finding Edith. Her looks of perplexity and dejection were more than sufficient to let him see that she had been disappointed.

Captain Heron had returned from Montague House, and now hurried from the breakfast-room to meet Lady Castleneau.

One glance at her was sufficient.

"You have been unsuccessful," he said. "The authorities would not aid you. Be it so! I will take this affair, in hand, then, myself; and I will not leave one stone standing upon another in Jonathan Wild's house until I find Edith."

"Alas!" said Lady Castleneau. "She is not there. I have had all facilities in looking for her, but she is not there."

"Then the villain Warringdale has played us false, and I must still wring the secret from his guilty heart."

"I know not what to advise—I know not what to do," added Lady Castleneau. "I regret, too, that we shall miss the counsel of our friend the Earl of Bridgewater, who probably would be able to look with calmer judgment into this affair, than either of us."

"No," said the young Earl, as he at this moment made his appearance in the room. "I have

JACK SHEPPARD MEETS WITH FLATTERING OVATION ON COMING
OUT OF NEWGATE.

Presented Gratis with No. 62, of the New Edition of Jack the Captive; or, the Robbers of Epping Forest.

EACH WEEK IS PRESENTED IS A COLOURED ENGRAVING.

yet an hour to spare, while my bride makes her preparations for her journey."

"An hour!" said Lady Castleneau,—"but an hour?"

"Less time," said the Earl, "has decided the fate of a kingdom. What is the news?"

Lady Castleneau quickly informed him of her disappointment in Newgate Street.

"One of two things, then, is certain," said the young Earl. "Warringdale deceives us, or his co-partner in villany, Jonathan Wild, plays a double game, and deceives him."

"But how are we to ascertain that point?" said Captain Heron.

"We have one, and we must now take the other."

"That's it!" said a voice; and Jack Sheppard, who had made his way into the apartment, made his appearance from behind the screen. "That's it! Take Jonathan Wild, and put a rope round his neck—give it a good hard tug at the other end, and he will confess anything."

"Who is this?" said the Earl.

"I think I know him," said Captain Heron. "Your name is Sheppard?"

"Yes; commonly called Jack. Her ladyship, here, came to Jonathan's house in Newgate Street to find a young lady, but as no such person was there, she took the nearest approach to it, and chose me."

"Yes," said Lady Castleneau. "I brought this boy away from the contamination of that dreadful house."

"Just so," said Jack. "I was losing my voice. But look ye here, gentlefolks all. It seems to me, from what I hear, that you want to catch Jonathan Wild, and I can tell you how to do it capitally. There has been a robbery in Blackfriars of some plate, and Jonathan is going to meet the fence who bought it to-night in Fleet Market. You see there's a reward of a couple of hundred pounds, and Jonathan will easily buy all the swag for fifty. That's the way he carries on his business. I heard it all from one of his men who brought me the pitcher of water and half a dozen ship's biscuits he allows to those he gets into his little jugs."

"This seems a strange youth," said the Earl of Bridgewater; "but if what he says is true, it may be a means of securing the person of Jonathan Wild; and, at all events, he must know the secret of the hiding-place of the Lady Edith."

"It shall be done," said Captain Heron with animation. "Pardon me for a moment; I am not in town in sufficient force, probably, to seize upon the villain, if he should chance to have some of his men with him. I shall have time yet to send Ogle to the forest for assistance."

"Oh, there's no need," said Jack; "Jonathan will be alone, you may depend. He never has anybody with him when money is in the question, for fear they should cry out 'Shares!' There's you and I, and Ogle, Captain; surely we three *men* can do the work."

"Men!" cried Lady Castleneau. "What will the times come to when children like you call themselves men?"

"Never mind, old lady," said Jack. "If there wasn't another crib to crack in all London, the doors of Castleneau House might be upon the latch all night before I would come near it."

"This scheme looks feasible," said the Earl. "I cannot stay to help you, Heron, for I'm off into Surrey in the course of another hour, with my wife; but before I go I have a word to say to Lord Warringdale."

"Ogle shall fetch him."

"Oh! I would that such a villain were no longer beneath my roof!" said Lady Castleneau.

"Bring him into the garden," cried the young nobleman. "In truth, when I am in a room with him, I feel as if the air was tainted by his presence. Come, Heron, step out with me, for I wish you to be present at this interview."

The Earl of Bridgewater opened one of the long French casements of the breakfast-room, and stepped out on to the terrace that ran along the back of the house.

Captain Heron followed him.

"If you please, my lady," said Jack Sheppard, "I've a very important question to ask."

"What is it?"

"Do you think there's anything to eat down below in the larder?"

"Anthony," said Lady Castleneau, "take this youth with you, and satisfy his hunger."

"Come, old brick," said Jack, "stir those stumps that, I dare say, you call legs, or I shall begin to eat you."

"You're an impertinent puppy," said Anthony, as they proceeded to the kitchen.

"I always was, my old tittlebat," said Jack.

"And you'll live to be hanged some day."

"Not a doubt of it. But in the meantime, if there's any cold mutton in the house, it will be quite a godsend."

Ogle was not long in producing Lord Warringdale from the cellar in which he had been confined, and with very little ceremony, he handed him into the garden.

Warringdale looked pale and anxious, for of course he was well aware how he had deceived Captain Heron and Lady Castleneau with respect to the destination of Edith; but in the solitude of his imprisonment, he had taken counsel with himself, and had resolved to adhere to his statement, throwing everything else upon Jonathan Wild.

Warringdale, however was somewhat surprised at the turn which affairs took in the garden, for Captain Heron merely stepped quietly up to him, and said, "Do you adhere to your statement that Jonathan Wild was to take the Lady Edith to his house in Newgate Street?"

"I do!"

Heron said not another word, but stepped back, and allowed the Earl of Bridgewater to take his place.

"My Lord Warringdale," he said,—"named such, as you are, by courtesy, and not by right,—I accuse you, as you well know, of the murder of my father. Had I sufficient legal proof, I would hand you over to the outraged laws of the country; but I have no real moral doubt whatever of your guilt, and therefore I have made a determination that whenever I meet you, be it in forest, field, or public street, I will not let you out of my power or my sight, until I have made you fight me."

"This is most monstrous!" said Lord Warringdale.

"Not so monstrous as to take the life of a man

who never really injured you, for the purpose of cancelling some debts of honour, and forging pecuniary obligations against his memory."

Warringdale could well see, now, that reflection had made the young Earl fully aware of the reasons which had induced him to commit the terrible murder in Paddock Hill Lane.

"I have nothing to say to you," he said. "You charge me with a crime: bring forth your proofs, before the proper tribunals, and I will meet you. I am innocent, but I cannot prove a negative."

"Nor do I ask you; but since you pretend to be a nobleman, and as I am aware that you hold the King's commission as a soldier, I challenge you to fight."

"I accept."

"You do?"

"Yes, at proper time, and in proper place; and when I am sufficiently recovered from some accidental hurts to be able to beat you. I should fence at great disadvantage."

"I do not ask you to fence. We will fight in the new-fashioned manner, with pistols. You can pull a trigger, and you have not lost your eyesight."

"I have no second—you are both my enemies."

"Here you are, my lord," said Jack Sheppard, as he came from behind a tree; "don't let that trouble you. I'll be your second!"

"Ah!" said Warringdale, "I can see that my assassination is half determined upon."

"Not so," said Ogle, as he, too, now advanced. "There are quite enough of us to see fair play; but if I were his lordship the Earl of Bridgewater, I would not put a pistol in such a rogue's hands. Why, my lord, what's his life compared to yours? If you shoot him, you do but rid the world of a great scoundrel; but if he shoots you, why there dies an honest and an honourable man. No, my lord, it is quite impossible there can ever be really fair play between you and such a man as Lord Warringdale."

"There never were truer words spoken," said Captain Heron, stepping forward. "Let me beg of you, my friend, to forego your purpose."

"No, no," said the Earl, "I cannot—I dare not. There is a something which seems to stop my breath—to stifle me, when I see this man. The spirit of my murdered father appears to hover about me. I have a raging desire to kill him, and I can only combat with it, by fighting him on equal terms. Do not try to dissuade me, or I shall commit some act of violence, which all who love me will regret."

"Be it so, then," said Heron.

"No," cried Warringdale, "I will not accept this boy as my second."

"As a matter of form, then," said Ogle, "I will stand by, and see a bullet put into you with all the pleasure in life."

Warringdale looked around him in despair. There was something so fiery and menacing about the eyes of the young Earl, that he saw there was no escape for him. To attempt flight would have been worse than useless. The garden wall was high, even could he have reached it. He stood like some savage animal at bay, who feels that escape is out of the question, and that he must turn and face the hunter.

"Be it so," he said. "This will be murder, although a dramatic one. Be it so. If I must

fight, the blood that is shed be upon your head, Lord Bridgewater, and not upon mine."

"There is innocent blood upon your head already, villain! Heron, my friend, I commend me to your good service. You have pistols, I fancy?"

"Yes," said Heron.

He turned aside, and whispered hurriedly to Ogle.

"No bullets," he said. "I cannot, dare not risk the life of the Earl of Bridgewater!"

"All right, Captain!" cried Ogle, with a look of pleasure.

Captain Heron measured out fifteen paces in the garden; and placing the Earl of Bridgewater at one extremity, he signified to Lord Warringdale that he was to take his situation at the other.

"No," said Warringdale. "There is a tree behind me. It directs the aim."

"Change places," said the Earl.

The change was instantly effected; and then Ogle advanced with a brace of pistols in his hands.

"How can I tell," said Warringdale, "but that there may be foul play yet? The pistol you give me may not be loaded with ball, while my adversary's may be fatal?"

"Take your choice, then," said Ogle. "You can have which you like."

Warringdale could have no more to say in the objection; but he took one of the pistols in his hand, and while he turned of a death-like paleness, he faced his young adversary.

"I will give the word," said Heron. "When I say 'Three,' you may fire."

Warringdale shook with fear.

The Earl of Bridgewater was firm and calm.

"One!" said Captain Heron.

Warringdale gazed about him like a man in a dream. He seemed as if he were taking leave of the old trees, the sky, the grass at his feet, and the old mansion, which cast its shadow over the scene of combat.

"Two!" said Heron.

A deadly fear came over Warringdale. He seemed to feel that, do what he would, Captain Heron would never take his life. He did not wait for the word "Three," but raised his pistol and fired full in the face of the Earl of Bridgewater.

"I was not too soon!" he cried. "I heard you say three!"

The smoke cleared away; and there, of course, stood the Earl with a proud smile upon his lips, and perfectly uninjured.

"That was a foul shot," he said.

Lord Warringdale uttered a yell of dismay.

"A most foul shot!" cried Heron; "and I now say 'Three!' It is your turn, my Lord Bridgewater."

"Yes; it is my turn now."

Warringdale crouched down close to the ground —he was as one who saw the very image of death approaching him with rapid strides. His limbs refused their office, or he would have fled from the spot. He uttered various discordant cries, and was altogether a frightful picture of abject and bodily fear.

The Earl of Bridgewater slowly raised his pistol, and pointed it full at the trembling Warringdale.

There came a cry from some one at a window of the breakfast-room. It was Lady Castleneau, whose heart at that moment relented even in favour of one whom she believed to be so utterly worthless as Lord Warringdale.

He heard the cry.

"Save me—save me!" he cried. "My life—my life!"

Bang! went the pistol, and Lord Warringdale, with a shriek, fell flat upon his back.

"I fancy I've killed him," said the Earl of Bridgewater, calmly.

"Settled, and done for!" said Jack Sheppard.

Ogle laughed, in his quiet way; and then Captain Heron, stepping hastily up to the Earl of Bridgewater, took him by the arm, saying, "My dear and excellent friend, make the best of your way to Montague House. Leave London with your charming bride, and we will see to all this business."

"Is he dead?"

"I think not."

"Well, at all events, my mind is easier. It was more than a fair fight for him, for the rascal took the first shot. Farewell, Heron, for the present. I shall be in town again in fourteen days, and shall hear of you through Lady Castleneau."

"Assuredly—assuredly! Farewell!"

The young Earl made his way, by the aid of the ladder, to the gardens of Montague House, and Captain Heron hastened back to where Lord Warringdale was lying on the grass.

He was not a little surprised that even his extent of cowardice could possibly delude him into the belief that he was struck by a bullet, when none had been in the pistol; but when he reached where he was lying, an expression of surprise came over Heron's face.

There was blood upon the forehead of Lord Warringdale, and trickling down his face.

Heron turned to Ogle.

"You misunderstood me—you put balls in the pistols."

"Not at all," said Ogle; "but Jack Sheppard here, who, like all London boys, is a dead hand at stone-throwing, flung a pebble at him, and hit him on the brow, at the moment the Earl of Bridgewater fired; so that, without a doubt, he thinks there is a half-ounce bullet in his brains."

It was a great relief to Heron to hear this, much as he had cause to wish Lord Warringdale dead; but now that he knew the exact state of the case, he had no hesitation in playing upon his fears.

Stepping close up to him, Heron gazed down upon his face, as he said, "So, my Lord Warringdale, it has come to this, at last."

"It is murder!" gasped Warringdale.

"It is death; but providence is kind to you."

"Kind?"

"Yes; it leaves you time for repentance—for repentance and confession of iniquity. Have you nothing to say now, in your last moments, which shall atone, in any degree, for all your wickedness?"

So impressed was Lord Warringdale with the idea that he was shot through the head, when in reality he had only received a little scalp wound with a pebble, that he made a wonderful difficulty in raising himself on his arm to look at Heron.

"No," he said; "danger and fear are past. The world slips from me; but I will die confessing nothing, saying nothing, fearing nothing!"

"Your time, then, has not come," said Heron, solemnly. "Still in the battle of life have I to fight with thee, oh, wicked brother, when I would gladly have—had you been true and good—strained you to my heart!"

Captain Heron clasped his hands for a moment over his face, and then, more in grief than in anger, walked slowly towards the house.

Lady Castleneau met him, and, as though she had been his mother, she placed her hands kindly upon his shoulders.

"You weep, Felix," she said,—"you weep."

"Nay," he said; "they are the tears through which the sunshine of happiness will yet make its radiant way!"

——

CHAPTER CXXXIX.

JONATHAN WILD PAYS A VISIT TO WHITCOMBE HOUSE.

NOBODY could know better than Ogle that Lord Warringdale was not in reality hurt. He saw that Lady Castleneau was much affected at what appeared to have taken place in the garden; and following Captain Heron, he spoke to him in a low tone.

"Captain, what is to be done? Shall I remove him to the cellar again?"

"Yes."

"Oh, no, no!" said Lady Castleneau; "surely not now. If he be badly hurt, enemy as he is to us all, it is our duty to be merciful to him, and lend him what aid we can."

Jack Sheppard began to laugh.

Lady Castleneau looked perplexed.

"My lady," said Ogle, with a respectful bow; "let me tell you—for I am sure the Captain has no objection that I should—that Lord Warringdale is very much frightened, but not hurt."

"Not hurt?"

"No," added Jack Sheppard, "except so far as a three-cornered stone I picked up from the garden path can hurt him."

"Pardon me, dear Lady Castleneau," said Captain Heron, as he turned now from the window towards her,—"pardon me that I did not tell you this at once. He is quite safe. I took care there should be no bullets in the pistols. I did not forget where we were, nor who he was."

"You never forget," said Lady Castleneau; and she took the arm of Captain Heron, and they went into the breakfast-room together.

Ogle marched up to Lord Warringdale.

Jack Sheppard followed him closely.

"Come," said Ogle, "since you have had your little fight in the garden, it is time you went back into the cellar."

"I am dying! I am dying!"

"What colour?" said Jack Sheppard, as he stood deliberately upon the breast of Lord Warringdale.

"Help! Murder!"

"I am a light weight," said Jack, as Ogle pushed him aside, "and I don't think I could do him any hurt."

"Fiends! Assassins!" gasped Warringdale.

"Don't use any bad language," said Jack Sheppard, "or you will aggravate us."

"Get up," added Ogle.

"You know well," said Warringdale, "that there is a bullet in my head! Why, or how, it has not yet killed me, I do not know; but I feel certain that the moment I attempt to rise to my feet, I shall be a dead man!"

"We will see."

"Oh, no, no, no!"

"Come!"

Ogle stooped over the prostrate form of Lord Warringdale, and seizing him by the cravat, he pulled him up to a sitting position.

Jack Sheppard got behind him, and gave him such a push, that he was compelled to scramble to his feet.

"Villains! wretches!" he said. "This will come home to you both, some day!"

"We will wait till it does," replied Ogle. "In the meantime, we will put you into the cellar again."

"Until when?"

"Until the Lady Edith is found, and herself orders your release."

"This is very strange."

"What is?"

"I feel no worse, and begin to think I have had one of those wonderful escapes, when a pistol bullet touches the head without making an entrance through the skull."

Ogle laughed.

"You may depend," said Jack Sheppard, "that the bullet is in your brains, but it don't make any difference to some people. Half an ounce, more or less, of lead in their brains, comes to much the same thing."

There was an odd, bewildered look about Lord Warringdale, which much amused both Jack and Ogle.

They hurried him onward, into the lower part of the house again, and soon reached the door of the old, disused, and neglected wine-cellar, in which he had been before imprisoned.

"Stop," said Warringdale; "I will tell more than I have told, if I am assured of one thing."

"What is that?"

"The departure of Lord Bridgewater, and my own release."

"Those are two things."

"Well, on those conditions, I will say where the Lady Edith really is."

"You will be released, then, I dare say, when she is found, but not before."

"Then, I will not say a word."

"In with you, then."

Ogle gave Lord Warringdale an impulse forward; and as Jack Sheppard had already gone into the cellar, and was stooping down just inside the door, where it went down a step, Warringdale fell over him, among a heap of old, damp sawdust.

"Where are you coming to?" said Jack.

"Murder! help!"

Ogle fastened the door.

"Ah, you may call out as much as you like, there," he said. "No one will pay any attention to you, I fancy. Come away, Jack."

Lord Warringdale was quite convinced, by this time, that he was not shot; and he commenced hammering at the cellar door with a wine bottle that he found in the cellar. It soon, however, broke in his hands, and then he could not make half so much noise.

Ogle and Jack went into the hall of the house, and waited for Captain Heron, who, after a conference with Lady Castleneau, came out to them.

"Ogle," said Heron, "I have quite made up my mind to attempt the capture of Jonathan Wild to-night, where Jack Sheppard says he may be found."

"You will easily take him," said Jack.

"I hope your information is correct."

"Quite certain, Captain! There is a sort of shed in the old market, just opposite to the gate of the Fleet Prison. It is kept by a man who professes to sell old clothes, and boots and shoes; but he is an agent for the sale of stolen goods, and Wild often deals with him. That is where he will be to-night, somewhere about ten o'clock."

"Then we will be there likewise."

"To be sure we will," said Ogle. "Keep up your spirits, Captain, for you may depend that when we have captured Wild, as well as Warringdale, we shall soon find out where they have bestowed the Lady Edith."

"I trust we shall! Indeed, I trust we shall! You make what arrangements you think proper, Ogle, and be here at nine o'clock."

Ogle and Jack Sheppard held a consultation together in regard to the best means of action, and Captain Heron again went into the breakfast-room to speak to Lady Castleneau.

While all this was going on, poor Edith was still a prisoner in Whitcombe House, and a prey to great anxiety.

Jonathan Wild, from the moment that he had heard Lord Warringdale was not at liberty, had felt that he alone had the management of the affair connected with Edith's imprisonment; and so, as we have stated, he made his way to St. James's Street, first to the chambers of Warringdale, and then to Whitcombe House.

Wild was in possession of a key which made him master of Whitcombe House, and watching an opportunity when no one was observing him, he stepped up to the door and rapidly let himself in.

As soon as he was fairly in the hall he listened intently for any sound that might indicate danger in the mansion; but it was as still as the grave, and Jonathan made his way towards the room in which he had imprisoned Edith.

It was always a fashion with Jonathan to affect a certain air and manner of brutality; so as soon as he opened the door of that mysterious apartment in which Edith had now been for some hours a prisoner, he shouted, "Hilloa! What now, my fair lady! What have you to say to your friend Jonathan Wild?"

"My foe!" said Edith.

"Ah, there you are!"

Jonathan opened the door wide, so that some daylight found its way into the room, making a kind of twilight.

"So there you are; and right willing, no doubt, to be released."

"I demand my release!"

"To be sure you do! To be sure you do! And you shall have it—on conditions."

"What conditions?"

"These!"

Jonathan Wild produced a written paper. He advanced right up to the table with which Edith had fenced herself into a corner of the room.

"Hold!" said Edith. "I will not allow you to come further towards me!"

"You will not?"

"No; I have said I will not!"

"Ha! ha!"

"Beware, Jonathan Wild!—beware!"

He seized the table, and was in the act of drawing it away, when Edith brought the sword-blade down upon his head with considerable force.

Wild staggered back.

The thick felt hat he wore, and some pieces of iron with which it was strengthened, had alone prevented him from getting a serious hurt.

"You are armed," he said.

"I am."

"What confounded fiend has given you the means of mischief?"

"It matters not, Jonathan Wild. I am armed, and can and will defend myself."

"There is no occasion for you to defend yourself. I do not want to interfere with you; and if you will sign this paper that I bring to you, you may be free as soon as you like."

Edith was silent.

"Perhaps," added Wild, "you prefer remaining here. If so, I will say as much to my Lord Warringdale, and he will come and see you."

"No, no! Read the paper."

"I will. You are getting reasonable. Hem! It is a very simple affair—very simple indeed. This is it."

Jonathan read rapidly—for he did not wish to dwell upon the words, so as to give Edith time to think seriously of their import:—

"'In consideration of various circumstances, I, Edith Heron, formerly Edith Tarleton, agree to use my best endeavours to persuade Felix Heron, my husband, to give up all his pretensions to the Earldom of Whitcombe, which pretensions I know, from the intimate relations I have with him, to be false——' "

"Hold!" said Edith. "You need not trouble yourself to read further. I will never sign any such paper as that."

"Do you know your own danger?" said Wild, in a strange, deep tone.

"No."

"Oh, you do not?"

"No," added Edith. "I know that just now I am a prisoner to you and to Lord Warringdale; but I believe that you love yourselves too much, and are too careful of your own safety, to be very dangerous to me. Well you both know that I should have avengers, from whom you could not escape."

There was so much truth in all this that Wild was proportionably provoked at it.

"Listen, then," he said. "I will tell you what will be the consequence of your refusal to make terms with us. You will be kept a prisoner until Felix Heron, worn out in mind and body by seeking you, will be glad to agree to anything, in order to effect your release. You will then rejoin him. You, however, will be a pale and wretched being, from your long imprisonment, and you will find him half a maniac, from the fever of his grief. All this you may avoid by agreeing at once to the conditions which will have to be agreed to at last."

"No, no! Never!"

"Be it so."

"I cannot commit such treason against the affections of Felix."

"You are mad already."

"Heaven, then, keep me so, if this be madness."

"Very well. There is your food for the next four-and-twenty hours. If you search well about this room you will find a sink and a water-tap, which was placed here for the convenience of the late——Well, well! I am not going to use a name which might give you a hint even of where you are."

"I know where I am."

"Indeed!"

"Yes; I am in Whitcombe House, the residence of the late Earl of Whitcombe—that house which, is in reality, the property of Felix."

Wild laughed a cold, sneering laugh, and then he flung a quartern loaf on to the floor.

"Much good may your information do you!" he said; "and as for Whitcombe House ever becoming the property of Felix Heron, the moon will fall into the Old Bailey before that will happen! Good day! I shall visit you again at this time to-morrow. Learn patience, for I have a presentiment that you will remain here until you are grey!"

He banged shut the door of the room, and Edith heard him double lock it on the outside, and remove the key.

It was with difficulty that she restrained her tears, but she did so.

"No, no!" she said; "I will not weep for aught that my enemies and those of Felix can do! So long as I live and he lives, I will hope!"

Edith felt the necessity of keeping up her strength; and she picked up the loaf, which Wild had flung to the floor, and partook of some of it.

It was with a good deal of difficulty, however, that she found a small brass knob in the wall, between two of the cabinets which opened a square door, within which was the sink and the tap with water that Jonathan Wild had spoken of. But she did find it, and was refreshed by a copious draught from the tap, which was of silver.

"Yes," she then said—"ah, yes; I will have patience, and out of that patience I will extort hope. I feel assured, even now, that Felix is not idle; but that he is, with his friends, at work to discover where I am, and to save me."

Edith was perfectly right in this supposition, as the reader is well aware; and so, after a prayer for him, she lay down on a couple of the huge old chairs, and fell into a deep sleep.

How long she slept, Edith had no means of knowing; but once or twice during her sleep, she had fancied she was not alone. When she opened her eyes, she started to her feet with some alarm.

There was a light in the room.

In a gilt candlestick there was a tall wax candle, which burnt with a steady, although very small flame. Still it was amply sufficient to banish the darkness of the place.

Edith looked about her in amazement. She fully expected to see some one in the room.

No; she was still alone.

But when her eyes fell upon the table on which the wax-light was placed, she was still more surprised than by its appearance.

On that table was a tray of silver, and on the tray were refreshments, consisting of a cold fowl, a plate of the most tempting ham—some exquisitely white, small rolls of bread—and in a decanter was some sparkling light-coloured wine.

The plates, the knives and forks, spoons, all were of silver glittering and bright, and the glass was most exquisitely cut.

Edith might well have been excused if, for a few moments, she had believed some supernatural agency was at work, to soften the rigours of her imprisonment in that gloomy, closed house.

"Oh, what can all this mean?" she said. "What am I to think of this?"

Then it seemed to her in another moment that there was probably some connexion between these viands, which were in so costly and inviting a fashion placed before her, and the mysterious voice which had spoken to her in such sympathising tones.

But how soundly she must have slept to permit some person or persons to come into the room, and lay a table with such refreshments, without disturbing her.

She approached the silver tray, and then she saw lying on it a small slip of paper.

There was something written on it; and Edith, taking it into her hand and holding it to the light, saw the following words:—

"The Lady Edith is entreated to believe that she is under the protection of a friend, who will see that she wants for nothing. Her release will be soon accomplished; and already the anxiety of him who loves her has been allayed by an assurance of her safety."

"Oh, thank heaven!" cried Edith. "Thank

heaven! and you, too, generous and unknown benefactor, who I owe so much to. The assurance that the anxiety of Felix has been removed gives me new life. Thanks! Oh, accept thanks —thanks and blessings!"

CHAPTER CXL.

JONATHAN WILD IS CAPTURED IN OLD FLEET MARKET.

CAPTAIN HERON did not entertain the slightest doubt in regard to the correctness of the information which he received from Jack Sheppard regarding where Wild was to be found.

It was a sad trial for him to continue all the remainder of the day in what had the appearance of inactivity at Castleneau House, while Edith was somewhere in the power of his foes.

But he was compelled to bring reason to his aid, and that told him that if he were to sally forth as his impatience would dictate, he could not tell whether to turn to the right or the left in search of the heroine of his heart.

To get possession of Jonathan Wild was the only and the most direct means of procuring the information he wanted.

So soon as that was procured, the release of Edith might be looked upon as a thing accomplished.

Captain Heron fully made up his mind that let her be where she might, he would storm that place with his whole band, if necessary, and release her. She was his—his wife; and no one had the right, or the semblance of a right, to step between them.

But the night seemed long in coming.

Captain Heron had left all the subordinate arrangements of the enterprise to Jack Sheppard and to Ogle, but of course it was necessary that he should be well acquainted with them.

It was about eight o'clock, then, and just as some rain began to fall in London, and give promise of a wet night, that on the steps of Castleneau House there appeared two persons, both of whom were enveloped in great-coats.

These two persons were Captain Heron, and his faithful associate, Ogle.

There was a dim light in the hall of the mansion, and by that dim light might have been seen Lady Castleneau.

She had just said "God bless and prosper you!" to Captain Heron, and there were the visible marks of emotion on her face.

Heron felt happier than he had done for the whole of that day, for now the period of action had come, and that, to him, was far preferable to the enforced repose that he had been compelled to endure for so many weary hours.

Just as Ogle reached the great gates of Castleneau House, however, there was a sharp ring at the old bell that hung above them.

Ogle stepped aside, to let Anthony see who was there, and Heron retired into the deep shadow of the old portico of the house.

He did not wish any extraneous adventure now to interfere with the expedition on which he was bound that night.

Anthony went at once to the gates.

There was no one there, although the ring at the bell had been loud and clear; but, fastened by a small piece of twine to one of the iron bars of the gate, was a folded paper.

Upon examination, Anthony found it to be a letter, folded into a very small size, and addressed to Captain Felix Heron.

Heron was naturally surprised at its receipt, but his first idea was that it must come from his friend, the Earl of Bridgewater. Upon reading it, however, he found that it approached his feelings much nearer than any mere missive of friendship could have done.

"Edith is safe, and watched over by one who values her happiness. Let this bring some peace to the heart of him who loves her."

Such were the words contained in this mysterious epistle, and such was the manner in which that personage who appeared to have a preternatural control over the events of Whitcombe House, kept his word, as he had pledged it to Edith, that some of the anxieties regarding her safety should be removed from the mind of Captain Heron.

Lady Castleneau was still in the hall, and to her Heron handed the note.

"I cannot say," he remarked, "if this be from a friend or an enemy; but it can make no difference in our expedition of to-night."

"And yet my heart seems lighter as I read it," said Lady Castleneau.

"And mine, too," added Heron, "and yet I know not why; for such means as these might well be used by my enemies, and by Edith's, to paralyse the efforts for her release. Farewell, then, once again, Lady Castleneau. You shall hear, by Jack Sheppard, of our success or failure."

The soft, small, spring rain which had begun to fall, still continued; but the night was calm, and heavy clouds obscured the sky. There were but few passengers in the streets; and as Ogle and Heron made their way towards old Fleet Market, the former explained the arrangements he had made for the capture of Jonathan Wild.

"Jack Sheppard," he said, "will be close to the corner of Holborn Hill with a light cart, that we have hired; and I propose that we make our way, before Jonathan comes, into the slop-seller's hovel."

"Be it so! Do you know the man?" asked Heron.

"Oh, perfectly! During the time I was with Wild, it was well known to us all that he acted for Jonathan in recovering, at a price, stolen property. He calls himself 'Nego,' although I believe that is only a portion of his name."

"Will he be alone?"

"Most assuredly. He admits no person to share with him in his gains; and no sooner has he completed a transaction, than he returns to his house in Field Lane, and secretes the money."

They walked rapidly; and it was considerably before nine o'clock when they turned into the old Fleet Market, which, with its long line of straggling booths and sheds, occupied the entire space from the foot of Holborn Hill to Blackfriars.

A light chaise cart was standing close to the kerb-stone at the corner, but no one was visible in it.

Ogle, however, looked in, saying, in a low tone, " Is all right, Jack ?"

" To be sure," said Jack Sheppard. " You're in capital time, and I've thought of such a dodge, only I was afraid you'd be too late to carry it out."

" What is it ?"

" Why, at the pawnbroker's, up there, at the corner of the next street, you will see in the window a whole collection of constables' staffs for sale. Go and buy two, and you'll frighten old Nego out of his wits."

" It will not be a bad plan. What say you, Captain ?"

" Anything that will facilitate our operations. Think you he will take us for officers ?"

" He must. We can easily say we've come from the country, to negotiate with him about the plunder from some pretended robbery."

Ogle went to the shop which had been mentioned by Jack Sheppard, and there he saw the small staffs for sale, which were at that period quite a common thing in the windows of miscellaneous dealers ; for any dealer who chose could get appointed a parish constable, and was entitled to an official staff. Hence, there was quite a manifestation of those symbols of authority ; and they were expensive or common, according to the means or taste of the amateur parish constable who chose to have one.

Ogle bought two, composed entirely of brass, and not above two inches in length, with a crown at the end of them, and then, returning to Captain Heron, he handed him one ; and they made their way through the mass of decayed vegetable matter, broken baskets, and heaps of matting, which was the characteristic, day and night, of old Fleet Market.

Among the most broken down and dreariest of the sheds on the side nearest to the Fleet Prison, was one so dilapidated, so one-sided, and so frail-looking, that it seemed to be at the mercy of the first gust of wind that might sweep down that thoroughfare from the river.

" This is the place," whispered Ogle. " It won't do for me to go in till Wild has made his appearance, for Nego has an eye like a hawk, and might know me. I will close in, however, upon Jonathan, so soon as I see him come into the street."

Heron assented to this arrangement, and tapped at the ricketty door, through many crevices of which there came very faint rays of light.

" Well," cried a voice from within in angry tones,—" well, what is it now ?"

" Say glitter," whispered Ogle. " Say glitter and glisten. That means jewels and plate."

Heron put his lips to one of the crevices in the door, and pronounced the words, " Glitter and glisten."

In a moment it seemed as if the receiver of stolen goods had recklessly torn down one of the pieces of planking of which the door of his wretched shed was composed ; but such was not the fact, since it was only an ingenious contrivance of his own, by a hinge and a button, to be able to look out upon his customers before he admitted them into the shed.

" Bless your soul !" he said ; " what is it ?" And a hideous countenance, which had not made acquaintance with the razor for many a month, presented itself at the opening of the door.

" It's a country affair," said Captain Heron, " down by Macclesfield. I'm told you would inquire into it. The swag's worth a thousand pounds. There's five hundred reward. Two men, they say, did it, with a gig ; and, of course, I should like to make something out of it."

" Ah !" said Mr. Nego, " it's in the way of business. Do you belong to the ' family ?' "

" No—a country constable."

" Ah, I thought so ! Well, come in—come in, and make yourself comfortable. I haven't heard of the little job, and I rather wonder at that ; but I shall know all about it in a few hours. Come in, and make yourself comfortable. What do you want for yourself ? Is it all glitter and glisten ?"

" All !" said Heron, as he stooped and entered the shed, the door of which Mr. Nego held open for him.

" Ah, well, I shouldn't wonder ! And so you're a country constable, and come from Macclesfield ?"

" Yes."

" Bless me, I've upset the light ; and candles are dear !"

There had been something about the eyes of this man as he admitted Captain Heron into the shed, which was not exactly in accordance with the easy manner in which he seemed to believe the tale which was told him by Heron ; and the evident purpose-like manner in which he overthrew the light, confirmed his visitor in the suspicion that some foul play was intended.

The hut was not above eight feet square ; and the moment the light was extinguished, the darkness in it was most profound. Heron had been standing close within the door ; but suddenly and noiselessly darted round a small table that was in the centre of the hut ; and the moment he did so he heard Nego cry out, " Take that, my hearty ! You don't put salt on an old hawk's tail quite so easy !"

It was evident Nego was too intent upon what he was about himself to have noticed the rapid movement of Heron. He thought him still standing close to the inner side of the door ; and a most unmistakable intimation of the danger he had run was conveyed to Captain Heron's ear by a sudden crashing noise, which resulted from the passage of a long, double-edged knife through the upper portion of the door.

Nego had intended that knife for the heart of his visitor.

The candle, although thrown upon the floor, and for a moment emitting no light, was not wholly extinguished. Some lingering bit of flame caught a small, jagged piece of the wick, and, although lying on the floor, it sent up a little, star-like refulgence, which was sufficient to let Heron see the interior of the hut, and Nego close to the door, with his hand still clutching the hilt of the knife he had passed through its panel.

Captain Heron made one stride towards him, and grasped him by the back of his neck.

" Murderous wretch !" he said ; " is this your fashion with visitors ?"

" Bless my soul !" said Nego.

There did not seem to be any apprehension on the part of this man, or the slightest desire to call for assistance, now he was in the hands of one whose life he had attempted. Murder must have

EDITH COMPELS JONATHAN WILD TO KEEP AT A RESPECTFUL DISTANCE.

Presented Gratis with No. 63 of the New Edition of Edith the Captive; or, the Robbers of Epping Forest.

EACH WEEK IS PRESENTED GRATIS A COLOURED ENGRAVING.

been a familiar idea in the mind of that man; but the clutch that Captain Heron had of his neck, began to be anything but agreeable; and Nego, with his eyes nearly starting from his head, succeeded in contorting his countenance towards Heron, and gasping out, "Now, my dear soul, don't! What do you mean? There, it's all right! How much do you want? What's the price?"

Heron flung him with such force against the back of the door, that, after making several grasps at the empty air, Nego fell heavily half-stunned to the floor of the hut.

Still, however, he had sense sufficient left him to try and grasp at something to aid in raising himself up.

A wretched piece of old felt carpeting, stiffened with grease and soil, was upon the floor of the hut; and as Nego, in the bewilderment of his half-stunned condition, grappled at anything within his reach, he tore up a considerable portion of this wretched covering on the floor.

Captain Heron had just succeeded in lifting the light before it actually expired; and stuck it, by its own grease, on to the corner of a narrow shelf which was in the shed.

"How much? What is it?" said Nego, evidently not half himself from the stunning blow he had received on the head. "What is it? How much? Where's the knife? Down! down! go down!"

The torn-up carpeting revealed beneath it a large iron ring, which could only belong to some trap in the floor.

Heron stooped, and exerting his singular strength, lifted Nego fairly off the ground, and flung him again as far as the narrow limits of the shed would afford. He struck against the jagged boarding of which the miserable structure was composed; and then, in either real or simulated insensibility, he lay profoundly still.

Captain Heron took hold of the iron ring in the floor, and with ease lifted a hinged trap about two feet square.

The moment he did so, he heard a rushing noise as of water, and strange noisome odours came up from below.

Then Captain Heron felt convinced that he stood over the fetid current of what had once been the Fleet River; but which had long degenerated from that name to be called Fleet Ditch.

Had Nego succeeded in taking his life, no doubt all evidence of the deed would have been engulphed in that terrible black weltering stream, which, crowded with thousand impurities, made its way to the Thames.

Captain Heron let the trap-door close with a shudder; and for a passing moment, he felt that it would be but a just retribution if he were to drag that man, who had made so atrocious an attempt upon his life, to the brink of the chasm, and plunge him into the unknown depths.

Heron's was not the kind of mind, however, to carry out such a suggestion; and he was rather abruptly recalled to a consideration of his errand in that place by a sharp knocking at the door of the shed.

Then Heron recollected how he had been answered by Nego when he rapped for admission, and he called out, in as good an imitation as he could improvise, at the moment, of Nego's voice, "Well, what do you want?"

"Open! open!" said a voice, close to one of the chinks of the door. "It's I—Mr. Wild! Confound you, don't you know me?"

"I'm coming," said Heron.

"The deuce take you! What's this? What have you stuck a knife through the door for? Is it to poke people's eyes out, idiot? Open the door, and be hanged to you!"

Wild dealt the door such a kick that its withstanding so much violence became evident proof it was not near so weak and crazy as it looked.

Heron stepped forward, and swung aside an iron bar which kept the door fast.

Wild pushed his way in, muttering as he came, "I tell you what it is, Nego, I shall have to hang you next sessions, to a certainty! There's some ugly stories about concerning you, and unless you make it well worth my while——Ha! ha!"

Captain Heron had sprung at his throat, and got a strong clutch at the voluminous cravat Wild was in the habit of wearing.

Another instant, and his wrists were seized and wrenched behind his back by Ogle, who had stepped into the hut behind him.

"Give an alarm," said Heron, "and you're a dead man!"

"Life is sweet," said Ogle. "Keep it while you can, Jonathan!"

Wild, with his mouth open and his eyes glaring, looked first at Heron, and wrenching his head round, managed to get a sight at Ogle.

"Nabbed!" he said.

"Oh, there is no doubt of that, Jonathan!" said Ogle.

"I'm a fool—an ass!"

"You always were!"

Wild kicked out savagely with his heavy boots, but Ogle soon taught him that was a dangerous game, and one which he, too, could play at with great advantage; for he saluted Wild with such a series of kicks that he was nearly doubled in two.

"Hang you!" he said, "that'll do! Leave off!"

"Have you had enough?" said Ogle.

"Quite!"

"Bring him along," said Captain Heron.

"Stop a bit," said Wild. "There is no occasion to bring him along."

"Yes, Ogle," added Heron. "Caution is necessary. Search him, and take his arms from him."

Ogle had produced a piece of stout whip-cord with which he now dexterously tied Wild's wrists behind him. The unscrupulous thief-taker was then quite helpless; and Ogle took from his breast pockets one pair of pistols, and from the skirts of his ample coat another pair, and a large clasped knife, with a blade at least six inches in length.

"That will do. Now bring him along, Ogle."

"Wait for the bag," said Ogle.

"The what?" said Wild.

"I've got a sack to put him in. You can't think how safe he'll go, Captain!"

"Stop! Stuff! rubbish!" said Wild. "I know what you want, Captain Heron. If you didn't want it, you and your man here would have knocked me on the head before now; but, you see, dead men tell no tales, and you want me to tell one. Now let me go, and give me my arms again, and you shall know all you want. It's a failure;

that's all that can be said about it. You want to know where to find Edith."

"Speak!" said Heron. "Give that information, and you will be safe so soon as it is verified."

"Oh! you won't let me go at once?"

"Certainly not."

"Then you endanger her safety. There is an old house at Knightsbridge which is called 'Pine Tree House.' You will find her there. Let me go at once, for you see I have trusted you."

"No. You shall be kept, Jonathan. We have your companion and employer, Lord Warringdale, and now we have you."

"Very well. Please yourself, Captain Heron. Do your worst, and your best. Warringdale don't know where she is. You may kill him, but he cannot tell you. And take this for your comfort, that if you keep me for four-and-twenty hours longer, Edith will starve."

"Bring him along!" said Heron.

"One moment more," cried Wild. "You're a clever fellow, Felix Heron. I did think to see you dancing on nothing at Tyburn; but I'm quite willing that you should be Earl of Whitcombe instead. It don't matter to me which side I'm on. Promise to give me what Warringdale owes me, if you come into the title and property, and I will help you."

"No. I will make no terms with such a villain, except these: If you give true information regarding where Edith is kept a prisoner, so that she may be released unharmed, you shall have your life; but if you give false information, and we find such to be the case, I will trust you no more, and you shall, without further parley or conditions, die the death you merit."

"That's hard," said Wild.

"Do you adhere to your statement regarding the place you mention as Pine Tree House, at Knightsbridge?"

"Certainly not."

"You are a most audacious villain; and it will be well for your safety that I hold no further converse with you for the present."

Doubled up, and strapped round his waist, Ogle had a large sack; and now, before Jonathan Wild could be very well aware of what he was doing, Ogle placed it over his head, and it unrolled down to his feet.

Wild uttered terrible imprecations, and engaged in a violent struggle with Ogle, who, however, flung him down, and tied the sack securely, in the process of doing which he dealt Wild so many punches and kicks, that the most ordinary exercise of discretion convinced the latter that it was safest to be quiet and enduring.

"Give us a hand up, Captain," said Ogle, "and follow close, as I carry him to the cart. If he begins howling, give him a dig or two with your sword."

Wild made an odd sort of noise in the sack, which probably he meant to signify that he would remain quiet; and then, Ogle, with the celebrated thief-taker on his back, walked out of the shed, followed closely by Captain Heron.

Nego looked up the next moment.

"Bless my soul!" he said, "they've got Mr. Wild! What a bit of swag! I wish I'd a known him! It's Captain Heron, the highwayman, after all! Bless me! what a bump on the side of my head! But I suppose it's all in the way of busi-

ness! Why didn't he say who he was? What's Mr. Wild to me? What's anybody to me—what's anything to me, but business, business, business?"

The distance was short from Nego's shed to where Jack Sheppard was in waiting with the chaise-cart; and the manner in which Ogle flung Wild into it, was something alarming to hear.

"Got him all right?" said Jack Sheppard.

"Oh, yes! Get in Captain, and drive on, Jack!"

Both Ogle and Captain Heron were in the chaise-cart in a moment. Jack Sheppard drove, and right through the City they went, past Jonathan's own house.

Then Ogle took the reins, saying, "We're going to Epping Forest, Jack; and as I know the nearest way, it's better for me to drive. I suppose you'll come with us?"

"Yes. I should like to see the end of Jonathan. A little trip into the country does one good now and then."

Wild made a curious kind of howl from the interior of the sack.

"What's the matter?" said Jack Sheppard, as he coolly put his feet upon him.

"Murder! Help! I smother!"

"Is that all?"

Another howl from Wild nearly frightened the horse.

"Release his head," said Heron. "He is more valuable just at present alive than dead. We shall, no doubt, find a means in the forest of getting the truth from him."

Ogle took Jonathan's own knife from his pocket, and ripped open that portion of the sack where Jonathan's head was supposed to be.

With a gush of relief Wild looked out, and inhaled the night air.

"I will give a thousand pounds," he said, "to be set down in the road!"

"It's no use, Jonathan," said Ogle. "We're all so rich that we don't want any more money."

"And you'd better keep still," said Jack Sheppard, "or you'll come to some bad end."

Wild felt how utterly hopeless was his situation. He spoke in all the bitterness of rage that was swelling at his heart.

"You may kill me, Captain Heron," he said. "You may do your worst. I know where Edith is, and could in two hours place her at liberty; but I will not tell you, and so I remain your master yet."

Heron made no reply, and in another hour the cart drove under the sylvan shades of Epping Forest.

————

CHAPTER CXLI.

JONATHAN WILD MAKES A FULL AND TRUE CONFESSION.

IT was not far from midnight when this chaise-cart, with its strange prisoner, reached Epping Forest; and it would seem that the journey had, in some measure, acted upon the fears of Jonathan Wild, for, as they entered amid the deep shadow of the old forest trees, he spoke in a less confident tone than he had done before.

"Captain Heron," he said, "you would do well

to listen to my proposals. I know as well as you do what your pretensions are—perhaps even a little better than you do; but it is only natural I should try and do something for myself. I can and will help you, but you ought not to let me lose by doing so."

"I have nothing to say to you," replied Heron, "on any subject but one. Declare, with truth, where the Lady Edith is to be found, and I will listen to you. The price of that truth shall be your liberation, and you may leave Epping Forest unharmed so soon as it is verified."

"No," said Wild. "You refuse all terms with me, and so I will keep my own secret."

"Whoop!" cried a voice from a tree, in imitation of an owl.

"Ah!" cried Ogle, "that's it. They can't make out what's the meaning of the chaise-cart."

"Give them the signal," said Captain Heron.

"Hawks abroad! Hawks abroad!" cried Ogle. "Hawks abroad, and home again!"

One of Captain Heron's band dropped from one of the branches of a tree, and amid the darkness he looked like some strange bundle falling from the clouds.

But this man had a lantern, which, although darkened at the moment, he soon made to give light enough to throw a broad beam upon the cart and its occupants.

"Any news?" said Heron.

"No, Captain. Not what you would call news, perhaps, but we have caught two strange birds in the wood. One pretends to be a deserter from the army, and the other, his master, a tradesman of some sort. We're a little suspicious of them, so we kept them close."

"I think I recollect such people," said Heron. "I cannot attend to them at present, for I have much to do."

"Hawks abroad, and home again," muttered Wild. "So that's the signal, is it?"

"Yes," said Ogle, who overheard him. "But we alter it often, Jonathan; and you may be quite certain *that* will never be used again, if you should chance to escape from Epping Forest with a whole skin."

Captain Heron now alighted from the cart, and turning to Ogle, he said, "You will keep your prisoner in security until the hour of five in the morning. Bring him then to the deep glade, and let all the band be there."

"Yes, Captain; and you may depend upon his safe keeping, for we will take it by turns to be with him. A good pair of eyes upon a man like Jonathan Wild is better than all the locks in the world."

Captain Heron made his way on foot to those secret foundations of old Hinchcliffe Manor which he had appropriated to the use of himself and his band; but it required all his force of character and self-control to enter the chamber which had been so lately in the occupation of Edith. Nothing was removed from it but herself, and yet what a scene of desolation it presented to the eyes of Heron.

A sensation of great fatigue came over him, and he dropped into a fevered sleep on a couch which was in the apartment.

While these affairs were going on in connexion with Jonathan Wild, Lord Warringdale's state of mind in the wine cellar, where he was confined in Castleneau House, was of the most gloomy and desperate description.

He raved and shouted, until, hoarse with passion, he was compelled to silence; and then, with his hands clasped upon his head, he, too, slept.

It must have been many hours that exhausted nature claimed her dues, even of the disturbed and seething brain of that man of many plots and crimes; for when he opened his eyes again, he became conscious of a faint light in the cellar, and he saw something white lying on the ground, which at first sight startled him.

It was but a small tray-cloth, on which he saw some meal-bread; and an earthen jug, containing either water or some more generous liquid.

It was evident, then, that while he slept, old Anthony, or some other person of the household, had been into that gloomy place and left the refreshments.

And now, as Lord Warringdale was really not materially hurt, notwithstanding all the recent rough adventures he had gone through, he felt keenly the need of some sustenance.

He had youth, and all its revivifying and invigorating powers about him; and as he rose and stretched his limbs, he felt that he was much stronger than he had been the day before.

He eagerly partook of the provisions that had been brought him; and then he turned his whole attention to find out from whence proceeded a singular kind of halo of light, which pervaded one end of the gloomy cellar.

An attentive observation of that portion of his dungeon let him see that near its roof there was an opening of the shape of a segment of a circle, the arched portion of which was upwards; and it was through that that the dim light streamed.

There could be very little doubt but that beneath Castleneau House there was a series of these vaults or cellars; but still the next one, inasmuch as some light came into it, seemed to Lord Warringdale more promising than that in which he was.

By great exertion, and after several failures, he raised himself up to this opening in the wall; and scrambling through it, he let himself drop into the cellar on the other side.

Then he saw, at once, from whence the light came. There was a grated window to this second cellar; and although nearly obscured by ivy leaves on the outside, yet sufficient of the morning light came through, to proclaim its existence.

A hope of liberty sprung up in the breast of Warringdale; but it was sadly quenched, by his finding the window was out of his reach. Advancing round this cellar, however, he found that it was tolerably stocked with old crates and barrels; and from that moment, he looked upon his escape as certain.

He soon succeeded in raising himself up to the grating, which was so old and rotten that it gave way before his touch. Separating the ivy leaves, then, he looked out into the open air, and saw a very retired and gloomy portion of Castleneau House.

"I'm all but free," he said; "and if ever I set foot in this detestable place again, I shall deserve all the ill fortune that may befall me."

Another moment, and he was in the garden; and crouching low, he ran along under cover of the wall, brushing the morning dew from the old ivy as he went, until he reached that portion of the garden, the inner wall of which was covered with very ancient espaliers.

He thought that he could get, by that means, into Bloomsbury Fields; but when he reached the top of the wall he was mistaken, for he found that immediately on the other side were the gardens of Montague House.

It was an easy thing, however, to run along the top of the wall until he came to the open fields; and having the good fortune to do so without being observed, he let himself drop down on very nearly the spot which had witnessed his encounter with the Earl of Bridgewater and Colonel Trelawney.

So elated was Lord Warringdale at his escape, that he ran as if Captain Heron and all his band had been at his heels, nor stopped until he found himself safely in the Oxford Road.

It was then that he begun to wonder what he had best do, for he had no exact means of knowing how affairs stood since his capture and incarceration at Castleneau House.

After some consideration, he made a determination.

"I will go to Jonathan Wild's," he said. "It is no longer of any use for me to set up any interest independent of him. I will promise him anything, and let him aid me in all my designs. It will be time enough to think of the readiest means of ridding myself of him when I have no further occasion for his services. Until then, I will not thwart or confuse him in any way."

The hour was very early, and no hackney coaches were as yet abroad, so that Lord Warringdale had to walk to the City. But he was so well pleased to find himself free and in the fresh open air, that he thought that no trouble, and soon reached Jonathan's house.

It was a little peculiarity of Wild's bull-dogs that having once seen anybody, they should always know him again, so that Lord Warringdale was at once recognised, and Blueskin came forward to speak to him.

"I wish to see Mr. Wild," said Warringdale. "Is he within?"

Blueskin shook his head.

"Something's happened. Mr. Wild went out, and hasn't come back again. Here, Nego, come here. Here's a gentleman wants Mr. Wild. Tell him all you know about him."

"Bless my soul!" said Nego, advancing with a large piece of bread and cheese in his hand; "you see, Mr. Wild went away with some gentlemen in a bag. Clever, very clever it was—very clever. Bless me, if ever that Captain Heron wants any business in my line, I shall be proud to deal with him. Quite a gentleman—quite a gentleman. Why did not he tell me who he was, and not try to fling the green grab to Nego?"

"What does he mean?" said Warringdale to Blueskin.

"Why a green grab," said Blueskin, "is a yokel nabster."

"Bless my soul!" said Nego; "the gentleman hasn't had the advantages of an education. A green grab is a country constable."

"I don't know what you're talking about," said Warringdale; "but if anything has happened to Mr. Wild, let me know at once what it is."

"Then Captain Heron, the highwayman, came last night, and took him away in a sack."

Warringdale looked at Nego in amazement.

"You jest, sir. This is some sorry joke."

"Bless my soul! Mr. Wild didn't think it a joke, for they carried him off head downwards, owing to putting the sack over his head, instead of asking him to step in civilly."

"Then all is lost!"

Mr. Nego stepped up close to Warringdale, and in an eager whisper said, "What's the reward? Business is business. What is it? Glisten, glitter, or spangles?"

"Keep your jargon to yourself; I do not understand you. I want no service from you."

Warringdale stepped hastily from Jonathan Wild's door with a feeling of dejection and despair.

"What a strange young man!" said Nego. "He must have come about business, and yet he wouldn't transact any business when he got here. Bless my soul! he's very ignorant, though."

Warringdale walked quite mechanically towards the West End of the town, and found himself in St. James's Street without a real intention of proceeding there.

And, in truth, he knew not what to do. For now that Jonathan Wild had fallen into the hands of Captain Heron, he scarcely thought it safe to go to Whitcombe House, since the secret of Edith's imprisonment there might have been extorted from the thief-taker by possibly the fear of death.

But when Lord Warringdale, from the other side of the way, observed the house, it looked so calm, and so still, so entirely undisturbed from top to bottom, that his inclination to assure himself if Edith were a prisoner there, grew too strong to be resisted.

"Come what might," he said, "Jonathan would be sure to hold out for a certain time; and if, now that I am at liberty, I could only succeed in removing her to some other place of secrecy and safety, I should still come out of this transaction with triumph, and achieve all I ever hoped, by holding Edith as a hostage or prisoner, for whose ransom I could exact any terms I please from Felix Heron."

This reasoning was acurate enough as far as it went, and time was an important element in it.

Crossing over the way, then, Lord Warringdale produced a key, which he, too, had to that house, and in another moment he was in its hall.

That was the first time he had stepped across the threshold of Whitcombe House since he had seen the vision in the late Earl's cabinet which had so greatly disturbed him; and now a feeling of terror and dread, which almost induced him to rush out into St. James's Street again, came over him.

The stir and turmoil of active affairs out in the world had tended, in a great measure, to distract his mind from dwelling too much upon the seeming apparition which had met his gaze; and at times, indeed, he had half-convinced himself it was but a freak of the imagination.

But now again that he was in the silence and solitude of that house, superstitious fear began to assert its dominion over him.

"No, no!" he said; "I can hardly stay here. If I should see it again, it might drive me to madness!"

He listened intently, and no doubt had he heard

No 64.—EDITH.

the slightest sound, he would have left the house at once; but all was so profoundly still that the desire to see if Edith were there, revived more strongly in his breast.

"I will see," he said, "I will see; and if she be here, I can speedily take her hence, and baffle Heron, notwithstanding all that has passed."

With a stealthy and rapid step, he made his way to the cabinet which he knew so well; and where it had been understood between him and Jonathan Wild, Edith was to be imprisoned.

On a bracket behind a statuette he felt for the key of that room, for there he had agreed that it was to be placed.

It was there. Another moment, and it rattled in the lock. The sound was of the every-day world, and it gave courage to Warringdale.

He flung the door wide open—for he guessed or knew that the apartment would be darkened; and even as he did so, there was a sharp noise like the click of a lock or spring.

"Edith," he cried, "are you here?"

There was no reply. The dim light from the open door streamed into the apartment.

It was vacant.

"She's gone," said Warringdale. "Wild has yielded to his fears, and she has gone!"

A heavy knock came at the outer door of Whitcombe House at this moment, and echoed strangely through the deserted mansion.

Lord Warringdale started in alarm, and stepped into the cabinet.

The heavy knock came upon the outer door again.

He knew not what to do. Fear and indecision took possession of him; and before he could free his mind from the thick-coming fancies that were taking possession of his brain, the door of the cabinet was suddenly shut with violence, and he heard the key turn in the lock.

Warringdale uttered a half-shriek of dismay, and hammered upon the inner panel of the door with his clenched fists.

Again there came that heavy knock at the outer door of the house.

CHAPTER CXLII.

THE MORNING DAWNS UPON A STRANGE SCENE IN EPPING FOREST.

It is morning in Epping Forest—dull, cold, and raw for the season, and a whistling wind is careering through the tops of the old trees.

In one of the most beautiful glades, where the patriarchs of the forest rear their giant heads to the sky, and where the soft, short grass is like a velvet carpet to the feet, a strange scene is being enacted.

The whole of Captain Heron's band is present, and he himself, standing somewhat apart, is addressing them.

"Our old enemy," he said, "and my most especial foe, Jonathan Wild, is in our power once again. I do not seek his life, except in fair fight; but by his machinations, the Lady Edith, my wife, is a prisoner in the hands of her bitterest foes. I offer him freedom for the disclosure of the place of her imprisonment. I threaten him with death, as

the consequence of his crimes, if he will not purchase his life with the information I seek. What say you, comrades—am I right?"

"Right! right!" cried the band. "Death to Jonathan Wild!"

"We have other prisoners, too, Captain," said the man who was called Atkins, stepping forward.

"So I heard. Bring them beneath the forest trees; they shall at least see that we perform justice beneath the shades of old Epping."

At this order, those two singular personages, which it will be recollected Captain Heron and Edith had met near the Maniac's Well, were conducted into the open space in the midst of the band.

"Who and what are you?" said Heron, sternly. "I doubt your errand and your pretences here beneath the greenwood tree."

"This is Tummus," said the substantial-looking person who accompanied the deserter.

"And this is master," said "Tummus."

"Is that all the account you can give of yourselves?"

"Well," said the deserter, "I did hear that there was a Captain Heron who was king of the forest, and I thought it would be a fine thing to join him, as I'm a faithful fellow."

"Which you attempt to prove," said Heron, "by deserting your regiment, if you've ever been a soldier. But stand aside—you have given a reason, and that is sufficient. Now, sir, what have you to say?"

"Why," said "Tummus's" master, "my affection for Tummus is so great, since he was my apprentice, that I couldn't help coming into the wood to look after him."

"Is that all you have to say?"

"Why, yes, friend; with the addition that I am a respectable man."

"Stand aside. Comrades, keep an eye on these men. And now send for Jonathan Wild."

"Jonathan Wild!" exclaimed Tummus and his master with one breath.

"Ah! you seem to know him!"

"We know him? No—that is—not at all. But we've heard that he's the greatest rascal that ever lived."

"A terrible rascal!" added Tummus.

"A rogue—a rogue!" said Tummus's master. "And if there's one thing worse than another about Jonathan Wild, truly, yea, and verily, it is that he pretends, at times, to recognise respectable people, with the mere object of damaging them by his affected acquaintance."

"I should not at all wonder," said Heron, "that he will recognise you."

"Yea, it is possible; but I know him not."

The deserter looked malignant, and rolled his eyes about in a strange fashion; at the same time that he plunged his right hand among his ragged clothes, as if he had some concealed weapon.

Ogle and one of the band had been for Jonathan Wild, who was well watched by another, whose turn of duty it had been, and in a few moments he was observed coming down the glade.

Tom Ripon had assumed part of the care of Jonathan during the night, and he had adopted a novel, and no doubt an efficient, expedient to prevent him running away.

Tom had tied a rope round one of Wild's ankles,

and by holding fast the other end, regulated any speed he chose him to walk at.

Wild had been allowed to have his hands at liberty under these circumstances, and as he came down the forest glade, he was relieving his wounded feelings by the utterance of the most diabolical expressions, at every one of which, however, Tom would give a pull to the string, so that Wild ran a great risk of measuring his length upon the green sward.

The looks of the pretended deserter grew more strange and savage still as Wild advanced.

Tummus's master became as pale as death, and trembled violently.

Jonathan Wild came each moment nearer and nearer to the spot on which were assembled Captain Heron and those bold companions of the road and the heath, who had shared with him so many adventures and so many perils.

The deserter cast a look of terror about him, as if then, surrounded as he was by so many persons, he could have possibly a chance of escape.

Captain Heron kept his eyes upon him in some amazement.

Then Wild was about twenty paces from the spot on which stood this man, who had played with so much art the part of a half-idiot, half-rogue, in the mazes of the forest.

Wild's eyes fell full upon him.

"Why, Wicketts!" he cried; "what do you do here? Have you, too, turned against me?"

The moment Jonathan spoke, the deserter made a rush towards him with a something bright and glistening in his hand.

"I don't know you!" he cried; "you don't know me! Take that, villain!"

Had Wild's hands still been tied with that piece of cord, which Ogle had found so efficient for the purpose in the shed of Nego, in the Fleet Market, he would no doubt have fallen at once a victim to the deserter.

But as it was, he stooped and avoided the blow with what was in reality a most murderous-looking, long-bladed knife or dagger.

Then Wild closed with the deserter, and there was a fierce struggle for a few seconds between them, which ended in the fall of the deserter with a deep groan on to the green sward.

"So!" said Jonathan. "You are here, I fancy, to do a little business on your own account, Mr. Wicketts?"

The men who were gathered on that spot had taken the most lively interest in this little affair, and they had all rushed forward to be as close as possible to its termination.

"Part them! Seize him!" cried Captain Heron.

He was too late!

The conflict was over, and the man who had been called Wicketts by Jonathan Wild lay apparently a corpse on the grass.

"What is the meaning of all this?" asked Heron, with an inquiring look at Jonathan.

"The meaning is that I have saved your life, while you threaten to take mine!"

"I do not understand you."

"This man, then, is, or was, one of my bull-dogs. He robbed me, and left me some time ago; and I fancy his errand here was on your account. He wanted to join you, and then take the first good opportunity to betray you."

"It may be so. Secure his companion, men! Do not let him escape!"

But the order was too late.

Tummus's master was nowhere to be seen. He had evidently taken advantage of the tumult, and of all eyes being concentrated upon Wild and his opponent, to leave the spot.

Whether he was still in hiding in the forest or not was a point to be considered when time permitted.

At present, Captain Heron was resolved that nothing should interfere with the purpose for which he had brought Jonathan Wild to Epping Forest.

"Let him go!" said Heron. "It is of no consequence. Let him go!"

Tom Ripon had let go the rope by which he had held Wild in such an ignoble kind of bondage, when he saw him attacked by the deserter, but now he had resumed it again.

"Come on," he said, "will you? Don't you see the Captain wants you?"

"Oh!" said Wild, "the time will come, I yet hope, when I shall have the pleasure of squaring accounts with you, my boy!"

"There is no hurry!" said Tom.

Wild looked as if he could with all the pleasure in the world have eaten Tom Ripon, but a sudden jerk of the cord let him feel how completely he was at Tom's mercy.

A few paces more brought him up to Captain Heron, who stood upon a slight elevation, which was made by the old thick roots of a huge chesnut-tree, which spread a gigantic arm far over the forest glade.

The band grouped themselves about in various attitudes of interest in what was about to take place.

Jonathan Wild looked dogged, obstinate, and resistive.

Captain Heron spoke in a loud, clear voice, which rung through the forest.

"Jonathan Wild, you are our prisoner. Your infamous accomplice and employer, who calls himself Lord Warringdale, is likewise in durance. Between you, and most probably known to you both, is a secret, which I will extract from your hearts, if I have to seek it there by force. I ask you now, where is the Lady Edith?"

Wild looked about him for a few moments in silence, and then he said, "Captain Heron, what will you give me for information that will do me a great pecuniary wrong?"

"Your life."

"My life? Humph! That belongs to me already, as it belongs to all men to live, unless some murderer chooses to take advantage of them."

"You shall depart from Epping Forest in peace and in safety, upon giving the information required. If you refuse it——"

"Well? If I refuse it?"

"You die!"

"We shall all die when our time comes."

"This is trifling. Ogle!"

"Here, Captain."

"Proceed!"

Jonathan Wild looked a little curious to know what exactly "Proceed" meant, but he soon had a tolerably clear notion on the subject.

One of the band had climbed up the huge

chesnut-tree, and was crawling along that branch which stretched so far over the green sward.

Over a fork of that branch, a convenient place, from which there shot up another powerful bough, this man placed a cord, and let down one end of it to the ground at which there was a loop.

"Oh!" said Wild, "I see!"

"You see!" said Heron.

The other end of the rope the man likewise flung to the ground, and then he hung for a moment or two, by his hands, at full length, from the extremity of the branch, before he dropped on to the grass below.

"That will do," said Ogle.

"Ah!" said Wild.

"Now," added Captain Heron, "I ask you once again, where is Edith?"

"Look you, Captain Felix Heron," replied Wild; "you are a bold fellow, but you have all along gone the wrong way to work with me!"

Heron made a gesture of impatience.

"Nay, hear me out," said Wild. "I like you a great deal better than I do my Lord Warringdale, and I make you a cheaper offer than I make him. I will help you for far less money."

"I disdain your help!"

"Come, come, Captain! You have objects, and high ones, too—why need you disdain any help that will enable you to reach them?"

"I should think the attainment of any object polluted which involved your assistance. I refuse all your offers, but I ask you again, where is the Lady Edith?"

"One might as well be hanged," cried Wild, "as lose more than forty thousand pounds! My Lord Warringdale is good for that sum so soon as he is safe and sure in the title and estates of Whitcombe. Come now, Captain, I will help you for say one-half the money!"

"Proceed!" said Heron.

Wild muttered something between his teeth which no one heard, and then Ogle, seizing him by the arm, brought him exactly under the bough of the chesnut-tree, over which hung the suspicious-looking rope with the loop at the end of it.

"Stop!" said Wild.

Heron made a sign with his right hand, and Ogle paused a moment, with the loop of the rope suspended over Jonathan's head.

"Why," added Wild, "have you not got the information from my Lord Warringdale? Why don't you hang him? Why am I selected to be the victim?"

"Go on!" said Captain Heron.

Ogle slipped the rope round Wild's neck, and then, retreating some half-dozen paces, he gave the other end into the hands of several of the band.

"Jonathan Wild," said Heron, "once more, and only once more, I ask you where is the Lady Edith?"

"If I won't tell?"

"You die!"

"Well—but—but——"

Heron made a sign.

"Pull!" said Ogle.

Jonathan was off his feet in a moment. He raised a yell that echoed far and wide through the forest.

"I will tell!"

"Down with him!"

With a heavy thud upon his feet, Wild was let down. He hung for a few moments listlessly by the rope, as if dead.

"Water!" he gasped—"some water!—I mean some brandy!"

"Where is the Lady Edith?" said Heron.

"In the Earl's private cabinet at Whitcombe House, in St. James's Street."

Captain Heron turned round with flashing eyes, and saw Tom Ripon.

"How is Daisy this morning?" he said.

"As well as ever she was," replied Tom.

"Quick! Bring her here! Ogle, you will follow me! See to this man, and keep him a prisoner until I return. I shall be gone perhaps three hours. If he cannot be kept without killing him, do so freely. Take him away!"

Jonathan looked cadaverous and weak.

The hoist that he had had off his feet had been rather unexpected by him, and it had half hanged him.

Still he had strength sufficient to utter such a string of invectives against Captain Heron and his band, that some of them had serious thoughts of actually hanging him, to put a stop to the scurrility of his tongue.

In about five minutes, Daisy was seen coming down the glade at a canter with Tom Ripon.

There was a gleam of pleasure in the eyes of Captain Heron, as he once more saw and welcomed his gallant steed.

"My Daisy," he cried, "welcome! Oh, most welcome, faithful heart!"

Daisy ran up to him, and placed her head caressingly upon his shoulder.

Then Captain Heron lifted the foot that had been injured, and was satisfied by a careful examination that all was well again, and Daisy was as fit for the road as ever.

"Let Ogle follow me!" he cried.

"I am here," said Ogle, as, mounted on the horse he usually rode, he came crashing through the underwood.

"That is well. Off and away to St. James's! And once more, my men, I commend the prisoner to your vigilance. Keep good watch and ward in the forest."

Heron waved his hand; and then, at a half-gallop, he started off to London.

Ogle followed him closely, and they very soon emerged from the trees and made their way, by leaping a gate, and going over some fields by a near cut, on to the high road.

Ogle then thought that Heron wanted to speak to him, as he glanced back, and he rode closer to Daisy.

"Ogle, you heard the villain," said Captain Heron. "Did he, in your judgment, speak the truth?"

"Yes, Captain."

"I am glad to hear you say so."

"I do not doubt it, Captain, for a moment. I think the rascal was really frightened."

"He was—he was! And yet what wonderful audacity he had even to the last moment in defying me!"

"That he was sure to have, Captain; but all's well that ends well; and if we find the Lady Edith in Whitcombe House, which I verily believe

CAPTAIN HERON HASTENS TO THE RESCUE OF HIS IMPRISONED BRIDE.

Presented Gratis with No. 64, of the New Elizabeth the Captive; or, the Robbers of Epping Forest.

EACH WEEK IS PRESENTED IS A COLOURED ENGRAVING.

we shall, she cannot have suffered much inconvenience."

"You comfort me, Ogle. Make your horse go at its best speed, without distress."

"I will. But it seems to me that there are some people yonder."

"Where? where?"

"Coming over the meadows, and I don't like the looks of them at all."

"Ah, I see them!"

"One, two, three, four, five, six. There are six of them," added Ogle; "and if they are not officers of the police, I never saw such people in all my life."

"What can be the meaning of their presence here, Ogle, think you?"

"I cannot exactly say, Captain, but I fancy that something is going on in connexion with those two men who were in the forest, and one of whom Jonathan was so good as to rid us of without any further trouble."

"It is probable."

"Ah! now I see I have made a good guess, for one of those mounted men is 'Tummus's' pretended master."

"Do they see us?"

"They do. They make their way over the fields, and now they raise cries and shouts."

"Then we shall have a fight for it, Ogle, and I would fain have avoided that, if possible. You are surprised to hear such words from me, but I grudge every moment that keeps me from Whitcombe House. Look to your pistols."

"All's right, Captain!"

The six horsemen came on over the two fields that separated them from Heron and Ogle with speed, but they kept well together, and it was evident that they were handling their pistols.

"Might I advise, Captain?" said Ogle. "I would separate them. They have had a trot from London, no doubt, and our horses are fresh."

"I understand you. Come on!"

Captain Heron gave Daisy a light touch on the neck, and she at once started into a gallop. The horse that Ogle rode, although not capable, as a general thing, of the speed which Daisy could put forth, was yet a good one, and for a mile or two could cover the ground quickly.

The moment the six horsemen saw Heron and Ogle take to flight, they set up a shout, and got into the field that was close to the high road.

"A highwayman! a highwayman!" they cried. "There he is—there he is! After him! A good reward! After him—after him!"

"This won't do, Ogle," said Heron, as he drew rein. "Since they will have a fight, why, the consequences of it be upon their own heads!"

"With all my heart, Captain!" said Ogle.

There was a low paling, on the other side of which was a farm-yard, at the part of the road where Captain Heron paused, and he there leaped Daisy over the paling just as the foremost three of the horsemen got through a gate into the high road.

Heron paused immediately on the other side of the palings, where Ogle had joined him, and cried out, "Now, sirs, if you are pursuing me, come on, or consult your own safety by taking your own way and letting me take mine."

"I have him!" cried one of the horsemen—"I have him!"

"Why, you are mad, fellow!" said Ogle.

"Don't kill him! I want to take him alive!" added this same man. "Now, you rascal, come here, and let me clap a pair of handcuffs on you, and I will guarantee you against any ill-usage."

Captain Heron felt inclined to laugh at this cool assurance; and as the man rode up close to the paling, Heron put out his hand and caught him by the arm, as he said, "Back, Daisy—back!"

"Hilloa!" cried the horseman; "what do you mean by that? Come, come, I shall be obliged to use violence! Help! help!"

Daisy had started back on the order so to do from Captain Heron; and as the latter kept a hold of the man by the arm, he was dragged off his saddle and over the palings before he could make any effectual resistance.

"See to this fool, Ogle!" said Heron, as he flung the man to the ground.

Then, drawing a pistol from the holster of Daisy's saddle, Heron fired right among the other horsemen.

A scene of ludicrous confusion immediately ensued, and they fled in all directions, leaving their leader as a prisoner in the hands of Heron.

"Who are you, idiot?" asked Ogle of this man, who looked very woful as he sat on the ground in the farm-yard.

"Who am I? Why, I'm Tonks!"

"What do you mean by Tonks?"

"That's my name, you see. Mr. Cuttles, you see, came and said that I had nothing to do but to ride to Epping Forest, and that there I should find Captain Heron, the highwayman."

"You have found him."

"But it seems to me that instead of my catching you—why—a—it seems to me——"

"That you are caught yourself," added Ogle, as he adroitly took from Mr. Tonks his purse, and watch, and a handsomely-mounted riding-whip.

"Come on," said Heron, in a tone of vexation. "We have lost, perhaps, invaluable time with this half-witted fellow. Come on, Ogle, at once!"

They set off for London once more, leaving Mr. Tonks in the farm-yard; and without further obstacle Heron and his friend Ogle found their way to St. James's Street.

Ogle paused at the corner of the street next to that which was nearest to Whitcombe House, and Heron went alone, and knocked that heavy knock at the outer door which had so much alarmed Lord Warringdale.

———

CHAPTER CXLIII.

CAPTAIN HERON HAS A MYSTERIOUS INTERVIEW IN OLD WHITCOMBE HOUSE, AND RESCUES EDITH.

THE proceedings of Captain Heron on his route from Epping Forest to St. James's Street, and the manner in which, after leaving Ogle in charge of the horses, he made his way at once to the door of Whitcombe House, afford a striking exemplification how strangely an all-absorbing feeling will obliterate every other consideration, and in its intensity break down all cautions which otherwise would attend particular acts.

There was Captain Felix Heron, the notorious and celebrated highwayman, with an immense reward upon his head, in the open face of day, without disguise or concealment of any kind, dealing those heavy blows with the knocker at Whitcombe House!

But it frequently happens that the very recklessness of courage brings with it its own security.

It was so in this case.

The entire forgetfulness of himself imparted such an air and manner to Captain Heron, that no one who had not the means of personally recognising him could have considered for a moment that he was inimical to the law.

And so many passengers passed him as he stood upon the door-step of Whitcombe House, and saw nothing in the transaction but a gentleman of unmistakable aristocratic bearing waiting for admission.

He avoided no gaze; any one might look at him who pleased, for from the moment that he had heard those words from Wild which convinced him that Edith was, or had been, at Whitcombe House, the spirit of his heart and mind, so to speak, had flown thither.

Readily, then, as a matter of course, had he followed that finer essence of his nature, and the great world, with all its hopes, and fears, and dangers, were forgotten in the all-absorbing feeling.

Heron had scarcely asked himself what he was to do, and he stood upon the door-step of his father's house, and gave those heavy knocks without other well-defined purpose than the one that, in some way, or in any way, he must search there for Edith.

It will be recollected that the state of affairs within that mansion was peculiar. Lord Warringdale had but by a very few minutes preceded Felix Heron: his errand too, likewise, had been to seek for Edith, but he found her not; and while he listened with intense alarm to those heavy blows against the outer door, he found himself a prisoner in that same apartment where he had expected to find Edith half dead with alarm and hunger.

But it never occurred to him for a single moment that the person demanding admittance to Whitcombe House was Felix Heron.

Nor did it occur to him, as a matter even of possibility, that those heavy knocks could be answered by any one within the house.

But they were.

Heron had raised the knocker for the fourth time, when he felt the door gently give way beneath his touch, and he at once stepped into the hall.

Well he remembered the last time he had crossed that hall to leave the mansion, after the agitating interview with the late Earl; but now he gave it only a careless glance of recognition, and closing the door behind him, he called aloud, "Edith! Edith! Edith!"

His voice echoed up the grand staircase, and seemed to die away in murmurs in the upper portion of the mansion.

Then Heron drew his sword.

"Woe be to those who now cross my path!"

he said; "I will leave no room unsearched in this place, and death shall be the portion of those who may have accepted the office of gaoler to my Edith!"

A sudden thought struck him that while he was searching one portion of the house, all his pains might be evaded by an escape through the hall and by the outer door. He turned to it, and elaborately fastened it: a chain, two bolts, a massive lock, all these would take time to remove, and he felt more secured, and greater freedom of action.

Then he paused for a moment at the foot of the great staircase, and again he called out aloud, "Edith! Edith! it is I!—it is Felix who calls upon you! Edith, if you be here, reply to me!"

There was one living being in that house who heard that call, and who trembled to hear it. Lord Warringdale knew the voice well, and with an accession of fear that deprived him almost of the use of his limbs for a minute, he crouched down in that room, the door of which had been closed upon him, and thought that in another moment, perhaps, the flashing eyes of Felix Heron would be upon him, and he could hear his voice demanding of him an account of Edith.

And this might well have been the case, for Heron was turning naturally to that suite of rooms at the end of which the Earl's private cabinet was situated, since those were the only apartments he had any knowledge of in Whitcombe House; but he was suddenly arrested in his progress by hearing a voice, which evidently came from some distance above him, and apparently at the upper portion of the grand staircase.

The voice sounded like an assumed one, and yet the tones were full of emotion, and had about them a tremulous earnestness which reached the heart of Heron.

"Felix! Felix!" said the voice. "Ascend! Your Edith is safe and well. Dismiss anxiety. He who sent you the billet to Castleneau House has watched over her. Ascend! ascend! ascend!"

Surprise at the moment prevented Heron either from moving or speaking; but then he hastily commenced his ascent of the grand staircase, calling out, as he did so, "Speak again—oh, speak again! I do believe your words—they reach my inmost heart! Speak again, and, be you whom you may, I will thank you from my soul!"

"Ascend!" said the voice again.

Heron reached the landing on the first floor of the house. He saw a door with richly gilded panels half open, and, from its size and ornamentation, he could well believe that it conducted to the principal saloons of the mansion.

But every shutter was closed, and beyond that door there seemed an impenetrable darkness.

It looked like a gilded and elegant entrance to some cavern, for the light that streamed into the hall, and up the grand staircase, came from a circular window over the outer door, and from the two side-lights, by which visitors could be reconnoitred, and which admitted two broad beams of light into the spacious vestibule.

"I am here!" said Heron. "Where am I to go?"

"Advance!" said the voice.

There was no doubt but that it came from the rooms into which the gilded door led; and as Heron never for a single moment doubted the friendly character of the voice, he replaced his sword in its sheath, and then strode forward unhesitatingly into the profound darkness of the suite of saloons which had so often glittered with the rich costumes of all that rank and beauty could collect to share the hospitality of a minister of State, high in the favour of his Sovereign, and almost absolute in the direction of the policy of the kingdom.

"I am here!" said Heron, after he had advanced some twenty paces.

"It is well!" said the voice.

"Ay, but better still far for this poor languishing heart, from which has been torn away its better portion, could I hear but one word, one grateful sigh, from the lips of Edith, to assure me of her safety."

"Hush!" said the voice.

Mingling with that "Hush!" Heron thought he heard another sound—a sigh, a light exclamation, a half-uttered word—and it fell upon his heart like a ray of sunshine, for it reminded him of Edith.

"Hush! hush!" said the voice again.

"Ah! she is here!" cried Heron—"here amid the darkness, and I cannot see her! She is here! Edith! Edith! Why this mystery? Speak to me?"

"No," said the voice, "she is not here. But be content—fond heart, be still! She is in safety!"

"I will believe it—and yet, why is this trial of my patience and my affection? and who are you that stand between me and my love?"

"Listen! You are not what you seem. The noble blood that flows through your veins should impart to you ideas and thoughts of high nobility. I am prophetic, and the time will come when on that breast, at which rude thrusts have been aimed by plebeian swords, the star of high authority shall glitter. Eagles mate with eagles. What say you, Felix Heron—if recognised as one of England's proudest nobles, and capable of commanding such an alliance as might give you cousinship with kings, is the weak fancy of your early days for a romantic girl to stand in the way of your high ambition?"

"Ah, now I know you!" cried Heron, and he drew his sword again—"now I know you for a foe, and yet so foolish an one that you would try to break your way into a fortress with a straw!"

"What mean you?" said the voice.

"You are one of those who would try to set up the weaker feeling against the stronger—worldly ambition against the heart's highest impulses. I tell you, mysterious being, be you whom you may, that the golden circlet of royalty itself would not tempt me from my faith!"

"Are you certain?"

"Ay, as certain as that bright sun to-morrow will chase away the mists of darkness."

"Reflect!"

"Reflect on what? Reflect on this puerile attempt to turn me from an adoration of a life? Edith! Edith! I call upon you—for, by some unknown influence I cannot fathom, you are kept silent, although I feel and know that you hear me. Edith, I have sought you through difficulty and through danger—I am here alone, to encounter all who would oppose our reunion. Speak to me, or by your silence leave me to think that you, too,

have been offered some glittering future which has beguiled and warped your better feelings!"

"Felix! Felix!" shrieked a voice.

It was the voice of Edith.

Among a thousand strains of music that voice, the sweetest melody of all to him, would have reached his heart.

It was Edith.

He seemed to feel her presence, although he could not see her. There was a light amid the darkness, which, although it had no earthly origin, in flame was present to his eyes.

"Edith! Edith!" he said. "You are here—you are here!"

"I am, Felix! This trial was not of my choosing, or of my making. I am here!"

He held out his arms—his sword dropped from his grasp, and in another moment his Edith was resting on his breast.

By accident, or by some means that had been contrived for the purpose, a long panel of one of the shutters of a window of the saloon swung slowly open, and a gleam of light made its way into the vast apartment, and was reflected in beauty from the heavy gilding of the walls and ceiling, from the rich lustres and chandeliers, and from many a glittering object of beauty and art which wealth had collected in that gorgeous saloon.

And there was Edith, well and happy, with a smile upon her face. and brightness in her eyes—no trace of suffering in form or feature.

Well might Heron look around him with bewildered eyes as he pressed her to his heart!

"What does all this mean?" he said. "Do we live in a land of dreams? What am I to think? Oh! Edith, speak to me!"

"Felix, I am here! I am yours again, and danger and distress have passed away. Amid the calamities that beset me when I was torn from you, I found a friend."

"Who, Edith? Who is it that has aided you?"

"Alas! I know not. In and about this house there is some mysterious being, who, almost from the moment that I set foot within it, has taken me under his especial protection."

"And you know him not?"

"I have not seen him. I have had communication with a voice, and a voice alone; but it has been one full of tenderness, of affection, and of pity."

"This is more than strange!"

Captain Heron looked around him, and for a moment a smile wandered over his face, as his eyes fell upon all the rich and rare appointments of that room.

"And this should be our home, Edith," he said.

"We will not sigh for it. We will be happy beneath the greenwood tree, if that be our lot. May we not, Felix?"

"Happier—happier far than with all this gilded pomp. But my mind is in a whirl of many emotions, and I would fain take you at once from this house, which, with all its beauty and magnificence, has still been, for a time, a prison."

"I am ready, Felix—I am ready!"

Joy was sparkling in the eyes of Felix Heron now, as he picked up his sword; and with Edith resting on his arm, he commenced again the descent of that grand staircase, up which he had been invited to so much happiness by the mysterious voice, which, without any corporeal presence, seemed to occupy Whitcombe House.

They crossed the hall.

With what wonderfully different feelings was it, now, that Captain Heron undid those elaborate fastenings of the door which he had thought necessary!

And then the thought of all the peril in which he stood—the recollection of how many people were armed for his destruction—came across him, as he and Edith stepped out into St. James's Street, and closed the door of Whitcombe House behind them.

She hung upon his arm, and he could feel her tremble as she did so.

He tried to reassure her by speaking lightly of the dangers which now began to rise up before him, and to force themselves upon his reflection.

"We have little to fear, Edith," he said. "We have but two great enemies, and they are both in my hands."

"Both, Felix?"

"Yes. Jonathan Wild is in Epping Forest, well looked after by my gallant comrades; and Lord Warringdale is a prisoner in the vaults and cellars of Castleneau House. Those two men alone knew the secret of where you were imprisoned, and I was determined to keep them until they disclosed it. They were hostages for your safety, Edith; and they must have felt the peril of their position."

Captain Heron now began to consider of the best means of getting to Epping Forest, for he seemed that he would never feel sure of the safety of Edith until she was once again in the recesses of the wood which had defied so much scrutiny, and so many dangers.

But Edith was anxious to proceed to Castleneau House, in the first instance; and upon their reaching the corner of the street, where Ogle was waiting with the horses, Heron placed his finger on his lips to deprecate any imprudent sally of satisfaction that might come from Ogle at the sight of Edith.

"A coach, Ogle!" he said,—"a coach at once! I will hold the horses."

"Hurrah!" said Ogle, in a low tone. "We're all right again, now! And here comes a coach lumbering along, just as if it knew it was wanted."

Ogle still led Daisy, and Captain Heron got into the coach with Edith, for he could not bear now to let her out of his sight even so far as a coach-panel might have intervened between him and her.

In this fashion they made their way towards Bloomsbury; but as Captain Heron did not wish to give a clue, even to the coachman, of where they went, he stopped the vehicle some distance off, and discharged it.

To the astonishment, then, and almost fright, of old Anthony, who happened to be in the fore court of Castleneau House, they all arrived, and Captain Heron rang the bell.

"Gracious providence!" cried Anthony. "Come in, come in!—oh, come in at once!"

"Yes, when you have opened the gate, Anthony," said Captain Heron; for the old man, in his astonishment, had quite forgotten to do so.

"Gracious me!" said Anthony; "I shall turn old and stupid some day! Oh, Miss Edith, it does my eyes good to see you! I beg your pardon—what am I saying? Mrs.—that is, Lady Edith, I mean. Come in, all of you—come in!"

"Woa, Daisy!" said Ogle, as they entered the gates, and Daisy amused herself by giving old Anthony a shake by the shoulder of his old livery coat."

"Bless us and save us all!" said the old servitor; "and this is the celebrated Daisy, is it?"

"Yes," said Ogle. "And you may be sure she has taken to you at once, or she would not have torn that bit out of your sleeve."

"How remarkable! Come round to the back of the house, Mr. Ogle, and we'll see what Lady Castleneau's cellars afford. Ha! ha! We've some prime old wines left yet, and some ale that is so strong, it nearly stands up on end when it comes out of the spigot!"

While Anthony was entertaining Ogle, Captain Heron and Edith had made their way into the mansion, and it may well be imagined with what extreme delight they were welcomed by Lady Castleneau.

"We must be off to the forest at once," said Heron, after he had told the old gentlewoman the story of the morning's adventures. "Jonathan Wild is a prisoner there, and I'm afraid that if I do not return in good time, my men will fancy something has happened amiss, and I do not want to have the villain's life on my hands in the manner that they might take it."

"And that wretch, Warringdale," said Lady Castleneau; "I suppose we must let him go now?"

At this moment old Anthony burst into the room, and elevating his hands, cried out, "He's gone—he's gone!"

"Who has gone?"

"My Lord Warringdale!"

Heron sprung to his feet.

"Then we live in an atmosphere of danger, Edith!" he said.

"Has he escaped?" said Lady Castleneau.

"Yes, my lady. I went down into the cellars to get some of the old ale for Mr. Ogle, and I thought I would just see what his lordship was about, but he has escaped through one of the narrow gratings that lead into the garden, just by the old ivy."

"There is the more reason that we should leave London as quickly as possible, Edith," said Heron. "I think you have that suit of apparel here of mine in which you came to town? You shall ride Daisy back to the forest, and I can take Ogle's horse. He will follow by any convenient opportunity he can find."

"Oh, yes," said Lady Castleneau; "be it so! For much, my dear Edith, as I would give to have you here, there can be no happiness in constant apprehension! Come, my dear child—come with me, and you will soon be ready to accompany Felix to Epping Forest."

Edith was soon equipped for the road. She took a tender farewell of Lady Castleneau; and even if any one had been upon the watch, they could hardly have supposed that the two mounted men, apparently, who rode out of the court-yard of Castleneau House, were the lady and gentleman who had arrived so short a time previously on foot.

Ogle promised that he would be at the forest

almost as soon as they were, for there was a stage-coach which would take him near at hand.

Edith and Captain Heron had been very happy before when they took their way from London to his sylvan home beneath the greenwood tree, but it is doubtful whether their present happiness was not of a higher order after their temporary separation and the many dangers which had beset Edith.

Daisy seemed proud of her fair burden, and soon the houses of London were left far behind them, and the open country spread out far, and wide, and beautiful.

In an hour and a half they plunged beneath the trees of the old forest.

"Home—home again!" cried Heron. "Home again, dear Edith, and in safety! My mind is full of rapture and content, and I could almost forswear all ambition, to live a life of sylvan repose beneath the shades of the ancient wood."

No. 65.—EDITH.

CHAPTER CXLIV.

CAPTAIN HERON AND HIS BAND RESUME THEIR ADVENTURES ON THE ROAD, AND FULFIL A NEGLECTED DUTY.

NOTWITHSTANDING all the suffering and all the persecution which Jonathan Wild had brought upon him, Captain Heron had no wish to protract the stay of the ruffian thief-taker in his forest-home.

No sooner, therefore, had some of his band made their appearance, welcoming him and Edith with shouts of exultation, than Heron issued his orders.

"Go," he said, "a couple of you, and take Jonathan Wild to the confines of the forest. Tell him distinctly from me that he is not again, on pain of death, to tread its grassy glades. Away with him at once! The free air that wanders through our sylvan home is tainted by his presence!"

No doubt Jonathan Wild was as surprised as pleased that he was let off so easily, and he made the best of his way to London, wondering, as he went, how it had fared with Lord Warringdale.

It was with a very vague hope indeed of hearing any news of him that Wild went to the chambers occupied by Warringdale in St. James's Street, opposite Whitcombe House.

There, however, to his astonishment, he found him.

They had each a long story to tell the other, but the only part of it which is not already known to the reader, consists in the means by which Lord Warringdale got free from his mysterious imprisonment in the cabinet at Whitcombe House.

That freedom was as easily achieved as his confinement, for the door of the room had suddenly swung open, with as little appearance of human agency as it had closed; and, without looking to the right or to the left, Lord Warringdale had been only too eager to embrace the opportunity of flying from the house.

We return, then, to Epping Forest, where, in the midst of his companions, upon whose fidelity Captain Heron knew he could so well rely, he found a happiness and contentment which more than once engendered the desire to banish from his mind all thoughts of contending for that peerage which seemed, notwithstanding all he had gone through, as far from his grasp as ever.

And now let the reader contemplate with us one of those sweet glades in the old forest, which looks as if it belonged to primeval times, and had scarcely ever been profaned by the foot of living creature.

Majestic trees on either side raised their tall summits to the sky, and, stretching towards each other, a thousand arms seemed to embrace in leafy fellowship over the soft bright turf beneath.

It was a glade in which the timid deer, with its dappled young, might pause, and believe itself free from danger—a spot in which the forest birds might teach their gentle fledglings to fly, and fear no footstep to make war upon the sweet retreat.

The sun is deep in the west. Islands of flame, and of gorgeous prismatic beauty, float around the radiant orb, and long streaks of golden light gleam through the trees like sheets of flame, and variegate the grass with many changeful tints.

The hum of insect life is still in the sunny air.

The evening carol of the birds makes vocal the light breeze that ruffles the tree-tops.

But soon that spot, so lovely, so abandoned, apparently, to natural sights and sounds, is invaded by many feet.

One by one the band of Captain Heron assembles until all are present.

Then there is a quick, short step of some one hastening through the trees, and the Captain himself appears amid his followers.

There is a murmur of satisfaction at his presence, and just as the sun begins to sink below the horizon line, and deeper shadows begin to creep over the scene, he speaks.

"Comrades and friends, you have borne well with me, and have allowed me to neglect our compact to follow the impulses of my own for-

tunes and my own wishes. I have done so to the full extent of my present means and present sources of information, and now I am with you once again as Captain Heron the highwayman."

A half shout of applause burst from the lips of the band, and died away in many cadences among the old trees of the forest.

"Yes," added Heron, "I am here as in time past to lead you to adventure. To take from those who have a superfluity of this world's wealth in any way we may, so that it be boldly done, that which we require."

"Bravo!" cried several voices. "Hear the Captain."

"Since, my comrades, we were all out upon the road together, I have been thrust into communication with many scenes of active life, and with all manner of men. I have noticed that fraud, chicanery, the arts of flattery and base dissimulation are the elements of many human actions. We will not stoop to those devices, nor emulate those intricate robbers, who hold themselves fairly to the world's face, and yet are greater plunderers than any bold rider who ever cried 'Stand!' upon the King's highway. We do not rob the widow and the orphan on pretence of friendship; we boldly take from the rich, and the rich alone, for the real plea of poverty never was made to us in vain."

"Never!" cried the band, as with one voice.

"To your horses, then!" added Heron. "To your horses, and see to your arms! for by yon star in the far east, I swear we will go forth upon the road to-night."

The delight of the band was excessive. They thronged around Captain Heron—they shook him by the hand—and showed all the exultation of men who were restored to the life they loved after long absence from it.

"To horse—to horse!" he cried. "But let not those whose turn it is to keep watch and ward in the forest envy their companions on the road, for their turn will come; and they are performing as good service here as if they stood by me in circumstances of the greatest danger."

The band raised another cheer, which echoed through the forest, and then they hastily departed to procure their horses; but Captain Heron called to Ogle, saying, "Let Tom Ripon bring your horse, Ogle, along with Daisy. I would speak with you."

"Tom is quite melancholy," said Ogle, "and thinks you will not take him with you."

"I cannot take him. Hark you, Tom, I leave you in a sort of authority in the forest, and if you wish really to serve me you will remain in content."

"Very well," said Tom; "but if you should go near Little Swallow Street, just inquire after the old gal, Captain, and tell her that as soon as a man can possibly do so, he will send her something."

"For your sake, Tom," said Heron, "I will take care she wants for nothing, although I have small thanks to give her for that affair when the house was burnt down. Now, Ogle, I would speak with you."

"I'm at your service, Captain."

"It is a long stretch of country between here and Highgate to the north of London, but I purpose scouring that whole extent with the band,

and taking what adventures we can on the road. When once there, my intention is to make a downright assault upon the asylum of those rascally Whalleys, for the purpose of rescuing poor Sir Dominick Browne, which I will do by sheer force of arms."

"It will be well done, Captain. I will take care that Atkins is not left in the forest as a scout, for he knows every in and out of the asylum."

"Do so; and now let us be off as quickly as we may. I have already taken farewell of Edith, and she is willing that I should go on this expedition to rescue Sir Dominick, whom she knows well as one of her own guardians, and to whom her heart warms for all his kindness to me when I was a youth."

Tom Ripon soon brought the horses, and although not over well pleased to be left behind, for he thought himself quite man enough to encounter anybody on the highway, he was rather flattered at the kind of confidence which Captain Heron reposed in him by leaving him in the forest.

In five minutes more the whole party was trotting down one of the glades, and as the twilight came rapidly on they emerged close to the old mill, and the roadside tavern at which Edith had asked her way on the occasion of her following Heron to Barnes Common.

But Felix and his band made no halt. Every stick, stone, tree, and rivulet of that neighbourhood, were to them well known. They formed a compact and strong body as they trotted along the highway; and Captain Heron felt that he had power enough to perform almost any exploit that might take his fancy.

The evening was so early, too, that he felt he had many hours before him in which to engage with such adventures as might present themselves. He felt, too, that consciousness which sometimes came over him when he sallied forth with his companions on the road, that something out of the usual routine of adventures would fall to his lot.

The presentiment on this occasion did not deceive him.

According to his usual custom, after getting some two miles or so from the forest, he divided his band into portions of two each, scattering them over the road, so that each couple was distant some hundred or two paces from another. In this manner about a quarter of a mile was occupied by the band, and Captain Heron and Ogle rode on in advance.

A pause of six or seven minutes on their parts would have been sufficient at any time to concentrate the whole force, by bringing them all up in successive couples to that point.

In this fashion they rode on until they crossed the river by one of the bridges high up the stream.

A long, shady road led towards the western portion of London; and as Heron and Ogle pursued it, they soon became conscious that a couple of horsemen were in advance of them, whose voices in conversation came rather loudly upon the night air.

"Is that a dispute, think you, Ogle?" said Heron.

"It sounds something like it."

"Let us listen. They ride slowly; and if we walk our horses we shall catch the sound."

So eagerly were these persons conversing, that it was evident they heard nothing of the horses' feet approaching them.

One voice rose high in remonstrance, so that every word it uttered could be plainly heard.

"I tell you, Sir Charles," it said, "my duty is to warn you. You stake your happiness as well as your fortune. The set, whom you think gentlemen, gay fellows, and *bon vivants*, are adventurers. Men of name and family, I grant you; but they are rakes and free livers, who have run through their estates and credit."

"Well, well," replied a voice, which was evidently that of a very young man,—"well, well; I will be careful, and not play high; but I have promised to go to the 'Brooklets' to-night."

"The 'Brooklets,' Sir Charles? What a name!"

"Nay, Mr. Revell, do not start at a name. It is after all but a pretty villa that belongs to the Count."

"What Count? Some foreign adventurer, I take it. I tell you again, Sir Charles——"

"Stop, Mr. Revell; I am of age. I have a large fortune, and if I choose to dissipate some of it in what staid and serious persons may call the follies of youth, I know not who is to call me to account."

"I am answered, Sir Charles—I am answered!" said the other voice. "Good night!"

Captain Heron and Ogle thought that this horseman would pass them when he left his companion, but such was not the case; for he only accelerated the pace of his horse, and rode onwards, leaving him whom he called Sir Charles on the road.

The young man seemed to have some compunction about the manner in which he had allowed his elderly mentor to leave him, for, after a moment's pause, he called out, "Mr. Revell! Mr. Revell!"

He was too late, however. The Mr. Revell who had given him such good advice was too far a-head to hear him, but this pause that he made in the road enabled Captain Heron to come up to him.

Before he did so, however, Heron whispered to Ogle, "Fall back to our men. Keep them well together, and don't lose sight of me unless I enter a house. Be then sufficiently close that my signal whistle may be heard, for I may want both you and them."

"Depend upon us, Captain," said Ogle, in the same low tone. "I know I can, as ever."

Heron gave Daisy a gentle impulse forward, and accosting the young man who had been named Sir Charles as he was riding on, he said, "A fine evening, sir. Do you ride to London?"

"No, I am a visitor at a villa close at hand, but it is a fair evening."

"Ah, I envy you, sir! You seek, probably, the hospitable board, and possibly the smiles of beauty; while I, a poor colonel in his Majesty's service, but newly arrived from foreign stations, scarcely have a friend in England."

"Sir," said the young man, "I am almost inclined to believe that Providence has thrown you in my way. I have lost of late such large sums at play that I am nearly desperate. An appointment has been offered me this night with those who have won so freely of me, that I might have what they call my revenge; for surely the blind goddess Fortune cannot be always against me—I must win, some day."

"Infatuation!" said Heron.

"Nay, call it not such. It is true, I mean to go on playing, and that, too, for such heavy, stakes that one piece of good fortune will redeem the past, and I play no more. Sir, I have a friend, who has been more than a father to me—I have a mother, sisters, and I only struggle to extricate myself from a vortex."

The young man's voice faltered.

"Look you here, sir," said Captain Heron; "I feel an interest in you. Suppose I accompany you to this appointment. I, too, will play. It is considered that I have amazing luck, and who knows but that my very presence may charm away the evil fortune that has beset you?"

"A thousand, thousand thanks!"

"Oh, it is nothing!"

"But are you rich enough, Colonel—I think you said you were a colonel—are you rich enough to bear possible losses?"

"I am the possessor of a priceless treasure. Money is to me as dross."

"I tremble with pleasure. There is nothing I could so much desire as to have one with me who, in the capacity of a friend, will be able to see, perhaps better than I can, that all is right and fair. My name is Sir Charles Chessington."

"And mine, Colonel Nox."

"Colonel Nox?"

"Yes; and I have come upon you like the night, have I not?"

"Nay, say, rather, like the daylight — for, without intending to play upon words, I feel lighter of heart since I met with you. And here, I believe, are the very gates of the villa. It is called the 'Brooklets,' and belongs to the Count Beltani, an Italian nobleman."

"As he says," replied Heron

"Oh, I assure you, Colonel, men of honour—men of honour, all!"

"Have they won much of you, Sir Charles?"

"They hold my acknowledgments for twenty thousand pounds, and I must needs part with my estate to pay them, if to-night I cannot save all by one happy stroke of fortune."

"But if you lose again?"

"Then am I a beggar, and perhaps a pistol-shot will settle all!"

"I think you said you had a mother and sisters?"

"Colonel, Colonel, do not speak of them! If you only knew what I have suffered! But here we are at the gate. Believe me, I will not play for a single doit beyond my means of payment, but I will lose all, or recover that which has gone!"

"We shall see," said Heron.

The young Sir Charles Chessington rang a bell, and the flash of lights across a beautiful flower garden began to show themselves.

"I have a little prejudice," said Captain Heron, "against placing my horse in strange hands. My servant is somewhere down the road; permit me to ride back and meet him. I will be with you again in a moment."

"As you please, Colonel. I will wait for you." Heron rode hastily back, and encountered Ogle.

"Be careful of Daisy," he said. "I'm going into yonder house, where you see the light among the trees. I may want you all, for aught I know, with the exception of one, who must stay with the horses. If you hear me whistle, be assured I require you promptly, and, in that case, make your way into the house in any fashion you can."

"Is it all danger, Captain," asked Ogle, "and no booty?"

"Nay, no danger I hope, and much booty."

Heron walked back to the lodge gates of the villa where Sir Charles Chessington had already dismounted, and they together walked through the gate, and across a lawn liberally bespangled with exquisite flowers, towards the villa.

The building seemed to have no upper storey, but it was raised upon a kind of terrace, and there were no less than five windows opening all from some room on the ground floor that seemed to be rather brilliantly illuminated.

One of these windows was open, and the room was only shaded from actual observation from without, by silken curtains that flapped gently in the night air.

As Captain Heron and Sir Charles Chessington ascended the three steps that led from the garden to the terrace, these curtains were pushed aside, and two gentlemen attired in the highest style of the prevailing fashion lounged out on to the terrace.

"Have we the pleasure," said one, in affected tones, "of welcoming our dear friend Sir Charles Chessington?"

"Ah!" cried the other, "I shall be more than happy."

There was a real or affected foreign accent about this last speaker.

"Yes," said Sir Charles Chessington, "I am here, and, I think, to my time. Permit me to introduce my friend Colonel Nox."

"Colonel who?" cried both the superbly-dressed gentlemen at once.

"Nox," said Captain Heron, as he advanced with a smile, and as vacant an expression of countenance as he could possibly assume. "Nox, gentlemen — N-o-x — without the K. It's one of the funniest things in life, but so many people spell my name with a K. And here's my friend Sir Charles, who tells me there will be some play; so, as I said to him, ' Why, Sir Charles, I doat on play; and what's the use of having a few spare thousands out of your annual income, if you don't play?' Eh, eh, eh?"

There was such a mixture of suavity and imbecility about the manner which Captain Heron put on on this occasion, that Sir Charles Chessington looked at him with surprise, and began to wonder that he had picked up so shallow a companion on the highway.

The two fashionably-dressed gentlemen exchanged glances; and Heron, who was particularly sharp of hearing, was quite certain that he heard the word "pigeon" pronounced between them.

"Any friend of yours, Sir Charles Chessington," said one, "is most deucedly welcome."

"Oh, yes, most deucedly," said the other, with the foreign accent. "Walk in, Colonel Nox—walk in, Sir Charles!"

The room that this open French window conducted them into was handsome enough almost to be called superb. In it there were four other per-

SIR CHARLES CHESSINGTON EXPRESSES HIS GRATITUDE TO HIS LATE DELIVERER.

Presented Gratis with No. 65 of the New Edition of the Captive; or, the Robbers of Epping Forest.

EACH WEEK IS PRESENTED GRATIS A COLOURED ENGRAVING.

sons besides the two handsomely-dressed gentlemen who had appeared to welcome Sir Charles Chessington.

They were all evidently men of fashion, but *roue* and libertine were stamped upon their countenances as with a seal.

"Colonel Nox !" announced one of those who had been at the window. "A harmless, inoffensive gentleman, and a friend of Sir Charles Chessington's, with a few thousands to spare."

"Oh, yes," said Heron, with an affected lisp; "I'm harmless and inoffensive enough. I went into the army ; but, would you believe it, gentlemen, they wanted me to be so ungenteel as to serve in the campaign in Hanover? I couldn't do it—I—a—couldn't do it ! I should like to ask you, gentlemen, how a gentleman, delicately brought up with the fashionable perfumes always at his elbow, could endure anything so vulgar as going to kill anybody, or being killed himself ?"

CHAPTER CXLV.

CAPTAIN HERON RESCUES SIR CHARLES CHESSINGTON FROM THE SHARPERS.

THE little party in the fashionable drawing-room of the villa was quite delighted at this acquisition to its strength in the person of the supposed Colonel Nox; for after his speech they could not but suppose him to be one of the fashionable fribbles of the day, who, with abundant means, and limited capacities, fall an easy prey to the social sharpers who infest society.

There was very nearly an acclamation of delight, with one exception, as Captain Heron made his appearance in the room, and that exception consisted of a man who lounged in an attitude of carelessness against the chimney-piece of the apartment.

He did not seem to be at all at his ease ; and by his manner, it was evident that he was repeating to himself the name of Colonel Nox with considerable doubts as to its authenticity.

"Yes, gentlemen," added Captain Heron, "my friend here tells me that he has lost a few thousands, and is willing to lose a few more. And what is life, gentlemen, without sensation ? Why, it tires you—sickens you—wears you out; and if it were not for dice and cards, I don't think I could live."

The utter serenity of expression with which Captain Heron spoke these words seemed almost sufficient to dispel the suspicions of the morose individual who leant against the chimney-piece.

The others were quite in ecstacies at the anticipation of additional plunder from this friend of Sir Charles Chessington.

"Come, we waste time," said one. "When gentlemen meet for a purpose, and that purpose is to enjoy a little play, every minute is lost that is not devoted to the enlivening pursuit."

"To be sure !" said another. "Let us arrange our game."

"Certainly, certainly !" said Heron. "What music is more musical than the rattle of the dice ! What works of pictorial art greet our eyes with more satisfaction than the honours in a hand at cards !"

"Bravo ! bravo !" cried the party, as they clapped their hands in approval of the sentiment.

Sir Charles Chessington looked uneasy. He placed his hand upon Heron's arm, and seemed as though he would draw him aside to remonstrate with him.

"Hush ! all is well !" whispered Heron.

The tone in which this brief admonition was given differed so entirely from the vacant kind of drawl with which the supposed Colonel Nox spoke to the gamblers, that Sir Charles Chessington started with surprise.

But there was no time for further conversation. The gentlemen of the dice, who held their appointment with Sir Charles Chessington, were too intent upon his absolute ruin, and upon fleecing his friend, to attend to much else than their preparations for the night's play.

"Come, Sir Charles," said one, as he rattled a dice-box, — "come, and take your revenge! I fancy I see good luck in your eyes to-night."

"Heaven grant——" said Sir Charles—and then he stopped abruptly.

"You're right, Sir Charles," said the sinister-looking personage who had been leaning on the chimney-piece. "This is no place in which to speak of heaven. But since we have met for play, gentlemen, let us commence."

"Cards or dice ?" cried one.

"Oh, the ivory—the ivory for me !" said another.

"Be it so—be it so !"

"But here are cards," cried the first speaker; "and perhaps Sir Charles would prefer——"

"I do," said Captain Heron. "Red and white for me! Place the pack in the centre of the table. I bet a thousand pounds on a majority of the first twenty cards being red !"

"Done !" cried everybody.

"One—two—three—four—five—six ! That is six thousand, gentlemen."

"Colonel, you must be mad !" cried Sir Charles Chessington. "You never will begin with such a bank as that?"

"Oh, yes ! Bet on me—bet on me !"

"What shall I bet ?"

"Another thousand on the issue !"

A slight flush of colour came over Sir Charles Chessington's face, and he beat the table nervously with his knuckles, as he said, "I do—I do !"

There was a general movement of chairs now, and the party seated themselves round the table in the centre of the room, which was covered with a green cloth, kept steadily in its place by heavy fringe and tassels.

It was the Count, or the pretended Count—the special enemy of Sir Charles—who immediately faced Captain Heron. The slightly foreign accent in which he had hitherto chosen to speak passed away from him, and he looked with cool effrontery into the eyes of Heron, as he said, "You really play in this fashion, and for such stakes ?"

"I do."

"Take your card, then, and I will follow you."

"Nay, do all these gentlemen elect you as their representative?"

"Oh, yes, with pleasure."

The others nodded assent, and a lurking smile was on most of their faces

"I never saw a game like this," said Sir Charles.

"Oh, but I shall win!" said Heron. "And if I lose, these gentlemen will still give me my revenge in any shape I please. Come, sir; I commence well!"

Captain Heron picked a card off the pack; it was a red one.

The Count picked another that was red likewise; and so on, for five cards in succession, the colour of red alone appeared.

"Double your bet, Sir Charles," said Captain Heron.

"Will that be fair now?"

"We will all agree to it," said the Count.

"Then I do."

The young man looked feverish and anxious, paling and flushing by turns, and breathing laboriously.

There was not a sound now to be heard in the room but the faint fall of the cards as they were lifted from the pack one by one, and placed in two distinct heaps—the red distinct from the black.

"Nineteen!" said Captain Heron; "and a black card. There are nine black, gentlemen, and ten red. What do you give now for your chances of the game?"

"Everything!" said the Count; and he lifted the next card, which was black.

"A tie!—a tie!" cried everybody.

Sir Charles Chessington breathed heavily.

Captain Heron picked up the remainder of the pack of cards, and began to deal them out singly, counting, as he did so, twenty-one—twenty-two—twenty-three—and so on, until he came to fifty-two, which, however, still left a card in his hand.

"Why, gentlemen," he said, as he held it up, "here are fifty-three cards in this pack; and if we did not know our illustrious friend the Count so well that we feel such a thing to be impossible, we might suppose that that twentieth black card which made the tie was, with the dexterity of a practical card-sharper, dropped from his sleeve."

The Count's face turned of a livid yellow. He dashed his clenched hand on the table, and glaring at Heron, he said, "Do you mean to charge me with cheating at cards, sir?"

"Not for the world," said Heron.

"A tie!—a tie!" cried everybody. "The bets are drawn!"

"Oh, well," said the Count, making an effort at composure, "I must say, Colonel Nox, that your language—that is to say, your insinuations—tended to—to——"

"My dear Count," said Heron, "don't disturb yourself in the least. I'm called Blundering Nox wherever I go, because I always say the wrong thing in the wrong place. But I've a proposition to make."

"What is it, sir?"

"That you and my friend Sir Charles decide this drawn bet by a cast of the dice. What say you all, gentlemen?"

"Agreed!—agreed!"

The Count's face resumed its ordinary colour, and he drew a long breath of satisfaction.

"Colonel Nox," he said, "you're a gentleman."

"So are you," said Heron.

"Nay," said Sir Charles. "Fortune may favour you, Colonel, but she always plays the jade with me. I pray you take the dice."

"No; I will look on, and get my money ready."

Sir Charles drew his chair a little closer to the table, and took the dice-box in his hand.

"Be it so," he said. "This cast makes me, or breaks me."

Amid a death-like stillness, he flung out the small solid squares of ivory, on which the name, rank, fortune, and life itself, of so many human beings had hung. They rolled on to the green cloth, and then settled, with a two, a six, and a four uppermost.

"Twelve," said the Count.

"There's no doubt about twelve," said Heron.

"It is my turn now."

The very lips of Sir Charles Chessington were white; and the Count seemed to take a malicious pleasure in protracting the agony that sat upon the young man's heart, for he rattled the dice a full minute before he flung them on to the cloth.

There were three sixes.

"Eighteen," said the Count.

"Eighteen!" gasped Sir Charles.

"There's no doubt about eighteen," cried Captain Heron; but, at the moment he spoke, he stretched forward his hand, and intercepted the fingers of the Count, which were about to lift the dice from the table.

"What do you mean?" said the Count, as Captain Heron laid his hand flat over the demoniac ivory cubes. "What do you mean, sir? Give me the dice."

"I think, as we pay eight thousand pounds between us for them, we may be permitted to take possession of such costly trifles."

"Never!"

"Never, say you?"

"No, it shall not be! Help, my friends! Hold him back! I will have the dice!"

The Count made a desperate blow at Heron, but it missed its aim, and was returned with interest, and the gambling swindler fell heavily over his chair. Heron immediately picked up the three dice from the table; and then, in a voice that rung through the apartment, he cried out, "Why, you are cheated, my dear Sir Charles; for these three dice have nothing but sixes on them, and it would be impossible to throw less than eighteen, cast them which way you might."

A yell of rage came from the Count's friends, and Heron waited calmly until it had subsided. Then, turning to the young Sir Charles, he said, "What do you propose to do? Your Count, you see, is a sharper."

"He shall fight me!" said the Count; "or you shall!" as he struggled to his feet.

"With pleasure," said Heron; "but I object to that gentleman leaving the room."

All eyes were turned to the morose-looking man, who was slowly making his way to the door. Sir Charles Chessington darted after him, and turning the key in the lock, took it out.

"Look to the windows, Colonel," he said,—"look to the windows, and see that the villain Count escape not. My worst suspicions have come true, my most terrible dreams are verified. I have been the victim of foul play. My fortune is ruined, my health shattered, and my home a wreck, by the arts of a villain!"

"We certainly look as if we had fallen into a den of thieves," said Captain Heron.

A general chorus of vociferations arose from

the Count's friends; but he interrupted them, and although ghastly pale, there was a bold effrontery in his looks, and a steadiness of nerve that could hardly have been expected under the circumstances.

"I am foully accused," he said; "and I retort the accusation. My friends here have nothing to do with this matter, and I challenge this stranger, who may or may not be a Colonel, to make his words good at the hazard of his life."

"You challenge me?" said Heron.

"No—me!" cried Sir Charles."

"Nay, my friend, I'm sure the Count means me."

"I do mean you, insolent braggart!"

"No bad language, Count. I don't like fighting in a room—it's close and confining, and your blood spoils the carpet; but if you really will fight——"

"I have said it."

"Then I submit. Sir Charles will second me; all your kind friends here will do the same by you; and as I'm always of opinion that these affairs are best settled if soon settled, I am ready."

"My pistols—my pistols!" cried the Count.

"Pardon me, sir, you wear a sword."

"No; I do not fight with swords with every chance ruffian who may come in my way, and who may be a fencing-master for aught I know. There are many cudgel-players, men of the sword, disbanded troopers, and bullies about the town, who make the use of cold steel their daily practice. I fight with the pistol."

"No," said Heron. "There are many cowardly scoundrels, sham counts, sharpers, and swindlers, who practise the pistol until they can snuff out the candle at twenty paces, but who have not the courage to face a drawn sword." (The livid yellow look came over the countenance of the Count again.) "And," added Heron, "as I am the challenged party, I have, by all the rules of arms, the choice of weapons. I choose the sword!"

"Then I will not fight with you!"

"Then I will pin you to the wainscoat, and leave you like a hawk on a barn door, as a warning to cheats and swindlers!"

"Look at my sword!" shrieked the Count. "It is small and light, while yours is a heavy weapon! Close in—close in, and end it!"

These last words were addressed to the dubious-looking personages who made up the company in the apartment; but young Sir Charles Chessington drew his sword as he said, "The first who closes in, or shows a disposition to do so, receives my sword in his breast!"

The gamblers hung back.

"Look you, sir!" said Captain Heron to the Count. "I see that your sword is shorter and smaller than mine, and that on that account you have cause of complaint. Yet, as I am the most accommodating man in the world, I will change with you!"

"No! If fight I must, I fight as I am!"

Captain Heron had watched carefully the eyes of his antagonist, and he saw the fell purpose which shone forth in them; so that when the Count, with a cry of rage, suddenly rushed forward, hoping to end the contest by inflicting upon Heron some grievous wound before he could place himself upon his guard against it, the treacherous villain found himself met steel to steel.

The swords rang together, and the Count stamped and uttered terrible imprecations, and darted to and fro, and strove by every art to confuse his antagonist.

Captain Heron never stirred an inch from the spot on which he stood, but calmly fenced the gambler off, and more than once he could have taken his life, but forbore to give the deadly lunge that would have ended the conflict.

His object was to disarm the Count, and that required waiting for. The opportunity, however, came at last, and the Count's sword sprung through the air, shattering in its flight some of the pendant lustres of the chandelier that hung from the ceiling of the room.

Captain Heron lowered his sword-point at once.

"That is over!" he said.

"No!" shouted the Count; and with a spring that cleared a full eight feet of space between them, he alighted nearly upon the breast of Captain Heron, brandishing a small triangular poniard in his hand, which he had taken from some concealed sheath in his apparel.

Heron saw the movement, quick as it was, and adopted the only plan which would secure him from injury. He stooped and swayed somewhat to one side, and the weapon that was aimed at his heart passed harmlessly over his shoulder.

Another moment, and Heron grasped the throat of the mock Count, and held him until insensibility crept over his frame, and he fell an inert mass at the feet of his conqueror.

Up to that moment the confederates of the Count must have had great confidence in the treachery or skill of their leader, for they had left the combat to take its own course; but now that they saw all was lost, and the people whose pockets they believed to be so well lined were about victoriously to leave the villa, they plucked up the courage of desperation. They were still five to two, and a sudden rush might overcome both the supposed Colonel Nox and Sir Charles Chessington.

The rush was made at the very moment that Captain Heron placed his silver whistle to his lips, and blew a blast so loud and shrill that it echoed not only through the whole building, but far and wide into the open air.

There was a crash of glass, and, heedless of framework or glazing, Ogle and half a dozen of Captain Heron's men dashed into the apartment.

"Seize them!" cried Heron, "and see that none escape!"

The gamblers found themselves in the hands of men too well accustomed to rough work to leave them any hopes of escape; and, while Sir Charles looked with perfect astonishment upon these proceedings, Heron turned to him with a smile, saying, "There cannot be the shadow of a doubt but that, from first to last, you have been robbed by these men, who have victimized you by the common arts of the swindler and the sharper. Should they have about them the gold and the acknowledgments which they have by arts extorted from you, it is your right to repossess yourself of that which is your own. My men will assist you. Ogle!"

"Yes, Captain."

"See what these fellows have about them; and, be it what it may, it belongs to this gentleman."

"I am lost in amazement," said Sir Charles, "but my heart already beats the lighter. I am saved—I am saved! Oh, demon of gambling, I escape thy clutches!"

CHAPTER CXLVI.

MR. WHALLEY AND HIS ASYLUM ARE TAKEN BY SURPRISE.

OGLE and his men emptied the pockets of the gamblers with a dexterity which, however creditable it might be to their culture in that line, was anything but pleasant to the persons operated upon.

The amount of money found was not so great as might have been imagined, but in the pockets of the Count a much more important prize was found—viz., the acknowledgments which young Sir Charles Chessington had given him from time to time, for large sums lost at the gaming-table, and to redeem which he must of necessity have parted with all his patrimony.

These documents, important as they were, formed the large bulk of the losses of the heedless young man.

"Behold!" said Captain Heron, "here is money, and here are these important papers, which, without a doubt, have been obtained from you by some such means as those we have discovered and exposed to-night. Take all, and for ever bid adieu to this haunt of iniquity!"

"No," said Sir Charles; "I cannot touch their ill-gotten wealth. It may, or may not, be my gold; but these written acknowledgments I know to have been in my own possession, and yet I have scruples."

"I have none," said Captain Heron.

As he spoke, he crumpled up the acknowledgments in his hand, and threw them into the fire.

The defeated gamblers raised a chorus of groans when they saw this operation take place.

Sir Charles Chessington smiled.

"You certainly," he said, "take a short and effectual method of relieving me from a scruple and a difficulty. I am saved, and satisfied. Let them keep their ill-gotten gold—I will have none of it."

"We will neither of us touch it," said Captain Heron, as he took the young man by the arm and led him from the villa.

"Other folks," said Ogle, in a low tone, "are not so scrupulous. Number Two, a bag."

"Here you are," said Number Two.

"In the name of our fraternity, take possession of this plunder. It will go into the common stock at the forest, and we shall each have our share of it. Now let us follow the Captain."

The gamblers were left in a very awkward position indeed, for Ogle and Captain Heron's men had tied them in such a way that they were each attached to some heavy piece of furniture, without the means of getting rid of the encumbrance.

Two were tied to heavy chairs—one to a couch—two others to separate small tables—and the Count himself was securely lashed to a what-not or a canterbury, which, although it might run glibly enough on its castors after him, could only have been removed from the room by the door or window if raised on one end.

And so they were left to their own consolations and resources.

"I know not what to say to you," said Sir Charles Chessington, when they were out in the open air, and mounted on horseback again. "I know not what to say you, in the way of thanks, Colonel Nox, if that be your true title and name, for you have saved me from great calamity, and perhaps from death."

"Think not of it," replied Heron; "but let me bid you here a fair good night. I am bound upon another errand of charity and mercy to-night, but still my pursuits are not those you would willingly consort with."

"Impossible! You must be both chivalrous and noble."

"Sir," said Heron, as he patted the neck of Daisy, "I am a highwayman."

"A highwayman?"

"Yes, Sir Charles. You start at the sound, but such, in truth, I am; and yet I would fain not be confounded with vulgar robbers. And should you ever see me in a higher station, and hear me called by another name, only think of me as one who was a friend to you in the hour of need, but who, even in that hour, would not deceive you in regard to his real condition."

Heron touched the bridle of Daisy, and was moving off.

"Stay—oh, stay yet a moment!" cried Sir Charles. "You will take with you nothing but my thanks, but leave me the pleasure of knowing that I have the means of communicating with you, should I wish to do so."

"Ride into Epping Forest," cried Heron, "when you will, and wait there until you meet with me. Farewell!"

"Farewell, and heaven speed you!"

Sir Charles remained motionless in the roadway, while Captain Heron and his men rode off at a brisk trot towards London.

After a time, then, Heron called to Ogle to send the man Atkins forward to him, and when that person rode to his side, he said to him, "I purpose assailing Whalley's asylum at Highgate to-night, for I am determined to rescue Sir Dominick Browne. What, in your judgment, will be the best mode of proceeding?"

"We must get into the place, Captain, without giving an alarm, or we shall fail entirely."

"Think you so?"

"I am certain of it. They have hiding-places, in one of which they will place him, and then make you welcome to search the place, in which you will be foiled."

"We will break in, then, abruptly."

"Not so, Captain, if you'll take my advice. I know the ways of the place and the people. Let me go forward, and they will open the door to me; after which all will be easy, for we can seize and make prisoners of every man we meet."

"So be it, Atkins. We will leave our horses in the care of a couple of the party, and follow you on foot; but some carriage must be procured

for the old man, whose strength would scarcely permit him to ride, even if we had a spare horse for him."

"That I will see to," said Ogle. "I suppose the asylum is not far from the village?"

"Close at hand," replied Atkins; "and at most there are not more than about half a dozen persons who can oppose us in it."

"Then, forward, comrades!" cried Heron, "at what speed you may; for this rescue of my old friend and benefactor is a duty which sits heavily at my heart, and by the aid of heaven it shall be done to-night."

Scarcely a stray word was now exchanged between Captain Heron and his band, as at a smart trot they made their way skirting the north of London towards Highgate.

Upon rising a considerable hill, Heron heard the sound of a church clock which struck the hour of two.

No. 66.—EDITH.

"Do you know where we are, Ogle?" he said.

"No, Captain; but Atkins says that is Highgate Church."

"It is so," said Atkins; "and the asylum is but half a mile from us. It will be well now that we make our arrangements, for a body of horse, even no larger than ours, looks formidable."

"We will ride on," said Heron, "until it would be positively unsafe to proceed farther, and then, Ogle, I think I would prefer leaving you in charge of the horses, with two of our comrades to assist you. You know how careful I am of Daisy's safety."

Ogle might be just a little disappointed at being out of the adventure at Mr. Whalley's asylum, but he knew the advantages of discipline too well to demur at the orders of Captain Heron.

At that dim and silent hour of the night they trotted through the whole length of the village of Highgate without attracting any observation.

the barking of a few dogs being the only notice taken of their progress, as they reached the northern slope of the range of hills in that direction from London.

There was a lane to the right of the road which led to Southgate; and it was so well wooded, that it formed a shadowy and secure retreat for Ogle and the horses.

"Now," said Heron, "go on, Atkins, and we will follow you sufficiently close that, when you get possession of the door of the asylum, we shall be able to back you against any force from within."

"It is an iron gate in a garden wall," said Atkins.

"Might we not climb it?"

"No, Captain, better not; for then they would know in the house that we were enemies, and we might get no further than the garden for a good half-hour."

"It is well.   Proceed!"

"Hush! There is the corner of the wall, and there is the gate."

Even as they spoke, to the great surprise of Atkins, the gates of the asylum were flung open, and a hackney coach came wheeling and rocking to and fro out into the open road.

"Hold back!" whispered Heron.

The coach paused for a moment when clear of the gates, and they were closed with a clatter.

"Justify me, then, to Sir John and to my Lord Warringdale, and I shall be satisfied."

"No fear of that," growled some one in reply.

It was a wonder at that moment that Captain Heron did not utter an exclamation of surprise, for in that voice he recognised the tones of his arch enemy, Jonathan Wild!

The voice had come from some one within the coach; and now the driver cracked his whip, and the pair of horses which drew it began to start off at a tolerable rate up the short, sharp bit of hill that led to the village.

"Wait here for me a moment," said Heron in an anxious whisper to his men. "Do not stir from this spot, for I have a suspicion which I must verify or dissipate."

Captain Heron ran swiftly after the coach, at a speed which soon brought him up to it. He clambered up behind, and projecting his head as far round to one of the panels as he could possibly do with any regard to not being seen from within, he listened intently.

He heard the well-known growling tones of Jonathan Wild.

"I tell you it's for him and his advantage," he said. "I have changed sides, and am all for Felix now. Ha! ha! What matters it to me, so that I am paid by one or other of them."

"If I could only be sure," replied a weak, moaning voice,—"oh, if I could only be sure! Anything for Felix—anything for my boy, Felix!"

Well did Captain Heron know the tones of that voice. They fell upon his heart with an emotion which brought tears to his eyes; and his thoughts flew back to the many kindnesses he had received from the old man who uttered those kindly words in regard to him.

He had not the shadow of a doubt but that it was Sir Dominick Browne himself who was in that coach with the villain Wild.

But what was the project? What was Jona-

than about to do? and whither was he carrying the old man?

These were questions which Heron found it impossible to answer; and as the coach was proceeding at a tolerable pace, he felt that his stay at the back of it was taking him too far from his comrades.

But he heard Wild speak again before he alighted.

"You're so suspicious!" said Jonathan.

"I suspicious?" said old Sir Dominick.

"Yes, to be sure! You won't believe a man when he tells you he has turned virtuous, and taken the right side instead of the wrong. Now you say that the certificate of the marriage of Amelia Staunton with the late Earl of Whitcombe is at your house close to Kingsbury, in a lac-Japan cabinet. Find it, and let me have it, and from that moment Felix is Earl of Whitcombe."

"Let you have it! For whom?—for what?"

"For the King!"

"Ah! The King!"

Captain Heron had heard enough. He dropped at once from behind the coach, for on the coachbox he saw two men were sitting, both of whom, no doubt, were Jonathan's bull-dogs, and armed to the teeth. He had but a pair of pistols about him, and it would have been madness to have compromised the safety both of Sir Dominick Browne and his own by an attack upon three such armed men as Jonathan Wild and two of his janissaries.

But Heron had heard quite sufficient to guide him on his course, and he knew that the good, kind old man was in no present danger.

"To horse! to horse!" he cried, as he reached the lane close to Whalley's asylum, where Ogle was in charge of the steeds of the party. "To horse!—to horse! we have no further business here!"

In less than a minute the whole party was mounted, and then Heron spoke briefly to his men in explanation.

"That coach we saw issue from the iron gates contains the object of my search. We have but to follow it, and I can lead the way. Forward! Trot!"

Captain Heron swept on in advance, but not so far that his men could not see him and Daisy amid the darkness of the night.

He knew perfectly well that the coach would turn down the lane to the right, which would lead it over Hampstead Heath, and his first intention was in that lane to surround the vehicle, and rescue Sir Dominick Browne.

But he had heard words which were to him of absorbing interest, and he longed for the opportunity of seeing unobserved, if possible, if Sir Dominick Browne really had the means of producing to Jonathan Wild the important document in question.

If so, the mere sight of it might produce in Wild's imagination an opinion of the utter futility of any longer aiding Lord Warringdale in his pretensions.

If this could be done without bloodshed, Captain Heron felt that he would be better pleased than as if he crushed his foes with the strong hand of physical power.

If otherwise, he thought it would be a terrible

lesson to Jonathan Wild to find that, go where he might, even amid the silence and secrecy of the night, he was not free from the interposition of him, Heron, at the most critical moments.

It was upon these considerations that he made up his mind to follow the coach to old Sir Dominick Browne's house before interposing in the matter.

The vehicle went steadily on its road, and it was evident that whoever drove it was well acquainted with all the highways and byways that lay between Highgate and Sir Dominick Browne's old deserted mansion.

Daisy had a particular swinging walk, which Captain Heron could put her to whenever he pleased, and which got over the ground at the full rate at which another horse could trot, while, at the same time, it was a nearly noiseless progression.

It was in that fashion, then, that Captain Heron followed the coach in which were Sir Dominick Browne and Jonathan Wild; while the band, led by Ogle, kept so far in the rear that the sound of their horses' feet, faintly as it might come to the ears of Wild, was not likely to be associated with the ideas of pursuit.

It was nearly four o'clock in the morning before the coach stopped at the old dilapidated gates, which shut in the fore-court and garden of Sir Dominick Browne's house.

Captain Heron rode swiftly back, and stopped his troop.

"Do not advance for five minutes," he said; "and then I shall leave it to your own ingenuity to take two men prisoners whom you will find on the coach-box with as little trouble as possible, and no bloodshed."

"Trust us, Captain," said Ogle. "We will do it."

"That I am sure of if it lies within mortal power. Look to Daisy now, and be careful of her as you would of my own life."

Heron then dismounted, and sped back swiftly to Sir Dominick's house.

Who could be more familiar with that old house, and all its intricacies, than he who had passed his youth about it? There was not a room, a staircase, an ancient gallery, or dim corridor, which he could not have traversed with his eyes blinded; and well he knew that corner of the old wall which would enable him to get into the fore-court, without troubling the gates.

It was well that the night was not further advanced, for another hour would have brought the first faint streaks of morning upon the eastern horizon, and the operations of Captain Heron and his men would then have been impossible. A short and sharp conflict must have settled the affair; but as it was, fortune had placed at his disposal that dim, dark, silent hour which always precedes the dawn.

He could just see the coach and horses, like a black cloud resting upon the earth.

One of the great gates was swinging open. Jonathan Wild had no doubt found among his multifarious picklocks one that fitted it, but that gate was so close to the door of the coach, that Captain Heron, even in the darkness, would not risk gliding into the court-yard through its opening.

He noiselessly climbed the dilapidated wall, and crept without observation towards the mansion.

When about half-way across the court, in which the rank grass grew in abundance, he saw the reflection of a light gleam past several windows in the upper floor of the building.

The old hall door was open. Wild had not thought it worth while to close it after him, since he was about, in his own estimation, so soon to return with the important document he had brought Sir Dominick Browne there to procure for him.

Little did he think that the man of all the human race whom he would the least wish to be cognizant of his proceedings on that night, was close upon his track, and had crossed the threshold of the old mansion within three minutes of the period when his own shadow had deepened the darkness of the ancient hall.

Captain Heron trod softly.

He could have closed his eyes and found the grand staircase, so well he knew the place; and keeping them closed, he could still have made his way towards that apartment which had already once baffled the researches of Jonathan Wild.

The lac-Japan cabinet was a familiar object to the youthful recollections of Captain Heron, and the room in which it stood had a further and higher interest to his imagination, for it was the one in which Edith had found a shelter after her daring escape from St. James's Church, when she was so nearly falling a victim to the duplicity of those who sought to convince her that by the sacrifice of self she was saving the life of Felix Heron.

Up the grand staircase noiselessly, two, and sometimes three, stairs at a time, went Heron. He glided like a spectre across the gallery, from the windows of which he had seen the light gleaming. He crossed two large apartments, and descended six small stairs; he laid his hand upon a door handle and listened.

The room he was about to enter was next to that in which the Japan cabinet was placed.

All was still within.

Cautiously, and without producing the slightest sound, Captain Heron opened the door, and glided into the apartment. A faint stream of light came from the half-open door that led into the next chamber, and from that chamber there came the murmur of voices.

One of those voices was that of Jonathan Wild, the other, in trembling and imploring accents, that of Sir Dominick Browne.

Heron loosened his sword in its sheath, and listened.

CHAPTER CXLVII.

THE RECOVERY AND THE LOSS OF AN IMPORTANT
DOCUMENT.

IT was with deep emotion that Captain Heron listened to the trembling accents of poor old Sir Dominick, who had played so much more the part of an earthly father to him than that real parent to whom he owed his existence.

The tone sufficiently indicated to Captain Heron how great had been the fear which was made upon the mind of the old man by the sad persecutions he had endured both on account of him, Heron, and of Edith.

It was a singular piece of evil fortune in the history of Sir Dominick Browne that his old age should be clouded and harassed with care, on account of transactions in which he really had no concern, except in the way of kindness and of sympathy.

It was to please his friend the Earl of Whitcombe that he had taken charge of the infant Felix, and it was his kindly feeling towards that fair, but unfortunate, being who had become the wife of Sir John Tarleton and the mother of Edith, which had induced him to consent to become a trustee for the fortune which had so much excited the cupidity of the evil-minded Judge.

No wonder that in the decline of his existence, and the decadence of his mental and physical powers, poor Sir Dominick Browne lost nerve and courage, and was at the mercy of such a man as Jonathan Wild.

"Yes, yes!" he murmured. "You tell me all that. I hear what you say, sir, quite well. You tell me you are a friend to my poor boy Felix, and that it is for his sake that you wish to find the certificate of his mother's marriage."

"I do tell you so," growled Wild; "and I tell you the truth. Why do you keep harping upon that, as if you doubted me?"

"I must doubt—I do doubt!"

"Ah! Say you so?"

"Yes, yes! But be not angry—be not angry! Do not take me back to the cell. You—even you do not know what I have suffered there. It would be a greater kindness for you to kill me—a greater kindness by far."

The old man began to moan and sob.

"This is childish folly," said Wild, abruptly. "You have admitted that here, in this house, in a lac-Japan cabinet, the certificate is to be found."

"Yes, yes—oh, yes, yes!"

"Find it, then, for I must and will have it. Here is the cabinet. It is large, and, no doubt, full of secret recesses; but you can, doubtless, easily place your hand upon that which contains the certificate."

"Oh, yes! With ease—with ease! The little drawer!"

"Quick, then!"

"But, sir—but, sir, you are that same Mr. Wild whose character is—that is to say, whose name has——"

Wild burst into a hoarse laugh.

"Say what you will, Sir Dominick!" he cried. "You cannot tell me worse of myself than I have heard from many lips. You mean that my character is notorious, and that my name has an evil repute. I admit it. What then? It has nothing to do with the certificate of Amelia Staunton's marriage. That I must and will have. You can help me to it, and it will be well that you do so quickly."

"But, sir—but, sir, listen! The Earl always said that, at his death, he would do justice to the boy."

"He is dead."

"Dead? The Earl of Whitcombe dead?"

"You surely knew it?"

"Alas! alas! My memory is weak; and of late so many horrors have crowded themselves into the short span of my existence, that I know not imagination from reality, or dreams from facts. The Earl of Whitcombe dead? Alas! alas!"

"Dead and buried," said Wild.

"And what has he done for Felix?"

"Nothing."

"Oh, do not say so! That is impossible. I have seen him shed tears. No, no! do not tell me that. It cannot, may not be!"

"I tell you it is so. The young Lord Warringdale, his son by the second marriage, claims the title and estates. He admits he's half-brother, to a degree, with Felix, but proclaims him a bastard."

"No, no! That is not true. The Earl married Amelia Staunton. I know it—I know it!"

"And I, too; and so you see, Sir Dominick Browne, as I can't sleep at nights if I see anything going on that is wrong or unjust—such as an orphan being deprived of its rights, or a poor widow being defrauded of her substance—I am anxious to confound this Lord Warringdale, and to prove his elder brother's legitimate right to the title and estates."

"He has the right—he has the right!"

"Then will you, Sir Dominick, be the man to deprive him of the proof? Find me the certificate in a moment, and Felix, from that time that I hold it in my hand, is Earl of Whitcombe!"

"I will—I will!" cried the old man, with sudden energy. "You swear to me that you are acting justly?"

"I swear!"

"Hush! I thought I heard thunder! Did you say you swore by heaven?"

Wild stamped on the floor passionately.

"Old man, you trifle with me! We are alone in this house. You are far away from any human aid. You trifle with me—with Felix—with your life—and with Edith!"

"Edith, Edith!" cried Sir Dominick Browne, as the name struck upon his senses,—"Edith, Edith! Is the dear child well and happy?"

"She will be when you produce the certificate which will prove the legitimacy of her husband!"

"Her husband?"

"Yes, her husband—Felix! Did you not know they were married?"

"Now, heaven, I thank thee! I am ready to die. Thy will be done with the old man, for the first wish of his heart is fulfilled! I am weak—weak—and yet joyful! My hands tremble, but my heart beats tuneful music!"

"Quick!" cried Wild. "The certificate!"

"Yes, yes; you shall have it—you shall have it! Hold the light, sir. Closer to the cabinet, dear sir. I tell you there are many secrets in this old piece of Oriental ware. Well I know where to place my hand upon the secret drawer—a secret within a secret; and which, to those who know it not, would remain in darkness and obscurity until the old cabinet would fall to pieces. Hold the light higher, sir—higher with the light!"

Captain Heron heard the creaking of the doors of the old Japan cabinet; and holding his sword firmly, so as to prevent it clanking on the floor, he stole as softly as foot could fall into the room.

One of the large, heavy doors of the cabinet was open, and cast a deep, broad shadow over the doorway of the apartment, completely shrouding the advancing figure of Captain Heron.

The light which Wild had was the small dark lantern he usually carried about with him. It had

CAPTAIN HERON EFFECTUALLY CHECKS THE MEDDLESOME INTERFERENCE
OF THE COOPER.

Presented Gratis with No. 66, of the New Edition of the Captive; or, the Robbers of Epping Forest.

EACH WEEK IS PRESENTED AS A COLOURED ENGRAVING.

a powerful lens, and a slide, by which at pleasure he could shut off the light, or moderate it to any degree.

The thief-taker was holding this lantern about the height of his face. Its lens was entirely uncovered, and it sent a broad stream of white light right into the cabinet.

Poor old Sir Dominick Browne was on his knees; and having taken completely out a shallow deep drawer, he had placed his hand in the cavity to feel for a button, which would enable him to draw out at right angles a secret recess.

"Quick!" said Wild. "You're very slow about it."

"It is here—I am sure it is here!"

"So much the better."

"The better for the good and the innocent, Mr. Wild?"

"Yes, Sir Dominick, and the better for you; for at your time of life you have little to live for but the benefit and happiness of your fellow-creatures like myself, and you won't care how soon you bid adieu to this world of troubles."

"I am quite ready to bid adieu to it," said Sir Dominick Browne, "now that I am sure those dear children, Felix and Edith, are happy. Ah, I feel it now!"

"The certificate?"

"No, the drawer which contains it."

Captain Heron had advanced step by step; and although he could not see Sir Dominick Browne, in consequence of his being too far within the cabinet, so to speak, he had a clear enough view of Jonathan Wild as he held up the lantern in his left hand, and plunged the right into the wide pocket of his coat.

When Jonathan produced that right hand again from his pocket, it had in it one of those short, stunted pistols, so much affected by officers of the police at that period.

Captain Heron could not doubt for a single moment now that the intention of the villain Wild was to take the life of the old man the moment he should actually produce the much-coveted certificate.

A feeling of deep thankfulness to Providence came over the mind of Heron, that he was permitted to be there at that critical moment to interpose for the protection of that true and affectionate friend to whom he owed so much kindness and obligation.

It is not too much to say that that generous gush of thankfulness on the part of Captain Heron was quite unalloyed by any thought of the importance to his own fortunes that certificate might be.

He only felt and saw the danger of Sir Dominick Browne; and had there been twenty assassins instead of one seeking his life, he, Heron, would have drawn his sword in his defence.

"The certificate!" cried Wild, fiercely.

"It is here—I am sure it is here," said the old man.

Captain Heron drew, silently and swiftly, his sword from its scabbard.

"Quick! Produce it!" added Wild. "Do you mean to keep me till daybreak?"

"Be patient, sir. The drawer is tightened by damp; but a little force—a very little force—and we have it."

Wild put the pistol upon full cock, and the click of the spring fell upon the ears of old Sir Dominick Browne, and caused him to look hastily round.

"Ah! Help! Murder!" he cried. "You would destroy me!"

One long step brought Captain Heron past the door of the Japan cabinet. He spoke not a word; but his long, bright sword-blade flashed in the light from Wild's lantern, as he placed its point right in the centre of the throat of the villanous officer.

"I am here!" he cried then. "I am summoned, and appear!"

Sir Dominick Browne uttered a cry of surprise and terror, and, still on his knees, fell back against the drawers of the cabinet.

But no pen can describe the consternation and astonishment that sat upon the countenance of Jonathan Wild. For more than a minute he was perfectly paralysed with terror; and, with the pistol in one hand, and the lantern in the other, he glared in the face of Captain Heron with all the alarm that he could possibly have expressed had he encountered a being of another world.

Captain Heron was not at all unwilling to enjoy, for a short space of time, this intense confusion of his implacable enemy.

Wild's eyes seemed to be almost projecting from their sockets, and his retracted lips exhibited his teeth in painful distinctness.

"You—you here?" he gasped, at length.

"Ever here," said Heron, solemnly,—"ever here, there, or anywhere, for the protection of those whom I love, against the villain Jonathan Wild."

Jonathan shrunk back a step. He was recovering, and Heron saw that such was the case. With his left hand he suddenly snatched the pistol from him, and, pressing the point of his sword still at his throat, he cried, "The time for forbearance is past! You would have committed a cold-blooded murder. Attempts upon my own life I have forgiven and forgotten, but——"

Wild saw and felt all his danger. With a cry of despair, he flung his head backward, and escaping the point of the sword for a moment, he turned and fled.

There was a door immediately opposite that by which Captain Heron had entered the apartment, and, fortunately for Jonathan Wild, it yielded to his touch. He dashed through the opening with all the speed of a man flying for his life; and Captain Heron pursued him, with a determination there and then, at once, to put an end to the career of a man so steeped in villany and crime.

Well acquainted with the mansion as he was, Heron thought he would have no difficulty in overtaking Jonathan Wild; but a man who flies for his very life has always an advantage over his pursuer; and Wild dashed along corridors, and down staircases, with a recklessness that might have met the death he felt to be at his heels.

Once Captain Heron dimly caught sight of him passing a window, and he fired the pistol he had wrenched from his hand at the dusky-looking figure.

There was no cry, however, to signify that the ball had taken effect, and finally Heron paused at the head of a flight of stairs which he knew led to the lower regions of the house.

This chase of Wild through Sir Dominick's

old mansion had gone far towards cooling down the first emotions of anger in the mind of Captain Heron.

He paused in his pursuit.

"We shall meet again," he said. "In the great world I shall meet that man again, and will exact from him the mortal retribution of his crimes. I will seek poor Sir Dominick, and calm his fears."

Captain Heron was, in a few seconds, back again in the chamber of the lac-Japan cabinet. The lantern, which Jonathan Wild had flung on the floor, was still alight, and Sir Dominick Browne was still in the same attitude Heron had observed when he left him.

The first impression of Felix was that the old man was dead; and then, when he saw that he still breathed, he feared he had fainted from excess of emotion.

Such, however, was not the case. Weakness, surprise, and terror, were all acting upon poor old Sir Dominick at once, and he could neither move nor speak.

"Dear, kind old friend!" cried Heron. "Do you not know me? I am Felix."

"Felix, Felix!" gasped the old man. "Oh, help, Felix!"

"You are safe now, and all is well. I have chased from you the ruffian who would have taken your life. He dare not approach you. All is well, and we will part no more, dear Sir Dominick."

The old man looked in the face of Felix for a few moments in silence, and then burst into a passion of tears.

"That is well," said Heron, gently. "It relieves the full heart."

"Felix, Felix!" said Sir Dominick, when he had somewhat recovered from this burst of emotion. "Is it indeed true that I look upon your face again?"

"Behold me well," said Heron, with a smile. "You, at least, Sir Dominick, cannot be mistaken in me."

"And Edith—our dear child Edith?" cried the old man. "What of her?"

"She is my wife."

"Ah! Then, Felix, you may kill me, for I have lived long enough to be happy."

"Nay, I have come to save you. Many, many happy days are in store for us. We have a sylvan home in the depths of old Epping Forest, which you shall share with us."

"But, my boy—my boy, you are an Earl."

"Yes, if the world would let me be one; for the Earl of Whitcombe, my father, is no more."

"Ah!" cried old Sir Dominick, as he clapped his hands together with sudden animation. "The certificate—the certificate! I did not give him that!"

"And is it indeed true," said Heron, sadly, "that such a document is in this antique cabinet?"

"It is so! Indeed, and in truth, it is so, Felix; and it is yours. It will clear up all disputes—it will reinstate you in your rights. You are the Earl of Whitcombe, Felix. Pride, Felix, pride, and the opinions of men—it was that that kept your father, the Earl, from doing justice to you in his life-time; but he declared to me at his death all should be known, and that you should be acknowledged as his only and true heir."

"Alas!" said Heron, "he has died and made

no such sign; but yet, if this certificate be really in existence——"

"It surely is—it surely is! I placed it here myself. Your mother gave it me. I promised her it should be yours. It was the only gift she had to leave you—the proof of her honour and your own condition. It is here—it is surely here."

Captain Heron held the lantern, even as Jonathan Wild had held it a short time previously; and old Sir Dominick, with eager, trembling hands, again attacked the secret drawer, which he succeeded in forcing from its place.

"Now—now I have it, Felix!" he said. "Behold!"

Captain Heron took the little drawer in his hand, with a feeling of reverence. It was of cedar, and the peculiar odour of the wood came strongly on his senses.

Lying flat at the bottom of it, was a piece of paper, or parchment, which occupied its whole extent; but, as Captain Heron turned the rays of Jonathan Wild's lantern upon it, he saw, to his dismay, in consequence of some dampness which had penetrated into the cabinet, and percolated into that secret drawer, the important document was almost in a state of decomposition.

Patches of blueish mould were upon it, and he could only faintly see some characters that imagination rather than fact helped him to make out as the name of Amelia Staunton.

"How is this to be preserved?" he cried. "It disappears even before my eyes! Oh, heaven! Are all my hopes thus to fly from me?"

It was contact with the open air of the apartment—a difference of temperature, probably occasioned by the concentrated ray of light that fell upon it, and a dryness of the atmosphere which was not to be found within the cabinet—that acted now upon this important certificate.

Even before the eyes of Captain Heron it crumbled up, and began to shrink into dust. The faint lines of writing disappeared from his sight, and as, with a deep sigh, he placed the little drawer upon a table, he saw that in half an hour more the certificate of his mother's marriage would have resolved itself to its elements.

"Fate and heaven are against me!" he said. "It is gone—it is gone!"

"No, no," cried Sir Dominick; "I am certain it was there."

"It was, indeed, dear friend; but twenty years and more of decay and dampness have been its destruction. That hope has passed away."

"But the bishop—the bishop lives!" cried the old man. "The Bishop of Worcester. He was but a poor clergyman when he married the then Lord Warringdale to your mother, Amelia Staunton. The Earl, your father, when he came to his title, and took part in affairs of State, was able to do much for him, and to seal his mouth by many favours. But he must, he will justify you."

"Then there is one more hope," said Heron. "The leaf of the registry has been torn away in the old church at Barnes that contained the record of my mother's marriage; and this certificate, which you thought so well preserved, has faded away before my eyes. But I will see the bishop."

"Yes, yes, dear Felix, see him, and surely all will be well."

A pistol shot from without, and which Heron guessed was in the direction of the coach Jonathan

Wild had left by the great gates of the mansion, at this moment interrupted the deeply-interesting conference between Felix and his old friend and protector.

_____

CHAPTER CXLVIII.

CAPTAIN HERON SENDS SIR DOMINICK BROWNE TO LADY CASTLENEAU'S.

At the sound of that pistol-shot which awakened the dull echoes of the early morning, Sir Dominick Browne uttered an exclamation of alarm, and crouching down to the floor, he seemed as if the courage and presence of mind which had come back to him in the presence of Captain Heron were all lost to him.

The persecutions which the poor old man had endured at the hands of the malignant and wicked Whalleys had completely prostrated his spirit.

He might recover, with associations of a favourable character; but as yet there had not been time to produce counter impressions, and any sound of alarm flung him back again into the midst of his excitements and his terrors.

"Heed it not—heed it not!" said Heron. "It is nothing. I have a strong force without, so be under no apprehension."

"Felix, Felix!" said the old man, trembling. "I have suffered so much."

"You shall suffer no more," cried Heron. "I pledge you my life for your safety. You shall suffer no more. Remain here in peace; I will return to you quickly."

"Oh, no, no! do not leave me—do not leave me alone! I shall be a prey to a thousand fears! Do not leave me, Felix—I pray you do not leave me!"

"Then I will not, dear old friend. You shall come with me. Lean on my left arm, so—that is well. My right will be free to defend you, if necessary."

"But the certificate—the certificate, Felix, of your mother's marriage!"

"It is gone—not a vestige of it remains. Damp and time have done their worst. It is gone."

"I remember—I remember! But the bishop, Felix—the Bishop of Worcester, he will do all that is right. It is a great thing that such a witness is spared to us."

Poor old Sir Dominick Browne leant heavily upon the arm of Captain Heron, and they together left that chamber in which for so many years had been slowly crumbling away so important a document as that which had greeted the eyes of Heron for a few moments, but to cheat all his hopes of its possession.

Upon arriving in the hall of the old mansion, Heron stepped forward a pace or two before the old man, and placing his silver whistle to his lips, he blew one low and plaintive note.

Ogle well knew that that was not a call for general assistance, but merely one that required his presence.

"I'm here, Captain," he said, as he ascended the steps that led to the hall door.

"Is all well? I heard a pistol-shot."

"Oh, yes, Captain, all is well; but who the pistol-shot came from we hardly know. We took the two men on the coach-box quite easily by creeping to them over the roof, while they were frightening each other by accounts of how this place was haunted."

"That was well done."

"Yes, Captain; but hardly had we succeeded when there came from out the shadow of the trees yonder one pistol-shot. The bullet went through the panels of the coach. We searched the place, but could find no one."

"It was Jonathan Wild, without a doubt."

"Think you so, Captain? Would he be content with one shot?"

"Doubtless he would, for he had but one pistol left; and after giving such an alarm, he would fly from the spot as quickly as possible."

Captain Heron turned to the hall, and addressing Sir Dominick Browne, assured him that no danger of any kind would attend his coming forth.

Sir Dominick answered him in so weak and low a tone, that Heron was afraid he would never live to get to the forest.

"I cannot take him so far," he said in an undertone to Ogle.. "Castleneau House is much nearer; and surely he will be in safety there for a few hours. Where have you bestowed Wild's men?"

"They're tied to a tree, back to back. That is to say, as nearly back to back as a stout elm tree between them can enable them to get."

"We will leave them there, then. Let Atkins mount the coach-box. Bring me Daisy, and I will proceed at once to Castleneau House."

"What is that, Captain?" said Ogle, starting.

The faint, low, wailing sound of a bugle-call, which had a very military echo about it, came upon the ears of Heron and his band.

"Quick—quick, Ogle, and get the old man into the coach! A feeling of danger is growing over my mind; and I fancy we shall yet have work to do to-night."

"Not to-night, Captain; for see, the dawn is coming, and in half an hour it will be twilight."

"Stop—oh, stop!" cried Sir Dominick Browne. "Death may seize me; and I must tell you, dear Felix, a copy of the registry of old Barnes Church is kept at St. Paul's. It is an old custom of the place, for Barnes was once a chapelry of the ancient cathedral in Catholic times."

"That is good news," said Heron. "And as your memory serves you, Sir Dominick, you seem capable of doing me abundant service. Forward, my men—forward! That trumpet-call is in our rear as we go to London, therefore that would be my post. Forward at once!"

Captain Heron had mounted Daisy, and the whole band were on their horses. The coach had just started, and Captain Heron himself was only lingering for a moment to let the cavalcade get a little ahead of him, when a horseman spurred up to the spot.

"If the scoundrels are here," he cried, "I will soon stop their proceedings! Murder and robbery on the highway, indeed! Ah, here is one of them!"

Heron had made Daisy give two bounds along the roadway, so that he met this horseman before, in the dim obscurity of that early hour, he could see the coach or Heron's companions.

The horseman was in military costume, and

dim as the morning light was, and notwithstanding a faint white mist which seemed to be rolling onwards from the east before the rising sun, Heron could see that he was in the costume of a cavalry subaltern.

The mystery of the bugle sound was cleared up at once. A troop of light horse, probably from Hounslow, was upon the road, and it was more than probable that Jonathan Wild, after his flight from Sir Dominick's house, had fallen in with them.

The officer regarded Heron for a few moments in critical silence, and then he said sharply, "At all events, my fine fellow, I have caught you. My party are close at hand, so I think I'll make my glove acquainted with your collar until they come up."

"You're a subaltern, sir," said Heron.

"What of that?"

"Simply that if you have any ambition to command a troop, you will consult your safety, and get out of my way."

"You're an impertinent fellow; and as I always chastise insolence when I find it, I will begin to-day with you."

The officer drew his sword smartly enough and charged at Heron, but he was no match for either the skilful swordsmanship of Felix or the rapid evolutions of Daisy. The two weapons clashed together for a few seconds, and then Heron's sword descended on the shako of the officer, and he bent right down to his saddle-bow, and dropped his sabre. His horse took alarm, and galloped off with him at a furious pace towards the country.

"Fools will thrust their heads into danger!" said Heron, as he sheathed his sword. "On, Daisy —on!"

This little conflict, short and sharp as it was with the subaltern, had certainly not lasted five minutes, but no one can have failed to notice how long a distance can be traversed in such a space of time on a straight road by a party travelling at a tolerable pace.

A good half-mile was between Captain Heron and his band, but that was nothing to Daisy, if he chose to put her to speed, and he rapidly cleared the distance; but as he saw the coach in front of him, he became quite certain, from the peculiar sounds a considerable distance on the road behind, that he was pursued.

It might be the party of light horse, or it might be persons much less to be feared; but Heron was so determined not to compromise the safety of Sir Dominick Browne, that he made a rapid resolve, and riding up to Ogle, he gave his orders accordingly.

"Tell Atkins," he said, "to make his way alone with Sir Dominick to Lady Castleneau's house in Bloomsbury Fields. It is not at all likely he will meet with any interruption. Let him say that I will be there as speedily as possible. We are pursued, Ogle."

"So I thought, Captain."

"It is so; and we must throw our pursuers off the track of the old man, for they may be as much his foes as mine, since he has become so much associated with my affairs."

All this was promptly done as Captain Heron ordered, but he did not omit to ride to the side of the coach to speak a few words to old Sir Dominick to assure him of his safety.

"Dear old friend," he said, "you have but to be calm, and still, and content. You are on your road to Lady Castleneau's house, and you know well that she will afford you a ready and kindly welcome. There is no danger in reality, so do not conjure up any in imagination."

"Thanks, Felix — thanks, my dear boy!—a thousand thanks!"

"Now, forward, Atkins," added Heron, "to Lady Castleneau's at as good a pace as you can, without making it so quick an one as to excite suspicion."

"Trust me, Captain. All's well," said Atkins.

The coach went on its way again towards London by the high road, but Captain Heron halted with his band until the clatter of horses' hoofs on the road announced that, whoever they were in pursuit, another minute would bring them to the spot.

Then Heron cried out in a loud voice, "To the right—to the right! Take to the lanes, my men, and you baffle them!"

There was a long straggling by-road to the right, and down this Heron and his band went, with quite noise enough to let his pursuers see and hear it was no ruse to keep them off the high road, but that the lane was actually the route taken.

It was probable enough that Captain Heron and his band might have turned and made a good fight with the horsemen who were following him, but it was never any part of his policy or his wishes to invite a combat in which blood would probably be shed on both sides.

Brave as a second Bayard, Captain Heron was ever tender in inflicting injury. When pressed too hardly, he could and would defend himself, as we have often seen, and woe, then, to those who forced the necessity upon him.

It would seem that Heron and his band were better mounted than their pursuers, for without making any very extraordinary exertions the relative distances between them seemed to increase.

The by-road was a very long one, and it seemed gradually to wind away, and to incline towards the north-east of London; and after an hour's good trotting, with the occasional episode of a gallop for a mile or two, Heron drew rein, and called out to Ogle to know where they were.

"Why, Captain," said Ogle, "I was puzzled at first to know myself, for we have come by a road I have never yet walked, ridden, or driven over until to-day."

"And do you know it now?"

"If I am not mistaken, we are near to Finsbury Fields."

The sun by this time had fairly passed over the horizon, and long, slant rays of grey light were spreading far and wide through the misty air.

The moment Ogle mentioned Finsbury Fields, Captain Heron knew the place at once, and all the neighbourhood seemed familiar to him.

"We have baffled our pursuers," he said, "and are scarcely a mile from St. Paul's."

Ogle looked puzzled at the latter part of this speech, for he had not the slightest idea what his chief could want at St. Paul's.

But those words which old Sir Dominick Browne had uttered were still ringing in the ears of Heron, and he felt how much more serene would

C.F. SARGENT

be his repose, when he could venture to lie down to seek it, if he were satisfied a record of his mother's marriage existed in the archives of the old cathedral.

"Ogle," he said, "come hither. I would speak with you."

Ogle was all attention.

"I have reason to believe I shall find a record in the registry of St. Paul's of the first importance to me; and if it be there, I would like many witnesses to depose to the fact."

"To be sure, Captain. Take us all with you."

"I have thought of doing so; but the horses? What shall we do with them?"

"Why, don't you recollect, Captain, old Ford, the farrier, who lives by the back of Smithfield? We can trust him."

"True—true! Is he there still, think you?"

"Not a doubt of it. He drinks his two gallons of ale a day; and a man who can do that, you know, Captain, finds the world too pleasant to leave it in a hurry."

Heron smiled.

"And yet—and yet," he said, "I am so loth to part with Daisy, even for an hour. I used to feel she was in safety when Tom Ripon was in town, and took charge of her at his mother's, in Little Swallow Street; but since our last escapade there, when Mrs. Ripon would really have betrayed us to Jonathan Wild, I have not fancied the place."

"Moreover, it's burnt down," said Ogle.

"Entirely?"

"Oh, yes! And my wife tells me that Mrs. Ripon has gone to be pew-opener at a chapel in the neighbourhood, and puts up prayers for us all to be hung three times a-week."

Heron laughed.

"Ogle, we will trust old Ford, the farrier, in preference, then, to Mrs. Ripon."

"To be sure, Captain. But do you know what Tom is doing?"

"No. What?"

"Why, by begging, stealing, and borrowing, he's getting all the gunpowder he can into a bag, and he says he's going to town then, when he's got enough to lay a train, and blow up the Rev. Jedekiah Jobkins, who he says has led his mother astray. He means to put two pound in the pulpit, and have a good train, so that just at the moment when prayers are put up for our destruction, bang will go the reverend gentleman like a thirty-two pounder!"

"You must stop those tricks," said Heron, "or he will get himself into mischief. Let us away to Ford's farriery at once, for the morning is creeping on apace, and my Edith will be anxious."

Old Ford, the farrier, whose powerful recommendation seemed to be an unlimited capacity for drinking ale, and a strong affection for highwaymen, occupied an ancient smithy and farriery close to Smithfield.

It was with perfect exultation that he took charge of the horses of Captain Heron and his band.

"Ford," said Heron, "be careful, on your life. In leaving Daisy with you, even for half an hour, I leave half my existence with you; and I want you to make one promise."

"A dozen, Captain—a dozen!"

"No, one will suffice."

"Just let me get a drop of ale, and I will promise anything in the world."

"That's just it, Ford."

"What's it, Captain?"

"The ale. I want you to promise not to take a drop until I come back to you."

Ford looked rather rueful.

"How long will you be gone, do you suppose, Captain?"

"About an hour."

"Then, suppose we say one quart only?"

"No, not a drop! Give me your word, or I will not leave Daisy with you."

"You have it, Captain—you have it! I like to give in to the little prejudices of my friends. But bless you, Captain, you don't know what good ale does you. I eat my ale—I drink my ale—I sleep on my ale—wake on my ale!"

Ford was still expatiating on the excellence of his ale, when Heron and his men, on foot, left the smithy, and took their way towards St. Paul's.

The hour was still an early one, and when they reached the cathedral, it was quite a matter of doubt if it would be open; and, in fact, it would not have been so, but that a couple of decrepit old women were sweeping out the aisles.

So formidable a body of men as Captain Heron and his companions entering the sacred edifice produced quite a sensation in the minds of the two old charwomen, and after in vain protesting that the cathedral was not open to any one, they ran off for the beadle, who, as he happened to fill another parochial office as well, which necessitated his being up at that early hour, soon made his appearance.

"Clear out—clear out!" he cried. "It can't be—it mustn't be! Not till half-past nine o'clock, gentlemen—it can't be! and then it's twopence apiece. Two—four—six—eight—ten—twelve—fourteen—sixteen—eighteen—twenty—one and eightpence lost to the dean and chapter of St. Paul's! The world's coming to a end—the world's coming to a end!"

"This guinea——" said Captain Heron.

"This what?"

"Guinea!"

"The world goes on agin—the world goes on agin! Gentlemen, your humble servant, Phineas Umblebug, the beadle, is at your service."

"I want to consult the registry of the cathedral," said Captain Heron, as he handed the guinea to the beadle.

"To be sure, sir. This way—this way! Mr. Simmons trusts me with the key, and well he may. I'm 'sponsible, sir—I'm 'sponsible!"

"I do not doubt it," said Heron, as he followed the beadle towards the sacristy of St. Paul's.

CHAPTER CXLIX

CAPTAIN HERON AND HIS BAND ENCOUNTER GREAT DANGER IN ST. PAUL'S CATHEDRAL.

IT was with a beating heart that Heron followed the parish official to the beautiful apartment beneath the roof of the cathedral, in which was kept a large collection of archives of all kinds and descriptions, not only connected with St. Paul's itself, but many suburban churches and chapels with which it was connected.

What if, after all, he was there to find an authentic and authoritative record of his mother's marriage?

How confounding to Lord Warringdale and to Sir John Tarleton would be such a document! How pleasing to Edith—to Lady Castleneau—to the young and chivalrous Earl of Bridgewater, and all others who had interested themselves in his welfare, would be the proof of his mother's honour and his own high destiny.

"What's the year, sir?" said the beadle; "and what's the name?"

The registry was on a shelf, and it was strange that the moment Captain Heron entered the sacristy his eyes fell upon the back of a bulky volume, on which he read the words—

"Copy of registry of Barnes Chapelry, from 1750."

"There is the book," he said; "the name is Amelia Staunton. She was married to the then Earl of Warringdale, in the year——"

Captain Heron had just got that length, when the beadle dropped on all fours, and tried in that attitude to crawl out of the sacristy.

"What is the matter?" cried Heron.

"I couldn't help it—it wasn't me! Murder! it wasn't me! He put two blunderbusses, one in each ear, and sawed away at my throat with a notched knife, and then he tore out that very leaf of the registry your worship asks for."

"Who—who did that act?"

"Somebody——"

"But who? Name the villain—and yet my heart can guess!"

"I'm glad to hear that, your worship; for I have not the least idea myself of who it was. But the leaf's gone—that very leaf; and what makes it more provoking is, that on it was likewise the blessed registry of Martha Jennings and Enoch Claypole, both of this parish; and I lost a half-crown, as I'm a sinner, as last Tuesday was a week, all in consequence of it. Good morning, sir, if you please! I suppose you don't want any change? I've a large family, and two more expected."

Captain Heron clasped his hands.

"Foiled again!" he said,—"foiled again! I might have foreseen this, and my heart half foretold it. My enemies are alert and skilful. Be it so—be it so!"

"Secure the door!" cried a loud voice at this moment from the body of the cathedral.

Heron placed his hand upon his sword.

Ogle ran out of the sacristy, to see from whom this loud command had come; and right down the long aisle of the building he saw six or eight men in a group, who seemed just to have entered it, and one of whom was closing and barring the wicket gate.

A glance was enough for Ogle. He saw directly that these were some of Wild's men, who most probably had seen Captain Heron and his party pass the end of Newgate Street.

With them, too, was a man in the costume of a military officer, for there were epaulettes upon his shoulders; and even as Ogle looked, he saw that the party was joined by three or four more persons, whose rank in life was considerably higher than that of Jonathan Wild's bull-dogs.

Ogle darted into the sacristy again in a moment.

"Captain," he said, "our enemies are in St. Paul's."

"Ah! say you so? How many?"

"They certainly exceed us in number."

Heron drew his sword. A faint flush of excitement came across his countenance.

"Look to the priming of your pistols, my men," he said.

When the beadle heard these words, he made a rush, on his hands and knees, and got under a bench; and, in his agitation, he seized Ogle by the ankle, who, thinking some dog had made a grasp at him, kicked furiously.

Then one of Heron's men spoke quickly.

"Captain," he said, "I know all the ins and outs of the cathedral. Follow me, and I will lead you to the crypt, where they will scarcely find us. I hid there once myself for three days and nights, and not a soul could light upon me."

Heron bowed his head gently.

"Lead the way," he said. "I avoid a conflict while I can. Let the mischief be upon the head of those who force me to it. Lead the way. We will follow you, Number Four."

Taken as Captain Heron's men were, from all classes of society, and some indeed from various professional pursuits, it would not have been easy to start any particular subject on which any information was required without finding some one or other of them fully equal to the occasion.

Heron made no remark in regard to the mode by which Number Four had acquired his information concerning the crypt of St. Paul's.

It was sufficient for him that the man knew the necessary route to take, and it was fortunate, too, that there was another door which led from the sacristy in the direction contrary to that which would have brought Heron and his band in contact with their foes.

This door was locked, but that created but a trifling impediment, for among the band there were two or three men so expert at picking a lock, that it seemed as though doors flew open before them with all the facility that Aladdin's wicked pretended uncle made his way into the cavern of lustrous jewels by simply pronouncing the words, "Open, sesame."

There was a slight rustle of a skeleton-key in the lock of the door, and it swung open.

The beadle made no opposition, for he was in a state of mental and physical prostration after the hearty kicks he had received from Ogle, and was not at all inclined to provoke a contest with Captain Heron or with any of his comrades.

The men who had entered St. Paul's in such numbers, with the determination to capture the robbers of Epping Forest, lost much time by the extreme caution they took to be certain of their prey.

Had they not delayed to fasten the little wicket gate of the cathedral, Heron and his band would scarcely have had time to leave the sacristy by the small door opposite to that at which they had entered.

The officers and their assistants saw their mistake too late, but the moment they found their prey was escaping them, they rushed forward with speed, not, however, succeeding in reaching the sacristy door before the opposite one had been banged shut and locked on the other side.

The officers began furiously hammering at this door, and then they encountered another delay, which was as unexpected as it was tantalizing.

The beadle did not gather courage, but, popularly speaking, he lost his head, and fear took such possession of him that he knew not friends from foes, but was only conscious of the one idea that it was necessary for his safety that he should make his way out of the sacristy as speedily as possible.

The officers were quite unaware of his presence, hidden, as he was, beneath a bench; so that when he suddenly dashed out, with a roar like an infuriated ox, and plunged among their legs in a frantic effort to reach the door, he created no little confusion, and a general skirmish ensued, which ended in his being brutally seized and dragged to his feet, and belaboured with blows right and left.

"Murder! Fire! Watch! I'm a lost beetle!"

"Hold him fast!" cried one of the officers; "it's one of the rascals in disguise. Perhaps the Captain himself!"

"I ain't a captain! Murder! help! Mercy upon us, what's the matter?"

It took a very few seconds now to believe in the veritable beadledom of this individual, and then that exalted personage himself began to have a suspicion that he was making a mistake, and that, after all, he was among those who would support the authorities, instead of defying them.

"I know all about it now!" he cried; "I know all about it! I was knocked down, like a lamb at the sacrifice, and somebody seized me at the back of the neck, gentlemen, if you'll believe it, like a Thomas cat hold of a rat! But I see it now—I see it now!—oh, be joyful—I see it now! They've gone through that door, and it leads to the *crip*."

"Leads to the what?"

"The *crip*."

"I suppose he means the crypt," said one of the officers.

"Well, I said the *crip!* A *crip's* a *crip*, I suppose! Have I been the beetle of St. Paul's a matter of thirteen years and three-quarters, and don't know what a *crip* is? I tell you they've gone through that door to the *crip*, and they'll have nothing to do then but pull out some old rusty iron bars, and scramble over the graves of some respectable parishioners, and away they are like that!"

The beadle illustrated how Captain Heron and his band were to go away, by snapping his fingers with a loud crack so close to the nose of the chief officer, that that personage chose to think himself assaulted, and with a flat-handed blow on the top of the beadle's cocked hat sent it at once down to his chin.

The parochial authority being thus extinguished, stood in the middle of the floor and fought fearfully—that is, he struck out right and left at the empty air, while the officers, with nearly as much adroitness as Captain Heron's men could command, opened the door of the sacristy, which led by some circuitous passages to the crypt of the cathedral.

The beadle, by a sort of instinct, made his way out of the sacristy, and still believing himself encompassed by hosts of foes, he struck right and left, and forward, and now and then turning, dealt a heavy blow rearward, until he reached the door, which having been opened by two affrighted old women, who had been dusting the hassocks in the pews, he knocked them both down at once.

Then sallying out into St. Paul's Churchyard, an unfortunate charity boy was the next victim of the blind rage of the beadle.

But this charity boy had a companion, who, feeling for his friend, adopted an ingenious mode of stopping the career of the parochial official.

He placed himself on his hands and knees exactly in the path of the beadle, who flew over him at once, sliding along the pavement to a considerable distance, and finally bringing himself up head foremost against a post—a process which further aided to fix the official cocked hat on his head so firmly that it took the united efforts of two men to wrench it off.

But much graver events were happening in the interior of St. Paul's Cathedral, while the beadle was pursuing so tremendous a career on its outside.

Captain Heron felt the full danger which this unfortunate visit to the sacred building had involved him in.

Had he but secured the certificate of his mother's marriage, he would gladly have risked his life ten times over to have carried it off in safety; but he was now incurring a world of danger for the barren satisfaction of knowing that his enemies with indefatigable rancour had been there before him.

But his was not the mind to succumb to circumstances, or to allow danger to disturb his equanimity, and he gave his orders calmly and judiciously to his men.

"Let every one look to his pistols," he said; "a miss-fire may be death. But do not use your arms needlessly, if you can escape without them. Number Four, are you sure of your route?"

"Quite, Captain."

"Where are we now?"

"We shall have to pass through a small chapel, and then a room that in old times used to be called the 'vestment room.' A flight of steps will then lead us to the crypt."

"Can we escape from it when there?"

"Yes, Captain, if we have time. There are some dozen or more small barred windows to it, which look into the grave-yard of the cathedral, and from which it gets light and air. I will warrant the old iron bars are rusty enough by this time."

"Forward, then, quickly! If we have five minutes' time, we are safe. If less, we will fight, and let the mischief light upon the head of those who follow us."

"Do you hear, Captain?" said Ogle, in a low tone.

"What is it?"

"They've got open the door from the sacristy."

"Quick! Forward—forward!"

Captain Heron and his men had considerably the start of the officers, but still he felt that whenever he should have occasion to pause, a couple of minutes would bring them up to him and his men. It was hardly to be supposed that so short a space of time would suffice to remove the iron bars from one of the gratings leading into the cathedral-yard, even were they ever so rusty.

Heron drew his sword.

He felt that there was now no resource but a

CAPTAIN HERON SURRENDERS HIMSELF TO THE SAFE CUSTODY OF HIS FOLLOWERS.

Presented Gratis with No. 67 of the New Edition of Edith the Captive; or, the Robbers of Epping Forest.

EACH WEEK IS PRESENTED GRATIS A COLOURED ENGRAVING.

contest of life and death with the officers, who were resolved upon the capture of himself and band. The short flight of steps that led down to the crypt was gained, and the officers were yet some thirty paces behind.

Ogle flew to one of the gratings, and made a vigorous tug at an iron bar, which came away with far greater ease than he had expected, but the next one, from some local circumstance, was not so decayed, and resisted his efforts. There was no time for further exertion in that quarter, for the officers now, with a rush, entered the crypt, and one who headed them cried out, "Captain Felix Heron, we know you! We saw you and your men pass the end of Newgate Street. You cannot possibly escape, and you had better surrender while you can count upon good usage."

"I warn all men," cried Heron, "who interfere with me, that they do so at their own peril!"

"You are mad, Captain Heron," cried the chief officer—"you are mad! You are like a rat in a trap!"

"Rats turn at bay!" said Heron. "Beware their bite!"

"Forward, my men!" cried the officer, furiously. "Take them all, dead or alive. That's your orders—dead or alive!"

The officers were a pretty strong party, and perhaps, after all, they hardly thought Heron and his band would, in the heart of the City of London, make a death fight of it, so they rushed forward at once with considerable boldness, most of them with a pistol in one hand and a hanger in the other.

The battle in the crypt began, and such a battle as surely never before had awakened the echoes of that solemn and gloomy precinct of the old cathedral.

There was the flash of pistols and the clash of swords—the cries and shouts of wounded and passionate men. Heron was surrounded by many foes, but several of the officers seemed exceedingly anxious to take him alive.

The only man who did not much interfere in the contest was Ogle; and, amid all the roar and riot of the fight, the measured clank of his sword against the iron bars of one of the gratings might have been heard.

But there was soon another sound, which overrode all before it.

With a yell, like that of some wild beast broke loose, a man leaped right down the flight of steps into the crypt.

He held a pistol in each hand; and, as he alighted in the midst of the combatants, he roared out, "Down with them!—down with them! Kill them all! I'm Jonathan Wild!"

Ogle heard this cry, and he immediately ceased his clanking noise against the iron bars, and sprung up upon a pile of wood which was behind one of the columns, from which elevated position he could command a good view of the whole scene of conflict.

At that moment Wild levelled both his pistols in the direction of Captain Heron, and fired.

Ogle drew a pistol from his breast-pocket, and through the smoke had, what he thought, a capital shot at Jonathan; but whether the shot took effect or not, he could not tell, for some suspended lights that had been burning in the crypt

suddenly fell—no doubt the concussion of the air caused by the firing produced this result; but in an instant, instead of being tolerably lighted, a dim, grey twilight only reigned in the place.

Ogle saw the advantage that this sudden catastrophe might produce to Captain Heron and his band. One other blow at the bar he had been at work upon sent it from its socket, and there was now a clear opening into the cathedral yard.

A sort of panic seemed to have taken possession of the officers, and before they had recovered from it, Ogle had darted like an eel through the opening, and then, crouching low down to it, he called out, "This way, hawks and herons—this way!"

His comrades needed no second invitation; and the celerity and speed with which they left the crypt was very much aided by Ogle from the outside, who, with his great strength, dragged them through as though they had been so many children.

Captain Heron came last; and his first cry was, "Are we all here?"

"All!" said Ogle, as he ran his eye rapidly over the group. Several, however, were rather badly hurt.

All this was the work of a minute; and then the officers began to recover from the stupor that had come over them at all the fierce resistance that had been made; and seeing their prey escaping before their eyes, and all their hopes of reward vanishing into thin air, they got desperate and vindictive, and made a rush to the opening from the crypt into the cathedral yard.

But Ogle stood there with his uplifted hanger, and, in a voice of great composure, he said, "Who'll put his head through first? Off it goes to a certainty!"

The officers drew back at this threat, for as Ogle stood just outside the grating, decapitation, if he so chose it, seemed to be the easiest thing in the world.

"That will do," said Ogle. "Now, Captain, be off, and I'll keep these fellows at bay. One man is enough for that."

"No," said Captain Heron; "we will all go together, or all stay. But I have a plan that will release you. Pick up some of these flat gravestones—hoist with a will, comrades, you that are not hurt, and place them against the grating. Two or three will suffice. It will need more power than they can muster from within to dislodge them."

This plan of proceeding was so obviously good, that Captain Heron's men set about it at once with energy, so that Ogle was, in a few moments, relieved from his post, and the officers fairly blocked into the crypt in that direction.

"Now," said Heron, "we have not a moment to lose, for they will run round, and get out into the churchyard by the front door of the cathedral, and give an alarm, so that we shall have to fight our way through a street mob. Follow me quickly."

Fortunately for Heron and his men, one of the numerous gates in the heavy iron railing which surrounds the cathedral court was open, and they sallied out close to Doctors' Commons.

"Now," said Heron, "take me into custody; and recollect, if we meet any persons inclined to interfere with us, I am the celebrated highwayman, Captain Heron, and you are officers. Collar me at once, Ogle, and let us proceed to Ford's smithy as quickly as we can."

"That's the very thing," said Ogle; "and will get us along nicely."

There was quite a mob of people in St. Paul's Churchyard, for the beadle, when rescued from what might be called the custody of his official cocked hat, had explained to an admiring throng that St. Paul's was full of highwaymen, and he had been nearly killed in trying to take twelve of them into custody with his own hands.

When the people, therefore, saw Captain Heron apparently in the custody of Ogle, who was flourishing one of those small brass constable's staves, which he was never without, they at once raised a shout of gratification, and a hundred voices, at least, cried out, "He's caught! he's caught!"

The beadle was in ecstacies. Some one had brought him his official staff of office, with a gilt ball at the end of it, and a cross above that, and, placing himself at once in a heroic attitude, he made a charge at Heron, which might have been serious, if Ogle had not warded off the weapon, and at the same time put out his foot, which brought the beadle with an alarming crash to the ground.

"Clear the way—clear the way!" said Ogle, as he walked deliberately over the beadle's back, an example which was followed by all Captain Heron's men. "Clear the way! It's a thousand pounds reward; and we've caught one of the most notorious highwaymen in the world! Clear the way—clear the way!"

After this process, the beadle was wrecked entirely, and made no further efforts; he only, in a weak voice, suggested that brandy-and-water would be acceptable, coupled with his firm belief that the world and the City of London were at an end.

Ogle kept a most anxious eye, and so did Captain Heron, upon the front door of St. Paul's, from which they expected to see, at any moment, the officers issue; and so they did at length, but they were just too late, for Heron and his men had turned the corner into Newgate Street, and the officers could not make out what the shouting and huzzaing was about, for the mob was cheering Ogle for his real or supposed valour in capturing so desperate a malefactor.

In this manner Captain Heron and his band made their way towards Ford's smithy, their great object being to get possession of their horses, after which they would have no fear of any pursuit that might be made against them.

The greatest danger now was in passing Jonathan Wild's house, in Newgate Street, and both Ogle and Heron regretted that they had come that way; for although the deception that was being practised might pass very well with ordinary people in the street, Jonathan Wild's bulldogs and janissaries were not so likely to be deceived.

In fact, the huge, bulky form of Blueskin was observable upon the very doorsteps—but, fortunately, he was too besotted with beer to be fully master of his senses, and he only glared at the tumultuous sort of mob that passed the door with stupid and senseless curiosity.

Ogle still held Captain Heron by the collar as they passed up Giltspur Street. The people then began to wonder where he was taking his prisoner; for after passing Wild's house, and leaving Newgate to the left, and then passing the Compter, in Giltspur Street, they were quite at fault as to any other place of security for the great highwayman. Five minutes more, however, brought them to Ford's smithy, and as Heron had whispered to one of his men to run on before and get the horses out, there was no delay, and as they reached the spot Daisy and the rest of the horses could be seen grouped about the door of the smithy.

"We are safe," said Ogle.

"I think so," replied Heron.

At this moment there came a roaring sound, swelling by degrees into a tumultuous shout, of more than a thousand voices. The officers were beginning to make themselves understood by the people, and a new host of pursuers would soon have been upon the track of Heron and his band.

Another moment, though, and they had mounted.

Then Heron turned and lifted his hat, and, with a smile, bowed to the crowd.

"Ladies and gentlemen," he said, "I wish you good day. You will find me at Epping Forest, if you wish particularly to see me, along with my friends and comrades here, who have had me in custody from St. Paul's."

At this moment, yelling and fighting with the crowd at the corner of Giltspur Street, appeared Jonathan Wild.

But Heron was off, and in a quarter of an hour the City Road was left behind them, and they were galloping through the then green lanes of Hoxton.

CHAPTER CL.

LORD WARRINGDALE CONSULTS HIS LEGAL ADVISER.

WHILE these important events were occurring to Captain Heron, and while, bit by bit, he was accumulating that evidence so essential to the substantiation of his just claims, Lord Warringdale began to sink into a state of despondency and despair.

That vicious and unscrupulous personage could not but see that the conflict between him and Heron would long since have been terminated, but that the latter, with chivalric generosity, never forgot the relationship that subsisted between them.

And now, as Lord Warringdale sat in his chambers in St. James's Street, reflecting over the events of the past year, the question could not but obtrude itself upon his notice of how he had succeeded in the advancement of his designs.

Unscrupulous and clever to a certain extent, utterly regardless of human feeling and even of human life—what had he achieved?

Nothing but danger and disaster to himself.

Indeed, there was a notable circumstance that had arisen and grown out of the exertions he had made—which was, that he found himself largely in the debt of Jonathan Wild.

It is strictly true that when Lord Warringdale

gave Wild acknowledgments for large sums of money, to be paid when he had fairly crushed all opposition and was fairly inducted into the Whitcombe estates, he intended to settle those claims in a peculiar fashion, viz., by the death of Wild.

But had he not made one attempt in that direction, and totally failed? Certainly he had.

Lord Warringdale found that the cunning and crafty thief taker was by no means so easy a prey as the unfortunate Earl of Bridgewater, in Paddock Hill Lane.

And so a kind of superstitious dread and undue estimate of Wild's powers of resistance began to come over Lord Warringdale.

He felt as though he were enveloped in the meshes of some net from which he might struggle to free himself in vain.

What was he to do?

Once, and once only, the idea came across him of abandoning the struggle and throwing himself upon the mercy of his half-brother, Felix Heron; and a sensation almost of peace and comfort came over him along with the idea.

But there were many objections to such a course. He was already deep in crime. The stain of murder was upon his soul; and what a world of persecution he might look forward to from Jonathan Wild, for it could hardly be expected that Felix Heron would impoverish the Whitcombe estates for the purpose of clearing Lord Warringdale's liabilities to the infamous Jonathan.

"No," he said, as he paced his room with anxious strides—"no! That will never do! I must fight the affair out to the last! Some lucky chance may deprive Felix Heron of life, and then I am safe! I have tried to kill him, but he seems to bear a charmed life, and ever to escape me; and surely, surely Wild is mortal! Surely there are bullets and there is steel to lay him low! Oh, if those two men were but dead! I should breathe again—sleep again—smile again!"

So delightful did the anticipation of this pleasant state of things appear to Lord Warringdale, that he almost smiled in expectation; but those little gleams of satisfaction were like the fleeting glimpses of sunshine on a winter's day—but momentarily lighting up a landscape, to leave it by contrast more gloomy than before.

And there was one want now which pressed itself heavily upon the mind of Lord Warringdale.

It was the want of human sympathy.

For good and for evil, it is an impulse of humanity to seek association—to yearn for some one with whom to consult, advise, and plan.

Jonathan Wild had to a certain extent filled up the void for a time in the mind of Lord Warringdale; but now, with his enormous claims against him, he assumed the aspect of a foe.

"I must speak to some one," said Warringdale. "I must make a whole or a half confidence somewhere. It requires the mind of a spectator of important events to take a calm and just view of them. The actors dress them up in the colours of imagination, and see all things through the medium of their own passions. I will go again to that attorney in the Temple who has professed a willingness to assist me. I will seek him and see if I can pit his subtle art against the villany of Jonathan Wild."

It was quite a relief to Lord Warringdale when he had made up his mind to some course; and he went his way at once to the Temple in search of the person whom, it will be recollected, had endeavoured to make a profit of Captain Heron, and then to betray him.

Lord Warringdale thought it fortunate that, immediately upon turning into the buildings of the ancient Temple, he encountered the very man he sought.

Addressing him by his name eagerly, he told him he came to consult him about important matters.

The attorney smiled in a peculiar manner.

"Your lordship," he said, "will be pleased to name me John Smith for the future."

"But that is not your name."

"Oh, no! I've had a difference with the Lord Chancellor about some points of legal practice, and he has, in a very coarse manner, requested me to withdraw my name from the roll of attorneys; but there are no less than one hundred and thirty-three John Smiths in the law in London, so I've adopted that name, and still continue to practise, leaving the Chancellor to discover, if he can, that I am not one of the John Smiths on the roll."

"It is ingenious," said Warringdale.

"I flatter myself it is successful. His lordship was very wrong to set his talent against mine. I have, however, removed from the Temple. I hope that my chambers in Essex Street will be honoured by your lordship's presence."

"I will accompany you at once; and I doubt not but I shall be able to tell you a tale that will interest you, and at the same time put money in your pocket."

"At once, my lord?"

"Oh, yes, I will tell you at once!"

"But the money?"

"So soon as I am fairly inducted into the estates of Whitcombe there will be no want of funds."

The attorney looked gloomy.

"My Lord Warringdale," he said, "I've heard much of your affairs of late. It is rumoured that a petition of right has been presented to the King, and that the present Earl of Bridgewater, who is on the committee of the Privy Council for such matters, takes a warm interest in a certain party."

"You mean Captain Heron, the highwayman."

"I do."

"Let us come into your chambers, and I will talk to you more of this. The street is not a proper place. I am in a sea of troubles; or rather, I am like a ship that needs helping into port; and those who succeed in doing so, will have a large claim for salvage. You understand me?"

"Follow me, then, my lord. There is no harm in talking the thing over; but if your lordship insists on likening yourself to a ship, I must confess the idea of a wreck rises up in my mind, and the port seems a long way off."

Warringdale bit his lips, and uttered a half groan; for he was very much of the opinion of the lawyer.

He followed him, however, to a gloomy set of chambers at the lower end of Essex Street, near to the river. The house had once been a noble residence, but the tide of fashion had set from that quarter, and it was suffered to fall much into decay. The rooms were large and grand-looking, and but ill-assorted with the few articles of modern furniture placed in them. The ceilings were richly ornamented, and the chimney-pieces had at one time been costly subjects of art, although now much defaced and injured.

Lord Warringdale looked about him with some curiosity, which Mr. Smith, as he chose to call himself, observing, he remarked, "This is a spacious lodging, my lord. It was the house of the young Lord Moffat, who, having some sixteen thousand a-year, was smitten with the idea of living to the extent of thirty-two. He is now in the Fleet, as his peerage is not an English one. I encountered him accidentally on a visit there; and he gave me the key of this house as the only and last possession left him."

"But why give it to you?" said Warringdale.

"It was to sell it for him, brick by brick and stone by stone, if in no other way. So here I am, waiting a purchaser. Now, my lord, be seated!"

The suite of rooms in the occupation of John Smith at Moffat House consisted of three apartments; but it was only in the outer one that so discrepant an aspect was presented by a few mean modern chairs and tables, the property of the attorney. The other two rooms had some of their ancient furniture in them. Huge old settees, with deep fringe, and multitudes of brass-headed nails—high-backed chairs, as comfortable as they could possibly be—oaken tables of great size and strength—very ancient tapestried carpets, leaving some six feet round the flooring, which had at one time been waxed and polished to excess;—these, and such-like articles, made up the furnishing of the _____ and the other one. The third apartment had in it one of those huge canopied beds, with a plume of feathers at the corner of each post; and it was into the second apartment that the attorney conducted Lord Warringdale.

A smouldering wood fire burnt upon the hearth.

"Be seated, my lord," said the attorney, as he pulled forward a chair covered with faded Utrecht velvet,—"be seated, my lord. We may yet see our way out of these difficulties."

"Heaven send we——No, I mean I hope we may, let the aid come from where it will."

"You're right, my lord. I fancy the assistance your lordship wants is more likely to come from the other place."

"It will be a relief to me to consult you," said Warringdale, drawing a long breath, and gazing at the embers of the fire.

"I'm all attention."

"You know that this Felix Heron claims to be heir-at-law to the titles and estates of Whitcombe, on account of what he states was the marriage of my father with his mother, Amelia Staunton. You, who acted for some time as solicitor to the late Earl of Whitcombe, must be aware of these facts."

"I am. The boy was brought up by Sir Dominick Browne, and still, while quite a boy, he got some inkling of the real state of the case, and came to me to know if, among the papers and documents I had in connexion with the family, there was anything which would substantiate the claim."

"Ah!" said Warringdale. "I know it."

"He was young, ardent, enthusiastic, and had no knowledge of the world. So when I told him a large sum must be placed in my hands before I could help him, I believe he took his first idea of going upon the road to procure it."

"Confound him! Another man on such enterprises would have had a bullet in his brain long since; but he escapes all dangers, and goes scathless through perils that should take a hundred lives."

"So it seems—so it seems! You will recollect, then, my lord, that I communicated with you, but you soon chose another confidant."

"No; I always trusted you."

"But ceased to employ me. You thought Jonathan Wild would go a quicker way to work, and that, in his character of a detected highwayman, Felix Heron would be put out of the world; but that has failed."

"It has failed," murmured Lord Warringdale, —"it has worse than failed; for in its failure it has brought circumstances to light which have nearly destroyed me. And then again the unfortunate complication of circumstances that brought Felix Heron into communication with Edith Tarleton upset all my plans."

"Very probably," said the lawyer. "And now, my lord, I have the honour to await your instructions."

"No—advise me. I have no instructions to give you. But if the knot of these difficulties could be cut asunder by two deaths——"

"Two deaths?"

"I have said two."

"But formerly it was but one. Felix Heron no more, there can be no opposition to you possessing yourself of the title and estates of Whitcombe."

Lord Warringdale spoke now in a low tone, as if he were afraid the very walls would overhear him.

"Jonathan Wild," he said, "under pretence of ridding me of Felix Heron by death, has procured from me acknowledgments, chargeable upon the Whitcombe estates, to the extent of nearly forty thousand pounds."

"Then he is number two?"

"His last sigh would be a receipt in full."

"Business," said the lawyer, crossing one leg over the other,—"business is always well conducted between principals, with one proviso."

"What is that?"

"That they are candid towards each other."

"I am candid."

"Speak out, then! What do you want me to do?"

"I want you, if you can, to rid me of Captain Felix Heron, as he calls himself, and Jonathan Wild."

"And the Bishop of Worcester?" said the attorney.

Warringdale turned ghastly pale.

"Why do you mention him?"

"Because, while a poor clergyman, and strongly under the influence of your father, the late Earl of Whitcombe, he married Amelia Staunton to him in Barnes Church, in Surrey. He has kept the secret well, and your father's political influence was sufficient to run him through all the grades of ecclesiastical dignity until he seated him in a bishop's chair."

"And surely he will keep the secret still?" gasped Lord Warringdale.

"Possibly."

"Do you doubt it? Can you doubt it?"

"Most certainly I do. Your father is no more —all motive for keeping the secret has passed away—the easiest thing for the Bishop to do would be to speak the truth. That cannot harm him; while to side with you, and to be discovered as having done so to the detriment of innocent people, would be his destruction, and break down the whole edifice of his existence."

A demoniac look came over the face of Lord Warringdale.

"I care not!" he cried with fierceness. "If fifty lives stood in my way, I would clear them from my path. I am as one now who passes through a wood, or crosses some dangerous ravine; there is as much, if not more, danger in retreating as in advancing."

The lawyer drew a piece of paper towards him, and began to write.

"You are never so mad," said Warringdale, "as to take notes of a conversation like this?"

No. 68.—EDITH.

"Certainly not," said Mr. Smith; "but it assists the mind to do as I am about to do. We will signify the Whitcombe title and estates by this mark."

"What then?"

"Here are three lines which bar the way, and by this other mark we signify your lordship. Now, the three lines separate the two marks one from the other, and they want to meet; that is to say, your lordship and the estates of Whitcombe. It looks as though you could go round the lines, and so reach the mark representing the estates, but then your lordship faces the lines which stand threateningly before you."

"What then?" said Warringdale.

The lawyer took a penknife in his hand, and began to erase one of the lines.

"You will have to scrape them out!" he said.

Lord Warringdale placed his hand upon the paper, as he said in a low tone, "There is nothing in the world I so much desire. Those lines represent Felix Heron, Jonathan Wild, and the Bishop of Worcester?"

The lawyer nodded.

"My dear friend," added Warringdale, "scrape them out, and name your own reward."

"Jonathan Wild has named his, my lord, and he becomes one of these lines to be scraped out. I have no ambition to make a fourth; so I will take so reasonable a compensation that your lordship will not think it worth your while to put me out of the world to avoid its payment."

"You are a clever man, Smith, and have given me more hope than I have had for many a day. Will a bond for ten thousand pounds content you, payable on the day I take my first seat in the House of Peers?"

"Entirely."

"Then that is agreed. I leave the affair entirely in your hands. Do with it what you can."

"But your lordship must assist."

"Ah, indeed!"

"Yes; but in no way to place you in any personal danger. I must be careful of the man who is to pay me ten thousand pounds on the day he takes his seat in the House of Peers as the Earl of Whitcombe. But still I say your lordship must assist, and the first person to be got rid of is the Bishop of Worcester."

Lord Warringdale looked terrified.

"I cannot assist you in that," he said. "I do not see how I can assist you in that."

"It is not with regard to the Bishop that I should require any aid from your lordship; but with the next person on the list."

"And that?"

"That is Captain Heron."

"Be it so—be it so!"

"Does your lordship know where he is to be found?"

"Perfectly well. He has made his home in Epping Forest; but so well contrived and secret is that home, that although several attacks have been made upon the place in force, he and his band, when hard pressed, seem to disappear, as if they had the power of diving down even among the roots of the old trees, and there waiting underground until their pursuers and enemies had left the spot."

"We shall not need to fathom that mystery, although it might be done. I shall want your lordship to go alone to Epping Forest, and there to seek out your half-brother, Felix Heron. I shall want you then to tell him that you repent of all the past, and are sick to the very soul of the fraternal contest. Tell him his petition of right, which you have spoken to me of, is looked upon favourably by the King and Council, and that you will put an end to all further trouble upon the matter, by introducing him at the next levee as your elder brother. Get him then to come to town on that proposition, and I will take care that he don't leave it in life. Leave the rest to me, and be assured all will go well."

"I can hardly think it possible that, after what has passed, he will fall into such a snare."

"He will have a thousand suspicions, which you can only set at rest in one way."

"What magical way is that?"

"By obstinately remaining with him, and therefore showing him that you are not in communication with his enemies."

"I will try it—I will try it. It is strange that some idea of the sort came over my own mind only a short time since; but then remains Jonathan Wild to be disposed of."

"I think you may leave him to me. I will furnish you a good account of him."

"Be it so—be it so. I feel wonderfully hopeful. I know well that I run no danger myself in visiting Felix, for he has some absurd and romantic notion about us being brothers, which prevents him aiming at my life."

Lord Warringdale rose to leave Moffat House.

"When shall we meet again?" he said.

"To-morrow, when I shall have some news to give you of the Bishop. Be here in the dusk of the evening, my lord, and knock thrice at the outer door."

"I will—I will! And if all this succeeds, and the weight of care that at present oppresses me passes away, I will not stop at ten thousand pounds to requite such excellent service."

Lord Warringdale left the chambers in Essex Street; and in a few minutes afterwards Mr. John Smith, as he called himself, with an old faded great-coat about him, walked up Essex Street to the Strand.

CHAPTER CLI.

CAPTAIN HERON PAYS ANOTHER FLYING VISIT TO LONDON.

AFTER the adventures he had gone through in connexion with Sir Dominick Browne, and the serious peril he had encountered in the crypt of old St. Paul's, Heron was most anxious to reach his verdant and beautiful home in Epping Forest.

The varied excitements he had gone through during the protracted contest with Jonathan Wild and his myrmidons had sufficed, for a time, to fill up his mind, so that his thoughts strayed not so exclusively to the glades of Epping Forest, and the hidden intricacies of Hinchcliffe Manor.

But now that he had baffled his foes—now that he was free, and, mounted on his gallant Daisy, felt the open breeze of the country playing upon his cheek, he began to count the hours that he had been absent from Edith.

It was not possible that his comrades could keep pace with Daisy, but as he was most anxious to proceed, he paused for a few moments on the brow of a hill overlooking Edmonton, and waited until Ogle came up to him.

"Ogle," he said, "I will ride in advance. Daisy seems to be fresh, and inclined for a gallop. There is no occasion to distress any of your horses, and it is my particular wish that you should not engage in any adventure on the road, if it can be avoided."

"Trust us for that, Captain. We shall be half an hour behind you,—although, for my part, I never like you to go alone back to Epping Forest."

"Why not, Ogle?"

"Why, one never knows what may have happened in twelve hours."

"Do not rouse up imaginary fears, Ogle, for

you know there is one dearer to me there than life itself."

"Nay, Captain, I have not forgotten; but I only meant that if you would let me ride on with you, I should be all the better pleased."

"No, no, Ogle. You know that I can place confidence in you. The men will be getting into some scrape without a leader. Do not hurry; I shall be safe enough."

The fact was, however, the words of Ogle had raised a presentiment of evil in the mind of Captain Heron, and he became haunted by a thousand fears for the safety of Edith.

Daisy seemed to partake of the ill-defined alarm which was in the mind of her master, and she flew along like the wind in the direction of those leafy coverts which had been her and his home for so long.

But we must precede Captain Heron to Epping Forest, in order to detail certain events which took place there prior to his arrival.

When Edith, on the preceding evening, could no longer hear the footsteps of Daisy upon the verdant turf, and felt assured that many hours must elapse before she could look upon the face of Felix Heron again, a feeling of great depression came over her.

It seemed to her, as the evening deepened into night, that the forest had never looked so gloomy, and as the wind sighed a requiem among the tall tree-tops, she thought the sound had never been before so mournful.

Soon, however, Edith found a cause for this unwonted depression of spirits.

In those deep forest recesses, where the phenomenon of nature take the place of the artificialities of city existence, the mind is more easily acted upon by external influences; and after Felix Heron had been gone for about an hour, Edith became aware that some abnormal condition of the elements had ensued, for a sharp flash of lightning shot over the forest, casting a lurid gleam of brightness into its deepest recesses.

For a moment the foliage gleamed and glittered with that peculiar metallic tint which artificial light lends to it, and then the darkness seemed to drop down among the old trees with tenfold gloom.

There was a pause for about half a minute, and then came the hoarse rattle of distant thunder.

"Ah," said Edith, "it was the coming storm that sat so heavily upon my heart."

Short as had been Edith's residence in Epping Forest, she had become tolerably well acquainted, under the tuition of Felix, with some of the mysterious narrow channels among the brushwood which led to the old ruins and foundations of Hinchcliffe.

When this storm, however, began, she was in one of the forest glades, and after gazing about her for a few moments, as if uncertain which course to take, she was startled by a second flash of lightning, much more vivid than the former.

The interval of space between the lightning and thunder was much less.

"The trees bring danger in storms," said Edith. "I will seek shelter."

"So will I!" said a voice.

Edith uttered a cry of alarm, as, after a rustling of branches overhead, some light, small object dropped from a tree on to the green sward a few paces from her.

"It's only me," said Tom Ripon. "I told the Captain I'd keep good watch while he was gone; and as the only tree in our shop in Swallow Street is a boot-tree, it is such rare fun to get up into one of these big ones, all among the birds' nests; and I like it above all things. Good gracious! what's that?"

A sharp pattering sound among the leaves gave the first indications of a heavy down-pour of rain.

"Come, Lady Edith," said Tom; "you'll soon get wet through if you don't find shelter; and I don't know that an umbrella would be much good—though that's neither here nor there, as we've not got one."

"You quite terrified me, Tom," said Edith. "But I am glad to see you here, for the darkness is becoming so great, that I fear I should scarcely find my way among the intricacies of the bushes."

"This way, then," cried Tom. "Bless you, I know every in and out of the old forest as well as possible! I don't mean to say, however, Lady Edith, that you could glide about the wood in the manner that I do."

"Why not, Tom?"

"Because, you see, Lady Edith, we men don't take up so much room as ladies. But this is the way; they're only nut-bushes, and won't scratch. I'll clear away the branches; though Ogle says I mustn't, because that, he says, will be making tracks to the old foundations of the Priory and Manor House."

"There is reason in that, Tom."

"Very likely, Lady Edith. But only listen to the rain!"

Some heavily-charged cloud was evidently discharging a swift and pelting shower over Epping Forest. For a few seconds the leaves of the old trees warded off the rapidly-falling rain, but soon they only acted as so many conductors to the water, which poured from the branches in little spouts; and had not Tom and Edith soon found a shelter in one of the cavernous recesses of the old Priory, they must have endured as much from the storm as though they had remained in the open glade of the forest.

We have before remarked that the old foundations of what had once been an ancient priory, and then, over a limited portion of the space, a manor house, extended for a considerable distance beneath the surface of the forest.

Various entrances had been contrived by Captain Heron and his band into these foundations, and such entrances were so artfully concealed by intricate, zigzag, narrow paths, and thick and apparently impervious brushwood, that no one without a clue to them would think of forcing his way into what looked like impenetrable coverts.

The only persons now inhabiting those ruins were Edith, Mrs Ogle, and Tom Ripon.

At the outskirts of the wood the usual scouts were posted, so that, in an ordinary way, no person could penetrate into the forest glade without being noticed by one or other of Captain Heron's sentinels.

It so happened, however, that just at the moment Tom Ripon and Edith succeeded in gaining the entrance of one of the cavernous recesses, they heard the sharp and sudden sound of a shot fired in the forest.

"What is that ?" cried Edith.

"A bullet for somebody," said Tom.

"Then it's for Ogle," cried Mrs. Ogle, as she started forward. "I dreamt last night of black-beetles and white mice, and that means a death in the family."

"Hush, female !" said Tom. "Let a man listen !"

"Why, you little wretched imp," said Mrs. Ogle ; "if you call me a female again I'll skin you !"

"Now, now !" said Tom ; "don't let men be interrupted in their duty by women's tongues. There's something amiss in the forest, and, as Captain Felix Heron is not here, Captain Thomas Ripon takes the command !"

"The end of the world's coming," said Mrs. Ogle, "when infants talk like grown people, and call themselves captains."

Edith was more alarmed than she permitted either Mrs. Ogle or Tom Ripon to perceive, and she made a determination at once to go into the forest, and ascertain if her own senses would serve her amid its sylvan solitudes sufficiently acutely to enable her to come to a conclusion if there were strangers at hand.

Tom divined her intention.

"No, no, Lady Edith !" he said ; "let me go. Indeed, I shall go safer. I'm sorry Jack Sheppard would go to London, for he is a capital fellow for a scout. He's just like an eel, is Jack Sheppard ; and then he jumps like a frog. But I'll go out and see what's amiss."

"I'm a widow !" said Mrs. Ogle,—"I'm sure I'm a widow ! I always thought I should be, and have told Ogle so a thousand times ; but he's the most obstinate man in the world, and comes back safe and sound when you least expect him. However, I believe, when you've dreamed twice of blackbeetles and white mice, it's a settled thing. Heigho ! Mr. Atkins is a fine man ! '

Tom made his way out into the darkness of the wood, and Mrs. Ogle adjusted a small hand-lamp, when, with a leap which certainly would not have disgraced Jack Sheppard, Tom came back again into the somewhat gloomy vault to which he had conducted Edith.

Tom's leap, however, had a special purpose in it, for he alighted full upon Mrs. Ogle, and dashed out the lamp within an instant after it had been lighted.

Mrs. Ogle opened her mouth to utter a scream, but Tom had in one hand a bundle of short grass, which he immediately crammed between her teeth, and the scream died away in an odd, stifled sound.

"Hiss ! hiss !" said Tom. "Be quiet !"

"Is it a bombshell ?" said Mrs. Ogle.

"What has happened ?" said Edith.

"There's men in the wood—there's men in the wood !"

"Who's afraid !" said Mrs. Ogle. " I never was afraid of the men in my life !"

"Silence ! Hiss ! hiss !"

"Don't be imitating a snake in that kind of way ! Who is it, and what is it ? I haven't dreamt about blackbeetles and white mice running about like coach-horses, for nothing ! Merciful providence ! what's that ?"

"Me !" said Tom.

"But you are holding my ankle."

"I know it," said Tom. "You won't be quiet ? Sit down, do !"

A sudden jerk at the ankle obliged Mrs. Ogle to sit down rapidly in the vault ; and then Tom turned to Edith, saying, "Having quieted this female, Lady Edith, I'm sorry to say there's a party of at least twenty men in the wood."

"It is Felix, perhaps."

"Oh, dear, no ! We've not so strong a party as that ; besides, I hooted twice like an owl, and there was no answer."

"Hush !" said Edith. "I hear sounds !"

They held their breath in the intensity of their listening.

There was a crashing and crackling among the bushes, and then a voice, that was completely strange to Edith, cried out, "We are too strong a party for concealment ; let everything be done by force. Light your links, and search the forest well through. Capture whoever opposes you, and be assured your reward is certain, and will be paid with no niggard hand by Sir John Tarleton."

"My father ?" faltered Edith.

"Her father ?" gasped Mrs. Ogle.

"The old 'un," said Tom.

"Hush—oh, hush !"

"Let me advise, my lord," cried another voice. "Offer a hundred pounds reward to every one of the highwayman's men who chooses to join our party."

"Very well ; be it so. I offer it, and will see it paid."

"Who can that be ?" whispered Edith to Tom. "It is not the voice of Warringdale."

Tom shook his head, but as Edith could not see that movement in the dark, she spoke to him again.

"Do you know the voice, Tom Ripon ?"

"No, Lady Edith ; but I feel quite certain of one thing, and that is, that somebody's crawling up here as close as possible among the bushes."

"We are lost."

"Not at all ; only don't speak, but listen."

The rain, which had ceased for a few moments, now came down with a rushing sound, and the wind howled among the tree-tops for a few seconds in a manner to overcome and obliterate to the most sensitive hearing any other sounds.

But the storm was of that fitful and squally character, that every now and then there would come a profound lull, during which a stillness and silence that was almost preternatural pervaded the forest.

It was during one of these lulls in the storm that Edith could distinctly hear a low rustling sound, and now and then the crack of some slender branch among the brushwood and bushes.

"You hear ?" she whispered to Tom.

"Yes, but there's lots of time to get away. This is only the beginning of the old ruins, and they're full of hiding places."

"But how can we see our way ?"

"Oh, I know all about that, Lady Edith. Trust to me ; but we must get rid of this fellow, who-ever he is, who is making his way through the bushes."

"How can that be done ?"

"I mean to try it. Wait here a moment, and

LORD WARRINGDALE ENGAGES THE SERVICES OF A FRESH CONFEDERATE.

Presented Gratis with No. 68, of the New Edition with the Captive; or, the Robbers of Epping Forest.

EACH WEEK IS PRESENTED WITH A COLOURED ENGRAVING.

I'll be back directly. I'll go and speak to him."

"Speak to him?"

"Oh, he won't know it's me."

"The boy's mad," said Mrs. Ogle.

Tom paid no attention to this reflection on his sanity, but crept very slowly to the mouth of the cavern; when there, he made a low snarling noise and gave one short bark, which was so exactly in imitation of a dog of some large and ferocious kind, that in a moment a tremendous scramble in a contrary direction from the cavern took place, and a voice cried out, "There's a dog as big as a lion, my lord. I saw his eyes, like two hot coals."

Tom growled again, and then, stepping back into the cavern, he gave two short barks, which so alarmed Mrs. Ogle, who was not at all aware of what Tom was about, that she started up, and in her effort to escape further into the ruins, fell down a short flight of steps.

"There you go!" said Tom. "Come along, Miss Edith. They will keep off long enough for us to get into some secure place now. Come, Betsy, pick yourself up, and follow us."

Mrs. Ogle was in a terrible fright, and kept turning round and saying, "Hisht!" fancying some ferocious dog was at her heels.

Tom Ripon, with a natural curiosity which always beset him wherever he was, had made himself perfectly acquainted with all the intricacies of the foundations of the old Priory, so that at any time he was a most efficient guide through its labyrinths.

Edith kept her hand upon his arm, and Tom proceeded for a considerable distance, until, with the rising character of the ground, it was evident they were emerging to some position on the regular level of the forest.

Suddenly, then, Tom halted, for a strange, fitful gleam of light was playing upon the face of a very ancient wall some distance in front of them.

"Ah!" said Tom; "they've got into the bit of ruin that's above ground."

"Then those apartments," said Edith, "which Felix and myself have occupied are discovered."

"Not a bit!" said Tom. "It's the cleverest ruin in all the world. There are three slips of rooms so built in among the old walls that you might live there a hundred years, and not find them out."

The murmur of voices now came upon the ears of the little party in the darkness of the forest.

Edith felt certain that, by some means, the secret of Captain Heron's hidden home in the depths of Epping Forest had been discovered, and that the intention was to make a thorough search throughout all the intricacies of the ruins.

"Tom Ripon," said Edith, "I trust much to you, but the danger is great. I do not mean to say that it is personal danger; and I thank heaven that Felix is not here! Yet I would not willingly be torn away from him who is my husband, to submit to any lawless imprisonment that my father, urged by the cruel and vindictive Lord Warringdale, might consent to."

The murmur of voices came nearer, and the gleam of light spread more and more over the dilapidated stone walls of those cavernous recesses.

"If we stay here we are lost!" said Edith.

"This way, then," said Tom. "Ogle showed me an odd looking hole in the wall here, which would lead out to a kind of grotto, a good way off in the wood."

"Do you mean the well cavern, where the poor maniac woman has her abode?"

"I fancy that's just it," said Tom.

"Let us hasten, then, at once, for our enemies approach."

"Betsy," said Tom, "I'd advise you to get up a' tree, and you can sit there chirping, you know, and attract everybody's attention till Captain Heron comes back."

Mrs. Ogle was too angry to reply, but she rained several swinging flat-handed blows in the direction she thought Tom's ears were likely to be.

CHAPTER CLII.

SHOWS HOW LORD BELESSIS THOUGHT TO MAKE AN EASY CONQUEST OF CAPTAIN HERON.

LEAVING for a short time Edith, Tom Ripon, and Mrs. Ogle amid the intricacies of the foundations of old Hinchcliffe Priory and Manor, it is necessary the reader should be made acquainted with the circumstances which induced this sudden and unexpected attack upon Epping Forest.

There was but one man of all Captain Heron's band of whom he had any suspicions, and it will appear that those suspicions were well founded.

Yet this man, who had been about twelve months a member of the fraternity, had not actually said or done anything which Heron could convert into a charge against him; nevertheless, from various little circumstances, the Captain so far suspected his fidelity that for a long time past he had kept him at outposts and as a scout, in order to prevent his becoming intimately acquainted with the innermost secrets of the forest.

This man had overheard a conversation between Edith and Captain Heron, in which the name of Lord Belessis was mentioned, for Heron had been relating to Edith all the particulars of that horrible adventure in the cage at Mortlake.

The moment, however, that this suspected member of the band heard the name of Belessis mentioned, he recognised it as that of a former master, and it confirmed him in the idea which had been floating in his mind for a considerable time, of making as much profit as he could by a betrayal of Captain Heron and his band.

This man, who went by the number Eight in Heron's band, was really named Fowkes; and he wrote to his old master, Belessis, stating that if he would be about the out-buildings of a deserted farm near Epping Forest, on the evening in question, he would meet him and give him such particulars of Captain Heron, the highwayman, as would ensure his capture.

Now it happened that Lord Belessis was well enough acquainted with Judge Tarleton, and after being defeated in the manner we have related by the young Earl of Bridgewater, aided by Captain Heron, he thought he would take the Judge's advice to see if the law had a long enough arm to reach the young Earl for taking away the young lady in question, and marrying her without her father's consent while she was under age.

The letter he received from his old servant, Fowkes, strengthened this determination on the part of Lord Belessis, and he repaired to Finsbury to see Sir John Tarleton, without being at all aware that the Judge was lying in a rather precarious state in consequence of the wound he had received in the garden of Castleneau House.

"You bring me new life," cried Judge Tarleton, when Lord Belessis had explained his errand to him. "This man, Felix Heron, is the bane of my life; he has stolen from me my child, my only child!"

"What! the fair Edith, whom we all admired so, only a year ago, at one of the Queen's drawing rooms?"

"Yes—yes! My child, whom I have brought up with such tenderness, and sacrificed so much for. Hem!"

"I heard somewhere," said Lord Belessis, "that Edith's mother had a competent fortune."

"Yes, yes—some means," replied the Judge, evasively. "The interest of the money has sufficed for Edith's education. But oh, my Lord Belessis, it is a sad thing for an old man like me to be robbed of his only child. She is not of age yet, and if this villain Heron could be only caught and delivered up to justice, and my daughter restored to me, I would take good care of her for the future."

"Then, Sir John, it appears," said Lord Belessis, "that we are both of a mind, and equally interested in this affair."

"Yes, both—both!"

"Lady Cleaveland, who honours me with her exclusive confidence, is as angry with the Earl of Bridgewater for carrying off her daughter, as you can be with Captain Heron for carrying off yours. For my part, I only feel like a nobleman and a gentleman in the matter."

"Oh, of course—of course!" said Sir John; "and I only as a father."

Lord Belessis coughed slightly.

"I suppose," he said, "when the Lady Edith comes of age, she can claim her mother's fortune?"

"Well, yes—she can."

"Ah! I thought as much!"

"And I suppose," said the Judge, fixing his little keen eyes upon Lord Belessis, "that when the young Lady Cleaveland comes of age, she can claim a good portion of the Cleaveland estates?"

"Well, I think I have heard she can."

"And you are so intimate with Lady Cleaveland?"

"I am. Her ladyship did me the honour to propose an alliance between me and her daughter, which has only been frustrated by this young Lord Bridgewater; and he would not have succeeded but for this Captain Heron, who, with unparalleled audacity, crossed me and my friends on Barnes Common."

"Be revenged on him, my lord, if you can! Seize upon him, and lodge him in Newgate! Bring me, likewise, my daughter; and I will then take care that the arm of the law is long enough and strong enough to do something in the affairs of the Cleaveland family."

Lord Belessis was quite willing to enter into this compact, which tended to satisfy his bitterly revengeful feelings against Heron. But he had no idea of going alone to meet his old servant,

Fowkes; and about the cockpit in Westminster, and the tennis-court in the Haymarket, he picked up a disorderly crew of seedy men upon town, broken-down gamesters, and adventurers, to the extent of about twenty, which with some trouble he got mounted and armed, and, at the head of which, on that very evening that Captain Heron started from Epping Forest to rescue Sir Dominick Browne, he made his way by a circuitous route to the place of assignation mentioned by Fowkes.

This man was one of the scouts or sentinels left in the wood by Captain Heron, for he had too little reliance upon him to take him upon any expedition which did not promise present and abundant booty.

Fowkes guessed very well that he would be left as guard at one of the entrances of the forest, and, for the first time, it suited him admirably, since he was thus enabled to keep his appointment with his former master, Lord Belessis.

It was this man, then, who conducted the formidable party into the recesses of the wood, after informing Lord Belessis that, although Captain Heron was absent, he might make quite as important a capture in the person of Edith, who certainly was somewhere in the intricacies of the forest.

The storm that had swept over the tree-tops had somewhat disconcerted Lord Belessis and his party, but still they persevered; and it was only the excellent imitation of a large fierce dog, on the part of Tom Ripon, that had prevented them making their way among the old Priory foundations by the same entrance as Edith.

And now again we join company with the three persons in whose fate we are interested, and who may well be called fugitives amid the dark and intricate recesses of the ruins, since they are pursued by so preponderating a number of enemies.

It was evident that Lord Belessis and his party had now provided themselves with lights, for there was a red glow upon the broken walls, and Edith fancied they were much closer at hand than they actually were.

"Are you quite sure, Tom," she said, "that you know your way from this spot to the well cavern?"

"It is easy," said Tom; "we've only to go on without turning to the right or to the left, and we shall get to the gun-room."

"What is that?"

"Ogle showed me that. It's where the Captain keeps some arms, and it's quite at the back of the old grotto. But come on, Lady Edith, the sooner we get there the better; for it may be some hours yet before the Captain comes back. I only wish he would come into the forest, those fellows would soon be started out of it. This is the way; it's rather a low entrance, and narrow at first."

The entrance was indeed low and narrow, being more like an accidental fissure in the wall than anything else.

It was intensely dark, too, and Edith could not forbear saying to Tom, "Are you certain that we may proceed in safety, heedless of our footsteps?"

"That you may, Lady Edith; it's all level walking, and the ground is as hard as possible, for no rain can get in here. There's more than thirty feet depth of old roots and forest earth above us."

"The place is like a dungeon," said Mrs. Ogle.

" Dear me!" said Tom ; " I forgot you, Betsy! Mind you put one foot before the other properly, for the holes at the side go down a thousand feet into the bowels of the earth."

" Gracious 'heavens! Bowels, did you say, Tom ?"

Mrs Ogle then uttered a faint scream, and declared that something had touched her foot.

" That's the worst of this place," said Tom, composedly ; " the toads are about the size of soup-plates, and if you happen to tread on one of their backs, don't he make a scuffle and spit a little!"

" I'm faint!" said Mrs. Ogle. " If I was once to put my foot on one of those toad's backs I should feel myself a lost woman!"

" Hush! hush!" said Edith. " Do you hear nothing? I fear we are pursued."

They all three halted, and then they heard a confused murmur of voices, but whether any persons were actually in the narrow passage, or the echoing sound of their words was only wafted there in the stillness of the place, Edith could not determine.

The intense darkness around her, however, began to have a depressing influence upon her, and she fancied the air felt thick and heavy.

" Let us hasten forward," she said, gently ; " it is not well to linger in this fearful place, so far beneath the surface of the earth."

" Come on!" said Tom ; " we shall soon be out of it."

Edith was only too well pleased to follow Tom quickly, and it was a great relief to her when suddenly she felt a rush of cold air upon her face, and found that they had cleared the narrow, tortuous passage.

" Now wait one moment, Lady Edith," said Tom, " and I will shut the door behind us. Ogle showed me all about it, because he knew very well he could depend on me in case he wasn't here himself."

" Surely we passed through no doorway," said Edith.

" Oh, yes, it was open, and lay flat against the wall. I will shut it up, and place the bar across it ; and it seems to me now that we can't do better than go out into the forest."

Tom's voice died away as he spoke, for he had gone back some distance into the narrow passage ; but he soon returned, and lighting a match, he held it up for a few minutes until it expired, so that Edith could just see the strange sort of cavernous place in which she was.

It was, in fact, a cave or excavation at the back of the well cavern, with which it communicated in an intricate fashion ; and through another low arched door of heavy planks of wood, so rugged, rough, and covered with earth and clay, that it would require a careful scrutiny to detect what it was.

The roof of the cavern was about twenty feet in height ; and some coarse kind of matting seemed to have been fastened by pegs of wood to the walls.

Running along a portion of it was a shelf, rudely constructed, but very substantial, on which were various articles, apparently appertaining to fire-arms ; and, in an indentation of the wall beneath the shelf, some ten or a dozen muskets were clustered.

Edith had barely time to make this brief survey of the place, before the match which Tom had lit went out.

Almost at the moment that it did so, a strange, hammering noise seemed to come from the very depths of the earth.

For a few moments Edith was perplexed to account for the strange sounds ; and Mrs. Ogle gave utterance to several expressions of alarm. Tom's tone, too, was much less confident, as he said, "They've got into the narrow passage, and are stopped by the door. I wish the Captain would come."

" But we can go out into the forest," said Edith, hurriedly.

" Yes ; and it's the only way now, Lady Edith. I must light another match, to look for the door that looks into the well cavern."

Just as the match was lighted, and a little, glimmering blue flame began to sputter at the end of it, there came a fearful yell from the direction of the wood, apparently close to the mouth of the well cavern ; and mingling with the echoes of the fearful cry, came a voice in screaming exclamations.

" Off—off, I say!" it cried. " Let the bell toll first! It is not time! Are you in such haste to drag him forth to death? Off, fiends that you are! You have no sons! Off, I say!"

" It is the poor maniac of the well," said Edith.

" I never heard such terrible noises in my life," said Tom.

" I'm turning into a jelly with fright," said Mrs. Ogle.

The match sputtered up into a slight flame, and Edith then saw the low, arched door, which led by a zigzag passage from one cavern to another.

" Let us hasten," she said. " I fear the poor creature is not alone, and that her wild delusions are not the only difficulties we shall have to contend with in reaching the forest."

The sounds that came from the outer cavern must have made their way into the inner one through some crevices, for they reached the ears of Edith distinctly.

" What is it ?" cried a man's voice. " Who is it you've let into the cave ?"

" It may be the fiend himself," said another, " for all I know. I made a grasp at some strange figure that tried to pass me, and you heard what an uproar took place."

" It's a mad woman," said a third voice. " I've heard of such being in the forest ; but we must hold our post for all that, since we are told that this is one of the secret outlets from the caverns."

" They know all," whispered Edith.

" Never mind," said Tom ; " they haven't got us yet."

" Come out!" cried a loud voice. " Mad, or not mad, you shan't stay in there! Light a link, my noble comrades! Lord Belessis is a Phœnix, and is going to turn all our lead to gold. Ha, ha! This is rare sport! A light! a light! We will have a look at the witch!"

" They will do the poor creature a harm," said Edith, compassionately.

" I think she can take care of herself," said Tom.

The poor maniac spoke, and her voice was now subdued, and imploring.

"Look you, sirs," she said; "you come to see the execution; but till the bell tolls, I tell you, it cannot be. It is cruel Judge Tarleton that has condemned my boy! Mark you that, sirs—hanging Judge Tarleton! But the time will come—oh! the time will come—when he will envy the poor, still form that swings on the rusted iron of the jibbet!"

"Come out, witch!" cried one of the men. "Come out, or I'll send a bullet after you!"

"Beautiful creature!" said another, in a bantering tone; "come out, or, in a lady-like manner, invite us into your den, for the rain is unpleasant. An elm-tree leaf may be a good umbrella for a gnat, but it's scarcely wide enough for a handsome fellow like me, so, good witch, don't be troublesome."

The steady blows upon the door of the narrow passage still continued.

"We must do something," said Tom.

"But what, you little wretch?" said Mrs. Ogle. "You brought us into all this mischief. I'm sure, from what I can hear, one of those gentlemen outside must be a very proper man. He's singing a song now about lovely woman; and, for all I know, it may be his delicate way of alluding to me."

The little light had gone out.

"Another match," said Tom.

"Well, I don't know," said Mrs. Ogle. "If it was to please providence to take Ogle, another match might do."

"Lady Edith," said Tom, in a whisper, "where are you?"

"Here."

"Don't be frightened!"

"I am not, but I am anxious."

"I mean at a noise?"

"What noise?"

"I'm going to fire one of the muskets."

"Then we're blown up into atoms!" said Mrs. Ogle.

A crashing sound at this moment proclaimed that that portion of Lord Belessis's party which had pursued the fugitives through the winding passage had succeeded in breaking through the door which Tom had closed.

At the same moment the sharp report of a musket rang through the cavern, and Tom called out, in as big a voice as he could assume, "Come on, there's bullets enough for everybody!"

The effect of this shot seemed to be all that could be wished, for the scuffle and the oaths that ensued as Lord Belessis's party cleared away from the door they had broken in, sufficiently indicated the panic that had seized upon them.

But still there came a strange red glare of light into the cavern from the narrow passage, and by that, as the smoke cleared away, Tom could see that Edith was standing by his side, calm and composed, although pale.

Mrs. Ogle had fallen into a remote corner, and seemed, by various starts and twitches, to be meditating a fit of hysterics.

"It's a capital thing," said Tom, "that the Captain keeps these guns always loaded."

"There's a light," said Edith.

"Yes; I can't make that out, as they seem all to have run away. But I'll go and see what it is."

"Be careful, Tom!"

"I will. But would you mind, Lady Edith, taking one of the guns, and if you see anybody try to lay hold of me, just fire away."

"I will arm myself," said Edith; "but I will be specially careful how I fire."

Edith took one of the muskets, and held it in such an attitude that Tom, as he crawled along towards the narrow opening, might be said to proceed under the protection of its muzzle.

"I see," said Tom. "They've thrown down one of their torches, and it's still burning. I'll bring it in."

"No, no!" said Edith.

The words were scarcely out of her mouth when the loud report of some fire-arm in the narrow passage drowned all other sounds, and a bullet came whistling into the cavern, and lodged in the wall, about six inches above Mrs. Ogle's head.

Edith darted forward. The fallen torch threw a lurid glare into the passage through the smoke of the discharge. She thought Tom was killed, as he lay at full length at her feet, and on the impulse of the moment she levelled the musket, and fired after a retreating figure she saw far away in the distance.

CHAPTER CLIII.

CAPTAIN HERON RESCUES EDITH FROM HER FOES IN THE FOREST.

IT was with a feeling of great anguish that Edith looked down at what she supposed to be either the dead body of Tom Ripon, or that faithful and courageous boy badly wounded, and it was with a sensation of intense relief that she heard Tom's voice in the midst of the smoke from the discharged fire-arms.

"All's right!" cried Tom. "They havn't hit me yet; but I rather think you've settled one of them, Lady Edith, by the noise he made."

"I sincerely hope not," said Edith. "I fired impulsively, thinking you were badly hurt."

"Not a bit—not a bit; and here's their link, that they threw down; so we shall be able to see about us in the cavern."

Tom did not trust himself exactly to rise to his feet, for he thought probably that Edith's foes might still be lying in ambush; but he crept along into the earthy cave, until he got out of the line of any fire into the narrow passage.

"I don't think at all they'll come up again this way," said Tom; "because, although they may know or think that only one will be shot, nobody likes to be the happy individual. But I do wish the Captain would come."

"And I," said Edith, "from my heart, wish it."

Loud cries, and all the indications of a serious scuffle taking place in the outer cavern that looked forth into the cavern by the old well, were now plainly heard; and the voice of the poor maniac woman swelled upon their ears, as she cried out, "Has the cruel Judge condemned me, too? Am I to be dragged to death, to please hanging Judge Tarleton? Let it be, then, on the same tree where swings my boy, and we will fight the carrion birds together."

"Silence, hag!" exclaimed a rough voice. "This madness may be feigned, for all I know."

"Oh, she's mad enough, my lord," said another. "I've heard of her often."

"Secure her, and see that she does no mischief, then. Now that we perfectly know those we seek are in these caverns, we must have them."

"What is to be done?" whispered Edith. "We are hemmed in now by enemies in both directions. The narrow passage by which we came here is no doubt well guarded; and if these men do but penetrate into this cavern, by the outer one, we are lost."

"They may not find the way," said Tom, "for it's not easy, and has rather a strong door, too."

It was quite evident now, from the tumult of voices in what might be properly called the well-cavern, that it was occupied by Lord Belessis and a portion of his party. The remainder of his men no doubt kept good guard in the narrow passage,

No. 69.—EDITH.

keeping, however, carefully out of the range of any bullet that might be sent down it on a death-dealing errand.

And now, as minute after minute passed, Edith hoped, even against probability, for the return of Captain Heron.

A sudden calm in the various noises which now betokened the presence of foes in the outer cavern became more alarming than the sounds indicative of their actual presence. This calm lasted for a considerable time; and then Tom, in a whisper to Edith, said, "Don't you hear anything, Lady Edith?"

"Yes. A sort of scratching noise."

"They've found out the old wooden door that leads into this second cavern, then."

"Do you think this link has betrayed us?"

"Hardly," said Tom; "but, after all, it may be as well to put it out."

"Oh, don't!—oh, don't!" cried Mrs. Ogle. "I

know we shall be killed, but it will be more satisfactory to have a light, if it's only just to see how they do it."

"We may be inviting another danger," said Edith, "by depriving ourselves of a light. The men may make a rush from the narrow passage again."

"If they do," said Tom, "it'll be worse for them; and before I put out the light, Lady Edith, I should just like you to take this little bit of string in your hand."

"String? What for, Tom?"

"Why, you see, I've laid down one of the muskets at the mouth of the passage; and the other end of this string is tied to the trigger, so you've nothing to do, Lady Edith, if there is any alarm, but give the string a jerk, and off will go the musket."

Edith rather mechanically, than with any wish to do so, took the cord in her hand; and, at the same moment, Tom extinguished the light.

It was not making any very great sacrifice to put out the light, for it was nearly burnt down to the end, and of its own accord would soon have left them in darkness.

The moment the link was extinguished, Edith saw the extreme danger of having kept it alight at all, since probably it had been the means of revealing the existence of the inner cavern—a fact which was sufficiently exemplified by the entrance through the minute crevices of narrow pencils of light from the torches with which Lord Belessis's party was provided.

The mysterious scratching at the door evidently resulted from some quiet mode of endeavouring to open it; and the caution with which this was attempted, sufficiently testified to the fear which the assailants had of the fire-arms of the fugitives in the cavern.

"What is to be done?" said Edith, in so low a tone to Tom that their foes could not possibly hear her.

"Well," said Tom, "it seems to me that I hardly know; but suppose we all three fire through the door on the chance of hitting some of them?"

"Not me," said Mrs. Ogle—"not me! You wretched boy, don't be asking me to fire guns. And, in fact, I won't touch one at all, for you never can know exactly which end the bullet is coming out of!"

"Silence—silence!" said Edith. "Do not speak so loud!"

At this moment there was a sharp knocking on the outside of the door, which was evidently to challenge the attention of those within the cavern.

"Do not speak," said Edith. "To parley with them is useless."

"Hilloa!" cried a voice from without, after the knocking at the door had continued for some seconds,—"hilloa, within there!"

Edith and Tom kept a profound silence.

"You will not speak," added the voice; "but I'm well aware, Edith Tarleton, that you are on the other side of this door. I am a nobleman, and you can have nothing to fear from me, as my sole object is to conduct you to your father, who is most anxious to receive you, and rescue you from present circumstances, which cannot be to your credit or to his."

"This should be evidence,' thought Edith, "that my father continues to get better from his wound."

"You had better answer," cried the voice, "or we will break down the door the moment the hatchets arrive we have sent for!"

Still Edith kept silent. Mrs. Ogle, however, wanted very much to say something; and it was only Tom who prevented her, for suspecting as much, he whispered to her, "They'll shoot you the moment you open your mouth. They can't see us, but they want to be guided by the voice where to fire."

This effectually silenced Mrs. Ogle, whose fear of fire-arms was decidedly in the ascendant.

Edith was perplexed to know what to do for the best; for although there were certainly some capabilities in those caverns for standing a kind of siege, yet she feared it could not be protracted long enough to procure the return of Captain Heron and his band.

And yet already some hours had passed away—for in rapid action the time flies swiftly—and the night was far advanced. It would seem indeed as if Lord Belessis and his party were anxious to convert their siege of the caverns into a kind of blockade; but the fact was, that since the firing, his lordship had become suspicious that the little expedition was not so easy or so safe as he had pictured it to himself.

From private motives and private hatred he had undertaken the affair, but now that it promised danger beyond his calculations, he sent off one of his men to a neighbouring justice, with a request that some regular constables might be placed at his disposal.

These his lordship waited for, because he wished to place them in the van of the battle, rather than risk his own person in that honourable position.

While he so waited, however, he adopted a plan which he thought might force affairs to a crisis.

The grinding, scratching noise which Edith had heard at the door connecting the two caverns, had resulted in the displacement of a portion of the upper part of it; and in the darkness it was not at all difficult for Edith and Tom Ripon to see that this result was produced.

Most effectually, however, did Tom prevent any further exertions in that quarter; for standing by the side of the door, so as to protect himself from a shot through its panels, he projected silently the barrel of a musket about a couple of inches through the opening.

This was a hint which Lord Belessis's men were not slow in taking; and the neighbourhood of the rough and rugged little door was at once abandoned.

"They're going to fire on us, my lord!" said one of the men.

"Let them alone then," replied Lord Belessis. "They will only too soon be glad to come out. Give me a link. That will do."

What it was that Lord Belessis declared "would do," remained for some minutes quite a mystery to Tom Ripon and Edith. Then, however, the meaning of the words declared themselves most unmistakably.

A dense, yellow vapour began to pour into the cavern through the opening at the upper part of the door; and it was accompanied by so strong an odour of damp wood smouldering and struggling with flame, that Edith could have no doubt whatever of what had occurred.

During that quiescent period when Lord Belessis had appeared to be doing nothing, he had ordered some of his men to collect from the forest a quantity of brushwood and old half-decayed leaves, to which he had set light; and, as the wind was in such a quarter that it blew right into the cavern, by far the greater part of the smoke made its way through the orifice at the top of the small door, very much as it would have taken its course through a regular chimney.

And, the very fact that the wood was green and damp made it answer Lord Belessis's purpose much better than though it had burned freely, for the smoke was thick and dense, and most antagonistic to human existence.

For a time it gathered in thick clouds at the roof of the cavern, from whence, as it accumulated in quantity, it slowly descended, coming down inch by inch towards the devoted heads of the three persons who maintained that place of refuge.

"Now, indeed," said Edith, "we are lost; but I would rather die than be torn in life from Epping Forest. It is my home, and the home of Felix. What have I endured in the world beyond it but misery, oppression, and despair?"

"Then," said Tom, "we'll fight our way out."

A loud scream from Mrs. Ogle at this moment proclaimed that either something had happened to awaken her fears, or that she had lost sufficient power over herself to keep silent any longer.

"What's the matter with you now?" said Tom.

"Murder!" said Mrs. Ogle. "I've gone through the wall!"

The green wood had been massed up against the lower part of the door; and now, as if it would perform a kindly office to those persons who were already beginning to feel the suffocating influence of its smoke, it shot two or three bright tongues of flame into the cavern.

By that light a most singular sight presented itself in regard to Mrs. Ogle.

Nothing, however, was visible, excepting her feet, encased in a pair of fashionable high-heeled boots which she had brought from London, and which she rattled together with a vehemence which sufficiently portrayed the mortal fear that was in heart and brain, wherever those portions of her animal economy might be.

"Why, where are you?" said Tom. "You've gone right through the wall of the cave!"

Edith sprung forward; and to her surprise, what had appeared a portion of the earthen wall of the cavern, and against which Mrs. Ogle had been resting, had been nothing more than a piece of coarse canvass stretched over an opening, and so bedaubed with clay and earth, as exactly to resemble the surrounding solid wall.

There could not be a doubt that whatever had been the original uses of those caverns in connexion with the old Priory ruins, secure and hidden modes of communication had entered largely into the motives of their construction.

Accident now revealed one of those curious secret passages, which, no doubt, communicated with other parts of the ruins; and it was at a fortunate moment for Edith, Tom Ripon, and Mrs. Ogle, that such an accident took place, for the dense smoke from the burning wood was collecting in alarming quantities.

A very few moments more, and the atmosphere of that cavern would have been quite unfit for human lungs.

The flames began to lick the inner side of the door, producing a strange, crackling sound upon the ancient wood-work, and throwing a strange, lurid glare over the interior of the cave.

Tom saw almost at the same moment that Edith did how important a discovery had been made.

"Lady Edith," he said, "we shall get away, after all."

"This is indeed providential," said Edith. "We will pursue this passage, let it lead to where it may."

"Now, mum," said Tom to Mrs. Ogle, "will you get up, or are we to walk over you?"

"Mercy upon me!" said Mrs. Ogle. "What has happened?"

The opening in the wall was not much above four feet in height, so that until Mrs. Ogle extricated herself from it, neither Tom nor Edith could pass from the cavern in that direction.

Fright, however, seemed so entirely to have taken possession of her, that she was quite incapable of understanding what she was required to do. But Tom and Edith, however, were warned of the necessity for immediate action by hearing an order given in a loud voice from the well-cavern.

"Give the signal," cried Lord Belessis, "for the other party to make a rush now through the narrow passage. I expect the smoke by this time has silenced opposition."

Upon hearing this, Tom laid violent hold upon Mrs. Ogle, and, in spite of her resistance, dragged her out of the narrow passage, where of her own accord she would neither have advanced or retreated, having in her fright some obscure idea that she was safe so long as her head was in it.

"Now, Lady Edith," said Tom; "off we go!"

Edith was about to enter the passage in the wall of the cavern, but Tom detained her for a moment by holding her arm.

"No," he said; "let me go first: there may be some deep hole, for all we know."

"And you would encounter that danger?" said Edith.

"To be sure!" said Tom. "When a man has the care of helpless females he don't mind trifles like that. Mrs. Ogle, come on!"

"I'm a dead woman!" said Mrs. Ogle.

Tom entered the narrow cleft in the wall quickly, and Edith, fully believing that Mrs. Ogle would follow them, kept close upon his heels.

The passage was very narrow indeed, but it was some satisfaction to find that at about six or eight feet from its entrance its height very materially increased, so that there was no longer any necessity for stooping in making progress through it.

It was not until they had gone a considerable distance that Edith felt certain Mrs. Ogle was not following them.

Any idea, however, of retracing their steps on her account would have been too absurd, since she certainly had every opportunity of availing herself of the same chance of escape which presented itself to them.

The fact, however, was, that Mrs. Ogle was so

terrified that she lost all conception of what she was about; and, after running twice round the cavern, she had plunged into the narrow passage, from which a portion of Lord Beleessis's men might be expected every minute to make the rush which they were to be signalled to take.

As Tom Ripon and Edith crept slowly onward, the various noises which they left behind them in the caverns died away into indistinct murmurs.

A death-like stillness reigned about them.

"Tom," said Edith, "I am apprehensive that if this narrow cleft in the hill-side continues much longer the air will be too close for respiration. Tell me at once if you have any fear on that head, and we will retrace our steps."

"No," said Tom; "I can breathe very well. But what's that, Lady Edith? Is it the moon?"

A considerable distance off, in front of them, appeared a very faint, white ray of light; but where it came from, or by what means it got into that cavernous recess, seemed to baffle conjecture.

Yet it was a something grateful and reassuring to feel that there was any communication, however slight, with the external atmosphere and that gloomy cleft beneath the surface of the earth, through which Edith and Tom Ripon were making their way.

It had been quite evident to Edith that for some distance their route had been on a gentle decline downwards; but, from about the time she had observed that faint ray of light, it was as evident that the incline had altered its character, and rose considerably.

Tom ran on now rather in advance, and Edith heard him calling out to her.

"Lady Edith, Lady Edith, I don't know where we are; but it's daylight, and here's a grating that looks up right into the forest."

Edith could hardly believe it possible that they had been in those gloomy-looking recesses—which made an intricate world of themselves—beneath the old trees of Epping Forest, during all the hours of darkness. But so it was—the dawn had come.

Long, slant rays of faint sunlight were beginning to penetrate the depths of the wood.

Edith, to her great surprise, found that Tom had halted beneath what appeared to be a grating let into the earth.

Grass, thistles, and some common wood-creepers, so nearly obscured it on the outer side, that it was only in consequence of the penetration of the subtle daylight through minute crevices that even they, looking from darkness to light, could perceive it.

"There's lots of fresh air," said Tom.

A keen, cool current rushed, with a slight sighing noise, through the crevices of the grating; and then both Edith and Tom started suddenly back, as a palpable dark shadow passed over its outer surface.

"What was that?" said Edith, in a low tone. "I fear that our enemies are even at this spot."

"It was a fox, or a hare," said Tom, "I'm quite sure; and I should say, Lady Edith, that the best thing we can do is to get out of here as quick as possible."

"Can we break our way through those bars?"

"Why, here's one of them," said Tom, "fallen in! I shouldn't wonder now, Lady Edith, that this grating has been here for hundreds of years. Why, it's as rotten as pieces of stick! Here it goes, and here I come! Whoop! Hilloa!"

Tom, as he spoke, clambered up to the grating,

and so old and decayed was it, that by the mere force of his hand striking against it, he was able to make his way through into a portion of the old crumbling ruins of the Priory and Manor House of Hinchcliffe.

It would seem that that part of the ruins was seldom visited, for a hare with a couple of leverets only made their way slowly from the place as Tom emerged from underground into the daylight.

"All's right, Lady Edith," he said. "There's nobody here, and I fancy we're far enough away from those rascals in the cavern, to be out of all danger from them."

With the assistance of Tom, Edith found it an easy task enough to get through the grating; but when Tom waved his hand over his head, and seemed to think that they had accomplished everything by their escape from the caverns, Edith checked his exultation by saying, "You forget that though we came through a passage which was concealed up to the moment of our accidental discovery of it, we were compelled to leave it open, and those who wish evil to us can easily traverse it in pursuit."

Tom looked grave, and whistled.

"To be sure, Lady Edith—to be sure—so they can—so they can—no, they can't!"

"What do you mean, Tom?"

"Why, look you here! We can't stop up the other end, but we can this."

Even as he spoke, Tom set to work with a will, and proceeded to lay branches of the brushwood, and every portable article he could lay his hand on, over the opening through which they had emerged from the cavernous recess.

"If we can only stop out the daylight," said Tom, "they will never think of trying how thick the covering is, but will fancy there's a regular roof over their heads. I only wish I had a spade, Lady Edith, but I suppose hands were made before spades, and the leaves of the trees here seem to be ever so many feet deep on the ground."

So lightly impacted was the surface soil of that part of the forest, that Tom had no difficulty whatever, by vigorously working with his hands, in making such a pile over the opening leading to the cavern, that from within, no one could possibly suspect that the trifling exercise of labour would carry them to daylight.

"What shall we do now?" said Edith. "We must not show ourselves in the ordinary glades of the forest until Felix returns."

"I know which way he'll come in," said Tom: "it'll be by the narrow glade, close by the spot that all the men call the 'Five Oaks.' It's daylight now, Lady Edith, and suppose we go there and wait for him?"

"It will indeed be wise to do so, Tom. Are the thickets dense? Can we hide well?"

"I should think so. Why, there's a complete little wood of nut-trees, that have the place all to themselves; and if once we get among them, nobody can possibly see us. Perhaps it won't be easy to get there, because, you see, Lady Edith, we can't take the open forest roads; but it's better to be scratched a little with the brambles, than fall in with those men, who want to burn us alive in the cave."

"Infinitely better," said Edith. "I shall not be afraid to follow you."

EXECUTION OF No. 5 FOR TREACHERY.

Presented Gratis with No. 69 of the New Edition of Edith the Captive; or the Robbers of Epping Forest.

EACH WEEK IS PRESENTED GRATIS A COLOURED ENGRAVING.

Tom led the way, and in the course of a quarter of an hour he and Edith were safely enough hidden in the midst of a complete grove of most luxuriant nut-bushes.

There they waited for the arrival of Captain Heron.

CHAPTER CLIV.

LORD BELESSIS HAS TO GIVE EVIDENCE IN A DISAGREEABLE CASE.

It was while Edith and Tom Ripon were concealed in this nut-grove, awaiting, with no small anxiety, the return of Captain Heron to Epping Forest, that that strange presentiment of something going wrong in his sylvan home came over Heron, as he gallopped ahead of his men, after their serious and dangerous adventure in the crypt of St. Paul's.

Captain Heron was not superstitious, but he was mounted on Daisy; and what so easy for his imagination, when once awakened to the supposition of fear for those whom he loved, to re-act upon his nervous system, and give the impulse of speed to the gallant creature he bestrode.

It was, then, that undefined feeling, that the nearer he approached Epping Forest the happier he would become, which induced a speed which soon left his companions behind somewhat more than a mile.

Alone, then, and at that striding half-gallop which carried Daisy over the ground with such amazing celerity, Captain Heron reached the confines of Epping Forest.

He drew rein about two hundred yards from those very nut-bushes among which Edith and Tom Ripon were concealed.

A confused murmur, as of voices in the wood, came upon the ears of Captain Heron; and instead of making his usual cry of "Hawks and herons," to challenge the attention of one of the scouts who should be on duty at that part of the forest, he was profoundly still.

Captain Heron seemed to throw all his senses into that one of listening.

The dense bushes, and the thick foliage of the tall forest trees, effectually hid him from the sight of Edith. True she had heard the swift beating of the horse's hoofs on the ground, but she could not recognise them with sufficient certainty to say that they bespoke the appearance of Captain Heron.

Yet there was both a hope and a fear in her mind that it might be him,—a hope, because it would have been a joy to look into his face again —a fear that he would be alone, and so unable to cope with his enemies in the forest.

And so, as Captain Heron listened for any sound, or rather that he might comprehend the meaning of the faint noises that came to his ears, Edith also listened, in the hope that the horseman, who had paused so suddenly a short distance from the place of her concealment, might utter some word that would enable her to decide if he were the dearly expected arrival, or not.

"Whisper to me, Tom Ripon," she said. "Is it the Captain?"

"It's not like him," said Tom, in the same tone, 'for he generally gallops right into the wood; and

besides, you know, Lady Edith, he went out with all the men but two."

"That is true."

"And so, you see, he's not likely to come back alone."

"No, no! He would not."

"The fellows have often told me he has sent them back without him, while he has stayed to finish some affair, perhaps, in town; but he never leaves them while there's anything to be done. However, I don't see why I shouldn't crawl through the bushes, and take a look at him."

"Do so, if you can with safety."

Tom was about to move from the side of Edith, when the faint murmuring sounds, which had come from the very depths of the forest, began to increase, so as evidently to point out the approach of Lord Belessis and his men to that part of the wood.

Tired out, and disappointed by their long and fruitless search, which had resulted only in the capture of Mrs. Ogle, they were leaving the forest in rather a tumultuous manner, fully believing that for them there was no danger beneath the overhanging branches of the beautiful glades which they had held possession of for so many hours.

Lord Belessis had utterly failed on his mission.

These sounds of an approaching throng of persons reached the ears of Captain Heron as quickly as they did those of Edith.

Alarmed for her safety, he darted forward; and clearing the trunk of a fallen tree, Daisy came to a halt close to the nut-bushes which screened Edith and Tom Ripon from observation.

Had Heron not been mounted, and had he not raised himself in the stirrups to get as extended a view as possible into the forest, Edith would even then not have seen him; but as it was, the hat and feathers and the upper part of his face were visible to her over the topmost branches of the nut-trees.

How welcome was the sight of those well-known features to Edith! The sparkling eyes—the youthful and ingenuous expression of countenance —the soft, full moustache that shaded the upper lip—and the few clustering curls that would escape from beneath the hat,—all spoke to her heart in the mental accents of recognition.

"Felix—Felix!" she cried. "You are there, and all is well!"

The sound of that well-known voice struck upon his ears; and the start that he gave made Daisy execute a curvet, which would have unseated a less skilful rider.

"Edith—Edith, can this be possible? You here, and on the outskirts of the forest! My presentiments, then, were not in vain. Something must have happened."

"I am here, Felix; but I am well and uninjured."

Captain Heron almost flung himself from his saddle.

"Still, Daisy—be still!" he cried, and in another moment he was beating his way through the nut-bushes, in the direction of the sound of Edith's voice.

"Hurrah!" cried Tom. "Here we are, Captain! All's right, now you've come back! I'll take care of Daisy!"

"Do so. Edith—Edith, what is all this? You

look pale and agitated; and your dress is torn by the briars of the forest."

Edith was so well pleased to feel herself clasped to the breast of Captain Heron, that it was some few minutes before she could summon words sufficient to inform him what had occurred in the forest during his absence.

And but a short time was allowed to Edith in which to render this necessary explanation, for Lord Belessis, and the party of men who were with him, disappointed of their chief prey, and fearful of the return of Captain Heron in force to the forest, rapidly approached the spot.

"Captain—Captain!" cried Tom; "I'm afraid we shan't be able to fight so many, for there are twenty of them at least!"

"Say you so?" exclaimed Heron, as he drew his sword. "I will, at least, hold this pass, Edith, while you gallop upon Daisy over the little waste ground adjoining the road. You will soon meet the band, headed by Ogle, and can hasten their approach."

"No, no!" said Edith. "With you, Felix—with you! I will share your danger!"

"Bravo!" cried Tom, as he clapped his hands. "Here they come!"

"Our foes?" asked Edith.

"No—our own fellows. And there's Ogle!"

"It is true," said Heron; "and they see that something's amiss, too. Behold! Edith, they set their spurs to their horses! Ogle points to this part of the wood. They see Daisy waiting without a rider. Retire, dear Edith, into the brushwood, and we will soon render an account of these marauders into our sylvan home."

But Edith still clung to him.

"They will kill you, Felix—they will kill you!"

"Nay—not so; and yet it is possible, if——"

"If what, Felix?—oh, if what?"

Heron smiled.

"If you, dear Edith, oblige them by holding my arm."

She released him in a moment.

"Now, that is well!" said Heron. "Would it become me, Edith, to allow my men, who follow me so faithfully, and whom I profess to lead, to engage in this conflict, while I stood idly by, lurking in the bushes?"

"No, Felix, no—a thousand times, no!"

"You bid me go, then?"

"Yes; and heaven protect you!"

Felix Heron darted to Daisy, and sprung to the saddle.

Up to that moment, Ogle and the band had not observed him, for the tall bushes and tree saplings had hidden him from their sight; but now, when they saw him fairly mounted, and turning to head them, they raised a cheer of satisfaction.

That cheer struck a cold chill to the heart of Lord Belessis and his party.

Then there came a screaming voice from among the trees.

"Ogle, you villain!" cried a voice. "Here's your natural born wife captivated by twenty men. Are you half a man, that you don't fly down all their throats, and rescue me at once?"

Lord Belessis's party halted, and for a moment he himself hesitated about engaging in the sort of conflict that seemed approaching.

Passion, however, got the better of a certain kind of cowardice which was lurking at the bottom of his heart.

"Forward, my men!" he cried. "They are but thieves and cut-purses, after all. They will fly before you, and we shall catch a few of the hindmost of them, as food for Tyburn tree."

"Halt!" cried Captain Heron to his men.

There was an ominous clicking of pistol-locks.

"Let no man fire," he said, "unless he hears the word from me."

For another moment there was a pause of expectation, and Lord Belessis called out in a loud voice, "Yield, you scoundrels! I call upon you to do so in the name of the law!"

"Charge!" cried Heron.

He dashed forward in front of his men with Ogle by his side, and although much inferior in number to Lord Belessis's party, the compact and ready manner in which the freebooters of the forest followed their leader struck dismay into the desultory crew that composed the other force.

They wavered—broke up into twos and threes; and then, as Captain Heron's party dashed in among the trees, Lord Belessis's men, in a state of perfect rout, sought individual safety in all directions.

Staggered and confounded by this desertion of the troop he had brought with him to Epping Forest, under such fine promises, Lord Belessis was a moment or two before he could gather his presence of mind to act for his own safety.

That moment or two brought Captain Heron to his side.

"So, my lord," he cried, "we meet again."

"Villain!" cried Belessis.

"Welcome to the shades of old Epping; and as for villain, were the word but a thing instead of a sound, I would cram it down your rebellious throat."

Lord Belessis's horse reared, or was made to rear by some trick of the rein, and at the moment that it did so, his lordship drew a pistol from the holster, and levelling it past his horse's neck, he fired, as he thought, full in the face of Captain Heron.

The bullet divided the stem of the long feather which so gracefully adorned Heron's hat, and the dissevered half fell fluttering to the ground.

Heron gave Daisy a slight touch with his left hand, and she cleared the distance to the side of Lord Belessis at a bound, for his lordship had backed away from his foe, before he fired, some dozen paces or so.

"Defend yourself, my lord," said Heron calmly—"defend yourself, or I cut you down in your saddle!"

"You bear a charmed life!" cried Belessis, in hoarse, choking accents,—"you bear a charmed life, or my bullet must have sped you to death!"

"Draw, sir, and defend yourself!"

It was with a feeling of desperation that his position could not be possibly worse, that Lord Belessis drew his sword, and aimed a deadly thrust at Heron.

That thrust, though well intended, was parried with ease; and for some few seconds the swords clashed together in deadly conflict.

With a yell of rage and pain, then, that rang through the forest, Lord Belessis dropped his sword, and fell back upon the saddle and crupper of his horse, but his feet were still in the stirrups, and he kept a convulsive grasp of the rein in his left hand.

By one well-directed, downward blow, Heron had inflicted upon him a serious wound; and blinded by the blood that streamed over his eyes, he saw not his way, or whither he was carried, while his affrighted horse tore madly with him through the forest.

Heron calmly sheathed his sword.

But the contest did not seem to be over, for crashing through the underwood close at hand there came another horse and rider, closely pursued by some one, who in a few seconds Heron saw to be Ogle.

The speed at which the first horse was proceeding would have carried it past the spot, but that the creature caught its foot in some tangled projecting roots of an old tree, and stumbled.

The consequence was, the burden it bore upon its back was projected a considerable distance in advance, and then Heron saw that that burden consisted of two persons, one of whom was Mrs. Ogle.

Ogle halted abruptly.

"Betsy's got him, I think," he said.

"Got him!" screamed Mrs. Ogle. "I should think so!"

In another moment she had seized the unfortunate rider by the hair of his head, and was holding him past all chance of escape.

"Got him, indeed!" she added; "I rather think I have; and a pretty fellow you are, Ogle, to leave your own wife, with her marriage-lines in her pocket, to be thrown off horses like a cannon-ball, with a wretch like this!"

"Murder!" cried the man. "Release me from this hag in human shape! Take away this she-dev——"

"What do you say?" cried Mrs. Ogle, as she at once inflicted ten scratches on the man's face.

"Come, come, Betsy," said Ogle; "that'll do! I'll take care he don't get away. Why, Captain, it's one of our own people!"

"Number Five!" said Heron, sadly. "I have long suspected him."

Mrs. Ogle released her prisoner.

With a bewildered look, the discomfited traitor struggled to his feet; then, by the glance he cast around him, it was evident he intended, as a last resource, to try flight even on foot.

But the voice of Heron stopped him.

"Number Five," he said calmly, "attempt to fly, and I fire!"

The traitor cowered down to the earth.

"Speak!" added Heron. "Do you confess to having betrayed us?"

"I deny."

"That is well. We must have evidence, then."

"Here it is!" said Tom Ripon.

Captain Heron's band had now assembled round the spot, and the discomfited Number Five saw nothing but hostile faces about him.

"Speak, Tom Ripon," added Captain Heron.

Tom pointed in the face of Number Five.

"I know his voice well," he said. "He was one of the scouts last night to the entrances to the forest, and it was he who led a party of men to the secret paths in the old foundations."

"I deny!" yelled Number Five,—"I deny! Is a man to be condemned upon his voice?"

"Did you see him, Tom?" said Heron.

"No, Captain."

Number Five drew a long breath.

"But I did!" said Mrs. Ogle, stepping forward. "And the villain that brought all the other villains here, that they called my lord, gave him charge of me; so he was quite clearly along with them."

"Guilty, or not guilty?" said Heron, turning to his band.

"Guilty!" pronounced every voice at once.

The word died away in melancholy cadences among the trees.

Number Five licked his parched lips.

"I could not help it!" he said. "I was taken prisoner."

"Search him!" said Heron.

A letter was torn from his breast-pocket, and one of the band read it aloud.

"We shall be at the forest shortly after dusk, and if you keep your word with us, and really can conduct a strong party to the secret recesses inhabited by Captain Heron and his gang, the reward named to you shall be doubled."

There was no signature to this paper, but its contents were fearfully criminatory of the traitorous companion.

Captain Heron then spoke in a deep, sad voice.

"Number Five," he said, "there was neither force nor persuasion used to induce you to join us; of your own free will you made one of this fraternity."

"Yes," gasped Number Five.

"It is well known," added Heron, "that excepting accidental good fortune in avoiding such a danger, the lives of all are at the mercy of any one. No oaths and no ceremonies bind us together. We believe in each other, so that we have no denunciations against treachery."

Number Five began to have a glimmer of hope.

"Such a case as this is special, and I will not judge it."

Number Five breathed more freely.

"I leave your fate in the hands of your own comrades. What say you, men?"

"Death!" cried every voice.

And this word, more fearful even than that of "Guilty," seemed to linger in dreary echoes above the old tree-tops, and to be whispered over and over again in the deep recesses of the forest.

Number Five raised a hoarse scream of terror.

Edith, who had approached the spot, clasped her hands.

"No, no!" she cried—"no bloodshed! Spare him—even him!"

A paleness came over Captain Heron's face.

"Edith, dearest," he said, "this is no place for you. Home, home!—to our secret and intricate home, beneath the gnarled roots of the old trees! Edith, leave us, if you love me!"

Edith tottered from the spot, and Mrs. Ogle sprang after her.

"Wait!" said Heron.

A deathlike stillness reigned in that old forest glade, and all eyes were bent upon the retreating figures of the two females, as they slowly made their way over the beautiful green sward towards the Priory ruins.

Then Heron spoke again

His voice was hoarse and low.

"Comrades," he said, "is there any one among you who wishes to speak a word in favour of this guilty man?"

All was still.

"Is there any one among you who feels a doubt of the justness of his sentence?"

No one spoke.

Then the abject wretch, trembling with fear, tossed his arms wildly in the air.

"Speak for me—speak for me!" he cried. "For the love of heaven, speak for me! I hear it in his tones, I see it in his eyes—he will spare me if but one voice speaks for me! I will be your slave, your servant—the slave and servant of you all—but spare my life! I only ask for life!—the life that you would take away, but cannot give!"

A deep and ominous silence reigned through the band.

"Is there no mercy in earth or in heaven? I ask but to be allowed to breathe! Hide me in a dungeon!—cast to me but the broken victuals from your table! Be merciful, and let me live!"

"Tom," said Captain Heron, "you are but a boy, and this is no scene for you. Follow me!"

Tom Ripon said not a word, but walked in the footsteps of Captain Heron.

Ogle ran after the Captain, and whispered hurriedly, "Fire or the cord?"

"Do not ask me!"

Ogle returned to the men, and Heron did not look back again. He had proceeded perhaps a hundred paces up the forest glade, when a rattling volley of pistol shots awakened the echoes of the forest.

One terrible cry mingled with them, and then all was still.

The traitor had gone to his account, and there was no Number Five in the band of Captain Heron.

CHAPTER CLV.

LORD WARRINGDALE MATURES HIS PLOT AGAINST CAPTAIN HERON.

THE more the villanous and unscrupulous Lord Warringdale considered the advice that had been given to him by his friend the attorney, at the old mansion in Essex Street, the more enamoured he became of such a mode of ridding himself of his half-brother, Captain Heron.

There was something at once subtle, deep, and attractive about the means suggested for the destruction of Heron; and he, Warringdale, set about the matter in a spirit of perfect accord with the diabolical suggestions of the lawyer.

His great object, however, was to prevent Jonathan Wild from knowing anything of the affair.

This would seem to be easy, inasmuch as it would, at first sight, appear that he had nothing to do but to abstain from informing him of what was on foot. But it was, in reality, not so easy as it looked.

If Warringdale was to induce Felix Heron to come to London in order that he might be cap-

tured, it would be necessary to have the authorities at hand to effect that capture.

How was that to be done, and Jonathan Wild at the same time be kept in ignorance of it?

That was the question.

It was one that Warringdale had not the wit to solve, but Mr. Smith, as the attorney now chose to call himself, volunteered to see to that part of the little treacherous affair.

While he, Smith, then, set about his preparations in regard to Jonathan Wild, Lord Warringdale called upon one of the Under Secretaries of State in order to procure his authority in the course he wished to pursue.

This Under Secretary was a man named Fitzroy—a coarse, truculent fellow, who was chosen by the heads of the Administration for his qualities as a bully, to whom could be turned over any disagreeable claimant upon the Ministry.

This man was poor and grasping, and Lord Warringdale was not without a hope that a promised bribe might induce him to lend his authority as far as he, Lord Warringdale, wanted it.

"You are aware, Mr. Fitzroy," he said, "that a change of Ministry is imminent; in which case, I do not see why you cannot join Lord Belphor, and retain your under secretaryship."

Fitzroy looked suspicious.

"Oh, you may speak freely to me," added Warringdale. "You know Sir John Tarleton will be Chancellor, and I am to be an Under Secretary."

"I have heard so."

"It is to be so."

"But," said Fitzroy, "there are ugly rumours."

"What?"

"About you, my lord."

"Indeed!"

"Yes. It is possible that the last person who hears these things is sometimes the person who is the most interested in them; but it is said that there is a claimant in the field for the title and estates of Whitcombe."

"Pshaw!" said Warringdale. "A claimant, indeed! I am sure, Mr. Fitzroy, that you will be the first person to smile at the character of the claim."

"I should like to do so."

"You shall, then, for I will tell you all about it."

"I shall be glad to hear," said Fitzroy, drily.

"You must know, then, that the late Earl, my father, had a sort of *liaison* with a person of the name of—of the name of——"

"Of what?"

Lord Warringdale hesitated a moment, for his suspicious and crafty nature began to doubt if it would be wise actually to give the name of Felix's mother before her marriage with the Earl of Whitcombe.

Fitzroy put on one of his ugly sneers, and said, roughly, "The name is Amelia Staunton."

"Ah! you know as much?"

"I do."

"Will you say how?"

"Freely. The young Lord Bridgewater——"

"Curses on his head!"

"Has been talking everywhere of a petition of right which has been presented to the King, and which has found its way into the hands of the Committee of Privileges of the Privy Council."

Warringdale turned a shade paler

"It is false!" he cried. "Amelia Staunton was never married to the late Earl."

"Ah!" said Fitzroy, as he drew up his tall, gaunt form to the full height, and rubbed his immense chin.

"I will explain."

"Do."

"The man who makes this absurd claim, founds it on the possession of some papers which, in his capacity as a highwayman and burglar, he has got possession of."

"Then there are papers?"

"Letters, I daresay."

"Well, my lord?"

"But this claim is an annoyance."

"No doubt."

"And I would willingly put an end to it."

"Still, no doubt."

"And if you, Mr. Fitzroy, would aid me so to

No. 70.—EDITH.

do, I would come under an obligation, along with Sir John Tarleton, to preserve for you your present situation."

"In writing?"

"Surely."

"Then count on me. I am well aware that the Whig Ministry is tottering, and cannot much longer subsist. What can I do for you?"

"I want you to sign a letter."

"Where is it?"

"Here."

"Read it to me."

Lord Warringdale read as follows:—

"Downing Street.

"MY LORD WARRINGDALE,—

"Your singular communication, in which you state that you intend to give up the title and estates of Whitcombe to a claimant of the name

of Felix Heron, has much surprised the Cabinet.
If, however, you wish to do so, no obstructions
will be cast in your way, and the King will give
a private audience to the person you name as Felix
Heron at the next levee, on Monday week.

"I have the honour to be,
"My lord,
"Your lordship's most obedient servant,
"HENRY FITZROY."

"The deuce!" said Fitzroy. "You have signed
it for me."

"No; there is a blank."

"But you said, 'Henry Fitzroy.'"

"I did; but that was only to signify that that
was where your name was to go."

"Very good."

"You will sign it?"

"I will, when you give me the letter you spoke
of."

"It is here."

"Read!"

Lord Warringdale produced a letter, and read
it.

"DEAR MR. FITZROY,—

"In the event of a change of Ministry, I, as a
gentleman, pledge myself that I will not myself
take office, unless you have the refusal of an
Under-Secretaryship.

"I am, my dear Mr. Fitzroy,
"Yours truly,
"WARRINGDALE."

"Will that do?" said Warringdale.

"It will."

"Then you will assist me?"

"With all my heart. That is to say, with all
my head, I mean."

"I prefer your head to your heart," said Warringdale.

"You are right."

"Sign this letter, then, Mr. Fitzroy, so that it
shall seem quite official; and then give me a
written order to the chief officer in command of
the troop of light horse, stationed at the King's
Mews, to obey my directions on the day of the
levee."

Mr. Fitzroy wrote the order.

"Is that all?"

"It is all. But I hope, slight as all this looks,
it will make up a net, in the meshes of which my
enemy will be entangled."

Warringdale left the office of the Under-Secretary, who chuckled and rubbed his hands together
when he was alone, as he muttered to himself,
"This is a good chance for me. Whether the Whigs
go out of office or not, I should have to resign my
place, since several members of the Cabinet have
chosen to complain of what they call my insolence
and my incapacity."

While Warringdale was thus laying the ground-
work of the snare in which he hoped to catch
Captain Heron, Mr. Smith, the ci devant attorney,
was not idle.

After his interview with Warringdale in the old
house in Essex Street, he had made his way to a
low, miserable-looking street at the back of Drury
Lane, and he tapped at the door of a house which
had all the appearance of having been shut up
and deserted for many a long year.

The tap, however, that Smith gave with his
knuckles at the door appeared to have something
cabalistic about it, for the door was immediately
opened.

"Enter!" said a voice.

Smith went into the passage of the house, and
the door was at once closed behind him.

All was dark.

"Speak!" said the voice again.

"I want Raphael," said Smith.

"Raphael hears."

"Is there any drug—any vapour—any subtle
and hidden means by which a man, crafty as a fox,
as well as with all the cunning of one who has had
long practice in treachery and crime, can be sent on
an errand to another world?"

"Yes."

"The price?"

"Ten golden pieces."

"Very well, Raphael. Here is the money."

The darkness was dissipated so far that Smith
could see an arm projected through a small,
round opening in the wall of the passage.

In the hand appertaining to that arm was a
little wooden box.

"Take this!" said the voice. "You place it
on a table, or a chimney-piece, or any odd corner
that will hold it, in the room of your enemy, and
on the powder that is in the box you place a small
live coal or red-hot cinder."

"Is that all?"

"Yes. You have but to hold the room door
shut for five minutes, and then, when you enter it
again, you will find a corpse."

"That is well!"

"The gold?"

"Here is the sum, Raphael; and I must say
that your art is wonderful."

The arm and hand were withdrawn from the
opening in the wall, and all was again intense
darkness for a few seconds.

Then the door was opened by some unseen
means, and the attorney passed out again into the
dim and wretched street.

He placed the box, which was not above an
inch in width, deep in a secret pocket.

"Surely," he said, "I hold the life of Jonathan
Wild now in my hands."

Mr. Smith's next object was to see Jonathan,
and for that purpose he repaired to Newgate
Street.

Wild was at home, but Blueskin declared that
for once in a way he had gone to bed.

No doubt such was the fact, for even Jonathan
Wild, with his iron frame, was but human, and he
had passed through so much lately, that he felt
the necessity for, at the least, four-and-twenty
hours' rest.

That period had nearly expired when the attorney called at Newgate Street.

"You can't see him, I tell you," growled
Blueskin. "He said as how he would shoot anybody who dared to disturb him before he rang his
bell."

Even as Blueskin spoke, the sharp tinkle of a
bell resounded through the house.

"That's it!" said Blueskin.

"Mr. Wild's bell?"

"To be sure it is. Wait a bit."

Blueskin was absent about five minutes, and
then he came back to say that Mr. Wild would

see his visitor; and the attorney was ushered up-stairs to a room on the first floor.

Jonathan Wild was in bed, with his wig off, and on his head were the marks of various cuts and slashes he had received in his different en-counters.

The thief-taker was sitting up in bed, and on his knees there lay an open book, which he ap-peared to have been attentively studying.

He was muttering to himself as the attorney entered the room.

"Ah! hem! To be sure! 'Abraham Peach, aged eighteen; clever at picking pockets. Been thirteen months a member of the family. Stole two watches on September the twenty-first, and said he would see Mr. Wild hanged first before he would bring to Newgate Street the regular per centage on the swag!' Ah, indeed, Mr. Peach! we shall see! You will be strung up at the Octo-ber sessions!"

Jonathan Wild had, fastened to the curtain of the bed by a tape that was round its neck, a little bottle of ink, and into this he now dipped a pen.

"To be hanged October sessions," he wrote opposite the name of Abraham Peach.

Wild then, having satisfactorily settled Mr. Abraham Peach's little business, turned his atten-tion to the next entry in his memoranda.

"Ah! who is this? Oh, I see! 'Charley Lockitt, aged twenty-two, cracksman. Been in the profession two years and a-half. Cracked Mr. Pope's crib in Holborn, and got fourteen pounds and a half of silver plate; sold it all to Travelling Mendoza, the Manchester fence, and is now carry-ing on business at the West End.'"

Wild shook his head.

"Charley Lockitt is a nice boy," he said, in re-flective tones; "but he is going too fast — too fast! I'm sorry for him—very sorry, indeed!"

Jonathan dipped his pen into the ink-bottle.

The memoranda was made.

"Charley Lockitt to swing next sessions."

"Hem!" then said Mr. Smith, the attorney, for he began to fear that his knowledge of Jonathan Wild's secrets might not be so wholesome or desirable a thing as a conference upon the actual business that brought him to Newgate Street.

"Hem!" coughed the lawyer again.

Wild looked up.

"What now?"

"Mr. Wild, I am glad to see you."

"Oh, that's you, is it? Ah!"

Wild ran his finger down an index cutting at the edge of the leaves of his memorandum-book; and the attorney saw with a twinge of apprehen-sion that the great thief-taker paused at the initial of his, Mr. Smith's, real name.

"Confound him!" thought the lawyer; "I do think and believe he has everybody down in that book."

"Well?" said Wild abruptly, as he turned over the leaves of the book.

"Mr. Wild, I have come to you on important business."

"Of course."

"Very important, indeed, I may say to you."

"And to you, too."

"Nay."

"I say to you, too!" roared Wild; "or you would not be here! What is it?"

"I am quite sure, Mr. Wild, that you will find

out, in some way or another, whatever is going on against you or your interests; so if anybody knows anything of either, the safest thing in the world is to come and tell you."

Jonathan glared at the attorney from beneath his knit brows as if he would read his very soul.

"Humph! Go on!"

"Then, Mr. Wild, I do hope and trust that you will see I am much devoted to you by what I am about to tell you."

"Go on!"

"I will, Mr. Wild. You know me?"

"Ha! ha!"

"I say you know me?"

"Of course I do! There is not a greater rogue——"

"Mr. Wild!"

"Unhung! Ha! ha!"

"You are pleased to be facetious, Mr. Wild."

"Not a bit. If you think it is a joke to be hung, it is more than I do."

"Well, well! To business."

"That's sensible. What is it?"

"Lord Warringdale——"

"Ah!"

"That name interests you, Mr. Wild."

"It does. Go on!"

"Lord Warringdale came to me at Moffat House——"

"I know the house. You have managed to get young Lord Moffat into the Fleet, where he will waste his life, while you have taken posses-sion of his house in Essex Street."

"Nay, nay."

"Go on! What is Lord Moffat to me?"

"Well, then, Mr. Wild, as I was saying, Lord Warringdale came to me and said that he was so involved with you that he was willing to do anything in the world to get out of your diabolical clutches."

Wild laughed.

"He said you were the greatest scoundrel the world had ever seen."

Wild laughed louder.

"And that you held his acknowledgments as a charge upon the Whitcombe estates for no less a sum than forty thousand pounds."

"Ah! He said that?"

"He did."

"Go on!"

"Then he offered me ten thousand if I would try any means to rid him of you."

Wild fixed a keen glance on the lawyer.

Possibly the idea may have crossed Jonathan's mind at that moment that he saw an assassin before him; but if it did, he dismissed it in a moment, as too incredible and ridiculous.

Wild laughed louder than before.

"I am glad you are so much amused, Mr. Wild," said the attorney.

"Of course I am amused, and of course you are glad that I am! Now, go on!"

"Well, I thought the best plan would be to pretend to agree to what Lord Warringdale pro-posed, in order that I might know all."

"Good!"

"So, Mr. Wild, I kept him in talk, and he thinks I am his confederate; and here I am, to tell you plainly and distinctly that he wants me to assist him in some attempt upon your life."

"Of course he does! And you?"

"I, by my presence here, and the information I bring you, show sufficiently that I am desirous of acting with you, and against him."

"You are right."

"I feel certain of that."

"You are not such a fool as you look—that is, I mean that you have more sense than I thought you had. Don't be offended at my plain way of speaking."

"Oh, dear, no! It sounds so sincere."

"Very."

"And now, Mr. Wild, what would you wish me to do in this matter?"

"When shall you see him again?"

"At ten o'clock to-morrow night."

"Where?"

"At Moffat House."

"I will be there."

The attorney could scarcely conceal his satisfaction at this announcement on the part of Jonathan Wild, for it was the very thing he wished to accomplish, only that he dreaded to propose it himself, lest Jonathan should suspect some deep-laid trick lay at the bottom of the whole transaction, as indeed there did.

If he once got Wild to Moffat House alone, the attorney looked upon the death of the thief-taker as all but certain.

Jonathan Wild was of a very different opinion.

"I will be there," added Wild.

"You will honour my humble rooms."

"Pshaw! Don't talk nonsense! I will come to you at half-past nine."

"Very good, Mr. Wild. But——"

"Oh, there is a but, is there?"

"No, no! I was only going to say that I had to go and meet Lord Warringdale in St. James's Street, and then we were to come to Moffat House together; so I shall have to leave you alone for some time in Essex Street."

"I shall not be afraid."

"Very good, Mr. Wild. I hope that in this affair you will see that I do you some service?"

"No doubt of it. Nobody does Jonathan Wild a service without finding a good paymaster; and you may be assured you shall receive your reward in full."

There was a kind of significance about the way in which Jonathan uttered these last words which rather alarmed the lawyer.

Were they merely what they seemed, or had they any hidden meaning?

That was rather an anxious question for Mr. Smith to answer, and answer it he could not, so he banished it from his mind.

Surely, he thought, come what might, he and Lord Warringdale would be a match for Jonathan Wild, if even he should get suspicious, and the curious mode of poisoning him that he, Smith, had purchased of the Jew chemist, should not be available.

"Is that all?" said Wild.

"Yes, Mr. Wild."

"Good day!"

The attorney lingered for a moment, and Wild began again, as if he was quite alone, to read the various memoranda in that book of human doom which he had upon his knees.

"'Johnny Mears. Has been once on the highway, and then took to foot-padding in the green lanes about Hornsey. Aged twenty. Says that he was brought to his present mode of life by Jonathan Wild, who, when he was apprentice with Mr. Chandler, the jeweller, got him to rob his master!' The rascal! I got him to rob his master, does he say? The villain! Why, all he took was about a couple of hundred pounds worth of general stock, and I recollect perfectly giving the villain a twenty pound note as his share! Well, there is no such thing as gratitude in the world!"

Wild dipped the pen into the ink-bottle.

"Johnny Mears to be convicted at the next assizes, and hanged in due course!"

The attorney left the room.

The moment he was gone, Jonathan Wild inclined his head in a listening attitude, and waited until he was certain that Mr. Smith had left the house.

Then Wild burst into a horrible peal of loud laughter, that rang through the room.

When Jonathan laughed in that fashion, he always left off abruptly, as if some piece of machinery had been wound up to execute a certain sound, and then ceased at a given period in the very midst of it.

Wild then got up and dressed himself.

"I'm afraid," he said, "that things have been neglected a little in this crib."

He placed a pair of loaded pistols in a belt that he buckled round his waist. Then going to a cupboard in the room, he took from one of its shelves a bottle of brandy.

Jonathan despised the refinement of a glass. He could drink out of the bottle.

The gurgling noise that now sounded in connexion with Wild's throat and the neck of the bottle, showed that his potation was no stinted one.

"Ah!" he said, as he drew a long breath, "that is decidedly good!"

Jonathan replaced the bottle in the cupboard, and then he girt on his hanger, which had been lying on a chair.

In one corner of the room rested one of those short, thick bludgeons, without which Jonathan Wild seldom stirred.

That he now took in his hand, and placed it, with the heavy loaded end downwards, in the wide, ample pocket of his coat.

The thinner end of the bludgeon projected about a foot, and was handy to his grasp.

He meditated a visit to the lower regions of his establishment.

Little Newgate!

That was the popular name which the great thief-taker's house went by.

"I will take a look," said Wild, "and see who is in the cells. I have rather neglected business lately, I'm afraid; but that can be put all right soon."

CHAPTER CLVI.

JONATHAN WILD VISITS HIS PRISONERS IN THE CELLS.

"BLUESKIN!" cried Wild.

"Yes, Mr. Wild. Here you are!"

"Your keys, and come with me!"

ONE OF THE MYSTERY OF LITTLE NEWGATE.

Presented Gratis with No. 70, of the New Edition of the Captive; or, the Robbers of Epping Forest.

EACH WEEK IS PRESENTED IS A COLOURED ENGRAVING.

Blueskin knew very well what Jonathan Wild was about to do.

"That's right, Mr. Wild," he said. "Lord bless you, sir, there's some of 'em down below will have it that you are knocked on the head, sir, and all because they haven't had the pleasure of seeing you for about a week!"

"It is a pity they should be so anxious."

"Quite! Ha! ha! Quite! The sight of you, Mr. Wild, will do them good!"

"Who have we in the cells?"

"Why, Mr. Wild, there's Jemmy Goodacre, the cracksman, and there's Tom Shears, who is as neat a hand in a crowd, where tickers are to go from one pocket to another, as ever I met with."

"I know."

"To be sure you do, Mr. Wild; and then there's that young girl, you recollect, who went up before Mr. Justice Bailey, and said that she saw you at her master's house, in Lincoln's Inn Fields, on the night of the robbery of the pictures, that were cut out of their frames so cleverly by Ned the Ugly One, as we calls him."

"Ah, yes! It was well to nab her."

"She's safe, Mr. Wild."

"Is that all?"

"That's about it, at present, Mr. Wild."

"Very good. Light the lantern."

Blueskin had opened that iron-cased door at the further end of the passage of Jonathan Wild's house, which conducted, by a gloomy flight of stone steps, to the dungeons under Newgate Street, which he had had constructed.

Well might the house of the notorious thief-taker be called "Little Newgate."

Just within that iron-cased door a lantern was always kept, but unlighted. It was easy to apply a match to it when it was wanted.

Blueskin did so now.

The keys which this ferocious assistant of Jonathan Wild carried, were massive and heavy, and they made an ominous gingling sound as he descended the stairs before his master.

"Who will you see first, Mr. Wild?"

"Jemmy Goodacre."

"All's right. Hoy!"

The shout which Blueskin uttered was meant as a kind of warning to the imprisoned cracksman that his cell was about to be visited.

Blueskin then turned one of the keys in the heavy lock of the cell door.

"Now, Jemmy!" he said.

"Now, ugly!" said a voice from within the cell.

Blueskin stepped aside, and Wild appeared on the threshold of the cell.

"Oh!" said the cracksman, "that's you, Mr. Wild, is it?"

"It is."

"Then what do you mean by keeping me cooped up here? What have I done to you?"

"Nothing."

"What do you mean, then?"

"Just this. If you want to breathe the fresh air again, my fine fellow, and to crack a crib once more, you must make terms with me."

"How?"

"I don't allow poaching on my manor."

"Your manor? What's that?"

"Every crib that a cracksman sees his way to

crack. You are a smart, clever fellow, Goodacre, but you must not think to work on your own account. Promise to bring all the swag you can lay hold of to me, and I will give you a price for it, and then you may work at your pleasure."

The housebreaker was silent for a few moments, and then he said, "Well, it is hard for a young fellow to waste his days and nights in a hole like this."

"It is hard."

"I consent."

"Let Jemmy Goodacre go free," said Wild to Blueskin.

"Now, Jemmy," said the assistant, "you are a made man, you are."

"And do you mean to say," cried the cracksman, "that you will take my word for it, Mr. Wild?"

"I do."

"But what is to hinder me when I am once free——"

The housebreaker paused. He thought that probably he was speaking in a very imprudent fashion if he desired his freedom.

"You mean," said Wild, "what is to hinder you from playing me false."

"Just so."

"Well, I will tell you. When a fledgling sparrow can escape a hawk by hiding its head in a bush, then you can escape me. Go! I am content with the bargain, if you are."

The housebreaker turned pale, and it was evident that he felt himself to be under the thraldom of Jonathan Wild.

"Wait in the hall above," said Blueskin. "We shall soon be up."

Jemmy Goodacre slowly ascended the stairs, and sat down in the hall with the patience of a lamb.

"Who next, Mr. Wild?" said Blueskin.

"Tom Shears, the pickpocket."

"Here you are, Mr. Wild."

Blueskin opened the door of another cell, and called out loudly, "Tom, Tom? Where are you? Asleep, lad?"

"No!" cried a voice in reply.

At the same moment the occupant of that cell darted forward and sprung upon Jonathan Wild, inflicting a jagged wound upon his neck with what turned out to be a long nail.

"Ah!" cried Wild, "you will have it, then?"

There was a struggle of a few moments' duration, and then the short, terrible mace-like bludgeon of Jonathan Wild fell with a sickening crash upon the forehead of the pickpocket.

The wretched man fell to the floor of the cell as if struck by lightning.

"That's done!" said Wild.

Blueskin held the lantern down.

"You have settled him, Mr. Wild!"

"He assailed me."

"To be sure he did that. He was a neat hand at a transfer, I will say. Poor Tom Shears! Poor Tom—poor——"

"Silence!"

"Yes, Mr. Wild."

"What do you mean by your confounded repetition of your poor Tom? Am I to be murdered in cold blood by any one who chooses to fly at me like a brute animal, eh?"

"No, Mr. Wild."

"Get rid of the body before night."

"Yes," said Blueskin, gloomily.

"Stay! It shall be done at once."

Blueskin looked black and sullen.

"If he should not be dead?" he muttered.

"Give me the lantern. No, you hold it. Down closer. There!"

Jonathan stooped right down to the prostrate body before him, and seizing the wretched pickpocket by the hair of his head, he turned the ghastly face upwards.

Death was upon every feature.

"Are you satisfied now?" said Wild.

"He's gone!"

"Of course! I don't need to strike twice. He shall be disposed of at once."

"At once?"

"Yes!" roared Wild; "and why not? Do you want to keep carrion like this above ground, to bring destruction on us all? Where would your neck be, Blueskin, if all was known that took place in Little Newgate, eh? Where, I say?"

"In a noose!"

"Of course it would! Come on!"

"I'm coming."

"Give me the keys."

Blueskin gave up the keys to Jonathan Wild, who, leaving the cell where the murdered man lay so still in death, made his way along the common passage from which all the cells opened to the extreme end of it.

Then appeared a door strongly clamped with iron, like the door at the end of the passage of the house above.

Wild selected one of the keys and opened this door.

A terrible noisome stench came immediately from the other side of it.

"The Fleet is in bad odour to-day," muttered Wild.

"It always is nowadays," said Blueskin. "They make it so about Bagnigge Wells."

Wild held the lantern now at arm's length before him into the cell which he had just opened, and its gleams fell upon a chasm in the floor which opened right down to one of the large City drains that ran down Snow Hill into the old Fleet River at Holborn Bridge.

A strange, washing, gurgling noise came up from the terrible and gloomy chasm.

"Bring the body," said Wild.

Blueskin turned and walked back to the cell of the pickpocket.

Wild went about a dozen steps after him to light him.

With glances that betokened anything but satisfaction at what had occurred, Blueskin soon reappeared with the dead body of Tom Shears, the pickpocket.

"Now, be quiet!" said Jonathan.

"I don't like to do it."

"You—don't—like——"

"No, Mr. Wild. You see, Tom was a sort of a pal of mine."

"What then?"

"Why, a fellow's feelings."

"What?"

"Feelings!"

Jonathan Wild burst into one of those awful peals of laughter which upon rare occasions he in-

dulged in, and which, as we have described, ceased always in so sudden and startling a fashion.

"Well," he said, "this is the first time I ever heard the word feelings uttered in Little Newgate. Perhaps, Blueskin, as you are so tender-hearted, you would like me to throw him in while you hold the lantern?"

"I would rather."

"Very well, I will do it; and since your feelings, Blueskin, are so very sensitive, you can hold the lantern."

Jonathan Wild spoke in a low, jeering tone of voice; but Blueskin looked grave and solemn, and was evidently not very well pleased at the whole transaction.

Probably, indeed, he might have taken some active notice of what had occurred in the way of direct opposition to Jonathan Wild; but it was too late to save the life that had been cast away. And then Blueskin could not conceal from himself the fact that the neat-handed pickpocket he had lauded so much had certainly been the aggressor.

From that moment, however, it might be said that the community of interests between Blueskin and Jonathan Wild had ceased; and we shall see, in the course of this narrative, how fatal it became to Jonathan Wild to lose the good will of a generally unscrupulous adherent like Blueskin.

The dead body had been brought to the verge of the abyss, beneath which gurgled and flowed the noisome stream communicating with the old Fleet.

Blueskin held up the lantern, and his hand shook a little as he did so. Then Jonathan Wild was about to stoop to lift the body, but he saw it was useless to do so, as, by pushing it forward with his foot, it must inevitably fall down the abyss.

"He's quite dead," said Blueskin.

"If you doubt it," roared Wild, in a passion, "satisfy yourself again."

"No; it's all over with him," added Blueskin.

Wild did not say another word, but urging the body forward a few inches with his foot, he brought it to the very brink of the cavern.

Another moment, and down it surged. There was a heavy splash. All was over with the pickpocket, whose skill in his profession had been so lauded by Blueskin.

"That's over!" said Wild. "It was the power to kill me, not the will, that the fellow wanted. I think you said, Blueskin, that the only other person in the cells was that young girl who made herself so dangerous before Mr. Justice Bailey?"

"That's all."

"I will see her. Take your keys."

Blueskin led the way willingly enough from that gloomy portion of Wild's domains which led to the Fleet River, and then, through its embrasure, to the Thames.

Another cell door was flung open, and a low, wailing voice issued from within.

"Oh, have mercy upon me, and let me go! I will say nothing—indeed, I will not speak! I will go away into the country—far away—and will not utter a word! In mercy let me go! I shall die in this dreadful place; and it is terrible to die so young, and so far away from all who know me and love me! Let me go, and I will swear to be silent! I am not one to break an oath, and you shall dictate it to me yourself, if you will ; but let me go ! Mercy, mercy !—oh, have mercy upon me !"

"Ha, ha !" laughed Wild. "So, my lass, you feel that your little expedition to Justice Bailey was rather ill-judged ?"

"Yes, yes, I repent it—indeed I do repent it, Mr. Wild ! I am truly sorry, and I will say no more ! Trust me, and let me go !"

"Trust you !" said Wild. "That's good ! Blueskin ?"

"Yes, Mr. Wild."

"Did you ever know me trust anybody ?"

Blueskin made a grimace, and held the lantern a little further into the cell, so that its rays fell upon the pale, emaciated face of the young girl, who was kneeling upon some straw, and holding up her hands clasped in an imploring attitude.

Tears were streaming down her face, and every now and then she uttered such a heartrending half-shriek, half-sob, that it should surely have evoked some compassion even in a heart of stone.

But Jonathan Wild's heart was harder than stone.

He laughed again.

"Hark ye, my lass !" he said. "It appears you were foolish enough to recognise me at your master's house in Lincoln's Inn Fields, on the night of the robbery."

"I could not help it. I saw you."

"Ah ! that's your misfortune ! And after that you were so far given over to your folly, that you must needs go before Mr. Justice Bailey, and say as much. I was then sent for, and the case was postponed for three days at my request "

"Yes, it was so ; and on that very evening I was assailed in the open square close to my master's house, forced into a hackney-coach, and brought to this dreadful place."

"Of course. The three days then expired, and I appeared again before Justice Bailey, who, remarking on your absence, said you had evidently fabricated the story, and were afraid to appear again, and there was an end of the matter."

"Yes, Mr. Wild ; and you will let me go now —I am sure you will ! Folks say that you are cruel and relentless, but I will not believe them ; for you will let me go now, and I will promise to offend you no more. I will go far away—indeed, I will !"

"There's no occasion," said Wild, drily. "Blueskin, you will see that this clever, observant young female is properly provided with bread and water. The expense is not great, and I'm a liberal man !"

"Mercy ! mercy !" screamed the young girl. "You are human yet ! You cannot mean to kill me—to keep me here until I die of weakness and despair !"

"Ha ! ha !" laughed Wild.

"Mercy—mercy ! Let me free !"

Wild laughed again.

"You jest with me—you mock me ! I will leave England even, if you will have mercy upon me, and let me free !"

"That'll do !" said Wild. "Shut up, Blueskin !"

The door of the cell was closed with a crash, and the smothered shrieks and cries of the young girl came but faintly upon the ears of her relentless persecutor.

Wild whistled a jocose, popular air, as he now ascended the stairs that led to the ground floor of his house, for he had finished his survey of those cells, which gave to his habitation the ominous name of " Little Newgate."

"That's finished," he said ; " and all being well at home, I can turn my attention to my kind friend Lord Warringdale and his affairs, and likewise to that pleasant and clever Mr. Smith, the attorney."

There seemed to be something that tickled the imagination of Wild immensely, whenever he thought of, or mentioned, the lawyer, who had recently visited him in so apparently candid and friendly a manner, for he burst out again into one of his loud laughs, terminating it as usual in that odd, abrupt manner, which made the mirth sound so deadly and artificial.

CHAPTER CLVII.

MR. SMITH AND LORD WARRINGDALE CONGRATULATE EACH OTHER.

"My lord," said the attorney, who inhabited Moffat House in Essex Street, Strand, as he rubbed his hands together, and looked smilingly in the face of Lord Warringdale,—" my lord, I think we may congratulate ourselves upon accomplishing the destruction of Jonathan Wild."

Lord Warringdale looked gloomy.

These two worthies had met at the chambers occupied by his lordship in St. James's Street, immediately opposite Whitcombe House.

"I see your lordship is haunted by doubts and fears," added the attorney ; " but I have every possible hope of success. If Jonathan Wild will but sit down for five minutes at Moffat House, he is a dead man !"

"I hope so—I hope so, indeed ; and at times I almost believe so—and then, again, at times there comes over my mind a recollection of the extreme subtlety of the villain. In truth, he has the suspicion and the craft of twenty men combined in his one person. Tell me, however, exactly how you mean to arrange, that I may play my own part properly."

"Be not doubtful, my lord ; all will go well. There are two things to do—that is, two enemies to dispose of, Jonathan Wild and Felix Heron. The latter your lordship will see to ; the former I will free you from. And in regard to Mr. Wild, I do not wish you to do anything, unless you would like to come to Moffat House and look upon his corpse."

"A most welcome sight !"

"You shall have it."

"I don't know anything that would lift a greater weight off my mind, for of one thing I feel confident—and that is, that even should I succeed in quenching all opposition to my being called to the House of Peers as Earl of Whitcombe, I should be harrassed to death by the villain Wild. His exactions would know no end, and the forty thousand pounds for which he actually holds my acknowledgments, swell by degrees into the value of the Whitcombe estates. He would hold my title—life—my reputation—my very name at stake, indeed ! I will come to Moffat House—hide me there in one of its most gloomy chambers, and I will wait with patience until you come to me with the most welcome words that ever saluted human ears, and they shall be, 'Jonathan Wild is dead!—Jonathan Wild is dead!'"

"Be it so, my lord. The old house has more than fifty rooms within it. Come, then, at about nine this evening; you will be then half an hour before Jonathan Wild arrives, and I will be there to bestow you somewhere in safety."

"And should you fail? Should that strange, subtle vapour, upon which you place so much reliance, turn out to be but a dream—a delusion?"

A malignant look came over the face of the attorney, and he replied in a low tone, "I have not left myself without other resources. It is neither pleasant nor desirable to get into trouble with the law, even about the death of such a man as Wild; so that if he can be put out of the world chemically and scientifically, you understand, so that there shall be no appearance of personal violence, it will be better, as then we can easily take his dead body into the streets at night, where it may be found, and there will be no inquiry, since no appearance of a violent death will be perceptible."

"But if your scientific means should fail?"

"Then I will resort to others. In the room which he will occupy, waiting, as he thinks, for my arrival with you, I have constructed a small orifice in the wall, through which the muzzle of a pistol can be quietly placed and safely directed. A bullet then will do the business, if other means fail."

"You cheer me—you cheer me!" cried Warringdale, as he started to his feet. "Rid of him, and rid of Felix Heron, what have I to fear? I shall be truly the Earl of Whitcombe, for no one will gainsay my assumption of the title. The approaching change of Ministry will bring my party into power; and, with rank, wealth, and political influence, I shall surely be able to find contentment."

"And do something for your friends," said the attorney.

"Yes; and you shall rank first among their number."

"Be it so, my lord; but I am tolerably satisfied with the document you have already signed, and which assures me, at least, of some reward for my arduous services."

That day sank but gloomily over London, for the summer was speeding away, and the weather was getting precarious. Essex Street, Strand—never a very lively place—was early involved in darkness; and Mr. Smith, as he called himself, sat in that large, ancient, and gloomy apartment in Moffat House, into which he had first introduced Lord Warringdale, upon their accidental meeting in the Temple.

A fire of logs burnt upon the low hearth, but there was no lamp or candle-light in the room, which was but dimly illuminated by the flickering flames that now and then coiled, like fiery serpents, around the large clumps of wood which lay one over the other.

The ancient apartment had an appearance of past grandeur, which was much more imposing by that flickering and evasive light, than as if the sunbeams had poured into the place, to make every defect glaringly visible.

The faded portions of the gilding upon the walls, panels, and ceiling might, by that flickering and uncertain light, have been mistaken for shadows merely. The old Utrecht velvet that covered the chairs and sofas, no longer looked colourless and threadbare in places; and a dim, ancient-looking Flemish portrait, which was over the richly-carved chimney-piece, seemed to catch the wavy firelight upon its eyes, and to be looking down upon the apartment in contemplation of its past splendours.

The attorney paced the room uneasily.

"It's sure to succeed!" he said. "It's sure to succeed! He suspects nothing—how can he suspect anything? He will be here to a certainty; and, one way or another, Jonathan Wild will be a dead man before another hour has passed away!"

The attorney flung himself into a high-backed chair, with something almost resembling a groan.

Despite all the security into which he tried to cheat himself, he felt anxious and ill at ease.

He stirred the logs on the fire, and they sent forth brighter flames.

"How is it to fail?" he said. "How is it to fail?"

He spoke in an interrogative style, as if he were addressing some one; and, as he did so, his eyes wandered up to the face of the old Flemish portrait; and it appeared to him as if the eyes of the portrait were looking right down into his, and as if the mouth curled with a mocking expression.

"I will have that old picture removed to-morrow," he said. "I hate the sight of it."

Even as he spoke, there came a heavy blow on one of the knockers of the ancient house.

The attorney started to his feet.

"It is Wild!" he said—"it is Wild!"

Eagerly he seized a pair of small chemical tongs that were hidden among the scroll-work of the chimney-piece; and lifting with them one of the large logs of wood that were burning on the hearth, he looked into a cavity which had evidently been designedly formed in the clump of wood immediately beneath it.

In that cavity reposed a lump of metal nearly of a red heat.

It was a copper button of large size, the shank of which being upwards, would enable it to be lifted with ease.

"It will do—it will do!" he said.

Bang! came the knock at the door again.

"He is impatient; but that is of no matter. I feel confident that the mysterious vapour must needs kill him. I will but detain him for a moment in the outer room while I make all preparations."

There were so many intricate carvings and mouldings, with animals' heads and scrolls of flowers, about the huge old chimney-piece, that the attorney felt no difficulty whatever in discovering a place in which he could snugly ensconce the little box in which he had been so thoroughly assured was the chemical preparation that would evolve, when heated, a deadly exhalation.

He placed the box in a secure crevice; and he felt that he had nothing to do then but to lift the red-hot copper button with the chemical tongs, and place it in the midst of the death-dealing powder.

But that must not be done prematurely.

Had he not been assured that the enervating influence of the vapour would be almost instantaneous, and that in the short space of five minutes it would carry death to heart and brain?

How careful—how exact—how precise and neat in his arrangements he had to be in such dangerous and deadly doings!

The knock came a third time.

The attorney hastened to the door to let in Jonathan Wild.

"My dear Smith," said Wild, with what he intended to be a smile, but which was a hideous sarcastic contortion of the countenance,—"my dear Smith, I have knocked thrice!"

"Is it possible?"

"Yes—and true. You were asleep, I fancy?"

"You've just hit it, Mr. Wild. Having nothing particular to think of, I sat looking at the fire, until it drew me to slumber."

"I expected as much; but as I'm in good time,

No. 71.—EDITH.

it matters not. Truly, in old times, this must have been a most pretentious residence, and might be still, only fashion has wended somewhat westward of Essex Street."

Wild looked and spoke quite amiably.

Mr. Smith preceded him up the once magnificent staircase of Moffat House, carrying in his hand a small hand-lamp, which had been burning on a bracket in the ancient hall.

"And so poor young Moffat is in the Fleet!" said Wild,—" rotting in the Fleet! Well off, though, I suppose?"

"No; starving!"

"Indeed!"

"That is to say, he would starve, but there was a young girl who loved him, although she met with but a wretched return for her affection, for he deceived and deserted her. She, however, now supports him in the Fleet."

"Touching amiability!" said Wild. "I almost

think, at last, I shall come to fall in love with human nature, and leave a large sum of money to found some almshouses, to be called 'Jonathan Wild's Refuge for Suffering Virtue.'"

Wild said all this in a sneering, sarcastic tone of voice, which jarred very much upon the spirits of the attorney. Much rather would he have heard Jonathan declaim angrily against Lord Warringdale; but all the preparations were made, and Mr. Smith had gone too far to retreat. He strove to gather confidence, and to assure himself that all would yet be well; and so he and Wild, step by step, ascended the grand staircase of Moffat House, and reached the landing, as large itself as a good-sized room, on the first floor.

There Mr. Smith paused, and strove to say something which would at once have the effect of restoring his own spirits to their wonted vigour, and of banishing all suspicion from Jonathan Wild's mind.

"Mr. Wild," he said, "I'm anxious and nervous, to tell the truth."

"Ah, indeed!"

"Yes. I am afraid that you meditate some mischief against Lord Warringdale; and before I go to fetch him, pray give me some assurance that you will not let your natural feeling of indignation get the better of your prudence."

This speech was made by the attorney to Jonathan Wild expressly for the purpose of impressing him with the idea that my Lord Warringdale was, without doubt, to be brought to Moffat House.

Mr. Smith was a good actor, and he played his part very well.

Even Jonathan Wild, adept as he was in all kinds of deceit, was almost deceived. It was but for a moment, though, that Wild yielded to the talent of the attorney, and then he was himself again.

"Oh, no!" he replied. "You may, indeed, rely wholly and entirely upon my discretion."

"I am delighted to hear it."

"And upon my temper."

"I am sure, Mr. Wild, you will believe that I spoke from the best of motives in this matter?"

"Of course you did. Who could doubt, for a single moment, the motives of a lawyer?"

This was rather an equivocal compliment, and Mr. Smith did not feel quite pleased or reassured; nevertheless, he put on a look of satisfaction, which he took good care to let Jonathan Wild see, by holding the little hand-lamp close to his face.

"This way," he said,—"this way. The old mansion is terribly dark always when the evening fairly sets in; and as for lighting it up, that would be an expense I am certainly not prepared to go to."

"It were needless," said Wild. "I, for my part, like these dark, dim old houses."

"So do I—so do I! This way, if you please, Mr. Wild."

The attorney led Jonathan into the room immediately adjoining that where the fire of logs was burning, and where the curious and interesting preparations were made for evolving the mysterious vapour from the little box that was in the niche amid the old rich carvings of the chimney-piece.

"I am to wait here?" asked Wild.

"One moment, if you please."

"Oh, certainly!"

The attorney put down the hand-lamp on a table in the room, and Jonathan paused close to it, and looked calm and contented.

Then the attorney passed into the next apartment.

Wild saw him close the door, and he bent all his energies to listen if he locked it.

Click! went the lock.

"Ah!" said Wild; "some nice little plan is on foot. What can it be?"

Then Jonathan Wild said, in a low voice, "Are you here, bull-dogs?"

"Here!" replied a faint voice from behind some faded curtains in the room.

"Here!" said another voice, in similarly low accents, from beneath a couch.

"Good!" said Wild.

CHAPTER CLVIII.

THE GOOD FORTUNE THAT ATTENDS JONATHAN WILD SAVES HIS LIFE.

WHEN Mr. Smith, the attorney, left Wild in that outer room, he felt that he was running a great risk.

The risk of at once arousing all the suspicions of the thief-taker that some foul play was intended.

But what else could he do?

The subtle nature of the poisonous gas which he intended to evolve from the little box, required that it should not be liberated until the very last moment.

Of course that button, which was waiting on the fire in a state of incandescence, could not be lifted on to the powder in the box before the eyes of Jonathan Wild.

There was no resource, then, but to leave him in the outer room for about half a minute, at all risks.

The attorney then locked the door.

He thought he had executed that measure of obvious precaution against such a man as Jonathan Wild, with a caution that prevented it being heard, but that, as we are aware, was not the case.

Wild had heard it.

The attorney then proceeded at once to the fireplace. He took the small chemical tongs in his hand, and although he shook a little as he did so, he succeeded in laying hold of the shank of the button.

The button was red-hot.

With a radiating glow it passed through the space between the log of wood, on which it had reposed for so long, to the niche among the carving of the chimney-piece, where nestled the little box.

Another moment, and the attorney dropped the red-hot button on to the powdered substance in the box.

He averted his face as he did so.

A peculiar odour at once impregnated the room.

It was not a disagreeable odour.

The attorney felt that it had saluted his senses before, but he could not at once say when and where. Then he recollected that it was something like the odour of the incense in Catholic places of worship.

But he had rapidly flung down the chemical tongs, and he flew to the door of the room.

"Now, now," he said, "I shall have him!"

He turned the key in the lock.

The attorney then uttered a hoarse cry of alarm.

He had immediately, upon turning the key in the lock of the door, placed his hand on to the latch handle, and jerked it round.

But the door would not open.

The attorney was locked into that terrible room with the red-hot copper button on the powder, that was to evolve the fumes of death.

He uttered another strange and terrible cry.

Alarm had got the better of all prudence now.

"Help! help! There is something the matter with the lock of the door!"

There was, indeed. The old lock had got over-shot, or some portion of it had given way. But be the reason what it might, the attorney had locked himself in, and there was no hope for him.

He had purposely chosen that room, because there was no outlet from it but by that one door —that one door at which he had intended to let in Jonathan Wild—that one door, from which he intended to adroitly take the key, and then slip out into the outer apartment, and lock Jonathan in.

The odour in the room became more powerful each moment.

But it was no longer the odour of incense alone.

Some much more pungent essense was mingling with it, slowly but surely.

The attorney gasped for breath.

He made another desperate attempt to open the door, but it was in vain.

It was the key.

Yes, the key had broken in the lock. It came out in his hand without the wards.

But there might be a hope yet.

The attorney sprang with two frantic bounds towards the fireplace. Surely he might extinguish the baleful combustion that was going on in the little box, and, if so, he would be saved.

He dashed the box off the niche in which he had so cleverly placed it. It fell on to the hearth —the powder scattered from it—but each individual grain of that powder seemed now to be a red-hot particle, which no power on earth could extinguish.

The attorney stamped upon it—he scattered it with his feet.

But still it burnt.

Still it sent up vapours which were gradually filling the apartment.

There came then a sharp knocking at the door of the apartment.

That was Wild.

"Hilloa! hilloa! What's the matter?"

Mr. Smith gasped and staggered. He had to lay hold of the back of a chair for support. A terrible pain began across his eyes.

The vapours of death were at work.

"Hilloa! hilloa!" cried Wild again.

He knocked furiously at the door.

The attorney tried to scream for help. He

meant to scream, but all he could do was to say something that was half-inarticulate in a faint whisper.

He staggered round the chair.

He fell with a groan into its recesses.

The terrible pain over his eyes spread over the top of his head.

It seemed as if his skull was being forced off by some tremendous pressure from within.

There was a convulsive movement of his hands, and then a gush of tears came from his eyes. His head sunk down upon his breast.

The attorney was dead!

In that old, deep-seated chair, by the fireside, he sat, a corpse.

The vapour from the powder that had been in the little box had done its terrible work, and it was nearly over. There had been but a small quantity, and that was now nearly consumed.

If the attorney could have lived until that time he might have began to recover.

It may appear strange that he did not fly to one of the windows for air, for there were two in the room; but he had anticipated—so clever and cunning was he—that Jonathan Wild would do that, and so he had taken most excellent care that the shutters were so well closed and fastened that no one could open them under, at the very least, ten minutes' trouble.

What care for self-murder!

What cunning and perseverance to compass his own destruction!

The lawyer was dead!

Wild knocked again at the door.

He could not imagine what had happened, and so, after knocking again and again, and hearing no response whatever, he turned to his two men.

Those two men had, hours before, upon Wild's instructions, made their way into Moffat House, and hidden to await his orders.

"Come forward, men," said Wild.

From behind the curtains, and from under the couch, came the two men.

"Here, Mr. Wild!"

"Break that door open!"

"I can pick the lock, Mr. Wild," said one.

"Very well."

Jonathan did not feel quite sure yet that all now taking place might not be part of the scheme of the lawyer for his destruction, and he drew a pistol from his pocket, and took good care to stand out of the line of attack from the other room when the door should be opened.

The bull-dog with the picklock was foiled.

The broken wards of the key that was in the lock effectually prevented him from opening it.

"No," he said; "there is something in the lock."

"Break it open!" said Wild.

"Yes, sir."

The man produced a thieves crow-bar—one of those small, hard, steel "jemmies" which the housebreaker carries with him,—and which, while deadly weapons of offence, will force open the strongest door, if skilfully used.

There was a creaking noise for a few seconds, which then increased to a sharp crackling one, and then the door flew open.

Jonathan elevated the hand in which he held the pistol.

No! there was no attack.

Wild himself then took the little hand-lamp, and walked slowly into the room—the room of the dead!

"A strange odour!" he said.

"Very, Mr. Wild," said one of the bull-dogs.

"Smith, are you here? Speak!"

Smith would never speak again.

The logs still burnt upon the ample old hearth, and still sent their flickering, flaming radiance over the room, with all its antique furnishing and appointments; but it was a few moments before either Jonathan or his two men saw the dead body of the attorney.

It was Wild himself, then, who, upon walking directly up to the fire-place, saw Mr. Smith apparently asleep in the chair.

"What does this mean?" he said.

The two bull-dogs advanced quickly.

"Smith!" roared Wild; "what farce is this?"

There shot up from the burning wood on the hearth at this moment a brighter flame, and as it played in mimic radiance upon the face of the dead attorney, Jonathan could no longer be in doubt that the seeming sleep was that which in this world knows no waking.

"Dead!" he said.

"Very dead, indeed, Mr. Wild," said one of the bull-dogs, as he looked curiously and closely into the face of the corpse.

Wild turned slowly round upon his heels, and took a long survey of the room.

He could not understand what it all meant.

That the attorney had in some way come by his own death by the means he had intended for his, Jonathan Wild's, destruction, was an idea likely to suggest itself, but the manner of the act was to Wild a perfect enigma.

Then the strange odour came across his senses again, and turning abruptly to his men, he said, "Do you smell anything?"

"Yes, Mr. Wild."

"What is it?"

The bull-dogs shook their heads, and then one said, "I don't know what it is, Mr. Wild, but it has given me a headache."

"That's it, then. I partly understand it now. Ha! ha! So that was the clever trick, was it? the fowler is caught in his own snare! Ha! ha!"

Tinkle! tinkle! tinkle! came at this moment the sound of a bell.

Wild started.

"Who is that?"

"Shall I go to the outer door and see, Mr. Wild?" asked one of the bull-dogs.

"No; stop a moment. Let me think."

The sound of the bell came again.

Then Jonathan Wild, with an imprecation, said, "That is Lord Warringdale, I'll wager anything. Here, you Jobkins! go to the door; speak quietly, and say to the person you will let in, these words: 'It's all done, my lord, and Mr. Smith will be glad to see you. Then you can show him up here."

"Yes, Mr. Wild."

The man departed on his errand.

"Mildew!" said Wild to the other bull-dog.

"Yes, Mr. Wild."

"Stoop down behind that chair."

Jonathan indicated the chair with the dead body in it.

Mildew obeyed him.

"I want you," added Wild, "when you find the head and face of the visitor who is approaching sufficiently close for the purpose, to reach round the chair and lay hold of him by the hair and ears, and hold him fast face to face with the corpse."

"Ah, Mr, Wild, will you excuse me?"

"What? Scoundrel!"

"No, Mr. Wild; I only mean that it will be much funnier if I sit in the chair with the dead body in my lap."

Wild laughed.

"So it will—so it will! You are ingenious, Mildew, and—and—you are not particular."

"Not a bit, Mr. Wild."

Mildew showed that he was not particular, for he lifted up the dead body of the attorney, and sat down in the chair himself with it in his lap. He held up the mortal remains of Mr. Smith by one arm round the waist.

Even Wild seemed to think that was a horrible spectacle, and he drew back a pace or two.

"Ah, he comes!" he said.

Wild then fetched himself a chair, and sat down on the other side of the fire-place.

The wood had very nearly exhausted all its flames, and it was now and then only that a faint, flickering, blue light played over the surface of the well-burnt logs.

The door of the room was abruptly opened.

Lord Warringdale spoke quickly and sharply.

"Smith," he said, "is it possible that you have succeeded? and was it possible, at the same time, that you required a confederate and *confidante?*"

"Oh, yes!" said Wild.

Lord Warringdale uttered a shout of dismay. He knew too well the tones of Jonathan's voice to doubt, even in the semi-darkness of that room, his identity for a moment.

And then Lord Warringdale would fain have fled from the room, and from the house itself, on the wings of fear; but the bull-dog who was behind him knew his duty too well to permit that. He had closed the room door, and had his back against it.

"My dear Warringdale," added Wild; "what is the matter?"

"The—the—matter?"

"Yes. You seem agitated."

"Agitated?"

"Well, perhaps I am wrong, for the light is but small in this apartment of our old friend."

"Our—old—friend?"

It seemed that the terror of Warringdale was so great, that he had lost all power of independent thought, and could only become the reflex of what Jonathan Wild said to him.

"Why," added Jonathan, "what can have happened to make you so strange?"

"Oh—nothing! I—I—that is——"

"My dear Warringdale, I met, you see, an old friend—the man who now calls himself Smith. He was good enough to say that you and he had an appointment here this evening; so, you see, I thought I would join the little party."

"You?—you?"

"Even I! And why not?"

"Oh, there is no reason; on the contrary, I thought—I fully expected that—that you would be here!"

TOM RIPON TAKES HIS LORDSHIP IN TOW.

Presented Gratis with No. 71 of the New Edition of Edith the Captive; or, the Robbers of Epping Forest.

EACH WEEK IS PRESENTED GRATIS A COLOURED ENGRAVING.

"To be sure you did! And here I am!"
Lord Warringdale, with slow steps, made his way now towards the fire-place. He was in a state of great surprise and astonishment, and wondered what had happened, and what was going to happen next.

"Here we are, you see!" said Wild.

"We?"

"Yes—Smith and I!"

"Oh!"

"Don't you see him? There he sits, but he seems almost ashamed to speak to you."

"Smith!"

The bull-dog who had the dead lawyer on his knees took hold of the dead arms with his disengaged hand, and made a gesture with it.

"For the love of peace and—and of common interests," said Warringdale, with a groan, "tell me what all this means?"

"Do you address me," said Wild, "or Smith?"

"Smith."

"Ah! then you must speak louder."

"Wherefore?"

"He is not well."

"Ah! Then he is hurt."

"On my soul," said Wild, "he is not hurt by me, for I have not raised a finger against him."

"Smith, tell me at once what is the meaning of all this!" said Warringdale in tones of despair and desperation—and, at the same time that he spoke, he seized the arm of the corpse and shook it to and fro.

"Don't!" said Wild's man.

"Eh?"

"Don't!"

Wild could only with the greatest difficulty control his laughter.

"Come—come, my Lord Warringdale," he said. "Bring yourself a chair."

"No, no!"

"But I say yes, yes! Bring a chair, and let us three hold a consultation — you, Smith, and myself."

Lord Warringdale hesitated for a few moments, and then he brought a chair, and sat down.

"That's comfortable!" said Wild.

"But——"

"One moment, my lord—let me begin. Smith has kindly informed me that you have proposed to him to get rid of me."

"No, no!"

"I appeal to you, Smith?"

"Yes," said the bull-dog.

"There—you hear—you hear, my lord. But I said, at once, to Smith, 'Perhaps you are not aware,' I said, 'that it is a very difficult thing to get rid of me, for his lordship has himself tried it, and failed.'"

"This is intolerable!" said Lord Warringdale.

"Nay, hear me out."

"Well, well?"

"Smith, therefore, began to dispute and argue, and would not be convinced without a trial. He has had it. Have you not, Smith?"

"Yes," said the bull-dog.

"Well, the result has been the death of Smith."

"Death!" cried Warringdale.

"Yes. Are you not dead, Smith?"

"I am."

"A farce! a farce!" cried Lord Warringdale, as he sprung to his feet.

"No, my lord; a tragedy. Get away!"

These last two words were whispered to the bull-dog who was in charge of the dead body, and then Wild called aloud, "A light!—a light, here! —a light!"

The bull-dog who had played the part of Smith adroitly moved from the chair, and replaced the dead lawyer in it.

Then the other man came from the outer room with the hand-lamp.

Jonathan Wild, too, at the same moment, gave the expiring embers of the wood fire a kick, which so changed the position of the logs, that several bright, long flames darted from them.

The room was no longer in that dim and obscure twilight condition which had made the preceding scene possible.

"Now," said Wild, as he pointed to the dead body in the chair; "see, my Lord Warringdale, if this be not more of a tragedy than a farce."

One glance at the dead face was enough.

There could be no doubt that the destroyer was there.

Lord Warringdale recoiled with horror.

"You see!" said Wild.

"Good heavens, I am mad!"

"Not in the ordinary sense," added Jonathan; "but only in imagining that you can do without me, or that you can ever compass my destruction. There, indeed, you are mad!"

Towards the end of these few words Jonathan Wild had raised his voice to a high pitch.

Lord Warringdale sunk back again into the chair he had previously occupied, and uttered a deep groan!

"Begone!" said Wild to his two men,—"begone! and take this carrion with you!"

"Where shall we put it, Mr. Wild?"

"Prop it up in some doorway."

This was just what had been intended to be done with Jonathan Wild, if the scheme for his destruction had been successful.

Lord Warringdale clasped both his hands over his face, and seemed to give himself up to despair.

The two men laid hold of the defunct Mr. Smith, and without the least ceremony hauled him from the room.

The door closed upon them.

Then Jonathan Wild burst into one of those terrible laughs of his, and this time it lasted longer than usual, although it ended in the ordinary abrupt and startling fashion.

Lord Warringdale shook in every limb.

Then, after a silence of some minutes, Wild spoke.

"My lord, you are slow to understand what you should know. Do you know me?"

"I do!"

"Well, you fancy every now and then that you can do without me. You take it into your head that I am expensive. You try to get rid of me by death."

Warringdale groaned.

"But it will not do—I repeat, it will not do; and until you are convinced of that, there will no good done in your affairs. You are your own ruin, and have yourself alone to blame."

Still Lord Warringdale did not reply.

"You are slow of apprehension," added Wild, "because you are disappointed. But that will wear away, and you will see your true interests. I may be expensive, but not dear, my Lord Warringdale; and it will be well that from this time forward we understand each other."

Lord Warringdale looked up now, and glared with suspicion and aversion into the face of Jonathan Wild.

"So you have killed him ?" he said.

"Killed who ? The lawyer ?"

"You know well who. A dead body is taken from the presence of Jonathan Wild by two of his men, and it needs no further question as to how it came by its death."

"And that is what vexes and disappoints my Lord Warringdale," sneered Wild. "It was the body of his friend Jonathan he wished to see taken from this room, and not that of his new ally, the attorney; and moreover he jumps to a conclusion, which is wholly and entirely wrong. I have not killed the man; and am now perfectly at fault as to how he came by his death."

"Can that be possible ?"

"It is true; for, although I am perfectly well aware that he meant to take my life by the same means that have been fatal to his own, I know not up to this moment what those means were, and probably shall never know, unless——"

"Unless what ?"

"Unless your lordship is kind enough to inform me."

Warringdale was silent for a few moments, and during that brief period he reflected upon his position. That Smith the attorney was dead there could be no doubt, and that Jonathan Wild probably knew of the plan for the capture of Felix Heron seemed likely enough, since, by some mysterious means, he had evidently found out that for his own destruction; much therefore as he mourned over the necessity of making yet closer companionship and community of interest with Jonathan Wild, he did not now see how it was to be avoided.

But what sort of communication, or what kind of confidence, could he and Wild now have in each other, after what had passed — after those two attempts upon the life of the thief-taker.

Lord Warringdale was not a man of quick sensibilities, but he felt how extremely awkward it was to hold confidential communication with a man whom he had twice attempted to murder.

Perhaps Jonathan Wild, with his usual keenness, saw this little difficulty.

"My lord, I am willing," he said, "that the past should rest. It is the future which interests us. In that I am willing to act with you, faithfully and well."

"Will you make one condition ?" said Warringdale, gloomy.

"Not blindly. What is it ?"

"An easy one. It is that the name of that man Smith is never to be mentioned between us."

"That is easy, indeed. I shall forget it in a day."

"You agree to it, then ?"

"I do."

"Jonathan Wild, then, I will now tell you all, and seek for your assistance in a plan I have for the capture of Felix Heron."

Lord Warringdale then detailed to Jonathan Wild the full particulars of that most insidious, crafty, and diabolical scheme, which was to draw Captain Heron to London, in the hope that it would end in his destruction.

Wild thought well of the plan, and promised to attend to some of its minor details; so that in the course of an hour any one who might have seen those two persons conversing together would have thought them the best friends in the world.

At all events, it would never have entered into the imagination of any one to conceive that so short a time before one of them had only escaped death, by the merest accident in the world, at the instigation of the other.

CHAPTER CLIX.

LORD WARRINGDALE PLAYS THE PART OF A VIRTUOUS PENITENT.

It is Sunday night—the Sunday preceding the levee at St. James's Palace, to which Lord Warringdale thought it would be possible to entice Felix Heron to his death.

In and about Epping Forest there reigned a sweet and holy calm. Far off there came the sound of evening bells upon the night air.

Then, as the change of temperature incidental to the night took place, there swept over the tree-tops of the wood a gentle breeze.

The wild birds were rocked lightly to and fro within cradle-like nests.

Then came the hoot of an owl.

Lord Warringdale, at least, thought it was the hoot of an owl, as he rode a beautiful hunter into one of the fair glades of old Epping.

He had ridden from London at sunset, and now had reached the green verdant home of his half-brother, Captain Heron.

In his pocket he had that letter which he had persuaded the Under Secretary of State to write at his dictation, and which was to be one of the means of overcoming the possible, and, indeed, probable, scruples of Captain Heron to venturing to London in the society of Lord Warringdale.

The face of the treacherous visitor to Epping was very pale, and he held the reins of the horse with a nervous clutch that showed his mind was ill at ease.

But Lord Warringdale had no fears for his present safety.

Well he knew that he contended with his generous and chivalric half-brother with all the odds in his favour, and all the seeming advantages on his side.

He was ready at any time, provided he could only do so with safety to himself, to take Captain Heron's life.

Captain Heron was only desirous that no accident ever should cause him to shed that brother's blood.

The one only remembered his hatred.

The other never forgot that the same father could call them both his sons.

And so Lord Warringdale, despite all the injuries he had done to his brother Felix, and despite all the injuries he had further tried to do him, but failed in accomplishing, was without personal fear as he rode into one of the fair glades of Epping Forest.

The hoot of the owl came again.

Then Lord Warringdale drew rein, for he heard a faint rustling sound in the branches of a gigantic elm-tree that was to the right.

"Halt!" cried a voice.

Lord Warringdale stopped his horse abruptly.

"Who want you here?" asked the voice. "And what are you?"

"I am a friend·"

"What friend, and a friend to whom?"

"A friend to Felix Heron."

A dark body dropped from the tree on to the green sward of the glade.

Then Lord Warringdale was aware that in the semi-darkness some weapon was pointed at him. It was a short carbine, with which the scouts of Captain Heron were usually armed.

"Your name?" said the scout.

"I am known by a name that may not be welcome in Epping Forest, but my errand is now one of peace."

"What name?"

"I am called Warringdale."

"Ah! the infamous Lord Warringdale?"

Lord Warringdale bit his lips; but he feared to give utterance to the anger that was in his heart, lest by some slight impulse the carbine should be discharged, and at once put an end to the nefarious scheme that had brought him there, by lodging a bullet in his heart or head.

"I am Lord Warringdale," he replied.

"Alone?"

"Quite."

"And what want you here?"

"I want to see and speak to Felix Heron, whom you call Captain Heron."

"Dismount."

Lord Warringdale was not well pleased to get off his horse; but an order to do so from a man who has the barrel of a carbine in a right line with the head of the person to whom he spoke, is not to be lightly regarded.

Lord Warringdale got off his horse.

Then the member of Captain Heron's band, who was there on duty, slung the carbine behind his back, and advanced from the shadow of the elms.

"Follow me," he said; and he took Lord Warringdale's horse by the bridle as he spoke.

"Why do you lead the horse?" said Warringdale, moodily.

"Because, now that you are here, I don't want you to have an opportunity of escaping."

"I have no such intention."

"That is very well. Come on!"

"My errand is one of peace and conciliation," added Lord Warringdale.

"Ah!" said the man.

"And if you have any apprehensions that I might make an attempt on the life of your Captain, pray dismiss them."

"I have none."

"You trust me, then?"

"Oh, no."

"And yet you do not think that Captain Heron is in any danger from me?"

"None in the least. You would be afraid to raise a finger against him."

Lord Warringdale was silent.

"Tu whoo! tu whoo! Whoot! whoot!" cried the scout, in imitation of an owl.

"Here you are!" replied a voice.

"Is that you, Tom Ripon?"

"To be sure it is, Number Eight! What's amiss?"

"Nothing, Tom. But here is some one who wants to see the Captain."

"Who is it?"

"Lord Warringdale."

"What, that rascal?"

The scout laughed.

"I think," said Warringdale, "that you might see what reception I get from your leader, before you venture to speak of me as you do."

"Oh, don't mind us," said the scout, "we are used to rogues of all degrees. Tom, you take charge of him. I will go back to my post. You know what to do?"

"Oh, yes."

"I mean with a visitor?"

"To be sure. Ogle told me all about that."

"All's right!"

The scout went back to his post; but while he had been talking to Tom Ripon he had tied Lord Warringdale's horse to the low branch of a tree, at a spot where there was a heap of soft grass and hay beneath, on which the animal might lie down, if so inclined, for the tether was long enough to enable it to do so.

"Now," said Tom, as he stepped up to Lord Warringdale, and before the latter was aware, he had adroitly from behind him slipped a rope over his neck, with a slip noose in it,—"now, if you please."

"Stop! stop! What is this?"

"Oh, nothing particular! It's only our way!"

"But—but——"

"Don't be vicious!"

"I cannot—I will not be treated in this fashion. I protest——"

"It's too loose, I suppose," said Tom.

As he spoke, Tom gave a jerk to the rope, which at once fastened it so closely round the neck of Lord Warringdale that any attempt on his part to get free from it would certainly be an ignominious failure; at the same time another jerk from Tom would go far to produce strangulation.

"Are you mad, you imp?" said Lord Warringdale. "What do you mean by this?"

"It's our way," said Tom.

"Your way?"

"Yes. If anybody comes into the forest, and wants to see the Captain, and we, his men, either don't know who it is, or do know it's a 'bad un, we always put a rope round his neck."

Lord Warringdale put his hand to his sword.

"You are a young rascal!" he said.

"I know that," replied Tom.

"I am half in the mind to correct you in a manner that will make you remember me as long as you live."

"I shall never forget you," said Tom, "as it is. Come on, won't you, eh?"

Tom gave another slight pull to the rope, and although almost bursting with rage, Lord Warringdale thought that discretion pointed out to him that he had better not make his situation any the worse by an useless resistance.

"Are you coming, or not?" said Tom.

"I am coming, but I feel sure that your Captain will not approve of this treatment to me."

"All's right!"

"And even you, boy as you are, must feel that I come here on a very friendly errand, or I would not put up with this indignity."

"Oh, I dare say you are as bad as ever," said Tom. "We all know what an out-and-out bad one you are."

"Insolence!"

"And there's no doubt, now, that we shall have the fun of hanging you."

"The fun?"

"Yes, to be sure. I dare say you will kick in the drollest way ever was seen. This way!"

Whenever Tom gave Lord Warringdale a direction or an admonition about his progress, he accompanied it by a jerk of the rope, which brought an unpleasant sensation to the neck of his lordship.

In this manner Tom led him through some very intricate paths of the forest, and then, as they were to all appearances going on more calmly, Tom suddenly went, as Lord Warringdale thought, mad.

With a sharp cry and a rush, Tom ran round the slender trunk of a tree that they were quite close to, and as he held the end of the rope in his hand, his progress three times round the tree effectually pinioned Lord Warringdale to it.

Tom then fastened the end of the rope behind the tree, so that Lord Warringdale, although he had his hands at liberty, would not find it a very quick process, or a very easy matter, to deliver himself from so troublesome a bondage.

"What is the meaning of this?" he cried. "What is the object of this? Help! help!"

"Oh, you are all right enough," said Tom.

"Murder!"

"Why, what's the matter?"

"Take this rope away, you young villain! Take it off, at once!"

"Oh dear, no! I will go now, and tell the Captain you are here."

Warringdale uttered an imprecation.

"Don't be in a passion," said Tom. "You can't possibly get away. The Captain will come and speak to you, I dare say, and order us to string you up to one of the trees. I have no doubt about that."

A sensation of fear began to creep over the craven heart of Lord Warringdale.

"No, no!" he said. "He will not—he dare not! That is, he will not have the inclination to take my life. I know Felix Heron better by far than that."

Tom was gone.

Lord Warringdale felt very lonely there in Epping Forest, tied to a tree, with no means of reaching any aid, if his situation should become still more desperate.

He began almost to repent that he had come on the errand of treachery that he had so carefully, and, as he thought, so skilfully, concocted.

There was a terrible silence, too, about the forest, which began to prey upon his imagination.

What if Captain Heron should be away upon some adventurous expedition? Would his men, knowing, no doubt, how great an enemy he, Lord Warringdale, had ever been to him, take his life?

It was possible.

A cold dew broke out upon the forehead of Lord Warringdale.

The abject fear, which always lies deep in a bad heart, took possession of him.

But he was in no danger.

Soon, then, there came a flash of light through the trees and bushes.

Then he heard the sound of voices and of footsteps.

Was it Heron who approached?

Yes; it was his half-brother, whom he had so greatly wronged, that Lord Warringdale heard speaking.

Another moment, and Ogle made his appearance, carrying a lantern.

The voice, then, of Tom Ripon could be heard.

"This way, Captain. At the end of this short path."

"I am all amazement," said Captain Heron; "and still cannot help thinking you are mistaken in the person you speak of."

"He cannot believe that it is I," said Warringdale to himself.

Then Ogle turned the corner of a bush, that brought him directly in face of Warringdale, and the young tree to which Tom Ripon had so cleverly tied him.

Captain Heron was but one pace behind him.

"It is Lord Warringdale, Captain," said Ogle.

"It is indeed."

Captain Heron paused opposite to his brother in both astonishment and sorrow.

Then Warringdale spoke.

"I have no doubt," he said, in a low tone, "that you are much surprised, Felix, to see me here."

"I am indeed. Can it be that there is a particle of remorse and repentence even in your heart?"

"There are true words sometimes spoken," added Lord Warringdale, "even accompanied by sarcasms."

Captain Heron made a gesture of impatience.

"Speak!" he cried,—"speak clearly and distinctly! What do you seek for here?"

"Your heart."

"My heart?"

"Yes, Felix, I seek a conference with you alone, for I have thought deeply, and am not what I was."

Lord Warringdale hung down his head as he spoke, and heaved a deep sigh.

Captain Heron regarded him for a few moments in silent amazement.

"What can all this mean?" he said.

"It means," added Warringdale, "that if you will please to remember who I am, and grant me an interview alone, I will say such things to you as will speedily make a great change in your fortunes."

The tone in which Lord Warringdale uttered these words was one of great apparent grief and contrition, and he sighed several times deeply.

Captain Heron was at once suspicious and surprised.

"No, no!" he said; "I want no conference with you. Take him, Ogle, and see him in safety to the outskirts of the forest."

"Yes, Captain."

"And then hang him!" added Tom Ripon.

"Silence!" said Heron. "Let him go in peace and safety. But now, Warringdale — as you wrongfully call yourself, for you have no right to any title of the sort—I warn you never again to

set foot in Epping Forest, for if you do, I will not know you."

"Hold! hold!" cried Lord Warringdale. "Pause yet a moment, Felix Heron!"

"No—no!"

"I beseech you to do so, for your own sake."

Heron made a rapid, deprecating gesture, and a look of scorn came upon his face.

"For Edith's sake!" added Lord Warringdale.

Fire flashed from the eyes of Captain Heron.

"Beware!" he said. "Beware, villain, how you profane that name by even mentioning it!"

"Nevertheless," said Warringdale, "I must tell you, Felix, that what I have come here all alone to say does greatly concern the safety and the happiness of Edith. If you send me away, you will be tortured by doubts and fears; if you hear me, you can but then decide that you care not for my words, and I will go at once and trouble you no further."

No. 72.—EDITH.

Heron considered for a moment or two; then turning to Tom Ripon, he said, "Is he alone?"

"Yes, Captain."

"Are you quite sure?"

"Oh, yes, Captain. It was Number Eight who saw him into the wood."

"Number Eight is careful and trustworthy, and could not be deceived. Ogle!"

"Yes, Captain."

"Bring him after me."

A lurking smile for a moment shot over the face of Lord Warringdale, but he suppressed it before it could be noticed.

Captain Heron walked slowly to a distance of about a dozen yards, and then he paused, while Ogle released Lord Warringdale from his state of bondage to the tree.

"Come on!" said Ogle, not very graciously; for if there was one man in all the world whom he might be said to have a meaner opinion of than even he had of Jonathan Wild, that man was most certainly Lord Warringdale.

But Ogle took the rope entirely off the neck of his lordship, and then walked by his side after Heron.

There was something about the looks of Ogle, as the lantern flashed upon his face, that did not dispose Lord Warringdale to speak to him, so they went on in silence.

Captain Heron plunged into one of those narrow, shadowy paths amid the brushwood, which were only known to the fully initiated into the mysteries of the old forest, and paused not until he reached a portion of the Priory ruins, which consisted of a couple of dilapidated portions of wall, over which the thick branches of a sycamore tree had spread themselves like a roof.

There Captain Heron paused.

And there, in a few seconds, Ogle brought Lord Warringdale.

"Set down the lantern," said Heron.

Tom, who was carrying it, set it down upon the the stump of a tree.

"Go!" said Heron.

Ogle lingered for a moment, and then approaching Lord Warringdale, he took hold of the handle of his sword, and half drew it from the sheath.

"He has no right to arms, Captain," said Ogle, "in our old forest home."

"It matters not," said Heron. "Let him be!" The sword fell back again into the scabbard.

There was a look of scorn upon the face of Captain Heron, as he added, "My faithful and good friend Ogle, you need be under no sort of apprehension. My Lord Warringdale would be as likely to try to eat his sword as venture to draw it against me!"

The look upon the countenance of Warringdale was for a moment demoniac.

Quickly, then, he hung down his head, so as to hide that expression.

They were alone.

Those two brothers, so widely different in every mental characteristic,—alone amid the shadows of the old trees, with only heaven as a witness to the words that should pass between them.

The lantern was so placed, accidentally, that its rays fell much more upon the face of Captain Heron than upon that of Lord Warringdale. Probably had chance not so disposed it, Warringdale would have taken some pains to change his position.

There was not the slightest sound to be heard in the forest.

The birds, and creeping things, and the wild creatures, that made the deep recesses of the wood their home, were either at rest, or stealthily creeping with noiseless steps among the bushes.

The light breeze now scarcely ruffled the treetops, and there stood those two men face to face: the one full of nobleness and chivalry, the other full of treachery and deceit.

May heaven protect its own!

Captain Heron was resolved that he would not be the first to commence a conversation, each word of which might possibly strike upon his heart like a wound; and he schooled himself to be stern and cold.

Then Lord Warringdale began to play the part he had sketched out for himself.

He felt that the time had come when it was

necessary for him to exert all his powers of deceit and pretended sincerity.

CHAPTER CLX.

CAPTAIN HERON AGREES TO ATTEND THE KING'S LEVEE.

THERE was a slight tremor about the tones of Lord Warringdale as he first spoke, for he could not conceal from himself that he was playing for a heavy stake, and it might, or it might not, be possible for him to induce in the mind of Captain Heron a belief in his sincerity or his repentance.

"I have come here," he said, "alone—alone and unarmed, with the exception of my sword, which is part of my dress—for the purpose of saying to you what I ought to say, since it has come into my mind to think it."

Lord Warringdale paused, for he wanted to hear the sound of Captain Heron's voice, in order that by it he might come to some judgment in regard to the state of mind with which Felix listened to him.

But Heron remained profoundly silent.

Lord Warringdale was compelled to go on without encouragement.

"It was perhaps natural for a time," he said, "and more than human nature could resist, that I should endeavour to set aside your fancied claims, which, by their substantiation, would deprive me of rank and life, and leave me a homeless, nameless man. Do you hear me?"

"I hear you," said Heron.

"I was fighting for all that makes life valuable, and I believed, up till very lately, that, although you might be the son of my father, the late Earl of Whitcombe, your mother had never been that father's wife."

Captain Heron made a slight movement of impatience.

"Bear with me," said Warringdale, hastily,— "bear with me for a moment, Felix. I would not come here beneath the shadow of the old trees of Epping Forest, seeking, to my own danger and detriment, this interview with you, were I not prepared now to admit that fact."

"You admit it?" said Heron, with surprise in his tones.

"I do," replied Warringdale, mournfully.

"This is indeed surprising."

"I thought you would find it so; and I deeply regret that, for some time even since I have come to that knowledge, I have carried on a contest with you—a contest of life and death."

"You have. And when did the knowledge dawn upon you?"

There was a slight touch of sarcasm in Heron's tone which Lord Warringdale did not like at all.

"I found some papers at Whitecombe House," he said, "which, although they do not prove the fact distinctly, do so by implication."

"Have you brought them?"

"No."

"It would have been wise to bring them, if this improbable sincerity, and almost improbable repentance, were true."

"They were too valuable, in truth, to carry

with me, for I knew not what kind of reception I should meet with in this neighbourhood; but they are at Whitcombe House, and are at your service."

"What more would you say?"

"You speak coldly to me," added Lord Warringdale.

"I do."

"It is possible you may be justified; but still I meet with but a cruel reception, when I come to abandon to you nobility and vast property, and consent to go forth into the world to seek my fortune, without a name, and with scarcely a hope."

"If it were indeed so," said Heron.

"You doubt me, and it is but natural you should. You will continue to doubt me, likewise, until I have, in some very public manner, taken the first step towards proving to you my sincerity. I wish to take that step before your face, and before the faces of others who will remember it, and by that remembrance render it irrevocable."

"And that you propose to do?" said Heron, still coldly.

"I do. His Majesty holds a levee to-morrow, at which, of course, I have the *entrée*. I have already sent in to the Lord Chamberlain a card, with the name of Mr. Felix Heron upon it, which, being unknown, will produce no remark, but will simply be accepted as the name of some private gentleman whom I wish to introduce."

"What then?" said Heron.

"Then I will take you by the hand when we reach the royal circle, and I will say, 'Your Majesty, this is my elder brother, who, with your Majesty's permission, will claim the Earldom of Whitcombe, and I surrender all right, and title, or claim, to that dignity to him.'"

"You will say that?"

"I will; and in a few words it will put an end to all contest between us. You will become Earl of Whitcombe, and Edith Tarleton, whose forgiveness I feel I much need, will be your Countess. The King will easily sign a complete pardon for all past offences, so that anything that has happened during your career on the road can never be brought up against you. Now, I think, Felix, you understand me!"

"I hear you, my Lord Warringdale; and if these words had been uttered before much treachery had made me doubtful of you, I should have been more credulous, but as it is——"

"Nay, pause a moment, and ask yourself if you are speaking justly. Does not heaven bestow a period of repentance upon the worst of men, and will you believe that it is impossible for me to have better and nobler thoughts than those which have hitherto actuated me?"

"I do doubt you. There was a time when, had you come to me in this fashion, I should have said to you, 'No; you have been brought up with the idea of being noble—you have been nurtured as a young patrician, and look forward to the inheritance of title and estates as your natural gifts, while I have been bred in obscurity. Knowing nothing, and expecting nothing, I will not deprive you of that which has seemed so long your own. Keep those gifts of fortune, and let Felix Heron strive to make for himself a name and fortune as best he may.'"

"You would have said *that?*" exclaimed Lord Warringdale.

"I would."

Warringdale uttered a groan, for he felt at that moment how utterly and entirely he had cast away all the pains, dangers, and difficulties he had been involved in for so long.

And here it will be seen how just an estimate even the villain Warringdale was capable of forming of a brighter, purer intellect than his own.

He believed implicitly what Heron said, because he knew that truth was as much the characteristic of his half-brother, as falsehood was of his own.

"And this is too late!" groaned Warringdale.

"Much too late," said Heron.

"Alas! alas!"

"You may well lament; but since the battle has began, and since it has raged between us with fresh violence and treachery on your part, the spoils of the field must remain with the victor."

"But you believe me now? It is to you that I surrender everything. I will do that which I promise—nay, indeed, I have already begun, and until this moment I had quite forgotten I possessed a proof of my sincerity which you will scarcely doubt. Here is a letter to me from one of the Under Secretaries of State, which will show you what I have been doing."

Far from forgetting for a single moment that letter, which he had so cunningly procured in London, and intended so artfully to use in Epping Forest, Lord Warringdale had never let the thought of it stray from his mind for a moment.

It was the one startling piece of evidence with which he intended to dispel all the doubts of Felix Heron, and he only waited till the most effective moment had come for its production.

That moment had now arrived.

He handed to Captain Heron the letter signed by the Under Secretary, and with the contents of which the reader is already acquainted.

Heron stepped towards the lantern, and calmly read the letter. As he did so, his back was turned towards Lord Warringdale; and a thought flashed across the villain's mind of how easy it would be there and then to slay Felix Heron, and so put an end, once and for all, to all trouble concerning him.

He only needed to have sharply drawn his sword from its scabbard, and then to have plunged it into him.

But fear kept his arm back.

How was he to escape from the forest? For all he knew, there might be watchful eyes even then upon him.

This last idea at once quenched all desire on the part of Lord Warringdale for violence, and he put on a hypocritical air of meekness and sadness.

Heron slowly turned round to him.

"May I keep this letter?"

"Oh, most certainly."

"And may I take steps to verify the signature?"

"Ah, if you will do that I shall be well pleased!"

"And will you remain here while those steps are taken, and abide the result?"

"With the utmost satisfaction."

Captain Heron drew a long breath, and twice paced to and fro within the confines of those dilapidated old walls, where this most singular conference had taken place.

There was a slight touch of emotion in his tones when he spoke again.

"I think your name," he said, "is Henry."

"It is."

"Well, I will not call you that as yet—but, figuratively speaking, I would almost give my right hand to feel assured that you were speaking the truth this night in Epping Forest."

"I am—indeed, I am!"

Lord Warringdale put on an appearance of great dejection, and even went the length of making an odd gasping sort of noise, as though he could scarcely control his tears.

"No more of this—no more of this!" said Heron. "Those can freely forgive who have nothing to regret."

"How true!" said Warringdale.

"Those can easily forget who have suffered, not inflicted."

"I feel that."

"And supposing this letter, then, to be verified, you will still wish me to appear at the levee?"

"I do."

"But why that needless and public mortification to yourself?"

"It is the only thing that will satisfy me. I shall fancy it is something like an atonement."

"I will consider. In the meantime, you shall lodge this night in Epping Forest, and be assured of your perfect safety."

"Brother!" said Warringdale, with a hypocritical air of deep emotion.

"Not yet," said Heron.

Felix then stepped some few paces from the spot, and placing a small silver whistle to his lips, he blew two faint calls which echoed among the trees like the notes of a bird.

There was a rustling among the underwood, and Ogle made his appearance.

Captain Heron spoke to him in a whisper.

"I give Lord Warringdale into your charge," he said. "See that he is well treated, and let him have a chamber among the ruins; but not such an one as will lead him to the knowledge of any of our most secret recesses. I shall have to go to town to-night; but do not let him, or any one else, know of my absence."

"It shall be done, Captain; but still I can't help thinking, after all——"

Ogle shook his head.

"What do you mean?"

"Why, Captain, when once you get hold of a fellow like that among so many nice boughs of trees suitable for the purpose, it's really best to hang him at once!"

"No, no, no! do not speak of that! My honour is now concerned that not a hair of his head should be injured; and were he ten times what he was, or perhaps what he still is, he is now my guest. So understand me, Ogle; there must be neither indignity nor rough usage inflicted upon him. I go to inform Edith of important matters, and shall be much guided by her advice."

Captain Heron then turned to Lord Warringdale.

"You will be well cared for, my lord," he said, "and you will be as safe here beneath the trees of Epping Forest, and perhaps even safer than at your residence in St. James's. Good night! I shall see you in the morning."

"Farewell for the present," said Warringdale.

"Dare I—ought I to believe him?" thought Heron, as he made his way towards those secret recesses of the ruins where he had fitted up a pleasant home for Edith. "What am I to think of all this? Can it be possible that this man, who has shown himself so vicious—who has not before exhibited a single spark of human virtue or feeling—can it be possible that there has yet lingered in his nature a latent sense of justice?"

Captain Heron was sorely perplexed.

He was young, and his naturally unsuspicious nature made him ever prone to believe any specious tale that had feeling and right for its basis.

He could not say but that it might be true. Lord Warringdale might, after all, have sickened at heart with the struggle that had been proceeding.

There was another view likewise to take of the question.

Lord Warringdale might be making a virtue of a necessity.

It was possible enough that some accumulated proofs had arisen of the marriage of Amelia Staunton with the Earl of Whitcombe, which he could neither combat with nor suppress.

"I will speak to Edith," said Heron,—"I will speak to Edith. She shall decide."

Captain Heron held a long conference with Edith upon this question, and although she had every reason to be doubtful of any statement whatever which was made by Warringdale, still she came to the conclusion, along with Heron, that if the letter which had been produced from one of the Under-Secretaries of State was really genuine, Lord Warringdale's contrition might be believed.

It was with great reluctance, however, that Edith consented to Captain Heron going to London for the purpose of making personal inquiries in regard to the genuineness of that epistle.

It was finally, however, agreed that he should go.

Captain Heron attired himself in a plain suit of Quaker cut, and as he had frequently before assumed that character with great success, he resolved that it should be his disguise on this occasion.

But probably Edith would scarcely yet have consented to his absence on such an errand, if he had not promised to take Ogle with him.

Mounted on Daisy, then, at nine o'clock on that night behold Captain Heron in full Quaker costume, and with Ogle following him, dressed as a very sober, steady-looking groom, such as a Quaker gentleman of fortune might keep.

Since the last hour a slight rain had begun to fall in the forest, and the night was very dark; the wind, which had been gradually rising for the last two hours, swept among the old trees, and seemed to be sighing mournful dirges for the brightness that had passed away.

Captain Heron had by far too much confidence in Ogle to keep from him what had happened; moreover, he had a high opinion of the practical good sense of his faithful follower; and as Ogle was an older man by a good ten years than himself, he had at all events seen that much more of the world.

CAPTAIN HERON FRUSTRATES THE EVIL DESIGN OF MR. WHALLEY.

Presented Gratis with No. 72, of the New Edition of the Captive; or, the Robbers of Epping Forest.

EACH WEEK IS PRESENTED IS A COLOURED ENGRAVING.

When he was possessed of the whole story, Ogle shook his head doubtingly.

"Captain," he said, "I don't half like it; it don't sound natural like: but still, if that letter is true, he must have committed himself so far."

"That is the point," replied Heron; "and before I sleep to-night I will at least make the endeavour to ascertain that fact."

"And what's to become of the band," said Ogle, "if you turn an earl?"

"I will make them all rich men—or you, Ogle, can be captain."

"Ah!" said Ogle, "I don't think that would do. But, however, it hasn't come about yet; and though I should like to see the Lady Edith a countess, yet I can't help thinking you would be much happier beneath the shades of old Epping Forest than as a stick-in-waiting, or something of that kind, about the King's Court."

"Perhaps so," said Captain Heron.

The ride to London was a sharp one, for Captain Heron let Daisy go at a good pace—in fact, as fast as was consistent with Ogle's horse keeping up to her.

A very little inquiry ascertained where the Under-Secretary resided, who had made the nefarious little contract with Lord Warringdale.

It was in Portman Square; but upon Heron and Ogle reaching the house, they saw that some entertainment was taking place at it.

All the windows were illuminated, and a great crowd of carriages waited at the door.

"This will suit us just as well," said Heron; "perhaps I shall be mistaken for a guest; for amid this confusion, I dare say almost any one may walk into the saloons, and my Quaker costume will excuse a more elegant evening attire."

"Look there!" said Ogle. "It seems to me that you may do better, Captain."

"How do you mean?"

"Why, ever so far down the row of houses I see an old gentleman getting out of a sedan-chair with a card in his hand, that I daresay is one of invitation."

"I see him."

"Shall I get the card for you, Captain?"

"I don't see how you can do that, Ogle."

"Oh, quite easy, if you'll be so kind as to hold the bridle of my horse for a moment."

"With pleasure. But be careful."

"Always careful, Captain—always careful."

Ogle dismounted, and met the old gentleman some few doors off the Secretary's house, for he was compelled to walk that distance, as indeed were many of the guests, who were gentlemen, and who did not like to wait the long, tedious time which the carriages took to file off before they reached the door.

Ogle intercepted the old gentleman by placing his hand on his arm and saying rapidly, "Sir, I am an officer of the secret police, and have been requested to speak to all the guests by way of caution, for there will be an attempt upon the life of the Secretary to-night with fire-arms, and it is desirable that every one should look sharp for a stray bullet."

"A stray bullet!" cried the old gentleman, giving such a start as he had not done for twenty years.

"Yes, sir; but the Secretary, being aware that you didn't mind a little danger——"

"Not mind it? But I do—I do, I tell you! I do mind it, and ever so much! Bless me! the bullet may hit me, instead of the Secretary! I won't go! Mine's a valuable life, and I won't go! I'll go home again directly, and I'm very much obliged to you, Mr. Officer, for putting me on my guard—very much obliged to you, indeed! I'll go home this minute!"

"Then, sir, you'll allow me to see you to your chair?"

"Certainly—certainly! Oh, thank you! That's all right!"

"And I will take your ticket, if you please, to show to Mr. Secretary, as a proof that I duly warned you."

"To be sure. There it is."

The old gentleman surrendered his card of admission to Ogle, who then politely saw him into his sedan-chair, lingering just sufficiently long to hear him, in tones of great trepidation, order the chair-men to take him home.

Upon looking at the card, Ogle saw that it was duly filled up; and upon handing it to Captain Heron, he saw that it was for the admission of Mr. Warren.

"This will certainly do," said Heron. "The servants will be sure to mangle the name sufficiently before it reaches the saloons, that it will not be recognised. Now, Ogle, hold Daisy, and be sure to keep near at hand. I fancy, Ogle, that the railings will be your best place, exactly opposite the house. I shall endeavour to transact the business I come about, and get away as quickly as I can."

CHAPTER CLXI.

CAPTAIN HERON IS SATISFIED WITH THE SECRETARY, AND VISITS CASTLENEAU HOUSE.

THE arrivals at the Under-Secretary of State's house were so numerous that not much attention was likely to be bestowed upon any individual, and Captain Heron was quite pleased to perceive that several of the guests were quite as plainly attired as he was himself, so that he was not likely to attract particular attention on that head.

Upon entering the hall of the mansion, however, he found the advantage of being possessed of a card of admission, since the very polite Groom of the Chambers, in plain attire, stepped up to him and requested to see it.

"Yea, friend," said Captain Heron, "some vain and unthinking person hath transformed my name from Waughan into Warren. Naithless, as I am here to partake of the vanities of this entertainment, take thou the card, and I will even ascend the staircase, although mine ears are not gratified at the reception of various speaking sounds from above to profane measures, and I much doubt me but that persons given to the gauds and vanities of this life are even now jerking up and down in what they call dancing."

The Groom of the Chambers was out of all patience long before this speech was ended, and after two or three ineffectual bows to bring it to a conclusion, he had left Captain Heron to attend to some new arrivals.

This was just what our hero required, and he ascended the staircase without further observation or question.

The spacious saloons of the Minister of State were thronged with company. The buzz of conversation was incessant, and the, in many cases, gay costumes and flashing jewels imparted great brilliancy to the scene.

Captain Heron found it impossible to get far into the saloon except by very slow degrees; and as he got wedged into a portion of the apartment close to a statue, he overheard an elderly beau say to a lady of fashion, "My dear Lady Cleveland, I can tell you all about it. You see, Edith Tarleton, the Judge's daughter, fell in love with the footman, who turned out to be a highwayman in disguise."

"Dear me! How romantic, Sir Jeremy!"

"Romantic, my lady, but low—deucedly low!"

"But how came Sir John to get so badly wounded?"

"That's the most curious part of the affair, my lady. You see, the highwayman——"

"Who was a footman?"

"Just so, my lady. A footman or a footpad, I'm sure I don't know which.'

"Lor'! Sir Jeremy, you're a charming wit!"

The old beau smiled and simpered, and could hardly stand upon his spindle shanks for a moment or two at this compliment.

"Well, Lady Cleveland, it appears that the footman, or the footpad, induced Edith Tarleton to elope with him; but the Judge pursued them round Finsbury Square, and just at the corner of Fore Street, by the silk mercer's, the rascal turned and demanded fifty thousand pounds of the Judge at once as the portion of his daughter."

"What assurance!"

"Oh, immense, my lady—immense; but upon Sir John very properly refusing, he shot him at once, and Sir John cried out——Murder! murder! good gracious! You heavy wretch, get off my toes, confound you! Murder! the deuce take you!"

At that interesting juncture of the narrative of the elderly beau, Captain Heron had surged up against him, and trod upon both his feet.

"Friend," said Heron, "what is the matter with thee? Art thou paid for making those strange contortions of the countenance?"

"Corns—bunions! Deuce—devil—get off!"

"Didst thou address thyself to me, friend?"

"My toes! my toes!"

"Yea, now thou mentionest thy toes, I am afraid I have even lightly placed my foot upon them; but thou needest not trouble thyself to apologise. I bid thee good even, friend."

Captain Heron left the elderly beau in an agony, and slowly worked his way up to the end of the room, where he saw a gentleman most accurately attired in black velvet, bowing urbanely to all comers.

That was the Under-Secretary of State, with whom Lord Warringdale had made the little political arrangement.

Heron slowly and insidiously made his way up to the side of the Secretary, and in courteous terms spoke to him.

"Having come far to ask a simple question, may I hope that, even at this inopportune moment, it will be answered?"

"What question, sir?"

Heron produced the letter, and pointed to the signature.

The Secretary turned a shade paler.

"Is this name in your writing, sir?" said Heron.

"It is."

Heron folded the paper, and bowed.

"I am quite satisfied, Mr. Secretary, and my object in intruding upon you is answered."

"May I ask who you are?"

"Perhaps you can guess, sir; but certainly I am not Mr. Waughan, the Quaker."

"Then you are the celebrated Captain Heron, the highwayman."

"I should be sorry, sir, to put you so out of conceit with your own penetration as to deny it."

At this moment there was a confused, but rapidly increasing, murmur of voices at the door of the principal saloon. Ladies began to scream, and gentlemen to bluster; it was evident that something unusual was occurring, and that some alarm was slowly spreading from one to another of the guests of the Under-Secretary of State.

Heron looked anxiously towards the door of the magnificent apartment in which he was, for there were at least three hundred people between him and it.

He addressed himself to the Secretary.

"Sir, if that commotion at the entrance to your saloons bodes mischief to me, is there any other mode by which I can leave this place?"

"Yes," said a voice suddenly, but it was not the Secretary's,—"yes, through one of the windows and on to the balcony, from whence it is but a light drop for an active man to the step beneath."

Both Captain Heron and the Under-Secretary of State started round at these words.

"My Lord Bridgewater!" exclaimed Heron, with pleased surprise, as he beheld that young nobleman.

"Ah!" said the Secretary, "you are known to each other, gentlemen?"

"Perfectly well," said the young Earl.

"I have that honour," said Heron.

The Secretary bit his lips, and began half to repent his bargain with the dissolute Lord Warringdale.

At this moment, however, the attention of every one was attracted by so great an increase of the commotion and disturbance at the doors of the saloon, that it was impossible to hear or attend to anything else.

Then above the waving sea of heads and feathers there rose the head and shoulders of a man, who had sprung upon a chair, in order that he might be conspicuous.

"Ladies and gentlemen," he said, "look to your pockets—to your rings, watches, diamonds, purses, and shoe-buckles! There is a robber in the room!"

Cries of dismay, and a tremendous rush to get from one saloon to another, took place.

"A robber! a highwayman!" yelled the man; "and I know him!"

"Who is that?" said the Under-Secretary, confusedly.

"I am surprised you do not know him," said Heron. "It is Jonathan Wild."

"What, the great thief-taker?"

"Even so."

"Then I'm afraid you will be captured."

"Oh, no, sir! Have no fear on my account. I have not come here to be taken by Jonathan Wild!"

"Ladies and gentlemen," cried Wild again, "you need be under no apprehension, for half a dozen of my bull-dogs are upon the staircase, and I will capture the ruffian!"

"The window!" hastily whispered Lord Bridgewater.

"This is very unlucky!" said the Secretary. "What will you do?"

"I must rid you of this troublesome fellow," remarked Heron, and then, raising his tall figure to its utmost height, he looked across the mass of heads and called out, "Jonathan Wild, get off that chair; you alarm the ladies!"

"There he is!" screamed Wild, with a dance of delight—"there he is! Ha! ha! I've got him at last!"

"Get down, Mr. Wild!"

"You insolent rascal! Now, my janissaries—now, my bull-dogs, this way! Ladies and gentlemen, don't be alarmed."

"I echo those words," said Captain Heron, in a clear, ringing voice. "Ladies and gentlemen, don't be alarmed. Mr. Wild and I have always a few scores to settle when we meet. Sometimes it is my turn, sometimes his. The last was his, and this is mine!"

As he spoke, Heron drew from his pocket a small pistol, and levelling it at once over the heads of the fashionable crowd that was between him and Jonathan Wild, he fired.

Even at the moment Jonathan made a frantic leap right over the back of the chair, into the midst of a tightly-packed and terrified throng of elderly ladies, who were impeding each other in their endeavours to leave the saloon.

The bullet from the pistol, though it missed Wild, struck a mirror, smashing it into a thousand fragments; and the concussion of the air from its discharge was so great, that many of the wax-lights were put out, and some of the frailest of the glass drops from the chandelier fell upon the heads of the Secretary's guests.

Some ladies screamed, others fainted; gentlemen swore and drew their swords; and then, amidst all the smoke and confusion, Captain Heron slipped behind a mass of curtains that hung before one of the windows, and opening the French casement with a touch, he stepped out upon the balcony.

The Earl of Bridgewater was perfectly right in his knowledge of the locality; a portion of the balcony was quite clear of the area in front of the house, and overhung the ample door-step.

A crowd of lackeys, with long malacca canes and most exaggerated liveries, were there, and in the midst of these Captain Heron dropped, scattering them in all directions, rolling several of them right out into the roadway.

"Ogle!" cried Heron.

There was a rush of horses' feet, and Ogle, mounted on his own horse and holding Daisy by the bridle, came at once on to the pavement, completing the discomfiture of the lackeys, who thought themselves charged by nothing less than a troop of cavalry.

Captain Heron was mounted in a moment.

"What's amiss, Captain?" said Ogle.

"Not much; but our old friend Jonathan Wild is above."

"Is that possible? He haunts us like an evil spirit."

A roaring sound now appeared to be coming down the grand staircase, and as Captain Heron had no desire to engage in a pitched battle in Portman Square, with he knew not how many people, he left the place at a swinging trot.

"I heard a pistol-shot, Captain," said Ogle.

"Yes; I fired it at Wild, but I must own that I cannot bring myself to shoot a fellow until after he has had a shot at me, and I purposely missed him; besides, I have a strong impression that Wild ought to be hanged, and that taking his life in any other way would be cheating the gallows."

"The last reason, Captain," said Ogle, "is much better than the first. But it's getting late."

"It is, Ogle; and much as I wish to get back to Epping, it must get a little later before I leave London, for I wish to make a call at Lady Castleneau's."

"That won't take us long, Captain. I'll see what the time is by this lamp."

"Why, Ogle, how did you come by that handsome watch?"

"The old gentleman in the sedan chair forgot to give it me out of gratitude."

"He forgot to give it you—but yet have it?"

"That's because I took it, Captain."

"Ogle, Ogle, that was hardly fair!"

"Oh, quite fair, Captain; for I frightened him about his personal safety—telling him there would be a pistol shot or so in the saloons, little fancying such would be the case. But here we are, in the Oxford Road, and ten minutes will take us into Bloomsbury Fields."

"Less time," said Heron, as he put Daisy to speed.

The gate of old Castleneau House was soon reached, but at that hour, for it was a little past midnight, no light was visible in any of the windows, and Captain Heron began to doubt, after all, whether he would disturb Lady Castleneau, or not.

The ancient mansion was dimly visible across the court-yard, as Heron halted close to the high old iron gates.

He was half disposed to make no appeal for admission, and was almost in the act of turning away from the gates, when he felt confident that he saw some dark object that looked like a human form upon the steps of the hall-door.

There was a very feeble ray of light, too, at the same time, and as the dark object ascended to the highest of the steps and then disappeared, Heron had a disagreeable suspicion that something was wrong.

"Ogle," he said, in a whisper, "do you see that?"

"Indeed I do," said Ogle; "and I see more, too. There away by the gates of Montague House, a horse and cart is waiting; and I can't help fancying that that's something to do with what's going on here."

"I would not get Daisy injured in a night brawl for anything I can mention," said Heron. "Wait for me in the shadow of the wall, and I will climb the gate, so as to give no alarm with the bell."

"I should like to see about the cart first, Captain."

"It is well advised. Go—I will wait for you."

Ogle dismounted, and walked without any concealment towards the cart, when a man, who was in it, holding the reins of the horse, said in cautious low tones, "Is that you, Phillipson?"

Ogle disguised his voice by a cough, as he replied, "Who else should it be, eh?"

"All right; but I hardly knew you. Have they got the old 'un?"

"Can't you call people by their names," said Ogle, pretending to cough again. "Anyone would think you meant the original old 'un; and I'm sure we don't want to catch him."

"Don't be frightening a fellow," said the man in the cart. "I mean Sir Dominick Browne."

"So do I," said Ogle; and swinging the heavy riding whip he had with him, he dealt the man such a blow with the loaded end of it, that he fell senseless into the bottom of the cart.

A watchman came drearily along at that moment on the other side of the way, and hearing some disturbance, paused in a half-sleepy announcement that it was "Past twelve o'clock, and a cloudy night," and turned the light of his lantern on the cart.

By that light, Ogle saw a name on the shaft.

"Peter Whalley, Highgate."

"Ah!" said Ogle; "now I know all about it. It's that rascal the madhouse keeper trying to get possession of old Sir Dominick again."

"Can't you move on?" said the watchman.

"Directly, my dear Charles," said Ogle. "Come, now! Hilloa! your'e *hobstructing* me in the discharge of my duty!"

"All's right! Good night!"

Ogle turned the horse's head towards the Oxford Road way, and set the animal in motion, so that it trotted off with the insensible rider lying at the bottom of the cart.

The watchman waved his lantern to and fro, and seeing nobody driving, he thought the whole affair too mysterious to take place upon his beat without being well considered, so he went at once to his box, and shut himself up, and went fast asleep until four o'clock.

Ogle made his way back to the gates of Castleneau House, and informed Captain Heron of the discovery he had made.

"It is the very thing," Heron said, "that suggested itself to my own mind; and thank heaven I am here at this lucky juncture, for, by defeating these rascals now, they will scarcely hazard another attempt, thinking the old mansion so well protected."

"I don't like you're going alone, Captain."

"It is nothing; they will only be too anxious to get out of my way. See to Daisy, Ogle, as you would to my own life."

Heron was about to climb the gate, but the moment he put his foot upon it, it began to swing gently open, so that it was evident the Mr. Whalley had found a means of picking the lock.

Captain Heron was across the court-yard in a moment, and ascending the steps, he laid his hand upon the hall-door, which yielded to his touch, and he stepped noiselessly into the house.

Amid the deep stillness of that midnight hour the whispered sound of voices from the breakfast-room could easily be heard, and Heron, with long, silent steps, crossed the marble-paved hall.

He had just time to shrink back as the door of the breakfast-room was opened slightly, and a faint gleam of light issued from it.

"Is that you, Owen?" said some one.

Heron kept profoundly still.

"I thought I heard Owen," said the voice again; "but it don't matter, there are three of us, and I dare say Phillipson and Owen are with the cart."

"Silence!" said another voice; "you talk too loud. Listen to me."

"Yes, Mr. Whalley."

"These old mansions have so many nooks and corners and hiding-places, that it would be quite out of the question to search it. The only thing would be to get hold of Lady Castleneau, and make her tell us where the old man is."

"I've heard she's obstinate, Mr. Whalley."

"She may be; but I will tie some oiled rags round her fingers and set light to them, and as soon as the flesh begins to frizzle she will tell everything. I have not been in the West Indies for nothing."

Captain Heron felt the flush of anger come over his face.

He drew his sword.

"Come on," said Whalley.

The breakfast-room door was opened a short distance; the light was very faint that streamed out into the hall. Heron saw a dark body before him; and silent as avenging fate he made a pass with his sword.

There was a shriek, and the dark body fell.

The light went out, and all was still.

It was the madhouse keeper himself who had thus met with his deserts, and two of his men, who were in the breakfast-room, shrunk back with fear of they knew not what, only they were certain something had happened to their principal.

Heron stepped then over the prostrate form of Mr. Whalley, and entered the breakfast-room.

It was profoundly dark.

Heron made passes with his sword in several directions, for he was so thoroughly excited and angry at what he had heard, that could he have done so on the first impulse of his indignation, he would have sacrificed both those men.

The probability was, however, that they had made their way to the remotest end of the apartment, and before Captain Heron could pursue them thither, a large triangular gleam of light came over the roof of the room, and old Anthony, with a candle in his hand, looked in from the hall, exclaiming, "Gracious heaven! Is it thieves! I'm sure I heard something!"

CHAPTER CLXII.

IN WHICH LADY CASTLENEAU MAKES AN IMPORTANT DISCOVERY.

THE light which old Anthony, the serving-man of Lady Castleneau, now threw upon the scene in the breakfast room, not only revealed to Captain Heron the whereabouts of Mr. Whalley's two men, but it let those two men see their own danger.

The sight of Captain Heron, with a flush of anger on his face, and his drawn sword in his hand, was not likely to inspire them with confidence or courage.

Moreover they had a tolerable guess that their master, the villanous madhouse keeper, had come to some bad end.

Thus, then, impressed with fear, a sudden panic took possession of them.

They both dropped on their knees, and roared out for mercy.

Captain Heron made a rush at them, with his long glittering sword in his hand.

The fright and panic of these two men became then so great, that they rolled over each other in frantic attempts each to interpose the other to the thrust of the sword which they fully expected each moment.

Heron dealt them several sharp blows with the flat part of the weapon.

No. 73.—EDITH.

"Scoundrels!" he cried. "Declare instantly who and what you are, and what brought you here, or I will take your lives."

"Have mercy upon us, good sir!" cried one, "and I will tell you all!"

"No, no!" shouted the other. "I will!"

"I spoke first!"

"You did not! I will bear evidence!"

"No, you won't!"

"But I will!"

"You shall take my life first!"

"You wretch!"

"Villain!"

"Rascal!"

The two men attacked each other with fury, for each seemed to be possessed with the idea that the one who should be fortunate enough to tell all he knew first would be certain of safety.

"Dear me," said old Anthony, "what does it all mean, and how came you here, Mr. Felix?"

"It is fortunate I am here, Anthony."

"It is always fortunate," replied the old man; "for everybody in this house is always glad to see you."

The two men from the asylum pummelled each other most vivaciously, and whatever might be their fears of Captain Heron, it was evident that they had none one for the other.

Finally, one, by a well-planted blow in the neck, put his companion out of the way of further interference, and he then cried out, "Sir, I will confess all, if you will be so good as to let me go free when I have."

"Speak!"

"You promise, sir ?"

"I do."

The man then, after clearing his visage from the blood which his contest with his fellow had produced, spoke.

"We are men belonging to Mr. Whalley, your worship, who keeps an asylum at Highgate, and he brought us here to recover a patient who had been taken away."

"His name ?"

"Sir Dominick Browne."

"I expected as much. But how did you know that he was here, if he be here ?"

"Mr. Wild, sir, wrote to Mr. Whalley."

"That is enough. You may go now."

"Thank you humbly, sir."

"But you must take, not only your companion with you, but what I suppose is the dead body of your infamous employer."

The other man at this moment recovered sufficiently to comprehend where he left off in reflection, just previous to the knock-down blow he had received, and he called out, "I confess—I confess all! Mr. Whalley——"

"Hold your row, stupid!" said his comrade. "I have told all, and his worshipful worship will let us go. Come on, stupid!"

The two men slunk out of the room into the hall.

There lay on the marble flag-stones what seemed to be the dead body of Whalley.

"Take your carrion!" said Captain Heron, as he pointed to it.

"Yes, your worship."

But Whalley uttered a groan when he was lifted up, and Captain Heron was well enough pleased now to find that he was not absolutely dead, although the sword had passed right through his body.

"Oh, you shall pay for this!" said Whalley, faintly,—"you shall pay for this!"

"Away with him!" said Heron.

"This is not a country," added Whalley, speaking with a pain and difficulty which, had he not been so enraged, would have kept him silent, —"this is not a country in which a man is to be run through with a sword by any one who chooses, and then no more said about it."

"No," replied Captain Heron; "nor is this a country in which a scoundrel, with three or four other ruffians at his back, can break into a gentlewoman's house in the dead of the night with impunity; and if the said scoundrel meets with a hurt in the affair, it is not a country which will say otherwise than that it serves him right."

Whalley uttered a howl of rage.

"Away with him this instant," said Captain Heron, "or it will be the worse for you all!"

The sight of the drawn sword, which Heron had still in his hand, was a cogent argument with the two men, and they dragged their wounded master out of Castleneau House.

Just as Heron had thus got rid of them, Lady Castleneau appeared on the staircase.

"Oh, what is all this ?" she cried. "Felix! Felix! Did I, or did I not, hear your voice ?"

"Dear Lady Castleneau," replied Captain Heron, "I am here, and very happy to say that it was my voice you heard."

"Yes, my lady," said Anthony. "There has been thieves in the house."

"Thieves ?"

"Yes, my lady; but the Captain has killed them all."

"Not exactly," said Heron, with a smile; "but I will explain all to you, dear Lady Castleneau."

"Tell me first, is Edith safe and well ?"

"Quite."

"Thank heaven! I will not ask if she is happy, because I know she is."

"You are kind and good to say those words," replied Heron. "And now let me ask of poor Sir Dominick Browne. Is he well, and with you still ?"

"He is, but far from well."

Lady Castleneau came down to the breakfast-room, on the hearth in which there was still the remains of a wood fire, the embers of which, when drawn together, sent forth some flickering blue flames.

Then Captain Heron explained to her how, being in London, he would not leave it without calling upon her to arrange about Sir Dominick and herself.

But the old lady was even more interested about the account which Heron gave of the visit of Lord Warringdale to Epping Forest, than in the foiled attack which had been made by Whalley and his men on Castleneau House.

"Oh, Felix, Felix," she said, "could you make up your mind to leave that wolf in the shape of man at Epping Forest with Edith ?"

Captain Heron rather started at this mode of putting the matter, for it had not before occurred to him.

"My Lady Castleneau, he is not with Edith in Epping Forest any more than as if they were both in London."

"Yet I tremble."

"Calm your fears. The whole of my men, with the exception of Ogle, are in the forest, and Lord Warringdale is as helpless and as harmless there as the meanest creature that roams beneath the trees."

"He is meaner than the meanest, Felix."

"He is, indeed, I fear."

"And can you for one moment believe in this sudden conversion of his to justice and goodness ?"

"I knew not what to think until I came to town and actually saw the Under-Secretary of State, who admitted his signature to the letter."

"It is very strange."

"It is; and yet by this document does it not seem tolerably evident that Lord Warringdale must have taken a step from which there is no possibility of his receding ?"

"It would seem so; and yet I feel quite convinced that there is some piece of deep villany lurking behind the whole transaction."

"If I thought that——"

"You do think it, Felix—you do think it, deep down in your heart, but you are reluctant to say you do, because you would always much rather believe in the goodness and the sincerity of any one than in their wickedness and deceit."

"I am afraid, Lady Castleneau, that you have by far too good an opinion of me."

"No, no! I know you well, Felix. I cannot say that Lord Warringdale's conduct is really treacherous, because I have no present means of proving it to be so, but I can truly say that I suspect it."

"There is cause, indeed, so to do," said Heron, in a sad tone of voice. "But I will no longer keep you from rest, Lady Castleneau. Edith will be much pleased when I tell her I have seen you !"

"Bless her! bless her !"

"That is indeed a prayer to which my whole heart says amen !" responded Heron.

Tears had started to the eyes of Lady Castleneau, and it was some few moments before she could control her emotion sufficiently to allow herself to speak. When she could do so, she said, "Felix, I want to know one thing."

"What is it, dear, kind friend ?"

"What is the latest hour at which you will leave Epping Forest with Lord Warringdale to-morrow, to come to the levee ?"

"I fancy about mid-day."

"Will you promise me that you will not start until mid-day ?"

"I will."

"Then I am more content."

"But what is it you mean to do, Lady Castleneau ?"

"I hardly know yet. I must think about it. But between now and then I will make an endeavour at least to get some information on the subject. You say, Felix, he told you he had left your name at the Lord Chamberlain's ?"

"He said so."

"That, then, is something. Go home now to Edith, who I am sure will by this time be a prey to much anxiety. Do not heed seeing Sir Dominick Browne, for no doubt he is asleep, poor man! He sleeps like a child, now that he is so happy to be free from those cruel men at the asylum."

"Then, dear, dear friend, I bid you good night; and if you have any apprehensions of a renewed attack upon the house, Ogle shall stay with Anthony."

"Have you, Felix ?"

"I must say I have not. The wound that the scoundrel Whalley has received will keep him quiet for a time."

"Then I am content. Take your faithful follower with you, Felix, and heaven protect you !"

Captain Heron did not believe for a moment that there was any real danger to be apprehended from either the Whalleys or Jonathan Wild at present at Castleneau House, or he would scarcely have permitted Lady Castleneau to be left with the meagre protection of old Anthony.

Taking, then, a kind farewell of the old gentlewoman, who loaded him with loving messages for Edith, he set off for Epping Forest.

And now a strange whirl of mingled sensations, of hopes and of fears, of irresolutions and regrets, came over the mind of Heron, and in good truth he knew not what to do.

Having the evidence of the authenticity of the letter from the Under-Secretary of State, could he rationally refuse credence to the repentance of Lord Warringdale?

Was he to cast aside the seeming opportunity for an amicable and speedy adjustment of the affairs of the Earl of Whitcombe?

That was the question which pressed itself upon the attention of Captain Heron, and he continued in such deep thought, that scarcely half a dozen words passed between him and Ogle during the sharp ride from London to Epping Forest.

It was not until they entered one of the glades of the ancient wood, and were challenged by one of Heron's scouts, that he seemed to shake off some of the oppression which hung so heavily upon his soul.

He then gave his well-known pass-word cheerfully, and Ogle trotted up to his side to take the bridle of Daisy.

"I suppose you will walk through the forest as usual, Captain ?" said Ogle.

"Yes; and I feel my mind much lighter, and a load of care removed from it, now that I hear the wind among these well-known forest trees."

"You speak like yourself again, Captain."

"And I feel more like myself. What is the time, Ogle ?"

"It is after three."

"So late! Edith will have a thousand fears. Give Daisy up to Tom Ripon : there is a kind of friendship between the boy and the horse which I'll be bound has kept Tom up even until this hour."

"That's true, Captain," said Tom, as he came from behind a tree. "I knew you'd come home this way. I'll take care of Daisy."

It always seemed to be, however, that Daisy appeared to think it was her especial mission to take care of Tom, for they generally went to the stable together, as if Daisy led him, since she frequently did so, by holding the collar or flap of his jacket in her teeth the whole distance.

"Edith shall decide—Edith shall decide !" said Heron to himself, as he plunged deep into the intricacies of the forest and sought his sylvan home.

The consultation was long and anxious, and Edith would not decide in favour of the visit to the levee, except conditionally.

"Do not accompany Lord Warringdale to town," she said ; "but promise to meet him where you will—say at the Palace, or Buckingham House ; and then let me, in that disguise which so much resembles you, and which even once made your eyes fancy you saw the double of yourself, proceed on this enterprise. If he be playing you falsely, he dare not let me cross the threshold of the Palace."

"And think you, Edith, I would let you fall into his hands in preference to myself ?"

"Yes, Felix, you should let me; for my danger, in comparison to yours, would be as nothing. What can they do to me ? I am so near of age, that my father has scarcely an excuse to claim authority over me."

"No, no—do not think of it," said Heron. "Let me chance it ; and if there be treachery, I will trust to that good fortune which has more than once saved me from much more perilous positions."

"Felix, I have made you a promise that I will not again follow you upon any expedition, as I once did, without your consent."

"Do not ask for that consent now, Edith; but rather take to yourself a full discretion to follow me or not, as circumstances may dictate, and your own judgment sanction. I have promised Lady Castleneau not to leave the forest until twelve o'clock to-morrow; and I fancy her object in getting that promise from me was, that she might have time to make some inquiries in substantiation or otherwise of Lord Warringdale's statement. But you look weary, dearest Edith, and I, too, have ridden far. The night wears on apace, and it will be well to snatch what rest we may until to-morrow."

Captain Heron then made a brief inquiry in regard to Lord Warringdale, and was told that he was sleeping soundly, although well watched.

Then a deep and holy stillness seemed to reign in Epping Forest; and until the first twitter of the birds at early dawn not a sound disturbed the repose of its leafy glades.

*　　　*　　　*　　　*　　　*

It is nothing new to the readers of this authentic narrative to find Lady Castleneau, despite her age and infirmities, acting in affairs that interested her with a vigour and a precision that might well have been envied by the acutest intellects and the most active frames.

By six o'clock in the morning immediately following the wretched attack upon Castleneau House by Whalley and his assistants, the old gentlewoman was fully attired for the open air, and her coach was in the court-yard of Castleneau House.

"Anthony," she said, "take your breakfast quickly; I wait for you."

"I've had all I want," said Anthony, "and am ready, my lady, to go whenever you please."

"Very well. Martha?"

"Yes, my lady."

"You'll attend to Sir Dominick Browne; and above all things, do not let him know of the disturbance last night."

"No, my lady; and I'm sure if anybody should come to attack the house, I shall scream till all the constables in the neighbourhood are in the court-yard."

"Do so. Now, Anthony, to Knightsbridge Barracks."

Lady Castleneau stepped into her coach, and Anthony got on the box.

"Knightsbridge Barracks!" said the old man. "What on earth can she want to go to Knightsbridge Barracks for? It's full of the Horse Guards! Surely they are not going to interfere about Captain Heron and Miss Edith?"

The ancient vehicle rumbled along, and Lady Castleneau sat as stiff and bolt upright in it as she had done in her younger days.

She had a settled purpose in her mind, which was to make every possible inquiry into the truth of Lord Warringdale's statement within sufficient time to allow of a messenger being despatched to Epping Forest, in case she should discover anything which it would be essential for Captain Heron to know.

Lady Castleneau was not without interest at Court, and some six months anterior to that day she had made it her special business to apply to a lady high in rank to procure for a young man of the name of Markham Amos a cornetcy in the dragoons.

This young man was a nephew of the Lord Chamberlain, but had been looked rather coldly upon by his official relative, because he was the son of a sister who had married for love—poverty, as in too many cases, being an ingredient in the match.

Lady Castleneau had known and esteemed the mother of the young man well, and hence she interested herself in his welfare.

When, by Lady Castleneau's interest, the cornetcy was procured for young Amos, his uncle, the Lord Chamberlain, condescended to take some notice of him, and appeared glad to receive him at all times.

Lady Castleneau's object, then, was to get this young officer to go directly with her to the Lord Chamberlain's, to ascertain, beyond a doubt, if Lord Warringdale's statement, that he had sent in the name of Felix Heron for presentation at the levee on that day, were true or not.

And so, in one hour after leaving Castleneau House, the ancient coach stopped at the door of the barracks at Knightsbridge, and the old lady sent in a card, on which was written in pencil:—

"Lady Castleneau, to take a cup of coffee with Cornet Amos."

The Cornet was rather taken by surprise, inasmuch as Lieutenant Dampier, of the Light Horse, and Captain Crawley, of the King's German Legion, were at that moment arranged in picturesque attitudes in his barrack-room, waiting to discuss the breakfast which his trooper-servant was actively preparing.

"Aw!" said Lieutenant Dampier. "Who the doose is it, Crawley? Lady Castle who? What's it all about? Shall we evaporate, Amos, my boy?"

Cornet Amos sprung rather hastily to his feet, and Captain Crawley flew to a cracked mirror, to arrange his rather dishevelled locks, and to put on as brisk an air as he could, which was rather difficult, considering that he had gone out for a stroll at nine o'clock on the preceding evening, and had only just come home.

"Don't be alarmed!" cried the young Cornet. "It's only an old lady."

"A what?" said Lieutenant Dampier. "An old woman? Aw! I thought they were abolished by Act of Parliament."

Cornet Amos ran out of the room; and, whatever might be his juvenile eccentricities, he was never unmindful of the obligation he owed to Lady Castleneau; and the manner in which he brought her into the room upon his arm was quite sufficient to convince the Lieutenant and the Captain that, be she whom she might, she was not a subject for jesting.

The officers bowed ceremoniously, and handed Lady Castleneau a chair. The chocolate was at that moment produced; and Captain Crawley, having a glass of *eau-de-vie* in his first cup, felt much revived, while Lieutenant Dampier whispered to him, "That—aw—he fancied the old gal had been a demmed handsome woman a hundred years ago."

Now, Lady Castleneau adopted the best possible mode of action, under the circumstances, that she possibly could by determining to give publicity to Lord Warringdale's pretended change of action, that he himself affected to be his wish. No sooner, then, had one cup of the unexceptionable chocolate been discussed, than with that comprehensive glance round the Cornet's breakfast table which let every one then present know that she spoke for the general information, she said, "Strange news at Court, gentlemen, if it be indeed true—that the Earldom of Whitcombe is about to fall into the hands of an unknown elder brother of my Lord Warringdale."

The officers looked surprised.

"By Jove," said one, "he owes me a couple of hundred on Blue Bell."

"And me four hundred at faro."

Lady Castleneau looked sharply from one to the other of them as she added, "You allude to the young man who has hitherto been known as Lord Warringdale?"

"Yes, madam."

"And is it possible that this news is true?" asked the Cornet.

"It is a rumour."

"Oh, only a rumour!"

"But yet one that I thought you might have heard something of."

The three young men shook their heads.

"Then," added Lady Castleneau, as she rose with that dignity of manner which was peculiar to herself,—"then, Mr. Amos, I must beg you to do me the favour to see me to my coach."

"With pleasure, dear madam, so far as it is a service rendered to you."

"Very well—very well! That is very prettily said! Are you on duty to-day?"

"No, Lady Castleneau; and if you will permit me to see you to town——"

"That is just what I was about to propose, for, to tell the truth, I meant you to be my friend this morning."

"By Jove," whispered Dampier to Crawley, "the old lady is going to fight a duel!"

"She looks an old trump," replied Crawley.

Lady Castleneau, leaning on the arm of the young Cornet, left the barracks, and so soon as they were in the coach together, she said gently, "My dear boy, I want you to go to your uncle's house, and inquire for me if there is to be to-morrow a presentation of a Mr. Felix Heron."

"With pleasure."

Lady Castleneau sighed, for she felt that even if such a card was lying at the office of the Chamberlain, it would not be conclusive of the honesty of purpose of Lord Warringdale.

But if there were no such card?

"Ah!" she thought, "then, indeed, Felix shall be warned by one whom I can trust!"

She meant the young officer who sat by her side, and who had been so much indebted to her kindly patronage and protection.

The old-fashioned vehicle rolled and wheezed over the ill-made road from Knightsbridge to town, and was in due time amid the streets of the West End of London.

CHAPTER CLXII.

JONATHAN WILD TAKES PRECAUTIONS. — LADY CASTLENEAU A PRISONER.—THE BILLET.

As Lady Castleneau's carriage neared old Buckingham House, close to St. James's Park, a ragged beggar-boy ran after it and got up behind.

Old Anthony was by far too busy with his horses to have the least idea that he carried more than his proper complement of passengers.

The ragged boy crouched down low about the hind springs of the carriage. What is he doing? Surely he has something in his hand which glitters like a knife!

Once, then, as the carriage turned into Pall Mall the boy made a rapid movement with the wretched old cap he wore, and from a half-open doorway a man's hand and arm was projected, as if in answer to the signal.

In that hand was a riding-whip, thick in the handle and heavy in the thong. This riding-whip was shaken, as if in recognition to the ragged boy, and then the hand and arm were withdrawn, but the door through which they had shown themselves still remained slightly open.

The carriage rumbled on.

Then the door opened, and a man led out of the dark passage of the house a horse. The animal was sleek and strong—the man was a thick-set, beetle-browed, villanous-looking personage, with a black patch over one eye, and a thickly folded, dirty scarlet cravat about his neck.

This man gave a hideous chuckle as he mounted the horse, and any one who had had the good, or the evil fortune, as the case might be, to hear that chuckle before, would find no difficulty in identifying it with Jonathan Wild.

In truth, this man was none other than Jonathan himself.

We may conclude likewise that the ragged boy, who was so busily at work at the back of Lady Castleneau's carriage, was one of the emissaries of the great thief-taker.

What was Wild's present object will only too soon be apparent.

He followed the carriage at a distance of about a hundred yards, and with a caution that would have made it a difficult matter for any one to have said positively that he even once cast his eyes upon it.

"Mr. Amos," said Lady Castleneau, "I want you to be very exact in the information you get me."

"My dear Lady Castleneau, you may depend most strictly upon the news I shall bring you; and here we are at the Lord Chamberlain's door. Without troubling him, I can get the news from one of the clerks at once."

"Do so—do so! I will wait here for you."

The young Cornet left Lady Castleneau in the carriage while he went into the office of the Chamberlain, and during the short time that he was absent it is not too much to say that the brave heart of Lady Castleneau suffered much anxiety.

When she had the information she sought would it be conclusive, provided she should really find that such a name as Felix Heron had been given in for presentation at the levee of that day?

That was the question.

But if, on the contrary, she should find no such name had been given in, what was she to do?

Would it be possible to carry out, with any safety to Captain Heron, the plan of operations she had managed in her own mind, in case of such a contingency?

"Yes, oh, yes!" she said, half aloud; "I am certain he will do it. I am certain that young Amos will reach Epping Forest in time. For me he will do it—for me!"

Jonathan Wild, when he saw the carriage of Lady Castleneau pause at the official residence of the Lord Chamberlain, was rather puzzled.

It did not at first occur to him what could be her object in calling there, or why she had with her a young officer whom she had brought from Knightsbridge Barracks.

Accident had enabled him to know of her visit to the barracks, for he had seen the coach as it passed the end of Piccadilly, and had set one of his scouts on its track.

But he held his hands to his head now in deep thought as to what she could want with the Lord Chamberlain.

Jonathan Wild was at fault.

But he edged nearer and nearer still to the coach, and watched.

Then the ragged boy beckoned to him.

Jonathan bent down low in his saddle, and thought that he would ride up to the back of the coach, and hear what the boy had to say. But the coach was still, and at that time in the morning —for as yet it was only nine o'clock—the streets of London had not assumed their ordinary day bustle.

Our ancestors took business easier than we do, and were not by any means in such a hurry for work as the present generation.

Wild dismounted.

He could depend upon the quietude of his own footsteps, although not on those of his horse.

A lad who was sweeping a crossing ran forward to hold Wild's horse, and in another moment the thief-taker was at the back of Lady Castleneau's coach, listening to the report of his ragged emissary.

"The young officer," said the boy, "has gone to see if one Felix Heron is a going to the levee."

"Ah!" said Wild. "I see it all now!"

In the excitement of the moment Jonathan had uttered the interjection half-aloud, and it reached the ears of Anthony.

There came a sharp slash of the whip over the coach-top, which lit upon the face of Wild and the hands of the boy.

Jonathan suppressed an imprecation.

The ragged boy uttered a howl.

"I had you there!" said Anthony.

"Show yourself!" said Wild, as he dealt the ragged boy a kick which produced another howl; but the lad knew Wild too to well dispute his orders, and he crawled round the coach, saying, in a whining tone, "What do you mean by hitting of a fellow in that ways, eh?"

"Be off!" cried Anthony.

"Eh? what do you mean, eh? Take that!"

A well-directed stone hit Anthony's hat, and sent it flying over the coach-top.

"Off!" said Wild.

The boy ran away as fast as his legs could carry him, while, as the young Cornet at that moment came out of the Lord Chamberlain's house, Jonathan crouched down almost under the coach to avoid being seen.

"There is no such card, with the name you mention, in the office," said the Cornet.

Lady Castleneau clasped her hands.

"I guessed it—I guessed it! You are quite certain?"

"Oh, quite!"

"And the name? You recollected the name?" The young Cornet smiled.

"Oh, yes! The name was Felix Heron."

"Yes, yes; oh, pardon my curiosity! And now I will tell you, my dear boy, why it is that, instead of making this apparently simple inquiry myself, I have brought you from Knightsbridge to do so. It was in anticipation of some such result as this. There is no name of Felix Heron in the office of the Chamberlain for presentation at the levee to-day; but there is one who owns that name, who thinks there is, and I want him to be warned not to come to London."

"Any service that I can be of to any friend of yours, Lady Castleneau, will be of real pleasure to me."

"I know it—I am sure of it, Amos; so you will ride to Epping Forest, and go through the the glades until some one meets you, and then you will give this slip of paper to that person, be he whom he may."

As she spoke, Lady Castleneau produced a packet, and on one of its leaves, which she tore out, she wrote the following words:—

"Ascertained treachery at the levee. Do not come, or you are lost.

                    "CASTLENEAU."

The young Cornet took the little slip of paper with surprise, but he did not hesitate for a moment about obeying the instructions of Lady Castleneau.

She laid her hand upon his arm, then, as she added, "You must reach the forest, my dear boy, before twelve o'clock."

"Must I?"

"Yes. It is a matter of life or death."

"I will, then."

The Palace clock of St. James's chimed the half-hour past nine at this moment.

"Oh, it will be quite easy," added the Cornet.

"But you have no horse here."

"I can borrow one at the King's Mews."

"Go, then, at once, and heaven speed you!"

"And when I have completed this errand, when and where shall I see you, Lady Castleneau? For it may be that I shall have some reply to bring back to you."

"Come to my house, at all events, in Bloomsbury Fields, that I may at least thank you for your diligence; but let me impress upon you again and again the necessity of being beneath the leafy screens of the trees of old Epping Forest before mid-day."

"Depend upon me. The distance is nothing; it is scarcely a forced march. I'm off!"

With rapid strides the young Cornet made his way towards the old King's Mews, at Charing Cross; and Jonathan Wild, perhaps, had never

JONATHAN WILD ARRESTS LADY CASTLENEAU FOR HIGH TREASON.

Presented Gratis with No. 73 of the New Edition of Edith the Captive; or, the Robbers of Epping Forest.

EACH WEEK IS PRESENTED GRATIS A COLOURED ENGRAVING.

been in so great a perplexity in his life to know what to do.

He had striven in vain to catch the purport of the conversation that had taken place between the Cornet and Lady Castleneau, and had failed signally; for, from excess of feeling and emotion, blended with the deep anxiety that had possessed her, Lady Castleneau had spoken in a very low tone of voice; so that the young officer had been compelled to put his head right into the carriage in order to hear what she said; and with that unconscious imitation, both of tones and gestures, which will come over people engaged in interesting converse, he too had spoken in subdued tones, so that Jonathan Wild was terribly puzzled.

And it could not be said that he was destitute of a vague suspicion of the truth.

But the one point upon which he had no real information was with regard to the whereabouts of Captain Heron.

He might be in town, or he might be in waiting somewhere upon the suburbs, until close upon the time to come to the levee—or he might even be at Castleneau House.

Jonathan Wild stretched out his arms with the evident earnest desire to grapple, as prisoners, both Lady Castleneau and the young Cornet; for one or other of them, he felt certain, would hold communication with Captain Heron, and warn him not to make an appearance at the levee.

But Wild was alone, and what could he do? The young officer was fast disappearing down Pall-Mall, and Jonathan's anger was beginning to find vent in volleys of strange oaths, when he saw three mounted men coming down St. James's Street.

One glance was enough for Wild. They were three of his own men, and once more he felt that he was master of the situation.

The shrill whistle of the thief-taker was too well known to his myrmidons for them to hesitate a moment in its recognition. In less than half a minute they were by his side; and then Wild issued his orders in that brief, energetic style, which, under circumstances of higher import, might have made him a great commander.

"Two of you," he said, "will follow that young man. You see him in the distance—he wears a military undress uniform. You will prevent him entering any house, or speaking to any person, unless in your presence; and should he attempt to leave London, you will arrest him, and take him to Newgate Street, there to wait my further pleasure. Be off!"

The two horsemen gallopped after the young Cornet.

The third man remained with Wild.

"I will have her now," muttered Jonathan to himself, "come of it what may. This blank warrant, signed by the Secretary of State, shall stand me in good stead. Now, my Lady Castleneau, you will have lodgings, I expect, for one night in a more imposing and historic mansion than even Castleneau House."

It was well known that Jonathan Wild at that period was the political officer of the Home Office. The alarm of Jacobite plots was but slowly subsiding in England; and it was believed that the Jesuits were at the bottom of those machinations, or at all events it was convenient for those who were not adverse to a little religious persecution to affect to believe so.

It was an undoubted fact that at that period even so venial and criminal a man as Jonathan Wild was in possession of blank warrants, which would enable him to search for concealed Jesuits, and to apprehend those charged with harbouring them.

It was one of these documents, so imprudently trusted in the hands of such a man, that Jonathan Wild now produced from the capacious pocket-book he always wore in the breast of his coat.

There was an indentation of a bullet in that famous pocket-book, which, but for its interposition with its multifarious contents, would have rid the world of Jonathan Wild.

With a pencil, the lead of which he wetted with his lips, in order that it should mark the blacker, he hastily inserted the name of Lady Castleneau in the blank warrant.

These proceedings of Jonathan Wild's took place while that brave and gallant gentlewoman was watching the receding figure of the young Cornet, as he walked rapidly down Pall Mall.

She did not associate in the slightest degree with him the two horsemen which she saw keeping together in the middle of the road.

"Heaven speed him—heaven speed him!" she murmured. "Felix will be saved, and with him will be saved Edith; for should he fall a victim to the implacable rancour of his foes, I feel sure that she would not be long behind him in this world!"

The Cornet was lost to her gaze as he turned a corner, and Lady Castleneau had just leant back in the carriage after crying out to Anthony "Home, home!" when there was a rush of horses' feet, and each window of the coach was darkened by a mounted man.

"Lady Castleneau," said a harsh voice, "you are my prisoner!"

She knew that voice in a moment.

"No, Mr. Wild, villain as you are, and bold as you are," she cried, "even your audacity cannot enable you to seize an innocent person in the streets of London!"

"We shall see!" cried Wild, with one of his hideous laughs.

"Drive on, Anthony."

The old servant tried to whip his horses forward.

"Knock that old fool off the box," said Wild; "and stand by the horses' heads, Ambrose!"

Poor old Anthony was assailed at once by Wild's man, and as might be expected the contest was brief; for the faithful servitor was dragged from the coach-box, and flung half-stunned on to a doorstep.

"Help, help!" cried Lady Castleneau. "Help! help! Who will stand by and witness this outrage unmoved?"

People began to run towards the spot from St. James's Street and Pall Mall.

"Yes," said Jonathan Wild, composedly, "let there be help, madam, if you wish it. We don't care how many witnesses there are that you resist the King's warrant."

Wild held aloft over the coach-top the Secretary of State's authority that he had just made so villanous a use of, and he kept repeating the words in a loud tone, "The King's warrant—the King's warrant!"

Hearing these words, and seeing the strip of

parchment, and the cool and confident air of Jonathan Wild, the people, who had rushed forward to the rescue of Lady Castleneau, shrunk back; and Jonathan Wild seeing at once the effect he had produced, again shouted out in still louder tones, "The King's warrant!—the King's warrant! Is there one here prepared to resist it?"

There was a crowd of some thirty people assembled, but no one stirred hand or foot now in defence of Lady Castleneau.

"It is false! it is false!" she cried. "This is the cruel villain, Jonathan Wild, and it is for his own purposes he seeks to make me a prisoner."

"The King's warrant!" said Wild again, and a sneering smile sat upon his face. "The King's warrant!"

A young man stepped forward.

"How are we to know that, Mr. Wild? The lady seems a lady, and King's warrants don't interfere with such as she is."

"My dear friend," said Wild, "upon giving me your name and address, so that we may know you're a seditious person, and apprehend you at our convenience, when his Majesty's Government wants some one of that sort to make an example of, you shall actually read the warrant."

The young man rushed over the roadway, and disappeared up a court.

"Ah!" said Wild, "that will do! Has anybody else any objection?"

No one spoke.

"Forward, Ambrose!"

"No!" cried Lady Castleneau, as she made an effort to open the door of the coach. "I will not be arrested in this insolent fashion at the will of such a man as Jonathan Wild! I know too well where it is his wish to take me: it will be to his own house, or to some pretended asylum, across the threshold of which justice and mercy never enter!"

"No!" said Wild, as he made a hasty motion to his man Ambrose to proceed. "No, Lady Castleneau; this warrant accuses you of complicity with the Jacobins: it authorizes your own detention, and a narrow and accurate search of your house for concealed Jesuits; where, no doubt, we shall find one who will answer to the name of Sir Dominick Browne."

"No, no; it cannot be! This is too wicked."

"As for your ladyship," added Wild, sneeringly, "you will sleep to-night in the Tower, whither this warrant authorizes me to convey you."

"The Tower?"

"Yes. It almost amounts to a dignity—does it not? Forward, Ambrose, to the Tower!"

Those words of Jonathan Wild's seemed to strike a kind of awe into the crowd; and the carriage dashed off, without a single word being uttered, or an arm being raised to stay it.

—

CHAPTER CLXIII.

THE FATE OF THE MESSENGER.—A SHOT AND A DEATH.—THE TERROR OF GUILT.

THE young Cornet of the Guard had been entrusted by Lady Castleneau with a much more hazardous mission than either he or she imagined.

That young officer might have taken part in many a battle, without one-half the risk he now ran from the unscrupulous myrmidons of Jonathan Wild.

The enterprise that he was upon was, however, as far as he could comprehend it, at the moment when he left Lady Castleneau in Pall Mall, anything but a disagreeable one. It had that great charm to the young and imaginative, of mystery. It was invested with a romantic character which recommended it to his attention.

Who was this Felix Heron, whose interests were evidently so dear to Lady Castleneau?

How was it that his presentation, or non-presentation at the levee, was to her a matter of such evidently vital importance?

These were the questions which must have interested the Cornet; but they were, at the same time, precisely those which he found it impossible to answer.

Nevertheless, the gallant young soldier made his way as quickly as he could on the errand which he little thought was one of life or death.

Once he paused, and looked back, as he heard the clatter of horses' feet in the road; and he saw those two men of Wild's coming in the same direction as himself, but he did not in any way associate them with the errand he was endeavouring to fulfil.

The gate of the King's Mews was reached.

The clock of St. Martin's Church struck ten.

"Ah! there is no time to lose," said the Cornet to himself, as he stepped up to the sentinel at the gate of the barrack.

The uniform he wore produced respect, and the sentinel stood at "attention."

"Is Captain Crawley's horse here?" he asked.

The sentinel was an infantry soldier, and knew little or nothing of cavalry movements. He was about to shake his head, and reply that he did not know, when a cavalry sergeant appeared at the wicket, who knew Cornet Amos, and saluted him.

"Well met, Sergeant Tully," said the Cornet. "You can tell me if Captain Crawley's horse, Marlborough, is here."

"Yes, sir."

"Then bring it out at once. I want to borrow it, as you know I may."

"Certainly, sir."

The Sergeant was prompt in his movements, and in five minutes Cornet Amos was mounted on his intimate friend Crawley's charger, and had turned the creature's head in the direction he wished to go.

But the young man was rather in doubt with regard to the best course to take; and reining in the horse for a moment, he called out aloud, so that not only the sentinel on duty, but several soldiers who were lounging about the barrack-gate, heard him—"Sergeant Tully! Sergeant Tully!"

"Yes, sir," said the Sergeant, as he marched in quick step towards the horse.

"Which is the nearest way to Epping Forest?"

"You will keep the Thames, sir, on your right hand, and ride through Stratford, and then to the north by any of the roads."

"Thank you—thank you; and how far is it?"

"Nine miles, sir, will take you right into the forest."

"That will do."

No. 74.—EDITH.

The Sergeant respectfully saluted the young Cornet, who returned it courteously; and then setting spurs to the horse, the officer galloped away.

That was the last time Sergeant Tully, or those soldiers who were listlessly hanging about the gate of the King's Mews, saw the young Cornet of the Household Cavalry alive.

But we will not anticipate. Sufficient for the hour let the event be.

Light of heart—thinking of a fair and gentle girl whom he loved, and who might yet, he fondly hoped, in the fulness of time be his, when he had won a higher rank than that of a mere subaltern, the Cornet galloped gaily onwards.

Onwards to death!

The two villanous men of Jonathan Wild followed him like fate.

It so happened that of all the gang of ruthless, reckless men who served Wild as a master, those two were the most unscrupulous and bloodthirsty. To them human life was as a thing only to be esteemed in their own persons, or in that of any one useful to them or their unscrupulous employer.

They took good care that, in their pursuit of the young officer, they should not be seen to be keeping him in view; and, indeed, as he made his way through the City, they occasionally went down a side street, which carried them out of sight for a few moments; but then they knew perfectly well that they would emerge on to the high road again, which he kept.

Then the chase was continued right through the City, until the sweet green lanes about Stratford were reached.

Additional caution now was requisite on the part of the officers.

Their instructions were quite clear. The young Cornet was not to be permitted to reach Epping Forest; and if it were necessary to leave him a corpse on the road, in order to prevent his progress, they were quite ready and willing to do so.

The route from Stratford to the Forest was almost entirely through verdant lanes, in many places with tall, majestic trees on either side, which shut out even the mid-day sun, and made a twilight while the bright luminary of day was still high in the heavens.

It was very strange—it felt strange to himself, that the young Cornet, as he rode on, should feel his thoughts carried far away from the present to his more boyish days.

It seemed to him as if the progress of human life and of human events had stopped, and he was flung back, so to speak, upon the memory of the past.

Once he turned upon his saddle, and looked back.

There were the two horsemen on the road, about a couple of hundred yards behind him.

For the first time, then, the idea came across his mind that the sight of those two mounted men was familiar to him.

For a few moments he was puzzled to know when he had seen them before, and where, but then suddenly he remembered.

"To be sure—to be sure!" he cried. "I saw those two ill-looking fellows in Pall Mall, and after that in the City. Are they after me?"

This was rather an important question.

The Cornet turned his horse completely round, and faced Jonathan Wild's two men.

They saw that the time was come at which they must either attack him or do something to ward off suspicion from them.

The former course was the most congenial to their feelings, if we may use such a word at all in reference to such men.

"Come on," said one,—"come on, Joe. Let us bring it to an end."

"With all my heart, Davies. Knock him on the head, and have done with it."

They were on the very point of putting their horses to a gallop, when an occurrence took place which at once altered the determination of the moment.

The unmistakable sound of horses' feet in some numbers, on a cross-road close to which they were, came upon their ears, and they paused at once.

"What's that, eh?"

"Somebody coming."

"A lot of somebodys I should say, Joe."

"Hold back."

Another moment made it sufficiently manifest who the new arrivals were, for from the cross-road there emerged a troop of about twenty persons in scarlet coats, followed by a goodly assemblage of dogs, that were with difficulty kept together by the whips of the huntsmen.

The two janissaries of Jonathan Wild wheeled their horses to the side of the road, and touched their hats as the cavalcade passed over the road at right angles, and continued the way down the cross-road.

When they were gone—when dogs, men, and horses had all left the spot, the two men of Jonathan Wild looked about them with some alarm.

The young officer was not to be seen.

"He's off!" said Davies.

"It looks like it."

"But he can't be far away. Let us ride on. We shall soon see him."

They galloped on for about half a mile, and then in a hollow of the road they saw the horse of the young Cornet, and for a moment or two they thought the horse was alone.

Then they saw him, the officer, come round the horse's head, and mount.

There had been a stone in the foot of the charger, which the Cornet had had some difficulty, by the aid of a small pocket-knife, in getting out.

The horse went a little lame for the next mile.

On the brow of the hill the young man looked back.

"By Jove," he said, "there are those two ugly fellows still on the road."

A countryman came across a stile by the roadside.

"Hilloa, my man!" cried Amos. "Am I on my right road to Epping Forest?"

"Quite right, sir, but not the nighest road."

"Then I am not on my right road. Which will be the nearer?"

"The first lane to the left, sir."

"Thank you."

The Cornet in two more minutes dived into a lane which was so shadowy with luxuriant vegetation, that to enter it from the high road looked like penetrating into the mouth of a cavern.

In a few moments, however, his eyes got more

accustomed to the darkness, and he was enchanted by the beauty of the lane.

Tall trees were on either side. The hedge-row was a perfect bouquet of wild flowers. From the meadows came the sweet scent of the clover; and birds in that sylvan spot twittered from bough to bough, as if questioning the right of man and horse to trespass upon their own leafy domain.

The Cornet drew up suddenly.

What does he hear?

There is a sound on the other side of the hedge.

An undefined feeling of anxiety came over him. He feels in the holsters of the saddle of the charger.

Ah, yes! He breathes more freely. The regimental pistols of his friend Captain Crawley are there. What, then, can he have to fear? Nothing—surely nothing.

A bird high up in one of the old elms was singing plaintively.

That song sounded like a dirge.

Again the young man hears a sound from the other side of the hedge.

"Stand!" he cried; "stand, or I fire!"

He was so certain that some one was there that he drew one of the pistols from the saddle and presented it towards the hedge.

"Hold, sir! Not yet!" cried a voice.

The thick branches of an alder were thrust aside, and the young Cornet saw a head and face.

"Who and what are you?"

"Why, sir, I have some advice to give you."

"To give me?"

"Yes, sir. It is that you will be so good and so wise, too, as to turn your horse's head towards town again."

"I will."

"That's the thing, sir."

"I mean to say I will when I have turned it in the direction I choose from town, so long as it pleases me so to do; but if you can give me a warning of any danger that I may guard against, I shall thank you."

"You must not ride to Epping Forest."

"Must not?"

"I said, must not."

"Good day, my friend. I am off for Epping."

"Hold, sir, on your life!"

The man in the hedge pointed full at the young officer one of those short, thick, stumpy pistols which at that time were so much the fashion with the officers of the police; but the moment he saw it, the Cornet smiled, and without moving a hair's breadth out of the line of fire, he said, "Blaze away, and then it will be my turn!"

As he spoke, he raised the holster pistol, and held it firm as a rock in the direction of the face of the man in the hedge.

Then there came upon the still air of that lane, so rich in verdant beauty, the sudden and sharp report of a pistol.

But it did not come from the short, stumpy weapon of the man in the hedge, nor from the holster pistol which the Cornet had drawn from the saddle.

It was from the other side of the lane—from the umbrageous hedge behind the officer and his horse—that the report emanated, and it was echoed by one short, sharp cry.

That cry came from the lips of the Cornet.

There was a bullet in his young and generous heart, and human nature could not forbear the scream of agony.

The startled birds flew from the trees in myriads—the timid hare rushed from brake to cover. A thin white wreath of smoke curled up from the hedge, and then there was a crashing of boughs on the side from which the foul and treacherous shot had come, and the other janissary of Jonathan Wild made his appearance.

The Cornet's horse was well trained as a charger, and the sound of a pistol-shot was not a matter of alarm to a creature educated to stand fire.

The Cornet reeled in the saddle.

The pistol he had taken from the holster fell to the ground. After that one extorted scream of agony he was silent. He fell over the neck of the horse.

There came then one shudder over his convulsed form, and slowly the half-dead hands let the reins and the flowing mane of the horse slip through the fingers, and so he fell heavily to the ground, where, with one last effort, then, he rolled over and looked up at the sun, which sent down a long narrow ray of light through an accidental opening in a tree-top.

Another moment, and that ray of light fell upon the calm face of death.

<hr>

CHAPTER CLXIV.

MID-DAY IN THE FOREST. — THE MYSTERY OF THE SHADOWY LANE.—AN ADVENTURE.

THE stillness in the lane was unbroken for the space during which, at moderate speed, one might have counted fifty.

There is something in death which has its effect even upon the most obdurate and callous natures.

Those two ruffians, hired as they were by the equal ruffian Jonathan Wild to perform any deed of iniquity that he might please to suggest to them—those assassins, who had thus in cold blood carried out the fell purpose of their master—could not speak for about the time we have mentioned, nor withdraw their eyes from a contemplation of the still form, which never again would rise and meet them until that awful day when earth's deepest caverns would not hide them from the accusing eyes of the murdered!

It was then by a great effort that the man who was named Davies spoke.

"Well," he said, in low tones, "that's done Joe!"

"It is done."

"Well, what then? You don't look pleased about it."

"Yes, I am."

"Then don't look about you in that scared kind of way."

"I am not looking about me. I'm like you."

"Like me? What do you mean?"

"I cannot take my eyes off the face!"

The other ruffian turned pale and trembled.

"No more can I!" he gasped. "Come away—come away! Don't touch him, or take anything he has about him. Come away! Why don't you say something, eh?—something cheerful! Come away! I—I couldn't look away from him for all the swag in Jonathan's house. Come on—come on! Where are you, eh? Let's get away at once."

With their eyes fixed on the face of the dead, these two men slowly made their way backwards down the lane to where they had left their horses. They felt it an immense relief when, by a turn in the lane, they lost sight of the terrible object which excited all their fears.

Then they ran as if they fully expected that the dead Cornet would rise up and chase them. They flung themselves on the backs of their horses, and urging the animals to speed, they made their way back to London.

But they might fly from the dim twilight of that shadowy lane—they might fly from the sight of that pale, gentle-looking face, which in the long pencil of sunlight that fell upon it might have been supposed to be sleeping—but never could they fly from the memory of that terrible hour!

*　　*　　*　　*　　*

And now in old Epping Forest the shadows are shortening, and the hour of mid-day is approaching.

There is a subdued kind of bustle in one of the deepest and most beautiful glades of the ancient wood. Tom Ripon is there, with the bridle of Daisy in his hand, and another of the band is holding a horse on which Ogle is to mount.

A third horse, at some short distance, is cropping the sweet herbage of the forest.

Various members of Captain Heron's companions of the road are scattered about, and from the tree-tops the scouts of the wood keep good watch upon the different routes by which old Epping Forest might be entered.

Slowly, then, and hand in hand with his darling Edith, comes Felix Heron himself, from one of those narrow and intricate paths in the thick brushwood which would seem only accessible to the fox, the hare, and the forest birds.

There are tears upon the fair face of Edith.

There is a deep seriousness upon the countenance of Captain Heron.

"Dear, dear, Edith, all will yet be well, believe me," he said, gently. "These undefined terrors that come over you are natural, but they will all vanish when you see me, before the sun has well commenced to decline in the western sky, return to the dear leafy glades of this old forest."

"Heaven grant you may, dear Felix; and yet —and yet——"

"You have a thousand fears," smiled Heron.

"I have—I have, indeed."

"Dismiss them—I pray you to dismiss them. I cannot well see what harm can come to me by attending the levee."

"The harm of treachery, dear Felix."

"I have thought deeply of that. I cannot believe it to be possible that, in the royal presence, I can be assailed in any way. If it be that my brother, Warringdale, means any foul play, it is of too subtle and deep a nature——"

"For you, in your generous and unsuspecting heart, to see, Felix," sobbed Edith. "That is just what suggests itself to me."

"Nay, dearest; I was not about to say that. I meant to say that his plot, if plot there be, is too intricate for success."

Edith would not, could not, be convinced.

"This," she said, "will be a sad and tearful day for me. Oh, Felix, Felix! we were happy here beneath the greenwood tree; and now, when there seems to be a chance or hope—call it which you will—of wealth and rank, I have suffered more anxiety in one night, than ever at our worst fortunes before!"

There was a shade of sorrow upon the face of Captain Heron. In his heart he devoutly wished that his brother, Lord Warringdale, had kept his real or simulated repentance to himself; but since the event had taken place, he felt he had no resource but to do what he was about to do.

For Edith's dear sake he was naturally desirous of assuming the rank which he felt truly belonged to him; although he did not expect to be one bit the happier, were he hailed by the common consent of mankind as Earl of Whitcombe, than he was amid the leafy glades of old Epping Forest as Captain Felix Heron.

Ogle now approached Heron, and said in a low tone, "It wants but a quarter of an hour, Captain, of noon. You told me to let you know when this time should come."

"Thank you, Ogle. I did—I did!"

"Alas!" said Edith; "then the time has come when I must bid you farewell."

"No, dear Edith, no! Not farewell—only good-day, and God speed for a few short hours."

"Heaven grant it may be so!"

"It will—it will! Bring Daisy, Tom—bring Daisy now; and, Ogle, you can now summon the Lord Warringdale."

Ogle muttered something to himself about his being quite as willing to summon a certain personage, seldom mentioned in genteel society; but he took his way towards the cavern by the little spring, and in the course of five minutes returned with Lord Warringdale.

Pale and anxious was Warringdale, for various doubts and fears had kept him awake the whole of the preceding night.

It was in vain that he had urged upon Captain Heron to let him go to London "to prepare matters for the presentation at the levee." Heron had turned a deaf ear to all such arguments, and had met them with but one remark.

"Brother, we will go together."

So Lord Warringdale had been compelled, much against his will, to stay that night in the Forest; and such had been the dread of any discovery taking place of the plot that he had laid for the destruction of Heron, that he had purposely avoided attempting any arrangement with Jonathan Wild, by which they might communicate with each other in case anything went wrong.

Thus, then, Lord Warringdale was full of anxieties; and it is possible enough that he had more than once bitterly repented of the plan he had commenced for the destruction of his brother.

But it was too late now to recede.

Warringdale felt, now, that he must stand or fall by the circumstances which he had himself created.

When Captain Heron saw him advancing with Ogle, he bowed slightly, but he took no notice of the somewhat ostentatiously offered hand of Warringdale.

It was only Edith, close to him as she was, who

THE DEAD CORNET.

Presented Gratis with No. 74, of the New Edition of the Captive; or, the Robbers of Epping Forest.

EACH WEEK IS PRESENTED ITS A COLOURED ENGRAVING.

heard Felix say in a low tone, "Not yet! Oh, no, not yet!"

"Ab, Felix!" she whispered, "you, too, suspect——"

"No, no, dear—no! But I would fain make assurance of his repentance doubly sure, before I can say freely I forgive. I do not wish to be cheated for a moment into so much of a brotherly caress as may be implied by taking his hand in mine."

Lord Warringdale now reached the spot on which Captain Heron and Edith awaited him; and he strove to put on a look of ingenuous hilarity, as he said with a forced smile, "My lord and brother, I wish you good-day. And you, too, Lady Whitcombe."

"Forbear!" said Heron. "It is too soon."

"Nay, brother, it cannot be too soon, since our poor father is no more. From that moment you were the Earl of Whitcombe, and your fair bride here is a countess."

"She is happier," said Edith, "as the wife of Felix Heron, than as if she were a duchess!"

"Oh, there can be no doubt about that," added Lord Warringdale, with a bow; "but yet we have none of us any right to forego our birthright."

"Twelve o'clock, Captain," said Ogle.

Heron started.

"It is time, then," he said. "I must wait for information no longer. It is time!"

Lord Warringdale turned a shade paler. There was a something in the manner and expression of Captain Heron which awakened all his fears. What could be the meaning of the time having arrived beyond which he need not wait? What communication could he expect which would be otherwise then detrimental to the plot, the successful progress of which lay so deep at his, Warringdale's, heart?

If he had been before anxious to leave the forest, he was doubly so now; for he felt a kind of assurance in his own mind that Heron had taken some steps to endeavour to unmask his villany, and that his position there in the forest was one of the most critical danger.

In the rustle of every leaf he fancied he heard the approach of some one who would uplift a warning voice to Heron; and, at the same time, denounce him, Warringdale.

When a small stray branch from a tree, broken by the wind, fell rustling to his feet, he uttered a sudden cry of terror, which made Captain Heron's band lay their hands upon their concealed weapons.

"What is this?" said Felix. "What is it moves you thus, Warringdale, and blanches your cheek with fear?"

"It is not fear—it is not fear; it is emotion, because I see I am still suspected."

"And can you wonder," said Edith, turning her gaze upon him and speaking with emotion,—"can you wonder, my Lord Warringdale, that you are still suspected after all the past? After the abundant treachery, the persecutions which we have both endured from you, can you wonder that your every word seems to have a covert meaning? Can you wonder that we may well be incredulous, when the wolf assumes the aspect of the lamb?"

"I feel that I deserve these reproaches," said Warringdale, striking his breast; "in fact, I rather rejoice in them, as part of the retribution on account of that past to which you allude. But, brother, the time has now surely come when we should proceed to London. Let not that act of justice which I propose carrying out to-day be too late. We have to ride some distance, and then we have to prepare for his Majesty's levee."

"I am ready," said Heron.

"Then I pray you let us go at once,"

"No; no!" cried Edith. "Even now, at the last hour—even now, at the last minute, I raise my voice against this enterprise, and I say to you, Felix, do not go!"

Lord Warringdale turned aside and bit his lips.

"Edith, dearest," said Heron, "do not withdraw your consent to this journey to London! I do not see the danger, and if I did, I could well see a mode of escape from it. Once for all, let this experimental test be tried. If there be such a thing as good feeling or repentant justice in the heart of Warringdale, I pray you let me go, Edith!"

"Go, then, and heaven speed you!"

Lord Warringdale drew a long breath of relief.

In another moment the little party was mounted. Ogle only was to attend Captain Heron and Warringdale to London; so that personal treachery on the road was out of the question. Edith would not trust herself to speak again, but waving her adieu with both her hands, she dived into the recesses of the forest.

And so, at about a quarter past twelve on that eventful day, since no messenger arrived from Lady Castleneau with news of danger, Captain Heron left his woodland home, with, for the first time, Lord Warringdale riding by his side, and every external appearance of concord and unity existing between those half-brothers.

Ogle followed at about twenty yards in the rear, and for the first half-mile he employed himself in drawing the old charges of his pistols and thoroughly and carefully reloading them.

As this process was going on, Lord Warringdale more than once turned his head in sudden alarm as the sharp clicking locks of the pistols came upon his ears, and on those occasions Ogle met him with a steady stare which much discomposed him.

"Is your man always fidgetting with those pistols, brother?" said Warringdale.

"No; but every day he puts in fresh charges, and he is more than specially careful of them when he rides abroad with me. In fact, he is so prompt and courageous, and withal so good a shot, that I scarcely need arm myself when he is within anything like reasonable distance of an enemy."

"He seems a troublesome—that is, an excellent fellow."

"He is an excellent fellow, and not at all troublesome," said Heron, drily.

"But it's rather dangerous to be clicking the locks of pistols in that manner. However, if you have confidence in him, brother, so will I. And now tell me, have you decided upon what to do when we get to town?"

"I think of riding direct to Lady Castleneau's, to dress for the levee."

Captain Heron could not possibly have announced a determination more at variance with the wishes of Lord Warringdale than this, but he dissembled his discontent at the statement, and putting on as careless an air as he could, he said, "Of course, that is just as you please, brother; and should you go there, I hope you will give my best compliments to her ladyship, and do your best to restore me to her favour, in which at present I fear I am sadly deficient; but I was about to suggest that you would probably be so good as to please me by going to Whitcombe House. There you will find every possible accommodation, and I must own it would give me some gratification to feel that you went from your own house—which that unquestionably is—to the first levee you attended."

"Be it so, then," said Heron; "be it as you wish."

It was by an impulse, then, that Felix turned in his saddle and faced Lord Warringdale.

"Henry, Henry," he said, "if this day you are playing a treacherous part by me, and attempting to lead me into any snare for my destruction, pity in my bosom will take the place of abhorrence, for I shall begin to believe that not in the whole confines of the world will be found so monstrous a villain!"

Lord Warringdale turned pale as death.

"Alas, alas!" he said, "have I done so much, and said so much, but at the eleventh hour to have such words uttered to me? Go back, Felix—go back. Since you have such feelings, return to your forest home, and I will ride to London alone. Alone I will seek the presence of the King, and utter those words which I would gladly have uttered with you by my side. I will add to them, too, that you mistrusted me after riding forth a mile from Epping with me."

"No; I will go on."

"Nay, I pray you do not. Go back, and mistrust me still—I deserve it all. It is a part of the retribution."

"No," said Heron; "I will proceed. Be the consequences of this day upon your head, not upon mine. And if I for a moment have wronged you by an unjust suspicion, I will find a means of making such ample amends that even the most sensitive heart must needs be satisfied."

"I am satisfied already."

"Say no more—say no more! I will go with you to Whitcombe House; I will there prepare for the levee. And you may yet find, Henry, that the greatest success you ever achieved over your brother Felix is by surrendering all to him."

Lord Warringdale pretended to be affected.

Ogle had ridden rather close when he saw Captain Heron turn towards Warringdale in the manner we have described; but he fell back again to his usual distance on finding the conversation was amicable.

Captain Heron turned and addressed him, crying out, in a loud, careless tone, "I think, Ogle, we will take Elm-tree Lane, if you know the bridge over the rivulet is replaced."

"Bless your heart, Captain—yes: The miller wouldn't leave it on any account. It's all right, and stronger than ever."

"Then we will take that route."

Heron rode down to a hollow, at the bottom of which grew a quantity of furze bushes, through which Daisy picked her way with dainty and accurate steps; and then, as the ground rose a little, there appeared a copse, in which the young timber grew so closely together, that it promised in a few years to be nearly impenetrable to mounted men.

It was from this copse, skirted as it was by a sandy little bit of road, that that shadowy lane emerged in which so fearful a catastrophe had taken place only one hour before Captain Heron and Lord Warringdale startled the wild birds by the tread of their horses' feet.

There was a chilling, damp sensation in the air of the lane; and as if with some instinctive feeling that all was not well within the precincts of that shadowy place, Daisy pricked up her ears, and glanced from side to side, curveting and uttering now and then strange sounds, indicative of some undefined alarm.

"Why, Daisy," said Heron, as he pressed his hand caressingly over the silken mane,—"why, Daisy, are you startled by a hedge-sparrow, or the rustle of a leveret in the foliage?"

"No, Captain," cried Ogle, who had observed these indications of nervousness on the part of Daisy,—"no, Captain; but you may depend there's something more in it than we can see at present. I never knew Daisy half so fidgetty about nothing."

"But what can it be, Ogle?"

"Yes," said Lord Warringdale, with apprehension in his look; "what can it be? I don't think there can be any danger to us."

"Nor I either," said Ogle. "But you may depend upon it, Captain, there's something wrong in the lane, and I should say that this is the beginning of it."

They all three stopped their horses, as Ogle spoke, for they saw approaching them a very handsome steed, but without a rider. The accoutrements of this steed were evidently of a military character; and if ever anxiety could be exhibited upon the countenance of a dumb animal, it was manifest in the face and about the eyes of this horse, which looked up to Captain Heron and his companions as though it had something to communicate which, if speech had not been denied, it would fain have uttered in a breath.

CHAPTER CLXV.

THE ROUTE TO LONDON.—THE DEAD CORNET IN THE LANE.—SUSPECTED TREACHERY.

IF the uneasy feeling about Captain Heron's horse, Daisy, was manifest and easy to be observed, the agitation that began slowly but surely to spread itself over the face of Lord Warringdale soon eclipsed the fears of the quadruped.

And yet, beyond the knowledge and sensation of his own guilt and treachery, my Lord Warringdale could have no special cause for alarm in that beautiful and shadowy lane. He had no ambuscade there in waiting to inflict mischief or death upon that brother whom he would right gladly have seen lying a corpse at his feet.

But who shall paint the thousand fears, the thousand false alarms, of the trembling wretch whose

"Conscience with injustice is corrupted?"

Who shall say how far transcending the pangs of death may be the agonies which such men as Lord

Warringdale endure from mere causeless apprehension?

In each circumstance, however trivial, they see food for despair. Nothing can happen—nothing can be said which bears not to them a double meaning: one that the mere words seem to carry—another which points, in a hidden fashion, to the discovery of some special guilt of their own.

Hence was it, then, that Lord Warringdale—as we still call him, for distinction's sake—was fearfully alarmed on finding that there was some mystery in the shadowy lane.

"Captain," said Ogle, "I think I had better go on in advance, and see what is amiss."

"Nay, Ogle. It may be danger."

"Just so. That is why I want to go."

"And that is just why I won't permit you. If there be danger it is I who will face it."

As he spoke, Captain Heron touched Daisy lightly on the neck, and she bounded forward.

Ogle, however, did not exactly like being left alone with Lord Warringdale, without more definite instructions than he at that present time had in regard to what he was to do.

"Hold, Captain! Hold! One moment!"

Felix Heron drew rein, and Ogle was the next instant by his side.

"Captain, if that—that——What shall I call him?"

Ogle indicated Warringdale.

"Call him by the name he has always hitherto been known by, Ogle."

"Very good, Captain. Then, if that rascal should try to go away, shall I shoot him?"

"By no means."

"Oh, very good!"

"And I did not mean you to call him by any name but that of Lord Warringdale. If he should choose to leave us, let him go. He is no longer a prisoner. He has been perfectly free from the moment that we left the shades of old Epping Forest behind us."

"Very good," said Ogle again; but it was evident that he did not think it was very good, and that he would have had no objection to send a bullet in pursuit of Warringdale if he should attempt to escape.

"Follow easily," added Captain Heron; "I will soon find what makes Daisy so uneasy, although I can already partly guess."

"Can you, Captain?"

"Yes; I have before seen her exhibit all this anxiety when in the vicinity of some one who has died a violent death."

As he spoke, Captain Heron again gave Daisy the impulse to proceed; and at a pace which would have prevented Ogle from following up the lane, had he determined even so to do, with any hopes of keeping up with Daisy, the noble creature sped onwards.

The shadows deepened as Captain Heron and his gallant steed advanced, until a gloom, almost equal to that which a lapsed hour of sunset would have produced, settled about that wild and shadowy spot.

Then Daisy uttered a short cry, and reared.

"Ah, it is here!" said Heron.

He turned on his saddle, and looked to the pathway before him.

A dark object was there lying.

Need we say who in life that dark object had

been? It was the young Cornet, who had fallen by that foul and treacherous shot from Jonathan Wild's men.

"A murder!" cried Captain Heron. "Stand, Daisy, stand!"

Daisy trembled, but she stood as still as a horse of bronze.

Captain Heron then dismounted, and stooped over the dead. Calm and placid lay that young heart now, and one glance at the still face and glazed eyes was enough to convince Captain Heron at all human aid was useless.

Not all the science—not all the humanity—not all the wealth the world ever saw—shall suffice to give life and motion again to that still form lying in the sleep of death.

There was blood upon the sandy pathway of the verdant lane.

Blood that had crept along and settled itself into a little pool, where it had coagulated, and looked ghastly and terrible.

Then Captain Heron almost uttered a shout of surprise, for at the moment he thought some one had touched him on the shoulder.

It was the charger.

The horse which the ill-fated and murdered young officer had ridden from London, and which, since his murder, had, with the instinct of the noblest of the animal kingdom, felt that there was something wrong, and had lingered about the lane.

The charger pawed the soft earth, and looked at Captain Heron and at its dead master.

Heron shook his head.

The creature then put its face close down to the face of the dead; then looking up, it uttered one of those strange cries which horses are capable of uttering on rare occasions, and in another moment it galloped furiously away.

"That horse will go now," said Heron, "to the home of its rider, or to the place where he mounted it. This has been some most dastardly deed."

Felix Heron then placed the silver whistle to his lips, with which he was in the habit of summoning his men, and blew one long, low call.

Ogle put spurs to his horse and galloped forward, quite heedless of whether Lord Warringdale chose to go on or retrace his steps.

In a couple of minutes Ogle was by the side of Captain Heron.

"It is a murder, Ogle!"

"Ah, I thought as much. Is it any one we know, Captain."

"No, no!"

"What shall we do?"

"Nothing. It is past doing anything now. And yet I would not that some careless rider should pass over this poor corpse. I will remove it to the road-side."

"I will do that, Captain."

"Nay, do not dismount. Your horse may not stand still, while Daisy is sure to do so."

Captain Heron dragged the dead body of the young officer to the road-side, and placed it among the trees, and the tall grass, and the wild roses, that made a screen of beauty between the trees.

"I will take some memorial of him, at all events," said Heron, "in case it should ever become necessary to say anything about this affair."

As he spoke, Heron twisted off one of the

buttons from the uniform coat of the dead officer, and in the effort to do so he brought with the button a small piece of the cloth of the coat.

"This will enable me to identify the clothing at any time," he said. "More I do not see that we can do at present."

"Here is a horseman's pistol lying in the roadway," said Ogle. "I will take it."

"Do so—do so! Is it charged?"

"Yes, Captain."

"Well, Ogle, you and I will remember all the particulars of this adventure; and you will keep the pistol, and I will keep the button. Here comes Lord Warringdale, and it will be as well, too, that he should be a witness to what we have here seen in Elm-tree Lane."

Lord Warringdale had not increased his speed, and only now, with some appearance of trepidation, rode up to the spot.

"Ah!" said Ogle, in a low tone, "it's a comfort to know that he could not have done this little murder on the road; but if he had been as far on before us as we were before him, I should not have been surprised at it."

"Hush! hush!" said Heron. "Wrong no man by, perhaps, unjust surmises of what he might do, Ogle. Sufficient for all of us to stand or fall by our own actual acts."

Warringdale called out in what he tried to make sound cheerful and indifferent tones, "Is anything amiss?—is anything amiss?"

"Only a murder!" said Ogle.

"A murder? No!"

"It is, indeed, but too true," said Captain Heron. "There you may see the body of one who has been most foully murdered!"

"It is, perhaps, a suicide," said Warringdale.

"No. There has been but one pistol found on the road, and that is charged."

Lord Warringdale made a circuit with his horse round the pool of coagulated blood, and seemed well pleased when he had got past both it and the dead body.

"Brother, brother!" he said faintly, "we shall be late!"

"We shall—we shall; and we can do no good here."

"Oh, no, no! None at all!"

"Forward, then, once more! Forward!"

Captain Heron gave one last look at the face of the young Cornet, and with a sigh he trotted onwards with Lord Warringdale by his side.

Little did he suspect that that young heart lay so still in death on his account; and that it was in an effort to bring him intelligence of the treachery of the very man who rode by his side, that that gallant spirit had been so instantly sent to eternity.

Had Heron searched the body he would have found that small scrap of paper, the leaf from the pocket-book which Lady Castleneau had given to the young officer to take to Epping Forest.

But neither the janissaries of Jonathan Wild nor Captain Heron disturbed that document, which virtually, when Lady Castleneau wrote it, had been the death-warrant of Cornet Amos.

Warringdale now turned a strange look upon Captain Heron, as he said, "Brother, do your men usually commit such deeds?"

Captain Heron checked Daisy, and looked full in the face of Warringdale.

"What do you mean, sir?"

"Oh, do not be offended; but I thought it only just possible, you see, that some of your men might have been out early, and had a contest with the young officer, and so it had ended in his death."

"If any of my men had been guilty of such a deed, I would hang them on the highest boughs of Epping Forest; and to remove from your mind the idea even of the possibility of their committing such an act, I can tell you that not one of them left the wood since last night, and this murder has but too evidently been done to-day. Ride more quickly, or we shall, indeed, be late."

There was no absolute necessity for riding very quick, but Captain Heron had an invincible and growing repugnance to conversation with Warringdale. There was a tone, a manner, an indescribable something about every word he uttered, which jarred upon the feelings of Heron, and he was glad when the rapid motion of the horses put anything like consecutive conversation out of the question.

The shadowy lane was passed through, and the wide, open country was before the horsemen. Then they reached the long straggling highway which would soon conduct them to London, and the houses that had been few and far between began to increase in numbers, until, passing through Stratford, Captain Heron and Lord Warringdale might be said to be in the suburbs of the metropolis.

Then Ogle, whose mind was never free from the apprehension of some foul treachery on the part of Lord Warringdale, rode a little closer still to his master, and kept one of his hands very near to the stock of a pistol.

There can be no doubt at all but that on any decided treachery from Lord Warringdale, Ogle would have shot him.

But the betrayer, and the treacherous brother, was too politic and too mindful of his own safety, to essay any such thing. Nothing was further from his thoughts than to commit any act that would entail the arrest of Captain Heron.

It was his death he wanted.

The mere apprehension of Heron would have filled him, Warringdale, full of a thousand fears. Indeed, he felt that so far as his material interests were concerned, he was much better off while Heron was a free wanderer beneath the glades of Epping Forest.

If, however, Heron was a prisoner, what would hinder him from telling his eventful history, and declaring who and what he really was? What would prevent Lady Castleneau from stepping forward to his protection? What would keep back the gallant young Earl of Bridgewater from using all his influence in the favour of one whom he already called a friend.

"No, no!" thought Warringdale to himself, as he saw that more than once they were so hemmed in by carts, coaches, and people, in the narrow thoroughfares of the City, that if he had chosen to shout out "Here is Captain Heron, the notorios highwayman of Epping Forest!" the arrest of Heron would have been more than probable,— "no, no! It is death alone that can give me assurance of safety."

And so they rode on towards the West End of London.

The idea certainly now and then could not but come over the mind of Captain Heron that he was running some risk. Once, when, in the Poultry, there was such a positive stoppage in the street from an overturned waggon, that it was impossible to make way in any direction, he could not but feel how dangerous to him would be a cry for his arrest.

But Lord Warringdale looked calm and placid; and hope, more than ever it had done before, found a place in the heart of Captain Heron, to the effect that, after all, Lord Warringdale might be acting fairly towards him.

It was this feeling that prompted the generous heart of Heron to look kindly on his half-brother, as they rode together down the Strand.

"Henry," he said, "you still, I can see, persevere in your purpose."

"I have never faltered in it, brother."

"I begin to believe you."

No. 75.—EDITH.

"You may indeed. The purpose for which I sought you, at some risk to myself, I fancy, in the glades of Epping Forest, I have never faltered in for a moment."

"Disabuse yourself of one thing, however," added Heron. "You ran no risk whatever in the glades of Epping."

"Indeed ?"

"Indeed, and in truth. From the moment that I found out our consanguinity, you were perfectly safe from me, and from all over whom I had any control."

"Well, well; I do hope that the next two hours will make a material change in both our fortunes."

"They cannot fail to do so."

"I hope not—I hope not! My mind will be at ease, and you, brother, will have no complaints to make."

There was a lurking malignity about the expression of Lord Warringdale which Captain Heron did not like to speculate upon; but he could not help seeing that there had come over the countenance of his half-brother a strange expression of devilish triumph, if one may be permitted to use the expression, since no other form of words would be sufficiently expressive of the fiendish light that glistened in the eyes of my Lord Warringdale.

He thought he had that generous, unsuspicious brother now at his mercy. He thought his death was all but certain.

They were now at Charing Cross.

Up the little steep bit of street that led to Pall Mall, steeper then by far than it is now, they took their way, and were soon close to the end of St. James's Street, and opposite to the old Palace.

Lord Warringdale reined in his horse.

There was much bustle and confusion about that part of the town; for the levees, at the period of which we write, were held at an earlier hour than at present.

The fashions of the day, along with its habits and customs, have changed greatly, and our immediate ancestors were by no means so late a race as the present fashionable and would-be fashionable world.

There was not the same disposition to turn night into day as now. The dinner hour in aristocratic circles seldom exceeded five o'clock, and the receptions at St. James's were generally over before three.

When, therefore, Captain Heron and his half-brother, the Lord Warringdale, reached the end of St. James's Street, the levee had not only began, but had made some progress, for it was then a quarter-past two o'clock by the Palace clock.

Coaches, sedan-chairs, the latter going out of fashion, but still sufficiently numerous to form a feature in the "crush" on such occasions, abounded.

The footways were crowded by sight-seers; and the windows, which commanded a view of the Palace, were crowded by ladies and children in gay apparel.

The royal regiment of Horse Guards did duty on the occasion, and the echo of the strains from their band, as it played just within the Palace gates, could be heard plainly by all in the open streets.

So different was all this noise, and gaiety, and splendour, from the deep stillness of his own leafy home in old Epping Forest, that Captain Heron, as he glanced about him, could not help saying to himself, "Shall I be the happier when I am forced to make one of all this glittering assemblage?—or shall I rather feel that it is I who will belong to, and be, so to speak, the property of my rank and my wealth, rather than they the additions to my consequence and felicity?"

Lord Warringdale touched him on the arm.

"Brother?"

"Yes, Henry."

"Will you go now, at once, to Whitcombe House and prepare for the reception?"

"I will. And you?"

"Oh, I propose going to my own lodgings, which, by the way, just face the windows of Whitcombe House, and no doubt I shall be ready as soon as you are."

"I will go, then. Come, Ogle."

"Ah!" said Ogle at this moment, as he pointed with his riding-whip at an attic window where a man's head could be seen. "Ah, who is that?"

"Jonathan Wild!" said Captain Heron, as he, too, looked in the same direction.

CHAPTER CLXVI.

THE TREACHERY OF LORD WARRINGDALE BECOMES APPARENT. — AN ESCAPE INTO THE PALACE.

LORD Warringdale fairly reeled in his saddle, as he found that Wild had had the indiscretion to show himself at such an awkward time and place. That Wild would naturally be anxious to note personally, as far as he could, the progress of the nefarious transaction which was on foot, Lord Warringdale could easily imagine; but that he would have had the imprudence to show himself in so marked a manner that the most casual glance might light upon him, he hardly thought possible.

And yet there was Wild's hideous countenance —the contour and expression of which could never be mistaken, showing itself over the parapet of the house, and glaring down upon the mixed throng of carriages, equestrians, sedan-chairs, and people on foot, which crowded the pavement and roadway of Pall Mall and St. James's Street.

"It is Jonathan Wild!" said Captain Heron; and there was the shadow of suspicion in the tones of his voice.

"Can it be possible," said Lord Warringdale, "that such a villain is here?"

"Oh, my lord," cried Ogle, "you should not be surprised at seeing one of your friends anywhere."

"Friends?" ejaculated Warringdale, who seemed glad of an excuse for getting up a grievance with Ogle. "Friends, say you? Jonathan Wild is no friend of mine; and, indeed, I may here remark, brother Felix, that this man of yours takes unwarrantable liberties, and says and hints things which you yourself would shrink from."

"Peace, Ogle, peace!" said Captain Heron.

A shade of care was upon the brow of the highwayman. He held the reins of the gallant Daisy gathered up tightly in his left hand, and he gazed about him as one might do who had a suspicion that he might be taking a last look of the objects of the earth.

"What is it to us—what is it to us?" cried Warringdale, with an assumption of energy and feeling that he hoped would carry all before it. "What is it to us that Jonathan Wild should be at a window?"

"He is," said Heron, "and has been, my bitterest foe!"

"Yes; the foe of Captain Heron, the highwayman of Epping Forest; but his enmity is aimless and absurd as against the most noble the Earl of Whitcombe!"

"It may be so."

"It is so!—it is so!"

"And yet what a look of triumph there is upon his face! How fiercely his eyes glare down upon us, or rather upon me! And see! now he claps his hands, and points full in my face! What should give Jonathan Wild such cause for triumph and exultation?"

"Nothing—surely nothing," replied Warringdale. "Heed it not, but make your way to Whitcombe House. You will find some of the old servants of our family there, who will gladly assist you, and hail you as their master. I will proceed to my own poor lodgings, and in a quarter of an hour from now we may both meet beneath the portal of the Palace, from which you will emerge as Earl of Whitcombe, although you cross its threshold as plain Mr. Felix Heron. Then, you see, you can laugh to scorn the utmost malice of Jonathan Wild."

The Palace clock at this moment struck the half-hour past two, and from somewhere in the immediate vicinity there came the faint sound of the cavalry bugle.

Lord Warringdale turned ghastly pale, and made a movement to ride off up St. James's Street; but in doing so he found himself face to face with Ogle, who had his right hand upon the bridle of his, Lord Warringdale's, horse.

"What is the meaning of this? Take your hand from my rein, sir."

"I can't help thinking," said Ogle, "that we'd better all keep together."

"This is unbearable. Brother Felix, has your man orders to make me a prisoner?"

"No," said Heron, musingly. "Take your hand from my Lord Warringdale's bridle."

Ogle did so, reluctantly; and, on the moment, Lord Warringdale struck the spurs deeply into his horse's flanks, so that the creature made a terrific leap, which carried him some fifteen feet from the side of Captain Heron. A sedan-chair had just turned from St. James's Street at the moment; and so heedless was Lord Warringdale of everything but the desire to get out of the immediate company of Captain Heron and Ogle, that he came against it with a concussion which threw down the bearers, and overset the sedan on to the pavement.

Then it was that the voice of Jonathan Wild, from his elevated position, could be heard above all other sounds, shouting, "Kill!—kill! Nabbed at last!—nabbed at last!"

Wild had made an artificial channel for his voice, by placing his hands about his mouth, so that the yelling sounds were projected right down to the pavement below.

The overturn of the sedan-chair frightened a pair of carriage horses, and a general scene of confusion began to ensue, in which might be heard the crushing of coach-panels—the oaths of coachmen—the screams of terrified ladies, and, mingling with all, another trumpet-call, of a different character from the first.

Captain Heron had not stirred from the spot on which he had held his brief conference with Lord Warringdale, and Daisy, with her fore-feet projected before her, and her ears startlingly erect, seemed to be waiting some impulse from the mind of her rider.

Ogle had drawn a pistol from his saddle, and, with lips compressed, turned his horse twice round, as if asking himself against whose breast he should level the deadly weapon.

There came, then, a faint flush of colour to the cheek of Captain Heron, as he still kept his horse's reins gathered up in his hand, and, with eyes that seemed each moment to flash with renewed fire, gazed about him.

"Danger—danger and treachery, Captain!" said Ogle.

"Where is the danger?" said Heron.

Then a voice rose from a short distance up St. James's Street, and in clear, loud, excited tones it cried, "Advance and seize the highwayman and murderer! He's armed to the teeth, and will be the death of some of you. There—there! on the black mare!"

"So, so!" said Heron, as he patted the neck of Daisy; "it is from that quarter, is it?"

"There they come!" said Ogle. "By heaven, it's a party of the Light Horse!"

Even as he spoke, there appeared riding four abreast down St. James's Street a party of the well-known cavalry of the period, known by the name of the King's Light Horse.

Captain Heron turned Daisy's head in the direction of Pall Mall, and there, too, appeared, stretching irregularly over the entire roadway, an officer's guard of the same regiment.

The authority which Lord Warringdale had procured from the Under Secretary of State had done its work, and by half-past two o'clock on that eventful morning every man of the King's Light Horse who was not engaged upon sentinel or barrack duty, surrounded St. James's Palace, as with an impenetrable military *cordon*.

The spot immediately in front of the old Palace was peculiarly well adapted for hemming in any one who might desire to escape. There were but two large thoroughfares to guard, namely, St. James's Street and Pall Mall, and they were both fully occupied by the Light Horse, while some four or five men were sufficient effectually to bar the narrow wing which ran parallel with the Palace in the direction of the Green Park.

The rush and crash of carriages began to hem in Ogle and Captain Heron in a most uncomfortable fashion. Another sedan chair was overturned, and Heron giving Daisy a slight impulse, which she well understood, at once leaped over the prostrate vehicle and its occupant.

Ogle followed, although with more difficulty; but the heels of his horse dealt the sedan chair a kick which sent the splinters of its panels flying in all directions; but Ogle was still by the side of Heron, who, turning to him, said rapidly but calmly, "It's an ambuscade, Ogle, and Warringdale is treacherous. Dismount, and let your horse go. Mingle with the throng of people on foot, and you will easily make your escape."

"And you, Captain?"

"I feel certain they want to kill me, but I feel equally as certain they will not succeed. Do as I bid you, Ogle, for my safety's sake."

"You order it?" said Ogle sadly.

"I do—I do! Behold!"

Just as Ogle slipped off his horse the party of cavalry in Pall Mall charged recklessly into the midst of carriages, sedan-chairs, and equestrians, in front of the Palace, and Captain Heron could not but perceive that the eyes of every soldier were fixed upon him, and that however recklessly they might be trampling the people under foot, and however gratuitously savage that charge of cavalry might seem to be, they all converged to the spot on which he stood, with the evident intention of taking his life.

"Kill! kill!" screamed Jonathan Wild from the attic window. "Cut him down! don't take him alive!"

"A hundred pounds!" shouted Warringdale from St. James's Street,—"a hundred pounds for the soldier who first does his duty!"

That that duty was defined to be the slaughter of Captain Heron, as he sat there upon his black steed, appeared to be well understood by the reckless cavalrymen, and as far as all appearances went a few moments now seemed as if they would be sufficient to witness the destruction of the bravest and most generous heart that ever beat in human bosom.

How was he to escape?

His foes were to the right—his foes were to the left—and more foes faced him. The Palace was behind him with its guards, its officials, its throngs of glittering guests attending on the reception of royalty. Hopeless as some shipwrecked man, who stands but for a brief space on the slippery verge of an isolated rock, over which the tidal waves are roaring and dashing, appeared to be the position of Captain Heron.

One of the Light Horse nearly reached him, and Daisy made another leap, which produced intense confusion amid a throng of people who had just issued from one of the entrances to the Palace.

The Light Horseman, with a brutal laugh, made a shot at Captain Heron, but missed him. Then was seen the strange sight of a man from the crowd leaping up on to the back of the horse immediately behind the soldier, and taking him so completely by surprise, that he wrested his sabre from his grasp, and brought it down with such slashing force upon the shako that the Light Horseman rolled from his saddle to the ground.

This was the work of a moment, and the man from the crowd who had achieved it had slipped off the horse again, and disappeared before any one could stretch forth a hand to save him.

Need we say that this feat was performed by Ogle?

And now Captain Heron felt that he had but one resource. He had come to London to enter the house of his father, and then the palace of his Sovereign; the one was barred against him, but not the other. Armed men stood between him and Whitcombe House, but the gate of St. James's Palace beneath the clock tower was open to him.

Turning Daisy's head in that direction, Captain Heron waved his right arm, and shouting aloud, "Good day to you, gentlemen," he, to the surprise of the Light Horse, and of Jonathan Wild, and of Lord Warringdale, dashed into the Palace.

One of the royal Guard of Yeomen made a dash at the bridle of Daisy, but he was ridden over on the moment for his indiscretion. Captain Heron darted at once to the right, and beneath that covered way which leads to another of the courts of the old building, he sought the narrow route which he knew would take him for the moment, at least, clear of his foes.

That he would attempt an escape by such a route no doubt had appeared, if it had occurred to the mind of Lord Warringdale, too visionary to be entertained for a moment.

But there he was, in one minute of time out of the riot, the bustle, and the danger of the front of the Palace, and making his way round to St. James's Park by that entrance so well known to Londoners.

The moment Heron had turned towards the Palace gate, the party of Light Horse in St. James's Street seemed to feel that their duty, which up to that period had been to hold the post, changed its character, and they, too, charged right down upon the Palace.

In the midst of them was Lord Warringdale, frantically excited at the apparent failure of his atrocious attempt to murder in cold blood, in the open face of day, his gallant brother.

He had lost his hat, and his hair was floating wildly about his temples. He was hoarse with rage now, as mingling with the Light Horse he rushed madly down towards the Palace gate.

"Kill him! kill him!" he cried. "This is treason, gentlemen! It is the death of the King he seeks! He is a mad, bold emissary of the Court of France! See you not he makes his way to the Palace? Kill! kill! kill! Cut him down at once! In sparing him you sacrifice your King!"

Jonathan Wild had removed his head from the attic window, and in a few seconds he appeared in the street, when his well-known face and figure were greeted with a yell of execration from the multitude.

"Hold!" cried Jonathan. "Shut the Palace gates, and we have him! A rat in a trap—a rat in a trap! We have him now!"

The Light Horsemen galloped into the Colour Court of the Palace; but except one of the Yeomen of the Guard looking very rueful and rubbing his head, which had been abruptly saluted by Daisy's heels, they saw no object upon which they could fix their attention. Some domestics of the Palace were running about impeding each other, and all vociferating together, so that to the reiterated questions of Lord Warringdale in regard to which way a man on a black horse had gone, there arose nothing but a confusion of cries and remarks from which no information could be gained.

Indeed, so great had been the consternation and confusion consequent upon the sudden invasion of the sacred precincts of royalty by Captain Heron and Daisy, that some of the officials of the Palace were really in doubt as to whether he had turned to the right or to the left.

It was Jonathan Wild who gave a new impetus to the pursuit by yelling out in his high snarling tones, "Idiots! Where could he go but to the Park, be it to the right or left?"

"Yes, yes!" cried Warringdale. "To the Park—to the Park! And yet now it is useless for he is mounted on that fiend of a horse, which once having a couple of minutes' start of us, will enable him to laugh to scorn the hottest pursuit. It is all over—it is all over, and Captain Heron has escaped!"

"I don't think so," said Wild, calmly. "I had not the least doubt in my own mind but that among you all you would let him go, so I took my own precautions. Every gate from St. James's Park is guarded by men on whom I can depend. Captain Heron has a large cage, but he is still a prisoner."

"I breathe again!" said Lord Warringdale. "You give me new hope!"

CAPTAIN HERON FINDS HIMSELF BETRAYED BY HIS TREACHEROUS BROTHER.

Presented Gratis with No. 75 of the New Edition of Edith the Captive; or, the Robbers of Epping Forest.

EACH WEEK IS PRESENTED GRATIS A COLOURED ENGRAVING.

"Pshaw!" said Wild. "When I make up my mind to lime a bird, I'm generally successful."

"And yet you have failed before with this one," replied Warringdale.

"I have; but my period of success was to come. Yours would never have arrived, my lord; and hence again and again, and for ever, you see how impossible it is to do without Jonathan Wild."

Warringdale leant down from his horse and whispered in the ear of Wild, "Let me be assured that he is a corpse before the sunset, and you may multiply the money named in the bond and securities you hold of mine by two."

"Do you mean that, my lord?"

"On my soul, I do!"

"Then give me till midnight."

"Be it so. You will come to me with the intelligence; and yet I know not where to go now, for, sleeping or waking, I shall be in fear of my life while Heron lives. He may forgive and forget much, but never the proceedings of this day. Those men of his in the forest of Epping will condemn me, and I shall walk about like a man waiting for execution. Where to go even now, for safety, I know not."

"Go to my house in Newgate Street. That is the last place in which they will look for you. You will be as safe there as many whom I have kept, and who would give half their lives to be where you are at present."

"I will trust you, Jonathan—believe, me I will trust you!"

"I wouldn't advise you," said Wild; "only as our interests happen to be in common just now, you see, my Lord Warringdale, we hang together."

CHAPTER CLXVII.

EDITH MEETS WITH A DANGEROUS ADVENTURE ON THE ROAD TO LONDON.

WE are compelled for a brief period to leave Captain Heron in St. James's Park, whither, although still hemmed in by foes, he had successfully made his way, while we once again conduct the reader to the sweet sylvan shades of Epping Forest.

There the gentle Edith had been left a prey to so much disquietude, that the step she took for the purpose of attempting to alleviate it must have been approved by the feelings of Heron, however he would have condemned it from fears for her personal safety.

Edith, then, in a word, resolved upon once again following her dear and devoted Felix, and endeavouring to ward off some of the dangers that might surround him, or if she could not do that, to at least share them.

Tom Ripon and Mrs. Ogle were the only persons that Edith took into her confidence on this occasion, and they were neither of them likely to oppose, to any very great extent, any wish of hers.

Captain Heron had probably been gone from the forest about half an hour, when Edith appeared, fully equipped for the road.

There was a flush of excitement upon her face, and her voice shook as she called to Tom Ripon, "Saddle the best horse left in the forest, Tom, for I cannot live and still endure the terrible suspense of the many weary hours of this day. Quick! quick! A horse! a horse!"

The nervous agitated manner in which Edith was pulling on the horseman's gloves she had in her hands, sufficiently testified to the state of excitement under which she was suffering.

Tom Ripon saw with instinctive quickness, which with him was nature, that all remonstrance against the going to town which Edith contemplated would be worse than useless.

"Yes, Miss Edith," he said. "It's all right. We will both go and look after the Captain and Daisy."

"No, no! You must stay here. Do you not know that it was his positive orders that no one was to stir from the forest until his return, or some authentic news came concerning him?"

Tom looked blank.

"And so, you see," added Edith, as she placed her now gloved hand kindly upon Tom's arm—"you must stay here, since I am the only person who may assume a discretion beyond the commands of Felix."

"And, besides," cried Mrs. Ogle, "I wonder what is to become of me, if you go, Tom?"

"Well, well," said Tom Ripon, "I'll stay; but I tell you what it is, Mrs. Ogle, I do hope the time will come when you will be able to take care of yourself."

"Marry come up!" said Mrs. Ogle; "I can take care of myself very well without the help of a little jackanapes like you!"

Tom placed his hands over both his ears as he ran off to get a horse for Edith, for he was well aware that Mrs. Ogle was about to open the floodgates of her eloquence, and that what she would say probably would be of an anti-complimentary tendency in regard to himself.

"Yes—oh, yes," said Edith, in a low tone, as she paced to and fro in the narrow darksome forest glade, where she waited for Tom Ripon to bring the horse;—"yes, it is my duty, and, heaven knows, it is my delight, to watch over him and his safety. Each moment that passes adds to my dread of some foul treachery on the part of the faithless Warringdale. Oh, that I may be yet in time to aid him!"

Each moment now to Edith appeared to be an age, until Tom came rushing through the trees with a horse which, from the good rest it had had, was fully capable of performing a sudden journey with excellent speed.

"Farewell!" said Edith, as she sprang lightly to the saddle. "Farewell!"

"Stop! stop!" cried Tom.

Edith paused a moment.

"You may miss the Captain, and what shall we say if he should get here first, Madame Edith?"

"Ah, that is well thought of. Say that I will assuredly return before sunset, and beg him not to leave the forest again in search of me."

"Very good," said Tom—"very good. That would be a pretty game, to be sure. Our Captain always going to look for our Edith, and our Edith always going to search for our Captain.

I think I'll just go a little way down one of the roads myself, and see what is to be seen. Who knows but I may meet the Captain as he comes back, and so be the first to see him and hear if all is quite right. Ah!—dear me! I was not to leave the forest, though! That's a little awkward. Let me see! What was it the Captain said to me? 'Tom,' says he,—and he pointed to the old double-trunked elm-tree as he spoke—'Tom,' says he, 'I know what a vagrant you are; so I leave you positive orders not to lose sight of the bark of that tree for more than five minutes at a time.' Good! I don't see why I should not manage that well enough. To be sure I can."

Tom stood contemplating the tree he had mentioned for some few minutes. Then, with a self-satisfied nod of the head, he went at once to where the horses were kept, and selected one for himself.

Tom shortened the stirrups until they were of a length to be useful to him, and then he managed to scramble on to the back of the horse, which was one of the tallest that Captain Heron had in the forest.

"That will do," said Tom. "Now I am off to town; and as I must not lose sight of the bark of the double-trunked elm-tree for more than five minutes at a time, why I don't see that I can do better than take a piece of it with me."

As he thus spoke, Tom rode up to the tree, and with his pocket-knife slivered off a piece of the bark of the tree, and put it in his pocket.

"Now," he said, "off we go. Hawks and herons for ever!"

Tom rode rapidly through the glades of the forest.

The scout who was on watch by the route which Edith took had been surprised to see a well-dressed young man, apparently, ride out of the wood, with a roquelaire cloak on him; but as the pass-word was duly given, it was no business of his to interfere, and so Edith was soon clear of the wood.

The next person who appeared was Tom, and the scout knew him on the instant.

"Hilloa, Tom Ripon," he said, "where are you bound to?"

"London."

"Oh, very well. I suppose its all right."

"Of course it is. But did you see a mounted—what shall I say?—a mounted individual pass this way?"

"A young fellow on a dark bay horse?"

"Yes, yes!"

"With a cloak, and a hat with a plain band around it, and well-polished boots, and——"

"Good gracious, yes!"

"Then I did."

"And which way did he go?"

"I watched him from the trees, and he went towards Elm-tree Lane, I should say."

"All's right. That will do. Good bye!"

Tom touched the horse sharply with his heels about the ribs, and off he went at a hand gallop.

Now Edith had taken that same route to London which had been so recently traversed by Captain Heron, Lord Warringdale, and Ogle—namely, by that shadowy lane in which so terrible a spectacle had presented itself.

The heart and brain of Edith were both too full of Captain Heron for her to do more than sharply tighten the bridle of her steed as the creature shied and swerved at a particular part of the shadowy lane.

That was where the dead Cornet was lying.

It is true that Captain Heron had dragged the body close to the hedgerow, and that it was partially concealed by the abundant vegetation of that spot; but there it was, and even amid the twilight obscurity of that place it would scarcely have needed a second glance to enable any one to see what it was that rested there amid the tall grass and the wild flowers of the hedgerow.

A cry of dismay burst from the lips of Edith as her eyes scanned the outlines of the human form lying so still in death in that lane. She dismounted in a moment, and with the name of Felix on her lips she flew to the spot.

One glance at the pale face was sufficient relief. And how great was the thankfulness that filled the soul of Edith to find that the face, though young and handsome to look upon, and scarcely even disfigured by the presence of death, was not that of Felix Heron!

A gush of tears came to her eyes, for at the moment her heart was full.

It was very strange thus to see Edith by the side of that poor murdered man, and to hear her, with a deep tone of thankfulness, cry out, "Thank God—thank God!"

Alas! are we not all selfish in our love?

Edith thanked heaven that the face she saw was not that of Felix; but soon the noble and gentle sympathies of her nature rose up in deep regret that, in the presence of death, she could for one moment have given way to a feeling of gladness and triumphant joy.

"Ah, poor, still heart!" she said; "I can pity you! Who shall say that there is not one who loves you even as I love my Felix?—one who, perchance, waits for you now, who longs to hear the voice that will never sound again, to look into the eyes for the beaming affection that will never more shine from them?"

Edith started, and listened.

The clatter of horses' feet approached.

She flew to her own steed, and was in the saddle in a moment.

There was a thin part of the hedgerow, where an old tree had been, some year or so before, struck by lightning. The vegetation had been scorched, and had withered, so that, piece by piece, it had given way.

Edith did not hesitate for a moment, but, urging her horse towards this gap in the hedgerow, she easily passed through it.

The meadow, on that side, was considerably lower than the level of the bank, so that the horse nearly fell as it crossed the hedge.

Edith was actually rolled from the saddle, but without any injury, inasmuch as it could scarcely be said that she was thrown, seeing that she only fell on account of the horse itself reeling for an instant right on to its side.

Both Edith and the horse rose to their feet at the same time, and then, without again mounting, Edith crouched down, and looked into the lane through the trailing leaves of some ivy that grew in great luxuriance about the spot.

The clatter of the horses' feet she had heard each moment came nearer, and hardly had she fairly assumed her post of observation, when two men drew up in the lane close to the gap in the hedge.

These two men were rough-looking fellows, with huge riding-boots, and truculent-looking visages. Just peeping up from their closely-buttoned coats was the end of a scarlet waistcoat. Their cravats were thick and large, as if intended partly for defence.

"Halt, Anthony!" said one. "We are now more than half-way down the lane, and I don't see anything."

"It's hereabouts, I know," said the other. "I tell you what it is, Mr. Blueskin, if you will look for it yourself, I will wait at the corner."

"Don't be a donkey," said the other. "Why, it almost seems to me, Tony, that you are afraid."

"I am not afraid of anything living; and at all events, since you see I have come here with you, I am not near so much afraid of anything dead as Joe is."

"Oh, you're a nice pair, both of you," cried Blueskin. "Here you meet a man on the road, and you put a bullet into his brain or his heart, and then you both run away. I am ashamed of you both."

"Ah!"

"What now?"

"Oh, oh!"

"What the deuce——"

"There, there! There he is—there it is—there!"

"Oh, I see! Hold my horse!"

"Yes, Blue—yes, I—I——But don't drag him out—don't! We left him in the middle of the lane. Do you think that a dead body could move itself, Blue, to the hedgeside?"

"Do you think a donkey can play the fiddle?" roared Blueskin.

As he spoke, he strode up to the dead body of the young Cornet, and at once, without betraying, or probably feeling, the smallest repugnance in the matter, he seized it by the cravat, and half turned it into the roadway again.

"There now—there now!" cried his comrade, who was one of the men who had murdered the young officer,—"there, now, you are bringing him into the lane!"

"Hold your row!"

Blueskin began deliberately to rifle the pockets of the dead Cornet, for to do that was the express object of that visit to the shadowy lane.

The two janissaries of Jonathan Wild, it will be recollected, had been too much scared at the result of their cold-blooded crime to remain for any such purpose. This one, however, who was now present, had communicated the little affair to Blueskin, who had accompanied him back to finish the piece of professional business.

"Is there anything? Do you find anything, Blue?"

"To be sure."

"What—what?"

"Here's a chain, and here's a watch. Here's a little bit of a purse with three guineas in it. Here's a comb, and here's a—a——What the deuce is this? Bless me, if it ain't a bit out of somebody's wig!"

"What, Blue?"

"A bit out of somebody's wig, and put behind a little bit of glass, with some filagree work and

stuff that ain't worth a guinea, to hold it all together."

"It's a lock of hair, Blue."

"Oh, is it?"

"Perhaps from his sweetheart, you know."

"Oh, that's it, is it? But what does he wear it for, eh?"

"It's what they call a sentiment, Blue?"

"What's that?"

"Oh, a sentiment, you know, is a—a—a—that is, a sentiment is—is just a sentiment."

"I shouldn't wonder if that wasn't what it was. Oh, here's a little bit of a pocket-book, too."

"Anything in it?"

"No—oh, yes! Here's a bit of paper with something wrote on it. Let me see. Why, that's it"

"What's it?"

"By golly!"

"What do you mean?"

"Why, I means, comrade, that we now, both of us, know why it was that Jonathan wanted to stop this young fellow from going to Epping Forest. I ain't much of a scholar, but that is plain enough."

Blueskin had found that little memorandum which the provident care of Lady Castleneau had entrusted to the young officer to carry to the forest, and which had, in truth, been the cause of his death.

Hardly, however, had the other man read the few words that were on the paper, when both he and Blueskin assumed attitudes of listening.

"What's that comrade, eh?"

"A horse."

"One?"

"Only one I should say, and it is coming from towards the country I should think. What shall we do, Blue, eh? What do you say, old friend? Suppose I mind the horses, now, while you ask whoever's coming if he happens to have any stray coin in his pockets, eh?"

"What!" cried Blueskin. "Do you want me to turn a highwayman? Do you want me to rob on the King's highway? Get out of the way, and I'll soon knock him over. Here he comes."

At that moment Tom Ripon dashed up on horseback, and as not far from where Blueskin and his companion had been rifling the dead there was a turn in the road, Tom had not an opportunity of seeing them until it was too late for him to think of retreat.

But Tom drew rein and came to a halt, and called out, "Hilloa!" and Edith, who with pain and anxiety recognised him, hastily stepped down from the portion of the root of the old lightning-stricken tree on which she had been standing, and took a pistol from the saddle of the horse which was by her side.

"Hilloa!" cried Tom.

"Well, old man," cried Blueskin, "who are you that cries hilloa before you are out of the wood, eh?"

"Blueskin—it is Blueskin!" cried Tom; for he knew Jonathan Wild's man in a moment.

"Yes, I am that illustrious individual," said Blueskin. "But you have the advantage of me."

"And I mean to keep it," said Tom.

Quick as thought Tom Ripon commenced such a drumming on the ribs of the horse with his heels that the creature darted forward, and he was past Blueskin before that personage could stretch out a hand, even if that would have been effectual, to stay him.

"Good bye!" said Tom. "If I should meet Jonathan Wild, I will let him know where you are."

"Fire!" shouted Blueskin. "Don't let the young imp go! Fire after him, Joe!"

There was the sharp crack of a pistol-shot, which was succeeded so quickly by another, that it almost seemed like the echo of it.

Joe uttered a cry, and it was one of pain, for a bullet from the pistol Tom had fired had found a lodgment in his shoulder.

Edith now thought the time for action had arrived, and she cried out in as loud and hoarse a voice as she could assume from the other side of the hedge, "Now, my men, down upon them at once, and you have them! Charge! charge!"

The wounded janissary at once gave up the reins of the horse he was minding for Blueskin, and set off at a gallop. It was in vain that Blueskin tried to seize the bridle of his horse. The animal was frightened by the firing, and in the most refractory manner swerved from one side of the lane to the other, so that Blueskin in a few seconds gave up the idea of mounting it, and set off on foot after his comrade as hard as he could go.

The horse then took it into its head to follow him at a good round trot, and Blueskin, hearing the clatter of the creature's feet behind him, was under the full impression for a time that he was pursued by some mounted man, and he expected each moment to be caught and apprehended.

When at last, however, he did look round and saw his own horse, he waited for it, and catching the bridle, mounted and was off for London at a gallop.

Edith had the old shadowy lane all to herself.

And now once more most mournfully did she gaze upon the face of the dead.

Lying trailing across that face was a small fluttering piece of rose-coloured ribbon, to the end of which was attached the little locket, with the lock of hair that had excited the contempt and derision of Blueskin.

"I will take this memorial of affection," said Edith, "with the hope that chance may some day bring me into contact with her to whom it should now be returned. Farewell, poor heart — you sleep calmly now!"

CHAPTER CLXVIII.

EDITH ARRIVES IN LONDON IN TIME TO BE OF ESSENTIAL SERVICE TO CAPTAIN HERON.

EDITH was fearful that the time she had lost in the lane might be so many precious moments abstracted from the usefulness she might have been of to Heron in London.

Urged by this idea, Edith started forward with all the speed her horse could put forth, and the shadowy lane was soon left far behind. It was about half-past two o'clock when, with Tom Ripon by her side, she fairly rode into London.

The dress that Edith wore was sober and serious enough with one exception, and that was the coat. Failing to find another which would answer her purpose so well, she had attired herself in one of those scarlet coats which Captain Heron had worn while conducting his band on more than one daring expedition.

But the brown cloak that she wore over all was, so long as she chose to let its folds overwrap her costume, an effectual means by which the scarlet coat was hidden.

The noise and bustle of London struck harshly upon the senses of Edith, after her serene residence in Epping Forest, and she turned to Tom Ripon, as they reached Northumberland House in the Strand, saying in a voice that in vain, for a few moments, strove to contend with the racket made by some carts passing, which in construction were far behind those in use in ancient Egypt, "Tom, I think you will do well to remain here, and let me go on alone."

"That's very odd," said Tom, "because I was just going to say that if you, Madam Edith, were to stay about here, I could go and look after the Captain."

It was at this moment that, from the direction of Pall Mall, Edith and Tom Ripon heard the shouts and cries, and other indications of alarm and riot, which had ensued upon the efforts made by the Light Horse to capture or to kill Captain Heron.

Those sounds fell ominously upon the heart of Edith.

"There is danger—I feel that there is danger!" she cried. "Forward! forward! I will at least share his peril, if I cannot avert it."

Edith galloped forward as she spoke, and heedless in the excitement of the moment of keeping the cloak wrapped about her, she let it fly loose, and the scarlet coat shone out most conspicuously from beneath it.

Taking her course towards Pall Mall, Edith soon saw the shakos of the Light Horse above the rout of carriages and sedan-chairs that was in front of the Palace of St. James's.

Terrible thoughts of what might be the danger of that dear idol of her heart came over her, and letting the bridle of her horse fell from her hand for a moment, she clasped her brows as she exclaimed, "Tom Ripon! oh, Tom Ripon! if you love me, ride forward now, and ascertain the truth!"

Tom was far from being backward in replying to this appeal, for his anxiety concerning Captain Heron could only be second to Edith's; but they were both spared the trouble of asking a question, for at the moment that Tom Ripon would have ridden forward to do so, there came a disorderly rout of men on horseback from Pall Mall.

Conspicuous in front of them, and on a big-boned, strong horse—it was said to be the same which had been used on the last occasion of any one being hung at Tyburn to draw the cart—came Jonathan Wild.

The face of Wild was inflamed by passion, and he was striking the horse with the flat side of his hanger to urge it to speed.

A troop—if we may use the expression in regard to so disorderly a crew—of his bull-dogs came after him.

Some of the janissaries of Jonathan Wild were anything but good riders, and the way in which

they swayed to and fro upon their saddles was strange to see.

"Forward! forward!" shouted Wild. "Follow me, and we have him! It will be a hundred guineas divided amongst you, and as much brandy as you choose to drink."

Edith shrunk back.

There before her was the unscrupulous foe, who had no touch of pity or of gratitude in his composition, inasmuch as he had been often spared by Captain Heron when the latter could have taken his life; but Wild was not a man to appreciate such acts. He looked upon sparing the life of an enemy, when once in your power, as a weakness.

That he now alluded to Captain Heron in his loud, brutal tones, Edith could not doubt for a moment.

The idea then crossed her mind that if he should see and recognise her, nothing would be easier in the crowded streets of London, at that time of

No. 76.—EDITH.

day, than for Wild to order some of his men to make her a prisoner.

In that case, she would only, by coming to London, have added to the dangers and perplexities of Captain Heron, without accomplishing for him one particle of good.

But Edith was not at that time aware of the precise state of affairs.

Had she known all, she would have played, perhaps better than she did, the accidental part which was soon bestowed upon her by Wild.

Concealment of her features, however, appeared to Edith to be the best plan she could now possibly pursue. She knew that in one of the tolerably capacious pockets of the scarlet coat she wore there was one of those silken and crape half-masks which Heron generally took with him in his excursions on the road.

It was but the work of a moment for Edith to place the mask upon her face.

Then, as Wild and his crew of desperadoes came roaring and screaming from Pall Mall, Edith backed her horse until it was a few paces up the Haymarket.

She hoped to escape his observation.

"On! on!" cried Wild. "We will go in by Spring Gardens, my men, and we are then sure to have him. Ha! ha! It is a big trap, is St. James's Park, but it has caught the rat! There is not an exit from it that is not doubly, trebly guarded! On! on! on!"

From these words, then, Edith fully comprehended that Felix Heron was at bay in St. James's Park, although how he had got there, when the entrances were so well guarded as Jonathan Wild declared them to be, she could not possibly divine.

The first impulse of her mind, on seeing Wild, was to shrink from him as one would naturally shrink from some noxious animal; but when she became aware of the danger of Heron, she forgot everything but that, and gave the horse an impulse forward that make it almost cross the path of Jonathan Wild.

Then, from behind some carriages, there darted forward a man who placed his hand upon the bridle of Edith's horse, as he cried, "Good heaven, Madam Edith, are you here?"

It was Ogle.

Edith uttered a cry of joy. She felt that she should now get authentic intelligence of Felix.

"Tell me—oh, tell me, is he—is he——"

"Safe and well!" said Ogle, hurriedly.

It was then that Wild, turning his ferocious eyes in the direction of Edith, saw her, with Ogle by her side, and with Tom Ripon close behind her.

In the dimmest twilight that ever gloamed, Wild would have known them both, but at sight of Edith he fairly staggered upon his saddle.

She was masked—she was booted and spurred —she had on a hat and feather belonging to Felix Heron—she had on his well-known scarlet coat.

Wild uttered a yell of rage.

"Escaped!—escaped! The idiots have let him pass through!" he shouted. "One shot, and then an end!"

As he spoke he drew a pistol from his pocket, and in the full belief that he was levelling it at Captain Heron himself, he fired at Edith.

She had seen the action; she had heard the frantic words of Jonathan Wild, and for the second time in her life Edith was thankful to heaven that she had been able to personate Felix Heron with a hope of saving him.

It was the horse she rode, however, which saved Edith from that dastardly pistol-shot.

The animal, alarmed at the unearthly, yelling voice of Jonathan Wild, had swerved so that Edith was out of the line of fire.

The shot took effect through the back panel of a hackney-coach, with a sharp crash, and then Ogle cried out, "Not yet, Johnny—not yet! Ha! ha! Not yet!"

"Charge!" shouted Wild.

But Edith was off.

Ogle had whispered in her ear but a few words. They were, however, important ones.

"Wild mistakes you for the Captain. Fly, and you will save him."

Would not Edith have galloped to the world's end on such an intimation?

She turned her horse's head in a moment, up the Haymarket. She struck the creature with those spurs she had hitherto worn for ornament, not use, and galloped towards the mass of streets, some of which, in all their original intricacy and acquired squalor, still remain about the neighbourhood of Soho.

Tom Ripon would gladly have followed Edith, but his horse stumbled, and poor Tom was flung off the saddle completely round the neck of the animal.

Jonathan saw his position, and made a savage slash at him with his cutlass as he passed him; but not only was the sword-blade warded from Tom, but Jonathan received himself such a blow across the back with a long weapon, which was, in truth, the handle of a hay-fork, that he bent down quite low on his saddle, and uttered a groan.

It was Ogle who thus had interfered for the protection of Tom Ripon.

The old coach-stand at the bottom of the Haymarket had furnished him with the weapon, which he had snatched from its recumbent position against a pump, and which he used so effectually on Jonathan Wild's back.

Edith had by this time got about half-way up the tolerably steep ascent of the Haymarket.

Wild saw the cloak flying loosely from her shoulders—he saw it float away entirely; for Edith as she went, feeling that it was in her way, had released its fastening at her neck, and let it go— he saw the scarlet coat, and the hat with the long slant feather; and combining all that with the presence of Ogle and Tom Ripon, he could not imagine for a moment but that it was Captain Heron himself who was before him.

Gladly would Wild have turned to capture or to kill Tom Ripon, and to do battle with the person who had nearly struck him from his saddle; and he would have yielded to those pleasures, but that the capture or death of the supposed Captain Heron was a far more important consideration.

And if he delayed in the pursuit now for such a space of time in which you might count ten, who should say that the figure in the scarlet coat might not be out of sight?

Jonathan just shouted out a brief command; and then, followed by two of his bull-dogs, he galloped up the Haymarket after Edith.

"Secure Tom Ripon and Ogle!" he yelled; "and relieve the men at the Park entrances. They are not wanted there now. Two only come with me."

Tom Ripon was made prisoner; but Ogle, in the confusion, scrambled under a hackney-coach, and got fairly away.

"Well," said Tom, when he found himself fairly in the hands of Wild's men, "what's the matter now?"

"You are our prisoner."

"I feel that, stupid; but perhaps you will be good enough to say what for?"

"That's Mr. Wild's affair."

"Oh, is it? Well, I'll be there—I'll be there!"

"What do you mean?"

"At Tyburn, when you are hanged!"

The other janissaries laughed at this; for

among Wild's men that "I'll be there," was a stock joke.

They all, however, bent their gaze up the Haymarket, where they saw Jonathan, and the two best mounted men of his troop, in pursuit of the seeming Captain Heron.

"Hilloa, boy!" said the officer, who was in charge of Wild's party, to Tom Ripon. "Is that, indeed, Captain Heron who is pursued by Mr. Wild?"

"To be sure."

"You know him?"

"I ought to."

With a rush now there reached the spot a man on a very fine horse, which was evidently a hunter of great value. This man looked pale and haggard, and in his right hand, with the stock half-hidden up his sleeve, he held a loaded pistol with two barrels.

"Ah!" said Tom to himself, "here comes my Lord Warringdale."

It was, indeed, Warringdale, who, from the stables of Whitcombe House had provided himself with its best horse; and with a savage determination to shoot his brother if he could but see him, had sallied forth thus armed.

"Where is he?" cried Warringdale.

"Mr. Wild, sir?"

"No, no! Captain Heron!"

"Oh, he's off!" said Tom Ripon. "He is half-way home by this time; and he says he intends to hang Lord Warringdale next Monday morning."

Warringdale turned a shade paler, and lifting the pistol in his left hand by the barrels, he was about to strike Tom on the forehead with the butt, when he suddenly uttered a cry of pain, and the pistol fell to the ground at his horse's feet.

A sharp-cornered piece of broken granite, flung by some one with unerring aim, had hit him on the wrist, and for the time disabled him.

"Death and fury!" cried Warringdale, "where did that come from?"

Tom saw that it came from behind one of the hackney-coaches, and he guessed that it was his friend Ogle to whom he was indebted for the friendly missile; but Tom looked right up into the sky, as he said, "Yes, I saw it coming."

Jonathan Wild's men, with some feeling of wonder and superstition, looked up likewise.

Lord Warringdale groaned with pain.

One of the janissaries picked up the pistol, and handed it to him, when turning the barrels towards Tom, he said, as he bit his lips with compressed rage, "At last I will now be revenged upon you for the indignities you put upon me in Epping Forest!"

It is probable enough that, suffering from pain as he was, and in such a state of rage that all discretion had fled from him, Lord Warringdale might have actually shot Tom Ripon; but one of Wild's men snatched the pistol from him, saying, "No, no, my lord. The boy is Mr. Wild's prisoner, and we cannot suffer you or any one else to interfere with him now."

"But—but—the boy—this wretch———"

"No, my lord. He shall not be killed or injured while I have him in charge."

Lord Warringdale saw that it was useless to contend the matter; and probably, as the murderous impulse of the moment subsided, he thought it best as it was.

"I will not harm him," he said, gloomily; "but I demand that he be kept in safe custody, for I have a serious charge to make against him of attempting my life in Epping Forest!"

"That's a lie!" said Tom.

"Ah!"

"That's a lie!"

"Peace, Tom Ripon!" said Wild's man, who had protected him. "Peace! Don't be aggravating, for that will do you no good; I knew you some time ago, and your mother, too."

"Oh, did you!" said Tom.

"Yes. When she kept the crib in Little Swallow Street."

"And how is the old girl?" said Tom.

"Oh, she is all right; she has gone into business again in St. Martin's Court."

"You don't say so! Hilloa! Oh, look there —there!"

"Where?—where?"

"There! Along Pall Mall! As far as you can see!"

"We are—we are! What is it?"

"Are you looking as far as you can, all of you?"

"Yes, yes!"

"Then look a little farther, and you will see what you shall see, and nothing more! Will that do?"

The janissaries of Jonathan Wild and Lord Warringdale looked suspiciously now about them, for there was a contented expression upon Tom's face, that they could not at all divine the reason of.

The fact was, that, at the moment he had got them all to direct their attention towards Pall Mall, he had seen Captain Heron, mounted upon Daisy, appear within sight from Charing Cross.

A glance had sufficed to let Heron see that there was a strong party of Wild's men at the bottom of the Haymarket, but he did not happen to observe Tom.

Heron turned and made his way up the Strand, much wondering in his own mind at the facility with which he was allowed to escape.

Upon making his way into St. James's Park, Captain Heron had sought a temporary concealment, as well as some slight pause to enable him to reflect upon what had happened, and arrange what he had better do, beneath the thick row of trees, which at that time divided the Green Park from that of St. James's.

He loosened the pistols in his saddle, and rather waited to see from what quarter an attack was likely to be made upon him.

Heron had no idea that the various gates of the Park were well watched; and, as time fled, he became more and more surprised at the extraordinary manner in which he was let alone.

The fact is, that Jonathan Wild was mustering his men; and as he had full conviction that Heron was in the Park, and could not leave it, he felt tolerably easy concerning his capture.

The false scent that Jonathan ultimately went upon, had the effect of leaving Heron at perfect liberty; and after a quarter of an hour's waiting in the Park, he rode out of it through the Horse Guards.

No opposition was made to his exit, for it was at the time of entering the royal Park, and not at that of leaving—which was of course inevitable—

that any question was ever raised regarding the privilege of a horseman to pass the gates.

"Very good," said Captain Heron, as he rode up the Strand. "Be it so. They choose to let me go, and I go. Ogle will take good care of himself; and the sooner I reach Epping the better, to relieve the mind of Edith from anxiety."

He spoke carelessly, but his heart was heavy.

With a deep sigh, he added, "And henceforward I have no brother, for Lord Warringdale knows not even the semblance of truth or of honour. Alas! alas! alas!"

It was indeed an affliction to the noble heart of Captain Heron to find that there could be so much duplicity and villany in the world, as had been exhibited that day by his half-brother, Lord Warringdale.

CHAPTER CLXIX.

THE COACH IN THE LANE, AND THE CAPTURE OF EDITH.—TOM RIPON'S GALLANTRY.

EDITH galloped up the Haymarket.

Tears stood in her eyes, and obscured her perception of all surrounding objects. Those tears trickled down from under the silken mask.

"Oh, what a wound will all this be to the heart of Felix!" she said, sadly. "Henceforth he will come to the belief that the evil of a human heart is fathomless!"

"Stop him!—stop him!" roared Wild. "A thousand pounds reward! Stop him!"

Edith's horse reared, for at that moment she checked its progress; and then a smile struggled with the emotion that agitated her lips, and she said, in low, sweet tones, "Is it possible, after all, then, I can be of such service to my Felix, as to draw off the pursuit of this implacable foe from him? Be it so, then—be it so! Hilloa, for a gallop! Welcome!"

There was but one person who made an attempt to earn the promised thousand pounds reward by arresting Edith. That was a man who darted out from a shop, and made a snatch at the bridle of the horse; but the road was wet, and his foot slipped upon the round stones with which the whole of London was then laid in its roadways, and he fell.

The horse walked over him; and then Edith, as she turned to the left, that direction being the furthest way from Epping Forest, put the creature to speed again, and was off at a gallop.

Jonathan Wild was about a hundred yards in the rear.

His horse was not so good an one for speed as that which Edith rode, and the horses of his two men were no better than his; but Wild knew that so long as he could keep any one in sight whom he was pursuing, that the horse he rode would inevitably at last succeed in reaching its prey, inasmuch as the endurance of the animal was wonderful, and transcended that of any other horse he had ever possessed.

Such a steed as Daisy would alone have got the better of Jonathan Wild's horse, inasmuch as by sheer speed it would have got out of sight, and round some half-dozen corners, so that the endurance of the other animal would have been at fault from not knowing in which direction to exert it.

But as it was, Wild and his two men kept Edith in sight; and they sped up some of the streets that led towards the Oxford Road with but little difference in the relative distance between them.

That any effectual pursuit would be made of Felix Heron, while Jonathan Wild himself with two of his best men were on her track, Edith had the satisfaction of believing impossible; and in proportion now as she began to think that the safety of her dear Felix was assured, her own desire to escape came fully and strongly over her mind.

Edith began to picture to herself the state of mind in which Felix would be if she were captured, and she urged her horse now each moment to increased exertion, in order to place as great a distance as possible between herself and her pursuers.

The Oxford Road was now passed, and Edith had thrown a piece of silver to the gate-keeper at Tyburn, and had gone through the gate.

The steep ascent of Bayswater Hill was before her, and still like fate Jonathan Wild and his two men clattered after her at not much greater distance than he had been a mile nearer to town.

Edith saw a turning on her right, and at haphazard she went down it.

For the moment she was out of sight of Jonathan Wild; and coming towards her, on the narrow by-road which this turning had led her into, she saw a coach.

An idea took possession of Edith.

As she neared the coach, she saw through the window of one of the doors that it contained only a couple of ladies. The driver was an old man, and the two horses that drew the vehicle were going at that sort of pace which showed that they had a most easy and comfortable situation.

Edith's idea was this.

"If I abandon my horse," she said, "now that I am out of sight of Wild for a few moments, is it possible that those two ladies will afford me shelter in the coach?"

This was not a matter to be argued about pro and con. There was no time to do more than think of it, and carry it out at once or abandon it.

Edith choose the former.

She swung herself from the saddle, and letting her horse go quite at liberty, she ran towards the coach, calling out as she did so, "Do not stop! do not stop!"

This mode of address, so different to what the coachman had expected, took him completely by surprise.

Edith's appearance and dress, with the half mask too on her face, so exactly corresponded to the popular ideas of a highwayman, that the words "Stand and deliver" were those which would have sounded more appropriate from the lips of the knight of the road.

No wonder, then, that the coachman was surprised to be told not to stop. He glanced over the roof of the coach, expecting to see further on the road some other vehicle, which the highwayman thought a better prey; but no such carriage presented itself.

Edith reached the coach-door, and at the slow pace it was going at, she had no difficulty in

JONATHAN WILD CHECKS THE INQUIRIOSITY OF THE PASSERS BY.

Presented Gratis with No. 76, of the New Edition of the Captive; or, the Robbers of Epping Forest.

EACH WEEK IS PRESENTED A COLOURED ENGRAVING.

opening that door, and springing at once into the vehicle.

The two old ladies uttered two screams.

"Murder!" cried the coachman.

Edith felt that her greatest danger now was from the fears of the driver, and she hastily let down the front glass which separated her from him, and pulling him by the cape of his coat, she said, "Give no alarm. There is no danger. I am a friend, and no highwayman. If you have a heart capable of feeling for one in danger, you will drive on as before, and say nothing."

These words served both for the purpose of calming the fears of the two ladies, as well as those of the coachman. But he had brought his horses to a standstill.

"For heaven's sake go on!" cried Edith.

The vehicle was in motion again.

"Gracious providence!" cried one of the ladies, "who are you, sir, and what does all this mean?"

"Ladies, you see in me an innocent fugitive."

"We don't see you at all, sir," said the other, "since you persist in keeping a mask on your face."

"Permit me still to do so for a few minutes, ladies, and to ask you one question."

"What is it?" they both asked together.

"Did you ever hear of Jonathan Wild?"

"Jonathan Wild, the notorious constable?"

"The same."

"Oh, yes, yes—the villain!"

"Good! I rejoice to hear you call him by his proper name, ladies. By permitting me to remain with you for a short time, you will save me from him; but I protest to you if you have any great objection, and would rather I should fall into his hands, I will alight from this coach at once, and take my chance on the road with him."

The two old ladies had scarcely patience to let Edith bring the speech to an end, so anxious were they to give a decided negative to the latter part of her proposition.

"No, no!" they both cried together. Indeed, those two ladies appeared to have a natural propensity both to speak at once, which, however it might save time, did not sometimes add much to the clearness of their memory.

"Then," added Edith, "accept from me a thousand thanks, along with the assurance, too, that you are doing a greater kindness even than you are aware."

"But," said one of the ladies, "where is that notorious villain, Jonathan Wild?"

"Yes," said the other one, "where is he?"

"He is——"

"Here!" cried Jonathan Wild, as at that moment he dashed his clenched hand through the glass of one of the side windows of the coach, and exhibited his hideous countenance through the fracture.

"Here!—he is here!"

The two ladies screamed.

Edith uttered a faint exclamation.

Jonathan Wild in another moment pointed with both his hands the barrels of two pistols at her head, as he said, "Captain, you are my prisoner, dead or alive! Which shall it be?"

These words, uttered in the coarse, brutal tones of Jonathan Wild, added greatly to the fears of the two ladies, who believed that nothing short of murder was about to take place actually within the carriage.

Edith was silent for a few moments, during which the beating of her heart could almost be heard, and during those few moments, too, it was more than probable that Jonathan Wild was debating in his own mind whether or not, after all, it would not be better to put an end at once to all his and all Lord Warringdale's troubles, with regard to Captain Heron, by at once discharging both those pistols, and so committing a deliberate murder, even before the eyes of witnesses.

But that was just the consideration which kept Jonathan Wild back.

The wholesale slaughter of Captain Heron, two innocent persons in a coach, as well as a driver, was not exactly what he could think of; and he had a special and particular dread that the young Earl of Bridgewater, and other good friends of Captain Heron, if he came by his death, would make a special and particular inquiry as to its mode.

It was quite a relief, then, to Jonathan Wild, when Edith said in a voice which she made as good an imitation of the tones of Captain Heron as possible, "I yield."

"You give me your word, Captain?"

"I do."

"Then remove your mask?"

"No!" added Edith. "That is the one condition, I retain my mask; but I yield as your prisoner, Jonathan Wild."

"And no violence?"

"No violence unless provoked."

"And no attempt to escape?"

"Yes. Every attempt."

"Never mind," said Wild. "I'll look to that. I take your word Captain. And now, ladies, as there is no danger, you can calm your fears, and look contented and happy. In about a fortnight, if you're coming down the Oxford Road, and see a crowd of people, you may possibly have an opportunity of seeing the last of your friend here, Captain Heron, the highwayman, at the end of a rope."

"He is no friend of ours," said one of the ladies. "But we would rather see you, Jonathan Wild, at the end of a rope, than him."

"I've not the slightest doubt about it," said Wild, raising his hat ironically, as though acknowledging some compliment,—"I've not the slightest doubt about it. Ladies see all things through their eyes only, and I was never accounted a beauty."

An altercation was now taking place between Wild's two men and the driver of the coach, but Jonathan called out, in his harshest tones, "Silence there! I've got my man; and if that old fool is at all troublesome, put a bullet through his head, and one of you mount the box."

Edith made up her mind to say as little as possible, and to keep the mask upon her face as long as possible. The fact was, the contingency of being taken by Jonathan Wild had scarcely presented itself to her, and she was in doubt whether to declare herself or not.

She could not but feel that her capture would be probably as welcome to Lord Warringdale as that of his brother, Felix Heron; and although she could not for a moment think that her life was really in danger, she could well guess how terrible a power would be exercised over Felix by Warringdale and Jonathan Wild, if they could manage to keep her from him in some place of security.

So long as he did not know her, Edith felt that there was yet a chance of escaping from the clutches of the villanous thief-taker.

For all she knew, Ogle and Felix himself might be upon the road, and rescue her. At all events she had nothing to gain by a declaration of who and what she was; and so long as Wild chose to delude himself into a belief in the identity of his prisoner with Captain Heron, it was possible that the latter had everything to gain by the mistake.

"Ladies," said Wild, with affected politeness; "I presume that there is ample room for four in this carriage. I will therefore make the fourth."

"Never!" cried one of the ladies; "I will never consent to sit in the same coach with such a man as Jonathan Wild!"

"Nor I," said the other.

"Then," said Wild, biting his lips, and uttering an imprecation; "you shall both go out of it, for sit in it I will; and upon consideration, as I have something to say to Captain Heron that I don't want any to hear but himself, you shall go out of it whether you like to do so or not."

"We are perfectly willing," said the lady who had first spoken, "as we have no desire to be comtaminated by your presence. Come, sister, let us leave. We will walk home, and make our complaints in the proper quarter of this man's conduct."

The two ladies instantly alighted; but Edith could not let them go without a few words expressive of her thanks to them, and her regrets at the inconvenience that they were put to.

Jonathan Wild, in a savage humour, sprang into the vehicle, and slamming the door shut, he roared out to his man, "Drive on to town!"

"To number one, sir?" asked the man.

"No; to Newgate!"

It was wonderful to see how carelessly Wild bestowed himself in the coach, apparently without the slightest fear of a prisoner whose prowess he had seen exhibited on more than one occasion. But this apparent indifference to his own personal safety showed the kind of apprehension in which such men as Jonathan Wild hold those on whose honour they can rely.

Edith—he at the same time believing her to be Captain Heron—had promised to use no violence; and from that moment Jonathan Wild had discarded every fear.

The two ladies were left in the road, either to walk home, or to proceed to town as they thought fit. The old coachman was terrified into submission by one of Wild's men who sat on the box with him; and so the vehicle started for London, not without considerable wonder in the mind of Wild that he had effected so easy a capture of Captain Heron.

It was quite true that Wild had something particular to say to his prisoner.

After regarding the supposed highwayman for a few moments in silence, Jonathan spoke: "Captain Heron, I once before made you a proposal, which you did not seem inclined to accept. Circumstances, perhaps, have altered since then, and you will listen to me now. At the same time I do not ask you for an answer. It is now nearly four o'clock, and I will give you till this hour tomorrow to decide."

"What have you to say?" asked Edith, still imitating the voice of Heron, and keeping her head as low as possible, in order that Wild should not see sufficient of the lower part of her face to make him suspect he had got the wrong person.

"You know well what I have said," he added. "It was that I would join you, and work for you, against Lord Warringdale, if you will pay me."

"Indeed!"

"Yes; and I'm glad to hear that you do not reply to me in exactly the same tones you used before. I'm going to be so candid with you, that perhaps it will surprise you; but, first of all, I will just tell you the reason why."

"Go on," said Edith.

She was desirous of hearing all she could from Jonathan Wild, since she was only personating Captain Heron, and therefore whatever encouragement she gave to Jonathan to proceed, could in no way commit Felix. At the same moment, she pulled down one of the little green silken blinds of the coach, so that the chances of her detection were somewhat lessened.

Wild looked a little suspicious at this movement; but, as nothing followed it, he went on talking.

"You want to know the reason why, Captain, I intend to be so candid with you. It is just this. You will either promise me upon your word and honour that you agree to the arrangement I wish to propose to you, or I cry 'done!' to a proposition on the part of Lord Warringdale."

"What is that?"

"To present to him your dead body, in return for an assignment of one-half the entire property in the Whitcombe estates!"

"Go on!" said Edith, again.

"You listen to me with composure, and therefore you entertain what I say. Now, I will tell you one secret. I hate Lord Warringdale, for he has sought my life, and would fain have paid the bonds which I hold of his with my blood; while you, Captain Heron, although you have more than once had the opportunity to kill me, have not done so. Therefore, I say, I will sell myself cheaply to you. I will place you in the way of the estates and title, and my Lord Warringdale shall hang at Tyburn, for half the money that he has offered me to sweep you from his path. Is this a bargain?"

Jonathan Wild projected his hideous face forward, until it was within six inches of that of Edith. She shrunk from him as far as she could, but the back of the coach prevented her from getting beyond a certain distance.

"Is it a bargain?" said Wild, again.

Edith was upon the point of crying "no!" with all the indignation and energy she could muster, but second thoughts came to her aid, and she said, in a still disguised tone, "If I were desirous of so much vengeance, how is it possible you would make Lord Warringdale suffer at Tyburn?"

"Because he murdered Lord Bridgewater in Paddock Hill Lane."

"Is that really so?"

"One of my men saw him. You see, Captain, I trust you with dangerous secrets."

Edith thought deeply to herself. "Can it be

possible," she considered, "now that Jonathan Wild is in this reckless communicative mood, that I may get from him information that will save Felix many a heart-sorrow?"

"You're meditating, Captain," said Wild. "Perhaps you mean to say yes at once, and to save us the trouble of waiting. Is it a bargain?"

"If I were to say yes, I have still the legitimacy of my birth to prove."

Wild laughed.

"That's easy, Captain. It is true that my Lord Warringdale, and his father, and your father, the Earl of Whitcombe, before him, has taken good care that there is no register of the marriage of your mother, Amelia Staunton, with the late Earl, who then bore the title of Lord Warringdale, as the eldest son of the family always does. The present Bishop of Worcester, however, actually solemnized the marriage, and there's an old mad woman now alive, who, I daresay, in some lucid interval, would be able to declare that she was present at it. It's odd enough, too, that she has taken up her abode in Epping Forest."

"Alas! I know her well."

"Of course you do, Captain. She goes raving through the wood about her son, who was brought to death by old hanging Judge Tarleton."

"Alas! alas! Can all this be true?"

"Oh, true as gospel, Captain! But here we are in the Oxford Road, and here, I see, are some of my men, come to tell me something."

Wild hastily drew one of his pistols again from his pocket, and presenting its muzzle close against the black mask which Edith still wore, he cried ferociously, "Captain Heron, give me again your sacred word that you will not attempt any violence against me while I may be off my guard, or I will pull the trigger at once, and put an end to all trouble about you."

"I promise," said Edith.

"Very well. On we go again."

Jonathan Wild projected his head out of the coach window, leaving his body quite defenceless within it, while he held a conference with his men.

Of that conference, Edith heard nothing but the last few words, which consisted in an order to proceed on to Newgate; and then Wild leant back in the coach again, and resumed his conversation with the supposed Captain Heron.

———

CHAPTER CLXX.

JONATHAN WILD CONTINUES HIS DANGEROUS
REVELATIONS TO EDITH.

EDITH had already learned so much of a deeply interesting character to Felix Heron, that she was greatly in hopes of hearing more, so she resolved, if possible, to continue that interesting conference, in which Jonathan Wild dealt so recklessly in information criminatory of himself and of Lord Warringdale.

"And you are sure," said Edith, resuming the discourse at the point which she thought was most interesting to Felix,—"are you sure that the present Bishop of Worcester will find himself in a position to prove the marriage?"

"Certainly, if I please. And there is some one else who will be able to call it to his recollection, should his memory fail him."

"Who is that?"

"The Dowager Countess of Whitcombe."

Wild, after uttering this name and title, laughed aloud.

"You do not seem to recognise her, Captain. The title sounds strange and startling to your ears; but there is a Dowager Countess of Whitcombe, who was once named Amelia Staunton."

"The mother of Felix!" exclaimed Edith, forgetting for the moment everything but the deep interest she felt in such a communication.

"What do you mean?" cried Wild,—"what do you mean by the mother of Felix? It is your mother, I mean. Your mother—Amelia Staunton! I tell you she lives!"

Edith was aware in a moment of her indiscretion, and how nearly she had betrayed herself.

"Oh, where?—where?" she cried, still imitating the tones of Heron. "Tell me where?"

"Ah, that interests you!"

"It does, indeed!"

"So soon, then, as you say 'yes' to my little propositions, I will tell you where. What the deuce is this?"

The coach had come to an abrupt standstill, for crossing the Oxford Road, in which they were still, was a regiment of the Foot Guards; which, during its progress, forced all carriages and equestrians to come to a halt.

Edith had been reflecting much upon her position as the coach had entered the crowded thoroughfare in which she now was, and she could not but feel that the information she now possessed was priceless to Felix Heron.

Could she, then, endure she thought of being immured in Newgate, or, what was still worse, possibly in the cells of Jonathan Wild's house, when there was a chance of her rescue?

She made her determination in a moment.

She tore off the silken mask which covered her face, and, to the astonishment of Jonathan Wild, presented the fair features of Edith, instead of those of Captain Heron. The window of the coach on Edith's side was down, and it required but a touch to remove the little silken curtain, in the shadow of which she had shrouded herself.

"Help! help!" she screamed aloud—"help! Will no one help me?"

Wild uttered a volley of oaths, but he was not a man to be taken much at unawares; and after the first shock of the discovery that he had been duped to such an extent, he adopted the only course open to him.

That course was to persevere in keeping his prisoner, under the affectation that there was no mistake at all in the matter, and that she was just the person he wanted.

Several people had rushed to the coach, but the first thing they met was Jonathan Wild's head projected from the window, armed with that small brass staff with the little crown at its end, which he knew would be regarded as the symbol of an authority few would be willing to encounter.

The few people who had made their way to the coach-window recoiled in a moment.

"Help! help!" cried Edith, again. "Rescue! rescue! Will no one save me from this man?— will no one save me from Jonathan Wild?"

"Yes," said Wild, "that's it! Is there any

one here who wants to cross me? I am Jonathan Wild, and I carry a prisoner to Newgate! Does any one want to try his hand at taking her from me, eh?"

The people tumbled over each other to get back again to the pavement.

"Oh, very good!" added Wild. "I think that'll do. Forward again, my men, to Newgate!"

He sunk back again in the coach, and Edith wrung her hands in despair.

"So," he said, "it is you, charming Edith—you who have so voluntarily and audaciously placed yourself in my hands! Why this is better and better; and I don't know if I had had my choice, but that I would have preferred your capture even to that of Captain Heron! Why, I must have been as blind as a bat not to know you!"

"Release me, for you have no right to detain me."

"Release you, indeed! Oh, no, my pretty hostage! The game is in my hands now, and I feel myself to be master of the situation!"

"You dare not keep me prisoner—you have no authority for so doing!"

"Oh, I do lots of things without authority; and as for daring, all I have to say is that my name is Jonathan Wild!"

"You cannot keep me prisoner: I will demand my release at Newgate. There must be some charge, and you have none to bring against me. Felix, Felix, where are you now—where are you, with your gallant band, to rescue me from this monster in human shape?"

"Well now, that's strange," said Wild, sneeringly. "I have always paid you most delicate attentions, and even went so far once as to negotiate with the old man, meaning your father, Sir John Tarleton, for your hand; but by one of those caprices incidental to the female head, you did not seem to fancy me."

Wild, at this moment, pulled off his hat and wig, and made one of the most hideous faces it was possible to conceive.

Edith shuddered with affright, and shrunk back from him as far as possible.

"But, as I say," added Wild, "I am master of the situation. The lovely Edith is my prisoner, and will remain so. She may beat her wings against the bars of her cage, and scream till she is hoarse, but she will not get out. Captain Felix Heron will be my humble servant, while I hold so fair and valuable a hostage for his good behaviour. Lord Warringdale lives, but at my good will. Sir John Tarleton still lives, but the breath of life in him is compelled to live, move, act, and speak, but as I desire. Lady Castleneau is in the Tower on a charge of treason and complicity with the Jesuits. Sir Dominick Browne is again in a cell of an asylum; and Amelia Staunton, the Dowager Countess of Whitcombe, occupies a similar position. I shall send one of my men to-night to knock that old mad-woman on the head, who roams about a great deal too freely in Epping Forest; and so, you see, Edith, I am master of the situation."

"But heaven is master of you," said Edith, "and in its own good time will scatter to the winds all your well-laid plots and plans."

"We shall see."

"We shall see. I live in hope—you in despair."

"In the meantime," said Wild, as he put on his wig and hat again, "here we are at Newgate; and I'm sure my good friend, Mr. Sharples, whom I have got reinstated as governor, will not refuse me the little favour I have to ask of him."

"I will tell you," said Edith, "since you have been so communicative to me, that you are not master of the situation, as you phrase it, while one honest heart lives to oppose you. There are still those in existence—free from your power—who will defy you, and release me. From the leafy glades of Epping Forest there will come brave hearts, in whose way not even the stones of Newgate will stand."

"Bravo!" said Wild. "When I have succeeded in hanging Captain Heron—which I assuredly shall—you will be a charming widow. It is not everybody who likes to marry the relict of a man who has been hanged; but I've no such prejudices, so you may count upon me."

"And upon me, too," said a voice, as at that moment, from the top of the coach, Tom Ripon slid down exactly before the window; and dealing Jonathan Wild a kick on the side of the head with not a very thin-soled boot, he dropped into the roadway, and, at a pace which defied all pursuit, made his way down the Old Bailey.

It was in vain that Jonathan Wild roared to his men to pursue and capture Tom Ripon, and offered fabulous amounts of guineas for that object. Tom was gone.

Then Jonathan fixed a cold, malignant look upon Edith, as he handed her from the coach, and growled, rather than said, "You will do well now to bethink you of all that I have said; and if you value liberty, and if Captain Heron values life, you will both of you consent to my proposals."

Edith made no reply to this speech, and in another moment the gate of Newgate shut her out from the world and from Felix Heron.

A pang shot across the heart of Edith, as she found herself in the dim vestibule of the prison, and she looked about her in vain for some pitying expression from the brutal men who lounged about.

"What, Mr. Wild?" cried one. "Have you caught a fine bird at last? Why this should be a gentleman of consequence, with his smart coat."

"Bah! Be quiet!" said Wild.

"What is the charge?" said another. "What has the dainty piece of goods been about?"

"Ay!" cried Edith, as she clasped her hands together, and looked imploringly around her. "What is the charge? Surely, no one can be kept here, unless they have committed some offence against the laws; and I again and again ask, 'What is the charge?'"

Wild laughed.

"I do not appeal to this bold, bad man, who has brought me hither," added Edith; "but I do to you all, who cannot have any personal wish to do me harm. I appeal to you, men, and ask if I can be kept here without having committed some offence?"

"Oh," said one, "that is Mr. Wild's business."

"To be sure," said another. "We have nothing to do with that."

"Is this possible?" said Edith.

"Quite possible," replied Wild; "but since you want to be charged with something, we will let it be robbery and murder on the King's highway!"

THE WARDER'S DAUGHTER.

"False! 'Tis false as your own bad heart!"

"Just so. Did you ever know comrades of any really guilty person by their own accounts being brought to Newgate?"

The turnkeys laughed.

The clerk of the prison then stepped forward, with a folio book in his hand and a pen behind his ear.

"What shall I put down, Mr. Wild?"

"Nothing."

"Nothing at all?"

"I have said nothing. It is an affair of State."

"Oh!"

"Are you all satisfied now?"

No. 77.—EDITH.

"Quite, Mr. Wild."

"And you, too?" added Wild, as he made a mock bow to Edith.

"I am satisfied that I am for the present in the hands of a remorseless villain, but I am likewise satisfied that it will not be for long."

"Ah," added Wild, "that puts me in mind of something. I offer twenty guineas reward for Tom Ripon, the son of Mrs. Ripon, who used to keep the fence in Little Swallow Street. I dare say some of you will manage to earn it."

"Trust us for that, Mr. Wild."

"Very well, then. Give me the keys of Number Ten cell below."

At this moment there was a loud knocking at

the door of Newgate, and a voice called out, "The Sheriff!"

"Then there is hope," said Edith.

"Not for you," cried Wild; and he clasped his arm around the slender waist of Edith, and hurried her from the vestibule of the prison before the Sheriff, who was making his daily official visit, could see her.

So repugnant was Edith to the slightest touch from Wild, that she ran on in advance of him, rather than be subjected to his hateful guidance. Two iron bound doors were opened and closed again, and she was soon far beyond the vestibule.

A turnkey accompanied Wild; and as they descended a flight of stone steps that led them below the surface of the street, they found the necessity for artifical light; and the turnkey, by the aid of one of those early chemical matches, which then went by the name of "thieves' lights," lit his lantern, which he had strung in the belt that was round his waist.

"Come on, now," said Wild. "Have you the right key, Davis, of Number Ten?"

"Yes, Mr. Wild?"

"Here we are, then. Who was here last?"

"Bless you, Mr. Wild, do you forget?"

"I do."

"It was Jerry Abershaw, then."

"Ah, yes. He made a good end."

"Well, Mr. Wild, if you call half strangling Mr. Snackman at the last moment, at Tyburn, a good end, perhaps he did."

"I recollect. By the by, Snackman is dead, is he not?"

"Yes, Mr. Wild."

"Who has his place?"

"Thomas Wright is hangman now."

"I know the fellow."

By this time the turnkey had opened the door of Number Ten, and Wild, who would keep his hand upon the arm of Edith, despite all her efforts to the contrary, said with mock politeness, "Now, if you please, and mind the step."

Edith paused a moment on the threshold of the perfectly dark condemned cell into which she was about to be placed, and in a loud, clear voice, she cried out, "A hundred pounds reward to any one who will make speed to Epping Forest, and tell Captain Heron that Edith is in Newgate."

Wild ground his teeth together with rage, as he gave Edith a push that nearly threw her on to her face in the cell, and then slammed the iron-bound door shut.

"Davis!" he said, hastily.

"Yes, Mr. Wild?"

"It is possible that you would like a hundred pounds?"

Davis coughed.

"But if you seek to earn such an amount in the way the prisoner has mentioned, you will not live one month after. You know me, and that in these matters I am a man of my word."

"Oh, Mr. Wild, I assure you I had no idea——"

"That is enough. Not another word, or I may come to suspect you."

Edith was in total darkness. For a few minutes she stood exactly where she had happened to be when Wild closed the cell-door. It could scarcely be said that she thought herself in any actual danger; but that she might be kept on one pretence or another a prisoner for an indefinite period she could easily imagine.

Edith, too, was too logical in her intellect not to perceive at once how completely her imprisonment would paralyze the actions of Felix Heron.

So long as she was in the power of his foes, all that he did, or attempted to do, would have some reference to her condition.

What course to adopt in order to obtain her freedom was at present all vague surmise. She had heard of such things even in free England as people being shut up for long periods at the desire of the authorities without being brought to trial. And was not Jonathan Wild an authority?

Most certainly, at that period, Jonathan had a very ample delegated authority from the Home Office, although it is not too much to say that his destruction was already determined upon, and his career was drawing to its close.

Wild was soon about to be found guilty of the greatest possible offence against a corrupt minister. The offence of knowing too much.

For years past he had been the unscrupulous agent of the Home Office; and, as a consequence, he was the depository of many little iniquitous State secrets, which could only be quenched with his existence.

Jonathan Wild did not know it, but he was, to all intents and purposes, a condemned man.

Edith stretched her arms as far as she could on all sides of her, in order to take in the dimensions of her cell; but, as she touched no walls, she began to think the place was larger than she had imagined.

The moment, however, that she took two steps in any direction, she found how confined a space she was in.

Her hands touched the damp, cold wall.

Edith, at that moment, could have shed tears, but she restrained them; for there came over her thoughts and feelings so strong a perception of the free air and the beautiful glades of Epping Forest, in contrast with that narrow, damp, noisome cell in Newgate, that it was almost enough to break her heart to fancy that even four-and-twenty hours might pass over her head in such a place.

And how many times, if Jonathan Wild had one-half the power which report gave him,—how many times four-and-twenty hours might be multiplied, before she should again see the light of heaven?

An impulse came over Edith to cry out aloud for help.

"Help! Mercy! Justice!"

Her own voice was the only sound that broke the terrible stillness of the place.

But, in another moment, Edith was aware that a faint ray of light had penetrated from some crevice into the cell.

CHAPTER CLXXI.

LADY CASTLENEAU BECOMES A STATE PRISONER, BUT FINDS A FRIEND IN THE TOWER.

LADY CASTLENEAU was on her route to the Tower, when last in the pleasant society of the reader.

Jonathan Wild had performed one of those audacious tricks that he considered stamped him as a genius. He had filled up the blank warrant of the Secretary of State in a manner which ensured a great deal of trouble to the gallant-minded gentlewoman.

But yet Lady Castleneau could hardly believe it possible that she was being conveyed on so vague a charge to the Tower.

It was true, though, for all that.

The fact was that Newgate was so full of ordinary malefactors, that one of the turrets in the old Tower had been by the Government turned into a prison for persons accused of political offences.

The bugbear of the Administration at that time was the real or pretended fear of Jesuitical plots. That no such fear existed, there has been abundant evidence since to prove; but the cry was one that enabled the Government to imprison at their pleasure what they called seditious persons.

A seditious person at that time would almost now be called a political reactionist.

It was quite sufficient, then, for Jonathan Wild to fill up the blank warrant with the word "Tower," and the further words "Complicity with the Jesuits," to ensure to Lady Castleneau a place in the antique fortress by the Thames.

The coach made its way with good speed now, for the officers of Wild did not spare the whip to the sleek, well-fed horses of Lady Castleneau. Tower Hill soon was in sight, and the carriage rumbled over one of the ancient drawbridges over the old moat.

The words "Secretary of State's warrant," which were called out by Wild's janissary, soon brought one of the authorities of the fortress to the gate.

Lady Castleneau was handed out of the vehicle politely enough, and there was such a look of pent-up wrath about the face of the old gentlewoman, that the Tower authority retreated a step or two.

"Sir, may I ask who you are?" said Lady Castleneau.

"Yes, madam. I am the chief warder of the Tower."

"Then, Mr. Chief Warder, I have to inform you that I am merely brought here to serve the purposes of that worst of villains, Jonathan Wild, and that the State, and their Majesties, have no more zealous supporter than myself."

"With that, madam," said the warder, "I have nothing to do—with this I have everything to do."

The chief warder indicated the Secretary of State's warrant as he spoke.

Lady Castleneau was much too proud to stoop to solicitation of any sort. Had she been told that the axe and the block were waiting for her upon the Tower green, she would neither have hurried nor retracted her footsteps. With a look of scorn, she said, "Then I have only to protest against a great piece of iniquity, and to regret that possibly a worthy man is by his duty compelled to aid in it."

The warder bowed, and merely replied, "This way, my lady."

Jonathan Wild's men chuckled to themselves, as Lady Castleneau was led away by the Tower warder, and she did not even turn her head to see what became of the carriage and horses.

The warder led the way along some narrow passages, and finally through a small arched door-

way, and up an ancient dilapidated circular staircase. They then reached a small room, in which there were some pieces of very antique furniture, and the warder, as he lingered by the door a moment, said, "I will send my daughter to your ladyship, if you please, to wait on you."

"I thank you. What part of the Tower is this?"

"Why, madam, this is the chamber in which they say the two princes were murdered, by order of their bad uncle, Richard the Third."

"Indeed!"

"Yes, madam; and now, if you please, I will leave you, for I have to see the warrant properly registered."

Lady Castleneau was quite calm enough now, and had quite discrimination enough to separate this man from the functions he had to perform. There was something, too, about his tone and manner that was evidently sympathetic, now that he found he was not treated by his prisoner with either contempt or rudeness, on account merely of doing his duty.

The slight bow, then, that Lady Castleneau gave him, as he left that deeply interesting historical apartment, quite won his heart; and from that moment Lady Castleneau had a friend in the Tower.

In the course of a quarter of an hour, the door of the turret-chamber was opened again, and the warder cried out from without, "This is my daughter, your ladyship."

Lady Castleneau was agreeably surprised to see a very pretty and lady-like young girl, of about sixteen years of age, enter the turret.

This young girl had a basket on her arm, which was covered over with a white cloth; and as she curtsied to Lady Castleneau, she said, "Madam, I shall indeed be happy to be of any service to you."

"And I shall cease to think the Tower a gloomy place, my dear, if I can see your pretty, cheerful face every day."

Lady Castleneau left a kiss upon the forehead of the young girl, who, much pleased with her reception from the prisoner, soon laid the table with a plentiful repast.

"Dear madam," she said, "I will do all I can to make your stay here as happy as possible, hoping at the same time that it will be short."

"It should be short, my dear. What is your name?"

"Annette, madam."

"Then, my dear Annette, tell me what you think a person ought to do who is a prisoner here, and yet wholly innocent."

"Madam, I do not understand."

"Then I will ask you if you do not think it right that such a person should do all in their power to liberate themselves; and would you not be glad to get any one to help you if you were a prisoner, and felt that you were unjustly so?"

"Oh, yes, madam."

"Then, Annette, I can tell you that I am merely put here to gratify the malice, and to carry out the bad designs, of one of the worst of men. You have heard of Jonathan Wild?"

"Oh, yes, yes!"

"It is he, then, who is my enemy; and you will be doing a kind and noble deed if you will assist me."

" But how, my lady ?"

" I want to write two letters."

" Oh, that you shall."

" And I want you to get them delivered for me."

Annette considered.

" Do you never leave the Tower ?"

" Oh, yes, sometimes, but very seldom. Yet I think—that is to say, I fancy I know that there is a plain—that is to say, a handsome youth here, who—who——"

" Who will do whatever Annette tells him," added Lady Castleneau, with a smile, " even if it were to jump off one of the battlements into the old moat."

" Yes," said Annette gently, " I almost fancy that Richard would do that for me."

" There cannot be a doubt of it, my dear. So will you engage his services in the cause of truth and right."

" Oh, yes, yes ! And I am so glad !"

" Glad of what, my dear ?"

" That you have asked this of me, madam, without offering me any reward, because I feel that then you speak truly, and that I shall be doing what is right for its own sake."

" You are a dear, good child," said Lady Castleneau with emotion ; " and when the sunshine of peace is again about me, which I hope and trust in heaven it soon will be, I shall be happy indeed to call you one of my dear friends, and to see you often and often at my house in Blooms-bury Fields."

Lady Castleneau partook now of the refreshments which the warder's daughter had brought her, with some satisfaction, and then she looked curiously about that old turret, which perchance had echoed with the cries and moans of those two innocents, who had so early in life tasted of that bitter and perilous cup, which in those days seemed ever to be filled for the high and powerful.

Lady Castleneau had no reason for a moment to suppose that the young Cornet Amos, whom she had sent to Epping Forest with the warning to Captain Heron, could possibly fail in his mission.

Little did she imagine that at that very time, when she rose from the first meal she had ever partaken of within the Tower of London, that young and gallant officer lay a corpse in the shadowy lane where he had met his fate.

And yet there was an uneasy feeling about the heart of Lady Castleneau, she scarcely knew why. She would have given much for some positive and authentic assurance of the safety of Captain Heron, and that all was well with Edith.

Such assurance, however, she knew that as yet, and situated as she now was, it was impossible she should have ; therefore she summoned as much patience to her aid as she could, and in comparative calmness waited.

Annette, the warder's daughter, was as good as her word. She brought to Lady Castleneau a pretty little fancy desk of her own, which "somebody" had given her, and which she rather ostentatiously, as regarded an exhibition of its ornamentation, placed before the prisoner.

Then Lady Castleneau wrote two letters.

One was to Edith.

The other was to the Secretary of State.

The first one was full of affection—the second

full of remonstrance, and concluded with a demand for instant release, or for some specific charge to be made against her, which she could meet.

The letter to Edith ran as follows :—

" The Tower, and the turret in which the Princes were murdered.

" MY DEAR, DEAR CHILD,—

" Jonathan Wild, to get me out of his way—in order, no doubt, that he may, as well as being avenged on me, again take prisoner poor dear Sir Dominick Browne—has had the audacity to fill up a blank warrant he had with my name, and I am here—here in the Tower of London.

" Tell your noble husband that he need not take any trouble about me—I can help myself ; but tell him of the danger of Sir Dominick Browne at Castleneau House, where he is hidden. Anthony and Martha know where to find him, but he had better now be removed to the forest.

" God bless you ever, my dear child, and believe me ever your loving aunt,

" CASTLENEAU."

The letter to the Secretary of State we need not transcribe. It was sealed by Lady Castleneau, with the aid of a massive gold seal, with the Castleneau arms, which she had appended to the old-fashioned watch she always took with her when she went from home, and which was about the size of a modern time-piece, such as would be placed on a chimney-piece.

In the corner of the letter she likewise wrote her name in full, so that, at all events, there could be no excuse for intercepting the letter on the part of any of the lacqueys of the Secretary of State.

Annette promised to see that these two letters were duly delivered by the young gentleman, " who, she rather thought, would do anything she told him."

Under such circumstances, Lady Castleneau might well be excused for having every reasonable confidence in the due delivery of the letters ; and, in fact, they both reached their respective destinations—one to the Secretary of State, the other to Epping Forest ; but the latter added only one pang to those sharp miseries which were gnawing at the heart of Felix Heron, to whom we now return.

It was somewhat late in the day when Captain Heron, still mounted on Daisy, made his way into one of the glades of Epping.

A confused feeling was about his brain that there was a something strange and unnatural about his escape from the deep-laid plot that had been got up for his destruction ; but he was far from suspecting what was the real cause of that escape.

With respect to the safety of Ogle he had no fears. Well did Heron know the thousand and one resources which his faithful follower possessed of baffling his enemies.

Indeed, it would not have surprised Heron much had he found Ogle in the forest before him.

The stillness of the leafy avenue in which he was now, for the first time in his experience of life beneath the greenwood tree, felt oppressive. He was wishful that some of his men would challenge him for a pass-word, but no one spoke.

The fact was, that he had been already seen by

THE WARDER'S DAUGHTER.

Presented Gratis with No. 77 of the New Edition of Edith the Captive; or, the Robbers of Epping Forest.

EACH WEEK IS PRESENTED GRATIS A COLOURED ENGRAVING.

two scouts, but as they could have no doubt of his identity they had not uttered a word.

The silence of the forest became, however, so painful to Captain Heron, that he himself called attention to his presence by a long, wailing blast upon the silver call that he always wore.

It was responded to in a moment.

From the midst of an old Spanish chesnut, one of the band dropped to the greensward beneath like an over-ripe berry.

"Here, Captain," he said.

"Ah, you are Number Four!"

"Yes, Captain."

"Any news?"

"None, Captain."

"That is well. No one has passed your post?"

"None but the Lady Edith and Tom Ripon."

"Ah! when was that?"

"One hour after noon, Captain."

"And when did they return?"

"They have not returned past my post."

A cold feel came across the heart of Felix Heron; and yet his reason told him there was as yet no positive evidence which should incite him to anxiety. There were at the least four entrances to the forest, by either of which, admitting that Edith with Tom Ripon had gone for a ramble in the outskirts of the wood, she might have returned. And yet—and yet, why was it that as he went onward at an increased speed he felt sick and faint?

Felix Heron galloped now along the remainder of the glade, and soon he made a halt at one of those narrow, intricate passes in the forest only known to himself and to his band, and which led to the most secret and secluded portions of the old priory ruins.

Then he blew another call on the silver whistle, and soon a ready hand took the bridle of Daisy.

"See to her well," said Heron; and then, without another word, he plunged among the tangled brushwood that concealed the narrow path he sought.

The timid hare fled before him. The wild birds flew from the deep recesses of the shrubs. A raven, with a hoarse cry overhead, startled him, as he went crashing on.

For the first time in his life, Felix Heron might be said to be getting superstitious, encouraging vague fancies, and a belief in omens; for, as he looked at this raven hovering over the tall trees of Epping Forest, and heard its dismal cries, he could not help fancying that it proclaimed or portended evil to him or his.

It was but for a moment, however, that so vague a fancy as this held possession of the vigorous intellect of Felix Heron. He smiled, although faintly, at his own superstitious fears; and then, knowing that he had reached far enough for his voice to be heard, he called aloud as he advanced upon that object of his tenderest affections, who, alas! was not there to hear him, "Edith! Edith! I am returned, and all is well."

There was no reply.

"Edith! Edith! I am here! There was treachery, but it has failed in its object."

All was still.

Felix Heron had now emerged completely from the brushwood, and was in a small cleared space immediately in front of one of the old portals of the ruin.

So completely overgrown with ivy was this narrow doorway, and the small oriel window above it, that they might have been passed twenty times, by even the most adventurous explorer, without detection; but it was from that window that Edith had been in the habit of welcoming the approach of Felix. It was now closed, however, and a feeling of blank despair began to creep over him.

He said not another word, but rushed into the ruin.

Five seconds could not have elapsed ere Felix Heron stood in that apartment which had been devoted to the service of Edith—an apartment into which all the luxuries of forest life had been accumulated; but alas! no Edith was there to adorn and make beautiful all things by her presence!

A few scattered articles of apparel lying about convinced him that once again she had made one of those changes in her costume which fears for his safety had induced her on a former occasion to adopt; and then his eyes fell upon a small scrap of folded paper.

His name was on the outside; and with trembling fingers he opened the little note, and read the following words:—

"If, my Felix, by any accident, you should return to the forest before I do, do not think me in difficulty or in danger. I could not bear to wait through the weary hours which must pass away until I saw you. So, accompanied by Tom Ripon, of whose fidelity and cleverness you are well aware, I am in town—not to seek adventures, or engage in any perils, but to obtain news of you, and then return. Believe me, all is well, and it may be that while these words meet your eye, you may hear my voice as I return beneath the old trees of our happy sylvan home."

There was no signature to this little epistle—there needed none; and then, for a moment, Captain Heron almost believed the words prophetic, and that quickly he should clasp his Edith to his heart, for there was a loud shout in one of the glades of the forest, and he could hear that his men were all astir.

Then it was the voice of Tom Ripon he heard, calling out, "Captain, Captain, where are you?"

"Here!" cried Heron—but a pang shot across his heart as he spoke, for although he strove to tell himself that Tom Ripon's return was surely indicative of that of Edith, yet how much rather would he have felt assurance doubly sure at his heart, by hearing one tone of her voice.

Tom made his way like a cat or a squirrel through the underwood, and in a few moments was at the feet of Captain Heron.

Then one glance told all that Tom could tell; all but the minute and special particulars of the disaster, which the expression of the boy, his torn and ragged apparel, and his jaded appearance, sufficiently testified had taken place.

"Speak!" cried Heron. "She is lost!"

"Master, she is."

"Where? How?"

"Jonathan Wild—Newgate!"

It was enough. For a fleeting instant it seemed as if some strong emotion was about to sweep in a fearful gust over the head of Heron; but by one of those wonderful efforts—which such men as he only can make—he overcame the disposition to a wild burst of agonized grief, and astonished Tom Ripon by taking him calmly by the arm and saying, "Come forth with me. The band must be called into instant action. You can tell me the minute particulars as we go of this terrible event."

"I will," said Tom.

"Speak freely."

"Yes Captain. We were in the Haymarket, you see, and we saw there was a bustle; and Lady Edith, although she had a cloak about her, let it fly rather wide, so that Jonathan Wild, as he came trotting along on his big brown horse, saw her, and took her for you."

"Ah! yes, yes, that was her object, of course, to save me—always to save me!"

"Then, Captain, Jonathan ordered his men to come off duty at the different gates of the Park, and off he went after Lady Edith."

"That accounts for all. Hence was it that I left the Park so easily, and not a soul questioned me on my way."

"We were hard pressed, Captain, and the Lady Edith got into a coach, where there were two ladies, while I got out of the way; but Jonathan happened to see her, and the long and the short of it was, that he took her prisoner, and off they went to Newgate. I got up behind the coach, and then on to the roof."

"To Newgate? Are you certain? What possible charge could be brought against Edith, that would warrant her imprisonment in Newgate? Well does Wild know that she is my wife, and that consequently, even by implication, she cannot be charged with any of my offences against the law."

"I don't know," said Tom; "but there she is, and I have pretty well ran all the way from town to let you know, Captain."

"You have done your duty, Tom, I feel certain, not only to the best of your ability, but you have done it well."

Felix Heron spoke firmly, and without the slightest tremor in his voice. He felt that it was now a time for action—not vain and hopeless regrets. Stepping forward into one of the most open glades of Epping Forest, just as the last lingering rays of the setting sun of that eventful day were fading away from the tree-tops, he blew thrice upon that silver whistle, the sound of which his men knew so well, and the triple call of which convinced them that the summons was one of no ordinary character.

In five minutes the whole of his band, with the exception of Ogle, was about him.

"To horse," cried Heron, "all of you! Take with you your best arms and ammunition, for we may have yet work to do to-night in London."

Then a low, wailing sound, which every one recognised as a signal from one of the scouts on the outer verge of the wood, came upon their ears. It was immediately followed by the dull beat of a horse's feet upon the verdant sod.

Captain Heron held up his hand, and listened for a moment.

"That is Ogle!" he said; "no one could ride so fearlessly through the glades of Epping Forest at such a time as this."

In another moment Ogle was in the midst of the throng. But the information he brought could add little or nothing to what had been related by Tom Ripon; nevertheless, Captain Heron heard all he had to say with an appearance of perfect calmness and attention.

"It is well," he said. "Every one has done his duty as best he could. Tom Ripon, fetch Daisy at once, and you, Ogle, see that my holster pistols are well charged. Let all be ready within ten minutes from this time."

The calmness with which Captain Heron spoke had something terrible about it, and his band felt convinced that he was bent on some purpose, which would perhaps call upon all its energies for support.

There was such a purpose, but as yet it could scarcely be said to have shaped itself in the mind of Heron; but shadowy and misty though it was, its presence in his imagination was probably the means of saving him from some great accession of despair.

The night air had began to creep in gusty volumes through the forest, as Captain Heron and his band, all well mounted and efficiently armed, trotted down one of the most verdant and beautiful glades, which led to the outskirt of the wood and the high road to London.

————

CHAPTER CLXXII.

HERON AND HIS MEN VISIT JUDGE TARLETON, AND FIND MURDER IN THE HOUSE.

THERE was no concealment now whatever in the march of that band of lawless men to the metropolis. They were strong enough and brave enough to effectually resist any obstruction that might come in their way, and what was of the most importance of all to such an irregular force, they had abundant faith in their leader.

They knew perfectly well that whatever Captain Heron ordered them to do—although it might be daring beyond all precedent—yet must to his mind present possibilities and probabilities of success.

They were all, too, greatly attached to Edith, for during the short time that she had resided in the midst of Epping Forest several opportunities had presented themselves to her for showing a kindly appreciation of their wants and wishes, and helping them through their little difficulties of forest life.

There were but four persons left in the forest—Mrs. Ogle, Tom Ripon, the poor mad inhabitant of the well cavern, and one scout, whose duty it was to take what cognizance he could of the outskirts of the wood.

Two and two, Captain Heron and his men rode onward, occupying a space of nearly a quarter of a mile; for after reaching the high road and proceeding about a couple of miles towards London, Heron had directed this open order to be kept; for although he felt himself quite strong enough to overcome any ordinary opposition to his course, he by no means courted a collision on his route to London, for the particular and special object which took him there.

Ogle had been very downcast when he arrived in the forest, but the calmness and firmness which

Captain Heron displayed raised his spirits considerably; and as he partook, in common with all the rest of the band, of that abundant confidence which they had in their leader, he could not believe that in the face of such a calamity as the arrest and imprisonment of Edith, Heron could be so cool and collected unless he had precisely known how to rescue her.

Ogle rode with Felix, and he was not a little curious to know what plan the Captain had in his mind for the accomplishment of what must be now the chief object of his existence.

There was not much *finesse* about Ogle, and when he asked a question, it was generally in tolerably direct terms.

"Captain," said he, "do you mind telling me where we are going, and what we are going to do?"

"I ought to tell you, Ogle, and I will."

"All's right, Captain; be it what it may, you know I am with you."

"I know that well. My first object, then, will be to go to Sir John Tarleton in Finsbury Square. He is a judge, although a bad one, and he has the power to liberate Edith at once."

"Good!" said Ogle. "But I fear the old gentleman is in a bad way since he came by that ugly hurt at Lady Castleneau's, when his precious friend, Lord Warringdale, either really mistook him for somebody else, or pretended to do so."

"Nevertheless, he is still one of the judges of the land, and can exercise the functions of one. Edith is merely under arrest, and it is in his power to issue an order that any prisoner be brought before him without delay, and liberated, unless good cause be shown to the contrary. I mean to give Sir John Tarleton now an opportunity of performing an act of justice before he closes his career."

"And should he refuse?"

"He dare not!"

"But still——"

"Well, Ogle, it may be possible. He may not, indeed, be in a state to sign such a document as we require of him; but, in that case, I have another resource."

"And what may that be, Captain?"

"I mean to go to Newgate, and take Edith out, whether they will or not."

Ogle whistled.

"You doubt my power to do so?"

"Newgate's an ugly jug to get into, Captain, and difficult to crawl out again. How do you mean to do it?"

"With the two weapons which do most things that seem impracticable."

"And what may they be, Captain?"

"Undaunted courage and unbounded audacity!"

"Then hurrah for Newgate! for I fancy that'll be where we shall have to go. But, indeed, if I were you, Captain, I wouldn't trouble the old Judge at all. You may fail there, and we shall just get somebody upon our track that will increase our difficulties at the Old Bailey."

"No, Ogle, I will go to Finsbury first, for I feel bound to try fair means before resorting to foul. It may be that human lives may stand in our way at Newgate, and it shall not be said, except in a last extremity, I resorted to violence, which we may be compelled to use at the prison."

"You're right again, Captain; so let us on to Finsbury."

There are circumstances which set all *finesse* and calculation at defiance. If Captain Heron had made up his mind, under any other condition than the present, to pay a visit to Sir John Tarleton, in Finsbury Square, he would, in all probability, have taken some precaution which might have been the very means of bringing danger and destruction upon his head. The present circumstances, however, over-riding all such considerations, he went boldly up to the Judge's door, accompanied by his band; and, while they collected in a group close to the verge of the pavement, Heron himself dismounted, and handing Daisy's bridle to Ogle, he strode up the steps and knocked loudly for admission.

It was eleven o'clock at night, and although the Judge's household was still astir, the streets of the City were getting thin of vehicles and passengers.

The long period now, too, during which Sir John Tarleton had been completely laid up as an invalid, had put an end to all visiting and socialities at his house. A startling knock, then, at eleven o'clock was quite an event, and the drowsy hall porter opened the door wide, expecting nothing less than to be told that the mansion was on fire.

"I want to see Sir John Tarleton," said Captain Heron, as he walked boldly into the hall.

"Sir John, sir? Bless you, sir, Sir John's too ill to see anybody, except the doctor and some particular old friend, such as my Lord Warringdale."

"Nevertheless, I must see him."

"But you can't, sir! He's in bed, and, I dare say, he's gone to sleep—though they do say he doesn't sleep much."

Captain Heron saw that in the pertinacity with which this man denied him access to Judge Tarleton there might be trouble, and there certainly would be waste of time. Stepping to the hall door, therefore, he called out, firmly and sharply, "Number One!"

"Here, Captain!"

"Give your horse in charge to Number Two, and come into the hall. Now, take charge of that man, and keep him quiet!"

The hall porter staggered back into his great leathern chair, while Number One, without saying a word, showed him the barrel of a pistol in a direct line with his right eye.

Captain Heron at once ascended the grand staircase of Tarleton House, and was about to pass the drawing-room door, in order to make his way to the suite of bedrooms above, when a moaning sound came upon his ears, and he likewise fancied that he heard voices in tones of remonstrance or contention.

Pausing, he listened until he felt certain that his ears had not deceived him, and then a vague recollection came over him that he had heard some one say how Sir John Tarleton, since he had been so great an invalid, occupied the first floor of the house.

This decided him, and he instantly opened the first door that presented itself, which conducted him into one of those elegant and spacious reception rooms which, in happier times, and before he had began scheming and plotting for wealth and power, had often, by Sir John Tarleton, been made the scene of innocent enjoyment.

A ruddy fire burnt on the hearth; and two long candles, which had been unsnuffed for a considerable period, lent a dim and uncertain light to the apartment.

Seated in a capacious easy chair by the fireside, and apparently fast asleep—under the influence of something a good deal stronger than water, which was in a tall glass by her side—was a female, who, at a glance could be seen, belonged to that tribe of professional nurses who are frequently paid extravagant sums for neglecting the sick.

Upon the thick, soft carpeting of this lordly apartment the footsteps of Captain Heron sounded noiselessly; but it is probable enough that had he come in with the tramp of a war-horse, the female in the easy chair would have been quite oblivious of his presence. It was from an inner chamber which must have looked on to the back garden of the house that the sound of voices unmistakably came; and as Captain Heron stood for a few moments intently listening, baffled perhaps a little by the heavy breathing of the lady in the easy chair, he felt convinced that he heard the voice of Judge Tarleton moaning out some feeble remonstrances to some one who was with him.

Who could it be that at such an hour had sought the house of the Judge, and was saying anything to him which required remonstrance or complaint?

Heron drew nearer the doors of communication, and as he did so, some accidental stream of air from the staircase, for he had left the door of the first saloon unfastened, caused the communication between the two apartments to sway gently open to the space of about five inches.

But that space, narrow as it was, was amply sufficient for the emission of the sounds of a voice, which sent a cold shudder to the heart of Felix.

There was a peculiar grating tone about the accents, which, once heard, could never be forgotten. They were those of Lord Warringdale; and as Heron stept back, and placed his hand upon the hilt of his sword, he could not help saying to himself, in accents of affliction, "Oh, that this man were not my brother!—oh, that this man were not my brother!"

"I tell you, Sir John," cried Lord Warringdale to the Judge, "I must be off—off at once! I will stay for some time at the Court of Versailles till our political intrigues are properly arranged, and the result may be depended on. You know very well that I have suffered a great deal for you, and through you; and in the list of that suffering, not the least item has been the total failure on your part to perform your promise that Edith should be Lady Warringdale!"

"Good heavens!—good heavens!" moaned the Judge. "He taunts me with not doing that which I tried in vain to do, and had set my heart upon!"

"Well, well, Sir John, it may be so! But the least you can do now is to sign the necessary papers which will place me in the possession of the remnant of Edith's fortune. I claim that of you as ordinary and equitable compensation."

"No, no; I dare not!"

"Dare not? You use such expressions to *me?*

How was it you were so daring when, from time to time for years past, you have appropriated thousands upon thousands of the money—signing your own name as one of the trustees, and forging that of Sir Dominick Browne as the other, while you kept him shut up in a madhouse, for fear the truth should come to light? And now you talk of dare not! when I only ask you to sign his name once, feeling certain that you must have signed it at least twenty times before!"

The only reply that the wretched Judge made to this taunt from the villanous Lord Warringdale consisted in a series of sobs and groans that, coming from any innocent person, would have been deeply affecting; but from one so stained with iniquity as Sir John Tarleton—the harsh Judge—the suborner of justice—the robber of his own child—they could scarcely be expected to awaken any such feeling of commiseration or sympathy.

"Come," added Lord Warringdale, after a pause. "Come, now. Do you consent? Will you sign the authority for me to get the money?"

Sir John Tarleton spoke in a much lower voice than he had done before, so that it was only with the greatest difficulty that Captain Heron could catch the purport of what he said.

The words were these:—

"My Lord Warringdale, there is much less money now in the public funds, standing in the name of Edith's trustees, than probably you imagine."

"Little or much, I must have it," replied Warringdale.

"And—and—and—if—if——"

"If what?"

"If I refuse?"

"Then your death be upon your own head; for I have made up my mind not to leave this house without the signature of yourself and Sir Dominick Browne being attached to this written authority to sell the Bank Stock in which the remainder of Edith's fortune is invested."

"I do not comprehend."

The Judge spoke confusedly; and Captain Heron, at that moment, might have echoed the words, and stated that neither did he comprehend how Lord Warringdale was to procure the signatures he wanted, even if he were to take the life of Sir John Tarleton.

But the explanation soon came.

"Look you here, Sir John," added Warringdale. "If you will sign the paper, well and good—I will leave you in peace, with every possible hope that you may recover from your illness; but if you will not, this hour shall be your last, and I will myself sign the paper in both your name and that of Sir Dominick Browne; and as I leave this house I will show it to the porter in the hall as having been signed by you, and that will be a kind of evidence that, should the paper ever be questioned, will tend to bear me harmless."

"But you would want a witness."

"I have one."

"No, no! What witness?"

"The woman who attended upon you as sick nurse is in my pay, and has been from the moment that she came to this house. She will be my witness, so that, you see, all is well."

The old Judge groaned.

"Sign the authority!" cried Lord Warringdale, "or by all that——"

"Hush, oh, hush! I find now that I must tell you all."

"All! All! What do you mean by all?"

"There is no longer any money standing to the account of the trustees of Edith's fortune."

Lord Warringdale uttered a yell of rage.

"Wretch! old monster!" he cried; "do you mean to tell me that you have taken it all?"

"All! Every farthing! All!"

"How can I believe you?"

"I cannot help it—I cannot help that, my Lord Warringdale. You can believe it, or believe it not, even as you please. It is the truth, for all that; and I only wonder that it seems so impossible to you that you should for a moment doubt it."

This was a home thrust. From that moment Warringdale had no doubt at all upon the subject; but although conviction—and a full and complete

conviction, too—came across his mind that Sir John Tarleton spoke the truth, he was none the more on that account reconciled to that truth.

That he really—partly from fright, and partly from his pecuniary embarrassments — meant to leave England for a time, there could be no doubt. He had fully relied upon extracting from the fears of the Judge, the necessary signatures to enable him to possess himself of the fortune of Edith, or at all events of that fragment of it which he believed remained, and which some time before had formed the basis of a nefarious bargain between him, Jonathan Wild, and the Judge.

Now, however, that he found such a chance had slipped through his fingers, he was frantic with rage.

"Well, my Lord Judge," he cried, "you have played me false, it appears; and the only wonder on my part now is that you have had the audacity to deny it while in your present enfeebled condition, and while I am here alone with you, possessed with the ability and the will to avenge such breach of faith and treachery."

Sir John Tarleton must have seen the savage gleam of murder in the eyes of Lord Warringdale, for he uttered a cry of terror.

"Forbear your cries," said Warringdale; "no one will hear them, and at the same time heed them!"

"Help! help! Oh, have some mercy!"

"None—none!"

"My Lord Warringdale, I am old and ailing— I am not long for this world."

"Too long for me. You will be venomous!"

"Let me die in peace!"

"Die, then! No human power can now save you; and as for any other, I have long since ceased to believe——"

"Hold, impious man!" cried Captain Heron, in a voice that rang through the apartment, as he flung the door of communication between the two rooms wide open,—"hold, impious man! Heaven hears you, and the eye of omnipotence watches you, and even makes me the humble instrument of its interference!"

The old Judge slipped from the chair on which he had been sitting, and fell in a swoon to the floor.

Lord Warringdale was so smitten with astonishment and terror at this sudden and unexpected appearance of the man, of all others, he least wished or expected to see, that he could only stagger back till stopped by the wall, and then, with both his arms outstretched before him, as though it was some spectre he would fain keep from nearer contact with him, he glared in the face of his much-injured brother.

Captain Heron, with the indignant flush of detestation of vice and villany upon his face, stood upon the threshold of the room, looking like some avenging spirit called from another and a better world to avenge a great iniquity. His hand was upon his sword-hilt, and his flashing eyes seemed to scorch the dull, trembling orbs of the villain Warringdale.

CHAPTER CLXXIII.

A COMBAT AND A CAPTURE.—LORD WARRING-DALE IS TAKEN PRISONER BY CAPTAIN HERON.

TRULY, that scene in the bed-chamber of old Judge Tarleton was one in which no dramatic element was wanting.

There was helplessness—there was terror and despair—and there was indignation. But Lord Warringdale could not for many moments remain passive, while Captain Heron fixed upon his livid countenance his indignant eyes. He felt that his life hung upon a thread. That he could successfully defend himself against Heron he could not hope; and yet to die then and there, without an effort at mischief, was what he could not reconcile himself to.

His hand strayed to the hilt of the sword by his side.

A scornful smile played for a moment about the handsome lips of Felix Heron.

"Villain! Worse villain," he said, "than

tongue can tell! Is it possible that, combined with such iniquity, there can be sufficient manhood left to enable you to make an effort to defend your noxious life?"

"I will not be murdered!" gasped Warringdale. "How, in the name of wonder, came you here?"

"I will tell you."

"I would fain know."

"After escaping from the most vile and treacherous snare that any human being—to say nothing of a brother—could ever lay for another, I found I had business with Sir John Tarleton, and so you see me in Finsbury."

The idea came across the mind of Lord Warringdale that Captain Heron was alone.

"Surely," he thought, "he has been in hiding all this time, and has come here for shelter, or on some sentimental errand to Sir John, as the father of Edith."

"Brother——" he began.

Fire seemed to flash from the eyes of Felix Heron, as he cried aloud, "If you dare to use that name towards me, I will at once put an end to your reptile life!"

"I will not—I will not!"

"Be careful that you do not."

"I will then say, Captain Felix Heron, I intend to go far away. Stand aside from the door; do not bar my path with such threatening gestures, and I shall, before three days are over, be out of England, and then you can carry on your suit for the title and estates of Whitcombe at your leisure, and without hindrance from me."

"No, no!"

"You say 'No,' Captain Heron?"

"I do say no. You came here to commit murder!"

"Oh, that was only an idle threat."

"I do not think so. You would have murdered Sir John Tarleton, whether you had succeeded in getting his signature to the document you have with you or not!"

"He has heard all!" muttered Warringdale to himself. "He has been a listener, and heard all!"

"Yes," said Captain Heron, whose acute ears caught the muttered words,—"yes, I have heard all—all your villany!"

"You probably mistake."

"That is impossible; and since I have discarded and cast off from my heart, once and for ever, that one word which has hitherto protected you from my vengeance, now is the time!"

As he spoke, Captain Heron, to the extreme terror of Lord Warringdale, drew his sword.

"No, no; you do not mean to say that you will murder me! You—you, of all men!"

"How can I murder a man who has a sword by his side, and when I pause to give him time to draw it?"

"No!—hold! I surrrender!"

"I do not want prisoners!"

Captain Heron's intention might be only to terrify Lord Warringdale, and if so, he certainly succeeded to the utmost; for as he advanced a step towards him, the most abject terror seemed to take possession of the villain, and it was with the greatest difficulty that he succeeded in tearing his sword from its scabbard, and in assuming even the aspect of defence.

The light sword trembled in his grasp, and the

little light that was in the room from a lamp that burnt but dimly in the tall sculptured chimney-piece shone along its blade with a shivering radiance, that sufficiently portrayed how uncertainly it was held.

Captain Heron stepped forward another pace.

Lord Warringdale opened his lips to utter a shout for help. How devoutly he wished that some of the household of the Judge would take the alarm and interfere!

How ardently, too, he hoped that Sir John Tarleton himself might awaken from the swoon into which he had fallen, and put an end to what he felt was an unequal contest.

But neither of these things happened.

"Help! Murder!" cried Warringdale.

The swords had clashed together, and he would not have been at all surprised to find in the next moment the long, keen blade of Heron's sword passing through his breast.

"Call out again, and you are a dead man," said Heron.

"Ah," said Warringdale, "then, if I do not call out, I shall be spared!"

Felix saw in a moment that he had said more than he intended; and although he would not take the life of Warringdale, he wished much that the villain should have for a few moments the terror of thinking that he was in imminent danger.

"You are wrong," said Heron, calmly. "I play with you, but you must die."

Feebly did Lord Warringdale defend himself against the attack of his brother. The swords did certainly clash together, and it appeared as if Warringdale warded off some thrusts aimed at his life. At length Captain Heron disarmed him.

The sword of Warringdale flew with a clatter to the further end of the apartment.

"I yield—I yield!" cried Lord Warringdale.

"Die, then!" said Heron.

He made a pass at Warringdale, so close above his head that the sword-blade ruffled up his hair as it went through it.

Warringdale yelled with terror.

A sword-pass ran across the side of his cheek, nipping the corner of his left ear as it did so.

Warringdale fell forward on his face to the floor.

He thought himself a dead man.

Captain Heron, in making those two sham passes at him, had put such fury into his looks that Warringdale began to think that at length he was in earnest, and that nothing but his death now would satisfy the vengeance he had evoked.

The last cry he uttered had echoed through the house, and some of the Judge's servants had heard it and caught the alarm.

There were audible sounds of some persons stirring in the upper part of the house.

Captain Heron then touched Lord Warringdale with his foot, as he said, "Rise, sir, if your coward heart will let you. I have always heard that the greater the villain the more manifest would be his fear of death when any real danger should come to him, and now I know it!"

Warringdale looked up.

"You spare me?" he said—"you spare me, bro——"

"Beware!"

"No, no! I did not say it!—I did not mean to say it! It was but a slip of the tongue!"

"Rise!"

"Yes, yes! I submit—I yield to you!"

"Sit there!"

Captain Heron indicated a chair that was far from the door, for he knew perfectly well Warringdale, if he only saw the opportunity so to do, would attempt to escape, since, by this time, he must guess pretty well that his life was safe. He sat down with a submissive look, and then Captain Heron gently raised Sir John Tarleton from the floor.

The Judge breathed faintly.

"Bless us, and save us all! what's the matter?" cried the extensive female, who, up to the last few moments, had been slumbering in the outer room, but who now appeared on the threshold of the inner room.

Captain Heron adroitly slipped between her and the door, and, in a voice of command, he said, "Go and sit there, woman!"

He indicated a chair next to that on which Lord Warringdale was sitting. But the nurse was obstinate at the best of times, and being now fortified by a good dose of ardent spirits, which she had just partaken of on awakening, "merely promiscous," as she said afterwards, and "because she found the bottle close to her mouth," she placed her arms akimbo, and shaking her head from side to side, she cried, "Marry come up! and who are you, I wonder, my saucy jay, that says sit down here, or there, or anywhere! Eh? eh?"

"I am the doctor!"

"You? you?"

"Am I not the doctor, my Lord Warringdale?"

"Y-e-s," said Warringdale hesitatingly.

The nurse looked from one to the other in a dreamy kind of way, compounded of semi-inebriety and doubt.

"Yes," added Heron, "I am the doctor; and I can see with half an eye that you require a stimulant. A good glass of brandy, now, would do you good."

"So it would."

"Fetch it."

The nurse at once fetched a bottle and a glass from the outer room.

"Drink!" said Heron.

She filled the glass, and tossed off the contents.

"Another!"

"You—you—order it. I—I—feel better—already. He's quite a nice man! Smother the patients, if so be as they is at all im-patients, say I! He! he! he! It's quite a joke—a connumdricum, as they calls it! Smother the patients! It's easy done, by sitting for a quarter of an hour on their faces! Where's the bag to put the things in? Take what you can, as soon as the deceased has breathed his last! Another? Oh, yes—I feel better—only the room will go round, and round, and round!"

The nurse was, with all her practice in hard drinking, not proof against the attacks of two large glasses of strong spirits in addition to what she had already had; and, after lurching up against Lord Warringdale, and then very nearly falling into the fire, she deposited herself in a corner of the room, and fell fast asleep.

But the house was alarmed. Various sounds began to be heard, indicative of the fact that the servants of the Judge were soon about to make their appearance.

And, as yet, Captain Heron had certainly not succeeded in the object which had brought him, at so great an amount of personal risk, to Finsbury; nor did it seem likely that he would succeed, for the swoon into which the violence of Lord Warringdale had thrown Sir John Tarleton showed no symptoms of substantially abating.

Lord Warringdale, too, heard those sounds in the house, which were indicative of the arrival of the servants of the Judge, and he began to think that surely he should see his way to revenge.

A malignant expression began to show itself in his eyes, in place of the humble one by which he had been trying to assuage the just indignation of his much-injured brother.

Giving the nurse a sudden push, which sent her reeling to the other end of the room, he glanced in the face of Captain Heron, as he said, with triumph in his tones and in his looks, "My time is coming!"

"No," said Heron, "do not deceive yourself. You are as much in my power as ever, should the entire household come to this apartment."

CHAPTER CLXXIV.

CAPTAIN HERON ADROITLY ESCAPES FROM SIR JOHN TARLETON'S MANSION.

BY the noise that now sounded from the staircase and the outer saloon, it would almost seem that the remark which had been last made by Captain Heron was far from being a mere figure of speech, since one might well fancy the entire household of the Judge was about to appear against the intruder.

"They come!" said Warringdale.

Captain Heron smiled contemptuously.

"You will be at my mercy in a moment," added Lord Warringdale.

"Again I say, do not deceive yourself."

"But you hear?"

"I do. I hear that, in consequence of the noise of our conflict, the servants of Sir John Tarleton are alarmed; but they know you, and do not know me; therefore I shall rely upon you to quiet their fears."

"Upon me?"

"Yes. Who else here is able to do so?"

"But——"

"You need say no more. You would say you would very much rather adopt quite a different course of action, and I know well that such is the truth; but, under compulsion, you will act as I desire."

"I cannot."

"Yet you will."

As he spoke, Captain Heron produced one of those small, elegant pistols which he carried, for last emergencies, in a pocket of his vest that just held them; and holding it in his hand, with the silver stock partially hidden by his sleeve, he added, "My Lord Warringdale, these pistols carry bullets not very much larger than peas, but they penetrate deeply, and, being of iron, they are not easily turned aside. One of them, lodged in heart or brain, is as effectual as would be a thirty-two pound cannon-ball, although probably more painful. Upon the least symptom of treachery on your part I will use one of these little rifled weapons against you, and your death will be upon your head."

"No, no!"

"I say yes; so if you have any desire to commit suicide do so, for it will amount to that; and at the same time you will not accomplish your object —that is to say, my arrest—since the force I have without far exceeds any power which the household here could resist."

Lord Warringdale shrunk back with dismay.

"You fully comprehend me?" added Heron.

"I fancy I do."

"You know you do. Now let them come."

The noise of the approaching servants of the house each moment increased in intensity. Probably there was so much fear among them that they were glad to make a considerable tumult in order to keep up their spirits.

Certainly, in no well-ordered household could some eight or ten servants have made so much uproar in proceeding from one part of the house to another.

In another minute the doors were flung open, and a motley assemblage presented itself.

Armed with whatever weapons happened to present themselves at the moment, the household of the Judge made an appearance. Shovels, pokers, broom-handles, stair-rods, anything which had the remotest aspect of being capable of conversion into a weapon of offence or defence, was pressed into the service.

But Captain Heron sat down on a chair near to the couch, on to which he had raised the still insensible Sir John Tarleton, and he looked as cool and composed as possible.

Lord Warringdale felt that he was in what might be called a critical situation.

In each hand of Captain Heron was one of those little suspicious-looking rifled pistols of which he had so recently spoken. The highly-polished barrels could just be seen, as, with his arms crossed over his breast, Heron nearly, but not entirely, hid the little weapons from observation.

Lord Warringdale would only have been too glad to point to Captain Heron, and to cry out, "Seize the highwayman!" but it was by far too hazardous a proceeding to think of; and, with some hesitation, he turned to the servants and said, "What is the cause of all this?"

"We heard somebody, my Lord Warringdale," said one, as he flourished a pair of fire-tongs.

"Yes, yes!" cried all the rest, "we all heard something."

"And we thought," added the first speaker, "that thieves were in the house."

"Go to rest," said Warringdale. "There is no cause for any alarm."

All eyes were bent curiously upon Captain Heron, and Lord Warringdale thought it necessary to say something; but before he could do so, Heron assumed a character which he, Warringdale, felt bound to support.

LORD WARRINGDALE FEELS THE HOPELESSNESS OF HIS SITUATION.

Presented Gratis with No. 78, of the New Edition of the Captive; or, the Robbers of Epping Forest.

EACH WEEK IS PRESENTED WITH A COLOURED ENGRAVING.

"No doubt," said Heron, "these good folks are surprised to see a physician not so accurately dressed in black as the faculty usually presents itself."

"Yes, yes," added Warringdale, "a physician! You disturb the doctor, all of you, by this tumult."

"The doctor?" cried every one, in chorus.

"To be sure," said Heron. "I hope yet to make a cure of Sir John Tarleton."

"Give us another bottle!" said the nurse. "Hurrah! Give us another bottle, and choke the patient!"

A sharp knock at the outer door of the house at this moment attracted attention from the inebriated nurse; and Captain Heron, looking keenly at Lord Warringdale, said in a low tone, that could only reach his ears, "Be careful!"

Warringdale heard and knew what he meant; and as Heron proceeded to the outer room, and was for a few moments out of his sight, he would have gladly betrayed him, but had not the courage so to do.

The member of Captain Heron's band who had charge of the hall-porter had closed the door, and thought surely enough that by so doing he was preventing any unnecessary alarm being given to the household.

Hence was it that when there arrived a little spare-looking man, attired in faded black apparel, he was compelled to knock for admission.

The band of Heron thought it better to allow so apparently harmless a person to knock at the Judge's door without interruption, than to make a disturbance in the square by preventing him.

The fact was that this individual, who at so late an hour arrived at Sir John Tarleton's mansion, was an apothecary residing in Fore Street, who had been commissioned by the physician, who paid, for a daily guinea, a daily visit to the Judge, to watch the case for him, and always to make a call the last thing at night after he had closed his shop.

Captain Heron leant over the balustrade of the staircase and listened.

The man whom he had placed on duty over the hall-porter below opened the outer door.

"Good evening, Mr. Jones," said the apothecary, who made sure it was the hall-porter who, as usual, opened the door for him. "Good evening, Mr. Jones; and how is Sir John to-night?"

Captain Heron's man thought it would be as well to secure this visitor; and accordingly he reached out his hand to the door-step, and pulled the small apothecary into the hall without any ceremony.

"Bless me, Mr. Jones, what ever is the matter?"

"Nothing," replied Heron's man. "Who are you?"

"Who am I? Why, of course, I am Mr. Jordan! But—but——Bless me! You are not Mr. Jones!"

"Oh, he is here!"

"Ah, yes, I see! Bless me, though, he don't look well, and my call now may be providential. Mr. Jones, are you poorly? You look in a bad way. It is my duty, both as a friend and as a professional man, to tell you that you look in a bad way."

"You are quite mistaken," said Heron's man.

"He was never better in all his life. Were you, Jones?"

"Oh, no, no! Never!"

"And you are quite delighted at the visit of your wife's cousin, meaning me?"

"Quite! Oh, dear me, quite!"

"Oh, that's it!" said Mr. Jordan. "Ha! ha! That's it! I see now with half an eye! You have both of you been enjoying yourselves with something stronger than water! Ha! ha!"

"What a conjuror you are!" said Heron's man.

"Ha! ha! Yes! I know a thing or two! But I will not say anything. I will just pop up-stairs to see how John is, and then be off."

"Do, sir."

The apothecary trotted up the grand staircase, and was soon at the door of the room which was still crowded by the servants of the household, and which contained Captain Heron, Lord Warringdale, and the insensible Judge.

"Bless me, what is all this?"

"Who is that?" asked Heron of Lord Warringdale, in a whisper.

"I don't know."

"Bless me!"

"Oh, Mr. Jordan!" said one of the servants, "I am so glad you have come, because you can find out if this strange doctor is a real one or not."

"Strange doctor? Where?"

"Here, sir," said Heron, "at your service."

"Oh, am I speaking to a brother professional man?"

"Well—a—yes, sir."

"Then, sir, I shall only be too happy to hold a consultation with you. My Lord Warringdale will you be so good as to have these rooms cleared of all intruders?"

"Certainly. The servants, seeing that there is now no alarm, will retire."

Lord Warringdale would have retired with the servants, but Captain Heron called out sharply and peremptorily, "We shall want you, my lord, therefore I beg of you to remain."

This request was an order, and Warringdale sat slowly down again. He felt that he was a prisoner to Captain Heron, and yet he could not make up his mind that he was in any real danger.

Such great faith had that bad man in the goodness and feeling of the person whom he had tried to injure in every possible way, and whose life he had done his best to sacrifice, only so short a time before.

The servants retired, and then Captain Heron, as he moved towards the door of the room, said, in cold, clear accents, "Sir, you no doubt will do all you can for Sir John Tarleton. I leave the case in your hands."

"But, my dear sir, you, as a physician——"

"I, as a physician, have a more urgent case to attend to, whither my Lord Warringdale, here, will accompany me. Come, my lord, come."

Warringdale looked vexed; and the little apothecary glanced from one to the other of them with a suspicious expression, as though he felt quite certain something was wrong, and he was being mystified in some way that was at present beyond his comprehension.

"My sword," said Warringdale, as he made a movement towards the end of the room where it was lying.

"Your sword, sir, will remain where it is," said Captain Heron. "It will be perfectly safe in the chamber of your old friend, Sir John Tarleton. Come, sir, come."

To the surprise of the apothecary, Lord Warringdale followed his strange companion from the room with the greatest possible docility. Captain Heron, so soon as they were fairly through the outer apartment, and on to the staircase, turned to Warringdale, and spoke in cold, clear accents.

"My Lord Warringdale—I still call you by that title, although I know, and you know likewise, that you have no right to it, but it serves to address you by for the present,—my Lord Warringdale, I tell you, then, that you are my prisoner; and when I say so much, it implies something else!"

"Nay, nay, brother!"

"Hush! Be warned!"

"Warned?—of what?"

"Have you so soon forgotten? Did I not tell you that I would never again permit you to address me by that name? I have no brother!"

Warringdale looked down, and shook with fear.

"I was about to say to you," added Captain Heron, "that when I choose to take a prisoner, it is with the full intention of keeping him. And my men all comprehend that there is but one alternative, should there be any insurmountable difficulty in keeping him."

Warringdale shuddered.

"You mean they would kill me."

"The alternative is certain death."

"Murder, you mean."

"You may please yourself in your choice of terms. No one will quarrel with you on that account. Now, follow me, and see that for your own sake you meditate no act of treachery; for, so certain as you do, you will fail, and the consequences will fall upon your own head."

With this caution to his prisoner, Captain Heron descended the staircase at Sir John Tarleton's house; and, as he did so, he did not look behind him to see what the villain Warringdale was about who was following him.

The dark thought of assassination was in the heart and brain of Warringdale. He had been deprived of his sword, but of late he had carried about him a concealed stiletto, for he still cherished the hope that some favourable opportunity might present itself for the death of Jonathan Wild by its assistance and agency.

And now as the villain followed Captain Heron down the grand staircase of Tarleton House, his hand was plunged into the breast of his apparel, and it rested on the hilt of that concealed dagger.

All he wanted was the resolution to draw it, and plunge it at once into the back of his brother.

What then, he asked himself, would be the result? That is to say, how could he escape any personal consequences of such a deed?

That was the respect which stayed the hand of the would-be assassin!

It was for himself he feared; and the easy confidence with which Heron preceded him down stairs was, in fact, what saved his life.

"What man, unless he knew himself so safe," thought Lord Warringdale, "would precede me in so satisfied a fashion,—knowing, too, as he does, what abundant cause I have to wish him dead."

The whole conflict of passion, and the desire to murder, with dread of the consequences, did not last half a minute, and then the opportunity had passed by.

They both reached the hall.

"Number Two," said Heron.

"Here, Captain."

"Gag that man."

The hall-porter was rendered incapable of giving any alarm in a moment, and this was ingeniously effected by a simple kind of gag which Captain Heron's men had invented, and usually carried with them when on any enterprise of finesse or difficulty.

The gag consisted of a new and good ordinary cork, such as would fit a wine-bottle, only a little longer than usual, and through the centre of it was run a stout cord, with tolerably long ends. The process of use was then simply to place the cork in the mouth of the person to be gagged, and to tie the strings tightly at the back of his head, and as no one was gagged without at the same time having his hands bound, the process was tolerably effectual.

"Now follow me," said Heron, when the hall-porter was put out of the way of giving any alarm.

They were in the square directly, and Captain Heron called to Ogle, who was some few doors distant, holding Daisy by the bridle.

"Here, Captain. Is all well?"

"No; Sir John is not in a condition to do what I required of him, any more than he was in a condition to do what my Lord Warringdale wished."

Warringdale bit his lips.

"Good gracious!" exclaimed Ogle. "You have that rascal a prisoner!"

"I have, Ogle."

"That is well. This square is very quiet just now, and we will manage him at once."

"What do you mean?"

"Why, Captain, I do trust and hope that, for once in a way, you will take my advice, and let me and the men hang him up to one of the lamp-posts. It's the only good thing that can possibly be done with him."

"He richly deserves it, and yet I dare not do it."

The cold drops of fear had started to the brow of Lord Warringdale, as he had heard the proposition of Ogle; and when the welcome reply which Heron had made to it came upon his ears, he drew a long breath of relief.

"Ah, Captain! Captain!" added Ogle. "You are too soft-hearted, by a great deal."

"Why should you seek my life?" said Warringdale. "I cannot but see you have an animosity against me, which will stop short of nothing but my murder."

"Silence!" said Heron, calmly. "Lord Warringdale well knows that there are few men who have suffered death for their crimes, for many a long year, who have been one-half so guilty as himself."

Warringdale was silent.

"But yet, Ogle, do not let us be his judges or his executioner. The time will come when the law must and will put an end to his career."

"You speak of the law!" muttered Warringdale;—"you, whose whole life has been an outrage to it—you, a robber——"

"Peace! peace! You are in danger, Lord Warringdale, and abuse the liberty of speech. Ogle, listen to me, and take my exact orders."

"I will, Captain."

"We are now about to make a march on Newgate."

"All right!"

"And it is proper and necessary that we should take my Lord Warringdale with us. You will depute two of the men on whom you can depend to take charge of him, with full instructions not to go after him, should he attempt to escape from them."

"Ah!" cried Warringdale.

"But," added Heron, "to shoot him down at once."

Warringdale shrunk back and groaned.

"Now, on to Newgate."

CHAPTER CLXXV.

LORD WARRINGDALE FINDS HIMSELF A FAST PRISONER.—THE ROUTE TO NEWGATE.

OGLE was quite delighted with the manner in which Lord Warringdale was given into the custody of the band; and he selected two of the men who would be of the least use, probably, in the dangerous expedition Captain Heron was on, but who would make capital guards to Lord Warringdale.

The two lightest weights among the band rode together, now, on one horse, so that there was a steed at the service of Lord Warringdale, which Ogle made him mount.

Ogle then whispered to Captain Heron.

"You have no sort of objection, Captain, to my taking such measures as I like for the security of the prisoner, so as to induce him to be quite sure you don't want him killed?"

"I certainly do not, Ogle; therefore do as you please in that respect."

"Very good."

Ogle, with this permission, set to work at once to secure my Lord Warringdale on the horse, and it must be confessed that he did so ingeniously enough.

Some of the band always had coiled around their waists a few yards of loose cord, and with that aid Ogle tied one of the wrists of Lord Warringdale to one of his ankles, but with such length of cord that he was perfectly at liberty, only as one of the band had the other end of the cord fastened round his waist, the escape of Warringdale was quite out of the question.

If he, Warringdale, were to start the horse forward rapidly, he would infallibly have been pulled off on to the road.

It was with great bitterness of feeling that Lord Warringdale found himself in the hands of men who knew so well how to take care of him.

What it was that Captain Heron wanted at Newgate he could not for the life of him divine, for as yet he was quite ignorant of the incarceration of Edith in that gloomy building by Jonathan Wild.

The affair had been too secret for any communication to take place between those associates in crime.

The fact was, that after the escape of Edith and of Captain Heron from the plans which had been lain for the death of the one, and the easy after capture of the other, the feeling of hopeless despair that had come over Warringdale had prompted him to make the last desperate effort at Judge Tarleton's to get hold of a sum of money, with which he really intended to leave England for a time.

If, then, during his absence in safety, Jonathan Wild could clear the way for him to the title and estates of Whitcombe, well and good; but he had had quite enough of the personal dangers of such attempts.

Now, however, his situation seemed to be worse than it had ever yet been.

He was the prisoner of his much-injured brother, and once and for ever his character was gone, and no affected repentance or desire to do justice would avail him again after the abounding duplicity of the last transaction.

Ogle rode up to Captain Heron now, and addressed him in low tones.

"Captain, we want another horse."

"Ah, yes; of course we do."

"Two of our men ride now on one, and that may prove very inconvenient provided we have to make a rapid flight."

"It may—it may! Surely, in all London a horse is to be got!"

"That is just what I was about to say, for there is one ready to our hand, if you have no objection, Captain."

As Ogle spoke, he pointed towards a door at the corner of the square from which they were just emerging, and there sure enough stood a horse with the bridle tied round a lamp-post.

"Take it," said Heron.

Ogle released the horse in a moment, and as he did so the door of the house close to which it was opened, and an old gentleman, who was hurriedly putting on his gloves, came out.

"Hilloa! hilloa!" he cried. "That is my horse!"

"Ah!" said Ogle; "you see it?"

"Of course I do."

"Then take a good look at it, for you will never see it again."

"But——Murder!"

Ogle had given the old gentleman a sudden push, which sent him at once back into the passage of the house, the door of which he, Ogle, closed sharply.

"Mount and away!" cried Heron.

The band turned the corner of the square, and was off at a trot, and had placed two streets between them and Finsbury Square in the course of as many minutes.

Then it was that Captain Heron, as he rode by the side of Ogle, gave him in low tones full instructions in regard to what he wished him to do.

The expedition he was on and the attempt he was about to make was one of those which, if successful, would live in the history of old Newgate while one stone stood upon another.

"Listen to me, Ogle," said Felix Heron, "and let every word I say find a place in your brain."

"They shall, Captain—they shall!"

"I shall know no rest—I shall eat not, drink not, until Edith is restored to me!"

"Oh, don't say that!"

"I say it because it is true."

"Alas! alas!"

"Nay, do not despair, Ogle, for I have a feeling here,"—Captain Heron struck his breast as he spoke—"I have a feeling here which tells me I shall succeed."

"Thank heaven!"

"You will understand, then, that so soon as we reach the Old Bailey the horses must all be put into the inn-yard immediately opposite. At this time of night there will be but one man in the yard, the night watchman, and he must not be argued with, or given the opportunity of making any scruples or giving any alarm. Gag him, and put him aside."

Yes, Captain."

"That, if done noiselessly, will give you possession of the inn-yard, for, no doubt, as long as we shall want it."

"Look on it as done, Captain."

"I do. Then you and I only will go up to the wicket of Newgate, and ask for admission."

"All right!"

"There will probably be about half a dozen men in the vestibule—certainly not more, and some three or four of them we shall get into the street—since, no sooner shall the man 'on the lock,' as they term it, open the wicket, but I will pull him out, down the steps. The others will come after him, and they must be secured at once."

"Trust our fellows for that."

"I do trust them, as I know full well I may do so; but they must be close at hand, and, if all goes well, we ought to be masters of the hall and the wicket-gate of the prison in five minutes' time."

Probably, in the history of Newgate, or in all the histories of all the adventurous men who have made life on the road a thing of romance it has become, had anything been attempted equal in audacity to this attack of Captain Felix Heron on the stony stronghold of the law, which, although it had often been the scene of exploits by which adroit and courageous criminals had escaped from it, yet, except by the wild lawlessness of a mob of rioters, had never been openly and daringly attacked from without.

But this was now to be done.

Not for the sake of spoil—not for the sake of saving any one from the penalties of the law—but because he, Captain Heron, felt that while she, Edith, was within the stony walls of the prison, his own heart and energies were there likewise confined, and he had neither mind nor purpose to do battle with the world without.

The night was dark.

A fitful, gusty breeze was dashing about the chimney-pots of the old City.

No rain was actually falling, but there was every probability that, should the slightest lull take place in the wind, such would be the case.

But all these conditions were favourable to the expedition on which Captain Heron had set his heart and mind.

The threatening aspect of the evening had chased the few passengers from the streets who might, by their lingering about the spot, have hindered in some degree the proceedings of Heron and his band.

By direction of Ogle, the horses were allowed to proceed down the Old Bailey at a walking pace only, and they halted at the gate of the inn-yard, which was exactly opposite the ordinary and small entrance of Newgate.

Ogle tapped at the wicket-gate of the yard, and in a few seconds it was opened by a man with a lanthorn, who said, in a half-sleepy voice, "Are you the horse-carriers from Gilford?"

"Just as you like, my friend," said Ogle; "but you're wanted outside here."

"Then I won't come!"

The words were scarcely out of the man's lips, when he was seized by Ogle, and a handkerchief tied about his mouth in such a manner that he could utter no articulate sounds. Ogle then put his mouth close to his ear, and whispered, "You need not be at all afraid—no harm is intended you, nor do we want to rob the yard; all we want is quiet shelter for a dozen horses, perhaps for ten minutes or a quarter of an hour, so you may sit down in a corner and make your mind easy."

The night watchman of the inn-yard kicked and plunged, and then managed, notwithstanding the bandage over his mouth, to make a sufficiently articulate pronunciation of Ogle's name, to convince the latter that he was known.

Had it not been that the name was one which could be pronounced with tolerable distinctness, notwithstanding the half-gagged condition of the man, Ogle would have failed to find that in this watchman he ought to recognise an old acquaintance.

Pushing aside the handkerchief for a moment, Ogle said, abruptly, "Who are you, and what do you know of me?"

"Why, dear me, Mr. Ogle, don't you know me? I'm Tom Davis, and left Jonathan Wild before you did!"

"To be sure you did! And I know you quite well!"

"Yes, Mr. Ogle; and you may trust me now, whatever's up."

"I know I may if you say as much; so, in plain words, will you take care of a dozen horses for us till we are ready to come back and mount?"

"Of course I will—of course I will; and are you still with Captain Heron?"

"I am; and he is here."

"What is that?" said Heron, advancing a step with the bridle of Daisy over his arm. "Who is it that mentions my name?"

"An old friend of mine, Captain," said Ogle; "and one who will take care of our horses right willingly, so that we shall be sure, at any moment, of a good retreat, which you know is one half the battle."

"It is—it is; and whatever assistance is rendered this night by any one, it shall, if I live, be the best night's work they ever did!"

Newgate looked cold, gloomy, and silent, opposite the inn-yard, as Captain Heron's band dismounted; and one by one the horses were kept ready at a moment's notice for the use of their riders.

There was but one faint light glimmering from the whole side of the prison, and that was in one of the windows of the Governor's house; but whether it indicated that some person was yet up, late though the hour was—or was left in case of being required on any sudden emergency, it was impossible to decide.

But there the light was shining dimly out, like some obscure beacon, into the night air.

The principal difficulty was to know exactly what to do with Lord Warringdale, for Captain Heron was very unwilling indeed, at such a juncture, when he required all the force he could muster, to deprive himself of two of his men, in order that there might be a guard over a prisoner.

He held a brief consultation with Ogle on this state of affairs, and the latter assured him that he might safely trust Lord Warringdale to the care of the night watchman of the inn-yard, who had not been in Jonathan Wild's service for nothing, and was well qualified to take care of the prisoner.

Captain Heron did not doubt for a moment but that Lord Warringdale would be well looked to by such a man, but he felt that to put such a task upon the night watchman would be to compromise him in a most unjustifiable manner.

No. 79.—EDITH.

"No, Ogle, whatever we do or seem to do must be of ourselves, and by ourselves. One man, no doubt, will be enough to take care of him, and his own fears of death will prevent him taking any steps which may jeopardise what we are about."

Ogle, however, took good care to put his old friend Tom Davis in possession of the fact that Lord Warringdale was a prisoner. And now, all these important preliminaries being settled, Heron was enabled to turn his attention exclusively to Newgate, which raised its cold frowning front before him.

It was with a strange sensation, and a choking feeling at his heart, that he looked upon those grim and blackened stone walls that separated him from Edith.

Perhaps not more than a hundred paces intervened between him and her, and yet, probably, as many difficulties had to be overcome, before he could again touch her hand, or clasp her to his heart.

But difficulty is the opportunity of courage, and well Heron knew that he could depend upon those brave spirits he had brought from the leafy glades of Epping to aid him in the almost fabulously audacious adventure he was now about to carry out.

In the deep shadow, cast by the wall of the inn-yard immediately opposite to Newgate, stood his men; and Captain Heron, as he passed down the silent and attentive line of his well-armed and hardy followers, gave them brief directions how to act.

He alone was to advance towards Newgate, and knock at the wicket-gate for entrance; they were to wait until by sound of voice he called upon them to act, and then whatever they did was to be under the special direction of Ogle.

And, above all, he warned them to discharge no fire-arms; and that whatever they did for the furtherance of his objects, would be best done if done most silently.

Feeling, then, that all this was well understood, Captain Heron with a deliberate pace crossed the road, and approached the steps leading up to the small entrance of the gaol of Newgate.

Heron then paused for a moment, for he heard the rapid pattering of footsteps, as some one turned in a hurried manner from Newgate Street.

It took but a trifling observation to perceive that the person approaching was a boy, and that he came apparently from some public-house in the immediate neighbourhood, since he carried one of those hand-trays for the convenient passage of beer and other liquor to the customers of the house.

The boy was much too intent upon his own business to pay any attention to Heron, and running up the steps to the wicket at Newgate, he rapped hastily.

Heron shrunk close to the wall of the prison, so that the turnkey, whose duty it was to attend to the wicket, was not in the least likely to see him.

"A pretty fellow you are," cried the turnkey to the boy, "to come now! Why, you're an hour late."

"I couldn't help it," said the boy. "Missus was out and had the keys; but here's the purl all smoking hot, and it's first rate! Mr. Wild came over to our house, and had it put down to him, and I heard him tell master it was to be the best!"

"All's right; but it was to have been here by twelve o'clock, and now it's one. There! Don't you hear it?"

The clock of St. Paul's struck one.

"Ah, to be sure," said the boy, "I do hear it; and it's a shame, it is, to keep a fellow up so late; but since Mr. Wild and master have been so thick, the 'King's Head' is never shut all night long, and I won't stay in the place!"

The turnkey laughed and closed the wicket; and as the boy passed him, Captain Heron stepped out from the shadow of the wall and arrested his progress, saying, "What's the reason, my lad, that such a crowd of turnkeys are in the hall of Newgate?"

"A crowd? There ain't no crowd!"

"I thought there was."

"Oh, dear, no! There's only Mr. Brand on the lock, and the two Jarvises, and Billingham, and Mr. Jobus."

"Oh, that's all?"

"Yes, to be sure. You don't call that a crowd, do you?"

"No—certainly not. Good night!"

"Good night, sir!"

The boy went his way, and Captain Heron had certainly obtained some important information; for he now knew that in addition to the man whose duty it was to attend to the lock, there were four other turnkeys in the vestibule of Newgate.

The time had come now for action. Heron, too, had heard that one o'clock boom forth from the old time-piece of St. Paul's, and he felt that a more appropriate hour could not be for the enterprise in which he was engaged. Another hour, and the early operations of Newgate and of Smithfield Market would commence.

An hour earlier, and the streets of London would still have been encumbered by those stray pedestrians which the taverns give forth at midnight, and who acknowledge that time as the most fit and appropriate for their amusements.

But now all was still.

The rain fell with a plashing, gurgling sound from the gutters of the house, and in long streams of inky blackness it soon made its way down the cold stony front of Newgate.

"Now," said Heron to himself, as he ascended the short flight of steps that led to the wicket-gate of Newgate,—"now heaven aid me, as my cause is just, for what has my Edith done that she should be enclosed in this prison-house?"

He rapped at the wicket.

The moment that Captain Heron struck the wicket-gate, he retreated down two steps towards the street. It was not that for one fraction of a second he hesitated about the enterprise he had commenced, but it was a part of his plan of operations so to retreat.

The turnkey "on the lock" looked out.

"What now, eh?"

"Oh," said Heron, "the Sheriff has sent me to say that he has it all, and don't mind."

This was a very enigmatical speech to the turnkey, and no doubt it will be as enigmatical a one to the reader; but since that was just what Captain Heron meant it should be, we must receive it as it was spoken.

"What?" cried the turnkey.

Captain Heron passed his hand to and fro over his lips for the purpose of confusing his words still more, as he replied, "Oh, if you please, the Sheriff says don't mind, and the remainder will do to-morrow."

Now there were but two words out of the whole of this sentence which we have recorded, that Heron meant should be heard distinctly and understood. Those two words were "Sheriff says."

They were quite sufficient to arrest all the attention of the turnkey, for the Sheriff for the time being is the greatest man in all the world to the officials of Newgate, and that so important a personage should send to say anything claimed the utmost attention.

"What?" cried the turnkey, in an aggravated tone. "What? eh?"

" That's it!" added Heron.

As he spoke, he descended the last of the little stone steps that led from the wicket-gate.

The turnkey was aggravated.

" Stop! stop!"

" Good night!"

" Confound you! You shall not go in that way. I shall get into trouble, for it is some message from the Sheriff, and I have not been able to comprehend a word of it."

As he muttered thus to himself, the turnkey flung open the wicket-gate quite wide, and made a rush into the Old Bailey, intent on the capture of the provokingly obscure messenger of the Sheriff.

This was just what Captain Heron wanted.

The moment the turnkey was fairly on the pavement, Heron made a rush towards him, and with one well-planted blow between the eyes, laid him prostrate.

Then two men sprang over the road from the inn-yard, and laid hold of the insensible turnkey.

" All follow me," said Heron, " and bring him along."

If a trumpet blast had aroused the energies of Captain Heron's men, they could not have obeyed its call with more alacrity than they did the sound of his voice on this occasion, for subdued and low as it was, yet there was a tone about it such as they had never heard before.

————

CHAPTER CLXXVI.

THE CAPTURE OF NEWGATE BY CAPTAIN HERON AND HIS BAND.—A SURPRISE.

THE two foremost of Heron's men had just lifted the turnkey from the pavement, when a stout, burly man descended the steps from the prison, calling out as he did so, " What's all this—what's the matter? This won't do! The lock should never be left! What?—where?"

Ogle closed with this man in a moment, and they both fell together. There was a brief struggle, and then Ogle managed to get a handkerchief into his mouth, after the fashion of a horse's bit, in such a manner that he was very tolerably gagged, since the handkerchief was tied tightly at the back of his head.

The hands, too, of this man were quickly secured behind his back with a piece of whipcord tied sufficiently tight only that so long as he submitted with patience it did not hurt him, but should he be foolish enough to engage in any desperate struggle to get free, the thin cord would cut into his flesh like a knife.

It was a particular fashion of putting people out of the way of doing any mischief, except to themselves, that Ogle might be said to have invented; and a long piece of stout whipcord was the very apparatus required.

First it was passed round the neck of the individual who had to be secured, and then round his wrists, as his hands were placed behind him.

If he pulled with his hands, the whipcord dug into his throat.

If he jerked his head, both throat and hands came in for a share of the suffering.

" Now, Captain," said Ogle, " that is done."

" Forward! Follow me!" said Heron.

He dashed up the steps to Newgate.

All that we have been at some pains to record as having taken place immediately outside the entrance to the prison, was transacted in much less time than it has necessarily taken to describe it; and Heron, with his men at his back, was at the open wicket before the other officers, who were in the hall, could make up their minds what was amiss.

Any idea of an attack upon Newgate did not occur to them for a moment. That was by far too bold, original, and extravagant an idea for them to entertain.

Hence was it that Captain Heron actually strode into the vestibule of the prison unimpeded.

Now, after what had happened, there were but three men then present in a condition to offer any resistance to Heron and his band.

These three men were in lounging attitudes, enjoying the leisure of being off duty, and sipping the hot compound which the boy had brought from the tavern opposite to Jonathan Wild's house in Newgate Street.

Captain Heron did not give them time for action—he scarcely gave them time for thought.

One, the most active, sprang to his feet.

" Hilloa! hilloa! An alarm!" he cried. " Ring the——"

This man meant to add " bell," but Captain Heron cut short the sentence by dealing him just such another blow as that which had felled the turnkey outside.

At the same moment, those of Heron's men who were not occupied by the two prisoners they had already made, sprang upon the remaining couple of officers.

There was a brief struggle, but it ended in the victory of the assailants ; and the vestibule of Newgate, in a few seconds, presented a very curious spectacle.

The four officers and the turnkey who had been upon the lock were all secured and gagged, and with so little noise, that in some half tipsy jollity of their own, they would have made quite as much.

Ogle closed the wicket, and took possession of the large bright key which belonged to the lock.

Then, with a flush upon his face which could well enough be seen by the light of the oil-lamp which was in the prison vestibule, Captain Heron held up his hand and said " Hush!"

Not a breath was heard.

Then Ogle could not refrain from saying, in a low voice, " Bravo! We have taken Newgate!"

" Hush!" said Heron again. " You know not what you say, Ogle, and what we have yet all to do."

The turnkey and the officers looked ferocious, for those who had been struck down by the well-planted blows of Heron were now recovering and glaring about them. One began to plunge with his feet.

" Will you be quiet?" said Heron gently.

The man plunged and kicked still more. It was evident that, at any price to himself, he wanted to make an alarm.

" Very well," said Heron.

As he spoke, he took a pistol from his pocket, and, lifting the pan, he carefully shook the priming; then, stepping up to the riotous officer, he fitted the muzzle of the pistol into his ear.

The officer turned as pale as death, and his eyes seemed to be starting from his head.

"Kick again," said Heron.

He was quite still.

"Kick once more."

Notwithstanding he was gagged, this officer now managed to say, "No—no—I—am—I will—quiet."

"That will do," replied Heron.

It was always a wonderful thing to see how Captain Heron managed to make people keep faith with him, simply by appearing not to doubt them. The manner in which he at once took the officer's word that he would make no more disturbance was as remarkable as, no doubt, it was efficacious in making the man keep that word.

And so it was that Felix Heron and his band from Epping Forest took possession of the outer hall of Newgate.

But yet they had much to do before penetrating to that cell in which Edith might be found.

"Ogle!" cried Heron.

"Here, Captain!"

"See that these men are so placed that any one coming into the vestibule may not take an immediate alarm."

"I understand, Captain. Now, my old pals, if you please,—just sit and lie as we want you."

The officers felt themselves vanquished. Further resistance was out of the question. The only hope they could now have was that some overpowering force might come to the hall and rescue them, but that, at such an hour, was a faint hope indeed.

Ogle made them all assume positions that gave them as free and unembarrassed an appearance as possible, in case any one should come into the vestibule, either from within the prison, or from without.

This precaution was not taken one moment too soon, for hardly was it achieved, when the sharp click of a lock was heard, and a man came from the interior of the prison into the vestibule.

This man spoke with his back to the party in the hall while he locked the door behind him through which he had passed; for it was a rule in Newgate—and is, probably, so still—that let the officials have to pass through a doorway as often as they might, it was never to be left for a moment unlocked.

"You can go now," he said. "I will take the lock. Is that something good to drink I smell?"

"Perhaps," said Captain Heron.

"Ah! Murder!"

"Silence! Another word, and the foolish cry you have just uttered will be a truth."

Captain Heron had stepped up to the man and clutched him by the collar at the back of his neck, twisting him round until they were face to face.

And now, but that the whole proceedings of that night at Newgate were so full of gravity that they overpowered all disposition to levity, Captain Heron might well have smiled at the ludicrous look of dismay that sat upon the face of the man he held in such an iron clutch.

But Heron was cold and stern.

"You comprehend me," he added. "A life more or less counts as nothing in that we are about to do. Be wise, and silent."

"Ye—e—s," stammered the turnkey.

"That is well; take good care of him."

Heron at once handed this new prisoner to Ogle, and then, he being well secured, as were the others, all was still again in the vestibule of Newgate.

But that stillness did not last many moments.

There was the sharp ringing of a bell.

"What bell is that?" asked Heron quietly.

No one replied.

Ogle put a pistol barrel right against the ear of the turnkey nearest to him, and then repeated Captain Heron's words—"What bell is that?"

The turnkey, under such pressure, replied in a moment, "The Governor's bell."

"And what does he want?" added Heron.

"The night report, up to twelve o'clock."

"Who takes it?"

"I do."

"Ogle?"

"Yes, Captain."

"I want that man's coat, waistcoat, and wig, for I see he wears the latter article."

"Yes, Captain."

The officers glared at each other with looks of spite and malignity, as Ogle quickly effected a transformation of Captain Heron into a very good likeness of that one whose duty it was to carry the night report to the Governor of Newgate.

To be sure, Heron was taller than the turnkey by some half a foot, but by stooping, he brought himself pretty near to the other's standard.

Not yet, however, was Heron permitted to leave the vestibule of Newgate without interruption, and that interruption now came from where it was least expected at such an hour. of the night.

It came from the outside of the prison.

There was a sharp rap at the wicket gate.

"Hush!" said Heron.

He held up his hand as he spoke, and no one dared to utter a word, while he went himself to the wicket.

"Who is there?" he asked.

"Yea," said a whining, canting voice from the outside,—"yea, I am here; and if verily I address the carnal mind of John Brand, I may say I come for the four pounds sixteen and twopence."

"Who is this man?" asked Heron, as he shut the wicket, and turned to the captive officers.

"I know," said Ogle.

"Who? who?"

"Don't you remember, Captain, a certain reverend gentleman who was on intimate terms with Tom Ripon's mother?"

"To be sure—to be sure!"

"That is the man."

"I recollect him well now, but his name has escaped me."

"It has escaped himself too," growled one of the officers; "for since he has married Old Mother Ripon, he calls himself 'the Reverend Mortification Ripon.'"

"What a name!" said Ogle.

"Yes; and they keep a fence together now, in Newcastle Street, Strand."

"I will admit him," said Captain Heron.

Even as he spoke, the Reverend Mortification Ripon made another appeal at the wicket gate of Newgate, for he was in great surprise at having it shut so abruptly in his face.

Heron opened the small hatch.

CAPTAIN HERON PAYS A VISIT TO THE GOVERNOR OF NEWGATE.

Presented Gratis with No. 79 of the New Edition Edith the Captive; or, the Robbers of Epping Forest.

EACH WEEK IS PRESENTED GRATIS A COLOURED ENGRAVING.

" Come in."

" Peradventure I shall come in," said the Reverend Mortification Ripon. " How are you all, eh? Have you seen Mr. Wild lately? because, if you have, you can tell him I have a plan for the capture of Captain Felix Heron, the notorious highwayman."

" You may as well tell it to me, then," said Ogle.

The Reverend Mortification Ripon staggered back a pace or two, right against the arm of Captain Heron, who then said, in his ear, " Or to me!"

The astonished visitor knew both the voices quite well, and at once dropped to his knees.

" Mercy! Have mercy upon me!"

" Scoundrel!" said Ogle.

" Villain!" said Heron.

" Murder! Oh, dear, sir! Murder! No, I don't mean that—I am not very well. Suppose we all join in prayer."

" Silence!" said Heron, in a voice of stern authority. " How dare a man like you talk of prayer? Be sure you do not mention such a word in my presence again!"

" No! no! Goodness gracious! I won't—I won't indeed!"

" Answer me, and speak the truth; for you are in peril if you do not."

" I will—I will! Oh, dear—I—I hope you are quite well, my dear sir. I always remember you in my prayers; I assure you I do."

" Ogle?"

" Yes, Captain."

" If this man utters the word ' prayer' again, shoot him."

" Certainly, Captain."

The Reverend Mortification Ripon turned ghastly pale, and, still on his knees, he looked in the cold, stern face of Captain Heron with the evident fear that his next words might be a death warrant.

Then the sharp tinkle of the Governor's bell came again.

Captain Heron laid his hand upon the arm of the officer who had said it was his duty to go to the Governor with the night report, and in a low, firm tone, he said, " You will guide me to the Governor's room."

" I can do that, Captain," said Ogle.

" No, no! I can leave no one in full command here of the vestibule of Newgate, but you, Ogle."

" He knows the way as well as any of us," said the officer, pointing to the Reverend Mortification Ripon. " He is on good terms with the Governor, and can show you the way."

" Good!" said Heron, as he dealt the reverend gentleman a not very gentle kick, as an admonition to get up. " Good! He will do."

" Oh! oh! oh!"

" Silence! Get up."

" Y—e—s. Oh, dear!"

" Conduct me to the Governor's room, and see that you contemplate no treachery; for however much the interior walls of Newgate may want plastering, I am not aware that human brains form the best; and yours will most undoubtedly be scattered over the old stones, if by word, look, or gesture, you give me cause to think you are trying to bring difficulty or danger about me."

The Reverend Mortification Ripon looked very rueful, but he fully comprehended his own danger, and strove, by a jerking alacrity of movement, to impress Captain Heron with the idea of how very willingly he obeyed him.

" Come now," added Heron.

" Yea," as the Psalmist says, ' I am willing to step into the furnace of affliction.'

" ' Here we go, both high and low,
    In billowy brimstone——' "

" Silence!" cried Heron, fiercely. " If there be one shade of hypocrisy more than another distasteful to me, it is that which assumes religion for its cloak. Silence, I say!"

The Reverend Mortification Ripon was dumb on the moment.

Then Captain Heron turned to Ogle, and spoke calmly and firmly: " You will let any one come into Newgate, but no one leave it. All, however, who do come in, you will make prisoners, and properly secure."

" It shall be done, Captain."

" Now, sir, you will for the sake of your life, at once conduct me to the Governor."

Captain Heron laid his hand heavily upon the shoulder of the Reverend Mortification Ripon, who, shrinking down until he was almost bent double beneath the touch, crept towards the door through which he had come into the prison vestibule, closely followed by Captain Heron.

The state of affairs now in the old gaol of Newgate was strange enough. Indeed, so entirely unprecedented a condition of affairs never could have been for one moment contemplated by the officers, who found themselves at the mercy of Captain Heron and his band, in the vestibule of the prison.

The door through which Heron and his guide made their way, conducted to a narrow gloomy passage, to the right and left of which were two rooms.

One of these rooms was named the Chaplain's Room; the other was named the Attorneys' Room.

Both of these apartments were in constant use during the daytime, but at this hour of the night they were dark and deserted, although the doors were open.

" Truly," said the Reverend Mortification Ripon, with a conventicle snuffle,—" truly, sir, you will not blame me if you meet with some misfortune."

" Yes, I shall."

" Goodness gracious, no! At the end of this passage there is a warder, who will stop us."

" Ah!"

" Yea, and you will remember that I told you, and so, I am sure, will take care that no harm befalls me."

" You must take care of yourself," said Heron.

At the moment he spoke, a door was flung open some dozen paces in advance of where they were, and a rough voice called out, " Is that you, Brand? Or who is it, eh?"

Captain Heron tightened his hold upon the upper part of the arm of the Reverend Mortification Ripon, as he whispered in his ear, " Answer, and say you have something very particular to communicate to the Governor, as indeed you have, if you could only get leave to say it."

—

CHAPTER CLXXVII.

HERON TAKES THE GOVERNOR OF NEWGATE
PRISONER.—A STRANGE ADVENTURE.

THE reverend gentleman was fully impressed
with the propriety of obeying without cavil the
commands of Captain Heron, and in a whining
voice he spoke to the warden on duty in the
narrow gloomy passage—"My dear sir, yea and
verily you know me, no doubt; and when I say,
in the words of the Psalmist——Oh!"

A sudden grip on the arm from Heron let the
Reverend Mortification Ripon know that he had
better not refer to the Psalmist; so he added,
"I want to see Mr. Governor on a matter of great
consequence."

"Then you cannot."

"Say you must," whispered Heron.

"Yea, I must."

"Then I say you shall not. Be off with you,
or I will come and lock you up. I cannot think
what the men on duty in the hall are about to let
you pass."

"Say you defy him," whispered Heron.

"Yea, I defy thee!"

"What?"

"Say you care nothing for him or any such
rascal," again prompted Heron.

The Reverend Mortification Ripon hesitated
about complying with this order; but another
sharp grip from the hand of Captain Heron on
his arm, which must have left a good impression
behind it, warned him that the danger of non-
compliance was present and tangible, while that
of obedience was, possibly, remote.

"You rascal," he said, "what do I care for
such a fellow as you?"

The warder was, no doubt, perfectly astonished
at such a speech from the person of all others he
would least have expected to utter such a defiance.

"Why I thought as much by your voice," he
said. "You have had a drop too much, as usual;
but I shall lock you up till morning, at all events,
my tipsy friend."

As he spoke, there was a faint flash of light
down the passage, for the warder had placed the
lantern he had on a moveable bracket, so that its
rays fell in the direction of the vestibule.

Captain Heron stooped low.

"Now, my joker," said the warder, as he approached the Reverend Mortification Ripon—"I
will soon get rid of your nonsense till the
morning."

He was within three paces of where Heron was
crouching down, when the latter sprung to his
feet, and with one movement—which took the
warder so much by surprise that he had no power
to speak—he clutched him by the throat as he
whispered, "Life or death—you can have choice
of either! Life if silent—death on the least
alarm!"

"Ah!"

"Hush! One more exclamation, and you are
a corpse!"

There was an odd rattling sound, which jarred
very much upon the nerves of the reverend gentleman, who could see, even by the dim light in
the narrow passage, what occasioned it. Captain

Heron had, in rather a regardless way of the
teeth of the warder, thrust the barrel of a pistol
into his mouth.

Hence the rattling sound.

Cold steel against ivory.

The warder was thoroughly terrified, and
trembled in every limb. Captain Heron felt quite
certain he was subdued.

"Go in there," he said.

It was to the Attorneys' Room that Heron
pointed, and the warder obeyed him with the
meekness of a lamb.

There were but two chairs in that room, and
they, with one heavy, strong table, made up its
whole furniture. To the table Heron—by the aid
of the man's own cravat—tied the warder by the
wrists behind his back, so that he was quite
secure. Then he whispered close to his ear,
"There is not the least occasion for you to
throw away your life. Newgate is in the possession of my men; and, upon any alarm, they will
kill you."

"I won't speak."

"That is wise."

"But—I should like to—to know, if you please,
who you are?"

"I am Captain Felix Heron."

"Oh!"

The way in which the man said "Oh!" was so
very expressive of his opinion of the hopelessness
of all opposition, that Captain Heron was tempted
to ask him a question.

"Tell me," he said,—"has a lady been brought
here a prisoner, who will be named, probably,
Edith Tarleton?"

"Oh, yes!"

"By whom?"

"Jonathan Wild."

"Then I may be sure to find her in Newgate?"

"To be sure, Captain."

"That is enough."

Heron left the warder to his reflections; and at
once resuming his hold upon the arm of the
Reverend Mortification Ripon, he said, "Now to
the Governor!"

"Yes—yea, I mean! As the Psal——Oh,
dear me, no! I did not say it; and, upon consideration, my dear sir, I don't think the Psalmist
said anything applicable to the present state of
affairs. And yet, oh, my brethren——"

"Silence!"

It was evident that the mind of the reverend
gentleman was scarcely proof against the accumulation of terror that had crept over it since his
capture by Captain Heron; but another, and still
tighter, grip from the hand of his captor ad-
monished him that he was letting his tongue run
too loosely, and he was silent again.

The door at which the warder who had just
been taken prisoner by Captain Heron had been
on duty was in immediate communication with
that part of Newgate in the occupation of the
officials who were not turnkeys or officers, and
from thence the route to the Governor's house was
easy and direct.

It was quite clear that Captain Heron had a
competent guide; for, with all his fright, the
Reverend Mortification Ripon went right on
without the least hesitation.

That door and that warder once passed, there
was no more obstruction to the advance of Heron;

and, finally, as they came to a door that was covered with green baize, and studded rather thickly with brass nails, Heron paused a moment, and spoke to his guide, for he felt certain that, from the appearance of that door, he was close to the portion of the prison in the occupation of the Governor.

"What is immediately on the other side of this door?" he asked.

"Yea, the Sheriff's room."

"And then?"

"Six steps. They lead to the Governor's own room."

"What do you call his own room?"

"Yea, where he keeps his books, and his papers, and his warrants—and, as the Psalmist says——"

"Hush! How often have I to warn you that you risk your life by such expressions?"

Captain Heron carefully pushed open the green baize-covered door, and found that it was about a foot from another door of the ordinary size, make, and appearance as might be found in any private house.

And now he knew that he had, so to speak, left Newgate behind him, and that he was in that portion of the building which was, for the purposes of habitation, rendered as unprisonlike as possible.

But no sound met his ears that could in any way be indicative of the presence of the Governor.

"Where is he?" whispered Heron.

"Yea, further on; for as the Psal——Oh, dear me, no! He don't say any such thing. This is the way—this is the way."

Exactly as the Reverend Mortification Ripon had said, there was a room, which, from its furniture and appointments, no doubt was at times officially in the occupation of the Sheriffs. It was lit by one of the prison lamps on a niche above the chimney piece. Passing then through a doorway opposite to that at which he had entered, Captain Heron came to the six steps ascending directly to the Governor's rooms in Newgate.

The steps were carpeted, and the footfalls of Heron and the reverend gentleman made no sound. There was another door, covered with green baize, and as Captain Heron pushed it gently open, he heard a strange sound, which induced him to pause for a moment.

It was only for a moment, however, that Heron paused to listen to that sound, and then he comprehended what it was.

Had he been in the far-off country instead of the metropolitan prison of Newgate,—had his attack been made upon a farm-house, Captain Heron would, upon hearing that sound, have come to the conclusion that he was making his way in the direction of the piggeries.

Now, however, he felt certain that he listened to an excellent imitation of the sort of noise made by a pig, but that it arose from some human animal in a state of repose.

"Ah!" murmured the Reverend Mortification Ripon; "he has taken his glass as usual, and it has been a little too strong."

"Who? who?"

"The Governor."

"Ah, indeed!"

As he spoke, Captain Heron strode at once into an apartment, on the table of which burnt two mould candles, lamentably long in the wick, and by the light of which could be seen the remains of an excellent supper.

The atmosphere of the room was full of the odour of spirits and water, mingled with a slight taint of tobacco. Glasses and bottles were upon the table, and seated on a low arm-chair, and fast asleep, was the Governor of Newgate.

But immediately opposite to him was another chair.

Close to the arm of that other chair—the arm which was next to the table—was an empty glass with a spoon in it, and close to the glass lay a tobacco pipe.

Leaning against this second chair was a riding whip, the handle of which was massive, and evidently loaded, so as to convert it into one of those terrible bludgeons, which are disguised by a thong to be made look the more harmless weapon—a whip.

It was quite evident the Governor of Newgate had had a visitor.

Who was that visitor, and where was he?

Captain Heron raised the heavy whip, and saw, roughly scratched on the handle, the initials J. W.

Could he doubt who had been the visitor of the Governor of Newgate?

"Jonathan Wild!" he exclaimed.

The heavy whip fell from his grasp as he spoke, with a dull sound, to the floor.

The pronunciation of Jonathan Wild's name probably reached the slumbering senses of the Governor of Newgate, combined with the noise made by the fall of the whip.

He spoke confusedly.

"All right, Mr. Wild! all right! Twenty guineas down! Take another glass! You can have her! you can have her! Five guineas a-week as long as you keep her! Good!—good! Take another glass, Mr. Wild!"

The colour went and came on the countenance of Captain Heron as he listened to these tipsy revelations from the slumbering Governor of Newgate. That he was speaking of Edith, how could Captain Heron doubt for a moment; and that some fearful and villanous compact had been entered into between the Governor and Jonathan Wild, in regard to her, appeared to be only too probable.

For a few seconds the heart of Captain Heron beat with such powerful violence that he was incapable of action; and had the Reverend Mortification Ripon but known that fact, then would have been his time to escape.

Heron, however, was not likely to give way for long to a feeling of despair when action was required of him.

Summoning all his strength and all his resolution to his aid, he murmured to himself, "I will save thee, my Edith, and waste no moments in idle lamentation. It is a time for action, not feeling; and I will have the secret of your hiding-place from this wretch, if I have to look for it in his heart's blood."

As he uttered the last two words, Captain Heron grasped the Governor of Newgate by the throat so tightly, that the sensation of strangulation must at once have got the better of all others.

A gurgling noise proclaimed that the Governor

was trying to speak—trying, perhaps, to cry out in such a tone as would soon have spread an alarm over Newgate.

But he found it impossible to carry out any such intention; and he could only glare in the face of Heron, while his reddening face and protruding tongue showed how near to strangulation he was.

Then Heron spoke.

In a low but clear voice he spoke; and although the thinnest partition would have sufficed to confine the sound of his voice to that one room of Newgate, yet the articulation was so perfect, that, confused and half choking as he was, the Governor could not but hear every word.

"You may or you may not know me, but I am Captain Felix Heron, of Epping Forest. I am aware that the villain Jonathan Wild has brought here, on a pretended warrant, my wife Edith, the daughter of Sir John Tarleton. I and my men have full possession of Newgate; and, on pain of death, I command you to conduct me at once to your prisoner whom I have named, in order that I may release her and carry her from the detested atmosphere of this place."

The Governor tried to speak, but the attempt was quite in vain while Captain Heron held him so firmly by the throat.

"Yea," said the Reverend Mortification Ripon, "the man choketh!"

The Governor kicked and plunged with his legs.

"I release you for a moment," said Heron, "in order that you may answer me. If you attempt even to give an alarm, you are a dead man!"

This time the reverend guide of Captain Heron did not hear that curious and uncomfortable rattling which the pistol-barrel had made among the teeth of the vanquished warder, but by the dim light of the unsnuffed candles he saw Heron place a pistol with the muzzle on the brow of the Governor.

The Governor felt it, too; and knew perfectly well what it was.

Captain Heron then took his hand from the half-choked man, so that he was able to draw a long breath of relief.

Then he spoke.

"I yield!—I yield! Don't kill me!"

"Your life is in your own hands."

"Don't—don't murder me! What—what good would it do you to murder me?"

"None, provided you are of more use to me living."

"What—do—you want?"

"Your prisoner—the young lady who was brought here by Jonathan Wild."

"The—the—that is, Miss Edith?"

"Call her by what name you will, we mean the same person."

"You—you want her?"

"I am here to rescue her; but since I find that you are inclined to parley instead of act, I will but exert a slight pressure upon the trigger of this pistol, and there will be no Governor of Newgate until a new one is appointed."

"No, no! Oh, no! I will do whatever you wish—whatever——Ah! Ah!"

The Governor held up one hand, and inclined his head in the attitude of listening.

"Yea," said the Reverend Mortification Ripon, —"yea, some one cometh."

"Who is it?" asked Captain Heron. "Who is expected here? Mr. Governor, you will do well to answer me at once, for I am in no mood for having my patience played upon."

"A man," faltered the Governor,—"a man to remove these things."

"Indeed! Is that all?"

"I speak the truth."

"Listen to me. Is it Jonathan Wild who is now approaching?"

"No—no—no!"

"You declare that,—and will accept death if you tell an untruth?"

"Mr. Wild has been here; but he has gone—gone—gone home."

CHAPTER CLXXVIII.

CAPTAIN HERON BAFFLES A GREAT DANGER, AND SECURES AN ASSASSIN.

THERE was a strange hesitation about the manner of the Governor which made it doubtful if he spoke the truth or not; but Captain Heron at once made up his mind to a course of action. He considered that he was tolerably safe in Newgate, as long as he held the Governor's life as a hostage for his security; and, likewise, he felt that if any one could lead him to the cell in which he should find his Edith it would be that high official, who, of course, by the exercise of his authority, could overcome all opposition to his, Heron's, taking her away with him.

The Governor's life, then,—along, however, with the Governor's silence and seeming concurrence in what he was about,—became of importance to Heron.

The sharp click of a key in a lock, however, warned him that there was no time to be lost.

Captain Heron at once flung himself into the chair which was opposite to the Governor—that very chair which he had every reason to suppose had been so recently in the occupation of his worst enemy, Jonathan Wild.

Then Captain Heron spoke in those low tones of command, which had already awed the Reverend Mortification Ripon, the warder, and the Governor to submission to his will.

"Mr. Governor," he said, "you will simply, when your servant appears, order more hot water, and then direct him not to interrupt you and your friends for the rest of the night."

"Yes—yes!"

"And you, Mr. Ripon,—since that is the *alias* by which you choose now to be known—you will sit down and be quiet."

"Certainly—yea, certainly; and as there will be some more hot water, don't you think it will keep up the delusion if we have a glass? for, as the Psalmist says——."

"Silence! On your life, silence!"

The door of the room was opened at that moment, and a sulky-looking man, whose duty it was to wait on the Governor, appeared.

There was a look of intense surprise upon his face when he saw that the Governor, whom he supposed by this time to be alone, had two persons with him as guests.

"Speak!" said Heron.

"Samuel," said the Governor, "you will bring some more hot water."

"Yes, sir."

"And pipes," added the Reverend Mortification Ripon. "And pipes, Samuel."

"Yes," said the Governor.

The Reverend Mortification Ripon then uttered a strange sound that might have been mistaken for the howl of a large dog, on whose toes some heavy substance had fallen.

The fact was that Captain Heron, to let him know that his interference with the orders given to Samuel was not wanted, had stretched his foot far under the table, and saluted the shins of the reverend gentleman by such a kick that, accompanied with the strange howl, it brought tears into his eyes.

"What's the matter?" asked Heron.

"Nothing—nothing! Only, as the Psalmist might say——"

No. 80.—EDITH.

An expressive look from Heron stopped further remark, and the Governor then added, "Be quick, Samuel! Be quick!"

"Yes, sir."

Captain Heron could not help seeing that Samuel looked at him suspiciously, and the moment he had left the room, Heron looked across the table to the Governor, as he said, "Does that man mean mischief?"

"No," replied the Governor. "He cannot possibly know you."

"That is well for you!"

"For—for me?"

"Decidedly; because I hold you to be responsible for my safety in Newgate."

"Me responsible? But is that fair? Is it right? How can I be sure what any one else may do?"

"I cannot help that. I am like some one who has assailed a city. I hold the Governor a prisoner. His acts are the acts of all the garrison; and I make him responsible after his own surrender for whatever may happen."

Samuel came back with a jug of hot water, which he placed on the table rather surlily.

"Anything else?" he said.

"Yes," replied the Governor; "you will see that I and my friends are not interrupted for the remainder of the night."

"Ha! ha!" laughed Samuel.

Heron regarded him with surprise.

"Ha! ha!" added Samuel, as he pointed at Captain Heron. "I know who this is."

"You do?" gasped the Governor.

"To be sure I do. It is Captain Heron, the great highwayman, and I can see with half an eye that you are afraid of him, sir. I've sent my wife round the corner to Mr. Wild's, and he will come and nab him, and I shall have half the reward. Ha! ha! How do, Captain? How do?"

"I am very well," replied Heron quietly; "but I am afraid that you are in a bad way, Samuel."

"Oh, dear, no! I'm all right. Ha! ha! I'm all right. What do you think of that, eh?"

Samuel made a dash at Captain Heron, producing, as he did so, a curious kind of half-knife, half-stiletto, from some concealed pocket of his coat, and brandishing it before the eyes of Heron.

"What do you think of this, eh? It's worth all the fire-arms, I think. An old master of mine, who was an Italian, taught me how to use it; and till my wife comes back with Mr. Wild, I hold your life, you must be aware, Captain Heron. Ha! ha!"

Heron, to the surprise of the Governor, and of the Reverend Mortification Ripon, sat quite unmoved, and looking up in the face of Samuel, he said calmly, "You are a great fool, Samuel."

"Oh, am I?"

"Yes, a very great fool: for if you had not sent your wife to Jonathan Wild's, you might have had all the reward of my capture yourself, whereas now he will pocket every penny of it; and if you so much as grumble, he will find a means of hanging you at Tyburn next sessions."

Samuel turned pale.

"Well," he said, "that may be; but I have not been such a fool as you think."

"Yea," said the Reverend Mortification Ripon; "I think, Mr. Governor, that it is our turn now."

"Silence!" said Heron sternly.

The Governor, with his eyes on Heron, began to rise to his feet.

"Sit down, sir!" said Heron.

The Governor sank back again into the arm-chair.

"Why, you are both afraid of him," said Samuel, as he with his left hand, which was disengaged, produced a pair of handcuffs. "Only see me put these bracelets on him, and you will manage him well. Ha! ha! These fellows are nothing when you fairly tackle them."

"Still you are a fool," said Heron. "A fool for sending to Wild."

"Then I have done no such thing, since you will have it, and since you see you have found your master. I am not such a fool; but I said I

had sent to Jonathan just to get you to give up without any fuss."

"Then you are a worse fool still," added Captain Heron.

"What for?"

"For holding that dagger so near to my eyes, when there is the Reverend Mortification Ripon standing up behind you to nab you."

"Ah!"

The man half turned, and on the instant, with the quickness of thought, Heron's right hand was flung upwards, and he caught Samuel round the wrist of the hand that held the stiletto.

"Now, idiot!" said Heron, "could you fancy for one moment that you, or such as you, could even be dangerous to me?"

Samuel uttered a cry, for Heron had twisted his wrist in a manner that made the bones crackle again.

With his left hand then Heron seized the fellow by the shoulder, and as he himself rose from the arm-chair, he forced Samuel down into it.

"Sit still," he said, "and wonder, as you do so, that I spare your worthless life; for I recognise you now as one of Jonathan Wild's men who came to Epping Forest on a mission to betray me."

The stiletto had dropped on to the table, and the fellow managed to get hold of it in his left hand, and made a savage stab at Captain Heron with it.

"A fool," said Heron, "will persevere in his folly, I perceive."

As he spoke, he wrested the stiletto from him, and dashing one of the hands of the would-be assassin on the table, Heron plunged the stiletto with such force through the back of it, that the blade went not only right through the hand, but through the table likewise, nearly up to the hilt.

The discomfited villain, who, but a few short minutes before, had been, as he thought, so triumphant, uttered a shriek of pain, the repetition of which was suppressed by Heron adroitly tying over his mouth, and indeed right into it, a silk handkerchief, the end of which he had seen projecting from the Governor's pocket.

The moment Captain Heron had thus secured Samuel, he strode across the room to the door at which that foolhardy personage had come in, and shot a large brass bolt into its socket.

"Now, Mr. Governor," he said, "further delay is useless. I command you to conduct me to the cell in which is imprisoned the purest and most innocent soul that ever crossed the threshold of Newgate."

The Governor looked ghastly now with terror, and could hardly withdraw his eyes from the hand and the dagger.

Samuel uttered low groans.

The Reverend Mortification Ripon had slipped off his chair, and was hiding under the table, in the vain hope that Captain Heron might forget him, and leave him in the room.

Heron, however, with Jonathan Wild's heavy thonged whip, hunted him out of his place of concealment; and the reverend gentleman sprang to his feet with ludicrous alertness.

The terror of the Governor was now very great, for about the eyes of Captain Heron there was a strange gleam, which spoke of mischief, and filled him with a thousand fears.

"Captain," he said, "I hope you feel that I

had nothing to do with the proceedings of that man, whom you have so effectually and so terribly fastened to the table."

Captain Heron made a gesture of impatience, and the Governor added, "Indeed, and in truth, Captain, I will keep faith with you, and conduct you to the cell of Edith Tarleton. I have but to get my master-key from this drawer, and I will come with you."

"Quick! quick!"

"As quickly as possible, Captain—as quickly as possible, you may depend."

The Governor was nervous, and could hardly manage to open the drawer in the table in which was the master-key he mentioned. He first pulled the drawer too much on one side, and then too much on the other, so that it was only by little jerks that he got it open at all.

"Here is the key; and, so far as I am concerned, you shall have nothing to complain of."

"And I will mind the room while you are gone," said the Reverend Mortification Ripon, "for I don't feel very well."

"Follow!" said Captain Heron.

That was all he said, but the tone in which it was said was quite sufficient for the reverend gentleman, and he followed Captain Heron and the Governor from the room without another word.

Heron had no doubt now but that the Governor would keep faith with him. He could not but see the state of almost helpless fear to which that official mind had been reduced, since the terrible example which had been made of Samuel.

The route taken for some part of the way was the same by which Captain Heron had approached the Governor's apartments. They turned into the Chaplain's Room, at the further end of which was a door which led into a narrow passage communicating with the chapel of Newgate.

"Is this the nearest way?" asked Heron.

"By far," replied the Governor; "and we avoid the night guards in two passages."

"Lead on, then."

Captain Heron was not at all displeased that the Governor of Newgate, acknowledging his defeat, and the power that he, Heron, had over him, should of his own accord wish to take a route that would avoid contact with the men on night duty in the prison, and he followed with more complaisance than he had yet done.

The chapel of Newgate looked dim and vast as the strangely-assorted party stepped into it on that eventful night, but that was owing to the darkness around, which was but slightly relieved by the small hand-lantern which Captain Heron made the Reverend Mortification Ripon take from the bracket in the Chaplain's Room.

"I shall lose my situation," said the Governor, "by this night's work."

To this remark Captain Heron had but one reply to make, and that was couched in the words, "Better to lose any situation than lose your life!"

The Governor was then silent, but the Reverend Mortification Ripon could not help now and then uttering sighs and moans, and occasionally muttering what "the Psalmist" thought of affairs in general.

The dismal, gloomy chapel was passed through, and by the aid of his master-key the Governor now opened a private door in one corner of it, and the little party found themselves at once in one of the darkest and coldest stone passages of the prison.

It was evident that this passage was on a considerable slope, and Captain Heron could not forbear from saying, with indignation in his tones, "Is it possible, Mr. Governor, that whatever excuse you may allege on the score of duty, you can have thought it necessary to immure a lady in the lower portions of Newgate?"

The Governor trembled, as well he might, at this question, and he replied with some confusion, "I have only done my duty."

"What duty, sir?"

"You must know the lady is here on a State warrant, and therefore I was compelled to take every care that she did not escape."

"Escape from Newgate, sir? A young and delicate girl escape from the stone walls of Newgate? Is it so easy, then, to break the wires of this dreary cage? But lead on, sir; we shall see what complaint there may be against you shortly."

"It is not my fault. Mind the steps, Captain, for here we have rather a steep flight."

"Lower and lower still!" said Heron, mournfully. "Oh, Edith — Edith! how utterly forsaken you might well think yourself by man and heaven!"

"Would you have any objection to a psalm?" said the Reverend Mortification Ripon.

"Every objection, sir, since here it is out of place."

"But, sir, the——"

"Silence, and be thankful for your worthless life!"

"Here is the cell," said the Governor.

They had descended sixteen damp and mouldy steps, and at the foot of them the Governor had walked on about twelve paces before he paused and held up the lamp, which he had taken from the hands of the trembling fanatic, towards a small grating in the wall.

"That the cell?" exclaimed Heron.

"I could not help it, Captain."

"Peace! I will reckon with you yet."

Heron sprung forward, and finding that he could just reach the grating in the wall with his lips, he placed them close to it, crying out "Edith, Edith! it is I—your own true Felix! Edith—dearest and best — speak to me! I can save you!"

All was as still as the grave.

"Good heavens!" exclaimed Captain Heron; "not a word! Edith, one sound—one sigh to let me know you are in life!"

Still there was no response; and the echo of Captain Heron's voice was the only sound that followed those impassioned and grief-stricken words he had uttered without that gloomy cell in Newgate.

CHAPTER CLXXIX.

CAPTAIN HERON FINDS HIMSELF CAUGHT IN A SNARE.—THE TERRIBLE NIGHT IN NEWGATE.

BUT that they wanted courage to do so, and but that they both had exaggerated notions of the power of Captain Heron, the famous highwayman and outlaw of Epping Forest, the Governor of

Newgate and the Rev. Mortification Ripon might have seized the opportunity of escape while he, Heron, called so passionately upon Edith through the bars of the cell.

But they let the precious moments pass away, and Captain Heron turned to the Governor with a calmness that was more terrible than rage, as he said, "Open the cell, sir—open the cell! I am now prepared for the worst!"

The Governor was so terrified, that his hands refused to obey him as he strove to put the key into the lock.

The Reverend Mortification Ripon, who had taken the lamp again, seeing the agitation of the Governor, began to shake the light to and fro in his own fear so confusingly, that the dim walls of that underground portion of Newgate seemed to be peopled by a thousand shadows.

"Give me the key!" cried Heron, firmly.

"Yes, Captain—yes. But——"

"Give it to me, I say!"

The Governor was loth to part with his master-key, which unlocked every door in Newgate, but the tone in which Captain Heron demanded it did not admit of denial, and he surrendered it.

It was wonderful now to see how apparently calm and cool Heron was as he opened the low iron door of the cell.

The grating through which he had already tried to look and call upon Edith was not really in the door, but above it, in one of the old thick stones of which the wall was composed.

The door itself was not above six feet in total height, and of solid oak, plated both within and without with iron.

"Edith! Edith!—heaven, where is she?"

No sound—no cry of joy to welcome him! No sigh even of suffering met his ears!

"The lamp—the lamp!" he cried.

"Yes, here it is; and as the Psalmist says——"

"Peace, fool!"

Heron snatched the lamp from the hands of the Reverend Mortification Ripon, and rushed into the wretched cell.

"Edith—for the love of heaven, Edith, if you be here, speak to me!"

The cell was not above twelve feet square, and the lamp which, in the chapel of Newgate, was quite insufficient to make more than "darkness visible," sufficed to irradiate that smaller space.

One terrified and agonized glance was sufficient for Felix Heron.

No Edith was there!

Some musty straw lay upon the cold flag-stones which formed the flooring of the cell, and Heron fancied he saw in a corner the shining eyes of some reptile, but the cell had now no human occupant but himself.

"Deceived!" he shouted, — "deceived and mocked! But I will pull Newgate stone from stone, ere I relinquish the search for my heart's treasure!"

He turned to leave the cell.

His foot was on the threshold.

His hand was almost on the door.

The Governor of Newgate, then, in the excitement of the moment, uttered such a yell, that it might fairly have been heard throughout the whole prison; and at the same moment, with all his force, he dashed the door shut, and held it with the strength of despair.

"Quick! quick!" he cried. "The bolt—the bolt! Shoot the bolt—confound you, shoot the bolt, or he'll be out! Ha, ha, ha! Nabbed at last! I have him! Hurrah! hurrah! The other bolt! The top one now! Idiot, be quick! Climb on me—don't mind me! There! It is done! He has the key of the lock, but the two outer bolts will defy him! Hurrah! hurrah! Victory! Nabbed at last—nabbed at last!"

Captain Heron had been struck on the chest and arm by the door as it was dashed shut, and the sudden blow had staggered him, so that he reeled back on the damp straw for a moment. That moment was fatal.

The cell door was closed, held fast for a dozen seconds by the Governor, and bolted both at the bottom and top by the Reverend Mortification Ripon.

Heron was caged!

A prisoner in Newgate!

Himself shut up within those stone walls within which he had penetrated to save Edith!

Oh, horrible conclusion! Oh, terrible fate! No wonder that, for a brief period, Captain Heron could do nothing but clasp his hands over his head and face, and moan.

The lamp had dropped from his hands, and lay upon the damp straw, but it was not extinguished by the fall.

The dim flickering light that it sent about it, seemed to reveal to him the full horrors of his situation.

Then, with the wild energy of despair, he made a terrible rush at the cell door. It shook upon its hinges, but it otherwise stirred not. The old doors of Newgate were constructed to withstand any kind of force that might be applied to them from within the cells.

Then the frantic prisoner knocked on the inner iron plate with the key.

"Ha! ha! I hear!" cried the Governor.

"And yea, so do I," said the Reverend Mortification Ripon; "but, as the Psalmist says, 'Safe bind, safe find.'"

Captain Heron knocked again with the key.

"Anybody there?" asked the Governor, in a jeering voice. "Anybody there, eh?"

"Yea!" said the Reverend Mortification Ripon, "it striketh me that the hot water in thy room, Mr. Governor, may still be a pleasant thing mixed with some ardent spirit; and with a certain modicum of sugar, and one small slice from a lemon —for, as the Psalmist says——"

"Hush! hush!" interrupted the Governor; "I want to hear what he says!"

Captain Heron had again knocked on the inner side of the door of the cell with the master-key.

The Governor put his lips close to the key-hole of the ponderous lock, and cried out sharply, "What now? What is it now?"

Heron spoke.

"Mr. Governor?"

"Well?"

"You like money?"

"To be sure I do."

"Yea, so do I," said the Reverend Mortification Ripon; "and as, friend highwayman, thou art quite certain of being hanged, it will bring comfort, yea, exceeding comfort to thy feelings, to inform us where thy swag——Bless me, I have

THE GOVERNOR OF NEWGATE ASSISTED BY THE REV. MORTIFICATION
EFFECTS THE CAPTURE OF THE REDOUBTABLE CAPTAIN.

Presented Gratis with No. 80, of the New Edition Edith the Captive; or, the Robbers of Epping Forest.

EACH WEEK IS PRESENTED IS A COLOURED ENGRAVING.

unwittingly given utterance to a word used by carnal-minded persons, who, at times, repair even into the shop of Mrs. Ripon with silver spoons."

"Hold your row, will you?" said the Governor. "We shall never hear what he has to say if you go on in that way."

"But, friend Governor——"

"I tell you what it is, Mr. Ripon—as you choose to call yourself—if you are any trouble to me, I will have an information laid against you for aiding and assisting Captain Heron to-night; and it will go badly with you, I can tell you."

It would appear that the Reverend Mortification Ripon thought this no idle threat, for he was silent, with the exception of muttering to himself very faintly, what he thought the Psalmist's opinion would be likely to be in the present juncture.

"Now, Captain!" cried the Governor, as he dealt the cell door a kick to summon the attention of Heron. "Now, Captain, what have you got to say?"

It was quite a forlorn hope in the mind of Heron to think that he could say anything to that man to induce him to release him, but yet he tried it.

"I am, it appears, your prisoner at present," he said.

"It looks like it," replied the Governor, with a laugh.

"But," added Heron, "it can do you no good to keep me."

"In—deed!"

"None in the least."

"How do you make that out?"

"You will lose a thousand pounds by letting any one know that I am in Newgate."

"On the contrary, I shall gain that amount; for that is about what is offered for your apprehension."

"Halves!—halves!" cried the Reverend Mortification Ripon,—"halves, Mr. Governor!"

"What do you mean with your halves?"

"Yea, did not I shoot the two bolts? Yea, did not I even scramble up on your back and secure the door of this cell? Yea——"

"Hold your row."

"You lose," added Captain Heron, "a thousand pounds each, I tell you, by my detention here. The reward is one thousand: and that, you know as well as I do, Jonathan Wild will try to deprive you of; whereas I offer three thousand for my liberation."

"Three—three——"

"Will you be quiet?" cried the Governor, as he hit the Reverend Mortification Ripon a blow on the top of the head,—"will you be quiet?"

"Oh, dear!"

"Hark you, Captain Heron. It's very easy for a man in a cell of Newgate to offer three thousand pounds to be let go—or three hundred thousand——"

"Good gracious!" cried the Reverend Mortification Ripon.

The Governor dealt him a savage kick, as an admonition to be silent; and then he added, "I say, Captain,—it is very easy to offer all that to be let go, but where is the money?—where is the security, eh?—that is the question. Where is the cash? Eh?"

"Yea, where is the tin—I mean the cash?

Yea, and truly, I get into bad habits of speaking at times, for I cannot say that I ever heard the Psalmist call money, tin."

"Come, Captain," added the Governor, "what do you say to that?"

Captain Heron was silent.

"That puzzles you."

"Yea, it puzzleth him."

Not a sound now came from the cell.

"Oh! very well," said the Governor, "if you are content, I am. I don't want you to speak; and you may remain where you are as long as you like without saying a word—ha! ha! But you had better, if you really have got three thousand pounds to offer, tell me how to get it, you know, because one might consider of it."

Still there was no reply.

The silence as of the tomb pervaded that wretched little cell into which Captain Heron had been so successfully inveigled by the Governor of Newgate.

"Yea," said the Reverend Mortification Ripon, "mayhap, he has gone into a swound?"

The Governor shook his head.

"Not at all likely, that. He thinks to confuse us—to bother our wits by keeping silence; because it is quite impossible that—that——"

"That what? Yea, that what?"

"Nothing—nothing."

The Governor was evidently disturbed in his own mind, and at that moment he would have given something to be quite certain that the silence in that gloomy cell arose from obstinacy or from despair on the part of Captain Heron. Twice he approached the little narrow wicket at the top of the cell door, and was upon the point of trying to look through it, but he recollected that, within the last year, a turnkey had lost an eye by such an action, as a prisoner in one of the cells had, in revenge for such a system of espionage, dashed between the iron bars a concealed key that he had.

Therefore the Governor was cautious.

But he was not, by any means, so careful of the eyes of the Reverend Mortification Ripon, to whom he said, "Just try if you can see him through the grating."

"Nay, friend Governor, I would rather not; for, as the Psalmist says—

'Cast thy mortal eyes around,
And lo! how sinners do abound.'

Now, truly, I might lose one eye, and so be unable to do as the Psalmist adviseth and wisheth."

"Bah!"

The Governor took from his pocket another key, and tapped on the door of the cell.

"Captain Heron! Captain Heron! Captain Heron!"

There was no reply.

The feeling of alarm which had began to creep over the mind of the Governor, deepened each moment, although the Reverend Mortification Ripon was rather at a loss to know from what it arose, since it appeared to him that whether or no Captain Heron was inclined to hold a conversation through the cell door, he was still, all the same, a prisoner.

But the Governor had a more accurate knowledge of the interior of Newgate than the hypocritical companion who was with him. He turned now abruptly to the Reverend Mortification Ripon, and, in a voice of some alarm, he said, " You must run round to Newgate Street, and tell Mr. Wild what has happened here, at once. If you do not, something uncomfortable will occur."

" Eh? Something uncomfortable?"

" Yes, more uncomfortable than you can have any conception of; for, instead of having Captain Heron on the other side of this cell door, we may find him on this !"

The Reverend Mortification Ripon was so confounded at this speech from the Governor of Newgate, that, in his dismay, he turned twice round on his heels, as though he fully expected to find Heron behind him.

" Fly at once !" added the Governor. " You don't know your own danger !"

" Danger ?"

" Idiot, I say ! Will you go ?"

" Yea, at once will I; but, as the Psalmist remarks, 'Safe bind, safe——' "

" Peace ! I know the rest; but if you or the Psalmist either think that Captain Felix Heron is safe bound in that cell, you will, I fancy, find yourselves mistaken."

The Reverend Mortification Ripon was incredulous; and well he might be, when he glanced at the powerful bolts which held the cell door close.

" Go at once !" roared the Governor. " Go, I tell you ! and do not take any denial at Mr. Wild's house : say you must see him, for it is a matter of life and death."

The Reverend Mortification Ripon now began to be seriously alarmed. There was no such thing as mistaking the tone and manner of the Governor of Newgate to mean anything else than that he thought there was abundance of danger somewhere; and although the reverend gentleman could not very well comprehend where it was, or in what shape it might show itself, he could not doubt of the genuineness of the Governor's alarm.

" Yea, I will even go at once," he said; " and notwithstanding I would as soon pay a visit to the——Hem ! Dear me, who was I about to mention ?"

" An acquaintance," said the Governor, as he pushed him down the narrow passage away from the cell door.

" Yea, verily, you may call any gentleman in an elevated position an acquaintance; but of a surety, I——"

" Look you here," added the Governor; " if you don't be off at once to Mr. Wild's, I will open the cell door, and push you in, either to keep company with Captain Heron, or to remain by yourself for a few days."

" Yea, I am gone."

The Reverend Mortification Ripon did not remain another moment, but made the best of his way from those narrow, damp, and underground portions of Newgate to the upper regions. He knew perfectly well that since the vestibule of the prison was in the possession of Captain Heron's men, it would be an act of madness to attempt to leave Newgate by that way.

The route, however, by the Governor's house might be open to him, and well acquainted as he was with the interior of the old metropolitan pri-

son, he soon made his way back to that room where so recently the Governor had sat conversing with Jonathan Wild.

To the surprise of the Reverend Mortification Ripon, the turnkey whose hand had been pinned in so terrible a fashion to the table by Captain Heron, was not there.

How he had contrived to escape was a mystery to the reverend gentleman, for the poniard with which that man—who had so quickly met with his deserts—had attempted the life of Heron, was still sticking to the table.

A pool of blood surrounded it.

" Yea, now," said the Reverend Mortification Ripon, " this is enough to produce of a surety various commotions about the regions of the stomach. Of a surety, I was ever a tenderhearted person, with by no means a strong digestion; and even now, yea, as I look upon that table——"

The Reverend Mortification Ripon gave a shudder, for the sight of the pool of blood about the dagger, which seemed as if it stood up by some strange power in the midst of it, was too much for his nerves.

But a smile crossed his features at the same moment that the shudder pervaded his frame.

The bane was there, but there likewise was the antidote.

The Reverend Mortification Ripon's antidote to all human ills.

A dark bottle, on which there hung a silver label, with the magic words " *eau de vie* " on it.

" Yea, I shall soon be better," he said. " I will not forget that my worthy and exemplary friend the Governor is exceedingly anxious that I should proceed to Mr. Wild with an account of the capture of Captain Heron, but I shall go all the quicker if my internal system is strengthened and comforted; so—ah! good! ah! uncommonly good! Better than good! ah !"

The reverend gentleman had possessed himself of the bottle with the little silver label, on which was the enticing and charming announcement of its contents.

He sat down with his back to the dagger and the pool of blood upon the table, and he took a deep draught from the dark-coloured bottle.

" Ah !—capital ! That will do. Only just enough to keep the dev——No, bless us and save us, what was I about to say ?—I mean to keep the wind out of my stomach. No—no—not another drop; or, if another, the—a—merest trifle, just to keep the dev——Eh? who is that? Oh, nobody ! It is good—first rate, I should say; and as the Psalmist remarks—

" When Claude Duval gave the nabs the sly,
       Tooraloo, tooraloo;
   'Hold fast,' says he, 'by the lash of my eye,
       Tooraloo, tooraloo.

" 'And if ever I sleep on Newgate straw,
       Tooraloo, tooraloo;
   Call me a lobster without a claw,
       Tooraloo, tooraloo.' "

Ha ! — ha ! Hoorah ! Hoorah for the Psalmist and a black bottle ! What do I care for you, Mr. Governor ? What do I care for you, old Jonathan Wild ? What do I care for you, old Mother Ripon ? Eh ? go to the dev——Eh? Coming !—coming ! This is good—decidedly good; and—and—the only pity is that—that the room will go round, and that there's no more of it. No more—no—no—more!

The Reverend Mortification Ripon fell from the chair on which he had seated himself with the black bottle in his hand; and after two or three fruitless efforts to rise again, he resigned himself to the deep sleep which came over him.

CHAPTER CLXXX.

EDITH FINDS HERSELF STILL IN THE POWER OF HER WORST FOE.

WE left Edith in a cell of Newgate.

After the agitating interview she had had with Jonathan Wild, and the hopeless appeals she had made to his cupidity and to his hopes and fears, she might well have been excused for thinking that she was lost beyond all power of rescue.

And Edith would in truth have thought as much, but that the mere utterance of the name of Felix Heron was, in itself, a tower of mental strength to her.

With the sudden closing of that cell door, which seemed so like a living tomb in old Newgate, it would seem that light, liberty, and hope had been for ever separated from the lonely prisoner.

But such was not the case.

We have mentioned that when Edith recovered sufficient equanimity to look about her, she was conscious that a strange ray of light in some way found a passage into the cell.

Whence it came was rather a mystery. If Edith had not felt quite certain that the cell door as she now stood was to her left-hand, she might easily have supposed that that ray of light came from the passage beyond, through the narrow crevice between the door and the wall.

But such could not be the case.

All was darkness in that direction; and, by merely stretching out her left arm, she could feel the ponderous lock of the door,—so that there could be no doubt in regard to its position.

And as she stood upon the damp straw of the cell, the light which attracted her attention came from the wall, or through the wall, which was at right angles to the door.

It was a long, faint slip of light, so to speak; and as Edith passed her hand now along it, she was certain there was some exceedingly narrow slit in the wall, through which it made its way.

Was it a door?

That was the question. But although Edith paid all the attention in her power to an accurate examination of the wall, she could not detect any appearance of a door, or opening of any kind.

The effect, however, of that narrow slip of light in the cell was to produce a dubious kind of twilight.

That was better than absolute darkness, for Edith was able to see the dimensions of her prison, and what it contained.

The floor was covered with damp straw. Along one side ran a wooden bench; and hanging from the wall immediately above it was a short thick chain, one end of which was embedded in one of the blocks of stone that formed the wall, while the other was terminated by an iron ring.

It would, no doubt, be quite possible to attach that iron ring to the neck of any one so that they would be compelled to sit or lie only on the wooden bench—doubly a prisoner—a prisoner to the stone walls of Newgate, and a prisoner to that iron manacle within them.

Edith shuddered.

A feeling of faintness came over her, and she was fain to rest upon the wooden bench until she could recover the even beating of her heart.

"Felix! Felix! Felix!" she said. "He will save me yet! Oh, yes, he will save me yet!"

Poor Edith pleased her imagination with these words. They came from the heart, not the head.

She would not reason upon them. Had she done so, she must have told herself how terribly hopeless would be the task of dragging her from that cell of Newgate.

Then she clasped her hands over her eyes, and sobbed.

It was not for long, though, that Edith gave way to tears. Probably, she could not help paying such a passing tribute to her woman's nature, and then she was firm again.

"No, no," she said, "I will not weep. I will hope for the best. While my Felix lives—while I live—he for me, and I for him—there should be no despair. All will be well—all must be well."

She looked up.

With a start, she sprung to her feet.

The cell, she thought, was surely much lighter than it had been.

The long, exceedingly narrow slip of light was certainly brighter, or her eyes had become better accustomed to the twilight which it produced in the cell, and so appreciated it more than they had done.

But speculations in regard to the character of that slip of light were soon dissipated by the sound of a key in the lock of the cell door.

Edith's first impulse was to fly towards that door, in the hope that it was opening the way for her to freedom; but her next feeling was to shrink back as far as she could into the cell, lest she should come into contact with some one whose touch would be a terror and a pollution.

The cell door was opened.

A flickering ray of light came into it, and a man appeared with a lantern in his hand, and a small basket on his arm.

Edith regarded him fixedly.

"Hush!" he said. "Do not speak loud; I am a friend, and will save you."

"The name of friend is welcome," said Edith; "but I do not know you."

"Oh, never mind that, lady. I am a poor, plain sort of fellow."

"Ah, I do know you now! You are the Governor of Newgate."

"Well, lady, and suppose I am? It only shows that I have the more power to help you."

Edith was suspicious, as well she might be, of any help or friendship coming from such a quarter as that.

"Yes," added the Governor; "I am full of pity and commiseration for you. I know all about you and Captain Heron, and why it is that Jonathan Wild wants to keep you a prisoner. But please — please the fates, lady, we will defeat him!"

"I think," said Edith, "you were going to say, 'Please heaven.' Why did you pause and hesitate at the utterance of that word?"

"That—that word? What word?"

"Heaven!"

"Oh, I have no objection to say it—oh, none in the least! But as I was saying, I should feel quite delighted to foil Jonathan Wild, and restore you to freedom and to Captain Heron."

"Do so, then."

The Governor shook his head.

"It is easy to say ' Do so,' but not so easy to do it. I am, it is true, the Governor of this prison, but you are not aware probably that I have to give a receipt for every one who is committed to my care within these walls."

"Well, sir?"

"So, you see, lady, I cannot take you by the arm and walk you out of the prison. That is to say, I could do so, but how would I be able to account for the act afterwards? You see that?"

"I hear you!"

"Very good; but there is no reason why you should not escape."

"Escape?"

"Yes, to be sure. You look about you, and you see the old black walls of Newgate, and you don't see how to do it; but if I want to let a prisoner go, it is easy for me to make such an arrangement, that he or she may seem to have escaped, in spite of the stone walls of Newgate, when in reality the affair has been as easy as possible."

"Well, sir?"

"You shall so escape."

"If you are sincere, I shall thank you with all my heart, and I shall beseech your pardon for my first suspicions of you."

"You will find me quite sincere."

"I hope in heaven I shall."

"Hem! Well, you see, lady, in this basket there are some refreshments, of which it is necessary you should partake, because, above all things, you must keep up your strength."

"Ah, sir, for how long do you mean that it will be necessary for me to take refreshments in Newgate?"

"Until to-morrow night."

"An age!"

"Pho! pho! The time will soon slip away, and by then Captain Heron will be waiting for you close at hand."

"What mean you?"

"Why, you see, the best way will be for you to write to him a note to wait for you, say at the foot of Snow Hill, or by the wall of the Fleet; so that when I manage to set you free, you will in a few minutes be with him, and under his protection."

"Ah!"

"You comprehend?"

"I do."

"Then that will be all right. Here is a pen, here is a sheet of paper, and some ink; and if I open my lantern, you will be able to write, using as a desk the old bench there."

"Yes—oh, yes!"

"You will do it, eh?"

"I will write to him."

"Why then you are simpler—that is to say, you are more innocent than even I thought you, lady; and it will be a great pleasure to me to set you free. You can perhaps tell me the best way of getting your note delivered to him?"

"I can."

"And you will?"

"I will."

The Governor chuckled and rubbed his hands together, as he placed the writing materials before Edith; and opening the lantern so that there was a good stream of light from it, he waited for her to produce the letter he had suggested.

Edith knelt down before the bench, and wrote.

"MY FELIX,—

"You will know my handwriting, so that these words, if ever they should really meet your dear eyes, will be authentic, as coming from your Edith."

"Capital! capital!" cried the Governor, who, shading his eyes with his hand, was able to look askance upon what Edith was writing.

"I am glad I please you, sir."

"You do indeed, lady; pray proceed."

Edith continued to write.

"I am a prisoner in Newgate, my Felix; and a proposal of escape is made for me, provided, at some particular hour to-morrow night, you will be close at hand to receive me."

"That's it!" cried the Governor. "That's the little arrangement. Nothing could be better!"

"And alone!" added Edith.

"Bravo!" shouted the Governor. "' Close at hand to receive me, and alone.' You write a beautiful letter, Lady Edith."

Edith continued to write, and, as she did so, a dark shade came over the face of the Governor of Newgate.

"But, my Felix, as you value life, hope, and the love of your Edith, pay no attention to such transparently treacherous proposals; make no such arrangement with any one; for, be assured, the object is to betray you, and make your Edith ten times more wretched than she can ever be, so long as she is assured of your safety."

"Confusion!" roared the Governor.

"Does not the letter please you, sir?" said Edith, quietly and gently.

"Please me? of course not. What the deuce? What? What? Can you suspect me?"

"Oh, no!—no!"

"No?"

"I am certain!"

"Confound your certainty! That is not the sort of letter you promised to write."

"It is the only one I will write. I said that I would point out to you how it could be best delivered, and I will do so. Send any one with it to Epping Forest, and let him fasten it to any tree he chooses, and then come away without turning to see who takes it, and Captain Felix Heron will have the letter."

"Bah! What good will it do me to let him have the letter? Good night, Lady Edith; I leave you now to your fate, and swear by—by——"

"Heaven?"

"No—no! Don't go on in that way! Bah! I won't stay any longer!"

The Governor then raised his voice to rather a high pitch, as he called out, " It's a failure !"

That he was addressing some one, who, no doubt, had been close at hand as a listener to the interview, was evident enough ; and Edith had no doubt in her own mind that that listener was Jonathan Wild.

The Governor, however, flung down the basket, with its contents ; and without waiting to hear another word from his fair prisoner, he left the cell.

Edith could hear him double-lock the door, and shoot the ponderous bolts into their sockets, and then she was alone again.

Mechanically she turned towards the wall, from which the long narrow strip of light had come.

It was no longer visible.

The cell was in the most profound darkness, and Edith was compelled to hold out both her

arms as she moved, for fear of striking herself against the jagged stones of the walls.

But it was not for more than half an hour that Edith was left to darkness and to solitude.

Suddenly the light that came through the wall, at right angles to the door, shone again, and she thought, this time, more brightly than before.

Edith could scarcely forbear from the utterance of a cry of surprise and terror, as the narrow strip of light suddenly widened, and she became conscious that some change was taking place in the wall of the cell. The narrow crevice, through which the gleam of light had passed, was rapidly widening ; and the dim and uncertain twilight which had pervaded the cell, was scattered before a broad ray from a lantern, the vivid reflector of which sent its light, almost like sunshine, into that gloomy precinct.

Then there came a great, black shadow, which spread itself over the opposite side of the cell.

No. 81.—EDITH.

That was the shadow of a hand, thrown out in bold relief, as it was placed over the lens of the lantern.

And then, if poor Edith had before felt inclined to utter a cry of alarm, how much more was she incited to do so now, when she saw the unmistakable physiognomy of Jonathan Wild peering over the top of the lantern, which he shaded with one hand while he held it in the other.

And by so shading it the concentrated rays were thrown upwards into the hideous countenance of the thief-taker. His eyes looked like pieces of glistening metal; and there was altogether a diabolical expression of fury and hatred upon his face as he gazed upon Edith.

"So!" he cried, "we are cautious and careful are we, and proof against little temptations! You know me, of course?"

"Who shall behold you, monster," cried Edith, "and ever forget you?"

"Good! I am no beauty, I know. I've no pretensions in that line; and, as I can't be admired, the next best thing is to be feared."

"Or defied!" said Edith.

"That's as it may be; but at present I like you better for the expression. When it's open, then I know what to do, and there is no perplexity; so I tell you, Edith Tarleton—calling yourself Edith Heron—you may fancy yourself badly off at being a prisoner in Newgate, but you little know that you in reality stand only upon the threshold of the real prison that is opening to receive you."

"It is needless," said Edith, "that I should understand you, Jonathan Wild, because, as I say, I defy you."

"That is well. Your enlightenment will come soon enough. Affairs between me and Captain Heron have reached that pass that it was absolutely necessary that I should have some hostage for my own safety. In you I have the best that I can possibly procure. He is mad not to make terms with me, because, if he would do so, I would at once place him at the summit of his ambition, and Lord Warringdale, in four-and-twenty hours, would be a hunted fugitive; but that, you will say, is idle talk."

"It is," said Edith, sadly. "Not for the world's diadem and the world's wealth could Felix Heron ever stoop to a compact with such as you."

"Very well," added Wild. "Every one to his taste. I could make him Earl of Whitcombe, and you a Countess; but since he prefers a swing upon nothing at Tyburn Tree, and you think that you would look well as a hempen widow, so be it. I'm perfectly willing. Now, my lady, if you please, walk this way."

Edith shrunk back to the furthest corner of the cell.

She had heard too much of Newgate, and its connexion with Jonathan Wild's house, in Newgate Street, not to come to the conclusion that there might be some communication between the two; in fact, she recollected, even in that moment of terror and alarm, that she had often heard Captain Heron say he was certain Jonathan Wild had some underground means of reaching the cells of the great prison.

From the first moment that she had been consigned to a cell in Newgate, Edith had felt a degree of surprise that it should be so, because she could not but be well aware that no charge of any importance could be brought against her.

Cruel, treacherous, and unfeeling too as her father, Sir John Tarleton, was, he could not, for his own credit's sake, as one of the judges of the land, suffer her to be made the victim of an illegal prosecution.

Hence was it that Edith had been somewhat surprised that Jonathan Wild should think of carrying her to Newgate.

But she was far from being aware of the good understanding there was between the villanous thief-taker and the Governor of the prison.

It was true indeed that she was taken there, but it was only for the purpose of placing her more securely, because by an indirect route, in the power of the villain Wild.

Measures could be easily taken, by which it would seem that she had escaped from that cell in Newgate, while all the time she would be in a much more secure one at the house of Jonathan in Newgate Street.

That cell, number ten, and which still exists beneath the surface of that portion of the prison now in use, although it has been long since locked up, was the means of communication between Newgate and Jonathan Wild's house, which often went by the name of "Little Newgate."

There was a narrow circuitous passage, not of any very great length, since the back of Wild's residence and that side of Newgate next to Smithfield were tolerably close together, which connected them.

A well-contrived door in the side of the cell, and another of a similar construction in one of the cells of Jonathan's establishment, answered all the purpose.

Hence was it that Wild found no sort of difficulty in presenting himself before the astonished eyes of Edith.

Well did the ruffian know that his victim was as completely at his mercy as heaven could ever leave one of its creatures at the mercy of another.

He set down the lamp he carried, and stepped into the cell.

He folded his arms across his breast, and burst into one of his hideous laughs—one of those laughs which he was in the habit of ending with such startling abruptness.

Edith shuddered as she heard it.

"Now," said Wild, "never yet, although you and I have met before,—never yet were you so completely in the power of Jonathan Wild."

Edith shuddered.

"Newgate is above you," he added. "The cell door is locked and bolted. I am here; and were you to scream and shout with fifty-human power, there would be none to heed you—none to listen to you."

A cold feeling crept over the heart of Edith.

"Ah!" said Wild, "you feel your pretty situation now. Ha! ha!"

Edith gathered courage.

"No," she said,—"no."

"No what?"

"You no more dare attempt any outrage here than elsewhere; because you know that there is one who would find you, and avenge me, were you hidden thousands of feet beneath this damp earth on which we stand."

"In—deed!"

"Ay, Jonathan Wild, 'indeed,' and in truth. You know well that I speak the truth; and even now your coward-heart trembles at what may be the consequences of holding me a captive for a single hour!"

"Now, by all that's good, you are a bold girl to speak to me in such a fashion in such a place as this! But come, Edith Tarleton, or Edith Heron, or Countess of Whitcombe, whichever you may please to name yourself, I will put an end to your suspense. I want to make some terms with you—I want to set you free if I can. You are not one of those with whom I dare—that is, with whom I wish to trifle; and as I say, I will make terms with you."

Edith felt her heart palpitate rapidly, as the idea of again looking into the eyes of her much-loved Felix, and that quickly, too, come across her fancy.

"What terms? What ransom do you ask for me?" she said, eagerly.

"I will tell you."

"Speak quickly!"

"No. That is not my fashion. But I will soon tell you. I have a number of bonds and bills signed by Lord Warringdale, to be paid so soon as he is called to the House of Lords as Earl of Whitcombe. Will you, in the name of Felix Heron, undertake that I shall be paid them by him when he is Earl of Whitcombe, if this night I ride with you to Epping Forest?"

"I cannot."

"You can easily; for I feel assured that whatever you solemnly pledge your word to, Felix Heron will abide by."

"It may be so; and because I feel that it would be so, I ought to be only the more careful what it is I pledge my word to."

Wild made a gesture of impatience.

"You forget—you forget that you are a prisoner here. You quite forget that."

"No, no! Oh, no!"

"Then decide at once. Shall it be so, Countess of Whitcombe who shall be, if I, Jonathan Wild, but choose to say the word?"

"I cannot promise."

"You will not?"

"If you prefer the expression, be it so,—I will not."

"You are mad!"

"No. But I should, I fancy, be mad to have faith in Jonathan Wild."

"Very well; so be it. You see I am in no passion; I am quite calm and cool—the calmness and coolness of conscious power. I will now tell you what will happen. Sir John Tarleton will die this night—that I know."

"No, no, you cannot know it! The issues of life and death are not with such as you."

"Well, you can believe me or not, as you please. I say he will die to-night. Lady Castleneau is a prisoner; and at her age, she will remain so until death."

"That will I not believe."

"I don't want you to say you believe. I am quite satisfied that, upon reflection, you will do so. Sir Dominick Browne is by this time in the hands of my men."

"Oh, no, no, no!"

"But I say, oh, yes, yes, yes! Captain Heron will soon be a prisoner, and he will be hanged.

Let me see. Oh, yes! In eighteen days from now, at the October Sessions. We will put him down for the first Friday, so as to bring him into the first batch for Tyburn on the Monday."

"False!—false!"

"Very good! There will, then, remain only yourself to look to; and if you don't go mad, which it is likely enough you will, why you can still remain cooped up at my house. But if you do get a little cracked, I will make you Mrs. Jonathan Wild the seventh——No—let me see—the eighth, I mean——"

Edith disdained to reply to this rapidly-uttered harangue, but yet each word of it fell like drops of molten iron upon her heart.

What if, amid an accumulation of horrors, such as he had painted, her reason were really to give way, and she was no longer to have mind enough to say nay to some terrible proposition from the villain Wild?

The thought itself was half-way towards madness.

But Edith still had presence of mind enough to conceal the effect which his words had upon her.

"I defy you," she said,—"and I trust in heaven!"

"Very good!" said Wild; "I merely point out to you that you bring upon yourself and all whom you hold dear these countless miseries, because you will not consent, out of the princely revenues of the Whitcombe estates, to pay a sum of sixty thousand pounds. That's all."

"No, no; I have no right——"

"Very well. Now, follow me!"

Wild's voice, which had been somewhat modulated up to this point, now assumed a grating sternness, which made it resemble the angry growl of some wild animal.

"Follow me, girl," he said. "We shall see what sort of fate obstinacy prepares for itself."

"I will not follow you."

"You say that?"

"I do. Help! ho! help! I am a prisoner in Newgate, but Jonathan Wild is not my gaoler, or its Governor. Help! help! I claim the protection of the law, which mistakingly holds me captive. Help! help! murder!"

Edith flew to the door of the cell, and grasping with her fair, delicate hands the rough jagged rusted iron grating over the top of it, she shook it to and fro.

The door made a hollow rumbling sound, which was echoed by the brutal laugh of Jonathan Wild.

"I can wait," he said; "you will soon exhaust your strength and your hope."

Edith felt that there was a terrible truth in those words. She ceased to shake the door, and turning to Jonathan Wild, she said, "I do not appeal to your justice—I do not appeal to your compassion, but I do to your fears; and I tell you that any oppression I suffer, or any injury you heap upon me, will be as assuredly visited upon you tenfold, as the light of heaven will shine to-morrow."

"Blue!" cried Wild in a tone that had growing anger in it,—"Blue, where are you?"

"Here you are!" said some one in a gruff voice from the passage that conducted from the cell to Jonathan Wild's house.

"Come here at once."

" Here you are !"

The giant form of Blueskin made its appearance in the cell. Wild glanced at him for a few seconds in silence, and then he said harshly, " You are drunk !"

" Not a bit of it, Mr. Wild ; but you know I was very bad and nearly killed, and ever since then I have had a cold feel from the top of my head down to my great toe, and there's nothing does me half so much good as old rum now. But I'm as steady as Newgate, I am."

" There is your prisoner."

" Very good !"

" She will probably refuse to go."

" Very good !"

" I do refuse," cried Edith. " I will not even willingly abandon a cell of Newgate, to trust to the tender mercies of Jonathan Wild."

" Blue ?"

" Yes, Mr. Wild."

" Carry her."

" All's right !"

" Hold ! hold !" cried Edith. " I will walk ; no one can resist brute force. I will walk, since it must needs be so."

" I thought as much," said Wild ; " but you will recollect that she called you a brute, Blueskin."

―――

CHAPTER CLXXXI.

EDITH FINDS A FRIEND WHEN AND WHERE SHE LEAST EXPECTED ONE.

BLUESKIN did not seem at all affected at Jonathan Wild's suggestion that Edith had called him a brute. He held open the narrow door in the wall of the cell for his atrocious master to pass through.

Edith, with a shudder, followed Wild, who let her pass him in order that he might himself close the cell door.

There can be no doubt of the fact that Jonathan Wild was exceedingly angry at what he called the obstinacy of Edith.

The arch conspirator and unscrupulous villain had begun to see how very hopeless Lord Warringdale's pretensions to the peerage and to the estate of Whitcombe were becoming, and he would gladly have sold him to Captain Heron for the price of the bonds and other money acknowledgments he held.

The refusal of Edith to pledge herself in the name of Heron to any such arrangement, was very exasperating to him ; and hence was it that he committed a folly, as he then stood at the door in the wall of the cell, which had very important results.

He slammed the door so sharply that he caught in it a small portion of the dress of Edith.

The fabric was not strong, and it gave way, leaving projecting into the cell number ten, a piece of cloth not more than half an inch in width, but still amply sufficient to point out the fact that there was some opening in the wall through which some one had passed with some garment, of which that small piece was a portion.

Edith herself thought that Jonathan Wild had touched her when she felt the sudden check to her

progress ; and she turned sharply as she exclaimed, with more of loathing than terror, " Wretch ! do not contaminate me by your touch ! I am your prisoner for a time, but not your victim !"

" Bah !" said Wild ; " you know not what you say. I touched you not ! Take her on, Blueskin, and see that the ' Lower Deep ' is well secured !"

" Why, Mr. Wild !" said Blueskin, " you don't mean to go for to say――"

" What, wretch ?"

" That you will have this chick of a girl put into the ' Lower Deep ?' "

" I will ! I will ! Who will dare to say me nay ?"

" Nobody, Mr. Wild, if you will do it ; but it's not safe, I say !"

" Not safe ?"

" No ! There's not one of the men but will know of it ; and as sure as rum is rum—and I only wish I had some now—they will speak of it. If you want to keep this dicky-bird in a good cage, stick to the house, Mr. Wild, and let the cells alone. Keep her up stairs, and nobody but you and me will know you have her, so nobody will quack about it, and bring the big-wigs about you."

Wild considered for a moment or two, and then he muttered, " There is some truth in what this thick-skulled fellow says. Hark you, Blueskin ! I want to keep this—this――"

" Chickabiddy !" said Blueskin, thinking Wild was at a loss for a word.

" Pshaw ! I want to keep her, for many reasons. As yet, only you and I know that she is in my power. If I place her in one of the strong rooms at the top of the house, will you be answerable for her safe keeping ?"

" To be sure I will !"

" Then be it so ; but remember, if she should escape, no one can possibly be to blame but you."

" I know !"

" And the consequences will be upon your own head, where you may be assured you will feel them."

" All's right !"

" Take her there ; you know the way as well as I do. Edith, I will visit you――"

Wild paused a moment, and then with a mock bow he added—" when you least expect me."

Edith did not reply, but followed Blueskin, who adopted an odd mode of being sure that she was coming after him. Between his thumb and finger he took hold of a corner of her sleeve, and so led her along the narrow gloomy passage which connected Wild's house with that number ten cell of old Newgate.

The distance was not great, and they soon came to a flight of stairs, which led to the ground floor of the house.

But in that short progress, Edith was terrified and afflicted by hearing cries, and shouts, and shrieks, and groans of distress.

The light which Blueskin carried no doubt sent some dim rays and pencils of illumination into the wretched cells where Wild kept his victims. Through key-holes and crevices, no doubt, that light found its way, and then there arose the cries, shrieks, and moans for mercy.

" Let me out ! Oh, let me out, Mr. Wild ! I will tell you where the booty is hidden ; I will,

JONATHAN WILD HANDS EDITH OVER THE TENDER GUARDIANSHIP OF BLUE-SKIN.

Presented Gratis with No. 81 of the New Edition of the Captive; or, the Robbers of Epping Forest.

EACH WEEK IS PRESENTED WITH A COLOURED ENGRAVING.

indeed! Oh, mercy! mercy! I am innocent—I am, indeed! Why am I kept here? Murder! murder! murder!"

Edith might well shudder as these and such-like cries met her ears; and Blueskin, who saw that she was affected, remarked, "The birds will sing sometimes in their cages, you see, and they hits their wings agin the bars, in a manner o' speaking. For, bless you, little 'un, some on em knocks theirselves to pieces agin the walls!"

Edith did not reply, but she felt in full force the terror of these remarks, and a feeling of thankfulness came over her that she was not compelled to make one of that miserable fraternity occupying those fearful cells in the foundation of Jonathan Wild's house.

And yet she knew not whether to be thankful to Blueskin or not, for his interposition in her favour; because she had no means of deciding in her own mind what had dictated it.

Still it was a great relief to find that she was ascending, instead of descending, a narrow flight of slippery stairs, and leaving behind her the noisome atmosphere of that subterraneous region.

"Ah!" cried Blueskin, "you'll be as snug as possible. You see, it's no use saying no to Mr. Jonathan Wild; and if so be as a drop of rum now and then will be any comfort, why, I dare say, the old 'un will get it for you."

Who the "old 'un" might possibly be, who was to be so gracious as to procure a drop of rum, if required, Edith had no means of knowing; but certainly as step by step she ascended that staircase, she felt as if she left a load of grief and care behind her.

Coarse and brutal as was Blueskin, she much more willingly followed him than she would Jonathan Wild; and indeed, even at that moment, Edith was not without a hope that there might be beneath the rough exterior of the huge animal, who appeared so willing to do Jonathan Wild's behests, some feelings of compassion, perhaps of tenderness, that might be acted upon for her advantage.

But she forbore to say anything to Blueskin until they began actually to ascend the staircases in Wild's house.

They met with no one in their progress, for it was that time of the night when only the watch —which, in imitation of the larger Newgate, next door to him, Wild kept in the hall of his house— was up and about.

Up two flights of staircases they took their way, and then they came to a door heavily studded with iron nails, and apparently cutting off all communication between the upper and lower portions of the house.

"Here you are!" said Blueskin: "there's nobody can come a-nigh you up here, and you won't have nothing to complain about. There's lots o' rats down below, but they never comes higher than the first floor! You'll be comfortable enough, and I'll send the old 'un!"

"Who do you mean?" said Edith, as Blueskin unlocked, with a master-key, which he had in his possession, the heavy door which had arrested their progress only for a moment.

"Who do I mean by the old 'un?"

"Yes. If it be any one who is to come in contact with me, I would fain know who it is."

"Why, it's old Mother Shackles, if you must know. She had a nice situation in the Stone Jug till she got the *rhumatiz*, and couldn't do the work, so she lives here now, and brings up hot water, and glasses, and spoons to Jonathan, when he wants a drop of comfort after a hanging Monday. Ah! she had a very tidy situation, indeed, in the Stone Jug."

"What was it?"

Edith thought it was as well to be on good terms with this man, and, even, in some measure, to encourage his garrulity.

"Why, you see, little 'un, it wasn't work, so to speak, but a kind of agreeable play and amusement. She had to lay out the *corpusses* of them as was hung at Tyburn, when they came back in the cart. Them as was owned then was given up, and the rest of 'em went to the doctors to be made skeletons of, and all that sort of thing. But here you are! This'll be the cage."

Blueskin had reached the top of Jonathan Wild's house, accompanied by Edith, and, lifting a heavy bar from the back of a door, he unlocked it, and pointed, with something like exultation, as though he were showing her quite a charming apartment, into a wretched attic, the closely barred window of which was so begrimed with dust and rain, that it was doubtful, even at mid-day, whether there would be anything but a dubious twilight within.

Edith could not then forbear from uttering an exclamation of surprise—perhaps, too, the exclamation had some slight element of gratification in it,—for she recollected, at the moment, that apartment as the very one in which she had before been imprisoned by Jonathan Wild, and where she had first made the acquaintance of Ogle, as he looked down upon her from the trap-door in the roof.

A feeling of hopefulness came over her at her recognition of the place.

Once again she was there a prisoner to Jonathan Wild, but might not Felix Heron find his way again to that prison-house, and, as before, rescue her?

She felt how admirable was the change from the gloomy cell in Newgate to that attic, although it was in the house of Jonathan Wild—her worst enemy. It was with a feeling something akin to satisfaction that she passed through its doorway, and then the idea came across her that if she could only make a friend of Blueskin, a speedy deliverance from the terrors and the perils of her present position might not be far off.

It was with this feeling that Edith turned to the rough janissary of Jonathan Wild, and spoke to him with that winning sweetness and gentleness which surely, if he were human at all, must reach his heart.

"I recognise this place," she said. "Once before I was a prisoner to Jonathan Wild; and then, as now, I was as innocent of any offence towards him, or any one else, as it was possible to be."

"Very good!" said Blueskin. "Nobody has ever done anything that's brought here—it's only suspicion, of course."

"But I want to tell you," added Edith, "that I am suffering from great oppression; and that although it may suit the private interests of Jonathan Wild to keep me here a prisoner, I am surprised that it should suit yours to assist him."

This speech was rather too much for Blueskin, and all he did in reply was to look vacantly round the room, and say that he thought it very likely.

"Ah!" cried Edith,—"if you would but be my friend!"

"All's right!" said Blueskin. "Anything you want, I'm sure you shall have."

"There is but one want to a prisoner."

"All's right! I'll send it up by the old 'un. A glass of rum-and-water, sweet and hot."

"You do not understand me. It is liberty I want."

"Eh?"

"It is freedom from this place. There is no possible reward that Jonathan Wild can give you which I cannot ensure you ten times over at the hands of Captain Heron, if you will but find a means of setting me free."

"Oh, that's it, is it?"

"It is, indeed! And if you entertain the proposition, say so at once, and lighten this poor heart of half its burden of care and sorrow."

"Can't do it, marm!—can't do it! Didn't the Governor say I was to be 'sponsible, and something would fall on my head if I let you go—consequences, or something of that 'ere sort, rather hard, I reckon. Can't do it, marm, for you're quite safe here; so all you've got to do is to make yourself comfortable."

"So be it," said Edith. "But the first guess of him who will fly to my assistance will most assuredly be that I am the prisoner of Jonathan Wild."

"Very good!" said Blueskin. "I'll send up old Mother Shackles, and she'll amuse you with an account of the last eight men as was hung for horse-stealing, and that she laid out when they came in from Tyburn. She'll be quite pleasant company, she will. Good night, marm! Can't do it! I only wish somebody would put me in a attic, with nothing to do but to drink and smoke all day! I s'pose you wouldn't like a pipe? Excuse me for offering it to one of the fair sex, but Mother Shackles, she smokes like a good 'un,—only I suppose none of you begins till you gets what you calls a certain age. Good night, marm! Can't do it!"

Blueskin left the attic.

Edith heard the lock shot sharply into the staple. She heard the heavy bar placed across the door, and a feeling of desolation began again to creep across her, although she could not be said to feel utterly hopeless.

The attic was intensely dark; for, if in daylight, in consequence of the begrimed state of the windows, but little light found its way to that little apartment in the roof of Jonathan Wild's house at that hour, the window had all the appearance of a blank wall through which the slight twilight of the night-sky had no chance of penetrating.

And yet the mere fact that she was there, in a place not wholly strange to her, seemed to have a grateful influence on the mind of Edith. She could not help associating the place with the gallant rescue achieved by Captain Heron, as well as with those kindly expressions of sympathy and friendship which had come from the lips of Ogle, dictated, though they were, at that time, by an eye to his own interests; for the very air of Wild's house had, for a time, vitiated all the better feelings of that afterwards faithful and attached follower of Captain Heron.

Edith was in this state of mind when she started to hear a noise above her, and could almost have believed that a repetition of the whole circumstances was about to occur, but that she heard a voice, the sounds of which were only too well known to her in their grating harshness.

It was the voice of Wild.

"Edith, Edith!" he said—"you seek in vain to corrupt the good faith of a man who scarcely understands the language you speak. Ogle was treacherous, and he will still pay for that treachery with his blood, but Blueskin I can trust: not that I mean to do so, for I never really trust any one; so, in order to put your mind quite at ease in respect of any attempt at rescue, I beg to inform you that I shall pass my time, except when otherwise urgently occupied—and you will never know when that may be—on the roof, here!"

The moment Wild ceased speaking, there was the sharp sound of the sudden closing of the small trap-door in the ceiling of the attic.

Then all was still.

Reply would have been useless to such a speech from Jonathan Wild, even if Edith had been left the opportunity to make it; and although it was contrary to reason to believe that Jonathan Wild spoke the truth, when he talked of passing the better part of his time on the roof of his own house, yet if he were sometimes there it might materially affect her chances of escape.

And now, what could she do but wait—wait and hope, in the expectation that Felix Heron would find a means of discovering her whereabouts, and rescue her from the perils of her situation?

And well, indeed, might Edith entertain this hope, for if by some strange accidents of evil fortune she fell into the hands of her enemies, yet amid those accidents there were ever some which pointed out to those who would befriend her, the path to her rescue.

This time it was a small fragment of woollen cloth in the crevice of an otherwise hidden doorway, upon which hung the liberty, perhaps the life, of Edith.

CHAPTER CLXXXII.

CAPTAIN HERON'S BAND FIND THEMSELVES DANGEROUSLY SITUATED IN THE VESTIBULE OF NEWGATE.

THE long delay which took place, while Ogle and the other companions of Captain Heron waited in vain for his re-appearance in the vestibule of Newgate, began to suggest serious and disquieted ideas.

The morning was coming, and although it was not that time of the year when the sunrise made itself manifest at its earliest hour, yet a comparatively short time must bring the dawn into the streets of London, and about the cold, grey stones of Newgate.

Various changes would then, no doubt, take place within the prison; and the position of those who held the vestibule for the present against all comers, both from within and without, would become untenable.

So soon as people began to pass in the street, the danger of discovery would be great; and no wonder then was it that Ogle listened with feelings of great disquietude for any sound from the interior of Newgate, which should indicate the success or failure of Captain Heron

But no sound came. The time occupied by Heron in enforcing the Governor's attendance to the cell where Edith was said to be imprisoned, had been considerable.

To Ogle it appeared to be an age; and, at length losing all patience, and almost all expectation of beholding Heron, he held a whispered consultation with those of the band who were nearest to him.

What was to be done? That was the question. Not as regarded their own safety, but what was to be done for the purpose of rescuing their Captain, if, indeed, any misadventure had befallen him in the interior of Newgate?

This consultation, however, had hardly proceeded beyond a few words, when it was abruptly put an end to by a circumstance which was at once a practical answer to the question regarding the success or failure of Captain Heron in his adventurous enterprise.

The alarm-bell of Newgate began to toll.

The moment its notes fell upon the ears of the officers who had been captured, and who lay so much at the mercy of Captain Heron's band, they could not forbear from making some slight movements of satisfaction; and Ogle, turning short to one of them, said abruptly, "Is there any change in the custom? or are all the men employed in Newgate to assemble here in the vestibule upon the ringing of the alarm-bell, as they used to do?"

The turnkey, to whom Ogle spoke, was gagged, and could not reply to him in words, but he nodded his head, which was equally satisfactory and significant.

"Then," said Ogle, turning to the band, "I fear that something has happened, and that our Captain is a prisoner. Ah! now we shall know more!"

Exactly at the entrance of the passage through which Captain Heron had left the vestibule, in company with the Reverend Mortification Ripon, there appeared the Governor of Newgate, who reached the spot with a sudden rush, and a strange yell of exultation, which betrayed an excitement of mind which said little for the discretion of his movements.

In each hand he held a large brass-barrelled pistol; and he cried out, in a voice that rung through the vestibule, "You're nabbed, all of you! —there's no chance of escape! Captain Heron is a prisoner, and orders you all to surrender!"

"That's not true!" said Ogle.

"That is, though!" cried the Governor, as he levelled one of the large pistols full at Ogle head, and pulled the trigger.

These pistols were a pair which always hung up in the Governor's room, labelled "loaded," and so, probably, they were; but they had been in that condition for so long a time, that the probabilities of their being useful at an emergency were few indeed. That one which the Governor levelled and fired at Ogle, would certainly, if it had done its duty, have deprived Captain Heron of that gallant and faithful follower, and this history of one of its characters.

But the pistol only flashed in the pan, sending up a dull flame for a moment, and a wreath of smoke.

Several of the band were upon the point of making a rush upon the governor; but Ogle cried in a loud voice, "Stand back—I'll see to him!"

Then Ogle saw that the Governor had turned, and was making his escape, which he would inevitably have done; for one of the officers, tied hand and foot as he was, managed to fling himself exactly in Ogle's way; and it was a hundred to one that the latter would fall over him, and permit the escape of the Governor.

But this was not to be.

Ogle saw the movement, and instead of rushing forward—which would have been perfectly futile—he gathered up all his energies into one tremendous leap, and alighting firmly on the back of the Governor, they both fell together, exactly at the entrance to the passage.

The pistol which had failed him had been flung on to the stone slabs by the Governor, but he had retained the other; and it was not until Ogle alighted on him with such crushing force that he parted with it, and then, on its fall, it immediately exploded.

"You used the wrong one!" cried Ogle, as he grasped the Governor by the throat; "a touch at that trigger, and I should have been a dead man!"

Mingled with Ogle's words there came a yell of dismay from the outside of the wicket gate of Newgate, and the Reverend Mortification Ripon, who had just reached the top of the steps, rolled backwards, right out into the Old Bailey, in the full belief that a bullet was in his brain, for that which had flown from the pistol just discharged, had struck his hat from his head, making at the same time a capricious kind of furrow, just skin deep, over the top of his skull.

The Reverend Mortification Ripon had been round to Wild's house, in obedience to the injunctions of the Governor; and when he met with so alarming a reception, he was upon the point of crying out "Mr. Wild is coming, and the wretches will all be taken!" but the words were smothered in their birth, and the reverend gentleman lay prostrate in the kennel.

Ogle had the Governor safely in his custody, and had fairly dragged him into the middle of the vestibule.

The alarm bell of Newgate, however, still continued to sound, and the position of Ogle, and the members of Captain Heron's band who were with him, was indeed most critical.

Ogle had but one hope.

The Governor might have the power and the immediate means to quiet the alarm; and fear might induce him to exercise that power, and bring those means into action.

Ogle did not rave at him; he did not even look angry, or use any violent expressions; but in a voice that was so cool, collected, and concentrated in its firmness, that it fell like cold water on the heart of the Governor, he said, "Choose, sir; choose between death, and the stopping of the sound of that bell."

232 EDITH THE CAPTIVE.

"I cannot."

"That is your misfortune."

"What do you mean?"

"Hold him by the back of the neck, number four, and I will blow his brains out."

"No! no!" yelled the Governor. "I will stop the bell. Ah, no! It is too late! too late! Help! murder! You may kill me if you like, but you shall swing for it."

It was positive desperation that gave the Governor of Newgate courage to speak as he did; and to that acquired courage of the moment, he, in all human probability, owed his life; for angry and excited as Ogle was, he certainly was the last man to commit a deliberate and cold-blooded murder.

If the Governor had had any weapon of offence or defence in his hand with which he could have "made a fight for it," no doubt that moment would have been his last.

As it was, however, Ogle saw, by the direction of his eyes, what it was that had given him the extraordinary courage and nerve to act as he did. That direction into which he glared was towards the wicket gate of Newgate, from the outer or street side of which several persons were looking into the vestibule.

That these were some of the officers who were non-resident in the prison, but who had heard the alarm-bell, and so sought its precincts to see what was the matter, Ogle did not doubt.

There did not, however, appear to be more than three or four of them.

Truly there was no time to lose.

Ogle let go his grasp of the throat of the Governor, and made a rush to the door that shut up the narrow vaulted passage from the vestibule to the interior of the prison.

He was only just in time.

The alarm-bell had rung for a space of about three minutes, and it had done its duty; for from all the stone passages and gloomy corridors of Newgate, the various turnkeys and officers on duty were hurrying to the vestibule, as was the understood arrangement whenever the alarm-bell was rung.

Ogle dashed the door shut, and secured it with an iron bar that went across it.

The passage, which was then closed, had an arched roof, but the door was rectangular; so that when it was closed there was, necessarily, a small open portion above it, between its straight top and the ceiling of the narrow, gloomy stone passage.

It was through this opening now that one of the turnkeys, who had hurried to the hall of Newgate upon hearing the alarm bell, looked, having mounted on the back of a comrade to enable him to do so.

"What's the row?" he cried. "What's amiss?"

"Open the wicket!" shouted those who were without.

"Help! help! Thieves! Murder!" yelled the Governor, who probably, by this time, began to think that, as he was not despatched at once, there was no real intention to kill him.

The confusion was great.

The peril was great.

And all these events, which have taken some seconds in the telling, did not take one quarter of the time in the acting, inasmuch as they were simultaneous.

"Silence?" cried Ogle.

The voice in which he spoke had that sudden effect upon anybody which a loudly uttered command will generally have upon a number of persons, who obey it before they have time to reason upon it.

There was a momentary lull, therefore, in the tumult of sounds, both within and without the vestibule of Newgate.

The only noise that still continued was the sound of the alarm-bell; and as the Governor, before he came to the vestibule, had set a boy to ring it, with orders to keep on until he saw him, the Governor, again, on it went.

Then Ogle spoke.

"Your pistols, comrades!" he said. "Shoot all who oppose you, and follow me!"

"Over you, you mean!" cried the turnkey, who was standing on the back of one of his fellows, and looking from the narrow vaulted passage into the vestibule.

At the same moment that he spoke, he fired a pistol at Ogle.

The couple of bullets that were in it tore past the cheek of Ogle, inflicting a slight wound only.

Then there mingled with the echoes of the pistol-discharge another loud report, and, with a yell of pain, the turnkey disappeared.

"Mine was the best shot, I take it!" said Ogle coolly. "Now, comrades, come on! Out of the way, will you, idiots!"

Ogle dashed open the wicket-gate, and the last words he spoke were addressed to the three or four men who were outside, and so completely astounded were they at his audacity, that they actually fell back for a moment or two. Then a sense of duty and shame came over them, and they closed with their assailants.

A brief contest took place upon the very steps of Newgate, but it ended almost as soon as it began in the discomfiture of the officers, and Ogle, with his comrades, were fairly in the open street.

Some clock struck four.

"Forward, men!" cried Ogle. "We shall have the dawn yet to light us to old Epping Forest, where we may find the Captain has arrived before us, after all, for he is not the man to remain long even in the Stone Jug."

Some early stray passengers, who had business at Smithfield Market, stopped aghast at the tumult and struggle of men that came tearing and toiling down the steps of the prison, but they had the wisdom not to interfere with what did not concern them, and what would, no doubt, have produced more blows than profit.

Ogle rushed over the way to the old inn.

"The horses—the horses!" he cried. "Once in the saddle, my men, and you are safe!"

The cry was heard by that old acquaintance of Ogle's who had charge of the horses; and in a moment the gate of the inn was flung open.

"All right and ready!" shouted the man.

"That will do," said Ogle. "Mount—mount, my men! For your own sakes, mount at once! On horseback you are safe!"

A yell, something like what might have come from the throat of a hyena, who by some carelessness of his keeper had contrived to escape from

his den, at that moment echoed through the Old Bailey.

It came from the throat of a man without a hat, who had just turned out of Newgate Street, and who was scampering along the pavement at full speed.

That man was Jonathan Wild.

"Kill—kill!" he yelled. "Kill them all! A hundred guineas for every dead body! Kill them all!"

"Not yet," said Ogle, calmly now, as the whole of the band sallied out from the inn-yard mounted and ready for the road.

Ogle had hold of a horse, on which the terribly bewildered Lord Warringdale was mounted, and he had whispered in his ear, "My lord, I want to carry you alive to Epping Forest; but if you would prefer to go there dead, it is at your own option, for alive or dead I intend to take you there."

No. 82.—EDITH.

Lord Warringdale did not reply to these words, but he shook in every limb.

"Forward! march!" cried Ogle.

Jonathan Wild saw that he was too late. He stopped about twenty paces from Newgate, and stooping down so as to command a good view before him, he fired at random among the band, in quick succession, two pistols he had with him.

"Shot for shot, and no more," said Ogle. "Fire at him, my men."

Bang! bang! went two shots at Wild, and then Ogle heard a strange sound close to him, and he saw that Lord Warringdale was hanging over the horse's neck, and groaning.

"What's the matter, my lord?"

"The villain Wild has shot me."

"That, indeed, is retribution," said Ogle; "and if you can only get him hanged, there will be a capital end of both of you."

"Oh, mercy! mercy! oh, agony!"

"Where are you hit?"

"The—the breast. Oh, I choke! Blood! blood! I shall die!"

Lord Warringdale slid from the saddle, and fell to the roadway; Ogle only holding by his coat as he did so with sufficient firmness to break his fall, and then he released his hold entirely.

"Be it so," he said. "If this is the end of my Lord Warringdale, I do not see that we need trouble ourselves further about him. Now, comrades, off we go!"

The band, with each a pistol in his hand, while the left held the horse's reins well gathered up, dashed up the Old Bailey, and amid shouts and cries from Jonathan Wild, and the officers, and turnkeys, they went up Giltspur Street, and so on into Smithfield.

The want of horses ready for any such service rendered pursuit perfectly useless, and Ogle was therefore able to bring off the band in perfect safety and apparent triumph. But his heart felt heavy, as the uncertainties regarding the fate of Captain Heron pressed upon it.

Ogle did not think proper, however, to dispirit the band by any such ideas. He rather sought to keep up the notion that Heron would be all safe, and probably at Epping Forest.

But, for all that, Ogle felt a reluctance to ride away from the old stone walls, which, for all he knew to the contrary, might contain Captain Heron as one of their prisoners.

Yet what else could he do?

To have remained in the vestibule of Newgate would have been absolute madness.

To have attempted to dive deeper into the prison would only have caused destruction to himself and to the whole of the band.

Ogle sighed deeply, and felt sick at heart; and yet he was quite sure he had done just what he ought, and Captain Heron would himself. How indeed could he, in the midst of all that danger and confusion, have made his voice heard?

That was a consolation.

After passing through Smithfield, and reaching the Goswell Road, all appearance or sound of pursuit had vanished, and Ogle called a halt.

It was half-past four o'clock then, and the only person who observed that strange troop of horsemen was a watchman, who had been suddenly awakened from a deep sleep in his watch-box, and who glanced at them in silent surprise, hardly being able to make up his mind if they were of this world or not.

Ogle and his comrades paid no attention whatever to this watchman. He was too insignificant a person to be of any account amid the more important affairs they had to consider. They therefore held a consultation not far from his box, and heeded him as little as though he had formed a portion only of its wood-work.

"Friends and comrades all!" said Ogle, "I want you to speak freely, and say what you think should be done. The Captain, you know, left me in full command; but you all have wits of your own, and I should like you to say what you think, since you know all about what has happened as well as I do?"

The men were silent for a few moments, and then one said, "It seems, Mr. Ogle, that the Captain has met with a misfortune, and has been nabbed, and is now in the Stone Jug."

"It may be so."

"Then we all give in to you; and whatever you think is best, by way of trying to get him out, we will do, won't we, comrades—eh?"

"All! all!" said the rest of the band.

"Then," said Ogle, "hear me, and I will tell you what I think will be for the best. It is not force now that will do any good, because all the traps are on their guard; but cunning may do something. I will stay in town alone, and get information;—I don't want a horse, it might only embarrass me, and prove dangerous. Leave me, all of you, and be off to the forest. I will find a means of sending for you, if it's for the good of the Captain you should all come to town again."

The band acquiesced silently in this plan of Ogle's, and the horses' heads were turned again towards the north-east, while Ogle dismounted.

"Be careful," he said, "of the approaches to the forest!"

"We will, Mr. Ogle, and we only wish we were all in the way to watch over the Captain's safety, and yours too."

"Watch the forest avenues: you will do as well, and better too, than in town. All that I can do for the Captain must now be done by finesse. I will watch Newgate well, believe me."

The watchman, who was the silent spectator of this strange scene, was each moment getting more and more wide awake; but still he was not so close to Ogle and the band as to catch distinctly all that they said. The word "watch," however, was one so familiar to his ears that, as it happened to be repeated several times, he caught it; and imagining at once that it referred to him, he set up a yell that was enough to alarm the whole neighbourhood.

The horses of Captain Heron's men started at the sound, and reared.

"Silence that fool!" cried several of them.

"Leave him to me!" said Ogle; "ride off at once, and leave him to me!"

The watchman, by this time, had disengaged his rattle, and began to spring it violently.

"Peace, idiot!" said Ogle, as he dealt him a blow that sent him, doubled up, at once to the bottom of the watch-box.

At that moment Ogle heard the sound of horses' feet coming up the Goswell Road at a great rate, and then a voice—which could proceed from no other lungs than those of Jonathan Wild—awakened the night echoes by shouting, "Forward! forward! We shall soon come upon their track! Forward! We are as well mounted now as they are!"

"Ah!" said Ogle quietly to himself, "so Jonathan has got a horse at last, has he; and, with some of his janissaries, is on the track of the band. It is not worth while that he should hinder them. I think I can play him a trick, to begin with, that will save me some trouble, if they should chance to see me, and put him off on a wrong scent."

Ogle turned to the watch-box, close to him, and opened it adroitly.

The moment he did so, the watchman rolled out on to the pavement.

To divest the "guardian of the night" of his huge box-coat, his red nightcap, his lantern, bludgeon, and rattle was the work of a few seconds to Ogle, who attired himself in these spoils of the field; and then, having dragged the still insensible watchman behind the watch-box, where, in the darkness, he was not likely to be seen, Ogle took his place within it to personate the watchman.

These preparations were scarcely complete, when up rode Jonathan Wild, with a couple of mounted men.

"Hilloa!" cried Wild, as he saw the glare of the lantern, which Ogle took good care to render sufficiently conspicuous,—"hilloa, watchman! Was it you who sprung your rattle?"

"Bedad, then, sir," said Ogle, who could imitate the Hibernian accent to the life,—"bedad, then, sir, it was my own self. The spalpeen just tipped me a crack on the head of me, and says he, 'Go to sleep,' says he; an' if my head had not belonged to the O'Keefes, it's small life would be left in me."

"Who did it?"

"A horse on a man—no, be aisy, I mean the t'other thing—a man on a horse; and a lot of the raparees there was, and one of 'em called the other Bogle, he did."

"Ogle, you mean."

"Bedad, an' that's it!"

"Which way did they all go?"

"They went to the left; and one on 'em said, says he, 'It's the New River we'll cross,' says he."

"That will do! This is the way!"

"Ah, thin, won't your honour give me a tester for the sake of the news I give your honour?"

"No, the credit is enough. I am Jonathan Wild."

"Bedad, thin your honour is the very gintleman they spoke of."

"Indeed! What did they say of me?"

"That your honour was the greatest thief, rascal, and murdering villain in the land."

Wild ground his teeth with rage, and, without a word more, spurred on.

CHAPTER CLXXXIII.

LORD WARRINGDALE HAS SAVED HIS LIFE BY A GOOD PIECE OF ACTING.

"THAT will do!" said Ogle, as he emerged from the watch-box, and looked about him in the silence and serenity of that hour in the Goswell Road. All was still; for the inhabitants, who heard the alarm given by the watchman, were too well used at that period of time in London to the sounds of street-rioting, to pay much attention to them.

And now, although Ogle had made up his mind for a time to return to Epping Forest, while Captain Heron was in London, and in danger, it could not be said that he had any very well defined idea what would be the best course for him to adopt.

Indeed, it would be impossible for him to lay down any plan of operations without some further information than he at present possessed, and how to get that information was his first difficulty—if it could be called a difficulty to one so fertile in resources and with so accurate a knowledge of London life as he possessed.

"I think I know how to set about it," said Ogle, after a few moments' communing with himself. "Yes, that will do! That will do excellently!"

What it was that was to do so excellently will be best seen in the action which Ogle was by no means slow about, for, throwing off the watchman's coat, he set off at a good round pace towards Newgate again.

But it was no part of Ogle's intention to show himself just as he was in the immediate neighbourhood of the prison; and so, by a number of cross cuts, diving down narrow alleys, and making his way skilfully through nests of courts, which none but one singularly well acquainted with the back thoroughfares of London could have threaded with anything like certainty or security, he reached the classic region of Field Lane.

That thoroughfare may still live in the recollection of Londoners, as well as of provincials, who may peruse these pages, although it has now been swept away.

Field Lane commenced at Holborn Bridge—that is to say, exactly at the foot of Holborn Hill, and proceeded in a narrow, ill-defined kind of fashion towards Clerkenwell.

There it was that the pickpocket, the footpad, or the burglar could, in a few moments, get rid of his spoils at a tariff of prices scarcely commensurate with the risk run by the children of Israel who purchased them.

There it was, too, if any gentleman of the road required safety for a short time, he could find it; for, upon pulling down the houses, it was discovered that no less than twelve of them adjoining had secret means of communication, the one with the other, in two directions.

Hence the strongest party of officers who might venture into that region in search of any gentleman who was "wanted" might be dodged most effectually.

There it was, too, that the perpetrator of any robbery might exchange, upon equitable terms, in a few minutes, all the outward apparel in which he had committed the depredation, and emerge quite a new man upon Holborn Hill.

Ogle had not exactly committed a robbery; but it was to effect some change of this sort that he repaired to Field Lane.

At that hour of the night, or rather of the early morning, the houses in the lane were apparently closed: we say apparently—because, in reality, every one was open—that is to say, open to the initiated, who knew how to knock for admission.

Of course but two classes of people ever repaired to these residences—namely thieves, and officers in pursuit of them. The former repaired there very frequently, the latter rarely.

No single officer of the police could have had the hardihood to venture, either by night or by day, sufficiently far across the threshold of one of those houses to be out of sight of the passing world without.

In fact, Field Lane might be called a place of sanctuary and security for depredators, and one vast warehouse of stolen goods.

There did not require any discrimination on the part of Ogle as to which door he tapped at—they were all alike so far as he was concerned—and within any one of them he would be quite certain of getting the accommodation he required.

The door of the house to which he made his way opened, as if by magic, in response to his knock for admission, and Ogle, stepping into a dark passage, cried out, "A change of togs, and no mistake! One gentleman wants to be mistaken for another!—spangles to pay, and lots of 'em!"

A light flashed in the passage instantly, and a gentleman of the Hebrew persuasion—who had certainly not thought it necessary to wash his face for the last twelvemonths—appeared, shading a lighted candle with one hand, while he looked over the top of it at his visitor.

"Don't you know me?" said Ogle.

"Blesh my soul, Mishter Ogles! I does; but, my dear, you got into a bad way, for you joined Mr. Wilds!"

"But I left him!"

"To be sure you did, and took to honest courses again like a gentlemans; and how ish Captain Heron, and all the other gentlemans? He's a peautiful youth; and if it should cost me sheven and sixpence for a hackney-coach, I'll go and see the last of him at Tyburns whenever it happens!"

"It will never happen!" cried Ogle; "but that's not the question now! Look at me well, Isaacs; I want an alteration; and such an alteration that nobody but you would know me."

"Goot! very goot!" said the Jew; "you're a nice man, Mishter Ogles, and we can alter you to anything. What do you say to being a sojer, now—a desertar, you know—or a sailor that's just left his ship at the Tower Wharf?"

"No, Isaacs—no! I want to be something quiet; I want to do a little of the sneak business in the way of listening, and must not attract attention."

"Goot! very goot! Then you shall be an old gentlemans with white hair, and very hard of hearing. Come thish way; there's nobody but a lady here with some shilver spoons and forks—a most respectable lady, and her name's Ripon."

"What?" cried Ogle; "you don't mean to tell me that Mrs. Ripon is here?"

"Yesh, my dear Mishter Ogles, and a most respectable lady. She used to live in Little Swallow Street, but the house was burnt down; and now she's taken a purty little crib in Star Court, St. Martin's Lane; but she keeps up the old connection, and brings any little bit of gilt or glitter here—'cos, you shee, Mishter Ogles, ladies don't understand the melting-pot so well as we do."

"I comprehend—I comprehend; and this is most fortunate!"

"Ish it?"

"It is indeed!"

"Then you won't mind paying a little more, my dear Mishter Ogles?"

"Certainly I won't. But are you aware, Isaacs, that Mrs. Ripon has taken into her confidence a man who has adopted her name, and calls himself the Reverend Mortification Ripon?"

"Yesh; we all know it."

"A dangerous man, I should call him, Isaacs; a man to put no trust in; one who would betray her, you, and the whole family, to the highest bidder, — ay, even to Jonathan Wild himself, with whom I happen to know he is in constant communication. He is a villain, who, under the garb of pretended sanctity, is capable of any treachery."

"My dear Mishter Ogles, we know it—we know

it. He ish useful just now; we suspect him, and as soon as we suspect a little more, a square hole will open, and down he will go in the Fleet Ditch, and then we will say 'good bye' to the Reverend Mortification Ripon."

Ogle had heard too often of those square holes, which led into the Fleet Ditch, to doubt of their existence; but the cool manner in which Mr. Isaacs spoke of the probable fate of the Reverend Mortification Ripon sent a shudder through his frame.

"Well, Isaacs," he said, "with all that I have nothing to do. If you find yourself betrayed by any one you have trusted, you must take your own remedy. I have business on hand of the greatest importance, and I suppose you have no objection to my speaking to Mrs. Ripon, for she may have information I want."

"Speak to her by all means. Thish way, Mishter Ogles—thish way."

Ogle thought it more than probable that Mrs. Ripon might have had some communication with the Reverend Mortification Ripon, even since the events in the vestibule of Newgate, which had been so recent, and were of such great importance to the fortunes of Captain Heron and of Edith.

That the sight of him would be anything but welcome to Mrs. Ripon, he could very easily imagine; but that did not concern him in the least, and of the two he would much rather see her at that house in Field Lane, than at her establishment in Star Court.

Mr. Isaacs opened a door at the side of the passage, and with an affectation of courtly ceremony, bowed Ogle into the apartment to which it communicated.

The room was a sufficiently wretched one; but it was lighted by a wax candle, which no doubt had found its way to Field Lane along with possibly some waifs and strays from St. James's; and it was no doubt cheaper to burn wax in Field Lane, than to purchase the lowest priced dip candles.

Mrs. Ripon was seated at a table, with a pair of scales and weights before her, by the assistance of which she was ascertaining the value to an ounce of some plate she had just emptied from a bag in which she had conveyed it from Star Court.

"Mishter Ogles," said Isaacs.

Mrs. Ripon uttered a scream, and either from excitement or nervousness at the moment, or from an actual desire to do some mischief, she threw half a dozen silver forks at Ogle, but he dexterously stooped, and the shower of missiles assailed Mr. Isaacs.

"Blesh us and shave us! What is the matter, Mrs. Ripon?—what is the matter?"

"Be composed, madam," said Ogle; "believe me, I am very glad to see you."

"Oh, my head! Oh, my poor nerves! What has happened? and who are you?"

"Do you mean to say for a moment you do not know me, Mrs. Ripon?"

"I don't know anybody. I never saw you before in all my life."

"Blesh us! Mrs. Ripon, that's a good un!" said Isaacs. "Not know Mr. Ogles? Dear! dear! dear! What a world we lives in! There's the forks, Mrs. Ripon—put 'em in the shcale,—there they are."

OGLE LOOKS UPON OLD FRIEND.

Presented Gratis with No. 82, of the New Edition of the Captive; or, the Robbers of Epping Forest.

EACH WEEK IS PRESENTED WITH A COLOURED ENGRAVING.

"Three!" shrieked Mrs. Ripon. "I threw six!"

"Eh?"

"I'm sure I threw the half-dozen."

"Perhaps they are shticking in the wall," said Isaacs, as he lifted the wax-light, and pretended to make a careful examination of the damp and mouldy plaister of which the wall was composed, and which was so rotten that no fork would have stuck in it for half a second.

"I'm robbed and swindled!" cried Mrs. Ripon; "a lone woman always is. There's nothing but thieves in the world, and they are continually dragging the bed from under her, and the victuals out of her mouth. Young man, what do you want with me?"

"Well, Mrs. Ripon!" said Ogle, "you may persist in pretending you don't know me as much as you like, but I know you well enough; and were it not out of regard for your son Tom, I would make you know me, probably, in a manner that would be anything but agreeable!"

"Fool!" said Mrs. Ripon; "I despise the likes of you! When are you going to be hung—next session?"

"I think not, Mrs. Ripon; but I want to know if you have seen the scoundrel who now calls himself the Reverend Mortification Ripon, within the last two hours—for although the last I saw of him was his lying in the kennel in the Old Bailey, immediately after a pistol bullet had flown in his face, I don't believe that a man like that, who is positively born to be hanged, can be otherwise mortally injured!"

"Gracious powers!" cried Mrs. Ripon, "perhaps I'm a widow again! Oh, Mr. Isaacs! Oh, Mr. Ogle! I'm but a young, artless thing, and you're both single men!"

"Go to the deuch!" said Mr. Isaacs.

"Answer my question, Mrs. Ripon," persisted Ogle; "and yet I fancy I need scarcely ask you, since I can gather from what you say that you have not seen the rascal!"

"Hush!" said Mr. Isaacs—and he put himself into an attitude of listening.

"What is it?" asked Ogle.

"Shome one's at the door!"

"It's him! oh, it's him!" cried Mrs. Ripon: "he was to meet me here. Perhaps you're not aware, Mr. Isaacs, that Mr. J. Wild offers fifty pound reward for that vagabond, Ogle, dead or alive? I claim half—give him up at once—and then we can come to a reckoning about the plate; and if he's hung, we can come on the Government for something beside."

"You're very kind," said Ogle; "but before you cook your hare, Mrs. Ripon, you must first catch it. Never mind me, Isaacs, I am all safe. There's another knock at your door—you'd better see who it is. I'll take care of the lady."

"No, you won't!" said Mrs. Ripon; "I'm going!"

"Not yet, madam; I bar the way. You don't leave the house till I do. I know I can trust Isaacs, but I'm pretty sure I can't trust you!"

"You're a wretch!"

"Very likely."

"A beast!"

"The Reverend Mortification Ripon!" cried Isaacs, as he flung the door open; and with a white handkerchief bound round his head, which was stained with blood, the reverend gentleman staggered into the apartment. At first he did not see Ogle, who dexterously slipped behind him so as to get possession of the door; and as the Reverend Mortification was rather confused by the chance pistol-shot which had passed so closely over his cranium, as well as by the deep potations he had indulged in as he paused in the Governor's room, on his route to give the alarm to Mr. Wild, he came into that apartment where Mrs. Ripon awaited him, in rather an eccentric fashion—that is to say, the Reverend Mortification Ripon came in head-foremost; and seeing, by the dim light of the one wax candle that his better-half was in the room, he overlooked the fact that there was a table between them of rather ricketty construction, on which were the scales and weights and the silver plate, which had already borne the deduction of three forks, that were snugly ensconced in Mr. Isaacs' pocket.

The Reverend Mortification Ripon then, in a lurching sort of way, dashed into the room, and, coming violently against the outer edge of the table, he shot it before him against Mrs. Ripon, who, being seated upon one of the not most trustworthy of chairs, went at once into a corner of the room, accompanied by the table, the scales, the weights, the plate, and the Reverend Mortification Ripon, in one crash of disorder.

"Blesh us and shave us!" said Isaacs: "what a smash!"

As he spoke, three table-spoons found their way to the companionship of the forks; and then Ogle took him by the arm, saying, "I will leave these people alone. I shall get no information from them upon which I can rely. Get me the disguise you mentioned, and I will be off at once; for, as I am a living man, I know not at this moment if Captain Heron be within the walls of Newgate or not."

"And you don't want them to go, Mishter Ogles, till you do?"

"Certainly not. Can you keep them?"

"Oh, yesh—easy."

While the Reverend Mortification Ripon and Mrs. Ripon were engaged in an apparently mortal combat in the corner of the room, one being armed with a silver gravy-spoon, and the other with a cheese-toaster of the same metal, Isaacs led Ogle from it, and closed and locked the door on the combatants.

And now, if any one had been curious enough, or interested enough, in Ogle to have watched his entering that house in Field Lane, they would never have recognised him when they saw him emerge from it in the similitude of a little shabby old man, in a very rusty old snuff-coloured suit of clothes, with a quantity of white hair hanging in a disorderly manner beneath his hat.

But it was Ogle, who had been dexterously disguised by Mr. Isaacs; and his object was, under cover of that appearance, so much at variance as it was with his ordinary one, to make his way to a public-house in Newgate Street, which he knew was frequented, not only by the turnkeys of Newgate, but by Wild's janissaries and bulldogs, as he frequently called them, and there ascertain, which there would be little difficulty in doing, if Captain Heron were really a prisoner in what was popularly called the Stone Jug.

The dawn had now come, and Ogle stopped at

Fleet Market, where he took his breakfast at one of the stalls, which were then to be found in abundance, and which had no lack of customers in such a neighbourhood.

Ogle supported his character well. He walked with all the feeble air and manner of a man who had very nearly reached the patriarchal period of existence; and, as he proceeded up Snow Hill towards the corner of Newgate Street, he took care never for a moment to forget the character he was personating, for he knew not what hostile eyes might be upon him.

It gave Ogle a slight start, though, when he arrived opposite St. Sepulchre's Church, to see no other than Jonathan Wild himself standing at the corner of Giltspur Street, gnawing the end of a heavy hunting-whip he held in his hand.

"He seems confused and angry," thought Ogle. "Surely, the Captain has escaped."

It was a piece of great audacity, now, on the part of Ogle to cross right over the way towards where Jonathan Wild was standing. He passed even before his very eyes; and as Jonathan started at that moment from his thoughtful position, in order to cross over to the Old Bailey, he fairly ran against Ogle.

"Out of the way, old fool!" he exclaimed.

"I humbly craves your honour's worshipful pardon!" said Ogle, in a whining voice.

"Go to the devil!" said Wild.

"After your honour!" said Ogle, "if you please."

Jonathan Wild darted a malignant glance at the seeming old man; and it certainly said a great deal for the disguise of Ogle, that it stood the scrutiny of such a pair of practised eyes as Jonathan Wild's.

It did do so; and when Jonathan had passed on, Ogle felt relieved from a danger; it was one he had courted in order to test his powers of personal concealment in the dress he wore, and he was abundantly satisfied with the result.

"That will do!" he said. "Jonathan Wild himself having failed to recognise me, I have no one else to fear."

With a perfect conviction, then, that he might with confidence make his way into any of the public-houses which were the resort of the turnkeys of Newgate or of Wild's myrmidons, Ogle slowly walked up Newgate Street.

The day was now beginning to show signs of the bustle of waking existence; and by the time Ogle reached the door of a public-house immediately opposite Wild's house, the streets were getting noisy and populous from the vicinity of Newgate Market and old Smithfield.

CHAPTER CLXXXIV.

CAPTAIN HERON MEETS WITH SOME CURIOUS ADVENTURES IN NEWGATE.

So many simultaneously acted incidents of one story call upon us for attention, that we are compelled, for a time, to leave sequent events unrecorded, while we step back a few hours in time to bring up to a particular point the adventures of some of our most important characters.

Hence we must at present leave the fair Edith in that dismal attic at Jonathan Wild's house, awaiting what good or evil fortune fate may send her.

Hence we must leave Ogle at the door of the tavern opposite to Jonathan Wild's house in Newgate Street, where he was going with the hope of obtaining accurate information regarding Captain Heron, regardless of the great risk he himself ran.

Hence we must leave that bad heart, my Lord Warringdale, in the kennel, opposite to the narrow entrance of Newgate, with a real or a supposed pistol-bullet in his head.

And we must likewise leave the daring and infamous Jonathan Wild to make his way over the road to the Old Bailey, after his brief interview with Ogle on some peculiar villany of his own.

It is then to that cell, number ten, beneath the ground-floor of Newgate, that we again with the reader repair.

That cell which had contained, for once in its existence, so fair a prisoner as Edith; and which —on the next occasion that its damp and noisome atmosphere assailed human lungs—was in the occupation of Captain Heron.

The shouts of exultation which had been given utterance to by the Governor of Newgate when he slammed the door of that cell shut, while Captain Heron was within it, rang most discordantly in the ears of our hero.

Well might he think that the time had come when evil fortune had determined to project at his head the most fatal arrow in its quiver.

He was a prisoner in Newgate. Locked and bolted into one of its most secure and detestable cells.

What hope could there be now of safety—of rescue—of escape—of life?

For the space of perhaps five minutes, Captain Heron felt himself enveloped in a cloud of despair.

Then it passed away.

It passed away, too, in the strangest manner that it was possible it could do so; and from the violent efforts he had made to burst open the door of the cell, and the hoarse shout he had uttered when he found that door closed upon him, Captain Heron subsided into silence and observation.

He had made a discovery.

It will be recollected that Captain Heron had carried into the cell with him the light, by the assistance of which he, and the Governor, and the Reverend Mortification Ripon, had managed to thread the gloomy passages from the upper portion of the cold stony pile of building to that underground region.

With that light in his hand, Heron had made his way into the cell in search of Edith.

It was only when he found no Edith there, and when he heard the cell door closed upon him, that he flung that light to the floor, and made a terrible effort to force his way out.

That effort failed.

But the light, although cast down, fell providentially in such a position that it was not extinguished. It still cast a tolerable refulgence over the cell; and from the position it now occupied on the floor the light was cast upwards, and caught objects that otherwise would have been left in impenetrable shadow, and so escaped observation.

Among those objects was a small piece of coloured cloth, which seemed, at the first glance Captain Heron gave to it, to be sticking to the wall of the cell.

He ceased his efforts to escape, and darted towards this object instantly.

Was it a memorial of the presence of his Edith in that cell? Had she, perhaps, placed it there with the express object and purpose that he might see it, should chance direct him to that gloomy place?

To lift the light now, and carefully trim it, so that it was in no immediate danger of going out, was a matter which Heron attended to carefully.

He examined the piece of cloth with eyes of eager interest.

There was a button—a small silver button attached to it. It was that which had caught in the edge of the narrow concealed door in the side wall of that cell.

Captain Heron might possibly have been unable to identify the little scrap of cloth thoroughly to his satisfaction, but the button he knew at once. It belonged to some of his own clothing, which he knew was accessible to Edith in the ruins which formed their habitation in the deep, verdant recesses of Epping Forest.

"Ah," he sighed, "she has been here! My Edith—my Edith! You have been, for a brief space, a prisoner in this terrible cell; but they have cheated me into coming here to take your place."

Captain Heron now jumped to the conclusion at once that Edith had torn that small scrap of cloth from her apparel with the button attached to it, and by some means fastened it to the stones of the wall of the cell as a memento of her presence.

He laid hold of the button, without a doubt on his mind that it and the piece of cloth would come away at once in his hand.

No, it was fast!

How could Edith have contrived to make a piece of cloth hold so tightly to the stone wall of that cell?

Surely, that was something marvellous.

Captain Heron held the light closer. He made another attempt to tear away the cloth, and he did so tear it away; and then he saw that a portion of it still remained in a crevice between two of the stones.

Slowly carrying his eyes upwards, and then downwards, he saw that that crevice extended in a straight line from the floor to about the height of five feet.

Then he traced it to a distance of about two feet in width, and in a straight line down again to the floor of the cell.

There was a door.

There could be no possible mistake upon the subject. There was a door there, and the piece of cloth with the silver button attached to it had caught in it as it was last closed. It followed, then, that if that piece of cloth was part of the dress of Edith, she had passed through that doorway on the occasion of its last opening.

Captain Heron felt that he had made an important discovery.

And yet for a moment his heart almost ceased to beat as, in an agony of apprehension, he asked himself whither does this small door lead, and where has my Edith been conducted by my foes and hers?

A sensation of weakness and coldness spread itself over his whole frame for a few moments, and the terrible apprehension that possibly at that time, when he required all his strength, all his resources both mental and physical, he was about to be prostrated by sickness, came over him.

It was only, however, for a few moments that this idea found a place in the mind of Felix Heron.

The cold, sick feeling which had been engendered by his sudden apprehensions in regard to the fate of his dearly-loved Edith passed away. The disturbed circulation resumed its ordinary healthful course, and his heart, although it beat quickly, no longer beat intermittingly, or laboured to perform its vital functions.

Captain Heron was himself again.

The circumstances that had brought him to that cell were peculiar. He was there a prisoner, locked and bolted in, but he had not been brought there as a prisoner; consequently, whatever arms, or implements of offence or defence, he had chosen to have about him when he came to Newgate, he still was in possession of.

That was most fortunate.

He had two pair of pistols; powder in a small copper flask, sufficient for about twenty charges; and bullets for the same.

He had a clasp-knife—half knife, half dagger—the blade of which was about nine inches in length, and which fitted to a sheath, which, when it was freed from, formed an efficient handle.

Surely with such weapons—with a strong hand and dauntless heart, he might do something for the liberation of his Edith.

At least he would try, and that at once.

Placing the light now on the floor, Captain Heron inserted the blade of the clasp knife between the stones which showed a crevice.

What an unexpected pleasure it was to him to find that, by exerting a little lateral pressure—which, however, tried the blade of the knife severely—the small door moved.

It moved inwards to the cell.

It was an oversight on the part of Jonathan Wild not to see that that door was secured on the other side; and yet under ordinary circumstances it would have been sufficiently secure without any fastening. If merely closed, it was likely to escape all observation.

There was nothing to lead to an idea of its existence from the other, or cell side.

In fact, it consisted of eight blocks of stone, held together by iron stanchions, and moving upon hinges concealed artfully, which enabled them to turn as a mass inwards to the cell.

The hinges were in good order—the points of contact were free, so that a small amount of power in the right direction was quite sufficient to turn the blocks of stone.

The pressure of Captain Heron's knife moved them sufficiently that he could get a hold with the points of his fingers.

Another moment, and he had the door fully open.

A profound darkness now reigned beyond.

There was no lamp there, as upon the occasion of Jonathan Wild's visit to Edith; and Captain

Heron, as he looked from the cell, might well hesitate before hastily leaving it to plunge into the unknown region that lay beyond it.

How could he know but that the whole affair might be only some artfully contrived trap, laid by Jonathan Wild for his destruction?

Captain Heron, therefore, judiciously enough controlled the desire he had when he got the door fairly open, to rush from the cell at once in search of the route which had been taken by those who held Edith a captive.

It was a great perplexity to him at that moment, to find that the light he had brought with him, was slowly expiring.

There was not a moment to lose.

Captain Heron brought the light to the doorway, and there were just sufficient rays from it to make him certain that, at all events, the path immediately before him was firm and reliable.

Then the light went out.

The darkness about him came up to the idea of "a darkness that could be felt." It seemed to move in solid, wavy masses around him.

But this effect passed away in a few minutes, during which he paused for it to do so. It was the sudden change from having a light to no light which produced it; and when his eyes got accustomed to that new condition, he no longer felt that confusion of darkness which had at first surrounded him.

Captain Heron then commenced an exploration of the gloomy passage before him.

There were but two suppositions in regard to it that could be entertained for a moment.

That secret door and secret passage either led to some of the most terrible hidden cells of Newgate—cells into which the foot of neither warder nor prisoner had trodden for years and years—or it led to Jonathan Wild's house in Newgate Street.

The direction of the passage favoured the latter supposition, and the more he thought of it the more he, Captain Heron, considered that it was the true one.

Still he proceeded with caution.

Step by step, never advancing one foot after the other until the foremost one had some solid and firm foundation to stand upon.

In this way it was not probable that if any snare for his destruction existed he would be caught in it.

Soon, then, he came to an obstruction in the shape of a door; but it was not fastened; and, after carefully passing his hand down the side of it, Heron found a lock, which enabled him to get a good hold of the door and pull it open.

Captain Heron then shrunk back a step or two, for some strange sounds met his ears.

Those strange sounds had met the ears of Edith likewise on her passage through that gloomy route from Newgate to the house of Jonathan Wild. They were the cries—the groans—the moans—and the sobs of the unhappy prisoners of the infamous Wild; for Captain Heron, when he opened that door, found himself in the region of "Little Newgate," as it was called—that is to say, in the underground part of Jonathan Wild's house, where, in defiance of all law and justice, he kept prisoners on his own account.

Captain Heron looked intently.

It was some few minutes before he could make up his mind as to the character of these cries and groans; but he was soon, in more ways than one, enlightened on the subject.

Then came the faint gleam of some approaching light to that dismal place.

Heron drew further back, and partially closed the door. He had felt that the lock was a heavy one, and he had no doubt the other side of that door was well enough supplied with bolts and bars. If it were to be closed and fastened by whoever it was who was approaching with a light, all progress of his in that direction would be indefinitely stayed.

Perhaps, whoever was coming, did so with the express purpose of fastening that door. If so, there was but one thing to do, and that was to take him prisoner; and in the event of too active a resistance, his death would be upon his own head.

Captain Heron was quite ready.

Not absolutely at once to court a contest, he closed the door all but about an inch. In that inch he laid flat on the ground one of his pistols, so that the barrel would effectually prevent the door from being closer shut.

The light approached.

The cries and groans from the cells in "Little Newgate" were more boisterous.

Captain Heron could just look through the chink he had left between the door and the wall; so, in a few moments, he saw the light and its bearer. The former was a small lantern—the latter was one of Jonathan Wild's janissaries.

This man was coarse and brutal-looking. He carried a rather large basket upon one arm, which, no doubt, contained provisions; and, from his air and manner, one might have taken him for the keeper of some menagerie, whose duty it was at that hour to bring food to the wild creatures he had in cages.

"Ah, you may grunt and growl, all of you!" he said; "it won't do no good. You don't get out till Mr. Wild pleases; and not always then. Hilloa! hoy! hoy! hilloa!"

The fellow had opened one of the gratings in one of the cell doors, and looked in.

"Mercy! mercy!" cried a female voice,—"oh, have mercy upon me! I will not tell anything about Mr. Wild and the case of watches—indeed, I will not!"

"Ha! ha! there is your food for the next twelve hours! You had better make the best of it!"

"Oh, mercy!—mercy!"

"Don't know what you mean."

Bang went the grating shut, and the man passed on to another.

Captain Heron had heard enough to let him know perfectly where he was, and what was going on. He made up his mind in a moment, and opened the door wide enough to enable him to pass through.

But by that time the man, who was, for his utter want of common humanity and unmitigated brutality, trusted with the duty of feeding the unfortunate prisoners in the cells, had advanced to another and opened the grating.

"Now you!" he cried.

"Help! help! Murder!" shouted the occupant of that cell. "Murder! murder! Jonathan Wild is a villain! Murder!"

"Go it—go it!" cried the man. "That will do it! Go it! Ha! ha!"

CHAPTER CLXXXIV.

CAPTAIN HERON TURNS THE TABLES UPON JONATHAN WILD.

THE occupant of the cell, at which Jonathan's man now was, seemed resolved to make all the noise possible. He shouted, yelled, and declaimed with a pertinacity which set all reason at defiance, and awakened all the echoes it was possible to awaken in that gloomy place.

"Ah!" said Jonathan Wild's man. "I hope that'll do you good! It don't matter to us a bit, and if you like it, why you can go on at it!"

No. 88.—EDITH.

"I will make myself heard!" cried the prisoner; "I am resolved to make myself heard!"

"No objection, my fine fellow—no objection in the world! Make yourself heard as much as you like—we're used to that here; but if you fancy that you'll make yourself attended to in consequence—that's quite another thing. You may make as much noise as you please: all the cries, and all the shouts of 'Help!' and 'Murder!' that may come from this place will be just as much attended to above, if they reached there, as the mewing of a cat!"

"That is well," said Heron to himself. "This fellow gives me a hint which I may improve upon."

Even as he spoke, Captain Heron stepped forward, caring little if he made noise enough at once to awaken the attention of Jonathan Wild's man or not, since he felt confident that even were he to make an attempt at escape, a rush of a few paces would speedily secure him.

The distance between them was not much above thirty feet, and so intent was the villanous gaoler of Jonathan Wild's upon mocking the misery of the prisoner, who raised such apparently vain outcries, that he heard nothing of the footsteps of Captain Heron, and knew nothing of his presence, until he felt himself seized by the back of the neck with a grasp of iron, while a voice sounded in his ears the words, "Which do you prefer—death or submission?"

Captain Heron then released the man from the grasp he had taken of him, so that the fellow could turn round, and with his back against the cell door, was face to face with Heron.

The look of consternation and surprise that set upon the countenance of the detected ruffian, would, under any other circumstances, have been positively ridiculous.

His mouth opened to its widest dimensions, and his eyes seemed staring from his head, as he looked in mortal fear and surprise to find any one but himself at liberty in that darksome and wretched region.

"Understand me," said Captain Heron calmly; "if you attempt to make the least resistance, or show even by a wandering look, or the movement of a muscle, any design to contend with me, or to escape from me, I will brain you on the instant."

The man shook in every limb, and a deadly pallor came over his countenance.

"Who—who are you?" he gasped.

"I am commonly known as Captain Felix Heron."

"Then I gives in."

"You had better."

"I knocks under, Captain; but don't kill a poor fellow as wouldn't do no harm to a fly."

"Silence! I want no remarks from you. I have promised you your life on conditions. Keep those conditions, and you live; break them, and you die!"

"Hilloa! hilloa! what's all that?" cried the prisoner from the cell. "Murder! murder! Help! help! I won't be quiet! I will make myself heard! Help! help! Thieves! thieves!"

"Stand aside!" said Captain Heron to Wild's man.

"Yes, Captain."

The fellow stood aside, and Captain Heron looked through the grating into the cell. He could just dimly see some human figure at the further end of it,—if the words "further end" could at all be applied with propriety to a miserable space, not exceeding eight feet in length.

"Be quiet," said Captain Heron, "whoever you are; you interrupt me. I will let you free in a few minutes; but until then, be quiet."

The prisoner in the cell uttered only the word "Free!" with a joyous shout, and then all was still.

Nothing could more prominently show the immense moral power which such a man as Captain Heron possessed over the mere brute force of Jonathan Wild's myrmidions, than the fact that it would have been extremely easy for the man who had come there with provisions for the prisoner, to attack Heron, and perhaps take his life, as he was looking into that gloomy cell, but he never attempted to do so. Fear kept him back, even as it had kept back the Governor of

Newgate and the Reverend Mortification Ripon, when they too had such an opportunity of being mischievous on the occasion of Heron looking into that gloomy cell, number ten, in which he believed Edith was a prisoner.

Captain Heron then turned to the myrmidon of Jonathan Wild, and, fixing his eyes upon him, he spoke coldly and sternly.

"You are still alive, therefore you can answer me what I have to ask you. How long you will continue in existence depends entirely upon the truth of those answers. I do not want you to reply as you think will please me, but simply and truthfully. You are here, no doubt, as you think, doing a duty to Jonathan Wild, your rascally employer; therefore I shall not take upon myself to punish you on that score. But I warn you, I am not to be played with; and even hesitation in replying to me may be fatal to you."

As he spoke, Heron took from his breast-pocket one of that small pair of beautifully-finished pistols he usually carried with him, and, throwing up the pan of the lock, he shook the powder, so that the weapon was ready for instant use.

Jonathan Wild's man glanced at him, with consternation depicted on every feature.

"Please, Captain," he said, "my name's Mobbs. I've been on the road myself once, and I hope you won't be hard with a poor fellow."

"I have nothing to do with what you have been, Mr. Mobbs," replied Heron. "I only wish you to understand that I shall certainly shoot you if you do not answer me truthfully and fully what I shall require of you."

"Yes, Captain."

"Where are we exactly now?"

"Underneath Jonathan Wild's house. These are the cells where he keeps his customers, as he calls those he puts into them."

"How many people are imprisoned here now?"

"Seven, Captain."

"All men?"

"No, Captain; five men and two women."

"How long," said Captain Heron, speaking huskily,—"how long have the two female prisoners been in the cells?"

"About a fortnight, Captain."

"You are sure?"

"Quite certain."

"Has Jonathan Wild any other prisoners in his house above?"

"Not that I know of, Captain; but——"

"But what? Speak out!"

"I've heard something among the men, that he has a prisoner up above he tries to keep all to himself—that is to say, old Mother Shackles and Blueskin are the only persons who know anything about it."

"But could you not know to a certainty in a moment?"

"No, Captain, there's an iron door, and it's only Jonathan, and Mother Shackles, and Blueskin who have keys to it. Ah, Captain! it'll be bad times with me now after this night's work. Jonathan Wild never looks over a thing of this kind. He says a man may be killed in his service, but never give in."

"What will he do?"

"He'll pay me regularly up to the very day and discharge me; but before I'm four and twenty hours older I shall be nabbed, and put on trial next session for anything Jonathan Wild chooses to say, and strung up at Tyburn without any hope of mercy."

"All that's nothing to me," said Heron. "I have let you wander from the point. How many men has Wild in the house at present?"

"Four or five, Captain."

Heron looked perplexed for a few seconds. He knew and felt that he had full courage enough to encounter any number of Wild's janissaries, but he was not so mad as to suppose that he could always have the good fortune to escape scathless in such encounters.

If he had only had his own safety to look to, he would have made a dash out of the house at once—chancing, perhaps, a few pistol-shots by the way; but it was Edith whom he was in search of, and for whom he had to preserve himself; therefore it was that he took a few moments to consider; and Mr. Mobbs thought it a favourable opportunity of adding something to his testimony.

"I think, Captain," he said, "from old Mother Shackles muttering and mumbling something to herself in the kitchen, that it's a lady who is imprisoned in one of the attics."

"You feel sure of that?"

"Pretty sure, Captain!"

"It must be so. Edith, surely heaven will assist me! I fly to your rescue, despite all obstacles that may stand in my path for a moment! Hark you, Mobbs! I have spared your life when I might have taken it. I will add to that as large a reward as you can in reason name, if you can devise any plan by which I can reach the upper part of Jonathan Wild's house without a positive fight with his men in the hall."

"It's easy enough," said Mobbs; "and I only ask one reward; and that is, that you'll let me join you, Captain, and become one of your band in the old forest of Epping."

"I know not that I can do so."

"You took Mr. Ogle, you know, Captain; and he was one of Jonathan's men."

"I inflict no one upon my band. They choose their own associates. If you wish to join them, you must come to the forest and ask them. It may be a recommendation that you are useful to me under the present circumstances."

"Then I feel quite sure that I've done with Mr. Wild; and if you'll be guided by me, Captain, I'll take you up by the iron staircase that Mr. Wild has had put at the back of his house for his own use; and you can get right up on to the roof, and look down into any of the attic cells that you like, for they've all got traps in the ceilings."

"Be it so; and be assured that, although you fancy this to be a bad night's work for you, if you are faithful it will be the best you ever did!"

Mr. Mobbs looked quite jovial and contented with this little arrangement; but Captain Heron was summoned to a recollection of the promise he had made to the noisy occupant of the cell by that person calling out, "Free! free!—you said free, and I'm not free yet."

"True," said Heron; "and I will keep my word. Have you the keys of these cells, Mobbs?"

"Yes, Captain. Here's one that opens them all."

"Let this man out."

"He's a dangerous fellow."

"Let him out, I say!"

With a cry and a rush, the prisoner bounded into the passage the moment the cell door was unlocked.

"Stop!" said Heron; "you're not quite free yet, whoever you are. Take this key: it opens the cells of other unfortunates who, like yourself, have been consigned to durance by Jonathan Wild. Release them all; and then take what measures you can among you to leave the house—I cannot help you further just at present. You will probably find two or three men in the hall; but if five of you—rendered desperate by imprisonment and oppression—cannot make your way to freedom I am sorry for it."

"We'll do it!—we'll do it!"

"But there is one thing I must say to you:— if you only look to yourselves, and do not release the two unfortunate females who are here likewise, I swear by heaven I will assist Jonathan Wild to capture every one of you again, and advise him to show you no mercy. Come, Mobbs, my own affairs now cry out aloud for my attention. I can do no more here, but must leave these people to whatever fate may befall them. I give them the chance of the freedom I should have been glad to have ensured them, but I can do no more. Lead on—I will follow you!"

With cries and shouts of gratification, the released prisoner flew from cell to cell, opening the doors, and permitting Jonathan Wild's victims to sally forth.

It is charitable to suppose he did so from purer motives than were attributed to him by Mr. Mobbs, who remarked, with a shake of his head, that he believed that man who had made so many outcries would have been glad to get away alone if he could, and only released his associates in misery, from the conviction that more force was required than he could singly bring to bear upon the enterprise.

"Who is he?" asked Heron.

"He is a witness," replied Mobbs.

"A witness! What do you mean by a witness?"

"He was employed, Captain, by Mr. Wild, to come forward at the sessions always, with any bit of evidence that was wanting to convict a prisoner. But last Old Bailey Sessions, Jim Danks, the cracksman, paid him better than Wild, and he took care to break down in the evidence; so Jim got off, though Wild had him on his list for execution, and then Jonathan nabbed the witness and put him in here."

"I regret releasing such a scoundrel," said Captain Heron; "but if he assists in the liberation of the others, it is as well."

"Quite so, Captain; and you may be sure of one thing—which is, that he'll come to Tyburn tree in good time."

Captain Heron had every reason to believe that this man Mobbs would keep faith with him. He knew well that what he had said concerning the way in which Wild would view what had occurred was perfectly true, and he therefore followed him with very few misgivings in regard to his good faith.

Wild's premises altogether were exceedingly intricate; no doubt purposely so, since the more difficult they were to comprehend, and for un-initiated persons to make their way through them, the better adapted they were for his purposes of concealment and oppression.

Avoiding altogether the staircase which led directly up into the hall, Mobbs opened two doors, which conducted them through some cellars strewn with broken bottles, and heaped up with old packing cases, crates, and such like matters.

These cellars opened by a very strong iron door into a small paved yard at the back of Wild's house, which not being above fourteen or fifteen feet square, gave any one who stood in it the impression of being at the bottom of a pit, since on two sides the actual walls of Newgate rose up to a great height, topped with some revolving spiked iron-work, as a safeguard against the escape of any prisoner in that direction.

The other two sides of this pit-like place comprised Wild's house, which was formed as of two buildings placed rectangularly together.

In the corner formed by the angle was the iron staircase, which Jonathan had purchased entire on the pulling down of a portion of old Whitehall, and had fixed as a convenient addition to his residence in Newgate Street.

This staircase was of a corkscrew shape, so that it occupied very little space: it passed within six or eight feet of several of the windows at the back of the house; and Jonathan Wild, who had a great fancy of being here, there, and everywhere with great celerity, and surprising his men by appearing downstairs when they thought he was high above, and upstairs when they considered he was quite in another part of the premises—had in the different rooms short sturdy planks of wood, which he could project from a window on to this circular staircase, and gain it with ease.

But this paved yard at the back of Jonathan's house, and the walls of Newgate, and the iron staircase, were all now enshrouded in darkness, for Mr. Mobbs had thought it prudent to put out the lantern, and he, with Captain Heron, stood amid such perfect obscurity that they could hardly see each other.

It was at that moment that the alarm-bell began to sound in Newgate.

Heron started.

"What is that?—what is that?" he cried.

"There's something amiss in the Stone Jug," cried Mr. Mobbs. "It's the alarm-bell; and it's never rung except in case of fire or the escape of a prisoner."

"I fear," said Heron, "that there is a third cause for that alarm at present, but I cannot help it now. Lead on—lead on!"

Heron felt a pang of regret and of apprehension as he thought of the precarious and perilous position of his men in the vestibule of Newgate; and but that he knew how fully he could rely upon the courage and the discretion of Ogle, he would almost have been tempted to rush back and attempt to bring them off scathless from that adventure, the dangers of which they had encountered solely from personal service to himself and her who was so dear to him.

But a moment's reflection told him that even although Edith would have been the first to counsel such a course of proceeding, it by no means followed that the route to the vestibule of Newgate was clear and open.

"No, no!" he cried, "I must take no step backward. On! on—to thy rescue, Edith, I must fly! Lead the way—lead the way! I pray you delay not another moment."

"Hush!" said Mobbs; "keep dark and close."

"What is it?"

"Look—look up!"

The circular iron staircase had been painted originally white, and although from various causes that had faded down to a dusky sort of colour, still, against the black and grimy brickwork of Jonathan Wild's house, the outline of that iron staircase could be perceptibly seen, even in the darkness which confounded most objects in the masses of obscurity.

The observation that Captain Heron was able to give to the staircase just sufficed to let him see that some object was at intervals darkening and rendering invisible portions of the iron-work.

It seemed as if at intervals of about three seconds each that some of the circular staircase had disappeared, or was cut away, leaving a blank through which only the blackened brickwork of the house was visible.

But this effect was but an optical delusion. Some one was coming down the staircase; and as he wound round and round its serpentine folds, he appeared to obliterate a portion of the faintly white railing of the iron structure.

Who was it?

Who was it? that was the question. Who was it that at such an hour descended that iron staircase in Jonathan Wild's premises?

CHAPTER CLXXXV.

CAPTAIN HERON HAS SOME CURIOUS EXPERIENCE FROM THE TOP OF WILD'S HOUSE.

MR. MOBBS was evidently greatly alarmed.

Captain Heron could feel that he clung to his arm with a tenacity and an abstraction of mind to all other objects but that strange dusky figure descending the staircase, that made him unconscious of the force he used.

"Who is it?" whispered Heron.

"Don't speak."

"But I must! Do you, or do you not, know who it is we see descending?"

"In a minute."

"What do you mean?"

"I mean that I shall know in a minute, Captain."

A minute was not long to wait, and Captain Heron curbed his patience for that length of time, during which the mysterious figure still slowly came down the iron staircase.

There it suddenly paused.

Mr. Mobbs held the arm of Heron, if possible, a trifle tighter than before, as he whispered, "It's Jonathan himself."

"I thought as much. Where is he going? Will he come all the way down to the yard?"

"I think not. Look!"

It was Jonathan Wild himself; and now that he had descended as far down as the level of the first floor of his house, he lifted one of the pieces of wood which we have already mentioned he was in the habit of making a temporary bridge or

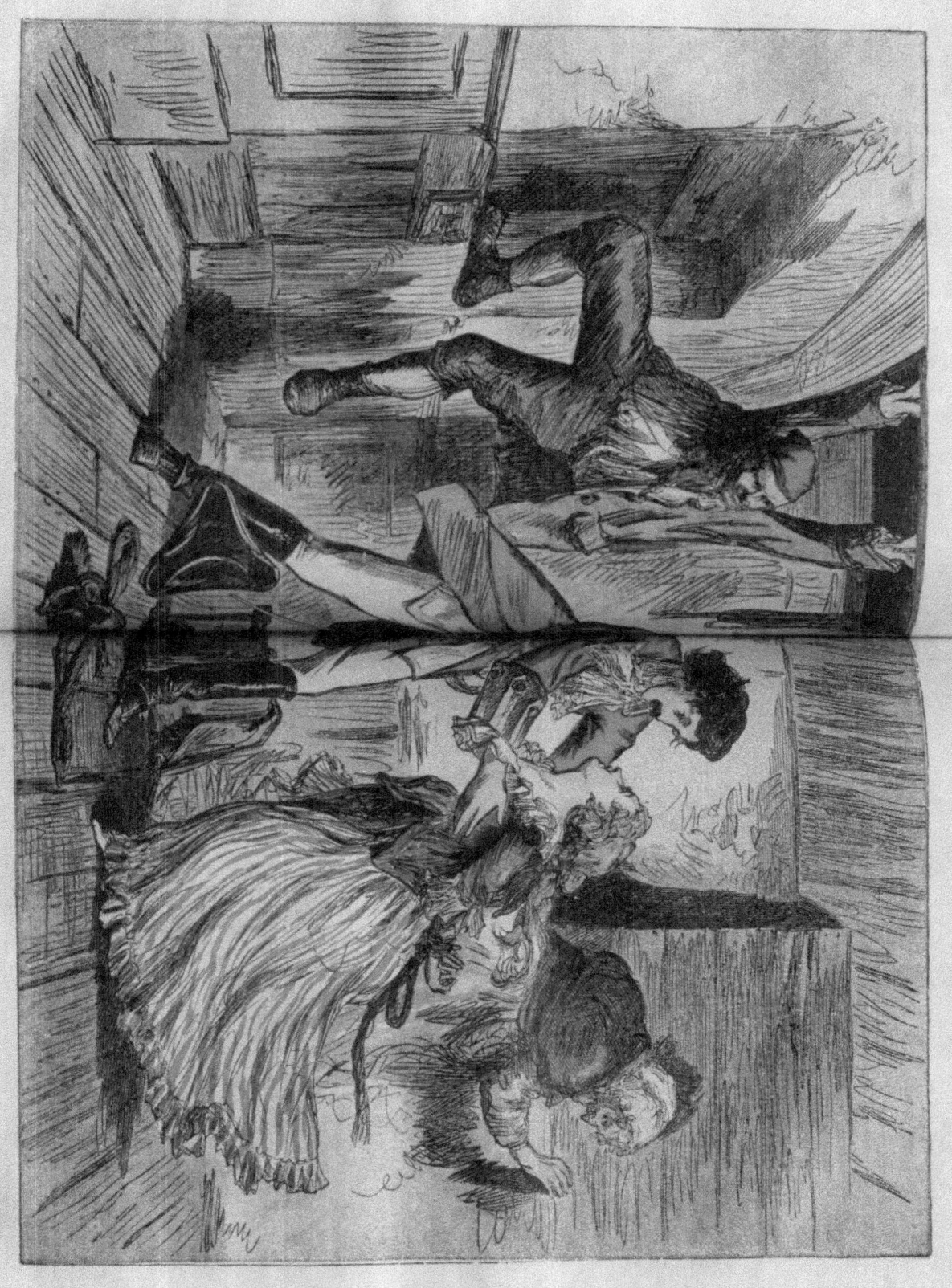

CAPTAIN HERON RELEASES EDITH FROER IMPRISONMENT IN LITTLE NEWGATE.

gangway of from the windows of the houses to the staircase, and reversed the operation.

That is to say, on this occasion he placed the board from the staircase to the window. He had no doubt drawn it after him when he left the house for the iron staircase, and had propped it up in the lattice ready for use to get back again when he should require it.

Like some black ghost, Captain Heron saw the figure of Jonathan cross this wooden bridge to the window he wished to reach.

It was rather a peculiar passage.

At that dim and dusky hour it required some nerve to cross a narrow plank, even although the distance was not above eight or nine feet, with no hand-rail, and with a consciousness that the end of it barely rested on the narrow edge of a window sill.

But Wild was a man of nerve, or he never would have been what he was, so he performed the feat easily enough, without thinking for a moment that it was one.

From where he and Mobbs were, Captain Heron could plainly hear Jonathan Wild open the window, and he could see the dim figure pass through the opening into the house.

The window was closed again, and all was still; but Wild had omitted to draw the plank of wood, which had served him for a bridge, after him.

Was that a signal that he was about to return quickly? It would appear so.

"Now, my friend," said Captain Heron to Mobbs, "it is our turn to ascend the iron staircase."

Mobbs was silent for a few moments, and it was evident that the sight of Jonathan Wild had filled him with a thousand fears.

"Captain," he said, "you may depend he will come out by the window again."

"I don't think so; and if he should, I am quite prepared for him. You can come with me or not, as you like; but if you wish my friends in Epping Forest to receive you as a comrade, it will be but a poor recommendation to state that you refused to accompany me for fear of Jonathan Wild."

"I am coming, Captain."

"Very well. Follow me, then."

Captain Heron at once commenced the ascent of the iron staircase.

Prepared as he was to reach the top of Wild's house, it was not in human nature that he should pass that window through which the great thief-taker had passed without looking in.

The view of the room from the iron staircase was direct and easy.

There sat Wild, at a small table, with some papers before him. He had lit a lamp, which however shed but a dim light on him and on the papers, some of which were thin and small, so that Jonathan had made a temporary paper-weight of one of those short, thick, dumpy-looking pistols which the police officers of that day were in the habit of using, and which are still to be seen for sale in some of the miscellaneous old property shops about Drury Lane and the New Cut.

Had Captain Heron been only one-half as unscrupulous when he had an enemy in his power, as Jonathan Wild would have been, nothing would have been easier for him than to have shot the notorious villain as he there sat, no doubt arranging some of his infamous and criminal memoranda.

But there was something so repugnant to the ideas of Heron to take the life of any one, except in fair fight, that with all the opportunity of ridding the world of Wild at once, the villain was perfectly safe.

The piece of plank was between the staircase and the window; and the notion did flit across the mind of Captain Heron, of crossing it and making Wild a prisoner; but upon a few seconds' closer consideration, he saw that that would not be so easy an adventure as it looked at the first glance.

The noise of opening the window would be sure to arouse Wild.

The pistol that he had made a paper-weight of lay within half a foot of his hand, with the little stumpy butt towards him. He would have but to lift it, and fire, and there would in all probability be an end of whoever might have his hands upon the window sash.

Captain Heron saw all this, and he merely let Jonathan Wild alone.

But all this time, and up to the moment when Captain Heron saw that it was impolitic to interfere with Wild, the alarm-bell of Newgate kept tolling.

Wild heard it well enough; and as he heard it, he made several impatient gestures, as though he were saying, "Confound that noise!—what is it to me?"

If Edith had been in Newgate, no doubt Jonathan would have thought any alarm in the prison something to him; but as he knew he held her securely in one of his prison attics, he cared nothing for the Newgate alarm-bell.

But he was soon to be convinced that he was wanted on the occasion.

A good deal of time had necessarily been occupied by Captain Heron in reaching so far on his route to the top of Jonathan's house; and during that time the Reverend Mortification Ripon had been indulging in the strong waters he found on the Governor's table, in his private sitting-room.

But for the entry into that room of one of the warders, the reverend gentleman might have gone on sleeping; but a jug of cold water dashed in his face aroused him, and he simultaneously with opening his eyes remembered that he was bound on an errand to Jonathan Wild.

With a rush, the Reverend Mortification Ripon then left Newgate by the front door of the Governor's house; and with the cold water dripping from his hair and face he reached Wild's residence, and convinced the "man on the lock"—as Jonathan's hall-porter was called—that he really had important business.

Hence was it that, just as Captain Heron had whispered to Mobbs—as they stood on the iron staircase—that they would proceed, he was tempted to linger yet a moment by seeing Wild give a sudden start, and lay a hand on the pistol that lay before him on the papers.

It was all dumb show in that room so far as Heron was concerned; but he could see Wild look angrily and inquiringly towards the door.

Then some one came in and nearly fell prostrate as he made violent gesticulations and spoke rapidly, and then tottered to a chair.

That was the Reverend Mortification Ripon; and no sooner had he spoken than Jonathan Wild uttered one of his harsh and discordant and yelling laughs, that was loud enough to reach the ears of Captain Heron and Mr. Mobbs.

"Gracious!" said Mobbs, "what's the matter with him?"

"He is pleased."

"Is he?"

"Yes, he has just received intelligence that I am in a cell of Newgate; and he is, naturally, quite delighted!"

"Oh, I understand now! He will be off to the Stone Jug at once, then, I suppose?"

"To be sure!—there he goes!—there he goes! He has given the Reverend Mortification Ripon a rap on the head with the iron barrel of the pistol he has in his hand, which one may hear even this far off. The reverend gentleman is howling and rubbing his head, but they leave the room together."

"Then we have this house all to ourselves for a time, Captain!"

"Yes. Edith, Edith, I come to you, now; and may, perchance, restore you to freedom within the next five minutes. Edith!—my Edith!"

Captain Heron made up for lost time; for he tore up the iron staircase with a rapidity that left Mobbs far behind him, and made his own progress look like that of some mechanical figure which rotated up that staircase from the impulse of some well-arranged machinery.

This was an exhausting mode, though, of getting to the top of the iron staircase.

Captain Heron was compelled to pause, as well for breath as to let his brain recover from the whirl which the cork-screw ascent had produced in it.

Then Mobbs joined him.

"The more haste, Captain, the less speed!"

"I know—I know—you are right; but all is well now. Can you tell me which is the actual trap on the roof that looks down into the attic we are in search of."

"No, Captain, but we shall soon find it; there are but four attic cells in all."

It was an easy thing to get on to Wild's house now, and both Mobbs and Captain Heron stepped from the iron staircase into a gutter which carried off rain water.

"Be careful, Captain," whispered Mobbs. "A loose tile would make a deuce of a clatter in the yard below."

"I will be cautious. Ah, here is some woodwork!"

"It is one of the traps in the roof."

"The one we want, perhaps."

"May be. Ah, look here!"

As Mobbs spoke, he showed Captain Heron that there was an excessively narrow thread of light on both of them, which must come from some crevice, and which betrayed the fact that there was a light in the attic immediately below them.

"I don't think," whispered Mobbs, "that Jonathan has any other prisoner just now up here, so if we lift the trap no doubt we can speak to the young lady; but I would advise caution."

"Yes—yes!"

Captain Heron drew back two bolts, and then very slowly and cautiously lifted the trap-door in the roof about a couple of inches.

There was a light in the attic, and he almost uttered a shriek of joy as he saw Edith.

But she was not alone.

A hideous old hag was with her, who, in a high, cracked voice, was speaking.

"I hope you will be hanged, that I do, and all like you. I suppose you call yourself a beauty. Ha! ha! Marry come up! beauty, indeed! I think the men be all crazy to be running after such as you. What's beauty? How long does it last, eh?—eh?"

Edith then spoke. Oh, what joy it was to Felix Heron to hear again the sounds of that voice which were so dear to him!

"My good woman," said Edith, "I do not wish to dispute with you. What harm have I ever done you that you should be so angry at me?"

"Good woman yourself," answered the hag. "I am no more a good woman than you are."

"I did not use the words offensively."

"I don't care whether you did or not."

"Very well."

"It ain't very well, Miss Jezebel. It ain't very well. Ha! ha! I'll take care the pretty bird does not get out of its cage. 'Mother Shackles,' said Mr. Wild, in his funny way, — 'Mother Shackles, you old wretch, I leave the young lady upstairs in your care, and if she gets away I'll knock your old head off.' So here I am, and so often as Mr. Wild is out I mean to come here and stay."

"As you please," said Edith.

"But I don't please."

"Go, then."

"I won't go."

"Then you please to stay."

"No, I don't. I won't be spoken to. Hold your tongue, hussey! I won't be spoken to. I'll—I'll—yes, I'll soon stop you from aggravating me with your talk, I will. I can put a handkerchief in your mouth; you can breathe through it, but you cannot talk. Ha! ha!"

"You dare not."

"We shall see. It's a good thing Mr. Wild thought of tying your hands together."

These words were too much for Captain Heron. The brief conversation that had taken place he had listened to with anger enough, but at the information that his Edith was at the mercy of such a being as the old hag who obeyed the villanous behests of Jonathan Wild, he could be patient no longer.

"Edith! dear, dear Edith!" he cried. "I am here! Here to save you, my own love!"

Edith uttered a scream of joy.

"Felix! my Felix!"

The old hag was so astounded at this sudden interruption to her proceedings that she could neither cry out nor make any attempt to escape for the very few seconds it took Captain Heron now to open the trap-door fully and drop into the attic.

Then Mother Shackles recovered her faculties sufficiently to make a rush towards the door; but Mr. Mobbs, who had followed Heron closely, judiciously put out one foot, and the old woman fell with a grand crash to the floor.

"Hope you haven't been and gone and hurt yourself, Mother Shackles," said Mobbs; "but you are always so hasty!"

"Murder! Murder! Mr. Wild! Mr. Wild! Murder! Murder! Thieves! Thieves! Mr. Wild!"

"Oh, you won't be quiet, I see," added Mobbs, "so here goes! You can breathe, you know, Mother Shackles, as you just now said, through a handkerchief, but you can't speak."

Mother Shackles could only now make a slight confused sort of murmur through the silk handkerchief which Mobbs gagged her with.

Edith was clasped in the arms of Captain Heron, and shedding tears of joy on his breast.

"You have come to save me, Felix! I knew you would come! My heart told me so, and I was hopeful and happy!"

"Yes, dearest! You in danger gave me but one object in the world, and that was to rescue you from it."

"All's right, Captain!" said Mobbs. "I think now we had better be off as soon as possible."

"Hark! I hear something!"

"And so do I."

The sound of some uncommonly heavy footstep on the stairs leading up to the attic came plainly upon all their ears.

"Who is that, Mobbs?" said Heron.

"Blueskin."

"Ah! one of Jonathan's most troublesome men!"

"Yes, Captain. No doubt he has heard the sounds of something like strife or noises from this attic, and has come to see what is amiss."

"No doubt."

Old Mother Shackles had no other way of expressing her satisfaction but by drumming with her feet upon the floor.

"Be quiet," said Mobbs, "or I shall have to put you up the chimney!"

Mother Shackles thought that would be rather an uncomfortable process, so she was quiet accordingly.

The heavy footstep approached nearer and nearer to the attic each moment.

"He is as strong as an elephant," said Mobbs, "and is afraid of nothing. The best way will be to let him come fairly in first, and then we can pounce upon him and overpower him."

"Yes. Keep back. Edith, dear, all is safe!"

"Oh, yes, yes! with you, always safe, Felix!"

Captain Heron and Mobbs drew back out of the way of the attic door, which in a few moments was opened by Blueskin, who made but one step into the room as he said, "Little 'un, I tells you what it is! Old Jonathan was on the roof when I spoke to you a little while agone, and I couldn't say what I meant all for to say; but now, little 'un, as I don't want to see your pretty little eyes getting dim, and your nice little face a-getting thinner and thinner, I means to let you out of here, and see you safe a bit of your way, whenever you likes to go. So come on; and I should just like to see the fool who will try to stand in our way—that's all, little 'un!"

CHAPTER CLXXXVI.

LORD WARRINGDALE THINKS PRUDENCE THE BETTER PART OF VALOUR.

WE left Lord Warringdale in an apparently serious predicament.

The stray shot from the Newgate officials appeared to have taken effect upon him; and for the moment Ogle and his companions were quite sufficiently deceived to fancy that a dead or dying man would be no longer a desirable prisoner.

Thus my Lord Warringdale was permitted to lie in the kennel of the Old Bailey while Captain Heron's band trotted off without him, feeling their position to be quite as gracious—if not a great deal more so—without the companionship of such a man.

The confusion in and about Newgate was very great; and what with the state of mind into which the Governor had been thrown, and the difficulty that Jonathan Wild had to comprehend the state of affairs, the turnkeys and officials were nearly driven distracted.

To be sure, Wild had been informed that Captain Heron was a prisoner; but although the Reverend Mortification Ripon could not exactly tell him what was amiss—inasmuch as he did not quite comprehend, himself, the cause of the Governor's alarm at the silence of Captain Heron within that cell number ten, in the foundations of Newgate—yet there was something about the message which implied quite as much disquietude to Jonathan Wild as triumph.

But now let us suppose one hour to have elapsed.

The Governor of Newgate has got over his fright.

My Lord Warringdale has raised himself from the kennel in the Old Bailey, and proved, by his activity, that no bullet had taken effect upon him.

Jonathan Wild is uttering awful language in the vestibule of Newgate, to which he has just returned from number ten cell, with but a doubtful conviction upon his mind in regard to the good faith of the Governor.

Captain Heron, upon leaving that cell by the secret door in the wall, had taken the precaution which Jonathan Wild himself had omitted, of shooting the bolts in their sockets on the other side; so that from Newgate Wild found his passage barred to his own house in that direction.

It was no wonder then, that, with his peculiarly constituted state of mind, Jonathan should jump to the conclusion that he was betrayed in some fashion.

He could not exactly recollect whether he himself had bolted that secret door on the side next his own house or not; but that he always intended to do so he knew perfectly well, and therefore the probabilities were strongly in favour of the act.

If, however, Captain Heron had really escaped from number ten cell in that fashion, Jonathan Wild considered that it would be but into a trap; for that he could get clear of his house in Newgate Street, he did not believe for a moment.

Pending, however, an investigation in that quarter, Wild adopted the plan, while at Newgate, of accusing the Governor of treachery towards him.

"All this affair is plain enough!" he said, fiercely.

"How do you mean by plain, Mr. Wild?"

"Why, that you have made something very handsome by the proceedings of this night!"

"I, Mr. Wild?"

"Yes, Mr. Governor! Captain Felix Heron

can afford to pay well; and would do so with no niggard hand, where life and liberty were at stake!"

"I do not understand you, Mr. Wild!"

"I think you do! But I will speak plainer! It appears to me that you certainly had Captain Heron a prisoner, and cleverly enough locked him up in number ten cell. You then sent the Reverend Mortification Ripon away under pretence of telling me; but, by comparing the time, he seems to have taken a good three-quarters of an hour to reach my house, when he should have done so in five minutes!"

"I cannot account for that, Mr. Wild."

"But I can. He was delayed in some way purposely, and during that time you had Captain Heron all to yourself. What has he paid you to let him go? Ha! ha!—every one for himself; but I think, as I have found it out, we may as well go halves, eh, Mr. Governor?"

"Mr. Wild, you wrong me very much by your suspicions. After Captain Heron was once locked and bolted in the cell number ten, I never set eyes upon him; but when he suddenly ceased to speak, and there was so profound a stillness in the cell, I must confess it did strike me that you might have left the secret door open when you took Edith Tarleton through it, and that he had passed that way into your house."

"Pshaw!" said Wild. "It's no such thing. If such had been the case he would have been a prisoner again before now. I have always force sufficient."

"It appears to me, Mr. Wild," said Lord Warringdale, "that I saw most of your force hereabouts within the last quarter of an hour. How many men had you at your little establishment this night?"

"Eight—eight!" cried Wild, as he glared about him—"and they are there now."

"Nay, Mr. Wild," said the Governor, with a gleam of satisfaction at Jonathan's discomfiture; "you ordered off six of them on horseback in pursuit of Ogle and Captain Heron's men."

Wild turned round twice upon his heels, and looked confused.

"What if I did? What if I did?" he cried. "I have two men still at my house round the corner, who are worth all the rest. Mobbs and Blueskin are there; and Captain Heron, although he is bold and lucky, would need to have the nine lives of a cat to get past them in safety."

"It may be so," said Warringdale; "but you were indiscreet, Mr. Wild, to leave your house so inefficiently guarded."

"Pshaw! my lord, my house is well guarded enough; and if it were not, there is no danger. I do believe that Captain Heron was in number ten cell safely secured; but I do not believe that he ever left it in the direction of Newgate Street. Mr. Governor here knows which way he went, and has no doubt profited well by the transaction."

"You're quite wrong, Mr. Wild," said the Governor, "and will find so in good time."

"I will go home at once," said Wild, musingly; "for danger or no danger, it is not well that a place like mine should only have two men to look after it."

"I advise you," said Warringdale; "and since I have suffered somewhat from the fatigues of this night, I will bid you farewell for the present."

"Nay, my lord," said Wild, with a sneering tone; "I should have thought you would be anxious to go round with me to Newgate Street, to see the state of affairs."

"No! no!"

"Can you be so indifferent?" whispered Wild, as they stepped into the Old Bailey together. "I have one bird in the cage; and, for all I know, there may be two."

"I'm afraid——"

"Ah! that's it—you're afraid, my lord—afraid!"

"Not in the sense you use the term, Mr. Wild. I was going to say I was afraid you reckoned too freely on your good fortune in fancying that Captain Heron was a prisoner."

"Ha! ha! Well! well! But have you nothing to say to the fine lady who I know to be safe in my house?"

"It is needless—it is needless. She would not listen to me. It is impossible that I can ever again say anything to Edith Tarleton that she will listen to with the patience of a moment. There was ever a gulf between us, which circumstances have widened until we seem as though we can scarcely see each other across the chasm."

Wild laughed.

"Women, my Lord Warringdale, find their way across wide chasms. But be it as you will. Good night!"

"Good night! You will find me at my lodgings opposite Whitcombe House; but still, if you are afraid, Mr. Wild, to go home alone, under the circumstances, I will freely accompany you."

"I afraid? No, my lord, I was never yet afraid of anything on the earth or out of it; and although there is a sort of impression on my mind that I have not yet seen the last of this night's adventures, I will go home alone."

Jonathan Wild strode up the Old Bailey without another word, and as the faint dawn was each moment getting brighter and brighter, he glared about him like some savage animal baffled of its prey.

He crossed over to the railings of St. Sepulchre's Church, from which spot he could command a view of the front of his own house, which seemed all perfectly quiet, safe, and secure.

"All is well—all is well!" he said. "I've nothing to fear. Nothing to fear at home. Blueskin and Mobbs are quite sufficient of themselves to look after the place. I gave strict injunctions to Mother Shackles to keep an eye on Edith; and the more I look about me, and the more I think, the more I am convinced that the Governor of Newgate has sold Captain Heron his freedom at a good round price. But it matters not—it matters not. I have a loadstone in the attic yonder, which will draw him safely enough. I shall nab him yet."

It was at this moment that Ogle, in his disguise of an old man, so nearly ran against Jonathan Wild as actually to touch him.

Some feeling was upon the mind of Wild which prompted him to go back to Newgate; but when half-way down the Old Bailey he changed his determination again, and, with very rapid steps, made his way to his own house.

Jonathan was in the habit of letting himself in without the ceremony of knocking; for, as we have hinted, he always wished, if possible, to take

his myrmidons at unawares. If he were going out for a whole day and a night, he generally left word he would return in half an hour; and sometimes, when he knew he would be but an hour absent from home, he would leave his janissaries to suppose he had several days' journey before him.

If Jonathan had only kept up this rule of contraries, his men would soon have found him out, and acted accordingly; but as sometimes he told the exact truth, they were completely puzzled, and knew not what to do.

Wild had his key with him on the present occasion, but he gave a quiet, timid single knock at the door, so that neither Blueskin nor Mobbs could have the least idea it was their imperious master who had arrived.

No notice whatever was taken of the knock.

"Ah!" said Wild to himself, "they think the applicant here is too humble; we will try something different."

Jonathan then perpetrated a startling rat! tat! But not the slightest notice was taken of that.

A vague feeling of alarm began to take possession of him.

Producing his key in a moment, Wild opened the door, and strode into the passage of his house.

"Hillos!" he cried, in a voice of thunder. "Thieves and scoundrels! where are you?"

The roaring voice in which he spoke echoed along the passage and up the staircase, but no reply came to him; and after those echoing sounds had died away, a silence as if of the grave seemed to pervade the establishment.

Wild staggered back until he was stopped by the street door, against which he propped himself, and, in a voice compounded of fear and anger, he yelled out, "Blueskin! Mobbs! Blueskin! Mobbs! By all the furies, I'll put a bullet in the first one of you I see! Blueskin! Mobbs! I say! Drunk, for a hundred pounds, I'll be bound! And yet, they dare not—surely, they dare not, when they knew I was about! They would never leave the place, strictly on duty as they were! Blueskin! Mobbs! Confusion take you both, where are you?"

The intense stillness of the house began to have an alarming effect upon the mind of Wild.

Could it be possible that Captain Heron had really made his way from the cell of Newgate, and had overcome both the men he had left in charge of his house? Was it possible that either above or below he should find the dead bodies of Blueskin and Mobbs, and ascertain that in his absence Captain Heron had achieved a complete victory, and carried off Edith in triumph?

Jonathan Wild could not suppress a roar of spite and anger at the mere supposition of such a state of things.

He got the better of all his fears in a moment, and made a rush up the staircase, for the purpose of ascertaining, in the shortest possible manner, if there were really any substantial foundation for them.

Should Edith be safe and a prisoner still, all would be comparatively well, and he would only have to make Blueskin and Mobbs account most particularly for their neglect, let the cause of it be what it might.

He reached the iron door which stretched across the staircase and cut off the topmost floor of the house from any visit from below, except such as was authorised by himself.

The iron door was fast.

That was a relief.

"Oh, it's all right enough," muttered Wild. "I can understand it all, now. Those rascals, Blueskin and Mobbs, thought I was booked for a long chase on horseback after Captain Heron's men; and so, I've not the slightest doubt, they are carousing over the way at the 'King's Head.' Edith, of course, is quite safe, and so are the prisoners below. The scoundrels will be back soon, and if I don't give them a pretty alarm, my name is not Jonathan Wild!"

Jonathan looked carefully to the priming of his pistols as he spoke, as if they would have something to do in the alarm he projected giving Blueskin and Mobbs.

He then, with the master-key he had, unlocked the iron door, intending to pay a visit to his fair prisoner in the attic, of whose presence he did not entertain the slightest doubt.

Still, however, Wild thought proper to herald his coming with a loud "Hilloa!" which he thought Mother Shackles—if she were properly on duty—would be sure to respond to in some fashion.

All continued still, however, with the exception of a dull, drumming sort of noise, apparently on the floor above.

That was Mother Shackles.

Wild reached the attic.

"Edith Tarleton!" he yelled out. "Answer to your name! You're a prisoner, and must cry out 'Here!' when the roll is called. Edith Tarleton or Edith Heron, which you will, answer to your name, I say!"

Edith did not answer: she was at that moment within sight of the leafy glades of Epping Forest.

The attic door was locked, but Wild's key opened it. He flung it wide, but the moment he did so, Mother Shackles made a rush upon him. Maddened by disappointment, imprisonment, and fruitless rage; and, perhaps, worst of all, in consequence of the silk handkerchief in her mouth preventing her from giving utterance to that flood of eloquence peculiar to her, she made a leap—like some wild cat of exaggerated dimensions—on Jonathan; and so astonished and terrified was he at the sudden attack, that he fell completely backward, and with Mother Shackles cuffing, screaming, and tearing at him—for she did not pause a moment to see who had arrived—they both rolled together down the stairs, stopping not until the iron door—which was partially closed—arrested their progress.

The shock with which Wild came against the iron door started the pair of pistols from just within his breast, where he had hastily placed them, and one of them exploded with a loud report.

Wild's immediate impression was that some one had fired at him from below; and, bruised and shaken though he was, he sprung to his feet, and dealing Mother Shackles a not very gentle admonition with his foot, which sent her past the iron door, down the remainder of the staircase to the hall below, he slammed that door hastily shut and locked it; after which, from that upper side of it, he listened intently, and was rather surprised that no further indication of any attack upon him took place.

Jonathan Wild was puzzled.

What could it all mean?

Why did the old woman—whom he had sufficiently recognised—fly at him in that fearful fashion?

Who had fired at him from below? For he still thought such to be the case.

These questions he put to himself rapidly enough; and although he was much shaken by his fall, he proceeded again to the attic and made a rush into it as he cried, "Edith! are you in any way concerned in the mysteries of this house?"

Then Wild lifted his hands above his head, and shrieked out the word "Gone!"

Edith was not there. His worst fears were but too true. Edith had escaped, and who could have had the audacity—who the courage—who the power to aid her in that escape, but Captain Heron?

"Lost! lost!" he yelled. "All my pains—all my skill—all my danger—gone for nothing! She has escaped me. Him I had not a prisoner, but her I had in such fancied security—such fancied safety—and now she is gone! gone! and all because I had the folly not to shoot a couple of bolts into their sockets! Fool! fool! fool! fool!"

Wild was beginning now thoroughly to believe the story told him by the Governor of Newgate. If he had but secured the secret door which led from the cell number ten, not only would Edith still have been his prisoner, but Captain Heron might have dashed himself to death against the stone walls of his cage without escaping from it.

All is lost by a moment's inadvertence.

He and the Governor alone knew that that cell, number ten, in the foundations of the old prison, had a communication with his (Wild's) "Little Newgate." It was never used to place any one in but for the express purpose of consigning them to the tender mercies of Jonathan Wild. Accident alone, as we are aware, had made Captain Heron for five minutes the occupant of it. No wonder, when Wild thought of all these things, that he should stamp, and wonder, and rave.

Then he became so suddenly calm that the startling alternation resembled much the extraordinary manner in which, after one of his loud and hideous laughs, he was in the habit of startling everybody by lapsing into perfect gravity.

"I'm a fool!" he said. I've been a fool; but that's no reason why I sho ld continue to be one. I suppose I shall find Blueskin and Mobbs shot in some hole or corner of the house. What's that— what's that? What strange noise is that?"

A confused, roaring sound came upon Wild's ears, as if a gale of wind were raging amid the tree-tops, or the waves of the sea dashing impetuously upon some pebbly beach.

What could it mean?

Wild listened, and began to tremble while he listened.

CHAPTER CLXXXVII.

JONATHAN WILD FINDS THAT THERE IS DANGER IN BEING TOO WELL SECURED.

THE strange noise that began to have an alarming effect upon the nervous system of Jonathan Wild increased each moment.

He could not divine what it was.

Neither could he satisfy himself why he should be so much alarmed at it as he was, and yet alarm was in every feature of his face, and in every attitude he assumed.

"Is it fire?" he asked himself. "It it an inundation? Is it a storm? Is it a—a riot of some sort?"

Jonathan Wild, when first he began to ask himself all those questions, had already began to come to the conclusion that the strange noise he heard was what he chose to call "a riot of some sort."

He was right.

A very few words will let our readers know how the riot began, and what were its objects.

When Captain Heron released so successfully the unfortunate victims of Jonathan Wild's dungeons beneath his house, they collected together those unhappy people in the vaulted passage, from which the various cells opened, with a determination to make a sudden rush into the hall of the house, and overcome all opposition, and so make their escape.

It was quite within the range of possibility that in that effort some one, two, or three of them might fall victims to the firearms of Wild's accessories; but they were rendered desperate by long imprisonment, the pangs of which were sharpened by a consciousness that it was not the laws of their country that held them in durance, but the arbitrary will of Jonathan Wild, a worse criminal himself than they.

In two or three instances it was, however, the absolute innocence of the parties which made them obnoxious to the notorious thief-taker.

These wretched people either would not lend themselves to Jonathan Wild's purposes, or they were accidentally in possession of secrets dangerous to his safety.

Such was the case in regard to the young servant-girl, who was aware of his complicity in a robbery of plate in Lincoln's-inn Fields.

Let us then imagine these persons, who only one brief hour before had little hope of ever leaving those dungeons of Wild's in life, released so far that they felt they had the power of making, at least, a struggle for the remainder of their liberty.

They armed themselves with whatever they could lay hands upon; and two of the strongest of the men succeeded in wrenching off the iron bars which formed an additional safeguard to the doors of the cells; and, with those formidable weapons in their hands, they took the lead.

The delay, however, which took place in the region below the house, before all the prisoners were collected, was of immense value to them, although each moment they groaned over it, and bitterly regretted it.

We are not always the best judges of the effect of incident, which at the moment of their happening seem to cross and perplex our dearest wishes and hopes.

That delay had the effect of completely dispersing their enemies.

Jonathan Wild and his men were, with the exception of Mobbs and Blueskin, all at Newgate.

Mobbs was busy with Captain Heron.

Blueskin had sought the attic where Edith was a prisoner, to make to her that extraordinary speech which had filled Captain Heron with so much surprise and pleasure.

The hall of Jonathan Wild's house was therefore completely empty and unguarded.

Probably such a thing had never before happened since that house was in the possession of the notorious thief-taker.

When, therefore, the prisoners from below made their rush up the narrow staircase, they were not a little surprised to find nothing in the shape of opposition.

In two minutes more they were all in Newgate Street.

In another minute they had dispersed in different directions.

The young servant-girl, who had been arrested by Wild, simply because she knew something about his criminality, fled across the way towards Giltspur Street; and such was the state of excitement that her unexpected release threw her into, that she commenced screaming and sobbing in a fashion that soon collected a crowd about her, so that by the time she reached Smithfield she was an object of great attention to the rapidly assembling people.

It was market day.

The whole area of Smithfield was gradually getting filled by animals, and drovers, and market people.

Then, with a scream, this young woman rushed into the arms of an old grey-haired man, who with astonishment, grief, and terror depicted upon his countenance, cried out, "Are my old eyes all wrong, or is this my grandchild, Sussy, I see?"

The girl fell sobbing upon the old man's breast; and then, when some hundreds of people had gathered about them, clamorous to know what was amiss, she looked up, and in a voice of great excitement shrieked out the story of her wrongs.

"It was Mr. Jonathan Wild — it was the villain Wild. I knew he had been one in the robbery. He had me seized, and taken to his house. I have been in one of his cells I don't know now how long. Oh, I have prayed for mercy, but found none. I have had from him kicks and blows. See here the livid bruises. Oh, God will surely not let that man go on in his wickedness! Justice, justice, justice! It is all Jonathan Wild's doings! The villain Wild—the villain Wild!"

A confused roar of execration at Jonathan's doings burst from the people; and then one tall and stalwart young drover, who had travelled a hundred miles to Smithfield Market, shouted out, "Let's go, and pull him out, like! Lets go, and pull out old Jonathan!"

"Hoorah!" shouted the mob.

It wanted yet a good half hour before the clock of the market would declare it opened, so they had time for any such little interlude as that suggested by the young drover.

"Hoorah! hoorah! To Jonathan's house! Pull it down! Drag him out! Hang him up by the market bell! Hoorah! hoorah!"

Those shouts and cries, from at least three hundred throats, had reached the ears of Wild.

It was that roar of human vengeance which had so much alarmed him.

The really coward heart of the ruffian felt that there was a danger approaching which he might find it difficult indeed to guard himself against.

And he was alone, too.

Alone in that house which he had always looked upon as a kind of baronial castle, within the precincts of which he could do what he liked, and commit any atrocity that his evil nature might suggest to him.

Alone in that house, which he had up to that moment believed to be impregnable, but which now appeared to his imagination to be little better than a house of cards against any mob attack.

What should he do?

He made his way into one of the front attics. He leaned his head and body out of the window, so that he got a good view in that dim and early dawn of the street below. For a moment he thought that surely all was well, and that he had allowed his fancy to delude him into an idea of danger, when none in reality was in existence.

It was only for a moment, however, that he was able so far to flatter himself.

Coming out of Giltspur Street, he saw a furious, excited crowd of men and women.

Drovers with their cattle-sticks—horse-dealers and pig-drivers with their whips and bludgeons—a terrible contingent of loose population from that neighbourhood about the north of Smithfield, and which had caught the alarm, and poured in to the aid of the drovers with a frightful celerity.

"To Jonathan's house! Pull him out! Roast him! Hang him! Tear him in bits! To Jonathan Wild's house! Hoorah! hoorah! hoorah!"

Wild looked over the parapet, just beneath the attic window, like a man paralyzed; and so, indeed, for all practical purposes, he was for a few minutes.

With a bewildered kind of fascination that prevented him, during that space of time, from taking the slightest care for his own safety, Jonathan Wild gazed over the parapet.

And yet each moment fled away with some of his chances of escape upon its fleeting pinions.

"There he is!" roared a hundred voices at once. "There he is!"

Wild slunk back.

A hundred hands had pointed upwards to him.

His face and head had been seen just over the coping-stone of the parapet beneath his attic window.

"Hoorah! Hoorah! There he is! There he is! Have him out! The villain Wild! Drag him out! Pull his house down! Hang him up! There he is!"

A yell and a moan arose from every throat just as Jonathan Wild withdrew his head from the window, stunned and bewildered by the sight he saw.

What could he do?

Escape! Of course, escape. Ha! ha! What could they do to him? Whatever had brought them upon him in that strange fashion he could not guess; but, at all events, he could foil them. There was surely time for him to get out of the house—out into Newgate-street—he, he!

Wild had come down the attic stairs. He had got past the iron door which cut off the topmost floor of his house from the others, and then he paused.

Such a furious knocking had commenced at the street door that it was a wonder the panel did not come in at once.

That was a practical answer to his idea of leaving the house in that direction.

But Jonathan was getting over his first fright. He was becoming cooler and more collected each moment.

"Ah!" he said; "too late, too late!"

The violent knocking continued—it was fast and furious.

The mob was on his threshold.

A hideous scowl came over Wild's face, and then he descended just low enough to see the top of the street door.

A greasy-looking fanlight was there, secured on the inside by strong iron bars, through which a cat might have squeezed herself, but no larger or less active creature.

"Hilloa! Come out, old Jonathan," roared a voice, as the fanlight was splintered into fragments, and a brazen face appeared at the bars, looking into the passage. "Hilloa! Come out, old Jonathan, or it will be all the worse for you."

"Or for you, my forward friend," said Wild.

At the same moment he grasped the pistol he had with him, and which was still undischarged, and fired full and fair at the fanlight above the door.

Simultaneously with the report of the pistol there was a yell of pain.

The face disappeared.

"I think I had you there," said Wild.

If anything had been at all wanting to thoroughly exasperate the mob without, certainly that was now supplied.

When the man, who, mounted on the shoulders of one of his comrades, had looked into Jonathan's house through the fanlight, fell back with blood gushing from his face, and in the throes and

JONATHAN WILD BAFFLES IE PURSUIT OF HIS FOES.

Presented Gratis with No. 84 of the New Edition of Isi the Captive; or, the Robbers of Epping Forest.

EACH WEEK IS PRESENTED GRAT A COLOURED ENGRAVING.

agonies of death, the mob, for a few seconds, recoiled in horror.

But the revulsion of feeling was as rapid as it was terrible.

The cry that arose from every throat was of quite a different character from any that had preceded it.

As many men as could act at once made a rush at the street door, and the concussion was so great that Jonathan involuntarily retreated upstairs a few paces.

"This cannot last," he said. "It cannot surely last many minutes. The constables will assemble; the Light Horse will be sent for. Such a riot as this will be put down. I don't think I need trouble myself to escape."

Even while Jonathan Wild thus spoke, he was considering what would be his best mode of flight from that house which was now so vigorously attacked.

"The secret way to Newgate," he said, at length, —"that will be the way—that will be the way! I will go through Number Ten cell into the prison. I have but to bolt and bar all doors behind me as I go, and I shall be safe enough. The fools! Do they think that I am to be caught quite so easily? No—no! Do your worst and best! I laugh at you. Ha! ha!"

The yells, shouts, cries, groans, and execrations outside the house combined in full chorus; and it was evident, from the volume of sound that met Jonathan's ears, that the mob had received a large accession of force, which it was sure to do.

There is nothing that recruits so quickly as a London mob.

By this time Newgate Street was completely blocked up; and the crowd extended quite up into Giltspur Street and down Snow Hill.

Wild slunk down stairs.

He had a fear, which he was loth to confess to himself, at descending; because, until he should have fairly passed the hall, and began a descent to the underground portion of his premises, each step he took really brought him closer to the roaring, shouting, yelling mob, who, if they could only just then have got hold of him, would, no doubt, tear him limb from limb.

But Wild was on nearly the last stair when he paused.

All the faculties of the crowd without seemed suddenly to be absorbed in one immense cheer of gratification.

What could it mean?

What popular person had suddenly appeared to head and, perhaps, organize the riot?

Jonathan was not left long in suspense.

With a tremendous force there came something against the door, which it had no power of resisting. Bolts, sock, all flew to pieces; and a huge, burly man, in his shirt-sleeves, which were rolled up above his elbows, and with a tremendous forehammer in his hands, fell into the passage.

Half a dozen of the foremost of the mob rolled over him.

That was the popular person who had received the cheering ovation from the people. He was a well-known blacksmith in the neighbourhood, who had brought the means of opening Jonathan Wild's door at one blow, and he did it.

Jonathan jumped the remainder of the stairs, and reached the hall.

"There he is!" yelled fifty voices, the voices of all who could catch a glimpse of him through the open door.

It was too late.

The terrible words—undoubtedly the most terrible ones that any language can give utterance to —rang in his ears as he himself pronounced them.

It would be an even race if he were now to try to reach the door at the end of the hall which led to the lower regions of his house; and what if it were fast?

What if he should be detained there half a minute—a quarter of a minute—a couple of seconds—in an endeavour to open it?

Fifty people would be upon his back.

Too late!

Wild turned and fled up the stairs.

The mob streamed into the house. They fought and struggled for precedence in the passage, and so they impeded each other.

Jonathan reached the iron door. He passed it. He closed and secured it; and then, panting and excited, he crouched down to listen.

The most terrible noises came roaring up from the lower part of the house into which had forced a dense infuriated mass of people.

Wild looked white as a piece of badly-bleached cotton, and he shook so that his teeth chattered like castanets.

CHAPTER CLXXXVII.

JONATHAN WILD ESCAPES FROM THE MOB, AND TAKES REFUGE WITH LORD WARRINGDALE.

ALL the terrible stories that from time to time Jonathan Wild had ever heard or read concerning men hunted by mobs, and torn limb from limb, came across his imagination, as he stood alone in his house, and listened to the shouts, cries, ravings, and maledictions of the infuriated mass of people who were vowing his destruction.

It is possible enough that there had been times in the career of Wild when he had thought the day might come which would see him dying of some fearful wound received in some encounter, in which, with his usual savage ferocity, he had engaged; but that was a very different mode of making an exit from the world, to being torn to pieces by an infuriated mob.

No wonder Jonathan Wild trembled.

"Pull him out! Drag him out! Hang him! Cut him in bits! Hanging is too good for him! Smash him! Out with him! Out with him!"

Yelling with rage, and the disappointment of not being able to lay hold of their victim at once, the mob, or the foremost of them, reached the iron door on the staircase.

Wild retreated.

He had great faith in the strength of that door, but not quite sufficient to induce him to stand still on the upper side of it.

So Wild retreated.

"Escape! escape!" he muttered. "I must escape, and that at once, too! The atmosphere of this house is now full of death to me!"

Still, shaking terribly by the fall he had had, and, perhaps, still more by the apprehensions that filled his mind, Jonathan slunk up the stairs that led to the attic.

How gladly now would he have welcomed any human voice that would have addressed him in hopeful accents, or promised him assistance, for after all the chances of escape from the upper part of his house were few.

And those few chances were dangerous.

There was a special reason why even Jonathan Wild, with all his strength, all his cunning, and all his dexterity, would find it difficult to get out of, or off his own premises.

The close proximity of the house to Newgate —that proximity which had recommended it to him as so desirable an abode—made it now all but a trap in which the thief-taker was himself caught.

The greatest pains had been taken, and the greatest skill had been used, to prevent people from escaping from Newgate in that direction.

The walls were covered with revolving iron-work, spiked and sharp.

The angles were protected by bayonets, fixed by their handles in deep mortar and cement, so that to get out of Newgate in that direction, even provided the top of the wall was gained, would be an enterprise fraught with peril.

All these precautions cut both ways.

If it were difficult to get from Newgate to Jonathan Wild's house, it was as difficult to get from Jonathan Wild's house to Newgate.

And where else could he, Jonathan, seek for a refuge?

The next door was quite inaccessible.

By order of the authorities, and at the suggestion of Wild himself, a brick wall, twenty-four feet in height, had been built between the roofs of the two houses. A fly could, no doubt, easily enough have walked up that wall, but not a human being.

Truly, the great thief-taker was in danger.

A roaring, shouting mob at his back.

Spikes, bayonets, and steep walls in advance of him.

And yet he must escape!

What chance of life had he otherwise?

Rapidly Jonathan Wild revolved all these particulars of his condition in his heated imagination, and for a time he could see nothing but destruction in the circumstances around him.

The noise, the outcries, and the shouts, and the racket made in the house by the mob, no doubt tended greatly to disturb the usually acute intellect of Wild; but who would have succeeded in the preservation of cool judgment with such sounds ringing in their ears?

The blows upon the iron door that shut the upper part of the house from the lower, now fell fast and furious.

The stalwart smith who, with one blow of his fore-hammer, had burst open the outer or street door of the house, was evidently now at work upon that iron obstruction.

Truly Jonathan had no time to lose.

He dashed into the attic in which Edith had been imprisoned. He closed the door, and did his best to fasten it on the inside. He scrambled on to the little moveable bit of wood on trestles which did duty for a table; he made an effort to reach the trap-door in the roof; but just missing it by a couple of inches, he overbalanced the trestles, and fell heavily to the floor.

We cannot transcribe the remarks that Jonathan Wild made at that moment in reference to his fall: they were rather too forcibly.

Then, however, as he half sat upon the floor of that prison attic, he heard one great shout of triumph from the mob, and he felt certain it was an announcement of the knocking down of the only important barrier that separated him from them—namely, the iron door.

Jonathan sprung to his feet as if some hidden spring had suddenly assumed immense power, and shot him up from the floor of the attic.

There was a chair in the room. It might scarcely be called a chair, since the back of it was broken away, and it had assumed the aspect of a stool. Jonathan seized it with avidity. It was his only chance now.

He replaced the board on the trestles; the stool-like chair he placed on the board.

The structure was tottery.

"Hoorah! hoorah!" shouted the mob. "Now we have him—now we have him!"

"No, you don't," said Jonathan Wild.

"Hoorah! hoorah! Throw yourself out of window, Johnny; there will be plenty to catch you! Hoorah! Lay hold of him! Have him out!"

The people impeded each other more on those narrow attic stairs than they had done on the wider ones at the lower part of the house.

Had Wild's pursuers only consisted of the stalwart smith and some half-dozen resolute men, he must have been taken.

As it was he found a certain safety in the multitude of his foes.

He clambered to the top of the broken chair.

He could reach the trap-door in the roof of the attic now with ease.

Another moment, and Jonathan Wild had managed, notwithstanding all his hurts and bruises, to scramble through the opening.

The attic door was dashed open by the foremost of his enemies, at the very moment that he closed from without the trap-door in the roof of the attic.

The one noise drowned the others.

Jonathan was in comparative safety on the roof of his house; but it was a perilous position—not ordinarily so, for he was used to it; but under the present state of things, it was doubtful if, with any degree of safety, he would be able to avail himself of his usual means of descent.

That was by the circular iron staircase.

There was a block of wood lying in the gutter of the roof, the end of which would crack the topmost slip of that iron staircase.

In peaceable and ordinary times, Wild could descend easily enough by that means.

Now the case was altered.

One glance over the parapet showed Jonathan that some dozen or two people were in the yard below.

That avenue of escape then was cut off.

Nay; the iron staircase, upon the acquisition of which he had so often, since he had possessed it, congratulated himself, seemed destined to become the means of his destruction.

With yells and shouts, several persons commenced the ascent.

Wild was desperate.

He poised the plank over the parapet in such a

manner that, by a slight impulse, he could project it down the staircase.

He waited a few moments, and then over he threw it.

The three or four persons who were first and foremost in ascending the iron staircase were shot down as if a battering-ram had struck them.

Those behind moved, and the plank of wood stuck fast in the ironwork, and barred the way as effectually as though it had been most artistically placed there for such a purpose.

For a moment, then, Jonathan Wild was free from attack in that quarter.

The mob in the attic had not yet noticed the trap-door in the roof.

At the first rush they had fallen headlong over the little arrangement of trestles, boards, and broken chair, so that they had failed to see that they had constituted a kind of pyramid to the ceiling.

But this state of security could not last very long. Crouching down in the gutter of the roof, Wild expected each moment to see some heads project from the trap-door.

What he should do then he had not the most distant idea.

Nothing but death stared him in the face.

Then he suddenly sprung to his feet. A new alarm had taken possession of him, and any one who could have noted and speculated upon the expression of Wild's face at that moment of time might well have wondered what it was that caused so strange and rapid a movement of his nostrils.

He smelt fire!

There could be no mistake about it.

Jonathan Wild smelt burning wood. The flavour came up to him strong—pungent and positive.

The house was on fire!

"Burn him out! Burn him out!" shouted a hundred voices in hideous chorus.

"Ah!" said Wild. "I have it. I fancy it's all over now."

Jonathan almost resigned himself.

It seemed a choice of pleasures.

Would he descend, and be pulled to pieces by the mob; or would he stay on the roof of his house, and be roasted?

Pleasant alternatives!

"Fire! fire! fire!" was the cry that resounded through the house.

That cry brought with it a sensation of alarm to those who were in the attic, and to those who were crowding the staircases, and unable to reach so far.

A violent retrograde movement immediately took place.

The mob fought, and kicked, and struggled to get out of Jonathan Wild's house, just as furiously as it had fought, and kicked, and struggled to get in.

But all that did no good to Wild. He was as badly off as ever.

Perhaps it may be considered that he was worse off than ever.

There was just the possibility that he might have escaped with his life from that infuriated mob; but how he was to do so from his own burning house, was a mystery,

Already the blood began to retreat to the heart of Jonathan Wild. Already he began to have those mortal shiverings which beset a man who sees death in some horrible shape before him, while he is otherwise hale and well.

The mind begins to feel as if its better portion were about to be released from its earthly casket, and makes vigorous efforts which shake the system, and produce sickness at the heart to accelerate its freedom.

Jonathan was very nearly giving way, without another attempt even to save himself.

"What can I do? What can I do?" That was the terrible question he kept asking himself, and to which there certainly appeared no very ready answer.

The odour of burning wood came each moment now more strongly to his senses, and accompanying it was a sharp crackling sound, which testified to the tolerably dry state of the panels, shutters, and balustrades of Wild's house.

Even where he was on the roof, he thought that a sensation of extraordinary heat came over him.

But that was imagination.

The fire had not yet made sufficient progress to develope heat enough to reach the position he occupied.

Suddenly, then, a loud ringing shout came from the throng of people in the street below—half a shout it was, and half a cry of dismay.

Something had happened, or was about to happen, inimical to the feelings and objects of the mob.

"Charge!" cried a loud voice.

There was a rush of horses' feet, and yells, and shrieks from the crowd, which were music to the ears of Jonathan Wild.

A party of Light Horse, from the King's Mews, had arrived on the scene of action, and the mob was melting away, like snow before a south wind and a warm shower.

The courts, alleys, and narrow streets on each side of the way of Newgate Street were most convenient for the dispersion of the people, and by the time the party of Light Horse had trotted the whole length of Newgate Street, and turned to come back again, no one was there to oppose them.

"Halt," cried the officer.

"Help, help!" shouted Jonathan Wild from the top of his house. "Help, oh help!"

At that moment a bright flame of several colours leaped up through the trap-door in the roof by which Jonathan had obtained his elevated position.

The house was fairly on fire, although, as yet, the flames did not show much in the front.

Wild heard a cry of consternation, and, as he looked over the parapet of the house, he saw the faces of the soldiers turned up towards him, and the officer said something which he did not hear.

But Wild had sense enough left to see that it was completely out of the power of the Light Horse to help him, if they had ever such an inclination to do so, and that was doubtful.

A fire-engine, from the direction of St. Paul's, then came dashing into Newgate Street.

Jonathan Wild gave himself up. He felt how utterly helpless he was.

To attempt, now, to rush through the burning house would be madness.

To attempt a drop on to the topmast portion of

the iron staircase, and a descent by that means, was now too late.

A volume of flame and smoke had come out of several of the back windows of the house; and that iron staircase resembled the flue of some great furnace, up which fire and vapour tore, and raged, and raved with fury.

"Lost—lost!" said Wild.

He flung himself down in one of the gutters of the roof, and gave himself up to despair.

"Mr. Wild! Mr. Wild!"

Jonathan sprung to his feet.

Who called him? Who was that? What voice was that? Whose voice?

Jonathan had at the moment a ridiculous and terrible dread that it was the voice of the arch enemy of mankind, or of some one from him, come for a legitimate prey.

"Mr. Wild! Mr. Wild!"

"What? Where? I am not dead yet!"

"Mr. Wild!"

"Help! Mercy!"

"It's behind you, Mr. Wild."

Jonathan fairly jumped round. He was close to that perpendicular wall which supported his house in Newgate Street from the next door—that wall which had been made so high and so smooth that it might not be scaled from below or descended from above—and, as he turned, something struck him on the back.

Wild screamed.

"No—no! not yet! Oh, not yet! Some few years more let me live!—live! Eh?"

It was a stout rope that was dangling from the top of the wall, and which, in its vibrations, struck him on the back.

Up above, just over the parapet of the wall, were the two hands and face of a man.

"Mr. Wild! Mr. Wild! If you can climb up the rope, you may get away this way easy enough, you know."

"Saved!" shrieked Wild. "Who are you?"

"Mr. Timms, the meat-salesman."

"You are rich?"

"Oh dear, no."

"You are! Hold on to that rope, and help me while I get to the top, and you are a thousand pounds richer than you were this morning—half an hour ago."

Jonathan was getting liberal.

He did not wait a moment for the answer of Mr. Timms, who was rather a slow-speaking personage, but, feeling all his strength and all his resolution restored to him, now that there was again a prospect of escape, he clutched the rope, and, heedless of the bruises and abrasions he got from the wall, he commenced its ascent.

Jonathan was not a bad climber, and he soon had hold of the hand of Mr. Timms, who helped him over on to the roof of that next house.

"All right, Mr. Wild."

"Yes," gasped Jonathan. "Yes; I am saved —saved!"

At that moment, with a hideous and alarming crash, a portion of the roof of Jonathan Wild's house fell in, and a shower of hot dust and sparks fell upon Mr. Timms and the rescued thief-taker.

The dull, heavy beat and clank of the pumps of the fire-engine was the only sound that mingled very audibly now with the roar of the flames, for the house was in full blaze.

The entire and total destruction of that detestable abode of Jonathan Wild was certain.

"They will roast," said Wild.

"Who, Mr. Wild?—who?" asked Timms.

"No; they will bake," added Jonathan.

"Who will, sir?"

"Nobody."

Wild said nobody; but he meant the prisoners, who, he thought, were still in the cells beneath his house, and of whose fate he spoke thus unconcernedly.

But he had himself escaped; and as the fear of death passed from him, all his old passions revived within him, so that in ten minutes more he was the same ruffian he had always been.

CHAPTER CLXXXIX.

RETURNS TO EDITH, AND TO CAPTAIN HERON AND BLUESKIN IN THE ATTIC.

THE necessity of following the fortunes of Jonathan Wild, so far as to see him clear of his burning house, has compelled us to neglect Captain Heron and Edith at a most important crisis of their fortunes.

It will be remembered that in the mind of Mr. Mobbs and of Captain Heron there had arisen an idea that Blueskin would be an obstruction to the escape of Edith that might cost, probably, a life to overcome.

What, then, was the surprise and pleasure of Heron to hear that remarkable speech—the longest one that Blueskin had ever made in his life— from this most important of all Jonathan Wild's myrmidons!

There was no doubt of the sincerity of Blueskin. He had not sufficient finesse in his disposition to have made such a speech if it had not been perfectly true and sincere.

Edith, too, was delighted.

"Ah," she said, "then I did not deceive myself, when I thought you looked kindly at me."

"Not a bit of it, little 'un. Come in, and I'll see you all safe. I don't seem to like these here goings on any longer, so I'm off, and you may as well be off, too, little 'un. Only say where you would like to go to, and I'll take jolly good care you get there."

Edith held out her hand, and placed it in the large—what shall I call it?—paw of Blueskin.

"I am as thankful to you, and shall be as grateful to you, as if you really had saved me."

"Eh?"

Edith smiled.

"Well," said Blueskin, "I can't make out what you mean, exactly; but if ever I seed such a little bit of a hand afore, I'm a Frenchman!"

Edith smiled again, and then raising her eyes to the roof of the attic, she said, "Felix!"

"Here, dearest."

"Bless us!" cried Blueskin. "Oh, I see! Here's the Captain! Hilloa! hilloa! I'll settle him! Out of the way, little 'un! Out of the way, Captain!"

"What do you mean?" said Edith and Captain Heron, both in a breath.

"Why, it's Mobbs. I thought I should have to settle somebody! Come here, Mobbs, and I'll

wring your neck for you, at once! You won't feel it much! Come here, Mobby—come along!"

"I'd rather not, Blueskin," said Mobbs; "and all the more particularly, that I have joined Captain Heron myself!"

"You have?"

"I have, indeed! And what I am here for was to get rid of you in some way!"

"No, Mobby, no! No, you couldn't do it—oh dear, no! But is it all true, and above-board, Captain, that Mobby has joined you?"

"Quite true. And I hope that, for the time to come, I may consider you as a friend?"

"Well, you may," said Blueskin. "But I tell you what it is, Captain Heron, if it hadn't been for the little 'un, I shouldn't have thought so much of Jonathan's doings, but I didn't like the looks of that 'ere transaction. What right had he to put the little 'un into one of the attic cells, eh? Why, no right at all, in course, eh?"

No. 85.—EDITH.

Blueskin, as he spoke, turned round twice, as if challenging contradiction to this opinion; and as none, of course, came, he felt abundantly satisfied.

Captain Heron now was conscious that nothing further had to be done now in Jonathan's Wild's house that could possibly interest him. His anxiety to leave it was great and immediate; the very atmosphere of that place—devoted as it had been to criminality and to villany of every kind and description—was hateful to him.

"Come, dear Edith," he said, " let us no longer linger in this house of crime. Thank heaven we can leave it now, and the episodes of this most eventful night are over. Let us fly to our own happy home, amid the shadows of Epping Forest; and henceforth, dear one, we will trust nobody but those whom we feel we can have faith in beyond a doubt."

It was quite impossible that Captain Heron

258

EDITH THE CAPTIVE.

could be more anxious to leave Jonathan Wild's
house than was Edith herself. The dangers, the
terrors, and the confusion of that night had been
greater than ever she could have thought it
possible to go through, even with the amount of
strength and judgment she had brought to bear
upon them.

It was to her, too, a subject of the greatest
felicitation that the escape from Wild's detestable
house would be accomplished without bloodshed;
—for, however little she might feel herself called
upon to feel in the way of sympathy for whatever
might happen to such a man as Jonathan Wild,
yet she naturally revolted from any scene of strife
or destruction.

Hence, to preserve the purity of that state of
things, Edith grasped the arm of Captain Heron,
as she exclaimed, "Yes, Felix; oh, yes! Let us
leave this place at once! It will be a mercy to
breathe the free open air of heaven once again!
Let us leave it at once; and as we do so we will
likewise congratulate ourselves that we have
made two friends instead of having to battle with
two foes."

Even while speaking, with Edith clinging
closely to his heart, Captain Heron left that attic
cell in Jonathan Wild's house.

Blueskin led the way, and Mobbs brought up
the rear; and as all this happened within the
exact cognizance of Mrs. Shakles—since she could
see what was taking place, although she had no
power to prevent it—the fury that glared forth
from the eyes of that disappointed female was
something terrible to behold.

It was well both for her and for them that she
was so effectually gagged as only to be able to
produce a strange gurgling kind of noise which,
accompanied by the drumming of her feet on the
floor, was sufficiently indicative of the state of
mind of Mrs. Shakles.

Nobody, however, paid the slightest heed to her
feelings or opinions upon the subject, and she was
left to settle matters in the best way she could
with Jonathan Wild, which she did in the manner
the reader is already aware of.

By the combination of circumstances which had
made the escape of Captain Heron and Edith an
accomplished fact, it was likewise a matter of
perfect ease for them to walk out into Newgate
Street unsuspected and unnoticed.

Mobbs pulled the door behind him and Jonathan Wild's house was closed, being left to solitude
and to Mrs. Shakles.

"If we could but get a coach," said Captain
Heron, "we might make, at all events, some progress towards the forest, even if we had to walk
the remainder of the way."

"There ain't no occasion for walking," said
Blueskin. "There's lots of coaches, and I dare
say, if we comes round the corner here, towards
Aldersgate, we shall find some one. You can
drive, Mobbs, can't you?"

"To be sure I can, Blueskin."

"Then we'll borrow a coach and horses; for I
suppose these here sort of little 'uns don't walk
much,—eh, Captain?"

Blueskin attended to Edith, whom he evidently
looked upon as a sort of natural curiosity, since
his experience of the fair sex had not extended
much beyond such specimens as Mother Shakles,
or, at the best, Mrs. Ogle.

"We will follow you, Blueskin," said Captain
Heron; "trusting to you entirely in this matter."

"All's right, Captain. Here you are."

They had turned the corner of Newgate Street
towards the City, and there, as Blueskin had predicted, they saw a hackney-coach and horses; but
the driver was, as is usual with men of his fraternity when not engaged, fast asleep upon the
box.

Blueskin paid not the least attention to the
driver; but opening the door and letting down the
steps, he said, "Now, little 'un, you get in there,
and you'll be as safe as a fly in a pot of treacle.
Mobbs 'll drive, and I'll sit on the roof and smoke
my pipe. Get in, Captain; it's all right. Off we
goes!"

The violent closing of the door was a familiar
sound to the driver, and roused him from his
sleep.

"Hilloa!" now he cried. "What's all this?
Where to? It's half a crown a mile at this time
in the morning. Murder! Help! Fire!"

These exclamations arose from the very sum-
mary manner in which Blueskin dislodged him
from the coach-box; that necessary feat being
effected simply and quickly by laying hold of the
coachman's leg, and dragging him to the pavement.

"All's right," cried Blueskin, again.

Mobbs was on the coach-box in a moment.
Blueskin scrambled on the roof, which Edith and
Captain Heron certainly thought was coming
through, when, with a tremendous concussion, he
settled himself comfortably, as he termed it, in
his elevated position. The coachman was so
encumbered with his heavy great-coat that he
floundered about upon the pavement like a
stranded porpoise, and was unable to oppose any
resistance to the departure of the coach, which
rattled over the stones of Aldersgate Street at a
good pace.

Edith, now, in the joy and congratulation of the
moment, could scarcely believe in the fact of her
own safety, and that Felix Heron, too, was unharmed and free.

With breathless attention she listened to his
account of the attack upon Newgate; and when he
came to that part of his narration where the
Governor and the Reverend Mortification Ripon
had closed the door of Number Ten cell upon him,
she was able to comprehend the full anguish of
the situation—for had not she, too, had that cell
door closed upon her; believing and dreading, at
the moment, that it shut her out from all communing with the outer world.

Then Edith was enabled to communicate to
Captain Heron how she had been visited by
Jonathan Wild in that cell; and how, with many
sneers and taunts, he had congratulated himself
upon being able to remove her from it to one of
the prison attics of his own house, as a place of
greater safety, but which very act had been the
very means of her present freedom and happiness.

If Wild had been content to leave Edith in the
cell of Newgate, whither she had been at first conveyed, and had kept the secret door of communication with his own house effectually closed, it is
possible enough that Captain Heron might likewise have been entrapped; but the villain, so to
speak, would be safer than safe, and the consequence was that both of those persons, whom he

would gladly have made his victims, escaped him.

Still, however, there was much to produce anxiety, both to Edith and to Captain Heron, as soon as the first congratulation of their escape from Jonathan Wild's house had passed away.

Those whom they loved were still in danger. Lady Castleneau and Sir Dominick Brown, both, for all they could know, were in the power of their worst enemies; and Captain Heron could not but likewise feel a continued pang of anxiety as regarded the fate of Ogle and his band of faithful followers who had attended him upon that perilous expedition to Newgate.

"Edith, dearest," he said, "I can but lodge you in safety in Epping Forest; there, in the deep recesses of our sylvan home, I shall feel that you are safe. Then I must return to the busy scenes of strife and anxiety which London still unfolds to me. Step by step, and bit by bit, we have now so much information to guide us, that I think, although but dimly at present, I can see the light of success before me. I have two anxieties: the greater of the two is for the preservation and safety of those who may be in danger and suffering on our account; the lesser is to procure, without the shadow of a doubt, such evidence of my birth and position as shall effectually confound the pretensions of Lord Warringdale, and end at once the unnatural strife that so sadly exists between the sons of the same father."

Edith was about to reply to these words, which had been uttered by Captain Heron in rather mournful accents, when Blueskin summoned attention to something he had to communicate by a series of raps on the roof of the coach.

"Ah," said Edith, "there is danger."

"Fear not," replied Heron.

"'From the nettle Danger, we pluck the flower Safety.'"

Blueskin continued exercising a series of double knocks on the roof of the coach, and Mobbs brought the vehicle to a standstill, just as Captain Heron put his head out of one of the windows, and demanded what was the matter.

"I rather think," said Blueskin, "there's some fellows coming across the fields, going to make fools of themselves."

"What do you mean, Blueskin?"

"Why, they're going to fall foul of us; and I rather take it, Captain, they'll come off second best."

"Here they come," said Mobbs. "I can count eight or nine of them, and they seem well mounted."

"Alas," said Edith, "how can we contend against such a number?"

"Simply, dearest, by the resolution to do so," replied Heron; "but let me beg of you not to leave the coach. It is in some sort a cidadel, which will protect you from a stray shot."

"I will follow your direction; but, oh, Felix, if this encounter could be avoided, and we could reach our happy home in the Forest, how much better would it be! It is these stray shots you speak of I dread; for might not one of them make me desolate?"

"Fear nothing—fear nothing!"

"They're coming over the fields, Captain," cried Blueskin. "I see the fellows now, and an ill-looking set they are."

Captain Heron sprung out of the coach, and

directed that it should be drawn to one side of the road, so that at all events it could only be attacked in one direction, since there was a tall hedge-row close to which one side of it could be placed.

The morning was certainly coming, but the dawn had not made sufficient progress to render objects fairly visible. Moreover, as the coach had made its way into the country in the direction towards Epping, it seemed to have travelled into a thick, white mist, which obscured all objects sufficiently to confuse their outlines, although not to prevent their being seen.

This mist, too, seemed to have a magnifying power about it. For when the coach had been placed in the best position to sustain an attack, Captain Heron, and Blueskin, and Mobbs looked with some surprise at the dim shadowy horsemen who seemed to be of colossal proportions.

"Bless us!" said Blueskin, "they're big 'uns."

"What does it mean, Captain?" said Mobbs. "I can't make it out."

"It's only the mist," said Heron.

"But they don't look like men on horses—they look like giants on elephants."

"Yes," said Heron, "and possibly the coach looks as big as a house to them, if they see it. It is a delusion of the morning fog. We shall find that they are men like ourselves, and I hope by the slant direction they are taking across the meadow, they may pass without observing us."

"Look out!" cried Blueskin; "here they come. They've taken a sharp turn now."

This seemed, indeed, to be the case; for the group of horsemen who thus so suspiciously made their way across the meadows, instead of pursuing the route they seemed to have been so industriously taking, suddenly turned, and made for the nearest point of the hedge which would conduct them into the high road where the coach was waiting.

"The time has come," said Heron. "Look to your pistols."

"All's right, Captain," said Blueskin; "we'll pop one or two of them off at once."

"Do not be precipitate," said Heron.

"What!" cried Blueskin. "Don't be what?"

"I mean do not be hasty."

"Lor' bless us, no! The idea now of anybody, when he wants to tell a fellow not to be hasty, coming out with such a crack-jaw word as princi-principate. Some people is so precious fine, they don't know what they are saying."

"Hush! hush!" said Heron; "they may still put us in the fog. Ah! no; that hope is over."

As Captain Heron spoke, the party of horsemen came one by one into the roadway; and it would appear, although no such thing could be observed from the coach, that there was a gate or gap in the hedge which the horsemen had observed, and which had enabled them easily to leave the meadows.

It was certainly a high road on which these occurrences were taking place. Although a narrow one, and, notwithstanding the mud which was rolling about in dense masses, it was sufficiently evident that the coach and its defenders had been seen, for a loud voice called out, "Halt, comrades; here may, or may not, be our game."

"Shall I blaze away?" said Blueskin.

"No, no; not yet," replied Heron.

"Heaven preserve you, Felix!" said Edith, from the window.

"Back, back, Edith,—for the love of heaven,

back! These fellows may fire upon us in a moment. Crouch down low in the coach, and you will be safe from harm."

"Speak out!' cried one of the horsemen. "Who and what are you, and what do you do upon the highway at such an hour as this?'

"I'll have that one," said Blueskin, "at all events."

Bang! went Blueskin's pistol; and then at the moment when Captain Heron had every reason to believe a general volley from the horsemen would be the reply to such rashness, their leader called out loudly, "Don't fire; there's no harm done. Close in upon them, and take all prisoners."

CHAPTER CXC.

CAPTAIN HERON FINDS THAT SEEMING FOES TURN OUT TO BE BEST FRIENDS.

THE excitement on the part of the small party in command by Captain Heron could not be said to be very great, with one exception, inasmuch as both Mr. Mobbs and Blueskin were persons who were not in the habit of putting themselves much out of the way about anything.

It was Edith who formed the only exception; for apart from some anxiety on her account, Captain Heron himself was cool and collected enough.

The rush now that the horsemen made would, in another instant, have brought on fatal events had not one of them suddenly called out, "Hold, hold! On your lives, hold! Good gracious, it's the Captain!"

Bang! went another pistol from Blueskin at the same time; but, like its predecessor, it did no harm, although nothing could be said against the aim; but the fact was, as Blueskin afterwards suspected, the bullets had dropped out of the weapons on account of the jolting they got on the roof of the coach.

Firearms, at the period of our tale, were by no means the "weapons of prisoners" they have since become.

The words which one of the horsemen had last uttered appeared as if they had at once torn aside some veil in which the perceptions, both mental and physical of Captain Heron, had been shrouded.

He spoke in a loud, clear, ringing voice.

"As I live, you are my own men!"

Edith, hearing this, uttered a cry of joy from the coach, and clasped her hands together with thankfulness.

Blueskin whistled.

Mobbs nodded his head several times, as much as to say, "So, so; that's all right."

"Halt!" cried Heron. "Are you there, Ogle?"

"No, Captain," said the member of the band who had been left in command by Ogle.

"Then is this night the most sad I have ever yet known?" added Heron.

"Captain, Ogle is all right, we hope and expect."

"Ah!"

"Oh, yes, Captain. He got us all safe out of Newgate, and then he brought us part of the way here; after which he left us to look to your safety, for he said he would never leave London while your fate was uncertain."

"I knew it! I was sure of it!" cried Captain Heron. "I have faithful hearts and faithful friends in you all; but in Ogle I have——Well, well, you are all good men and true. I thank you. Edith, Edith, you have heard?"

"I have, dear Felix," said Edith; "and I hear more than is yet spoken."

Captain Heron smiled.

"I can hear your heart, dear, dear Felix, and it says that you will not abandon the man who has remained behind, and risked all to save you."

"Dearest and best!" cried Captain Heron, in a voice of enthusiasm. "Who shall read my heart as you read it?"

"No one knows you, Felix, so well as I know you."

Captain Heron clasped the hands of his Edith as they were projected from the coach window; and as he did so that morning mist, which had shrouded so many objects in a dim obscurity, and which had, by its accidental convex character, made Heron's companions look so monstrous on their apparently elephantine steeds, began rapidly to change its colour.

From a dull hazy grey it assumed a yellow tinge; from that again it visibly whitened, and began to roll away, or rather, perhaps, to the greatest extent, to condense,—for something that resembled a small rain fell upon the coach, Captain Heron, Blueskin, Mobbs, and the band.

Then the morning mist vanished.

It was daylight.

The birds began to sing in the hedgerows, and a large, pleasant, although rather watery, gleam of sunshine lit up the whole landscape.

"Dear Edith," said Heron, "look around you now! The night of violence has passed away."

"Yes," said Edith; "and the night of our evil fortunes, I hope, Felix."

"Amen to that hope, dear one!"

Captain Heron, then glancing at his band, could scarcely forbear from a smile, as he saw the wonder and amazement with which they regarded Blueskin, as he sat on the top of the coach.

Probably there was not one among them who did not know him well as one of the oldest and most effective of Jonathan Wild's janissaries.

To see him, therefore, in the company of Captain Heron, and quite calmly seated on the roof of the coach that contained Edith, appeared to them little short of a miracle.

Blueskin, when the appearance of a fight was so apparently obvious, had laid down his pipe; but now that peace, happiness, and concord seemed to be the order of the day, he began coolly to re-light it.

But, while Blueskin did this, he kept one eye guardedly fixed upon Captain Heron's men, and now and then gave a slight nod, as much as to say, "Ah, I see, you can't make it out yet; but you will in good time; and if you don't, what matters?"

Mobbs was not so well known, and, therefore, did not produce the same amount of curiosity and conjecture as Blueskin.

"Friends, all," said Captain Heron, indicating Blueskin and Mobbs; "these are two candidates for places in the band. I propose them."

"You, Captain?"

"Yes, Number Four; what have to say?"

"Nothing, Captain; but that I am astonished."

BLUE-SKIN PROVES HIMSELF A MAN OF VAST RESOURCES.

Presented Gratis with No. 85 of the New Edition of the Captive; or, the Robbers of Epping Forest.

EACH WEEK IS PRESENTED A COLOURED ENGRAVING.

"You looks it," said Blueskin.

"I can silence all objections," added Captain Heron; "by stating, at once, that but for Blueskin here, and Mobbs, I do not think that either Edith or myself could possibly have been in life this morning."

These words were more than sufficient.

The band dashed forward, and each strove to see which should be the first to shake hands with the two new comrades.

Blueskin and Mobbs, therefore, might be said to be elected members of Captain Heron's band by acclamation.

"All's right," said Blueskin; "I ain't good at making a speech; so all I says is, has anybody got a drop of anything to drink, for I am as dry as dust?"

One of the band at once won Blueskin's heart by producing a small case-bottle of that particular old cognac of which he was specially fond; and while Blueskin and the band were thus "fraternizing," Captain Heron bent down his head to Edith, and spoke in a low tone.

"Dearest Edith, you have guessed my wishes, and told me my duty."

"It is a duty, dear Felix."

"A paramount one."

"Yes; and never will the day come when your Edith will counsel you to desert a friend and comrade."

"That I am certain will never be, Edith; but you will now, with no fear for me, since I will be careful of myself for my own dear Edith's sake, go home to our home in the forest."

"Ah! Felix, Felix, I read your heart, but you have failed to read mine."

"Have I, dear?"

"Yes, Felix your heart said, 'I must not desert my friend Ogle.'"

"It did, indeed."

"And mine—what did it say?"

"It approved."

"And ——"

"My dearest Edith I can read no more."

"Then I will translate it to you, Felix. My heart said, 'I will not desert my husband.'"

"Ah! I comprehend."

"Yes, Felix, you do comprehend; and you will let your Edith be with you."

Captain Heron hesitated, and was about to say a something that might have taken the form of a serious objection; but Edith hastily spoke again.

"Nay, dearest, it is not to encumber you with the presence or care of a woman that I would accompany you; but I would go to Castlenean House, whither you or Ogle, or either of you, can fly for refuge at any time, that you may call half an hour of safety your own,"

"Alas! I fear that Castlenean House is even now beleagured by Jonathan Wild."

"He may have been there, but he would have no temptation to remain. Sir Dominick Browne may be there still in hiding. Ah! you do not know how unhappy I should be in the Forest, alone now!"

Captain Heron spent some few moments in consideration; and then he said, "Dear Edith, it shall be so! We will go to Castlenean House and ascertain the state of affairs there; and if you can take possession of it with anything like safety, you shall do so."

"Oh, thanks—thanks, dear Felix!"

Captain Heron then turned to his men. "I want two of you to accompany me to London again," he said.

"Let me be one," said Blueskin; "I don't think the country air agrees with me. I hears now some frogs a-croaking in a ditch, and they puts me in mind of a Frenchman, and all the world knows I never could abide one."

"Be it so, then. You, Number Two, will come with us. I will explain to you both what I shall expect of you as we proceed. I will ride your horse, Number Two, and you can drive the coach in which Edith will ride; and Blueskin can, if he pleases, still occupy his place on the roof."

"All's well!" said Blueskin. "It's a fine, open situation. Only tell me who you wants smashed, Captain, and you may look on it as good as done."

Captain Heron smiled as he explained to Blueskin that just at that present time he did not want any one smashed; and then, all the arrangements being made, the horses' heads of the coach were turned again towards London, and the little party —the same in number that had left it—again sought the metropolis.

The band pursued its way to Epping Forest; and, mounted upon the horse he had appropriated, Captain Heron rode by the coach window, in painful thought as to what had become of Ogle.

That the faithful and attached fellow would run into any danger without a thought of the personal consequences so long as it promised to be of any benefit to him, Captain Heron, he well knew; and his great hope was that he would be able to find out where Ogle was, and what he was doing, in time to save him from any gallant and reckless effort in his, Captain Heron's, supposed behalf.

Occasionally, too, conversing with Edith through the coach window, Captain Heron found the time pass quickly enough.

It was about a quarter past eight o'clock when they reached London again; and halting the coach at a quiet, retired portion of Bloomsbury Fields, Heron resolved to make what might be called a reconnoissance of Castleneau House before he would permit Edith to approach nearer to it.

Few people were astir at that hour in the morning; for our ancestors were by no means in the same hurry that we are to commence the troubles and the vexations of a new day, so that Captain Heron reached the old gate of Castleneau House without attracting any particular attention.

The mansion bore that strange, deserted aspect which by some means a house contrives to put on so soon as it is deserted by its regular inhabitants.

There was an indescribable something about the look of Castleneau House which brought a feeling of great depression upon the heart of Felix Heron.

"Where," he said, "is the kind, dear friend of my boyhood, and the counsellor of my maturer years—the ever-consistent, ever self-denying, courageous, wise, and noble Lady Castleneau?"

He had rung twice at the massive old gate-bell, and there was no response.

The stillness of the tomb appeared to be in and about that mansion.

A feeling of impatience, that would not be controlled, came over Heron, and he commenced to climb the old iron gate.

To one like him—an adept in athletic exercises

—the task was one of ease; and Heron soon leaped lightly into the old courtyard.

There were two distinct drops of blood upon the old worn stones exactly before him as he alighted.

The heart of Felix Heron accepted those drops of blood at once as a bad omen. He was very pale; but his compressed lips, and the fire in his eyes, sufficiently pourtrayed the character of the feelings he did not attempt to give utterance to.

Heron crossed the courtyard.

He reached the house.

He made an appeal to the knocker, which must have sent its echoes to every corner of the mansion; and then he waited one — two — three — four minutes.

No one came.

Then Captain Heron spoke in a low voice of concentrated feeling, for he was much affected at the possibilities of what might have taken place at Castleneau House.

"I must and will find a way into this house," he said, "if I live for another quarter of an hour."

But as he glanced about him he saw, now that the day had made such progress, that not only would it be out of the question to make any efforts to break into the house by the front without the risk of search and observation, but it was just possible Edith might attract some unfriendly scrutiny in the coach where he had left her.

A moment's consideration decided Heron what to do.

"I will bring her here," he said, "and we will get rid of the coach. Yes; I will bring her here at once."

Hastily, then, crossing the courtyard again, Heron unbolted the iron gates and sallied out, only closing them, so that they might seem fast without being in reality so.

A sharp run of three minutes brought him to the coach door.

"Dear Edith," he said, "the house seems deserted. I think we may, however, effect an entrance in some way, and we had better do so together."

"Oh! yes, yes."

"Come, then, dear. We will dispense with the coach now. You, Blueskin, and you, Mobbs, follow us."

"In a minute," said Blueskin. "A marciful beast is marciful—no, I don't mean that. A marciful man is marciful to two beasts."

"What do you mean, Blueskin?"

"Just this here, Captain. Look at these two bags of bad bones in a mangey skin, each of 'em that the coachman, no doubt, called osses."

"They are poor creatures."

"Starved, Captain."

"No doubt of that."

"Good!"

"Do you call that good, Blueskin?"

"No, Captain; not the starving, but the idea. I say, Mobbs, old boy."

"What now, Blue?"

"I've got an idea."

"No?"

"Yes, I have. You know old Bayley, as keeps the livery-stables close by here?"

"To be sure."

"Well, if Jonathan Wild was to come to him and say, 'Bayley, buy a hundred osses, and keep 'em till I come for 'em, he'd do it.'"

"To be sure he would."

"Then here goes."

"What goes?"

"These here two hanimals. I shall take 'em out of the coach and out of the harness, and then, naked as they was born—excuse me, Mrs. Heron —I shall take 'em to old Bayley; and, as he knows me well enough, he will believe me when I says to him, 'Take care o' these two osses; never mind their looks; keep 'em well with three feeds of corn a-day for Mr. Wild, and he'll come for 'em and pay when he thinks proper. That's the idea, 'cos, you see, a marciful beast—no, not a marciful beast—a marciful man, I mean."

"Be quick, then," said Captain Heron. "When you have pleased yourself by having those two poor half-starved creatures in clover for an indefinite period, follow us to Castleneau House."

"All's right, Captain, I'll come; but I doesn't like them new-fangled horse-feeds."

"What do you mean?"

"Didn't you say as the osses clover was to be mixed up along of some 'definite periods,' or some such stuff?"

"No, no; go along with you, and rejoin us as soon as you can."

"Very good, Captain."

While Blueskin pleased himself by carrying out his "idea" in regard to the two miserable hackney coach horses, Captain Heron, with his Edith upon his arm, and closely followed by Mobbs, made his way again to Castleneau House.

They met with no obstruction, and Mobbs remained close to the gate waiting for Blueskin, as Captain Heron wished, then halted, while he and Edith went up the stone steps to the house.

All was still.

They both tried to look through the narrow window on each side of the door which commanded a view of the hall, but for a few moments they saw nothing. Then, however, they uttered a simultaneous exclamation,—for, from the old breakfast room, usually in the occupation of Lady Castleneau as a sitting-room, they saw come forth a dim, shadowy figure, which was, in another moment, lost in the gloom of the spacious old hall.

CHAPTER CXCI.

EDITH AND CAPTAIN HERON ARE INITIATED INTO SOME OF THE MYSTERIES OF CASTLENEAU HOUSE.

On the impulse of the moment, when Captain Heron saw this strange, shadowy form in Castelneau House, he rapped smartly on the glass of the small side Hall windows, and called out aloud, "Who goes there? Speak, if you be mortal man!"

But the figure took no notice of his words, nor of the violent rapping on the window-pane.

"This is strange, indeed," said Heron. "One would have thought that, be that person friend or foe, some notice would have been taken of our presence."

"It is indeed strange," remarked Edith; "and my mind is full of sad forebodings."

"At all events, dear one," added Heron, "this

will be no place for you to wait in while I proceed to the City to get news of my friend Ogle."

"I know not—I know not, Felix. It may be that my presence in this house will be a comfort and a consolation, but there will be a difficulty in getting into it."

"Let me think," said Heron, "how that difficulty may be best overcome. "Ah, yes—by the garden and some of the old windows at the back we shall have the best chance of effecting an entrance. Come, dear Edith, come."

By this time Blueskin had carried out his "idea" in regard to the hackney coach horses, and had found his way to Castleneau House, so that the great gates were fastened by Mobbs, who, with Blueskin, reached the steps of the Hall door just as Edith and Captain Heron were deserting them.

"Do you want to go into the house, Captain?" asked Mobbs.

"I do."

"Then, unless some one has fastened the Hall door on the inside, that is soon done."

Mobbs, after a little rummaging in his pockets, produced some picklocks, and commenced operations on the door, which Captain Heron was well enough pleased to await, because, as he whispered to Edith, "Dearest, if the door can be opened from the outside here, it will afford good presumption that whoever left the house last considered there was no one behind him, but if it be fast we may conclude that some living beings are in the mansion."

Mobbs now shook his head.

"It won't do, Captain."

The door is fastened then, by some means, on the inside?

"Yes, Captain. The bolts are shot."

"Then Castleneau House is still inhabited?"

"No doubt of that, Captain, unless somebody who shot the bolts has got out some other way."

"Come, comrades," said Heron, after a moment's thought, "follow me, and we will try to effect an entrance from the garden, where, at all events, we shall not be exposed to observation."

Having quite made up his mind that he would not leave Edith in Castleneau House unless he was well assured that he could do so with perfect safety, and as the little party made its way from the front to the back of the house, he spoke to her gently.

"My Edith, with two such efficient guards as Mobbs and Blueskin I can safely leave you for a few minutes."

"Leave me, Felix?"

"Yes, dearest, while I make an examination of the mansion, to see if it will be safe for you to remain in it."

"Oh, no! Rather let me go with you, dear Felix. Do you not know that an old esteemed friend, Sir Dominick Brown, should be here."

"Alas! I fear he is here no longer."

"And I, too; but as I only can conduct you to one of the secret rooms in which Lady Castleneau hid him from the villain Wild, I pray you to let me accompany you on this expedition."

"Be it as you will, Edith."

"Ah, that is well; and see, Felix, there will be no great difficulty in gaining the broad sill of one of those windows, and then it will, surely, be easy to get into the house."

"I will try, dear."

They had reached the garden of Castleneau House now, and the range of windows to which Edith alluded were quite accessible.

It was easy enough to reach one of them from the terrace that ran along the back of the house; and Captain Heron soon stood upon the broad stone window-sill, and applied all his strength to opening the window, but it resisted.

Then he though he had better break a pane of glass, and so endeavour to get in.

He did so; and although the opening did not appear nearly of size sufficient to enable him to pass through, he succeeded in doing so, and with an ease and agility that excited the admiration of Blueskin.

But Edith was full of fear when she saw Felix Heron disappear into the house.

"Felix! Felix!" she called out, "do not forget your promise that I am to go with you."

Another moment, and Captain Heron appeared at the window again, and began to open it slowly, for it was of great weight, and from not being opened probably for a very long time it stuck in the frame.

"Come, my Edith," he said, "reach up to me, and I can assist you."

Edith willingly did this; and she was soon by the side of Captain Heron in one of the large saloons of her aunt's house.

Heron then spoke to Blueskin and Mobbs as they looked up at him for orders from the garden below.

"Keep good watch and ward," he said, "round the house; and should you hear a pistol-shot you will know that I want you, and, in that case, come in at once by this window."

"All right, Captain," said Mobbs.

"To be sure," said Blueskin. "That will do; only I have broken my pipe, and don't know how to get a comfortable smoke nohow."

Captain Heron did not close the window by which he and Edith had obtained admittance to Castleneau House, for he could not tell how suddenly he might wish for the assistance of his two comrades from the garden.

"Now, dear Edith," he said, "let our first care be to seek Sir Dominick Browne "

"Oh, yes—oh, yes! This way, Felix—this way."

Edith, owing to her several periods of residence with her aunt, was tolerably familiar with the interior of Castleneau House, and she was able to conduct Captain Heron to a small apartment, connected with which was a secret room of minute dimensions, but, upon that account, all the more safe and secure from discovery.

There was a picture on the wall of an old lady in a tremendous ruff and farthingale; and Edith, by running her finger down a portion of the ornamental part of the frame, soon found a spring, which, when pressed, caused a strip of the frame, of about six inches in length, to fly up on a concealed hinge.

This disclosed a small loop-handle, similar to those usually found upon old-fashioned trunks, and on last century chests of drawers.

By simply pulling this handle the whole of the picture, with its frame, opened from the wall like a door, disclosing behind the small secret apartment which the provident care of Lady Castleneau had devoted to the security of Sir Dominick Browne.

"Alas! It would appear that it had been anything but secure to him."

The devilish ingenuity of Jonathan Wild, or of some of his myrmidons who had visited Castleneau House must have contrived to discover the place, for it was vacant.

It is true there were some indications and appearances of recent occupation, but the occupier whom they sought was no longer there.

There was an overturned chair.

There were some viands scattered on the floor, which seemed to have been swept off a small tray that was half on and half off a table with a marble top, and which was no larger than those small tables used for a chess-board.

"Gone! gone!" cried Edith. "The villain Wild has surely been here."

"Yes, Edith; and behold, too, there has been some violence."

Captain Heron, as he spoke, pointed to the door composed of the portrait on the wall, which, having swung half-shut, showed by the light on the other side of it a jagged sort of hole in the panel.

"What is that?" asked Edith.

"A bullet has passed through that orifice."

"Are you sure, Felix?"

"I have seen too many to doubt it, dearest."

"Then who shall say that our old and dear friend may not have been murdered by Jonathan Wild?"

"No, Edith; no, I do not think so. There are no indications of such an act here. I am rather disposed to think that Wild has fired through almost every suspicious-looking panel he came to, on the chance of making some discovery. On this occasion it would probably have required stronger nerves and a rude, self-possessed judgment than his many sufferings had left poor Sir Dominick Brown to prevent him from calling out."

"Yes, oh yes! You must have guessed it all, Felix, and he is in the power of the villain Wild."

"I fear so."

"But you will rescue him, Felix?"

"If I live."

"No, no! Oh no! I do not mean what I say. You must live for your Edith, and encounter no dangers that may be avoided. No, no! Oh forget that by a single word I incited you to any perilous adventure."

Edith clasped the hands of Captain Heron, and fell upon his breast in tears.

At that moment, and before Felix could utter a word in reply to this sudden occasion of feeling on the part of his beloved Edith, the loud and unmistakable sound of some door violently closed in the mansion came upon their ears.

Edith started, and cried out, "Ah, there is some one in the house!"

"No doubt of that, dear one," said Heron, as he made a rapid movement of one of the butts of his pistols, so that he could get at it handier than before.

All was still again, but they could not for a moment persuade themselves that the noise they had heard was anything but a reality.

Captain Heron, however, was rather puzzled how to set about an examination of the mansion which was so large, and had so many corridors and staircases, that it would be quite easy for any

one who was well acquainted with the place to dodge any pursuit for an indefinite period of time.

It was Edith who made a suggestion that promised to get rid of some of the difficulty.

"Felix," she said, "there are pieces of chalk in abundance in the garden. It will be but the work of a few moments to get one, and then I should propose that every door we pass through we lock and remove the key, and mark the panel with chalk, so that we may not search the same apartment twice."

"I will do so, Edith. Let us seek again the room which we reached by the open window."

This was now done; and Captain Heron called to Mobbs, who he saw leaning against a tree in the garden.

"Mobbs! Mobbs!"

But Mobbs did not stir.

"Mobbs! Mobbs, I say!"

The man appeared to be looking right up to the window, but he did not take the least notice of Captain Heron's calls to him.

"Can it be possible," said Heron "that he has gone to sleep against a tree?"

"It is strange," said Edith. "There is a look about him that—that——"

"That what, Edith?"

"That I cannot comprehend if we were not quite sure that he must be asleep. I should regard him with a shudder, and fancy he was no more."

"Good heavens! that is not possible?"

"Let me go and see, dear Felix."

"You, Edith! Oh no, no!"

"Stay! oh stay! There is danger! I am certain there is danger."

"What danger?"

"I know not; but my heart tells me there is. Where is Blueskin, Felix."

"Ah, yes,—where is Blueskin?"

Captain Heron looked carefully about the garden as well as he could from the window, but no Blueskin was to be seen; and there, leaning against the tree, was Mobbs, as still and as calm as ever.

The distance that Mobbs was from the house no doubt extended a couple of hundred yards, for the garden was large; so that it was not possible to see him more minutely from the window than scarcely sufficed to enable Captain Heron and Edith to feel certain, or wholly certain, of his identity.

Why he did not move or reply to them was a profound mystery.

"Remain here for a moment, dearest," said Heron; "this must be cleared up."

"I dread to let you go."

"You shall see that I will not proceed out of your sight."

Edith was compelled reluctantly to allow her reason to consent to what her love dreaded; and Captain Herom was about to jump from the window into the garden, when, pausing, he handed to Edith one of the pocket pistols to which such frequent allusion has been made in consequence of the elegance and beauty of their workmanship.

"Take this weapon, dearest," he added. "It will be some company for you when I am in the garden; and it will speak loudly enough if requisite."

Edith took the pistol and stood quite close to the window; while Captain Heron jumped into the garden.

As soon as he touched the ground he called out again, "Mobbs! Mobbs, I say!"

But Mobbs never stirred.

Captain Heron, then, waving his arm to Edith and giving her an assuring smile—although in his heart he began fully to believe that something serious was the matter,—ran forward towards the tree against which Mobbs was leaning.

And now Felix Heron might well have turned and sought the house again before he reached the spot where Mobbs was waiting; for as he neared it he saw what was the matter.

Mobbs was dead!

There was no such thing as mistaking the look of the dead face.

The expression of it was terrible—an expression to haunt the imagination for months—ay, for years—when once the eyes had conveyed the terrible object to the brain.

Captain Heron did wait a moment; but then a

No. 86.—EDITH.

wish to see, if such were possible, how this terrible and unexpected catastrophe had been brought about came over him, and he conquered his repugnance to approach the tree.

When close, he saw how Mobbs had come by his death, although the human agency which had been at work was nowhere visible.

A piece of stout wire was round his neck, and likewise round the tree. It was that which held up the dead body.

The wire was secured behind the tree by a piece of rough wood, which had been turned round and round, and so, tightening the wire, had produced death by strangulation to the unfortunate Mobbs.

But who had done the deed?

Where was Blueskin?

Was he, too, dead?

How had such a tragedy been enacted without noise or alarm, and who could be the perpetrators of it?

There was an awful depressing stillness in the garden.

The twitter of some young birds in the branches of what might be called the "death tree" then broke the silence, and Captain Heron started and drew the fellow-pistol to that he had handed to Edith.

Then he heard his own name.

It was Edith, from the window.

"Felix! Felix!"

She had seen, by the attitudes he assumed, and the strange manner in which he had been turned completely round upon his heels, that something was amiss.

But what it was Edith had still to learn.

At the sound of her voice, however, all the possible peril to which she might be exposed flashed across his mind, and he turned and ran towards the mansion again with hurried steps.

"Edith! Edith!" he cried, as he reached the window, "there is murder and there is treachery in the very air of this house!"

"Murder?" said Edith.

"Yes, dear one; he whom we now look at yonder by the tree is a dead man."

"Oh, heaven!"

"Come down, Edith—come down! Leap into my arms—I will abandon the search of this house. Who shall say what perils may environ you even now? Come down, dear one, I will catch you as you leap! Come down, my Edith — come down!"

Edith could well guess, by the tones of Captain Heron's voice, that something very terrible had happened; and she was in the act of making a spring into the garden, when an indefinable sensation that she was not alone in the room caused her to turn her head behind her.

The moment she did so she uttered a cry of alarm, and levelling the pistol she held in her hand, she fired it at once towards the further end of the saloon.

Simultaneously, then, almost with the discharge of the pistol, Edith sprung into the garden, and was caught in the arms of the gallant Captain Heron.

"What was it? Who was it, Edith?" cried Heron, quickly.

"I do not know. Some strange, unsightly object."

"What? What?"

"A man, I fancy, in a mask."

Edith was trembling violently.

"Now, by the heaven above us," cried Heron, "I would give something to get at the bottom of all this mystery; and but that your safety, my Edith, is the paramount object of my heart, I would not leave a square inch of old Castleneau House unexplored."

"Look! oh, look!" cried Edith, pointing to the window.

Captain Heron cast his eyes up to the window from which Edith had just leaped, and he saw at it a tall figure enveloped in a dark grey cloak, and with a half mask upon the face.

"Ah!" cried Heron, "if one shot has failed, another may be more fortunate."

CHAPTER CXCII.

EDITH AND CAPTAIN HERON RECEIVE ADVICE AND CONSOLATION FROM A SHADOW.

It was among the singularity of the proceedings of that hour that Captain Heron did not fire his pistol at the dim shadowy figure in the window; but there was a something at the moment—he could not define what—which stayed his purpose, and kept that light pressure of the finger from the trigger of the weapon which would have sped the bullet on its fatal journey.

There was nothing revolting about the appearance of this mysterious personage, who looked like a portrait framed by the window of that old house, gazing out into the garden, and assuming an attitude of courteous friendship.

"Was that the form at which you fired at, Edith?" said Captain Heron.

"Oh, no, no; it was something much more terrible!"

"And in this person," said Heron, "there is nothing terrible. If it be a shadow from the grave it is a beneficent one, and has come to warn us, not to threaten."

There could be no doubt whatever, from the aspect of this shadowy-looking personage, that it wished to impress both Captain Heron and Edith with the idea that, as regarded them, it was filled with friendly emotions.

The attitude which the figure assumed, and the way in which it gently waved its hands, were sufficiently indicative of the fact that it wished to be at peace with those below in the garden.

They saw its lips move, although they could not catch the exact sounds that issued from them.

"Dear Edith," said Captain Heron, "I have no fears of this figure; and whether it belong to this earth or that to which we are all hastening, I will trust it."

Edith was clinging to Captain Heron's arm, so that as he advanced towards the window she accompanied him, and there could not possibly be a greater proof of the fact that he considered there was no danger than his allowing her to approach with him so close to the window that if the shadowy figure had any evil intentions there could have been little difficulty, although, perhaps, at personal sacrifice, in carrying them out.

But the figure, still waving one hand, courteously uttered but two words, and they seemed to be uttered constrainedly, as if in a feigned voice.

"Fly!—fly! Danger! — danger!" were the words uttered by this mysterious monitor.

There was a strange and most unaccountable feeling at the heart of Captain Heron as he heard the tones of that voice, which prompted him to acknowledge it as those of perfect truth and friendship.

"You hear, Edith—you hear!" cried Heron. "There is danger—danger to you, dear one, which I dare not encounter. Yes, courteous shadow—be you whom you may — your admonition shall not be given in vain. We will leave this place, which is now one of horror, and seek for safety in some purer atmosphere."

Then the figure spoke again, and the one word it uttered was " Farewell!"

With a courteous inclination of the head it

moved them away from the window, as though it had done and said all that it cared to do and say, and was quite satisfied that its injunctions would be fulfilled by those whom it wished to save placing themselves out of the reach of danger.

Captain Heron was now as anxious to leave the precincts of Castleneau House as he had been before to reach it. With Edith clinging to his left arm he rapidly traversed the garden, or, at all events, that portion of it which it was necessary to traverse in order to get round into the front court.

A very few minutes sufficed to bring them to the iron gates; and Captain Heron then did what he never intended, considering the many dangers which surrounded himself and Edith, namely, walked out in the open face of day into the streets of London with her upon his arm.

What had become of Blueskin was a perfect mystery; and although there could be no doubt about the fate of the unfortunate Mobbs, yet how he had come by that fate was as mysterious as the disappearance of Blueskin.

Captain Heron and Edith were, however, not left many minutes in doubt as regarded the wisdom of the advice which had been given to them by the shadowy form at the window; for just as they reached a small street in the neighbourhood of Bloomsbury Square, they heard the rapid trampling of horses' feet, and Heron only had time to draw Edith into a doorway when a troop of horsemen galloped past, in the leader of which there was not the slightest difficulty in recognising Jonathan Wild.

And, indeed, as if fate would have it that Wild should proclaim his intentions to the ears of the very persons most interested in knowing them, he called out in his violent snarling tones as he rode past, "Quick, my bulldogs—quick! Put the spurs to your horses; it's fifty guineas among you for the morning's work, and Castleneau House is close at hand."

"Ah!" cried Edith, "this, then, was the warning of that friendly spectre."

"We cannot doubt it," said Heron. "It is clear, by some means, the villain has found out our presence at Castleneau House; and in another five minutes it would have been surrounded by him and his myrmidons—possibly enough to our capture or destruction."

"Felix! Felix!" said Edith, with considerable agitation of manner, "let us try, at least, to make one effort to discover the fate of Ogle, and then seek for safety and security in our forest home."

"It shall be so—it shall be so, dearest! There is a man whom I can trust, who resides not far from Charing Cross. We will take that direction, and I will send him into the City, and I have no doubt he will bring us accurate intelligence of what has taken place."

With this arrangement Edith was well content; but as it was now ten o'clock in the morning, and the business day of London might be said to have fairly commenced, it was somewhat a hazardous thing for Captain Felix Heron, with a high price set upon his head and so many private interests involved in his destruction, to walk with any degree of composure in the midst of that broad, open, daylight from Bloomsbury Fields to Charing Cross.

But still it was possible to do so with safety. After all there were but three or four persons sufficiently familiar with his appearance and sufficiently vindictive against him to wish to interrupt him; and surely malignant fate would not so persecute him as to conduct them across his path in that brief quarter of an hour from the whole of the rest of London.

Edith trembled occasionally, but it was not for herself. She dreaded that each chance passenger who would cast a more curious eye than usual upon them might be upon the point of calling out, "This is the notorious Captain Heron, the highwayman!"

But as they traversed street after street and no such sounds met their ears, Edith gathered courage and strength of heart.

Heron, himself, moved along without the alteration of a muscle of his countenance. He felt that if danger came it had to be met, and that it would be none the less, and none the more easily met, by being terrified at it beforehand.

"Courage, dear Edith—courage!" he said. "If it be, indeed, an act of audacity for me to walk the streets of London, knowing how many enemies I have breathing the air, I will hope that the audacity of the act may bring with it its own safety."

These words had scarcely left Captain Heron's lips, when, from out of one of the streets in the Strand, there emerged a horseman, who trotted diagonally right across the roadway towards St. Martin's Church, close to which Edith and Captain Heron had paused for a moment.

There was traffic and there was noise in London streets at that period of time; but it was no more to be compared to the noise and traffic which at present beset them, than is the profound silence of the great desert to be likened to the din and tumult of a populous colony.

Therefore it was that the clattering sound of this horse's feet attracted the attention of both Edith and Captain Heron.

They both looked attentively.

They turned, and, unconscious of danger, presented their features full for recognition to the approaching horseman.

And of all persons that London could produce at that inopportune moment, there was no one better qualified to recognise them both, or to make that recognition full of mischief.

The horseman was none other than Lord Warringdale.

He and Captain Heron knew each other simultaneously, and each pronounced the name of the other.

"Felix Heron!"

"Warringdale!"

Edith uttered a cry of despair, and on the impulse of the moment clung so closely to the left arm of Captain Heron, that if Lord Warringdale had had that nimble and speedy courage which is so rare a gift, and in which he was so remarkably deficient, it might at once have ended all disputes between himself and his brother, by taking his life.

But Warringdale had a special terror and respect for the prowess of Felix Heron, as he called him, so that nothing was further from his intention than to risk a personal encounter.

But surely now, in the open broad daylight and the thronged streets of London, he had his highwayman brother at his mercy.

And more than that, too, there was Edith; she who had defied him, scorned him, and set at nought all the villanous schemes concocted between him and Sir John Tarleton, her father, for the destruction of her happiness.

A double prize seemed to be in his grasp, which he had but to shout out to secure.

Lord Warringdale was not backward, then, in calling for assistance.

With a loud yelling voice, in which was concentrated all the anger, rage, and despair which from time to time he had suffered, in consequence of the warfare he had waged with Edith and with his brother, he screamed to the passers-by to aid him.

"Help! help! Seize him! Heron, the highwayman! A thousand pounds reward! A thousand pounds for him dead or alive! There is warrant for any injury you do him! Seize him—seize him!"

Warringdale himself began hastily to dismount from his horse as he uttered these cries; and after the bewildered pause of a moment—in order to comprehend what it was that had rung in their ears with such frantic vehemence—passengers about the spot began to rush forward,—rather from curiosity to know what was the matter, than with any decided intention of assisting Lord Warringdale in the capture of Captain Heron and Edith.

Heron had just the advantage of that momentary pause, and no other. It was fortunate that the hazardous recognition had taken place just at the spot it did—which was at the mouth of one of those narrow courts, now pulled down, but which at one time so completely surrounded St. Martin's Church that they formed a perfect colony, hiding almost everything but its front entrance and the spire, and abounding in so many intricacies that a person might be lost or lose themselves in that nest of courts with incredible rapidity.

Captain Heron flung his arm round Edith, and before the bewildered people and the half-maddened Lord Warringdale could stretch out a hand to seize him, he dashed down the court.

At twelve paces distance there was another narrow turning, and Heron took that—and then another, and then another; so that before any one with moderate speed could have counted twenty, Captain Heron and Edith were as completely lost and bewildered themselves in the intricacies of those courts, as they were lost and out of sight of their enemies.

" Safe again! Safe again!" cried Heron. "They will scarcely find us here."

"It was Warringdale," said Edith, faintly.

"It was, indeed, dearest. By a most unlucky chance he crossed our path. He knows his own safety from me, or even in the midst of crowded streets he would scarcely have dared to challenge my progress, for he is a coward as well as a villain."

"Qualities, Felix," said Edith, "which ever go together. But hark! what noise is that?"

A commingling of cries and shouts came upon their ears, to which in silence they listened attentively for a few seconds. Rising above the surge of many voices and unmeaning shouts they began to hear some distinct words, and there could be no doubt but that those words were suggestive of danger to them.

"Block up the courts! He can't escape. My Lord Warringdale will see to the money! Follow him in! Seize the highwayman!"

"So—so!" said Captain Heron. "My Lord Warringdale, it appears, has found those who are willing to engage in a man hunt for the price of blood; but it shall go hard, Edith, if we do not foil him yet."

It was quite evident, though, that these shouts and cries, indicative of a determination to pursue Captain Heron and Edith into the intricacies of the courts, were approaching nearer.

Their situation was getting critical.

It was quite possible for Heron to resist one, two, or three persons, and probably achieve a victory over them; but to be overridden by a crowd, such as the streets of London so readily produces, was a thing fraught with all the wildest aspects of danger.

There was not another moment to lose.

With his arm still flung round the waist of Edith—half carrying her, so that the speed at which he went was no trouble to her to keep up with,—Heron turned rapidly into another of the courts; but that seemed to be an unfortunate movement, since the moment he did so the cries and shouts of the rapidly gathering mob came more distinctly to their ears.

He turned to retrace his steps. But now it seemed to be as perilous to retreat as to advance; and Captain Heron and Edith felt for a few seconds what it was to be hemmed in and surrounded by great dangers, from which—unless they had had the wings of birds—there seemed no possibility of extrication.

Heron looked about him with eyes of flame.

If Edith had not been with him there can be no doubt but that he would have chanced life and liberty upon one rush through the midst of his foes; and in the consequences of that rush many of them would have suffered for their temerity in taking up the cry of destruction which was yelling around him.

But Edith was with him, and such a course could not be thought of. There was, perhaps, the space of half a minute left for reflection and for action; beyond that time his foes would be upon him.

Close at hand there was a wretched little shop—a miserable collection of second-hand apparel fluttered at the door. The window was grimy and dingy with dust and rain, but heaped up within with every possible portable article that could be bought or sold.

There could be no doubt about the character of this shop, considering the locality in which it had set up its sign. Probably in any locality an inhabitant of London would have had no trouble at once of declaring that this was one of those pernicious establishments which offer an incentive to crime from the facility with which its proceeds are disposed of.

In the language of thieves and of the police, this was a "fence."

It was not for Captain Heron to be very particular about the refuge which presented itself to him. The keepers of that little thieves' establishment were sure to be at war with the authorities; and either for sympathy or for money, or probably from both, would be sure to afford him all the assistance in their power.

"This way, Edith—this way! We may yet baffle them!"

CAPTAIN HERON AND EDITH FIND THEMSELVES IN A POSITION OF
GREAT DANGER.

Presented Gratis with No. 86, of the New Edition of the Captive; or, the Robbers of Epping Forest.

EACH WEEK IS PRESENTED GRATIS A COLOURED ENGRAVING.

To reach this little shop door was the work of a moment.

It was fast.

The upper panel of the door was of glass—that is to say, four miserable little panes of dingy green glass, each one not above four or five inches square, were let into the woodwork.

The flash of a light from within came upon the eyes of Captain Heron as he looked through one of these little squares of glass; but the light was not precisely in the shop—if such a miserable den could be called a shop. It seemed to be in some room beyond it, through the open door of which it passed, or through some corresponding panes of glass, more probably, since it was dim and faint.

Heron rapped hastily at the door, but no notice was taken.

The whole house was rickety and frail, and it was not probable that the door would resist him for a moment, should he really have the wish to force it.

The notion of breaking one of the little squares of glass did occur to him as a means of attracting the attention of those within; but even then there might be time wasted in a parley; and, besides, the broken pane of glass might be suggestive to his pursuers that he had taken refuge in that particular establishment.

Captain Heron, therefore, adopted the much simpler expedient of putting his shoulder to the door, and, by one vigorous push, bursting it open.

The lock, or latch, whichever it was, which kept it closed, flew off with a crash; and so suddenly, too, that Captain Heron was nearly precipitated into the shop.

Some cries of indignation and alarm issued from the back room, whence the reflection of the light had proceeded; but Heron paid not the slightest attention to them.

Turning rapidly, he closed the door again; and as the light shone more fully on that side he speedily laid hands on an iron bar which effectually secured it.

"Wretches," cried a voice, "what do you mean? If you've found anything, and want to sell it, couldn't you ring the bell?"

Heron turned from fastening the door and faced a tall, gaunt female, who stood on the threshold of the inner room with a lighted candle in her hand.

One glance was sufficient for Captain Heron; and he said, with a smile, "I have the pleasure of speaking to Mrs. Ripon?"

CHAPTER CXCIII.

THE REVEREND MORTIFICATION RIPON FINDS THIS LIFE FULL OF TROUBLES AND DISASTERS.

MRS. RIPON, perhaps, would not have uttered a scream one half so shrill, had the unmentionable gentleman himself from below suddenly announced himself, as he now did, at sight of Captain Heron.

If the aforesaid unmentionable gentleman had only made an appearance, and said, "Mrs. Ripon, here are some silver spoons for sale!" there can be no doubt whatever that he would have been abundantly more welcome than Captain Heron.

Mrs. Ripon therefore uttered a scream.

Mrs. Ripon therefore dropped the candle, and trod upon it at once.

Mrs. Ripon opened her mouth to utter another scream, but Captain Heron stopped it on the threshold of her lips, by saying, in his sharp, short tones—tones which in a moment he could assume to such people,—"Mrs. Ripon, if you cry out again I shall be compelled to lodge a couple of slugs in your head."

Mrs. Ripon was silent.

There came from the inner room the faint flashes of a fire, by the side of which, no doubt, Tom Ripon's exemplary and affectionate mother had been assuaging her troubled feelings with rum and water, for a strong and sensible odour of that compound made its way into the shop.

There came, too, an odd scuffling noise from that back room, which awakened suspicion in the mind of Captain Heron that Mrs. Ripon was not alone.

"Who have you there?" he asked.

"Who have I,—eh?"

"Yes, woman; who is in the parlour? Answer at once!"

"Thomas."

"Thomas who?"

"The cat."

Mrs. Ripon shook as if she had been suddenly attacked with the worst ague that ever afflicted poor human nature.

Probably Captain Heron would scarcely have been satisfied with this reply, but his attention was drawn off from the back room of Mrs. Ripon's establishment by the sound of some of the mob seeking him in the court.

A gang of desperate ruffians—petty thieves, who had not the courage to cry "Stand" on the highway to a traveller, but who swarmed about the courts of St. Martin's Lane, and four or five together would attack any low person, or even a child, for the sake of its boots and clothing—had been incited to hunt Captain Heron for the magnificent reward promised by Lord Warringdale.

These persons reached the court in which was the "Fame" of Mrs. Ripon.

"Where is he? Have him out! A thousand pounds reward! He must be hereaway!"

"Oh, good Lord, deliver us!" said Mrs. Ripon.

An attempt was made to open the shop door, but the bar that Heron had put up at the back of it was an effectual safeguard and barrier.

The door was however shaken fiercely, and a voice cried out, "Open! open! Open locks, Mother Ripon! Open, I say! There is not a crib in all the rookery but must be well looked into tonight!"

"Who is that?" asked Captain Heron of the terrified and bewildered Mrs. Ripon.

"Oh, dear me, it is Tom Bonus."

"Who is he?"

"They well say he's a footpad."

"Send him off."

"How can I? Oh dear—oh dear! For a respectable lone female, who has seen better days, to be so bullyragged by a set of ragamuffins! Oh dear—oh dear! A weak, poor, meek creature, now, as I am! Oh! I should like to twist some one's neck, I should!"

"Open! open! open!" cried the voice. "It

may be a good double-handful of guineas in your way, Mother Ripon."

"Mrs. Ripon," said Captain Heron, "it appears to me that it is suspected I am here."

"Oh dear, yes; and if you would only be so good, as they are there to have you, to let a poor lone woman, who has seen better days, have the reward——"

"Silence! Send that man and his rascally comrades away, or I will——" Captain Heron looked about him as he spoke, and then added: "Yes, that will do."

"What? Oh, what?"

"I will set the place on fire, and roast everybody in the flames."

A confused noise came again from the inner room.

"Drat that cat!" said Mrs. Ripon.

"Open! open! open!"

"Who's there?"

"I told you, old Mother Jazebel, it is I, Tom Banes. Open! open! open!"

"In a minute."

Mrs. Ripon flew into the back room; but what she was about Captain Heron could not imagine until she entered with a large iron kettle of boiling water.

"There's a swinging-point just above the door," she said, "but I'm afraid——"

"You cannot exactly reach it," said Captain Heron.

"I will distribute the hot water if you will say something appropriate to the occasion."

"Go along, you wretches!" screamed Mrs. Ripon.

At the same moment, Captain Heron had mounted on a chair, and, opening the panel at the top of the door, which was a sort of window fanlight swinging on a centre, he tilted over the iron kettle, and a shower of boiling water fell on the assailants without.

Yells, shouts, and shrieks of pain came from the disagreeable fellows who were close to the door; and then Mrs. Ripon bawled out, "I'll teach you to disturb a lone woman at her prayers, you wretches! There are no highwaymen here, I can tell you."

"I think that will do," said Heron. "Do not be alarmed, Edith, dearest."

A third time the odd sound came from the inner room, and it would appear it had come this time at the sound of the name of Edith.

"Drat that cat!" said Mrs. Ripon, again.

"Oh, Felix! Felix!" said Edith, in low, whispered tones, "this is a terrible place! It is as dark as night here, although without it is nearly noonday. Let us go now at once, if our enemies have given up the search for us in despair."

"Yes, my pretty lady," said Mrs. Ripon, "its best to go at once."

"By no means," said Captain Heron.

"Then I will stay, cheerfully," said Edith.

"But you cannot," said Mrs. Ripon. "Nobody can stay here. I cannot have it. Besides, the Captain would be sure to be found out, and this is the worst place in all London for him."

"I am of a different opinion, Mrs. Ripon," said Heron; "and, to prove it, I intend to stay here for the present."

"Oh dear! oh dear!"

"I only wonder that you don't ask me what has become of your son Tom?"

"The reprobate!"

"Not so, Mrs. Ripon. He is brave and faithful, and I mean to take good care of him, and to see to his future, if it be in my power to do so. Come, Edith, dear, we will further trespass upon the kind hospitality of Mrs. Ripon by sitting down in her parlour."

"No—no—no!"

"Wherefore not?"

"The—the cat."

"Oh, we won't interfere with him; only if it be a cat upon two legs, whose continued existence is not compatible with my safety, I would not be in its shoes for a trifle this day!"

Captain Heron had his own suspicions as to the identity of the cat who was in the back room of Mrs. Ripon's little establishment at Star Court, and he walked into the wretched apartment with a pistol in his hand.

A fire was burning in the grate, and, as accident would have it, at the moment Captain Heron, with Edith on his arm, entered the room, a bright little flame burst up from the fire, so that the room was well illuminated.

Without some artificial light that parlour of the "fence" would have been in total darkness, for its only window was closely blocked up by shutters, which did not permit a ray of daylight to pass them.

Probably this arrangemnnt was necessary, in order to prevent the possibility of any of the little transactions in stolen goods, in which Mrs. Ripon was frequently engaged, being overlooked from any of the houses which were in such close proximity at the back.

To the surprise of Captain Heron no one was there, and he came to that conclusion at a glance, for the room was small and had no perceptible hiding places.

To be sure there was a cupboard in one corner, which, from the outside, could not, of course, be judged of in regard to extent, but Captain Heron stepped up to it at once and flung open the door.

It was but a shallow cupboard, and when he opened the door some old baskets rolled out on to the floor.

"Your cat has taken a hasty departure, Mrs. Ripon," said Captain Heron.

"Oh dear, no—yes!" was the only reply.

Edith, with a sigh, partly of relief, for she was tired, and partly of apprehension, for she was full of fears on Captain Heron's account, sank into a chair by the fire.

There stood a table, covered with not the choicest of clothes, in the middle of the room; but the cloth, although it would have been much improved by a visit to the laundress, was one of great size and beauty, and had a coronet marked at each corner.

No doubt it had been "found" by some one of Mrs. Ripon's "clients" in some nobleman's house

On this handsome cloth was spread the materials for a supper.

The repast was not choice.

Some sheeps-heads, oysters, and an indescribable-looking dish that might have been tripe cooked in some odd fashion, together with a bottle from which issued the powerful odour of old rum, completed the bill of fare.

But Captain Heron could not help seeing that there were plates for two.

"Does your cat sup with you, Mrs. Ripon?" said Captain Heron.

"Oh dear, oh dear! Dont be joking a poor defenceless female, don't. We live in wicked times, Captain, and I cannot help thinking that a great tribulation is coming. There's a light, and I am sure you are vastly welcome to anything you want here. You are not the man, Captain Heron, as I have often said, when people wondered when you were going to be hanged,—you are not the man to eat a poor lone woman out of house and home, and then go away without paying."

"Certainly not," Mrs. Ripon.

"And how is Tom?"

"I told you he was all right and well."

"That's a mercy."

It was quite evident that Mrs. Ripon was in that state of mind in which a person may speak vaguely to the purpose, and yet repeat the same thing over again from a kind of preoccupation or absence of mind at the moment.

What it was that so particularly distressed Mrs. Ripon, Captain Heron could scarcely say; but he quietly made up his mind that from that place he would send a messenger to discover something of the fate of Ogle, and he was resolved that Mrs. Ripon should not only find that messenger, but be a security for his faithfulness.

"Fear nothing," he whispered to Edith. "I will take care that this woman, with all the disposition in the world to betray us, shall yet be faithful."

"Felix! Felix!" whispered Edith. "How can you ensure that?"

"Simply by never letting her out of my sight. But do not let us forget one thing, Edith,—strength of body is strength of mind. You require refreshment. I do not know that there is much here to tempt you, but this loaf looks pure and wholesome."

Edith took a small quantity of bread; and then Mrs. Ripon, who had been fidgeting about the room in an odd, darting, spasmodic sort of manner, suddenly exclaimed, as if she had just thought of it, "And how is Tom?"

"I have told you twice, Mrs. Ripon," said Captain Heron, "that he is well."

"That's a mercy."

"It will be greater mercy still if you contrive to collect your scattered wits, and attend to what I have to say."

"Oh, yes, Captain. I'm sure anything that I can do—a poor lone woman as I am; for, as I often remark, when people wonder when you're a-going to be hanged, you always pays your way if you has your say."

"Mrs. Ripon, you said all that before, or something very like it. But do not forget, if I have something to pay, that I have also likewise something to forgive. You no doubt remember a certain occasion upon which you and that abominable canting hypocrite—who now calls himself, I understand, the Reverend Mortification Ripon—laid a nice little plan to betray me into the hands of Jonathan Wild?"

"Oh dear! oh dear!" said Mrs Ripon. "I feel poorly; let's all go to bed."

"But," added Heron, speaking sternly and slowly, "I am willing to forgive the past, provided there is no more treachery; and I have something for you to do which will be a test of your faithfulness and sincerity. By heaven! woman,

if you attempt to play me false, now that I have this dear partner of my hopes, and fears, and joys, and sorrows with me, I will not leave so large a piece of this house standing and clinging to another as you might measure with your finger."

"Mercy upon us!" said Mrs. Ripon. "I feel worse. I'm going a-swimming—I mean a-swimming's come to me—a swimming in the head."

Captain Heron was determined to show Mrs. Ripon that he was in earnest, and he began trying his pistols with the ram-rods, to see if the charges remained intact.

Finding them, or fancying he found the priming of one of them was, somewhat damp, he shook out into his hand a small quantity of gunpowder, speaking all the time slowly to Mrs. Ripon.

"I want you to find some one," he said, "who can be relied upon—apparently as your messenger, not as mine, for I of course must not be mentioned—who will go to the City, and make cautious inquiries, both at Newgate and Giltspur Street Compter, if there be any news of my man, Ogle."

As he ceased speaking, Captain Heron flung from his hand on to the fire the small quantity of gunpowder he had shaken from the pan of the pistol.

A large piece of wood was on the top of the fire, every particle of which, to its very centre, was in a state of red heat; and the moment the gunpowder fell upon it a considerable portion of it burst into a million of red-hot sparks, crackling, hissing, and flying out into the room with a force that sent some thousands of them under the table.

Mrs. Ripon screamed in chorus with a loud howling row that came from some one who had hitherto been concealed by that large and handsome tablecloth with the coronets in its corners.

"Ah!" cried Captain Heron, quite composedly, as he gave two hearty kicks under the table with his heavy horseman's boots. "I thought, Mrs. Ripon, your cat would make his appearance at last."

"I'm a lost woman!" cried Mrs. Ripon, as she fell at once into a corner of the room.

"And I'm burned to death!" cried the Reverend Mortification Ripon, as he rolled from under the table with some hundred of the once red-hot sparks from the wood speckling his face with black particles.

Edith looked alarmed at the moment, but a glance from Captain Heron calmed her, and let her see that he was fully prepared for what was happening. Balancing, then, one of the pistols in his right hand, he contrived that the muzzle should oscillate somewhere in a right line between the eyes of the Reverend Mortification Ripon, who, on his knees with his hands uplifted, presented a ridiculous appearance of pain and terror.

"I was perfectly aware," added Captain Heron, "that you were somewhere concealed here, although I could not take upon myself to say where. And now, reverend sir, if you give me the slightest cause for suspicion, I will repay some of the favours I owe you with—let me see—half an ounce of lead, for these pistols carry thirty-two to the pound."

"Mercy upon us!" said the Reverend Mortification Ripon. "Recollect, young man, what the Psalmist says."

"We will leave the Psalmist alone for the present, if you please. Get up, sir."

"Get up! Oh! yes, yes! Here I am."

"And how's Tom?" murmured Mrs. Ripon.

"Yea," added the Reverend Mortification,—"how is the blessed youth?"

"The blessed youth," replied Captain Heron, "is well, and happily out of both your hands."

"That's a mercy," said Mrs. Ripon.

"Yea—amen!" said the Reverend Mortification.

It was quite evident that these two persons, with the full consciousness of the dastardly treachery of which they had been guilty on more than one occasion to Captain Heron, considered themselves, now that they were at his mercy, in the greatest possible danger. The very calmness and coolness of his manner alarmed them much more than if he had been furiously angry. Indeed it was quite evident that they were rapidly losing all command of themselves from sheer fright and panic.

When Captain Heron had cried to the Reverend Mortification Ripon to get up, Mrs. Ripon took it as an order to herself likewise, and at the same moment scrambled to her feet; and such was the state of agitation they were in, that they ran against each other, and knocked their heads together with a violence that must have been anything but reassuring, or calculated to increase their mental perceptions.

"I hardly know," said Captain Heron, "what hinders me from putting you both out of the world."

Down plumped the Reverend Mortification on his knees again, and Mrs. Ripon again resigned herself to the corner, faintly murmuring, "Will you be so good as to say how Tom is?"

"Yes," groaned the Reverend Mortification, "how is the blessed youth?"

"Wretches!" said Captain Heron, "you infuriate me by asking the question!"

"That's a mercy!" said Mrs. Ripon, pretending at the same time to shed sentimental tears, as though she had received the most amiable answer in the world.

"Tell me," said Heron, sternly, "as some ransom for your worthless lives,—tell me by what means you can find some one to go on the message I have mentioned."

Both Mrs. Ripon and the Reverend Mortification opened their mouths to reply; but before they could utter a word there came a heavy blow upon the outer door of the house and a sharp ring at the bell, which stopped with an abruptness suggestive of the wire breaking in consequence of the violence with which it had been pulled.

"Be calm, Edith," said Captain Heron, gently; "we are together, and there will be no danger."

————

CHAPTER CXCIV.

TOM RIPON ASTONISHES HIS MOTHER, AND IS OF GREAT SERVICE TO CAPTAIN HERON AND EDITH.

THE different hopes and sensations that that violent knock and ring at Mrs. Ripon's door produced among the persons in the back parlour may be easily imagined.

No doubt the Rev. Mortification thought it just within the range of possibility that something was about to occur which would enable him to take a very different position in regard to Captain Heron and Edith to that which he at present occupied, and which had filled him so full of fears.

Perhaps, too, Mrs. Ripon was of the same opinion.

Edith looked pale and distressed, but she never for one moment thought of any personal danger to herself. It was Felix alone she thought of, and it was for his safety alone she had a thousand fears.

And he repaid all this self-abnegation and affection in the only way it could be repaid, namely, by bending all his thoughts and all his energies to considerations of her safety and of her happiness.

There was a pause perhaps of half a minute's duration, and then the knock came again.

No doubt the violent ring would have come again if the bell-wire had not been broken.

Both Mrs. Ripon and the Rev. Mortification made a movement, as though they would go to the door, but Captain Heron stopped them.

"No," he said; "that is now my business."

"But," said Mrs. Ripon, "I——"

"I know what you mean," added Heron. "You don't like me to have the trouble; but in this case it is both a duty and a pleasure."

"But," said the Rev. Mortification, "the Psalmist frequently remarks——"

"No doubt he does," interrupted Heron; "but as I don't want to trouble the Psalmist in the matter, I will go to the door myself."

Captain Heron handed Edith one of the pistols, and said but one word—"Guard!"

Edith pressed his hand for a moment, and then he left the room, and strode with three strides over the shop floor to the outer door.

At the moment he did so, the person who had in so violent a manner demanded admission spoke in a loud angry tone, "Mrs. Ripon! Mrs. Ripon, I say! Is this the way you keep people waiting? How do I know that the grabs are not at my heels? And here am I with a bag of glitter that is groaning to find its way to the melting-pot. Open the door quick, will you!"

"Goodness gracious!" cried Mrs. Ripon, who, in consequence of the piece of wood above the door that acted as a fanlight being open, heard these words quite plainly. "Goodness gracious, it's business!"

"Keep where you are," said Heron.

"But I can't! It's a customer—it's business. I'm a lone woman, and poor as Job's mice."

"Edith."

"Yes, dear Felix."

"Shoot this woman."

"Murder!" cried Mrs. Ripon, as she at once subsided into the corner from which she had emerged.

Captain Heron had spoken in low tones, scarcely above a whisper, so that his voice did not find its way outside the shop; but Mrs. Ripon's did; and whoever was listening must have been somewhat surprised to hear such disjointed sentences as "Goodness gracious! it's business—but I can't—it's a customer—it's business—I'm a lone woman, and poor as Job's mice—murder!"

Then all was still.

Captain Heron went close to the door of the shop and put his ear to the panel, and listened. He then heard some one say in low tones, "I feel sure of it now."

"Well, Mr. Wild, if that's so, break in at once, and take him; and, if I might advise, by far the best way will be to shoot him at once—the moment you clap your eyes upon him. I mean it."

"All's right; I'll knock again."

"Do so; and I will, under cover of that noise, of which you can take care to make enough, find a means of getting in by the window."

One of these voices was unmistakably that of Jonathan Wild, but who the other man was Captain Heron had no means of knowing.

He felt, however, that the danger to himself and Edith was now imminent.

It would take Jonathan some little time to effect an entrance by the window of the shop, so that Captain Heron went back to the parlour with a motive to extort from either Mrs. Ripon or the Rev. Mortification a piece of information which he was quite certain they must possess.

No. 87.—EDITH.

That piece of information was with regard to the mode of leaving that room without going through the shop.

There was no appearance of any such mode; but Captain Heron knew quite enough of the kind of establishment kept by Mrs. Ripon to feel certain that there was some such means by which a customer, who might be hard-pressed by the police, might escape.

Without a word, Heron made a rush upon the reverend gentleman, and, dragging him to his feet, he clapped the muzzle of a pistol to one of his eyes.

So completely astounded was the Rev. Mortification at this attack, that his tongue refused its office; and, much as he desired to yell out for mercy, he only glared in the face of Heron with a look of terror that was becoming more and more tragic each moment.

Then Heron spoke.

"Show me," he said, "how to leave this room without going through the shop, or I will blow out your brains, and trust to chance scattering them in the right direction."

"The cupboard!" gasped the Rev. Mortification.

"The cupboard!" yelled Mrs. Ripon.

"Be quiet; I don't want all London to know. Go, then, and prove your words, rev. sir, or, as the Psalmist don't say, I will make short work with you, and there will be one scoundrel less in the world."

"Oh dear! oh dear! I shall never get over this dreadful day," groaned the Rev. Mortification.

A precious knocking at the time commenced at the other door, and Captain Heron felt certain that Jonathan Wild, under cover of the noise, was commencing his operations on the window.

But the Rev. Mortification, with the fear of sudden death upon him, was powerful and vigorous in what he set about. He opened again the cupboard door, and clearing away the baskets and old rubbish with which it seemed to be filled, he quickly reached the back, of which by a peculiar touch he opened, disclosing to Captain Heron a little miserable back yard, which seemed to answer all the purposes of a permanent dustbin, for it was chocked up with refuse of all kind.

"Where does this lead to?" said Heron.

"Yea, through that window yonder to the next house, which goes round the corner to Ann Court."

"That will do. Ah! betrayed!"

The window to which the Rev. Mortification Ripon had alluded was fastened by an old shutter that seemed to be all away, and hanging only by one hinge; and now as Captain Heron had his eyes upon it he saw that shutter make a suspicious movement, and he felt confident some one was on the other side of it.

Who could it be but a foe?

The Rev. Mortification Ripon fell upon his knees in a moment, in that most unsalubrious yard, and cried out, "I didn't know it! I don't know it! Don't say it's my fault! I didn't know there was any one there!"

Captain Heron, in the brief moment he had for thought, had come to the same conclusion, but he considered the best way to settle the question would be by a pistol-shot.

Levelling the pistol he had in his hand, he said, sharply, "Come out from behind that shutter, whoever you are, or I fire!"

The shutter fell to the ground.

The moment it was unloosed from some flimsy fastening it was seen to fall.

"Hoorah!" said a voice. "All's right, hoorah!"

Any one with less self-possession than Captain Heron perhaps would have fired his pistol when the shutter fell; but he never allowed himself to be hurried, and the adventurous life he had had for so long had cultivated a kind of self-possession and coolness which could not have been attained by any other means.

It was well that such was the case; for if Heron had fired, it would have been a shot he might have regretted as long as he lived.

It was no other than Tom Ripon who appeared on the other side of the shutter, with a face beaming with delight at the sight of Captain Heron.

"Tom?" cried Heron.

"Yes, Captain, here I am."

"Or your ghost?"

"Oh no, Captain, it's me—I'm all right."

"How is the blessed child?" said the Rev. Mortification Ripon, still on his knees.

"Quite well, thank you," said Tom. "How are you, old friend?"

"Tom," added Heron, "I have no time to ask you how you came where you are, but tell me if the route is clear through that house."

"Quite, Captain."

"Where does it lead?"

"To the court round the corner, Captain, where Ogle is keeping guard."

"Ogle, say you?"

"Oh, yes, Captain. Your scout was on the look-out for all of you; so I saw Ogle in Newgate Street, and I made up to him, and then Jonathan Wild he comes like a madman to the 'King's Head,' and calls out his men; and I heard him say, 'To Star Court, St. Martin's Lane; I will lay a life he is there.' Well, Captain, then I thought, and so did Ogle, that by 'he' he meant you; so off we came; and I left Daisy at the 'Pied Bull' in Maiden Lane."

"Daisy?"

"Yes, Captain. It's all right."

"I know all is right if you have left Daisy there, Tom. But do you hear that knocking?'

"Yes, Captain."

"That is one of Wild's men making a noise on purpose to cover Jonathan's operation in forcing the window of your mother's shop."

"Mother's shop!" said Tom, with unfeigned surprise.

"Yes, yes," said the Rev. Mortification. "Come to my bosom, blessed babe!"

"Get out!" said Tom.

"I am your father."

"Go to the deuce!"

"Sir, I am."

"Bother!"

The Rev. Mortification made repeated efforts to enfold Tom Ripon in a voluminous embrace, but Tom avoided him; and, darting past him, made a rush into the back parlour, where his mother was on her knees, peeping through the room door in an endeavour to see into the shop, and note what progress Jonathan Wild was making.

Mrs. Ripon, no doubt, would have gone into the shop and saved Wild a deal of trouble by taking the bar down from the door, but that Edith kept her in awe with the loaded pistol Captain Heron had left with her.

Now, when Tom saw his mother in that position, with her back towards him, he made but one leap and alighted just between her shoulders, where he set up such a capital imitation of some gigantic cock crowing, that Mrs. Ripon was petrified with astonishment and fear.

Jonathan Wild, too, heard that loud and well-executed crowing, and, for a moment or two, suspended his operations upon the window.

The man, likewise, who was knocking at the outer door, paused.

Then Tom crowed again, for he feared that he was producing unexpected effects.

Mrs. Ripon fell flat.

"That will do," said Tom.

"Oh! Tom, Tom!" said Edith, "how came you here?"

"Come, dear, come!" said Captain Heron, at this instant appearing from the cupboard. "Come, dear Edith! The route to escape seems more plain and fair before us, thanks to Tom, here."

Edith uttered an exclamation of joy, and darted to the side of Captain Heron.

"A minute—only a minute!" said Tom.

"What for?"

Tom made some antic gestures which, no doubt, he intended should be quite explanatory, but, unfortunately, they were not so; and all that Captain Heron could see was that he took a little canvas bag from his pocket and ran into the shop with it, opening it as he went.

"What is he about, Felix?" asked Edith.

"I cannot guess."

Tom was back in a moment, and, as he came, he was sprinkling something on the floor.

"All's right," he said; "Jonathan has nearly made an opening big enough to get through into the window."

"But what have you done, Tom, and what are you doing?"

"That was a bag with a pound of gunpowder in it, that Ogle gave me to mind, you see, Captain. I have put it in the window among mother's stock, and there's a nice train now all the way to the fire here."

"Ah, now I comprehend, Tom."

"Oh, do wait a minute more, Captain! Won't old Jonathan jump!"

"Surrender!" yelled Wild, at this moment; and there was a crash of glass as he made his way impatiently into the shop by the window.

Tom finished his train by sprinkling the last of the powder he had in his hand on to the fire, and then the same effect ensued as when Captain Heron had unentionally contributed so much to the scorching of the Rev. Mortification.

The incandescent wood sent out a plentiful shower of red-hot sparks, some of which fell on the powder sprinkled on the floor.

There was a flash of light, and a curling wreath of white smoke as the flame flew along the lines. Then there was a tremendous report as the bag with the remainder of the powder exploded.

Jonathan Wild uttered a yell of rage and terror.

There was a crash of glass, and then a red flaring light began to show itself.

The miscellaneous stock in trade of Mrs. Ripon's was in flames.

"Now, Captain," said Tom, "off we go!"

Edith clung to Heron, and Tom followed; but in his progress he stood once more upon his mother's back, and uttered a terrifically loud, exultant crow, which nearly threw Mrs. Ripon into a swoon.

When Tom and Captain Heron and Edith reached the yard, they found that the Rev. Mortification was not there. No doubt he had taken the opportunity of making his escape; but as he could only do so through the house, which communicated with Ann Court, round the corner, Captain Heron was in hope that Ogle would secure him.

The house they now made their way into was uninhabited, except by rats and mice, and spiders, and other crawling things. Dust lay in abundance upon the floors, and the whole air became so full of it, owing to being disturbed by the feet of the little party making a thoroughfare through

it, that Heron and Edith were glad to get clear of it.

Tom ran on before and opened the outer door, where they found the Rev. Mortification sitting on the step, with Ogle keeping guard over him.

"Ogle," said Captain Heron, "I am rejoiced to see you!"

"God bless you, Captain, and you, Lady Edith!" replied Ogle. "It does my heart good to see you both alive and well."

"And you, Ogle?"

"Yes, Captain, and you, too. Please heaven, we shall all soon be beneath the boughs of the trees of the old Forest."

"On, on, then!"

"But what shall I do with this fellow?"

"Murder! murder!" said the Rev. Mortification.

"Hang him to the knocker of the door," said Tom. "It won't take long."

"No, no," said Heron.

"We have no authority," said Edith, "to take his life."

"Begs pardon, Lady Edith," said Tom, "but I have. He says he's my father-in-law; and if a fellow maydent hang his own father-in-law, it's hard lines, indeed."

"Bring him along," said Heron,—"that will be the best plan,—bring him along, Ogle!"

"I can't walk, I have hurt the small of my back," said the Rev. Mortification, and as the Psalmist remarks——"

"I know," added Heron. "He remarks that if a man can't walk, or won't walk, and it happens to be dangerous to leave him behind, he must be got rid of."

Captain Heron produced a pistol.

"Oh dear, no," said the Rev. Mortification, as he scrambled to his feet. "I will try."

"I thought you would. Now come on, Ogle. Tom tells me that Daisy is at Martin's, in Maiden Lane."

"Yes, Captain, and my horse, too."

"We shall manage capitally, then."

Ogle made the Reverend Mortification take his arm; and so, like two dogs linked together, one of whom has serious objections to the companionship, they proceeded some five paces in advance of Edith and Captain Heron.

Tom Ripon brought up the rear; and he took care to keep a good look out that they were not followed.

Poor Edith's spirits were in a great flutter now, for she saw the chances of escape from London with Felix Heron fairly before her.

It seemed a terribly long way, short as it was in reality, to Maiden Lane, where the horses were put with an old acquaintance of Ogle's, and where he knew they would be perfectly safe.

"Dearest Edith," whispered Felix, "what a sad life my love for you prepares for you!"

"Oh, no, no; not a sad one!"

"But all these terrors—all these alarms?"

"I would not exchange them, my Felix, for the calmest existence under heaven without your love."

"My own, dear Edith!"

Edith looked up into his face with a smile of ineffable affection.

"Ah!" added Heron, "I will hope that the time will come when I can stand forward in the face of all the world, and, placing a coronet upon your brows, cry out, "Behold, the priceless treasure of my life!"

The distance from Star Court, St. Martin's Lane, was passed, and Ogle pulled the Reverend Mortification Ripon after him at a most uncomfortable pace, until they reached the door of the little old-fashioned public-house named the "Pied Bull," which was kept by Ogle's old friend, Daniel Martin.

"Hilloa!" cried Ogle. "Dan! Dan!"

The landlord ran to the door.

"The horses, where are they?"

"In the best parlour, Ogle. I thought they would be safest there, and readiest to get at."

"All's right. Here's the Captain."

"Ah, Captain Heron, your humble servant. Daisy is as fresh as a lark. I have given her a pint of old ale, and no end of biscuits."

"A thousand thanks, Martin," replied Captain Heron. "I am not the man to forget favours of this kind, as you shall find at the proper time. It is not the few guineas I might hand to you at the present moment which could testify to you how much I feel your faithful kindness; but the time will come—the time will come, Martin."

"It don't need to come, Captain I'm quite pleased if you are; and here's Daisy."

The landlord quickly brought out both the horses; and it was something grateful and pleasant to see Daisy's instant recognition of her master—for she went up to him at once, and placed her head caressingly upon his breast.

There was a flush of gratification upon Captain Heron's face as once more he laid his hand caressingly upon the silken mane of his dumb friend and favourite.

How many dangers had he passed through since he had last looked into the large, liquid eyes of that gallant steed!

Pistol-shots had whistled about his ears, and the strong, doubly-ironed, doubly-bolted door of a cell in Newgate had closed upon him.

But now he was free again, and, if all went well, an hour and a half more might see him perfectly safe and free from all pursuit amid the leafy glades of Epping Forest.

"Listen, all of you!" said Tom, suddenly. "I hear something."

A confused noise of cries and shouts came upon their ears.

"I almost fancy," said Captain Heron, with a smile, "that if Jonathan Wild was blown up, he has come down again. But we are quite safe from him now. Mount, Edith, mount, and we will be off at once!"

"There is no danger now," said Ogle; "we shall distance them in half a mile."

"But we will not bring danger upon the 'Pied Bull' by lingering unnecessarily at its door."

Captain Heron, while he spoke, had assisted Edith to Daisy's saddle, and, springing then lightly behind her, he held the bridle with both hands, so that she was perfectly secure from the chances of a fall.

Ogle mounted his own horse, and Tom sat in lady-fashion on the crupper.

The Reverend Mortification Ripon stood at the door of the "Pied Bull," looking, with a bewildered air about him, as though he expected somebody to take him up, and ride off with him likewise.

"Beware, sir!" cried Captain Heron, as he fixed his eyes upon him for a moment,—"beware of your future conduct. You may make friends of my foes if it so please you; but beware of treachery to me or mine, for I will seek you out and punish you if were you hidden fathoms deep within the earth. Now, Ogle, off and away!"

There was a row of posts at the end of Maiden Lane, to signify that it was no thoroughfare except for foot-passengers, at that period, but those posts were not so close as to prevent a horse being guided with some dexterity between them.

Daisy passed them with a mincing, delicate step, without touching them in the least; and, although Ogle's horse did not go through quite so neatly, still the obstruction was passed, and they both set off at a half-kind of gallop to the north-east of London.

The smoke of the great city, and the faint shouts and cries of those who would have pursued them to the death, were alike left behind. The open country appeared before them, and, after a night and day of perilous adventures and hair-breadth escapes, Captain Heron and Edith found themselves rapidly nearing a haven of safety.

CHAPTER CXCV.

LORD WARRINGDALE HOLDS A CONFERENCE WITH JONATHAN WILD UPON THINGS IN GENERAL.

LORD WARRINGDALE had promised his arch-tempter and confederate in iniquity that he would be at his chambers opposite Whitcombe House, in St. James's Street, whenever he (Wild) should wish to see him.

That it would be absolutely necessary now to hold some conference and decide upon some plan of action, which should hold out greater chances of success than any they had hitherto attempted, was a self-evident proposition.

Lord Warringdale felt himself in the position of a general, who had not only lost a campaign, but with it had lost his honour.

Every scheme, whether artificial or violent, which he had attempted for the destruction of his brother, had hitherto signally failed.

The causes of those failures were at once inscrutable to him, and full of suggestive terrors.

He knew that he himself had tried to take the life of Felix Heron, and he felt that there had been no shrinking on his part in the wish and intention so to do; but, signally failing—failing from want of strength and want of courage,—he thought, when once he had made the necessary arrangements with Jonathan Wild, that he might look upon his object as accomplished.

But Wild, too, had failed.

And now, as Lord Warringdale paced up and down with uneasy steps and a mind full of a thousand perplexities, it was that failure of Jonathan Wild's which vexed and annoyed him more than his own, because for his own want of success he could find causes, while for Wild's repeated failures he could find none.

Lord Warringdale could not bring himself to believe that Jonathan Wild was playing the

LORD WARRINGDALE CONTEMPLATES AN ACT OF GREAT VILLANY.

Presented Gratis with No. 87 of the New Edition of the Captive; or, the Robbers of Epping Forest.

EACH WEEK IS PRESENTED GRATIS A COLOURED ENGRAVING.

double game throughout which had in reality suggested itself to the prolific brain of the great thief-taker.

The vast estates and revenues of the earldom of Whitcombe were the prizes upon which Jonathan fixed his earnest gaze; and if it were possible to induct into the property a wrongful possessor, such as Lord Warringdale, there was no exactly conceivable limit to the demands which he, Jonathan Wild, might make upon those estates and those revenues.

Hence we find that in bonds and securities of one kind and another, Wild had procured from Warringdale a sum which was rapidly swelling up to the amount of a hundred thousand pounds.

But that was all upon paper.

It was all contingent upon Lord Warringdale being put in possession of the earldom and estates.

Now, Wild knew perfectly well that Captain Heron, as being the real first-born and legitimate son and heir of the late Earl of Whitcombe, was entitled to the rank and the property.

But what good was that to Jonathan Wild?

What necessity was there to the possessor of an earldom and sixty thousand a year to make any bargain with Jonathan Wild, the thief-taker? None whatever. It was the man who was nefariously endeavouring to possess that which was not his own, of whom a profit and a property could be made.

But there was this consideration always weighing heavily on the mind of Jonathan Wild. He might succeed in keeping out of the estates of Whitcombe their rightful possessor, but it did not by any means follow that he should succeed in inducting into those estates and properties their wrongful claimant and aspirant.

Then Wild had the hope that Felix Heron would be so perplexed, so hard-driven, so worried, so surrounded by dangers, both on his own account and on that of Edith, that he would be glad to make any terms to end such disastrous conditions; and he (Wild) might then stand in as good a pecuniary position with the right heir to the earldom as with the wrong one.

If so, Wild felt that his position would be infinitely safer and better.

Whatever the force of circumstances might induce Felix Heron to give him, he might feel that he really possessed; while, as regarded his transactions with Lord Warringdale, he would, so to speak, be living on a mine which might explode in danger on the accident of any half-hour.

This, then, was the real secret why Jonathan Wild broke down so repeatedly in carrying out his engagement with Lord Warringdale. There is very little doubt that if Jonathan had set his mind deliberately upon the murder of Felix Heron he must have succeeded; but he spared him, because there was always the lingering thought that he might be valuable.

And now the sun is about to set on that eventful day when Captain Heron and Edith had made so adventurous an escape from the nefarious little establishment of Mrs. Ripon.

They are safe in Epping Forest, and have the happiness of serenity and mutual affection.

But Lord Warringdale, as we have said, is pacing his apartments to and fro, with a heart brimful of bitterness, excitement, passion, and remorse.

His temper had become so capricious and violent, that no servant could live with him for long; and the man he had now waiting upon him in those chambers was an old, worn-out valet who, because he could get employment nowhere else, was willing to put up with the caprices and wild rage of even Lord Warringdale.

This man, too, had the advantage—and it was one under the circumstances—of being a little deaf; so that a good two-thirds of the abuse levelled at him by Lord Warringdale was completely lost.

There had come a sharp knocking several times repeated at the door of the chambers, but to which the old valet had paid not the least attention until Warringdale himself, with roaring vehemence, informed him of the fact.

When the door was opened, then, Jonathan Wild, with a look of sharp suspicion upon his countenance—for he could not comprehend why he had been kept waiting,—entered the chambers.

"Oh! you're come?" cried Warringdale. "And it is well, for I am sick at heart and brain."

"And when I do come, you keep me waiting," said Wild.

"It is that idiot. He is deaf, or pretends to be so."

"Indeed?"

Wild looked scrutinizingly and suspiciously at the old valet. Then, diving his hand into his pocket, he put on a smiling countenance as he looked at the old man, and said, in quite ordinary tones, "I have been commissioned to bring you five guineas, which you can have at once."

There was not the slightest spark of intelligence on the face of the old valet, and it was quite evident he did not hear what was said.

"I am satisfied!" growled Wild. "He is deaf, indeed. And now, my Lord Warringdale, let us walk into your inner room; for I want to ask you, in plain language, what is to be done."

"It is I," said Warringdale, as he followed Wild, and, closing the door of the inner room, sunk down with a look of exhaustion into the recesses of an old-fashioned, high-backed chair,— "it is I who should ask you what is to be done."

"How so?"

"Because you have miserably failed."

"Ha! ha!" laughed Wild.

"You laugh; but remember, Jonathan, that although your failure is my failure, mine is likewise yours; and the bonds and money obligations you hold of me are but as so much waste paper if I have not the means of discharging them."

"Land," said Jonathan, "don't run away. All those matters you speak of are charges upon the Whitcombe estates."

"Give me the estates, then, and I will pay them."

"Fair and softly," said Jonathan. "I don't mind owning to you, my Lord Warringdale, that I have had some little difficulties in the matter— some little disappointments and some perplexities."

"And what have I not had?" cried Warringdale passionately. "In what a strange position do I not present myself to the world? The Earl of Whitcombe has been dead a considerable time, and I who ought to have been called to the House of Lords, and easily become possessed of the title and estates, am still no more than Lord Warringdale, which I was in my father's lifetime.".

"That's true."

"And, indeed," added Warringdale, speaking yet more vehemently, "I am scarcely that: for if my claims upon the earldom of Whitcombe are not valid or acknowledged, I am not, and never was, Lord Warringdale."

"That's true," said Wild.

"And I am not blind to the fact that members of the old nobility of England, who used to be my father's frequent visitors at Whitcombe House, shun me when they see me in the street. They are seized with a partial blindness, or they cross over the way, or they go into a shop; indeed, my position has become unbearable."

"And the reason of all that?" said Wild.

"Is your failure."

"Not exactly."

"What then?"

"If the young Earl of Bridgewater had not been on the standing committee of privileges of the House of Lords, you would have been called at once to the title."

"My malediction be upon him!"

"But," added Wild, "as he chose to make acquaintance with Felix Heron, and adopt his course, he was just in a position to obstruct yours."

"Curses on him!"

"Ah!" said Wild, as he drew the heavy hilt of his hanger further forward, and leant his arms upon it; "curses are all very well in their way. They relieve the mind occasionally, and, perhaps, prevent a surfeit of the blood; but for all other purposes they leave us just where we were."

"What can be done, then?"

"How?"

"Why are you so oracular and mysterious to-day, Jonathan?"

"Am I?"

"You know you are. Speak out, if you have anything to say to me!"

Jonathan bent down his head and looked out curiously from the top of his eyes at Lord Warringdale, and then in a voice that sounded more like the hissing of a serpent than anything human, he said, "The young Earl of Bridgewater had a father."

A death-like paleness came over the face of Lord Warringdale, and he staggered backward to a seat.

"No, no!" he gasped.

"On my faith!" sneered Wild, with one of his hideous laughs. "Can you deny it?"

"Hush! No, I don't mean that."

"What then?"

"I mean that I don't want to speak of—of that father."

"Oh, that's it? I suppose that may be called the weakness of human nature. Well, my Lord Warringdale, you need not speak of him; but that need not hinder me saying what I have to say in regard to that worthy and departed individual."

"Hush! hush!"

"Stuff! Hear me out. Do you fancy that when one kills a man that for all future time he is at your elbow?"

"No, no! but there have been times when I have fancied, knowing that it was but fancy, I—I saw him."

"Oh, indeed?"

"Yes, Jonathan Wild, it is but too true."

"Well, different people take different views of matters. I've lost count a good while ago of how many people I've put out of the way; but, be they more or less, I never found any of them to come back to trouble me, and never expect; but that is not the question. We don't meet to talk of dead men and ghosts, do we?"

"No, no! heaven forbid!—that is, I hope not."

"And yet you are pale and ghastly, as if you had seen a spectre."

Warringdale covered his eyes with his hands, and groaned as he rocked to and fro on the chair on which he had seated himself. Well might he have said—although with very different feelings and emotions—with the philosophic Hamlet, that he saw such images in his "mind's eye."

Wild regarded him for a few moments in silence, and then cried out, boisterously, "Come, my Lord Warringdale, you're a cup too low, and I should not object to something of a cheering character. Have you no wine in these fancy chambers of yours?"

"Yes," cried Warringdale. "Wine! wine! Let us drink! Were it not for wine, I should be dead — dead — long ago! When these thick-coming fancies oppress me, I am forced to fly to the rosy bright delusion, which steeps the senses for a time in forgetfulness, and drowns reflection."

"Very good!" said Jonathan, "but don't get out any of your wishy washy stuff from France—your clarets, which no more agree with an English stomach than would a frog's hind leg for breakfast, and a fricasseed puppy for dinner. Have you none of the generous, deep red wine of Portugal, purple with the grape, and full of power?"

"I have—I have."

Lord Warringdale did not trouble his deaf valet; but opening a bureau, he himself procured a couple of glasses, and a bottle of that port wine since so popular in England, but which was at that period hardly known.

In silence, then, these two worthies—or, rather, unworthies—drained a couple of glasses to the dregs.

"You're better?" said Wild.

"Much."

"And that mind's eye of yours that you spoke of don't look with such terror back to the past?"

"It does not."

"Very good! Then I must continue what I was about to say. The late Earl of Bridgewater came by his death in order that that death might give a receipt in full for a few thousand pounds' worth of gambling debts. The present Earl of Bridgewater stands materially in the way of the earldom of Whitcombe and the revenue of sixty thousand pounds a year."

"Ah!" gasped Warringdale, as he poured out for himself and drank another glass of the rich red wine.

"And, moreover," added Wild, as he, likewise, helped himself from the bottle—"and, moreover, this present young Earl of Bridgewater has some ugly suspicions touching his father's sudden decease."

"I will kill him!" cried Lord Warringdale, with flashing eyes.

"That's it!" said Jonathan Wild.

CHAPTER CXCVI.

LORD WARRINGDALE MAKES AN ATTEMPT ON THE
LIFE OF THE YOUNG EARL OF BRIDGEWATER,
AND SIGNALLY FAILS.

THERE was an ominous silence of some three or
four minutes' duration between Jonathan Wild and
Lord Warringdale, after the former had fairly
given speech to the villanous proposition for the
assassination of the Earl of Bridgewater.

It took even Lord Warringdale some short
space of time to get familiar with the idea, notwithstanding he had in so apparently prompt a
fashion signified his readiness to do the deed.

Wild looked at him through his half-shut eyes,
over which his brows were drawn down low, and
waited for him to speak again.

But Warringdale found it necessary to partake
of two glasses more of the strong bright wine before he uttered another word.

Then he spoke.

"I have said I will do it, and it shall be done!"

He glanced round him as he uttered the words,
as though he feared that the spectre of the murdered man, whom he had left in death in Paddock
Hill Lane, would appear visibly before him.

"Good!" said Wild.

"Yes. It shall be done."

"When?"

"So soon as time and opportunity shall serve
me."

"Good again!"

Wild rose as if to go.

"No, no!" cried Lord Warringdale. "Don't
be leaving me alone now, after this."

"After what?"

Wild put on quite a look of surprise, as though
the conversation which had just taken place between him and Warringdale had been of the most
non-exciting and innocent description.

"You know well what I mean, Jonathan."

"Hang me, my lord, if I do! I have merely
pointed out an enemy to you—one who I think
is the greatest present obstruction to your progress
in life; and you naturally say that you mean to
get rid of him."

"Yes, but——"

"And the sooner the better, I add. That is all;
and so now good day, or rather good night, for I
see the night has come. I am weary, and must
needs, my lord, leave you to yourself."

Jonathan Wild tightened the hilt of his hanger,
and then tossing off the last glass of the rich,
generous port wine, he bestowed a nod upon Warringdale, and strode out of the chambers.

Warringdale was alone.

If there be anything that may fairly be called
retribution in this life, it certainly is to be looked
for deep in the hearts of evil men.

The greatest punishment that could possibly be
inflicted upon such a man as Warringdale, was to
leave him to think.

Alone! No companionship, no human, gentle,
tender sympathies! Alone with his own terrible
thoughts of the past!

Alone with the as terrible thoughts of the future!

No wonder that now he should lift his hands
above his head, and groan out, "I have embarked
in a sea of crime! Fain would I steer back to the
port from which I started, but the adverse currents
of destiny hurry me on; and if I end in a wreck,
I cannot retreat, or help the catastrophe."

Miserable, mistaken man!

Is it ever too late to retreat from evil?

Never! never! A higher wisdom and a
higher mercy than are to be found upon earth has
given such assurance; but those who will close
their ears cry out that they hear not.

Lord Warringdale was one of those.

He would have been glad and willing to carry
out his views, if possible, without committing himself to great crimes; but if the great crimes were
necessary, why then he consented to look upon
them as things which must be accomplished.

He made up his mind to the death of the young
Earl of Bridgewater.

To the murder of the son of the man whom he
had from such paltry and slight reasons hurried
from the world.

But how to set about it?

That was the question.

Lord Warringdale rested his head upon his
hands, and thought long and earnestly upon this
part of the question. Many plans and schemes
suggested themselves to him, for murder has
many phases, and it may be imagined that the
enemy of mankind would find some mode of sug-
gesting the readiest mode by which a human soul
could be dragged to perdition.

Lord Warringdale, however, could not for a
time make up his mind to any of the plans that
suggested themselves to him.

Some were too personally hazardous.

Some depended too much upon the good faith
of other people.

Some were too complicated, and depended upon
the accurate adjustment of too many small circumstances, so that the failure of any one would have
a tendency to break up the integrity of the whole
scheme of operation.

But the more Warringdale thought over the
means of carrying out his murderous intentions
the more faint-hearted he became with the idea of
the contemplated assassination.

In the course of another hour he began to look
upon the affair as a something that of necessity
must be done, and which merely had to be considered with reference to the mode of doing it.

Poison would have been a congenial mode for
him to adopt.

But how was he to bring that about?

How would he induce the young Earl to drink
from any cup that he, Warringdale, would present
to him?

How was it possible to infuse any deadly drug
into the food or the wine of a man who looked
upon him with such eyes as the young Earl of
Bridgewater regarded him?

But the more he thought the more he became
enamoured of the idea of putting the young Earl
to some death which should puzzle the medical
faculty, and, probably, be believed to be what is
called natural.

Then, as he thought back—back to several
incidents of his life—he remembered how some
attempts had been made upon the life of Jonathan
Wild, and how signally one of those attempts had
failed in the house by Milford Lane.

Then the name of Raphael occurred to Warringdale as the name of the chemist, or alchemist, as he recollected the attorney who had been outwitted by Wild had called him, who had purchased that subtle and death-dealing powder in the small box, whose fumes were to be the death of Jonathan Wild, always providing he would sit still and inhale them for a sufficient length of time.

"Raphael!" he said to himself. "Raphael! Yes, that is the name of the man who concocts such subtle poisons, that he rivals the Medici, and might have been the favourite chemist of a De Brinvilliers."

The idea that in some way this man would and could help him, for a consideration, quickly grew in the mind of Lord Warringdale into a desire to seek him.

At all events it would be progress of some sort. It would be a movement in the right direction for the accomplishment of his designs.

"I will seek this man out," said Warringdale to himself. "I will go to him at once, and ascertain if he can suggest some mode for the safe use of those dangerous commodities he deals in."

Warringdale accordingly had to assume an appearance of ordinary composure which he was in reality very far from feeling, and bawling in the ear of his deaf valet that he would " soon return," he left his chambers.

There was a wretched street leading from the Strand to the river, which was nearly uninhabited.

The houses were going to decay, so that even the poorest of the population of the neighbourhood hesitated to reside in them.

It was in the last house on the right hand side of the way of this street that Raphael the alchemist and vender of poisons resided.

Lord Warringdale sought the house with a quiet, noiseless step.

To be sure no one was in the street to observe him, but the errand on which he went imparted to his aspect an appearance of suspicion.

It was quite a relief to him when he stood in the deep doorway of Raphael's house, and felt that no one looking down the wretched street from the Strand could see him.

There did not seem to be any visible means of summoning the chemist to the door, so Lord Warringdale was forced to kick at the panels with his heels as he stood with his back to it.

The door opened in a moment.

"What now ?" cried an irritated voice. "Whom do you seek here ? Rats or mice ?"

"I seek Raphael the chemist."

"Dead!"

"Dead, is he ?"

"To be sure he is. All people die, I fancy, at some time or another, and it would be a hard case if a man could not be dead when he pleased."

"Cease those words," replied Lord Warringdale. "I infer that Raphael is dead or alive as it may suit him."

"And what then ?"

"Then I have only to say that if twenty pounds are worth the having——"

Lord Warringdale had only got so far in what he was saying, when the voice interrupted him by calling out in much more bland accents, "The first door to the left along the passage. Close the outer door; you will know it is fast by hearing the snap of the lock."

It was not a very usual thing for Lord War-

ringdale to be told to shut the street door after him when he visited a house ; but under the present circumstances, provided he succeeded in the object he came about, he was not disposed to be very critical about the mode of his reception, or to stand upon any of the minute ceremonies of life.

He did as he was directed.

The outer door closed with a sharp snap, and he went down the passage and took the first door to his left, which door yielded to the touch, and conducted him into a room which was very much impregnated with the odour of ether.

A spirit-lamp, the pale, sickly-looking flame of which flickered and waved aside at even the slightest movement of the air of the room, was the only light that it contained, for, if there were a window, its shutters were fast closed, so that no wandering daylight could find its way into the apartment.

At the other end of a table sat Raphael, the chemist. A glass mask was on his face, either from the fact that he was engaged in some distillation, the fumes of which were noxious to life, or because he wished to interpose that semi-concealment between him and his visitor.

"Well ?" he said.

The voice of Raphael sounded strange and hollow behind the mask.

Lord Warringdale was silent for a few moments because he could not exactly make up his mind how to frame the request he came to make.

When he did speak it was with a hesitating tone and manners.

" I have an enemy," he said.

The alchemist laughed behind the glass mask.

"I have an enemy, and know not how to dispose of him. He is a great enemy."

"No doubt! no doubt! But human life is so very frail and uncertain a possession, that people take ill and die at times when least expected."

"Ah, yes! If that could be done !"

"Give him this."

The alchemist handed over the table a small packet. It looked like one of the ordinary powder packets such as chemists make up, and was enveloped in a green paper.

"How ?"

"That is your business."

"Mine or not, it cannot be done, for I have no means of administering any medicament or potion to him—no means whatever."

"Neither in food nor in drinks."

"In neither."

"Can you scratch him ?"

"Can I what ?"

"Can you give him on his hand or face so much of a scratch as the chance point of a pin would produce ?"

"I fear not."

"Then I cannot help you."

"Nay, I hope you can. Let me think. It is possible. Perhaps I may be able."

Lord Warringdale was trying now to see his way.

"Do you mean to tell me," he added, "that you can furnish me with a something which, if it be introduced into the system by so slight a wound as the scratch of a pin, would be fatal ?"

"I do."

"Give it to me. It will suffice."

"You said twenty guineas ?"

"I did.   There is the sum."

Lord Warringdale flung a purse of gold upon the table; and then the chemist presented him with so minute a vial that it was quite a wonder where it could be manufactured.

"In that vial," he said, "there are just three drops of a pale yellow liquid.   If you dip the point of a pin in them and then let it dry when taken out, a scratch from that pin will, in a few hours, produce death."

Lord Warringdale held the little glass nervously in his hands.

"Then the whole three drops," he said, "would, I fancy, be fatal to a great number of persons."

"You hold the lives of a hundred men in your hands."

"I am content, and thank you, Raphael; but now tell me, and tell me truly, one thing——"

"Speak."

"Do you know me?"

No. 88.—EDITH.

"No."

"Are you quite certain?"

"I make it my business to know nobody, and nobody ever comes here from one year's end to the other."

"I comprehend you, Raphael, and believe you to be a man of most admirable discretion.   Good day, and thank you."

The chemist made no reply; but Warringdale did not want one.   He had that which he came for, and he hastened to leave the house, and make his way up the narrow street into the Strand again.

Deep in the corner of a secure pocket he held the little vial which he hoped would aid him in putting an end to all his trouble in regard to the young Earl of Bridgewater.

And as Warringdale took his route towards his chambers, in St. James's Street, he began to reflect, that if he really held the deadly instrument of destruction in his possession, which Raphael had announced it to be, he might find a means of making a path to all his desires over the dead bodies of all who opposed him.

As people passed him, bustling and active in all the freshness of health and strength, Warringdale grasped the little vial he had in his pocket, and began to fancy himself a sort of fate, or arbiter of death or life, to all who passed him.

But what was this idea that he had of compassing the death of the young Earl of Bridgewater?

What diabolical plan was he now elaborating in his complex intellect, to enable him to make a deadly use of some portion of the three drops of death he had purchased of Raphael?

We shall quickly see.

No sooner had Lord Warringdale reached his own chambers, than he sat down, and wrote the following letter :—

"To the Right Honourable the Earl of Bridgewater.

"MY LORD,—

"It has pleased you to make an accusation, or to imply an accusation against me, which is so odious to a gentleman and an innocent man, that I cannot endure it.

"You have more than once hinted that you still believe I had some hand in an occurrence which I know nothing of personally, and you have made a parade of the fact that we have met once with our swords opposed, and that you were the conqueror.

"Make that boast no longer, for I am willing to meet you again with my sword, so soon as you may be able to muster courage to accept the invitation.

"I have the honour to be, my lord,
"Your foe,
"WARRINGDALE."

This was step one in the means by which Lord Warringdale thought to render useful the three "death drops" which he had purchased of the villanous old dealer in such murderous preparations.

The second step was one that was sufficiently significant of what he meant to do.

Lord Warringdale shut himself up in one of the rooms of his chambers; and carefully opening the little vial, he just managed to insert the extreme point of a very thin, slender Court sword he had in it.

Keeping the point of the sword there for the space of about a minute, Warringdale then withdrew it, and saw that there was a pale yellow stain upon the bright steel, for the space of about a twentieth part of an inch from the point of the weapon.

Then he looked at the vial.

There was still sufficient of the death drops to be effectually seen.

"Of this I will be careful," he said, as he unlocked a cabinet, and hid the vial in a secret drawer. "Who knows but it may be useful to me on some other occasion? I forgot to ask Raphael how long the power of the poison would last upon the point of a pin, or of a sword. Perhaps I have a hundred deaths here about me, as I carry this slender steel weapon at my side. If it be so, woe be to him who offends me!"

Lord Warringdale had still a little difficulty to encounter, and that was to find some one to carry this challenge to the young Earl of Bridgewater.

That it would be accepted he had no doubt in the world, but still he felt that he must get some apparently respectable person to be the bearer of it.

Lord Warringdale's acquaintances had somehow fallen off from him of late, and for a time he could not think of any one whom he would like even to ask to go to the young Earl on the errand.

The room in which Lord Warringdale now was, happened to be a front one. It immediately faced Whitcombe House, the house of his father, opposite —that father for whom he had cared less in life than he did in death; and in the latter case he only cared because he was superstitious enough to have been dreadfully terrified at what had happened to him in Whitcombe House.

As he was now in deep thought, his eyes happened to stray over to Whitcombe House.

Now, Lord Warringdale knew perfectly well that the mansion of the late Earl of Whitcombe was deserted. The few domestics who had lingered there after the Earl's death had left, when they found that something was amiss about the succession to the title and estates, and that they need not look to Lord Warringdale for wages.

So the house was shut up.

It was a great surprise, then, to Lord Warringdale to see a light pass one of the windows.

At first he could scarcely believe his senses, and thought that it must be the reflection of some light on the side of the way he was on; but in a few moments he was convinced that such was not the case, by not only seeing the light again, but the sudden closing of a shutter, or the portion of a shutter, which had permitted it to be seen by staying accidentally open.

There could be no doubt that some one was in the house of the late Earl.

Who was it?

Lord Warringdale asked himself that question with a shudder.

Had his mind been free from the taint of deep iniquity—had his conscience not been contaminated by crimes already committed, and by those he was contemplating the committal of—nothing would have been more natural than to have ran out into St. James's Street, and summoned a constable to go with him over his late father's house.

But Lord Warringdale did not do that.

It would have required something very much more strange than seeing a light at one of its windows to induce him to cross again the threshold of Whitcombe House.

CHAPTER CXCVII.

CAPTAIN HERON COMES TO LONDON, AND VISITS THE BISHOP OF WORCESTER.

WE must now leave Lord Warringdale contemplating the magnificent mansion opposite to his chambers, and thinking upon who he could get to carry his challenge to the Earl of Bridgewater, while we repair to the glades and deep recesses of Epping Forest once again.

Without any cross accident, the little party

who had galloped from London so successfully, reached the forest, and at the sight of the glorious trees, and the feel of the fresh and fragrant air, Edith could not help exclaiming, "Ah, Felix! Felix! Why do we ever wander from this peaceful sylvan home? We are always happy here, and we never leave it without encountering many dangers and anxieties."

"Fate, my Edith, fate! We have all in this world a certain part to play!"

"Let ours be a part, then, of peace, of serenity, and of love!"

Captain Heron sighed deeply.

"I would that it could be so!" he said. "But I am inclined to think, dear Edith, that a higher power than we can hope to contend with, when he allotted to us all our parts in the great drama of existence, took means of preventing any one from drawing aside and allowing the play to go on without him."

"It may be so," said Edith, with a sigh.

"But cheer up, dear one," added Captain Heron. "We will not let any gloomy philosophy mar the pleasure of a return to our home."

"No, Felix; and for a time, at least, we will be calm and happy."

"Yes, dear one, yes. As calm and happy as love and mutual confidence can make us."

The scout, whose duty it was to keep watch upon the confines of the Forest, had seen Captain Heron and Edith, with Ogle and Tom Ripon, approaching, and the signal had been given to the band of the approach of its well-loved leader.

It was strange to hear how full the old forest of Epping seemed to be of owls.

The whooping and hooting of those creatures appeared to come from every tree.

Edith looked at Heron for a moment, as though she were puzzled by the sounds.

Felix smiled.

"Dear Edith," he said, "you have seen enough of our woodland home to comprehend its signs and cries."

"Ah, yes!"

"Well, my faithful men—or rather my faithful owls—will soon show themselves when I give the signal."

They had ridden among the trees right into one of the forest glades, and then Captain Heron pausing for a moment, cried out, "Hawks without, and the owls sleep well!"

No sooner had he so spoken, than, like over-ripe fruit from the surrounding trees, there began to drop down the various members of the band.

"Hurrah!" cried Tom Ripon. "Here we are, all right, my brave fellows! I have brought off the Captain and Lady Edith all right and safe, as I told you I would!"

"And," said Ogle, "if you had not brought off something else, Tom, it would have been just as well!"

"What's that, Daddy Ogle?" said Tom.

"Why, the end of your tongue, for it's all the last inch too long."

Tom Ripon looked a little downcast for a moment at this rebuke; and the band laughed at him when Captain Heron and Edith had retired hand in hand through one of those narrow and almost inaccessible paths which led to the foundation of old Hinchcliffe Priory.

There it was that the longest, and perhaps the most deeply anxious, consultation that had ever yet occurred between Captain Heron and his dearly loved Edith took place.

Edith flung herself upon his breast, and while the tears sprung unbidden to her eyes, she spoke to him.

"Oh Felix! Felix! what are titles, wealth, all that the world can bestow, compared with one dear look, one kind word of love? Let who will seize upon the Earldom of Whitcombe and its properties, we will be happier far with youth and dear affection."

"Alas, alas!" replied Heron. "I would that it could be so!"

"Let it be so," my Felix.

"How, dear one—how?"

"We will leave England. There are many climes far away, where, to breathe the free air and look upon the glorious sunshine, are delights of themselves. Let us seek some such home, and our lives will glide away in the peace and the joy of mutual affection."

"Oh, that I could say yes to such a proposition, my Edith, but I dare not."

"Dare not, Felix?"

"Just so, dear one. Remember that I have already—by the slight assertion I have made of my rights and claims—stirred up many enemies."

"Heed them not! oh, heed them not! Forgive them and despise them."

"Would that I could do so! But there is yet another thing to be remembered."

"And that, Felix—what is that?"

"Our friends."

"Ah, yes!"

"Remember that we have stirred up those who love and wish us well, and that by so doing we have brought upon them many dangers."

"Felix, Felix, how selfish I have been! I thought at the moment but of ourselves, and our peace, serenity, and happiness, when I should have thought of others who are at present suffering for our sake."

"Yes, Edith, we may regret that we commenced the strife; but having so commenced it, it is not for us to fly from the battle. We must now see all these matters to an end, for in so seeing them is involved the rescue of those who have jeopardized safety, and even life, for our sakes."

"You are right, Felix, you are right!" sighed Edith; "and we must yet be brave and strong."

"Recollect, too," added Captain Heron, "how much more we know now than we did previously. The revelations that the villain Wild made to you, when he was conveying you in the coach to Newgate, are most important. Upon that information we can act."

"Oh, yes—yes, Felix, we now know all."

"I think we do, Edith, and there is but one favour I would ask of you."

"A favour of me, Felix? Say one command to give me."

"No, dear one, it is a favour. Let me feel for the future that, whatever I am encountering in London, and whatever efforts I am making in the cause which now I must carry out to an end, I leave you safe here in our forest home."

"I comprehend you. My presence perplexes you."

"That is scarcely the word, Edith; but I will say that when I have you with me, anxiety for your safety overcomes all other considerations, and I am more anxious to reach again the green glades of Epping Forest, than to carry out those views, and make even those discoveries, that might create me Earl of Whitcombe."

"Go, then, Felix, and my prayers will attend you. I will believe that right and justice, although they may be trodden down for a time, cannot be trodden out; and I will believe that heaven will hold a watchful care over you, and save you from those who would destroy you."

"I shall go courageously and hopefully. I cannot leave Lady Castleneau's fate longer in a state of doubt and uncertainty. My heart too is wrung with anguish, when I think of old Sir Dominick Browne, and all that he has suffered for my sake. But my first visit to London, Edith, will be so peaceful a one, that I do not believe it possible to evolve any danger from it."

"Ah! Where is it possible, Felix, that you can go, surrounded as you are by such implacable enemies, and by so many persons who seek your destruction? Where is it you can go, and yet find safety?"

"We are well convinced now, Edith, that there is every probability in the story that the present Bishop of Worcester is the clergyman who actually united my poor mother to the late Earl of Whitcombe. It is that personage I will seek, and his memory must surely be treacherous indeed if it fail to remember the marriage of Amelia Staunton with the then Lord Warringdale—for that was the title of the late Earl at that period, since his father was still living."

"Go, then, Felix; but you will not go alone? You will take some one with you who is able to aid you in critical circumstances?"

"I have already, in my own mind, selected one, Edith.

"I can guess who that will be. You will take Ogle?"

"Nay, dearest, I thought of leaving Ogle in charge of the forest; and I think, of the two, the most useful person I can take with me will be Tom Ripon."

"Alas!" said Edith, with every appearance of disappointment; "I would fain some stronger arm had been by your side than that of a mere boy."

"I do not think, Edith, that it is strength I shall want. I rather think that finesse and management will do more good for me now than any real force I could bring to bear upon any special occasion. Tom is clever and acute, his very youth makes him unsuspected, and I can make use of him in a thousand ways, where a man would be challenged and hindered at once."

Edith could not but agree with this reasoning on the part of Captain Heron, and she was well pleased to see the pains that he took in perfecting a disguise in which to proceed to London.

Heron's idea was to leave Daisy at the forest, and disguising himself as a bluff country gentleman, half yeoman, half farmer, take Tom Ripon with him in the appearance of foot-boy, or servant.

One of the effects of the depredations which had been committed from time to time by the band of highwaymen of Epping Forest, had been to supply them with various trunks, valises, and mails, as a certain kind of travelling box was then called, from which clothing of every kind and description had been procured.

There was one apartment amid the ruins of the old Priory and Manor House which was well stocked with every possible disguise that, under ordinary circumstances, Captain Heron or his band could require.

That happened to be the period, too, when a great number of persons still adhered to the practice of wearing wigs, and although that barbarism was rapidly going out, yet to see anybody with one of those appendages created no remark or surprise whatever.

In the way of disguise this was an immense advantage.

Behold, then, Captain Heron, on the morning following his arrival so happily and safely at the forest, fully equipped as a country gentleman.

It had not been difficult for him to find a means of imparting to his cheeks a much more ruddy glow than they usually possessed.

The small silken moustache, which had been a distinguishing feature in his countenance, he ruthlessly sacrificed; and, attired in top boots (rather large for him), a very voluminous coat with huge lappels, a cravat wound many times round his neck, and a three-cornered hat of formidable dimensions,—Captain Heron, instead of the slim and elegant figure he usually presented, came very well up to the general notion of a bluff, hearty country gentleman.

He took care to be well armed, however; and although he wore no sword, the pistols, upon which he could depend at a moment's notice, were handily within his reach.

The change in Heron's appearance was so perfect that when Ogle saw him he fairly started, and was about to raise the peculiar cry of danger, which would soon have brought plenty of the band to the spot.

Of course, it was but for a moment that the eyes of Ogle could be deceived in such a matter but that he was deceived at all, even for an instant, put Captain Heron in good conceit with his disguise.

But when Tom Ripon appeared, prepared for the journey to London, Ogle, and those members of the band who saw him, could scarcely refrain from a shout of gratification and amusement.

Tom was attired in a suit of livery—a full size too large for him—which gave him a loutish, clumsy appearance, as foreign as anything could possibly be from the neat, lithe activity which in reality characterized him.

But when Tom, in broad country dialect, gave a pull to a bit of his hair that he let stick out in front of his hat, and said, "I be a goin' to Lunnun town along o' measter!" the band burst into a roar of laughter, and declared Tom's disguise to be perfect.

Then Captain Heron held up his hand, and there was an expression upon his countenance which let them see that serious business was to be now the order of the day.

The sun was high in the heavens, but in the shadowy, leafy spot where they were assembled, but a green and misty twilight made its way.

Heron, in a calm, distinct voice, addressed his comrades: "It may be said that the time has again arrived when you fancy that I am paying more

CAPTAIN HERON SETS OUT ON AN EXPEDITION TO THE METROPOLIS
IN A NEW CHARACTER.

Presented Gratis with No. 88, of the New Edition Edith the Captive; or, the Robbers of Epping Forest.

EACH WEEK IS PRESENTED GRATIS A COLOURED ENGRAVING.

attention to that which concerns Felix Heron alone than our whole fraternity."

"No, Captain, no!" was the cry that came from every lip.

"It is well," added Heron. "I am glad to hear you say so much. But yet I cannot but feel I have, to a certain extent, ceased to be your leader in those expeditions on the heath and on the road, the conduct of which you chose to trust to me. Bear with this sort of inactivity yet for a time, and I promise you nothing shall be lost."

"All's well, Captain—all's well!"

"I am content, then; but if I live, I will yet lead you upon some expeditions which shall remind us all of old times, and let the world still know that Captain Heron, of Epping Forest, with his band of gallant men, are in the land of the living."

This announcement was hailed with shouts of gratification; and as Captain Heron had already taken leave of Edith, he turned to Tom Ripon, saying, "Follow me, Tom, then! We will strike into the high road, and meet one of the stage coaches somewhere about Woodford, which will take us to London without suspicion and without trouble."

Tom was eager to be gone, for he anticipated fun, excitement, and mischief as certain to arise out of the new part he was about to play.

Heron waved his hand, and the band disappeared as if by magic among the trees and thick growth of underwood around.

With a look of thoughtfulness—if it were not indeed one of sadness—upon his countenance, Captain Heron went mechanically, rather than observantly, towards the confines of the forest.

Tom Ripon saw that his master was in much too meditative a mood to be spoken too, so he contented himself by following Heron in silence at some dozen paces distance, and accurately copying every attitude he saw him assume.

This was not done on Tom's part from any feeling of ridicule or impertinence, but simply because he thought that everything that Captain Heron did, was the wisest, best, and most admirable thing to do in the world.

But when they emerged into the open road, and it was likely they would soon be overtaken by one of the coaches travelling to London, Heron shook off his thoughtfulness of demeanour, and glancing behind him, he cried out, "Tom, come hither!"

"Yes, Captain."

"Do you know what you have to do?"

Tom looked confused and puzzled for a moment, and then he shook his head.

"It is very easy," said Heron, with a smile.

"I'll do it, Captain," said Tom, "if it was ever so difficult."

"Very likely you would, Tom; but in this case it is all summed up in one word."

"A long word, Captain?"

"No, a short one. All you've got to do is nothing."

Tom did not seem much more enlightened, so Captain Heron added, "What I mean you to understand by that, Tom, is just this—that you are not to try to do anything. That to support the character you have assumed, the less you say, and the less you do, the better; and you may be assured that whenever I require any special service of you, you will understand what it is quite distinctly. You comprehend all that, Tom?"

"Quite, Captain. You mean that I'm not to think of any cleverness of my own, for fear it should interfere with some cleverness of yours."

"That will do, Tom. And now I think I can see, some half-mile off, a four-horsed mail coach, coming along at a rattling speed."

"Captain," said Tom, "there's only one thing I should like to do."

"What's that?"

"Why, Captain, if there's lots of time, and you shouldn't happen to want me for an hour after we get to London, I should like to call upon the old gal."

"The who?"

"Oh, I call mother the old gal; and ever since you see, Captain, that Reverend Mortification has been there, I feel as if I should like to go twice a-day, and twice every night, to kick up some disturbance; and I don't think, either, the old gal would know me know in this dress."

"I rather think, Tom, that the last disturbance you kicked up there must have demolished the establishment."

"Well, it was a bit of a blow up, Captain, and I don't think it improved Jonathan Wild's beauty. Bless us, how the old clothes did fly about!"

"Very well, Tom, if I can find time to give you, you shall pay your visit; but be careful, for although there is a kind of buffoonery, and almost silliness, combined with abject cowardice, about that Reverend Mortification Ripon, as he call himself,—yet I am convinced that those are but the outward coverings of a heart capable of any villany, treachery, or cruelty. So beware of that man, Tom, lest he get you in his power."

"I'll look out, Captain. And here comes the coach. It's one of the North mails."

"Yes; I will stop it. And now remember, Tom, that I am Squire Arden, of Arden Hall, Shropshire; and as for you, you shall still remain Tom, since the name is quite sufficiently common to require no alteration."

"Yes, measter," said Tom, in country dialect again.

CHAPTER CXCVIII.

CAPTAIN HERON MEETS WITH A STRANGE ADVENTURE IN THE COACH TO LONDON.

THE coach which was now so rapidly approaching the point in the high road where Tom Ripon and Captain Heron were waiting its approach, looked heavily laden.

If the state of its living cargo could be judged of from the outside, it seemed a doubtful case whether there would be room for Captain Heron and Tom, either outside or in.

"I fear, Tom," said Heron, "we shall have either to wait for the next coach, or walk to London."

Heron, however, took the chance of hailing the coach, and it drew up with an alacrity that he did not expect.

"Going to town, sir?" cried the coachman.

"Yes, if you have room."

"All right, sir—only one inside; and your boy can find room on the roof."

The guard alighted, and opened the coach door for Captain Heron to get in.

The moment the door was open, a sharp-visaged sinister-looking man, with pinched up features and straggling grey hair, and who was attired in a rusty suit of black, cried out with tones of considerable irritation, "I thought you told me I should be sure to have the inside all to myself, and I promised you a shilling, eh, didn't I ?"

"So you did, sir."

"Well—well? and now you put people in upon me?"

Captain Heron contorted his countenance into a broad smile, as he said, with only a slight touch of the country dialect in his tones, "Never mind me, sir. I am Squire Arden, of Arden Hall. Everybody knows me, sir. I won't tread on you. Oh, dear, no !"

"Murder ! You elephant ! What do you mean ?"

Captain Heron had purposely come with all the force he could, upon the toes of this irritable and obtrusive personage, who wanted the coach all to himself.

"Bless me, sir, was that really your foot ?"

"You know it was."

"Now I do."

"Guard ! Mr. Guard ! I cannot suffer this—I will not suffer this ! I was to have the coach inside all to myself—you know I was !"

"Beg pardon, sir," said the guard; "but I don't know any such thing. You asked me if you were likely to have any fellow-passenger, and I told you no ; nor would you have had any, if this gentleman had not wanted to be taken up."

"Then he must get down."

"Ha, ha !" laughed Heron.

"You should have paid for all the inside places, sir," said the guard, "if you wanted it all to yourself."

"And if he wanted to do so," said Captain Heron, " it is too late now. Ha, ha ! I am Squire Arden, and I don't budge, not I."

"But you shall, sir."

"Look here, my little man," added Captain Heron. "If you think you can put me out, do so. Try now, will you."

The idea of the little wizen-faced occupant of the mail coach putting out Captain Heron was too ridiculous, and the guard could not help laughing.

"Now then, Jack," cried the coachman, "are we to wait here all day ?"

"All right !" cried the guard, as he mounted to his place, and then blew one shrill blast upon his horn.

Off set the mail coach again, with Captain Heron fairly seated inside, and Tom Ripon in a very crooked position outside among the luggage.

The thin, wretched-looking individual, who had so strenuously objected to the presence of Captain Heron, uttered many groans ; and Heron could see that he kept up a tremulous motion of his feet, from some cause or another.

"What's the matter with you ?" said Heron.

"Nothing—nothing."

"Then don't be so fidgetty."

"I will be fidgetty if I like. I have a right to take care of my property."

"Oh, it's your property, is it ?"

"Well, sir, what's that to you ?"

"I tell you what it is, my ill-tempered friend," said Heron. "If you cannot be a little more civil, I will open the coach door and drop you into the road."

"Drop me?—me ?"

"Yes, you. Who else is there to drop ?"

The strange passenger made a sudden dive with both his hands under the seat, and drew up a leather portmanteau, which was secured with several locks, and placed it on his knees, as he looked defiantly at Captain Heron, and screamed out, "You will drop me on the road?"

"I said so."

"Do you know who I am?"

"No. And I may add that I don't care."

"Then, my name, sir, is Wright."

"It may be Wright or wrong, for all I care."

"I am, sir, an attorney at law."

"Very likely."

"And therefore, sir, I would advise you to be very careful indeed what you say or what you do."

"I mean to be."

"Then, sir, you are wiser than you look."

"Thank you, Mr. Wright, attorney at law. I am sorry I cannot return the compliment, for up to the present moment you have been quite as stupid as you look."

"Beware, sir !"

"What's the matter ?"

"Nothing, sir—nothing. Don't speak to me. I hate casual conversation, sir. Pray don't address me."

"As regards that," replied Heron, "I shall please myself. If I think proper to do you the honour of speaking to you, I shall certainly speak."

"Bah !"

"And so, to begin with, what have you got in that portmanteau, Mr. Wright, attorney at law ?"

"Bo !"

"Oh, that's it, is it ?"

"No, sir, that is not it."

"Come, come," added Captain Heron; "you will make me wish to go back to Arden Hall, if you go on in that way, instead of going to London, to look for an honest lawyer, for my thirty thousand pounds I want to put out in some way."

"Sir ?"

"Sir to you !"

"Hem !"

Mr. Wright, attorney at law had to put on a bland look, which made him resemble strongly a laughing hyena about meal-times.

"Hem ! I am sure, Squire Arden, that as a man of the world——"

"What ?"

"As a man of the world and a man of business, you will excuse any little—what shall I call it ? —caution, or—or what you might think unpoliteness in my manner."

"Oh, don't mention it."

"You are very good, sir."

"Not at all. All beasts act according to their nature. The goose cackles, the dog barks, and the donkey brays. They can't help it."

"Sir, permit me to apologize."

"Don't. It's nature."

"But, sir,—Squire Arden I think you named

yourself,—will you permit me to say that, if your going to London is for the purpose of finding an honest professional man, who will assist you to put to good use your thirty thousand pounds, you have found him."

"Sir?"

"Hem! hem! hem!"

Mr. Wright, attorney at law, dealt himself three little blows on the breast, to intimate that there was the honest man, and that within that breast was to be found the incomparable professional heart that Squire Arden, of Arden Hall, wanted.

"You don't mean that?" said Captain Heron.

"I do, sir."

"Then give me your hand."

"Sir, you—you are too kind! Oh—oh! mercy upon us, how strong you are, sir; my fingers are squeezed one into the other!"

"Never mind. Let us talk of business."

"Oh, dear, yes!"

"The Arden estates have a clear income of forty-seven thousand a-year behind them."

"Dear me, sir! A most magnificent property."

"Pretty well. I spend the odd seventeen thousand, so that every year there are thirty thousand pounds that I don't know what to do with."

"My dear sir!"

"Now, can you tell me?"

"Of course I can, my dear sir, my client, and my friend. Excuse me, sir; one's feelings at times are too much for one. Thirty thousand every year that he don't know what to do with! Oh! oh!"

Mr. Wright, attorney at law, took out a very faded old blue handkerchief with white spots on it, and applied it to his eyes.

"Why, what's the matter?" said Heron.

"Feelings, sir, feelings! that's all."

"Ah! I don't grow 'em."

"Sir?"

"I say I don't grow 'em. I've no end of swedes, mangold wurtzel, and beetroot, but I don't know anything about feelings."

"Ah, Squire, you are pleased to be facetious."

"What's that?"

"Ha! ha! ha! ha! Well, Squire Arden, all I can say is that, if you will trust to me, I will take care of your thirty thousand a-year, and find you first-rate investments for the money."

"I'm delighted."

"And I."

"Your hand again."

"Quietly!"

"As a dove."

"Murder! murder!"

"Hilloa!" cried the guard: "there's something amiss with the insides! Pull up, Bill."

"Woa! woa!"

The mail coach came to a standstill, but Mr. Wright, attorney at law, was in such a state of mental agony at the idea of anything putting a stop to the deeply interesting conversation he was having with Squire Arden, of Arden Hall, that he put his head out at the coach window, and cried out, "Go on! drive on! It's only a little joke! a story that this gentleman is telling me! Go on—it's nothing at all!"

The coachman, with not a very complimentary remark regarding the general anatomy of the passengers in the inside, drove on, and Mr.

Wright looked as pleased as the crushed condition of his hand, from the terrible grip Captain Heron had given it, would permit him. Tears, real tears were in his eyes; but as he had quite made up his mind that Squire Arden, of Arden Hall, with thirty thousand pounds a-year, surplus income, should pay handsomely for every word that was uttered, he suppressed his emotions, and spoke quite blandly. "My dear Squire," he said, "if you have nowhere in particular to go to when you reach London, pray do me the favour of making my house, in Bloomsbury Square, your home."

"Stop! stop!"

"Eh?—what?"

"My old mother used to say, 'Never trust a stranger.'"

"My dear sir!"

"How do I know you are an attorney at law? —how do I know you are Mr. Wright?—how do I know you are a respectable man?—how do I know——"

"My dear Squire, stop! stop! I will soon convince you I am all that."

The attorney, whose imagination was quite dazzled by the vision of thirty thousand pounds a-year passing through his hands, hastily produced a bunch of keys, and proceeded to unlock the portmanteau which was upon his knees. He then took out a letter, and giving it a kind of flourish before his eyes, he said, "You will see by this, Squire Arden, that I am all I say I am, because it will assure you that I am the confidential agent of one of the first noblemen of the land."

"What nobleman?"

"The Right Honourable the Earl of Whitcombe."

"Ah!"

"You—you know him?"

"No. But I had a fancy I had heard the name before, and that somebody said he was dead."

"Ah, my dear sir, you allude to the old Earl. He is certainly dead; but my client is, or was, Lord Warringdale, who now, of course, is Earl of Whitcombe."

"But somebody down our way told me, or I heard it somewhere, that Lord Warringdale could not get his title."

"Yes, my dear Squire, you heard some rumour, but the whole truth is this: there is an outrageous, murderous scamp and villain, who is named Felix Heron."

"Really!"

"Yes, one of the greatest scoundrels unhung, although, thank heaven, that won't be for long."

"He is reforming, then?"

"No, no! I mean he won't remain unhung for long."

"Oh, I beg pardon!"

"Well, Squire, this unmitigated scoundrel, who I only wish I could once hold by the collar, has the unparalleled effrontery to pretend that he has a prior claim to the title and estates of Whitcombe, to the sweet, amiable young nobleman, my Lord Warringdale, who is the real heir to the title and properties. He is a sweet youth."

"So I have heard."

"You have?"

"Oh, yes! But somebody told me something about this rascal Heron."

"Hanged, my dear Squire, hanged! He must and will be hanged! I only wish, as I say, I could meet the villain face to face!"

"Would that be very difficult?"

"I am afraid so; because, of course, he would take good care to keep out of my way."

"But accident may favour you some day!"

"It may—it may! But now that I know who you are, Squire, and that you are a very respectable man, I will prove to you the trust that the amiable and excellent young Earl of Whitcombe puts in me, by explaining what business I have been upon for him."

"I should like to hear that."

"You shall. Well, you must know that owing to the vile proceedings of the villain I have mentioned to you, there is some little hesitation on the part of the Standing Committee of Privileges of the House of Lords, in calling the sweet young nobleman to his seat."

"Oh, is there?"

"Yes, and it is all on account of a troublesome, half-mad young man, who has taken the part of the wretch."

"Of Lord Warringdale?"

"No, no! That Felix Heron."

"Oh, ah! To be sure!"

"I mean the young Earl of Bridgewater, who no doubt has had some rascally dealings with the villain Heron, who is a highwayman; and we really and truly believe—that is, I and the amiable and exemplary Lord Warringdale—that between them they murdered the late Earl of Bridgewater."

"What, Lord Warringdale?"

"No, no! This Captain Heron and the present Earl of Bridgewater."

"Oh, yes! I see."

"Well, then, the dear young Lord Warringdale, owing to this most unnatural delay, became short of money. I have, therefore, been to Bedfordshire to some of the tenants of the Whitcombe estates to collect for him; and as I was empowered to offer a very handsome abatement, and to assure them that there could be no doubt of the issue of the whole proceedings in the Committee of Privileges in the House of Lords being in his favour, I have to some extent succeeded."

"I am glad to hear it."

"Thank you."

"For the sake of the Earl of Whitcombe!"

"Thank you."

"And how much have you got?"

"Four thousand pounds."

"Really!"

"Every farthing."

"Then, that is rent from tenants of the Whitcombe estates, so that it really belongs to the present Earl of Whitcombe?"

"It does."

"I am delighted to hear it."

"Upon my word, Squire, you really do seem delighted. One would almost think you were a dear friend of the sweet, amiable young Earl."

"I am."

"You—you are?"

"I am, indeed. No one knows him better. Is the money in that portmanteau?"

"Every farthing of it."

"Then I will trouble you for it, since, to tell the truth, I am rather short of cash, and don't

know how much I may want for many occasions in London; and I am glad the tenants have responded to your persuasions to so liberal an extent."

A slight paleness came over the face of Mr. Wright, attorney at law, as he said, "Eh? eh, Squire?—you are fond of a joke!"

"I never was more serious in all my life."

"But—but——"

"I want my money!"

"Your money?"

"To be sure! Whose else's should it be?"

"Oh, this is a madman, after all!" thought the attorney.

"Come, sir—be quick! Where is the money?"

"Help! help!"

"Quick, sir!"

"Murder! murder!"

"Oh," said the coachman, "you don't catch me pulling up my 'osses again, if you cry murder till you are as hoarse as twenty ravens, my fine fellow. Do you hear him, Joe, old fellow?"

"All's right."

"To be sure it is. He wants to sell us again, don't he? but it won't do."

"Not a bit of it."

"Play a 'hair' on the horn, Joe!"

"I will."

The guard began to bray out a melancholy tune on his horn, and as one-half the notes were absent, the effect was not enlivening. While it was going on, Captain Heron had placed the muzzle of a pistol exactly between the eyes of Mr. Wright, as he said to him in the calmest possible tones, "I don't want too much noise, and therefore will trouble you now to be still. If it be any satisfaction to you to know who I am, permit me to state that my name is Felix Heron—my title Earl of Whitcombe."

CHAPTER CXCIX.

CAPTAIN HERON CALLS ON THE BISHOP OF WORCESTER, AND OBTAINS A PROMISE.

IT would be quite impossible for any set of words to paint the consternation that sat upon the countenance of the attorney, when he heard the little speech from Captain Heron with which the last chapter concluded. A kind of paralysis seemed to come over all his faculties, and exactly in the attitude which he was accidentally in at the moment Heron spoke, there he remained for the space of about two minutes.

Heron kept his eyes fixed upon him all that time, and the silence within the mail coach was something profound and strange.

Mr. Wright then let the portmanteau slip from his knees to the floor of the coach. Then he stooped after it, and uttered some hideous groans.

"If you make that noise," said Captain Heron, "I shall certainly leave you on the road!"

"Mercy! mercy!"

"Why, what do you mean? Only a little time since, you were offering something very liberal if you could only have the good fortune to be face to face with Captain Felix Heron; and now that you are so, you don't seem to be in the least pleased."

"I am a dead man!"

"You may be so, if you are indiscreet"

"Have mercy upon me, and let me go! Oh, do let me go, with—with the money! If I don't take it to Lord Warringdale, he will certainly kill me! He is the most outrageous, villanous——"

"Hilloa! what do you mean by that? I thought just now that you informed me Lord Warringdale was the incarnation of everything sweet and amiable, while Captain Heron was the villain, interrupting the felicity of so delightful a young nobleman?"

"No, no—I didn't mean it—indeed I didn't mean it! My dear sir, I assure you I didn't mean it! only, you know, in speaking to supposed strangers, one must say something; and if you will only have the goodness now to let me go, and take my little portmanteau with me, I shall always pray for your welfare; and if at any time you want any little professional business

No. 89.—EDITH.

done, I shall only be too glad to do it for costs out of pocket, which is what I never did for anybody else in all my life."

"But, my dear sir," said Heron, "you seem to mistake the position of affairs. It is surely you who are now master of the situation, and according to your own account, if you recollect, you have just reached what you desired."

"What—oh, what, my dear sir? But it don't matter; only let me go, and I have no questions to ask."

"Stop a bit: I have some questions to ask."

"Oh, dear! oh, dear!"

"You are premature; nor would 'oh, dear!' be any answer to me if I had already spoken. Do you mean to tell me that you were really conveying four thousand pounds to Lord Warringdale, which, by lies and misrepresentations, you had induced the tenants of the Whitcombe estates to pay you?"

"Half of it—half of it! I was to have half—we were to go shares in whatever I could get: for so long as the affair could be kept to ourselves, and a certain person knew nothing of it, it was likely to turn out well."

"By that certain person you mean me!"

"Oh, no—oh, dear, no!"

"Why, you do not mean your other friend?"

"What other friend?"

"Why, the gentleman below, with whom you will be so exceedingly intimate some of these days."

"Oh, no! I mean Mr. Wild."

"Ah, indeed! Jonathan Wild?"

"Yes. I don't know exactly why, but my Lord Warringdale was exceedingly anxious that he should know nothing about it."

"Without a doubt. I think I can understand, and I presume you can likewise. There is a community of interest between Jonathan Wild and your infamous client, Lord Warringdale; and along with that community of interest there is, at the same time, a singleness of purpose, in so far as one of them is always trying to overreach the other. But since I am the real owner of the Whitcombe estates, I claim this money which you have kindly collected for me, unless, indeed, you wish to make an extra profit of this morning's transaction in another way."

"How—oh, how is it possible?"

"I think that, first and last, there is about a thousand pounds offered for my apprehension, and that, you know, added to the two thousand you were to get from Lord Warringdale, would make a respectable sum, which seems to me to be wholly in your power, if you carry out your idea of seizing me by the collar and delivering me up to justice. Now, sir, what say you?"

"You—you, that is—I mean—I'm afraid you won't let me."

"I should resist, certainly; but as I like to give every man a fair chance, and as even you shall not say that I took unfair advantage of you inside a coach, with fire-arms in my possession, I will hand this pistol to you, assuring you that it is well primed and loaded."

"Hand it to me? To me?"

"Certainly, to you."

A slight flush came over the countenance of the attorney at law, as he seemed to think it possible the advantages might turn in his favour, in consequence of the romantic generosity of Captain Felix Heron.

But it was only for one instant such an idea found a place in the imagination of Mr. Wright, for when Captain Heron produced the fellow pistol to the one he had handed to him, the notion vanished in a moment.

"Now, sir," added Heron, "we are equally armed, and if you choose to run your risk, why, we will fight the matter out even within the narrow precincts of a mail coach."

"I beg your pardon," said the attorney, faintly, as, in a very delicate and tender manner, he laid the pistol on the seat of the coach next to him,—"I beg your pardon, sir, I never fought anything out, except in the precincts of a court of law. But," he added, with a sigh, "there is one proposition I have to make to you, which I think you cannot but consider equitable."

"What is it?"

"Simply this: that if you are really Captain Felix Heron, and considering yourself entitled to the Whitcombe estates, lay claim to this money, you will, at least, treat me as the other claimant, Lord Warringdale, would have done, and let me take the two thousand pounds for my half share."

"If I had employed you on those conditions," said Captain Heron, "I would have abided by them, and that, too, probably with a far greater certainty than Lord Warringdale would have done; but as I made no such conditions, and simply find you in possession of some of my property, I take it, and you may think yourself fortunate if I merely do so, without visiting upon you some punishment for an attempted robbery."

"I am lost! I am lost!"

"Not at all, my good friend, for here the mail coach is coming into London, the streets of which are tolerably familiar to you."

"Ah, yes—the streets of London! Passengers, constables, throngs of people! Any outcry now, Captain Felix Heron, must be to you fatal."

"Possibly."

"So, you see that, after all, you have delayed too long in the open country; you should have carried out your little project."

"Not at all. I was coming to London; wherefore, then, should I have troubled myself to alight from this mail coach, which was conducting me there so comfortably?"

"Because you can see danger. Why, here we are in Bishopsgate!"

"It is Bishopsgate."

"I cannot help thinking, then, Captain Heron, that you are in great danger; you, a celebrated highwayman, with, as you admit, a thousand pounds reward upon your head—you, alone, too, in the City—that is to say, you have no one with you but that lout of a country boy, now on the roof. Why, Captain Heron, you're in great danger; and, after all, it seems, I might ask what you are going to give me to keep quiet, and let you go about your business?"

"Have you done? Have you said all you wish to say?"

"Well, Captain Heron, and if I have, what reply have you to make?"

"Simply, that you are greatly mistaken, and that it is you who are in danger, not I; since, if you attempt now to give the slightest alarm, I will blow your brains out as you sit opposite to me, and then adopt some means of escape, peculiarly my own, of which you can have no conception."

The attorney at law shrank back aghast, and as the coach at that moment drew up at a well-known inn, in Bishopsgate, Heron spoke a few earnest words to him.

"Look you here, sir," he said: "of course you do not want to throw away your life, for I have ever found, in my career, that that is a possession which always appears most valuable in those cases where, in reality, it is most worthless. You will, therefore, alight with me, and arm-in-arm we will proceed together for some distance. The lout of a boy, as you call him, that I have in attendance upon me, will carry this portmanteau with my money."

"Your money?"

"Certainly, sir. Am I not the Earl of Whitcombe? and has not this money been collected from the tenants of the Whitcombe estates?"

The attorney was silent.

"I see you are convinced," added Heron; "so now we will alight, if you please; and for your own sake—not for mine, since I care little about it—you had better be discreet."

Pale and haggard—for he was suffering from a thousand fears, while the loss of the two thousand pounds he had hoped to call his own seemed to have had such an effect upon him, that one would have imagined as many drops of blood had been abstracted from his veins—the attorney alighted with Captain from the coach.

The coachman and guard looked curiously at their inside passengers. There seemed to be a sort of suspicion upon their minds that there was something amiss; but what it was, they had evidently not the least idea, since the two insides were, to all appearance, upon amicable terms.

The lawyer, with a groan, paid his fare, and Heron likewise paid his, adding at the same time so liberal a gratuity for the coachman and guard, that they would both have been ready to swear to his respectability at a moment's notice.

Heron slid the arm of the lawyer underneath his own, and took care to hold him tight, while he called to Tom on the roof of the coach, who looked rather astonished at the companionship.

"Come down, Tom."

"Yes, measter," said Tom.

"Take my portmanteau, and follow us."

"'My portmanteau!'" thought Tom to himself: "the Captain's been doing a little business on the road."

Tom was alert in his duty; and while Mr. Wright, the attorney at law, looked at him with eyes of anguish, he shouldered the portmanteau, and followed the strangely assorted couple, who walked arm-in-arm towards the heart of the City.

"You might let me go," whined the attorney. "I can't do you any harm now, and you might let me go."

"I don't know that. It is just possible that I might have a mob at my heels in five minutes' time. But I have a few words of directions to give to my lout of a boy here; and as the truest philosophy, Mr. Wright, is to avoid as long as possible even the knowledge of things that may be disagreeable to us, I advise you not to listen."

"But what do you mean? What do you mean? What are you going to do?"

Captain Heron beckoned to Tom, and whispered a few words in his ear, which the attorney in vain tried to catch, for he was in a state of great nervousness to know what they could possibly be, feeling tolerably sure in his own mind that they in some manner concerned him.

Tom nodded.

"You quite understand?" said Heron.

"Yes, measter."

The attorney looked after Tom Ripon with curiosity, and once or twice he vainly strove to disengage his arm from that of Captain Heron.

And certainly Tom's conduct was such as to excite a great deal of surprise, and to give food for a great deal of speculation to the mind of that miserable man.

After the few words he had had with Captain Heron, Tom preceded the party instead of following, and with the small portmanteau still upon his shoulder, kept looking about as if in search of something, and particularly upon reaching any corner did Tom Ripon glance down the streets in all directions, as if in search of some particular one.

At length, with a nod of satisfaction, Tom proceeded down a narrow turning, which led to a gloomy sort of thoroughfare near Alderman's Walk.

The City of London is ten times as populous now as it was then, and yet you may now stand in this silent and out-of-the-way street, and in five minutes not see five people.

At the period of our tale, you might stand there ten minutes, and not see one person.

Tom turned and glanced at Captain Heron, as he said, "This'll do, measter."

"I think so," said Heron.

"Help! Murder! Have mercy upon me!" said the lawyer, whose fears by this time had reached so alarming a height, that they could no longer be controlled.

"Be quiet," said Heron.

"But I can't be quiet, and I won't be quiet! I may as well be murdered with a noise as peaceably. I am brought here to be disposed of in this quiet way; but I will scream and shout, and the windows will open, for there are inhabitants here, lonely and silent as the place seems."

"You are hasty," said Heron.

"No, no, no!"

"It is necessary to dispose of you."

"I knew it! I knew it! Help! Murder!"

"Another word, and you are a dead man. I did think of disposing of you with safety to yourself, as well as to me; but since nothing but your actual death will satisfy you, it is much more your own act than mine."

"Oh, no! Spare me! Save me! What do you mean?"

"This'll do, measter," cried Tom at this moment.

The attorney had been so intensely occupied with his fears of Captain Heron, that he had taken his eyes off Tom Ripon for the last few minutes, and it was not until Tom thought something would do, that Mr. Wright, with a sudden jump, began to regard what he was about.

And even then, the attorney could not see very well what should particularly interest him in Tom's proceedings, for, to all appearance, Tom was merely standing in the middle of the pavement, and remarking that something would do, although what that something was remained a mystery.

Coldly and quietly, then, Captain Heron bent his eyes upon the trembling lawyer.

"I told you," he said, "it was necessary you should be disposed of, and I have thought it advisable that you should go into one of these houses in this quiet street, and there remain until I shall have had time to remove from this neighbourhood, so that you can no longer affect me by any outcry you may make, or any hue and cry you might bring at my heels."

"Oh, my dear sir," cried the greatly relieved attorney, "with pleasure—with pleasure! I will knock at the first door we come to, and request them to let me stay for—what shall I say?—half an hour."

"No, sir."

"But you said——"

"Yes, I know I said that I wished you to remain in one of these houses; but the difference of opinion between us is in regard to the manner in which you get there. Is that one loose, Tom?"

"Yes, measter."

Tom stepped aside, and then the astonished attorney understood the whole business, for he saw that Tom had succeeded in picking up one of the round iron covers to a coal-cellar; and he understood that that was the mode by which he was expected to effect an entrance into one of those quiet-looking, silent, dingy houses.

"You will go down there," said Heron; "you will fall upon the coals, and that will shake you a little. You will, perhaps, find the cellar-door locked, and if not, it will take you some time to scramble into the house. You will be suspected of burglary, and all sorts of nefarious intentions, and it will take you some time to explain yourself; so that the half-hour I promise myself as time sufficient to get out of all danger of anything you may say or do, will, according to all reasonable calculation, expire."

The attorney licked his parched lips, and looked terrified.

"Quick, sir, quick—there is not a moment to lose!" cried Heron.

"I cannot—I cannot! Yes, I will—I will!"

The sight of the pistol—the long, bright barrel of which flashed in his eyes—quickly convinced Mr. Wright of the propriety of doing as he was desired.

He put his feet down the narrow, circular orifice, but it was with such a woful expression of countenance that he performed the action, as to excite laughter, loud and boisterous, from Tom Ripon, and a smile from Captain Heron.

"Silence, Tom! This is a quiet street, but not an uninhabited one."

Tom was quiet.

"Put him down," added Captain Heron, convinced that Tom would adopt some signal mode of convincing the lawyer that it would be better to descend to the cellar at once, of his own will, than be made to do so by any of Tom's modes of persuasion.

Tom went a short distance off, and lifted a loose stone of some ten or a dozen pounds in weight; and then, as he bowled it along the pavement, he cried out, "Heads!" and in a moment Mr. Wright disappeared.

The stone rolled down into the cellar after him, and loud cries and a great scuffle were heard among the coals; but those sounds got dim and indistinct when Tom put on the iron cover.

"All's right, Captain! He won't come out again quick: and I can hear a dog barking in the house and a watchman's rattle springing, so I dare say they will take him for a housebreaker."

"It is likely. Follow me quickly."

Tom did so, and Heron left the street with such rapidity that he was, no doubt, half a mile away before the discomfited lawyer could enter into any explanation with the people of the house as to who and what he was, and how he got into the cellar.

A hackney-coach was passing, and Heron hailed it, and ordered the man to drive to St. James's Street.

Captain Heron's intention to call upon the Bishop of Worcester was unchanged; and as Parliament was then sitting, he considered there was every probability the Bishop would be in town.

It was a hazardous thing to ask for the address of the Bishop at the door of the House of Lords, but Captain Heron thought that the most direct way of getting it; so leaving Tom in a doorway of St. James's Street, he went leisurely down to the Park.

Captain Heron procured the address he wanted, but he was gone half an hour.

During that time Tom had waited on the doorstep of Whitcombe House, for it was there his master had left him.

"Captain," said Tom, "I have seen Lord Warringdale while I have been here."

"Doubtless. I believe he resides opposite, Tom."

"And he looks as vicious as ever."

"Of that there can be no doubt, Tom."

"Would you go over, Captain, and give him a bullet?"

"No, Tom. That may not come from my barrel; but I am now about to go to a house in Clarges Street, Piccadilly—so follow me."

Tom rather reluctantly gave up the idea of going over the way to have something to say to Lord Warringdale, but the commands of Captain Heron were paramount; and shouldering the portmanteau, in which so large a sum of money was to be found, he trotted up St. James's Street, a few paces from Captain Heron.

The Bishop of Worcester was in town, and Captain Heron had been informed that he would be found at his town house in Clarges Street.

It was with feelings of considerable excitement and hope that Heron made his way to call on the man whose memory, if it served him right, might go so far towards substantiating his claim to those honours and those estates he had now got so much in the habit of contemplating as the joint property of himself and Edith, that he was far more eager in the pursuit of them than he had been in days gone past.

"I must and will foil these people," said Heron to himself, "who seek to deprive me of my birthright and of my life! I can be as merciful as I please when once success has crowned my efforts, but I will not relax in them while I have life!"

Heron made a sign to Tom to wait on the doorstep of the Bishop's house while he went in.

The hall-porter received Heron respectfully enough, for there was an air of the gentleman so much about him, that had he announced himself by any title, it would have been conceded to him.

"If the Bishop is within," said Captain Heron, "tell him that Sir Felix Arden desires an interview."

Captain Heron knew well the magical effect of any title at the fashionable houses of London, and he added the "Sir" to his assumed name, from a thorough conviction that it would procure him the interview he sought.

Captain Heron was right.

In a few minutes a servant out of livery came to the hall to say that the Bishop would see Sir Felix Arden with pleasure.

"I beg pardon, sir," said the hall-porter, "but is that your servant, sir?"

"Oh, yes!"

"He can come into the hall, sir. He seems

CAPTAIN HERON RELIEVES HIS FELLOW TRAVELLER OF A HEAVY RESPONSIBILITY.

Presented Gratis with No. 89 of the New Edition of Edith the Captive; or, the Robbers of Epping Forest.

EACH WEEK IS PRESENTED GRATIS A COLOURED ENGRAVING.

quite a country lad, and there are so many thieves and sharpers about London streets."

"Thank you. Come in, Tom."

"Yees, measter. Here I be."

"Come in, I say."

"Yees, measter."

"Dear me!" said the hall-porter, half-aloud, "what a stupid fellow he seems! I suppose you came from Worcestershire, my boy—eh?"

"I dunna," said Tom.

"You don't know?"

"Noa—I bean't no scholard."

"Well, I never! Was there ever such a greenhorn? There—sit down and make yourself comfortable."

"Ees, I wool."

Captain Heron followed the servant who had come to conduct him to the Bishop, and was soon ushered into a handsome library, where a venerable-looking man with very white hair was sitting reading, and who looked up curiously at Heron as he appeared.

That was the Bishop,

CHAPTER CC.

JONATHAN WILD IS BOTH PUZZLED AND ALARMED AT THE PROCEEDINGS OF CAPTAIN HERON.

In reply to the look of inquiry on the face of the Bishop, Heron bowed and spoke.

"My Lord Bishop, I have come to you in the hope that I shall be able, by reminding you of a circumstance which took place many years ago, to recall its particulars to your full recollection."

"Pray, sir," said the Bishop, in a quiet and gentle tone of voice, "be seated, and inform me, if you please, what the circumstance is to which you allude."

Captain Heron took a chair—and a load appeared to be lifted off his heart as he looked in the face of the venerable man before him; for it was that of one who had grown old in charity, and it beamed with intelligence and kindly feelings.

Captain Heron felt as if half his task was already done, and in his heart he blessed the thought that had brought him to that venerable man, and the accidents that had made him aware of the fact that it was through his ministration his father and mother became united.

It seemed to Heron as if at that moment he was brought almost into the presence of his parents by looking upon the priest who had joined their hands together at the altar.

A gush of feeling came over the heart of Heron, and for a few moments he could not speak.

There was before his mental vision that little old church at Barnes, by the altar of which stood the cold, stern Earl of Whitcombe, together with Amelia Staunton, whom Felix Heron had been brought to think of as a mother.

Perhaps the Bishop thought that it was from some excess of emotion that his visitor did not immediately speak to him, and he said, kindly, "Sir Felix Arden—for I believe that is your name—pray take what time you please to compose yourself. Let us talk a little upon indifferent subjects, if that about which you come specially to converse so much distresses you."

"Nay, reverend sir, I will speak at once; but you have given me so kindly a reception that it touched me closely."

"Is kindness then so rare to you, young as you are—for you are very young?"

"I, sir?"

"Yes; I can see that, for some motive which I have no right to pry into, you are disguised to look a much older man than you are."

"Sir, I will not deceive you: I feel that I ought not—that I dare not. I am a young man, and my name is not Sir Felix Arden."

"I am sorry."

"Sorry, sir?"

"Yes; sorry that you should have thought it necessary to approach me by any name but your own."

"There are reasons, reverend sir."

"Then I can guess that the story you have to tell me is one of crime."

"It is."

"Alas! alas! And so young, too!"

"You mistake me, my Lord Bishop. The crime is not on my heart or brain: the suffering has been mine, but not the crime. I have much to complain of, little to repent of; and now, reverend sir, I will ask you a question, if you please?"

The Bishop inclined his hand in assent.

"Do you remember, sir, when you were but a parish clergyman, performing marriages at Barnes Church?"

"Certainly; I did duty there, and consequently solemnized marriages."

"Among those marriages was there one in which the bridegroom was a Lord Warringdale, and the bride Amelia Staunton?"

The Bishop placed his hands over his eyes, and was silent.

"Oh, sir, tell me!—tell me, I beseech you. I call upon you as a minister of that heaven from which no secrets are hidden, and which——"

"Hush! Hush, young man!"

Captain Heron was silent.

"I am endeavouring," added the Bishop, "to settle with myself a case of conscience."

"How, reverend sir?"

"It is this. I made an imprudent promise to keep secret that which I ought at any time to be ready to proclaim to all men; and yet I did promise."

"I understand you, reverend sir. You promised to keep secret the marriage I spoke of?"

"I did."

"Death, reverend sir, absolves you from that promise."

The Bishop was silent.

"Death," added Captain Heron, "has taken from the world the only person to whom the revelation of that secret marriage could produce a pang. You know that the Earl of Whitcombe is no more?"

"I do know it."

"Then let me ask you if you do not feel yourself in safety absolved from all obligation to keep a secret which should never in reality have been one?"

"Your reproach is just. The secret should never have been one. I was but a young man when I made the promise. I had newly gone into the Church, and was anxious for preferment. The Lord Warringdale, as the late Earl of Whitcombe was then called, was a man of rank and influence, and I yielded to his solicitations."

"How far, sir! Oh, how far?"

The Bishop was silent for a short space, and then, in a voice of emotion, he added—"The Lord Warringdale asked two favours of me. The one was to seem to perform the marriage ceremony, but to do so in such a fashion that its legality would be doubtful."

"Ah!"

"Stay—stay! Hear me out, sir. The other favour was that I would keep secret, until he absolved me from the promise, even that marriage, informal though it might be."

"And you——"

The Bishop looked earnestly in the face of Captain Heron, as he cried, "What am I saying? What prompts me to speak to you in this fashion—I who know not who you are, nor what use you may make of my words? Speak to me, sir, and tell me why you came to me to rouse up the memory of other years?"

"Alas, reverend sir! I am one who may plead a right which none other can possess."

"What right?"

"I am the son of that marriage!"

"You—you?"

"Even I. Oh, sir, you saw my mother—my poor persecuted mother! Look into my eyes, and tell me if you can trace any likeness there to the Amelia Staunton you saw at the altar with the late Earl of Whitcombe?"

The old Bishop looked long and fixedly at Captain Heron, and then, with a deep sigh, he said, "This must be true—too true! I now comprehend why it was that I was induced to speak to you so freely."

"Indeed, my Lord Bishop!"

"Yes. It was because there is something about your face which carried me back to that moment when I stood by the altar as the officiating priest on the occasion of the marriage you speak of."

"That is well, reverend sir," added Heron. "And was it possible that any hopes of preferment, or any dreams of earthly ambition or prosperity, could induce you to desecrate heaven's altar by acting as the Earl desired you?"

"No—no!"

"No, say you?"

"I do say no. I refused the Earl's first request, but I kept the second."

"Then the marriage——"

"Was well and truly performed between Amelia Staunton and the Lord Warringdale."

"Pardon my doubts!"

"They were natural. I well deserved them, and I found out too late that even in paying such a price as keeping secret the marriage, I was purchasing a shadow—a hollow fruit, like those by the shores of the Dead Sea, full of naught but bitterness."

"I do not comprehend you."

"You will, easily, when I tell you that through the influence of the Earl of Whitcombe, who was one of the chiefs of a powerful party in the State, I rapidly rose in the Church. I thought that would be happiness, but I have discovered the delusion. I am a bishop, but I was in reality far happier as a humble curate, for then I had the bright visions of hope about my heart; but now they have all fled, and I am but a miserable,

anxious old man waiting — waiting — waiting!"

"Waiting for what?"

"For death!"

There was something inexpressibly sad about the tone and manner of the Bishop; and as he rested his head upon his hands and sighed deeply, even Captain Heron, young and full of life as he was, with all the world before him, felt a pang as the idea of the worthlessness of worldly things came across his mind, and he could have exclaimed "Vanity—vanity!—all is vanity!"

But then he thought of Edith.

His own dear Edith!

"Yes," he cried,—"oh, yes, I have yet much to live for!"

The Bishop started, and looked inquiringly at him.

"Pardon me," said Heron; "I spoke in answer to my own thoughts."

"I, too, have thought deeply."

"Well, reverend sir, will you now bear witness to that marriage?"

"Most cheerfully; although I cannot comprehend what good it can do to you, since the Earl of Whitcombe being dead, and Amelia Staunton likewise——"

"What do I hear? How know you that?"

"Is it not well known, since the Earl married again a noble lady?"

"That is no proof. Good heavens, sir! can it be possible there is more wickedness in this transaction than I ever imagined?"

"It is possible; and, I regret to say, is more than probable."

"I am the son of that marriage of the late Earl of Whitcombe with Amelia Staunton. The Earl is no more, and I claim my birthright."

"The earldom?"

"As you say, my Lord Bishop, I claim the earldom."

"And the vast estates of Whitcombe?"

"And, as you likewise say, the vast estates of Whitcombe."

"The patronage of eight good benefices."

"I was not aware of that," said Captain Heron, with a slight smile.

"Pardon me—pardon me," said the Bishop. "It is difficult for the mind of a Churchman not to dwell upon such things. But is it possible, young man, that all you state is true?"

"It is most strictly true. My father, no doubt, thinking it safe to do so, repudiated his poor victim, Amelia Staunton. I, an infant, was confided to the care of a friend of his, by name Sir Dominick Browne."

"Yes—oh, yes!"

"You knew it?"

"No, no! I only know that your father, as you say he was, had such an intimate friend."

"I was then brought up under the name of Felix Heron, until I found out some clue to the mystery of my origin; and the moment I did so, there commenced a persecution of myself and of all who showed an inclination to befriend me. Sir Dominick Browne has so suffered."

"But there is a Lord Warringdale."

"Yes. There is a shameless, worthless villain, who so names himself."

"Your brother?"

"I grieve to say yes. He is my brother. Had

he not been, he would, long ere this, have been called to his account."

"But have you seen him? Have you explained to him his and your position?

"I have. He knows all only too well; and his aim has been—from the moment that he did know all—to take my life."

"Fratricide?"

"Ay, reverend sir, fratricide. That is the name that would have belonged to the ready act of Lord Warringdale, my brother, if heaven had not preserved me from his deadly malice."

"This is terrible."

"It is as true as it is terrible; and now, my Lord Bishop, I call upon you, as a high priest of heaven, to do me justice!"

"I will—I must."

A glow of joy came over the heart of Captain Heron.

"You will depose to the marriage?"

"I will. It is my duty. I deceived your father."

"Deceived him?"

"Yes. I performed the marriage ceremony in so full and ample a manner, and with such perfect accuracy, that it would be quite impossible to find a flaw in it; while he thought it was so performed that he could, at his own will and pleasure, break the bond. When, however, he one day told me that Amelia Staunton was no more, the whole matter seemed to be at an end."

"And you knew not there was a child of that sad union?"

"I knew it not."

"And now you will do me justice? Oh, reverend sir, you will perform a gracious act before high heaven, and you will feel the happiness!"

"I shall—I shall. Come to me to-morrow at this house. I will go to the old church at Barnes myself, and search for the entry in the registry, which I myself carefully wrote."

"You will seek in vain!"

"Wherefore shall I so?"

"It is abstracted. There is no such entry now. The leaf of the registry is torn away. The name of Amelia Staunton is not there to be found. I have looked for it, and looked in vain."

CHAPTER CCI.

CAPTAIN HERON AND TOM RIPON ARE EXPOSED TO GREAT DANGER AND TREACHERY.

A FLUSH of indignation came over the countenance of the old Bishop, when Captain Heron informed him how the registry at Barnes Church had been tampered with. He half rose from his chair as he said, "I ought to see the Bishop of London at once."

"Ah, my Lord Bishop, if you would!"

"I will, to-day—I will, to-day. But tell me more. Tell me more. The leaf, you say, of the registry, is lost, or stolen?"

"It is gone."

"That is rank villany."

"It is, indeed!"

"But stay! stay! Let me think. Yes—yes. To be sure—my private diary. That will be strong evidence."

"It will, indeed!"

"I will find it. Come to me to-morrow, young man—come to me to-morrow, and justice shall be done. I will prove the marriage of one Amelia Staunton with the late Earl of Whitcombe, while he held the subsidiary title of Lord Warringdale; and it will be for you to prove you are the son of that marriage."

"A thousand thanks and blessings attend you!"

"My blessing be upon you, too, young man. I will do that which is right in this case, you may be assured, let it cost me what it may."

"Ah, reverend sir, it will cost you nothing. You are too high for the anger of Lord Warringdale to reach. You will be the only one able to serve me without the risk of any consequences."

"I do not know that, but I will do my duty all the same. Come to me to-morrow, young man—come to me to-morrow."

"At this hour?"

"Yes, at this hour. Now leave me; I will find my diary, and all will perhaps be well."

Captain Heron saw that the Bishop was much exhausted by the agitating nature of the interview that had taken place, and he took a kindly leave of him.

Tom Ripon was well pleased to see Heron again; but he had some news to tell him.

A knock that had come at the Bishop's door soon after Tom had taken his seat in the hall had awakened Tom's attention, he hardly knew why, because that could not be a very unusual circumstance at such a house.

The house-porter went to the door, and Tom took care to keep out of sight of any one who might be on the threshold when the door should be opened.

No sooner was the door half open, when Tom Ripon nearly jumped off the portmanteau he was seated on, to hear the voice of Jonathan Wild himself.

"Is this the Bishop of Worcester's?"

"Yes."

"Is his lordship within?"

"Well, he is."

"Then be so good as to say that Mr. Smith would be glad to see him."

"I cannot disturb his lordship. He is busy, and not very well, too. You must come again, or see the secretary."

Wild spoke in quite an amiable tone of voice, as he added, "I think I will see the secretary."

"Very well—step this way."

Tom, therefore, had just time to dart behind the great leather chair which the hall-porter passed most of his lazy hours in, as Jonathan Wild stepped into the hall of the Bishop's house.

Tom Ripon had heard quite enough, and knew quite enough, to feel convinced that let Jonathan Wild's errand be what it might to the Bishop of Worcester's house, it could not possibly be in any respect favourable to the views and wishes of Captain Heron.

Indeed, Tom's first idea was that Wild must have found out their actual presence there, and that some personal danger was to be apprehended.

How to warn Heron of what was taking place was the proposition that presented itself to him; but Tom Ripon did not see how exactly to do that without raising an outcry which in all probability would do more harm than good under the circumstances.

Hidden, then, most effectually behind the great easy leathern chair of the hall-porter, Tom Ripon made up his mind to wait a little to see what would come of a transaction that could not be otherwise than dangerous.

The hall-porter had no means of connecting the visit of Jonathan Wild, or Mr. Smith as he chose to call himself, with that of the gentleman who was holding a private conference with the Bishop; so without the slightest notion of knowing that he might be on the eve of some rather violent transactions, he politely showed Jonathan Wild into a room devoted to the use of the Bishop's secretary.

Hardly had this state of things taken place, when that interesting interview which Captain Heron had had with the Bishop terminated; and full of thought, with an anxious expression upon his face, Heron slowly descended the staircase of the Bishop's house, little imagining that beneath the roof at that precise moment was to be found one of his most implacable foes.

Tom Ripon then saw how very possible it was for Captain Heron to effect what might be called a narrow escape.

If the thing were done promptly, nothing would be easier than to cross the hall and leave the Bishop's house before Jonathan Wild could catch a glimpse of him or even dream of his presence in it.

Therefore was it that Tom Ripon, darting forward and clutching Captain Heron by the lappel of his coat, whispered eagerly to him, "Jonathan Wild is here."

If Tom Ripon had announced that an earthquake was about to take place in Clarges Street, the words could scarcely have excited more surprise in the mind of Heron.

"No, Tom," he said; "you are mistaken!"

"Not at all. He's there!"

Tom pointed to the door of the room leading from the hall, where Wild had been conducted by the porter; and Captain Heron, with an almost involuntary movement, plunged his hand into the bosom of his apparel, to feel for the butt of one of those pistols to which he had so frequently owed the preservation of his life.

But as it happened, there was not the slightest occasion for any violence.

Jonathan Wild had not the most remote notion on earth that he was anywhere in the vicinity of Captain Heron; and, notwithstanding his visit to the Bishop of Worcester materially concerned the fortunes of our hero, their presence there, at one and the same time, was one of those accidental circumstances which are out of the sphere of all calculation.

The hall-porter thought that the gentleman who had called to see the Bishop, and his country servant, were a little distracted, for the rapid interchange of words that had taken place between Tom and his master, as he had recently called Captain Heron, had been in too low a tone to reach his ears, and he was somewhat surprised now at the celerity with which they both darted from the house.

So soon as they had got a sufficient distance to render open conversation at all safe, Heron turned to Tom Ripon, and with surprise and incredulity in his tones, exclaimed, "You must have been mistaken, Tom! It is impossible that Jonathan Wild could have been in that house!"

"Oh, he was there, Captain," said Tom, "fast enough."

"How can you be sure?"

"I saw him, and heard him speak."

"That is very strange!"

Captain Heron paused in thought.

What could be the meaning of Jonathan Wild's presence at the Bishop of Worcester's house? for, admitting the fact, that he, Jonathan, was well aware as any one could be of the important testimony that the Bishop could bear, in regard to the marriage of Amelia Staunton with the late Earl of Whitcombe, surely it would do no good to Lord Warringdale or his prospects, to awaken such recollections in the mind of the Bishop.

"Well," said Heron to himself, "let the villain take his course. I have the promise of the Bishop that he will bear testimony to the fact of the marriage. It was not an extorted promise, but one voluntarily given, and I will rest upon it as upon a thing not to be doubted. Tom, I fancy you will have to go back to the forest and explain my absence, for I shall have business still in London that will detain me past this hour to-morrow, and Edith will be anxious."

Tom did not seem half to like this arrangement, and he made a counter proposition to Captain Heron.

"Let me go and come back again, Captain," he said. "I shall know where to find you, if you tell me."

"I shall stay, then, at the Golden Cross, Charing Cross. Leave the portmanteau with me. It is now nearly two o'clock, and let you make what speed you may, Tom, it is scarcely possible for you to return before midnight."

"Oh, I'll be back before that."

"As you will, then—as you will. I need write nothing, for you can explain to Edith that I am unexpectedly detained, but that there is no danger."

"You leave all that to me," said Tom; "I'll manage it. And now I'll be off, for it seems to me the sooner I go, the sooner I shall get back."

"Go, Tom, and may good fortune attend you."

If the truth must be told, Tom Ripon had another object in getting off with all the celerity in his power. He had made up his mind to pay a visit to his mother, if possible, and to the Reverend Mortification Ripon, in Sun Court, St. Martin's Lane.

Perhaps Tom had no very precise idea as regarded his object in paying that visit, and if his feelings on the subject had been carefully analysed, it would probably have been found that the perpetration of some boyish frolic, or the playing some alarming trick upon the Reverend Mortification, was at the bottom of his desire to visit her whom he called the "old gal."

But we shall leave Tom Ripon for the moment to carry out his own particular views and objects, while we follow the fortunes, during that night and day in London, of Captain Heron.

As soon as he was alone with the portmanteau in his possession, Captain Heron thought it would be as well to house himself as quickly as possible, and the idea came across him that it might be prudent to make some change in his apparel; since his encounter with the attorney, both in and out

of the mail coach, had made his appearance in the character of Squire Arden, rather perilous.

But there was a feeling of great exultation and pleasurable satisfaction in the mind of Heron, for the promise that the Bishop had made him appeared to him to comprehend all that he could wish in the way of proof of the marriage of his mother with the late Earl of Whitcombe.

Had he been merely consulting his own personal feelings and safety, he would have walked through the streets of London to Charing Cross heedless now of any dangers that might assail him; but Heron thought of his Edith, and he felt that he had no right to throw away even a chance of safety of a more absolute character than his own ardent courage presented, by running the slightest risk. Hailing therefore a hackney-coach which stood disengaged at the corner of Piccadilly, Captain Heron got into it, and was driven to the ancient hostel at Charing Cross, which he had

No. 90.—EDITH.

named to Tom Ripon, and which was then one of the oldest houses in London for the accommodation of travellers, although it is now so modernised that it presents nothing of the appearance it did in the days of which we write.

There it was that Heron found himself soon comfortably situated in a small apartment that, for the time being, he could at all events call his own; and he proceeded to make an examination of that portmanteau which had strangely enough fallen into his possession, and which contained the first instalment due to him from the estates of Whitcombe.

He found the amount as stated by the attorney and agent of Lord Warringdale to be perfectly correct; and often as Captain Heron, in his adventurous career, had availed himself of the resources of other folks, without any claim so to do, he could not help feeling the novelty of the sensation of being now in possession actually of means which, without a doubt, belonged to himself.

Captain Heron was re-packing the portmanteau and re-considering the question of making some alteration in his apparel, when there came a slight rap at the door of the apartment.

It is not too much to say that Captain Heron, surrounded as he was with many dangers, was always on what our Gallic neighbours call the *qui vive* on every occasion, and the tap at the door of the room he occupied at the "Golden Cross" was quite sufficient to awaken his caution.

While he was investigating the interesting contents of the portmanteau that had belonged to the legal agent of Lord Warringdale, Captain Heron had taken the precaution to lock the door of the room.

Hence he was not taken by surprise.

"Who is there?" he called aloud.

"Me, sir," was the unsatisfactory reply.

"Who?"

"I am Peter, sir."

"Peter who?"

"Peter Simms, sir, if you please. Beg pardon, sir, but you are in the wrong room, sir."

"What do you mean by the wrong room? How can there be a wrong room or a right room in an hotel?"

"But you are in number eight, sir!"

"Well?"

"And number eight, sir, was engaged beforehand. If you don't mind, sir, moving into number seven."

"Not a bit—wait a moment."

Captain Heron thought it would consume less time, and be less trouble to make the change as requested, than to argue the point; so he packed up the portmanteau again, and opened the door with it in his hand.

"Very sorry, sir," said Peter Simms, "but it was all the fault of one of the under-waiters, sir. I am the head-waiter, sir, if you please. That door leads to number seven, sir. Quite as good a room as this, only the gent who had engaged this likes number eight; and so you see, sir, we don't like to say he shan't have it."

"Do not mention it," said Heron; "it is of no moment."

"All right, sir! Now, sir, you can come up! Number eight is vacant now, sir!"

Some one from below now began slowly to ascend the stairs, and Captain Heron, as he stood upon the threshold of number seven, was rather surprised to hear that the particular "gent" who was so attached to number eight kept uttering hideous groans as he came up.

"What is the matter?" asked Heron, of the urbane Peter Simms, the waiter.

"Why, sir—if you please, sir—the gent has been robbed and nearly murdered by a ferocious highwayman."

"Oh, indeed!"

"Yes, sir. He was assailed in a mail coach, and robbed of a portmanteau with I don't know how many thousand pounds in it."

"When was that?"

"Oh, only to-day, sir. I heard him telling master and missus all about it. But I daresay he will give you all the particulars, sir, and here he comes."

Captain Heron just advanced sufficiently close to the stair-head to see the upper part of the face of the groaning traveller who was approaching.

That slight glance was enough.

In the pertinacious occupant of number eight, Captain Heron recognised at once the professional personage who had been left by himself and Tom Ripon in the cellar of a house in the obscure street in the City.

"That will do," said Heron, as he made his way at once into number seven, and closed the door. "That will do. I have no interest in other people's affairs."

Another moment, and the man who must instantly have recognised him was on the landing. He was speaking as he came up.

"And, Peter, you won't lose an instant. Oh, dear me, I have not a bone in my body that is not aching most desperately; but you will not lose an instant, Peter—mind, now."

"Certainly not, sir."

"Say the messenger is to ask for a shilling."

"Yes, sir."

"And mind there is no blunder about the name and the address."

"Oh no, sir. 'Lord Warringdale, at number eighteen, St. James's Street, opposite Whitcombe House.'"

"Yes, that is it. Oh, dear! oh, dear! I am all aches and bruises. Let me have some more wine with honey in it, as soon as possible."

"Yes, sir."

The waiter took his departure, and the door of number eight was closed.

Captain Heron then began to think it was time to take his departure likewise.

And yet, since he had heard that his infamous half-brother, Lord Warringdale, was to be sent for, he was seized with an irresistible desire to see if he would come; and, possibly, Captain Heron might confront him, even in that public hotel.

CHAPTER CCII.

LORD WARRINGDALE COMMITS A DREADFUL MURDER AT THE GOLDEN CROSS.

WELL would it have been for the peace of mind as well as for the safety of Captain Heron, if he had obeyed the first instinct that came over him and at once taken his departure from the Golden Cross Hotel and Tavern when he found that it was likely to be in the occupation of persons antagonistic to his safety.

But his destiny would not have it so.

Heron had to pass through a great danger, which was just gathering around him.

By stooping, and applying his eyes to the keyhole of the door of number seven, Heron found that he could command a tolerable view of the corridor and the head of the stairs.

The desire then to see if the false and wicked Lord Warringdale would arrive came strongly before Captain Heron, and he kept his post with the object of arriving at some certainty on that head.

Half an hour, probably, had passed away when Heron heard the sound of footsteps ascending the staircase in haste, and in another moment he saw his bad half-brother appear.

A deep sigh came from the heart of Captain Heron as he saw that man whom he would have been glad to make so happy, would he only have permitted it.

Lord Warringdale paused at the top of the stairs, as if in doubt which door to go to, and it was a wonder, and quite a chance, that he did not apply to the very room where his noble and gallant brother had taken refuge.

There was, however, a kind of timidity about Lord Warringdale which prevented him from opening any door at random, and he called down the staircase, "Which is the number?"

"Number eight, my lord!" replied a voice. "I will come, my lord, if your lordship pleases."

"No—no! It is here. I see the number on the paint."

As he spoke, Lord Warringdale turned the handle of the room door in which the bereaved professional personage awaited him, and went in.

All that Captain Heron could hear was a loud exclamation from some one, and then another voice, as if in entreaty or supplication.

The old panelling was thick between the rooms, and Captain Heron sought in vain for some place in it by which he would be enabled to hear what was going on. None such presented itself, and all he could hear was that the interview was far from being gentle or harmonious.

Then there was a sharp, sudden cry, and the door of number eight opened quickly.

"Very well, sir," said Lord Warringdale, "I will send to you."

There was no reply to this speech, and it looked rather suspicious that Lord Warringdale should take the trouble to close the door of the room very carefully, making several rattling efforts at the lock before he fully succeeded in doing so.

Captain Heron saw that proceeding through the key-hole, and as he had not fully made up his mind to present himself to Lord Warringdale, he now let him go without making his presence known to him.

Warringdale indeed descended the stairs with such haste, that if Heron had desired to speak to him, he would have had to call after him.

As it was, however, he let him go.

But the intense stillness in number eight was suspicious,—nay, it was something more than suspicious, coupled with the extraordinary conduct of the villain Warringdale.

A terrible idea took possession of the mind of Captain Heron.

Had Lord Warringdale, inflamed by rage and disappointment, actually murdered his agent?

This was an idea that such a mind as Heron's could not long support without seeking to arrive at the truth. The corridor was silent and deserted. There was no one on the stairs. It would be but the act of a moment to put all doubt at rest by one look into number eight.

Captain Heron, with three long strides, was at the door. He tapped at it.

No reply.

He pulled the handle of the latch, and looked in. The sight that met his gaze was not one to look twice at if it could be avoided.

Partially propped up by a chair was the dead body of Lord Warringdale's professional agent. The aspect of the dead face was a terror to be remembered in dreams. A thin stream of black blood was slowly pouring from the chest and collecting on the floor.

"It is murder, then!" said Heron, as he closed the door of number eight, and stood for a few seconds on the threshold in a state of irresolution what to do.

Then his impulse was to fly from that ill-omened house, and seek for any other shelter which, until the morrow, might present itself.

This was a resolution which grew in strength each moment, and Captain Heron at once fetched the portmanteau from number seven, and hastily descended the stairs.

It cost him a painful effort of self-control to hinder his voice from making itself heard in startling accents in that hotel, and from crying out "Murder! murder!"

But Captain Heron was peculiarly situated.

How could he put himself into contact with the police and the magistracy, as he would be compelled to do if he became the accuser of Lord Warringdale?

No! There was no resource for him but flight from a house which would surely be soon full of danger to him.

Nay! Who should say that if he remained he might not himself be suspected of the crime? And if so, how was he to clear himself from that suspicion by avowing who and what he was?

No! Nothing but flight from the inn of the "Golden Cross" was now open to him.

And so Captain Heron reached the hall.

The waiters looked surprised, and Peter Simms came bustling up to him to know what he wanted

"I find I must leave," said Heron.

"Oh, sir! Quite sorry, sir! Perhaps you don't like number seven, sir! Daresay if I go to the gent in number eight and say so, he will change, after all."

"No! no! I—that is I have thought of some business. There's a guinea—keep the change. It will pay for my short stay."

"Oh, yes, sir! Very sorry, sir!"

"Good day."

"Good day, sir! Glad to see you again, sir!"

The waiter snatched up a clothes-brush, and followed Captain Heron officiously right on to the steps of the inn, brushing his coat.

It was with a feeling of exquisite relief that Captain Heron felt himself once more breathing the open air, and free from the atmosphere of that place, which seemed to him tainted with blood.

He could have no doubt whatever of the exact state of affairs, which had induced this seemingly gratuitous and cold blooded assassination on the part of Lord Warringdale. No doubt he had thought to steal a march upon Jonathan Wild by this little manœuvre in respect to the tenantry of the Whitcombe estates, and much in want of money as he was, the rage at finding himself foiled had only found vent in the death of his agent and victim.

But Captain Heron was now at a loss where to go, and the idea came across him more than once that it would be a pleasure—although, perhaps, a melancholy one to him—to spend the night he had to pass in London, before he could again see the Bishop of Worcester, in either Castleneau House, in Bloomsbury Fields, or in the mansion of his father, the late Earl of Whitcombe, in St. James's Street.

There was quite sufficient of mystery about both those houses to induce a disposition to seek either of them on the part of Captain Heron.

Pausing, then, at the corner of one of the narrow streets leading from Pall Mall, Heron asked himself which should be his course, and he was nearly deciding in favour of Castleneau House, because he felt how great would be the hazard while daylight yet maintained itself, in effecting an entrance to Whitcombe House.

Surrounded as it was by so many other mansions, it was almost impossible that any one should be permitted to ascend its doorsteps unobserved.

A hundred hostile eyes might be upon him, and he might find himself besieged in that house of his father, without the means of keeping off his foes beyond a very limited period of time.

Captain Heron might then be considered to have decided in favour of Castleneau House, but as he turned his footsteps in that direction, he became conscious that a white fog was settling over London.

Gradually the ends of the streets seemed to be receding from his vision, and then even the houses on the opposite side of the way grew dim and misty, as though they had moved far off to some plain loaded with vapours through which only their outlines could be faintly visible.

For almost the first time in his life, a superstitious feeling came over the mind of Captain Heron.

"Surely, surely," he said, "this is a mute yet eloquent signal from nature to bid me seek my father's house, which I can now do in safety under cover of this gathering mist."

Without hesitating for another moment, Heron made his way hastily towards St. James's Street; once only he paused in his progress, because he heard, coming on the thickened air at some distance behind him, shouts and cries, as if either some accident had happened, or as if some excited pursuers were on the track of a fugitive.

Heron paused, and bent his ear down to listen.

"Stop him! stop him! Murder! murder!" were the cries that came distinctly to his senses.

But those cries had no disturbing power over the heart and brain of Felix Heron. He in no way connected them with himself, and he stood within the arch of a doorway, listening with a vague curiosity to the cries until they died away in the distance.

"Some crime has been committed," he said, "in the streets, perhaps of nearly as black a dye as that which Warringdale has been guilty of, within the last hour, at the 'Golden Cross.'"

It is only to be accounted for by the feeling of entire innocence which pervaded the heart of Captain Heron, that the thought never occurred to him for a moment of the possibility of these cries being upon his own track.

But such was indeed the fact.

A discovery of the murder in one of the upper rooms of the "Golden Cross Inn" had taken place, and the strange traveller who had at first declared his intention of sleeping there that night, and then had so hastily left, after paying an extravagant sum for the slight and temporary accommodation he had had, was at once suspected.

And so, still in happy ignorance that the inn of the "Golden Cross" was in a state of agitation and convulsion from attics to cellars on his account, Captain Heron made his way through the rapidly increasing fog to St. James's Street.

The arts of the London "cracksman" had been too often described to Captain Heron for him to be ignorant of them, but he was by no means possessed of the skill of the accomplished housebreaker. The adventurous life, however, that he had led, made it necessary that he should possess sufficient efficiency in the use of a skeleton key, to enable him to open any ordinary lock that might be opposed to him.

The fog seemed to thicken in St. James's Street.

It was in vain that Heron strove to define to his eyes the outlines of the old Palace, as he stood upon the doorstep of his father's house.

And then his eyes were naturally cast over the way, where he knew the lodgings of Lord Warringdale were situated.

All was darkness there. Heron could but dimly see the houses and trace the outlines of the windows, but as he looked, he saw a dull red colour through the mist.

That was a light in a room of the house exactly opposite to Whitcombe mansion; and with a dull, fiery gleam, its reflection came through the mist and fell upon the figure of Captain Heron, as with little difficulty he opened the outer door and passed into the hall of his father's house.

It was a tolerable proof that the house was untenanted, since the door could be opened with such facility from without; but Captain Heron was not a little startled the moment after he had closed the door and stood alone, as he thought, in the spacious hall, to hear a deep and most audible sigh, evidently not many paces from him.

Involuntarily he started back, and placed his back against the massive door.

"What is that? who is here?" he cried. "Friend or foe, answer me, for I have the right to be here, and will maintain it!"

"The right! the right!" said a low, whispering voice, which seemed, as it repeated the words, to retreat far away up the spacious staircase.

There was enough in this to try the nerves of so stout a heart as Captain Heron's; and that species of shuddering terror which human nature can never divest itself of, upon the slightest suspicion of a communion with the beings of another world, crept over him.

And why should he stay there to have his heart, perhaps, frozen up with some strange terror?

Why should he linger in the still dreamy atmosphere of that gloomy mansion, beneath whose roof more crimes might possibly have been committed than it had ever entered into his imagination to conceive the existence of?

He was more than half inclined at that moment to open the door and sally out again into the fog.

His hand was on the lock.

"Felix! Felix!" sighed a soft and gentle voice. "No harm to thee—no harm to thee, Felix! Felix!"

It would seem as if the supernatural inhabitant or inhabitants—if such they were—of Whitcombe House had divined what was passing in his mind, and had uttered these words to induce him to remain in safety, if even at the same time in imaginative terror.

Then Heron cried out aloud, "Let me see you, be you what you may. Come to me in any form that has the aspect of humanity, and I will not shrink from you. If—as my heart would dictate to me—it is the spirit of my dead father that speaks to me, let me see the gracious shadow, and I will still accord it the duty of a son."

"Peace! peace! peace!" cried the voice again. "Peace will come, and happiness to Felix. Felix and happiness!"

It seemed as if the spirit—if spirit indeed it were—played upon the signification of Captain Heron's name; and as he listened to the tones of the voice, which at some moments appeared close to him, and then again far away, the cold feeling that had crept through his blood-vessels passed off, and a spirit of daring—not mere animal courage, but a strange desire, accompanied by a species of recklessness to danger—came over him, to fathom the depths of the mystery.

"Speak to me again," he said: "I will listen, and fear not."

"Hush!" said the voice. "Listen!"

Captain Heron's attention was, at this moment, attracted as much to cries and shouts from the outside of the house, as to the apparently supernatural voices within it.

That some concourse of people were making their way up St. James's Street in a tumultuous fashion, was evident.

They seemed to pause even at the door of Whitcombe House, but that was a mistake of Heron's.

It was at the lodgings of Lord Warringdale, opposite, that the crowd paused; and then Heron heard a violent knocking; and it would appear that Lord Warringdale had said something from the window of his lodgings, for some man cried out loudly from the street, "My Lord Warringdale, I am a constable, and we want your testimony about a gentleman who has been murdered at the 'Golden Cross.' It's the gentleman who sent for you, my lord, a little while ago, and whom you visited there. We want your testimony, my lord, if you please."

Lord Warringdale, doubtless, made some reply from the window, but it was too indistinct to reach the ears of Captain Heron.

Another voice, however, soon took up the cause of contention in the street; and so soon as it was discovered to whom that voice belonged, every one deferred to it with a kind of habitual terror.

Perhaps that voice was recognised by Captain Heron as quickly as by any one.

It was the voice of Jonathan Wild himself, who was on a visit at that opportune moment to Lord Warringdale; and who, the moment he saw a crowd collected, thrust himself into the midst of it, roughly calling out, in his snarling, savage accents, "What's the matter? If it's anything but a drunken brawl, speak to me—I'm the man to see to it!"

"Mr. Wild! Mr. Wild!" cried several people.

"Yes, I am Mr. Wild—Jonathan Wild's my name—and if you don't clear off, all of you, you'll find me Wild by nature!"

Captain Heron heard the sharp cracking of a whip—for Wild had been recently riding upon some expedition, and was armed with a heavy whip, similar to that used by postilions, the handle of which was heavily loaded with at least a pound of lead.

"It's a murder, Mr. Wild," said the constable.

"Ah! that's something in my line—because a good forty pounds blood-money may come of it when the condemned murderer takes a ride to Tyburn in the Government carriage."

A confused murmur of voices then ensued, intermingled with the sharp cracking of Jonathan Wild's whip—after which all was comparatively still.

But Captain Heron now thoroughly understood that the hue-and-cry through the streets of London was in consequence of that fearful murder, perpetrated, apparently, on the spur of the moment, by Lord Warringdale.

Heron felt all his danger; but if he had had to do over again what he did in consequence of that atrocious deed—which was committed, so to speak, within his immediate cognizance—he knew not how he could have acted otherwise.

And now he turned his whole attention again to the mysteries of Whitcombe House, which seemed to be thickening fast about him.

CHAPTER CCIII.

CAPTAIN HERON FINDS THE MYSTERIES OF WHITCOMBE HOUSE THICKEN AROUND HIM.

THE mysterious voice which had addressed Heron in his late father's mansion, filled him with a thousand vague conjectures in regard to its character.

The superstitious element in the character of the bold and ingenuous knight of the road had never been very powerful, and Heron would have been far better pleased to find some natural explanation of the strange phenomenon, than be compelled to resolve it to supernatural agency.

And now that the tumult in the open street had died away, Heron strove to pierce with an ardent gaze the darkness of the hall in which he stood.

But the evening was rapidly approaching, and the London fog without was thickening.

Captain Heron might as well have striven to look into the deepest and darkest cavern in the world with the hope of distinguishing objects, as across that hall and up that spacious staircase.

He felt a natural reluctance to move away from the advantageous position he occupied close to the outer door, but at the same time he could not but feel that so long as he remained there he was not in the way to find any explanation of the strange voice or voices of the deserted house.

The silence in the mansion was now most profound; and Captain Heron, although he was wont to laugh at such stories, could not help at the moment thinking of the old superstition or idea that the beings of another world can only speak to mortals by way of reply or rejoinder to something said to them.

If, then, such an enforced silence was upon any such existence in that house, Heron was resolved to enable it to break it, and speak again.

"Tell me," he said, "who and what you are, and what can be your object in shrouding yourself in gloom and mystery?"

Again the stillness about him was broken by a deep and long-drawn sigh.

"Do you suffer?" asked Heron.

"Suffer! suffer!" said the voice.

"Can I aid you?"

"You will? Oh, you will?"

"With all my heart, if I can! Only tell me how!"

"The time has not yet come."

"When will it, then?"

Another deep sigh was the only answer to this question.

"If, then," said Heron, "I may not aid you now, and I may not know when I shall have the opportunity to do so, at least let me know who and what you are?"

"Your friend."

"I know not that."

"Your best friend!"

"Nay, that will I dispute; for my best friend under heaven is the pure and gentle heart that, despite all the evil fortune that surrounded me, joined her hand to mine, and has become the angel of my destiny, my own dear, loving Edith!"

Captain Heron uttered these words with a fervour that was amply sufficient to stamp them with an air of deep sincerity.

There was no reply or remark for the space of half a minute or so from his unknown and unseen companion in the solitude and darkness of that house, but then, in low, tender accents, the voice spoke again—"Love her fondly, love her dearly, for aye and for ever!"

"I do—I will! It needs no ghost to tell me so to do!"

"Follow! follow!" said the voice.

At the same moment Captain Heron saw a faint glimmer of light at the further end of the hall.

It could hardly, however, be called a light, inasmuch as it was rather a kind of radiance in the black darkness, which, as it spread from a small speck, showed him the dim outline of a hand.

That hand looked not as if belonging to this world.

There was a semi-transparency about it, and a strange flicker of its whole substance, which imparted to it something most unearthly in aspect.

Captain Heron shrunk back for a moment.

Then the voice spoke again.

"Follow, and fear naught!"

That word "fear" probably did more towards lending Captain Heron fixedness of purpose than would any other expression. It was a word he knew, but never would acknowledge as entering into his calculations in regard to anything he had to do.

"I will fear nothing," he replied.

"Follow! follow!"

"I am strong in the integrity of my purpose. I came here to do wrong to no one. I have forgiven as many crimes and sins as I have committed; and even the worst foe I ever had—namely, the treacherous and murderous brother who has so often sought my life—I have spared."

"Follow! follow!" said the voice again, and this time there was a tone of impatience in its accents.

"I come—I come!" said Heron. "Lead where you will, I follow you!"

The strange, illuminated hand was raised so that the fingers assumed now the attitude of beckoning, and Captain Heron at once left his post at the back of the street door, and slowly stepped towards it along the hall.

The marble flag-stones echoed to his tread, and in the silence of the deserted mansion, those sounds, light and faint as they were, seemed to travel right up the grand staircase, and to lose themselves only in the silence of uninhabited chambers above.

Captain Heron kept his eyes fixed upon the hand which beckoned him onwards.

In a few seconds he saw that it was slowly rising higher and higher in the black darkness around it, and then he began to conjecture that whatever form that spectral-looking hand belonged to, was ascending the grand staircase of the mansion.

A feeling of satisfaction came over the mind of Heron at the fact that the route of the real or apparent spectre-hand was upwards, to the large saloons of Whitcombe House, in preference to its lower regions.

He followed with more alacrity.

The hand still preceded him, and he counted the stairs as he ascended them, rather mechanically than because he had any spirit or desire so to do.

There were thirty steps.

Then Captain Heron was certain he had reached the landing of the grand staircase, and was on the first floor of Whitcombe House.

"Speak, now!" he cried; "and tell me for what purpose I am guided hither?"

The hand disappeared.

Captain Heron was alone in the darkness.

He thought, then, that he heard a door close; and the feeling which had begun rapidly to grow upon him as he ascended the staircase—that he was being made the victim of some villany—induced him to say in loud accents, "I am armed, and by the aid of my pistols I daresay I can procure a light."

Hardly had these words escaped his lips, when he started on one side, for his impression at the moment was that some one stood close to him.

That, however, was but a natural delusion of the senses, contingent upon the fact that a long, narrow, bright pencil of light suddenly streamed through the key-hole of a door close at hand, and fell upon his arm.

Heron saw what it was immediately after the first start he had given.

"So," he said, "that is to be my route! There is light, at all events; and, come what may, I will seek it!"

He took two steps to the light, which brought him close to the door. He could see the polished ivory handle of the lock, and he turned it without trouble or opposition.

The door opened, and Captain Heron looked with surprise into one of the largest reception-rooms of Whitcombe House.

The room was one in which the late Earl, as one of the Ministers of State, was wont occasionally to receive the *elite* of the fashionable world of London.

Imagine a magnificent saloon over seventy feet in depth—for it went far back from St. James's Street—and the middle of the whole front of the house.

Eight tall windows gave light in the day-time. Four in the front of the house, and four looking into a garden at the rear, for at that time there were real gardens to be seen, even in the heart of London.

There were trees in Piccadilly even then famous for a particularly beautiful and toothsome pear they bore.

But what astonished Captain Heron more than anything, was to find that this magnificent apartment in the apparently uninhabited Whitcombe House, was lighted.

Hanging from the centre of the ceiling was a glass chandelier that carried about thirty wax candles.

They were all alight.

This display of lights was not sufficient to give anything approaching to brilliancy to the vast saloon, and there were girandoles in every compartment of the richly ornamented walls, each one of which bore four lights.

These additional wax candles were, however, upon this occasion, not lighted.

The effect of the thirty-light chandelier was to Captain Heron very magnificent — perhaps even more so than as if all the lights of that saloon were in a blaze; and coming as he had out of the extreme darkness of the hall and of the staircase, it was, to his eyes, a scene of dazzling and gorgeous magnificence.

Across the windows the crimson silk hangings were drawn closely.

Upon the gilt furniture, and upon the many mirrors, the light danced in beautiful reflection; and, amid all the silence and stillness of the saloon, gave to it a strange and magical charm.

No wonder that Captain Heron stood for some few seconds on the threshold of that apartment, and gazed about him with a growing doubt in his mind that he was dreaming.

"Speak to me again!" he said. "Speak, spirit, if you be one, and tell me what part I am expected to play in the midst of all this display of magnificence?"

"Welcome!" said the voice.

"How mean you?"

"Welcome home!" said the voice.

"Home! Yes, this is, was, or should have been my home, but wickedness and heartlessness prevented me from sharing it!"

"Alas! alas!" sighed the voice.

Captain Heron looked keenly and eagerly about him, in order to discover, if possible, from whence the voice came. He thought that surely now, in the midst of so much illumination, he would certainly be able to discover the person who spoke so sadly and yet so kindly to him.

But he could see no one.

Alone, quite alone he appeared to be in that saloon, and the voice that now and then addressed him seemed to float in the still atmosphere about him.

"Welcome! welcome!" it said again.

Heron advanced.

The portmanteau that he had brought with him from the "Golden Cross" he had still in one hand; and now that he could see so well about him, he placed it on the silken cushion of a chair near at hand, and strode forward towards the centre of the saloon.

There was a table there, just beneath the great glass chandelier with its thirty lights, and upon that table Captain Heron saw that there was something that glistened and caught the light with great brilliancy.

His surprise was very great on getting close to the table, to see that there was laid upon it a repast all served in silver and in beautiful cut glass, which accounted for the glitter that had met his eyes.

"Welcome!" said the voice again.

"Why, this is surely all a vision!" said Heron. "I have stepped out of the common-place streets of London, into a region of magic enchantment."

Twice he turned completely round upon his heels, and cast his gaze into the remotest corners of the saloon, but he could see no one.

Once only, for half a moment, Captain Heron thought he had caught sight of a human form.

He darted forward on the instant, and then he found it was but his own reflection, in one of the numerous mirrors of the apartment.

And there, before him, was that elegantly-laid repast, to which he felt each moment more and more inclined to do justice.

Captain Heron was young, and he had not tasted food since he had breakfasted with his Edith, in Epping Forest. It was now many hours since then; and unromantic as it may sound in the midst of the mysteries of Whitcombe House, truth obliges us to confess that Captain Heron began to look with longing eyes at the silver covers and the rich wines in the sparkling decanters before him.

That the repast was laid for him he could not doubt, and that he was in the hands of beings friendly to him, whether they were of this world or not, was sufficiently evident.

"I will dine," said Heron, "let the issue of this adventure be what it may."

"Welcome!" said the voice again.

"Thanks!" said Heron. "I will partake of your hospitality in the spirit that it is intended I should."

"Intended!" said the voice.

Captain Heron had now ceased to start and look about him every time the voice reached his ears, for he had made up his mind that the spectre was either invisible to mortal eyes, or if human like himself, was too well concealed for him to discover.

He therefore sat down at once to the table.

Some exquisitely cooked chickens, a loaf of the whitest and finest bread he had ever seen, and various other dishes, invited his appetite.

Captain Heron made a good meal, and then he poured from one of the decanters a glass of sparkling amber wine, and held it up about the height of his eyes as he cried out, "To the giver of the feast!"

"Amen!" said the voice.

"A thousand thanks!" added Heron.

He drank the wine, which was of the highest possible quality, and then, as he sat down the glass, the voice spoke again: "Discretion," it said, "keeps the heart and brain free from confusion and danger!"

Heron comprehended what was meant.

"Dear, unknown monitor," he said, "I am not one apt to fall into excesses. This bright wine is no temptation to me, and I drink no more."

"Joy—joy and happiness, Felix," said the voice.

"Was I expected, then," said Heron, "to be intemperate?"

A deep sigh was the only reply.

"Come, beneficent spirit," added Heron, "trust me, and speak to me. Say—oh, say, now and at once, what is the meaning of all these strange scenes?"

"I may not, yet."

"Wherefore not?"

"Because——"

The voice paused.

"Because what?" added Heron. "You trust me by halves, and far better would it be to trust me wholly."

"The trial is not complete."

"How so?"

"Drink!"

"No. I never exceed what I have now taken. I do not call it a virtue, but I have no taste for those coarse pleasures of the appetite which make up so large a portion of the every-day existence of so many persons. I often have a deep regret that human nature is compelled to sustain itself upon meats and drinks, and think that if beneficient heaven in its goodness had made the mere air sufficiently revivifying and vital for all our wants, how happy a state that would be."

The deep sigh came again.

"You disagree with me," said Heron.

"Whatever is, is best," said the voice. "A higher wisdom than ours directed all."

"Amen!" said Heron. "I do not repine, neither do I challenge the designs of Omnipotence. I do but utter the careless thought of the creature, without a doubt of the better wisdom of the Creator."

"Listen!" said the voice.

"I do, I will, with all my power."

"You are deeply injured?"

"I am, indeed."

"You are deprived of your birthright?"

"I am—I am."

"Revenge is human. You should kill the man who stands between you and the same."

"What man?"

"He who miscalls himself Warringdale."

"Never—never!"

"Have you no feeling?"

"I have, false and malignant spirit. It is because I have feeling, I can never imbrue my hands in the blood of Lord Warringdale. He is my brother. The same father belongs to both of us. No, no! Oh, heaven be thanked that I can suffer, but not inflict!"

Captain Heron was silent, and the moment he was so, he felt certain that he heard a sound closely resembling half-suppressed sobbing.

"Is this possible?" he said. "Do the beings of another world feel human sympathies? Have they tears to shed?"

"They have," said the voice.

"That is more than strange."

"And you will not be avenged upon the bad, wicked brother who is so great a foe to you?"

"I will not."

"Think again. Drink deeply of the red wine, and then you have but twenty steps to take from this house to that on the opposite side of the way, and you may take his life."

"Never! never! So help me heaven—no!"

"And there is another," said the voice, "whose memory ought to be to you an aggravation and a detestation."

"Who is that?"

"Your father."

"My father? Oh, no! no! Wrong he may have been. Deluded and deceived he may have been. But he was my father, and I will not—I cannot think harshly or unkindly of him. Speak not to me in such a strain, I pray you."

The sound of weeping came more decidedly now upon the ears of Captain Heron.

CHAPTER CCIV.

EXPLAINS WILD'S VISIT TO THE BISHOP'S HOUSE, AND WHAT CAME OF IT.

MOST reluctantly are we compelled to leave Felix Heron in the midst of all those mysteries which had found a home at Whitcombe House, while we proceed now to detail some important movements of Jonathan Wild and the villanous Lord Warringdale.

We left Jonathan Wild at the Bishop's house, passing Captain Heron and Tom Ripon so very narrowly, that, had any accidental circumstance induced him to pause for a moment, he must have seen one or both of them.

It was fortunate that such was not the case; for although there can be very little doubt in the event of a personal contest between Heron and Jonathan Wild, which would be the victor, yet in the very confusion of the battle danger might have surrounded Heron of a character impossible to evade.

It was not at all probable that Jonathan Wild would have desired an interview with the Bishop's secretary if that person had been completely a stranger to him.

Such, however, was not the case. Wild knew perfectly well who and what he was.

The Bishop of Worcester was one of those good, easy kind of men, who are the subjects of the most transparent deceptions.

Anything approaching him with the external indications of piety or of repentance, was sure to receive a ready welcome.

This secretary of his, then, had belonged to a Catholic seminary at St. Omer, from whence he was expelled on account of his irregularities.

It suited, then, this person—whose name was Lejeune, and who, although of French parents, was born in England and spoke the language perfectly—to become a convert to the Anglican Church.

After some inquiry, he found out the most credulous of the whole bench of bishops, and made such an impression upon him that he became his secretary.

The story of Jonathan Wild's acquaintanceship with this man is very simple.

Wild was regularly in the commission of the Ministry for the purpose of hunting recusants, Jesuits, and Jacobins; and it was by the assistance of this apostate that Wild was enabled to hunt many innocent persons to destruction, whose only crime consisted in the fact that they adhered to the religion of their forefathers and of their consciences.

Now Jonathan Wild was perfectly well aware that he had said quite enough to Edith in the

coach when he mistook her for another person, to let her and Heron know how important the Bishop of Worcester's testimony would be in regard to the marriage of Amelia Staunton with the late Earl of Whitcombe.

Wild's errand, then, was to call upon his old associate Lejeune, and consult with him what was best to be done.

Hence was it that he had passed so narrowly Captain Heron and Tom Ripon, and little suspecting the importance of the interview which the former had already had with the Bishop, he appeared before the eyes of Lejeune as not the most welcome visitor in the world.

"Ah! I perceive," said Wild, as he seated himself without ceremony, "you would rather not see me now that you are secretary to a Bishop; but I never forget old friends—ha! ha!—nor old foes either!"

"I am sure," said Lejeune—who had an un-

fortunate obliquity of vision, and seemed at that moment to be looking quite over Wild's shoulder, instead of looking into his face—"I'm sure I'm always glad to see you, Mr. Wild; and if I can be of any service to you, I shall be very happy."

"You'll never be happy," said Wild, "so long as you keep that hang-dog expression of yours."

"Sir?"

"Oh, don't mind me; you know I'm a plain speaker."

"If," said Lejeune, "it came to a question of expressions, I don't think that of Mr. Jonathan Wild would be esteemed the most desirable in the world."

"Bravo!" said Jonathan; "you're improving. "But elegant and handsome as we both are, that gratifying subject is not what I came to talk about."

"What then?"

"I'm afraid the Bishop will be called upon to

try to remember something which a friend of mine would rather he forgot."

"What do you mean? You speak in riddles, Jonathan Wild."

"I'll be quite plain with you. A good many years ago, some twenty or more we will say, the Bishop—then the incumbent of an ordinary living—solemnised—I believe that is the word in use for the every-day folly—a marriage between two persons, one of whom was a man of rank, and the other a young girl of respectable but poor parentage. The man of rank, in a short time, began to think he had played the fool."

The Bishop's secretary made a hideous grimace.

"I understand you. You mean to say 'So he had?'"

Lejeune nodded.

"Well; we and the man of rank are all agreed upon that point. He wanted to contract a semi-political marriage with one of the great families of the kingdom; but this poor young person, whom he had wedded for her beauty, was in the way."

"Of course," said the secretary. "It's a very old story, Mr. Wild."

"Probably. But it is a true one in this instance, and one which will be repeated over and over again, in many instances to come."

"Oh, there's no doubt about that. And what did the man of rank do?"

"He shrunk from murder."

"Ah, some people are weak-minded!"

"But he disposed of the young person from humble life, in one of those receptacles for people who are decidedly in the way in the open air, and in the great world, and which are called asylums."

"For the insane?"

"Just so. She was insane enough to be very much in the way of the man of rank!"

"I see."

"Of course you do. If she had been sensible enough in the first instance to consent to become his mistress, he would in due time have pensioned her off handsomely, and she might have acquired a character of vestal purity, and lived in the greatest respectability, but she must needs insist upon being married, and she took the consequences."

"Foolish young person!" said the secretary.

"Oh, decidedly silly!"

"But, my dear friend, Mr. Wild, that being the end of the story, what do you come to me about?"

"Oh, you shall soon hear. The man of rank gave out that she was dead; and your patron, the Bishop of Worcester, who had married them, was far too simple-minded to doubt it for a moment, and therefore said nothing to the second marriage of the man of rank with a titled lady, heiress to a large fortune, and belonging to one of the first families in the kingdom."

"What then?" cried Lejeune, with some asperity in his tones.

"By the first marriage there was a son."

"Oh!"

"You begin to see?"

"I think I do."

"That son was obstinate and healthy. The man of rank by no means acknowledged him, but he gave him into the care of a personal friend, and the boy had grown up to manhood; and such a

kind of manhood, too, as makes him a—very—troublesome—customer—indeed."

"Oh!" said the secretary.

"Moreover," added Wild, as he stretched out his feet and rapped one of his boots with the riding-whip he carried in his hand—"moreover, this troublesome customer, by one means and another, has become acquainted with some of these particulars I have now narrated to you; and he is very likely to call on your patron, the Bishop, just to ask him if he remembers solemnising such a marriage as I speak of."

"Ah!" said the secretary.

"Now what would you do, Lejeune, in such an emergency?"

"Is that all, Mr. Wild?"

"Nearly so. I may as well, however, mention that there is a son by the second marriage likewise, and he claims the titles and estates. The only obstacle to his possession of them being this son by the first marriage, who knows too much, and who is a very obstinate fellow."

"I think I do see now. The son by the second marriage is a friend of yours?"

"You have said it."

"Then I must say it appears perfectly extraordinary to me, Mr. Wild, that a man of your ready resources does not dispose at once of the very troublesome fellow, and so put an end to the latter difficulty."

"I thought you would say that," cried Wild, as he rose and paced the room to and fro, slashing his boots with the riding-whip as he did so—"I thought you would say that; but there have been difficulties, and there are reasons which I cannot very well explain to you. Tell me what you think had best be done in order to make the Bishop of Worcester forget entirely he ever performed this marriage between the man of rank and the poor young girl whom he believes to be dead?"

"Believes to be dead?"

"Of course he believes it, since the man of rank told him so."

"Then she is not dead?"

"Bah! what matters? I care not if she be or not. I have ceased long ago to trouble myself about her. She is scarcely in question; and if she be not actually dead at this present moment, she can be so at any hour when it shall be desirable for her to leave this troublous world, and seek the repose of another—where, I suppose, there will be neither Lejeunes nor Jonathan Wilds admitted."

"You're quite profane, Mr. Wild; and holding such a situation as I do, I really ought not to listen to you."

Wild laughed hideously.

"Come, come, Lejeune; we understand each other. I ask you what is to be done to make the Bishop forget?"

A strange, blanched look came over the face of the secretary, and he shook his head.

"No, Mr. Wild—no—not on any consideration. I think I understand what you mean; but the next Bishop of Worcester may be provided with a secretary, or, if not, he may take some exception to me. No, Mr. Wild, unless the Bishop actually forgets, I don't see how it is possible to make him do so."

"What's that?" cried Wild, as a bell rung sharply at this moment.

"It's the Bishop's bell."

"For you?"

"Probably. Wait a moment, and we shall soon know."

The door of the secretary's room was opened in about a minute, and a servant announced, respectfully, that the Bishop wished to see the secretary.

"Pump him," said Wild, "and I'll wait for you."

"Do what?"

"Pshaw! You were not always so particular about phrases, Lejeune. Find out, in some circuitous sneaking way, particularly your own, whether he does or does not recollect the marriage I speak of."

"You're very plain, Mr. Wild!"

"I always was," said Wild, with a horrible grimace. "I am plain with friends, but rugged with enemies. Distrust me when I'm civil, Lejeune; but not when I say to you just what I think, and do not mince my phrases or study my words."

"Well, well!" interrupted the secretary; "we know all about that. But how can I pump the Bishop, as you elegantly term it, unless I know the names of the parties?"

"I will tell you, then. The man of rank was the late Earl of Whitcombe, who at the time of the marriage was called by the title always in use by the eldest son of the family, and heir presumptive to the earldom—namely, Lord Warringdale."

"And the name of the young person in humble life?" interposed the secretary.

"Amelia Staunton."

"And——" cried the secretary, as he bent a look full in Wild's face, but seemed in reality to be looking out at the window.

"And what?"

"What is all this to me?"

"My excellent friend, I quite forgot. It's a thousand pounds, if the Bishop forgets. But go; your right reverend patron will be impatient."

"Not at all; he is never impatient: but I will go, and hope to bring you some news, although I must be very cautious that in trying to discover if he recollects or not, I do not awaken the very memory we wish to slumber for ever."

"You're a clever fellow, Lejeune, and I will wait for you here. Have you got any brandy?"

"Certainly not, Mr. Wild; recollect where you are."

The secretary left the room, and Wild, as was always the custom with him, when he waited anywhere alone, put the back of his chair against the wall, and kept a tolerably steady eye upon the door.

But we must leave Jonathan to his cogitations while we follow the secretary to the presence of the Bishop, whom he had no occasion—to use the phraseology of Wild—to pump, inasmuch as the subject of his recent conversation with Jonathan was the very one upon which the Bishop desired his presence.

Little did Jonathan Wild and the Bishop's secretary suspect that within that very hour Captain Heron himself had refreshed the memory of the Bishop upon the important subject in question, and had obtained from him all the promised satisfaction in his power.

The Bishop was sitting with his eyes closed, as was the custom with him when he looked back into the past, and was striving to recal, in all their *minutiæ*, circumstances which were slowly fading away from his memory.

Probably he saw, in his mind's eye, that little ancient church at Barnes, in which he had performed the ceremony of marriage between Felix Heron's father and mother.

Looking back through the vista of those long years, he probably saw the Earl of Whitcombe standing at the altar at the side of that victim whose union with him had led to nothing but desolation and despair.

The secretary stood for some few minutes within the apartment without being noticed by his reverend master, and it was only when he coughed slightly that the Bishop looked up and observed his presence.

"Oh, my good Lejeune," he said, "you are there!"

"Ever at your service, best of masters. I should have answered your summons sooner, but was at prayers."

"You are quite right, my good Lejeune; never neglect prayer for any earthly consideration."

"Ah, dear and reverend sir, I never will."

"I thought they said some one was with you."

"Yes, reverend sir. A friend of mine who calls now and then to join with me in pious exercises, and in beseeching blessings on all men"

"I am very glad to hear it," said the Bishop; "we live in a very irreligious, and I may almost say sacrilegious, age."

Lejeune uttered a dismal groan as his testimony to the truth of that statement.

"I have had," said the Bishop, "a singular visitor this morning. A young man has called here, with whose looks I must say I am very much prepossessed, and has wished me to look back into what records I may have of the past—or if I have no special records, into my memory—in order that I may bear testimony to a marriage solemnised by me long ago."

Lejeune fairly staggered. His face—usually the colour of indifferent parchment—became livid, and he was glad to hold by the back of a chair for support; for the idea came over him that the Bishop had, in some incomprehensible manner, overheard every word which had passed between him and Jonathan Wild.

"My good and pious Lejeune," said the Bishop, "you don't look at all well."

"Well! Oh, yes—that is—I—pump—brandy—Jonathan——"

"What?" said the Bishop, in intense surprise.

"I'm a little faint."

"My good Lejeune, I am very much afraid that you still cling to the idea that physical austerities are necessary to propitiate the goodwill of heaven. You are not strong, Lejeune; and you may depend that the good things of this life would not have been presented to us in such boundless profusion if they were not for our use. You shall have a glass of wine now, Lejeune, and then I shall want you to help me in this rather important matter."

The secretary was recovering. His first fright had passed away, but he was glad of the glass of wine which the Bishop rung for, since it helped to compose his spirits, and likewise gave a pause during which he had some time to think.

Thought, however, did not do much towards

clearing the confused faculties of the Bishop's secretary, for still he could not help reverting in imagination to the terrible idea that his right reverend master really knew something more of his interview with Jonathan Wild than was desirable.

After a few preliminary coughs he said, "Hem! —dear and reverend sir, I have no doubt—that is to say, I have a great hope that you will be able to assist those who are deserving in this transaction."

"I have no doubt I can."

"Hem!—and—and—may I venture to ask when you will set about it?"

"This day."

"This—this very day?"

"Yes, Lejeune, this very day I will set about looking for my diary of the proceedings of the year in question, so that when the young man, in whose fortunes I confess I feel much interested, calls to-morrow——"

"To-morrow?"

"Really, my dear Lejeune, I cannot comprehend you. You seem to me to be strangely disturbed, and you repeat my words as though your mind was in a state of great pre-occupation."

"Oh, no, no, dear and reverend friend!—oh, no!"

"Well, as I say, the young man, who I verily believe, from the air of truth and of candour that was about him, to be the son of that first marriage of the late Earl of Whitcombe, will be here to-morrow at about this hour, and I hope then to be able to hand to him the memoranda he requires."

"That will be a great and good work."

"I hope so. At all events, my good friend, it will be a just and equitable work, and one that I, of all men, should not shrink from for an instant. But I am very remiss—oh, I am very remiss."

"In what, dear sir?"

"You said you had a pious friend with you."

"Yes. Oh, yes."

"He is probably waiting?"

"He is."

"Go to him, then, at once—go to him. He longs, no doubt, for some more of that secret religious communion of soul with soul, which, to my thinking, is the only thing in this world which can give us a foretaste of a blessed immortality. Go—go at once!"

"With your kind and gracious leave, dear sir, I will."

"Do, and take with you this book, as a present from me to your friend. It is a copy of 'Pious Meditations addressed to the Pure Thinker.' Take it."

"Oh, he will be rejoiced! I take my leave. Bless you, dear friend and spiritual guide!"

"Bless you, too, my good Lejeune!"

————

CHAPTER CCV.

JONATHAN WILD CONSULTS UPON NEW INIQUITIES WITH LORD WARRINGDALE.

"WELL?" cried Jonathan Wild, as the Bishop's secretary made his appearance in the room where he, Wild, had been waiting. "Well, what's the news?"

"Wonderful!"

"Stuff!"

"It is wonderful stuff, then! The Bishop knows all about the affair!"

"Confusion!"

"And he has seen, and is mightily smitten with, the young man who is the son of the first marriage of the late Earl of Whitcombe."

"What? He seen him? He seen Captain Felix Heron, the notorious highwayman of Epping Forest?"

"Oh, indeed!" said the secretary. "So that is the man, is it, who has proved such a very— troublesome—customer—a very—obstinate—fellow, eh?"

"I don't mind owning it," said Wild; "and should scarcely have gone away without telling you. That is indeed the man."

"Then—indeed and in truth—the marriage between this Amelia Staunton and the late Earl being perfectly legal, Captain Heron, the well-known highwayman, is Earl of Whitcombe?"

"He is."

"Ah!"

The Bishop's secretary wore a curious expression on his face; and Jonathan Wild, stepping close up to him, touched him slightly on the arm as he said, "I, too, thought of all that."

Lejeune started.

"All what?"

"All that now engages your thoughts."

"But——"

"Pho! pho! It is quite natural. You ask yourself whether, after all, it would not be safer to make terms with the real heir than the false one, but I tell you no! If that were the game to play, it would have been played by me long ago. It won't answer, my friend."

"Why?"

"I will tell you. Captain Felix Heron is one of those men who would not give one pound to be placed, wrongfully, in the possession of three."

"Well?"

"But if he thinks himself entitled to the three, he will not see that he ought to employ gentlemen like you and me to give him his own. Lord Warringdale, on the other hand, will expend one-half the estate, if necessary, to secure the other half."

"I see."

"Of course you do."

"Then I am with you."

"Of course you are."

"The Bishop has seen the young man, then, and he is to come again to-morrow for the proofs of the legal marriage of Amelia Staunton with the late Earl of Whitcombe."

"To-morrow?"

"Yes; at this hour, or about this hour."

"Good! You have already earned your thousand pounds, old friend."

"Have I so?"

"Even so have you. I, too, will be here to-morrow; and I will take good care that Heron, the highwayman, makes but a rapid journey from this house to Newgate, and then from Newgate to Tyburn tree. I should like if my presence here, and that of Lord Warringdale likewise, could be managed with the good will and cognisance of the Bishop."

"I have a plan, Jonathan."

"You have?"

CAPTAIN HERON RECOVERS A LONG-LOST AND PRICELESS TREASURE.

Presented Gratis with No. 91, of the New Edition of The Captive; or, the Robbers of Epping Forest.

"Yes, a simple one, because it will be played off upon a simple person."

"You mean the Bishop?"

"I do."

"Well, the plan? the plan? What is it?"

"The great delight of the Bishop is in healing family feuds and family dissensions, and in inducing people who have an idea of doing wrong, to turn aside from that path and do what is right."

"Well?"

"I can, acting on that little peculiarity of his, induce him easily to send for Lord Warringdale."

"Ah, I see, now!"

"And Lord Warringdale can bring you with him as his friend, Mr. Smith—a professional friend!"

"Excellent!"

"Do you like the plan?"

"Amazingly. Set about it, and let me know of its success as soon as possible. I will be at my Lord Warringdale's lodgings until a late hour to-night, and shall expect a communication from you."

"Which you will assuredly have, Mr. Wild, and I hope my thousand pounds will not be forgotten."

"Make yourself easy upon that score. Good bye for the present. I am inclined to think—ha! ha!—quite inclined to think that this is a good morning's work! Ha! ha!"

Jonathan Wild left the Bishop's house in a frame of mind that had more certainty and contentment about it than had for a long time past belonged to any of his thoughts, in which Captain Heron was concerned.

The villain thought that the fate of Heron was sealed, and that there could be no possibility now of his escape from capture and death.

We shall see.

The secretary of the Bishop, when he was alone, spent some time in consideration, during which the original idea which had come over him, and which had been so cleverly divined by Jonathan Wild, namely, of making terms with Felix Heron, for a few minutes returned to him.

But with it returned all Wild's reasoning upon the subject.

"No, no," he said, "I see that would not do. If I assist a man into the wrongful possession of honours and estates I have ever a claim upon him through his fears, whereas the rightful possessor gives me no such power over him. I will help Jonathan Wild and my Lord Warringdale."

Having arrived at this decision, the secretary again sought the Bishop, and found him rummaging among some old documents and papers.

"Ah, reverend sir, I fear I intrude!"

"Not at all, Lejeune—not at all."

"I came, with all the humility possible, to hazard a kind of suggestion."

"What is it, my friend?"

"It is so sad a thing to see two brothers at war with each other, that if anything could be done to make peace between them, and heal the discord that rages, it would surely be an acceptable work in the sight of heaven."

"Very—oh, very acceptable, Lejeune."

"Then, reverend sir, if this young man, the son of the first marriage, would forgive his brother, Lord Warringdale, all the wrongs done him, and if Lord Warringdale would repent him of the evil

he had committed, what a gracious thing it would be to see the brothers hand in hand!"

"It would—it would. But, but—dear me, how came you to know so much about it?"

"Ah, reverend friend and pastor, did you not tell me?"

"I—I did not think—I did not fancy I had said quite so much as you seem to know."

"How else could I know?"

"Ah, to be sure—that is true. I must have told you, and forgotten. I of course must have told you, and I rejoice at your happy and Christian suggestion."

"I was certain you would."

"How shall I carry it out?"

"Suppose you were, dear sir, to commission me to seek out this Lord Warringdale and ask him to come to you to-morrow, say one hour before the—the—other son is to be here: then you would have time to exhort him."

"Yes, yes. Capital!"

"To exhort him to repentance."

"Let it be so. Let it be done, Lejeune. I will receive Lord Warringdale to-morrow at one o'clock, say; and I will show him my memoranda concerning his father's first marriage, and I will urge him to do what is right and just by his elder brother. Seek him and bring him here, my good Lejeune, and let me assure you you are about a work which you will receive your reward for."

"I shall, I hope."

"In eternity!"

The secretary rather shrank from this termination to the Bishop's speech. It was the reward in this world he looked for; and he would rather the transaction was forgotten when he should come to balance his accounts with eternity.

He hastened from the presence of the simple-minded Bishop, and made up his mind, when the dusk of the evening should serve him, to seek Jonathan Wild at the lodgings of Lord Warringdale, in St. James's Street.

The remainder of that eventful day, we are aware, was spent by Captain Heron partly at the inn of the "Golden Cross," which he left with such precipitation; and now we will seek him at his father's mansion, where he was so mysteriously received.

The repast which Captain Heron had partaken of had wonderfully renovated his strength, and he felt an ardent desire to continue the strange conversation which at first had struck him with so much surprise in the deserted mansion.

There was a tone and a manner about the expressions used by his invisible friend that came very close to his, Captain Heron's, heart. He longed to hear again those tones, that seemed as if they evoked within him some tender recollections, to which, while he could give them no name, he clung with a fondness he could not define.

"Speak to me further," he said. "Why am I thus questioned about the inmost secrets and feelings of my soul?"

"Because," replied the voice, "the questioner would fathom the depths of those feelings."

"It is strange," added Heron, "how I feel a secret and gentle compulsion to reply to you."

A deep sigh again sounded in the air.

"Speak to me again!—oh, speak to me again!" added Heron.

"Yes; upon one more theme."

"What is it?"

"The future of the man who calls himself Lord Warringdale."

"I do not comprehend."

"What would you do as regarded his fortunes if you were Earl of Whitcombe?"

"I should recollect that he was my father's son."

"And then?"

"Then I would forgive him."

"Oh, noble heart! Oh, noble heart!"

Captain Heron now began to be conscious that the large saloon in which he was, and in which he had dined or supped—let him call the meal he had partaken of by which name he chose—was gradually growing darker.

At first, Heron had some difficulty in finding out what was the cause of this diminution of light in the saloon, but upon looking up to the chandelier he soon discovered the cause in the fact that the wax-lights in it had all been cut into short pieces, none of which were likely to last above one hour of time.

Captain Heron rose from the chair on which he had been sitting at the table.

Then the voice again addressed him.

"In light or in darkness you are equally safe. Heed not the passing away of the partial illumination of this saloon: no hostile hand dare be raised here against the eldest son of the Earl of Whitcombe."

"I have no fear," said Felix Heron, "but I have much amazement; for I can well perceive that but few minutes must elapse before I shall again be left in darkness; and I would fain have remained in this house until to-morrow, if I could do so with peace and safety."

"In peace and in safety!" said the voice; "oh, remain!"

"But, it appears, in absolute darkness!" exclaimed Heron; and, as he spoke, the last of the thirty little ends of candles, which had lit up the magnificent chandelier, went out.

The darkness that fell upon the great saloon was most profound; and Captain Heron could well conceive that—by whatever agency that apartment had been lighted up for the special occasion—that same agency had been careful to close all the windows, both with their shutters and their curtains, so that no rays from the illumination should make their way, either into St. James's Street, or into the gardens at the back of the houses.

Hence, when the last light had expired, the vast saloon was like a cavern.

It was an artificial darkness only to be found within some of earth's caves, or created by man in consequence of the exclusion of that faint, wandering twilight which is never totally absent from any portion of the earth's surface.

Captain Heron moved a pace or two from the chair on which he had been seated; but he thought it would be as well to recover that chair again, as it happened to be a large one with ample arms; because in it he considered that he might pass the night with some degree of comfort.

Slowly he felt his way in the direction of the chair, but just as he touched its tall back, his eyes were attracted in another direction by a small, star-like light, which appeared about six feet or so from the floor, at a considerable distance from him.

Heron, as he gazed at this light—which was exceedingly minute, and sent but few and faint rays about it—thought that he could discover beneath it the dim outlines of a human form.

But of that he could not by any means feel sure; for imagination, under such circumstances, might well aid him to such a perception.

"Do I see you?" he cried; "or is it mere fancy, that, out of the darkness, shapes to my eyes a figure?"

"Be it fancy or reality," said the voice, "learn at least to respect the mystery and the obscurity in which one who wishes you well chooses to shroud himself."

"But, surely," cried Heron, "it is a sort of right prescriptive in human nature that one should feel at liberty to fathom such a mystery as this."

"Felix Heron," said the voice, sadly, "thou hast crossed this threshold and been made welcome; thou hast eaten and thou hast drank; and here thou may'st pass a night in safety and security. Be not ungrateful, but respect the secrets of thy friend and entertainer."

"I admit the justice of the appeal," said Heron, "and will hold by it. I will seek to know nothing, and to discover nothing, but what it may please you to impart to me."

"Follow! follow!"

"From this apartment would you lead me?"

"Ay—follow! follow!"

"Freely and willingly I place my life within your grasp—and yet I feel no fear; for in the voice that has addressed me in this mansion, there has ever been a something which has made me feel a sensation of rest and security—such as, since I became a man, and mingled with the strifes of the world, I never felt before."

"Follow! follow!" said the voice again; and this time the words seemed hardly capable of being uttered, from some earnest and deep emotion that came over the speaker.

Captain Heron did not hesitate a moment; indeed, as he spoke, he advanced in the direction of the little star-like light.

The light receded before him, and in a few seconds he became conscious that he had passed out of the saloon through some doorway different from that at which he had entered it.

He no longer trod upon the soft carpeting of that magnificent apartment, and by the cold, sharp feel, he fancied he walked over something like tesselated pavement.

Then, still preceded by the light, he passed through another doorway, and the moment he did so the door was closed upon him, and the star-like light disappeared.

But Captain Heron was not in darkness.

To his surprise he found himself in a small apartment, the walls of which were covered with book-cases, while each corner was adorned and set off by a full-length statue from the antique.

A rather small round table occupied the centre of this room, and drawn up close to it was a very wide and ample couch, upon which were heaped up a number of cushions, with rich silken coverings; and thrown carelessly among them, trailing partially upon the ground, was a magnificent and beautifully prepared lion's skin trimmed with costly velvet.

Captain Heron had a sort of intuitive perception that this apartment was intended to be his bed-chamber, and that couch the place on which he was to pass the night.

The accommodation was far from mean to one who had passed through the adventurous life that had been Captain Heron's for the last few years of his existence.

We have stated that this room was not in darkness, but the light which illumined it was a peculiar one.

On the round table in the centre stood a small hand-lantern, through the lens of which issued a broad, fan-shaped sheet of light.

This light fell upon the table and its contents, which appeared to consist of several papers and documents, and of one book, which was open and turned down upon its face.

Captain Heron approached this table and its contents with intense curiosity. He sat down upon the ample couch, and casting his eyes upon the papers and documents before him, he saw one above all others.

On that one paper was written the following words:—"It may not be possible to forget, but there is much to forgive."

From the appearance of the writing upon this paper, it seemed to have been but recently executed; and upon lifting it, Captain Heron saw immediately beneath it a document, which transfixed all his attention, and made him forget for the moment where he was, and all the strange mysteries and excitements of Whitcombe House.

The document was a formal certificate of the marriage of Amelia Staunton with Lord Warringdale, afterwards Earl of Whitcombe, at the little church of Barnes, therein stated to be a chapelry of St. Paul's, and the whole was duly signed by the present Bishop of Worcester.

"Ah," cried Captain Heron, " beneficent being, be you whom you may, you have discovered for me a document I searched for long in vain. I hold my birthright and my name now within my grasp. Speak, oh, speak to me again, and say to whom I am indebted for this great happiness."

"Peace! peace!" said the voice, sadly. " It is retribution. Look further, oh, Felix!"

"What!" cried Heron; " can it be that I shall find further confirmation of my dearest hopes?"

"Look! oh, look!"

It would seem that it was the earnest desire of the mysterious and invisible being who thus held strange converse with Felix Heron, that he should continue his search or investigation among the papers which were on the table before him.

"Be it so," said Heron. " I obey you."

It was with trembling eagerness that he now looked at the next paper which presented itself to his gaze.

That one was scarcely less important than the one which had preceded it.

It was a certificate of the baptism, in an obscure church in Essex, of a child named "Felix," and said to be the son of Amelia, Lady Warringdale, and Stephen Clare de Warringdale, commonly called Lord Warringdale.

"I am saved!" cried Felix Heron. " Henceforth I am, indeed and in truth, the veritable Earl of Whitcombe!"

"The veritable Earl of Whitcombe!" said the mysterious voice; and at that moment the light went out.

Felix Heron was in profound darkness. But it was strange that notwithstanding all the mysteries that were about him he felt no fear.

CHAPTER CCVI.

TOM RIPON VISITS HIS MOTHER AND DISCOVERS A SECRET AND A PLOT.

WHEN Tom Ripon left for a brief space of time, as he thought and meant it to be, the company of his friend and master, Captain Heron, he had no idea of the consequences that were in reality to flow from his projected visit to his mother and to his father-in-law, the Reverend Mortification Ripon, who had paid the Ripon family the compliment of adopting its name.

Perhaps, though, after all, that compliment was a doubtful one, and would never have been thought of, if the patrimonial name of the reverend gentleman had not became so badly odorous that the desirability of changing it was patent.

But be this as it may, our business now is to follow Tom Ripon on his expedition to Star Court, St. Martin's Lane.

An ordinary person would, on the occasion of this visit, have been content to walk in at the door of Mrs. Ripon's little miscellaneous repository, but Tom, as the reader is aware, was not an ordinary person.

" I should like to come on the old gal at unawares," said Tom to himself.

This was, therefore, an idea which Tom set about realizing as best he might.

Many of the houses in and about Star Court were in a sad state of dilapidation—so sad, indeed, that even destitute poverty feared to inhabit them, lest the tread of even a light footstep should have the effect of being just those few pounds too much for the stability of the building.

It is, as the proverb says, "the last feather that breaks the camel's back;" and really some of the houses in that group of courts about St. Martin's Lane seemed only to want the mystical feather's weight to bring them down in one rush of ruins.

"If," said Tom, " I could only get into one of the old houses, I would soon make my way to the attic windows of the old gal's crib."

The difficulty was not insurmountable.

Tom tried several doors; they were all fast; and although they were only on the lock, he was not in possession of the requisite means to open them.

Then Tom adopted another expedient.

Some of the houses had little narrow areas, with dilapidated wooden railings in front of them, and into these areas there looked small windows, now, however, quite opaque with dust thickened into mud with many rains, and then baked into cement by the heat of summer.

"Here we go," said Tom Ripon, as he descended one of these small areas.

The space in which Tom found himself was very small indeed, not much larger than sufficed to hold him.

" Now, for the window!" said Tom

There was no real appearance of glass about the kitchen window of the house into which he wished to penetrate, but Tom knew that glass must be there.

" Here goes !" he added.

Wrapping his cap carefully round one hand, he made a good forward blow, and the crash that followed was sufficiently satisfactory.

A pane of glass was gone.

Tom put in his hand and felt for the fastening of the window. It was a very ordinary one, and in a very few minutes more he was in the kitchen of one of the old condemned houses of the court that was exactly at the back of Star Court.

" It's only a scramble over the tiles," said Tom, " and I shall get to the old gal's attics."

It was not everybody who would have liked to make a dreary, lonely way through that shut-up house, but Tom had few fears either of the natural or of the supernatural world.

As for the insecurity of the house as a structure, Tom never thought of it.

" Hilloa ! What's that ?"

Tom paused when he got into the old house, for there came upon his ears a scuffling sound as of many feet.

" What is it ? Hoy ! Hoy ! Who are you ?"

The scuffling noise of feet died away ; and as it did so, it was accompanied by some squeaking tones, which at once opened Tom's eyes to the truth.

" Rats !" said Tom.

They were rats. The old, dilapidated houses were infested with them.

How these vermin live in such places is a mystery. Is it upon each other ?

Tom had no affection for rats, and he almost gave up his purpose with the knowledge that the place was so infested.

Indeed, Tom had one foot and one arm out at the kitchen window when he paused, and almost held his breath as the sound of voices in the narrow court came upon his ears—the sound of voices that he knew.

" It's Lord Warringdale," said Tom,—" and that rascal, the Reverend Mortification."

Tom was right. The footsteps that paused quite close to the wretched, dingy area in which Tom Ripon was crouching, and the voices he heard, belonged, most unquestionably, to the two persons he had just named.

What could they be doing there ?

What could two men, moving in such widely-different spheres of existence, want with each other ?—or, rather, why had the proud, haughty, insolent Warringdale stooped to hold a conference with a man whom he must despise, in one of those dingy and despicable courts close to St. Martin's Church ?

Tom was as still as the night-wind on that evening, which had not a breath to waste on those dreary courts, where crime had set up its ensigns, and where the free air of heaven scarcely could be said to find a home.

Still, with that one foot upon the window-sill, and still with that one arm grasping the casement-frame, Tom listened—not to the rats now—not to the scampering, nor to the squeaking, but to the tones of those human voices, which were much more noxious, and full of evil purposes.

It so happened that a short question from Lord Warringdale, and its reply from the Reverend Mortification Ripon, had occurred at the moment they paused exactly in front of the area, so that Tom had heard both the voices, and had no doubt about the identity of either.

" No eaves-droppers—are you certain, sir ?" said Warringdale.

" Yea, I say none," replied the Reverend Mortification Ripon.

" That is well. The place sounds and feels lonely."

" Yea, of a surety is it ; and I can say most truly that—for the consideration your lordship has been pleased to name—it would content me much to do any service that may be in my humble power—ahem ! hem !"

" The service is one you can easily perform."

" And the reward ?"

" One hundred guineas."

" One hundred ?"

" Nay—that should be a sufficient sum for the service I require of you, which is rather one of secrecy than of an active nature."

" One hundred ?"

" Plague take your avarice !" cried Lord Warringdale, with considerable irritability of tone. " It shall not be one hundred, nor two, that shall stand in the way of making you contented with the job."

" Hem ! Then yea, and truly, if it be all the same to your lordship——"

" Hush ! Not even here—where you say there are no ears to listen to us—would I have you pronounce my name."

" Yea, then, I will not ; but I was about to say that the troubles and the difficulties of the affair, be it what it may, do not appear to me one-half so great, when two hundred pounds are forth-coming, as they did with only one."

" Then say two."

" Yea, then, I will."

" Now, listen to me, so that you may fully comprehend what I require of you."

" Yea, will I."

" You are tall and thin, and, for a time—that is to say, for half an hour or so—you can hold yourself upright, and with the carriage of a young man."

" Yea, I can."

" And, in a befitting costume, you might manage to pass—with those not very intimate with him—as Captain Felix Heron, the highwayman."

The Reverend Mortification Ripon gave a very uneasy start at this suggestion.

Tom Ripon pricked up his ears, and was determined that not the slightest word of the conversation should escape him.

All the desire which Tom Ripon had started with to play some boyish trick upon his mother and the Reverend Mortification Ripon, became at once absorbed in the real, serious interest of this dialogue, in which the name of Captain Felix Heron was so strangely introduced.

" Come, sir !" added Lord Warringdale. " Come, sir ! do you decline a part in the little comedy, or not ?"

" Comedy ?"

" Yes ; I say comedy. You do not suppose, for one moment, that I would trust a man like you to make it a tragedy ?"

" Tragedy !"

" Why do you echo my words ? Is it possible that your craven spirit is cowed at the very mention of the name of Heron ?"

"Yea; he is a dangerous man!"

"Yes, to meet in arms; but you are not asked to do so."

"What then?"

"It is as I tell you, but a comedy. I will so contrive, that you shall be brought to a place under some trees——"

"Under some trees?"

"Yes, under some trees; where you will see, lying, a man who will, perhaps, pretend to be dead."

"Pretend to be dead?"

"I have said so."

"Pretend?"

It was tolerably evident that the Reverend Mortification Ripon had his suspicions that what Lord Warringdale called a "pretence," would be much more likely a reality.

Tom thought so, too.

There was a rather ominous pause of a few

seconds. It was Lord Warringdale who broke through it, by saying, in tones of well-assumed coolness, "It is tolerably evident that the sum of two hundred pounds is not of sufficient importance to you to induce a compliance with my wishes."

"Nay, nay!"

"Good night, sir!"

"Yea, good my lord, you are in a wondrous hurry. I will do it."

"You will?"

"Look upon it as done. Only tell me the way to set about it, and yea, as the Psalmist says——"

"Stuff! Don't talk nonsense!"

"Yea, it is surprising the objection that everybody has to hear what the Psalmist has to say."

After this little passing reflection upon the perversity of human nature, the Reverend Mortification Ripon listened intently to what Lord Warringdale had to say in elucidation of the little job he had on hand.

"You must know," said Warringdale, "that it is necessary you should endeavour, as much as it may be in your power, to imitate the gait and general appearance of Captain Felix Heron, the notorious highwayman."

"I will."

"It shall be my care to provide you with the requisite disguise, which you shall put on at my lodgings, in St. James's Street; and then I will conduct you, in safety and in secrecy, to where you will find, lying, as I have said, in a wood, an apparently dead man."

"A real one?"

"Well, real or apparent, it will make no difference to you."

"I don't know that; for, as the Psalmist——"

"Nonsense! In a word, I want you, in the dress of Captain Heron, and having in every possible particular his appearance, to be taken for the person who has killed the man."

"Me? Me?" said the Reverend Mortification Ripon, in defiance of grammar. "Me taken?"

"I do not mean apprehended, by that word taken."

"Oh!"

"But I do mean that you should be seen; and that then you should fly from the spot."

"Fly from the spot!" said the Reverend Mortification, as he moved his long arms in a flapping sort of way, as though he were practising how they would serve him in lieu of wings.

"Yes. You will wear the suit of highwayman's clothes entirely over your ordinary apparel, so that the moment you get out of sight of those who will see you, and fancy that in you they will recognise Captain Heron, the highwayman, you can slip off the disguise and dispose of it where you please."

"I see—yea, I see!"

"Of course, you do. You can, then, from the moment you have got rid of the disguise, appear in your own proper person, without the least danger."

"Yea, I can! Two hundred pounds?"

"Two hundred."

"Done!"

"Come with me, then."

Lord Warringdale and the Reverend Mortification Ripon rapidly left the spot.

Tom was rather bewildered.

"What does all this mean?" he said to himself. "It is danger to the Captain; but I don't very well understand it. A dead body, and old Mortification disguised among some trees. What does it all mean?"

Tom could not make it out at all.

But although Tom Ripon found it rather difficult thoroughly to comprehend what Lord Warringdale meant by those mysterious instructions he had given to the Reverend Mortification Ripon, he had no doubt at all about what he ought to do.

That was to acquaint Captain Heron with all that he had so providentially overheard.

"Yes," said Tom, "I will be off at once and tell the Captain. Who knows but he will understand it better than I do?"

Tom thought he would have no difficulty in finding Heron by going to the "Golden Cross Inn;" and giving up completely his original idea of vexing his mother and Mortification by some unexpected appearance, he got out of the area of the dismal house in the court, and ran all the way to the "Golden Cross," and as the distance was very short, Tom was soon close to the inn.

A crowd of people was on the steps, and various loud voices were descanting upon some transaction which Tom thought—as he had already been fortunate in what he had paid attention to on that evening—he might as well listen to.

"A cold-blooded murder!" said one man.

"Yes," said another; "and if it be true that the fellow was a notorious highwayman, I only hope that I shall see him swing for it."

"What's the matter?" asked Tom, of a lad about his own age, who was gaping at the house.

"Oh, it's a murder!"

"Who did it?"

The reply was on the lips of the boy, when a harsh voice yelled out, "Seize that lad there! A guinea to the first person who lays hold of him!"

Tom did not wait to ascertain who was the speaker, but darting between two men, and then under a cart that was at rest close to the kerbstone, he was off, and in two minutes had made his way to the nest of courts at the back of St. Martin's Church, where he felt himself tolerably safe.

"What has happened now?" said Tom to himself, as he rubbed his forehead, with an idea of quickening his wits by the process.

But Tom was all abroad about the events of the night; and although he seemed quite convinced, in his own mind, that it was no longer prudent to seek Captain Heron at the "Golden Cross," yet he knew not where else to light upon him.

"I ought to go to Epping," said Tom. "But! —but——"

Tom was right—he ought to go to Epping; but he could not quite make up his mind to leave London without finding out—if such were possible—something more of the transaction between Lord Warringdale and the Reverend Mortification.

This idea brought Tom back to his original notion of going to his mother's house, and, by some means, effecting an entrance into it.

That he could still do this by the roof, as he had originally projected, Tom had no reasonable doubt.

All he assuredly had to do was to get down that area again, and defy the rats, and make his way through the condemned house and out on to its roof, and so scramble to the roof of that house in the occupation of Mrs. Ripon.

"I will do it," said Tom. "Perhaps I shall find out really what it all means before I go back to the forest, and then the news will be worth ten times as much as I can only tell now."

Tom Ripon was a person of action, and even as he spoke he made his way down that area again, and through the still open casement that led to the lower regions of the house he made an entrance.

Then Tom heard the scuffling noise of the feet of the rats, as they again fled before the human intruder into that region which had been so long their own.

But Tom did not pause now. He knew perfectly well what those sounds meant, and although he could not be said to be wholly indifferent to the circumstance that he had to make his way through an army of the reptiles, yet he would not give up his expedition on their account.

Tom clapped his hands together, and made various wild and unearthly noises with his mouth, in order to scare the rats from his path.

The scampering and the squeaking that ensued let Tom see that he was so far successful.

At all events, the vermin did not attack him, which possibly they might, had he not seemed to take the initiative in offensive operations.

It was a great relief, however, to the boy, when he had fairly ascended the dull, gloomy old flight of steps that led from the lower regions of that deserted house to the passage.

Tom wiped the drops of perspiration from his brow as he said, "I don't think I'll come back this way."

Who knows? The rats might hold a consultation and lay in wait for him, should he venture to return among them.

"Oh, dear, no!" added Tom. "You may have it all your own way now, and the rain and the wind will come in upon you from the open kitchen window now. You don't catch me down there again!"

Tom's eyes had got a little accustomed to the darkness of the old house, as those of prisoners who have been for long periods confined in dark dungeons are said to do.

And as Tom, with this more accustomed power of vision, peered down into the abyss-like place from which he had just emerged, he was at first puzzled to account for a phenomenon which presented itself in the darkness to his observation.

There seemed to be a multitude of little sparks of a phosphorescent character,—although Tom Ripon did not call them by such a name; and these sparks seemed to be dancing over and about each other in the wildest state of confusion.

Tom considered for a few moments, and then clapping his hands together, he cried out, "I know what it is now—I know what it is now! It's the rats' eyes!"

CHAPTER CCVII.

TOM RIPON ARRIVES AT A BETTER COMPREHENSION OF THE PLOT BETWEEN LORD WARRINGDALE AND THE REVEREND MORTIFICATION.

If our friend Tom Ripon had had any doubt whatever concerning the character of the little luminous spots he saw in the lower regions of that house, such doubt would have been dispelled by their instantaneously vanishing when he clapped his hands loudly.

"Oh, yes," said Tom, "it's the rats' eyes, and no mistake! I dare say now they're expecting me to come back, and then they'll make supper and breakfast of me, I do believe. I should like to make believe I'm coming."

Some hundreds of the luminous eyes again appeared, and from the position which some of them occupied, it was evident that an advanced guard from the army of rats was beginning to creep up the staircase.

"They mean to be after me through the house," said Tom. "I wish I'd anything to throw at them."

Tom felt in his pockets, but he only had there the usual collection of odds and ends which he was in the habit of carrying with him.

A four-bladed knife, a number of nicely coiled-up little bits of string, three or four pistol bullets, which Ogle had given him at different times, some chesnuts and oak-apples from Epping Forest, and such like matters, made up the contents of Tom's pockets, so that he had nothing of a very formidable character about him to throw at the rats.

There might, however, be something in the old house; for the idea of being chased, possibly right up to the roof, by the vermin, was distasteful indeed.

Tom turned his attention to the passage, looking about him as well as he could in the darkness, and feeling right and left if there were any portable articles which would answer his purpose.

He had just concluded that his search would be in vain, when he nearly tripped over something which lay upon the floor close to the outer door, and upon examination Tom found that something to be a long iron bar, which, no doubt, was the fastening on the inner side of the door, but which had rotted away from its place, and fallen into the passage.

"That'll do," said Tom, as he picked it up. "I'm coming, my dears; you shall eat me up as soon as you like. I dare say I shall last you a week, if you don't quarrel over me. I'm coming!"

When Tom reached the head of the stairs again, he was startled for a moment to see that a large body of the rats was actually half-way up, so that his notion of being actually chased through the house by the noxious vermin did not seem altogether so wild a one.

"Below, there!" said Tom.

He flung the iron bar down with an awful clatter.

The scampering and squealing that ensued was prodigious; and in the course of a few seconds the dense body of rats had taken to flight, hiding and burrowing, no doubt, in every available nook and cranny of the basement of that deserted house.

"That'll do," said Tom. "I fancy I've got rid of you all; and now I'll go and look after the Reverend Mortification, who, after all, is worse than any of you; for it's your natures to be nasty vermin, and he's only so just because he wants to be."

Tom had a full conviction that he had scattered his enemies below; but still, the higher he ascended in the condemned house, the better pleased he was to feel that he was the further removed from the haunts of the rats.

The stairs leading up to the first-floor of the ancient residence creaked ominously beneath his tread; and, perhaps for the first time, Tom began to have a notion that the roof—by which he purposed to reach his mother's house in Star Court—was not the safest in the world.

One stair made so suggestive a creak, as he trod upon it, that Tom reached out his hand to clutch by the balustrade.

He did get hold of it—damp and clammy as it was—but it nearly proved fatal to him; for about a couple of yards of it came away in his grasp;

and he was nearly falling right down, perhaps among his old acquaintances, the rats, in a manner which—although it would have given them again considerable alarm—might have crippled him, and left him to die by inches—as the saying is—alone and uncared for in that wretched place.

But Tom was light and agile.

He shrunk back from the broken balustrade until he touched the wall, and being then at the strongest part of the staircase, he found a better support; so that after waiting for a few minutes, and finding that the house was not actually coming down about his ears, the adventurous boy slowly proceeded.

But Tom made up his mind that, come what might, he would not return into the open air by that route.

"I'll get out by the old gal's shop, somehow," he said; "and if I can only find out what that rascal Lord Warringdale meant he was to give old Mortification two hundred pounds for, I shan't mind all the trouble."

Tom was better pleased, as he ascended the house, to find that the ominous creaking of the staircases ceased; but, even in the darkness, he was quite conscious of the fact that each stair was an inclined plane from the walls in which the ends of its supporting timbers were inserted.

Truly it was time that house was condemned: but in old times that was a process gone through frequently without anything further coming of it than the mere fact that the habitation was deserted, and left to fall down at its own good will and pleasure.

Tom drew a long breath of relief when he crept out at the attic window, and found himself fairly in the open air.

To be sure, he was still on the top of the condemned house, and if it were there and then to fall, fall he must with it; but the danger did not seem to be so great with the open sky above him, as upon the creaking, tottering staircases which his light weight had almost hurled to destruction.

The houses in that nest of courts at the back of St. Martin's Church were built in eccentric-shaped clumps, about which the narrow courts ramificated in all possible directions, and with a confusion of design, which, if it were intentional, did great credit to the architect.

Tom took an observation from his elevated position, and then he saw that he had but to scramble over two or three roofs, and he would find himself in the same relative position to his mother's house, as he then was to the dilapidated residence he had passed through—namely, in the garden outside one of the attic windows.

To any one of unsteady nerves and giddy inclination, who looked over those roof-tops, it would have been a thing of dismay, but to Tom Ripon it was an amusement.

Slates were not in use when those old houses were built, so that it was over the old red tiling that Tom crawled; and, now and then, one of the tiles would get displaced, and, with a rushing, scraping sound, would make its way down the sloping roof into the old leaden gutter, which was choked up with blackened mud and the *débris* of many seasons.

But Tom made his way manfully—perhaps we ought to say boyfully; for those old roofs were, probably, in too great a state of decay for any

man of ordinary weight to have passed over with impunity.

"Here we are!" cried Tom. As he glanced down into Star Court, he felt confident he was on the roof of his mother's house; and, probably, Tom spoke in the plural on account of a couple of tiles coming down into the gutter, outside the attic window, along with him.

How black that attic looked as Tom peered into it through the small diamond-shaped panes of its lattice!

No danger was apprehended from such a quarter; so that the difficulty of opening the window from without was nominal; and Tom Ripon, in a few minutes, found himself actually beneath the maternal roof without any difficulty.

The attic did not look so dark when Tom was fairly within it as it had done from without, and he could see that in one corner was one of those stump or truck bedsteads which were generally to be found in the upper rooms of houses of the class of Mrs. Ripon's.

Then Tom fell over a chair, which had but three legs upon which it artfully stood—no doubt for the express purpose of betraying any one who might venture to sit down upon it.

This made a noise, so that Tom had some fears he might be giving an alarm of a different character to what he had intended in the old gal's house. He listened intently, with his head over the balustrade at the top of the attic stairs, but nothing came of the noise.

Then Tom crept down softly.

As he neared the lower regions of the house, a faint murmur of voices came upon his ears, and proceeding lower still, Tom came to the first floor, from whence he thought the voices proceeded, but he was mistaken.

The house was in a bad state of repair. The floor boards were shrunken, and numerous knots had fallen out.

Large masses of plaster from the ceilings had tumbled in from time to time.

This deterioration of the building had taken place in almost every room of the house; and it was owing to the ceiling of the room at the back of the shop having suffered in this way, and owing to the boarding of the small back room of the first floor being in a very disorganized condition, that Tom heard so plainly the voices he had, at first, thought to be nearer at hand than they were.

In fact, various minute pencils of light made their way from the room at the back of the shop right through apertures in its ceiling, which corresponded with similar ones in the flooring of the back room of the first floor.

"That'll do!" whispered Tom.

He laid himself down quite flat on the floor of that back room, and applying his eye to the oval orifice, left in one of the floor boards by the slipping out of a knot, he was, to his great contentment and satisfaction, enabled to obtain a view of the very penetralia—the *sanctum sanctorum*, so to speak—of the little establishment kept by Mrs. Ripon and the Reverend Mortification.

The savoury steam of some appetizing compound that had been prepared for supper came through the orifices in the roof, and Tom could see that both his mother and the Reverend Mortification were in the room.

With the humming sounds of some monster bee the tones of the Reverend Mortification's voice came up to Tom's ears, and it was some little time before he could distinguish the actual words he spoke, since the Reverend Mortification was addressing Mrs. Ripon in a voice of mystery, as though he feared his communication might reach from that place some profane ears for which it was not intended.

And so it did very shortly; for as the reverend gentleman proceeded he spoke a little louder, and Tom, by paying great attention, and inclining one ear to the hole in the floor-board, caught pretty well the purport of the conversation.

"Yea," said the Reverend Mortification, "as the Psalmist says, look after yourself, for nobody else will; and, therefore, my dear Sarah Maria Jane, I advise thee to be a countess."

"But I never could abide foreigners," said Mrs. Ripon.

"Yea, my charming Sarah Maria Jane, we're all the sons and daughters of Adam; and as the Psalmist says, why can't we believe as such? Taste a little of this ragout, and then tell me really how much money you've got."

"You're an insinuating man," said Mrs. Ripon. "How much did you say?"

"I didn't say anything, and I didn't believe it, that you could take me to France or Portingale, and for a matter of fifty guineas make a countess of me!"

"It's to be done—it's to be done!" said the Reverend Mortification. "Yes, it's to be done; but, as the Psalmist says, you ought to tell me how much money you've got, and where it is."

"Six hundred guineas," said Mrs. Ripon, in a faint voice.

"Six hundred?"

"Six!"

"Dearest Sarah Maria Jane, the chair's hard; sit upon the lap of your own Mortification."

"Go along with you, do!"

"I'm sure you're thirsty. Let us imbibe another glass of that compound, which yea and truly cometh from Jamaica, and, when old and good, warmeth the heart of man, and, as the Psalmist says, is only eightpence-halfpenny a quartern. I think you said six hundred, Sarah Maria Jane?"

"I did. But, oh, Mortification——"

"What?"

"Can I go to France, or to Portingale, and leave that little limb of——"

"Satan," interposed the Reverend Mortification. "You allude to Tom?"

"I do—I do! I can't forget I'm his mother; though heaven knows that boy's been an iron chain to me, and a hammer with two heads."

"And can I forget," cried the Reverend Mortification, holding his hands above his head, and making a howling sound to signify the extent to which his feelings were touched,—"can I forget that I am his father?"

"His father?"

"In law, which is the same thing, only a little better. No, Sarah Maria Jane, you're a handsome woman, and I'm not going to have you spoil your good looks, by tears of compassion for that hardened little sinner. We will take him with us, or send for him; and then as you walk abroad with your title as a countess, and people bowing before you, and glorifying you, and playing cym-

bals, he will be mistaken for your little brother, for, nobody would believe, as the Psalmist says, that so young and still charming a woman could be mothery!"

The Reverend Mortification knew that this was a weak point of the sex generally, and the words had all their effect upon Mrs. Ripon, who made several devious attempts to catch a glimpse of herself in the cracked looking glass that hung over the chimney-piece.

Now, whatever ideas the Reverend Mortification might attach to looking "mothery," certainly the aspect of Mrs. Ripon at that moment might have carried them out, for she wore an immense mob-cap, which projected at least eighteen inches above her head; and catching a glimpse of this appendage in the cracked glass, Mrs. Ripon, inflamed by the praises of the Reverend Mortification, fancied that she would look better if the crown were lower.

One sudden movement and a pressure of the hand effected the object, but the crown of the mob-cap was stiffened and elastic, so that for the moment, although it was completely flattened, it began slowly to rise again as if instinct with life.

"Gracious goodness, what's that?" said the Reverend Mortification.

"What's what?"

"The crown of your cap."

"Merciful Providence!" screamed Mrs. Ripon; "he's guessed it!"

"Guessed what?"

"You knew it all along, you deceitful man. I tell it you to your face, and that's flat!"

"But it isn't flat now," said the Reverend Mortification, "for it's sticking up as high as ever."

"My money—I mean my savings—they're all in good, crisp bank-notes, in the crown of my cap."

"No?"

"Yes!"

"And they made it go up again. Beautiful and accomplished being, come to the arms of your faithful Mortification. Oh, Sarah Maria Jane! did you say crisp, new bank-notes? Let me embrace you, dearest! Six hundred charms—amiable and excellent being!"

The Reverend Mortification rose to his full height, which, being considerably above that of Mrs. Ripon, enabled him—as he clasped his arms, apparently with the intention of folding them around her—to secure the mob-cap.

But Mrs. Ripon was not quite satisfied to be thus easily despoiled of the accumulations of her industry in keeping a "fence" for so long, and seizing a fork from the table, she presented its two prongs so close to the throat of the Reverend Mortification, that—feeling his danger to be imminent—he put on what he meant to be a fascinating smile; but which was, in reality, a ghastly sort of grin, as he said, "Lovely Sarah Maria Jane, I will not only take care of this money, but I shall be able to put two hundred golden guineas along with it, and then we will be off together."

"No!" said Mrs. Ripon; and she advanced the prongs of the fork the eighth of an inch, which—short as the distance was—made so serious a difference to the Reverend Mortification, that he jerked his head backwards, and hit it a sharp crack against the corner of the mantelpiece. "No, deceitful wretch! give me my cap and my money!

Men were deceivers ever, and we, poor tender creatures of women, are always being taken in and done for. Give me my money—I can take care of it myself."

"But, my sweet angel——"

"My money! my money!"

The fork advanced another eighth of an inch; and those two eighths were more than the Reverend Mortification could bear—particularly as he could not get his head any further back; therefore he surrendered the mob-cap with a sigh.

"My own lollipop," he said, "I did not intend to keep it. Take it, and be careful of the crisp bank-notes. Let us mix another glass, and I will relate to you how I shall be able to add two hundred golden guineas to what I suppose I may call our little store."

"That's just what I want to hear," said Tom to himself, as he looked through the oval hole in the floor-board.

CHAPTER CCVIII.

TOM RIPON ARRIVES AT THE HEART OF THE MYSTERY, AND MEETS AN ENEMY.

THE Reverend Mortification seemed still reluctant to speak of the little arrangement he had made with Lord Warringdale, which was to bring him in the two hundred guineas; and yet he did not see how he could avoid a confidence with Tom's mother, which might involve a corresponding reliance upon him in regard to those crisp and tempting bank-notes in the mob-cap.

"Hem!" he said. "Hem! I am now about to disclose to you, my charming Sarah Maria Jane, a circumstance that—ahem! Really, I hardly know how to begin."

"Deceitful wretch!"

"Nay! nay! Say not so—I will tell all—I mean to tell all. You must know, then, that my Lord Warringdale——"

"The ugly monster!"

"He is not altogether what the Psalmist would call good-looking, but I feel sure he is about to kill some one."

"No!"

"Yes, I am certain of it, and he wants somebody else to be accused of the murder."

"The murder?"

"That's the right name of it."

"But—but who? Who is it to be murdered? Who is to be the somebody else who will be accused? Who——"

"Patience, admirable creature, and I will tell you all I have been able to find out upon the matter. The Lord Warringdale has read the old saying of 'killing two birds with one stone,'"

"One stone?"

"My dear Sarah Maria Jane, do not jump so. As the Psalmist says, my nerves will not stand it."

"I won't. Go on."

"In plain language, then, my Lord Warringdale has somebody he wants to kill, and then he wants to put the guilt upon no other than Captain Felix Heron, the highwayman."

"Oh!" said Mrs. Ripon.

"Ah!" said Tom, above; "I fancy I begin to understand now what it all means; and if I could only find out who the somebody was that my Lord Warringdale intended to kill, I would be off to the forest at once, and tell Lady Edith all about it."

Tom lingered where he was, in the hope of yet getting this desirable piece of intelligence.

"You comprehend now?" added the Reverend Mortification.

"I think I do."

"Of course you do, charmer."

"But I should still like to know who is the person that will be murdered."

"So should I."

Those words were spoken by the Reverend Mortification with a truthful emphasis that left no doubt upon the mind of Tom of the ignorance of Mortification on that part of the subject.

Tom could have echoed the words, "so should I," but the pause that now ensued in the little conference about human life below, produced a silence that warned him to discretion.

The Reverend Mortification then briefly related to Mrs. Ripon how he was to be attired in the costume of Captain Heron, the highwayman, in order that some one might see him in contact with the dead body, and so be able to swear to that seeming fact, to the great detriment of Felix Heron.

"There will be two hundred pounds, my charming Sarah Maria Jane, to add to your six hundred, and then we will be off at once."

"Off at once!" said Mrs. Ripon, in a musing manner

"Now," said Tom to himself, "if the old gal won't have anything to do with the villany, I will take her into favour again."

Mrs. Ripon continued silent, but she little suspected that she had two auditors of that silence, during which there was certainly a struggle taking place in her mind between her natural cupidity and her reluctance to add even two hundred guineas to her store, in the way pointed out by the Reverend Mortification.

If Mrs. Ripon had been a romantic individual, which certainly she was not, we might here say something about the good and evil spirits which are said to attend mankind, and to whisper their opposite counsels to the vexed intellect.

But Mrs. Ripon was a matter-of-fact person—of the earth, earthy—and the only spirits she knew anything about or cared anything about were those, the odour of which at that very moment mingled perceptibly with the air of that room she was in.

If the proposition had comprised merely the felonious abstraction of some silver plate, or even of money, Mrs. Ripon would not have hesitated a moment, for that would have been all in the way of business; but since the last attempt by treachery to effect the capture of Captain Heron, and the magnanimous manner in which he had allowed it to pass over without seeking for vengeance, Mrs. Ripon shrunk a little from adding even two more crisp bank-notes, of a hundred pounds each, to those which were in her mob-cap.

Tom, with a delicacy of apprehension far transcending that of the Reverend Mortification, gave his mother credit for the real scruples that possessed her.

The unscrupulous Mortification, on the contrary,

flattered himself that considerations for his own personal safety alone made Mrs. Ripon hesitate.

"I don't think there's any danger," he said.

"I don't suppose there is," said Mrs. Ripon; "I must think of it—I must think of it."

"Think nothing of it, but that it shall be done; and then, Sarah Maria Jane, with your money and mine, we will take our departure. There is a little place called Grays, in Essex; and when the tide is running quick down the river, it's easy to get there in an open boat. There are always some small Dutch vessels lying there, trading to and fro with cheese, fruit, and grain. What is to hinder us, then, getting over to Holland, and baffling all pursuit?"

"Pursuit!" said Mrs. Ripon, for it was a new idea. "You think, then, there will be pursuit?"

"I cannot say so. I do not know; but it is possible. My Lord Warringdale may not be able to arrange everything quite to his satisfaction, and I should much prefer that we left in that fashion, so as to leave no trace behind us."

The Reverend Mortification spoke these words in a very peculiar way—indeed, so entirely different from his usual style and manner, that if anything had been wanting to convince Tom of the entire insincerity of his usual canting, conventicle style, the tone in which these words were uttered would have supplied that want.

At the same time, there came over Tom's mind an undefined idea that the Reverend Mortification had some deep-laid plan in hand which, in all probability, he intended to eventuate in his own entire and exclusive possession of the contents of the mob-cap, as well as of the two hundred pounds he expected to get from Lord Warringdale.

The more Tom considered the whole of the circumstances that had come to his knowledge, the more he felt convinced that there was treachery in the mind of the Reverend Mortification towards his mother, as well as towards Captain Heron.

"Lucky!" said Tom, in a low voice,—"lucky, a hundred times over, that I am here to know all about it!"

The Reverend Mortification now rose to his feet, and swinging his long arms about him in what he, no doubt, thought an imposing manner, but which, in reality, only gave the idea that he was imitating a windmill, he said, "I leave you now, my charming Sarah Maria Jane, in the blessed keeping of the Psalmist, and shall return shortly—ahem!"

"I suppose," said Mrs. Ripon, "you are going sotting, as usual, to the 'Marquis of Granby?'"

"Nay—nay; it is but that I know you dislike the delicate perfume of tobacco."

"Delicate perfume, indeed!" responded Mrs. Ripon. "But be off; I expect some customers yet to night."

"My angel, I go!"

The Reverend Mortification, after casting another glance of admiration, which Mrs. Ripon thought was at her, but which was, in reality, at the mob-cap, departed from the back parlour.

Tom heard him going in a lumbering sort of way through the shop; for, to tell the truth, the reverend gentleman had already imbibed as much of the old rum as was good for him—and perchance a trifle more; and then, as Tom listened for the sound of his actual departure into Star Court, he was startled,—and so was Mrs. Ripon,—by something that was between a shriek and a howl, from just outside the house.

The noise sounded scarcely human.

Mrs. Ripon uttered an exclamation, and sprang to her feet.

Tom listened intently.

The sound was not repeated.

"Goodness gracious!" said Mrs. Ripon, "what was that?"

Tom might have uttered a similar speech, for he was quite at a loss to comprehend the odd sound.

The stillness, however, which succeeded it in Star Court began to have an effect upon Tom's imagination, and to make him think that, after all, no such sound had met his ears, or that it was the echo of some noise a long way off.

"Some dog run over, perhaps," said Tom. "It could not have been here."

It was strange that Mrs. Ripon was possessed of the same idea at that same moment, and almost in chorus with Tom, she said, "Some poor animal in trouble, I shouldn't wonder. Oh, dear me, we live in a world of woe—of woe—of woe!"

Mrs. Ripon, as she spoke, finished the contents of the glass before her, and the last time she said "woe," it had a deep and sepulchral sound from the interior of the glass.

Then Mrs. Ripon sat down and sighed.

Tom began to consider whether he should at once make his presence known to his mother, or not.

"I think I will speak to the old gal," he whispered to himself; "for I am quite sure that the Reverend Mortification is up to no good."

Another moment, and Tom would have carried out his resolution to call out to his mother, but Mrs. Ripon commenced communing with herself in a half-tearful voice, and the desire to know as much as possible before he declared his presence, kept Tom for a time silent.

"I don't know what to think," said Mrs. Ripon. "I feel, at times, all over of a cold shiver."

"Serve you right," whispered Tom.

"He's a fine man," added Mrs. Ripon.

"Who the deuce does she mean?" said Tom.

"A very fine man, I may say, although not strictly handsome."

"Good gracious!" thought Tom. "She means old Mortification!"

"Oh, dear, no!" added Mrs. Ripon. "He is not strictly handsome; but, as I say, he is a fine man."

"Oh, bother!" said Tom.

"And yet my mind misgives me, and I am afraid he means something that gives me this cold shiver."

"So do I," said Tom, still speaking in that low whisper with which he had been communing with himself, and which—above her, as he was—had no chance of reaching the ears of Mrs. Ripon.

Mrs. Ripon then leant her head upon her hands, and with her elbows on the table before her, she, apparently, gave herself up to deep and anxious thought.

Tom had never before seen his mother in so thoroughly contemplative a mood.

"What does she mean, I wonder?" said Tom. "What can the old gal be thinking about now, I wonder?"

" Murder !" said Mrs. Ripon.

" Eh ?"

" Murder !" she added.   " It would be murder.
I don't mind a little business in the way of plate,
or other valuables, but I don't like murder."

" That's right !" said Tom.

" I have a good mind," added Mrs. Ripon—" I
have ever so good a mind to let Captain Heron know
all about it ; and yet—and yet I don't want to get
him into trouble. He says he will marry me,
and it's a sad thing to be a lone woman. I don't
know what to think, and I don't know what to
do."

" The old gal," said Tom, " is not so bad,
after all."

" No ! no !" suddenly said Mrs. Ripon. " I
won't have it done, and so I will tell him. He
no more dare do it—if I threaten to let Captain
Heron know—than he dare to try to jump off the
house-top. He shall not do it. We will go to
France or to Portingale without the two hundred
pounds, and he shall not do it. I wonder—oh,
dear ! oh, dear ! I wonder——"

" What does she wonder ?" said Tom ; for Mrs.
Ripon at that moment began to cry.

" I—I—wonder where my boy Tom is now ?"

" Oh, that's it !"

" At times I—I only wish—that—that I didn't
know that man Mortification, and had my own
boy here with me ; but I won't now let anything
be done to bring danger to Captain Heron ; for
if he has misled Tom, he has been kind to him—
I'm sure he has been kind to him ; and that's more
—more than he will ever think his mother has
been."

Mrs Ripon went on crying. The flood-gates of
that corrupt and seared heart were open and old
feelings, and old sensations that had long slumbered there, came welling up to the surface.

" God bless him !" said Mrs. Ripon.

" Now," said Tom, " is that me or Mortification ?"

" God bless my own boy Tom !"

" All right ! Mother ! mother ! mother !"

Mrs. Ripon uttered a scream.

" Murder ! Fire ! Who's that ?"

" It's me, mother—it's only me !"

" Me ?"

" No, not you ; me—Tom. I am up here. It's
all right ; go and bolt the shop door, for I don't
want old Mortification to come in."

Mrs. Ripon was too much astonished for a few
moments at the sound of Tom's voice, to have the
least apprehension of where he was ; and, in fact,
from the fright depicted on her countenance, it
might almost be inferred that she thought she
was listening to a voice from some incorporeal
spirit.

This idea, however, did not last many seconds,
and it was succeeded by another of an exceedingly practical and common-place character.

Mrs. Ripon was seized with the idea that Tom
was up the chimney, and in a delirious kind of
way she projected the mob-cap some distance into
the flue, and brought down an immense quantity
of soot which nearly blinded her.

" What are you at ?" cried Tom. " I'm up here
—I'm up here, in the ceiling."

Upon this, Mrs. Ripon looked upward, but
seeing nothing — for although Tom's eye, from
being close to the oval hole in the floor-board,

commanded a good view of the room below, Mrs.
Ripon had no such advantage, and she was
rapidly reverting to her original idea of the supernatural character of the transaction, when Tom
again called out loudly, " I tell you I'm in the
room above, and looking through the floor."

This was sufficiently explanatory.

" Come down at once ! Oh, Tom, come down
at once !"

" The hole in the floor is rather too small for
me to get through," said Tom ; " but I'll come
down in a minute, if you'll bolt up the shop
door."

Mrs. Ripon by this time had got rid of all her
fears, and while she went to obey the request to
keep out intruders from this shop, Tom made his
way down-stairs, and by a side door into the
parlour.

" Come, mother," he cried. " don't be all night.
I've heard all that that old Mortification has said,
and I want to speak to you quite particular
about it. You may depend upon it, mother, he
means some harm to you, as well as to the Captain."

Mrs. Ripon made no reply.

Tom ceased speaking, but he put himself into
an attitude of listening intently, for the moment
the sound of his own voice no longer prevented
him from catching other sounds, he became cog-
nisant of an odd scuffling sort of noise either in
the shop or immediately beyond it, in Star Court.

" What's that ? what's that ? Come here, mother. Where are you ?"

The odd noise ceased.

A vague apprehension that something had happened came over Tom, and he flung open the door
of the back room, which communicated with the
shop, and looked out into the darkness.

Then Tom recollected that when he had passed
his mother's establishment about an hour and a
half before, on his route to the deserted house,
through which he had made so dangerous a progress, there had been a light in the window of the
shop. But all was darkness now.

" Speak !" cried Tom. " Where are you, mother ?"

There was no reply.

Tom rather shrunk from walking directly into
that dark shop, which looked like a cavern,
viewed from the room behind it—for, in fact,
that room, too, was but dimly illuminated.

The lighted candle which had enabled the Reverend Mortification and Mrs. Ripon to partake of
the dainty repast which had been placed before
them had burnt down very low ; and while Tom
was coming down the staircase, from his post of
observation to that room, and while Mrs. Ripon
had gone to fasten the outer door, that bit of
candle, in a very dissipated manner, had guttered
all down on one side, and disappeared with a
sudden flop to the bottom of the candlestick.

The fire was but a small one.

A few red cinders only remained in the grate,
and the dubious, dull sort of radiance they cast
into the room was not sufficient to penetrate into
the shop.

" What's the matter with you ?" cried Tom.
" Can't you speak, mother ?"

He drew back further into the room as he
uttered these words, for a notion came across him
that there was danger in that shop.

And then Tom recollected the strange cry—half human, and half like the echo of some animal in distress—which had so quickly and so mysteriously succeeded the departure of the Reverend Mortification.

Tom coupled that with the mystery of his mother's apparent disappearance; and no wonder, then, that he shrunk back further and further from the door of communication, and began to wish himself anywhere but where he was.

Tom was brave, however; and added to that was a spirit of curiosity which prompted him to ascertain what this seeming mystery was all about.

Among the miscellaneous articles upon the mantel-shelf, a candle-end was not difficult to be found; and, by the aid of a match—the blue, sputtering, brimstone flame of which shed a lurid light over the wretched-looking room—Tom lit the candle.

No. 93.—EDITH.

Holding it as high as he could above his head, he stood once more upon the threshold of the back room.

Brighter and brighter grew the flame as the tallow thawed about its base, and then Tom's eyes encountered a sight in that front shop, which, for a moment, sent the blood rushing tumultuously back to his heart, and blanched his cheeks with terror.

A man was seated on the counter, carelessly swinging his legs, and looking as much at home as if he had called in for a half-hour's chat with the proprietress of the establishment.

A ray from the candle-light fell full upon his face.

It was not a face, once seen, to be ever forgotten.

It was the face of Jonathan Wild.

CHAPTER CCIX.

TOM RIPON FINDS HIMSELF A PRISONER, WITH
BUT LITTLE CHANCE OF RESCUE.

THE mystery of the odd noise which had so
quickly followed the departure of the Reverend
Mortification, and the mystery of the as odd
scuffling sounds which had ensued on Mrs. Ripon
going to bolt the outer door, were explained in a
moment.

Escape—flight, rapid, instant, and immediate—
was Tom's only chance.

He flung down the light.

He made a rush to the small door which opened
on to the staircase. If he could only get half a
dozen yards' start, he would surely be safe.

No. He was too late.

A rough hand clutched him at the back of the
neck.

"Bring a lantern here!" cried Wild, in his
most harsh and grating tones. "We have nabbed
the last bird of the nest, now. Bring a lantern
here!"

Tom writhed in the grasp of Jonathan Wild,
and twisting round, was face to face with his
captor.

At the same moment there was a gleam of
light from the shop, and one of Jonathan's myrmidons made his appearance, having opened the
darkening shade of a lantern.

"So," said Wild, "this is you, my beauty!"

"Yes," said Tom; "but I can't say that of you,
Mr. Wild."

"What do you mean, whelp?"

"Why, you're uglier than ever."

"Ha! ha!" laughed Wild. "Quite a sharp
lad, this! I suppose you're fourteen years old
now, Tom Ripon, because we hang after that
age."

"No, I ain't," said Tom.

"Oh, we'll see about that. Glummy, you'll
swear he's fourteen, won't you?"

"Certainly, Mr. Wild. I'll take a davy I was
present at his christening—fourteen years, two
months, and one day ago, come next sessions."

Wild laughed in his peculiar fiendish style—
that high, half-*falsetto* laugh, which always ended
so abruptly that it seemed as if stopped in the
middle.

"Bring him along!—bring him along, Glummy!
Our business is over here. We have cleared the
nest, and needn't stay in it any longer."

"Now, young 'un," said Glummy, as he laid
hold of Tom Ripon in a scientific manner by the
cuff of one hand and the back of the neck,—
"now, young 'un, trot."

"Pooh! pooh!" said Wild; "give him a pair
of bracelets—boys are fond of finery."

Tom's last hope of escape vanished, as Jonathan
Wild roughly twisted his arms behind him, and
held them in that awkward position while Glummy
put on a pair of handcuffs, which completely disabled him, and left nothing but his feet at
liberty.

Tom had a strong inclination to kick at Wild,
and at Glummy, but he wisely abstained, considering, as there were four legs to two, that the
kicks in return might not be very pleasant.

Tom was down at heart; but he was determined not to let Wild see that such was the
case.

"Well, Johnny," he said, "what do you want
me for?"

"Anything that'll hang you," said Wild.
"Bring him along!"

Glummy, in not the most gentle manner, led
Tom right through the shop, and out into Star
Court. Any attempt to escape in his present
helpless condition Tom felt would have been quite
out of the question; but he longed to ask Wild
or Glummy if his mother and the Reverend Mortification were their prisoners. It was not likely,
however, that he would get any satisfactory reply
to questions, and his curiosity was excited by
seeing with what coolness and dexterity Mr.
Glummy secured the now vacated establishment
from intruders.

Wild kept an eye upon Tom Ripon while
Glummy took from one of his capacious pockets
a hasp, a staple, and a padlock, which, with singular dexterity and quickness, he attached to the
outer door of the shop.

"All right, Mr. Wild!" he said. "It's pretty
secure now."

"I'll make it more so," said Jonathan; and
taking from his pocket a piece of chalk, he wrote
upon the door:—

"Shut up.   By order,
                    "JONATHAN WILD."

"That'll do! Now, come along!"

"Where to?" said Tom.

"I don't see that that can matter to you a
bit," replied Jonathan. "But if you have the
least fancy to save your neck at the next sessions
—and they commence on Monday—you will do
all that I ask you."

"You haven't asked anything yet," said Tom.

"But I will now. I want to capture Felix
Heron and Edith Tarleton. It's likely enough
that you could help me to that; and if you do
honestly, you shall go clear whether you succeed
or not."

"I might have done it," said Tom.

"What do you mean?"

"Why, you see, you want it done honestly,
Jonathan; and as that can't be, I decline."

"Bah! you're a nice little brat—but, however,
you're troublesome; and the Chief Justice always
leaves everybody for execution who is convicted
of sheep-stealing."

"Sheep-stealing?" said Tom. "I never stole a
sheep in my life."

"That don't matter in the least," said Jonathan.
"I can get a conviction, and you'll be hanged.
Bring him along, Glummy!"

Tom Ripon found he was gaining nothing by a
conversation with Jonathan Wild; and although
he was rather curious to know where he was
about to be taken to, he did not utter another
word for some time—and, in fact, might have
continued silent until the little party reached one
of the round-houses—as watch-houses were then
called, which term of "watch-houses" has in turn
given way to the modern police-station—had not a
voice from a doorway suddenly called out, as the
party passed, "Why, that's Tom Ripon!"

"Ah!" cried Jonathan, starting; "who are you,
my fine fellow?"

"Bless you!" said the voice, as a slim, youthful-looking figure emerged from the doorway, "don't you know me?"

"I do now. You are that young rascal, Jack Sheppard. Nab him, Glummy!"

"Not yet," said Jack Sheppard, suddenly dropping to the pavement in a squatting posture, at the moment Glummy made a movement to clutch him by the neck; "not yet, Jonathan; I've a good many nuts to crack before you net me!"

Jack Sheppard, as he spoke, made a rush—still crouched down as he was in an inconceivably small compass—right at the ankles of Jonathan Wild, who fell heavily.

"Run, Tom, run!" cried Sheppard.

Tom Ripon felt how exceedingly inconvenient it was to run, with his hands manacled behind him, but still he made the attempt, although in vain, for Glummy—missing his hold upon Sheppard—pounced upon Tom, with a celerity that made escape impossible.

Wild gathered himself up, uttering the most terrible imprecations; but Jack was off, and having turned the corner, was not to be seen.

"That settles him! that settles him!" cried Wild. "I meant to let him run on a session or two longer, but Jack Sheppard shall swing, or my name's not Jonathan Wild. Look out for him, Glummy! It's five guineas to you when you can lay hands on him!"

"And I'll give you more than that," said Tom, "to shut your eyes when you see him, Glummy!"

"Peace!" said Wild; "the less you say, the better for yourself!"

"I think, Mr. Wild," said Glummy, "we might put him in one of the cells of Little Newgate, though the house is being put to-rights after the fire."

"No, said Wild; "let me get the workmen out first. There was a good deal of flame, and a good deal of smother, but less damage done than I expected. He'll be safe till to-morrow night in St. Martin's round-house."

It came over Tom Ripon with a feeling of some satisfaction, to hear that he was not to be taken to Jonathan Wild's house, in Newgate Street—that terrible home of the wretched—over the portal of which might well have been written, "Let not hope enter here."

The round-house of St. Martin's parish could not, Tom thought, be anything so secure as Little Newgate; but the fact was that, at that present time, Jonathan Wild's establishment was in anything but an efficient condition.

The assault of the mob, and the fire that had taken place within it, had necessitated reparations that could not be done in a moment.

Then was it that Wild had to distribute his prisoners where he could.

Newgate—that is the big stone prison—was certainly open to him, but the Governor had given him an intimation that one of the Sheriffs was getting disagreeable, and therefore Wild preferred lodging Tom Ripon in St. Martin's round-house, which was in keeping of a man of the name of Jenkins, who he knew dare not disobey him.

In ten minutes more Tom Ripon was in one of the cells of the round-house, and as he occupied it alone, he guessed that he was put there by the special orders of Jonathan Wild, to prevent his sending any messages to Captain Felix Heron.

But Tom had a friend outside who did not seem inclined to desert him in this extremity of his fortunes.

Jack Sheppard, with all the daring subtlety of his character, was determined to make an effort for the rescue of Tom, and he set about the project with great ingenuity.

Any direct attempt by force to rescue Tom Ripon, Jack knew would be absurd; but if he had not the lion's strength, he certainly had the fox's cunning.

Dogging the footsteps of Jonathan Wild and Mr. Glummy, Jack Sheppard soon found out where Tom Ripon was to be placed for temporary security.

Wild was perfectly satisfied that he had his prisoner securely, and with rapid stride took his way towards the Giltspur Street Compter, in a private room of which he already had two prisoners, in whose company the reader has before been on this evening.

Those two prisoners were the Reverend Mortification and Mrs. Ripon; and as this history owes but little to concealments and mysteries, but rather gathers its interest from the force of its events, we may say at once that Jonathan Wild, suspecting that Lord Warringdale was about to engage in some little plots and manoeuvres without his assistance, was resolved to thwart him.

Wild had no objection whatever to the character or the amount of iniquity which Lord Warringdale chose to indulge in.

But the thief-taker had the greatest possible objection to Warringdale being permitted to accomplish anything without his—Jonathan's—cognizance and assistance.

Hence Wild had followed Lord Warringdale in his expedition to Star Court, and had been, from a dark corner, a spectator and listener to the conference with the Reverend Mortification.

At the same time then that Tom Ripon—with one foot in the condemned house, and the other hanging out of the kitchen casement into the area—had listened to what Lord Warringdale and the Reverend Mortification were arranging, Jonathan Wild—wrapped up to the chin in a dark-coloured great coat—likewise was a secret party to the conference.

It did not, then, take Wild five minutes to get into Mrs. Ripon's shop; and—by another singular combination of circumstances—while Tom Ripon was playing the spy upon his mother, through the ceiling of the back-parlour, Wild was peeping through the key-hole of the door of communication between that room and the shop.

Thus, then, Jonathan became acquainted with the fact of Mrs. Ripon's possession of six hundred pounds.

To resolve, consequently, upon her capture, and the appropriation of those crisp bank-notes to himself, was but natural to Wild.

He had but one man with him, but he sent him in hot haste for several others of his janissaries, so that before the conversation between Mrs. Ripon and the Reverend Mortification was over, in that little back-room, Wild had quite a respectable force in Star Court, St. Martin's Lane.

When the Reverend Mortification sallied out of the house, he was seized and carried off at once.

That was the first odd noise that Tom Ripon had heard.

The second was occasioned by the arrest of his mother, by Jonathan Wild, on the occasion of her going to bolt—by his desire—the shop-door on the inside.

Thus, then, as Wild himself had expressed, he "cleaned out the little nest in Star Court."

It was not competent of Wild to make use of Giltspur Street Compter as a private prison of his own, but he lodged Mrs. Ripon and the Reverend Mortification there, on the true charge of keeping a "fence" in Star Court, St. Martin's Lane.

The mob-cap of Mrs. Ripon, Wild had snatched from her head, and had in his pocket.

He intended to pay them both a visit as soon as he had time.

To Mrs. Ripon he meant to offer liberty, and immunity for the past, if she would say nothing about his appropriation of the contents of the crown of the mob-cap.

To the Reverend Mortification he intended to offer pardon, as the condition of his betraying to him every movement of Lord Warringdale.

If they were both, or either of them, so very obstinate as to refuse such conditions, all Jonathan had to offer them was the certainty of being, by his management, hanged at the next sessions of the Old Bailey.

Certainly, Jonathan Wild had the best of the argument.

But now we return to Jack Sheppard, and the means he took to be of some service to his old acquaintance, Tom Ripon.

Jack waited quietly in a doorway in St. Martin's Lane until it was about twelve o'clock; and then he waited a little longer, until he saw a watchman come along, in a dreamy sort of way, as though he were but half awake.

"Past twelve o'clock and a—eh? what sort of a night is it?—cloudy night! I feels cloudy; but perhaps it's the purl has got into my eyes a bit? Well, it don't matter. Past twelve o'clock and a cloudy night!"

The guardian of the night, as an old, superannuated watchman used facetiously to be called, was evidently a little the worse—or, as he would have said, the better—for some strong compound.

"Past twelve o'clock, and a cloudy night! Past cloudy and twelve—eh? no! that isn't it! Move on, will you! Move on! Bless me, it's only a post!"

"Hoy!" said Jack Sheppard, as he emerged from the doorway.

"Eh? Who are you? Move on!"

"I say, old Blunderbuss, do you belong to St. Martin's parish?"

"What's that to you? Mind I don't knock you down, and then take you up, young fellow!"

Jack Sheppard's only reply to this threat was to stoop until he brought the top of his head to a horizontal position; and then, like some ancient battering-ram or catapult, he brought it with stunning force against the stomach of the watchman.

The guardian of the night uttered that sort of sound by the aid of which paviours beat down stones in a roadway, and in a moment he was prostrate.

Jack Sheppard coolly stood upon the watchman, and cried out, "Past twelve o'clock, and the Charley is floored!"

"Murder!"

"What's the matter?"

"Murder!"

"Come, now, don't make a row! What do you want!"

"My rattle."

"Oh, is that all? There it is."

The watchman got hold of his rattle. He raised himself partly on one arm, and, with the other elevated in the air, he sprung the rattle.

Then from dark streets, and still darker courts, came hobbling the white-coated watchmen, their lanterns gleaming, and their staves resounding on the hollow pavement; and this irruption of the watch was just what Jack Sheppard wanted.

The fact was that the first part of Jack's plan consisted in being taken prisoner, and conveyed to St. Martin's round-house.

"Murder! murder! Help!" cried the prostrate watchman, as he still continued to spring his rattle, which, had Jack Sheppard been so inclined, he could have stopped in a moment.

But Jack now flung himself down, and completed the confusion and fright of the watchman, by rolling over him several times, as if he, the guardian of the night, had been a piece of dough, which he, Jack, was bound to play the part of a rolling-pin to, and flatten out as quickly as possible.

"Murder! murder!"

"That's the villain! Seize him! Down with him! Take him up!"

Such were the cries with which the other watchman reached the spot.

Jack was still on the pavement, and he managed to make a dart at the ankles of the foremost of the reinforcement, and in a moment there was a confused mass of white great coats, lanterns, rattles and staves, all on the pavement together.

"Hurrah!" cried Jack, assuming a tipsy tone. "Hurrah! There's nothing like egg flip! Hurrah! I'm a lord—I'm a lord!"

Jack lay on his back, and made no further attack upon the watchmen, who gathered themselves up in great wrath.

"He's drunk!" said one.

"The villain!" said another. "The villain has smashed my lantern!"

"And my nose!" said a third.

"Bring him along! bring him along! You shall have a night in the round-house, my fine fellow, and pay for all damages in the morning! Bring him along!"

Jack began to sing —

"Wine fires us and inspires us—
Rosy, rosy wine, ha! ha!"

The watchman made repeated efforts to get Jack Sheppard on to his feet again, but Jack as pertinaciously resisted those efforts.

He was determined they should carry him to the round-house.

"What's the row now?" said the night-constable. "What's the row now, eh?"

"Drunk, that's all, and 'salting the watch."

"Oh, that's it, is it?"

"I'm a gentleman," said Jack Sheppard. "Hurrah! I'm a gentleman, although I haven't got any money, and never had any! I'm a gentleman, and must have a cell all to myself; do you hear, you low lot! Ha! ha! All to myself!"

"Call yourself a gentleman," said the night-watch, "and have no money!"

JACK SHEPPARD DIVERTS HIMSELF AT THE EXPENSE OF THE WATCH.

Presented Gratis with No. 93 of the New Edition of Edith the Captive; or, the Robbers of Epping Forest.

"Not a sixpence, old pudding-head."

The night-watchman was not a handsome man, and, perhaps, on that account, had more serious objections to be called old pudding-head, than as if he had been an Adonis.

"I tell you what it is, young fellow, you may be drunk or not drunk, for all I know!"

"Give me a cell to myself," said Jack Sheppard, "I'm a gentleman, and insist upon it."

"That's just what I was going to say," added the night watchman. "You want a cell to yourself; and, just because you do, you won't have it. I shouldn't at all wonder but you'd try to burn down the blessed round-house. Put him along with that boy that Mr. Wild brought here."

This was just what Jack Sheppard wanted; and in order to confirm the night-watchman in his determination, Jack made so many kicks and plunges, and such a general amount of obstinate and vigorous resistance, that the same four watchmen who had brought him to the round-house, were compelled to take him by the legs and arms again, and carry him to the cell.

There they flung him in without any ceremony, and much to the discomfort of Tom Ripon, who cried out, "What do you mean by bringing a drunken man here? You must have plenty of places to put him in without bothering me with him!"

"That's no business of yours," said the night watchman, who was superintending the proceedings.

The door of the cell was banged shut; and then, just as Tom Ripon was doing all in his power to get as far off from the unwelcome visitor as possible, Jack Sheppard caught hold of him by the arm and whispered in his ear, "All right, Tom. Don't you know me? I'm Jack Sheppard!"

"Bravo!" cried Tom; "that's all right. I feel as good as free now; for if they do keep me, Jack, I'll tell you what to say to Captain Felix Heron, and how to see him at Epping Forest, and say it."

"You shall go yourself, Tom. Make yourself easy about that. I haven't come here to talk to you, and leave you then behind: we will go to the old forest together. I want a little country jaunt for the good of my constitution. Give us your hand, old fellow, and believe me when I say——Eh? where's your hand? It's so plaguy dark here."

"Jonathan has put what he calls his bracelets on me," said Tom Ripon; "and I'm afraid, unless somebody can borrow the key of him, I shall never get free from them again."

"Now, how you talk," said Jack Sheppard. "Who do you take me to be? And how do you suppose I live, Tom?"

"By cracking cribs, I suppose, Jack."

"To be sure I do. And how do you suppose I should get on if I wanted to borrow keys. No, Tom: give me a bit of wire, or an old rusty nail, that I can bend into a hook, and I don't think there's a lock in all London can resist Jack Sheppard."

"You don't mean that, Jack?"

"Stand still, and I'll show you. They brought me in here, thinking I was far gone in tipsyness, but I have got some of my best tools in my pocket."

As Jack Sheppard spoke, Tom Ripon heard a sharp, clicking sound, and in another moment his hands were free from Jonathan Wild's "bracelets."

With the use of his hands and arms, Tom Ripon felt as though freedom was more than half achieved; and, in imagination, he could almost hear the wind among the waving tree-tops of old Epping Forest.

CHAPTER CCX.

LORD WARRINGDALE ARRANGES THE PRELIMINARIES OF A GREAT CRIME.

"YES," said Lord Warringdale to himself, as he paced, with an exultant look, the larger room of the three which he occupied, as chambers, in St. James's Street, immediately opposite to old Whitcombe House,—"yes, I shall now most assuredly succeed. No man should look for success in the great affairs of life, until he relies entirely on himself."

Lord Warringdale clapped his hands together as he spoke, to give emphasis to the opinion he had uttered.

That opinion was correct enough as an abstract proposition. The only difficulty he was likely to experience was in the carrying it out.

"Now," he added, "I have surely my two principal enemies almost within my grasp."

Lord Warringdale was so well pleased with the idea of his approaching triumphs, that he now paused, and took a deep draught at that port wine, which was just coming into fashion.

"If," he added, "I can successfully rid myself of Felix Heron and of the young Earl of Bridgewater, I get rid of, I think, the only two persons who can keep the coronet of the Whitcombes off my brow, and the ermined robes of a peer from my shoulders."

Lord Warringdale was tired of parading his room to and fro, and he sat down.

Then he took from his pocket a small memorandum-book, and carefully turned over the leaves.

In his way he had become almost as methodical as Jonathan Wild, in keeping an account of the persons whom he intended to make his victims.

In a low tone Warringdale read his little memoranda.

"Ah, yes, that will surely do. The young Lord Bridgewater will or will not accept the challenge I have sent him. If he refuse, it will answer my purpose just as well as if he accepts."

Rat-tat-tat! came a sharp summons at the outer door of the chambers at this moment.

That knock from without was followed by a strange lumbering noise within the chambers, which arose from the fact that the pretended old deaf servant, upon the acquisition of whom Lord Warringdale prided himself, fell over a chair in his hurry to get off his knees, at the keyhole of the door of the room were Warringdale was.

"What is that? what is that?" cried Warringdale.

There was no reply, but he heard the outer door of the chambers opened.

Some one spoke, and then the old deaf valet brought in a card upon a salver.

"Sir Wentworth Miles."

Lord Warringdale could have no doubt whatever but that his visitor came from the young Lord Bridgewater.

He made a sign to the deaf valet, as he thought him, to show the visitor in.

A gentlemanly-looking man, of about fifty years of age, showed himself.

They both bowed.

"Pray be seated, Sir Wentworth," said Lord Warringdale. "Your name is not strange to me, although I have not had the honour to be introduced to you."

"I came," said the Baronet, "on behalf of my friend the Earl of Bridgewater."

Lord Warringdale made a half bow.

"He is quite willing to meet you when and where you please, and with what weapons you choose to name."

"Swords, sir," said Lord Warringdale, sharply.

"Swords, and Kensington Gardens."

"Be it so."

"And as soon as possible!"

"The sooner the better. You have only to put me into communication with the person who is to act on your behalf, and I will take my leave."

"That person, said Warringdale, "who may be supposed to be a gentleman, will wait on you within the next two hours, where you please."

"At the 'Thatched House Tavern,' just below here," said Sir Wentworth Miles, with the same frigidity of air and manner with which he had conducted the entire interview.

Without another word, then, he turned his back upon Warringdale, and stalked out of the chambers.

"He insults me!" said Warringdale, when he was alone. "But he will find it dangerous play, as all, now, who stand in my way or incur my resentment, shall find it."

Warringdale slightly touched the secret pocket he had himself constructed in the breast of his apparel, where he had secured that small phial with the deadly contents which he had purchased so recently.

Then he wrote upon a slip of paper the following words:—

"Go to the Cockpit, at Westminster, and ask for Major Redgky, and say I want him at once."

This slip of paper Warringdale placed in the hands of the deaf valet, and motioned him to go directly.

The old man made a low obeisance, and left the chambers.

Then a terrible and malignant smile came across the face of Warringdale.

"I have them—I have them!" he said. "A life or two, more or less, shall be as nothing now in my estimation. This Sir Wentworth Miles had better make his will, for he is in danger! Ha! ha! He don't know how ill he is, and how soon he will be a candidate for the family vault, if he have one!"

Truly, Lord Warringdale was making his little arrangements, and human life was becoming in his hands a plaything.

It was with strange and terrible deliberation that he set about the details of what he meant to do on the occasion of the duel with the young Earl of Bridgewater.

Those details he actually wrote down in the little book he had with him.

The terrible memorandum was as follows:—

"Get rid of Major Redgky, so soon as I reach Kensington Gardens, so as to reach Bridgewater alone. Take care to have Mortification in a tree, ready, in the costume of Felix Heron. Take care to have the two rangers of the Gardens close at hand, that they may see Mortification rifle the bodies. Take care——"

A rattle of a key in the lock of the outer door of the chambers stopped the further reading of the memoranda, and Lord Warringdale hastily put up his book.

"Ha! ha!" cried a loud, swaggering voice. "Ha! ha! where is my noble friend? where is my illustrious friend and patron, the Lord Warringdale? Ha! ha!"

"That is Redgky," said Warringdale, "than whom a greater scamp does not live. I am not over solicitous of being of any benefit to what is called society, but I shall certainly do it some good by ridding it of Major Redgky, black-leg, bully, thief, and villain. Ah, my dear Major, how are you? Take a seat—take a seat!"

"Thunder and fire!" said the Major. "It does me good to see you, my lord; and I only hope your lordship has thought of some service that Adolphe Redgky can do you."

"I have."

"You have? Give me your lordship's noble hand, and let me swear, by the mortal gods, that I am rejoiced—Adolphe Redgky is rejoiced!"

"I am about to fight!"

"A duel?"

"Just so."

"I'm just the man, then. Your lordship may find it difficult to credit, but I have fought no less than seventy duels."

Warringdale smiled.

"Seventy! as I am a gentleman—seventy!"

"Then you are, indeed, just the man for me."

"I am—I am. Who is the opponent? Who is the unfortunate individual whom we shall leave the inheritor of six foot of cold earth."

"Lord Bridgewater."

"Humph! There will be a hue and cry—a—a—riot and a—warrant from the Privy Council!"

"My dear Major, I have so arranged everything, that it will be impossible you can suffer the least inconvenience about the result of the duel."

"Indeed, my lord!"

If the Major had, at the moment Warringdale was speaking, caught a good, full look at his eyes, he might not have liked their expression.

"Yes," added Warringdale; "and the service you will render me will be so fully appreciated, that I mean to take some steps, as a return for it, to provide for you for life."

"Oh!"

The Major did not exactly like that term "for life."

"But," added Warringdale, quickly, "we will talk of other things now."

"Ah, yes—other things."

"You will first of all taste a glass of this good,

strong. Portugal wine, and then you will go to the 'Thatched House Tavern' and ask for Sir Wentworth Miles, with whom you will arrange the little affair, only remember it is to come off with swords."

"Yes—yes. By George, my lord, this is the prince—the king of all wines!"

Bang! came a knock at the door of the chambers.

The valet brought in a crumpled-up piece of paper, on which was the name, "The Reverend Mortification Ripon."

"An acquaintance of mine. Major, that is all," said Warringdale. "He will be gone by the time you come back from the 'Thatched House.'"

The Major took this as it was intended—namely, as a hint to go at once, and he nearly ran against the Reverend Mortification at the door of the chambers.

Now, the reader will kindly bear in mind that this scene at the chambers of my Lord Warringdale was taking place on the morning after Jonathan Wild had made such a complete clearance of Mrs. Ripon's establishment in Star Court.

But yet the Reverend Mortification was here, in St. James's Street, and at liberty;—that is to say, he looked as if he were at liberty; but, in reality, he was as much in the clutches of Jonathan Wild as he had been only a few short hours before.

A very few words will suffice to explain the tactics of Jonathan Wild in this affair.

Convinced, as he was, that Lord Warringdale was making some vigorous effort to act independently of him, Wild was resolved—in some manner that should have an effect upon the imagination of the false Lord—to let him see that he could not do so.

Hence Jonathan had captured the Reverend Mortification, and put him into the Compter, in Giltspur Street.

Wild's argument to Mortification had been short and simple.

"Tell me everything, and act in all respects as I direct you, or, as sure as the sun will rise to-morrow, I will get you hanged next Old Bailey sessions."

Nothing could be more conclusive or more argumentative.

The Reverend Mortification shook in every limb, and declared himself the slave, the vassal, the humble and devoted creature of Jonathan Wild, then and for all time, in this world and in the next, if it were possible.

Jonathan had overheard all that Warringdale had to say about the sort of service he had expected from the Reverend Mortification; but still there was one part of the mystery that he could not comprehend.

He could see that the success of Warringdale's scheme all depended upon the fact of his killing Lord Bridgwater.

"How does he purpose doing that?" said Wild, to himself. "My Lord Bridgewater is the better man of the two; and in a fair fight would have much the fairer chance of victory."

Jonathan Wild did not, as yet, know of the small vial and its deadly contents, which Lord Warringdale had purchased of Raphael—if he had, the mystery would have been all explained.

That Warringdale meant to kill the young Lord Bridgewater, and then that the Reverend

Mortification was to be seen, accurately disguised as Felix Heron, rifling the body; and that Mortification was to escape; and then such a hue and cry be raised for Heron that his life would be no longer a tenable possession in England, Wild could see.

That Lord Warringdale might find difficulty in the minor details he could likewise see, but that difficulty might not be insurmountable.

But how was he to kill the young Earl of Bridgewater in a duel, with seconds to see all fair?

That puzzled Jonathan.

However, he liberated the Reverend Mortification, and told him to call on Lord Warringdale, and try and find out as much more of the plot as he could.

"Yea," said Mortification. "Mrs. Ripon will be anxious about me, since I was not home last night."

"She will be much more anxious about herself," said Jonathan. "She is a prisoner."

The Reverend Mortification started.

"Yea, she—she—had on—a mob-cap."

"I know it," replied Wild; "and in the crown of it were six hundred pounds in bank-notes. I have not looked at them, but I have them all safe, and shall return them to her and to you."

The Reverend Mortification groaned, but he felt that remonstrating with Wild was like going to Rome to argue with the Pope, so he said not another word.

"Now," said Wild, as on the following morning he led the Reverend Mortification out of the Compter,— "now, I have only one word of warning to give you. It is possible that you may think of playing the double game."

"The what?"

"Oh, you know what I mean, well enough. You may think of betraying me to Lord Warringdale. But, if you do——"

"Yea, I——"

"Silence! I don't want any protestations; I only want to let you know what will happen, if you do. It is just this. The moment I meet you, let it be where it may, I will blow your brains out, and then prove that you had a design to assassinate the King."

The Reverend Mortification opened his mouth to say something, but Wild gave him a push as he added, "Be off. Go to Warringdale; get all the news you can, and then go to the 'Spotted Dog Tavern,' in Fleet Market, and sit down in the bar parlour, till I come to you."

The Reverend Mortification had no resource but to obey Jonathan; and hence was it that we find him tapping, in rather a disconsolate manner, at the door of Lord Warringdale's Chambers, while Major Redgky was there.

In a few moments more, the Reverend Mortification was in the presence of his infamous employer.

CHAPTER CCXI.

MY LORD WARRINGDALE HOLDS QUITE A LEVEE OF INIQUITY AT HIS CHAMBERS.

EVENTS were thickening around the head of my Lord Warringdale, and if we might hazard a con-

328 EDITH THE CAPTIVE.

jecture, one might almost say that he had too much to do.

The complicated means by which he was seeking the destruction of his brother, Felix Heron, and of the young Earl of Bridgewater, were quite sufficient to occupy his attention fully.

But there was another affair to which he was called by Jonathan Wild, which was certainly rather perplexing.

That affair had connexion with the proceedings at the house of the Bishop of Worcester, and a very slight consideration of the circumstances connected with that matter will show how exceedingly indiscreet it is for men, seeking their objects by such nefarious practices as those which suggested themselves to the wicked intellects of Lord Warringdale and Jonathan Wild, to act otherwise than in strict concert.

The arrangements that Jonathan Wild had made at the Bishop of Worcester's looked as though they might eventuate in the capture of Felix Heron, and that, too, by a much easier and less complex means than the affair of the duel which Lord Warringdale had on the *tapis*.

But then Warringdale's plan had advantages peculiar to itself.

It tended to involve Captain Heron in a crime of much greater magnitude, to all appearance, than any which Wild, as an agent of the law, could accuse him of.

It likewise seemed to involve—although that, as we have remarked, was puzzling to Wild—the death of the young Earl of Bridgewater.

Therefore was it, that Lord Warringdale's plan of operations, if it could only be carried out, was a much stronger one than that accidental entanglement of the Bishop of Worcester's, in which Wild proposed to entrap Felix Heron.

But as yet Lord Warringdale knew nothing of Jonathan's arrangements with the infamous secretary of the Bishop.

It may be supposed, then, that Wild felt a malicious satisfaction in confusing the perceptions of Lord Warringdale, by calling upon him on that eventful morning to engage his presence at the Bishop of Worcester's.

But Jonathan took care not to interfere with the visit of the Reverend Mortification Ripon, and he hovered about in a doorway some short distance from Lord Warringdale's chambers until he saw Mortification leave them.

It may well be considered, then, that Lord Warringdale was holding on that morning a kind of levee, and that every person who came to him had some iniquitous object in view.

The Reverend Mortification easily excused his visit by affecting to be more than ever anxious that he should fully understand the details of the affair in which he was to be useful to his new patron.

Warringdale was impatient, and half angry at this unexpected call on the part of the Reverend Mortification; and but for the fact that it would have been indiscreet at that moment to quarrel with the man whom he was about to employ as a prime agent in a piece of villany, he would have given the Reverend Mortification but a very rough reception.

"Be easy," he said, "and leave all further details to me. But since you are here, it may be as well that you stay a short time, for it may be

possible for me to get information enough to tell you when exactly I may want you."

Warringdale was anticipating the return of the Major from the Thatched House; but since that worthy did not make his appearance, he dismissed Mortification, with an intimation that he should expect to see him again in the evening some hour or two after dark.

Thus was it that Wild saw Mortification come out of the chambers; and believing Lord Warringdale then to be alone, Jonathan, with his usual calm, impassible manner, and with one hand upon the hilt of his hanger, strolled up the door-steps of the large house in which Warringdale occupied the three rooms we have so frequently mentioned.

Jonathan Wild had reached the top of those steps when—as was always the custom with him before he actually entered a doorway—he turned, and took a glance right and left to see who might be observing him.

The glance to the right showed him a figure familiar enough to him, for there was not a gentleman who lived upon his wits, in all London, that was unknown to Jonathan Wild.

It was the Major, who was to act as Lord Warringdale's friend on the occasion of the projected duel, that Wild saw slowly pacing up from the Thatched House Tavern, as if with an intention of ascending the very steps at the top of which he, Jonathan, was stationed.

Wild drew back a little.

The Major reached the top of the steps, and then Wild confronted him.

"You know me, sir?"

The Major did not look happy in the recognition.

"You, sir?" he said: "well, I suppose I—I—may recognise you as the famous Mr. Jonathan Wild."

"And I recognise you," said Wild, "as Mr. O'Rourke, who quitted Ireland under circumstances——"

"Hush, my good fellow, hush! Don't fly at game like me. I'm doing you no harm, and why should you seek to do me some? At the same time, if I can ever be of any service to you, Mr. Wild, pray command me."

"That's just it!" said Jonathan. "You are now on a visit to Lord Warringdale—what's the object?"

This was merely a guess on the part of Wild, but it was one of his happy ones, and the self-styled Major at once replied, "I'm to be his second in a duel with the Earl of Bridgewater."

"Ah, indeed! And who acts for the Earl of Bridgewater?"

"A certain Sir Wentworth Miles, whom I have just arranged matters with at the Thatched House. He told me that Colonel Trelawney was to have seconded the Earl, but as he is on duty at Windsor he couldn't do it. I suppose now, Mr. Wild, you'll stop the affair?"

"Not I. But when and where is it to be?"

"To-morrow morning at eight o'clock, in Kensington Gardens, at the back of the old Palace, close to the King's new conservatory."

"That will do. Go and make your report to my Lord Warringdale; but stay as short a time as possible, for I too have business with him. In fact, I will give you ten minutes, after which I

shall arrive, which will be a signal for you to take your departure."

The Major, in a very humble manner for so fire-eating an individual, who—according to his own account—had fought such an alarming number of duels, promised strict obedience to Wild's commands, and then took his way to the door of Lord Warringdale's chambers, at which he knocked with not one-half of the confidence that had characterised his former visit.

Lord Warringdale received the intelligence regarding the time and place of the proposed duel with an exultant kind of satisfaction; for now that he had made up his mind to walk over the dead bodies, so to speak, of all who opposed him towards the completion of his designs, he felt a strange rage for murder, and was anxious for the hour to come when, stretched in death, he would see some of those persons who stood between him and preferment.

NO. 94.—EDITH.

"You will be here," he said, "at a sufficiently early hour to accompany me. Until then I have no need of you."

"Perhaps," said the Major, "you've got a stray guinea or two, for I really have come out without my purse."

Warringdale, with a sneer, flung him a few gold pieces, and just then there came a loud single dab of a knock at the outer door of the chambers, which, while it said nothing for the gentility of the person demanding admission, seemed to imply that, be he whom he might, he felt that he had a right to be there.

"Mr. Jonathan Wild!" announced the valet.

Lord Warringdale bit his lips.

"I'll be off," said the Major.

"Do you know him? and does he know you?"

"Oh, no, no!—that is to say, we've all heard of Jonathan Wild; but that's all. I will be off! Depend upon me, my lord, in good time in the morning. Let me recommend a cup of chocolate and a little burnt brandy in it before we go. That and a dry toast are the very things to fight upon."

"Hush! So you want to baulk me by proclaiming to all the world what I'm about to do?"

"No, no, my lord! Mum's the word—mum's the word!"

The Major nearly ran against Jonathan Wild in his hurry to leave the chambers; and then he bowed obsequiously, while Jonathan Wild uttered a low, snarling sound, like some dog in possession of a bone which he is afraid may be wrenched from him.

"Ah, Wild!" said Warringdale—"that's you. You're an early caller."

"Business!" said Jonathan.

Wild seated himself familiarly, and rested his arms over the hilt of his hanger.

"Business—business!"

"With me?"

"To be sure! What should I come here for else? I'm as good as a father to you."

"What do you mean?"

"What do I mean? Why, that I'm always plotting, planning, scheming for you—always having your interest at heart."

"Oh, I'm sure of that," said Warringdale, with a slight smile.

"Of course you are sure of that. What do you say, now, if I tell you there is just a chance of seeing the dead body of Felix Heron before the clock strikes one to-day?"

"The dead body of Felix Heron?"

"Yes. Are you alarmed at the prospect?"

"No, no! But how can it be? how is it possible?"

"I will tell you. The Bishop of Worcester—some twenty years ago, or more, when he was but a poor clergyman, solemnized a certain marriage."

"Yes," said Warringdale, "we know that. It was a piece of information we got among us from that troublesome old man, Sir Dominick Browne."

"It was so; and that marriage so solemnized was between Amelia Staunton, the mother of Felix Heron, and the late Earl of Whitcombe."

"Hush, Jonathan Wild,—hush! Walls have ears, they say."

"Perhaps so."

"And what is all this to me? There can be no doubt that the late Earl, my father—if he ever said a word to the Bishop upon the subject—told him that Amelia Staunton had died childless; and so long as we can keep the information from Felix Heron, there is no danger from that quarter."

"But Felix Heron has been to the Bishop."

"Ah, say not so!"

"I should be willing enough not to say so, but it happens to be a fact. The old Bishop is enchanted, fascinated with him. His noble appearance, his ingenuous, manly, truthful manner,—all his fascinations, which made Edith Tarleton fall so desperately in love with him, and contrast you so unfavourably with him, told upon the Bishop."

"Confusion take him!"

"Heron has related his story, and has won the full credence and confidence of the aged prelate."

"Jonathan Wild, what is to be done? Because—because even if within the next four-and-twenty hours Felix Heron were to stand accused of some hideous crime that would deprive him of his peerage, this meddling old Bishop might be the means of proving my illegitimacy."

"Exactly so. For, on my conscience, my Lord Warringdale, as I sit, I not only believe that Amelia Staunton was alive when the Earl of Whitcombe contracted his second marriage, but I further believe that she is *alive still*."

"You never told me that," said Lord Warringdale, while his very lips were blanched with fear.

"No; I reserved that."

"Another, and yet another!" murmured Warringdale.

"What do you mean?"

"I mean that living beings rise up like spectres before me to bar me from my inheritance."

"Oh, my dear friend, if they were only to rise up like spectres, you would be safe enough. I never heard of their evidence doing any good in a court of justice. But come, now. What say you? The Bishop of Worcester has an appointment with Felix Heron at mid-day."

"To-day?"

"Even so; and that is what has brought me to you. Come, sit down and be calm. Don't be pacing the room in that disturbed fashion. Be calm, and listen to me."

"But what is to be done?"

"I will tell you what is intended to be done. The Bishop of Worcester has instructed his secretary, and, in fact, himself assisted in the matter, to find an old diary of his, a sort of private registry of all the ceremonies and sacraments administered by him from the first day that he was qualified to act as a clergyman. That he intends to place in the hands of Felix Heron, so that one of the two difficulties with which your half-brother has had to contend, will vanish."

"The two difficulties?"

"Yes. He had to prove the marriage, and then that he was the son by that marriage; and, upon my faith, I think he is in a fair way of doing both."

"I will kill him—kill him! I must have his life!"

"How?"

Lord Warringdale looked fiercely in the face of Jonathan Wild, and was silent for a few moments. When he spoke again, it was in a low, husky sort of whisper that he said, "I will be at the Bishop's house. I have a means. I ask for no assistance—no help from mortal man. I am strong now—terribly strong!"

Wild gave his hanger a slight rattle, which loosened the blade in its sheath, for he could not tell what this terrible strength, which Lord Warringdale spoke of, could possibly mean, and, for all he knew, it might be exerted in some uncomfortable fashion against himself.

"I think, my lord," he said, "it will be the best for both of us that you speak more clearly."

"Look ye here, Jonathan Wild," replied Warringdale. "I do not exactly want to be the—the personal executioner of Felix Heron."

"Oh! I perceive you're getting sentimental."

"If you think you have sufficient power in the

law, considering his past acts, to sacrifice him, do so; and if you can apprehend him at the Bishop's——"

"Oh, easily."

"Then take him."

"But the Bishop—the Bishop! A man of rank, power, and influence—a man with the *entré* to the monarch at any period. Why, my hold upon Felix Heron would be with a pack-thread."

"I—I think I could dispose of the Bishop."

"Ah, that, indeed! Now, look you here, Warringdale. By going to vast expense—which of course you will repay me—I have succeeded in making a friend of the Bishop's secretary, who has suggested to his right reverend master to see you and reason with you upon the whole affair; so that at length, amid a penitential flood of tears, you shall surrender to your brother his birthright, acknowledge him heir to the title and estates of Whitcombe, and for the future get your own living in some useful and industrious manner."

"Perdition seize me if I do!"

"Well, I didn't think you would, but the Bishop expects you. His secretary was to communicate to you his desire to see you, and must have done so, but that I told him I would save him the trouble. So, now, what do you think of doing?"

Lord Warringdale could not sit in calmness and peace as Wild advised him; but now again he paced the room with anxious strides, while Jonathan kept a wary eye upon him, for he had not forgotten how Lord Warringdale had boasted of the possession of some unknown power; and although he could not divine what it could be, yet he thought there might be something in it, and it behoved him to be upon his guard.

Then Warringdale stopped abruptly before Jonathan Wild, and spoke rapidly.

"Take your own measures, Wild," he said, "to secure Felix Heron. I will see the Bishop before the hour you have named, and his testimony will not trouble us."

Wild shrugged his shoulders.

"Very well," he said. "All you've got to do is to go to the Bishop's house, and you'll be admitted to see him. I expect Felix Heron there at mid-day, and shall be quite prepared for him; but still I do think, among friends, now, that you show a want of confidence. You boast of some unknown power—you talk of a means of silencing the Bishop. What are the means?"

"Ask me not—ask me not; but be assured that whatsoever means I may possess of the kind will ever be used against my foes and for my friends. Hark! St James's clock strikes eleven. I will go at once."

"It's about time; and I, too, have some little arrangements to make."

Lord Warringdale threw a cloak about him, and issued out into St. James's Street, accompanied by Jonathan Wild.

They both stood for a few moments on the stone steps, and as they did so, it was but natural that they should glance over the way at Whitcombe House.

"It is very strange," said Warringdale, "but last night I am certain that I saw a light in Whitcombe House."

"Who keeps it?"

"No one. It is deserted."

"Then you imagined you saw a light? It was some reflection in the windows from this side of the way."

"I cannot say that that is impossible, but yet I still think I saw a light, and that it seemed to move from window to window, as though some one carried it the whole extent of the principal saloon."

"It may be well," said Wild, "to see to that; but at present we are both busy."

"True—true! I will to the Bishop's."

"And I will look up some of my janissaries, for we may want them."

If Lord Warringdale and Jonathan Wild could have seen through a very narrow crevice in one of the shutters of Whitcombe House, they would have seen what would have attracted much more attention than any light could have done; for Felix Heron himself was on the other side of that crevice, and saw the departure of his wicked half-brother from the chambers opposite; and the reader will recollect how Heron was left in that mansion of his father, and how, after being conducted from room to room, by mysterious invitations and mysterious lights, he was at length placed in possession of some documents of material interest to his fortunes.

And now, in order that we should bring up the incidents of that night of mystery in Whitcombe House to the period when Felix Heron felt that the time had come when it was necessary for him to keep his appointment with the Bishop of Worcester, we once more repair to that richly-appointed chamber where Felix Heron seemed to be waited upon by invisible attendants, cheered and advised by the voices of the dead, and surrounded by a supernatural atmosphere, which, while it interested all his feelings, was of too benign a character to awaken any of his fears.

CHAPTER CCXII.

CAPTAIN HERON MEETS WITH A PERILOUS ADVENTURE AT THE BISHOP OF WORCESTER'S HOUSE.

THE two most important documents which in so strange and mysterious a manner had been placed in the hands of Felix Heron in Whitcombe House, seemed for the moment all-sufficient to substantiate every claim he wished to make and to ensure every happiness.

"Ah," he exclaimed, "now indeed shall I be able to prove my birth and rank, and my Edith shall rank with the noblest and the highest of the land."

The first thought of Felix Heron was sure to be of Edith.

But when the sound of his own voice had died away in the apartment of old Whitcombe House, in which such extraordinary revelations had been made to him, he heard a deep-drawn sigh.

Then Felix Heron found that either the invisible and mysterious being who had been holding converse with him was displeased at something he had said or done, or, what was more probable, had some disastrous information to give him which would damp the ardour of his joy.

"Speak, oh, speak! unknown monitor and

friend!" cried Heron. "Let me know all that you can have to communicate, for something seems to tell me you have not yet reached the end of your mission to me."

"Alas!" said the voice; "I have not."

"Let me know all, then."

"I will—I will! Oh, fond and foolish heart, you have much to forgive!"

"I? What have I to forgive but what I shake from my heart and memory at once and for ever?"

"Will you judge so leniently the father who left you to the care of a stranger?"

"That stranger was the kindest and noblest of human beings. My father placed me with the good Sir Dominick Browne."

Another deep sigh seemed to come from an almost broken heart.

"The father," said the voice,—"the father who has passed away, cannot accept, even for his memory's sake, such undeserved commendation."

"But such was the fact."

"No, no—alas, no!"

Captain Heron could not comprehend this, for his own recollection of his childhood and boyhood told him that both of those periods of existence had been made happy by the unvarying kindness of Sir Dominick Browne.

"I cannot understand your words," he said.

"You shall know all," added the voice, which seemed to hover in the air of the apartment,—"you shall know all. Your father, when the charms of Amelia Staunton no longer sufficed to hold him to the vows he had spoken——"

"Hold! hold! no more!" exclaimed Felix Heron. "I can forgive, and I can forget, all that I do know. Let not my heart and brain be encumbered by aught else that can tend to make me think harshly of that father who has passed away!"

The voice was silent for a few moments; but when it spoke again, there was evident in its tones a painful and terrible effort at calmness and composure.

"Hear me, Felix! Hear me—hear me!"

"If it must be so, I listen."

"That father really deserted both you and your mother!"

"No, no—oh, no!"

"He did. But as the whole transaction was known to Sir Dominick Browne, it was that great and good heart which interposed; and all that has seemed considerate—all that has seemed merciful in the time that followed—was by him suggested, and by him arranged."

"Heaven bless him!"

"Amen!"

"Amen a thousand times!" added Heron; "but heaven needs no blessings from mortal lips to remind it of the great and good."

"Felix! Felix! Felix!"

"I listen."

"Can you still forgive?"

"I do."

"With your lips only?"

"No, no! with all my heart! I am not one to forgive in words, and cherish such feelings in my thoughts."

"Alas! alas!"

"You still sigh!"

"There is more still to tell."

Felix Heron now sighed, for he would fain have heard of the future, since the past was so full of sadness.

The voice continued.

"Your poor, poor mother was deserted to want —to misery!"

"Oh, heaven!"

"That want and that misery preyed upon her brain until her imagination became filled with wild fancies, and she lost the very remembrance of who and what she was, along with the memory of her wrongs."

"Oh, horror! horror!"

"Then came the opportunity of the destroyer. It was in vain——"

"Stop—stop! No more!"

"Your father——"

"I will not hear it. Oh, spare me!"

"It is nearly spoken. Amelia Staunton was mad; but in a lucid interval she proclaimed to all who would listen who and what she was, and then, as I say, came the opportunity of the destroyer."

"Death, mean you?"

"No; Death is merciful."

"Who else? What else?"

"Your father—he affected to pity the poor demented wretch who called herself the Countess of Whitcombe—for he had just come to his titles and estates—and he had no difficulty in consigning her to what may be called a living tomb."

"What?—where?"

"A madhouse!"

"Oh, poor, poor mother!"

"Ay, poor, poor mother!"

"And then?—and then? What happened then?"

"The excitement of brain that had produced the insanity of the moment passed away, but she was not allowed again to walk forth into the world; for the Earl of Whitcombe had again stood by the altar, and pledged his troth to a daughter of one of the high and mighty magnates of the land!"

"I see—I see!"

"You do see, and can you still forgive?"

"Heaven help me! the task is difficult."

"Too difficult?"

"No, no! Father that is in heaven aid me, and look down upon this poor heart! I do—I will forgive, as—as——"

"As what?—as what? What would you say?"

"As I hope to be forgiven."

There was a stillness now in the room as if death itself had taken up its abode within it.

Felix Heron had let his head droop upon his hands, and his soul was full of sad and heartbreaking thoughts as he reflected upon what must have been the sufferings of his poor mother.

It was a good ten minutes before he looked up again, and spoke.

"She died?" he said, faintly.

"No. Amelia Staunton, Countess of Whitcombe, still lives!"

"Lives! My mother—my own mother—lives! Oh, heaven, spare me! my brain reels—this poor mind will surely burst its confines! My mother still in life?—still breathing, despite all her sufferings?"

"She lives!"

"Oh, gentle spirit! beneficent being, who, by permission of high heaven, now makes to me these revelations, add but the last words which shall tell me where to fly to her arms, and I will bless thee!"

"Look further. You are possessed of two documents—the certificate of your mother's marriage, and of your own baptism. Look further, and you will find a third."

What pen can describe the eagerness with which Felix Heron now turned his attention again to the papers lying on the table for him.

The two important documents he was already in possession of lay under his hands, but they both seemed to him to sink into insignificance in comparison with the third one which was promised him.

There was a small sealed packet just under the other papers.

The sealed packet was addressed as follows:—

"To the Right Honourable the Earl of Whitcombe."

Felix Heron felt at the moment that there was no one entitled to break the seals of a packet so addressed but himself. Was not he the Right Honourable the Earl of Whitcombe by every evidence that could be brought to bear upon the subject?

He broke the seals.

Several letters fell from the packet, and there was one open, and in a different handwriting to the others, at the top. It contained but a few words, and most eagerly did Felix Heron read them.

"MY LORD,

"The poor woman, Amelia Staunton, whose delusion that she was the Countess of Whitcombe caused her to be placed in our care, managed, with great ingenuity, to effect her escape some time back, but we put forth all our energies, and captured her in London, in the Strand, and we have her now securely.

"We write this, lest your lordship should hear some exaggerated statement on the subject, and fancy we had been guilty of neglect.

"We have the honour to be, my lord,

"Your lordship's most obedient servants,

"ALLANBY AND PARKES."

"The Asylum, East Sheen."

By there being no address at the top of this letter, Felix Heron had been terribly fearful that he should get perhaps every information but that which was most important—namely, the place of his mother's imprisonment.

But there it was at the foot of the letter, and upon looking lower down he saw a postscript.

"P.S.—The enclosed letters are various ones which Amelia Staunton has tried to get sent to various people, but which, in pursuance of our duty to your lordship, we hand over to you."

A hasty glance at these letters let Felix Heron see that they were passionate and earnest appeals for liberty.

"Mother! mother!" he cried, as he sprang to his feet. "your son will fly to your rescue—your son will save you!"

"Be patient," said the voice.

"Patient, patient, when my own mother suffers a thousand torments?"

"Rest—oh, rest this night! Remember that you have another's happiness to look to, and that that other's happiness is bound up in your safety! You can, and you will, rescue Amelia Staunton; but that you may certainly do so, you will go so strong that bolts, nor bars, nor armed men shall stay you."

"Ah, yes!" cried Heron. "You are right—you are right, kind spirit! I will take with me the devoted band that owns me as its Captain, and then no ordinary force can stay me. To-morrow I have to see the good Bishop of Worcester. I will not leave to-night."

"Rest, rest, and the blessing of heaven hover over you!" said the voice.

The light which up to this moment had shone with tolerable brilliancy in the room, now slowly faded away until it went entirely out.

A feeling of drowsiness came over Captain Heron, and after murmuring a prayer for his poor mother, his head sunk upon the table, and he fell into a deep sleep.

It was a ray of daylight coming through a narrow chink in the closed shutters of that room that awakened Captain Heron.

He started in a moment to his feet.

"What is all this? Where am I?" he exclaimed.

There was in his mind a confused perception of all that happened the night before; and as the various circumstances rose up to his memory, his decided impression was that he had only had a vivid dream.

"Visions—visions, all!" he said, sadly. "Oh, would that these dreams were but the precursors of realities!"

He went to the chink in the shutters and looked out.

Captain Heron found that through that narrow crevice he had a view of St. James's Street; and knowing that Whitcombe House was exactly opposite to the mansion in which his bad half-brother, Lord Warringdale, had chambers, he naturally cast his eyes over the way.

As he did so, he saw, pausing for a few seconds on the steps, before descending them, his brother, Warringdale, and Jonathan Wild.

Then Captain Heron heard the clock of St. James's Palace chime the quarter past some hour, but from his position behind the shutters of Whitcombe House he could not see what the hour was.

Holding, however, his watch exactly in the narrow pencil of light that made its way through the crevice, Captain Heron saw that it was a quarter past eleven.

"Ah!" he cried; "so late! It is time that I bethought me of repairing to the good Bishop."

He opened the shutters about another half-inch, which would not be observed from the outside, but which would make a very material difference in the amount of light within the room.

When he had done this, and had turned round with his back to the window, Felix Heron saw that the broader and brighter ray of daylight he had admitted into the room fell full upon the table upon which he had rested his head in repose.

For a moment he could scarcely credit the evidence of his own waking senses, so fully impressed was he with the idea that he had dreamt all that had really happened to him.

But there, lying exactly in the full ray of light, were the documents he had never thought really to possess, save in imagination, while the reason slumbered.

The certificate of the marriage.

The certificate of the baptism.

The packet, with its broken seals, from the keepers of the asylum at East Sheen.

All lay before him, and he clutched them in both hands, as though he feared that they might fade away before his eyes even with that ray of daylight upon them.

"Then it was a reality!" he cried; "and there are, in truth, more things in heaven and on earth than are dreamt of in our philosophy."

The chimes of St. James's clock struck the half-hour past eleven.

Felix Heron felt that he had no time to lose in repairing to the Bishop of Worcester's house; for although now he had become so mysteriously and strangely possessed of all the information the good Bishop could give him, he was more than ever anxious to see him, to lay before him the evidences he was in possession of.

With a full reliance upon the single-hearted goodness of the Bishop, Felix Heron was exceeding anxious to have the opportunity of relating to him all that had taken place at Whitcombe House.

Another glance from the window let him see that his brother, Lord Warringdale, and Jonathan Wild were gone.

"The way is clear," said Heron. "I will to the Bishop's at once, and then to Epping Forest, where I have a tale to tell my Edith which will move her tenderest sympathies."

CHAPTER CCXIII.

TOM RIPON ESCAPES FROM THE ROUND HOUSE OF ST. MARTIN'S PARISH.

"WHAT shall we do next?" said Tom Ripon, when he found himself so far at liberty in the cell of the round-house of St. Martin's, that Jonathan Wild's bracelets, as he called them, no longer confined his wrists,—"what shall we do next, Jack?"

"Get out of here as quick as we can," said Jack Sheppard.

"But how can we do it?"

"Do you think there's a round-house or gaol in all England can keep me in when I want to get out? No, not one. I dare say the time 'll come when they will put me in Newgate, and fancy they've got Jack Sheppard all secure, but then they will find out that their biggest and strongest stone jug is no match for me. I shall make an escape which will be talked about while one stone of old Newgate remains upon another."

Tom Ripon looked with evident admiration upon his friend Jack Sheppard, and Jack was not at all idle while this little conversation was going on—he was indeed at work upon the door of the cell.

"There goes the lock!" said Jack, as a grating noise proclaimed that he was successful in forcing it back.

"Then we can get out?" said Tom.

"Not quite yet; there's an iron bar."

"Then," said Tom, as he sat down with a despairing look, "you can't get rid of that. You may pick a lock, I know, quite well, and I've heard some of our fellows at Epping Forest say that the bigger and stronger a lock looks the easier it's opened."

"That's true."

"But you can't pick an iron bar, you know, Jack?"

"Wait a bit, Tom, and you'll see what you'll see."

The cell was intensely dark, and all Jack's operations had to be carried on by sense of touch. That circumstance, however, did not seem to make much difference to him; and while Jack Sheppard was still speaking, he had set about effective operations with a simple little bit of apparatus, which was then his own invention, although it has since been improved upon, and very elaborately and expensively constructed.

First of all, there was a short sort of bradawl, rather stumpy and thick, around which Jack Sheppard looped a piece of exceedingly strong catgut.

The bradawl was then inserted deep into the wood of the door.

The bit of catgut that hung round it by a loop was not above four inches in length, and it had a similar loop at the other end, into which Jack Sheppard inserted a piece of exceedingly sharp, finely-tempered steel, with two cutting edges.

This steel was about three inches, or rather more, in length, and was fastened into a short, thick wooden handle, forming an excellent grasp for the hand.

By the aid of this little piece of machinery, Jack Sheppard could cut a circular hole through any woodwork of about eight inches diameter; and so dexterous was he in the use of the implement, that as he worked away little was heard, save a hissing sort of sound as the sharp steel cutter was whirled round and round in the deep groove it soon made for itself.

"What are you doing, Jack?" said Tom.

"Making a hole."

"In the door?"

"Yes, to be sure, Tom. I must get my arm through, you see, and lift the bar."

"Jack," said Tom, "you're a capital fellow, and almost a conjuror. But I tell you what it is—the bar was lifted and let drop when I was brought in here, and so it was when they pushed you in; and each time that it fell, it struck against something iron, and made such a clatter as never was known."

"Now do you think, Tom, I'm such a goose as to let it down in that sort of way?"

"Well, but——"

"Shut up, Tom—shut up! Come along, the door is open."

Not the least sound of the falling bar had been heard, and yet it was removed from its place, and the door of the cell swung open.

While he had been talking to Tom, Jack Sheppard had made the circular hole in the panel of the cell door just above the bar. Through that he had put his arm, and having a piece of string in his hand, he, with that delicacy of finger and dexterity of touch for which he was famous, fastened the end of the string round the bar.

Jack had nothing to do then but to lift it from its socket and let it down gently by the string until it hung perpendicularly by the side of the door.

Nothing could exceed the ease, dexterity, and smartness, so to speak, with which all this was accomplished, and from that moment the estimation in which Tom Ripon held Jack Sheppard was of the highest order.

Still there was something to do before they got out of St. Martin's round-house.

There was a short flight of steps to ascend, and then another door to pass through, which led directly into the apartment in the occupation of the night constable, beyond which was the open street.

The ascent of the steps presented no difficulties, and the door at the top of them was only on the latch; but to rush out and attempt to gain the street, in defiance, probably, of several watchmen and of the night constable, was to run a risk not only in the round-house itself, but of a hue and cry through the streets, which would be anything but agreeable.

"I tell you what we must do, Tom," whispered Jack; "we must wait until some more night charges are brought in, and then in the bustle and confusion we will easily escape."

A loud clamouring at the door of the round-house at this moment attracted the attention of the officials of the place, and also of Jack Sheppard and Tom Ripon.

"We've not had to wait long," whispered Jack Sheppard; "for here's a rough lot coming."

"Hush! Keep close and stoop low."

The outer door of the round-house was flung open, and some half-dozen watchmen appeared, dragging in three or four tipsy personages, who had been amusing themselves by what they called making a night of it about Pall Mall and the Haymarket.

Several watchmen, who seemed to have been tolerably well knocked about in the affray, were vociferous in their description of the assault, and a great exhibition was made of broken lanterns and torn great coats.

"Lock them up!—lock them up!" cried the night-constable. "Down to the cells with them!"

"What do you mean, you scoundrel?" said one of the tipsy prisoners, in a tone of voice which sufficiently betokened how far gone he was in inebriety, — "what do you mean, you rascals? Can't a gentleman with money in his pockets enjoy himself? Where's the liberty of the sub—sub—subject, if a gentleman can't beat a watchman in his own parish when he means to pay for it?"

"Pay for it?" said the night constable, in a considerably mollified tone.

"Pay for it?" cried the watchmen in chorus.

"Is it pay for it, your honour's glory?" cried an Irish watchman; "it's kilt intirely I've been, beside my lantern torn all up the back, and the inside of my coat knocked all to smithereens!"

"Hoorah!" said the drunken gentleman. "The liberty of the sub—sub—subject for ever! Here's ten guineas; divide them among you. Hip! hip! hoorah! we'll all return thanks for the ladies!"

"Ten guineas?" cried the night constable. "I see it's all a mistake, and your honour's a perfect gentleman."

"A perfect gentleman!" chorussed the watchmen.

"A gontlemon! a gontlemon"! cried the Irish guardian of the night; "and his father and mother were both old Irish gontlemen before him."

"Good night, sir," said the night constable, with great urbanity. "I hope the time will never come in this world—leastways, not in St. Martin's parish—when a gentleman mayn't amuse himself when he's willing to pay for it. Come, boys, here's five guineas for me, and the rest among you. Now, fellows, what have you got to say for yourselves? Are you gentlemen, too?"

There were three other prisoners, but not one of them made the least offer to pay for his amusements.

The night constable put on a look of severe majesty.

"This is intolerable," he said, "and not to be borne. Peaceable and respectable citizens and parishioners of St. Martin's-in-the-Fields are wakened up by Mohawks and vagabonds in the middle of the night—it's too bad! I hope it'll never happen in this world—at least not in St. Martin's parish — that such goings on can be winked at—I say, winked at! Take 'em into the cells, Barney, at once!"

The watchman pounced upon the unlucky transgressors of the peace, who had not money to pay their way out of the round house, and with the smallest amount of tenderness and ceremony, hauled them towards the door leading down to the cells, and behind which Tom Ripon and Jack Sheppard had been amused spectators of all that had passed.

"We shall be nabbed now," said Tom, in a whisper; "for they're coming this way."

"That's just what I've been waiting for," said Jack.

"But what shall we do?"

"Keep close and lie still. Stoop down, Tom, and tuck in your head; keep your back just level with the top stair. Here they come! Look out—they'll catch it! But we're all safe."

The five watchmen and the three disturbers of the peace reached the top of the stairs in rather a confused mass; but no doubt the watchmen—who were well acquainted with the steps—would, under ordinary circumstances, have hauled their prisoners down in safety, but the foremost watchman, instead of putting his foot upon the second step, placed it upon Jack Sheppard's back.

Jack immediately uttered an awful howl, and flattened himself completely down at the same moment, so that away went all the watchmen and the three charges headlong down the short staircase, without either Jack or Tom Ripon sustaining the least injury.

"Now for it!" cried Jack. "Follow me, Tom."

Sheppard rushed into the night constable's room of the round-house, and there sat that worthy in his easy chair, grasping the two arms of it, and livid with apprehension; for that fearful howl that Jack Sheppard had uttered was ringing in his ears, and which had been followed by the united yells of the five watchmen and their three charges as they rolled down the staircase.

Jack Sheppard knew perfectly well that it would never do to let the night constable recover in the slightest degree from his fright; so, rushing forward, Jack seized hold of the two front legs of the chair, and by a sudden jerk precipitated the night constable, chair and all, into the corner behind him.

"Come along, Tom," cried Sheppard.

"One moment," said Tom.

"No, Tom; a moment's a life! Are you mad?"

Just over the mantelpiece of the round-house was one of those old squat, brass-barrelled, bell-mouthed blunderbusses, for which the immediate ancestors of the present generation seemed to have a special affection and veneration.

These weapons have been known to go off at least once in five minutes, and it was always a question whether they were most dangerous to the person who fired them or to the depredator against whom they were pointed.

Up to the last thirty years they were still to be seen suspended over the chimney-pieces in ancient and respectable banking-houses, in bullion dealers' and money-changers' offices, with a faded label underneath, on which was the word "loaded."

There was such a label under this very blunderbuss in the old round-house of St. Martin's parish.

Tom only paused sufficiently long to take the unwieldy weapon off its hooks, and then he rushed out into the street after Jack Sheppard.

The door of the round-house swung shut behind them, and then the springing of rattles that took place within it was something tremendous to hear.

"Good gracious, Tom!" said Jack Sheppard, "what do you want with that blunderbuss? It won't do for a pocket-pistol, and it won't sell for sixpence."

"Here goes!" said Tom, and he dropped upon one knee as he spoke. He levelled the blunderbuss clearly at the door and the window of the round-house, and pulled the trigger.

That was surely the one time out of five when the unwieldy weapon might be supposed to go off.

A tremendous report followed, and Tom might have been seen on his back in the kennel with his feet in the air.

The smash of glass and the crash of panelling in the round-house window and door was perfectly alarming.

"What a mad trick!" said Jack Sheppard, as he seized Tom by the collar, and dragged him on to his feet. "Come on at once, will you?"

A very few seconds sufficed to place them both in temporary security in one of the courts at the back of St. Martin's Church.

Then Tom rubbed his head, and looked very much confused.

"I'm quite sure," he said, "that blunderbuss fires at both ends; for it knocked me over at once, if it knocked over the round-house."

Jack Sheppard held his sides and laughed, and when he recovered himself sufficiently, he said, "Now, Tom, what do you mean to do, and where do you mean to go?"

"I want to go to the Golden Cross Inn, to look for Captain Heron."

"Then you won't find him there. I don't know what has happened, but there's been a hue and cry from the Golden Cross, and some talk of a murder. The 'runners' were there, and after that it's not likely Captain Heron will be found beneath the roof."

"I don't know what to do," said Tom, holding his head with both his hands. "I feel rather confused, and somehow wish I hadn't fired off that blunderbuss. The Captain's got to go to the Bishop of Worcester's to-morrow at twelve o'clock."

"It wants a good while to then, Tom."

"I suppose it does. But my best chance of seeing him, and telling him what roguery there is afloat between Lord Warringdale and the Reverend Mortification, will be to hide about the Bishop's house until I see him coming."

"Well, Tom, you can please yourself; but you'll be half stupid to-morrow if you don't get a bit of rest. Come along with me, and I'll find some crib where we can turn in for the remainder of the night."

"There's an old condemned house," said Tom, "in one of these courts: we can easily get into it by the kitchen window."

"A condemned fiddlestick!" said Jack Sheppard. "Do you think I'm going to sleep in condemned houses? Come along with me; the Duke of Queensberry's house is to let in Pall Mall. It's beautifully furnished, and there's nobody minding it. There's some beds there, Tom, that when once you get into them they come up upon each side of you like two hills of down and feathers, and you wonder how you'll ever get out again."

"But——" said Tom.

"Oh, stuff! there's no danger; the house is empty of people, and as there's nobody inside, you see they're forced to leave the street door on the lock; they think there's nothing to take away, for all the plate and small things are moved off. Come on! don't talk to me of condemned houses while I've got this in my hand."

Jack Sheppard held up in the night air one of the wiry-looking pick-locks which formed his master-keys to any establishment into which he chose to make his way.

Tom was certainly not reluctant to exchange a hard lodging on the floor of the condemned house for one of those peculiarly soft, mountainous beds which Jack Sheppard mentioned; so they proceeded together towards Pall Mall, and without encountering a single watchman to question their proceedings, they soon stood upon the door-steps of one of the large mansions in that aristocratic portion of London.

Jack Sheppard was not above two or three seconds in picking the lock, and in another moment these two juvenile defiers of the law were in the stately hall of the magnificent town residence of one of the richest, although not one of the most respectable, peers of that time.

The night was tolerably far advanced, and what with the fatigues and excitements he had undergone, and the heavy knock-down blow he had received from the blunderbuss, Tom Ripon was not at all sorry to follow Jack Sheppard up the grand staircase to the floor above the reception-rooms, where from a long corridor, richly carpeted and hung with full-length portraits, the principal bed-chambers opened.

Jack Sheppard paused a moment and lit one of those matches of phosphorus, which then, and for a considerable time afterwards, went by the name of "thieves' matches," so that they could see about them.

The magnificence of the place struck Tom with admiration.

"It's a beautiful house," he said; "but I don't see the beds."

"Oh, they're not here; this is only the passage

to them. Come on, through this door, and you'll see one of them."

Jack Sheppard opened a door, the panels of which were richly embossed, and they made their way to what was, in truth, the state bed-chamber of that lordly mansion.

If Tom had had eyes of admiration for the hall and its costly contents, he was perfectly entranced by the luxurious fittings and furniture of this chamber.

"Take a good look at it," said Jack Sheppard, "for we must be off before daylight, or some of the neighbours may see us. There, you can see it all if I hold up the match. Look at the velvet curtains and the gold tassels—look at the big looking-glasses and the state bed!"

The match went out. A profound darkness reigned in that magnificent room.

"Find your way," cried Sheppard, with a laugh. "I'm going to bed."

No. 95.—EDITH.

Tom Ripon was not sorry to do so likewise, and after some stumbling about, he managed to climb into that magnificent state bed, where—as had been described by Jack Sheppard—he lay with a mimic mountain of down and feathers on each side of him.

"Good night!" cried Jack.

Tom made no answer.

"Good night, eh? Don't you hear? Why, I declare he's off to sleep already!"

Mrs. Ripon had not nearly so comfortable a night's lodging as her son Tom, for she slept, or rather moaned and groaned, in Giltspur Street Compter.

Jonathan Wild paid her an early visit. What he had to say was short and simple.

"Never, Mrs. Ripon, by any accident engage in any transaction in which Captain Heron is concerned without letting me know, or you shall be banged as a receiver of stolen goods!"

"Merciful Providence! Me a receiver of stolen goods?"

"Never," added Wild, "allow yourself to be drawn into any transaction with my Lord Warringdale without telling me, or you shall be hanged as a putter up of robberies."

"Me put up robberies? Goodness gracious!"

"Surrender to me without another word of complaint the contents of your mob cap, or you shall be hanged, Mrs. Ripon, for conspiracy, and any other offence I may think proper to name and prove against you."

"And if I promise?" said Mrs. Ripon.

"You will be free this moment."

"Well, Mr. Wild, I suppose needs must when the—hem!—drives! Let me go now, and promise never to interfere with me again, and I'll agree."

"You're a sensible woman, Mrs. Ripon. I'd rather deal with you than with many men, who go on making a fuss about what they still know to be inevitable. Take my arm, Mrs. Ripon, and I'll carry you past the lock."

It was an odd sight to see Jonathan Wild escorting Tom's mother from Giltspur Street Compter; and, in fact, Wild himself was rather surprised at the facility with which Mrs. Ripon had fallen into at least one of his arrangements — particularly that one which involved the unconditional surrender of the contents of the mob cap. But Jonathan Wild, cunning and artful as he was, was not quite equal to Mrs. Ripon.

She bade adieu to Wild at the corner of Snow Hill, and then, as she trotted homewards, she congratulated herself.

"We live in a vale of tears," she said, "and Providence looks after us all; so we're bound to look after ourselves as a common return. It's a mercy I've had so many dealings with Starlight Jem, the footpad of Bagshot Heath, for the dear fellow was dreadfully took in the other day, and thought he had robbed a Jew money-lender of no end of bank notes, but they all turned out to be on the Bank of Elegance instead of England, which makes a wonderful difference; and it seems to me quite a providence that I've got my own six hundred pounds at home in a yellow bag, all in guineas, but the Bank of Elegance was in my mob cap. I mistrusted Mortification, and meant to take him in; but Mr. Wild's took in himself, and he lives in a vale of tears. Amen!"

CHAPTER CCXIV.

SHOWS WHAT HAPPENED AT THE BISHOP OF WORCESTER'S HOUSE IN CLARGES STREET.

JONATHAN WILD and his evil employer, the Lord Warringdale, made haste on their nefarious mission to the residence of the good Bishop of Worcester.

Wild was full of curiosity.

Curiosity to know what was the nature of that unknown power of which Warringdale boasted.

Warringdale himself looked ghastly.

The shadow of murder was upon his face. The idea of murder looked out from his eyes. It was manifest in every one of his movements.

Wild was on his guard.

Not for one moment did he permit Lord Warringdale to get behind him.

Not for one moment did he take his eyes off those of the associate in wickedness whom he certainly had good cause to suspect.

Had not Lord Warringdale already attempted his life?

Had he not artfully and systematically endeavoured to free himself from the encumbrance of the man who now held bonds, bills, and securities on the estates of Whitcombe, all signed by him, Warringdale, to the tune of sixty thousand pounds?

Was there not a high rate of interest on those bonds, bills, &c., &c., running on day by day, hour by hour?

Truly Jonathan Wild was a man to be got rid of as soon as there should appear any very good chance of the Whitcombe title falling into Lord Warringdale's possession.

And he meant—always meant—to get rid of the thief-taker.

And Jonathan knew it.

What a delightful feeling to be upon the minds of two men who drank together—talked, walked, and schemed together!

But so it was.

"I wonder," said Wild to himself, as they went towards the Bishop's house,—"I wonder if it be poison, or steel, or gunpowder Lord Warringdale relies on."

"I wonder," thought Lord Warringdale, "when I shall find it quite desirable to try the effect of Raphael's poison upon Jonathan Wild."

And so they reached Clarges Street.

They stood upon the doorstep of the good old Bishop; and no voice whispered in their ear that his residence was there.

"So, said Wild, "here we are."

"Yes. Where will you wait?"

"While you arrange matters with the Bishop?"

"Yes."

"Oh, I will stay with my friend the secretary in his private room."

"Very well. Be it so. I will then come down for you. What men are those?"

"What men?"

"There are some half-dozen men skulking about the different doorways of the street."

Wild laughed.

"Don't you know who they are?"

"How can I know?"

"They are my men. I picked them up as I came along. My fellows generally know pretty well where I am."

"Jonathan Wild, you are a wonderful man!"

"I know I am."

Lord Warringdale knocked at the Bishop's door, and then Wild said rapidly, "This will be the plan of operations. So soon as you have settled matters with the Bishop, and got possession of the papers or books he would give to Heron, you can come down stairs to me, and then we will wait the arrival of Felix Heron."

"That will do, and I fancy there is no time to lose."

"Not a moment."

The door was opened, and Jonathan Wild looked for the Bishop's secretary, and was shown with Lord Warringdale into the room in the occupation of that person.

"Well, old friend," said Wild, "how is the Bishop disposed this morning?"

"He is more than ever pleased with the idea of making peace with the two brothers."

"Amiable idea!" laughed Wild. "Ha! ha!"

"And I presume," added the Secretary, "that in this gentleman I have the honour to see my Lord Warringdale?"

"You do—you do. His lordship will see the Bishop at once, and try to persuade him to let him have the papers and diary."

The Bishop's bell rung at this moment; and the secretary, as he moved towards the door of the room, said, "He has heard the knock, and is all impatience to know if Lord Warringdale, on whose feelings he hopes to produce some impression, has arrived?"

"Tell him I am here," said Warringdale, "and most anxious to wait on him."

Jonathan and Warringdale were left alone in the library for a few minutes, during which they regarded each other strangely.

"You still keep your secret!" said Wild.

"What secret?"

"Your death secret!"

"Do not ask me yet to disclose it to you. The time will come when, believe me, you shall know all about it."

"Thank you."

The secretary returned.

"The Bishop will be delighted to see you, Lord Warringdale; and he says that he is quite pleased that you have got here before your brother, the Captain."

"So am I," replied Warringdale. "I will follow you, sir, if you please."

Lord Warringdale, as he followed the secretary from the library, cast a reproachful look at Jonathan Wild; for from the few words the Bishop's Secretary had just uttered, he could well comprehend that Wild had told him much more than he, Warringdale, was at all pleased at.

The old Bishop looked with a benign aspect at Lord Warringdale as he entered the room, and held out one of his hands as he said, "Welcome young sir—welcome! Believe me, I am right glad to see you."

Lord Warringdale touched little more than the tips of the Bishop's fingers with his own as he bowed low.

"I attend your Grace," he said, "with great pleasure, since you desired to see me."

"Come, come, sit down—sit down close to me, and let me talk to you."

Warringdale did sit down close to the old Bishop, who, laying his hands upon some papers on the table before him, said, in tones of emotion, "Heaven knows we are all the children of our Father who is above us, and so we may well call ourselves brethren, but the accidents of birth bind together by closer ties of brotherhood many of us; and inasmuch as we should all be kind, and good, and just to each other, as being all children of heaven, it follows that where these special ties of consanguinity exist, we should more specially strive to be just, loving, and affectionately desirous of peace."

Lord Warringdale coughed.

"So, you see," added the Bishop, "I want to make peace between you and your brother."

"My brother?"

"Even so! Your brother, the young man with the kind eyes and the ingenuous countenance, who is named Felix Heron."

"Ah, if I could only feel sure!"

"Sure of what?"

"That his poor mother and my father were not living in sin when he was born."

"Ah! is that your doubt?"

"It is indeed!"

"And if you felt sure now that the father and the mother were duly united in the sight of heaven and according to the ordinances of the Church?"

"If I were sure of that there would be but one course to pursue."

"And that?—and that?"

"That would be to hold my dear brother to my heart, and restore to him all that belonged to him!"

The old Bishop, who had been alternately looking under and above his spectacles at Lord Warringdale, now pulled them off, and looked him full in the face, while tears glistened in his aged eyes.

"Admirable young man!" he said; "I misjudged you, but I now see that all will be well. I am in possession of such proof."

"You, reverend sir?"

"Even I! Behold! here is the very volume of the parish diary and registry in which is recorded the marriage of your father, the late Earl of Whitcombe, with Amelia Staunton. He was then, as his father was alive, only Lord Warringdale, you comprehend, that being the second title of the family, and borne by the eldest son."

"As I bear it."

"As you bear it—but as Felix Heron, wrongly so called, ought to have borne it."

"Just so!"

"This will be a happy day to me!" added the old Bishop, as he looked about him in the room he knew so well; "a very, very happy day to me!"

The cadaverous hue that had been upon the face of Lord Warringdale deepened to a sickly yellow, and his hands shook.

That bad and cowardly man was about to try an awful experiment with human life.

"And so," he said, "this book is the only evidence of the marriage of Amelia Staunton with my late father?"

"I almost fancy it is."

"Almost only?"

"I use that term because, of course, I must have given a certificate at the time to either the Earl himself or to Amelia, his wife."

"Ah! yes!"

"But those kind of documents are so easily lost, so easily destroyed; and your brother informed me only yesterday that the leaf of the registry in the church at Barnes, which had borne the record of the marriage, was missing."

"Then, probably," said Lord Warringdale, as he laid his hand on the old Bishop's diary, "this is indeed the only evidence?"

"Yes—together with my personal testimony."

"Exactly!"

"Here is the entry."

"Oh, that is it!"

"You can read it, but by right I should of course give it to your brother."

"Of course—of course! I am so near-sighted that I have to point to small writing with something to lead my vision."

"And have you the habit of pointing with an ordinary pin?"

"I have."

Lord Warringdale had taken from a piece of paper, in which he had it carefully wrapped up, a common pin. His fingers shook as he produced it. *The point, to the depth of about an eighth of an inch, had been dipped in Raphael's poison vial!*

Warringdale pointed to the writing on the page of the old diary; and then as he rapidly withdrew his hand, he, apparently quite accidentally, inflicted on the back of the Bishop's hand a slight scratch from the point of the pin.

The poisoned pin—that slender and fragile-looking toy that was more harmful than the most trenchant falchion ever wielded by warrior's hand!

The Bishop held up his hand.

There were some very minute beads of blood following the course of the slight scratch that had been made upon it.

The eyes of the murderer and his victim met at that moment.

"I am afraid I am very careless," said Lord Warringdale.

The Bishop shook his head and sighed, "God help you, young man!"

Warringdale pushed his chair back, and half rose.

A sob, that if there had been one spark of humanity in the heart of Warringdale would have melted it to the very agony of contrition, came from the lips of the old Bishop.

"Help!" he said faintly. "This darkness!"

"Ah, it works!" cried Warringdale.

"Help!"

"Hush! hush!"

The Bishop tried to rise, but with a deep-drawn sigh he fell back into his chair again, and then he beat the air for a few seconds with his hands.

"It is done!" said Warringdale.

The Bishop spoke once more.

"I am in the shadow of the valley of death, but I see the radiant light which is behind the clouds. Oh, heaven! forgive this man! Pardon! Pardon! Pardon!"

The old Bishop had inclined gently forwards as he sat; and with one more sigh, his pure, and gentle, and kindly spirit was wafted to eternity!

Happy—happy—happy spirit! Well might that good, unsoiled soul rejoice in its escape from the thraldom of humanity!

"This will be a very happy day for me!"

Such had been the words of the Bishop; and they had come true to the very letter.

The unhappy wretch was he who still in life gazed with blanched cheek and trembling lips upon the relic of humanity that sat so calm and still in that chair before him.

Nervously, Lord Warringdale clutched the diary and placed it in his pocket.

"I am safe! I am safe now!" he said; and he glanced round him as though he feared he was not quite alone with the dead.

It took him quite an effort to pick up the pin and wrap it carefully in the paper again, and place it in his waistcoat-pocket.

"I am safe!" he said. "I am safe! I will keep my secret; and I shall, when I please, be the—the"—he was going to say "angel of death," but he altered the phrase and added, "spirit of destruction!"

He thought then that he heard some slight noise in the lower part of the house, and he listened with an awful fear about his eyes.

No. It was nothing.

"I must not be found with the dead," he whispered. "Let it be supposed that nature had reached its limit, and that this old man has given up the—the—ghost. No—not ghost. There are no such things; for if there were, surely I should be haunted to madness! There are no such things!"

Lord Warringdale turned twice round upon his heels, as though to challenge some contradiction to his words.

No. He was alone!

Alone with the dead!

How still the air of the room seemed! What a change in the aspect of everything within it that calm, motionless form seemed to make!

Warringdale trod on tip-toes to the door.

Tread boldly, O assassin! You will not now awaken your victim. Step harshly and noisily as you may, no shouts or cries that you can make, or all the world can make, will stir a muscle or make quiver an eyelid of the still form that sleeps the long sleep of death.

It was with a feeling of great relief that Warringdale got out of the room.

The air was to his perception of a different character only one pace from the threshold of that chamber of death. He almost ran down the staircase; and when he reached the hall, the strange, lambent light in his eyes, the whiteness of his lips, and the dry, parched way in which he breathed could not but invite the attention even of the hall porter.

"Good gracious, sir!" he said; "is anything the matter?"

"The matter?" responded Warringdale, in a high, harsh, cracked voice. "What should be the matter, eh?"

"Nothing, sir."

"Then nothing is the matter."

Both the secretary and Jonathan Wild heard these words which passed between the hall porter and Lord Warringdale

They were close at hand in the library.

Jonathan opened the door a little way. He did not speak, but he looked full into the eyes of my Lord Warringdale; and if the word murder had been written in legible characters across the countenance of Warringdale, it could not have been more easily read than was the expression of the awful deed he had just committed.

Probably from that moment Jonathan Wild begun to have a kind of respect for Lord Warringdale which he had never had before. He knew he was a weak-hearted, shrinking villain; but now that he really had taken a life, Wild felt that he was a something to be feared, and that was the only kind of respect that Jonathan felt for anybody.

Lord Warringdale staggered rather than walked into the library of the Bishop's secretary. When he looked in his face he was alarmed at the expression he saw there.

JACK SHEPPARD INTRODUCES TOM TO SNUG QUARTERS.

Presented Gratis with No. 95, of the New Edition of Jack the Captive; or, the Robbers of Epping Forest.

But he did not translate it quite so easily as Jonathan Wild had done.

"What has happened?" he said; "what has happened?"

"Nothing—nothing! Who says anything has happened?"

"I suppose the Bishop is still bent upon letting your brother, the highwayman, have the title and estates?"

Warringdale gave Wild another of those looks which implied his entire disapproval of the manner in which he must have made a confidante of the Bishop's secretary; but Jonathan looked perfectly indifferent, and before another word could be spoken among those persons, there came a sharp demand for admission at the street door of the Bishop's house.

Any one might have thought by the simultaneous start which Jonathan Wild, the secretary, and Lord Warringdale gave, that the knocker of the Bishop's door had struck each of them personally.

The fact was, that although but one member of that trio of iniquity had actually upon that morning committed murder, they were all three as much implicated in the deed as though they had been present at its awful consummation.

The person who knocked at the door of the Bishop's house was Felix Heron.

CHAPTER CCXV.

TOM RIPON OVERSLEEPS HIMSELF IN THE LUXURIOUS BED AT THE DUKE OF QUEENSBERRY'S.

IT was Felix Heron who knocked at the Bishop's door.

Twelve o'clock had passed about ten minutes, so that Heron was a little late for his appointment.

What terrible consequences sometimes hang upon ten short minutes! How little could Felix Heron have supposed it possible that during so brief a period of time which had expired during the time he was delayed by an accidental crowd in Piccadilly, the Bishop of Worcester would be swept away from the place of the living, and that diary, which contained the registry of the marriage of his mother with the Earl of Whitcombe, would be in the possession of his deadliest foe.

But so it was. Ten minutes had done all that; and but for that mysterious, and to all appearance supernatural, communication which Felix Heron had held in Whitcombe House, the evidence upon which his birth and legitimacy depended would have passed away like a shadow.

But before we admit Felix Heron to the Bishop's house, it will be necessary that we take a glance at another of the personages of our history.

Tom Ripon found the state bed in that magnificent mansion in Pall Mall so great an inducement to repose, that notwithstanding all his determination to rise at so early an hour that it would be impossible he could fail of meeting Captain Heron before he reached the Bishop's door, he overslept himself, and the sun was gleaming e the ap artment before Tom opened his eyes.

Somewhat to his surprise, too, Tom found himself alone.

Why and under what circumstances Jack Sheppard had left him in that house to shift for himself he could not make out; but certainly no Jack Sheppard was there; and Tom Ripon, as he sat up in bed, above the billowy waves of which his head only appeared, looked round him with dismay.

The room was perfectly light, and yet it was an odd sort of light, for it streamed between the green laths of Venetian blinds, which were down to their full extent over each of the tall windows.

But still the room looked gorgeously magnificent in Tom's eyes.

"Jack! Jack! Hilloa! Jack!" he cried.

There was no reply. Jack Sheppard was certainly gone. He had left the room, if not the house; and Tom Ripon—as, after many scrambles, he succeeded in getting out of the bed—began to fancy himself in a very dangerous situation.

He heard the rustle and bustle of the living tide of humanity without. The rumbling of carts —the sharp, rushing rattle of carriages and waggons—cries and sounds indicative of the fact that the day was far advanced—came up to that chamber, and terrified Tom with the consciousness that he must have taken but one step in sleep from the stillness and darkness of past midnight to the light, the roar, and the riot of mid-day in London.

"Too late!" cried Tom; "I shall be too late!"

He hustled on his clothes as though he had been dressing for a wager.

"Too late! too late!" were the only words he kept crying out to himself, and as he did so a feeling of bitterness came across his mind.

"Too bad! too bad!" said Tom. "He has left me sleeping here, and gone off by himself, as he said he would, before daylight. If he were not gone his clothes would be here. Oh, he's off fast enough! I suppose when I see him again he will tell me he didn't like to wake me. I made sure I should be up of my own accord long before this. He's a very good fellow is Jack Sheppard, and got me out of the round-house; but he oughtn't to have left me here. Oh, dear! he oughn't to have left me here."

Tom Ripon had just completed his toilet when he assumed an attitude of listening.

What sound is that that comes up sharp and clear in the morning air above all duller noises?

It is a clock striking.

"Hush! hush!" said Tom, as though he could have stopped all the carts and coaches of London, and the trampling of horses, and the pattering of feet, and the hum of human voices in the great hive of humanity, while he listened to those sounds.

After all, he might not be too late. How could he tell as yet? The sun might shine brightly, and London be all alive, at ten o'clock, or at eleven.

Tom counted the strokes of St. James's clock with the most eager attention.

"One—two—three—four—five—six—seven—eight—nine—ten—eleven—twelve!"

Tom Ripon clasped his hands together.

It was mid-day, the hour at which Captain

Heron was to be at the Bishop's—the only place now at which Tom could hope to see him, except in Epping Forest, and then it might be too late; if ever, indeed, Heron so far escaped his enemies as to stand again beneath the boughs of the ancient trees.

What to Tom Ripon now was all the gorgeous furniture of that splendid mansion? How much rather would he have passed the night upon some straw, or even upon the hard boards of the condemned house near to Star Court, and exposed to the attacks of his old acquaintances the rats, so that he should have been up betimes and ready to warn his friend and master of the danger that threatened him.

Tom dashed out of the state bed-chamber. He flew rather than ran down the grand staircase; in fact, for the greater part of the way Tom Ripon took the more expeditious way by sliding down the balustrades. He reached the hall, and open the street door in a moment, heedless whether he was seen or not, he dashed out into Pall Mall.

He might yet be in time.

Small of person and fleet of foot as he was, the distance from there to Clarges Street was nothing. Tom could dart about among the passengers with the dexterity of a mountebank, or he could take to the open roadway if the pavement became too dense for rapid progress.

Certainly five minutes could not have elapsed from the time when Tom Ripon set foot upon the pavement in Pall Mall to that when he arrived at the corner of Clarges Street, Piccadilly.

Then Tom raised a half cry of exultation, for not above twenty or thirty doors before him he saw Captain Heron.

And here Tom lost some of his caution; for making a dart forward to overtake his master before he could have time to ascend the steps of the Bishop's house and knock at the door, Tom was heedless of an obstacle in his way.

This obstacle was an elderly gentleman, of the class commonly called "fogy," who had just issued from his own house to take a constitutional walk in the Park.

The fogy was accurately attired, and got along pretty well with the assistance of a thick malacca cane, gold mounted and with an ivory handle.

"Stop! stop!" cried Tom, as he darted forward with as much velocity as if he had been discharged from a mortar. "Stop! stop! Don't knock!"

The fogy had been rapping the pavement with his malacca cane, and a dim idea took possession of his mind that these words were addressed to him—although Tom undoubtedly meant them for the ears of Captain Heron.

Not for more than the space of two seconds, however, had the fogy time to think about the matter, for Tom's head flew into his stomach, and fogy, and malacca cane, and Tom then flew into the road one over the other, in most admired confusion.

Then Tom Ripon cried out again, "Too late!" for he felt that this encounter with the fogy had put an end to his hopes at once of a communication with Captain Heron before he found his way into the Bishop's house.

The battle with the fogy did not last many seconds. Tom, after rolling right out into the

carriage-way, gathered himself up and at once darted into a very deep doorway.

The old gentleman sat in the kennel for a few minutes, entertaining the idea that the end of the world had come.

Then some compassionate passers-by helped him up, and he returned home in a very dilapidated and disconsolate condition.

Tom, as we have said, darted into a doorway; but the moment he got there he found himself on somebody's toes, and a gruff voice growled ont, "Be off! What do you want here?"

Tom cleared out of that doorway at once and darted into the next one.

"Be off, will you!" growled out some person, who was there likewise.

Tom tried a third doorway, and a third voice muttered, "Get out! You can't stay here!"

Tom began to feel like Morgiana, in the "Forty Thieves," when she visited the different oil jars in the yard, and found that each one was tenanted by a robber.

The fact was that these persons who so morosely objected to Tom's presence in the different doorways of Clarges Street were Jonathan Wild's men, who were, by his direction, waiting to apprehend Captain Felix Heron.

And the capture of Heron surely now looked like a fact accomplished; since so to speak, when he thought, metaphorically speaking, he was making his way into a dove's nest, he was in reality going into the lion's den.

The good old Bishop's house was in the possession of Jonathan Wild, Lord Warringdale, and the infamous hypocrite who had filled the situation of the Bishop's secretary.

The street without was well guarded by Jonathan's janissaries.

Little did Captain Felix Heron suspect the true state of affairs when he calmly knocked at the door of the Bishop's house.

The noise of the encounter between Tom Ripon and the fogy had certainly reached him, and he glanced in that direction at the moment the door was opened to him. All he saw, however, was that some scene of confusion was taking place, but he had no means of connecting it with himself or his fortunes.

"Is the Bishop within?" asked Heron cautiously of the hall porter.

"Yes, sir."

The door was opened wide, Captain Heron stepped into the hall, and the heavy door closed behind him.

Truly the Bishop had been within, but he was within no longer.

The earthly casket that had been the abiding place of the pure spirit was still there; but the Bishop was with his Maker.

The door of the library in which were Lord Warringdale, Jonathan Wild, and the secretary was not quite closed. Sufficient of a crevice was opened to enable them to see that the intended victim was there.

Of course Jonathan and Lord Warringdale were specially careful to keep out of sight.

"There he is!" whispered Warringdale.

"As good as nabbed!" said Wild.

"What shall I do?" asked the secretary.

"Show him up to the Bishop!" replied Wild.

"But why not take him now?"

Wild laughed in low tones like a hyena who feels certain of its prey.

"You do as I tell you," he said, "and the thousand pounds promised you will perhaps grow into two."

This was sufficient inducement for the secretary to act, and he forthwith sallied out into the hall.

It is doubtful if up to that time the Bishop's secretary fully realized the fact of the murder of his reverend master. He had, it will be remembered, objected to that mode of avenging the affair, and that objection was partly on personal and interested grounds.

The next Bishop might not want him as a secretary.

But from the manner of Jonathan Wild a suspicion began to dawn upon the mind of the man that the Bishop was indeed disposed of in the most effectual way.

"Good morning, sir," he said to Captain Heron; "you wish to see the Bishop?"

"I do. I come, indeed, by appointment."

The secretary bowed.

"If you will be so good as to follow me, then, sir, I will take you to his room."

The secretary preceded Captain Heron up the staircase of the Bishop's house, and the higher they got the more boldly did Lord Warringdale and Jonathan Wild open the library door, to look after them.

"Now," said Wild, "we must be prepared to act."

"Yes—oh, yes!"

"You are quite sure the Bishop is dead?"

"I did not say he was dead."

"But you looked it."

"He will probably die soon."

"Pho! pho!"

"He is an old man, and may alter his mind at the last moment, and refuse to help Felix Heron, and then some scuffle may be supposed to take place, and the old man may die."

"I see. If Heron can be thought guilty of the death of the Bishop it will save trouble."

"A world of trouble."

Lord Warringdale thought that if what he had just suggested could be brought about, it would save him all the trouble of the complicated plot in which he had secured the services of the Rev. Mortification Ripon.

But if Jonathan Wild had had the least idea of the important character of the documents Captain Heron actually had in his breast coat pocket at that time, he would have been too anxious for his capture to lose sight of him even as he went upstairs to the Bishop's room.

Not only had Captain Heron knocked at that door and walked into the very hands of his foes, but he had with him the documents which were more important to them than his life or death.

From Whitcombe House he had brought with him those papers that had been so mysteriously placed before him by the apparently supernatural and beneficent being who had spoken to him.

The very certificate of the marriage of Amelia Staunton with the late Earl of Whitcombe, which the Bishop had spoken of and surmised was lost or destroyed.

The certificate of his own baptism.

The letter from the keeper of the asylum at East Sheen, with all its enclosures.

Such were the documents with which Captain Felix Heron so innocently made his way into that house in Clarges Street.

His life—the evidences of who and what he was —the hopes of an existence—the happiness of Edith—all seemed now to be involved in one common ruin.

Heaven protect the right!

Captain Heron passed out of sight of Warringdale and Jonathan Wild as he ascended the stairs after the Bishop's secretary, and then Wild and Warringdale looked at each other, and there was triumph on their faces.

"Nabbed!" said Jonathan.

"Better dead!" said Warringdale.

"No, no! Leave him to me. When I can, I like to do things in the regular way. Never have I been so thwarted by living man as by this Felix Heron. I want to see him hung!"

"Hush!"

"Ah! he has, then, made a little discovery above!"

An exclamation—almost a shout of alarm—had come from the room above.

In another moment the secretary came down the staircase with a rapidity that he had probably never before exhibited.

Fear was the acting agent of that man. What he dreaded and expected was a contest, in the course of which a stray bullet or two might fly about, and before that began he wanted to get back to the library, where he intended to remain in safety until the capture was effected.

What made Captain Heron utter the exclamation he had done may well be surmised.

When he and the secretary reached the Bishop's room, the latter opened the door wide, and allowing Heron to pass him, he said, "Your Grace, this is Mr. Felix Heron, who attends you by appointment."

Heron bowed and advanced.

The secretary had taken but one anxious look into the room. His worst fears were confirmed. He saw by the attitude of the Bishop what had happened, and that it was a corpse which sat in that large padded chair, which alone prevented the dead from falling to the floor.

The secretary then dashed down stairs in the precipitate fashion we have recorded. He was full of fear mingled with rage.

The murder of the Bishop was not what he wanted or had advised, and he was prepared to reproach Lord Warringdale with the deed, not on account of the deed itself, but because it was likely to be contrary to his wishes.

Meanwhile Felix Heron advanced into the Bishop's room.

"I am here," he said, "kind and generous friend, to avail myself of your promise of yesterday."

Captain Heron suddenly paused.

The attitude of the old Bishop was peculiar. His head was resting on the table before him, and there was that complete and strange stillness in the room which the most profound repose can alone produce.

Captain Heron advanced another pace or two, and in a voice of deep emotion he spoke: "Is this sleep, or is it death?"

CHAPTER CCXVI.

JONATHAN WILD FOILED AT THE MOMENT HE THINKS HIMSELF CERTAIN.

WELL might Captain Heron doubt for a few short moments if it were death or its mimic presentment, sleep, which he saw before him.

The destroyer had indeed been there, but he had left no traces of his presence. So calmly and so gently did that good man rest after a long life of charity and gentleness, that even when Heron was so close to him that he could have stretched out his hand and touched the white locks which serenely hung over his brow, he could scarcely persuade himself that it was indeed death he saw before him.

Again Heron spoke. "Is this death or sleep?"

Another step forward, and he saw it was in truth death!

He lifted up the head of the old Bishop, and he saw the unmistakable aspect of the destroyer upon the venerable features.

"It is death!—it is death! Help!—oh! help!"

That was the cry which had been heard by those below.

For another half-minute, then, Captain Heron remained in the Bishop's room, and during that time he turned partly round twice, in order to see if there were any traces of violence in the apartment, or if he could discover how the good old man had come by his last sleep.

All was calm-looking and undisturbed in that room. Death had been there, but in no violent form. Captain Heron had no means, then, of forming the least judgment in regard to how the good Bishop had been sent from the world.

But that apartment was now no place for him. The secretary had shown him up, and had introduced him in a manner which showed him that the shock of the Bishop's death was yet to come upon his household.

It was a grief to him to know that he had to make the announcement, but yet he felt that it was his immediate duty to do so.

"Farewell, kind and generous man, farewell!" he said, as he took another glance at the Bishop, and then he left the room and stood at the stairs' head, as he cried out, "Help! help! help! The Bishop is dead! The good Bishop is dead!"

Now if we say that the surprise and the shock which Captain Heron had experienced upon finding himself introduced to the dead Bishop of Worcester, instead of the living one, were great, we shall be saying no more than the simple truth.

And yet, as he stood a few steps down that staircase, so that he could command a view of the hall, he was much more surprised at what he saw taking place.

Loud cries came up from that hall, and Captain Heron saw two people, one of whom was most unquestionably the hall porter, rolling over one another on the door-mat.

Who the other person was Captain Heron could not at the moment determine.

At the same time there was a furious knocking, apparently from the inner side of some door of a room leading directly from the hall.

The singular thing was that all this fracas below seemed to have sprung up as if by magic, for only the instant before all seemed to be at peace.

It is our duty to explain the meaning of all this to the reader.

When Tom Ripon found that the doorways in the immediate vicinity of the Bishop of Worcester's house were occupied so very pertinaciously, he set about asking himself who the men were likely to be. He ran round the next corner, and then stopped to think.

Tom was not long in coming to a sound conclusion.

The growling voice of one of those men had sounded to his ears as if he had heard it before; and in a few moments Tom, as he clasped his hands together in dismay, said, "They are Jonathan Wild's men; and the Captain is lost!"

This perfectly correct supposition filled Tom's heart with grief and affliction.

What should he do? What could he do?

There was no time to lose if he would do anything whatever; and yet how could he hope now to be of the slightest use?

Forewarned would have been to be forearmed in the case of Heron, but Tom had just been two minutes—perhaps only one minute—too late.

He was desperate.

"I don't care," he said,—"I don't care a bit what becomes of me. I can't make matters worse. I will do something, and see what will come of it."

The something which Tom Ripon made up his mind to do was to go at once and knock at the door of the Bishop's house, and get into it if possible, trusting then to chance to enable him to be of some use to Heron.

It so happened that if Tom Ripon had reflected for a month he could not possibly have done anything wiser or more opportune than this.

The knock that Tom gave at the door was a single dab, but it was sharp and decisive, and the hall porter at once opened the door.

It is the custom of hall porters to fling their portals wide open for a rapid and important double rat-tat, but the way in which they just open the door wide enough to look out to the single knock, is as common as it is peculiar.

Tom Ripon, however, marched in.

"What is it, eh?" said the hall porter.

"Nothing!" said Tom, as he stooped a little, and so dived into the hall.

"Come!—come! What do you want here?"

Tom's eyes fell right before him on to the partially opened library door,—that door within which now all three villains who were foes of Captain Heron were to be found. It was not open above an inch, but Tom's eyes were sharp, and although that inch of space only disclosed a narrow slip of a face, Tom at once recognised it.

It was a narrow slip of the face of no other than Jonathan Wild.

Perhaps the recognition was mutual—no doubt it was—but Tom certainly could not now be accused of hesitation. The door opened outwards towards the hall, and on the instant that Tom saw it was Jonathan Wild who was on the other side of it, he made a dash across the hall with a speed of desperation that cleared the space he had to pass in half a moment, and with both his hands, his head, and the whole accumulated force of his body he came against the door.

The manner in which it was slammed shut was was quite alarming to see.

Was it Wild's nose—one of his fingers—or had he so narrow an escape of a jamb of one or both, that extorted a yell from his lips? Certainly he did utter such a yell.

Tom had not had time to observe that there was a key in the lock of this door, but as he dashed it shut the handle of the key touched his hand rather roughly, and Tom welcomed the touch with almost as loud a cry of exultation as Jonathan Wild had uttered of startled fear when the door was slammed so violently in his face.

Tom turned the key instantly.

Lord Warringdale, Jonathan Wild, and the Bishop's secretary were prisoners in the library.

It was not likely that such men—particularly as one of them was Jonathan Wild—would continue for long prisoners in a room simply because the door was locked upon them; but, under the

present circumstances, passing moments were precious, and life or death certainly hung upon the events of a minute.

Tom left the key in the lock—perhaps he only did so accidentally,—but it baffled Wild, who, with a skeleton key that he immediately produced, strove to liberate himself and his rascally associates.

The key was an effectual bar to the use of the ingenious instrument, which otherwise, in the accomplished hands of Wild, would have unlocked the door almost as quickly as it had been locked.

From the moment that Tom Ripon had struck that single decisive dab at the Bishop's door, to that at which he moved the key in the lock of the library, was such a fleeting interval of time that the hall porter was perfectly bewildered.

It was not until Tom turned round and faced him again that he at all recovered sufficiently his presence of mind to attack the daring intruder who seemed thus to be taking the whole establishment by storm.

Then the hall porter rushed at Tom, who met him half-way; for Tom's object was to prevent him unlocking the library door, on the inner side of which Jonathan Wild, Lord Warringdale, and the secretary commenced a furious hammering.

Tom and the hall porter fell down together upon the door-mat, and that was just the juncture at which Captain Heron appeared a few paces down the great staircase.

"What is all this?" cried Heron in a high voice, which rose above all other sounds.

Tom heard Heron's voice.

"Fly! fly!" he cried. "Escape! escape! Not this way Captain—not this way! The street is full of Wild's men. Find some other way, Captain. Escape! escape! Don't mind me—they'll nab me,—but don't mind me!"

Captain Heron was quite at a loss to know what all this meant; but that Tom was warning him—for now he recognised him both by voice and appearance—of some true and tangible danger he did not for a moment doubt.

He (Heron), however, was not the sort of person to leave even the humblest of his followers to capture and danger for his sake; and quickly re-ascending the staircase—heedless of what might be the consequences to himself—he at once put an end to the contest between Tom Ripon and the hall porter by watching his opportunity to deal the latter a knock-down blow, that sent him in a very doubled-up and melancholy condition to the further end of the hall, where certainly for a time he was perfectly harmless.

Heron had had no time to inquire into the merits of the fight between Tom and the Bishop's porter; it was sufficient for him that he saw it raging, and that one of the persons engaged was a follower of his own.

"Hoorah, Captain!—hoorah!" cried Tom. "We'll beat them at last. Jonathan Wild's in that room. The street's full of his men. Ah! who are you?"

This sudden and unconnected manner in which Tom Ripon concluded his speech might have given rise in Captain Heron's mind to doubts of his sanity—more particularly, too, as Tom at the same moment dashed past him and slammed shut another door which led into the hall, and which was just being slowly opened by a terrified footman, who, hearing the riot and racket overhead, was coming up from the domestic regions, followed by the cook, scullery-maid, three housemaids, and the under footman, to see what it was all about.

This door luckily likewise could be fastened from the hall, so that Tom when he had done that was really master of the situation.

The position of affairs at the Bishop's was now most peculiar.

The street door was shut, so that Wild's men had no means of getting in to the assistance of their master even had they wished to do so, which they certainly did not; for not only had they no idea that he was in any danger, but they were so accustomed to act only under his direction that it is doubtful if they would have stirred an inch had they been perfectly aware of all that was taking place.

They waited for orders.

The only danger that Captain Heron ran from them was that if he appeared in the street they certainly would pounce upon him; for Jonathan Wild had told them to let anybody into the house without molestation, but to take prisoner everybody who came out of it excepting in his company.

The hall porter either would not or could not get up from the corner into which he had been flung by the straightforward blow of Captain Heron.

The domestic establishment of the Bishop were shut out from participation in the affairs taking place in the hall.

Jonathan Wild, Lord Warringdale, and the secretary were still prisoners in the library.

And the dead Bishop sat up-stairs in his easy chair, as the only occupant of the upper portion of the house.

Thus that establishment in Clarges Street, Piccadilly, might be considered a sort of fortress, of which Captain Heron and Tom Ripon had got possession, while it was so beleaguered without that they dared not stir from it.

"What on earth is all this about Tom?" cried Heron—"what can it mean? Are you—or am I—or are all these people mad?"

"All right, Captain! I overslept myself, you see, in the Duke of Queensberry's state bed—that's all; and now you know all about it."

Captain Heron was quite convinced now that Tom's wits had departed; but he was quickly aroused to the fact that he occupied rather a dangerous position in the Bishop's hall, for Jonathan Wild, finding his efforts with the picklock perfectly futile in consequence of Tom having left the key in the lock, adopted a rough and ready mode of clearing away the obstruction.

Placing the muzzle of a pistol against the key-hole, Jonathan Wild fired, and a portion of the iron-work of the lock flew past Captain Heron's head like the fragment of a shell.

"There they are!" cried Tom. "They'll be out directly."

Heron saw the danger.

With that quickness of mental adaptation to the circumstances of the instant which characterized him, he seized the huge leathern chair, with its ample canopy—in which the hall porter was wont to doze away his time at night—and wheeling it backwards with a rush, the door of the library was slammed shut again with tremendous force just as Jonathan Wild had cautiously opened it about an inch.

"Bring those fire-irons here," said Heron, pointing to the grate that was in the hall.

Tom obeyed him; and Heron propping them up slantways against the indentation made by the lower panel of the door, jammed the other ends so hard and close against the floor that the library door was most effectually barricaded.

Jonathan Wild fired another pistol through one of the panels; and this shot Captain Heron thought he might as well return, so he sent a bullet crashing through the same panel.

There came a loud cry from within the library; but whether from fear, or because one of its occupants had received a wound, Captain Heron had no means of telling.

"Come up-stairs, Tom, with me," he said; "and, for the love of liberty and life, tell me truly what all this is about."

"Jack wouldn't stay to wake me up," said Tom; "and I overslept myself in the Duke of Queensberry's state bed."

"My dear Tom, you said that before, but it don't enlighten me in the least. What brought you here? Tell me that."

"My legs," said Tom, "as fast as I could put 'em to the ground, only I ran against a fogy, or else I should have caught you just before you came in at the door. The Rev. Mortification is up to some tricks—and so is mother—and so is Lord Warringdale. The rats nearly eat me up; and Jonathan Wild's men are in the doorways of the street. I got out of the round-house, and the blunderbuss sent me sprawling in the gutter; and what's become of Jack Sheppard I can't think. But here we are—hurrah!"

If Captain Heron was rather at a loss before to understand exactly the meaning of all that was taking place, he was certainly not much more enlightened by the fragmentary manner in which Tom Ripon detailed his adventures for the last twelve hours.

"I can understand," said Heron, "that there was some plan on the part of Jonathan Wild to capture me here, but how it came about I can hardly tell."

"Yes, that's it!" said Tom.

"Are you certain Wild's janissaries are in the street?"

"Yes, Captain. There's one in every doorway, I do believe."

"Then an attempt in that direction would be madness."

Captain Heron and Tom had reached the top of the staircase, and certainly if ever there was a situation full of difficulties and fearfully un-suggestive of any means of escape, it was that of Felix Heron upon this occasion.

There was temporary safety just for the period of time that the present singular state of affairs lasted, and it was not possible that could be for long; and as Heron paused at the door of the room where the good Bishop slept the sleep of death, he felt that a new aspect was about to be put upon his position, for a loud knock came at the street door of the house.

It might have been habit—which exercises so strong a control upon human nature—but certainly the hall porter, who, up to that moment, did not seem capable of moving hand or foot, gathered himself up instinctively to do his duty.

The door was opened.

The Bishop's coachman made his appearance, to know if his master required the carriage, as he had not received the usual message concerning it.

Jonathan Wild, Lord Warringdale, and the secretary had recommenced their assault upon the panel of the library door.

They accompanied their assault this time with cries and shouts to be released, for they had heard the knock at the street door, and that it had been opened.

The barricade was removed, and flushed, heated, and angered, Jonathan Wild—like some savage animal escaping from a trap or cage—rushed into the hall.

He was closely followed by Lord Warringdale and the secretary, who looked extremely pale.

CHAPTER CCXVII.

CAPTAIN HERON AND TOM EFFECT THEIR ESCAPE THROUGH A REMARKABLE INTERPOSITION.

FELIX HERON kept Tom silent, while he himself leant over the balustrade of the staircase of the Bishop's house, to hear what was taking place below in the hall.

Indeed, by descending a step or two, Heron was able to look over sufficiently far to see Jonathan Wild and Lord Warringdale.

Had his revenge then been unscrupulous, and his intentions murderous, he might easily, from where he stood, have shot one or other of those enemies to his peace, his happiness, and his life.

But no such idea came into the mind of Captain Heron. It was only in actual self-defence that he could have brought himself to commit such an act.

He saw Wild make a rush to the street door, and then he heard a whistle blown loudly and fiercely, which was the signal for Jonathan Wild's myrmidons without to join him in the hall.

No less than eight of his janissaries were soon assembled, and then in a loud, passionate, ring-ing voice, he cried out, "My men, the famous Captain Heron, the highwayman, is in this house! There's a thousand pounds reward upon his head, and you shall have every penny of it among you!"

Jonathan's men did not seem quite so enthu-siastic as probably he would have wished them to be, for they bore a deep-rooted conviction in their minds that Captain Heron was by no means an easy capture; and the idea that two or three of them might be shot in the affray rather damped all their energies.

No one wished exactly to encounter death, in order that his surviving companions might inherit his share of the thousand pounds reward.

"Cowards!" cried Jonathan, "do you all shrink from one man?"

"No, Mr. Wild," said one, "we'll do our duty, and follow you."

"Yes, Mr. Wild, we'll follow you!" said the others.

Wild understood what this meant very well. "Confusion seize you all!" he cried; "this is the first time that my bull-dogs have shown fear. Come on, then, since you must follow me! I'm not afraid of a bullet, and never was! I'm scarred and seamed enough, or I shouldn't be Jonathan Wild the Great, as I am—as I am! Come, my Lord Warringdale—for you at least will accompany me."

"I think I'll sit here," said Warringdale, "for I don't feel very well."

"What, my lord, do you too shrink?"

"No, Mr. Wild; but I think I've done enough for one day."

There was a significance in these words which enabled Wild fully to understand them. They alluded to the murder of the Bishop, which had certainly been accomplished by Warringdale, and which, if by any means it could be fixed upon Captain Heron, would surely accomplish his de-struction.

The hall porter now put in a word. "Gentle-men all!—gentlemen all!" he said, "didn't you hear an outcry that the Bishop was dead?"

"The Bishop dead!" cried Wild, with a well-affected expression of intense surprise.

"The right reverend and admirable Bishop no more!" exclaimed Warringdale.

"My friend and master departed!" cried the secretary, who, now that the fact was accomplished, felt that his best interests would be to accept it, and play upon the terrors of Lord Warringdale for all time to come for payment and profit.

"I heard him say so," said the hall porter. "There was a cry from the top of the stairs of 'Help! help! the Bishop is dead!'"

"Then that villanous Heron, the highwayman, must have killed him!" said Wild.

"Undoubtedly," added Lord Warringdale.

"Oh, it's beyond all dispute!" said the secretary; "and to prevent us going to my good master's assistance, we were all three locked in a room by one of the associates of the villain!"

"Seize him!—seize him!" cried Wild, as he commenced ascending the staircase. "It is not now a highwayman that we are after, but the murderer of the Bishop!"

Captain Heron had heard all this, and some idea of the plot which was formed against his life began to be clear to him; although how the good Bishop had come by his death, he, Heron, had no means of coming to any conclusion regarding.

"Come, Tom," he said, "we will at least interpose what obstacles we can between ourselves and our enemies. Follow me, and let us see what fortune will do for us."

"We ain't nabbed yet, Captain!" said Tom, "and I somehow seem to think we shan't be. This is a fine house, but I would give it all for one of the dear old glades of Epping Forest."

"And so would I—and so would I!" said Heron with a sigh.

The Bishop's house was a large one; but Captain Heron was utterly ignorant of the topography, and he felt that he must trust to chance to prevent —at least, as far as possible—what seemed to be his inevitable capture.

Taking Tom by the arm, he led him into the room where sat the dead Bishop in his chair. He closed the door, and locked it on the inside; and then addressing Tom, he said, "Do not be alarmed. The Bishop is indeed dead!"

"Dead!" cried Tom, as he shrunk back with that instinctive fear of dissolution which generally affects the young.

"Yes; but there is nothing to fear. In life, he was a man who would not have trodden upon a worm; in death, he is but a picture."

But still Tom took care to give the dead Bishop an ample share of the room; and he was much pleased when Captain Heron turned the handle of another door, and called to him to follow.

There was, in good truth, no time to lose.

At the moment when Captain Heron opened that other door, which led he knew not where, there was a violent effort to get into the room in which the dead body of the Bishop was lying.

That effort was made by Jonathan Wild.

The little altercation and delay that had taken place in the hall of the house was over; and, inflamed with passion at the cowardice of Lord Warringdale and the lukewarm manner in which his own men took up the pursuit of Captain

Heron, Jonathan was prepared to commit any violence and any atrocity.

Locked doors, however, in even an ordinary house, although they might be most ridiculously ineffective in withstanding such a man as Wild, still were obstacles.

It took some minutes to break one down, and during those minutes Captain Heron had not been idle.

The other door which he opened in the Bishop's room led into a smaller chamber, in which was a plain little tent bed, and a table, on which were some devotional books.

For the first few seconds that Captain Heron was in that room he thought that there was no outlet to it.

"Tom," he said, "I am grieved to the soul that you are here!"

"And I'm glad!" said Tom.

"Do not say so. You will be taken with me; and not only shall I have the affliction that I have brought danger upon you, but you will not be able to proceed to the forest, as I would fain wish, and let Edith and my gallant comrades know what has happened."

"I don't see," said Tom, "why I might not get out at the window."

Captain Heron shook his head.

"The depth is too great, Tom."

"But here is another small door in the wall, behind the head of the bed."

"Ah, say you so?"

There was a loud crashing sound in the outer room at this time, which was occasioned by Jonathan Wild breaking his way into it from the landing at the head of the stairs.

Captain Heron had fastened the door of the small retiring-room he was in by a bolt that was on its inner side; but now that Tom Ripon had found another door in the wall, he eagerly hurried to avail himself of it.

The door was evidently a supplementary one, which had been made in the wall after the house was built; and being merely cut in the wainscot, it resembled so much the rest of the panelling that Captain Heron might well be excused for not noticing it.

Tom flung this narrow door open, and then they both saw that it led into a small but prettily appointed bath-room, which no doubt had been built out from the back of the house since the Bishop had been in the occupation of the premises.

Scarcely had Captain Heron and Tom Ripon crossed the threshold of the bath-room when they heard Jonathan Wild thundering at the door which was defended by the bolt.

His voice rose loudly and harshly above all other sounds, as he cried, "Surrender! surrender! Surrender, Captain Heron, upon fair terms! I do not seek your life; but if you force me to take it, I am not the man to hesitate, for my name is Jonathan Wild."

The door at which Wild was hammering now offered to him a much greater obstruction than the other which he had passed through; for the brass bolt which held it was a powerful one, and not easily acted upon from without. Probably, too, Wild was baffled to guess for a few moments what kind of fastening it was that resisted him; and if there had been any present means of escape for Captain Heron and Tom Ripon, those few moments would have been quite invaluable.

There was, however, no outlet from the little bath-room but by the same door through which they had entered it; and Captain Heron, as he glanced about him, and saw the apparent hopelessness of his situation, drew out his pistols—that exquisite pair of highly-ornamented weapons to which we have more than once alluded.

One of these pistols he had discharged through the panel of the library door, in reply to the shots from within that room, which had been levelled at him; but the companion pistol he had still loaded.

It was a wonder that Captain Heron could speak with the calmness he did while Jonathan Wild was hammering at a door within fifteen paces of him, which must soon give way, and which alone stood between the unscrupulous thief-taker and his victim; but if there was any mental quality which more than another characterized Heron, it was that calmness and presence of mind in circumstances of great peril, which exhibits the truest courage.

"Tom," he said, "I suspect that it is my life they aim at; for that will put an end to a world of trouble, which otherwise, I fancy, they will have with me. I do not think, however, that they will murder you; and perhaps, indeed, in their anxiety to destroy me, they may pay little attention to you, so that you may escape."

"But I won't," said Tom. "If they take you, Captain, they may take me; and if they murder you, they may murder me. We celebrated highwaymen, Captain, ought always to live and die together."

A faint smile crossed the lips of Captain Heron.

"No, Tom, no," he said; "that must not be. Let what may happen, I hope still that you will be free, and able to perform for me a great service. Take these papers, Tom, and hide them securely about you; and whatever happens to me, if you can but live, and find your way to old Epping Forest, tell Edith all that has happened, and place them in her hands."

Felix Heron's voice faltered slightly as he pronounced the name of Edith; and he felt that his heart was too full at that moment to permit him to add any expression of endearment to that name, or to send even by Tom Ripon a message the very utterance of which might unman him.

As he spoke, Captain Heron had handed to Tom those important documents which he had brought from Whitcombe House, and which—could but Lord Warringdale have guessed his possession of—would have overcome even the cowardice of that villanous spirit, and induced some bold attempt to seize them.

Tom's hands trembled, and the tears stood in his eyes, as he took those papers, which were the proofs of who was the real Earl of Whitcombe, and the possessor of its magnificent properties.

"Captain! Captain!" he said; "don't let them kill you."

"Not if I can help it."

"Shoot Jonathan Wild, Captain. Who knows but that may frighten the others?"

"I will not die tamely, like some timid hare. I have one pistol loaded, at all events, and may send a bullet into that villain's heart before I breathe my last sigh."

"And give me the other, Captain," cried Tom; "it may help me to get away, and carry these papers to Lady Edith."

"It is unloaded, Tom, and useless. But I will put a charge in it for you."

A slight cessation had taken place in the thundering blows Jonathan Wild had been dealing at the door with the bolt; and as Captain Heron, without the shaking of a muscle or the tremor of a nerve, loaded, from a small powder flask he had with him, the discharged pistol, he half stepped into the centre room of those three that had evidently been in the private occupation of the Bishop, and heard Jonathan Wild call out, in a loud screaming voice, "Are you sure of that? Will you take your oath of that?"

Then another voice, which probably belonged to one of the household of the Bishop, replied, in tones which betrayed considerable trepidation, "Quite sure, Mr. Wild—quite sure. Bless you, sir, we ought to know the house."

"Then you tell me," added Wild, "that through this door there is a small chamber, sometimes occupied by the Bishop after he has studied late at night, and that beyond that there is nothing but a bath-room, from which there is no outlet?"

"If you please, Mr. Wild, that is it."

"It isn't as I please, blockhead! Is it a fact?"

"Yes, Mr. Wild."

"Then," yelled Wild, "the rat's in a trap!"

"Tom," said Captain Heron, quietly, "I find that, by some accident, I am without bullets."

Tom, with an air of satisfaction, dived his hand to the bottom of his pocket and produced one.

"There you are, Captain—lots of ammunition!"

"How came you by bullets, Tom?"

"Ogle gave me some to fling at the crows when I'd nothing else to do."

"Then, Tom," said Captain Heron, as he wrapped the bullet in a piece of paper, and rammed it home in the barrel of the pistol—"then, Tom, you have a life in your hands; but I charge you, as you wish to obey my orders—and they may be the last ones you will get from me—do not recklessly, or without abundant cause, shoot any one. But remember, if it be necessary for your escape that you should do so, you must not hesitate, for in those papers I have given you are comprised the fortunes of Edith and the confusion of her enemies."

Tom was about to make some reply when he and Captain Heron were both startled by a crash of glass; and upon turning to a small, narrow window which was in the bath-room, and through which they had both previously looked, and seen, at a glance, that it descended a sheer twenty-five feet or more, and so was not available for escape, they observed one of the panes of glass shattered, and that some portion of what had once been a china ornament lay upon the floor of the bath-room.

Then Captain Heron uttered an exclamation of joyful surprise, for glancing from that window, across a space of about thirty feet, he saw another window, of similar size and shape, belonging to the next house, projecting from which was a similar bath-room to that which the Bishop had appended to his residence.

That other window was open, and at it stood the young Earl of Bridgewater, with a look of excitement and surprise upon his face, and making signs to Captain Heron that it was his hands which had thrown the piece of broken ornament to attract his attention.

"It's all right!" cried Tom. "We shall get away now!"

"Yes, Tom, if we were birds and had wings. But how are we to cross this chasm?"

The actions of the young Earl of Bridgewater were now, for a few seconds, quite unintelligible to Captain Heron, for he saw him rushing about the room as if hard at work about something, but what it was he had no means of observing.

Time passes quickly under such circumstances, and the young Earl of Bridgewater soon appeared at the opposite window with something in his hands that Tom was the first to observe consisted of a coil of rope.

The young Earl made various gestures then to indicate that he did not wish to call out lest his voice should be heard, but that he wanted Captain Heron to open the window of the bathroom.

That there was now some rational prospect of escape from the apparently hopeless condition in which he and Tom Ripon had found themselves, warmed the heart of Captain Heron, and brought fresh light to his eyes.

"Tom, Tom!" he said; "all are not lost who are in danger. We may yet be free."

"Hoorah!" cried Tom.

Crash at that moment went the door with the bolt, which had hitherto withstood the attacks of Jonathan Wild and his janissaries.

Perhaps those attacks had not been quite so furious as they would have been if Wild had thought that Captain Heron and Tom Ripon had any chance of escape from the bath-room.

CHAPTER CCVIII.

CAPTAIN HERON ADDRESSES IMPORTANT COUNSEL TO HIS BAND AT THE FOREST.

THE movements of the young and noble-minded Earl of Bridgewater from the opposite window quickly explained themselves.

He had a stout and trustworthy rope, one end of which he wanted to throw across the space between the two windows.

The other end he could easily make fast on his side.

That rope, then, would form a kind of bridge, although but a frail one, from one window to the other.

But the position of Captain Heron was too critical and dangerous to permit him to occupy himself wholly with this effort at rescue, for when Jonathan Wild had forced the door with the bolt, he really seemed to be on the point of laying his hand upon the arm of Captain Heron.

The bath-room door had but a very frail little latch on the inside as a fastening, which was not intended for security at all, but merely to keep the door shut from draughts of colder air than ought to be in the bath-room while in use.

One kick from Jonathan Wild would have put an end at once to any opposition which that door would have presented.

"He's coming, Captain—he's coming!" cried Tom. "Shall I shoot him now?"

"No, Tom, no—not yet! Help me!"

Captain Heron placed his shoulder against the side of the bath, which was of a grey, slaty-looking marble. The weight of it was great; but although it would have taken half a dozen strong men to lift it, yet, as it rested on the floor, it was by no means so difficult a thing to push it along.

On the impulse of some powerful feeling people can exert for a few moments power of muscle that under ordinary circumstances they would not be able to persuade themselves they possessed.

The bath moved about six inches.

"That will do," said Heron.

The slight space through which the marble bath had passed had been sufficient to bring one corner of it about half an inch over the edge of the room door.

From that instant that door was more securely fastened than any of the others had been, and nothing but breaking it absolutely down would remove it.

"Captain Heron — Captain Heron!" cried Wild from the other side of the door.

"We are safe, Tom," said Heron.

"How so, Captain?"

"He stops to parley, and that gives us all the time we want."

"Captain Heron, do you hear me?" cried Wild again from the other side of the bath-room door, which all the while he was making vigorous attempts to push it open, and wondering what could possibly hold it so tight.

"Who speaks to me?" cried Heron.

At the same time that he thus answered Jonathan Wild, he caught the end of the rope which the young Earl of Bridgewater flung from the opposite window to him, and tied it securely round a portion of the bath.

"It is I, Jonathan Wild. You are my prisoner, Captain Heron, just as much as if I had you in my hands. You cannot escape."

"I can fight!"

"Pho! pho! You are a man of sense, Captain. You will give in, trusting to good luck and better times, when you find there is no chance of getting away."

Heron pulled the rope quite tight when he found that the Earl of Bridgewater had fastened what might be called his end of it securely. He thought it no bad plan, at the same time, to keep Jonathan Wild parleying on the other side of the bath-room door.

"I am armed, Jonathan Wild," he said; "and an armed man does not feel inclined to surrender."

"What's the good," said Wild,—"what's the good of your shooting me or my shooting you? There are handy to a dozen of my men here, who will be sure to nab you."

"Tom!" whispered Heron. 'The rope is all right and tight—go across!"

"After you, Captain."

"Go, I say! It is my order."

Tom would as soon have thought of denying his existence as a positive order from Captain Heron; and he accordingly launched himself on to the rope from the bath-room window.

To twist his legs and arms round the rope, and go across to where the Earl of Bridgewater waited to help him in at the window at which he stood, was child's play to Tom Ripon. He would have gone to and fro a dozen times for the fun of the thing.

"Come, come, Captain!" said Jonathan Wild, in rather impatient tones. "Open the door, and yield like a sensible man, or I will fire through the panels; and the room you are in, they tell me, is so small, that I don't see how I can miss you."

"Fire away!" said Heron.

"I don't want to behave unhandsomely to you, if you will give in."

"What do you call handsome behaviour?"

"I will take your word."

"For what?"

"Not to escape; and then I will not even put the handcuffs on you."

"You are too kind!"

As Captain Heron uttered these last words, he swung himself gently out at the window on to the rope.

"What do you say?" cried Wild.

Heron, just as he commenced pulling himself over the chasm which the rope crossed, spoke for the last time on that occasion to Jonathan Wild.

"Good bye—good bye!"

"What?"

Captain Heron was gone.

Wild rapped still at the bath-room door with the butt-end of one of his pistols, and called out that he would certainly fire through the panel if Heron did not yield.

Then Jonathan stepped on one side, so that, if the shot should be returned, which he fully expected, it might pass him harmless; and only putting one hand and arm forward, he fired through the middle panel of the bath-room door.

Captain Heron was at that very time being assisted in at the opposite window by the Earl of Bridgewater and Tom Ripon.

"Dear friend," said Heron, "you have saved me!"

"Thank heaven I had the means and the opportunity!"

"But the rope will betray to Wild the route I have taken—for of course we have no means now of disengaging it on the other side."

"But," said Tom, adroitly, "we have on this, Captain;—and there it goes hanging right down into the yard, and Jonathan may fancy that is the way we have gone."

"Capital! capital!" cried the Earl of Bridgewater, as he closed the window rapidly, but carefully. "I think we have foiled the ruffian now, Heron—or, rather, my Lord Whitcombe, as I feel I ought to call you."

"Call me anything," replied Heron, "so that you permit me always to call you my friend."

The rope swung right down to the paved yard at the back of the Bishop's house, so that it did not appear ever to have had the slightest connexion with that window of the adjoining residence, where the young and gallant Earl of Bridgewater had appeared so opportunely to the aid of Captain Heron and Tom.

But by this time, as might well be supposed, the patience of Jonathan Wild, of which he never had a very large share, was quite exhausted.

The non-return of the pistol-shot, too, which he had sent into the bath-room, combined with the continued silence of Captain Heron, began to fill him with undefined fears, and he called aloud to his men.

"Smash this door! In with it!—in with it! Open! open!"

There was a crash of splintered wood, and the frail door of the bath-room gave way.

Jonathan at once, with a pistol in each hand, rushed through the aperture; and then he uttered one of those peculiar and terrific yells of rage and disappointment which were so appalling to hear.

"Gone! gone! Escaped! By all the fiends, he has fled and foiled me!"

Wild ran to the window, and looked out. He saw the rope hanging down to the paved yard, and he did not for an instant doubt but that, in so seeing it, he looked upon the means by which Heron had left the bath-room, as well as the route he had taken.

From the window opposite, hidden themselves from observation, Captain Heron, and the Earl of Bridgewater, and Tom Ripon, saw Wild's hideous countenance projected from the bath-room window, as he gazed down into the yard of the Bishop's house.

"I could easily settle Jonathan, now," whispered Tom. "Wouldn't it astonish him, Captain? May I send a bullet across at his head?"

"No, no, Tom—not now. We have foiled the rascal, and let that suffice."

Jonathan Wild was puzzled. The more he looked down to the paved yard of the Bishop's house, the more he was confounded to know what had really become of Captain Heron and Tom. That they had effected an escape from the window of the bath-room by means of that rope, which went down to within a foot or two of the pavement of the yard, seemed clear enough.

That was not exactly what puzzled Jonathan Wild.

It was what had become of them after they got there, which was a matter of doubt and reflection to him.

The yard seemed to be something like a pit, into which, if you once got, there did not seem any means of leaving, except through the Bishop's house.

The lower part of that house Jonathan Wild knew to be well guarded by his janissaries, for he was too old a campaigner in such matters as that he had now in hand to take all his force with him up-stairs.

If Captain Heron, then, attempted to leave the yard of the Bishop's house by the only apparent means he had of leaving it—namely, through the house itself—his capture was certain.

Jonathan Wild placed his hand to his ear, and withdrew his head from the window, to listen if any sounds came from the lower part of the house indicative of the capture of Heron.

But all was still in that quarter, and then Jonathan crammed his head out of the window so far to take a still better survey of the yard, that his hat fell off, and his wig followed it.

There he stood, like some hideous portrait, framed by the outlines of the casement, and little suspecting that he was full in the view of Captain Heron, Tom Ripon, and the Earl of Bridgewater.

How easy it would have been for Heron, at

that time, to have got rid at once and for ever of that determined and unscrupulous foe, by sending a bullet on its errand of death across that limited space, to the head which presented so fine a mark! But Heron was not the man to commit such an act secretly, and from a window, and in cold blood. He looked upon Wild with loathing and detestation, and ample cause had he, indeed, to wish him dead, but he was not the man to kill him.

"The rascal will tumble out at the window," said the Earl of Bridgewater.

Felix Heron shook his head.

"No, my lord—no. Wild will look after himself too well. But he is perfectly astonished to know what has become of me; and I, too, may say that I am equally astonished to find your lordship here, and would fain know to what most fortunate accident I am indebted for your presence."

"This is my sister's house," said the young Earl. "I and Lady Bridgewater are here on a visit; but hearing that there was some disturbance taking place at our neighbour's, the Bishop's, curiosity led me to this window, where I was soon delighted to remain to be of service to you. But come down stairs. Lady Bridgewater and my sister will be delighted to see you; for they both know sufficient of your history, and that of Edith, to feel the deepest interest in all that concerns you both."

"I will follow you, my lord, with pleasure," said Captain Heron; "although it would hurt me to the soul to think for a moment that I might bring some trouble upon the household. I am scarcely, too, in fit trim to be introduced to ladies, for, you see, I am in a sort of disguise."

"I see—I see! But that matters not. Follow me, and you can explain all to them. I can assure you, Heron, that I have had some difficulty in persuading my sister, the Countess of Chester, and Lady Bridgewater from taking a drive over to Epping Forest on purpose to see Edith. Pray pardon me for speaking of her so familiarly."

"She will be ever better pleased to be plain Edith to such a dear friend as yourself," replied Heron.

"It's very true, what you say, Captain," interposed Tom. "We ain't hardly fit to go to the presence of the ladies; but I've cleaned my face as well as I can; though spitting on the corner of your handkerchief isn't the best way."

"Go right down stairs, Tom, as far as you can," said the Earl, "and say that you come from me, and that you are to have something of the best the kitchen affords."

"That'll do," said Tom. "It seems to me as if I hadn't had any dinner for a month, and no breakfast for six weeks."

Tom sallied out at the door to which the Earl of Bridgewater pointed, and which led, by a back staircase, down to the domestic portion of the house, where, guided by some savoury fumes of cooking, he soon arrived.

The Earl and Captain Heron passed through two rooms, which were en suite with the small back apartment in which they had so opportunely met; and then, without encountering any of the household, they reached the door of a small reception-room, from within which came the tinkling sound of a spinet, as the rudimental pianofortes of that day were called.

The Earl of Bridgewater opened the door and said, in a low tone, as he stepped into the room, followed by Captain Heron, "Ladies, will you be quite discreet, and neither scream nor faint away, when I introduce to you the Earl of Whitcombe —commonly called Captain Felix Heron, the highwayman of Epping Forest?"

The wife and sister of the young Earl were, indeed, surprised; but they were not so foolish as either to scream or faint away, but received Captain Heron with kindness and courtesy.

Briefly, then, Heron related to them all that had happened to him in relation to the Bishop of Worcester, and during that relation he bethought him of the fact that he had still left in Tom's possession those important documents which substantiated all his claims, and without which, now, he felt, he must ever remain an outcast.

"My friend, who is down stairs," he said, "holds the earldom of Whitcombe in his pocket; for I gave him the three important packets, which, I am bound to think, were supernaturally delivered to me in Whitcombe House."

"I will get them myself," said the Earl; "for they should be in no one's possession but your own."

"Or yours, my lord," said Heron; "for I was about to ask you the favour of taking possession of them for me."

"That I will do with pleasure; for, to tell you the honest truth, Heron—and without any disparagement to you—they are anything but safe in your possession, considering the adventurous life you lead."

"I know it, and feel it. But I scarcely think Tom will deliver them to you. And he had better come up here; for if by any means we can alter his appearance, so that Wild and his men do not recognise him, he will be able to sally out, and bring me intelligence of what Wild is doing."

This was instantly agreed to; for the ladies had a particular curiosity to see Tom Ripon.

Before, however, the Earl could proceed to the door to ring for Tom, a confused noise upon the staircase aroused their attention.

The Earl's wife and sister turned pale, thinking that some danger was at hand to Heron, and that, surely, Jonathan Wild had attacked the house.

The Earl of Bridgewater lifted his sword from a side table, on which he had laid it, and half drew it from its scabbard.

Captain Heron, with his hand plunged into the breast of his apparel, stepped boldly forward; for he thought it not impossible that Jonathan Wild had by some means found out where he was, and was about to make an audacious attempt at his capture even in the house of the Countess of Chester, the sister of the Earl of Bridgewater.

For a few seconds this tumult upon the staircase and the landing, just opposite to the door of the apartment in which the party in whose fortunes we are interested was anxiously waiting, increased rather than diminished.

The sounds of some female voice, in remonstrance loud and shrill, predominated over all other noises, and it was evident that some scuffle of no ordinary character was taking place.

"What can this mean?" said the Earl of Bridgewater, as he unsheathed his sword wholly, and stepped towards the door.

"My lord!—my lord!" exclaimed Heron, "you shall not run into danger on my account."

"Nay, there will be no danger to me, although much to you. Let me go"

"I cannot!—I cannot!"

The result of this friendly contention was that the Earl of Bridgewater and Captain Heron reached the door of the room together.

Just as Heron had his hand upon the handle of the lock, the door was opened from without, and a curious spectacle presented itself.

There stood Tom Ripon, unable to disengage himself from the hold of one of the female servants of the house, who called out loudly, "Thieves! Thieves! He's a housebreaker and a robber, my lady; and my best gown, and bonnet, and my reputation, are all gone together!"

But it was the appearance which Tom presented which was the most remarkable and suggestive of laughter. He was attired in a woman's

No. 97 —EDITH.

dress, and had on his head a bonnet, which being, according to the fashion of the time, of very ample dimensions, flapped right down over his face; and if it were intended to conceal his features, certainly most effectually answered that purpose.

———

CHAPTER CCIX.

THE EARL OF BRIDGEWATER ARRANGES HIS DUEL WITH LORD WARRINGDALE.

ALL idea of danger vanished from the mind of Captain Heron, when he saw Tom Ripon in the curious disguise he had assumed; but it was in a tone that had some anger about it that he cried out, "Tom! Tom! what is the meaning of this absurd and extraordinary mummery?"

"Now, young woman," said Tom to the servant, "be so good as let go my hair, or you will have it all out by the roots."

"You villain, give me my bonnet!"

Tom Ripon, perhaps, by this time began to perceive that Captain Heron was not well pleased with him, and he at once turned towards him to explain his conduct.

"Captain, I meant to go out into the street to see what was going on, that was all; and as I didn't like somebody you know to call out, 'There goes Tom Ripon!' I thought I might make myself look like a respectable young woman; and on going to the top of the house, I found this gown and this bonnet."

Felix Heron shook his head.

"Tom! Tom! I cannot disapprove of your motives, because I know they are kind and good ones."

"Then I'm off!" said Tom Ripon. And before either Captain Heron, the Earl of Bridgewater, or the young girl, who was so enraged at the felonious abstraction of her gown and bonnet, could prevent him, he ran down the stairs, and was out of the house.

"Let him go," said the Earl. "I wish I had, among all the pampered tribe that fatten on the revenues of Bridgewater, one who would do me half the honest service that lad is evidently disposed to do you."

Tom Ripon was absent about a quarter of an hour; and then he returned, to say that it was quite clear Jonathan Wild was thoroughly foiled in the attempt to capture Captain Heron.

There were none of his janissaries in the street; but yet neither Heron nor the Earl of Bridgewater were disposed to think that such a man as Wild was got rid of quite so quietly and so easily.

"He may still," said the Earl, "be lurking about; and I should recommend the utmost caution in your leaving this house."

"I cannot doubt but he has taken steps to watch the street," replied Heron; "and if you will bear with me until sunset, I would fain increase my chances of escape by waiting till that time."

"We shall only be too happy to entertain you; but whither do you purpose going then?"

"To the forest!—to the forest!"

"You will then," said Lady Bridgewater, "give my kindest love to Edith."

"And mine, too," added Lady Chester; "and say that we shall certainly come to see her at Epping if she be not soon in London."

"Those kind messages I am not likely to forget," replied Heron. "My Lord Bridgewater, I will remind you of your promise to take charge of these most important papers for me."

Captain Heron alluded to the three packets he had brought from Whitcombe House, and which Tom Ripon had delivered up to him; and now Felix Heron handed them to the young Earl of Bridgewater, as he added, "All my hopes, and all the hopes of Edith, lie now, my good friend, in your hands."

"I will be as careful of them as of my life; and if—if——"

The young nobleman hesitated; for at that moment the recollection came across his mind that he had to meet Lord Warringdale in the morning to fight that duel which Warringdale intended

should be so fatal to him, and so treacherously dangerous to Captain Heron.

Up to that moment the Earl had said not a word to Heron about the duel; for, like a brave man as he was, he naturally shrunk from speaking of such an affair being in contemplation.

And Captain Heron had but a vague idea of something Tom Ripon had said in which Lord Warringdale and the Reverend Mortification were mixed up strangely with some plot that was to be carried out to his detriment.

After a pause, the Earl, however, made up his mind to tell Heron of the duel; for if he should fall, those most important documents which he, Heron, had placed in his hands for security, might be in more jeopardy than as if he kept them himself and took them to Epping Forest with him.

But the Earl of Bridgewater had no desire to make either his sister or his wife acquainted with the fact that he was about to have a hostile meeting with anybody; so, after a few minutes' reflection, he took Captain Heron by the arm and led him from the room, saying, "Ladies, excuse us; I have something to talk to my friend about, and will take him to my own room."

When alone with Heron in the apartment which was always kept for him and called his in his sister's house, the Earl of Bridgewater spoke rapidly.

"My dear friend, since you have thought proper to make me a depository of these most important papers, it is fit that I should tell you I am not altogether to be depended on."

Captain Heron was astonished at these words, for at first he could not comprehend exactly what they meant.

"You not to be depended on!" he exclaimed. "Believe me I would not contentedly hear any one else say that of you."

"Let me explain. It is just within the bounds of possibility, although I do not think it at all probable, that there may be no Earl of Bridgewater to-morrow, for at present the title would become extinct with me."

"What do you mean? What can you mean?"

"Simply that I have a duel on hand."

"Ah!"

"I have indeed, and it comes off to-morrow morning in Kensington Gardens."

"May I ask with whom?"

"Yes; it is with Lord Warringdale."

"Warringdale! That infamous coward and traitor?"

"Even so."

"But how have you induced him to fight with you?"

"He has challenged me!"

"You surprise me more and more, my lord."

"Yet it is so. You know well, and so does he, that in my heart, although I cannot legally prove it, I believe him to be the murderer of my poor father, who came by his death in so tragical a manner in Paddock Hill Lane."

"I do not doubt it."

"Nor I—and he is aware that I have not scrupled to avow my convictions; and upon that ground and provocation he has challenged me. There is his letter. All is arranged, and I meet him with swords in the morning."

Captain Heron read Lord Warringdale's letter to the Earl of Bridgewater with unfeigned surprise, and when he had concluded it he said, "Treachery! treachery! There is some awful treachery in all this!"

"How mean you?"

"I can hardly tell—but before we say another word about it let me have up Tom Ripon, for he has a story to tell, which, to my mind, has a strange connexion with your forthcoming fight with Warringdale."

It was now the turn of Captain Heron to surprise the young Earl by telling him what he as yet knew; and upon sending for Tom Ripon, they got from him a full detail of all that he had overheard, while he was in the area of the condemned house, between Lord Warringdale and the Reverend Mortification.

Tom now added to his relation a full account of how he had looked from the first floor of his mother's house in Star Court upon the interview between Mrs. Ripon and Mortification, and how he had there and then, from that advantageous position, heard still more of the affair.

From all this, both Captain Heron and the Earl of Bridgewater could come to no other conclusion than that some most elaborate piece of villany was intended; but from want of one piece of information they could not have, they wanted the key to the whole transaction.

That piece of information was what Lord Warringdale had trusted no one with. It was the secret of the poison.

That secret lay deep in his own bad heart, and he meant to keep it there.

"What are we to think of all this?" asked the Earl.

Captain Heron shook his head.

"It is a maze," he said, "in which I am puzzled, and seem to lose my way."

"Well, let him do his best. I am, at all events, not so confident as he seems to be, that I shall lie in death upon the greensward of Kensington Gardens."

"Heaven forbid it!"

"But if I did, there can be no doubt that by some means he intends to get you accused of my death."

"That seems the plan. I will not go to Epping Forest to-night."

"Nay, I shall be safe enough."

"No, no! I will not leave you alone."

"But can you think for a moment, Heron, that the sword of Lord Warringdale will have any effect upon me? Surely I can conquer him? He cannot be so inflated with the vanity of his own prowess as to suppose he has nothing to do but to meet me in arms to conquer me?"

"No, no, my lord; he does not think so! He cannot think so for a moment!" exclaimed Heron. "But there is some treachery, which, at present, I cannot comprehend, by which your fall is hoped to be accomplished."

"Can it be possible?"

"Any wickedness, I fear, is possible when Lord Warringdale is concerned."

"I must be wary."

"Indeed, you must! And those who love you must be wary likewise."

The Earl was evidently much disturbed by all this, and he paced the room twice before he spoke again, when he said, "Tell me, my friend—tell me what, in your better judgment, I ought to do?"

"I scarcely know; but I can say what I will do on the occasion."

"What!—what!"

"I will be present at the duel."

"You, Heron?"

"Even I. Do not seek to turn me from my purpose, I pray you!"

"Nay, you forget your own dangerous position. And although I know you would be ever ready to jeopardize your life at the call of friendship, I cannot allow you in this case to run any risk. My second in the duel is an honourable gentleman upon whom I can rely; and his presence will surely be sufficient to protect me from any open treachery."

"It may, and yet it may not. I pray you to let me have my own way in this case."

"Tell me the exact spot where the duel is to take place, and I will manage to hide myself in such a way that I shall be present, and yet at the same time not be known to be there. No doubt there will be trees near at hand, which will enable me to take up a position."

"Oh, there are plenty; for the spot of the encounter is to be the back of the Palace, near to the conservatory."

"I know the place, and will be there in time. And now I would fain send Tom Ripon to Epping Forest; for well I know that by this time Edith will be a prey to a thousand fears on my account."

Tom was summoned again, and Captain Heron gave him his instructions.

"Go home, Tom, at once—home to the old Forest, and tell Edith I am safe and well, but shall not be able to leave London until to-morrow morning."

"I'm off!" said Tom.

"Not with one-half your message, Tom."

"Oh, no, Captain! What else?"

"Tell Ogle to come to town, and to be at the old posting-house, at Kensington—'The Anglers' it is called—not later than eight o'clock, well mounted himself, and with Daisy for me, and there he is to wait till I send for him, or come to him."

"Ah, Captain!" said Tom, with a sigh; "would not another of your men do instead of Ogle?"

"Another of my men? What do you mean?"

"Hem! I mean one of the name of Ripon, Captain?"

"No, no, Tom; you have done enough in London for the present. Go, and carry out the orders I give you, and be off at once."

Tom Ripon no longer hesitated. He knew that prompt obedience to whatever Captain Heron required was the first virtue of the band.

"Take care of yourself," added Heron; "for if you fall into the hands of Jonathan Wild, he will have scant mercy upon you now."

Tom nodded, and was off.

"Now, my dear friend," said Heron to the Earl, "I will remain with you until daylight to-morrow morning; and then I will find my way to Kensington Gardens, with the hope of unravelling—or, at all events, of foiling—what I fear is some diabolical plot against your life and mine."

While Captain Heron and Lord Bridgewater are thus waiting for the new day, we may briefly state that Jonathan Wild, Lord Warringdale, and the Bishop's secretary were intensely puzzled and confounded at the mysterious escapes of Captain Heron and Tom Ripon from the bath-room.

Wild himself, accompanied by two of his most acute and experienced men, made a thorough examination of the lower part of the Bishop's house, to which only Heron and Tom could possibly have access had they descended to the yard by the rope, which seemed to say, almost in intelligent language, that they had done so.

All this search, however, was of course of no avail.

Wild looked ferocious and gloomy.

Lord Warringdale was evidently alarmed.

The secretary shook in every limb, and turned white and flushed by turns.

"He's a clever fellow," said Wild, as he bit his lips; "and I don't mind owning that, for once in in a way, I can't at all make out how he has managed matters."

"He has vanished," said the secretary.

"Into the air," added Warringdale, "or into the earth."

"Pho! pho!" sneered Wild. "It's all natural enough, of course, if we could but hit upon it. But it's clever; and I am, I admit, quite at a loss to understand it, as yet."

"What is to be done?" asked Lord Warringdale, anxiously.

"Why, make a rant about the Bishop's death, and lay it to Captain Heron."

"Yes! Oh, yes! But how?—how?"

"I will have bills posted in the street, offering a hundred pounds reward for the murderer of the Bishop!"

"No, no!"

"But I say yes! They won't suspect you!"

"Me! me! I did not kill him!"

"Ho! ho!"

"Hush! Oh, hush, Wild! Don't laugh in that way! The Bishop was old; and I am inclined, after all, to think that his death was natural. I would advise that we let Captain Heron alone as regards it; and—and—I think I shall be able to think of some other way of meeting him."

"Indeed!"

"Yes; I will think."

Lord Warringdale was thinking of the duel which was to take place on the following morning.

"You seem wonderfully squeamish all of a sudden," said Wild.

"Not so—not so, Wild! If we had caught him here, nothing would have been better than to have at once accused him of the murder of the Bishop, and then there would have been no further trouble; but, as it is, I counsel that we let him alone, and the world may assume that the Bishop died from natural causes."

"That's unlucky,'" said Jonathan.

"What's unlucky?"

"What I did."

"What did you do? I do not understand you. You alarm me by your looks and expressions."

"Why, you see, making quite certain of the capture of Heron, and understanding that we were to charge him with the murder of the Bishop—since he appeared to be the last person in his company while he lived——"

"Wild, you torture me! What did you do? Tell me at once."

"Well, I was anxious to be of all the assistance to you in my power; and believing, as I tell you, that we had the fellow in our grasp, and seeing the old Bishop in his chair, looking so calm and cheerful——"

"Cheerful? He was dead."

"Oh, yes; I know that. You didn't do the business by halves."

"Hush—hush!"

"Oh, we're among friends here, and it don't matter. Seeing him, then, as I say, looking so cheerful—with no marks of violence upon him,—I first gave him a slight nip of the throat—to give an air of reality, you know, to the act of murder. The marks of a hand will be found; and who shall say it will not fit that of Captain Heron?"

"Or mine!" said Lord Warringdale, gloomily. "I wish that you had left him alone. But Heron has escaped, although so mysteriously, that it fills one with a thousand alarms."

"I can't make it out. It's more than strange."

"Jonathan Wild, will you call upon me at midday to-morrow? I shall be glad to see you."

"With pleasure," said Wild; "and if I can only nab Heron in the meantime, I will let you know."

Jonathan Wild placed one of his men in the hall of the Bishop's house, with directions to stay there till he sent for him; and then he went off to St. Martin's round-house, where the riot he made, and the horrible language he used, in consequence of the escape of Tom Ripon, may be imagined, but cannot be described.

CHAPTER CCX.

STRANGE EVENTS HAPPEN IN KENSINGTON GARDENS AT AN EARLY HOUR IN THE MORNING.

LORD WARRINGDALE would have been quite as well pleased to have compromised Captain Heron in the death of the Bishop of Worcester, as by that of Lord Bridgewater, but since the one had failed, his mind reverted back to its original plan.

That original plan he hoped to carry into effect, as we are aware, with the assistance of the Rev. Mortification.

The apparent complication of that plot against two lives, and perhaps more, did not exactly recommend it to the mind of Lord Warringdale, and hence was it that he felt a proportionate degree of disappointment at the failure to capture Heron, with the murder of the Bishop of Worcester hanging as a charge over his head.

Had Wild succeeded in making Heron a prisoner upon that occasion, there can be no doubt that he and his men would readily have sworn that they saw the fatal struggle take place between Heron and the Bishop.

Then Lord Warringdale could have stepped forward and supplied the apparent motive for the murder, by falsely stating that the Bishop had informed him Heron had used the most deadly threats towards him should the Bishop refuse to give false testimony in regard to an alleged marriage between Amelia Staunton and the late Earl of Whitcombe.

All this would have looked wonderfully feasible, and Captain Heron might have found con-

LORD WARRINGDALE CALCULATES HIS CHANCES.

Presented Gratis with No. 97 of the New Edition of Edith the Captive; or, the Robbers of Epping Forest.

siderable difficulty in freeing himself from the complication.

The escape of Heron, however, had broken down the whole plan; and we now request the reader's presence at Lord Warringdale's chambers in St. James's Street, late in the evening of that same day, where he sat alone, revolving in his mind the probable of the following morning.

"I shall kill him!" he said. "I shall certainly kill the Earl of Bridgewater. I am now convinced, after the experience I have had with the Bishop of Worcester, that I'm in possession of a deadly agent of destruction, the slightest touch of which to a wounded blood-vessel, or even to a scratch upon the skin, is instant death. Surely, I shall kill him!"

Lord Warringdale, however, was not without some fears; for, to a man of his disposition, the mode in which he purposed giving the Earl of Bridgewater that slight wound, which was to produce his death, was not one that he could reflect upon with perfect equanimity.

It was just possible that he might, in the encounter which he had taken such pains to bring about, be put out of the world himself, before even he could inflict the scratch upon his opponent which would suffice for death.

This was an uncomfortable reflection.

Lord Warringdale drinks some of the port wine of which he is getting fond. He tries to sit still composedly, and to think, but he cannot do so, and it is only by pacing his room to and fro that he can find any mental ease.

Then he tries to reason with himself that all will be quite safe.

"Oh, yes—yes, I cannot fail! It is quite an axiom of the fencing schools, that if you like to take a wound you may give one."

This was true, so far as it went in words, but it did not go far enough in explanation.

An indifferent swordsman may run in upon his much more skilful adversary, and inflict upon him a wound, but at the same moment that adversary's sword may be through his heart.

Now, what Lord Warringdale wanted to do in his duel with the Earl of Bridgewater was, to run in upon him, and perhaps take and give a slight wound.

That slight wound, probably in the left arm, would do him no harm, but it would be death to the Earl.

"Yes—oh, yes!" added Warringdale to himself—"I shall surely succeed! I will use my left arm as a guard, and his sword will wound it, while at the same time I touch him with the point of my weapon!"

As he spoke, Lord Warringdale took from a corner of the room the sword he usually wore, and slowly and cautiously unsheathed it.

He held the long shining blade to the light.

On the extreme point, about half an inch in extent up the blade, there was a dull, filmy something, which, by the artificial light in the apartment, had a slightly yellow tinge about it.

That was the poison.

That was a small portion of the dried-up potion which was in the vial. He had dipped that sword's point into it, and then patiently held it at arm's length until it had dried.

"Surely, surely," he said, "here is death!"

Lord Warringdale thought of how effectually he had disposed of the Bishop of Worcester by the mere scratch of a pin, the point of which had been immersed in the poison, and he felt confident that the much larger quantity on the point of the sword would do its work.

"He is a dead man!" he added. "The Earl of Bridgewater is a dead man! Could he but know it, he has but such a time to live now as may be easily counted by hours."

There was an awful look of gratified villany upon the face of Lord Warringdale as he spoke.

He was getting familiar with the contemplation of the terrible power he now had in his possession of clearing the path to his objects.

He had committed one murder, and others were to follow.

"Who now shall stand in my way?" he muttered. "Let them beware who do so."

A knock came at the door of the chamber.

Lord Warringdale assumed an attitude of defiance with the sword.

Let it be whom it might, he felt certain that, if he chose, he had the life in his hands.

The deaf valet flung open the room door, and the Rev. Mortification Ripon made his appearance.

"Oh, it is you!"

"Yea, as the Psalmist says, I am here, although it rains, and I am wet."

"Ah—well—I am glad to see you."

Lord Warringdale carefully sheathed the sword, and replaced it in the corner of the room.

"Hem!" coughed Mortification. "I thought I would come early; for, truly, I am not only anxious to do the service your lordship spoke of, but I am desirous of better comprehending it than, as yet, I have been able to do."

"You will comprehend quite enough of it by simply doing what I order you."

Lord Warringdale took up his hat as he spoke, and made preparations for going out.

"I interrupt your lordship," said the Rev. Mortification; "and I will call again."

"Not at all—not at all. I want you to come out with me."

"Yea, is it now that your lordship is so good as to want me?"

"Yes. Did I not tell you that you were to wear a certain disguise?"

"Yea, you did."

"Well, then, it is necessary to procure it at once; for you will want it now before many hours are past."

Lord Warringdale put on his sword—that fatal sword—one slight touch, that would draw blood, from which would be instant death.

How like a personification of fate he felt himself! How easily he felt that he could take the life of that miserable wretch who was with him—how easily he could strew St. James's Street with corpses!

Truly it was a terrible power for any man to have, and more terrible still to be in the hands of such an one as Lord Warringdale.

The Rev. Mortification Ripon, when he sallied out into St. James's Street with Lord Warringdale, could not help looking about him, to the right and to the left, most anxiously.

He knew perfectly well that Jonathan Wild was watching the house, and he was afraid that Warringdale would see him.

But the Rev. Mortification Ripon might have made himself quite easy on that score, for Wild was not quite the sort of person, with all his experiences, to be seen if he did not happen to wish it.

It was perfectly true that Jonathan was taken a little by surprise at Warringdale and Mortification coming out of the chambers so soon; but he only shrunk back a little deeper into the doorway in which he was hiding.

"What is he up to now?" growled Wild to himself.

It happened that the route taken by Lord Warringdale and the Rev. Mortification Ripon passed quite close to the doorway in which Wild was hidden; but the latter made no trouble about that.

He turned his face to the door, and shrunk down some inches, and elevated his shoulders, so as to present a very different figure to what would be recognised as his.

Then he knocked at the door at which he stood.

Jonathan had before, more than once or twice, when he had been hiding in doorways, practised this manœuvre of knocking at the door when he thought there was the slightest chance of his being looked upon as hiding or watching.

He knew that nothing could be more convincing to any one having suspicions of that sort than to see the supposed spy knock at the house, in the doorway of which he would otherwise have undoubtedly had the appearance of hiding.

Lord Warringdale cast but a passing glance at the figure of Wild, and he heard the knock, which put all doubt at rest about the object of the dim-looking person in the doorway.

A servant opened the door, to whom Wild said abruptly, "Who lives here?"

"Mr. Strangeways."

"Then tell him to look to his bolts and bars to-night. My name is Wild. Good night!"

Jonathan thus got over the awkwardness of knocking at a door where he had no business, and at the same time achieved the credit of having given a friendly warning of some projected burglarious attack.

No doubt Mr. Strangeways did look to his bolts and bars. Perhaps he sat up all night in his hall with a blunderbuss; but, at all events, he felt very much obliged to Mr. Wild.

Jonathan then began, in his artful and well-practised manner, to dog the footsteps of Lord Warringdale and the Reverend Mortification.

"You will comprehend now," said Warringdale, "that there is to be a masquerade to-night at the Opera House."

"A masquerade! Yea, as the Psalmist says, such things are all vanity and vexation of spirit!"

"Probably; but the circumstance is so far fortunate, that it enables you, without, in the least, attracting suspicion or awakening speculation, to hire or purchase a dress which shall make you resemble a 'knight of the road,' in his full professional costume."

"Yea, I see."

"Of course, you do! It will be better to purchase the dress entirely, for that will prevent any troublesome inquiries on the part of the wardrobe people to whom we are going about it, when it is not brought back to them."

"Yea, yea; but—but——"

"But what? Have you any silly scruples suddenly?"

"Yes, I have one serious scruple about the purchase of such a costume."

"What is it?"

"I have no money."

"Pshaw! Did you fancy I intended you to put your hand into your own pocket on my account, when I am going to pay you a hundred pounds for the little affair?"

"Two hundred! Yea, two hundred! You said two hundred."

"Did I?"

"Yea, on my oath, you did; and as the Psalmist narrates, I'll be hanged if I do it for less!"

"Well, well, let it be two hundred. There is my purse. Put it in your pocket. You can pay for the dress out of it, and then give it back to me. But remember that the dress must be sufficiently large to be put on entirely over your own clothes."

"Yea, I will remember."

"There are two reasons for that."

"Two?"

"Yes. Captain Heron, for whom I want you to be taken——"

"Taken!—taken! Yea, as the Psalmist says, if I am taken, I am certainly hanged!"

"Peace! peace! You do not understand me. I should have said, perhaps, mistaken. It is in order that you should not be taken in the sense you mean, that I want you to have your ordinary clothes under the highwayman's suit, and that makes the second reason."

"But the first is not clear."

"I meant to say that Heron is stouter than you are; and that, consequently, you will look more like him with two suits of clothes on than with one."

"Yea, I comprehend that. So I shall."

Lord Warringdale paused in the Haymarket, which then, as now, was very much devoted to shops which had a connexion with refreshments, and to those which contributed to the theatrical conveniences of the metropolis.

Masquerades were at the period of our tale fashionable amusements.

The state into which they have now fallen, as the resort of ruffianism and vice of the lowest description, was not then dreamt of.

In the Haymarket there were, at the least, half a dozen shops carrying on the trade of theatrical and masquerade costumiers; and it was at one of those that Lord Warringdale paused with the Reverend Mortification.

The evening was not far advanced, and yet the streets of London wore a much duller and shadowy aspect than they can ever possibly do now; for that was the period when the whole metropolis was lighted—if we may use the term in anything of a real sense—by miserable oil lamps.

Within a couple of hours of their being lit, one-half of these lamps either went out, or burnt so badly, that it came to the same thing, so far as their illuminating powers went.

Thus was it that when two or three or more of the lamps got into so bad a state, all succeeding each other, a whole street, or a great part of it, would be as dark as some common in the country.

The footpad then had it all his own way, and could boldly attack the traveller, and maltreat and rob with impunity.

That portion of the Haymarket at which Lord Warringdale paused on this occasion was very dark, and but for a faint glimmer of light that came through the eye-holes of a huge, hideous mask in a shop window, it would have been difficult for any one to distinguish the pavement from the roadway.

That light that came through the eye-holes of the huge, hideous mask announced that the shop was one of the sort which Lord Warringdale wanted.

It was a masquerade and theatrical costumier's, doing more business in the former line than in the latter.

CHAPTER CCXI.

JONATHAN WILD TAKES HIS MEASURES TO SURPRISE MY LORD WARRINGDALE.

"I WILL wait for you," said Lord Warringdale to the Rev. Mortification — "I will wait for you here."

"Yea, shall I put on the clothing of the highwayman?"

"No, no! But be sure that you purchase a large sad-coloured cloak, which, when you do put on the disguise, will cover you up completely."

"Yea, I will."

"You can wrap the costume you purchase in the large cloak, and bring the parcel with you. I will be here when you come out. Keep me as short a time as possible."

The Rev. Mortification, being provided with Lord Warringdale's purse, had no objection to make the purchase in the wardrobe shop; and, while he went to do so, Warringdale flitted about the Haymarket like some disturbed spirit.

Jonathan Wild had not for a moment lost sight of them; and from the entrance of a court on the other side of the way he kept an eye on their movements.

Jonathan Wild did not expect to acquire any particular information by thus dogging the footsteps of Lord Warringdale and the Rev. Mortification; but what he wanted to do was thoroughly to verify information that Mortification had given him before he took his own measures to be present at the duel in Kensington Gardens.

When he (Wild) saw the strangely assorted pair stop at the theatrical costumier's, he felt that he could no longer have any reasonable doubt upon the subject, and the only aggravation that remained in his mind was that Lord Warringdale should be carrying out an intricate and complicated plot without his countenance and support.

"It shall go hard," muttered Wild, "but I will read his lordship such a lesson that he will be afraid to eat, drink, and sleep for the future without consulting me. Ah! there comes that rascal Mortification out of the shop again, and he carries with him a bundle, which is a sufficient proof that what he has told me is the truth. Farewell, then, for the present, my Lord Warringdale; you may kill your man to-morrow morning in Kensington Gardens, but be assured that Jonathan Wild will be in at the death!"

Wild did not think it worth while to cast another glance at Warringdale or the Rev. Mortification; but, turning his back to the Haymarket, he at once dived down the narrow court, at the mouth of which he had been keeping watch, and, by circuitous routes well known to him, he made his way towards Newgate Street, where he had some arrangements to make of importance to the part he intended to act in the transactions of the morrow.

The Rev. Mortification had a large bundle under his arm when he came out of the masquerade warehouse, and he stood for a moment irresolutely on the pavement, until he was joined by Lord Warringdale.

"You have the dress perfect, I hope?"

"Yea, have I."

"That is well. And the cloak?"

"Yea, truly, as the Psalmist says, a cloak covereth many things."

"Follow me, then. You must spend the remainder of the night in my chambers, for what you have to do in the morning is of too important a character to trust to the chances of your punctual arrival to set about it. But stop a moment; give me my purse."

"Yea, there it is."

"Why, it is empty; and it was well furnished with gold!"

"Of a truth," said the Rev. Mortification Ripon, assuming his most snuffling tones, "it was the purse you asked me for, and not its contents. Does your lordship want me to bestow money upon you?"

"But you cannot have spent the whole of the contents of the purse in the purchase of a highwayman's suit of clothing?"

"Yea," added the Rev. Mortification Ripon, speaking right on, as if he did not hear this last remark of Lord Warringdale's—"yea, does your lordship actually want me to pay you?"

"But you're absurd."

"Yea, as the Psalmist says, don't be mean."

"Hark you, Mr. Mortification, or whatever your name may be; you are a cunning and elaborate rogue. There were twenty guineas in the purse; and, if you don't return me at once the difference between that amount and what the clothing cost, I will break your head, as the Psalmist says."

"Yea, I am certain that the Psalmist could never have made such a remark; but, since your lordship wishes it, there are the two guineas change."

"And so a highwayman's dress, from an ordinary masquerading warehouse, has cost eighteen guineas?"

"Yea, you have said it."

Lord Warringdale might easily have verified the falsehood of this statement if he had thought it worth his while—which certainly it was not; and as he carried on this conversation with the Rev. Mortification while hastening towards his chambers, they reached the doorstep by the time it was concluded.

On that doorstep was a lounging, slouching-looking figure of a man, with his hands plunged deep into the pockets of a huge-skirted coat.

Immediately upon the appearance of Lord Warr ugdale this person sprung forward with an air of vulgar familiarity, and was recognised by his lordship as the disreputable individual who was to second him in the morning in his duel with the Earl of Bridgewater.

"Ah! my good lord!" cried the Major; "I thought you would be glad to have me with you for the night, seeing that we have that little affair to come off in the morning. Friends should stick together! Ha! ha! And, as I once said to the Elector of Hesse-Embourg, when I was his second in a duel with one of the Austrian Archdukes, 'Elector,' says I——"

"Stuff!" cried Lord Warringdale, angrily. "I cannot accommodate you, Major, in my chambers. Be here by seven o'clock, and you shall have breakfast. There, take these—there are plenty of nice houses about St. James's where a man like you can get a bed."

The touch of the couple of guineas which Lord Warringdale, since they had been handed to him by the Rev. Mortification Ripon, had carried loosely and abstractedly in his hand, completely mollified the Major.

"Sink me, my lord," he said, "and clap me in the bilboes, but you're a gentleman, every inch of you; and at some other time I'll tell you what the Elector said to me, and how we got on in that duel with one of the Palatines of Bavaria!"

"Yea," said the Rev. Mortification, "I thought it was one of the Archdukes of Austria even now?"

"Zounds! sir! Who are you? Do you give me the lie, sir? Eh, sir? Cut me into small bits, sir! but I'll have you out, sir!—I'll have satisfaction, sir!"

"Yea, but I won't come!"

"Then, sir, I've a foot, sir!—a foot, sir!—and I kick—kick with the toe, sir!"

"Yea, and I with the heel!" said the Rev. Mortification, as at the same moment he dealt the Major such a crack on the shins that that gallant individual uttered a howl of rage and pain, and struck out heartily at the Rev. Mortification, whose possession of the bundle from the masquerade warehouse, however, enabled him effectually to ward off the blows.

"Come, come," said Lord Warringdale, "I must have no quarrelling among those who are serving me. When my business is over, you may cut each other's throats if you please, but not till then. Be here at seven o'clock, Major, but until then I am busy."

The Major retreated, muttering fearful imprecations against the Rev. Mortification, whose courage in so assailing the gallant son of Mars with his heels quite surprised Lord Warringdale, but a remark that Mortification made as he entered the chambers explained it.

"Yea," he said, "I knew he was a poltroon, for I saw him kicked and pumped upon at Charing Cross."

"Well, well," said Warringdale, who could not help feeling some degree of humiliation that even the Rev. Mortification should know so well the character of the man whom he had chosen as his second—"well, well; I wish to hear no more about it. Here is a large easy chair, in which you may comfortably enough pass the night, for I do not choose to lose sight of you again; since,

if you failed me at the appointed hour, all my trouble will have been in vain."

"Yea, I will sleep," said the Rev. Mortification; "but the inward man rejoiceth not without supper—and, yea, I am a-hungered."

Lord Warringdale stamped impatiently.

"There, cormorant!" he said. "Take that key; you will find refreshments of various sorts in yonder buffet; but keep sober, or, by the heaven above us, I will be your death!"

The Rev. Mortification made himself quite comfortable, for in the buffet he found a number of appetizing things to which his palate was a complete stranger; and, to do him justice—although he certainly had a weakness in that direction—he abstained from taking more wine than was good for him.

In the course of about an hour he fell asleep contentedly enough in the large easy chair which Lord Warringdale had pointed out to him, and with his feet resting upon the bundle he had brought from the theatrical wardrobe warehouse, he awakened the echoes of the chambers by snoring at an awful rate.

It was in vain that Lord Warringdale, in an adjoining apartment, sought repose.

The anxieties that pressed upon his mind and the tumult of his passions were for a long while effectual foes to rest.

At last, he fell into a light slumber, which was abruptly terminated by the Rev. Mortification making more hideous noises, with the assistance of his nose, than ever.

Warringdale made a rush into the room, and flung the circular bolster of a couch at him.

"Yea," said the Rev. Mortification, "the flies are troublesome here, and seem of a large sort."

Then he fell asleep again, and Lord Warringdale saw how utterly futile it was to stop the noisy character of his slumber.

And so passed that night, until towards morning, when, thoroughly exhausted, Lord Warringdale dropped into another short sleep.

This slumber was of a more disturbing character than the former.

It was from the imagination and conscience of Lord Warringdale, however, that the disturbance now came—for, no sooner had he closed his eyes, and his senses had yielded themselves up to sleep, than busy fancy flew back to that apartment at the Bishop of Worcester's, where he had been for a brief time alone with the living, and for a still briefer time alone with the dead.

There he thought he saw the old Bishop again, but by some strange means their relative positions seemed changed.

Lord Warringdale fancied he was seated in the Bishop's chair, from which he had not power to stir hand or foot.

It seemed to him as if hundreds of pounds weight of lead rested upon every limb.

He could not have wagged a finger to save his life.

He felt as if he were a statue of iron, screwed and bolted down to a chair of bronze.

The only thing vital about him was his heart, and that beat with a heavy, laborious pulsation, as though confined in ribs of steel, which were each moment contracting and impeding its action.

Then he thought the door of the room opened,

and the old Bishop came in—even as he himself had entered the apartment of the ancient ecclesiastic.

In one pale, thin hand, grasped in the long taper finger shrivelled with age, which he had observed as it rested upon the papers on the Bishop's table, he saw that the spectre had a pin.

Surely it was the same pin which, dipped in the poison, had enabled him, Lord Warringdale, to hurry from the world the generous and gentle-hearted old man!

But the tables were turned : it was he, Lord Warringdale, who sat in the chair.

It was the Bishop who approached him, with the small, poisoned weapon.

Step by step he came nearer, and Lord Warringdale had to cry for help. He tried to shout "Murder!"—he tried to scream in the midst of his dismay—but the only sounds he could utter were faint and inarticulate whisperings.

No. 98.—EDITH.

Then his eyes fell upon the other hand of the Bishop, which was held up threateningly.

The fingers were curved ; and it struck Warringdale, at the moment, that there was a terrible difference between those two hands.

The hand holding the poisoned pin was white, fragile, and delicate.

The other resembled nothing so much as the coarse, vulgar hand of Jonathan Wild.

Then Lord Warringdale seemed to understand exactly what was going to happen.

He was about to be scratched with the poisoned pin, and then finished by strangulation with the other hand.

Thus his fate was to be a kind of imitation of that which had overtaken the good old Bishop.

Step by step the spectre crept towards him, and then, with a sudden rush, flew upon him.

Lord Warringdale sprung to his feet, and uttered a yell of dismay.

"Help! help! What fiend is this? Help! help!"

A faint ray of daylight was gleaming into the apartment. A clock on the chimney-piece gently and sweetly struck the hour of six. Lord Warringdale looked about him with a sigh of relief as he dashed the heavy beads of cold perspiration from his brow.

"So—so!" he said; "that is well! It was but a dream. It was but a dream, after all. 'Twere better not to have slept. The mere physical exhaustion and fatigue of a night's watching were nothing in comparison to the encountering these hideous images. My very soul is shaken by them!"

There came a strange, lumbering sound from the next apartment.

For a moment, then, so partially only was Lord Warringdale recovered from the terrors of his dream, he almost imagined they were about to become realities, for he had forgotten the Reverend Mortification.

The fact was that that cry from Lord Warringdale had wakened up Mortification at once, and so alarmingly, too, that he fell headlong from the easy chair, and rolled over several times along with the bundle from the masquerade warehouse, fancying he was attacked by some wild animal of that shape and size.

Lord Warringdale, however, quickly recovered from this new alarm, and the memory of all the past came back to him.

He sought the deaf valet, and, shaking him lustily, let him know that breakfast was required.

He then went into the room where the Reverend Mortification had slept; and although very pale, and trembling in every limb, he assumed an air of sharp decision as he spoke to him.

"The time has come," he said. "Dress yourself at once in that costume which, within two hours from now, will, I hope, make you be mistaken for Captain Heron, the highwayman. Quick! quick! for there is no time to lose."

"Yea, I shall soon be ready; but breakfast is a meal——"

"Pshaw! Nonsense!"

"That I have a partiality to partaking of."

"Stuff! stuff!"

"Never miss your meals, as the Psalmist says, if you can possibly help it."

"There is abundance left in the buffet. Take some refreshment hastily, if you must have it, and then dress, for I want to see how you look in your new costume. Remember that, within the next two hours, you earn two hundred pounds; and it will scarcely fall to your lot again in life to spend so short a time so profitably."

This last argument seemed to have considerable effect upon the Reverend Mortification Ripon. He snatched a few mouthfuls of pleasant-tasting preserves from the buffet, and tossed off a tolerable bumper of canary; after which, with a speed and judgment that Lord Warringdale hardly expected from him, he proceeded to array himself in the highwayman's costume he had in the bundle.

The Reverend Mortification Ripon was tall and lank in figure; but the people at the costumier's were so in the habit of fitting all sorts of persons, that, at a glance, they had handed him a dress suitable for him.

Completely over his other apparel, then, the Reverend Mortification put on the highwayman's costume.

The tall riding-boots—the buff-leather smallclothes—the gold-laced waistcoat—the scarlet coat, with its ample facings—the lace cravat—the ruffles and the three cornered hat, with its half-hidden feather, confined by a sparkling sham jewel—the belt—the riding-whip—the gloves, fastened to a swivel at the waist,—all was perfect.

The Reverend Mortification Ripon stood in the middle of that apartment—a personification of the dashing knight of the road—the highwayman of Hounslow or Bagshot Heath.

Lord Warringdale was delighted.

"The very thing!" he cried,—"the very thing!"

"Yea, as the Psalmist says, I think it 'll do."

"Give me that hat."

The Reverend Mortification handed the threecornered hat to Lord Warringdale, who, with the assistance of some pen and ink from a side-table, placed in the lining of it the initials "F. H."

"Now, wrap yourself up in the cloak," said Warringdale, "and take my instructions."

"Yea, I will; and but that I know myself to be a pious individual, I could almost fancy I was going on the road.

"'Hark! the sound of wheels approaches;
    Quite a cavalcade of coaches.'"

"Why, you are a veritable highwayman! But put on the cloak at once; and see that you cover yourself up well with it, for you have to walk from here to Kensington Gardens, and must not let a glimpse of that scarlet surtout be seen."

"Yea, will I cover myself up, so that the Philistines shall be deceived!"

The Reverend Mortification wrapped round and round him the ample cloak, which was one of those used on the stage when a disguise is necessary, and which seems to have such an unlimited quantity of cloth in them.

"Yea, I am ready. And now, my lord, be so good as to tell me precisely what I have to do; for as yet I am even as one travelling in a darksome valley."

"Your instructions shall be precise."

"Amen!"

"Be you as precise in following them, and all will be well."

"Amen!"

"Peace!—peace! Do not be repeating 'Amen' in that absurd fashion, but attend to me."

"Yea, I will."

"Do you know the conservatory and the flowergarden, at the back of Kensington Gardens?"

"Yea, I do."

"Then all you have to do at once is to go there and hide in the thick foliage of one of the trees, and wait there until I clap my hands together thrice in this way."

"But how shall I know it is you, my lord? Yea, some one else may clap his hands, and down I may come, and fall at once into the clutches of the Moabites, and the Hittites, and the——"

"Silence, and listen to me. You will easily know that it will be no other than I who summon you, because you will see me."

"Amen!"

"Now, go."

"Good my lord, have you a particular wish that I should get up a tree?"

" Yes."

" Yea, let me observe that at that same spot there is a deep hole—a pit—a valley—an excavation, from which gravel has been dug; and it is interwoven with weeds and sucklings of trees, and creeping plants, and bushes, and——"

" Good heavens! bring your catalogue to an end, and say what you mean."

" Yea, then, I mean, I would more gladly hide me in that place than up a tree; and with a wonderful deal more security, too, as to me it seemeth."

" Do as you please, then, in that respect. Tree or pit, it matters not to me, so that you be hidden until I want you, and so that you then appear."

" Yea, I go!"

The Reverend Mortification Ripon gathered his cloak more closely still about him, and departed from the chambers.

On the stone steps that led from the outer door into St. James's Street, however, he met the Major, who was to be Lord Warringdale's second.

That disreputable individual looked more tired, and used up, and out of condition, this morning, than even he had done the day before. He did not evince any disposition to renew his quarrel with Mortification, but growled out some defiant epithets as he passed him.

Mortification took no notice of him, but went his way.

CHAPTER CCXII.

CAPTAIN HERON FINDS HIMSELF AWKWARDLY SITUATED IN THE GRAVEL-PIT.

WE leave the Reverend Mortification Ripon to proceed to Kensington Gardens.

We leave Lord Warringdale to make his final arrangements for the approaching duel.

We leave, too, Jonathan Wild to take those measures which he intended to astonish Lord Warringdale, and no doubt would do so, while we repair once more to the house of Lady Chester, the sister of the Earl of Bridgewater, and place the reader in communication with that nobleman, and with Captain Heron.

Felix Heron knew perfectly that he could depend upon Tom Ripon obeying the directions that had been given him.

When he, Heron, sat with the Earl of Bridgewater at an early breakfast, he could have there and then taken his oath that Ogle, well mounted himself, and with Daisy's bridle in his hand, was at the old inn at Kensington.

That assurance gave to Felix Heron a confidence in the proceedings of the morning which he could not otherwise have had.

He knew perfectly well that the old road-side inn he had mentioned was only about eight or ten minutes fast walking from Kensington Palace.

It was not likely that he should be so hard pressed by his enemies as not to be able to compass that distance in despite of all the opposition they could bring to bear against him.

Captain Heron had fully made up his mind to be present at the duel, either in hiding or openly.

But for the opposition of the Earl of Bridgewater Heron would have found some means of disguising himself, and gone openly, as a friend of the Earl: but the young nobleman, with that nice sense of honour which characterised him, had an objection to such a course.

" No, Heron," he said. " If I have two friends with me, Warringdale may well complain if he has but one."

" Be it, then, as you wish," replied Heron. " I will find some hiding place from which I can be a spectator of all that passes."

" Do so—do so. It seems to me that, with fair play, the result of this duel is certain. I shall, in all probability rid you, at once and for ever, of Lord Warringdale."

" I would that that riddance had been achieved by some other hand than yours, my dear friend; but he has challenged you, and it is not to be supposed but that he seeks your life, so you are right to take his."

" Of course—of course. And you should always remember, Heron, that I have my poor father's murder to avenge!"

" True—most true!"

Captain Heron rose from the breakfast table of the Earl of Bridgewater about a quarter of an hour before the Rev. Mortification Ripon left Lord Warringdale's chambers, in St. James's Street.

The destination of these two persons was the same.

They were both bound to Kensington Gardens, in order to be spectators of the duel between Warringdale and the Earl of Bridgewater.

It was a strange coincidence, too, that, inasmuch as the Rev. Mortification had met Lord Warringdale's second as he left the chambers, so did Captain Heron, as he left the house of Lady Chester, meet the gentleman who was to be the second of the Earl.

But no recognition passed between the two latter.

They only bowed as gentlemen might do who encounter on a door-step.

Captain Heron, then, it will be observed, had the start of the Rev. Mortification in proceeding to Kensington Gardens; and, as he walked faster than the reverend gentleman, he reached the back of the old Palace a good twenty minutes before Mortification.

The morning was raw and chilly, but the day promised to be fine.

There was that faint kind of yellow halo in the misty air, which bespoke a bright sunshine when the night vapours should entirely fade away.

The little shady spot, with its beautiful trees and its flower garden, at the back of the old Palace, was so silent and serene that it would have been difficult to have convinced any one who did not know it of his own knowledge that he was within two miles of Charing Cross.

The birds were twittering from tree to tree, and the bright morning air was making a pleasant rustling among the leaves, which at times sounded like the wash of the sea upon some sandy beach.

To Captain Felix Heron, who was so well accustomed to the deep leafy shades of old Epping Forest, and who so much loved and admired those natural solitudes of nature, this pretty spot in Kensington Gardens had many charms.

" Ah!" he said. " My Edith, I will hope that

before this day's sun has set I shall be hand in hand with you in our forest home, which I would fain remain in, for ever leaving the great warring world without to fight and jangle as it pleased."

Felix Heron sighed as he thought of how happy he might be in some humble cottage with his Edith, with nothing to think about but "the seasons' difference," and love—dear, lasting, gentle love—to shed the charm of its radiant beauty about even the sterile winter time.

Heron was startled from these reflections by seeing a wild rabbit run in a startled manner past him at a short distance.

His forest lore let him know at once that some human footstep was near.

The rabbit took a leap down the old gravel-pit.

"That is a good hint and suggestion to me," said Heron to himself. "Where shall I find a better hiding-place than the sagacity of that wild creature has chosen?"

Heron approached the edge of the pit, and he saw that there would be no serious difficulty in scrambling down into it, while in its depths there were hiding places for a troop of horse, if necessary.

Just as the Reverend Mortification Ripon crossed the path which skirts the trees close to the Palace, Captain Heron swung himself over the edge of the gravel-pit, and found a sure shelter behind a tall and broad bush which had been formed by suckers from the roots of a fallen tree, the huge original stem of which lay like a bridge across a still deeper part of the gravel-pit.

From where he was, Heron could command a very good view of the edge of the pit in the direction of the Palace, and he saw a tall figure, closely wrapped in a brown cloth cloak from head to foot, pause on the brink of the excavation.

"Who can that be?" thought Heron; for the disguise of the Reverend Mortification effectually baffled Heron at the moment.

But that failure of imagination was not to be for long.

Mortification took off his hat and wiped his brow, for he had walked fast.

"Yea," he said, "here I am!"

The voice, and the appearance of the head and face, were conclusive.

Captain Heron at once recognised the husband of Tom Ripon's mother.

The presence of the Reverend Mortification was quite in accordance with the information that had been given by Tom in regard to the conversation he had overheard between Lord Warringdale and that unscrupulous and eccentric personage.

As Mortification wiped his brow, the cloak became naturally deranged a little; and, to the surprise of Heron, he saw that Mortification had on a scarlet coat and tall riding-boots.

Heron shrunk down closer still amid the bush-wood.

"Yea," said Mortification, "this is the place. Here is the pit."

"What on earth," thought Heron, "can he want with the pit?"

Captain Heron was not left long in suspense in regard to what the Reverend Mortification wanted

with the gravel-pit. He required it for the same purpose that he, Heron, found it so useful—namely, as a place of hiding and espionage.

It would have been an odd *contretemps* if Mortification had sought to make his hiding-place those same tree-root suckers and that same stem by which Heron had ensconced himself.

Indeed, it seemed as if such was about to be the case by the route which Mortification first took; but then he took a turn to the left, and without descending quite as low as Captain Heron was, he found a kind of hole in which grew some fine fern, and then he paused.

In the solitude of that spot every sound was very clear and distinct, so that when the Reverend Mortification spoke, although it was in low tones, Captain Heron did not lose a word that he said.

"Yea, I will even remain here until my Lord Warringdale maketh the signal for me to sally forth. This is some comfort. Ah!"

What the Reverend Mortification meant by the latter part of his speech, Captain Heron was at a loss to comprehend, for he could only catch a very indistinct sight of him among the ferns and the underwood.

Had Heron been able, however, to see the strange companion he had in the gravel-pit better, he would have observed that when he uttered those last words, he lifted to his mouth a flask, and let some of the contents gurgle down his throat.

That flask he had found in the buffet at my Lord Warringdale's chambers, and had at once appropriated it and its contents, which consisted of choice eau de vie.

"Good! Amen!" said the Reverend Mortification. "Truly is Providence good to its creatures, and the invention of eau de vie and case-bottles shows that——Eh? What's that? Get along!"

Some wild bird had flown so close to the face of the Reverend Mortification as almost to flap him with his wings.

Captain Heron was in deep thought now as to what he should do.

Should he wait where he was the order of events, or should he at once take one prisoner in the person of Mortification, and force him to disclose what part he had to play in the drama of that morning.

Upon the whole, Captain Heron thought it best to let Mortification alone.

He was the more inclined to this course because he felt certain that at any moment he chose he could capture him.

And now we must, having disposed of Heron and Mortification both in the gravel-pit, pay some attention to what Jonathan Wild was about.

Jonathan was resolved to take some means of being master of the events which were to take place that morning in Kensington Gardens, and he thought the best way to do that was to take possession, so to speak, of the ground.

Wild was daring enough to suppose he could do all that was required with a very small force; so he only, at six o'clock on that morning, took three of his men with him to the gardens.

No man was better known, more feared, and, we may add, more implicitly obeyed, than was

Jonathan Wild at that time by all constables and inferior officials.

It was a matter of tolerable notoriety that he was in the confidence of the "Home Office"—that he was the jackall chosen by the highest authorities of the kingdom to hunt down such prey, political or otherwise, as they wished to bring into jeopardy.

Hence Wild knew perfectly that his orders were sure to be obeyed.

Those orders on the present occasion were rather peculiar.

Jonathan purposely took his way to one of the entrances to Kensington Gardens the furthest removed from the Palace, and with his three bull-dogs at his heels he rapped sharply at the porter's lodge.

At first, the official who resided in that lodge was inclined to receive his visitors in rather a brusque manner, but this idea soon subsided when he saw who it was that disturbed him so early.

"You know me?" said Wild, in his sharp, short accents.

"Oh, yes, sir!" replied the lodge-keeper.

"Good! I'm Jonathan Wild; and, knowing that, you will attend to my orders—because, by doing so, you attend to the orders of his Majesty's Government."

Whenever Jonathan Wild had any of his own affairs specially to carry out, he always talked more largely of the authority he held under his Majesty's Government than he did when he really had something to do for the venal Administration then in power.

The lodge-keeper, in a few words, expressed then how happy he should be to oblige Mr. Wild and his Majesty's Government.

"Very well," said Wild. "You must send for three of your rangers, for I want to borrow their green coats for my men here; it will not be above an hour, and then they can have them back again. Do you understand me?"

"Perfectly well, Mr. Wild."

"Then set about it at once, for there is no time to lose."

"It's just their time to come on duty, sir; and you may see them straggling across the Park."

"What's o'clock?"

"A little over the half-hour past six, Mr. Wild."

"Then there's plenty of time."

Wild strode up and down, whistling an air hideously out of tune, as he waited for the arrival of the rangers.

There was much more royal state and dignity kept up in regard to Kensington Gardens at the period of our story than now.

The old gardens were for a long time actually a private and royal domain, and it was only by special grace that visitors were permitted to wander amid its leafy recesses.

From that time, however, the gardens were what is called neglected, and few and far between were any draughts upon the Privy Purse on their account.

The trees grew at their own wild will and pleasure, high up into the sunny air, spreading their huge branches in all directions, and mingling together, sometimes for half an acre in extent, in one mass of vegetation.

The underwood grew thick and deep—the wild rose and the yellow gorse seemed intent upon stopping up every available avenue—and twenty years of what was called neglect made Kensington Gardens a charming, romantic, shadowy wood, amid the deep recesses of which it was somewhat of a struggle to make one's way, but which was full of delightful little bits of real forest scenery.

Troops of deer lived a free and undisturbed life beneath the gigantic chesnuts.

The common squirrel leaped from bough to bough, and many a bird which is now only to be found far away from the hum of cities and the haunts of man, took up its abode and reared its fledglings in the old neglected gardens of Kensington.

But since then the gardens have been "improved"—cleared, popularized, and spoilt.

But to our story.

Jonathan Wild had not to wait long for the appearance of some of the rangers; and they had nothing to do when they did arrive but to obey orders, and to lend their coats to Wild's three janissaries, who, among the trees, and at a casual observation, when so attired, might very well have been mistaken for some of the real rangers of the gardens.

"That'll do," said Wild.

Without another word of explanation, he marched into the gardens, followed by his three men, and was soon completely lost to sight from the lodge among the tall trees and thickly-growing underwood.

Then Wild turned abruptly to his men.

"You will go," he said, "to that woody spot at the back of the old Palace. You will make your way there cautiously, and hide; but be ready at a moment's notice, when you hear my whistle, to appear, for I may want you. Now, be off."

Wild waited where he was until his men had disappeared; but he had no intention of not being at the spot when the duel was to take place—only he knew he had plenty of time before him, so he took a circuitous route, which led him through some of the thickest and deepest recesses of the old gardens towards the Palace.

It was quite a blot upon the sylvan beauty of that place to see such a man as Jonathan Wild making his way through the brushwood, and beneath the low-hanging boughs of the ancient trees.

Sometimes he startled a timid fawn, which, with a few bounds, would hide itself in some brake, or plunge into one of the deep hollows, where the decaying leaves of half a century lay thick and soft.

Many a bird flew hither and thither in the fancy that this intruder upon the solitude of the place was prying about for its nest, and intent upon the destruction of its home and habitation.

But Jonathan Wild cared nothing for the stately trees. He cared nothing for the many-hued parasitical plants that climbed about their branches. He cared nothing for the graceful bounds of the deer, or the nimble rush of the little squirrel that scrambled up the barks of the old trees.

Nature had no charms for Jonathan Wild.

With his hat slouched down over his eyes, and his hands deep in the skirt-pockets of his ample coat—from one of which projected the end of a stout bludgeon, heavily loaded with lead,—he took his way towards the Palace, only now and then casting his eyes upwards to note the position of the sun, in order to be certain that he was pursuing the right direction.

CHAPTER CCXLII.

DETAILS WHAT HAPPENED AT THE DUEL IN KENSINGTON GARDENS.

WHAT were the fearful and deadly thoughts that found a home in the mind of Lord Warringdale on that eventful morning?

Did he intend to commit wholesale murder?

Was it possible that he contemplated wading through such a sea of blood to his objects?

How else could he achieve them?

If his plan of operations were worth anything, it involved, not only the destruction of the Earl of Bridgewater, but of that nobleman's second in the duel.

It involved, too, the death of that dissolute and disreputable man who was to play the part of "friend" to Warringdale himself on that occasion.

Remotely, too, it involved the murder of the Reverend Mortification Ripon;—for was it likely that he, Lord Warringdale, would strew corpses around him, and hesitate to add one more to the group who, if left in life, might be the most dangerous witness against him of all?

Besides, Warringdale had agreed to pay two hundred pounds to the Reverend Mortification for his assistance on this occasion. How much easier was it to kill him! It was like being paid two hundred pounds for his death; and Lord Warringdale was not the kind of man to forego such a sum of money to keep any one in life.

The Reverend Mortification was in danger, although he knew it not.

The plan of Lord Warringdale was clearly and distinctly to get rid of the troublesome accusations against him by the Earl of Bridgewater, as well as his enthusiastic advocacy of the cause of Felix Heron, by killing him.

He meant to manage that killing in such a fashion that there should seem incontestable evidence that Captain Heron had done the deed.

How he set about this, the reader has already some idea; but in the events which we are now about to relate, the whole diabolical agency of the plot will be seen more clearly.

Warringdale and his second, the Major—who, according to his own account, had fought more duels than any man breathing,—started from the chambers in St. James's Street very soon after the Reverend Mortification.

And here Lord Warringdale felt that he had the most delicate part of his plot to carry out; and he took some time to consider how he should do it.

He thought it would take him a quarter of an hour to kill the Earl of Bridgewater—to kill the Earl of Bridgewater's second, and to kill the Major, his own second,—for all these three persons were doomed to death, in the imagination of Lord Warringdale.

The power to dispose of three men thus coolly and easily he considered he fully possessed by having the point of his sword steeped in that fearful poison—a specimen of the power of which he had had in the death of the Bishop of Worcester.

Over and over again he repeated to himself—but not with the faintest whispered sound that could reach another ear,—" I have but to touch them, however slightly. I have but to inflict the merest scratch upon them, one by one, and they will fall dead around me, as if struck by lightning. I can do it before they've time to think of opposition. I shall be among them like Fate, which cannot be resisted."

It was an awful and hideous thing that Lord Warringdale should walk composedly by the side of a man whose deliberate murder he contemplated, and that man coming with him in the semblance of a friend, and with whom he held as quiet converse on the way as though no such terrible thought had found a home in his breast.

But Lord Warringdale thought there was but one little difficulty to surmount in regard to that morning's proceedings, and that was to procure witnesses at the precise moment he wanted them, neither too soon nor too late.

When he had committed the murders, and was left alone upon what might be called the field of battle, his intention was to summon the Rev. Mortification from his hiding place in the gravel-pit, and direct him, in the full costume of a highwayman, to make himself busy among the dead, in rifling them of their purses and jewellery.

At that moment he wanted some witnesses to come upon the scene—some independent witnesses with whom he had no connexion—who would be able to swear that they saw a tall figure, with a scarlet coat and horseman's boots, rifling those who had, apparently, become his victims.

Then so soon as these witnesses had made their observation—but before they could get sufficiently near to arrest the Rev. Mortification—he, Lord Warringdale, was to give him the signal to escape into the gravel-pit again.

When once there, a minute's space of time would suffice for him to strip himself entirely of the highwayman's suit, and make his appearance again in his own clothes, which he wore under it.

But Lord Warringdale meant him to leave behind him, on the ground, the hat in which he had marked the initials F. H.

From all these circumstances, Warringdale thought he would be able to turn the tide of suspicion against Felix Heron, who, as a highwayman and wholesale murderer, would be hunted to the death, and no man pity him.

What terror would have blanched the countenance of Lord Warringdale had he known that Felix Heron himself was to be a spectator of these proceedings, and that Jonathan Wild was actually in Kensington Gardens, determined to take part in them!

As he walked along, Lord Warringdale made up his mind in regard to the best course to be pursued to get the witnesses he wanted, and at the precise time he wanted them.

"My dear Major," he said, "you will, perhaps, be surprised at what I am going to say to you."

"Thousand bombs! no," said the Major. "I'm surprised at nothing. A man who has fought and conquered on every battle-field in Europe, is far beyond being surprised! Speak, my illustrious friend, speak!"

"Well, then, Major, I really do not want to kill this young man."

"Ah! Say you so?"

"I do say so, and I will tell you why. He fancies that he has some ground of complaint against me. It is but a fancy; and, in reality, he should pursue another person in regard to the subject which fills his mind with hatred against me. Sooner or later, of course, he will know the truth; and then I shall be glad I have spared him."

"But you mean to fight?"

"Oh, yes! And perchance I may wound him; but he is so hot-headed a man that he will not be satisfied unless I kill him, or he kills me."

"Very likely."

"Now, if I kill him I'm sure I shall live to be sorry!"

"Ah! Hem!"

"And if he kills me I shall not have an opportunity, in time to come, when I have full possession of the estates of Whitcombe, to make a handsome provision for you, in consideration of the service you do me this morning."

"My dear friend—my illustrious friend!" cried the Major. "You must not be killed! Perish the thought! Thousand bombs!—no!"

"Then I tell you what I will do—or rather, my dear Major, what I want you to do."

"Speak, and look upon it as done. Ha! ha! I guess—I guess!"

"What do you guess?"

"You want me to join in—tierce—carte—passado—in comes a third sword. Ha! ha! there you have it! Away goes his guard, and you pink him under the fifth rib!"

"You forget——"

"What do I forget, my illustrious friend?"

"That the Earl of Bridgewater has a second, who would immediately draw upon you, and the duel would become a melee, in which we might get the worst of it."

"Gad! that's true! Thousand bombs!—yes! What's to be done?"

"Just this. I will precede you to the place of encounter, while you stop at one of the lodges and inform the keepers there that you have reason to believe a duel will come off, at a quarter past eight precisely, at the back of the old Palace. It is their duty to prevent it; but warn them, if they come too soon, that the parties will just go to another part of the gardens, and they will lose all credit for their vigilance. I will keep the Earl of Bridgewater in fence until I see them arrive, and then the affair must come to an end. You can tell them that some persons, high in rank and authority, will be much pleased with them if they reach the spot at a quarter past eight, and not before."

"I will do it—I will do it at once. Odds, culverins and pistolettes! we mustn't have your lordship's honour or your life sacrificed, and this is a course which will save both. I'll do it at once. And if you walk slowly, my illustrious friend, I shall overtake you."

"I will!—I will!"

While the Major hastened to one of the lodges to make this little arrangement—which he was just the sort of man to carry out with an immense quantity of bluster and pomposity—Lord Warringdale slowly continued his route towards the spot appointed for the encounter.

"Surely, all is well!" he muttered. "Surely, I shall succeed this morning in making a great step in advance towards the realization of all my hopes! The Earl of Bridgewater stands as much in my way as Felix Heron can; and if I dispose of one this morning by death, and place such a ban upon the name of the other, that he dare never again show himself without abundant testimony surrounding him to hurry him to the gallows, I shall feel myself a free man."

He stood amid the shadow of some trees, and gazed around him on the silence and beauty of the old gardens.

How still and calm the world seemed at that time in the morning, when even that undefined, subdued roar, which betokens the presence of a large city close at hand, had not commenced.

But no such tender and gentle thoughts as those which had found a home in the breast of Felix Heron came across the imagination of his bad half-brother, Lord Warringdale.

His heart was full of bitterness and scathed in crime.

The past for him was but a recollection of accomplished vices, or attempts at cruelties and crimes, which had failed none of them from want of will.

Any one, to glance at him from a distance, would have thought they saw a man pleased with the beauty and the verdure about him; but such was far from being the case.

His mind was intent on murder.

Slowly and carefully he drew the long, slender sword he wore, and passing the blade across his gloved hand until he came to the point, he looked earnestly at it.

That filmy yellow stain was there.

A gleam of satisfaction lit up the malevolent eyes of Lord Warringdale.

"I shall succeed," he muttered; "surely, I shall succeed! I have but to draw blood, however slightly, and the deed is done. Why, it is killing, but no murder. How easily they slip away from mortal toil, and all the perils and pains of human existence! They ought to be obliged to me—but human nature is perverse. Yet shall I be their fate. You have bearded me once, my Lord Bridgewater: you and your prime bullying friend, Colonel Trelawney, covered me with confusion and disgrace in Bloomsbury Fields. But my time has come now. Yes, my time has come now?"

Lord Warringdale walked very slowly, for he wanted to be overtaken by his friend the Major, and soon he saw that individual bustling after him.

"I've done it, my illustrious friend—I've done it!" cried the Major. "Mines, bombards, and scaling-ladders! but I've done it!"

"They will not come too soon?"

"No, no! I've arranged all that. You will have time to cross swords with your opponent, and show him a trick or two of fence, before they make their appearance. But the time runs on, my illustrious friend; know you not that it is near upon the stroke of eight? And egad! it seems to me we're not alone in this wilderness of trees and bushes."

Approaching diagonally as regards the path which Lord Warringdale and the Major were making for themselves through the brushwood towards the Palace, appeared two other persons, who Lord Warringdale had no difficulty in recognising at a glance to be the young Earl of Bridgewater and his second.

"It is our opponent," said Warringdale. "Let us hasten. I would not have them say they were first on the field."

It would appear that the Earl of Bridgewater and the gentleman who was to second him had recognised the Lord Warringdale and the Major at the same moment they were themselves seen, by the gestures they made towards them.

It was curious, then, to see these two parties approaching the same spot by different paths, but yet as quickly as they could, so that they were pretty sure to meet at a point which would be the commencement of an avenue among the trees leading to the pretty little romantic spot at the back of the Palace.

Warringdale twice loosened his sword in its sheath, although there was in reality no occasion for going through that process, and, turning to the Major, he said, in low tones, "I think it would be proper for you to go on, quickly and alone, and speak to the Earl's second. I will try and reach the spot of encounter between the trees."

"I'm off—I'm off! But by that, illustrious friend, they will reach the ground first."

"It don't matter now, as I've been seen."

"Certainly not!—certainly not!"

Lord Warringdale was nervously anxious to avoid as much as possible any personal communication with the Earl of Bridgewater. Well he knew his frank and heedless style of discourse; and that, in all probability, he would at once, and to his face, accuse him of the murder of his father.

Therefore it was that Warringdale deviated from the direct path, and left the Major to be as ceremonious as he pleased to the Earl and his second.

But still it was impossible for Warringdale to delay the meeting beyond two or three seconds; and upon consulting his watch, he saw that it wanted only one minute to eight o'clock.

"Now," he muttered, "I fancy the earldom of Whitcombe hangs upon the arrangements of the next twenty minutes."

He hastened his footsteps, and in a few minutes more emerged from a little clump of elm-trees on to an open space, which looked more like the well-kept lawn of some pretty garden, than merely one of the public nooks of green and spring-like vegetation beneath the trees of old Kensington Gardens.

On this spot stood the Earl of Bridgewater and his second.

A few paces apart from them was the Major, with his head inclined towards the elm-trees—evidently waiting for the appearance of Lord Warringdale, which taking place on the moment, induced a slight bow on the part of the second of the Earl of Bridgewater; but the young Earl himself vouchsafed no such courtesy to Lord Warringdale.

"No!" he said; "no!"—and he spoke in tones of excitement—"I do not bow to the murderer of my father! For here I declare to all present, let the issue of this contest be what it may, that I firmly believe this false and wicked man to be the murderer of the late Earl of Bridgewater!"

A malevolent expression shot from the eyes Lord Warringdale, and he replied, sneeringly, "You are free in your accusations, my Lord Bridgewater. And it is because you are so that I have cited you this morning to appear upon this spot, that I may punish your falsehood and your insolence."

"Villain!"

"Gentlemen, I fancy it is eight o'clock, and I would rather fight with the Earl of Bridgewater than undertake a contest of railing and abuse with him."

"Mille bombs!" cried the Major; "that's well said."

"I can well comprehend," said the Earl, "the reluctance of my Lord Warringdale to hear me speak; but I cannot comprehend his willingness to fight."

"What mean you, my lord, by those words?" said Warringdale angrily.

"I mean that a willingness to fight is a new trait in your character."

"My lord!—my lord," interposed the impetuous young Earl's second, "an altercation of this kind is unworthy of you."

"You are right, Miles!—you are right! I thank you. My feelings for a moment hurried me away; but I will say no more."

"Zounds! gentlemen," said the Major; "enough has been said, in all conscience! Let us to work; for, as I had the honour to remark to the Elector of Bavaria, on the occasion of his duel with the Duke of Alencon, the sooner we hear the clank of sword-blades the better."

"I am ready!" said Lord Warringdale.

"And I!" said the Earl of Bridgewater.

"Then heaven protect the right!" cried the second of the young Earl.

It was now just five minutes past eight o'clock; and what Lord Warringdale had to do, he felt must be done quickly, or not at all.

Casting a glance in the direction where he expected the rangers, who had been warned to appear by the Major, he drew his sword.

As he did so, he cast a last rapid look towards the point, where the poison had been allowed to dry into that yellow film which he knew was so deadly.

There it was still; and the savage gleam that shot from the eyes of Warringdale might well have awakened the suspicions of all present that some terrible treachery was intended.

The position of the different parties now within sight and ear-shot of that little green spot in Kensington Gardens deserves from us a slight glance.

The moment the parties to the duel came upon the ground, the Reverend Mortification shifted his position a little, so that he could see over the edge of the gravel-pit.

As he did so, Captain Heron, who was some short space lower down in the pit, saw that he dropped the flask of eau de vie—or rather, as it might now be spoken of, the flask that had contained the eau de vie.

It was evidently now empty.

It was evident, too, from the movements of the Reverend Mortification, and the tipsy leer that sat upon his countenance, that he had taken more of the contents of that flask than was at all good for him at so early an hour.

Captain Heron, however, in consequence of Mortification shifting his position in the gravel-pit, was able to make a change in his own, and he reached the brink, where, concealed by some bushes, he could look over on to the scene of contest.

There was yet another spectator of the affair which Lord Warringdale thought he had so snugly all to himself.

That was Jonathan Wild.

Jonathan closely followed his three men, attired in the rangers' coats; and while he himself ascended to a forked branch of a tree, where he could sit quite comfortably, he hid his men among the underwood, with directions not to stir till they heard his whistle.

Such, then, was the state of affairs at the back of the old Palace in Kensington Gardens at the moment that the gallant young Earl of Bridgewater drew his sword, and stood upon his guard.

The duel was about to commence.

No. 99.—EDITH.

CHAPTER CCXIV.

LORD WARRINGDALE FINDS HIMSELF CONFRONTED
BY A MOST UNEXPECTED ENEMY.

THE two seconds stepped a little aside.

The Earl of Bridgewater cast his hat to the ground, and looked Lord Warringdale calmly and steadily in the face.

Warringdale was in the most careful attitude of defence that the fencing school could teach.

He wanted the hot-headed and heedless Earl of Bridgewater to begin the duel by attacking him.

In the course of such an attack, he hoped to inflict the slight wound which would be sufficient for death.

And as yet Captain Heron could see no sufficient reason for interfering with the duel. The combatants seemed to be equally armed. The seconds were there. What excuse had he for even showing himself? None whatever. That some foul play was intended he did not doubt, but until he saw some real indication of it, and comprehended somewhat of its nature, he could do nothing.

He could only watch and wait.

Now, it was the etiquette in duels with swords that he who was the challenger should commence the assault; and as Lord Warringdale stood in that relation to his noble and brave opponent, the Earl waited to give him his opportunity.

But Lord Warringdale waited likewise, for fear was at his heart.

Now that he stood fairly opposed to the Earl, he seemed to have a greater dread of the result of the combat than had ever before possessed him.

The long, bright blade of the poisoned sword trembled in his grasp.

But time was passing away. The rangers, if they were to make their appearance at a quarter past eight, would in five minutes more be upon the spot.

There was no time to lose.

"Come on!—come on!" cried Lord Warringdale hoarsely. "Why do you tarry there to gaze upon me?"

"Be it so, then!" replied the Earl.

He made a spring forward, and the sword-blades encountered each other with a light clashing sound.

"Bombs and pistolettes!" cried the Major. "You will be run through, my lord!"

Warringdale had made a shield of his left arm in the most outrageous manner as regarded all principles of fencing and, as was to be expected, he received a wound in it on the instant.

But he had an object, and that object he succeeded in.

It was to take a wound and give one.

He took his wound, which extorted from his lips a sharp expression of pain, and at the same moment he slightly touched the Earl of Bridgewater in the neck with his sword's point.

With his sword's poisoned point!

"You are mad, sir!" said the Earl,—"you are mad! or heaven has given you up to my vengeance!"

As he spoke, he shortened his arm, and in another moment he would have plunged his sword through the breast of Lord Warringdale; but, to the surprise of both the seconds, and to the surprise of Jonathan Wild, and of Captain Heron, the Earl paused, and stood as if suddenly turned to stone.

The poison was doing its terrible work.

So sudden had been the attack upon Lord Warringdale of the Earl of Bridgewater, and with such rapidity, for a few seconds, had the swords entwined like living things in mortal strife around each other, that neither the disreputable Major nor the second of the Earl could decide if a wound had been given or not.

But the attitude and manner of the Earl of Bridgewater were suggestive of serious mischief.

It was well for Lord Warringdale that their eyes were upon the Earl, and not upon him, at that time, or they would have seen what a fiend he looked, and must have suspected some foul play.

Slowly the Earl of Bridgewater lowered the point of his sword.

With a gasping sound, as though he drew a last breath with infinite difficulty, he tried to overcome the effects of the poison, which, through that slight wound in the neck, was mingling with his blood.

He tottered two or three paces backward.

His sword trailed along the grass as he went.

"You are hit, my Lord Bridgewater!" said Lord Warringdale.

At the conclusion of these words, Warringdale could not refrain from a loud exultant laugh.

The Earl's second sprang forward and caught him in his arms at the moment that the sword dropped from the relaxed grasp of the young nobleman; and but for that support from his second, he would have fallen to the ground.

"By heaven, he is killed!"

"I—I faint!" murmured the Earl; "I faint! but—but surely am not killed."

Then, as if death had struck him on the instant, to give a practical contradiction to his words, he rested so heavily upon the arm of his second, that that person was compelled to let him slide gradually to the grass, where he supported him on one knee.

A very curious circumstance, indeed, now took place.

Lord Warringdale suddenly darted forward, exclaiming, "I cannot think that I have hurt him! The point only of my sword touched in something of this fashion!"

As he spoke, he made a deliberate pass with his sword at the Earl's second.

"Villain!—assassin!"

"Ah! say you so? Ha! ha!"

Lord Warringdale sprang back again to what might be called his own place on that field of battle; and as he did so, he caught the astonished Major by the arm with his disengaged hand, while with the other he still held out the sword at full length.

The sword which had already done so much mischief!

The poisoned blade which seemed to carry death upon its point!

The Earl's second let drop the insensible form of his principal and sprang to his feet.

He laid his hand on his own sword-hilt.

"Wretch!" he exclaimed; "I know not if you be a demon or a mortal man; but be you which you may, I—I——"

He paused.

He had drawn his sword about half a foot from the scabbard. Then it seemed to stick fast as though it were riveted to its position.

It was the arm of that gentleman and brave man which refused to obey the will.

"Ha! ha!" laughed Lord Warringdale. "Look, Major—look! Saw you in all your experience of mortal combat, so easy a victory as this?"

"Bombs and sabretaches! what does it mean?" said the Major, looking pale in the face.

He made an effort to free himself from the vice-like grasp which Lord Warringdale had of his left arm.

That effort was in vain.

"Why, Major," added Warringdale, "I did but touch them so slightly, that when I show you practically, you——"

The Major uttered a cry of horror.

Warringdale, still holding him by one arm, had

turned the point of that horrible sword upon him.

"You will no more regard it, than the scratch of a pin."

"Help! help! Murder!" shouted the Major.

Lord Warringdale made a pass at him with the sword's point, but missed him.

The second of the Earl of Bridgewater fell heavily over the body of the young Earl.

The Major uttered scream after scream—"Help! help! Murder! murder!"

He clutched the feet of Lord Warringdale, and they both fell on the green turf together.

Then there came with a rushing bound on to the scene of action, a tall and lithesome figure; and a voice that sounded like that of destiny in the ears of Lord Warringdale—a voice which, of all others, he least expected to hear in that place, rang in his ears.

It was the voice of Felix Heron.

"Rise, villain worse than human language can describe!—rise, and behold the avenger!"

Heron had seen all that took place from his place of espial in the gravel-pit; and on the instant that the young Earl of Bridgewater had fallen, he had made an attempt to rush forward and interpose.

The very speed that he wished to exert was, however, for the moment fatal to his purpose, for his foot slipped upon the very brink of the pit, and he fell half-way down its entire depth before he could stop himself.

The Reverend Mortification had then become, for the first time, aware that he was not alone in the gravel-pit; and between alarm and inebriety—for his devotion to the flask of eau-de-vie had not been without its results—he knew not what to do.

Active, and light, and energetic as Felix Heron was, the fall was only sufficient to delay him some half-minute or so.

He was then at the brink of the pit again, and gaining his feet, he dashed forward in the way we have described.

But during that half-minute important events had taken place on the green-sward above him.

The Earl of Bridgewater was, to all appearance, a dead man.

That sudden and dastardly attack had been made upon the second, which had sent him to keep company with his principal, and the struggle between Lord Warringdale and the terrified Major was in full progress.

At the sound of Felix Heron's voice, Lord Warringdale uttered a yell of dismay.

"Rise, fiend in human guise!" cried Heron. "The time has come when I must cast mercy from my heart!"

Warringdale struggled to his feet.

He had still his sword in his hand, and he made another effort to inflict a wound upon the Major, but the latter rolled over and over, and escaped him. Springing to his feet, then, he made a rush through the underwood, and escaped.

Captain Heron picked up the sword of the young Earl of Bridgewater, and brought it with a clash across the blade of the poisoned weapon in the hands of Warringdale.

"Be it so!" yelled Warringdale. "This is providential, and I shall accomplish all my desires at once!"

"Defend your worthless life!" said Heron. "I would not have it on my thoughts in time to come that I did not give even to you a fair field!"

"Ah!"

Lord Warringdale's eyes wandered to the left, where he could see rapidly approaching several of the garden rangers.

They were the officials who had been warned by the Major, at the instigation of Lord Warringdale himself, to come to that spot.

Now, if by one breath he could have brought sudden death upon them all, he would most gladly have done so.

They were too soon, or too late.

Too soon, if he should have the good fortune to wound Felix Heron.

Too late to stop the contest from being serious to him, provided the skill in fencing of Heron should be so superior as not only to protect himself from the point of the poisoned sword, but possibly to mortally wound him, Lord Warringdale.

But the rangers were at some distance.

There might still be time.

Warringdale gave ground. Step by step he went back before the sword of his brother; and as he did so, he watched the opportunity when he might possibly dash in and pass his guard.

But this opportunity did not come.

Then Warringdale thought of another expedient. Well he knew the generosity of his opponent, and he cried out suddenly, "You do well to attack me now that I am faint and bleeding!"

Heron paused, and partially lowered the point of his sword as he cried, "Then yield, thou murderous wretch—yield thou at once! and let the consequences to myself be what they may, I will place you in the hands of justice for this morning's work."

While Captain Heron was speaking, Lord Warringdale, who knew he was for the moment safe from his sword, clapped his hands sharply together, letting the poisoned weapon he had hang by the silken cord and tassel which was about its hilt by his wrist as he did so.

That was the signal for the appearance of the Reverend Mortification.

He heard it.

"Hoorah!—hoorah! As the Psalmist says—

"'When the heart of a man is oppressed with care,
The gloom is dispelled when a woman appears.'

Ha, ha! I ain't drunk! Eau-de-vie for ever! Here you are! as the Psalmist remarks. Any little iniquity wanted, eh? Amen!"

The Reverend Mortification staggered on to the scene of action.

The cloak was hanging loosely from his shoulders; and beneath it there appeared his highwayman's dress, from which Lord Warringdale had expected so much assistance.

Well might Captain Heron look at him with the most intense surprise.

"Cross his path!" cried Warringdale. "A thousand pounds for you, Mortification, if you do but entangle him in your arms for a moment!"

Mortification had just sense enough left to comprehend what Warringdale wanted him to do; and he knocked up heavily against Heron, as he said, "Do you mean this one? Do you mean this one, eh?"

"Yes."

Warringdale was in the very act of darting

forward, when a sword-blade came over his shoulder and across his breast with a sudden gleam; and a hand was laid upon the very hilt of the poisoned weapon.

"Hold!" said a voice. "I restore thus the balance of the combat!"

Warringdale shrunk back aghast.

"It is now again two to two!" added the voice. "You will engage with me, false, perjured murderer!"

The person who had thus suddenly darted from among the trees, and interposed at the instant when Warringdale was about to rush forward and take the life of Captain Heron while he was disentangling himself, so to speak, from the Reverend Mortification Ripon, might well strike Lord Warringdale with terror and amazement.

The stranger wore a mask of black velvet, so that he could not see the face; but the costume was that of a knight of the road, with the addition of an over-coat of some light material, which was flung back, and exhibited the scarlet coat, the tall boots, and the various ornaments and *et ceteras* of the well-known costume of Captain Heron.

CHAPTER CCXV.

JONATHAN WILD THINKS HIS GOOD FORTUNE TO BE IN THE ASCENDANT, BUT MEETS WITH A GREAT DISAPPOINTMENT.—LORD WARRINGDALE IS IN DANGER.

AFFAIRS in general, upon that little green spot in Kensington Gardens, were turning out in anything but the fashion Lord Warringdale desired.

The fine-drawn plot—upon the fitness of the various parts of which he had so plumed himself—was evidently scattered to the winds.

People whom he knew, and people whom he knew not, seemed to have made that spot a rendezvous on that particular morning—momentarily to his exultation, but eventually to his despair.

A multitude of questions rushed upon the mind of Lord Warringdale, as he found himself so suddenly seized upon and prevented from perpetrating another murder.

Who could this individual be with the black vizor on his face, who so suddenly interposed between him and the long-cherished vengeance of his heart?

How came Captain Heron himself there, upon that same spot, on the occasion of a duel the secret of which seemed to have been confined to so few persons?

How was it that the Reverend Mortification Ripon—who certainly had started from the chambers in St. James's Street in tolerable, if not perfect, sobriety—was now in a state of wild excitement, alternated by the very depression of stupidity, in consequence of strong potations?

Why was it, too, that those rangers of the royal gardens, who had been so specially warned by the Major to come to that spot by a quarter past eight at the latest, suddenly paused at a considerable distance off, as if spellbound, and advanced not another step?

These were the bewildering queries which Lord Warringdale's imagination suggested to him.

He could find no answer to them; but the reader will see how they all came about, in the regular order of events.

And to take the last first, we may state that the reason the rangers, who had been warned by the Major, did not persevere in approaching the spot was, that Jonathan Wild, with his three bull-dogs, whom he had succeeded in so artfully disguising, emerged sufficiently from the trees to be seen, and energetically waved them back.

The rangers then, seeing, as they supposed, some of their own comrades in their official green coats upon the spot, paused instantly, lest they should be doing some mischief by an interference with what was going on, and which was already supervised officially.

But of this, Lord Warringdale could know nothing; nor could he know anything of the circumstances that brought Captain Heron to the place.

Quickly, however, Warringdale had to dismiss from his mind all speculative matters—since he was engaged hand to hand and sword to sword with one who called for his utmost attention.

So soon as he recovered himself sufficiently to make an effort to free himself from the grasp of the stranger with the vizor—who had come so suddenly upon the scene,—he did so with an energy which seemed upon the point of being successful.

It might have been chance, or it might be that there was some inward admonition or conviction in the mind of this stranger that the great danger lay in the sword-blade of Lord Warringdale, for he still kept his hold upon the hilt with his left hand.

It was in vain that Warringdale strove to disengage himself from that grasp, and it was not in its tenacity or its strength that the difficulty lay, but because he had no power in his hand to shake off a hold that moved as he moved, while his other arm was engaged in trying to defend himself from the sword that gleamed before his eyes.

It would seem, however, that the attack made upon Lord Warringdale by this stranger was not altogether so aggressive as it might have been, for nothing could have been easier, on his arrival, unobserved and unknown, than to have plunged his sword through the body of Warringdale; but, on the contrary, the stranger had grappled with him, rather obviously intent upon preventing him rushing forward against Captain Heron, than upon taking his life.

The struggle, however, lasted scarcely a few moments, for Captain Heron flung the Rev. Mortification so heavily upon his back that he lay at full length upon the grass, as if with the greatest disinclination ever to rise up again.

Three strides brought Captain Heron to the spot where his unknown ally was struggling with Lord Warringdale.

The first thing Heron did was to grasp the sword-blade which, in Warringdale's hands, had already done so much mischief, and to wrench the weapon from his grasp.

"Now, villain," he said, "your doom is sealed!"

"Mercy!" shrieked Warringdale, as he sunk upon his knees.

"Yes, such mercy as you have shown, you shall receive. That which is infinite, and not in this world, you must seek of heaven!"

LORD WARRINGDALE SHOWS THE WHITE FEATHER.

Presented Gratis with No. 99, of the New Edition of Edith the Captive; or, the Robbers of Epping Forest.

"No, no! Oh, do not kill me!—do not kill me!"

Heron still had the sword of the young Earl of Bridgewater in his hand, and at that moment he certainly drew back his arm for the purpose of making a lunge at the breast of Warringdale; for the seeming treacherous manner in which the young Earl of Bridgewater had been murdered, along with his second, had obliterated all feeling of compassion from the mind of Captain Heron.

"Die, villain!" he said. "Time and circumstances justify me in ridding the world of a monster of vice, ingratitude, and crime!"

Probably that moment would have ended the career of Warringdale, but the unknown person in the velvet mask interposed.

With a rapid motion of his sword he parried the thrust which might have reached the heart of Warringdale, and as he did so he cried out, "No, Felix, you would repent—you would repent! Felix, Felix, remember still this man is your brother!"

Heron's sword passed swiftly along the side of Warringdale, ripping both coat and vest in its progress, so near was it in accomplishing its fatal purpose.

And then if Warringdale had been armed—which he was not, for his sword was wrested from him, and lay on the turf at his feet—he might still have accomplished his terrible purpose, for in that voice which had so remonstrated with him Heron recognised the dearest one to him on earth!

It was Edith who spoke!

It was Edith who, thus disguised, had come from Epping Forest, in consequence of the tale that Tom Ripon had told upon his arrival there the evening previous.

It was Edith who had thus availed herself of the permission given her by Captain Heron, that she should not think herself bound to exercise no discretion in any enterprise that suggested itself to her—who, thus disguised, had made her way, with Ogle, to London.

She had been convinced, in her own mind, that there was much more in the narration of Tom Ripon than, at the first blush, appeared to the understanding. What it was she could not tell; but that some fearful treachery was at work, which, in all probability, would involve the life of Heron, she could not doubt.

Was she, then, to remain in safety and security amid the recesses of Epping Forest while such things were going on in London?

She could not think of it; and gathering from Tom Ripon that a shady, grass-grown spot, at the back of Kensington Palace, had been mentioned casually in his hearing by the Earl of Bridgewater, she guessed that there the interest would concentrate.

Mounted on Daisy, she had ridden to London with Ogle; and leaving him at the ancient ruin at Kensington—where Heron had appointed him to wait—she had walked among the shadows of the old elm-trees until the arrival at the spot of the encounter so opportunely to prevent Warringdale from adding, in the person of Felix Heron, a third victim to those who already lay upon the greensward in that spot of sylvan beauty!

And now Heron shouted aloud the name of Edith, for it sprung up from his heart to his lips; and, notwithstanding the presence of Lord War-

ringdale, from whom it would have been wise, perhaps, to keep the secret of her incognito, he cried out, as he stretched his arm towards the velvet mask, "Edith, Edith! If you be not my Edith, some spirit has borrowed your voice and hastened hither to aid me, as well as to save me from the commission of an act I should, indeed, have bitterly repented, for, in truth and in sadness, this man is my brother!"

Edith herself removed the velvet mask, and Captain Heron looked with delight upon the fair features of the much-loved partner of his soul.

"Can you forgive me, Felix," she said, "that I have availed myself rather of a permission frankly given than a wish on your part that I should ever follow your footsteps?"

"Dearest Edith, you have saved me!"

Lord Warringdale was still upon his knees, with his body wrenched back and his eyes staring wildly, for he felt that he had been very near death.

The surprise of seeing Captain Heron and Edith there before him so confused him that he might have been excused, almost, for supposing that he had really received some mortal wound, and that he was gazing about him through the mists of futurity.

"Edith, Edith!" cried Heron, "what am I to do? Look upon this spot, and behold its terrors! The Earl of Bridgewater is killed—I think I ought to say murdered!"

"Alas! alas! How has this been possible, Felix?"

"I cannot tell—it is a mystery. Some hideous treachery lies hidden beneath the appearances of this morning's work, for not only is the Earl of Bridgewater no more, but by some strange fatality the gentleman who came here to second him is stretched in death by his side."

"Let me go—let me go!" said Lord Warringdale, faintly. "Let me go. Give me my sword, and let me go. I do not want to fight with you, Felix Heron—nor with you, Edith. Let me go—let me go!"

"Wretch! confess all!"

"Felix! Felix!" cried Edith, "do not again let your rage master your judgment."

"I've nothing to confess," said Warringdale. "I know not what you mean. I've nothing to confess."

"Speak, monster! How came those two corpses to fall before you?"

"I am skilful and cunning of fence."

"It is false!"

"Nay; you contradict me when the evidences of the fact lie before you."

"But how," said Edith, "should the Earl's second be involved in his death?"

"Speak, villain! Answer that! Rise not from your knees, but answer that!"

Lord Warringdale thought it was just possible Felix Heron might not have seen the dastardly attack upon the second, so he hazarded a specious explanation of the fact.

"When the Earl fell before my sword," he said, "the gentleman who was his second—a complete stranger to me—became inflamed with fury, and rushed upon me at unawares. It was by the greatest good fortune I got upon my guard and killed him."

The look that passed from the eyes of Felix

Heron to those of Edith, and the return glance she gave to him, showed Warringdale that he had hazarded a safe assertion, and that they were actually not in a condition to contradict him.

"What else could I do?" he said; "what else would any man have done, having the power to do it?"

The fact was, the little episode of the attack upon the Earl's second had taken place just at that period when Captain Heron fell partially down the gravel-pit, so that he had escaped seeing it.

But it had been seen by other eyes, for the reader will not forget that during all this time Jonathan Wild, bit by bit, and incident by incident, was very much enjoying all that took place.

His surprise at the appearance of Captain Heron was as great as Lord Warringdale's, although it was not accompanied with the same amount of panic.

But when Edith made her appearance, Wild was quite delighted, and rubbed his hands so hard together, that it seemed as if he were trying to elicit sparks from them.

No doubt Jonathan thought he had his two victims safe; and in perspective he saw the Earl of Bridgewater got rid of, who had always been an eye-sore to him, Captain Heron and Edith both his prisoners, and he with a stronger hold than ever upon Lord Warringdale.

And by this time, too, Wild had got up a theory of his own in regard to the sudden and mysterious deaths of the Earl and his second.

It said something for the ingenuity of Jonathan Wild, that he should have hit upon the truth.

Perhaps he had seen the play of "Hamlet," where Laertes poisons his sword-point to slay the vacillating and philosophic Dane; but, whether or not, Jonathan had certainly hit upon the fact.

"I must look out for myself," he muttered, "for Warringdale is evidently in possession of some poison that does its work quickly. He has anointed his sword-blade with it, and that explains all. I must look out, or he will be becoming dangerous to me."

It was Edith who broke the pause of irresolution and doubt in the mind of Captain Heron as regarded what to do next.

"Let us fly from this spot, Felix," she said; "let us seek our own home, beneath happier shadows than those cast by these trees."

"But this man, Edith—this man?" said Heron. "What shall we do with him?"

"Unarmed, he is harmless; and even armed, he dare not raise his coward hand against you, Felix?"

"If such is your opinion of me," said Warringdale, in a low tone, "give me my sword, and let me go. As regards the deaths of those two men, I shall have to answer to the law, and the law will know where to find me. Give me my sword, and let me go. I will promise not even to turn my head to look which road you take."

The poisoned sword lay almost within reach of Warringdale, as he knelt now only upon one knee upon the grass—for he had raised the other. He stretched out his hand towards it, and the life of Captain Heron might be metaphorically said to have hung upon a thread.

If Warringdale had but got hold of his poisoned sword, he would no doubt, on the moment, have succeeded in inflicting some slight wound upon Captain Heron; and, slight as it might have been, it would have laid him low in the same manner as the young Earl of Bridgewater and his second were laid low.

Then he would have had no one to cope with apparently but Edith, and the strong probability was that the murderous instinct which had been awakened in the breast of Warringdale would not have hesitated at her destruction.

The death, too, of the inebriated Mortification Ripon would have been easy; and then what a monarch of all he surveyed might not Lord Warringdale have thought himself!—what a fate—what a spirit of death, standing in the midst of his victims!

But this was not to be.

Captain Heron struck his arm sharply with the Earl of Bridgewater's sword, and at the same moment Edith picked up the poisoned blade.

Warringdale saw that the opportunity was gone.

Rage flashed from his eyes.

"Who is the coward now?" he cried. "You—you, Felix Heron! You, whom I now challenge to a match of life or death! I will fight with you—once and for all, I will fight with you! You have a second here, in Edith—I have none! I will fight with you, and if you deny me I will brand you coward!"

A flush came upon the face of Captain Heron.

"Heed him not, Felix," said Edith—"heed him not. He raves as one who has played a game of villany, and lost the stake."

"No," said Warringdale; "I have won it!" (he pointed to the bodies of the Earl of Bridgewater and his second as he spoke)—"I have won it!—I have won it! And it is because I have won it, the politic and careful Felix feels his bastard blood circle in alarm round his heart at the idea of crossing swords with me!"

Captain Heron turned pale.

"You have uttered a word," he said, "which has several times hovered upon your lips."

"I will utter it again!"

"I advise you not, for your own safety's sake. This is the first time you have gathered courage to give a voice to the falsehood and malevolence of your heart, which coined the word."

"I will repeat it!"

"Oh, heed him not! oh, heed him not!" cried Edith; "he is unworthy, Felix, even of your anger!"

"Edith, dearest, grant me one favour!"

"No, no; I know what you would say!"

"There is no danger."

"Do not—oh, do not! I know what you would wish to do."

"Let me cross swords with this vile wretch for a minute's space; I will not kill him."

"I implore you not!"

"Ha! ha!" laughed Lord Warringdale; "that is well. Felix Heron can be excused from defending his honour and his name, because Edith is fearful for his safety."

Edith looked disdainfully at Lord Warringdale.

"No, sir," she said, "it was for your safety I was fearful. I did not wish the shadow of a moment's grief to stain the pure mirror of my husband's thoughts. He is so tender, true, and gentle, that to kill you would be an everlasting regret—because his father was your father. To wound you, even, would hurt him to think of. Therefore I spoke. But now, since you goad him to it—since you strive to hurt him, and to hurt me, through those feelings and those affections which such men as you know nothing of, I say to my Felix—I say to my husband, fight this man!"

CHAPTER CCXVI.

EDITH SUMMONS ASSISTANCE TO CAPTAIN HERON WHEN ALL APPEARS LOST.

THERE was something so noble—something so beautiful and majestic about the tone, the look, and the manner of Edith, as she uttered the words with which we concluded the last chapter, that Captain Heron took his eyes off Lord Warringdale, to gaze upon her with delight and love.

"My Edith!" he cried,—"my own brave and noble Edith! oh, how can I be ever worthy of you?"

Lord Warringdale slowly rose to his feet.

"The time has come!" he muttered to himself.

He had no doubt whatever, now, but that Captain Heron would engage in combat with him; and if so, he had no doubt of being able to inflict upon him some wound which would lay him low by the side of the Earl of Bridgewater and Sir Wentworth Miles.

"The time has come!"

But if Captain Heron took his eyes off the movements of Lord Warringdale, Edith did not. She had a full appreciation of all his possible treacheries, and she would not allow him to feel that he was for an instant unobserved.

"Fear not, my Edith!" added Felix Heron; "I will fight this man, and I will conquer him."

"I know it," said Edith.

A bitter, mocking smile came over the face of Warringdale as he made a bow, which had more of insolent defiance about it than any other feeling.

"Pray, please yourselves," he said; "I am content to abide the issue."

"My father's blood that flows in your veins," said Heron, "cannot be all cowardly, and that gives you now the courage to die."

Lord Warringdale did not like the tone in which Felix uttered these words, and he began to feel that he had staked, perhaps, really his life for the second time that morning.

The insolent flush of colour that had come upon his face as he had looked upon Heron and upon Edith as both in his power, began to fade away.

But he could not now retreat.

He did not in fair truth wish to do so, for the chances were so greatly in his favour as regarded inflicting some trifling hurt upon his brother which would be sufficient to let the poison into his veins.

"I am ready!" he said; "I am ready!"

"Be it so," replied Heron. "Edith, dear one, let him have his sword."

Edith cast the poisoned sword at the feet of Lord Warringdale with disdain and aversion in her looks and actions.

He made a dart at it as though it were the prize of his existence—and so, indeed, he felt it to be at that moment.

So soon as he had the hilt fairly in his grasp, he astonished both Captain Heron and Edith by the half-shout of exultation that he uttered.

There could not seem to their minds any possible occasion for so strong an expression of satisfaction on the part of Lord Warringdale.

Little did they suspect the cause of that satisfaction.

Little did they suspect the black and hideous treachery which filled his heart.

"Come on! come on!" he cried, as he put himself upon his guard. "Come on, thou false and base impostor, who would wrench from me the title and the fair lands of Whitcombe,—come on, and meet your doom!"

Heron was perfectly surprised at this apparent exhibition of courage on the part of Lord Warringdale; but he raised his sword to a guard, as he said, "Witness, heaven, that from time to time I have spared this man!"

"Spare him, then, no longer!" cried Warringdale. "Do your worst, rather?"

"You are mad!"

"Ha, ha! And what are you?"

"Your brother."

"Yes; and you are one who would parley when he should fight!"

A scornful smile, that had in it likewise something of pity, came across the handsome features of Captain Heron.

"Be it so, then!" he said, in a tone of sadness. "I am to be the avenger; and I will not shrink from the appointed duty!"

Heron stepped forward one long pace.

With great excitement of manner—for although he thought himself so dangerous, Lord Warringdale could not but feel that he was himself likewise in danger—he, too, stepped forward a pace upon the grass.

They were now within fair fighting distance of each other.

Edith clasped her hands together; and only in a low murmur uttered the words, "Heaven protect my Felix!"

The swords clashed together.

Lord Warringdale stepped back a pace. He kept his eyes fixed upon Heron. He was calculating how he might, with the greatest certainty, inflict upon him some wound.

No one was there present to object to the unfairness with which he might conduct the combat—for the laws of such conflicts could scarcely be expected to be known to Edith.

And he thought Edith was the only spectator of the fight.

Lord Warringdale, therefore, stepped back a pace, because he had just made up his mind what to do.

He intended to stoop suddenly, and try to hit Heron with the point of the poisoned sword upon the foot or knee.

But Heron was wary and watchful now; and something in the eyes of his opponent let him suspect that some mischievous mode of action was intended.

Darting forward as Warringdale stepped back,

Captain Heron kept him so engaged that he had not time to stoop. If he had tried to do so, he might have received some serious wound.

Then Warringdale added to his plan another piece of artifice.

He thought if he could, by startling his brother, withdraw his attention for a moment, he should be able at once to accomplish his fell and dastardly purpose of slightly wounding him.

"Ah!" he cried, suddenly, "what do I see above us?"

Certainly, nineteen men out of twenty would involuntarily have looked upwards on such an exclamation; but Captain Heron was the twentieth one, who did not.

Keeping his eyes steadily fixed upon Lord Warringdale, he still pressed onwards as he, Warringdale, retreated step by step.

The swords twined round each other for a few moments like serpents; and then, as Lord Warringdale uttered a cry of rage, fear, and despair, his sword was wrenched from his hand, and flew, tearing through the air, to a considerable distance from the spot.

"Yield thee, villain!" cried Heron.

"No—no! Yes! I do not mean no! Spare me!—spare my life!"

"Coward!"

"Coward and vain, boaster!" added Edith.

Lord Warringdale cowered down before the presented sword-blade of Captain Heron, and trembled in every limb.

"Spare me!" he said. "This is a trick of fence! My sword is shorter than yours, or it would not have happened."

Captain Heron held his bad half-brother at his mercy; but when was he ever known to take advantage of such a power? He forbore to make that one thrust which would have ridden the world of Lord Warringdale, and himself of the worst enemy human life could ever present to him.

"Let me go now," added Warringdale. "The chances are yours."

"Chances, villain! Call them not chances!"

"The swords were unequal in length. You had the advantage."

"Say you so?"

"I declare it. I will always declare it, or else the issue of the combat had been widely different."

The look of scorn and loathing that came over the face of Captain Heron was beyond all description.

"Edith, Edith," he said, "what am I to do with this man?"

"Leave him," replied Edith—"leave him, my Felix, with such contempt as honour, courage, and truth may leave falsehood, cowardice, and villany!"

"You hear?"

"I do hear," replied Warringdale.

"Edith," added Heron, "have you a writing tablet with you?"

"No, Felix, no."

"Then this must suffice."

Captain Heron picked from among the grass a small piece of chalk that lay accidentally among it, and then tearing from the breast of Lord Warringdale's apparel a shred of cloth, he wrote upon it one word.

That word was "Bastard!"

"You will please," he then said to Warringdale —"you will please to swallow this!"

"What do you mean?"

"What I say! You will please to swallow this, or fight again!"

"Ah!"

"I say it; and, by the heaven above us, I will keep my word!"

"I will, then, fight again."

"Be it so. But beware; for this time I will not spare you!"

"Nor I you!"

Lord Warringdale was gathering fresh courage. Again, he thought, everything might chance to turn out in his favour. He began to look about him more and more confidently.

"I will fight—I will fight again!"

"No, Felix—oh, no!" said Edith. "Remember that time is fleeting. The day has commenced, and there may soon be many foes around us."

"Have no fear, Edith, dearest! This man now courts destruction."

Captain Heron flung down at his feet the shred of cloth on which he had written the word which he had proposed to Warringdale to swallow; and then, as he cast his own sword at the feet of his opponent, he said, "You shall not this time complain of an inequality in the length of the weapons with which we fight, for you shall have my sword, and I will use yours."

Lord Warringdale uttered a yell of affright.

No possible form of words could have issued from the lips of Captain Heron, or from those of any human being, that could have given him such a shock as they did.

Caught in his own snare—sacrificed to his own arrogance and villany, he saw nothing but certain destruction, without the shadow of chance to the contrary, if Heron should persist in fighting with the poisoned sword!

"No, no!—oh, no, no!"

"You refuse?"

"With all my voice—with all my heart—with all my brain!"

"But you shall fight!"

"Ay, with my own sword."

"No!"

"Help, help! Murder!"

"Look to him, that he stir not, Edith."

Edith, with the quickness of thought, drew a pistol from the ample pocket in the skirt of the scarlet coat she wore, and presented it at the head of Lord Warringdale.

"Attempt to move from the spot—ay, even attempt to alter the attitude you are now in, and I will fire!"

Lord Warringdale cowered down before her, and he turned pale as death.

Some dozen of rapid strides brought Captain Heron to the spot where lay the poisoned sword, and he brought it back in his hand.

"Now," he said, "take up the weapon I have cast at your feet; and, by your own showing, you renew this combat with the advantage of the longer sword of the two!"

"No, no!"

"You will not?"

"I—I—that is——"

"He dare not!" said Edith.

"I decline!"

Captain Heron turned aside with a gesture of contempt.

"I—I will eat he—the word. I will eat it, if you will have it so."

"This is indeed passing strange, Edith," said Heron. "This villain is at one moment the slave of abject fear, with cowardice shining forth from every feature of his face, and the next he is full of fire and fury and desire to fight."

These rapid alternations of feeling were naturally quite inexplicable to Edith and to Captain Heron.

The one sufficient explanation of the phenomena, which the reader is in possession of, they wanted to enable them to comprehend that which struck them with such complete surprise.

But now Captain Heron added greatly to the terrors of Lord Warringdale; for, in lieu of picking up, as he (Lord Warringdale) expected, the shred of cloth with the word "bastard" written upon it, and presenting it to him to swallow as

the price of his life, the mode by which Heron raised it from the grass filled Warringdale with a thousand agonies.

Instead of stooping, Captain Heron, with the poisoned sword—with the very point of that dreadful weapon which seemed to carry death and destruction on its glittering blade—Heron picked up the shred of cloth by the simple process of thrusting the point through it, and so raising it to a level with the face of Lord Warringdale.

Heron did not speak, but he presented the before not very tempting morsel to the shrinking wretch who was cowering before him, and who now regarded it as he would have regarded a death-potion pressed upon his lips.

For all he knew, the mere contact of the sword-blade, as the poisoned point passed through the shred of cloth, might communicate sufficient of the deadly fluid to stretch him in death upon that green-sward.

"No!" he cried; "not that, now—not that,

now! I cannot!—I will not!—I dare not! Spare me!—spare me!"

Every one of these extraordinary and contradictory actions of Lord Warringdale's filled Captain Heron and Edith with more and more surprise.

"He is mad, Edith—he is mad! He is surely mad!"

"This is very strange," said Edith.

"In mercy, spare me!" faltered Warringdale. "Oh, forget, from this moment, all that I have said and all that I have done."

"I have spared you."

"No, no! You do not know—I cannot tell you——Help! murder! mercy!"

He shrunk down upon the ground, and in the most abject attitude he could assume, he trembled before the glance of the man whom he had so deeply injured, and whom he had met that morning with the full intention of destroying.

But Captain Heron could have no notion of the extent of the villany to which he had been exposed. A feeling of contempt and loathing took the place of all other sensations in his breast as regarded Lord Warringdale, and he turned from him with the sort of shudder that might come over any one at sight of a noxious reptile.

"Edith! Edith!" he said, "I can bear this no longer. It presents human nature in an aspect too humiliating either for you or for me to contemplate."

"Come, Felix, let us fly to our home amid the deep shadows of the trees. There are hearts there that love you; and if the old forest were a wilderness, better, far better, would be the companionship of the wild creatures that make it their home, than that of such a man as this."

"Go, go!" said Heron.

He motioned to Lord Warringdale that he might depart.

Scarcely, then, daring to raise himself to his full height, lest that permission should be retracted, Lord Warringdale commenced slowly to crawl away from the presence of his injured brother, and from the bodies of the slain.

Then Captain Heron, as though he had forgotten in a moment the very existence of Lord Warringdale, turned to the spot where lay, so still, so patient, so calm now, all that remained of his young friend, the Earl of Bridgewater.

"Alas! alas!" he said, "and has it come to this? The good, the great, and the noble-hearted fall, and the vile and despicable still lingers on the earth! This is a sad sight, my Edith!"

"Most sad—oh, most sad!"

"My gallant friend, you have fallen, and fallen for my sake, and I see not how to avenge you!"

"Felix! Felix! do not linger here. The dead are in heaven, but you live, and the very air is thick with enemies."

"That is too true, my Edith."

"Fly with me—fly! One hour's time takes us far from this spot, to the safety and security of our sylvan home."

"I come—I come!"

Both Captain Heron and Edith at this moment started and drew back a pace or two, for, amid the silence and solitude of that spot, which seemed so sacred to the dead, there came a jarring and most uncongenial sound

Some one was whistling, not altogether unskilfully, and yet with a certain jarring harshness of tone.

The air whistled was one of those well known at the period among the footpads, cracksmen, and other celebrities of Newgate.

The sounds came nearer and nearer each moment, and it was evident that whoever was disturbing the solitude of that leafy spot with such desecrating tones, was rapidly approaching.

The heavy footsteps could be heard, and the whistling tones became louder and louder.

Slowly, then, from among the trees, with an easy, careless manner, as though he were out for a morning walk, appeared a man, with his hands plunged deep into the pockets of his huge-skirted coat.

From one of these pockets projected the end of a bludgeon, to which a piece of leather hung, in order to secure it to the wrist.

"Jonathan Wild!" exclaimed Captain Heron and Edith, both in a breath. "It is Jonathan Wild!"

"Good morning, Captain—good morning!" cried Wild, in a loud voice. "Good morning, madam! It's pleasant to meet old friends—very! Good morning—good morning! Ha!"

CHAPTER CCXVII.

JONATHAN WILD IS BAFFLED AT THE MOMENT OF SUCCESS.—THE ESCAPE TO THE FOREST.

EDITH clung to the arm of Captain Heron, and at the sight of Jonathan Wild uttered a cry of despair.

Captain Heron stepped back a pace and stood upon the defensive, with the poisoned sword-blade pointed towards Wild.

"Come, come!" added Jonathan. "You know me, Captain, and I know you. A wise man accepts, without kicking, a defeat when it comes. I have a force of twenty men yonder, among the old trees."

The heart of Captain Heron would not have sunk for a single moment at these words of Jonathan Wild's, but for one circumstance.

Edith was with him!

Had he been alone, in all probability Wild would scarcely have had time to utter them.

The statement, however, was perfectly false;—for beyond the three men he had with him in the coats of the rangers, Wild had no force at hand

Still it may be presumed that three of his unscrupulous myrmidons, in addition to himself, should be sufficient to overcome one person.

But perhaps we should say two persons; for Edith was courageous now and defiant, when Felix Heron required an arm to aid him.

Jonathan Wild now paused. The suspicions he entertained in regard to the sword of Lord Warringdale had by no means dissipated.

So Wild paused.

"Come, Captain," he said, "you are brave enough to yield when you see resistance is useless."

"No, no!" cried Edith.

Jonathan just lifted his hat for a moment about an inch from his head, in mock politeness to

Edith, as he added, "And I am sure, madam, you are wise enough to advise a surrender in safety, in preference to a capture that may be stained with blood."

Wild pronounced the word "blood" with such a startling distinctness that it had all the effect he had intended upon the nerves of Edith.

She started, and turned pale.

Captain Heron drew her still further back, so as partially to shield her by the interposition of his breast and arm.

"Show me your twenty men, Jonathan Wild," he said.

"Oh, dear, no! You can do as you please, Captain; but have you I must."

"I will not yield to you, Jonathan Wild; and I defy your power! Edith, keep close to me; and if the villain should assail us, it will be the last time he shall do so in life!"

Wild placed the whistle he had with him—and the sound of which he knew would summon his men to his assistance—to his lips.

"Captain," he said, "the consequences of your obstinacy be upon your own head!"

But Jonathan did not yet blow the whistle.

"Will you yield," he added, "and so spare the lady the possibility of getting hurt in a contest which can have but one ending?"

Heron rapidly whispered to Edith.

"Walk quickly, dearest; I do not believe he has the force he says."

"Stop!" cried Wild.

Captain Heron waved his arm and hand in which he held the sword.

"Advance, Jonathan Wild! Advance, at your peril!"

Wild at once, then, blew a long, shrill whistle, which echoed among the trees.

That whistle-sound was immediately answered by his men appearing from behind the trees; and at the same time, then, there came a sound upon the green turf of the old gardens as if some one were beating the bushes and the underwood for game.

It was the rapid beat of horses' feet.

Then there was a shout, as a mounted man emerged from among some tall trees close to the round pond.

What was the strangest sight, though, was to see, following this man, another horse, but without a rider. Neither was the loose horse held or led in any way, but followed of its own will and purpose the rider and the steed that went before.

Then the horseman raised another shout; and Captain Heron and Edith could distinguish some words, that sounded like "In time—in time!"

Wild uttered a howl of rage.

"Seize him, bull-dogs!—seize him!" he shouted, "or it will be too late!"

The three men made a rush towards Captain Heron; but, flinging his left arm around the waist of Edith, he still retreated, waving the sword around him.

Wild's men did not look well at what might be in the way; and two of them fell over the prostrate form of the Reverend Mortification Ripon, who, from the moment that he had been flung upon the bank by Captain Heron, had not stirred hand or foot.

Now, however, the spell, whether it was fear or eau-de-vie, that kept the senses of Mortification so

locked up, was suddenly dissipated; and he rose to a sitting posture, as he cried out, "Yea, yea, the Philistines are upon us! Murder! murder! Oh, for a pot of small ale, as the Psalmist says; for I am athirst! Yea, I am athirst!"

The horseman, followed by the steed without a rider, came tearing over the green turf. Whenever any obstacle in the shape of a bush or the stump of some old broken-down or fallen tree presented itself, the horses leaped it, one after the other, with a precision and ease which was charming to see.

"Captain, Captain!" cried the horseman; "I am yet in time!"

It was Ogle who spoke.

It was Daisy that followed so closely in the wake of the steed which had borne Ogle from Epping Forest.

"We are saved!" said Edith. "Oh, thank heaven—thank heaven, we are saved!"

A happy, triumphant smile beamed upon the face of Captain Heron.

"Daisy! Daisy!—oh, my gallant Daisy!" he cried. "Come hither, friend and companion! Ho, Daisy! Daisy!"

The noble creature heard the voice it loved. Daisy saw the form of its kind and gentle master, and with one bound it shot past the other horse; and then, with a succession of leaps that were alarming and yet beautiful to see, Daisy reached the side of Felix Heron.

"Not for your life's sake, Jonathan Wild!" shouted Ogle at that moment.

Wild had drawn a pistol from his pocket, and presented it towards Heron.

Ogle, with a long holster-pistol that he snatched from the saddle of his horse, kept Wild at bay. The two men who had fallen over Mortification had scrambled to their feet, but they paused then irresolutely. The third one slunk back close to Wild.

"You are foiled, Jonathan," said Heron.

"Yes," said Edith; "and a wise man accepts a defeat which is inevitable."

This paraphrase of the very words he had addressed to her seemed to drive Jonathan Wild to the verge of madness.

"No, no," he cried, "I am not yet foiled; and I may not be! Since you will have it, take the bullet that fate has marked with your name when it was cast!"

Wild fired.

There was a report at the same moment, that mingled its echoes with those of his pistol; and then immediately a third shot, and then a fourth.

A regular fusillade seemed to be in progress at that spot at the back of the old Palace in Kensington Gardens.

The first of those shots was rather recklessly fired by Jonathan Wild, but whether at Captain Heron, or at Daisy—we should be loth, indeed, to think it could possibly be at Edith—it is impossible to say, but it missed both, or all; for in those days, certainly, fire-arms were not weapons of precision.

The next shot was from the holster-pistol of Ogle, who levelled it as nearly as he could at Jonathan's head; but that was a great mistake, for, from long practice in such-like encounters, Wild was in the habit immediately when he fired his own pistol of almost dropping to the ground, in order to avoid a return shot, whether he really expected one or not.

Jonathan, however, was not so quick upon this occasion but that the two bullets in the holster-pistol of Ogle nearly caught him.

His hat and wig both flew off, as if some gust of wind had caught them and whirled them from his head.

And this little circumstance completed the confusion of Wild's bull-dogs; for that one of them who had slunk back close to him, and avoided falling over the Reverend Mortification, as his two companions had done, received the hat and wig full in his face, which had so much the effect of a shot upon him, that, although the bullets actually missed him, he fell backwards with a shout of fear.

Then came the third shot.

That was from Edith.

Wild was hit this time.

It was but a flesh-wound, but he felt as if a red-hot iron had suddenly run up his arm and come out at the elbow.

Rage, which had been growing and swelling at his heart for the last few minutes, now got the better of all prudence.

Drawing his only remaining pistol, he levelled it, and fired. It was through the smoke and the smother of those rapid previous discharges—so that well it was for Jonathan Wild, so far as his human existence was concerned, that Captain Heron did not actually see, and could not take upon himself to say with certainty that the shot was levelled at Edith.

Many hours elapsed since this important minute when death-dealing bullets flew about so recklessly in old Kensington Gardens, before Edith herself discovered the partial loss of one of those wavy ringlets which had escaped the control of the hat and wig she wore as disguises, and through which the hot bullet must have winged its way.

But of that neither she nor Captain Heron knew anything at the moment.

Heron's voice, however, rose above all the tumult.

"Ogle," he cried, "to you for the next minute I commit the safety of Edith; for I must take this ruffian prisoner, if I have to hang him on the highest tree in old Epping Forest."

"He is killed, Captain," cried Ogle. "See, he falls! No man could fall like that without a shot."

"Ah! say you so?"

"Yes, Captain; farewell to Jonathan Wild, and let's be off."

Ogle had every reason to believe in the truth of what he stated in regard to the fate of Jonathan Wild; but he was entirely mistaken, for all that, and ought not to have trusted to appearances.

The sudden headlong fall of Jonathan Wild was entirely to be attributed to the Reverend Mortification Ripon.

When Jonathan's two men fell over Mortification, and roused him so effectually from the real or pretended state of insensibility he had preserved for the last ten minutes, he sprang up to a sitting posture, as we have related, and then the rapid interchange of pistol-shots which took place above him and about him, filled him with so much fear, that but one idea of a rational character remained to him, and that was to get away from so dangerous a place as quickly as possible.

The shortest and safest mode of doing this appeared to the Reverend Mortification to be in anything but the ordinary erect posture of man; so, dropping forward upon his hands, he made a rush across the green-sward upon hands and knees in so wild and reckless a manner that in a few seconds his head encountered the legs of Jonathan Wild, and the thief-taker was precipitated to the ground head-foremost in that sudden and violent manner, which made Ogle think that surely one of the shots had taken effect in his brain.

"Help!—murder!—fire!—thieves!" cried the Reverend Mortification; "let me alone! Get out of the way! Murder! Everybody for himself, as the Psalmist says! Oh!"

The next object the Reverend Mortification ran his head against did not yield to his furious charge quite so easily as Jonathan Wild, for it happened to be a tree against which the Reverend Mortification brought his head with a force that one or the other must give way to.

The tree took the attack quite calmly; but the Reverend Mortification rolled over upon his back, really stunned and insensible this time.

And, now, if Ogle was deceived, and thought that Jonathan Wild had been shot; and if Captain Heron and Edith were disposed to take Ogle's opinion upon trust,—there was another personage upon the scene whose acuter senses appeared to come to a juster conclusion.

That personage was Daisy.

With one of those terrific leaps, which spread always alarm and terror in the minds of those who saw them, Daisy reached the spot where Jonathan Wild lay, and before he could attempt to rise, she placed both her fore-feet upon his back, holding him down to the earth with a force it was in vain to resist, and with a look of proud hostility and defiance as terrible as it was beautiful to see.

If ever fear took entire possession of the breast of Jonathan Wild, it certainly did at that moment.

He uttered half-stifled yells and cries; and every time he did so, Daisy lifted one of her feet, and brought it down with a blow upon his back that must have left its mark behind it.

The smoke from the pistol-shots had flown away in blue, misty wreaths, and Captain Heron could see about him.

"You are unhurt, Edith—you are unhurt?" he cried.

"Perfectly. And you, Felix?"

"The villain missed me."

The two myrmidons of Jonathan Wild, who had been checked by falling over the Reverend Mortification, were now so alarmed at the turn affairs had taken, that they fled precipitately, calling out, however, as they went, in loud tones for assistance, so that they were likely to prove dangerous, if Heron, Edith, and Ogle lingered many minutes more on that spot.

The small party of rangers, too, that had been warned back by Jonathan Wild, but who kept in sight, now began to think it was time to interpose, and in a cautious, flurried sort of manner, began to straggle towards the spot.

"We must be off," said Heron. "We have time enough, and that is all. Mount Daisy, Edith, and make good speed to the forest."

"And you, Felix?"

"I will make my way, never fear. There is a weight at my heart, for my best friend has fallen by treachery, and lies yonder in death."

"Captain, Captain," said Ogle, "take my horse. I shall be able to look after myself, and you may be assured I shall find my way to Epping before sunset."

"We will go together," said Heron. "Daisy will carry us both for a few miles, Edith, as she has done before, and seemed to care but little for the additional burden."

"Help! Help! Death and murder!" cried Wild. "Take the mad horse off me! Kill me some other way, and don't let this beast pound me to death with its hoofs."

"Daisy! Daisy!" cried Heron. "Hither! hither!"

Daisy left Jonathan Wild, and trotted up to Heron. But so strong was the impression her fore-feet had made upon Wild's back, that even when they were removed, he still thought he felt them, and did not attempt to rise.

Captain Heron sprung to the saddle, and then assisted Edith to mount behind him, where, by clasping his waist, she could sit easily, and not obstruct him in the free management of the gallant creature that bore them.

"Off and away!" he cried. "The air of cities is hateful to me—the toilsome rush of human life, where all its treachery, deceit, and falsehood, shall be no more for me. Welcome the old glades and deep leafy recesses of my forest home! Farewell, farewell!"

He cast one glance to the prostrate form of the Earl of Bridgewater, and then with an audacity that surprised them, he turned Daisy's head full on the advancing party of rangers.

Men on foot were not likely to have much success in atttacking two such mounted persons as Ogle and Captain Heron; and no wonder, therefore, was it that the rangers scattered right and left, and only one of them made a feeble attempt to catch at Daisy's rein.

The sagacious creature was quite on the alert for such a circumstance, and repaid the attempt by such a sudden grasp at the man's arm with her teeth, that it was a thousand mercies to him that she only caught the sleeve of his coat.

Going at the speed she was, Daisy carried the green cloth sleeve with her—tearing it away from the ranger's arm as though it had been tinder; and so, with that trophy in her mouth, the noble creature, carrying its double burden, dashed out of Kensington Gardens by the small gate leading into the High Street of the royal village of Kensington.

Ogle followed close at hand; and when they both emerged into the open roadway, Captain Heron felt that their escape by no means hung upon the issue of an event which might have completely frustrated it.

Had that small and narrow gate been closed, they might have found the greatest possible difficulty in leaving the old gardens, for Jonathan Wild's discomfited bull-dogs had raised such a hue and cry that assistance was pouring into them to aid them in retrieving their lost ground.

But Heron and his Edith were safe; and Ogle, as he galloped up to the side of Daisy, lifted his hat and waved it triumphantly, as he gave a cheer, and cried out, "Captain, Captain, I did not wait for you at the old ruin in the Kensington Road, because I guessed pretty well the route by which you would come to it. I thought it would be as well to meet you. I found no one at the gate of the gardens, so in I trotted, and Daisy followed me like a dog!"

"You saved us, Ogle!"

"Hurrah for that, then!—and I do think, too, Captain, that Daisy has done the business for Jonathan Wild!"

CHAPTER CCXVIII.

RAPHAEL, THE CHEMIST, PLAYS A DOUBLE GAME, AND WINS.—THE STRANGE SCENE IN KENSINGTON.

PURSUIT of Felix Heron, and Edith, and their friend and companion, Ogle, was quite out of the question.

If the Park and Garden rangers and woodmen had been in possession even of horses, they would have had but a poor chance, indeed, against Daisy; but as it was, on foot as they were, the least attempt to stay the flight of Heron was not to be considered feasible for a moment.

Jonathan Wild's men might have been troublesome, but their courage had rapidly given way, and it was not until the last faint sounds of the retreating horses' footsteps that carried away Heron and Edith had died away, that they took courage to show themselves again upon the field of operations.

The position of Wild himself was suggestive to his men that he had received sufficient injury to make it necessary for them soon to look for a new employer.

The villanous thief-taker seemed to be at his last gasp.

Lying on his back, with his mouth wide open, and his eyes fixed on vacancy, Jonathan might be supposed to be ready to bid the world at once adieu, and to seek for mercy for his numerous offences of a justly offended heaven.

Close to him was the Rev. Mortification Ripon, who had now dropped off into a comfortable sleep, which he gave sufficient evidence of by prolonged nasal intonations that were enough to make all the birds and small wild creatures of Kensington Gardens imagine that some terrible and unknown foe had taken possession of the sylvan spot.

The apparently lifeless forms of the young Earl of Bridgewater and his second lay at the distance of about fifty yards from Jonathan Wild.

The real rangers of the Gardens came up to the interesting spot of the conflict at about the same moment that Wild's men, in their borrowed costumes, reached it.

No wonder that the former stared at the latter in undisguised amazement.

"Why, who are you, eh?" asked one of the real rangers. "I don't know one of you!"

"Never trouble your stupid head about that," was the reply. "Hilloa, Mr. Wild; how do you feel now, sir?"

Wild made no reply.

"He's right down dead!" said another. "What shall we do with him?"

"Get a chair and carry him to town, I should say; but, to look at him, one would think he is one of those cocks who is done crowing!"

"You lie!" said Jonathan Wild, hoarsely.

The change in the manner of Jonathan's men when they found he could hear and speak, was very great.

They gathered round him at once, and one lifted him to a sitting posture, while another said, with a great appearance of sympathy, "Dear me, Mr. Wild, we all hope you are not hurt, sir!"

"Not a bit!"

"Then——"

The man was going to say, "Then why do you lie there for, looking as if you were," but he thought better of it, and only coughed. Jonathan Wild, however, caught his meaning, and replied to him just the same as if he had spoken his thought.

"Because I choose, idiot!"

The janissaries shrank back a step or two. They saw that their nefarious employer was not only in anything but the best of humours, but they began to have a pretty clear idea that he was in the worst.

Then Wild made an effort to rise to his feet, but he failed in that.

He fell back with a groan.

A smile came over the faces of his bull-dogs, as he delighted to call the disreputable men who were in his pay.

"Listen!" cried Jonathan, sharply.

"Yes, Mr. Wild."

"Fetch a sedan chair. You will easily get one at Kensington or Bayswater, whichever may be nearest to here."

"Yes, Mr. Wild."

"Go you, Snaresbrook, at once."

The man named by Wild went on his errand, and then the rangers of the gardens began to raise a clamour about the dead bodies that lay upon the scene of action, which Wild hearing, induced him to utter a strange sort of howl that drowned all other noises, so that general attention was directed towards him.

"Be quiet, all of you!" he then said. "This is my affair. Leave all this to me—I am Jonathan Wild."

The rangers had heard the janissaries use the name of Wild, but still they needed this confirmation from his own lips that the person they saw before them was in truth the notorious and much-dreaded officer; and now that they had such confirmation, they did not attempt any action of their own.

"Look you here, all of you!" added Wild. "This is an affair of state—an affair of Government—of treason!—being drawn in hurdles, hanged, and quartered! So I will trouble you, if you have any regard for yourselves, to leave it all to me!"

The rangers drew back in fright.

"You comprehend me?"

"Oh, yes, sir; we do."

"Very good. That's enough! Let no man dare to touch those dead bodies without my consent."

The rangers began to think they might as well, under these circumstances, get out of the society of the dead duellists and the living Jonathan Wild as soon as possible; so they, after a few words

with one another, fairly turned, and made the best of their way back to the Lodge, by Kensington.

Only one of them, who was a loquacious man, and who liked to say something, turned and called out.

"Then, Mr. Wild, we leave it all to you."

"Bo!" roared Wild.

Then, as he sat up—for he could manage to do that—Jonathan looked about him on the field of battle.

His men remained, silent spectators of his thoughts and movements.

"Ah!" he muttered. "So! so! That's it, is it? Well, it was perhaps not a bad plan; though I can't say I yet understand it in all its details. However, it has so far succeeded——"

Jonathan pointed to the two still forms of the Earl of Bridgewater and his second.

Then his eyes fell upon the Reverend Mortification Ripon, who, in the costume which, at the instigation of Lord Warringdale, he had put on, lay still, sleeping off the effects of the liquor flask he had so prudently, as he considered, brought with him from the lodgings of his villanous employer.

"Kick!" said Wild.

"This one, Mr. Wild?"

"Yes; kick!"

One of the bull-dogs went up to the Reverend Mortification, and dealt him, as he lay, two or three such hearty kicks, that no mortal sleep could possibly withstand the assault.

With cries of "Murder!" the Reverend Mortification rolled over and over, and then assumed a sitting posture, and looked, in a scared, terrified fashion, about him.

"Idiot!" said Wild.

"Yea, he means me!"

"Dolt! Fool!"

"Yea, he means me again; but the Psalmist beautifully says:—

"'If thy brother donkey prove,
Bestow on him celestial love.
If thy——'"

"Peace, scoundrel, and reply to me!"

"Amen!"

"How came you here?"

"The bottle——"

"The what?"

"And it was not all a bottle."

"Knock him down again," added Wild. "I see he is not in a fit state to give me any information."

"No—no! Don't—don't! I can give information! As the Psalmist says, I——"

"Silence! Tell me——No, no! On second thoughts, no—do not!"

"I won't," replied the Reverend Mortification—"I won't; and it's all the more easy not, because I don't know myself! Yea—Amen!"

"If you please, Mr. Wild," said one of the men, at this moment, "here is the sedan-chair you sent for."

"Ah! That is well! Let me think."

Jonathan clasped one hand over his eyes for a moment, in order to shut out external objects while he arranged his thoughts;—for, to tell the truth, although he spoke so imperiously, and had, to all appearance, such a will of his own, in regard to the whole of the strange events that had taken place in the royal gardens of Kensington on that most incidental morning, he was in reality puzzled to know what to do.

Should he leave the two bodies as they lay, or should he make some effort to remove them? Should he try to keep the whole affair private and mysterious, or should he make a great parade of doing his public duty as a police-officer in regard to it?

These were questions that Wild put to himself very rapidly.

The second one was soon answered, for the natural sagacity of Wild told him that, firstly, the young Earl of Bridgewater was too important a person to be quietly killed and no fuss made about; and secondly, too many eyes had already seen what had happened to hope for secrecy.

As regarded the question of leaving the dead bodies where they were, or taking them with him, that was not so easy to reply to.

At one moment, Jonathan had an idea of devoting the sedan-chair he had sent for for himself to the reception of the young nobleman and his second, and so carrying to town the sad memorials of the conflict that had taken place.

There was but one objection to this.

Jonathan could not walk.

Daisy had given him one kick that had disabled him by what, he thought, was the fracture of a rib; and when he tried to get upon his feet, he found, too, that he had a sprain about the region of the ankle, which effectually prostrated him.

It was, therefore, necessary that he should have the use of the sedan-chair for himself.

Jonathan then made up his mind to another course.

"You, Moggsley," he said, "come here!"

"Yes, Mr. Wild."

"You are armed?"

"Oh, yes!"

"Then you will stay here on duty."

"Yes, Mr. Wild."

"You will guard this spot, and these two bodies; and let no one, in any way whatever, interfere with them until you get an order from me. I am going to the Secretary of State on this subject. Now, my men, help me carefully into the sedan-chair, for the sooner I am off the better."

Two men had come with the chair, and they were so amazed and terrified at all they saw and heard, that they were scarcely capable of doing their work.

Jonathan's own janissary, however, picked him up, and put him into the chair.

The oaths and imprecations he gave utterance to as he did so were of the most awful description, for the pain he suffered was great.

At length, however, Jonathan was fairly seated in the sedan; and then he called out once again, "Moggsley, on your life, do the duty I have set you!"

"All right, Mr. Wild!"

"Start!"

The sedan-chair was put into motion, and Moggsley was in a few moments left alone with the dead.

The Reverend Mortification Ripon was made to follow the chair containing Wild by the gentle admonitions of one of the janissaries, who goaded him on in the same manner that inhuman drovers goad on cattle—namely, with the end of a stick from which projected a nail or bradawl.

In this fashion, then, Jonathan Wild, like some great potentate surrounded by his slaves, and with a prisoner in his train, proceeded to London.

The silence of that verdant spot among the trees in which Mr. Moggsley found himself would have been irksome under any circumstances to that personage. It was Newgate Street, and the public-house, to which he paid his respects.

But when superadded to the stillness of nature—to the solemn, majestic waving of the trees—to the twitter of the birds, and the faint sighing of the wind—there were two dead bodies on the spot, the situation became doubly uncomfortable to Mr. Moggsley.

At first he tried to whistle.

That did not succeed. The echo of the tones himself had made had a strange and terrifying cadence about it.

Then Mr. Moggsley made up his mind to walk up to the dead bodies, with the idea that there might be something in the pockets of their apparel that might reward him and reconcile him to his lonely watch.

Mr. Moggsley thought this a very bright idea—and so, indeed, it was, if he could only have carried it out.

"Ha! ha!" he said, "I wonder that old Jonathan forgot to see if there was any plunder to be had from these dead men. However, I am not going to be such a fool as to neglect the opportunity; so here goes! Hallo! yah! murder! Oh!"

A sharp, jagged stone, flung with some force, had hit Mr. Moggsley on the ear, and cut a piece out of it.

Where did the stone come from.

From earth, or from air—from the living, or from the dead?

The stillness around him when he ceased speaking and yelling was as profound as before. No wonder that the "bull-dog" crouched almost to the rails, and felt such an amount of alarm that he was nearly bereft of his senses.

He put up his hand to his ear.

Blood was trickling down his neck.

What could it be? Why could it be? Mr. Moggsley could almost have cried from sheer vexation. He spoke in a low, whining tone.

"What have I done? Why should a fellow be served out in this way? Eh? eh? what have I done?"

All was still. The invisible agent of the punishment of this man of Jonathan Wild's gave no indication of its presence, so that in a little time—say ten minutes—Mr. Moggsley began to gather courage. He asked himself how near he was, after all, to the Kensington Road, or to the Bayswater Road, or to some other road from whence, at that opportune moment to make it seem preternatural, the stone might have come, perhaps flung from the hand of some mischievous urchin.

There was consolation in the idea.

Mr. Moggsley gathered courage.

"There must be a something in their pockets!" he said. "They look both like gentlemen, and they are quite sure to have purses—and, perhaps, pocket-books. Ha! ha! I don't want the purses and the pocket-books—I can put them back; but I do want what may chance to be in them.

That's what I want; and that's what I mean to have, too! Yah! Oh, don't! Oh, Lord! oh, Lord! Yah! boo! boo! Oh! oh! oh!"

Something hard had hit Mr. Moggsley right on the top of the head, and with such good will, too, that for the moment he thought it had gone right into his brain. He rolled on the ground, and yelled with the pain; and then, as he sat up, he put his hand to his head, and found that his hair was becoming matted with blood; for the scalp was divided by the something that had hit him, although he had not the remotest notion what it was.

"Murder! murder! I'm as good—no, I mean I'm as bad as a dead man! I shall never leave this place alive!"

Mr. Moggsley then uttered a succession of groans, and then a succession of oaths; and then he felt that blood-clotted as was the hair on his head, it had a disposition to stand up on end; for a deep, solemn voice, floating apparently in the air, uttered the one word "Beware!"

Mr. Moggsley felt too choked to speak.

"Beware!" said the voice again.

By a great effort, the janissary found breath sufficient to ask the pertinent question, "Beware of—of—what?"

"Fly!" said the voice.

"A fly!"

"Begone! It comes! it comes!"

"Oh, does it? Then Jonathan Wild may say what he likes, or do what he likes. I am not going to stay here to be eat up, and knocked into blood and bits, by all the devils in the world!"

Mr. Moggsley scrambled to his feet, and took to his heels, and ran from the spot with a speed that soon placed pretty nearly the whole width of Kensington Gardens between him and the verdant spot on which the fatal encounter had taken place between Lord Warringdale and the young and gallant Earl of Bridgewater.

Scarcely had the janissary of Jonathan Wild left the place clear of his presence, than a human foot and leg hung down from the thick branches of a tree close at hand.

This foot and leg was soon followed by a companion; and then, after swaying about for several moments, the two feet came plump to the earth, bringing with them the body to which they belonged.

The person who thus made his appearance upon the scene of action was an old man, with a white beard and moustache. The reader has seen him before.

This person was no other than Raphael, as he called himself, the chemist or alchemist who had sold to the Lord Warringdale the poison with which he had anointed his sword-blade.

CHAPTER CCXX.

JONATHAN WILD GIVES SOME ADVICE TO LORD WARRINGDALE, WHICH APPEARS SUPERFLUOUS.

THERE was a very peculiar look upon the old, worn face of Raphael the chemist, when he thus descended from the tree, where he had kept up an espial upon all the strange proceedings that had taken place during the last hour beneath it.

The look was one partly of alarm, and partly of gratification.

No doubt this man hardly up to that period of time knew whether he was on the eve of being involved in the consequences of great crimes, or in a fair way of making a fortune.

A fortune from the fears of one person, and from the gratitude of another.

"That is well—that is all well!" muttered Raphael, when he had recovered himself from the slight shock of the drop on to the soft grass from the old tree, amid the umbrageous foliage of which he had lain concealed. "That is well! It was quite a mercy I happened to have about me those specimens of minerals, which have done such execution to that man of Jonathan Wild's. Let me see—let me see! I must not lose them here. They have done their work, and I may as well possess myself of them again."

Raphael looked closely among the grass at his feet, and he soon picked up the jagged stone which had just hit Mr. Moggsley on the ear, and then the bit of metallic ore which had assailed him with such force on the top of his head.

"That will do—that will do," said the chemist to himself, as he carefully put the two minerals in his pocket. "So far, so good; and now for these seeming dead men."

Raphael approached the still and unconscious forms of the Earl of Bridgewater and his second.

As the alchemist reached them, he still muttered his cogitations to himself.

"Well, well! This will pay—this will pay. It is true enough that I sold my Lord Warringdale a poison, but I kept the antidote to myself. If used within twelve hours, the antidote is certain in its effects. After that——Well, after that time, death, or seeming death, has had it too long its own way. No human art can set the life-blood flowing again."

He took from a secret pocket a small packet, which he carefully unwrapped, exhibiting, within its innermost folds, about a pinch—as much as might be taken up by the finger and thumb—of a light violet-coloured powder.

Then he produced one of those small glass tubes which chemists use, and call test-tubes. They are about six inches in length, open at one end, and not above three-eighths of an inch in diameter.

This little tube was securely corked, and was about half-full of distilled water. Into the tube, then, the chemist carefully introduced the pinch of violet-coloured powder.

A slight commotion, like a partial effervescence, ensued in the tube.

"That will do," said Raphael. "The power of this antidote is fleeting and evanescent. In ten minutes it would not act, but now it is safe and certain."

He knelt down by the side of the young Earl of Bridgewater, and lifted the head of the apparently dead young nobleman on to one of his knees. Then, carefully, he poured from the little glass tube some few drops of its contents between the partially-opened lips.

"That will do," he said.

The Earl of Bridgewater did not make the slightest movement, as the chemist laid his head down again upon the grass.

Raphael then went through the same process and ceremony with the apparently dead gentle-

man, who had been the second of the Earl in the seemingly most fatal and disastrous duel.

"It is done," he said.

The chemist appeared to be perfectly satisfied with what he was about.

If he had any anxiety at all, it was that he should not be interrupted; and that feeling he manifested, by putting his hand behind one of his ears, and occasionally listening.

"It is done," he said again; and he carefully flung out of the little test-tube all that remained in it of the antidote on to the grass, and put the tube again in his pocket.

It was just as Raphael had finished these arrangements that the seeming dead Earl of Bridge-water uttered a sigh.

"Ah!" said the chemist. "It is in good time."

He paid no other attention now to either the young Earl or his second than just to cast a casual glance at them now and then, while he walked up

and down upon the still dew-bespangled grass, chafing his hands; for the man of skill was cold.

Raphael the chemist was in possession of many wonderful secrets, but the one which he would most have coveted—namely, that which would have enabled him to ward off the insidious approaches of old age—had eluded him.

Then he stopped abruptly in his walk.

The Earl of Bridgewater had made a movement.

It was a struggling effort to rise.

The chemist at once then approached him, and stooping over him, he said, in low, earnest tones, "Rest—rest for a few brief moments. All is well, but all will be better of some further rest."

The tones were deep and gentle, and they seemed pleasantly to reach the senses of the young nobleman, and he obeyed the injunction.

Then Raphael looked towards the Earl's second, whose eyes were open, and who seemed, as he lay upon the grass, to be listening to what the chemist said to the Earl, and to be regarding him with fixed attention.

"You are better, sir?" asked Raphael.

The reply was an inclination of the head.

"Ah, I comprehend! You feel weak?"

The second inclined his head again, and at that same moment the Earl of Bridgewater, who was a good bit the younger man of the two, and therefore probably possessed of more vital energy, spoke.

"What has happened?" he said, "and what is the meaning of all this?"

"Ah!" said Raphael. "That is well."

"What is well?"

"It is refreshing."

"Explain to me who and what are you?"

"Why, my young sir, I meant that it was well to hear your voice so strong and clear, and it was at the same time refreshing not to hear you say what ninety-nine men out of a hundred would have said, in your situation."

"What?—what?"

"Where am I? That was what I expected to hear you say; but as you did not, I gather that you have an original mind."

What object the chemist could have, at such an important moment, in speaking with such frivolity, it is difficult to say, unless he wished merely to arouse the awakening senses of his patients before they had time to think of anything distressing or disastrous.

The Earl of Bridgewater smiled.

"Better and better," said the chemist.

Then the young nobleman without being checked by Raphael in so doing, rose to his feet and looked about him, as he said, "I feel like a man who has had some strange and very troubled dreams."

"And I, too," said the second, as he also rose to his feet; but he did not look so strong nor so completely recovered as the Earl of Bridgewater did.

Raphael gazed at them both for a few seconds in silence. Then, with a cautious movement, he placed his finger on the wrist of the second, and looked at him fixedly.

"All will be well," he said. "In five minutes more you will have as completely recovered as this gentleman."

The chemist pointed to the Earl, who, now that his full senses had come back to him, along with the memory of the past, was full of wonder in regard to what had happened during that hiatus of the intellect that had so suddenly come over him on receiving a slight wound from the sword of Lord Warringdale.

"Speak to me, sir, and speak fully and freely," he said. "Tell me all you can of this mystery."

"I will. You came here to fight a duel."

"I did—we did."

"You fought it."

"Well; but—but——"

"You interrupt me, sir. You were by far the better swordsman and the better man, but your opponent was armed by science."

"By science! What mean you?"

"The explanation is simple; and if you will, both of you, gentlemen, walk with me out of these gardens, I will let you into a secret, as we proceed, that will surprise you."

It was evident to both the Earl of Bridgewater and his second that the intentions and objects of the strange man who spoke to them were friendly, and they walked by his side willingly, from the royal gardens into the old Bayswater Road.

In a few brief sentences the chemist then explained to them that the sword which was wielded by Lord Warringdale had been poisoned, and that they would both have fallen victims to it had he not, suspecting the designs of Warringdale, kept a watch upon his movements.

"I hid, at an early hour this morning," added Raphael, "in one of the large trees, which would give me a good view of all that was about to take place; and I descended with an antidote, which I administered to you both in time to save you."

"Then we were left for dead?" said the Earl.

"You were."

"But—but—I——"

"Say on—I say, say on; although I have a shrewd guess that what you are about to say will not sound complimentary to me."

"You are right. I was going to say that the person so ready with the antidote may have been as ready with the poison."

"You are perfectly correct."

"Is it so, then?"

"Certainly. I sold the poison to the Lord Warringdale."

"You did?"

"I did. Nay, young sir, do not recoil from me, but please to remember that I might have left you in that deep sleep which would have known no waking; but that, on the contrary, I have chilled my old blood almost past recovery to save you."

"That is true—that is true."

"It is not only true, but there is another truth involved in it, which is this: Lord Warringdale, if I had refused him the deadly potion he sought of me, would have, probably, procured it of some one else, who might not have taken the trouble to counteract its effects as I have done.

The Earl of Bridgewater felt that he was, in a measure, constrained to forgive this man, although he shrunk from him with a feeling of aversion.

"You shall not find me ungrateful," he said; "but I would rather that the obligation I owe you was not associated with the fact that from you such a man as Warringdale can purchase the means of so much mischief."

The chemist smiled.

"It matters not—it matters not, young sir. Better of me than of another, should he get those means, since I take it into my head to foil him."

The Earl's second, who was now perfectly recovered, fully coincided in this view of the matter, and he said, with some emphasis, "It is necessary now, my Lord Bridgewater, to decide upon some course of action which shall bring the murderer, or would-be murderer, to justice."

"Yes, my friend—yes. But, before anything is done in that matter, there is a dear friend whom I must consult."

"You mean Captain Felix Heron?"

"I do—I do."

"Ah!" said Raphael. "The famous highwayman of Epping Forest?"

"That is the man. And now, sir, tell me one thing—will you henceforward place yourself at our disposal, so that you may assist in seeing justice done both to the innocent and to the guilty?"

Raphael smiled.

He turned towards the southern sky, and waved his arm, as he said, "I am going there."

"Where do you mean?"

"South—far away south, where there are fairer skies and softer airs than blow in this fog-encumbered climate. It is some pleasure to me that the last act of my life in England has been to save you two from Warringdale. I would advise you both to look to your future safety, so far as he is concerned; but, as for me, I bid you adieu, gentlemen."

"Nay. Stay—stay!"

"Wherefore?"

"To receive, at least, the pecuniary reward which it is in my power to offer you."

The strange alchemist smiled again, and then, in a voice that had more of human emotion and feeling in it than he had before exhibited, he said, "I thank you for the intention, and it shall rank in my mind the same as the deed; but, in good truth, I am more rich than I know of—I want for nothing; and when, after proceeding south as far as I may think proper, I turn my steps to the east, I shall be glad to forget that the pilgrim has more gold than the meanest beggar who, with staff and wallet, he meets on his weary way."

As Raphael turned towards the east, when he mentioned it he made some strange movements with his hands, and bowed his head as if he was murmuring a prayer.

Without another word, he then left the Earl of Bridgewater and his second, and was soon lost to sight in the shadows of a well-wooded lane leading from the high road.

The two men who had been so singularly preserved from death looked after his retreating figure as long as they could see it; and then, as if by a mutual feeling which at the same moment found a home in their hearts, they turned towards each other and shook hands.

"It seems," said the Earl, "that we have both been on the confines of the grave together."

"Indeed, it is so."

"Can you forgive me for leading you, by a quarrel of mine, into so much danger?"

"Name it not—name it not. This morning's events only seem to draw my heart closer to you in friendship. Only decide what you wish to do, and depend upon me in all things."

"Then," said the young Earl, "I will remain for the day at some country inn; and when the shades of evening come again, I propose that we go to London. If the villain Warringdale really thinks me dead, which no doubt he does, he will take some action upon that same fact, which it will be well to discover, and glorious to defeat."

"Be it so. We know something of all this affair; but yet there is much of it involved in mystery, which, perhaps, we shall come at with greater ease if we are considered to be out of the world than in it."

"No doubt of that; and here is an inn."

The inn that Lord Bridgewater stopped at was the well-known "Old Hats Inn." He and his second had taken the direction and way from London; and having passed through Shepherd's Bush, then a real village, and not, as now, a straggling suburb of London, they had with rapid walking got so far down the old Western Road as to reach the inn in question.

And there we will leave the young Earl and his friend to their reflections, while we pursue an inquiry into the proceedings of Jonathan Wild and his villanous associate, Lord Warringdale.

On his route to London, Wild had had time to consider and reconsider the whole affair in every possible light; and the result was that he determined to make some capital out of the affair before he saw Lord Warringdale.

Jonathan Wild ordered the bearers of the sedan-chair to take him at once to Whitehall; and then he halted at the official residence of the Secretary of State for Home Affairs.

Jonathan had felt all along that the duel in the royal gardens was known to too many people to afford any chance that it could be kept a secret, and so he considered it would answer his purposes to be the first to reveal it.

Besides, by so doing, he could put what complexion upon the matter he chose.

Now, Mr. Wild was still, at that juncture, sufficiently in the employment of the Government, if he was no great way in its confidence, to make his request for an interview attended to by, at all events, one of the Under-Secretaries of State.

Jonathan just managed to hobble along out of the sedan-chair to one of the reception-rooms, and there he seated himself.

"Well, Mr. Wild, what is the matter now?" asked a gentlemanly-looking man, who entered the room.

"Oh, Sir George Armitage, that is you!"

"Well, sir?"

"Sir, some of my ribs are broken. I am bruised, and battered, and wounded."

"Well, sir?"

"And so, sir, I ask permission to keep seated."

"I will stand, Mr. Wild; so you can remain seated."

The tone of contempt in which these words were uttered was quite translatable. It meant that, so long as he (Sir George Armitage) did not sit down with Jonathan Wild, it did not matter whether he, Jonathan, were seated or not.

Wild thought, then, that he would make a sensation; and he said, abruptly, "Do you know the young Earl of Bridgewater, sir?"

"Of course I do."

"Dead!"

The Under-Secretary started.

"Killed!"

"No, no!"

"Oh, yes!"

"What? When? Where?"

"Pray, take a chair, Sir George, and I will tell you all I know of it."

"No; you can tell me as I am."

"Very good. My spies—of whom I have so many that every penny I receive from the Government goes to pay them, leaving me a poor man, and the worst paid of all—informed me that the young Earl of Bridgewater was about to fight a duel, but they did not know with whom, and could not possibly find out."

"Well, sir—well?"

"I thought it might be with some disreputable

person, who had forced him into a quarrel; and I thought it my duty to prevent the encounter, if possible. I had some difficulty in finding when and where the thing was to come off; but at last I got, at a great expense, the information."

The Under-Secretary made an impatient gesture.

"Well, Sir George, Kensington Gardens was named; and I went there. I got there a little too late. The Earl lies dead there, along with his second."

"Along with his second?"

"Just so."

"His opponent, you mean?"

"No—his second."

"How do you know that?"

"I knew it the day before. That is, who was to be his second, I mean, I knew. I have not told all."

"What more, then?"

"While I was deploring what had happened, and wondering what I ought to do, I was set upon by some ten or twelve men, who left me in the state you see me. Being, then, quite unable to do anything further personally in the matter, I came here direct to give early information."

"That was right! That was right! The affair shall be seen to at once. Where lies the Earl?"

"Close to the Palace; at the back of it, by the new conservatory and the gravel-pit."

"I know the place. Good day, Mr. Wild! I will get you an order from the Secretary for any amount that may be due to you."

Wild was satisfied that he had done the best thing he could in the matter. Without giving a particle more information to the Under-Secretary than was comprised in the mere fact that in Kensington Gardens would be found the dead body of the Earl, he had shown his efficiency as an officer, and along with that had placed himself in a capital position to prey upon Lord Warringdale.

CHAPTER CCXXI.

THE EARL OF BRIDGEWATER PAYS A VISIT TO EPPING FOREST.—THE PROJECTED ROYAL INTERVIEW.

JONATHAN WILD was, no doubt, very much bruised and hurt, but he was not nearly so much injured as he really himself thought at first.

When he got to his own house, which was still in a very dilapidated condition, he felt very much better; and a lay up for the rest of the day enabled him, towards the evening, to feel that, although not quite in as good a trim as usual, he was ready enough for such action as might be required of him.

Wild made no inquiry now about the supposed dead men in Kensington Gardens. He did not forget that he had left Moggsley there in charge; but he knew that, if the Secretary of State took the affair in hand, and sent a messenger from the Home Office with such assistance as might be required to remove the bodies, Moggsley would have no resource but to come to him with such a report.

But he did not come.

That surprised Wild a little; but his interest was in the living, not in the dead, and he did not trouble himself about it.

He did, however, trouble himself about the Lord Warringdale; and if Jonathan Wild had been in reality as bodily hurt as he had pretended he was, or thought he was, he certainly would have made an effort to pay Warringdale a visit at his chambers, in St. James's Street.

With that intent, Wild hired a hackney-coach, on Snow Hill, at about nine o'clock in the evening, and ordered that he should be driven to Pall Mall, close to the corner by the Palace.

Then, as coolly and as calmly as if nothing had happened very particular, Jonathan walked up St. James's Street, with his hanger by his side, and peeping out of the skirt pocket of his ample coat, the end of one of those formidable short bludgeons which he was in the habit of depending upon more than upon either sword or pistol.

There was a light in the chamber of Lord Warringdale.

"Good!" said Wild. "He's at home!"

Bang went the end of Jonathan's bludgeon against the door!

To his surprise, it was Warringdale himself who opened it.

There was a strange look of exultation struggling with terror on the face of Lord Warringdale; and Wild thought, by his looks and manner, that he had been indulging in more of that newly imported Lisbon wine than was good for him.

"Ah, Mr. Wild, is that you?"

"Look! I am easily identified, my lord?"

Wild made one of his most hideous grimaces.

Lord Warringdale still held the door in his hand as he spoke again.

"I am afraid——"

"Ha!—you generally are!" interrupted Wild, coarsely

Lord Warringdale bit his lips

"I was saying I am afraid I am busy, Mr. Wild."

"So am I!"

"Well, then——"

Lord Warringdale began slowly to close the door, keeping Jonathan on the outside; but Wild had put one of his feet within, as he always had a custom of doing whenever a door was opened before him, which effectually prevented it being shut again.

"Mr. Wild?"

"Well, my lord?"

"I will see you to-morrow."

"No! To-night!"

"Sir?"

"Bah! Bo! I said I was busy, but it was with you, my Lord Warringdale! I must and will see you! Come, now, do you mean to put on black for the Earl of Bridgewater?"

Lord Warringdale recoiled a step or two.

Jonathan Wild took immediate advantage of the moment to make good his entrance to the chambers, and close the door.

"What—what," stammered Warringdale, "do you know about the Earl of Bridgewater?"

"Not much."

"How much?"

"Why that you, with a sword, the blade of which had poison upon it, killed him this morning in Kensington Gardens, and his second likewise."

JONATHAN WILD STRONGLY OBJECTS TO A TRESPASSER ON HIS PRESERVES.

Presented Gratis with No. 101 of the New Edition of Edith the Captive; or, the Robbers of Epping Forest.

Warringdale was defeated. He staggered back into the room, and sunk upon a chair with a groan, for he felt himself deeper and deeper still in the terrible power of Jonathan Wild.

Jonathan sat down opposite to him and laughed.

"Fiend!" said Warringdale.

"Ha! ha!"

"Leave me! leave me!"

"What for? What for, I say?" roared Wild. "Leave you, indeed! Oh, dear, no! But I tell you man, you are a fool—a double distilled fool! For what? you will naturally ask; and I will tell you. It is for thinking for one moment that you can act without me—that you can keep me in ignorance of what you are about—that you can scheme a plot, and try to get on in your projects without me! You cannot—you shall not; and from this day, I will add the words, you dare not!"

Wild's voice rang in hoarse cadences throughout the apartment; and he finished by dealing the table a blow with his open hand that made the glasses upon it dance again.

That blow on the table seemed to have an echo outside the door of the chambers, or else some one else was demanding admittance.

Wild sprang to his feet.

"Who is that?"

"I don't know," replied Lord Warringdale, so faintly, that all strength and power of resistance seemed to have departed from him at once.

Rap! rap! came the appeal for admission at the outer door of the chambers again.

"Who did you expect?" asked Wild.

"No one."

Rap! rap! came the knock again, and then Wild went to the door, and listened. There was a voice from the outside.

The voice was to the well-practised ears of Wild sufficiently expressive of two facts.

One was that the owner of it was making an effort to appear courageous, while fear was clutching at his heart.

The other was that the voice would not have been there at all, but for a certain infusion of Dutch courage, in the shape of some strong potations.

"Hilloa! hilloa! Open the door!" cried the voice. "I am a friend. The good friend of my Lord Warringdale, I say! Open the door! I must and I will see him!"

Wild stepped back to the room in which the trembling Warringdale sat.

"Do you know that voice?" he asked.

"I do—I do!"

"Whose is it?"

"The voice of the man who went with me this morning to Kensington Gardens."

Wild struck his forehead as he said, then, in tones of vexation, "To be sure it is—to be sure it is! How could I be so foolish as not to recognise it? Of course, it is the voice of that penniless adventurer who calls himself a Major, and who boasts more than any two men living."

"It is he," added Warringdale faintly. "He calls himself Captain, or Major, just as the word comes uppermost to his memory; but he is neither the one nor the other."

"Pho! pho! I know that."

The voice grew louder, and the knocking at the outer door of the chambers more demonstrative.

"Open! open! I will and I must see my lord! Open, open, I say!"

"Now, my Lord Warringdale," said Jonathan Wild, sneeringly, "what do you suppose that man wants with you?"

"What everybody wants."

"And that?"

"That is to prey upon me! He knows too much."

Wild nodded, and his countenance assumed one of its most diabolical expressions, as he leant over the chair in which Lord Warringdale was sitting, and whispered in hissing accents, "Do you suppose for one moment, my lord, that I am going to put up with anything of the sort?—do you imagine that I will let anybody prey upon you but myself? No; you are my property—you are my estate—my funds—my annuities—my dividends. Let those look out who attempt to trespass on my property! I will admit this man."

"Oh, no, no!"

"Peace! You must hear what he has to say, and you will then please to leave the rest to me."

Lord Warringdale shuddered.

"What?" added Wild; "you pretend to shrink, and shudder, and grow pale, because you comprehend that I am about to rid you of a troublesome and dangerous visitor by the best possible means."

"No, no!"

"What do you mean?"

"Nothing!—oh, nothing! Will you do it at the door, and let me avoid seeing it?"

"Pho! You are growing too particular and tender-hearted. The fellow wants to speak to you, and I want to hear what he shall say. I will open the door to him, and then quickly retreat behind yonder screen. You have nothing to do but to sit where you are, and look, and listen."

Jonathan Wild did not wait for any further acquiescence on the part of Lord Warringdale to this mode of operations, but just as the disreputable acquaintance of Warringdale—who had accompanied him, in the capacity of second, to the duel in the morning—recommenced his demands for admission, he, Wild, opened the door and rapidly retreated, and hid behind a screen which was in the room in the occupation of Lord Warringdale.

"Hilloa! hilloa!" cried the second, when he found the door was open, but saw no one. "Bombs and pistolettes! What does this mean? I want to see his lordship, and I will see him."

The "second" was decidedly the worse for what he had been imbibing, or he would hardly have ventured a call upon the man who had made so atrocious an attempt upon his life in the morning.

"I am here!" said Warringdale,—"I am here!"

"Oh! you are there, are you? Bombs and carronades! Ha! ha! Well, my lord? No tricks upon travellers, my lord. Ha! ha! Marshal Saxe always used to say to me, 'Colonel,' said he, 'you are the life and soul of the army,' said he. 'What will you take to drink?'"

"Come in!" said Lord Warringdale.

The outer door of the chambers was so called because it did not immediately open to the room which was the principal one of the suite, and in which the occupier of the apartments might be supposed to sit. There was a small ante-room, and then a short passage, not above eight feet in length; so that the "second" had to pass through two doorways before he reached Lord Warringdale.

Guided, however, by the voice that bade him "come in," and by the light, he advanced, and was soon in the prescence of Warringdale, whom he saluted with a mock bow.

"Ha! ha! Well, my lord?—well, my lord? What shall the first soldier of the age say to you, and what do you propose to say to the first soldier of the age?"

"I do not understand you?"

"Well, we shall find a means of jogging your memory. Ha, ha!"

"In plain language, sir," said Warringdale, "what do you want with me?"

"Do you forget this morning, sir? Do you forget this morning, sir—my lord, I mean? Do you forget that you tried to settle with me, at the sword's point? Do you forget that—that—— Good, by Jove!"

The already sufficiently inebriated man poured himself out a glass of the Lisbon wine which was on the table before him, and drank it off.

"Sir," said Warringdale, "you must be dreaming.

"Dreaming? I dream? I never dream. Come, my lord, I know too much for you, and enough for myself. I must be paid. Money—money! Gold—gold, in pretty good abundance, seals my mouth; for, as the Prince of Orange said to me, 'Comrade,' says he—he always called me comrade —'comrade,' says he, 'you are the pink and model of discretion.'"

"And so, sir, calling yourself the pink and model of discretion, you venture here, alone, to threaten me."

"Ha! ha!"

"What do you mean by laughing at your own danger?"

"That is just it!"

"What? What?"

"I am not alone!"

Lord Waringdale gave a start.

Jonathan Wild projected his head from the screen. He had in his right hand the short, leaden-headed bludgeon, and in the other a large hand-kerchief, curiously held, and with a knot tied at each corner.

"Not alone?" ejaculated Warringdale.

"No, my lord. Do you think so meanly of my intellect as to suppose I would venture into this lion's den quite alone?"

"But—but——"

"Oh, I comprehend. You would say that you see me here alone, and that that fact is worth a thousand assertions to the contrary; but know that there is a friend of mine waiting at the corner of Pall Mall, and that he has in his pocket a sealed letter, addressed to the chief magistrate of London, which letter contains an account of the transactions of this morning in Kensington Gardens, and if I do not join my friend within one hour of coming here he delivers that letter."

"Indeed!"

"Yes, indeed, and in truth!"

"Of course, then, he has to be paid likewise, since you have made him a confidant?"

"No, no!"

"You say no?"

"And I mean no. Thousand bombs! Do you think I am a fool? No; he is a blind agent, and knows nothing!"

"Are you sure of that?"

"Quite! The letter is sealed; but as, from this time forth, owing to your lordship's kind liberality ——Ha! ha! We may as well be polite. As, I say, I shall now be a rich man, I like to have my humble friend—my led captain—my sycophant— who follows me about; and that will be the man who now waits for me at the corner of Pall Mall.

"I understand."

Of course you do! A hundred pounds, now, and I will let you off for a few months!"

"You are kind!"

"I always was! Come, now, my lord, give me my reward."

"Take it!" said Jonathan Wild, in a voice of thunder.

He darted out from behind the screen; and, casting the handkerchief over the head and face of the unhappy man, he completely hid him from view, and prevented him from taking another look upon the world he was about to leave.

Two sickening blows of the heavy bludgeon— one on the top of the head, the other on the face— and the man fell to the floor a corpse.

Lord Warringdale sprang from his chair, and retreated as far as the wall of the room would permit him.

"That is done!"

"No, no, Wild! You forget, or you did not hear——".

"What?"

"That this man has a comrade waiting for him."

"Oh, I know all that. I will keep the appointment with the comrade, my Lord Warringdale. In the meantime, where can this carrion be bestowed. Have you any good hiding-place here?"

"None—none!"

"Let me see! Yes, this will do quite well!"

In those old houses there was at or beneath each of the windows a seat, about the width of a couch. On this seat was a well-stuffed cushion; but the top of the seat opened like the lid of a box, and, in fact, the whole arrangement was something like a box ottoman, only that it was a fixture, and belonged to the architectural construction of the house.

It was the lid of one of those window seats that Jonathan Wild opened.

"This will do!"

"No!—oh no! Do not leave him here."

"Not leave him here? Why, you don't suppose, Warringdale, that I am going to do your murders, and walk away with the dead bodies on my back. I tell you, he must be left here."

"But the place is too—too small."

"We can double him! He will be limp for some time yet!"

Lord Warringdale would fain have turned away from the hideous spectacle; but he was, so to speak, fascinated and compelled to look upon the operations of Jonathan Wild, which consisted in cramming the murdered man into the window-seat box without any ceremony, and by main force.

"There!" said Jonathan, as he shut down the lid, and then jumped upon it to make it flat,— "there, that job is done! I will call on you to-morrow, my lord, but just now it is important that I should go to the corner of Pall Mall. By the bye, I would advise you to sit upon this window-seat as often as you can; it will keep things snug, you know. What a fortunate man you are to have such a friend as I am!"

Warringdale was as pale as death. He could only incline his head, as Wild, in a hideous tone of ribald jesting, thus spoke of the terrible murder that had been committed in those chambers.

In another minute he was alone!

Alone with the newly dead!

CHAPTER CCXXII.

JONATHAN WILD TAKES A PRISONER. — THE EARL OF BRIDGEWATER ARRIVES IN LONDON.

WILD was as fully alive as any one could possibly be to the necessity of acting promptly in regard to the friend or comrade of the murdered "second," who was said to be in waiting, with the dangerous sealed letter in his pocket, at the corner of Pall Mall.

He did not think that an hour had elapsed since the arrival of the "second" at Lord Warringdale's chambers, nor did he think that, if it had, the "comrade" would be inclined to act very strictly, as regarded a few minutes, up to his instructions; so, if the whole affair was not a mere threat, Wild fully expected to find the man there at his post.

The night had turned to rain while Jonathan was with Lord Warringdale.

St. James's Street was almost deserted, and that was a state of things that suited Wild's purposes much better than as if the streets had been populous, and the night fine.

The habits of our ancestors were by no means so nocturnal as ours. It was then about eleven o'clock, and the town was quiet enough, so that no notice was taken of Jonathan Wild when he stopped at the corner of King Street and blew three peculiar calls upon the silver whistle he always had with him.

In a few seconds two men stepped up to him, coming out of the shadows of the houses and deep doorways like spectres.

"Here, Mr. Wild," said one.

"Here, sir," said the other.

"That is right! Two more and a sedan chair, or one more and a hackney-coach."

The two men seemed to vanish into the gloom of the deserted street.

Wild himself stepped into the deep recess of a doorway. He did not notice, at the moment, that it was the large doorway of Whitcombe House, but he soon recognised it.

"So, so!" he said. "This is the family mansion. I wonder if there is any truth in the ideas of Lord Warringdale, and in what my own eyes have observed from opposite, in regard to this house? I saw, or thought I saw, a light in one of the windows; and Warringdale says he has seen as much frequently; yet we may both have been deceived by some reflection."

Jonathan Wild, as he spoke, turned his face to the massive street door of the house; and, as he did so, he started back a pace.

A very small pencil of light came through the keyhole, and fell upon his breast, where it looked like a faint star for a moment or two, and then vanished.

That was conclusive.

That could be no reflection from opposite lights.

"Very well," muttered Wild. "I must see to this. There is a mystery about this which I must solve."

The rumbling of the wheels of a hackney-coach now came upon his ears, and he stepped out of the doorway, and stood close to the kerb of the pavement.

The coach stopped.

"Here, Mr. Wild," said a voice.

"Oh, that is you, Wigglets?"

"Yes, Mr. Wild. The coachman is in a public-house, so we did not trouble him, but brought off the coach, as you wanted one."

"That is right. Follow me."

Wild strolled down St. James's Street quite coolly and quietly, and when he arrived at the corner of Pall Mall, he glanced warily about him. For a few seconds he could see no one; and then he fancied there was something that looked darker than darkness, in a doorway just opposite to Marlborough House.

Was that the man he sought? He would soon ascertain.

Walking up to the doorway, Wild said in a low, cautious tone, "Hist! hist! Have you got the letter?"

The dark figure emerged at once.

"Yes. But you are not——"

"That will do," said Wild.

The man uttered a cry, and fell to the pavement. Wild had hit him on the back of the head with the bludgeon. Stooping then over him, he tore open his vest, and snatched at a letter that was there.

"A match," said Wild.

One of his men lighted one of the thieves' matches which they were never without, and Jonathan was by the feeble flame enabled to read the address on the letter.

"To the Chief Magistrate at Bow Street."

"That will do. Take this man to the cells, and see you keep him safely."

The man, in a state of insensibility, was flung into the coach, and off it went to Newgate Street with him, while Jonathan strolled along, whistling a tune, as if nothing had happened.

After walking some short distance along Pall Mall, Wild altered his mind in regard to the direction he chose to take, and returned towards Marlborough House, to make his way by that entrance to the Park. He knew that the exhibition of that small gilt staff, with the crown at the end of it, and which he always had with him, as the symbol of his authority, would enable him to pass the sentinel. Otherwise, it was beyond the hour to allow unprivileged persons to make a thoroughfare of St. James's Park.

But just as Wild was on the point of passing through the gate at Marlborough House, he heard the sound of approaching footsteps from the Park.

He drew back out of the faint rays of light

which the oil-lamps at that spot cast about them, and he could see without being seen.

Two gentlemen approached from the Park, at an easy pace, arm-in-arm.

Another moment, and they were within the light of the lamps, and Wild was able to see both their faces.

What was his astonishment, not unmingled with fear, to recognise in one of them the young Earl of Bridgewater, and in the other his second, both of whom he, Wild, had seen, as he thought, lying in death that morning in Kensington Gardens.

So intense was the astonishment of Jonathan Wild, that he quite lost his presence of mind; and the two gentlemen had passed on, and disappeared from his observation, before he sufficiently recovered to rush after them.

But they were gone.

He could see nothing of them. Whether they had turned to the left, or to the right, or had gone up St. James's Street, or vanished into the night air, he could not determine.

Here was food for all sorts of conjecture on the part of Jonathan Wild.

On the whole, he thought that they had gone right on up St. James's Street; and he went to the top of it as fast as he could go, without making the noise of actually running.

The two spectres—which he began to think them—were nowhere to be seen.

Then Wild began to doubt the evidence of his own senses, and he rubbed his eyes savagely.

"Surely I saw them—surely I saw them. They passed me closely, and they passed the sentinel closely; but did my eyes deceive me in the darkness? No—that was not possible. Ah! there is a sure and easy mode of determining if two people did come out of the Park, although their identity must still be kept to myself. The soldier on duty must have seen them."

Wild thought this a good idea, but it was a most fallacious one.

Twelve o'clock had struck while he was at the top of St. James's Street, and the guard in and about the Palace was changed.

By the time Jonathan Wild got back to Marlborough House, a new sentinel was on duty there. One soldier, however, was too like another for Wild to notice that it was not the same man; and he addressed to him the question which he thought would put an end to all doubt upon the subject.

"Did two gentlemen, arm in arm, and both rather tall, recently pass your post, sentinel?"

"Where from?"

"From the Park."

"No, then. Not a living soul has passed my post from the Park, since I have been here."

Wild walked away without another word. It appeared to him that there was something solemn and strange about even the accidental words that the sentinel had used.

"Not a living soul has passed my post!"

Wild shuddered.

"Are there such things as spectres, after all?" he said to himself, in low tones. "Are there dead men walking about at night? No, no, no! I was mistaken—I cannot be well. Something is amiss with me: I have been too long awake, I suppose. I want sleep. I have heard that long

wakefulness and watchfulness will have such an effect upon the brain, that it will begin to reproduce to the eyes images that have seemed to have faded away; and perhaps that is the explanation of one-half the ghosts that people fancy they see. I will go home, and have some rest."

It was neither wakefulness nor watchfulness that had conjured up to the eyes of Jonathan Wild the sight he saw.

The Earl of Bridgewater and his second in the duel had waited at the "Old Hats" inn until night; and then they had quietly walked to London, and had, as we have seen, been accidentally met by Jonathan Wild.

The Earl was intent upon taking counsel with his sister and his Countess, who were both in Clarges Street. He could well conceive the state of anxiety they would both be in by that time about him, but he had not quite made up his mind what course to pursue in respect to Lord Warringdale; so he thought that he would make no public appearance until the whole matter had been well considered and talked over at home, in that house next door to the Bishop of Worcester's.

It cannot be said that it was from any special tenderness towards Lord Warringdale that the Earl of Bridgewater acted in this case, but it was that he recollected well the close relationship there existed between the base and bad Warringdale and the high and noble-minded Felix Heron.

"If," said the Earl to himself,—"if Felix Heron wishes me to say nothing, and do nothing, in this affair, now or never, indeed I will obey his wishes."

The Earl of Bridgewater was quite chivalrous enough to do this.

As he approached his sister's house, the young nobleman quickened his steps; for well he knew there were those there who loved him, and to whom his absence was a distress—an agony far beyond the reach of consolation.

Soon was he clasped in the arms of those who loved him; and then it was that, turning to his second in the duel, he clasped the hand of that gentleman, saying, "Dear friend, will you do me a favour?"

"A hundred, if in my power," was the prompt and ready reply.

"Then, will you lie by for a few days, or until you hear from me?"

"Certainly I will. I have a small estate, as your lordship knows, at Oxford, and I will go there at once."

"Be assured I shall send for you. And now, dear wife, and you, dear sister, advise me what to do, for I have made up my mind to go at once to Epping Forest."

The wife and sister of the impetuous young Earl could not but smile at the way in which he asked for advice, proclaiming at the same time that he had made up his mind what to do.

But in this case they happened to be of the same opinion as himself; and after he had narrated to them all that had happened, they were quite as ready to urge him to seek an interview with Felix Heron as he was to set out on that errand.

After snatching a few hours' repose, the Earl started from home just before the dawn of another day. He did not wish to encounter any one whom he knew, as he had no desire to consult, or even to

converse, with any one upon the subject of his duel with Lord Warringdale, until he had held a long and confidential chat with Felix Heron.

The Earl, therefore, warned his groom, who had been ordered to bring his horse to the corner of Clarges Street two hours before daybreak, to say nothing to any one of his being in town.

Mounting quietly the hunter which the groom brought him, the Earl of Bridgewater started at once in the direction of Epping Forest.

The mind of the gallant nobleman, who had been rescued from death by such a mere chance, ran over the strange events of the morning with increased interest, as, for the first four miles, he took his solitary ride to Epping.

His way then lay over a small common, which terminated in a lane, where the trees grew so luxuriantly on each side that they made a positive dark arch beneath their overspreading branches.

The Earl of Bridgewater had not advanced

more than a quarter of a mile down this lane, when he became aware that there was another horseman within it.

The unmistakable beat of horse's feet, going at an easy trot, came upon his ears; although, for a few minutes, he was in a state of doubt as to whether the horseman was advancing towards him or receding from him.

That he was in advance the Earl was quite well aware, but no doubt some turnings and windings in the lane confused the sounds.

The best way of putting an end, however, to all doubts upon the subject was to press onward.

The Earl touched his horse lightly with the riding-whip he had with him, and the animal darted onward at a pace which—if the other horseman in the lane did not happen to be wonderfully well mounted—must soon overtake him.

That result was speedily accomplished, and all the more speedily that the horseman who was in advance at first slackened his pace, and then came to a dead halt.

The young Earl reined in his steed; and as by this time the faint grey light of early dawn had began to show itself, he was, even in that shadowy lane, able to see that both steed and rider that he had overtaken were of great size and apparent strength.

Then a loud voice cried, "Stand! Stand! On your life, sir, stand!"

The Earl of Bridgewater placed his hand on one of the holsters of his saddle, where he knew a pistol would be ready to his grasp, and prepared to defend himself.

CHAPTER CCXXIII.

THE EARL OF BRIDGEWATER IS ROBBED OF ONE SHILLING BY AN ECCENTRIC HIGHWAYMAN.

THERE was something in the tones of the loud voice that called upon the Earl of Bridgewater to stop in that beautiful shady lane which was pleasant and kindly, imperious though the command was.

It was partly those tones, and partly from a consideration of another fact peculiar to his present position, that the Earl was induced not, on the instant—as his hasty nature would have otherwise prompted—to fire one of his holster pistols at the highwayman.

The other fact to which we allude was that he, the Earl, was actually bound on a visit to a renowned highwayman, and therefore he could not exactly feel so acutely on the subject as he might.

This man, likewise, who stopped him in the lane might be one of Felix Heron's own men, for aught he knew to the contrary.

The Earl did not wish to inaugurate his presence in Epping Forest by sending a bullet into the brain or heart of one of Felix Heron's band, desperadoes though they were.

This, then, was the consideration which made him pause.

During that pause, the highwayman spoke again.

"Sir," he said, "I hope you are a gentleman."

"I hope so, too," replied the Earl. "But I fancy there is no doubt whatever in regard to what you are."

"None in the least, sir."

"A highwayman?"

"Just so!"

"You are candid, at all events."

"Heaven knows I wish to be so; and therefore it is, sir, that be you whom you may, I stop you on the King's highway, to rob you of the smallest coin in this realm!"

The Earl of Bridgewater could not well comprehend what the highwayman meant by speaking in so strange a style. There was a tone, likewise, of such deep sadness and feeling about his voice, that the half-formed intention of resisting him in any way was at once dissipated.

"Pray speak more clearly," said the Earl, "and explain to me the mystery which most evidently envelopes you."

The highwayman was silent for a few seconds;

and then it was, in a voice that had still more of emotion in it than before, that he replied, "Sir, I have no explanation to offer; but I ask you as a gentleman, which I see you are, have you a farthing about you?"

"A farthing?"

"Just so, sir! If you have such a coin, I want to rob you of it. If you have not a piece of money so small, let me rob you here, on the highway, of the next smallest and least consequential coin you possess."

"Mad!" said the Earl of Bridgewater to himself. "This man, whoever he is, is mad!"

The highwayman shook his head sadly. He seemed to be aware of what was passing in the mind of the Earl of Bridgewater, for he said again, in those deep, sad tones in which, after the first cry to "Stand!" he adopted, "I am not a madman, sir, nor have I any purpose hidden in my apparently strange request that can in any way injure you."

"Well," said the Earl, as he took a shilling from his pocket, "this is the smallest coin I have about me. Will it content you?"

"Perfectly, sir!"

"Take it, then!"

"No, no!"

"You refuse, now, when I give it to you freely?"

"Ah, sir, that is it!—that is just it! I do not want you to give it to me freely. It is necessary that I should rob you of it!"

"Well, certainly, you are the strangest knight of the road I ever heard of. Rob me of it, in heaven's name, if it so please you, and let me go my way, for I am in haste!"

"A shilling, or your life!" said the eccentric highwayman, as he produced a pistol, and held it at the head of the Earl.

"There it is!"

"That is well, sir! You are prudent. Now pass on. That is all I require of you, sir!"

The Earl of Bridgewater was lost in surprise at this conduct of the highwayman, and he strove all he could to get a glimpse of his face; but that was impossible, in consequence of a half-mask which the latter wore.

There was no resource but to let him have his own way, and to ride on; yet the Earl could not do so without a suspicion that he had not seen the last of the strange adventure.

In that suspicion, however, he was wrong—for nothing further came of it; and the eccentric highwayman rode off in the direction towards London at a quick pace.

Musing over this odd adventure, the youthful noble went on his way towards Epping Forest.

There he was destined to make a sensation which very much puzzled him, until he found out that Felix Heron had such good reason, from ocular demonstration, to believe him dead.

The morning was growing bright and fair by the time the Earl of Bridgewater reached the confines of the forest.

Plunging into one of the long green avenues of the ancient wood, he hoped that he would soon see something of Heron, or of some of his men, who would conduct him to the retreat of the highwayman.

Captain Heron had not thought it necessary to conceal anything from so good and faithful a friend as the Earl; and he had accordingly informed him that the security he found in the old forest was in consequence of discovering a complete network of underground passages and vaults beneath the ruins of the old mansion that had once stood there, and the still older priory.

At that time, when in London at the house of his sister, Heron had said this much, he had not had any idea that the Earl would so soon be amid the leafy glades of the forest, and consequently he had given him no special directions how to seek him.

Still there was a kind of recollection on the mind of the Earl that Captain Heron had once said, if any one wished to see him in Epping Forest, it would only be necessary to ride into it and call upon him by name.

Seeing, then, no one in the long glade into which he had ridden, and hearing no sound among the trees save the hoot of an owl, the young Earl resolved to try the effect of calling out the name of Heron in loud accents.

Pausing, then, in his ride, and letting his horse crop some of the sweet herbage at his feet, the Earl said, distinctly, " I am a friend, and I desire to see Captain Felix Heron."

In a few seconds he heard again the hooting of an owl.

It was then that he began to suspect that hooting came from human lips, good as the imitation of the solitary bird of night was.

Again he spoke.

" As a friend, I want to see Captain Heron."

Then there came a sharp crackling noise among the bushes some distance from him, and a man appeared.

This man had on a rough great-coat, and a hat pulled down rather low over his eyes; and as he made his way into the forest glade from the thick brushwood, among which he had been concealed, he made gestures to the Earl of Bridgewater to keep silent.

The Earl obeyed the signals, although he could not imagine what was the object of them.

The man then approached him in a crouching attitude, and when he got close up to him he said, " Sir, sir, I beg you won't make a noise, and we shall nab him."

" Nab who ?"

" Captain Heron, sir, the notorious highwayman."

" Indeed !"

" Yes, sir. I am a constable. Here is my staff. I suppose, sir, you are on the same lay ?"

" The what ?"

" I mean, on the same errand, sir ?"

" I am rather surprised how you can think that, after hearing what I said just now. Did I not call out that I was a friend to Captain Heron ? How, then, can you suspect that I am here with any such design as that you impute to me ?"

The man shook his head, and then nodded and smiled knowingly.

" Oh, that's all right of course; but, between us, you know, sir, there need be no concealments, and I am quite willing to help you in his capture."

" You mistake; I have no thought or desire to capture him. I am what I said I was—the friend of Captain Heron."

" Then," replied the man, suddenly altering his tone, and putting the constable's staff he had produced back again into his pocket—" then, sir, if you will be so good as to walk your horse slowly up this glade, we will see what can be done."

This conduct of the pretended officer opened the eyes of the young Earl at once to the fact that he was one of Heron's own men, who only adopted the character of a constable for the purpose of ascertaining the object of the horseman who called out the name of Felix Heron in that forest glade.

The Earl rode on.

The glade was about half a mile in length, and seemed to terminate in a dense mass of tall old trees, through which there might be some difficulty in making way with a horse.

The Earl was not, however, destined to test the difficulty, for he had not proceeded above two-thirds of the distance when he heard a voice behind him.

" Turn, sir !" cried the voice. " I will conduct you to him you seek."

The Earl knew the voice at once to be that of Heron himself, and he wheeled his horse round with a joyous exclamation.

Captain Heron, with the bridle of Daisy hanging over his arm, stood about twenty paces from him; and the moment he saw the Earl of Bridgewater, he uttered an exclamation of the greatest astonishment.

" You ?—you here ?—you ?" he shouted.

" Yes, my dear friend," replied the Earl. " Are you so very much surprised to see me ?"

" From death—yes ! From death !"

" No, Heron,—no ! From seeming death, if you please. But let me touch your hand, and you will soon perceive that it is a living, breathing man who greets you."

Captain Heron was not superstitious, and he at once flew forward and grasped the Earl of Bridgewater by the hand, instead of flying from him, as some would have done, in the belief that he was a visitant from another world.

" You live ! you live !"

" Indeed, and in truth, I do !"

" Heaven be thanked for this mercy ! I thought I saw you lying in death on the greensward of Kensington Gardens !"

" Were you there, Heron ?"

" I was, indeed ; and the seeming fact that I was too late to save you has sat so heavily upon my heart ever since, that I have known no peace or rest."

The two young men clasped each other's hand, and tears started to their eyes, as, for the space of about half a minute, they were silent from emotion.

Seldom had human friendship attained so full a growth as it had in the minds of those two persons, who, the more they knew of each other, felt that they had the more occasion and justification for esteem.

" Edith," said the Earl,—" dear Edith, is she well ?"

" Quite well, but unhappy."

" Unhappy ?"

" Yes ; but that will pass away when she sees again, in life, the friend of her husband."

" Thank heaven—thank heaven ! Oh, Heron, I have much to tell you ! The villain, Warringdale !"

" Alas ! alas !"

"It was he who thought, by diabolical schemes, to take my life; and, at the same time, I make no doubt, involve you in destruction."

"My dear friend, I fancy I know more of this affair than you do; for while, by some means, you lay in such a trance that I mistook it for death, I discovered a great deal which now I can communicate to you, and which, with what you can tell me, will enable us to form some accurate conclusion in regard to the whole affair. But come with me; I must lead you at once to Edith, who will exchange tears for smiles when she sees the friend of her husband has not fallen on his account—for well I know that it was because you favoured me the villain Warringdale sought your life."

Edith was, in truth, delighted to see the Earl; although, like Heron, it was some time before she could believe her own eyes, and acknowledge that he was really alive.

Then ensued a long and earnest consultation in regard to what was to be done.

It was the advice of the Earl that Captain Heron and Edith should both come to town again.

"Things have reached such a pass now," he said, "when some energetic course must be adopted. My privilege as a peer enables me to ask, and to obtain, an interview with the King, and I will lay the whole affair before him, without the least reservation."

Heron sighed.

Edith looked wistfully around her upon the tall trees of the forest.

"Do not hesitate," said the Earl. "There is surely such a thing as justice to be obtained even at a Court!"

Edith crept closer to Felix Heron; and, as he kissed her fair brow, he said, gently, "It is our destiny and our duty, my Edith. When we thought this dear friend was torn from us by death, we felt that we must either avenge or forgive—no, no—not forgive—we meant to be quiescent, and to leave vengeance to heaven, which surely, in its own good time, and in its own good way, would visit upon the head of Warringdale his crimes!"

"Yes, ah, yes!" said Edith; "and we meant to try to look for peace."

"Peace," continued Heron, "in obscurity, where I fancy it is most to be found."

"You affect me deeply," said the Earl, "by speaking in this way."

"We had but two duties," added Edith—"two duties unfulfilled."

"I had not forgotten, dear one," said Captain Heron tenderly, as he took Edith's hand in his. "We meant not to rest until we had rescued Lady Castleneau from her enemies, and until we had placed, if he be still in life, poor old Sir Dominick Browne in a position of peace and happiness."

"But now," added Edith—"now the world calls to us again."

"And you will obey the call, Heron?" said the Earl.

"I will."

"That is right. You are the real and true Earl of Whitcombe, and it is a duty to yourself and to society that you should not hide one of the few hereditary nobles who will be a credit to his order, even amid the peaceful glades of a forest."

"You are right—you are right. Edith, dear one, we will go to London."

"With you, anywhere, Felix."

"It is well resolved," said the Earl. "Come once more to the house of my sister. I will write to the King at once, and ask for a private interview, at which he shall know all. Let the consequences of all his acts of wickedness fall upon the head of the villain Warringdale."

"To horse! to horse!" cried Captain Heron. "We will go to London at once, my Edith; and this time we will go openly, and without any concealment. I will go, as the Earl of Whitcombe; for the papers and documents which so mysteriously have come into my possession at Whitcombe House enable me to do so. Come, my Countess, we will emerge from our low estate; and if it be that we must seek happiness in high places, we will try to find it and adorn it."

CHAPTER CCXXIV.

DETAILS SOME PROCEEDINGS WHICH TOOK PLACE IN LONDON, CONSEQUENT ON THE SUPPOSED DEATH OF THE EARL OF BRIDGEWATER.

LEAVING Captain Heron, Edith, and the Earl, their most welcome visitor, in the forest, to partake of the morning meal before they took horse for London, we repair to the cabinet of the Secretary of State, in Whitehall, where there is rather a strange collection of visitors.

Lord Warringdale.

Jonathan Wild.

The Reverend Mortification Ripon.

Those were the persons to whom the Secretary of State had been induced to give audience on that morning following the one on which the duel had been fought in Kensington Gardens.

It was the full impression of the villain Warringdale that the young and chivalrous Earl of Bridgewater was no more. What else could he think but that the poisoned sword had done its work?

Jonathan Wild, too, was of the same opinion; —for the man whom he had left to guard the supposed dead bodies had not thought proper to show himself to his imperious and angry master, the great Jonathan, after his ignominious flight from Kensington Gardens and defeat by Raphael, the chemist.

What the Reverend Mortification Ripon had to do was just to swear to anything that was suggested to him, either by Wild or Warringdale.

The reverend gentleman was quite willing.

And the object of this visit to the cabinet of the Secretary of State was sufficiently transparent.

It was to complete the ruin of Captain Felix Heron, if possible, by accusing him of the deaths of the young Earl of Bridgewater and the gentleman who was his second in the duel.

It will be borne in mind that the fact of a duel being fought at all was generally confined to the four persons engaged as principals and seconds in the transaction; and in this case—as out of that four Lord Warringdale really believed himself to be the sole survivor—he felt he could put what complexion upon the affair he liked.

It was a quarter to eleven o'clock when there

glided into the room in which Jonathan Wild, Lord Warringdale, and the Reverend Mortification sat, waiting the leisure of the Minister, a very polite, fashionable-looking young gentleman.

That was the private secretary of the Minister.

He addressed himself to Warringdale.

As for Jonathan Wild and the Reverend Mortification Ripon, they were far beneath his polite notice.

"My lord," he said, "the Secretary of State will see you in five minutes."

Warringdale bowed.

The little villanous party of three were alone again.

"Remember," said Warringale to the Reverend Mortification—"remember what you have to say."

The Reverend Mortification groaned, and looked confused.

"Yea, as the Psalmist says, I feel the want of some slight stimulant."

"Peace, wretch!"

"Peace, idiot!" added Wild.

The Reverend Mortification looked hopelessly from one to the other of his revilers; and then Wild said, in a hoarse whisper, "He will ruin all!"

"Beast!" snarled Warringdale. "Remember that your life is in our hands."

"Yea, I do—I do!"

"Listen to me," added Wild, after a few moments' reflection. "We must represent this man to the Secretary of State as a harmless idiot."

"Thank you, Mr. Wild. I'm sure, as the Psalmist says somewhere—

"'Wisdom is but foolishness;
Folly often wise:
None so blind as he who closes
Wilfully his eyes.'

Yea, too, the Psalmist goes on to say——"

"Silence, fool!"

"Nay, he says no such thing."

The door of the apartment was flung open at this moment; and a messenger cried out, "Lord Warringdale, to his lordship's cabinet!"

Warringdale rose.

"Follow me," he said; and Jonathan Wild walked close to him, followed by the Reverend Mortification Ripon.

There was a strange look upon the face of the Secretary of State, as, with his back to a small wood fire that smouldered in the grate, he faced his strange visitors.

Lord Warringdale advanced and shook hands with the Secretary—for in the polite and great world of fashion in which they both lived they had met before often.

Jonathan Wild stood by the door.

The Reverend Mortification Ripon propped himself up in an angle of the room.

"Well, my Lord Warringdale," said the Secretary of State; "I hear that you have very strange things to communicate to me."

"I have."

The Secretary pointed to a chair.

"Pray be seated."

"It matters not," said Warringdale. "I know your time is valuable, and therefore will take up as little of it as possible."

"Thank you—thank you."

"You are well aware that I have not been called to the House of Peers, notwithstanding the death of my lamented father, the late Earl of Whitcombe, because there arose a pretender to the title and estates in the person of a highwayman."

"I have heard so much."

"That person has pretended that he is the legitimate son of the late Earl by a previous marriage to that which, in the face of all the world, was solemnised with my mother."

"Really, my Lord Warringdale," said the Secretary, "I think you make the mistake of supposing that you can advance your peerage claims by arguing them before me. It is the Committee of Privileges of the Privy Council alone who have any power in that case."

"I am well aware of that fact, my lord; but what I have said was a necessary preliminary to what I have to say."

The Secretary slightly inclined his head.

"You will recollect," added Warringdale, "the mysterious murder of the late Earl of Bridgewater?"

"Certainly."

"Suspicion pointed to this very man who claims the title of Earl of Whitcombe; but up to yesterday, it was only suspicion."

"Ah! Have you a certainty, now?"

"I have."

"Then that fact would, I fancy, very much jeopardize the claim of this—this——"

"Highwayman!"

"Yes; this highwayman, Captain Heron, to the Earldom of Whitcombe."

"I fancy so. But when to the murder of the father is added the murder of the son——"

"Ah!"

"The murder of the son, I say, no one can view this man Heron but as a monster of iniquity."

"Certainly, certainly! But where is the evidence?"

"There!" said Warringdale, as he pointed to Jonathan Wild; "and there!" as he then pointed to the Reverend Mortification.

Wild advanced a few paces, and made an awkward bow, as he said, "Yes, my lord, I have the honour to be evidence."

"Oh, we know you, Mr. Wild, well enough; but who is that—that person?"

"A sinful vessel!" said the Reverend Mortification Ripon.

"A what?"

"Yea, a vessel of wrath!"

"A fool!" said Wild.

"A weak-minded, but honest man," added Lord Warringdale. "But he is so truly truthful, that whatever he says may be most implicitly depended upon. He goes by the name of Honest Ripon."

"Oh, dear!" said the Reverend Mortification.

"Yes," added Wild. "The poor fellow has no art. He does not know what deception means!"

"Upon my word," said the Secretary of State, laughing, "in these degenerate days, it is quite refreshing to meet with such a mirror of honesty and probity."

"It is, my lord," added Warringdale. "But it so happens that Mr. Wild, too, can confirm the statement of this pure and simple-minded soul; and that, to some extent, accident enables me to confirm Mr. Wild."

"Well—that is all very satisfactory. What may the precise statement be?"

"Simply this. After the villain Felix Heron had murdered the Earl of Bridgewater—that is, the old Earl, I mean——"

"Stop! stop! You have not quite proved yet that he did so."

"He was seen close to the spot," said Wild; "and after that he was in possession of a remarkably valuable diamond ring, which the Earl was known to have worn on the day of his murder."

"Well, go on."

"By an exercise of the strangest arts of deception and insinuation, Felix Heron contrived to quench the suspicions entertained against him for the murder of the Earl of Bridgewater, by making a kind of—I know not what to call it—acquaintance or intimacy with his son."

"Indeed!"

"Yes. He assisted the young Earl in some intrigues, and that formed a bond of union between them."

"But do you mean to say, my Lord Warringdale, that the young Earl of Bridgewater willingly consorted with his father's murderer?"

"He did not know it."

"Ah! That indeed!"

"But the time came when he did know it, and then a quarrel arose between them. A challenge was the result."

"What! Would a nobleman fight a duel with a common highwayman?"

"No, my lord."

"But you say so!"

"Permit me to explain that this Captain Felix Heron, the highwayman, had, by a well-concocted tale, actually persuaded the young and inexperienced Earl of Bridgewater that he was the first and legitimate son of my late father, and so, the only true and veritable Earl of Whitcombe. It was in that belief that the Earl of Bridgewater consented to fight with him as an equal."

"I see. Go on."

"They met in Kensington Gardens, yesterday morning, at an early hour. The Earl of Bridgewater took with him a friend of the name of Miles; but lurking among the trees was a band of the villanous associates of the highwayman, Felix Heron, and they, aided by him, fell upon the two unfortunate gentlemen, and murdered them."

"Murdered them?"

"Yes, in cold blood, murdered them."

"I had the honour," said Jonathan Wild, at this juncture—"I had the honour to make an official communication that the two dead bodies were lying in the Gardens."

"Yes," said the Secretary of State, "and that communication was attended to instantly."

"You found the bodies?"

"No!"

"No!" ejaculated Lord Warringdale and Jonathan Wild in chorus.

"Yea!" said the Rev. Mortification, "as the Psalmist says——"

"Silence!" roared Wild.

"Hush!" said Lord Warringdale, while his face turned of a livid paleness. "Do you mean to say, my lord, that your messengers found not the two dead men in the Royal Gardens?"

"I do. Nothing of the sort was there. The grass, they tell me, was trodden, and there were suspicious indications, even to the appearance of blood upon the ground, that some contest had taken place; but there was not the vestige of a dead body to be seen there."

Lord Warringdale looked disturbed.

Jonathan Wild, with the usual ready boldness of his character, came to his relief.

"This," he said, "is only what might have been expected. There is no doubt but that the murderer has removed the evidences of his crime."

"Yes—oh, yes! That is it," said Warringdale.

"It may be so," said the Secretary. "But what is the evidence of this Felix Heron's guilt, for as yet I have heard nothing but assertions?"

Lord Warringdale pointed to Wild.

"Speak!" he said. "Speak!"

"I will. Hem! From information I had received, I had a suspicion that such a duel was about to take place. Not much of that sort of thing, if I care to know it, escapes me, although people sometimes think they are cunning enough wholly to elude my vigilance."

Jonathan Wild gave Lord Warringdale a very significant glance as he uttered these words.

Go on, sir," said the Secretary.

"Well, my lord, I went to the spot alone, and there I saw the whole affair."

"Describe it."

"I will. The young Lord Bridgewater came on to the ground first, with his second, to whom I heard him say that he was now convinced Felix Heron was the real murderer of his father. The words were hardly out of his mouth when they were both set upon by Heron and his band."

"And what did you do?"

"I am no coward. I rushed out from my place of concealment, and engaged with the ruffians."

"And then?"

"They killed the Earl and his second."

"But how came they to spare you?"

"They did not spare me. They left me for dead on the grass; but after they had gone I recovered, and hope to be yet useful to his Majesty's Government."

"Then you were not hurt, after all?"

"Not hurt!" said Wild. "I have a pistol bullet wound in my shoulder, and look at my head."

Wild snatched off his wig, and exhibited his hideous bald head covered with strips of sticking-plaster.

"That will do, Mr. Wild. Put on your wig."

"Thank you, my lord."

"But in so serious a matter as this, some corroborative testimony would be very valuable."

"There it is," said Warringdale, as he pointed to the Rev. Mortification Ripon.

"Well, sir, what have you to say?"

"Yea—I—a—know not."

"Let me question him, my lord," said Jonathan. "I know how to get the truth from him."

"If what you have already said of him be true, Jonathan Wild, you will get nothing else from him."

"Exactly, my lord; but he will keep us here

all day, with his roundabout way of telling the story, if not questioned."

"Go on, then."

"Now, Ripon, attend to me!"

"Yea!"

"Were you in a state of rum-and-water on the evening before last?"

"Yea, I had some eau de vie."

"Oh, eau de vie, was it?"

"Yea, it were."

"And what did you do then?"

"I wandered into the wilderness."

"My lord, he means Kensington Gardens by the wilderness."

"How do you know that?"

"We shall see. Speak up, Ripon. What do you mean by the wilderness?"

"Yea, I went into the Park, and from the Park into the Gardens called Kensington; and I lay me down to repose, like the children of Israel, in a gravel-pit."

"Ah! A gravel-pit. My lord, there is but one gravel-pit in the Gardens, and that is close to the spot where all this affair took place."

"Let him proceed."

"Well, Mortification Ripon? What did you do then?"

"Yea, I was aroused by a contention, and I bethought me of the beautiful words of the Psalmist—

"'Birds in their little nests agree——'"

"Oh, stop him!—stop him!" said the Secretary. "Don't let him go astray in that way. To the point—to the point!"

"Silence, fool!" cried Wild.

"Yea, I am silent."

"What did you do, and what did you see, when you were aroused in the gravel-pit?"

"Yea, I saw my Lord Warringdale."

"Villain and liar!" shouted Warringdale.

"Ah!" said the Secretary. "So you were there, my lord?"

"No, no! It is false!"

"But he says so."

"Ha, ha!" laughed Wild. "Ha, ha! Pardon me, my lord, for laughing, but your lordship will comprehend. It was Felix Heron, the highwayman, he saw; but as he—Felix Heron—affects to be the eldest son of the late Earl of Whitcombe, why, if he were so, he would be entitled to be called Lord Warringdale."

"But——"

"Nay, my lord. I will ask him. Speak, Ripon —was it this gentleman, or Heron, the highwayman, you saw?"

"Oh, the highwayman."

"Ah! Just so!"

"And you called him Lord Warringdale, because you perhaps heard some one else speak of him by that title, I fancy?"

"Yea, the Earl of Bridgewater so spoke of him."

"Just so! Ha, ha! That explains it. Ha, ha! This idiot, now, might have led us astray."

"Ha, ha!" said Warringdale, with a forced laugh. "So he might."

"Go on!—go on!" added Wild. "What happened then?"

"The Earl of Bridgewater and his friend were slain, and I was knocked down, and hid among the bushes to save my life."

"Is that all?"

"Yea, that is all."

"Well, my Lord Warringdale," said the Secretary of State. "What do you want me to do?"

"Nothing, my lord—nothing. I merely wished that these facts should be known to you; so that whatever Mr. Wild here, in his capacity as a constable, may think proper to do, in his exertions to apprehend this Felix Heron, may be justified."

"Any man, constable or not, can arrest a felon," said the Secretary, drily.

"But," added Lord Warringdale, "it would materially expedite the march of justice, if your lordship, in your official capacity, would feel justified in offering a handsome reward for the apprehension of the villain who has made a noble family desolate, by the murder of two of its successive representatives."

"Be it so," said the Secretary of State. "I am sure I can take upon myself, in the name of the Government, to offer a reward of five hundred pounds for the apprehension of the murderer of the Earl of Bridgewater."

"Of the young Earl, your lordship means."

"Let us leave it in the terms I have stated, my Lord Warringdale, and then it will apply to the murderer of either father or son. If it be found that they are both combined in one person, it will come to the same thing. We need make no distinction; and you, of course, can have no motive in the transaction, but that justice should be done."

"None in the least, my lord—none in the least," said Lord Warringdale, rising. "And now I will trespass no further upon your attention, which I know is fully occupied."

Lord Warringdale bowed, and the Secretary of State returned it with interest.

Followed by Jonathan Wild and the Reverend Mortification Ripon, he left the official residence, and in a few moments they were all three standing together in Whitehall.

Lord Warringdale beckoned Jonathan Wild aside.

"I don't half like the aspect of affairs," he whispered; "nor do I like the manner in which the Secretary carried on the investigation."

"Nor I."

"What is to be done?"

"Let me think a moment."

CHAPTER CCXXV.

JONATHAN WILD'S REFLECTIONS SERIOUSLY IMPEDE THE LIBERTY OF THE REVEREND MORTIFICATION RIPON.

WILD'S reflections were short and to the purpose.

"Look you here, my lord," he said; "there is something amiss, but I don't know what it is exactly."

"The mysterious disappearance of the bodies," murmured Warringdale.

"Yes, I can't make that out—although, if I had not seen Felix Heron gallop off, accompanied by that infernal Ogle, and Edith, Judge Tarleton's daughter, I should have thought that, in some sentimental way, he had removed the bodies."

"And now, Jonathan?"

"Now I don't think any such thing; but I will find it out. In the meantime, however, there is one person who may be very dangerous to us."

"Who is that?"

"Why, your friend, the Reverend Mortification, who is getting away from us as fast he can down Whitehall."

"Ah! I see. He is so, indeed! Would it be prudent, Jonathan Wild, to let him escape?"

"Let him escape!" sneered Wild. "Do you suppose for a moment that I mean to let him escape?"

"But you see he is going!"

"As he thinks!"

Wild, with his hands in his pockets, walked slowly after the Reverend Mortification, who, by a sidelong glance, saw Jonathan following in his footsteps.

The reverend gentleman quickened his pace.

So did Jonathan Wild.

Arriving just opposite the Admiralty, the Reverend Mortification seemed to be seized with a sudden desire to alter his slow walk into a rapid one, and then to alter that rapid one into a race.

Jonathan Wild did not pursue him. He paused instantly, and blew a shrill blast upon the silver whistle, the sound of which his myrmidons knew so well.

A couple of men instantly darted out from the archway of the Admiralty.

Wild pointed after the retreating form of the Reverend Mortification Ripon.

"Quick!" he said. "That man!—secure him! Hackney coach—quiet cell—close and solitary till I come. Away!"

Jonathan Wild turned his back upon the proceedings of his men, and quietly rejoined Lord Warringdale. He had given his orders, and he did not think it at all necessary that he should trouble himself to wait to see them carried out. It was Warringdale, however, who kept his eyes fixed upon the retreating figure of the Reverend Mortification, and while Jonathan Wild paused for a moment, as if good-naturedly to allow his friend the gratification of harmless curiosity, Lord Warringdale saw the particulars of the apprehension of the terrified Mortification.

The two officers run him down in a few moments.

A hackney coach, from a stand which was then to be found close to the King's Mews, was hastily summoned, and the Reverend Mortification was bundled into it as though he had been nothing more than a parcel of old clothes.

"Help! help!" he cried. "Murder! They are going to murder me! Help! help! I'll tell everything to everybody! Murder! murder!"

There was a rush forward of a few chance passengers, and the usual crowd, upon anything out of the way happening in London, would soon have congregated, but the two bull-dogs of Jonathan Wild produced their constables' staves, and the words "Prisoner of State" awed the crowd in a moment.

Then one of the officers sprung on to the coach-box by the side of the driver, the other got inside the vehicle along with the Reverend Mortification

Ripon, and the coach soon left the crowd behind it as it rattled up the Strand.

"You have him?" said Warringdale.

"Oh, yes, safe enough," replied Wild.

"What will you do with him?"

"Keep him for the present quietly in one of the cells beneath my house, which people call Little Newgate."

"Then it was not so much injured by fire as was supposed?"

"No; it's pretty well to-rights again. I drew upon the Government a hundred and forty pounds for repairs. Ah! they know the value of Jonathan Wild. I fancy I stand pretty strong with the Administration. The fact is, I know too much for them to refuse me anything. I am a power in the State, my Lord Warringdale. I have said that you shall have the title of Whitcombe and its properties; and, as far as you are concerned, it is better for me to say that much than as if a privy counsellor had assured you of it."

"I believe you, Wild—I believe you. But I am troubled."

"About what?"

"About everything—but, perhaps, most of all about the singular disappearance of the dead bodies of the Earl of Bridgewater and his second."

"Leave that to me. I cannot quite make it out at present, but I will; and, at all events, Warringdale, you know the adage holds good that 'dead men tell no tales wherever they may be.' But come, now; you've often manifested a desire to visit me at my own house. Shall it be this morning? I have an hour to spare; and after that I mean to take such measures for the destruction of that one life that stands between us both and fortune, that they must succeed."

Lord Warringdale hesitated a moment, and then he said, "Well, Jonathan, I will visit you. It seems to me, now, to be dreadful to be alone. I do not think I shall venture into those apartments again opposite to Whitcombe House, where so fearful a sight is to be seen."

"Pooh! pooh!" said Wild. "It's only to be seen if you look for it. The sight is hidden safely enough; and if you did see it, what is it, after all, but a dead man?"

"Do not speak of it. I will come with you to the City, Jonathan."

"Do so; and, after that, let me advise you how to act.

"In what way?"

"Go and take possession of Whitcombe House at once. You've got rid of the Earl of Bridgewater, who was, probably, the only member of the Committee of Privileges of the House of Lords who cared two straws who came into the possession of the Earldom of Whitcombe."

"I think I will do so."

"Do not think, but act."

Lord Warringdale shuddered.

"There seems to me something awful," he said, "in the atmosphere of that house. I have had a fright, as you know, in it."

"Pshaw! pshaw! Visions of a disturbed imagination. But for fear that you should be dull when you get there, I will take up my abode with you for a time, and cheerfully keep you company. A West End house will be handy and agreeable to me; and, as I am naturally of a lively disposition,

you will, of course be delighted to have me with you."

Lord Warringdale made no reply, but a slight groan came from his lips; for if ever human being felt himself oppressed with the society of another, certainly he did with that of Jonathan Wild.

And here we may say that Lord Warringdale felt none of that exultation and lightness of spirit which he thought would be his could he but contrive the death of the Earl of Bridgewater.

He had always considered that that young nobleman was as great an obstruction to his acquisition of the title and estates of Whitcombe as Felix Heron himself.

Nay, had it not been for the partisanship of the Earl of Bridgewater, Felix Heron would have been comparatively helpless.

Therefore was it that Lord Warringdale was surprised that he did not feel more at ease now that he had accomplished the destruction of one

of the three persons he had in his own mind condemned to death.

Those three persons were Felix Heron, his brother, the Earl of Bridgewater, and Jonathan Wild.

The Earl, he believed, he had himself disposed of; and he believed, too, that Wild would now have but little difficulty in ridding him of Heron.

Jonathan himself would still remain; and, notwithstanding his want of success on previous occasions, Lord Warringdale thought that surely a man that made up his mind to assassinate another could not be long without an opportunity of accomplishing his purpose.

Wild had a particular motive in persuading Warringdale to accompany him to the City.

What it was we shall see.

They hired a hackney-coach in the Strand, and together they made their way to Jonathan's house, in Newgate Street.

Wild made no inquiries about the Reverend Mortification Ripon. He felt quite confident his orders had been obeyed; but he conducted Lord Warringdale to the private apartment in which he himself usually sat, and slipping a small brass bolt into its socket which was beneath the lock of the door, he turned sharply to Warringdale, and said, in a harsh, grating voice, "Now, my lord, let's settle accounts, if you please."

"Accounts, Jonathan? What do you mean?"

"You know what I mean perfectly. The prospect of your possession of the estates and title of Whitcombe brightens. I will charge myself with the destruction of Felix Heron, and then there will be nothing in your way at all except——"

"Except what?"

"One solitary fact, of which I mean to keep the proof in my own hands."

"What is that?"

"The fact of your illegitimacy."

"Say not that—say not that! Felix Heron may be my elder brother, and a marriage may have taken place between the Earl and Amelia Staunton, his mother—a secret marriage; but my mother was married to the Earl in the open face of day, in the presence of a hundred witnesses. I am not, I cannot be, illegitimate, although I may be a younger brother."

"Ah! You say so?"

"I say what I think and feel."

"Stuff! What if Amelia Staunton lives?"

"She does not live. That is a bugbear to frighten me. I say she does not live."

"Very well. We will say no more about it. But here are pens, ink, and paper; and now, my lord, to business."

"What business is it you require of me? Already you hold bonds of mine to the tune of about eighty thousand pounds, which I shall have to meet by the sale of some portion of the Whitcombe estates."

"Undoubtedly," said Wild. "I have made some careful inquiries, and I find that if the whole of the Whitcombe estates were sold they would produce half a million of ready money."

"Half a million?"

"Yes. A tolerable sum, is it not? And that makes my half come, you know, to two hundred and fifty thousand pounds."

"What?"

"My half, I say, comes to two hundred and fifty thousand pounds."

"Are you mad, Jonathan Wild?"

"Never was more sane in my life."

"Your half, did you say?"

"Yes, my Lord Warringdale," shouted Wild, as he dealt the table a blow with his fist that made everything upon it jump again,—"yes, my Lord Warringdale—that shall be Earl of Whitcombe—my half; I say it again. Do you think I would work, toil, lie, murder, and jeopardise my life itself, to permit you to carry off the lion's share of the booty. No, my lord; we will be both lions, and share and share alike; or tigers, if you please. You shall sell one-half of your patrimony, and hand over the ready money to me."

"I refuse."

"Oh, you refuse?"

"I do! You are a villain, Wild!"

"Stale news, my lord. As if I did not know that!"

"Your proposition is monstrous.

"Oh, is it? That is your present opinion; but a little familiarity will enable you to see it in quite a different light. Think again, my Lord Warringdale, and remember who I am, and, likewise, *where you are!*"

Lord Warringdale sprung to his feet, and laid his hand upon his sword-hilt.

"Oh, there's no danger yet," said Wild.

"Yes, there is," said Warringdale.

As he spoke, he plunged his hand into the breast of his apparel, and rapidly drawing it forth again with a pistol in its grasp, he levelled it across the table at Wild, as he cried out, "Villain! you are now at my mercy! Stir from your present attitude, move but a finger, and you are a dead man!

"Blaze away!" said Wild.

Even as he spoke, he flung himself clean backward upon the floor.

Bang! went Lord Warringdale's pistol, for his finger was upon the trigger; but as far as any danger to Jonathan Wild was concerned, the bullet might have been winging its way over Hounslow Heath.

"Missed, by heaven!" cried Warringdale, with a shriek of despair.

He started back as he spoke, forgetful of the chair from which he had just risen; so that, in fact, he fell into it again.

The moment he did so, the square portion of the floor on which the legs of the chair stood, opened in the form of a trap-door, and down went Warringdale, chair and all, through the opening.

Then was a yell of dismay from the aperture, and then all was still.

The trap-door closed of itself by some powerful spring acting on its hinges, and then Wild sprung to his feet.

"A close touch, that!" he said. "It's well I've practised that kind of fall—they don't do it better at the old theatre in Duke Street; and it enabled me to reach the bolt close under the skirting-boards here, that set the trap free. I wonder, now, if that dear Warringdale has hurt himself? That would be a pity. He's a valuable piece of goods, and must not be entirely destroyed; but he will break out now and then in this extraordinary fashion, and then of course he must take the consequences. This will have been a rough lesson, but I hope it will do him good."

Jonathan Wild, with all the composure imaginable, left the room, and proceeded down the stairs immediately outside its door.

He felt in his pocket for a key as he went, with which he unlocked a door upon the floor beneath.

But Jonathan Wild was much too cautious to put his head into the room, through the ceiling of which Lord Warringdale had fallen.

He was not aware of the exact state of affairs.

But Jonathan was equal to every little emergency of this kind.

Taking off his hat and wig, he balanced them both on the end of the short bludgeon he carried in his pocket; he then suddenly projected both hat and wig into the room, when another pistol-shot sounded sharply in his ears, and the hat spun round as a bullet perforated it.

"That'll do," said Jonathan. "I could have sworn he had a pair of pistols with him; and now he has fired them both, we can proceed to business."

Wild fitted on his wig and hat again, as if nothing particular had happened; and then, with his hands in his pockets, he strolled into the room with quite a careless air.

Lord Warringdale was crouching down upon the floor, amid the fragments of the chair, which had broken to pieces in its fall.

There was a wound upon his forehead, from which the blood was trickling; and he looked ghastly, lividly pale.

"Well, my lord," said Wild, "how do you find yourself now? This sort of thing is foolish—very foolish—and exhausts your strength—makes you look ugly, and might break a limb."

Warringdale groaned.

"Ha! ha!" laughed Wild, "it's an ugly tumble, although not above ten feet. I generally find people more tractable after it: it shakes their obstinacy a little."

"Fiend!"

"Come, come, my lord, this house goes deeper still. There is another floor below this; and a series of short cuts, from room to room, through the floor of one and the ceiling of the next, might be uncomfortable."

"Spare me! spare me!"

"Spare you? What *do* you mean, my good friend? Spare my excellent friend Lord Warringdale!—my illustrious acquaintance, who is about to give me his written acknowledgments for a sum of two hundred and fifty thousand pounds! Spare you, indeed!"

"This is cruel irony!" moaned Warringdale.

"Not at all—not at all! Pray get up, and take my arm. Spare you, indeed! Long may you be spared! Long may both of us be spared, to be the ornaments of society and the props of religion!"

Warringdale shuddered.

"Ah! you feel a little shaken?"

"I do."

"No bones broken?"

"I think not."

"There's nothing like luck. The last person who took that tumble broke his back. I kept him till nightfall, and then had him put in a wheelbarrow, and trundled to the door of St. Bartholomew's Hospital, and shot out. I don't know what became of him; but it didn't matter."

Lord Warringdale shuddered, and his teeth chattered in his head. He was fain to accept a potent glass of brandy from Wild; and within the next half-hour he had signed acknowledgments to the thief-taker to the sum of two hundred and fifty thousand pounds.

CHAPTER CCXXVI.

SIR JOHN TARLETON, IN HIS LAST MOMENTS, REPENTS OF HIS EVIL LIFE AND DEEDS.

WHILE these occurrences—in regard to the villain Jonathan Wild, and the unhappy and criminal wretch, Lord Warringdale, who might now be called his victim—were taking place, a singular scene was enacting in an apartment in Lincoln's Inn, which had a great effect upon the fortunes of some of the persons of our story.

The then Lord Chancellor of England was a cold, austere man, who had little sympathy for human failings. His justice was all of the harsh description, untinctured by an infusion of human charity.

He used to sit in the old dingy Court at Lincoln's Inn, with a look of inflexible pride and coldness; and when he rose from the chair of dignity, and retired to the private room in the ancient building, which was known by the name of "The Chancellor's Chamber," the suitors in the Court—the counsel, the attorneys, and the spectators—felt as if the weather had suddenly changed from winter to spring.

The relief from his presence was great.

And no one ventured into that private room, unless his rank made a justification for the intrusion.

The judges, the Vice-Chancellors, and now and then the Attorney-General, or Solicitor-General, would be there, waiting to speak to the Chancellor.

On those occasions, the Chancellor's secretary would send a slip of paper into the court, with the name of the visitor upon it.

That slip of paper would have to pass through three or four hands before it reached those of the great man.

Then, perhaps, within the next five minutes, he would rise, stopping some mumbling, hesitating advocate in mid-career. He would make a slight bow to the bar—the curtain that shielded him from the cold air of the old hall would be jerked aside, and he would retire to his private room, to commune with the visitor.

But woe be to any one, let his rank be what it might, who interrupted the Chancellor on any pretence but that of urgent business.

It was the second morning, then, after the duel in Kensington Gardens, that a slip of paper took its course in the Court of Chancery, until it reached the hand of his lordship.

On that slip of paper was merely a name—Sir John Tarleton.

The brows of the Chancellor settled down in an anxious frown.

He did not like Sir John Tarleton.

They were political foes. He knew—or he thought he knew—that Sir John Tarleton had been, for a long time, scheming and plotting to effect such a change in the Ministry as should place himself in the chair of the Chancellor.

But still this cold, austere man was more punctilious about his conduct to his enemies than to his friends.

Holding, then, the slip of paper in his hand for a few moments, he waited until the counsel who was addressing the Court was in the midst of a long sentence, and then he abruptly rose.

"Silence!" cried the usher.

The curtain was drawn aside. Everybody breathed more freely. The Chancellor had left the Court.

The private room was a gloomy apartment, the floor of which was covered by an old faded Turkey carpet, which had once been most costly.

The ceiling was blackened by age, and the carving, and painting, and gilding upon it could be but faintly seen.

Some massive chairs, covered in morocco leather, and some couches to match—a table of huge proportions, littered with papers—and the heavy crimson silk curtains to the casement, completed the getting-up of the room.

The obsequious attendants of the Chancellor flung the heavy door wide open, and then closed it behind him.

The Chancellor heard a deep groan from some one in the room.

For a few seconds, then, he could see no one; and he turned twice round, shading his eyes with his left hand, so as to concentrate what light there was on the floor, before he saw that there was—huddled up upon one of the massive arm-chairs—a bundle of something, that might be a human being.

The deep groan was repeated.

"Who is there?" asked the Chancellor.

He could not believe that it was in reality Sir John Tarleton.

"Who is there?" he repeated.

"I," said a feeble voice, in reply.

The Lord Chancellor moved with a slow and stately step to the window, and flung aside the silken curtains.

Some more light came into the room.

Then he saw, huddled up in that strange fashion in the huge arm-chair, Sir John Tarleton, one of his Majesty's Barons of the Exchequer.

Limp and listless, with apparently no power to raise his head, with his arms hanging down as still and nerveless as though they belonged to a corpse, sat Sir John Tarleton.

His eyes alone seemed to be full of a more than natural life, and he glared into the face of the Chancellor with an expression of such abject woe and misery that it would soon have melted a more susceptible heart.

"You know me, my lord?" said Sir John Tarleton, faintly.

"I do."

"That—is—well. It is now half-past twelve o'clock."

The Chancellor turned his eyes mechanically to a time-piece that was on the chimney-piece, and then, gravely inclining his head, he replied, "That is a statement, Sir John Tarleton, that I am not in a position to dispute."

"At one o'clock," added Sir John Tarleton, "I shall be no more."

The Chancellor shook his head.

"You doubt it?"

"I cannot know it; but if it is to be the fact, I would fain suggest, Sir John Tarleton, that your own home, and not my private room, would be the more appropriate place for the ceremony."

"The ceremony?"

"Yes—of death."

"That is true, my lord; but there is a reason."

The Chancellor gravely bowed, as though he would have said, "Well, let us have the reason."

Then Sir John Tarleton made a great effort, and raised his hands, and clasped them together; and while the tears rolled down his cheeks, he said, "I have come to you, my lord, to make a confession of a breach of trust."

"Ah!"

"Yes—oh, yes! Along with Sir Dominick Browne, I was trustee for the fortune of my daughter Edith. I have taken possession of the whole of that fortune, and dissipated it."

"Is this possible?"

"It is true."

"And you are one of the judges of the land?"

"It is true—it is only too true."

"And your co-trustee—is he equally guilty?"

"No, no!—oh, no! A thousand times, no!"

"Only negligently criminal?"

"Not criminal in any form, shape, or way. I placed his name to the necessary papers. He is an innocent and a persecuted man, neither criminal nor negligent."

"Ah! You depose to that?"

"I do! I do! 'Tis I alone who am guilty!"

"Well, Sir John Tarleton, and what is it you propose to do?"

"I propose that from this hour your lordship should interpose in this matter, by virtue of your authority over all trusts. Whatever property I die possessed of can be taken possession of by your lordship's authority."

The Chancellor inclined his head.

"And," added the wretched Sir John Tarleton, "I have no accusation to make, but I have a caution to give to you."

"Say on."

"Beware!—oh, beware of the man who calls himself Lord Warringdale!"

"The son of the late Earl of Whitcombe?"

"The same. And, oh, beware more than all of Jonathan Wild!"

A look of contempt passed over the face of the Lord Chancellor.

"And save Sir Dominick Browne—save Lady Castleneau."

"What mean you? Save them from whom and from what?"

"From persecution! perhaps from murder!"

"Sir John Tarleton, it seems to me that you have come here to make a revelation which you have not well studied beforehand; and that, consequently, you are making it in a very inconsequential and illogical manner."

"My lord, I am a dying man!"

The Chancellor glanced at the clock; for the statement Sir John Tarleton had made that he should die at one o'clock came to his remembrance.

It wanted ten minutes to one.

"Oh, if it were possible for me to make full restitution!" moaned Sir John Tarleton. "If I could only do a something that would, in some measure, condone the past! But I cannot—I cannot! I am a poor, lone, wretched man, and I feel the hand of death approaching my heart."

The Chancellor gravely approached the chimney-piece, and placed his hand upon the silken cord of a bell.

"No!—oh, no! Do not summon assistance!" half screamed Sir John Tarleton. "It will be of no avail. I must die—I will die!"

"But the impropriety of dying here, Sir John Tarleton, is very great."

"Oh, cold heart—cold heart! Have you no human feeling? Ah! it comes—it comes! Death—death! Edith—Edith! My child—my own Edith! Oh! heaven spare—spare——Forgive!"

A cold gloom came over the face of the old Judge. The eyes no longer gleamed with the fire of life.

The clock struck one.

Sir John Tarleton was dead!

"Exceedingly improper conduct in every way," said the Chancellor, as he gave the bell-pull a jerk.

LORD WARRINGDALE MAKES PREPARATIONS FOR A SETTLEMENT OF
ACCOUNTS WITH HIS FRIEND JONATHAN WILD.

Presented Gratis with No. 103. of the New Edition of Edith the Captive; or, the Robbers of Epping Forest.

Some of the attendants immediately appeared.

"Sir John Tarleton is dead," said the Chancellor. "See that the body is removed to his own house at once."

In two minutes more the Chancellor was sitting in Court again, as if nothing particular had happened; but there he wrote a note, and addressed it to the Attorney-General, with a request that he would be at St. James's Palace, to meet him—the Chancellor—at three o'clock.

Before, however, he left the Court, a folded paper was handed up to him, with an intimation that it had fallen from the pocket of the deceased Judge Tarleton.

The paper contained the following words:—

"In case death should seize me before I can communicate what I have to say to some one of the high law-officers of the Crown, let this paper be considered as my confession.

"I have—by forging the name of my co-trustee, Sir Dominick Browne—taken possession of the whole of the fortune left by my deceased wife to my daughter Edith.

"I have connived at the persecution of Sir Dominick Browne, and his confinement in a lunatic asylum, lest he should discover what I had done, and expose the wrong.

"I have reason to believe that my wife's sister, the Lady Castleneau, has been likewise persecuted on the same grounds, and that she is now somewhere most unjustly imprisoned.

"My assistants in all this villany have been the Lord Warringdale and Jonathan Wild.

"JOHN TARLETON, Knight."

The Lord Chancellor looked grim and cold, as he read this statement.

By three o'clock, his carriage halted at the gate of St. James's Palace.

There were at that time a suite of rooms in the old Palace, to which the ministers and great officers of State could always proceed, without any ceremony; and the Chancellor took his way there, and was soon in close confabulation with the Attorney-General.

These two luminaries of the law, after conversing together for some time, both nodded their heads, and the Attorney-General said, "Yes, my lord; that shall be done immediately. It is quite time that the career of Jonathan Wild should come to an end."

"It is."

"And, as your lordship says, if it be found to be a fact that the Home Secretary has entrusted Wild with blank warrants of committal, it is high time that His Majesty should be advised to dispense with the counsels of so dangerous a minister."

The Chancellor almost smiled.

He hated the Home Secretary.

"I should not be at all surprised," added the Attorney-General, "at finding that the mysterious disappearance of the Earl of Bridgewater and Sir Wentworth Miles had some connexion with these transactions, since I hear that it was Jonathan Wild who first gave some information on that matter at the Home Office."

"It is probable."

The door of the apartment in which the Lord Chancellor and the Attorney-General were conversing at this moment opened, and Lord Warringdale made his appearance.

Pale and ghastly as he looked, yet there was about his eyes a glance of exultation; and, upon observing the occupants of the room, he made a low bow, as he said, "My Lord Chancellor, I hope soon to have the aid of your lordship's voice, to call me to my proper rank in the House of Lords. I languish in vain for a decision, and hope——"

"Sir," said the Chancellor, almost fiercely, "it is most improper to speak to me in private on the subject."

"And, besides," said the Attorney-General, "what we now know——"

"We mean to keep, for the present, to ourselves," added the Chancellor, directing a look of caution at the Attorney-General.

The latter bowed, and Lord Warringdale glanced from one to the other of them, with fear—of he knew not what—gathering at his heart.

In a few moments more he was left alone.

"What has happened?" he said. "What can have happened amiss? Surely all is well. The mysterious disappearance from Kensington Gardens of the two dead bodies would perplex and terrify me, but that I suspect Wild to know all about it; and while he is easy, I need not be alarmed."

But Lord Warringdale was alarmed, for all that he tried to reason himself into something like composure.

Lord Warringdale had thought it good policy to show himself in and about the Court; and now that he thought there was no danger of encountering the Earl of Bridgewater, he was the more inclined to do so than before.

Hence his present visit to that suite of apartments in St. James's common to the use of all persons who had any official standing.

Sinecure posts and places, at that period, were more common than even at the present day; and, although he did no duty whatever, Lord Warringdale, as the son of the Earl of Whitcombe, held no less than two such situations connected with the Court and the Administration.

It was the fact of his having this fallacious official existence which enabled him to show himself in that suite of rooms; although, if he had believed, for a single moment, that the Earl of Bridgewater was really in existence, he would have shunned St. James's Palace, even as he would have shunned it had it continued to be the hospital it once was, before it became the abode of royalty.

But yet he felt uneasy.

How suspicious does every circumstance appear to those in whose hearts and brains dwell the consciousness of secret guilt!

Safe as Lord Warringdale had reason to think himself, every little circumstance that occurred about him seemed suspicious, and possibly full of disaster.

Did that evidently private conference between the Lord Chancellor and the Attorney-General concern him?

That was a question he asked himself, and he trembled as he asked it.

He would have trembled still more, had he but known the events of the next hour.

Those events were important and troublesome to Jonathan Wild.

CHAPTER CCXXVII.

JONATHAN WILD UNDERGOES AN EXAMINATION
BEFORE THE PRIVY COUNCIL.

WHEN the villain Wild had forced, from the fears of Lord Warringdale, the acknowledgments for so large a sum as two hundred and fifty thousand pounds, a feeling of contentment came over him.

Yes. For once the cupidity, the greed, the grasping nature of Jonathan Wild was sated.

He actually thought he had enough!

There was a glow of satisfaction at the bold, bad heart of Jonathan. It seemed as if the concentrated refulgence of all that large sum of money, in bright, new gold pieces, was shining in his eyes.

He paced the apartment, in which Lord Warringdale had had such a tremendous tumble, with quite the step and the look of a conqueror.

Jonathan Wild almost looked majestic.

Two hundred and fifty thousand pounds seemed to him a kind of pinnacle on which he could stand and overlook his fellow-men.

"Yes," he said, in a loud, exultant voice,— "yes; that will do! I have achieved something at last! Ha, ha! I have done the trick; and one-half the estates of the Whitcombe earldom are mine—mine—my own—the veritable property of Jonathan Wild!"

He clapped his huge, hard, heavy hands together in the rapture of the moment.

"Capital! capital!" he cried. "Nothing, after all, could have turned out better than all that affair in Kensington Gardens! Lord Warringdale saved me a world of trouble. He was quite right in thinking that to get rid of the young Earl of Bridgewater, was as great an object as to get rid of Captain Heron himself?"

Wild went to the window, and looked through the dingy panes of glass.

He never had his windows cleaned. He was of opinion, that the more difficult it was for people to see in from without, the better it was for him.

So it was difficult for Wild to see through the grimy panes.

But still he could see, although dimly; and he was a little surprised to observe a hackney coach draw up opposite to his house, and two men get out of it, one of whom he knew by sight as a messenger of the Home Office.

The other was a constable of the name of Larkins, who was permanently attached to the House of Lords.

"What do they want?" muttered Wild.

Then he altered the phrase; and he said, "Who do they want?"

But it never, for one half-moment, occurred to him that they "wanted" him, in the police acceptation of the word "wanted."

He could see that the constable, Mr. Larkins, looked to the priming of his pistols, and then put them back into his pocket, with the air and manner of a man who should say, "Be at hand; I may want you both."

All this was mysterious to Wild.

"What is in the wind now, I wonder?" he muttered again. "I am half in the mind of going down to ask them."

Jonathan Wild soon found that he had no occasion to do that.

The messenger from the Home Office, accompanied by the constable, crossed the way towards his house.

Bang! came a heavy knock at the outer door.

"Ah!" said Wild, "that's it, is it? I might have guessed as much. They would hardly be so near me without calling upon me for my help."

Bang! came the knock at the door again.

Then Wild heard voices below.

The man he had upon the lock, in lieu of Blueskin, after reconnoitring the visitors, had opened the door.

"Is Mr. Wild at home?"

"Ah! yes," said Jonathan to himself, as he slowly walked down the stairs; "it is always Mr. Wild if the service be one of danger. I wonder if it is after Heron now that they are? Who knows? Perhaps they may have got some information that may enable them to capture him; and, if so, of course, they want me to help. Ha! ha! I may yet sleep to-night in the consciousness that all who can stand between me and my fortunes are safe—ha! ha!—safe between four walls. It may be so."

Wild reached the hall of his house.

"Well, Mr. Larkins, who do you want now?"

"You, Mr. Wild!"

"Of course you do! There is not an officer in all London but wants me so soon as he gets in his hands a warrant against any one who is likely to give trouble."

"Now, sir!" said Larkins, to the messenger from the Home Office.

Jonathan Wild could not comprehend what this "Now, sir!" meant; but the messenger nodded, and passing Jonathan, he proceeded towards the staircase.

Wild naturally turned right round to look after him, and that was just what was wanted, for then his back was towards Larkins, the constable.

With a sudden rush, Larkins flung himself upon Jonathan Wild, and got such a grasp of his collar at the back of his neck, that it could not be shaken off.

For a moment or two Jonathan Wild was perfectly still. The surprise of this sudden attack seemed as though it had literally stunned him.

Then, with a roar like that of some wild beast who finds it has fallen into a trap, Jonathan wrenched himself round.

He was face to face with the constable, at the expense of the collar of his coat, which was half ripped off.

"What do you want?" he yelled.

"You, Mr. Wild—you! Resistance is the worst folly you can be guilty of."

"What?—what charge?"

"We have nothing to do with that," said the Home Office messenger. "I produce a Privy Council warrant for your apprehension."

"A warrant?"

"Yes. Here it is."

"Stop! stop! Let me think. I—I——Arrest me?—me? It is some mistake—I am Jonathan Wild."

"Just so, and that is the name on the warrant."

Wild had had time to think. His first impulse was resistance, but his second told him what folly that would be. Moreover, he had in the house—actually upon the table up-stairs—the acknowledgments for the two hundred and fifty thousand pounds he had forced from the fears of Lord Warringdale.

"Have you any objection," said Wild, "to let me see the warrant?"

"None in the least. There it is!"

"Ah, I see! It is quite correct. Well, I am Jonathan Wild; and, of all men living, it would least become me to offer resistance to a warrant."

"That's sensible, Mr. Wild," said Larkins.

"I," continued Wild—for now that he had made up his mind to play a part, he was resolved to play it well—"I, who have been the man who has carried out so many warrants—certainly I should ever be the man, of all others, who is ready to submit to the law. I obey the warrant at once, and I trust you will report my conduct."

"Oh, yes, Mr. Wild!"

The officer was quite delighted to find an affair of which he had had the most grievous forebodings go off so pleasantly.

It would not have surprised him in the least if Jonathan Wild had engaged in a contest with him and the Home Office messenger, in which some wounds might have been received.

But this lamb-like forbearance of Wild was quite charming.

"All I ask of you," said Jonathan, "is leave to lock my desk."

"Where is it?"

"Up-stairs."

"We must go with you."

"Oh, of course. I always made it a rule myself never to let a prisoner out of my sight for a moment. It would be very wrong of you, Larkins, to let me go up-stairs by myself."

The officer began to be actually frightened and uneasy at the facility with which the redoubtable Jonathan Wild had allowed himself to be apprehended in his own house; and if the messenger had not been with him, he would scarcely have ventured up-stairs with his prisoner.

But Wild had only one idea in his mind at that moment.

That idea was to secure about him the precious documents with the name of Warringdale to them.

So soon as they all three reached the rooms above, Jonathan put the acknowledgments into a secret pocket of his waistcoat; and then, as he locked his desk and put it into a cupboard, which he likewise locked, he said, "Now I am ready."

Larkins, the officer, would fain have put handcuffs upon Wild's wrists, but he was really ashamed to propose such a thing to a man who took so patriotic a view of his own arrest.

They left the house, therefore, without that ceremony being gone through.

Wild turned to the bull-dog who was on the lock in his hall, and said, with an air of great suavity, "I shall soon be back. Be careful—on you life, I say, be careful of all here!"

"Yes, Mr. Wild."

"Now, sirs, I am ready."

Wild's imagination was busy asking himself what could be the charge brought against him;

but he could not come to any rational conclusion.

That it was no ordinary police affair he felt conscious, or he would have been taken on a much more common-place warrant. It was a consolation to Wild to be, in his own mind, convinced that the affair had no reference to his atrocious proceedings in the way of compromising felonies.

Then an idea came across him on the moment that he was stepping into the coach.

"Oh, of course," he said, "that's it!"

"What, Mr. Wild?"

"Nothing—nothing."

Wild kept his own counsel; but his opinion now was that he owed his arrest to some suspicion that he was the person who had removed from the royal gardens, at Kensington, the dead bodies of the Earl of Bridgewater and Sir Wentworth Miles.

The more Wild thought over this idea the more he was convinced, in his own mind, that he had hit upon the true cause of his arrest.

He became quite composed.

What could the Privy Council say or do to him in the matter? For once in a way Jonathan Wild relied upon his actual innocence, and felt all that confidence which a man may feel in the impossibility of proving an act against him which he had never even dreamed of committing.

Wild got cheerful.

The coach rattled on, and he found that he was taken to Downing Street.

"Very good!" he said. "Larkins, you are a good fellow, and I hope you will dine with me to-morrow."

"We shall see."

"Say you will."

The officer shook his head.

"I wish you well, Mr. Wild, but I can't make any promises. You do your duty, and I will do mine."

"Very good," thought Wild. "I will think of some plan for getting Larkins hanged some session, soon."

A pleasant acquaintance was Jonathan Wild.

There was just a slight feeling of apprehension in the mind of Jonathan when he found that he was taken charge of by two officers whom he did not know, and conducted into a room, down the centre of which was a large table so nearly touching the walls at each end as only to leave sufficient space for one person to pass.

Each of those narrow openings between the table and the wall were occupied by a constable.

Behind the table, at that side of it furthest away from the prisoner, and from the door, were six or eight elegant chairs covered in very fine Morocco leather.

Two of those chairs were occupied.

In one of them sat the Lord Chancellor, and in the other the Earl of Arranmore, who was well known as an active member of the then existing Administration.

In another moment, a door opened, and the Secretary of State for the Home Department made his appearance.

"My lord," said the Chancellor, "we have requested you to favour us with your presence, because what Jonathan Wild is accused of concerns you."

The Secretary bowed.

"Indeed, Mr. Secretary," said Lord Arranmore, "it concerns us all—for who is safe if blank Home Office warrants are to be in the hands of such a man as the notorious Jonathan Wild!"

"Oh, that's it, is it?" said Wild to himself.

A flush of anger was upon the face of the Home Secretary.

"My lords," he said, "I certainly, on one occasion, when the names of suspected traitors were unknown, entrusted to Wild some blank warrants. He is responsible for any use, other than that intended, which he has made of them."

Wild began to tremble a little. That the Home Secretary would throw him over, was a matter of course; and he listened anxiously as the Chancellor said, "What is your name?"

"Jonathan Wild."

"What are you?"

"An officer of police."

"Have you had blank warrants entrusted to you by the Secretary of State; and how many?"

"I have; but I can't say how many."

"Have you any now?"

"I have."

"Produce them."

Jonathan Wild took from one of his capacious pockets a large black leather pocket-book, and took from it two blank warrants, which he laid on the table.

"Is that all?"

"It is, my lord."

"But you had more?"

"Certainly."

"Then what did you do with the last one, to which you appended the name of some person, who no doubt has been apprehended?"

"The last one?"

"I said the last."

"May it please your lordships, I filled it up at the request—indeed, I may say at the order—of a member of the Privy Council."

"What member?"

"Let me explain, my lords. There was a member of the Privy Council who had become accidentally acquainted with treasonable practices on the part of a lady."

"Her name?"

"Lady Castleneau."

"Go on."

"This member of the Privy Council, my lords, had a kind of struggle in his own mind between his duty to his country and his King and his private sense of honour."

"As how?"

"Why, my lords, what he knew of the treasonable practices of this Lady Castleneau he had found out by going to her house, and it might be almost said that his knowledge was confidential. Therefore was it that the struggle to know what to do arose in his mind."

"His name?"

"Please you, my lords, I will tell you that directly, but I wish to explain. That nobleman came to me at my house in Newgate Street, and, said he, 'Mr. Wild, I'm in a difficulty, which, from your great experience as a police-officer, you may be able to relieve me from; but you must consider what I am about to say to you as strictly confidential.'"

"And yet you tell us this without scruple?" said the Lord Chancellor.

"My lord," said Wild, audaciously, "I think it is a little too bad to bring a man by force of a warrant before a Privy Council, for the purpose of making him submit to interrogations, and then quarrel with him because he's too candid."

The Secretary of State smiled, and a dark frown settled on the face of the Chancellor.

"You are not only too candid, Jonathan Wild," he said, "but you are too insolent."

"My lord, I have no desire to be so, but being here before your lordship, my impression was that I ought to make a clean breast of everything I know."

"Go on, sir—go on. We hear you."

Jonathan Wild's countenance looked almost radiant. He was quite in raptures with his own cleverness, for on the spur of the moment catching a true sense of his situation, he had determined on throwing upon the dead—as he supposed—young Earl of Bridgewater the whole blame of the transaction.

Wild was fully of opinion that, by some means, Lady Castleneau, whom he had consigned to the Tower of London, had made her situation known; and he felt convinced that this examination before the Privy Council was on account of his filling up one of the blank warrants with her name.

How triumphantly, then, would he not only bring himself through the transaction, and at the same time save the Secretary of State from further trouble about it, by putting it upon the shoulders of a dead man.

"Yes, my lords," added Wild, "I feel myself bound to tell you the exact truth in this matter. The Earl of Bridgewater told me that his duty to his King and country called upon him to accuse Lady Castleneau of corresponding with disaffected persons of traitorous designs; but at the same time he was tormented with a consciousness that he had acquired the information actually beneath the roof of Castleneau House, and in the familiar confidence of a friend."

"You will swear to this?" said Lord Arranmore.

"Most willingly, my lord."

"Will you take a voluntary oath here before us."

"With pleasure."

"Swear the man, then," said the Lord Chancellor. "We are quite competent to receive a voluntary oath, although we are not sitting here now in a judicial sense."

One of the persons who had been guarding the narrow passage which led round the table, and who had been taking notes of the examination, now stepped forward, and administered the oath to Jonathan Wild.

"Now, go on, sir," said the Chancellor.

"Well, my lords, finding the Earl of Bridgewater in this difficulty, I mentioned to him that I had some blank warrants; upon which, with a feeling of great relief in his tones and manner, he requested me to fill up one of them with the name of Lady Castleneau, as though from information I had myself discovered."

"And you did?"

"I did, my lords; and lodged her ladyship in the Tower; but I cannot say I have discovered anything since to confirm the matter; and it is a thousand pities that the Earl of Bridgewater, being no more, cannot himself step forward and exonerate me."

"It is indeed," said the Secretary of State; "because it would then be shown that the blank warrant was most judiciously used for the public service; although I am not at all prepared, my lords, to defend the practice of entrusting such documents to any one, and it shall not occur again in my department."

The Chancellor bent his brows upon Jonathan Wild, and said, in a cold, harsh voice, "Upon your oath, you depose to all this?"

"Upon my oath, my lords, I do."

There was a small silver bell upon the table before the Lord Chancellor, who now touched it slightly, and hardly had its soft tinkling sound ceased when the door at that side of the room opened, and another person entered.

Jonathan Wild was ordinarily self-possessed enough, but at the sight of that other person he uttered a cry of dismay, for he recognised him at a glance.

No. 104.—EDITH.

There, in life, in health, calm, resolute, and cheerful, with a smile of disdain upon his face, was the young Earl of Bridgewater.

CHAPTER CCXXVIII.

CAPTAIN HERON AND EDITH REMAIN IN REFUGE IN THE HOUSE OF LADY CHESTER, AND AWAIT EVENTS.

THE determination to proceed at once to London, with Edith in his company, and to rely upon what the Earl of Bridgewater could immediately do in the cause of truth and justice, when once fixed in the mind of Captain Heron, was a resolve in which he never faltered.

The little party started from Epping Forest on horseback, and consisted of Captain Heron himself, the Earl of Bridgewater, Edith, Ogle, and Tom Ripon.

That day, so fresh and fair, imparted a joyousness to the spirits of the party, which seemed the presage of a happy issue to the expedition on which they were bent.

The young Earl had related to Captain Heron the singular adventure he had on his route to the forest; but neither Heron nor Edith could perceive any connexion between that adventure and their own fortunes, therefore they could only express their surprise at its singularity.

Tom Ripon and Ogle trotted on some hundred paces in advance of the three principal personages of the party; and it was with deep emotion in his tones that Captain Heron, addressing both Edith and the Earl of Bridgewater, said, "I now proceed to London, my dear friend, in compliance with your advice, because I feel that what you advise ought to be done without delay; but I cannot let another four-and-twenty hours pass over my head and leave a most sacred duty unfulfilled."

"There is no duty which you consider sacred," replied the Earl of Bridgewater, "that you may not ask me to assist you in carrying out."

"I mean so to ask you. I have already related to you the mysterious and seemingly supernatural circumstances that occurred to me during some nights' residence in Whitcombe House, and you are aware of what precious documents came into my possession."

"I am, indeed."

"Yes," said Edith; "and I have those documents in saftey. You have entrusted them to me, Felix; and you know I would not part with them except with my life!"

"They are, indeed, most precious. The certificate of the late Earl's marriage with my mother, Amelia Staunton, is one of those documents. The registry of my own baptism as their son is another; but the third has an absorbing interest which transcends them both, for it points to the place where I may seek my mother."

"Ah, yes!" said Edith. "May my prayers be heard, and that mother be found still in life, and know the joy of a reunion with you, my Felix."

"Let me say amen to that prayer," interposed the Earl of Bridgewater.

"To-night," cried Heron, holding up his hand, as though making a solemn appeal to heaven to attest the truthfulness of his words—"to-night, if I live, I will ride back to Epping Forest, and, collecting around me all those brave hearts which have followed me through so many dangers, perils, and difficulties, we will ride to East Sheen; and if I have to take the house to pieces, brick by brick—which has been indicated to me in those papers—I will find the unhappy, much-wronged Amelia Staunton. But why do I call her by that name? Amelia, Countess of Whitcombe, is her proper title."

"It is well, dear Felix," said Edith, "for her who was the mother of Lord Warringdale, that she has passed away from this life before these—to her—terrible discoveries took place."

"It is well, indeed," said the Earl of Bridgewater, "for she might have been called the second victim——"

"Of my father," interposed Heron, sadly.

The young Earl saw that the conversation was painful.

"Let us speak no more," he said, "upon that theme. You did but justice to my friendship, Heron, when you supposed I would accompany you on the expedition you name. Nevertheless, I cannot help thinking that it will be unnecessary."

"Unnecessary, my friend?"

"Yes; for no sooner shall I have lodged you in comfort and security at my sister's—Lady Chester's—house, in Clarges Street, than I will seek an interview with the King, and his Majesty shall become possessed of the true particulars of all this affair. You can entrust to me the two documents you speak of—that is, the marriage and baptismal certificates; and I really do not anticipate any difficulties."

"You are kind and good; but yet——"

"Your expedition to East Sheen will not be required, for the agents of the law will do all that is necessary."

"No," said Heron. "That is a task which belongs to me, and I alone will perform it."

"Then I am not the man to baulk you, but rather to assist you."

"And the King, you think, will listen with patience," asked Edith, "to this strange story?"

"I think so; but, from what I know of his disposition, I fancy I shall have a great deal more trouble in getting him to pardon Captain Heron, the highwayman, than in getting him to acknowledge Felix Heron as Earl of Whitcombe. But fear nothing, Edith. I see you change colour. Fear nothing; it needs but a little perseverance, and all will end well."

The ride from Epping to London was quickly performed, and the party arrived—without molestation or adventure—at Lady Chester's house, where Edith and Captain Heron found a kindly welcome, and where Ogle and Tom Ripon remained; while the Earl of Bridgewater hastened to St. James's Palace, with the hope that the leisure of the King would admit his claim to an interview, as a peer of the realm and a member of the Privy Council, to be immediately acceded to.

The Earl of Bridgewater was more fortunate than his expectations, and he succeeded in reaching the Lord Chamberlain—who happened to be at the Palace—before any one was really aware of his presence.

He had every reason to suppose that the rumour of his death would be in the mouth of every one; and his sudden appearance again in life would, he was sure, gain as soon an extensive popularity.

What he wished was that neither Warringdale nor Jonathan Wild should be put upon their guard, and hence he was delighted that he so far made his way into the Palace without creating a commotion.

The Lord Chamberlain carried the request for an interview to the King; and within a quarter of an hour of his arrival at St. James's, the Earl of Bridgewater found himself in the private cabinet of the monarch.

The young Earl, as he entered the apartment, felt confident that he heard some one leave it rather abruptly by a door immediately opposite to that through which he was ushered.

But it was not for him to pry into the secrets of royalty; and, with a low bow, he waited, as otiquette demanded, for the King to address him.

There was a visible embarrassment about the manner of the King; and the Earl of Bridgewater, coupling that with the fact that some one had certainly been in close communication with the monarch just before his arrival, began to think it possible some secret enemy was at work.

After rather a long pause, the King spoke.

"My Lord Bridgewater," he said, "it is a great pleasure to us to see you alive and well, after what we have heard of you."

"Your Majesty does me infinite honour," replied the Earl; "but it is to explain certain affairs that have some connexion with the duel I was supposed to have fallen in, that I have ventured-respectfully to solicit this audience."

"Have you any objection, Bridgewater, to put what you have to say in writing?"

"None, if your Majesty desires it."

"Very well, then. I shall be glad to look over any statement you send to me. Let it be sent to-day; and to-morrow morning, at one o'clock, my answer will be at your disposal."

"At one?"

"Yes, Bridgewater—at one; and be assured that—let it cost what it may to pre-conceived ideas and prejudices—justice shall be done."

There was a marked emphasis about the tone of the King, as he uttered these last words, that —combined with an air of feeling, too, pervading them—gave the Earl of Bridgewater the best hopes of a successful issue to the affairs of his friend, Captain Felix Heron.

The young nobleman was perhaps a little disappointed that he had not then and there brought the matter to some satisfactory conclusion, but still he had the best hopes for the proceedings of the morrow.

The Earl of Bridgewater would have had better hopes still if he could have seen what took place in the King's cabinet immediately after his departure.

No sooner had he left it than the King uttered a slight "Hem!" and then the door through which the Earl of Bridgewater had felt certain he had seen some one hastily leave the cabinet, upon his entrance, opened, and there came forth, from the adjoining apartment, an elderly man.

The hair of this person was of that perfect silky whiteness which is seldom seen when the colour has fled from the natural decay of years. His dress was the plainest of the plain.

And yet about this man there was an air of nobility and courtly ease, which would at once anywhere have stamped him as belonging to the highest class of society.

The King smiled as he spoke.

"Well, my lord," he said, "I have got rid of the warm advocate and the impulsive heart."

"Your Majesty is ever good and gracious," replied the gentleman with the white hair.

"We wish ever to be just, and there is but one deep regret at our heart in all this matter."

The King shook his head as he spoke, and then the white-haired gentleman bowed low, as he said, in a faltering tone of voice, "Oh, your Majesty, it is so much greater to forgive than to punish."

"It is, abstractedly. But yet there are many criminals in this fair land of England who would justly complain, if they knew we had yielded in this case. But be it as we have arranged and promised. We will not take away the grace of mercy, by making too many words about it Go, and take your own mode of warning this bad, bold man—this Lord Warringdale—of the danger he is in."

"It shall be done; and doubtless he will be wise enough not to show himself again in your Majesty's dominions."

"It will be unwise should he do so."

The personage with the white hair bowed again, more lowly than before; and then the King, with a smile, held out his hand to him, saying, "We wish you and yours many years yet of happiness, my lord. Be here punctually at one o'clock to-morrow, and then we hope that all these complexities will be over."

"At one," replied the white-haired gentleman; and, from the tone in which he spoke, it was very evident that his heart was too full of many emotions to permit him to say another word.

There was some secret mode of leaving the old Palace of St. James's, by the apartment from which this gentleman had issued, adjoining the royal cabinet; for it was by that way the mysterious visitor left, closing the door carefully after him.

When the Earl of Bridgewater left the royal closet, he made his way towards that apartment in which the Lord Chancellor and Lord Arranmore were sitting in judgment—or rather in an accusatory spirit—upon Jonathan Wild.

As he proceeded along one of the long galleries, he took an opened letter from his pocket, and read it quickly.

The letter ran as follows:—

"MY DEAR LORD BRIDGEWATER,

"My relative, Lord Arranmore, informs me that he has had a visit from the Chancellor, who has made to him a very singular revelation.

"The Chancellor states that Sir John Tarleton came to him at the Court of Chancery in Lincoln's Inn, and accused himself of appropriating to his own use the whole of the fortune of his daughter Edith. In addition to that self-accusation, he likewise stated that Lord Warringdale, in conjunction with Jonathan Wild, had been committing many iniquities. It appears, too, that Wild has had blank warrants entrusted to him by the Home Secretary, of which he has made the most infamous use.

"Wild will be arrested, and examined before the Council. Will you at once communicate with my relative, Lord Arranmore, and the Chancellor?

"I advise that you should, in the interests of your friend, Captain Heron.

"Believe me to be, my dear Lord Bridgewater, yours ever truly,

"WENTWORTH MILES."

"Yes," said the Earl, when he had read this letter through again,—"yes. Circumstances now come to a head. It is time that the villanies of Jonathan Wild and his associate, the so-called Lord Warringdale, should be exposed to the world. I have time now to attend to the instructions of the Chancellor."

This letter, which we have just now found in the hands of the young peer, had been received by him before he went to the Palace; and, consequent upon the receipt of it, he had had an interview with the Lord Chancellor and Lord Arranmore.

The result of that interview was that he, Lord Bridgewater, was to repair to the room adjoining that where the examination of Wild would take place, and make his appearance at that examination if the Chancellor should think it wise and well that he should do so.

The signal of the wish of the Chancellor to that effect was to be the ringing of the small silver bell on the table before him.

Let the reader, then, travel back with us to that room where Jonathan Wild had so glibly taken an oath, that the presence of the Earl of Bridgewater was to scatter to the winds in a moment.

The cry of dismay that Wild uttered, at the sudden appearance of the man whom he verily believed to be dead, echoed through the suite of apartments.

Then he struck his own forehead with his open hand,- as he exclaimed, "Oh, fool! fool!—fool that I am! I did see him at the gate by Marlborough House!"

"Probably you did, Jonathan Wild," said the Earl of Bridgewater. "And now you see me again, to your confusion."

"The game is up," said Wild.

"Are you not a most consummate villain?"

"My lord," replied Jonathan, recovering some portion of his audacity,—"my lord, it is not at all generous to press too heavily upon a fallen man."

The Chancellor turned to the clerk, who had written down what Jonathan Wild had deposed to on his oath, and, in his deep, stern accents, he said, "Read to the Right Honourable the Earl of Bridgewater the statement made just now, upon oath, of Jonathan Wild."

"It is needless," said Wild.

"Why so?"

"Because now that the Earl is alive and well—on which I congratulate him—I give up the statement as one still perfectly true, but yet one that he will not like, and therefore I retract it."

"Villain!" cried Bridgewater. "Were it not that your rascally blood would be an indelible stain of disgrace upon my sword, I would thrust that lie, with its point, down your throat!"

"Peace!" said the Chancellor. "My lord, you do but lower your dignity by holding discourse with this perjured man."

The Earl bowed, and said not another word.

The Chancellor scrawled some words on a slip of paper, and then passed it to Lord Arranmore, who likewise signed it.

It was a warrant for Jonathan Wild's committal to Newgate.

Then the Chancellor touched the silver bell again, and a pursuivant, with a couple of officers, appeared in the room.

The warrant was handed to them, and the Chancellor, indicating Wild, said, sternly, "You will remove this man, and be answerable for his safe lodgment in the gaol of Newgate."

The pursuivant laid his hand on Jonathan Wild's shoulder.

"May I humbly ask," said Wild, "of what I am accused?"

"Murder!" said the Earl of Bridgewater.

"And robbery!" said Lord Arranmore.

"And perjury!" said the Chancellor.

"Thank you, gentlemen!" said Jonathan Wild, with a low mock bow. "You are too good! I have the distinguished honour to bid you all good day, and to hope that you will in time to come get some one who will do as much good service to the State as Jonathan Wild."

The two officers who were with the pursuivant clapped, with professional dexterity, a pair of handcuffs upon Wild, and in a few minutes more he was hustled into a hackney-coach, and driven off to Newgate.

"Ah, my game chickens!" said Wild to the officers, "I am not quite done for yet; so look out for squalls another time!"

CHAPTER CCXXIX.

LORD WARRINGDALE RECEIVES A MYSTERIOUS WARNING, AND GOES INTO HIDING.

"FLY while you can! Justice will not be always blind! Already she slips the bandage from her eyes, and looks upon my Lord Warringdale as a criminal who may not be saved! Fly while there is time!"

Such were the words upon a slip of paper which Lord Warringdale found, about the dusk of the evening, in his chamber on the day of the arrest of Jonathan Wild by the Privy Council warrant.

As may well be supposed, the greatest possible alarm took possession of the consciously guilty man.

The terror that shone forth from his eyes was something awful to see, and looked more like incipient insanity than aught else.

His knees knocked together; an universal weakness came over him, and he would have fallen had he not contrived to stagger to a seat.

Then, with a cry of fright, he made an effort to spring to his feet again; for the seat to which he had staggered in his weakness was that window-seat within which reposed in death the murdered man who had had the ill fortune to second him in his duel with the Earl of Bridgewater.

The wretched Major Ridgkey, *alias* O'Rourke, lay there waiting the discovery that, sooner or later, must take place of the terrible end he had come to.

No wonder that Lord Warringdale should recoil with horror from that part of his chambers.

"Save me!—oh, save me!" he cried. "Have mercy, heaven!"

Too late—too late was it for that man of many crimes to call upon heaven to save him.

Besides, it was fear that spoke, not repentance.

The hot tears that started to his eyes were produced by personal apprehension.

The cold dew that settled upon his forehead, and seemed to spread over all his limbs, was the result of fear.

Yes; that man of deep iniquities felt not real remorse.

That agony—that salutary agony of the soul had not yet come. It was to come.

"Save me!—oh, save me! What shall I do?"

A knock came to the door of the chamber.

Lord Warringdale echoed it by a scream.

CAPTAIN HERON RECEIVES A FULL PARDON FROM THE HANDS OF HIS
GRACIOUS SOVEREIGN.

Presented Gratis with No. 104 of the New Edition of Edith the Captive; or, the Robbers of Epping Forest.

He sprang to the further end of the room, and placing the hilt of his sword against his breast so that the blade projected before him, he gasped out in half-smothered accents, "No, no! I will not be taken! Not in life!—not in life! Kill me; but I will not be taken!"

The knock sounded again.

"Help! help! Have mercy upon me!"

The knock came a third time.

The first paroxysm of terror was passing away from the mind of Lord Warringdale, and he was able to reason with himself a little.

There might, after all, be no danger.

It was possible—nay, it was probable enough that whoever was at the door might have come there on some very simple errand not all inimical to him.

Then a bright idea at the moment struck him. He would answer the door, but he would deny himself.

In a wardrobe, which stood in a recess of one of the rooms, he knew he should find livery coats which had belonged to different servants he had had while residing in those chambers. His idea was to put on one of them, and, in fact, to play the part of his own footman.

With trembling eagerness Lord Warringdale set to work to carry out this scheme. He was soon attired in one of the livery coats. He flung back his hair, and tried to look as little like himself as possible.

The person at the door was persistent without being impatient.

He still, at intervals of about half a minute, kept up the single knocks, and at length Warringdale went to the door.

The last quarter of an hour had deepened the approaching darkness of the evening very much. It had happened to be that quarter of an hour in which the twilight was flashing its last tints upon this hemisphere, and the darkness then seemed as if it came all at once.

Lord Warringdale was glad of that.

Darkness and his deeds well agreed.

But still the guilty man shook like a leaf in autumn as he placed his hand on the lock of the door.

The knock came again at that moment.

"Who is there?" asked Warringdale.

"Is this Lord Warringdale's lodging?" asked a voice from without.

Warringdale was silent for a few seconds. He could not make up his mind which to do—to deny his residence there, or admit it.

But now the man outside grew impatient.

"Can't you answer? Is this Lord Warringdale's lodging?"

"What do you want with him?"

Warringdale thought it the best and wisest plan to answer the question from without by asking another from within.

"I have a letter."

"For him?"

"Yes, to be sure, it's for him, and it's from Newgate."

"Newgate?"

"Yes. From Mr. Wild."

"Jonathan Wild in Newgate!" exclaimed Lord Warringdale, as he flung open the door in an agony of apprehension. — "Jonathan Wild in Newgate! No, no! It cannot be! And yet—yet,

perhaps, I mistake you, and he only dates a letter from Newgate. You do not mean to say that he is in Newgate as a prisoner?"

"Yes I do, though!"

"No, no! That cannot be!"

"Well, you may say it cannot be as long as you like, and as much as you like; but it is, for all that."

"Gracious powers! Then there is danger!"

"I don't know about that. All I want to know is if this is the lodgings of Lord Warringdale or not?"

"Yes!—oh, yes!"

"You are his servant, then?"

"I am."

"Then that will do. You are to give him this letter as soon as you can—now, at once, if he is at home."

"He—he is not."

"Very well. My duty is done. There's the letter. It's from Mr. Wild, to Lord Warringdale. I'm paid to deliver it, and there it is."

"But—but will you—eh?—will you be so good as tell me how—that is to say, why Mr. Wild is in Newgate?"

"A warrant."

"A—a warrant? Then you mean to say he is a prisoner?"

"To be sure he is! I don't know rightly what for, but there he is; and I heard one of our people say it would be a hanging affair."

Lord Warringdale licked his parched lips.

"Thank you—thank you!" he said. "The Lord Warringdale shall have the letter. Thank you! Good night!"

"All's right! Good night!"

The messenger from Newgate carelessly left the door of the chambers; and in two minutes more Lord Warringdale had a light, and was reading Jonathan Wild's letter.

It contained these words:—

"Newgate.

"MY LORD,

"I'm nabbed. It won't be for long, though. The Stone Jug is not yet built that will hold Jonathan Wild much longer than he chooses to stay in it.

"I rather fancy, though, that things have taken a wrong turn; and, if so, it will be well that both you and I go into hiding for a time.

"Perhaps you don't know where to go—I do. We must be saved together, or we must hang together; and therefore I will tell you just what to do. You need not do it, however, unless you see—or think you see—there is absolute danger.

"Go into the old Abbey of Westminster, during the time that it is shown. Give one of the vergers a handsome fee, and say that you want to roam about among the old monuments and chapels alone. He will, for the handsome fee, let you do so. You will then make your way to one of the chapels, where you will see a monument, consisting of a large flat stone, supported at each corner by kneeling, armed figures, sculptured in stone. On the eastern side of that small chapel, and close to the floor, you will see a square stone, forming apparently part of the wall, and composed of a blue kind of slate, or stone, that will easily enable you to identify it.

"That stone is about four feet square; and if

you push it hard at either end, it will turn on its centre, disclosing an opening in the wall, and a narrow flight of steps.

"Those steps lead to one of the vaults of the old Abbey.

"Take some provisions with you, and go down and wait for me. I intend to be there to-morrow night. We must consult upon what is best to be done. Let me find you there, in that vault, at all events, at midnight to-morrow.

"This—which you will burn as soon as you shall have read it—is from

"JONATHAN WILD."

Lord Warringdale trembled excessively when he had completed the reading of this letter from his villanous associate.

He was filled with a thousand fears. What was he to think? What was he to do? What discoveries had taken place, which had involved Wild in the meshes of the law? How far did those discoveries affect him, Lord Warringdale?

These were pertinent enough questions to put to himself; but, amid them all, he felt one conviction that he could not shrink from, and that was that, come what may, he must obey the orders of Jonathan Wild.

The consciousness of mutual iniquity bound him and Wild too closely together for him to venture now to have an opinion or a wish of his own.

What Wild chose to dictate to him, that he, Lord Warringdale, must do. There was no escape from that condition of affairs.

Lord Warringdale, while life remained to him, was, so to speak, the bond-slave of Jonathan Wild.

"Yes—oh, yes!" he said; "it must be done, even as he says. There is no other hope for me now. I feel that something most disastrous must have happened, or this advice never could have come from Jonathan Wild."

Lord Warringdale coupled now in his imagination the order he received in this letter with the mysterious anonymous warning that had reached him in his chambers.

"Surely," he said,—and he trembled as he spoke,—"surely, all this must mean something serious."

Even as these words passed his lips he heard a confused sound of footsteps at the door of the chambers.

The echo of voices, apparently subdued to tones of cautious consultation, likewise came upon his attentive ears.

Was the danger he had been warned of close at hand?

The question was a terrible and anxious one for Lord Warringdale.

Crouching down close to the inner side of the door of the chambers, he listened with an intensity and anxiety that was soon positively painful.

The whispering tones continued.

Nay, he could have sworn that he heard his own name uttered.

Then there was a smart rap at the door—such an one as might be made by some person who was assured of a welcome as an acquaintance.

What was the agonized, trembling wretch,

who was crouching down on the inner side of that door, to do?

Was his fate certain now? Was detection, exposure, arrest, and perhaps death, to come to him, in fearful order, as the consequences of his many and deep iniquities?

How was he to escape?

The sharp rap came again.

Then a thin pencil of light shone through the keyhole of the door, the key in which happened to be turned aside, so that there was a space, of some half an inch in width, through which so subtle a thing as light could make its way.

That pencil of light, which no doubt came from a lantern, fell upon the shrinking form of Lord Warringdale, and was at the moment a terrible alarm to him.

Then, as there is no such thing as unmixed evil or unmixed danger, that very pencil of light, which at the moment of its appearance had sent the blood back to his heart with a gush of fear, brought to him a new hope.

It fell upon the gold lace of the cuff of the livery coat he had on.

Lord Warringdale uttered almost an exclamation of delight.

A new hope had sprung up in his heart.

He might escape. In disguise as his own servant, he surely had a chance—something more than a mere chance—of escape.

Hanging on a peg above the door was an old livery three-cornered hat, which the last valet of Lord Warringdale had discarded for shabbiness. How welcome it was now, in all its dust, and in all its dilapidation, to the master!

Lord Warringdale reached down the old hat at once, and put it on.

Something soft was in the crown of it. A wig —one of those coachmen's wigs, with the rows of curls on each side, tier above tier.

Could anything be better? Could anything be more fortunate?

At any other time, Lord Warringdale would have looked upon that old hat and the still older wig with abhorrence and contempt.

Now he put them both on his head with quite a joyful expression.

The knock came a third time.

Warringdale flew to that buffet from which the Reverend Mortification Ripon had, on the morning of the duel in Kensington Gardens, taken the bottle of eau de vie; and he rapidly filled the pockets of the long coat he wore with raisins and various other dried fruit, as well as some biscuits, which were there in store.

He had upon his mind the advice contained in Jonathan Wild's letter—to take some provisions with him.

Then, just as the knock came to the door a fourth time, Lord Warringdale summoned all his courage to open it, and all his firmness to play the part of his own footman when he should do so.

With an affectation of hurry, he flung the door open; and then giving his arms a formidable stretch, and yawning in the faces of four men who were without, he said, in half-sleepy tones, "Egad! I thought I heard a knock!"

"You thought you heard a knock, stupid!" said one of the men. "Why, you might well think so; for we have been knocking for this half-hour!"

"No!—have you, though?"

"To be sure we have! Is this Lord Warringdale's?"

"Oh, yes!"

"All's right! Sir, sir! this is the proper door. This way, if you please!"

An individual, who up to this moment had kept himself some distance in the background, now made his appearance.

"Then take your prisoner!" he said. "I hold the warrant. Be quick about it!"

The four men dashed past Lord Warringdale into the chambers; and he put on a bewildered look as he stood at the door.

"Not here, Mr. Pursuivant!" cried one of the constables, for such they were.

"Not there? Lord Warringdale not there? Hilloa, you, sirrah! Where is your master?"

"Oh! you want my master, Lord Warringdale?"

"Yes, yes! Where is he?"

"Oh, he has gone to Epping Forest, to see if he cannot apprehend the notorious highwayman, Captain Felix Heron; and he won't be home till quite late. He was late last night, too, and that's what makes me so—ah! ah!—very—sleepy now, though it is early in the morning. If you have no objection, I'll just finish my nap."

"Kick that lazy rascal out into the street, at once!" said the pursuivant, angrily, pointing to Lord Warringdale, who, however, rapidly left the house, saying as he did so, "Well, well, gentlemen all, I don't want to be kicked out. If I must go, I must."

"No—stop! On second thoughts, he may warn his master. Stop!"

It was too late. Lord Warringdale had reached the pavement of St. James's Street; and then, with all the fleetness which fear could lend to him, he fled, and was in a few seconds completely lost amid the intricacies of some of the back streets. The pursuivant and the constables sat down in the chambers to await the return of the man whom they hoped to capture. A Privy Council warrant had been signed for the apprehension of Warringdale; and it was hoped he would pass the night in Newgate.

CHAPTER CCXXX.

THE CONCLUSION.

At the moment that Lord Warringdale slunk down St. James's Street in the disguise of a footman, the clock of the Palace struck the hour of nine; and in the ancient breakfast-room at Castleneau House an old time-piece echoed the sounds. Lord Warringdale was a trembling fugitive; but in that breakfast-room we present to the reader a group of happy faces.

Lady Castleneau, released from the Tower, is there, with the hand of Edith in her own. Captain Felix Heron, the Earl of Bridgewater and his Countess, and Lady Chester, his sister, are there present; and close to the door may be seen old Anthony, with tears of joy in his eyes.

It was the Earl of Bridgewater who was speaking; and his voice, although with a tincture of sadness in it, was soft and melodious.

"This night," he said, "surely should end the fears and the perplexities of Edith, who has suffered so much, and with such fortitude endured persecutions. At one o'clock to-morrow the King consents to receive both you, Heron, and your fair bride in his private cabinet."

Captain Heron grasped the hand of the young nobleman who had done so much for him; and while his voice was broken by emotion, he said, "One more effort—one more expedition, on which you, dear friend, shall accompany me—and Felix Heron can have no more to hope—no more to fear. Come with me to that asylum at East Sheen, where my poor—poor—mother——"

The voice of Heron was broken by a sob.

It was Lady Castleneau who then spoke, and the tears chased each other from her eyes as she did so.

"Felix," she said, "I have already told our Edith, and it is fit and proper that I should now tell you, that that asylum has already been visited. Here is one who will tell you all."

Lady Castleneau rose, and removed a portion of the tall screen by the fire; and on a couch, in the last stage of feebleness, appeared Sir Dominick Browne.

"Good heaven!" exclaimed Heron; "what means this?"

"This dear old friend, who, in common with all who loved you, has suffered much for you," added Lady Castleneau, "was found a prisoner in that asylum, but Amelia Staunton had escaped."

"Escaped! When?—where?"

Lady Castleneau pointed upwards, solemnly, and Captain Heron understood the action. His mother was in heaven!

We draw a veil over the grief of the gallant Captain Heron. Oh! how he had longed to embrace that mother; but it was not to be. He is young, however, and the world lies before him, fair and bountiful. His Edith will tread the flower-decked paths by his side. Let that night, then, pass away, O friend and reader, who thus far have followed with us the fortunes of Edith and Felix, and repair with us now, at one hour past the mid-day of the morrow, to that cabinet in St. James's Palace, where the monarch of these realms had appointed to see the gallant Earl of Bridgewater and Felix Heron, with his Edith.

A soft summer's sun is shining in at the gorgeous painted window; and we look into that apartment at the moment that Felix Heron, on one knee, has done homage to his Sovereign.

The King spoke.

"We fancy, sir, that we have heard the whole of your most romantic story. You have been foully wronged; but although we have heard some things of your character in Epping Forest that we must not approve, yet we have never heard of one cruel or reckless action as against the life or feelings of any of our subjects."

"That, your Majesty, I can answer for," said the Earl of Bridgewater.

"My Lord Bridgewater," said the King, with a smile, "is always ready to answer for his friends. We are right glad to see the Earl of Whitcombe."

The King extended his hand to Felix Heron; and by that action, and the words he uttered, Heron felt that his rank was acknowledged, and that he was a Peer of England.

"My Countess—my Edith!" he cried, with emotion.

Edith burst into tears.

"Hold! Yet a moment, hear me," added the King. "We said that we could not pardon Felix Heron, the highwayman; but it seems we have signed a pardon in full to the Earl of Whitcombe for all the offences committed up to that date. Take it; and be happy with her who now graces this old cabinet of St. James's with a presence of beauty that seldom has adorned it."

The King handed a folded paper to Captain Heron, and a small slip, with a few words on it, fell out and lit upon his breast. It was Edith who looked at the words on that slip of paper, and found them to be as follows:—

"The blessing of God, and of the earthly father, be upon the Earl of Whitcombe and his fair Countess, ever and ever."

"Gracious heaven!" said Felix Heron. "These words are written in a character that so strongly resembles the writing of the letter from my father to my mother, that but for the fact that the grave has closed over that father, I might believe that he yet lived and watched over me."

"Forbear!" said the King—"oh, forbear! We will not deny that there is a mystery yet unsolved in regard to the fate of one who has inflicted much misery and suffered much retribution. Be happy, my Lord Whitcombe, and leave the rest to heaven!"

The Earl rose to his feet. He turned to Edith and opened his arms. Etiquette, forms, ceremonies, the royal presence in which they stood—all were forgotten, as Edith, with a cry of joy, flung herself into his arms, and sobbed upon his breast.

"My Edith! My own!—my beautiful!"

"Yes, dear, dear Felix! Your own Edith, ever—and still Edith the Captive, because her heart is held in chains of dear affection that never may be riven. Oh! happy, happy Edith!" she smiled amid her tears. "Happy, happy Edith! How have I deserved such a heart as yours, my Felix?"

The folding-doors that led into one of the reception saloons of the Palace were thrown open by the royal pages at a sign from the King. There was a clash of martial music, and as the monarch took the hand of Edith, he said, "Let us be the first to welcome the Earl and Countess of Whitcombe to the Court of St. James's."

THE END.